OF WAR
AND RUIN

By Ryan Cahill

THE BOUND AND THE BROKEN

NOVELS

Of Blood and Fire
Of Darkness and Light
Of War and Ruin

NOVELLAS

The Fall
The Exile

OF WAR
AND RUIN

BOOK THREE OF
THE BOUND AND THE BROKEN

RYAN CAHILL

OF WAR AND RUIN

Book Three of The Bound and The Broken Series

Copyright © 2023 by Ryan Cahill

First Published in 2023 by Ryan Cahill

ISBN 978-1-7396209-3-6

www.ryancahillauthor.com

Cover Design by: Stuart Bache

Edited by: Sarah Chorn

Map by: Keir Scott-Schrueder

To all those we've lost.

Vir'uva niassa du i denir viël are altinua. Må Heraya tael du ia'sine ael. Indil vir anarai andin.

We will love you in this life and always. May Heraya take you into her arms. Until we meet again.

THE STORY SO FAR

The following is meant only as a quick, high-level refresher of the events in *Of Darkness and Light* and *The Exile* rather than a full synopsis. As such, I will gloss over many important occurrences and characters during this recap, and some – in a few cases – are not mentioned at all. I will try to catch you up on the events and characters that are the most important to Of War and Ruin

This refresher will contain spoilers.

OF DARKNESS AND LIGHT

Five days after Daymon's coronation, the imperial forces laid siege to the city of Belduar. All four Kingdoms of the Dwarven Freehold fight alongside the Belduarans, after Kira had come to Belduar's aid when the Fade attacked. Calen fights on the city's walls alongside his companions, but during the chaos, he gets separated from all but Erik and Valerys.

Three of the Dragonguard appear and, with many of the Bolt Throwers destroyed by the Fade's attack five days prior, tear the city apart with fire and fury.

Calen, Erik, and Valerys fight their way through the Lorian soldiers to find aid in the form of King Daymon, Lord Ihvon Arnell, and Lord-Captain Tarmon Hoard. They try to mount a defence but the Dragonguard are too powerful. With the city lost, Tarmon tries to convince Daymon to sound a retreat through the Wind Tunnels, but Daymon is furious at the suggestion of retreat. It takes both Calen and Tarmon to convince Daymon that he needs to sound the retreat to save the lives of his people.

Calen stays back on a Wind Runner platform and covers Tarmon and the Kingsguards' retreat once the last of the last of the Belduarans have retreated down the tunnels. He finds Vaeril – one of the elves that swore an oath to protect him.

When the Kingsguard retreat, and the Lorians flood into the courtyard after them, Calen leaps from the platform to aid the retreat. Vaeril joins him and the pair attempt to bring down the entrances to the courtyard using the Spark. Vaeril destroys three of the entrances, while Calen almost burns himself out attempting to do the same. He brings down two entrances, but Lorians flood through the third. As Vaeril helps Calen back to the Wind Runner, Valerys soared through the courtyard and poured fire over the Lorians.

When they get to the Wind Runner, they find that the Falmin Tain is the navigator. In the scramble to board, Tarmon takes an arrow through his lower abdomen. Calen and the others drag him aboard and Falmin pilots the Wind Runner into the tunnel. While Vaeril heals Tarmon, Calen discovers Falmin has also been struck by an arrow. Weak from battle, Calen assumes control of the Wind Runner. The Wind Runner crashes in the depths of the mountain.

Meanwhile, Ella, Faenir, Shirea, and Farda sail for Antiquar. Ella tells Farda her name is Ella Fjorn, and Farda draws connections to Rhett's uncle Tanner Fjorn, who is revealed to be the High Captain of the Beronan Guard. Ella spends time with Shirea, who is suffering badly from seasickness, but also with the loss of her partner – John.

Hours later, Farda strolls the deck of the ship at night and finds Shirea. He has already decided he needs to 'deal' with her. A flip of his coin makes up his mind, and he snaps Shirea's neck and dumps her into the ocean.

In the tunnels below Lodhar, Calen and the others awake after the crash to find the Wind Runner is destroyed and many Kingsguard and dwarves are dead. Tarmon, Vaeril, Erik, Valerys, and Falmin have all survived along with sixty-two other dwarves and humans. Vaeril heals Falmin's wounds and they set about planning how they are going to find a way through the tunnels and back to Durakdur. It is here that Calen notices the others are looking to him to make the decisions as he is now 'the Draleid'.

As they walk through the tunnels, Vaeril tells Calen the reason the elves of Aravell – the Darkwood – have disavowed Therin is because he refused to choose sides during 'the Breaking' where the elves of Lynalion abandoned the rest of the continent. Therin refused to pick a side as his duty was to all elves, but the elves of Aravell saw this as cowardice. After some time searching, Calen and the others discover the ruins of a lost dwarven city known as Vindakur.

In the rubble of Belduar, Inquisitor Rendall finds a one-handed elf amongst the ruins and orders the elf brought to his tent for interrogation. Above the city, Eltoar Daethana and Helios land beside the Dragonguard command tent where they meet Eltoar's two companions, Lyina and Pellenor, along with the dragon to which Lyina is bound, Karakes. They talk of the other Dragonguard. Jormun, Ilkya, and Voranur all remain in Epheria. Erdin and Luka left the continent years ago, and Tivar hasn't left Dracaldryr in nearly a century. Eltoar sets Pellenor to watch Rendall.

In Durakdur, Daymon vehemently urges the Dwarven rulers to help him retake Belduar, but they deny him. Too many have already died, and they collapsed the Wind Tunnels after the retreat. Instead, they offer the Belduarans refuge. Daymon is furious. Aeson informs the rulers of his plan to search the tunnels for any signs of Erik, Calen, and the others. Asius goes in search of clan Fenryr of the Angan – a race of shapeshifters – to aid in finding Calen and the others. Therin tells Asius that if he has trouble with clan Fenryr that he is to tell them 'the son of the Chainbreaker is lost, and he needs them.'

Later that night, Ihvon foils an attempt on Daymon's life after Dahlen alerts them to a shady man he'd seen in the courtyard. The assassin reveals he was sent by the dwarven queen Elenya. The next day, as Dahlen is waiting for Aeson so they can start the search, Alea and Lyrei – two elves who swore to protect Calen, tell Dann that Vaeril and Gaeleron never made it to Belduar either. Aeson arrives with fifty dwarves in tow, along with a dwarven guide named Nimara. Aeson tells Dahlen that he cannot join, as, in light of the attempt on Daymon's life, Aeson needs him to watch over the young king.

In the palace of Al'Nasla, Rist, and three sponsored apprentices of the Circle of Magii – Neera, Lena, and Tommin – are being instructed in histories by High Scholar Pirnil. Rist is punished by Pirnil for losing his focus. After his lessons, Rist goes to meet his sponsor, Brother Garramon. Garramon gives Rist a letter from his parents but tells Rist he hasn't received a response from the letters sent to Calen and Dann in Belduar. Garramon reveals Belduar has been defeated, and that a newfound rebel Draleid is causing havoc. Rist is careful with his questions, aware that he is no longer in The Glade. Garramon grants Rist his brown apprentice robes, which are adorned with a black stripe – the colour of the Battlemages.

In the Temple of Achyron, Brother-Captain Kallinvar watches the knights of his chapter practice in the sparring pits. Brother Lyrin, who had been sent to Camylin to build connections, returns in time to spar with Kallinvar. After the sparring, Grandmaster Verathin visits Kallinvar and informs him that the first dragon has hatched since The Fall. They agree that if the Draleid and the dragon hatchling aren't loyal to the empire, they need to be protected.

Lyrin and another knight, Brother Arden – who was only granted the Sigil of Achyron two years ago – visit the Tranquil Garden to recuperate in the Waters of Life after the sparring. While there, Verathin along with Watcher Gildrick inform the pair that they are needed to combat a convergence of the Taint.

Arden and Lyrin travel through the Rift to a town called Helden. Here they battle against a horde of Uraks that are attacking the town. Arden faces a Bloodmarked Urak, which comes very close to killing him before he is saved by Lyrin.

In the north, Ella's ship approaches Antiquar, and Farda tells her that a deckhand saw Shirea throw herself overboard the night before.

Below the mountains of Lodhar, Calen and his group of survivors move through the ruins of Vindakur in search of a Wind Tunnel that might lead them back to Durakdur. Amidst signs of a past battle, Calen sees a building with the symbol of the order engraved above the door. Valerys senses something inside the building and swoops through the broken roof to find a chest of shattered dragon eggs. In the same room as the shattered eggs, Calen finds a pendant and a letter written by Alvira Serris. After Calen finishes reading the letter, he and the other survivors are set upon by a swarm of kerathlin – spider-like creatures with chitinous bodies – that had turned the city into their nest. The kerathlin tear through the survivors, killing humans and dwarves alike. The group run towards an island of rock in the centre of the city, connected to the streets by several bridges. They make it to the island and Calen collapses one of the bridges, buying them time. They take a tunnel into a chamber at the centre of the island where they find a Portal Heart. As Falmin tries to activate the portal, the others ready themselves to face the kerathlin that are swarming down the tunnels into the chamber. Falmin uses Korik's hand to active the portal and they escape, but many of the surviving dwarves and soldiers are killed.

On the other side of the portal, the group wander through tunnels in search of a way out. The sound of kerathlin causes Valerys to panic, and he almost brings the tunnel down until Calen calms him. In the aftermath, Calen finds a way out of the tunnels. They emerge onto a snowy mountain to find they are now in Drifaien with an old friend, Alleron, who Calen met in the Two Barges. Alleron provides the group refuge and reveals he is the son of Drifaein's High Lord, Lothal Helmund.

In Valtara, Dayne Ateres returns home after twelve years in exile. The Steward of House Ateres, Marlin Arkon, brings Dayne to see his brother, Baren, who is now head of House Ateres. Initially overjoyed, Baren grows furious when Dayne shows him a letter from Aeson Virandr. Later, Baren betrays Dayne to the empire, and Dayne only escapes with the help of his sister, Alina. Alina takes Dayne to the hidden fortress of Stormshold, built inside the island that once held the city of Stormwatch – where Dayne had once watched his parents die.

In Stormshold, Dayne sees Valtarans of all the Major Houses – Ateres, Deringal, Thebal, Herak, Vakira, and Koraklon – all working together in opposition to the empire. Alina tells Dayne that while he was gone Baren had her partner, Kal, killed, and also agreed to having her newborn son taken and inducted into the Lorian army – as the Lorians did what all

Valtaran firstborns. Alina agrees with Aeson's request to start a rebellion, but is still furious.

In Antiquar, Ella discovers that Shirea's body was found with her neck snapped. She and Faenir agree to travel with Farda to Berona. Far north, in the Beronan dungeons, Inquisitor Rendall takes his new initiate, Fritz Netly, to aid in the interrogation of the one-handed elf they found in the rubble of Belduar, while Pellenor secretly watches them.

Tempers fray in the tunnels of Lodhar as Aeson, Dann, and the others reach a dead end in their search for Calen and Erik, and are forced to turn back.

In Durakdur, Dahlen spars with Ihvon while Daymon has a private meeting with Queen Pulroan. Later, Ihvon takes Dahlen to the refugee quarters of Durakdur, where the Belduaran refugees are being housed within the city. The people are hungry and living in squalor. Dahlen experiences a traumatic episode at the sight of all the injured, and he helps distribute the sparse food.

Resting in the town of Katta, Calen has a vivid, almost real, dream that he experiences in tandem with Valerys. Vaeril teaches Calen of the Spark and a sword movement called 'fellensír'. Calen convinces the others they should travel with Alleron to Arisfall, where he can arrange a ship to take them back to Durakdur.

In Al'Nasla, Rist bonds with the other apprentices while reading as many books as he can find, and Neera tells him of the goings on in the South.

On their way to Berona, Ella, Faenir, and Farda find themselves in a town attacked by Uraks. Farda saves Ella's life, and she and Faenir return the favour. Ella learns Farda is a mage and an Imperial Justicar.

Rist trains with Garramon in Al'Nasla and sees the scars the man has on his back from his own apprenticeship. After training, Rist takes a forbidden trip into the city with Neera. While there, Rist sees an Alamant. Rist and Neera sit on the docks, talking of their past, and eventually share a kiss.

Back in Durakdur, Ihvon and Dahlen debate who is behind the assassination attempt and Ihvon introduces Dahlen to Belina Louna, who is to help them investigate the attempt on Daymon's life and unravel the web of plots taking hold of Durakdur.

After being left under watch in Stormshold by Alina, Dayne finds that the women he has always loved, Mera Vardas, is now a wyvern rider. That night Dayne climbs to the Rest of Mera's wyvern, Audin, and there he learns Alina is gone to Skyfell to start the war against the empire and to kill Baren for what he has done.

Trekking through the snow in Drifaien, Calen and his group are attacked by wyrms. Valerys displays his incredible destructive powers by ripping the wyrms to pieces, but not before many are killed. One of the surviving dwarves, Lopir, loses an eye.

In the Temple of Achyron, the knights debate over their next steps. Arden suggests reaching out to find allies and is ridiculed by the captains as the knights, historically, do not become involved in the politics of the continent. Kallinvar explains the history of the knighthood to Arden and Lyrin. The knights rush to intervene when Uraks attack Calen's home in The Glade. They manage to thwart the Urak attack, but not before the village is destroyed and many of its inhabitants killed, including Erdhardt Hammersmith's wife, Aela. After the battle, Kallinvar comforts Arden, who seems particularly traumatised by the scenes.

Dann, Aeson, and Therin finally arrive back in Durakdur having failed to find Calen and Erik. While in Durakdur, Dahlen tells Aeson that he suspects deeper machinations within the dwarven city. When trying to arrange another expedition to search the tunnels for Calen, Aeson and the others are visited by Baldon, and Angan of Clan Fenryr, who reveals that Calen and Erik are alive and in Drifaien. Dahlen decides to stay behind to help Ihvon and Daymon.

Having finally arrived in Arisfall, Alleron arranges ships for Calen, who is waiting with the others near a small town. Alleron goes to Arisfall castle to speak with his mother, and on the way runs into Leif. After speaking to his mother, Alleron is cornered by his father, who threatens him.

When Alleron meets back up with the others to inform the ships have been secured, they are ambushed by an Imperial Battlemage by the name of Artim Valdock and Lothal Helmund, who throws Leif's severed head into the snow. In the fighting that follows, Artim Valdock kills both Falmin and Lopir. To save Valerys's life, and those of Erik, Tarmon, Vaeril, Korik, and the others, Calen surrenders.

Calen awakens in a cell in Arisfall, his wrists bound with rune-marked manacles that cut him off from the Spark and his connection to Valerys. Alone, and distraught from the loss of his friends, Calen is tortured by Artim Valdock.

While riding across the continent, Dann tries to apologise to Alea and Lyrei for losing his temper in the tunnel, and learns that his horses's name in the Old Tongue is Drunir – Companion. While camping for the night, Therin tells Dann about his valúr – the elven tradition of learning to create before learning to destroy. As Therin tells the tale of what happened after The Fall, Lyrei becomes enraged and tells him he is no better than the Astyrlína – the Faithless; those elves who turned their back on the continent and withdrew into Lynalion. Aeson, furious at her disrespect towards Therin, tells her that her honour is forfeit. After the argument, Baldon tells them that Calen has been captured.

Meanwhile, Ella finally arrives at Berona, the city where she and Rhett had planned to start their new life. Ella and Farda argue, and he brings her to meet Tanner Fjorn, Rhett's uncle – who she has pretended is her own uncle. Tanner plays along with the ruse. When Farda leaves, Tanner comforts Ella and asks how his nephew died. Later, it is revealed that Tanner is aligned with Aeson's rebellion.

Farda meets with Grand Consul Karsen Craine, who tells him he is too close to Ella and is to join the Fourth Army to relieve Fort Harken of Urak attacks. Karsen plans to capture Ella that night.

When Karsen's men come for her, Ella and Faenir kill them and are bundled from the city by Tanner, a woman called Yana, and a Rakina elf named Farwen.

In Arisfall, Alleron is approached by his old friend Baird along with a Fenryr Angan, Aneera, both of whom are allied with Aeson. Alleron and the others break Calen out of his cell, along with Erik, Vaeril, and Tarmon, but Korik was killed during torture. Asius, the Jotnar also aids during the escape. While fleeing, Calen's manacles are removed and his eyes glow purple. He bonds deeply with Valerys and the dragon lays waste to their pursuers, then flies Calen to safety.

Meanwhile, in Valtara, Dayne and Mera sneak back into Redstone. Dayne stops Alina from killing Baren, then lets his brother go free, telling him to wait at the farm near Myrefall. Dayne then witnesses hundreds of wyverns freeing Skyfell from Lorian control, and Alina is revealed to be a wyvern rider.

As the wyverns fly over Valtara, Calen reveals his plans to find Rist. If he goes back to Durakdur, Aeson will stop him from going after his friend. Calen and the others sail north with Captain Kiron on The Enchantress. Valerys flies alongside the ship.

While Calen sails, Ella travels with Farwen and Yana, discovering that she may in fact have the blood of the old druids in her veins.

Within the walls of Al'Nasla, Rist studies and practices the Spark using A Study of Control, by Andelar Touran. He also learns about the different divisions of druid – Aldruid, Skydruid, Seerdruid – from Druids, a Magic Lost. Garramon brings Rist for his Trial of Will. In the trial, Rist enters the Well of Arnen, where, in a dream-like state, he sees a faceless man who kills Neera, his mother, and many others, along with destroying Al'Nasla and The Glade. The faceless man, who now has a massive, white-scaled dragon by his side, is revealed to be Calen. In the trial, Rist chooses to kill both himself and Calen to prevent Calen from destroying everything. He awakens from the trial and is granted the brown-trimmed black robes of a Battlemage acolyte for passing the trial. Rist is unsure whether the trial was simply a trial or something more. Was it a glimpse of the future?

Still searching for Calen, Dann and Aeson visit one of Aeson's contacts in Argona, a man named Arem. They learn the state of the continent and that Calen has escaped the cell in Drifaien.

Ella arrives in Tarhelm – a hidden rebel outpost in the Firnen mountains – and meets one of the rebel leaders: Coren Valmar. Tanner is brought in badly wounded and clinging to life.

Calen, Captain Kiron, and the others debate what route to take north and eventually settle on landing at Kingspass and crossing The Burnt lands instead of sailing the Lightning Coast.

Back in Durakdur, Dahlen and Belina meet with a dwarf who knows something about an assassination attempt on Daymon. But before the dwarf can reveal too much, he is poisoned. Dahlen kills the assassin, then goes in her place to meet with her superior. Belina saves Dahlen from death and learns there are assassins moving for every ruler of the Freehold, and Daymon. They both rush to stop the attempt on Daymon's life to find Ihvon bleeding out on the floor and all the assassins either dead or incapacitated.

Calen and his group arrive in Kingspass and find a room. They awake at night to an Urak attack on the city. Calen, Valerys, and the others fight alongside the Lorian defenders. Bloodmarked, Fades, and even a Shaman crash down on the city's defences, tens of thousands of Uraks flooding into the city. Calen and the defenders make their last stand. At the last moment, Kallinvar, Verathin and the other Knights of Achyron rush through the rift, which appears above the city, and drop from the sky. The knights help the defenders push back the Uraks. Grandmaster Verathin is killed by the Urak Shaman, which is, in turn, killed by Kallinvar.

As Kallinvar holds Verathin's body in his arms, Calen discovers Arden is, in fact, his brother, Haem.

THE EXILE

In the year 3068 After Doom, the fortress of Redstone is attacked by the Lorian Empire in an effort to stop a Valtaran rebellion before it starts. A young Dayne Ateres rescues his little sister, Alina, from Lorian intruders and sends her and Baren to wait in a safe cave, watched over by Marlin Arkon.

Accompanied by several Redstone guards, Dayne rushes to the defend the fortress's walls. In the Garden below, Dayne's father, Arkin Ateres, leads the elite Andurii against the besieging Lorians. While Dayne fights on the walls, his mother, Ilya Ateres, arrives astride her wyvern, Thandril, and turns back the attackers. A Dragonguard, Sylvan Anura, arrives on her soulkin, Aramel, and kills Thandril. There is no choice but surrender.

His hands bound, Dayne watches from the deck of a ship as three Dragonguard bathe the city of Stormwatch in dragonfire, burning and suffocating everyone within. A fight ensues on the ship, in which both Ilya and Arkin Ateres are killed by Sylvan Anura. It is revealed that Loren Koraklon, the head of House Koraklon, betrayed the Valtarans to the Lorians.

Sylvan Anura exiles Dayne and throws him from the ship with his hands bound. Dayne swims ashore. The cave he sent Alina, Baren, and Marlin to is empty. Dayne moved to his quarters to gather supplies and is surprised by Iloen Akaida, a young boy he works as a porter in the kitchens. He gives Iloen a knife and sends him to hide. Dayne decides not to damn Mera to his own fate and leaves without telling her. Sylvan Anura catches Dayne before he can leave. She reminds him if he ever returns, she will erase his bloodline, then throws him from the window of his father's study.

Two years later, Dayne is hunting down the people who were responsible for what happened that night in Redstone. He finds one, Harsted Arnim, in Winter's Keep. To avoid the keep's defenses, Dayne purposely starts a bar brawl to be brought to the dungeons below the keep. Once there, he makes his way to Harsted Arnim. He kills the man, exacting revenge, but not before finding out Sylvan Anura's name so he can continue his path of retribution.

After killing Harsted, Dayne goes to clean himself up in a local inn. While there, Belina Louna approaches him in the baths. She recognises him by the Sigil of House Ateres tattooed on his chest, and she has been sent to kill him. Instead of killing him, however, she gives him an offer: join her, help her kill those who control her, and she will in turn help him kill the people who harmed his family.

Five years later in 3075 After Doom, Dayne and Belina kill the last of the people who had tethered her to the Hand – an order of imperial assassins. The man they kill is Belina's father.

Dayne and Belina go to Gildor to meet an elf by the name of Therin Eiltris. They must first help Therin to free some of his kind from Lorian imprisonment, so he will bring them to meet the man who knows how to kill Sylvan Anura. They enter a seemingly abandoned fortress to discover the empire are running experiments on elves by carving blood runes into their skin. Many of the elves are twisted and broken. The group kills the Lorian Mages and soldiers running the facility and free the two surviving elves: a child, and an elf who has runes carved into her chest.

Therin takes Dayne and Belina to see Aeson Virandr – who was responsible for pushing Dayne's parents to start a rebellion. Dayne believes Aeson will lead him to Sylvan Anura and also show him how to kill her and the Dragonguard. But Dayne is shocked to find that Aeson has not only hunted down and killed two of the three Dragonguard who burned Stormwatch, but he has Sylvan Anura captive. After the death of Sylvan's soulkin, Aramel, the once-powerful woman is now blind and deaf, the heat has been pulled from her bones and an unyielding tremble has set into her hands. Dayne decides not to kill her, understanding that her fate – to live for years with only half a soul, unable to see or hear – is crueler, and therefore more fitting, than death would ever be.

Aeson then convinces Dayne not to rush straight home. He asks Dayne to let him put Valtara in a position to truly win its freedom. If Dayne starts a war now, Valtara will lose.

Five years later, Dayne receives a letter from Aeson telling him the time has finally come to go home. There is one name left on his list: Loren Koraklon.

Contents

PROLOGUE

Easterlock – Earlywinter, Year 3081 After Doom

Captain Teera Linar folded her arms, dragging a lungful of frost-touched air in through her nostrils. Even armoured in her full plate she felt the sharp bite of the storm winds moving inland from the Lightning Coast. Above her, clouds of obsidian-black blanketed the sky, blocking out all but a few stray strands of pale moonlight. Shadows flickered along the battlements, soldiers moving about in the dim glow of the lanterns that hung from poles.

Easterlock was ringed by two walls, each fronted by a spike-filled trench that sank thirty feet into the ground. The city's walls were manned night and day. Always ready, always waiting. The elves rarely strayed from the cover of Lynalion and only ever in small numbers. But Easterlock was the first line to hold back the tide should that ever change.

A dense layer of fog coated the land that lay before the city's outer walls, tendrils of grey snaking over the River Hurin, creeping ever closer to the city. The river was almost six hundred feet wide, running from the mountains of Mar Dorul and outward into the Veloran Ocean. No bridges traversed the river, no fixed point of crossing – it wasn't meant to be crossed.

On the other side of the river, the immense woodland of Lynalion rose through the thick fog, each tree climbing hundreds of feet, their branches sweeping outward, thick with leaves of dark green. The woodland was as vast as an ocean, stretching over a thousand miles around the foothills of Mar Dorul, hugging the coastline on the other side.

"It never gets any easier, does it?"

Teera turned at the sound of the familiar voice, nodding to Galow as the man ascended from the shadow-covered stairs and stepped into the light of the lantern that hung on a pole to Teera's left. Galow was no taller than her, with a thick beard of black stippled with white and a helm strapped firmly under his chin. He wore a steel breastplate emblazoned with the black lion of Loria, a sword at his left hip. He, too, was a captain of the guard, though he was ten years Teera's senior. He had been a captain when she had first arrived at Easterlock. She had only seen eighteen summers then. "Not when you never get any younger, old man. You've come from the inner wall?"

Galow nodded, casting his gaze out at the oozing layer of fog that crept across the ground before the city walls. "Aye, 'tis quieter there than a funeral. I left Duris in charge. Thought you'd appreciate the company. How goes the watch?"

Before Teera could answer, a shiver ran the length of her spine, a faint sound touching her ears, like a whistle in the wind. She tilted her head sideways. "Did you hear that?"

"Hear what?" Galow asked, raising an eyebrow.

"I... I'm not sure. Something." Teera unfolded her arms, stepping closer to the battlements, narrowing her gaze as she studied the creeping fog. She looked along the ramparts. Lanterns illuminated the length of the wall, spots of warm orange light stretching off into the distance until they were nothing but dim flecks, partly obscured by the silhouettes of the soldiers who huddled around them.

"The night's playing tricks on you, Teera." Galow laughed, clasping his hand on her shoulder.

"Maybe..." Teera continued to stare along the ramparts as she spoke, not bothering to shrug away Galow's hand.

"It's what this place does," Galow said, leaning against the battlement, staring out at Lynalion in the distance. "Here." Galow produced a small metal flask from within his cloak, taking a swig before passing it to Teera. "Something to warm the body and soothe the mind."

Teera took the flask, raised the opening to her nose. The smell of the sharp spirit burned her nostrils. She knew the noxious liquid would do little to soothe her mind, but she would take every drop of warmth she could find. Lifting the flask to her lips, she took a long draught, relishing the burn as the spirit slid down her throat. She tilted her head back and let out a long sigh, watching her breath mist in the air.

"That stuff isn't cheap, you know," Galow said, laughing. He snatched the flask out of Teera's hand, took another swig, then slid it back inside his coat.

"I know," Teera said, smiling. "That's why I drink yours..." Teera's voice trailed off, the hair on her arms and neck standing on end as she saw one of the lanterns go out further along the wall. Her heart stopped. Had she just seen that or was the night truly playing tricks on her?

"What is it?" Galow asked, following her gaze into the distance. A sense of urgency picked up in his voice. "What are you looking at?" As though in direct response to Galow's question, another light went out, another lantern snuffed. Then another, and another. "Did that just..."

"We need to sound the alarm!" Teera yelled, pulling at the horn that hung around her neck.

"Teera, hold on we need to—"

Teera whipped her head around at the sudden stop in Galow's words. She found herself staring into her friend's eyes as they bulged. Galow's hands were clasped either side of his throat, his fingers wrapped around the shaft of an arrow that had punched through his neck from right to left. He stood there for a moment, surprise painting his face, blood pouring over his fumbling fingers, his lips moving but no sound escaping his throat. Then, he stumbled sideways, the surprise in his eyes supplanted by fear before they rolled to the back of his head, and he fell from the ramparts.

Dread slithered through Teera's veins, her blood turning to ice as she watched her friend fall into the darkness. She staggered, resting her hand against the battlements, steadying herself. Taking in a deep breath, she pulled the horn to her lips and blew as hard as her panicked lungs would allow.

A chorus of horns answered her call.

After a few moments, the deep, sonorous ringing of the city bells echoed through the night, joined by the sound of armoured boots as the city's garrison mobilised. Thousands of soldiers emptied out into the streets, reacting to the alarm with an efficiency bred from repetition and time, flooding the ramparts of both the inner and outer walls.

Shouts and screams rang out all along the walls, lanterns going dark, soldiers plummeting to their deaths. Her mouth going dry, Teera pushed herself away from the battlements, standing to her full height as soldiers swarmed around her, bows gripped in their fists, swords at their hips, taking up their positions.

It took Teera a moment to gather herself, pushing the images of Galow from her mind. She cast her gaze over the flickering mass of torches that now filled the city and illuminated both the inner and outer walls.

"Steady!" A voice called in the night. "Hold your positions!"

Teera turned to see a tall man marching towards her. He had a face that looked as though it had been chiselled from rock, and a long black cloak with silver markings billowed behind him as he moved. "Captain Linar, report. What's happening?"

"Exarch Dradkir." Teera inclined her head, as was proper, shifting so some of the soldiers could take up position along the walls. "I…"

"Spit it out, Captain."

"I don't know, Exarch. Everything was quiet, and then… We've taken casualties from arrows. But visibility is too low to tell how many."

The Exarch narrowed his eyes, held Teera's gaze for a moment, then nodded. "Nock arrows!"

Dradkir strode over to the battlements, his eyes fixed on the fog-covered ground below. Teera didn't have to look to know that more Battlemages had taken up position along the length of the wall.

Orbs of light burst into existence across the landscape at the base of the walls, floating off the ground, slicing through the thick fog, illuminating the night. Teera's heart hammered against her ribs. Within moments, every inch of ground within a hundred feet of the city walls was bathed in white light as though it was mid-day. But there was nothing to be seen, no attackers, no army, only damp grass and shrubs.

The echoing clang of city bells pierced the heavy silence. But after a few moments, even the bells faded; the garrison was roused, the people sheltered.

Exarch Dradkir looked to Teera, but she was as perplexed as anyone else. She had seen the arrows. She had seen Galow fall to his death, blood spurting from his neck. She had seen the lights go out.

"Exarch!"

Both Dradkir and Teera turned at the sound of the soldier's voice. It took a moment for Teera to realise what the man was pointing at, but then she saw it. On the ground below, standing at the edge of the orbs' light, was an elf.

It was nearly impossible to gauge the elf's size or build, but it wore a full suit of smooth-flowing golden plate that glittered in the light of the orbs, a red cloak knotted at its shoulders. The elf held a teardrop shaped shield in its left hand that stretched from its neck to its knees, a long shafted battleaxe in its right fist.

"What's it doing?" one of the soldiers whispered.

"Waiting," Dradkir answered, causing the soldier who had spoken to jolt upright, straighten his back, and stare ahead. "But the more prudent question is what is it waiting *for*?" Dradkir stared at the elf for a moment, casting a cursory glance further along the ground. No other elves stood in the light; Teera had already checked.

"Should we wait?" Teera asked, glancing towards Dradkir.

Dradkir held Teera's gaze for a beat. Around him, the soldiers' erratic breaths misted in the air, their eyes fixed on the elf, their hands twitching on their bowstrings. "This is not the time to wait and see, Captain Linar. Draw and loose!"

The sound of hundreds of arrows being loosed cut through the air, and Teera watched their flight, the light from the baldír on the ground below dispelling any shadows. Anticipation knotted in her gut. The hairs on the back of her neck pricked when she saw the arrows parting before the elf, splitting like water breaking against the bow of a ship. One after another they plunged into the ground around the elf, leaving it unscathed and unmoved.

Fear set like ice in her veins. She had witnessed the Spark being used countless times. She had grown up around it. She had been trained around it. But it had only ever been the mages who had wielded its power. She had seen the Battlemages rip holes through enemy lines, Healers set broken bones, Craftsmages build bridges in minutes. But she had never seen an enemy wield the power of the Spark. She had never had to face it in battle.

As Teera's eyes remained fixed on the armoured elf, arrows studding the ground around it, more elves stepped from the fog-obscured darkness, their golden armour sparkling like stars in the white orb light. In a matter of moments, one became ten, became a hundred, became thousands.

Teera swallowed hard, her throat tightening. A shiver swept through her, starting in her chest then moving through her arms and legs, until even her fingers trembled. She could hear the shuffling of armoured feet around her, the mumbles and gasps.

"What are they waiting for?" Teera whispered, more to herself than anyone else, but she saw Dradkir glance towards her, trepidation in his eyes. That worried her even more. She had never seen Dradkir so much as flinch. In fact, she had never seen any Battlemage show even the slightest hint of hesitancy.

Whoosh.

Teera's blood turned to ice.

Whoosh.

She had heard that sound before, many times.

Whoosh.

But she had never heard it come from behind enemy lines.

The air felt heavy. The night was still. Nothing but breaths and wing-beats. Then the world shook.

A blood-chilling roar ripped through the sky. Teera's heart plunged into her stomach, her limbs stiffening. The dark erupted with a series of blazing flashes as orange-red fire poured over the ramparts, sweeping from east to west, snuffing out hundreds of lives in the blink of an eye.

It was only then Teera connected everything: why the elves had feigned the first assault and why they had waited. *They were drawing us out, pulling us onto the walls.*

All around her, soldiers scattered, screaming, shrieking, running for the stairs, knocking each other to their deaths. Teera stood rooted in place, her gaze fixed on the sky. There was no point in running. Two blazing orange eyes stared back at her, glistening in the light of the roaring fire as the great dragon plummeted, its jaws open wide. Wisps of flame formed in the creature's gaping maw, flickering.

Taking a deep breath, Teera exhaled through her nose, then closed her eyes.

Heraya embrace me.

CHAPTER ONE

OATHS AND BLOOD

Kingspass – Earlywinter, Year 3081 After Doom

The screams and howls of the dying filled the air as the incandescent light of dragonfire washed over the central plaza, casting shadows of the dead across the stone. The Bloodspawn were in full retreat, minds shattered at the sudden loss of their Shaman, the imperial soldiers cutting them down as they fled. But even as the chaos raged around Arden, it blurred at the edges of his vision, his gaze focused on one singular thing. "Little brother…"

Arden took a step towards Calen, a weightlessness filling his chest, his hands trembling. When Arden had been granted the Sigil, Calen had seen only sixteen summers. He had been a boy, bright-eyed and eager to learn, following Arden around like a shadow. But it wasn't a boy that stood before Arden now. Calen's shoulders had broadened, a stubbly beard now adorned his face, and he had grown taller. But the true difference in Calen was in the way he held himself, the way those at his side looked to him. Arden had seen how he had fought, carving through the Bloodspawn like a maelstrom of death, the dragon moving at his side, scales gleaming. Even now, his face coated in dirt and blood, his body looking as though he'd been to the void and back, his left arm hanging limp by his side, and the luminescent purple glow of his eyes fading, Calen still gripped his blade in his fist, defiant. He was a warrior. But more than that, he was the Draleid.

All this time, Arden had never thought to ask the Draleid's name. What had it mattered? It was inconsequential. The thought that it could have been Calen had never crossed Arden's mind. He had always hoped his family was all right. It was easier to imagine that they were living on without him. When the knights had stopped the Urak attack on The Glade, he had wanted to search through every single body, to know for sure who had died and who had lived. He had wanted it more than anything else in the world. But he had sworn an oath. *'If we save you, are you willing to forgo your past life and everything that holds you to the person you are now? Are you willing to bear the Sigil of Achyron? To follow his creed and serve The Warrior until the day you are taken from this world?'* Brother-Captain Kallinvar's words resounded in Arden's mind.

A gust of wind swept over him, spirals of dust and debris whipping into the air, fires flickering as the enormous frame of the white dragon dropped from the sky. The dragon alighted on the stone behind Calen, its claws crushing broken bodies, its black-veined leathery wings spread wide, lavender eyes fixed solely on Arden, weighing, measuring. The creature was the perfect blend of majesty and power. It stood at least thirty feet from head to tail, the orange-red glow of the city's fires glistening off its snow-white scales. Its body was layered with thick muscle that rippled with every movement, and ridges of horns framed its jaws and snout. Two frills ran from the base of its skull, down its back, and along its tail, which tapered off before turning to a spear-tip at its end. The creature stared at Arden with an intensity that left a nervous knot in his stomach, its neck craned over Calen's head, a deep rumble resonating from its chest.

Arden could hear people calling his name – Ruon, Lyrin, Ildris. He could hear them, but the words were muffled.

Calen took a step from underneath the dragon's shadow, his gaze boring into Arden, the defiance fading from his eyes, replaced by utter disbelief. In a fraction of a moment, all hesitancy evaporated from Calen's face and he dropped his sword, steel clattering against stone. No sooner had the blade hit the stone than Calen was running, slamming into Arden with a force that sent him stumbling backwards. Calen wrapped his one good arm around Arden, pulling him tight, resting his head on the chest of Arden's Sentinel armour, and for a moment Calen was the boy Arden had remembered. "Haem… you… you're alive."

Haem. Arden had not heard that name in such a long time. It had almost slipped entirely from his memory. A remnant of another life. A life he promised to leave behind.

Arden rested his chin on the top of Calen's head. He had always been far taller than Calen, but in his Sentinel armour he stood even taller again. As he looked down at his brother, a tangible pain ached in his chest, squeezing like a fist gripping his heart. Drawing a deep breath, he leaned into Calen's embrace, wrapping his arms around his brother. He released his breath in a sigh. "I've missed you. So much. I'm so sorry, Calen."

Even in his Sentinel armour, Arden could feel Calen pulling tighter and tighter, as though he was trying to squeeze the air from Arden's lungs. Arden closed his eyes, savouring every second before the moment was torn from him as he knew it would be, for this was no longer his place.

"How?"

Arden opened his eyes to see Calen staring up at him, his eyes blood-shot, his irises a pale purple in colour. *What happened to your eyes?* Arden pulled Calen in tight once more, letting out a sigh. Where could he even begin?

Before Arden could think to answer, a shiver rippled through him, emanating from the Sigil fused with his chest. It moved like a wave of ice, surging through his Sentinel armour, washing over his skin, filling his bones. He stumbled backwards, releasing Calen, his head spinning, pulse racing.

"Haem. What's wrong?"

Arden reached out, pushing Calen away, the sudden sensation shaking his knees and causing his balance to waver. But then, as quickly as it came, it was gone, replaced by a low thrum that resonated through his Sigil. The thrum had a source. He could feel it. Dazed, he turned away from Calen, his heart pounding against his ribs.

Lyrin, Ildris, and Ruon stood before him, other knights from The Sixth and The Third scattered around the plaza, stumbling through the mass of bodies. They all looked as shaken as he felt, their helms already receded into their armour, their eyes wide, bodies trembling. It was only then Arden's gaze fell on the origin of the thrum that resonated through each of them: Kallinvar.

Brother-Captain Kallinvar knelt where Arden had left him, Grandmaster Verathin's armourless body in his arms. It was strange to see Verathin's body that way. Unnatural, even. Grandmaster Verathin had been a tower of a man. Unyielding, unbending, unbreaking. Yet there he lay, lifeless, his soul sheared by a níthral, destined to wander the void restlessly, never to dine in Achyron's halls. It wasn't right.

Gradually, Arden's gaze moved from Verathin's body, to Kallinvar, the hairs on the back of his neck pricking up, the air fleeing from his lungs.

Where once Kallinvar's Sentinel armour had been identical to Arden's with overlapping plates of flowing green, golden ornamentation now trimmed the Sigil of Achyron on his breastplate, accented his pauldrons, and ran along the edges of his helm. The golden markings continued all over his armour, shimmering in the firelight.

Arden watched as the other knights dropped to one knee, putting a fist to their foreheads, then holding it to their chests, each bowing their heads, each uttering one word: "Grandmaster."

Arden followed suit, a vibration running through his armour-clad knee as it hit the stone. He brought his fist to his forehead, then held it across his chest, his eyes fixed on Kallinvar. "Grandmaster."

Arden watched as Kallinvar's helm turned to liquid metal, receding into his Sentinel armour, revealing the man's tear-streaked face and despondent, bloodshot eyes. Becoming the Grandmaster of the Knights of Achyron should have been Kallinvar's proudest day, but Arden could see only anguish and loss in his eyes.

For a few moments, all was silent. Even the men and women of the empire had stopped to watch with barely a murmur between them as the knights knelt. Men and women in leather armour; soldiers in full plate and coats of mail; warriors astride obsidian-black mounts, curved swords in their fists; a handful of Battlemages, cloaks billowing behind them. They stood, watching, their eyes wide and mouths ajar. Many had never laid eyes on a single knight in Sentinel armour. But on that night, they had watched near thirty fully-armoured knights drop from the sky, Soulblades shimmering. And now those knights knelt before them, witnessing the rise of Grandmaster Kallinvar.

Kallinvar lifted his head, his gaze lingering on Verathin's lifeless body for a few moments before taking in the scene before him. Letting out a subdued grunt, he lifted himself to his feet, nestling Verathin's body close to his chest like a mother would nestle a newborn babe. Kallinvar stumbled slightly, his body trembling. Out of the corner of his eye, Arden saw Ruon begin to rise, her face painted with concern, but she held, watching as Kallinvar regained his footing.

Arden was still kneeling, his fist pulled across his chest, his heartbeat thumping through his veins, when a shiver swept over him, tickling the back of his neck. A deep thrum resonated from his Sigil as a green orb flickered into existence before Kallinvar, spreading outwards, turning to deep black at its centre.

Arden rose to his feet at the sight of the Rift, glancing towards Calen who stared back at him, the white-scaled head of the dragon arching above him with pupils narrowed to black slits. Three emotions vied for control over Arden's heart: relief, regret, and pride. Relief in seeing that Calen still drew breath; that he had not been in The Glade that night the Bloodspawn attacked. Regret for not being there when Calen had needed him. And pride in seeing the man his little brother had become. A Draleid. A warrior of legend. A leader.

He wanted to pull Calen close and hold him until the walls crumbled around them. In truth, he had never thought he would lay eyes on his brother, or his family, again. And he had come to terms with that. He had made that choice when he accepted the Sigil. It had been that or death. But now, looking at Calen, seeing the wounds that laced his body and the dark circles that ringed his eyes, Arden's heart broke. His brother needed him. But he couldn't be what his brother needed.

"Arden."

Arden turned at the sound of Ruon's voice and the touch of her hand on his shoulder. As he did, he caught sight of Kallinvar walking through the Rift without a word or a glance, Verathin's body still in his arms.

"We need to go." Ruon's regret swam in her eyes. "Kallinvar needs us."

"I just…" Arden looked back at Calen, who simply returned Arden's stare. "I need more time, Ruon. I—"

"No." Ruon shook her head, her eyes cold and hard. "This is the choice you made, Arden. It is the choice we all made."

Arden nodded, his throat tightening. There was so much he wanted to say. So many things that needed to be said. So many questions that needed to be asked. But he had spoken his oaths. He had pledged his life to The Warrior.

"I'm sorry." Drawing in a deep breath, Arden cast one last look at Calen, then turned, following the other knights towards the Rift. "I promise I will come back."

"So that's it? You're just going to leave?"

Arden stopped at the sound of Calen's voice echoing through the plaza. Fury seeped into each word.

"They're dead, Haem. Mam, Dad, Ella, Faenir. They're all dead!" Calen's voice shook as he shouted, a tremble setting in.

Arden's heart stopped, numbness sweeping through his body, an iron grip closing around his throat. He turned back to Calen, his lungs struggling to drag in air. "Calen… I didn't know…"

"Where were you?" Tears streamed down Calen's cheeks. "I needed you… I still need you. Haem, I need you."

"Pain is the path to strength, Arden," Ruon whispered, resting her hand on Arden's shoulder, urging him to keep walking. "We fight for Achyron to protect the ones we love. That doesn't make it easy."

Gritting his teeth, Arden nodded. "I will be back, Calen. I promise."

Arden drew in a deep breath, turned. The Rift's icy embrace washed over him, his heart aching.

Pain is the path to strength.

KALLINVAR DROPPED TO HIS KNEES on the stone floor of the Heart Chamber as the other knights stepped through the Rift behind him. He could hear voices, echoing, calling to him. At the edges of his vision, he saw the Watchers rushing towards him, their motions panicked and frantic. But he ignored them; he ignored everything. Instead, he focused on the aching hollow in his chest and the emptiness of his hands.

He released his Sentinel armour, watching as the now gold-flecked, green metal turned to liquid around his fingertips and receded, flowing back towards his Sigil. As the armour melted away, Kallinvar's gaze remained on his empty hands, clean and untouched by blood. Only moments before, he had cradled his oldest friend's lifeless body to his chest, but now his hands were empty. Verathin's body belonged to the Rift.

CHAPTER TWO

FOUND AND LOST

Calen's hands shook as the rippling gateway of black and green collapsed in on itself, the air distorting around it as it flickered from existence. He could feel the cold paths his tears left as they rolled down his cheeks. White-hot anger seared through him, numbing the edges of his mind to the point that words deserted him, and he could do nothing but stare at the empty space where his brother had been, a tremble spreading through his chest with each breath.

Haem was alive. He had been right there. He had not been a dream or an apparition or some figment of Calen's imagination. Calen had heard his voice and felt his embrace. Watched him walk away as if it were nothing. As if *Calen* were nothing. In that moment, Calen felt more alone than he ever had. Memories of his family flashed across his mind. Faenir saving him from Fritz, Kurtis, and Dennet; Ella sitting with him on the porch before the Proving; his dad handing him his sword; his mam hugging him when she had stepped into the feast tent.

They were dead. Gone. Saying it out loud had hit him like a hammer in the gut. He would never see their faces again, never hear their voices. But of everything, he could never have prepared himself for watching his brother turn his back on him. Haem had seen him, held him, spoken to him. And then he left.

When Calen was a child, Haem had always been the one he looked to. The strongest, the kindest, the most caring. All Calen had ever wanted was to be like Haem.

As Calen's thoughts threatened to consume him, an ocean of warmth flooded through his mind from Valerys's, filling the cracks, soothing the pain. The dragon craned his neck down, nudging Calen's shoulder with the flat of his scaled snout, a low rumble resonating in his chest. Anger had always been the emotion that Valerys amplified most, the dragon's rage feeding off Calen's, giving them both strength. But as they stood in the plaza of the still-burning city, death and loss all around them,

Valerys's warmth tempered the fires of Calen's anger, allowing sorrow to seep through and touch depths Calen had never known existed.

Closing his eyes, Calen leaned his forehead against Valerys's snout, wrapping his right arm around the side of the dragon's head as his left arm hung limp at his side, the pain burning brighter as the rush of battle ebbed. He ran his hand along Valerys's scales, his fingers brushing the ever-growing ridges of horns that framed the dragon's face. Calen's voice shook as he spoke, starting as a hushed whisper, then fading to nothing. "He was right there…"

A low rumble resonated from Valerys's chest in response. The dragon pushed his head harder against Calen, trying his best to comfort his soulkin. Calen could feel the loss filling Valerys's mind as much as it did his own. The dragon felt the fullness of Calen's sorrow. Every moment of longing, every lingering doubt. And yet, every thought, every sensation, and every image that flowed through the dragon's mind was to ease Calen's pain, conveying a single message: *You will never be alone.*

They stood like that for a few moments, wrapped in each other's minds as though they were the world's only two occupants. And that was precisely how Calen would have stayed had he not felt a hand on his back.

Calen took a breath in through his nostrils as he opened his eyes, turning to see Erik standing before him. Erik looked as though he had been dragged through the void and back. Cuts and wounds laced his body. Dirt and blood crusted into his clothes and skin. Tarmon and Vaeril stood by Erik's side, neither looking any better off than Erik. But they were alive, and that was all that mattered.

"I know it's a stupid question, Calen, but are you all right?"

Calen shook his head, tears burning at the corners of his eyes. "No."

Erik reached out, pulling Calen into a tight embrace. After a few moments, he spoke. "Back in Ölm Forest, when I asked of your family, you never mentioned a brother."

"Because he died over two years ago." The words echoed in Calen's mind as he pulled away, a lump catching in his throat, his mouth going dry. *Haem is alive.* Calen should have felt relief, comfort. His brother was still alive. But instead, it was all he could do to keep his anger smouldering below the surface. He'd had so many questions, needed so many answers. And Haem walked away like it was nothing, leaving him there.

Before Erik could ask one of the many questions Calen knew he had, a familiar voice broke through the silence.

"Draleid."

Calen's first instinct was to reach for his sword as soon as Arkana Vardane's voice touched his ears, but he had dropped it when he ran to Haem. He reached out to the Spark, but the pulsating strands floated just out of reach, the drain sapping at him for even trying. His knees trembled, struggling to keep him upright. In the rush of battle, with Valerys's power flowing through him, he had felt almost unstoppable. But now, his blood cold in his veins, his body laced with cuts and wounds, his left arm dangling at his side, he was reminded just how weak he truly was.

"Don't take another step." Calen poured as much strength into his words as he could muster, feeding on the rage that burned within. He held his chin high, turning to face Arkana. The woman had promised she would let them leave unharmed, but people broke promises, and Calen's trust was thin at that moment.

As soon as he turned, Arkana dropped to one knee, bowing her head. Calen would have been surprised had he not felt Valerys looming over him, wings spread, teeth bared, a low rumble resonating from his throat. Even then, weak as he was, Calen could feel the dragon's heart thumping and anger swelling. He could sense the smell of blood thick in his nostrils. Valerys moved his head so close to Arkana that his breath swept her hair back over her shoulders.

Arkana lifted her head, her azure eyes striking against her pale, bloodstreaked skin. Despite the scene that lay before her, she didn't flinch. She held Calen's gaze. "I mean you no harm. I seek only to honour my word."

Calen's chest trembled as he looked down at the woman, his jaw tensing. Images of Artim Valdock flashed through his mind. Of the cell, the hunger, the emptiness. His rage redoubled; Calen could hear the low rumble resonating from Valerys's chest, the dragon's nostrils flaring.

Calen glanced back at Tarmon, who gave the slightest nod, grimacing in pain as he did. There was no council he trusted more than Tarmon's. He had no doubt Erik and Vaeril would follow him to the void and back, as he would them, but Tarmon always seemed to know the right course, even when the path ahead was clouded.

Taking a deep breath, he forced his rage down, burying it in a dark corner of his mind. When the Bloodmarked had leapt from the buildings, and the Urak horde had poured into the plaza, Arkana had charged at Calen's side. She had stood by them. And Calen knew in his heart that she had been willing to die alongside them as well. *She is not him. She is not Artim Valdock.* Even as his mind warned him away, Calen extended his hand, offering it to Arkana. "Then keep your word, Mage."

He thought he could a hint of a smile curl the woman's lips as she reached forward and took Calen's arm, wrapping her fingers around his forearm and pulling herself to her feet, a flash of pain passing through her eyes as she did.

"Thank you." The words took Calen by surprise. Of all the things he had expected to leave the woman's mouth, a thank you was not one of them. "Every soul within this city owes you a debt, Draleid. Had you and your companions not been here, we would have died long before those warriors arrived. It was an honour to fight by your side. Thank you for trusting me."

If the woman's thanks had caught Calen off guard, those words took the air from his lungs. An honour? Calen looked around the plaza, illuminated by the light of the moon and the dying fires. It was in ruins. Bodies lay everywhere, twisted and broken, armour torn to ribbons, blood staining almost every inch of shattered stone. They may have won, but it felt nothing like a victory.

His gaze slowly shifting from the dead, Calen watched as groups of Lorian soldiers surrounded them. Men and women in the red and black of Loria; soldiers garbed in heavy plate and coats of mail. Many carried bloody wounds and scars from the battle, pain etched into their faces, dirt and blood marring their skin. Twenty or so feet behind Arkana, a clutch of riders sat astride the Varsundi Blackthorns, their gazes fixed on Calen. At any other time, Calen would have feared for his life. But as he looked out at the soldiers, he felt no fear. Many closed their fists across their chests, nodding as his gaze met theirs. Calen could hear Tarmon's words in his head. *'Tonight, those men and women are not empire soldiers. They are just people. People who don't want to die. And they need us. They need you. They need a Draleid.'*

"I don't know where you are heading, Draleid, and it is better if I do not," Arkana continued, pulling Calen's attention back towards her. "All I know is that you arrived alone, burned a path through the Uraks, and escaped in the chaos as the creatures were routed."

Calen let out a soft sigh, shaking his head. He looked into Arkana's eyes, understanding the meaning of her words. "Thank you."

The woman nodded. "I only wish I could do more. But word of this battle will reach the other cities soon, and I cannot guarantee anything once that happens."

"You have already done more than I would have expected from any Lorian."

The words cut into Arkana. Calen could see as much, but she didn't argue, and he didn't apologise. "There is a house a few days' ride north of here, nestled into a small wood near the fork of the river Kilnír. The man who lives there will give you sanctuary, at least for a few days. His name is Rokka. Tell him I sent you. I would offer you to stay a night here, but even with everything you have done, it isn't safe. I will have horses arranged and left at the gates for you, along with food and supplies. If you stay along the river, you should be safe. The soldiers will follow the Uraks back towards the mountain, and I will set patrols through the night."

"I…" Calen couldn't find the words. This woman was his enemy. Her robes alone embodied everything he wanted to destroy, and yet there she was, treating him as though he were an old friend.

Arkana smiled, her eyes softening as though she had read his mind. "I will leave you to gather yourselves. The horses will be ready when you are."

With that, the woman gave a short bow before turning and striding towards a group of men and women who stood waiting for her, black robes draped over their shoulders. Battlemages. At the sight of the group, Calen once again felt the urge to reach for the Spark but stopped as each of them inclined their heads before turning and matching Arkana's stride.

"She was true to her word," Tarmon said as Calen turned to face his companions.

"She was." A look passed between Calen and Tarmon. It wasn't something that needed words.

"I still don't trust her." Erik limped closer to Calen, his left leg dragging a little, a gash along his calf.

"We don't have a choice." Calen grasped Erik's shoulder. "We'll take the horses and go. We don't yet have to decide whether we seek shelter with this… Rokka. For now, we can follow the river north and make for the Burnt Lands."

"As good a plan as any," Vaeril said, nodding at Calen. "But whatever we do, we will need to find somewhere to rest and lick our wounds. If we enter the Burnt Lands in this condition, there is no chance we will emerge on the other side."

"Agreed."

Calen turned to Valerys, patting the scales on the right side of the dragon's neck. "You will need to fly alone," Calen said, tracing his hand along the dragon's neck and under his winged forelimb. Valerys had gotten so big that Calen actually had to duck beneath the dragon's wing to reach the long wound of fused scales that ran from just below Valerys's right wing, along his side, and down to the joint of his hind leg. A shiver ran down Calen's spine as the memory of purple lightning crashing into Valerys's side filled his mind. The pain. "You're not strong enough to carry us both."

A rumble of disagreement drifted from Valerys. The dragon snarled as he craned his neck around, nudging Calen with his head.

Calen pushed down on the throbbing wound in the dragon's side, wincing as Valerys whimpered, their pain shared. Valerys let out another snarl, but Calen rested his forehead against the flat of the dragon's snout. "I'm sorry," he whispered, running his hand along horns that trimmed Valerys's jaw. "But you're too stubborn to admit when you're hurt. You're not strong enough to carry me."

Valerys snorted, pushing his snout into Calen once more, baring his teeth.

"Fly north along the river. Find a place to sleep for the night. Don't go too far. I'll find you."

Were it up to Calen, he would have climbed onto Valerys's back in a heartbeat, but he could feel the dragon's strength ebbing. Even aside from the wound, the battle had taken a lot from him. He wouldn't make it past the city walls with Calen on his back.

"Go, Valerys. Haryn asatrú en mir." *Have faith in me.*

For a moment, Calen thought Valerys might continue to argue – the dragon was certainly stubborn enough – but then a defiant acquiescence touched his mind. A jolt of pain struck Calen as the dragon stepped backwards, spread his wings, and lifted into the air, the light of the dying fires glimmering on his scales.

"Is he all right?" Erik asked, his gaze following Valerys's flight until the dragon disappeared into the clouds above.

"He's weak. He needs rest." Calen looked towards Vaeril, who inclined his head.

"I will do my best to heal what I can when we find him, Draleid. But I must recover my own strength first."

Calen nodded. "Du haryn myia vrai, Vaeril." *You have my thanks.*

Vaeril gave a weak smile, inclining his head once more.

Calen tilted his head back and let out a sigh, grunting as a flash of pain ignited from a wound in his side. Valerys wasn't the only one who needed rest. Calen was tired enough to sleep for days on end, and he had no doubt that he could eat enough food to fill the belly of a horse. He cast a cursory glance across the ground, his stomach twisting as his gaze passed over the ocean of death and blood that filled the plaza before finally finding what he was looking for: his sword. Walking past the others, Calen knelt beside the sword his father had given him. The intricate spirals that ornamented the blade scintillated in the ebbing firelight, dulled only slightly by the blood that coated the steel. He wrapped his fingers around the emerald-green handle, feeling the familiar touch of the leather against his skin. For a moment, he was back in The Glade. Back in his father's forge the day Vars had given him the sword. *'There is no need to thank me, Calen. You have filled me with more pride than I ever thought possible. The man you have become is thanks enough.'*

Calen's grip tightened on the handle of the sword. He could feel his eyes welling up once more. Shaking his head, he rubbed the corner of his eye against his shoulder, then wiped both sides of the blade against his trousers, taking off as much of the blood and dust as he could. Standing, he slotted the sword back into the scabbard at his hip. "Let's get moving. We still need to gather our things from the Cosy Daisy."

As Calen made to turn, Vaeril grasped his wrist, a look of concern on the elf's face as he looked Calen over.

"I'm fine," Calen said, shrugging Vaeril away. But the elf simply gave Calen a knowing look. "I'm not fine. But I can hold until morning. You need rest."

Vaeril's eyes were heavy and tired, but he shook his head. "Your arm is dislocated. We need to reset it before we do anything else."

Calen grunted as he attempted to move his arm. Reluctantly, he nodded. "All right. But anything else can wait."

The simple fact the elf didn't argue was a sign of just how much the battle had taken from him. "Lie on the ground."

MADAME OLMIRA HAD ACTUALLY SMILED at each of them when the group returned to the Cosy Daisy. Calen had been surprised the muscles in the old woman's face remembered how to form such an expression. Judging by the glassy look in her eyes and the drunken stupor of the other patrons, Calen had guessed the woman had been drinking from the moment they left the inn.

The group didn't linger in the Cosy Daisy. They stayed long enough to gather their supplies into their satchels and head back towards the central plaza, then onwards to the northern gate where the Uraks had destroyed the section of wall. It wasn't as if Calen had much to carry; his satchel, the coat and spare clothes Alleron had gifted him, the coin purse – which Alleron had also gifted him – along with the pendant and letter he had found in the abandoned dwarven city of Vindakur. He still hadn't figured out if the pendant and the letter were of any use, but something told him they were important. He just didn't know for what.

As the group made their way down the long street, Calen felt a physical pain aching in his chest, his heart twisting as his eyes fell on the sheer number of the dead. It was the same street they had retreated down when the wall had collapsed. The smell of burnt flesh and leather clung to the air, heavy as fog. The stone was a mixture of black char, blood, and shards of bone. The mangled bodies of men and Uraks alike decorated the ruined path, their bodies twisted and burnt, some barely recognisable as to what they once were. *So many dead…*

Without a word between them, the group trudged through the long corpse-filled street, the fetor of death filling their nostrils, their silence only broken by the tortured cries of those clinging to life. After they traversed the small chasm Arkana and the mages had created with their lightning during the retreat, they stepped into the square that fronted the city gates.

If Calen had thought the plaza destroyed, he didn't have words to describe the devastation before him now. Men and women, some in the colours of the empire, others in simple shirts, coats, and nightgowns, ran about, pulling soldiers from beneath rubble, carrying the injured on stretchers of wood and tarp, and releasing those who could not be saved from their pain. Each of the statues that had once bounded the grass periphery of the square lay shattered, indistinguishable from the rest of the rubble.

Past the dead and the dying stood the broken remnants of the city walls. The gates themselves still stood, the pair of crenelated bulwarks framing the massive arch. But the section of wall to the left of the gates lay in ruins, the moonlight illuminating a mound of crumpled stone.

"They will be helpless if the Uraks return." Calen moved his gaze along the walls as the group passed through the gates, noticing other collapsed sections that must have come down after the first blast.

"They will," Erik said, following Calen's gaze. "But if they don't have any Craftsmages left alive in the city to repair the walls, I'm sure some will be sent by ship. If not, I won't cry over spilt Lorian blood."

"Blood is blood." Calen was taken by surprise at his own anger as he rounded on Erik. He slowed his breathing, shaking his head. "These people aren't responsible for the suffering the empire has caused," Calen said, gesturing out at the men and woman who lay weeping over their dead. "They are burying their children, their fathers and mothers. Theirs sisters... brothers..." Haem's face flashed in Calen's mind, but he shoved it away, buried it. "They suffer too."

"I'm sorry." Understanding filled Erik's eyes as he looked over the square. "You're right."

"Come on," Calen said, resting his hand on Erik's shoulder. "We all need rest."

Just as Arkana had promised, the horses were tethered to a fence no more than twenty feet from the outside of the gates, saddle bags brimming. Four bay geldings, each standing at least seventeen hands tall, coats sheening in the soft light of the moon.

"She holds to her word again," Tarmon said, running his hand along one of the horse's muzzles, touching the flat of his head against its cheek. "And these are no pack horses either," he said, pulling away from the horse and patting its neck. "They're fine animals."

"Hidranians," a small voice said, a young boy emerging from behind the farthest horse. He could not have seen more than fourteen summers. His hair was black as night. The beaming smile on his face seemed at odds with the misery within the city walls. "My mistress told me to tell you that her mistress says thank you. Although, I don't know why her mistress didn't just say it herself."

On any other day, Calen might have laughed at the boy's candour, but not this day. Calen let out a grunt, a flash of pain tweaking in his ribs. "Tell your mistress she has my thanks."

"Will do, m'lord."

The boy was about to make himself scarce when Vaeril called out. "Child, have you any need of a horse?"

The boy froze, his eyes flitting from Vaeril, to Calen, to Tarmon, then to Erik, and back again. Calen knew the look of confusion on the boy's face. He knew it well. It was the same look he was sure he had given his mother every time she offered him something too good to be true. Were these horses a gift, or a trap?

"I ehm…" The boy's eyes narrowed at Vaeril, his back straightening. "I was told to run if I ever saw an elf."

A flash of anger rose within Calen, but Vaeril's face was the picture of calm.

"We are often told to fear the things we don't understand," the elf said, untethering the horse from the fence. He rested his head against the flat of the animal's cheek, whispering something to it, before leading it towards the boy. "But it is from those things we learn the most."

The boy tilted his head, his expression shifting, more than a hint of scepticism filling his eyes. "What do I have to do in return?"

The elf looked down at the boy for a moment, contemplating, then held out the reins. "Take care of him, feed him, bring him water when he is thirsty, and give him shelter. Understood?"

"That's all?" the boy asked, his eyes narrowing even further.

"That's all."

The boy nodded, still seeming slightly hesitant at a deal that was too good to be true. "I'll take good care of him, I promise."

"On your honour?"

"On my honour," the boy said, stuttering.

"Where I come from, there is nothing more important than your honour. But honour is not determined by the perception of others. It is in how you see your own deeds. Treat him the way you believe he should be treated." Vaeril reached down, handing the reins to the boy. "You should never mount an animal without first knowing their name. Without forming a bond. His name is Elminsûl. It means 'heart's pillar', or 'pillar of the heart'. But you can call him Min if you like."

"Min," the boy repeated, staring at the horse that towered over him. "I like it." He took the reins, patting the horse on its muzzle, then nodded and made to leave. He stopped and turned back towards Vaeril, bowing his head. "My lord elf… thank you."

With that, the boy led the horse back through the gates, the clip-clop of hooves slowly swallowed by the crackling of fires and the wails of the dying.

"Oh," Erik said, swinging himself up into the saddle of his horse. "My lord elf?"

42

A melancholy smile rested on Vaeril's face as he pulled his gaze from the boy and looked up at Erik. "The damage between our two peoples runs deep here. Children can be taught to hate, but they can also be taught to think. I have no use for a horse. I simply hope the gift gives him something to think upon."

The sound of horse hooves against the stone drew Calen's attention back towards the gates.

Seven riders approached them, armoured in dark steel, curved swords strapped to their hips, their helms tied to the saddles of enormous obsidian-black mounts. Blackthorns. Even amidst the ruin and destruction of the city, the horses somehow lost none of their majesty. Their black coats shimmered in the moonlight, heavy muscle rippling with each step. Before him, unobscured by the rush of battle, they seemed somehow even more gargantuan. He was now certain he had been correct in his initial judgement before the battle; the horses were at least nineteen hands tall, some of them even larger. The crest of the animals' shoulders easily stood as tall as Calen, some even higher.

"Maybe the mage changed her mind," Erik whispered, his eyes fixed on the advancing cavalry, his hand hovering near his sword.

The rider at the head of the group looked to have seen nearly fifty summers. Patches of greyish white dappled his thick head of dark hair, dried blood stained his scarred face, and he held himself with the composure of a man who had seen more battles than warm meals.

Calen fixed his gaze on the man, his hand dropping to the thick coin pommel of his sword. A sense of calm touching him as his fingers brushed the steel. He could feel Valerys in the back of his mind, the air rolling over his scales. The dragon wasn't far. *Wait.* A roar of defiance was Valerys's only reply as the dragon swept around, riding the currents of wind back towards the city.

Back through the gates, Calen could see some of the people in the square lift their heads to the sky, searching for the source of the roar. He wrapped his fingers around the leather handle of his sword, a knot tightening in his chest. Both Vaeril and Tarmon did the same, and Calen could feel the elf reaching out to the Spark.

To Calen's surprise, the lead rider inclined his head, fixing his gaze on Calen, greeting him with a gruff, "Draleid."

The other six riders followed suit, inclining their heads towards Calen and calling him by his title before riding into the night, their obsidian mounts blending with the darkness.

The air left Calen's lungs in a heartbeat, as though a hundred coiled ropes had just come loose. He lifted his hand from his sword and rested his palms on his knees, pulling air into his lungs.

"Come," Tarmon said, heaving himself into the saddle. "It's best we leave this place."

CALEN WASN'T SURE HOW LONG they had been riding – maybe an hour. Barely a word had been exchanged between them as they rode through the dark. The constant *clip-clop* of the horses' hooves becoming nothing more than a dull drone in the back of Calen's consciousness, blending seamlessly with the burbling of the river that flowed to his right, dark water rushing over smooth stones.

Calen closed his eyes, gripping the reins in his right hand, his left arm tucked against his body. His shoulder burned with a dull pain that twinged with every step the horse took. He swayed in the saddle, moving with the motion of the horse, not having the strength to keep himself steady. He didn't need his eyes to find Valerys. He could feel the dragon's soul pulling him, drawing him in. They weren't far apart now.

Over and over, Calen played the same scene in his mind: Haem stopping for a moment before walking through that shimmering gateway. His brother was alive. All this time. More questions took residence in Calen's mind than there were flakes of snow in all Drifaien. But one rose above them all. *Will I ever see you again?*

"Is it much further?" Erik's weary voice pierced through the monotony of clopping horse hooves and running water.

Calen let out a soft sigh before opening his eyes. "Just ahead," he said. He could feel Valerys's soul pulsating from a dense patch of trees that hugged the river ahead and to the right. The dragon's heart beat with a slow thump, pain burning in his side.

Erik only grunted in response.

As they reached the trees, Calen slid from the saddle, stumbling as his feet hit the ground, a jolt of pain running up through his arm. He groaned.

Leading his horse into the clutch of trees, Calen glanced around, looking from Vaeril, to Erik, to Tarmon. Dirt and blood crusted their clothes and matted their hair. They each looked like they could sleep for weeks. They had nearly died. And were it not for those warriors who fell from the sky – for Haem – they likely would have. And it was Calen who had brought them to Kingspass. Brought them on a wild goose chase. He wasn't even sure Rist was in Berona. That was just where Aeson and Therin had said he would likely have been taken. The thought of it left a sour taste in Calen's mouth. When he had told them he was travelling north to find Rist, none of them had even hesitated. They had stood by him. And in return, he had almost cost them their lives.

No more than fifty feet inside the dense wood, they found Valerys curled up, his wings folded, his snout resting on the ground, his lavender eyes watching them. Calen could feel the pain surging through Valerys's side with every draw of his breath.

Letting go of the horse's reins, Calen dropped to his knees beside Valerys, resting his forehead against the flat of the dragon's snout. "I'm here."

A low rumble resonated from Valerys's throat, and comfort touched Calen's mind.

"The sun will rise soon." Tarmon tethered his horse to a nearby tree before doing the same to Calen's without a word of complaint. "We should get some rest. It will take at least two days to reach the house the Battlemage spoke of. Even with horses."

"Are we really going to keep trusting her?" Erik unfurled his wool-lined sleeping sack, unbuckling his sword belt from his shoulders. "I say we just keep going."

"She's kept her word so far." Tarmon shrugged. "Get some sleep. We can decide our course when we wake." With that, Tarmon turned his attention back to the horses, inspecting the contents of the saddlebags. He rummaged through the bags strapped to his own horse and produced strips of dried meet, some hard cheese, and some bread, passing them around to the others. "Eat. We'll need the strength."

Erik grunted and took some of the food from Tarmon, chewing on a strip of meat, shuffling himself into his sleeping sack. He let out a long sigh. "I would do horrible things for a fresh meal. Horrible, horrible things."

Calen let out a soft laugh and unfurled his sleeping sack beside Valerys. He climbed into the sack and lay with his head resting against Valerys's hind leg, ignoring the aches and pains that assaulted his body. A sense of calm washed over Calen as Valerys's wing extended over him, blocking out all but the faintest glow of moonlight. *Am I doing the right thing?*

CHAPTER THREE

ONCE MORE INTO THE DARK

The Darkwood – Earlywinter, Year 3081 After Doom

Dann leaned forward, patting the side of Drunir's neck, the touch of the horse's hair soft against his fingers. He could feel the apprehension radiating from Drunir. Those kinds of things were easy to sense in animals: emotions. It was part of the reason Dann figured he understood animals more than people most of the time; they were always clear about what they felt and what they wanted. And right then, as they trotted down the sloping hill, the sun high in the cold sky, an endless ocean of dark green before them, Dann couldn't help but agree with Drunir's unease.

The Darkwood didn't look as menacing as it had the first time Dann had been there – not arriving in the dead of night had a lot to do with that – but still, it wasn't a particularly inviting scene. Even in the light of day, the dark forest still sat beneath a blanket of greyish-black thunderclouds, streaks of lightning tearing through the skies above the dense canopy. Dann had heard the stories, of course. The voidspawn. The monsters. The living forest that consumed human flesh.

He hadn't spent long enough within the confines of the woodland to know truth from fiction, but in the short time he had spent beneath the forest's aphotic canopy, he had taken an Urak's spear through his shoulder – which didn't exactly lead to fond memories. Vaeril had healed that up nicely. But of course, the Fade had ruined that. Dann lifted his hand, touching his fingers to the leather of his coat, tracing over his collarbone and up along his shoulder where the Fade's lightning had scarred his flesh.

"Are you well?"

"Hmm?" Dann shook himself from his thoughts as Therin drew up beside him, his hands resting either side of his horse's neck. That was a question Dann needed to ask Therin – Dann loved asking Therin questions, just to see the irritation on his face – why did Therin ride horses when the other elves didn't? He had intended to ask Alea, but he was only just beginning to get back onto her good side. It would be better to tread carefully in that regard.

"You look troubled." Therin raised an eyebrow.

"Well, I'm not exactly excited about coming back to this place. It didn't go so well for me last time, did it?" Dann glanced down towards his shoulder, pouting.

"How's it feeling?"

"Not too bad," Dann said with a weak smile, tapping his fingers against the outside of his coat. "Can't feel a thing where the scars are, but I've got full motion."

Therin turned down his bottom lip. "That's not bad at all. You're lucky. Few people walk away from a Fade's lightning."

"You know, I'd been searching for a word to describe myself recently, and 'lucky' is just what I'd been looking for."

Both Dann and Therin let out a laugh. Therin shook his head as he looked back at the Darkwood before them. Hearing Therin laugh was a rare thing – it didn't quite match the joy of irritating the elf, though.

"Are *you* all right?" Dann couldn't help but notice the shift in Therin's demeanour as the elf looked out at the woodland. An uneasiness had set over the group since Lyrei and Aeson's argument near Argona. Therin, for his part, had become quieter than usual. But Lyrei hadn't spoken a single word.

Therin nodded, giving a weak smile. "All I've ever wanted was to do right by my people. But what is right is almost never easy." Therin looked towards Alea and Lyrei, who walked in silence about twenty feet ahead, their hoods drawn, green cloaks rippling in the wind, white wood bows strapped across their backs. Aeson rode beside the two elves, with Baldon walking beside him. The Angan's willowy fur-covered arms swept back and forth, his legs covering large swaths of ground in long strides. Dann still wasn't entirely sure what to make of the creature. Every word that passed Baldon's lips sounded as though it was foreign to his tongue. One thing Dann knew he would never get used to was waking up and seeing a wolf the size of a war horse sitting beside the campfire.

"Therin," Dann said, pulling his gaze from the shapeshifter, "the night Lyrei and Aeson argued, what was that word Lyrei called you – Astyr... Astyr something?"

"Astyrlína," Therin said with a sigh, his gaze not shifting from Alea and Lyrei. "It is the name given to those who retreated to Lynalion, leaving the rest of the continent to their own devices. It means 'Faithless'."

Dann nodded to himself, gazing towards Aeson, who sat silent in his saddle. Up ahead, the trees of the Darkwood seemed to grow taller the closer they got, casting a shadow over the land before them. They had to be at least a hundred feet tall. "And what Aeson said? What did that mean? Lyrei hasn't spoken since."

"Aeson said something he should not have." Therin let out a sigh. He was flipping a small, round-backed knife along his fingers. "*Din haydria er fyrir.* He told her that her honour is forfeit."

"That's it?" Dann looked at Therin in bewilderment. "She hasn't spoken in nearly two weeks because he said she has no honour? If I acted like that, I wouldn't ever be speaking. I'd be a mute. Silent as a drowned frog."

Therin raised an eyebrow. "Are you sure that would be a bad thing?" A smile touched his lips before fading. "Honour means something different to elves. It is the cornerstone of everything we are. To be told your honour is forfeit is akin to being told that you do not exist. If Alea were to say it to Lyrei, it would hurt, but she could disregard it with rational thought. But from Aeson, a Rakina whose honour she believes to be above her own, it is a hammer blow. For a man of such honour would never say something of that magnitude unless it were true."

"But… why does she remain silent? What does it gain?"

Therin laughed, patting his horse's neck. "Do you ever run out of questions?"

"Does a bear shit in the woods?"

"Yes."

"Well then." Dann hadn't realised until after he had spoken that his analogy made little to no sense, but he was committed already. Better just to see it through.

Therin sighed, shaking his head. "Lyrei is… reflecting. For lack of a better word. Our people call it *Holmdúr.* It means to search within oneself. She must think on Aeson's words, decide whether she has acted without honour, and if so, find a way to regain it."

Dann nodded, his enthusiasm for the conversation waning as the shadow of the Darkwood swept over them, the sun's light retreating as the forest engulfed them. Dann straightened in the saddle, shivering. "I hate this place…"

Nothing had changed since the last time Dann had set foot within the Darkwood's bounds. It took no more than a few minutes for the faint glow of the sun to disappear entirely, absolute darkness taking its place. And with the darkness came the scents and sounds of the ancient woodland. The heavy aroma of earth and damp, accented by what Dann knew could only be the smell of animal shit. The creaking and groaning of branches meshed with the rushing wind, the snap and crack of twigs, the rustling of leaves. He broached no complaints when two orbs of white light formed in front of him, one floating beside Aeson at the head of the group, the other floating to Dann and Therin's left. The pure white light from the orbs – *baldír*, Dann was fairly sure they were called – lent the forest an otherworldly glow, casting shadows in all directions, illuminating beady eyes that hid in the darkness. In this particular case, otherworldly was not a positive trait.

As the forest grew denser, the undergrowth rising high, gnarled roots twisting and lifting from the forest floor, the group dismounted, leading their horses by the reins. Alea and Lyrei led, moving through the forest with ease. Dann had a feeling the two elves would have been able to find their way through the woodland even if they were blindfolded and bound. Such was the effortless grace with which they moved, never showing even the slightest hesitation as they chose their path.

Barely a moment passed where Dann couldn't hear the snap of twigs and branches in the darkness, the rustle of trodden leaves, the low growls of creatures he could not see but knew to fear. Whether or not the stories were true, Dann was certain that Uraks were not the scariest things lurking in the depths of this woodland.

"How much farther to Aravell?" Aeson asked, dropping back beside Dann and Therin.

"Two full days of walking, at least," Therin replied, light from the baldír causing his silver hair to scintillate as though it were a gleaming coat of mail. "We should rest soon. Alea, Lyrei, and I can take shifts on guard. We should make it to the first line of *Nithrandír* by the time we grow weary tomorrow. It would not be wise to be caught deeper in the Aravell without their protection."

"Agreed," Aeson said with a nod and a sigh. He ran his tongue across his teeth, then marched on ahead, calling to Alea and Lyrei.

"Do I want to know?" Dann asked, a shiver running through him at the idea of anything that might strike fear in the hearts of Therin and Aeson – an elven mage and a centuries old warrior who had once been bonded to a dragon.

Therin shook his head. "If I say run, just run."

"Therin, that doesn't make me feel any better."

"It wasn't meant to."

DANN SAT ON THE THICK, unearthed root of a nearby tree, his elbows rested on his knees, his head bent over, eyes closed. Sweat streaked his forehead, rolling down his cheeks and dripping from the tip of his nose.

Hours had passed before the group had finally stopped to set up camp for the night. How many hours, he wasn't sure. Tracking the passage of time was near impossible without the rise and fall of the sun. If he were to go with his gut, he would have guessed five or six, but it just as easily could have been three or ten. Keeping up with Aeson, Baldon, and the three elves was no mean feat. His lungs felt as though they had been lit on fire. With a heavy sigh, he lifted his elbows from his knees and leaned backwards, stretching out the knotted lumps of muscles along his spine.

He glanced at Drunir, who stood with the other horses, happily drinking from a brook that cut through the forest floor at the edge of the camp. The horse was a fine animal. Fifteen hands, maybe fifteen and a half, with a black mane and a black coat dappled with grey and white – a colouring Dann had never seen before. The horse was quick, powerful, and even as it stood by the brook in the heart of the Darkwood, Dann could see little fear in its eyes or in the language of its body. Unease, yes, but no fear. Aeson's and Therin's horses moved around anxiously, unsettled, their ears flicking back and forth, the occasional snort leaving their nostrils. The creatures had every right to be fearful. This place set an unease into Dann's bones.

A few feet away, by a small clearing at the base of a tree, Baldon sat with his fur-covered legs crossed, his arms resting in his lap; he had been sitting like that since they set up camp. From what Aeson and Therin had told Dann, the Angan could communicate with their kin from over a hundred miles away, and as long as there were enough of them in a long chain, they could extend that distance endlessly, like a chain of messengers. Dann didn't understand how that could even be possible, but then again, he didn't understand most things that had happened in the past year.

How in the gods did I get here? Dann turned his gaze from Baldon, running his fingers through his sweat-soaked hair, slicking it back over his head. If someone had asked him a year ago where he thought he would have been now, roaming through the Darkwood with three elves, a fallen Draleid, and a half-man-half-wolf thing in search of Calen, who was now also a Draleid wouldn't have even been a contender. It sounded ridiculous. Nobody had believed him that time he had seen a horse with a horn growing from its head or the time he had dropped a tankard only to catch it on his foot without spilling a drop, so why in the gods would anyone ever believe *this* story?

Dann jerked backwards as a fire burst into life before him, casting a warm orange glow over the forest floor. "A little warning next time?"

Therin sat on the ground beside the fire, to Dann's right. There was a smug look on the elf's face, as usual. When Dann had first met Therin properly, after they had gone back to The Glade, the elf had been colder than a naked morning in the snow. Dann could count on one finger the number of times the elf had smiled. But since the battle at Belduar, Therin had seemed… warmer. He even told jokes. Not many, but some. Progress was progress.

"Are we *sure* Berona is where Calen is going?" Dann stared into the newly born fire before lifting his gaze towards Therin. He had asked the question four or five times already, but it wouldn't hurt to ask again. They had been riding across Illyanara like headless chickens since leaving the Lodhar Mountains, and all Baldon had been able to tell them was the general direction Calen had been travelling when he had left Drifaien.

Therin looked towards Aeson, who sat beside the fire, his legs folded beneath him. Alea and Lyrei were off gathering fresh fruit and berries – they knew the forest flora better than any of them.

"We're as sure as we can be." Aeson stared absently at something on the ground. He lifted his head. "According to Baldon, Asius and Aneera helped Calen and the others – Erik amongst them – escape from Drifaien. They then boarded a ship heading north, around the Arkalen coast. My contacts in Drifaien informed Aneera that Calen was intending to rescue someone."

"Rist."

Aeson nodded. "When Rist was first taken, we suspected he would be brought to the High Tower in Berona to be trained by the Circle. If I were to place a bet, it would be that Calen is heading there."

"Then that's where we go."

"It is. If we can cut through the Aravell, we may reach them before they make it to the Burnt Lands." Aeson let out a sigh, and Dann could see the man's jaw clenching. "I don't understand how Erik could be so senseless. There is more at stake than one man's life. If something happens to Calen, then all that we've worked for could be destroyed."

A knot twisted in Dann's chest. All he wanted was to find Calen and Rist. If Calen was trying to get to Rist, then finding Calen could kill two birds with one stone – without the killing, of course. Dann's only other worry, though, was what Aeson would do if they found Calen. Dann didn't think for a second that Aeson would let them travel north to look for Rist, never mind travelling through the Burnt Lands. That was a bridge they would have to cross when they came to it. For now, Dann just needed to focus on not dying. Which he figured would not be as easy as it sounded.

He looked up at the sound of rustling leaves to see Alea and Lyrei stepping into the light of the fire, their arms full of strange fruits and berries, a bulging sack over Alea's shoulder.

Alea greeted them all as she sat beside Dann. But Lyrei said nothing, her gaze never leaving the forest floor.

Silence descended as they ate, the flickering light of the fire casting eerie shadows around the camp. Dann would get little sleep that night, the sounds of the forest serving only to fuel his restless thoughts.

The snapping of branches. The howls, the snarls, the whispers that drifted on the wind.

Brushing imaginary dirt off his trouser legs, Dann rose to his feet. "I'll take first watch."

Chapter Four

War Under the Mountain

Durakdur – Earlywinter, Year 3081 After Doom

Dahlen drew in a trembling breath, holding the air in his lungs as long as he could before setting it free. He stood by the window in Daymon's office, one hand resting against the wall, his eyes closed, images flashing through his mind: dragonfire pouring over Belduar; the Heart of Durakdur filled with the dead and dying; Ihvon lying on the floor, his skin cold and pale. Muffled sounds drifted around Dahlen, voices, footsteps, the clamour of people arguing. It all sounded as though he were underwater.

His throat tightened, his breathing becoming rapid, images of death and blood still dominating his mind, clanging steel and screams of the dying reverberating in his ears. His shoulders trembled as the smell of charred flesh touched his nostrils. *It's not real.*

"Dahlen."

Dahlen pushed his hand harder against the wall upon which he leaned, the stone smooth against his fingertips. He clenched his jaw, his chest shaking.

"Dahlen."

Focus. They need you. Give your mind a task.

Dahlen drew in another deep breath, holding it in his chest.

"Dahlen!"

A hand rested on Dahlen's shoulder, and the sounds around him became crisp and clear: Belina's voice calling to him, a man and a woman arguing, the sounds of servants scurrying about the room. He opened his eyes and turned.

The room was chaos. Ihvon lay on a stretcher of cloth and steel near the centre of the space. His blood had seeped into the cloth, staining it a murky crimson. His skin was pale, almost white, but there was still a near-imperceptible rise and fall to his chest. Two healers – a stout, black-haired man and a red-haired woman – fussed over him, while servants darted about with strips of cloth, wet rags, and small tins of what could only be brimlock sap.

Nearer to the door, another man, the assassin who had survived his encounter with Ihvon, lay flat on his back, his face coated in blood, his nose shattered, shackles around his wrists. Dahlen loathed keeping the man alive, but it was the prudent thing to do. He might have information they needed. And in what was to come, information would be worth its weight in gold.

Daymon was seated on the floor near Ihvon, his back pressed against a bookcase, his eyes fixed on Ihvon, his hands shaking.

Six Kingsguard stood about the room, their purple cloaks hanging from their shoulders, their burnished plate glistening in the bluish-green flowerlight from the lanterns.

It took a moment for Dahlen's mind to push back the chaos and focus on the people who stood before him. Beads of sweat dripped down Belina's forehead, her deep purple dress marred by patches of Ihvon's blood. Beside her stood Oleg Marylin – the Belduaran emissary to the dwarven freehold – and a woman in the burnished steel plate of the Kingsguard, her purple cloak knotted at her pauldrons. The woman looked no older than thirty summers, her chestnut hair tied back, her face all planes and angles. He recognised her. She had been on his Wind Runner during the retreat from Belduar.

After the healers had arrived to take care of Ihvon, Dahlen had asked Belina if she could find Oleg to see if the emissary could bring him the closest thing the Kingsguard had to a Lord Captain. Daymon hadn't chosen a new Lord Captain after Tarmon Hoard was lost at the battle of Belduar, and right now they needed a leader. This woman looked to be the one Oleg had chosen.

"Dahlen Virandr." Oleg bowed deeply, attempting to grab Dahlen's attention. The man was usually relentlessly boisterous, but standing before Dahlen now, he held not a single shred of mirth in his eyes. Oleg glanced towards Ihvon, grimacing. "As requested, this is Lumeera Arian, Captain of the Kingsguard's fourth regiment."

Dahlen did his best to compose himself, straightening his back and breathing out slowly. He wasn't quite sure how he had come to be the one taking charge. He didn't have much of a choice, though. Ihvon was unconscious, Daymon was useless, there was no Lord Captain, the Belduaran nobles seemed nothing more than a pack of squabbling dogs, and Dahlen's father had gone after Erik and Calen. "It's a pleasure to meet you, Captain Arian."

"The pleasure is mine, Lord Virandr. It was an honour to fight beside you in Belduar."

Lumeera's response was something Dahlen was going to have to lean into. 'Lord Virandr'. Dahlen's father was a legend. The mighty Aeson Virandr. His name carried weight. "Lumeera, how many Kingsguard do we have here in Durakdur?"

"By my estimate, we have just under two thousand Kingsguard here in the Heart. We lost many in the retreat from Belduar, but not as many as we would have if the Draleid and the elf hadn't collapsed the entrances."

Dahlen nodded, rubbing his cheek and chin with the fingers of his right hand. That wasn't close to enough. If the dwarves moved on them, the Belduarans would be crushed. "How many regular soldiers? Swords, cavalry, archers, mages. What are our numbers, Lumeera?"

The woman hesitated, looking towards Oleg.

"Less than four hundred in Durakdur," Oleg said, stepping forward. "Most of the soldiers are spread throughout Ozryn, Azmar, and Volkur. In Durakdur, it's mostly citizens. The old and infirm, those who couldn't travel further on the Wind Runners. We have nine mages, but no cavalry. The horses weren't a priority when evacuating."

Dahlen puffed out his cheeks and ran his hands through his hair as he nodded absently. Now that he thought about it, he realised he hadn't seen a single horse the entire time they had been under the mountain. He just hadn't made the connection. "Dammit... fuck."

"What is it?" Oleg asked.

"They spread us out on purpose, Oleg. This has been their plan all along." Dahlen let out a sigh, composing himself. "Oleg, can you arrange for messages to be sent to our people in the other kingdoms? It needs to be done quickly and quietly. We need them to know what happened here and to be ready. There are moves being made, and we still don't know who all the players are."

"I will see to it personally," Oleg said with a nod. "I will ask my contacts in the Wind Runners Guild to carry the messages."

There was a momentary silence before Dahlen leaned a little closer to Oleg, raising an eyebrow. "Oleg?"

"Yes, my lord?"

"Now."

"Oh, right. Of course. My apologies." Oleg glanced once more towards Ihvon, scratching nervously at his beard. "Will he be all right? Lord Arnell that is."

"I'm not sure, Oleg. But you do need to go. We don't know what time we have. Take one of the Kingsguard with you. No more than one – we don't want to draw attention."

"Quite right, my lord. Quite right. I will leave right away." Oleg nodded repeatedly to himself before he straightened his back and gave a slight bow. "Your Majesty."

Daymon approached as Oleg scuttled from the room. The king's eyes were red and raw, ringed by dark circles. He rolled his shoulders, pushing his chest out as he stopped beside Dahlen, letting out a singular inward sniffle – the aftermath of tears. "Where is Oleg going?"

Dahlen needed to handle the situation carefully. Whatever Daymon had done, he was still the king of Belduar. And Dahlen was the only person who had heard him admit to working with Pulroan. He didn't think Daymon would do anything rash, but he dared not underestimate what the man might do to save his skin. Even if Dahlen wanted to wring the man's neck where he stood, he would need to tread lightly. "I sent him to deliver messages to your people in the other kingdoms, to warn them that the dwarves might attack, and to learn what we can. It seemed the right thing to do, given the situation."

Daymon looked from Dahlen to Belina before his eyes finally settled on Lumeera. "And you saw fit to summon a captain of the Kingsguard, I see."

"I did, Daymon." Dahlen refused to refer to Daymon by his title, which only caused the irritation in the man's eyes to flare. "We don't know how much time we have. We need to gather ourselves and choose the path forward. As it stands, we have no idea who is truly behind any of this. The Belduarans in the refugee quarters are defenceless, but there is a lot of ground between us and them. We need to—"

Daymon held up his hand. "The Kingsguard are under *my* command. And the people of Belduar are under *my* protection. Know your place, Virandr."

Dahlen clenched his jaw. Out of the corner of his eye, he saw Belina looking at him, her face twisted in silent warning – 'Don't do it'.

Dahlen knew she was right. It would all be easier if he kept his mouth shut and bided his time. But as he looked at Ihvon lying on the floor, the life draining from his body, a surge of anger rippled through him, blood boiling, hands shivering. He did his best to temper the flames, to slow his breathing, but he failed. "My place, Daymon? *You* are the reason Ihvon is lying on that floor." Dahlen stepped closer to Daymon, lifting his arm, extending a finger out to where Ihvon lay. Lumeera and the other Kingsguard stepped closer. "*You* are the reason eight Kingsguard died in that hallway. They were ready to die for you, and you made sure they did. You struck a deal with the dwarves to retake your kingdom without a thought for the lives it would cost. We don't have time for your games. If we don't make the right moves, more people will die." Dahlen leaned closer, lowering his voice. "You are a king in nothing but name."

As the words left Dahlen's lips, he saw Lumeera's hand drop to her sword, her gaze moving between Daymon and Dahlen, her shoulders tense. The sound of rasping steel from elsewhere in the room let Dahlen know that the other Kingsguard set to protect Daymon had done the same.

"I…" Daymon hesitated, taken aback by the ferocity in Dahlen's words. Dahlen could hazard a guess that the man had expected him to back down. "I will give you one chance to take that back."

It was only Dahlen's word against Daymon's. A warrior's against a king's. "Tell them, Daymon. Tell them the truth. Tell them about your dealings with Pulroan."

Daymon held Dahlen's gaze. The calm on the man's face sent a shiver down Dahlen's spine. Daymon was many things, but calm was not usually one of them, and it was the last thing Dahlen expected after what he had just said. Dahlen could feel the eyes on him. Everyone in the room had stopped what they were doing to watch Dahlen and Daymon. With their helms on, he couldn't see the expression on the faces of the six Kingsguard who stood about the room, but he could see a hesitancy in the way they held themselves. They looked at each other, their hands pulling away from their swords, their legs straightening. Whether or not they believed what Dahlen had just said, he had most definitely planted the seed.

Captain Lumeera stepped forward, her hand still wrapped around the hilt of her sheathed sword. "My king, I—"

Daymon raised his hand, his eyes narrowing as he stared at Dahlen. "Lumeera Arian. You fought in the Inner Circle during the first attack on Belduar. Then again, in the Wind Runner courtyard during the second attack. Ihvon mentioned your name as one of those on the last Wind Runners to leave the city." Daymon paused, drawing in a deep breath. "I had hoped Tarmon would have returned by now. But it seems I was waiting on a ghost. In times like these, I need strong people around me. Loyal people who would do anything for their kingdom and their king. People like you. It is my great pleasure, Lumeera Arian, to name you Lord Captain of the Belduaran Kingsguard."

Lumeera dropped to one knee without hesitation, her steel plate clanking off the stone, her head bowed. "My King, I will serve with honour."

An uneasy feeling filled Dahlen's stomach.

"Rise, Lord Captain."

When Lumeera stood, she held her head higher, her chest puffed out, a suppressed smile on her face. Whatever doubt Dahlen's words had given her was now gone. She was Daymon's. Dahlen turned to Belina to find she no longer stood beside him. She was gone. She must have slipped out while he was speaking. The woman always had a knack of being able to do that. *Dammit, Belina.*

Dahlen clenched his jaw, feeling the tension rise in the room.

"Lord Captain." Daymon stepped forward, clasping his hands behind his back, his lips puckering, his face twisting into a smug glare. "As your first act, you are to take Dahlen Virandr into custody for collusion with the Dwarven Freehold, and the attempted assassination of the King of Belduar. Were it not for Lord Ihvon Arnell, he would have succeeded."

Dahlen could feel the vibrations of his heartbeat, hear the thump in his ears. He could see the hesitancy in Lumeera's eyes, but it wouldn't last long. The other Kingsguard were already moving closer, pulling their swords from their scabbards, the rasp grating in Dahlen's ears.

"He's lying," Dahlen said as he stepped back, pulling both his blades free. "Lumeera, think. Why would I do that? We were on the same Wind Runner back from Belduar. We fought together. Why would I risk my life then and throw it away now?"

Lumeera swallowed, her fingers gripped around the hilt of her sword, which still sat in its scabbard. For a moment, Dahlen thought she might refuse the command, but that hope was dashed when her gaze hardened and she pulled her sword free. "Dahlen Virandr, you are accused of the attempted assassination of King Daymon of Belduar and will be taken into custody by the word of King Daymon himself." Lumeera's voice grew a touch softer. "Please, there has been enough bloodshed. Put down your weapons. You are surrounded and outnumbered. More of my guard are in the hallway, on the staircase, and in the street outside. Please."

Dahlen's breath trembled. The Kingsguard had begun to close in around him, each moving slowly and purposefully, keeping their distance while encircling him. He could probably kill four or five of them before they took him down. But where was the logic in that? What would he achieve? He would be dead and Daymon would be free to continue spinning his lies. Besides, Dahlen had fought beside these men and women at Belduar. He had bled for them, and they had bled for him. He had no desire to spill their blood. Lumeera was right, there was no way out. A knot twisted in his chest, and he tossed his swords to the ground, the clang of steel on stone reverberating through the room. He fought back a surge of fury at the satisfied look on Daymon's face.

Lumeera stepped forward and grasped Dahlen's wrists, pulling his hands behind his back in a far gentler manner than he had anticipated. "I'm sorry," she whispered before handing him to two of the other Kingsguard, who were not quite as gentle as she was.

"I told you that you needed to learn your place." Daymon moved to stand directly in front of Dahlen. "Find something to bind his hands," he said to the two Kingsguard before turning towards Lumeera. "Lord Captain, please see to it the Kingsguard are ready to march on my order. We leave for the refugee quarters immediately. We cannot stay here – we are too exposed. The refugee quarters can be fortified, and our people need us."

"Yes, Your Majesty. It will be done."

"Daymon, please." Dahlen pulled away from the Kingsguard. "You can't just march an army through the Heart!"

"I will not show weakness," Daymon said. "Get him out of my sight."

As the Kingsguard bound Dahlen's wrists with a length of rough-cut rope and shuffled him out of the room, he glanced back, watching as Daymon dropped to his knees beside Ihvon, resting his hand on the man's chest.

DAHLEN'S WRISTS CHAFFED AS HE walked, the rope scratching his skin. Around him, almost two thousand Kingsguard marched through the streets of the Heart, the crashing of their boots against the stone echoing like thunder, their polished steel plate glistening in the dim bluish-green flowerlight that emanated from the lanterns set about the city. There was no day or night in the Dwarven Freehold. No rising or setting of the sun to mark the passage of time. But when the city slept, covers were draped over many of the lanterns that stood in the streets, creating an ethereal twilight.

Along with the Kingsguard were the nine Belduaran mages who had been stationed in Durakdur, the nobles who had been given accommodation in the Heart, some craftsmen, servants, porters, cooks, and healers. Dahlen hadn't seen Oleg Marylin return, but he was sure the man would be somewhere at the front, near Daymon. Somehow, Dahlen was going to have to get a message to Oleg. The emissary may have been slightly stranger than most, but he was one of the few people beneath the mountain who Dahlen trusted.

Dahlen walked in the front third of the column, two Kingsguard on either side of him, each watching him with cautious sideways glances. To his right, two men carried Ihvon on a stretcher, the healers at his side. The surviving assassin walked on Dahlen's left, hands bound. The man moved as though he were half dead, swaying back and forth, his nose a bloody mess of torn skin and broken bone.

As the column marched through the streets, windows began to illuminate throughout the Heart, glowing with uncovered flowerlight. Dwarves emerged from their tiered homes carved into the stone, curious to see what was happening. But even as the city woke, the column marched onward.

But the more they marched, the more Dahlen's concern grew. The streets of the Heart were a maze of stone. Dahlen had spent a long time memorizing each twist and turn, each corner and alleyway. But the

Kingsguard had not. They meandered their way towards the enormous gates that separated the Heart from the rest of the city. But if they didn't pick up the pace, and the dwarves truly did want them dead, they would be like lambs to the slaughter.

"How is he?" Dahlen asked the taller of the two healers beside Ihvon – a red-haired woman with broad shoulders, a narrow waist, and high cheekbones. The woman wore a white gown covered by a red mantle.

"Alive. But barely. We were able to remove the knife, bandage his hand, and stop most of the bleeding. We did all we could, but we're both Alamants. Our strength with the Spark is weak at its best. Only time will tell."

Alamants. Dahlen had heard that word before. It was the name given to those mages who were not deemed strong enough to serve the Circle in the North. "Thank you."

"Just doing what we can," the woman replied.

Dahlen could see his guards eyeing him askance, but they didn't move to stop him talking. That was good. It meant one of two things: they either had sympathy for him or respect. Whichever it was, it didn't matter. He could use either.

After a vast number of wrong turns and wasted time spent tracking back, Dahlen eventually spotted something ahead: the statue of Heraya with the Waters of Life flowing from her jug. Dahlen had seen that statue enough times to know precisely where they were. They had reached the gates of the Heart.

Within a few moments, the column of Kingsguard had filled the square that fronted the gates, stretching back for hundreds of feet down the street, the sound of their steel boots echoing off the stone walls. Ahead, Dahlen could see the upper half of the enormous wooden doors that marked the divide between the Heart and the rest of Durakdur. The doors were still open, the low drum of the city's waterfall drifting through the archway, the refugee quarters lying on the other side.

"Who goes there?" a voice called. Dahlen couldn't see the foot of the doors, but the voice belonged to a dwarf, of that much he was sure. It seemed their unobstructed march had come to an end.

"Lord Commander Lumeera Arian of the Belduaran Kingsguard, escorting King Daymon Bryne," Lumeera replied. "We are marching to our people who reside in the Refugee Quarters across the waterfall bridge. Is there a problem?"

Lumeera's voice was strong and calm, only the slightest tremble betraying what Dahlen was sure was inner panic.

"May your fires never be extinguished and your blade never dull, Lumeera Arian. And yours, King Daymon. There is no problem. I simply question why so many armed soldiers march through the Heart."

Dahlen's pulse quickened, his chest tightening. Everything balanced on a knife edge. If chaos broke out, he was all but helpless, his hands bound. The tension in the air about the Kingsguard was a palpable thing. He could see those around him shifting restlessly, many of their hands drifting to their pommels.

"There has been an attempt on the king's life. Two assassins lie dead in his chambers." Dahlen noticed Lumeera neglected to mention the third assassin who now stood beside Dahlen, gagged and hands bound. "The Heart is no longer safe, and we are taking the King and his servants to the refugee quarters so he may be with his people. Does this sate your curiosity?"

A long moment passed before the dwarf's response came. "Carry on through, King Daymon. I will send word to our queen of what has happened. May Hafaesir guide you."

Every muscle in Dahlen's body relaxed and he felt the tension drain out of the air around him at the dwarf's words.

The column had only started moving through the doorway when the drumming sound of armoured boots echoed from the streets around them. Dahlen didn't have to look to know that the streets behind them and to their left were teeming with dwarven soldiers.

"King Daymon!" Even through the clamouring feet, Dahlen recognised the voice of Queen Kira. The dwarf's voice usually held a sweetness to it that belied her ferocity – and by the gods was she fierce – but now it simmered with fury. "Stand down, and order your guards to lower their weapons."

A murmur swept through the Kingsguard, feet shifting, steel clinking. The guards closest to Dahlen pulled their swords free a few inches.

"We will not stand down!" Daymon called out.

"Then you will be stood down."

A shiver rippled through Dahlen's body. There was no room for movement in Kira's tone. It wasn't a suggestion or a last attempt at discussion. It was a cold fact.

Dahlen had a feeling Daymon wasn't the only one whose life had been threatened that night. He also must not have been the only one who thwarted that attempt. If Dahlen were a gambling man, he would bet his life that the assassin had laid the blame at Daymon and Elenya's feet. Daymon had said Pulroan promised she would help him retake Belduar, her and Kira. The man Belina had interrogated below The Cloak and Dagger – even the thought of what she likely did to extract the information made Dahlen sick to his stomach – had said that Elenya was moving against the others and had sent an assassin after Daymon. There were a lot of moving pieces, but none of the moves made sense. Whatever was happening here, it was clear that everyone knew less than they thought they did, and the small amount they did know was likely wrong.

"By Hafaesir's hammer!" The cry was greeted by a chorus of shouts, steel drumming against steel. "Take the king alive!"

"Form up!" a voice called out. "Protect the king!"

Shouts rang out all around Dahlen as the Belduaran Kingsguard dropped into formation, moving seamlessly like cogs in a well-oiled machine. Purple cloaks drifted left and right; the rasp of swords being drawn crashed against the thunderous sounds of steel boots beating against the stone.

"Get behind me," the Kingsguard closest to Dahlen said, his words aimed at Dahlen, the healers, the assassin, and the men carrying Ihvon's stretcher. "Bunch together and stay with us. Understood?"

"Yes, sir," came the reply from the two men carrying the stretcher.

The four Kingsguard who had been set to protect them – or guard them – fell into a tight square around Dahlen and the others, their swords gripped in clenched fists, thick heavy rimmed shields on their left arms. A moment of calm fell over the square, and then the dwarves crashed into the Belduaran lines from the left and the rear.

"Through the gates!" Dahlen heard Daymon call. "Forward!"

That was probably the first intelligent decision the king had made. Dahlen had seen the Kingsguard hold the line at Belduar. Their training and skill were particularly aligned with a slow tactical retreat. If they stayed where they were, they would be overrun, but if they could make it to the walkways, the mages could collapse some bridges, giving them time. If they could make it to the refugee quarters, the dwarves would likely put them under siege, but it would at the least buy them the one thing they didn't currently have: time.

Slowly, step by step, the column of Kingsguard and Belduarans moved through the gates, feet shuffling, bodies crushing together.

"It's all right," Dahlen said to the healers and the two men who were carrying Ihvon's stretcher. He bent slightly as he walked, looking down at Ihvon, who still lay unconscious. "Just keep moving. They won't break through."

Screams and howls echoed off the rock and stone, turning in on themselves, colliding with the harsh ringing of steel on steel and the crunch of bone. The iron tang of blood tinged the battle-warmed air, leaving a foul taste on Dahlen's tongue. The Kingsguard around him began to move closer, the crush of bodies closing. Instinctively, he tugged at his bonds as he walked, the rough rope digging into his skin. The helplessness made his skin crawl. What good was he if he couldn't hold a sword, if he couldn't defend himself? Even if he could, his swords still lay on the floor in Daymon's quarters – the swords his mother had forged for him. *Keep moving. Give your mind a task. One foot in front of the other.*

A series of blood-curdling screams rang out, and Dahlen leapt backwards as an enormous bolt ripped through the air, slicing into the lines of soldiers before slamming into the chest of the Kingsguard who stood next to Dahlen. The bolt punched through the man's breastplate in a plume of blood and gore, the sheer force lifting the Kingsguard into the air, sending him crashing to the ground a few feet away, his body limp, blood pouring freely onto the stone.

What the fuck was that? Dahlen stared at the man's body for a few moments before it was swallowed by the retreating mass of Belduarans. More screams rang out, and another bolt cleaved through the column of Kingsguard, pinning a man against the stone wall of the building to the right, blood spilling over his lip and out around the bolt that was embedded in his gut. The enormous wooden shaft of the bolt looked to be about eight feet long and almost two handspans wide. *The Bolt Throwers from Belduar!*

Dahlen had forgotten it was the dwarves who had made the Bolt Throwers that had been mounted on the towers of Belduar. Those machines had been built to slay dragons. It was no wonder the bolts tore through men with such ease. But Dahlen hadn't seen any Bolt Throwers in Durakdur, which meant the dwarves must have built mobile versions.

Dahlen heard a loud snap followed by screams. The hair on the back of his neck stood on end and he leapt into the two men beside him that carried Ihvon's stretcher, knocking them to the ground. A gust of wind passed over Dahlen's head as they hit the stone, along with a sharp *whoosh*. A shriek rose beside them, and Dahlen looked up to see the bolt had struck one of the healers – the stout, black-haired man. The woman who wore the red mantle stood beside him, shrieking, her hands clasped to her chest, her shoulders convulsing. The man swayed left and right, his eyes wide, his mouth open. A stump sat where his left arm had been, broken bone protruding from the mangled flesh of his shoulder, blood sluicing onto the stone. The healer dropped to his knees, his body trembling, then collapsed, blood spraying in spurts.

"Get him up," Dahlen said to the two men carrying Ihvon's stretcher. "Get him up, and keep moving!"

The man closest to Dahlen stared at him for a moment before scrambling to his feet and darting ahead, pushing his way through the crush of Kingsguard. The second man looked at Dahlen, then glanced after his fleeing companion. He shook his head. "I'm sorry." He only made it a foot or so before a bolt crashed into the side of his head, the impact pulverising the bone and flesh into a cloud of gore. The mangled body collapsed.

Fuck. Fuck. Fuck. Dahlen's hands trembled as his breaths grew ragged and sharp, the rope around his wrists seeming to grow tighter and tighter. *Get up. This is not where you die.* Drawing a deep breath in through his nostrils, Dahlen dragged himself to his feet. The other healer was gone by the time he stood upright, but the assassin and the three remaining Kingsguard who had been set to watch them still drew breath.

Dahlen could see the assassin's eyes glancing between the three Kingsguard, his gaze resting on a sword that had been fallen on the ground. The man dropped to his knees, reaching for the weapon. Dahlen swung his hands back and slammed his wrists into the back of the man's head, feeling the *thump* as bone collided with bone. The man dropped to his side, howling. Dahlen grabbed him by the scruff of his neck and dragged him back to where Ihvon lay. "Stay down!"

The assassin wrapped his fingers around Dahlen's throat, but Dahlen swung his hands again, smashing them into the bridge of the assassin's already broken nose. The man's fingers loosened around Dahlen's neck, his hands falling away. Dahlen struck him again, ignoring his own pain as blood sprayed across the ground. He raised his arms once more but stopped himself. The man was unconscious, and Dahlen needed him alive. He needed whatever information was locked inside the man's head.

Another bolt tore through the Kingsguard to Dahlen's left, breaking bones and armour as it flew. A series of howls and shouts followed the bolt, and Dahlen turned to see a clutch of dwarves in heavy, sharp-cut plate charging through the gap created by the weapon, swinging their axes in pendulum-like sweeps, forcing the Kingsguard to step back further, widening the opening. With a gap now open in the Belduaran lines, Dahlen could see the full might of the dwarven forces attacking from the left. Past the force of charging dwarves was a long, wide street filled with heavy armour and crimson cloaks. Three Bolt Throwers jutted above the dwarves' head, sitting atop elevated platforms. Dahlen had little doubt that the force attacking their rear flank was similarly armed. Queen Kira had been decisive in her choice to stop Daymon, picking the one point in this labyrinthine city where she could use her numbers to her best advantage.

As the charging dwarves pushed further inward, sliding a wedge through the lines of Kingsguard, Dahlen noticed the Kingsguard weren't engaging. They were stepping back, letting the dwarves bounce off their shields, allowing them to push further in. It only took a few seconds for Dahlen to realise what was happening.

They're letting them in.

Almost as soon as the thought touched Dahlen's mind, a shout rang out from the left and the lines of Kingsguard pushed hard, cutting the charging dwarves off from the rest of their forces. Then, with the dwarves fully encircled and trapped within a wall of steel, the Kingsguard pressed inward.

Dahlen couldn't help but feel an immense sense of loss as Daymon's Kingsguard and Kira's Queensguard tore into each other. They should have been on the same side. More screams sounded, more bolts tearing into the Belduaran forces. The Belduaran column was still moving, shifting more towards the doors with each passing moment. With a quick glance, Dahlen guessed he was no more than forty feet away, but looking back down the street, there were still hundreds of men and women behind him: Kingsguard, servants, cooks, porters. No matter how this ended, Achyron's halls would be full that night.

"Get down!" An armoured hand shoved Dahlen in the chest, sending him stumbling over Ihvon, who still lay unconscious on his stretcher. Dahlen crashed to the ground in time to see a wicked double-bladed axe plunge into the chest of the Kingsguard who had pushed him to safety. The dwarf who had swung the axe shifted his feet, heaving the blade free in a spray of blood. He let the Kingsguard fall to his knees before pushing the man to the ground. More dwarves followed after the first, howling battle cries as they fought like caged beasts. Trapped as they were within the column of Kingsguard, death was but a certainty. Still, Dahlen couldn't help but admire their sheer unwillingness to give in. That admiration quickly faded, turning to fear as a stout dwarf with a crimson cloak set his gaze on Dahlen.

The dwarf hefted his axe and charged, throwing his momentum forward. Scrambling, ropes cutting into the skin on his wrists, Dahlen grasped at a bloody sword that lay on the ground. He threw himself backwards, bringing the sword up to meet the swing of the axe. The force of the dwarf's swing wrenched the sword free from Dahlen's grasp, knocking him backwards as it did. Without his hands to brace himself, he hit the stone hard, his back first, then his head. The light in his eyes flickered, the world swimming.

Moving to stand over Dahlen, the dwarf swung his axe above his head, readying the final blow. Through the slits in the dwarf's angular helmet, Dahlen could see the battle rush in the dwarf's eyes, the bloodlust. He pushed himself sideways as the axe fell, waiting until the last moment so the dwarf couldn't adjust his strike. The axeblade collided against the stone with a furious *crack*, the momentum carrying the dwarf forward, shifting him off balance.

Just as Dahlen had found another fallen sword and gripped it in his bound fist, something sliced through the dwarf's neck, leaving a trail of blood streaming out over his chest.

Something hard crashed into Dahlen's wrist, forcing him to drop the sword, then a hand clamped down over his mouth and pointed steel pressed against his side. Whoever held him dragged him backwards, pulling him away from the fighting.

"Don't try anything," a voice whispered in his ear.

DAHLEN DREW IN SLOW BREATHS as whoever was behind him pulled him backwards through the fighting, their hand still clamped over his mouth, a blade still pressed against his back. They pulled him through a low archway connected to the street, the shadows washing over them as they left the flowerlight that illuminated the main street.

The stranger pushed Dahlen forward, turning him so his back was flat against the wall of the alley they were now in. They pulled their hand from his mouth, moving the blade to his neck. In the dim light that shone from the main street, Dahlen saw a face he recognised. "Belina?"

"That went well." The woman suppressed a laugh as she pulled the blade from Dahlen's throat. "You shit yourself, didn't you? I can smell it."

"I didn't shi—Fuck, Belina, where did you go?"

"Where did I go? You stood in a room with a king whose ego is only slightly outweighed by his clumsy desire to fill his father's boots. And then you decided to spill his secrets for his guards to hear and tell him he was 'a king in nothing but name', I believe were the words. Anyone with half a brain knew what was coming next. Which says a lot about you. Come on, we need to get higher." Belina grabbed Dahlen by the shoulder and shoved him down the alley, away from the fighting.

Dahlen looked back, trying to see Ihvon in the mass of blood and flowerlight-tinted steel.

"Come on, move." Belina said, pushing him forwards again.

"We can't just leave them."

"They'll be fine. Most of them are through the doors already, and there's nothing we can do. With any luck, that arsehole of a king will die in the fighting. I know a navigator in the Wind Runners Guild. I can get us to the Southern Fold Gate and out of here before this entire place collapses into chaos." Belina looked back out at the fighting on the main street. "Well, into more chaos."

Dahlen stopped. "I'm not going, Belina. I'm not leaving the Belduarans here, backed into a corner with nowhere to turn."

Belina turned, incredulity in her eyes. "That idiot king made his own mess, Dahlen. And I'm not dying for him."

"I don't give a fuck about Daymon, Belina. But there are nearly forty thousand souls in the refugee quarters and almost twice that many spread throughout the other kingdoms. They don't deserve to die for what Daymon has done. They don't, Belina."

Belina tilted her head back, drawing a slow breath through her nostrils before letting it out in a sigh. She ran a hand through her black hair, shaking her head. "You and Dayne would get on like a barn on fire. Two peas in a fucking pod. Two pigs in a steaming pile of—"

"Belina?"

"What?"

Dahlen just shook his head, an incredulous look on his face. "Who in the void is Dayne?"

"A friend," Belina said, defeat in her voice. She sighed again. "All right. I'll help. But only because I have nothing better to do, and you'll get yourself killed without me. I have some contacts throughout the Freehold who might be able to fill in some missing pieces. Come on, let's make ourselves scarce."

CHAPTER FIVE

ARBITER

Al'Nasla – Earlywinter, Year 3081 After Doom

Duran Linold, Ark-Mage, Year 1807 After Doom

Today I met a rather peculiar man. Tall and broad of shoulder, but as gaunt as a tree branch. His complexion and overall appearance was that of a man who had witnessed the passing of no more than thirty or so summers, but his demeanour told a different story.

Why is this of any importance, you ask? Why is this one man worthy of a mention in the pages of this book? Well, I believe he may, in fact, have been a druid. Ah, but this raises more questions, doesn't it? It does indeed. But they are questions I will answer. Fear not.

The first question is, how did I meet the man? Well, I came upon him on the road from Ilnaen to Amendel. I did not meet him as two travellers passing one another. No. As I travelled the road with my retinue, we came across the man sitting cross-legged in our path. He wore nothing but a long, brown, hooded robe.

Now we move to the second question. What made me suspect this man might, in fact, be a druid? This is the pressing question indeed.

When I asked him why he was sitting in the middle of the road, he told me he was waiting.

"Waiting for what?" I asked.

"For you," he replied.

Needless to say, my interest was piqued. He may have been a wandering vagrant, but that didn't seem to be the case. His hair was meticulously groomed, his skin scrubbed clean. Were I any other man, I may have marked him an irritation and ridden on, but I am not any other man, and it is a good thing I am not, for if my interest had not already been piqued, what he said next brought it to new heights.

"You are Duran Linold, Ark-Mage of The Order." *It wasn't a question; it was a statement.*

Now, based on my research, as noted in my entry on page 153 of this book, dated year 1798 After Doom, if this man was in fact a druid, he was a Seerdruid, one capable of glimpsing future events. I do believe it is needless to say that the prospect left me more than a little excited. Sightings, rumours, and whispers of druids are not all that uncommon. But confirmations? Not one in nearly four hundred years.

But another question remained. How do you have a conversation with a man who already knows what you're going to say? At first, I thought that mayhap I simply never say the first thing that comes to mind, but I dismissed that utterly. Pure idiocy. How am I to get answers to questions I never ask?

And this is where the peculiarity truly began.

"How do you know my name?" *I asked the man as I dismounted, eager to study him more closely.*

"Why, you told it to me. On a different path."

Rist reached the end of the page and reluctantly lifted his eyes from the book, glancing at the wrought iron clock that hung on the wall at the far end of the enormous library hall. If he didn't leave soon, he'd be late. And it was best not to think of what Garramon would do to him if he was late. Garramon was a kind man, or at least, he was kind to Rist. He had believed in Rist, sponsored him into the Circle. But as Garramon's apprentice, Rist was a reflection of his sponsor, and Garramon did not tolerate tardiness.

With one last reluctant glance at the page, Rist folded the corner and stuffed the book into his pack. Contemplating, he picked up the two other books that sat beside him on the table. One, he had found tucked away in the far corners of the library, slipped behind a row of books on the bottom shelf of a bookcase. He had not been looking for it specifically, but once his gaze had fallen on it, he had snatched it up right away. *The Spark: a study of infinite possibilities.*

He had sought the second book out purposefully – *The Forging of an Empire*, by Orduro Alanta. The embassy's library contained many detailed accounts on the formation of the Lorian Empire after The Fall – or 'the liberation of the free peoples of Epheria' as it was named in the North – but the vast majority of those accounts were written by Scholars and historians who Rist had already learned not to trust. From reading their work, he had determined they were far from objective in their recounting of events. Their works were always overly praising of the empire, which in itself wasn't a problem, but they lacked any critique, and Rist didn't trust a historian who lacked critique.

It was quite an interesting thing really, how hundreds of years of history could differ so greatly from one place to the next. The stories he had heard growing up in the South were nothing like the stories that were told here in the North. He supposed it was similar to paintings. If ten artists were asked to paint the same flower, ten vastly different paintings would be produced. And the only way to find a true-to-life idea of what the flower originally looked like would be to examine each of the ten paintings for commonalities and then build a new picture. Which was exactly what Rist intended to do.

It had taken him quite some time to decide where to start, though. But once he learned that Orduro Alanta had been sent to work the mines in Dead Rock's Hold not two years after finishing *The Forging of an Empire,* his decision was made. If a man was cast aside for his ideas, that generally meant there was merit to them, merit that others did not wish to see the light of day. Of course, he might just as easily have been a raving lunatic.

Rist shoved the two books into his pack, careful to ensure nobody was watching him, then slung it over his shoulder. He pulled in a thin thread of Air, snuffing out the candle that sat on the table to his left, and exited the library in as swift a manner as he was able without drawing any pointed glances from the librarians. Irritating the librarians didn't bother Rist – they were grumpy and irritable at the best of times – but he didn't want to draw any undue attention. He wasn't strictly permitted to remove books from the library, but he had a lot to read, and there were distinctly too few hours in the day.

The sun sat high in the cloudless sky when Rist stepped from the library, lifting his hand to his face to shield his eyes. Earlywinter was not as frosty in Al'Nasla as it had been in The Glade, but the air was still cool enough to send a shiver across his skin. He pulled his second-tier apprentice robes tighter about himself. He would be a far happier man when spring finally arrived.

Rist made his way from the library through the embassy grounds, then through the winding palace gardens. He paused only for a few moments to chat with Tommin, who was on his way to meet with his own sponsor, Sister Danwar of the Healers. Both Tommin and Lena had undergone their Trials of Will a week after Rist and Neera. They had both passed and joined the affinities of their sponsors, the Healers and Consuls respectively. Rist had been curious to know if the Trials of Will for the other affinities were similar to what he had undergone, but neither Tommin nor Lena had been willing to talk about them. He didn't blame them. He still hadn't told anyone about what he had seen in his own trial, not even Neera. The memories of it still swirled in his mind, still haunted his dreams: the faceless man, Neera's dead body, the blood spilling from his mother's throat – Calen.

'You should have been by my side,' Calen's voice echoed in Rist's head, sending a shiver through him. Rist pushed the memories from the Trial of Will from his thoughts, picking up his pace.

When he finally arrived at the practice yard, he had worked up enough body heat that beads of sweat had formed on his brow and his shirt had grown tacky. The practice yard itself, one of four courtyards gifted to the embassy of the Circle of Magii, was over a hundred feet in both length and breadth. Four sparring squares of hardened clay framed by red brick sat at its centre, each about fifteen feet by fifteen feet. A number of benches sat around the perimeter of the squares, along with four weapons racks laden with a variety of blunt-edge swords and long wooden staffs. The courtyard was framed on all sides by the grey stone of the palace walls, and several large oak trees were set about its perimeter, providing shade. Brother Garramon stood at the centre of the courtyard, between the four squares, his silver-trimmed black robes neatly folded on a bench beside him – not a good sign. That meant he had been waiting. Garramon was talking to a woman who stood about a head shorter than he did, Exarch robes draped over her shoulders, blonde hair tied into an unmoving bun.

Garramon threw Rist a sideways glance as he approached, a frown touching the man's face.

"Tell him I will be there as soon as I am finished here," Garramon said to the woman.

"As you please, Arbiter."

"Fulya, please. That title is long gone."

The woman gave a placating smile, inclining her head in a way that seemed more submissive than respectful, then turned and strode from the yard, glancing towards Rist as she made for the archway he had just come through. It wasn't the first time Rist had seen another Exarch act strangely towards Garramon. And then there was that title – Arbiter. As Garramon let out a sigh, Rist turned towards the palace walls, pulling his robes from his shoulders, trying his best to make it look as though he hadn't been eavesdropping.

"You're late."

"I'm sorry, I got caught up in the library." Rist turned to find Garramon staring at him. "I—"

Garramon gestured for Rist to stop. He shook his head, letting out another sigh. "It doesn't matter. From what I've heard, Brother Pirnil has been disciplining you enough for the both of us. Need I remind you that your insubordination to other mages reflects on my ability as a sponsor?"

"No, Brother Garramon." Even as Rist stood there, he could feel the fresh scabs on his back pulling at his skin. If he didn't graduate to Acolyte soon, his flesh would look like a wicker basket. "Brother Pirnil and I simply have differences of opinion, which he doesn't like." *Because he's wrong.* Rist wanted to say that part out loud but figured it wouldn't go down well.

A flicker of a smile betrayed Garramon's otherwise stony façade. "Come, you have already wasted enough time."

Rist nodded, following Garramon to the nearest weapons rack, where the man handed him a dull-edged longsword with a brown leather-wrapped handle and a plain, flat-bar crossguard. Rist took the weapon, loosening and tightening his fingers around the hilt, gauging the weapon's weight and balance. Since the Trial of Will, when he had seen how helpless he truly was with a blade, Rist had made a point of improving his swordsmanship. He knew it took years to be considered even a reasonably capable swordsman, and years more to be proficient, but Rist often found that most obstacles of time and learning could be significantly reduced through strict, single-minded dedication. Or, more simply put, working harder than anybody else. He had never been strong like Calen, or quick like Dann, or even particularly charismatic, but one thing Rist prided himself on was his commitment and refusal to give up. That was something unique; it was something he was in complete and utter control of.

Most nights, after his lessons were finished, he would continue practising sword forms and movements long after the sun had set, when the courtyard was illuminated solely by baldír light. He did his reading after that, followed by exercises with the Spark from Andelar Touran's *A Study of Control*. The secret to rapid progress, he had discovered, was reducing his hours of sleep to the absolute minimum his body required to function and then shaving a sliver of time off that as well.

He actually found himself enjoying the sword forms far more than he had anticipated. But that had more than a little to do with the fact that every time he practised his forms, it made him think of Calen and Dann – more Calen than Dann, as Calen had often practised in the mornings long before their worlds were turned upside down. He was starting to understand the peace that Calen seemed to find in it.

Neera had joined him on more than a few occasions, but she didn't share his enthusiasm for what she called a 'layman's weapon'. She instead preferred the Spark and its 'elegance'.

"You look tired," Garramon said, stepping into the sparring square nearest them, turning his foot back and forth in the clay. "You're not sleeping."

"I'm fine," Rist lied. Well, it wasn't quite a lie. He was tired but not tired enough for it to be a problem.

Garramon nodded. His expression let Rist know the man didn't believe him. "Set your feet. We will go through form one, movement six before we begin."

"That Exarch," Rist said, shifting his stance a little wider, following Garramon through the sixth movement of the first form. He liked that the forms were numbered. When Aeson had taught Calen and Dann, he had always used obscure names that seemed unnecessarily difficult to remember. Numbers were simpler, more structured. "Why did she call you Arbiter? I've not heard that title."

"A story for another time, apprentice."

Rist wasn't letting Garramon get away that easily. "If I land a blow, will you tell me?"

There was no mistaking the amused smile that sat on Garramon's face. Rist had not landed a single blow in any of their sparring matches. In fact, he hadn't even come close. "You have a deal. Land one blow, and I will tell you. Starting now."

Rist nodded in acknowledgement, rolling his shoulders back and forth. One deep breath and then he charged towards Garramon.

For what felt like minutes but was in actuality only seconds, they traded blows in a whir of steel, the constant vibrations jarring Rist's arms. Then, Rist felt a jolt of pain as Garramon's foot crashed into the inside of Rist's right knee, not hard enough to break bones, but enough to cause Rist's leg to give way. His heart pounded as his knees hit the hardened clay. Garramon swung his sword. *He's not going to stop!*

In a panic, Rist lifted his left arm, reaching out to the Spark. He pulled in threads of Earth, driving them into the clay beside his knee. He shattered the clay, lifting it with threads of Air, then reformed it into a solid shield that hovered over his left arm. Garramon's sword collided with the makeshift shield, shattering it into a thousand pieces and sending Rist sprawling to the ground. Falling backwards, Rist caught the fragmented shards of clay with threads of Air, separating them. He flung half the shards at Garramon's left foot and the other half at the man's hand. Using threads of Earth, he melded the clay together, encasing Garramon's hand and the hilt of his sword while also binding his foot to the ground. The manoeuvre led to Garramon's arm dropping flat by his side due to the combined weight of the clay and sword, while stumbling sideways as his foot broke free from its temporary prison with a jolt.

No sooner had Rist hit the ground than he threw himself back to his feet, lunging after Garramon. *I just need to land one blow.* He drove his sword forward, aiming for Garramon's torso, only for the man to step sideways, slam his palm into the flat of Rist's blade, and proceed to drive his elbow into Rist's nose.

Blinding pain was accompanied by stars flitting across Rist's eyes as his head bounced backwards. He stumbled, only just stopping himself from falling. Rist's nostrils felt as though they'd been stuffed with cloth. The coppery taste of blood touched his tongue, dripped down the back of his throat, and rolled over his lips. He shook his head, doing his best to clear the dizziness.

Rist brought his blade up, deflecting a swing of Garramon's sword, then another, and another, until a heavy blow crunched into his right hip, then again into the outside of his right leg, above the knee. The edge of Garramon's blade might have been dulled, but the weight of the steel still hit like a horse's kick. Rist staggered backwards, his jaw clenched, his blade raised defensively. He was under no illusions that Garramon was putting in any effort. If the man had wanted, he likely would have had his sword to Rist's throat within the first ten seconds. But the sparring wasn't about Rist beating Garramon, it was about progress. Every day, progress. And today would be the day Rist would land his first blow.

Rist shifted his feet into the stance of form two, movement three. He needed to go on the offensive. At the same time, he reached out to the Spark, feeling the elemental strands pulsate in the back of his mind, their energy radiating through him, filling him with a sense of calm. He pulled on threads of Air, Fire, Earth, and Spirit, dividing them into the segments he would need. He saw Garramon raise a curious eyebrow and felt the man open himself to the Spark, preparing for whatever Rist might attempt.

Rist drew in a deep breath and let it out slowly, then charged. He wove threads of Air, Fire, and Spirit into a baldír, closing his eyes for only a fraction of a moment as he allowed the orb to pulse with a harsh burst of light before letting it flicker from existence. He opened his eyes to see Garramon stumbling, one hand gripping the hilt of his sword, the other covering his eyes. *Perfect.*

With Garramon staggering, Rist took a single thread of Earth and formed a lump of clay at the Exarch's feet, no larger than three or four inches off the ground – a technique he had seen in *A Study of Control.* The Spark didn't always have to be grandiose and extravagant, just effective.

Stepping forward blindly, Garramon's foot hit the lump of clay, which was enough to knock his already precarious sense of balance. The man fell forward, and a surge of pride rushed through Rist's body. *Progress.* He lunged.

As Rist swept his sword towards Garramon, the man swung his blade in an arc. It wasn't a targeted strike, but it was moving straight for Rist's head, meaning Rist would either have to deflect it or get out of its way – meaning he would miss his opportunity to land his blow. Luckily, he had prepared for this. Keeping his blade on course, he sent a whip of air towards Garramon's sword, intending to knock it off course. But then threads of Spirit wound around him, forming into a barrier, his grip on the Spark vanishing, his whip of air dissipating.

Garramon side stepped, his blade sweeping through where Rist's whip of Air had been.

In only moments, everything had shifted. Rist now stood with his weight on his right leg, his sword extended through the space where Garramon had been only seconds before. Garramon stood to Rist's left, the cold steel of his dull-edged blade resting against the nape of Rist's neck.

Rist let out a deep, regretful sigh. "A ward of Spirit."

"Indeed." Garramon lifted his blade.

Rist shook his head, lifting himself back to full height. He shouldn't have been so stupid. Wards were something he had dedicated little time to as they were complicated and intricate. He needed to master the basics first. Had he been paying more attention he would have been able to put a hole in the ward before it was formed.

"You're thinking of the ways you could have countered my ward," Garramon said, walking back towards the weapons rack. "That is not the line of thought you should be taking. You know better than that."

"Excuse me, Brother." Rist handed his sword to Garramon, wincing as he wiped his bloodied nose with his shirt. The combination of the throbbing pain and his inability to breathe through his nose was rather irritating. "But what line of thought should I be taking?"

"Your ingenuity is not your problem, apprentice." Garramon set his sword back on the rack, doing the same with Rist's. He then reached into a pack that sat beside his robes on the nearby bench, producing two waterskins. He tossed one to Rist, then sat on the bench. Upon closer inspection, Rist noticed Garramon was slightly short of breath, and a bead of sweat rolled down the man's brow. Rist might not have landed a blow, but this was also the first time he had made Garramon sweat. *Progress.* The surge of elation caused him to snort blood onto his hand. "You demonstrated that with your little trip hazard – page one hundred and twelve from *A Study of Control.* Well executed, I might add."

Rist popped the stopper from the waterskin, taking a deep, longing draught of water before using the remainder to wash the blood from his face. He had long since grown used to Garramon's blunt nature. In fact, he had come to appreciate it. "What is my problem, Brother?"

"Well, there are two. The first is your unwillingness to deviate from your established plan. No plan survives contact with the enemy, apprentice. Real battles change in an instant, turn on their heads with the flash of a blade. When you realised I had warded you, you should have adapted. Commitment to a broken plan is often the reason commanders send their men to their deaths. Refusal to adapt is fatal. Second, you rely too heavily on the Spark. I felt your doubt as soon as you were cut off. If you are to be a Battlemage, you must hone your body as well as your mind. Your sword must be as much a part of you as the Spark. Though, from what I have seen, you are working to rectify that issue."

Rist nodded, doing his best to steady his breathing. As the pain from his nose dulled, the rest of his body called out, reminding him of the numerous places Garramon had laid steel against skin. "I will improve, Brother."

"I know you will."

Silence descended over the courtyard as Rist dropped to the ground. He crossed his legs and leaned back, his hands pressing against the hard clay. Sweat had tacked his shirt to his skin, and his lungs burned. The only sounds that drifted through the open yard were the rustling of fallen oak leaves in the breeze and the trill of birdsong. It was quite peaceful. If Rist closed his eyes, he could imagine he was still sitting on that fallen tree near the edge of Ölm Forest the day he, Dann, and Calen had gone hunting before the Moon Market.

"You didn't land a blow," Garramon said, breaking the silence, "but you impressed me."

Rist looked towards his sponsor, raising an eyebrow.

"Four hundred years ago, after the liberation, Emperor Mortem and Primarch Touran granted me the title of Arbiter." Garramon gave Rist an amused laugh, letting Rist know he must not have hidden his surprise at Garramon's age as well as he'd thought he had. "Yes, I am that old. I was once a Battlemage of The Order. But that is a tale for another day. The years that followed that first battle at Ilnaen were tempestuous at best. The political landscape had been irreparably changed, power was in flux, and we faced enemies from outside and within. Trust was a commodity in scarce supply. For the empire to succeed, it needed loyalty. It needed men and women who believed in it. As Arbiter, I was charged with determining that loyalty and rooting out those who sought to do the empire harm. It was a necessary task but not an easy one. I am not proud of the things I had to do. It was almost a century before the position of Arbiter was no longer deemed necessary." Garramon stared towards the sky as he spoke, a pensive sadness filling his eyes. "The Exarch you saw, Fulya. She was once my wife. She has never forgiven me."

As always, a hundred thousand questions ran amok in Rist's mind. But he could see by the look on Brother Garramon's face that now was not the time to ask them. That in itself went against Rist's very nature. How could it ever not be a good time to ask a question? But Calen had always admonished him for not understanding that not everyone thought that way; it was something he was working on.

So instead of asking the questions, Rist simply sat in silence, letting his emotions percolate. It was strange, blending sympathy and anger. Sympathy for the task Brother Garramon was given, and anger at him for following through. But Rist knew he had no right to be angry. A man could not judge another until he has walked in their shoes. "I'm sorry, Brother."

Garramon shook his head, seeming to pull himself back into the moment. "What is done is done, apprentice. We cannot change the past, only move forward with its lessons." Garramon lifted himself to his feet. "We will have to keep it to one bout today. I have somewhere I must be. But from what I remember, you are to meet Sister Anila soon."

It was not a question, but Rist knew Garramon well enough to know he expected an answer. "Yes, Brother. Neera and I are to meet Sister Anila at the palace gates. She is taking us outside the city walls to where the First Army is barracked."

"Good." Garramon unfolded his silver trimmed robes, shrugging them on over his shoulders, then replaced the two waterskins into his pack. He inclined his head, his gaze lingering on Rist for a moment before he turned and left.

PARTICLES OF DUST FLOATED IN the beams of sunlight that drifted through the arched windows along the wall to Garramon's right as he walked through the corridors of the Imperial Palace. Birdsong and the constant chatter of servants and porters drifted up from the gardens outside, filling the quiet emptiness of the corridor.

Two guards dressed neck to toe in black plate trimmed with red steel stood at the entrance to the Imperial Chamber. Each had a large square shield strapped to their back and a longsword at their hip. The doors they guarded were forged from gold-plated steel, each emblazoned with the image of a roaring black lion facing inward. Each door stood over fifteen feet high and ten feet wide, meeting in an arch at the centre.

"Guinan, Karka." Garramon nodded to the two palace guards who stood watch at the doors to the Imperial Chamber. He had made it a point to memorize the names and faces of each guard, which included taking the time to introduce himself to any new recruits. It was a time-consuming task but one worth completing should there ever come a time he might need their favour. *Old habits die hard.*

"He awaits you inside, Exarch Garramon," the man on the left of the door, Guinan, said, inclining his head.

"My thanks."

Garramon stepped past Guinan and Karka, pushing open the door on the right and entering the Imperial Chamber.

The chamber was enormous, at least a hundred feet wide and double that again in length, with ceilings that stood taller than thirty men atop one another's shoulders. A long red rug embroidered with gold thread ran along the stone floor from the entrance to a raised stone dais at the far end of the chamber. A solid oak desk sat atop the dais and an enormous red banner, running from the ceiling to the floor, adorned the wall behind it. At the centre of the banner was the symbol of the Lorian Empire: the black lion of Loria. Garramon's eyes fell back to the desk for a moment. When they had taken the city and sentenced King Eric Ubbein to death, the first thing Fane had done was dismantle the throne room and have it rebuilt brick by brick. The throne had been melted down and sold, and Fane had chosen that desk to take its place. *'A throne is built to support the weight of those who have grown fat on their own incompetence and inaction. The Order's council sat on thrones,'* he had said. *'A simple desk is far more practical.'*

A marble fireplace was set into the wall on the left side of the chamber. Much like everything else in the room, the fireplace was at least twice the size of any other Garramon had laid eyes on. Two marble statues of roaring lions on their hind legs framed the fireplace, an ornately carved mantel of thick marble balanced atop their heads.

Light drifted into the chamber through a number of long windows set into the upper half of the wall on the right. Below the windows was a bookcase carved from solid oak that stood almost ten feet high and ran the entire length of the wall from the front of the chamber to the back. Ever since Garramon had known Fane, the man had been obsessed with books – with knowledge. It was knowledge that had driven Fane to seek out that Urak Shaman at Mar Dorul. And it was from that Shaman that Fane had learned the truth of the gods. The truth of The Saviour.

Garramon found his old friend sitting in one of two leather couches by the bookshelves, one leg crossed over the other, his back pressed into the firm cushion behind him, a book in hand. Fane wore a simple, black cotton shirt; light trousers; and a pair of black, thick-soled boots. His red-trimmed black robes lay folded on the cushion beside him.

Without a word, Garramon made his way over and dropped himself onto the couch opposite Fane. He knew better than to interrupt Fane while he was reading. Tilting his head sideways, Garramon took a closer look at the book in his friend's hands. It was bound in black leather, its edges beaten and worn, its pages stained with what looked to be blood.

"The research papers of Kiralla Holflower," Fane said without lifting his gaze from the book. "You remember her, don't you?"

"A member of the Scholars, was she not?" Garramon said, trying to picture the woman in his mind. Dark hair, reasonably pleasant face, no sense of humour whatsoever. From what he remembered, she was a religious zealot, utterly devoted to The Saviour. Garramon was a believer, but Kiralla Holflower was something else entirely. "It's been quite a while since I've seen her."

"She's dead," Fane said matter-of-factly, turning the page. "She was killed six years ago, along with three others and their retinue."

"That would explain it, then."

Fane lifted his gaze from the book for a moment, shaking his head at Garramon, a half-smile on his face. "She had been conducting research into Essence Runes and summoning, in an old fortress south of Gildor, just within the bounds of Mar Dorul – Kragsdenford."

"I've heard of it. It was abandoned almost a century ago, was it not?"

"For a time, yes. Whoever took it upon themselves to kill Kiralla also decided to burn the place to the ground. It was only by Efialtír's grace that the woman had carved protective runes into the inside of this book. Even at that, some pages didn't survive, but there's enough to be of use."

Garramon nodded, catching Fane's gaze over the top of the book. "I dare say, you didn't summon me here to talk about a dead woman's experiments."

"No. I did not." Fane leaned forward, snatching a long, thin bookmark of red steel from the low table that sat between the two couches. He slid it into place, then closed the book, setting it on the table. He folded his arms, and, leaning back into the couch, turned his full attention to Garramon. "Tell me of the boy's progress."

Garramon shifted in his seat. "His strength grows each day," Garramon said, trying his best to keep his tone flat and level. "He is intelligent, quick to learn, and as stubborn as he is wilful. It has been a long time since I've seen an apprentice with such potential."

"Good. He will be a powerful instrument against the Draleid. His Trial of Will went as planned?"

Garramon nodded. "It did. He is discerning, and he asks as many questions as breaths he draws in a day, but I believe he is beginning to let his walls down."

"He would be a good candidate for Ascension."

Garramon's chest tightened. "If he ascends, he will be of little use when it comes to the Draleid."

Fane let out a laugh, shaking his head. "You've grown fond of him, Garramon. Do not worry. He is far too valuable, particularly with the Blood Moon coming."

Garramon cursed himself for not seeing what Fane was trying to do. He often forgot Fane was no longer simply his old friend. He was the emperor. There was always more to his questions than met the eye.

"To that end, you are to commence his Trial of Faith by the next moon."

"So soon?" Garramon could do little to hide the surprise in his voice. He had always known Fane would want Rist's training accelerated, but to commence the Trial of Faith so soon, particularly in one who was not raised in the ways of the North, would be complicated indeed.

"Indeed." Fane leaned forward. "I will command the same of other sponsored apprentices as well. Primarch Touran is also under instructions to accelerate the training of all Battlemage apprentices in the High Tower. The Blood Moon is fast approaching, old friend, and we must be ready. I need not remind you that this opportunity has been four centuries in the waiting and will not come again for another four centuries. The Uraks grow bolder with each passing day. They seek to be the ones who strengthen Efialtír's hand in this world. Even now I receive reports of heralds aiding their cause. He tests us, and we cannot fail."

Garramon drew in a deep breath, then released it as he nodded. "I will make the arrangements. The trial will begin before the new moon touches the sky."

"Good. Between the unrest in the South and the Urak attacks, we are spread thin. I have spoken to Eltoar, and the full strength of the Dragonguard will be assembled. We must crush this uprising before it begins. We cannot allow it to distract us from our purpose."

As the words left Fane's mouth, the chamber dimmed as though the light had been pulled from the room, darkness encroaching from all corners. Garramon sat up straight. There were some things in life it was advisable to carry both a respect and a healthy fear of – a herald of Efialtír was one of those things.

"Brother Garramon, a faithful servant of the true god." The words echoed in the chamber like the rasp of steel.

Clenching his jaw, Garramon pulled himself to his feet, turning to see the herald standing at the end of the couch, its skin as pale as stretched parchment, its eyes as black as jet, its short hair bone-white. Swirls of vivid blue adorned the herald's black, light-drinking robes. There was only one herald Garramon knew that bothered with that kind of ornamentation, but Azrim's host had been destroyed during the first battle of Belduar. It seemed he had found a new one. Garramon inclined his head. "Herald Azrim, The Saviour's light upon you."

Azrim's attenuated lips pulled into a brittle smile. It was only then Garramon looked closer at the herald's face, or rather the host's face – the high cheekbones, the sharp jawline. Garramon tried to imagine him with bronzed skin and blonde hair. *Artim Valdock.*

Artim had risen to the rank of Battlemage almost two centuries ago and to the rank of Exarch fifty years after that. Garramon had fought many a battle at his side and shared many a bottle. He had certainly counted Artim as a believer, but he had never for a moment thought he was the kind of man who would have put himself forward for ascension. Artim was too arrogant, too focused on his own progress to give himself over to such a cause… at least, that's what Garramon had thought. Perhaps he had judged too quickly. As much of an honour as it would be to share his body with a herald of Efialtír, ascension was not something Garramon himself would have considered. There were far too many unknowns, and he had long questioned how much sentience the host truly retained. It had been a few years since he had last talked to Artim, but he was sad to know they had shared their final conversation.

"Azrim." Fane was slower to rise than Garramon. Looking more closely at his old friend, Garramon couldn't help but notice the weariness that wore dark circles under Fane's eyes. "What news do you bring?"

"Your city of Kingspass was besieged by Uraks who sought to harvest." Azrim's voice was harsh and sharp, each word drawn out longer than it should have been, his breaths a rasping hiss.

If Kingspass had fallen, that would mark the first major city the beasts had razed. The fury in Fane's eyes was plain to see, the twitch of the muscles in his jaw. "And what was the outcome?"

"The city still stands." The herald's bluish tongue crept across its brittle lips as though savouring the words that would soon touch them. "The people speak of a Dragonguard who saved them."

"Dragonguard? Eltoar could not have mobilised so quickly. He is…" The fading of Fane's words mirrored Garramon's own realisation.

"A dragon of white scales," Azrim hissed. "A man with eyes that gleamed purple. They are calling him the Warden of Varyn."

GARRAMON RESTED HIS PALM AGAINST the solid wood of his office door for a few moments, his gaze lingering on the shimmering gold insignia of the Circle – two thin, concentric circles with six smaller, solid circles set into them at evenly spaced intervals – that adorned the wood. Letting out a deep breath, he pushed the door open.

The familiar scent of parchment and burnt wood filled his nostrils as he stepped into his office, the subtle aroma of the candle on his desk lingering in the air. He moved past the rumara wood bookcase that covered the near wall, then dropped onto the wooden chair behind his desk. It wasn't a comfortable chair – far from it. It was sharp and solid, with no cushion, and it creaked every time he sat or stood, but that was the way he preferred it. If the chair had been comfortable, he would have been inclined to sit in it more often – which was precisely the reason the leather chairs by the fireplace had claimed so much of his time.

He reached down, opening the drawer on the right side of the desk, revealing two crystal glasses and a mid-sized crystal flask three-quarters full of Drifaienin whiskey. The tension that had knotted in his muscles during Fane's outburst at Azrim's report loosened at the sight of the mellow brown liquid. He grabbed one of the glasses and placed it on the desk in front of him, then pulled the crystal stopper from the flask and poured a healthy measure of the sweet liquid into the glass before replacing the stopper. He breathed in the earthy aroma as he raised the glass to his nose, holding it there for a moment before pouring every drop into his mouth.

As he held the whiskey in his mouth, the initial sharpness dulled, the earthy flavours distilling, slowly replaced by a sweetness. He drew in another breath through his nostrils, savouring the taste, then swallowed. The liquid burned on its way down, but the sweetness of its aftertaste lingered.

Garramon tilted his head back, closing his eyes. He stayed like that for a few moments before letting out a sigh, opening his eyes, and placing the glass back down on the desk. Reaching into the pocket of his robes, he produced a small iron key, the bow of which was wrought into an open circle with six small balls set at evenly spaced intervals – an imitation of The Circle's insignia. He inserted the key into the lock that was set into the front of the drawer on the left side of his desk, then turned until he heard a distinct *click*.

The drawer held a number of things: a gilded box of blackened oak that held an Essence vessel, a purse full of gold coins, a silver necklace with an emerald pendant, and a cream envelope sealed with beeswax. Garramon's eyes lingered on the gilded box and the Essence vessel within. It had been quite some time since he had felt the rush of Essence flowing through him. He was tempted to tap in, just to feel it, to taste it, but he resisted. As sweet as the power was, it was precious, and it shouldn't be wasted.

Looking past the small box, Garramon picked up the envelope, placing it on the desk in front of him. He ran his fingers across the rough paper, then over the smooth wax that sealed the top.

When Fane had first come to him and told him of Rist, of a young man the herald Azrim had found who not only had the potential to be incredibly powerful but was also a close friend of the emergent rebel Draleid, Garramon hadn't hesitated to do what was asked of him. His duty was to the empire, to Fane, and to The Saviour – as it always had been. Besides, the boy was lucky. Back when Garramon was first brought to The Order, to be trained as a mage was amongst the highest honours possible for a human child – second only to being chosen as a Draleid.

Garramon tapped his finger against the wax seal, producing a solid clicking sound along with a slight flutter as the paper of the envelope repeatedly pressed against the wood of the desk. The boy reminded him of his son, Malyn. They both held the same thirst for knowledge. The same drive. The same dogged determination.

Once more, Garramon removed the flask's stopper, poured a glass of whiskey, emptied the contents into his mouth, and swallowed. "We do what must be done."

CHAPTER SIX

SPIRIT OF THE WOODS

Dann drew in a deep breath, the heavy, damp-soaked air of the woodland clinging to his throat like a wet sock. Cracks of thunder rumbled in the skies above the sweeping forest canopy. The group trudged through the dense foliage, thick vines, and enormous roots that coated the forest floor, with only the light of the baldír to guide them. At that moment, Dann was certain of one thing and one thing only – he fucking hated the Darkwood, or the Aravell, or whatever it was truly called.

There wasn't a single redeemable thing about the place, and of all the questions that burned in him, the one for which he was most eager to gain an answer was why in the void had the elves chosen this place as their home?

"I don't see it, do you?" he whispered, tightening his fingers on Drunir's reins as he leaned closer to the horse who walked along beside him. The horse didn't answer, which, of course, Dann had expected. But even without words, the animal was probably one of the most talented conversationalists in the group.

Therin and Aeson both walked to Dann's left, each with their horse's reins in hand. Ahead, Alea and Lyrei made their way through the dark woodland like kats, an orb of white light floating in front of them. The Angan, Baldon, was in his wolf-like form, keeping pace with the elves, walking on Alea's right, the crest of his back stretching an inch or so above the elf's head.

"Therin?"

The elf stared straight ahead.

"Therin?" Dann raised his eyebrows. "Therin, that's not going to work. I know you can hear me."

Aeson shook his head, a rare laugh escaping him. "Therin, please, for the love of the gods, answer him. You know he won't stop."

Therin turned his head, looked at Aeson for a moment, then at Dann, letting out a sigh. "This better not have anything to do with elves and beards."

For a moment, Dann was tempted, but he thought better of it. "No, but I still have questions about that."

"You always have questions, Dann."

"Fair point. What is it you're so afraid of here? The bards back home always told stories of Voidspawn and dark creatures that stripped flesh for fun and ate bones. If that's true, why in the gods are we here?"

Therin drew in a breath, tilting his head to the side, pondering. "There is truth in every tale, Dann. It is that truth upon which the foundation of myths and legends are created. An old magic permeates this woodland. It was here long before the elves built the city of Aravell. In fact, it was part of the reason they chose this location – an extra line of defence, if you will. There are... spirits that dwell in the forest's depths. In the Old Tongue we call them Aldithmar. They are neither benign nor malevolent. They simply *are*. How they came to be, I truly do not know. But whatever their origins, they defend this place with an unrelenting ferocity. Even the Aravell Rangers only travel the wood safely when accompanied by Angan of the clan Dvalin. The Dvalin seem to have an understanding with the spirits. While it is only the Nithrandír that keep the spirits from the city."

"You mentioned them earlier, Nithrandír."

Therin dipped his head beneath a low-hanging branch, coaxing his horse on after him. "Soulguard, in the Common Tongue. It will be easier to show than tell."

"Mysterious as always, Therin," Dann said, shaking his head. The elf always had a way of turning one question into a hundred and then had the audacity to be irritated when Dann asked for more answers. "Therin... one more question?"

Much to Therin's misfortune, Dann continued to ask as many questions as was humanly possible. Some for curiosity – others for fun. Even if Dann hadn't enjoyed seeing the annoyance on Therin's face, the questions were a welcome distraction from the world around him. But after a while, the questions dried up and the sounds of the Darkwood took over: snapping branches, whistling wind, deep rumbles, and the occasional cries of animals that had suffered the same fate he eagerly wished to avoid.

Dann tightened his fingers on Drunir's reins. "I'm not worried, you're worried."

The horse let out a soft neigh, but otherwise continued onwards, his hooves leaving an impression in the ground with each step.

Dann reached back, brushing his fingers along the fletchings of the arrows that sat in his quiver. He already knew there were twenty-seven; he'd checked them that morning. It was more a comforting habit than anything else. He touched his index finger to the string of his bow, then dropped his hand to the pommel of the sword that hung at his hip. He could wield a sword as well as any, well, perhaps not *any,* but most. Present company excluded. It was Calen who was the true swordsman. He always had been. Dann could barely remember a morning he hadn't seen Calen going through his forms before helping his dad in the forge. And then again most evenings. Particularly after Haem. Something had changed in Calen after Haem died.

Dann pulled himself from his thoughts, looking ahead to where Alea and Lyrei strode through the dark-shrouded wood, Baldon loping along beside them, his enormous frame blocking out most of the baldír light. Dann had spent a lot of time thinking on what Therin had said about elves and honour – about Lyrei. She still hadn't spoken a word. Not one. That in itself seemed like torture to Dann. It also seemed a strange sort of punishment. Back in The Glade, if Dann had done something wrong, his mam might have refused to speak to *him,* but him refusing to speak to her would've been a very short road to a very hard spank with a wooden spoon. And his mam was a kind soul – one with a wooden spoon of retribution.

Dann ground to a halt as something pushed against his chest, and he looked down to see Therin's hand pressed against him. "Therin, what—"

"Shh." The elf kept his hand on Dann's chest as he looked around, a tightness in his stance. Beside Therin, Dann saw Aeson's hands rise to the pommels of his swords.

He hadn't noticed it before, so lost in his thoughts, but now Dann could hear something drifting on the wind. It wasn't the sound he thought he would hear. No snapping, cracking, or vicious snarls as Voidspawn tore through the woodland. It sounded like… a song.

There were no words, only a melody, barely audible. Sweet, soft. It actually brought a smile to his face.

Up ahead, he saw Alea and Lyrei had stopped, the light of the baldír illuminating the raised hackles on Baldon's back.

Therin slapped his horse on the rear, doing the same to Drunir. Both horses took off like bolts of lightning, tearing through the forest in the direction of Alea, Lyrei, and Baldon, Aeson's horse following behind.

"Why in the gods did you do that?" Dann stared at Therin incredulously.

"They won't make it far with us on their backs. Now run." When Dann didn't move, Therin wrapped his fingers around the front of Dann's shirt and threw him forwards. "I said run!"

Dann stumbled forwards, still unsure as to what was happening. Aeson and Therin followed him, pushing him onwards, their swords now drawn, their pace increasing. Up ahead, Alea, Lyrei, and Baldon were doing the same, flitting through the undergrowth like kats, a baldír floating along beside them, matching their speed.

"Therin, what's going on?" Dann pushed the words out through heavy breaths, constantly swivelling his head around to see what they were running from, his pulse racing, his mouth going dry.

"Keep moving." Aeson looked behind them as he spoke, leaping over the trunk of a half-rotted, fallen tree. "Don't stop until we say."

Dann's heart thumped in his ears, each heavy step sending vibrations through his legs, the crunching of branches and shifting of foliage beneath his feet suddenly sharp and crisp. The light from both baldír grew dimmer as they ran, Aeson and Therin's attention drawn elsewhere, allowing Dann to see no farther than a few feet from his face before darkness swallowed everything. Ahead, through the dark, he could still make out the others' outlines, the second baldír causing their shadows to dance as they moved. Fear coiled in his stomach, twisting and turning. He could barely see, he didn't know the ground beneath his feet, and he had no idea what he was running from, but he was absolutely certain if he stopped, he would die.

"The first line isn't far!" Alea roared back, turning her head only slightly. "Just keep—"

Whatever words the elf had intended never left her lips as a shape erupted from the dark, crashing into her, a swipe of its long limb knocking her to the ground. One look at the creature, and Dann's heart stopped.

It stood at least seven feet tall. Its limbs, long and thick, looked as though they had been carved from shattered segments of tree bark. Its arms reached as far as its knees and ended with long broken-ended fingers. Its eyes, set into a head of gnarled, moss-covered wood, pulsated with a pure white light that misted into the air like fog. A shroud of black smoke moved with the creature, mimicking its shape.

The edges of the creature's bark-covered arm shifted and changed as it moved to strike at Alea, sharpening to a fine edge. Lyrei swung her sword, slicing through the bark-forged blade. Carrying her sword through its arc, she brought it back down, dropping to one knee as she cleaved through what looked to be the creature's calf, causing it to unleash an inhuman shriek as it stumbled forwards. The noise sent shivers down Dann's spine. As the creature staggered, roots that coated the forest floor lifted from the dirt, tangling around themselves before connecting to the stub of the severed leg. When the roots had twisted into place, the creature pulled itself free with a snap, its leg renewed.

What in the name of Heraya and Varyn...

Another spirit – that was what Therin had called them, but how true it was, Dann had no idea – stepped from the dark of the surrounding forest, only for Baldon to crash into it, tearing at its chest with his claws and fangs, ripping it to pieces while Lyrei heaved Alea to her feet.

As two more of the spirits stepped into view, Aeson charged, his blades shimmering in the light of the baldír. The spirit closest to him reached out its bark-covered arm, its fingers launching forwards, spiked roots flying through the air. Aeson sidestepped, the roots crashing into the ground where he'd stood. The creature let out a roar, only for it to be cut short as Aeson took its head from its shoulders.

Before the spirit's head had hit the ground, arcs of blue lightning streaked from Therin's fingertips, crashing into both spirits, their bodies igniting in a blaze of orange-red fire.

"Can you run?" Aeson roared as he reached Lyrei and Alea.

Alea nodded, her chest rising and falling in heavy sweeps, her breaths laboured. "The Nithrandír are only a few hundred feet. We can make it."

"Go," Aeson said, pushing Alea forwards. "Go!"

Dann stumbled over a low root, catching himself with his hand before he hit the ground, scrambling forward. As they ran, Aeson turned, pausing so Dann could pass him, before a column of roaring fire erupted from his hands, illuminating the dark-obscured woodland like a signal fire. The blood in Dann's veins ran cold. Dark shapes loomed out of the forest, eyes of misting white, charging towards them. More than he had the time to count.

What the fuck am I doing here? His lungs burned as he begged his legs to keep running – to run faster.

As they ran, Aeson turned sporadically, hurling pillars of fire, casting shadows in bursts of orange-red light. But as Aeson turned once more, roots erupted from the dark, plunging into the man's calf and bursting through the other side, burrowing into the ground. Aeson let out a howl, stumbling and crashing to the ground. Dann stopped, his heart clapping like thunder. A fraction of a second, and Lyrei streaked past him, her curved elven blade glinting in the blended light of Aeson's fires and the baldír.

Every bone in Dann's body told him to keep running. He wasn't a mage. He wasn't a ranger of the Aravell. *Run.* He glanced towards Therin, Alea, and Baldon. The three were still running; they hadn't noticed Aeson fall.

Dann's foot twitched, urging him to turn. *Neither of them even like me that much.* He couldn't just leave them. "Fuck."

Dann shrugged his bow from his shoulders, nocking and loosing three arrows in quick succession. All three found their mark, gliding over Lyrei's head and crashing into the gnarled face of the spirit charging towards her. A burst of white light erupted as one arrow sank into the spirit's pulsating eye. The spirit roared, the blow causing it to hesitate for only a moment before it continued its charge. But that moment was enough for Lyrei to cleave through its legs, take its head, and reach Aeson.

Dann slung his bow back over his shoulder and charged towards Aeson and Lyrei. The elf had sliced through the roots that held Aeson in place and was lifting him to his feet.

Two more spirits erupted from the darkness, crashing into Aeson and Lyrei. Shouts rang out behind Dann, drowned out by the thumping of his heart.

Dann's hand reflexively went for his sword, but he stopped himself. *Steel only slows them. Fire. Fire kills them.*

Not stopping, Dann leapt into the air, bringing his foot down hard on one of the fallen creatures' burning limbs. Like any branch, it broke away with a *snap*. Snatching the burning limb with one hand, Dann rushed towards Aeson and Lyrei, who had managed to drag themselves to their feet, blood pouring from their wounds.

Dann charged past his companions. Heaving as much force into the swing as he could, he slammed the makeshift weapon into the closest spirit's face. A plume of sparks and flames burst into the air, and the creature howled, reeling backwards. Dann slid forward, his legs coming out from under him as his momentum and the damp earth betrayed his footing. He hit the ground with a slap. His fingers carved furrows in the muddy soil as he scrambled to drag himself back to his feet, panic burning in his veins. *What a stupid fucking idea. Get up. Get up. Get up.*

A flash of light burst into life above his head. Arcs of blue lightning. Piercing shrieks scratched at his ears. Fingers wrapped around the back of his shirt, heaving him, pulling him. Lyrei's face was streaked with blood as she pushed him forward, her mouth twisted in pain. Dann stumbled and staggered, catching his feet on vines and upturned roots. Ahead, Alea and Baldon stood beside Aeson, who lay crumpled in a heap, his face pale. *They're not moving. Why aren't they moving?*

"Run!" Dann roared, his throat dry and cracking. "Run!"

He glanced over his shoulder, Lyrei's fingers still clutching the back of his shirt. Therin ran amidst a sea of glowing white eyes that hung in the dark of the forest, illuminated by arcs of lightning that streaked from the elf's hand. More shrieks rang out behind Dann.

Lyrei's hand tightened, clutching the back of Dann's shirt into a clump, then she heaved him forwards, knocking him off balance. He staggered, his foot kicking something hard on the ground, sending him careening towards the others, his arms flailing. The dirt and mud rose to meet him, slamming into his face and chest with a wet slap, knocking stars through his eyes, his lungs gasping for air.

Get up.

His head spinning, Dann pushed himself up from the dirt and scrambled to his feet, slipping and sliding as he did. Lyrei lay face down in the mud beside him, her breathing laboured, dirt and blood coating her face and body. Dann ripped his sword from its scabbard, turning towards the creatures that loomed from the dark. There was no chance of him outrunning them now. If this was where he died, the least he could do was slow them down. *Therin better tell stories about this.*

His chest heaved, his body shook, and the sound of his own breathing was heavy in his ears. The misting white eyes of the spirits pulsated in the dark before him, the outlines of their bark-like faces visible in the dim baldírlight.

"Come on!" he roared, willing his legs to stop shaking.

But the spirits didn't move. Dann tightened his grip on the hilt of his sword. He glanced down at Lyrei. Blood pooled around her.

"They won't cross the line, Dann," Therin said, dropping to the ground beside Lyrei. The calm in his voice was unsettling. "Help me with her."

"What line?" Dann looked to Lyrei, then back at the host of spirits that stood no more than six or seven feet away, black smoke shrouding their frames, their white eyes glowing.

"Dann." Therin's voice was firm. "She's going to die if I don't heal her. I need you to hold her down while I pull this out."

"Pull what out?" Panic set in as Dann turned and dropped to his knees to see a long snapped-off segment of intertwined roots jutting through Lyrei's stomach, blood spilling from the wound. *When did that happen?* Dann let go of his sword, dropping to his knees in the mud.

"Hold her wrists," Therin said, not taking his eyes off Lyrei.

"How bad is it?" Aeson stood over Dann, Therin, and Lyrei, drawing in short, faltering breaths, one hand held against a wound just below his ribs, the other around Alea's shoulder. The muscles in his jaw were twitching as he ground his teeth, the wound in his leg still leaking blood.

Therin ignored Aeson, catching Dann's gaze. "Dann. Wrists."

Dann nodded, swallowing hard in an attempt to grant some moisture to his cotton-dry throat. He slowed his breathing, in through his nose, out through his mouth, just as his dad had taught him. The spirits still stood in the same place, but now Baldon stood only a few feet in front of them, his hackles raised, his lips pulled back in a vicious snarl.

Dann wrapped his fingers around Lyrei's wrists holding, gripping them tight. The elf groaned. "Please… Gahh!"

With no warning, Therin yanked the gnarled section of root free, tossing it over his shoulder in the same motion. Lyrei howled. Dann looked down to see a gaping hole in her leather armour, a hole that carried through into her flesh and deeper into her body. But blood didn't spray or spurt from the open wound. It didn't so much as trickle.

Therin held one hand to Lyrei's side, the other over her wound. "It's going to be all right, my child." The elf's jaw clenched. "It's going to be all right."

Coils of dread turned in Dann's stomach. It didn't look like it was going to be all right.

"Therin." Aeson pulled his arm from around Alea's shoulder and dropped beside Therin, grunting in pain as he did. "Therin, that wound is bad, and you're already weak."

"I'm not letting her die," Therin growled. "You hold back the blood flow. I'll knit the wound."

Aeson looked between Lyrei and Therin, closed his eyes for a moment, then nodded, his expression cold and stoic. To Dann, Aeson looked far weaker than Therin.

Dann softened his grip on Lyrei's wrists and looked up to see Alea standing over them, her eyes wide and bloodshot as she looked down at her sister.

"By the gods," Dann whispered as he watched Lyrei's wound knit itself together from the inside out, blood vessels pulling together, muscle fibres stitching, tissue and skin weaving. Dann had seen Therin heal before – Therin had healed Dann's shoulder – but he had never seen anything like this. How in the name of Heraya was it even possible?

Lyrei groaned, her eyes flickering beneath closed lids.

Therin dropped forward into the mud, his breathing heavy. "We need to get her to Aravell," he said, squeezing the bridge of his nose and shaking his head as though trying to keep himself awake. He leaned back, bringing his arms around his knees and tilting his head back, allowing his breathing to slow. "Aeson, we need to close the wound in your leg. We're going to have to use fire."

Alea knelt beside Lyrei. She brushed her sister's hair aside and ran her fingers along Lyrei's cheek.

Drawing a deep breath, Dann hauled himself upright, picking up his sword and wiping the mud from the blade with his trousers. He slid the blade back into its scabbard as he turned towards where the creatures had been standing and found nothing but darkness and the faint outline of trees and undergrowth looking back at him.

Baldon still stood watch, though he was on two feet, having taken his more human form – *more* being the operative word. Blood and dirt matted the shapeshifter's grey fur, which was tangled with strips of wood and bark. A low growl emanated from his throat.

"Why did they stop?" Dann asked, still trying to calm his breathing and slow his heart. He had barely exchanged two sentences with Baldon since the Angan had appeared at Durakdur. Now was as good a time as any to change that.

"The Nithrandír keep them at bay," Baldon said, his voice harsh and cold. He turned his head, gesturing towards something to the right, his golden eyes gleaming in the white light of the baldír that hovered around Aeson and Therin.

Dann followed the Angan's gaze, finding himself lost for words, which didn't happen often. He wasn't sure how he had missed it at first – likely the lack of any natural light – but before him was what looked like an enormous statue, at least ten feet tall, wrought from thick roots that wrapped around each other like coiling snakes. The roots took an almost human-like shape, though the shoulders were disproportionately large, and the chest broad and deep. Thick silver plates of decoratively ornamented armour covered the statue's back and shoulders, along with its chest, arms, and legs. The plates looked almost twice as thick as any Dann had ever seen, their edges trimmed with gold. "What is that?"

"The souls of old elves who gave themselves to protect their descendants. They ring the entire city."

"I don't—"

"Dann, now is not the time," Aeson called out. "We need you to help carry Lyrei. Aravell isn't far. We need to hurry."

Dann rolled his neck, groaning as his bones cracked and his muscles ached. He carried Lyrei in his arms like a small child. Though she was no small child, and his arms were not built for carrying. He had initially made to toss her over his shoulder, but that had elicited a sharp look from Alea. He had tried to protest but, for the first time in as long as he could remember, he was the only one *not* suffering an injury. On any other occasion that would have been cause for celebration, but at that time, with his arms and shoulders burning from Lyrei's weight, it seemed more a punishment.

"Why can't you carry her?" Dann rolled his shoulders, shifting Lyrei so he could look at Baldon, who walked along beside him with a languid gait, long arms swinging.

"I'm not one of your pack animals," the Angan replied, his golden eyes gleaming, the movement of his mouth showing his razor-sharp teeth.

"And I suppose I am?"

Baldon gave an almost imperceptible shrug, turning his attention back to the path ahead.

"It's not far now," Alea said, walking with a slight limp. "Just up ahead."

"Just up ahead? I think we need to work on your idea of what that means." All Dann could see past the roots, vines, bushes, and trees illuminated by the baldír, was all-consuming darkness. "I'm going to have to put her down soon. She's heavier than she looks." Dan squinted, turning his head away as a blinding light filled his vision. He shook his head, shifting Lyrei in his arms so as not to drop her. As his eyes adapted to the newfound brightness, blurred images and lines began to take shape. The rhythmic sound of running water filled his ears, mixing with birdsong. He felt as though he had been tossed upside down, his stomach threatening to empty its contents. When the sharpness of the light faded and Dann's vision returned, he stumbled backwards, the breath fleeing his lungs. "What in the gods…"

The Darkwood was gone. Above, the sky still held dark clouds, but the sun rested along the western horizon, illuminating the world in a soft glow. Before him was an enormous platform of white stone that spread out in a semicircle, framed by a low white-stone wall. A chasm-spanning bridge connected the platform to a truly gargantuan set of gates that looked as though they had been carved from solid bone and inlaid with an intricate vine-like pattern of gleaming azure stone. The gates rose almost two hundred feet into the air, their tops curving like the antlers of a stag. Two cylindrical, flat-topped towers framed the gates, connecting directly to a wall of smooth natural stone that spread for miles in either direction, rising and rising, connecting to cliffs on either side, as though the city contained within was protected by the landscape itself.

"This can't be possible…" Dann trailed off as he looked around. The forest still stood at his back, as dark and gloomy as ever, but it now lay on an enormous incline as though they had been walking downhill for hours. "I've lost my mind. That's the only explanation," Dann said, gazing towards the massive bone-wrought gates, where there had once been an endless sea of woodland. A sense of relief flooded him as his eyes fell on Drunir. The horse's grey and white dappled coat glistened in the light of the sun as he and the other two horses stood by the low stone wall. "I'm very happy you're all right, but I've finally lost my mind."

He caught Therin's eye, cursing himself at the pure smugness on the elf's face. Therin hated answering Dann's questions, but he delighted in Dann relying on him for explanations. It was a bit of a paradox, really, now that Dann thought about it.

"The most powerful glamour in all Epheria," Therin said. His shoulders were still drooped from healing Lyrei, his eyes sunken and bloodshot, his breathing slow and heavy. But he managed to form the makings of a grin. Dann knew that Therin knew that Dann was going to need more of an explanation than that. "You remember Belduar? The cave in the mountain pass."

Dann nodded. He remembered being just as irritated at the lack of explanation back then as well.

"The magic is similar, though far more powerful. It has kept the Aravell safe for centuries. Even from dragonback, the Darkwood is all that can be seen unless the dragon's underbelly scrapes the forest canopy. The main drawback with glamours of this magnitude is they cannot be locked with a key – as the one at Belduar was. It is a sight-glamour and not a touch-glamour, to put it crudely. Smaller, more concentrated glamours can be gifted with true physical manifestation."

"I see." Dann didn't have a clue what Therin was talking about but Therin didn't need to know that. The elf was smug enough as it was.

The sound of steel on stone drew Dann's attention towards the bridge. His first instinct was to reach for his bow, but since his arms were currently preoccupied with the dead weight of an unconscious Lyrei, he decided against dropping her to the stone.

Ten figures walked across the bridge. Six wore gleaming steel plate, smooth and sleek, looking almost too light to be of any use, swords strapped to their hips, spear-like weapons with long curved blades gripped in their fists. One wore the same leather armour as Alea and Lyrei, green cloak flapping behind them, white-wood bow slung across their back. Another wore long green robes embroidered with gold along the collar and cuffs of his sleeves, and his snow-white hair fell past his shoulders. The last two, who marched either side of the elf in green robes, were garbed in plain white tunics and loose green breeches, their hair cut short.

"Alea, Lyrei!" The elf who wore the leather armour broke into a run at the sight of Alea and Lyrei. "What happened? Where are the others?"

The elf met Dann's gaze, holding out his arms to take Lyrei. His left eye was a milky white. Dann recognised him from the last time they had been in the Darkwood. His scarred face and glassy eye would have been hard to mistake. He was the one who had ridden the black-antlered stag. Taking as much care as he could, Dann let the elf slide his hands under Lyrei's back, taking her into his arms.

"High-Captain." Alea bowed her head, her posture stiffening. "From what we know, Vaeril is still with the Draleid." She paused, her words catching in her throat. "Ellissar and Gaeleron have been welcomed back to the earth."

The High-Captain shifted Lyrei so her head rested on his shoulder. His jaw stiffened. "You have lost the Draleid?"

"We were separated at Belduar, Thalanil," Aeson said, grimacing. "That is why we are here. We require escort through the Aravell, to the Svidar'Cia. We must leave as soon as possible."

Thalanil looked down at Lyrei, who lay in his arms, then towards Alea. He made to respond but was cut short as the other elves reached the group.

"Welcome." The elf in the green robes spread his arms in greetings. He glanced towards Lyrei, then turned to the elf in the white tunic, who stood on his right. "Inform the healers to be prepared." The elf turned his attention back towards the group. "It is truly an honour to lay eyes upon you all." He inclined his head towards Aeson, enough to be a show of respect, but nothing more. "Rakina, your brothers and sisters will have full hearts when they hear of your arrival. And Baldon of the clan Fenryr, may the spirits of the gods guide your light. Clan Dvalin will be most warmed by your presence."

"Halmír, we don't have time for pleasantries," Aeson said, interrupting the elf as his eyes fell on Dann. "We need an escort through the Aravell towards the Svidar'Cia. The Draleid is in danger. As is my son. Please."

The elf held his gaze on Dann for a moment, then reluctantly nodded to Aeson before letting out a subdued sigh. "Very well, Rakina. I will bring you directly to the Ephorí."

CHAPTER SEVEN

SLEEPING DRAGON

Tarhelm – Earlywinter, Year 3081 After Doom

The clash of steel rang out through the enormous atrium of brown stone, bouncing off the walls, echoing in Ella's ears. Her eyes could barely follow as Coren and Farwen danced back and forth across the dusty sparring yard. The sweeps of their swords were little more than shimmering blurs, illuminated by the sunlight that poured through the near-perfect circular hole at the top of the chamber.

Over a hundred people occupied the sparring yard at that particular moment, but most of them had stopped to watch Coren and Farwen, including more than a handful who had ceased their own sparring matches to do so.

Ella didn't blame them. Many of the people Ella had watched spar were at least as capable as any of The Glade's town guard, most even more so, but Coren and Farwen were on another level entirely. The only other person Ella had seen who could move like that was Farda. Perhaps it was something that came with being a mage? Ella wasn't sure, but all she knew was that all three were mages, and all three wielded swords like they were born gripping steel in their fists.

Leaning forward, Ella rested her left elbow on her knee and reached down with her other hand, running her fingers through Faenir's coarse grey fur. Ella sat on a stout wooden bench, one of many that lined the walls of the atrium, with Faenir curled up at her feet, his snout resting on his paws, his gaze following Coren and Farwen as they moved back and forth. "What do you think, boy?"

Faenir let out a low rumble. His ears pricked, and he lifted his head, tilting it sideways as he watched the pair exchange blows. *The two are powerful predators.* A shiver ran through Ella's body, and she shook her head at her own observation. Ever since Farwen had said that Ella might be a druid, something had felt different. It wasn't a dramatic change, but

Ella had begun to notice things. Things that, upon reflection, were likely always there but which she simply didn't question. But now, when she actively leaned into those *feelings*, those sensations, they seemed stronger somehow.

Ella had always known when Faenir was hungry, but she had simply put that down to understanding him. But now, if she tried, she could feel… *more*. She could sense his emotions, his intentions, and in this case, his opinions. The feelings that touched her mind were still obscure enough for her to believe they might be nothing more than an over-active imagination on her part, but she couldn't shake the notion that was not the case.

A round of applause pulled Ella from her thoughts, and she looked back out over the sparring yard to see Coren standing over a kneeling Farwen, her blade resting on the elf's shoulder.

Since she had arrived in Tarhelm, Ella had witnessed Coren and Farwen spar six times, with each of them taking three victories apiece. This was Coren's fourth.

"How are you feeling?" Coren asked as she walked over towards Ella, sweat glistening on her dark skin. Her black hair was tied into a ponytail of intricate braids at the back of her head. The woman was slender, but every inch of her body was lean muscle. She moved with the poise of a kat, her eyes always watching, her body always prepared to move. Faenir respected her deeply.

"Well enough," Ella replied. "Yana insisted I get some sleep last night."

"And she was right to insist so," Coren said, pulling a waterskin from her pack that she had left by the bench before sparring. Lifting the skin to her mouth, she took a deep mouthful, tilting her head back and puffing her cheeks out when she was done.

"She needs sleep as well." Ella did what she could to hide the irritation in her voice. She wasn't truly angry with Coren. The woman had done nothing to deserve her anger. She was angry with herself. It was for her that Tanner had risked his life. And because of her, he now lay in the infirmary. In the ten days since Farwen had returned with Tanner, the man had woken only once and even then for no longer than a few minutes. Apparently Coren had been keeping him alive with her magic, which raised more questions than it did answers. But from what Ella had gathered, that wasn't something Coren could keep doing long term. Yana had stayed with him almost every minute of every day, leaving only to relieve herself, and even then, Ella had caught her eyeing a bucket.

Ella had wanted to argue with her, to drag her out and drop her in a bed instead of the cot she had been using in the infirmary. And she had come close to doing so on a number of occasions, even though she was sure she didn't have the physical strength to drag Yana anywhere, and Ella herself would most likely end up in the infirmary if she tried. But every time she had come close, one thing had stopped her: Rhett. If it had been Rhett lying on that cot, it would have taken the gods themselves to drag her from his side. And she would have fought tooth and claw.

"I will go and see to the scouts," Farwen said, approaching Coren and Ella. The three long scars that ran from the elf's jaw down past her collarbone were even more prominent than usual, flushed with blood from the sparring. Her white-streaked brown hair was twisted into a bun, and much like Coren, sweat slicked her skin, causing her loose shirt to cling to her stomach and sides. "They were due back at least an hour ago."

Coren nodded, taking another swig from her waterskin, handing it to Farwen. "Where are they returning from?"

Farwen took the waterskin, her eyes narrowing as she gauged its weight, hearing the dregs sloshing around at the bottom. She tossed the skin back at Coren with enough force that had it been Ella on the receiving end, it probably would have left her with a black eye. But Coren just snatched the skin from the air and laughed.

Farwen shook her head, not a hint of mirth touching her face. "Fort Harken. The fortress has been under constant Urak attack for weeks now. The fighting has caused disruptions to our supply lines to Catagan and our contacts there. We have more scouts due back from Steeple and Arginwatch by day's end. Juro has been busy."

The hair on Ella's arms pricked, and Faenir lifted his head, his ears sticking straight in the air. Fort Harken. That had been where Tanner had said Farda was going with the Fourth Army.

"All right," Coren said, lifting herself to full height, stretching out her back and arms. "You go. Ella and I have a few things to talk about."

Ella raised an eyebrow at that. If they had things to discuss, it was news to Ella. Though, if she took a moment to think about it, it likely had to do with her place here in Tarhelm. How long had she been there now? Two weeks, perhaps. Ella had known this conversation was coming. Coren had given her longer than Ella had expected. And yet, Ella still wasn't sure on how she felt. She supposed it all depended on the questions Coren asked.

"Here." Coren walked over to a weapons rack that stood between two benches, running her fingers along the pommels of a few of the swords before stopping at one: a short sword with a blade about eighteen inches long, a concave crossguard, and a squashed oval pommel. She pivoted, tossing the blade to Ella. A flash of panic jolted Ella as the blade soared through the air. She jerked forward, snatching the handle as she did, almost tumbling over Faenir. She made to snap at Coren for throwing the sword, but the woman had already stridden past her and now stood about ten feet away in the sparring area.

In truth, Ella was more annoyed that nobody had been there to see her catch the blade. She had surprised herself with that one.

She reached down and scratched the top of Faenir's head as she walked past him. The wolfpine rose to his feet, following her, then dropped in a heap a few feet away, his golden eyes fixed on Coren.

Ella sighed, looking from the blade in her hand to Coren. "You want me to spar with you?"

Coren inclined her head.

"Why is everyone here always sparring?"

"An unused mind grows dull, and unused steel rusts."

In the ten days since Ella had met Coren, she had spent an abnormal amount of time trying to work the woman out. Usually, Ella figured herself for a good judge of people. She had known from the start that Farda was hiding something from her, but she also knew that there was more to him than he let on. Either way, he had served his purpose: he had gotten her to Berona quickly and in one piece. She had also known she could trust Tanner within moments of meeting him. But with Coren, it wasn't that easy.

"Yana tells me you can handle a sword," Coren said, stepping closer, her stare hardening.

"And how would she know that?" Ella tightened her grip on the string-bound handle, moving to her left, her eyes fixed on Coren.

The woman darted forward with no more warning than the slightest shifting of dust beneath her feet. Ella stumbled backwards, just about managing to bring her sword up in time to knock Coren's blade off course.

"She tells me when Tanner brought you to her, you were covered in the blood of the men sent to kill you." Coren swept forward once more, her blade a shimmering blur. Each swing pushed Ella backwards. Within a minute, sweat rolled down Ella's brow, stinging her eyes. It took all her effort to stay on her feet and keep Coren's blade from her skin. The worst part was that Coren wasn't trying particularly hard. Ella had seen more effort on the woman's face when she was practising sword forms.

A glint of steel flashed low, and Ella brought her blade down to meet it, but the force of the collision sent her arm swinging backwards, carried by the weight of the sword in her hand. She gasped as Coren's foot crashed into her stomach, wrenching the air from her lungs.

She released her sword involuntarily, collapsing to her knees, the clattering of steel on stone nothing more than a muted drum compared to the thumping of her heart in her ears. "What..." The words fought against her, refusing to obey until she could drag more air into her lungs. "What was that?"

Coren didn't respond. She simply stood there, looking down at Ella curiously.

Out of the corner of her eye, Ella saw Faenir rise to his full height, his lips pulling back in a snarl, his nostrils flaring, the hackles on his back raising. The wolfpine took two careful steps towards Coren, his head low to the ground. Ella could feel the wolfpine's blend of caution and alertness. It filled her as though it were her own, her heartbeat slowing, her breathing returning to normal. He knew the woman would likely kill him if he attacked, but he would not let her harm Ella.

Ella shook her head, her gaze moving between Faenir and Coren. Had she imagined it? Surely. Grunting, she grasped the handle of the sword and dragged herself to her feet. As soon as she did, Faenir's snarling ceased and the wolfpine stopped, his gaze still locked on Coren. Ella clenched her jaw, taking in a deep breath through her nostrils as she stared at Coren. The dark-skinned woman smiled, nodding slightly and gesturing for Ella to continue.

Ella took a tentative step forward, her throat tightening. She could hold a sword well enough. But she could see no point in sparring with Coren. It was like a mouse sparring with a hawk. Was the woman testing her? If so, what was she testing? Drawing in a deep breath, Ella moved forward, striking twice at the woman's right. Coren deflected the first and sidestepped the second, letting Ella stumble past her, hammering her across the back with the flat of her blade. Ella dropped to one knee but quickly pulled herself back up, turning in time to catch Coren's next strike with the edge of her blade.

After a few minutes, Ella was dripping sweat, her knees were scratched and bleeding, and she could already feel the bruises forming along her arms and back. She stumbled backwards, avoiding a lunging strike from Coren. The woman was only toying with her. She could have had Ella on the flat of her back with ease. Ella tried to relax her shoulders, tightening her grip on the handle of the sword. She could feel it slipping, her hands already slick with sweat. Ella stepped sideways, parrying two swipes of the woman's blade, one at the hip, one at the shoulder, only to feel cold steel on her neck. She swallowed involuntarily.

"What will you do when Tanner wakes?" The tone in Coren's voice was sharp, her eyes locked on Ella's, her arm unwavering as her sword rested against Ella's skin.

"I... I don't know," Ella stuttered, dragging breaths into her exhausted lungs. "I haven't thought that far ahead."

It was the truth. She genuinely hadn't thought that far ahead. For a long time, she hadn't thought any further than getting to Berona. That had been her sole purpose.

"You have family, aside from Tanner?"

The question tied knots in Ella's stomach. She did have family, but how far away were they now? Two thousand miles? Three? Four? Ella had no idea. Even then, it would take her years to gather the coin to pay for a ticket south. How would she ever get back to them? Was going back even what she wanted? She loved her family deeply, but The Glade had always felt so small. Nothing ever changed there. Ella wanted more. But that kind of eye-opening revelation wasn't something she was going to share with Coren, who, for all intents and purposes, was a complete stranger. "I do. But they're a long way away right now."

Coren nodded. "So, you wish to stay? You wish to fight?"

"I don't... I don't know," Ella replied, still very aware of the steel resting against her neck. "I need to speak with Tanner. He's all I have here."

Ella felt Faenir grumble at that. *Aside from you. There is nobody like you.*

"You're going to have to make decisions eventually, Ella."

Ella bit the inside of her cheek, trying to keep down the irritation that was bubbling within. She failed. Reaching up, she swatted the flat of Coren's blade away, glaring at the woman. She held her tongue for a moment, twisting it in her mouth as her mother had taught her. Though her irritation was enough that she didn't bother counting to five. "What is the damn point of all of this? What are you hoping to find by beating me black and blue?"

Silence answered while Coren stared at her as though weighing up what to say. After a few moments, she slid her sword into the scabbard at her hip. "I needed to know your intentions."

"You could have just asked!" Ella threw her arms in the air, doing nothing to hide her frustration.

"Conversations are often more honest when steel is involved." Coren shrugged. "It's harder for that quick brain of yours to come up with an answer when you're swinging a blade." Coren grabbed her pack from the bench where she had left it and slung it over her shoulder. "I hope Tanner wakes soon, Ella. But whether or not he does, you will have decisions to make. For now, I have some things to attend to."

"What? You didn't even..." Ella let her voice trail off as Coren walked away, leaving Ella standing by herself. Even Faenir was confused. The wolfpine watched after Coren for a moment before strolling over to Ella and rubbing his head up against her hip. "Come on. Let's go check on Yana."

YANA WAS PRECISELY WHERE ELLA had left her the night before, sitting on the cot beside Tanner's in the infirmary. Her coal-black hair was tied up with a piece of string, dark circles ringed her eyes, and her legs were folded in front of her with scraps of paper laid out over them and covering the rest of the cot.

The woman didn't so much as lift her head when Ella entered the infirmary, Faenir at her side. Instead, she picked through the scraps of paper, her eyes narrowed like a hawk hunting for prey.

"How is he?" Ella asked, standing by Tanner's cot, watching the slow rise and fall of his chest. He looked a far cry better than he had when he had first arrived. He wore fresh clothes, and the blood had been cleaned from his skin. Most of the smaller cuts on his body had scabbed over and healed, while some of the larger gashes looked as though they were old scars.

Yana lifted her gaze from the papers, staring at Tanner for a few moments before looking up at Ella. "Better," she said, a weak smile touching her lips. "I see his eyes moving beneath his lids from time to time, which means he is dreaming. He'll come back to us soon. He's not done here yet. He's strong."

Ella nodded, resting her hand on Tanner's wrist. "That he is. Just like Rhett."

The coldness that had taken home in Yana's eyes since that night they escaped from Berona faded a little. "If he was anything like Tanner, then he must have been a very good man."

"He was." Ella felt tears threatening her. She shook her head slightly, twitching her nose. She had done enough crying. "What are those?"

"Letters." Yana shifted some papers in front of her, lining them out beside each other. "We've started intercepting the communications from the eastern cities along the Lightning Coast."

"Doesn't the empire get suspicious?"

Yana smiled, more a satisfied grin. "They're a little busy right now with the Urak attacks and the rebellion brewing in the South. They'll likely notice soon, but for now, we get everything that comes this way. We let the ones we have no interest in slip through and add a few of our own, so as not to arouse suspicion too quickly. Everything else we keep. Though, in truth, I'm not sure what to make of it."

"Why?"

"Come here," Yana said, not lifting her eyes from a piece of paper she held in her hand. "Look at this."

Ella moved beside Yana's cot, looking over the letter the woman held out in front of her.

Commander Olivan Karta,

Brother, I hope this letter reaches you before it is too late. Last I heard, you were camped north of Arginwatch with the Second Army. I pray to Efialtír that you are still there. We lost contact with Easterlock and Ravensgate a few days past. Every scout we send fails to return. Twenty good men and women lost.

There have been reports of lone travellers telling stories of armies and dragons, burning and razing everything in their path. My head tells me that is not possible, but with everything that has been happening of late, I dare not discount the notion. I have sent letters to Berona and Al'Nasla in the hope of reaching High Command and the Dragonguard, but you are closest. Brother, whether it be dragons, elves, Uraks, or foreign invaders, something is coming. The air has changed. It tastes of blood and death.

My forces are stationed five miles north of Gildor. We make for the city in the morning. I request immediate support.

Commander Giana Karta, Sixth Army

"Dragons? Surely that's not possible." Ella read the letter again, checking she had read it correctly.

"Is it not? What of the new Draleid that torments the empire in the South? What is possible and what is not seems to have been flipped on its head of late."

Ella shook her head. "But... where would armies even come from? From the ocean? A foreign invasion?"

Yana let out a sigh, giving a slight shrug. "I don't know. Armies from Karvos, maybe. Though that is unlikely. The Karvosi haven't troubled these shores in centuries, and even then, the Order made short work of them."

"But The Order haven't existed in four hundred years. And all I've seen of the Dragonguard are stories."

"Oh, the Dragonguard are very real, girl. Believe you me. But you are right, they are not as common a sight as they once were. All this conflict might change that. We are always fearful of poking a sleeping bear, but what happens when you poke a sleeping dragon? Either way, it could be Karvosi, maybe the Ardanians. I can't see why they would attack the western coast, though. There is always the chance the elves might have finally decided to leave Lynalion. Now there is a scary thought..." Yana's voice trailed off as she read some of the other letters, each from a different person, each saying much the same thing: people are dying, cities are burning.

"The elves? I thought Lynalion was a fairytale. Cities hidden by thousands of miles of forest. Armies of elves waiting for their revenge. It's a common one amongst the bards. I have never doubted that many elves lived within Lynalion, but armies? Numbers great enough to destroy cities?"

"You Southerners believe everything is a fairytale, don't you? The elves of Lynalion are both very real and very dangerous. The cities of Kingspass and Easterlock suffer greatly from raiding parties. And no man nor woman has ever returned once they set foot in that woodland. But stories aside, Farwen has spoken of them, once or twice. It is the only time I hear fear in her voice."

"Fear? But they are her kind."

"Things are... not always so simple. Farwen has not set foot within the bounds of Lynalion since The Fall. Nobody has. At least not anybody I've met."

"Since The Fall? The fall of The Order?" Ella couldn't help but laugh. "That would mean she would have seen at least four hundred summers. That's not possible..." Ella narrowed her eyes as Yana stared at her, a knowing look on the other woman's face. "Is it?"

"You have a lot to learn, Ella Fjorn. Farwen was once one of them, a Draleid." A soft laugh escaped Yana's throat, likely at the look of surprise on Ella's face. "She is not the only one. Coren too. They fought at The Fall, watched their brothers and sisters die before their eyes, their world shattered. I'm not sure when, but sometime between then and now, they lost their dragons to the Dragonguard. I'm sure you've heard stories, but once, when Farwen and I were drowning our sorrows in a bottle of Wyrm's Blood, she described the loss of her dragon like a shattered pane of glass. Like every piece of her was broken at once, with no way of putting it back together. I might not have believed her had I not seen her hold her hand over a flame until her skin blistered. She can't feel pain, or touch, or anything really. She says her dragon took that with him when he died. The ability to feel – I've never quite been able to wrap my mind around that. If you or I think we have endured sorrow, we are sadly mistaken. All we have endured is loss."

Ella's heart ached. Physically. A pain twisted in her chest. The thought of that kind of anguish was incomprehensible. Images of Rhett flashed through her mind, images of Haem. "How... how can they still go on?"

"For the same reason you do," Yana said, resting her hand on Ella's arm. "Because we are more than what we think we are. We are more than the sum of our parts."

"I…" A strange sensation tickled the back of Ella's mind. She could hear something, but she wasn't sure what it was. Beside her, Faenir got to his feet, his ears pricked up.

"What is it?" Yana looked between Ella and Faenir, then towards the infirmary door. "Ella, what's—"

A coughing, spluttering sound came from the cot beside them, and both Ella and Yana nearly leapt from their skin.

"My love!" Yana jumped from her cot, sending letters and sheets of paper pluming into the air.

Ella's pulse raced, her heart pounding like a hammer.

"It's all right, I'm here. It's all right. Try to breathe."

"Alari!" Ella roared, screaming for the infirmerer. "Alari, we need you! He's awake!"

"Ella." Tanner's voice was dry as sand. It croaked from his throat, scratching at the air.

"Ella?" Yana turned towards Ella, her eyebrows raised, then turned back to Tanner, who still lay in the bed. "She's here, my love. What is it? What's wrong?"

Her heart beating even more fiercely, Ella put one foot in front of the other, making her way around Tanner's cot. The man's eyes were wide open and bloodshot, looking straight at Ella as she came into view. His skin was pale, as though the blood had been drained from his face. He swallowed repeatedly, trying to find moisture for his cracked lips and dry throat.

"He needs water," Yana said, her hand cradled behind Tanner's head. "Ella?"

Reluctantly, Ella pulled her eyes from Tanner. She knew Alari kept more than a few waterskins in the infirmary for just this reason. After searching every corner of the room with her eyes, she spotted a leather waterskin sitting on a shelf near the door. She snatched it and pulled out the stopper, sniffing the contents – better safe than sorry. Her mother had often kept diluted brimlock sap in waterskins at home. Ella had forgotten to sniff once; it had not been a pleasant experience.

Once she was sure the waterskin contained water, Ella darted to Tanner's side, pressing the nozzle against his cracked lips. "Drink slowly, otherwise you'll choke."

Tanner spluttered a bit as the first few drops went down, but after a few seconds, he relaxed.

"That's enough for now," Ella said, lifting the nozzle from Tanner's mouth. "I'll give you more in a few minutes. Best to take it slow. How are you feeling?"

Tanner ran his tongue over his lips, spreading the moisture across the dried, cracked skin. He attempted to sit up but grunted in pain, giving up on that idea swiftly. "Ella…" He swallowed hard, closing his eyes for a moment. "I know why—" Tanner gasped in pain, grimacing and clasping his hand to the left side of his ribs.

"Easy," Yana said, resting the backs of her fingers against Tanner's cheek. "You've been asleep for a while. Just breathe with me. In…" Yana drew a deep breath in, holding it. Tanner did as he was asked, closing his eyes and drawing a deep breath in. "And out…" Yana and Tanner both exhaled at the same time.

"Good," Yana gave a soft smile. "Good, my heart. How are—"

Ella's heart almost stopped as the door behind her slammed against the wall, and Alari the infirmerer bounded into the room, her eyes wide and manic, her apprentice, Halea, behind her. "What's wrong? Oh god, Tanner! Halea, get Coren, now!" With Halea dashing from the room, Alari ran to Tanner's side, almost knocking Ella off her feet. "What happened?" she asked, her eyes flitting between Yana and Ella.

"Alari," Tanner croaked, wincing as he turned his head towards the panicked infirmerer. "Please, wait. I'm all right. Just give me some space." With every passing second, Tanner seemed to grow that little bit stronger. He didn't, by any means, look as though he was ready to even sit up straight, but his words became clearer, his focus sharpening.

But before Tanner could say anything else, Coren threw open the infirmary door, Alari's young apprentice walking sheepishly behind her. Without waiting for anyone to speak, Coren cleared the space between her and Tanner in the blink of an eye, resting her hand on his chest. "It's all right, my friend. We weren't sure if we'd ever hear your voice again, but we forgot who we were talking about, didn't we? Lie back, I'll help."

Ella had expected Tanner to argue, or at least for Yana to, but neither said a thing. Tanner simply nodded weakly and lay back in his cot.

Ella had heard of Coren's ability to heal, but she had never actually seen it. The woman had often stood over Tanner for minutes at a time and stepped away weak and weary, but Ella had never seen any improvement in Tanner. This time however, as Coren stood over Tanner, a look of intense focus on her face, Ella could see Tanner's expression change as the pain was lifted from him. More than that, Ella watched as a cracked scab on his left cheek knitted itself back together before falling onto Tanner's pillow, leaving nothing but pink skin behind.

Ella had seen Farda use magic when they had fought the Uraks and when he had dragged the air from that man's lungs at Berona, but this was somehow different – watching a magic that could save a life, instead of taking it.

Coren stumbled, grabbing onto Alari as she did. "That's… that's all I can do for now." She nodded towards the infirmerer, giving a smile of thanks, before looking back to Tanner. "How do you feel?"

Tanner stretched his head back, eliciting a series of – surprisingly satisfying to hear – cracks. Pushing his hands against the base of the cot, he lifted himself into a seated position, allowing a smile to touch his face for just a moment. "Much better. Thank you, my friend."

"Your thanks have been given in your deeds." Coren bowed her head, sitting back on the cot behind her. The woman's eyes held a tiredness that had not been there previously. Ella noticed her shoulders were slumped, her head drooping as though it was now too heavy for her neck.

"Ella."

Ella turned her head at the sound of Tanner's voice.

The man drew in a deep breath, wincing as he exhaled. "Before they got to me, I spoke to some of my contacts within the keep. I was looking for anyone who might know why Farda was interested in you."

Ella sighed, doing her best to hold her frustration down. "Tanner, I don't think—"

"It's your brother, Ella."

A shiver swept across Ella's skin, every hair on her body standing on end. A lump formed in her throat, as though she had tried to swallow an apple whole. "… Calen. Tanner, please tell me he's all right."

A deep sadness filled Tanner's eyes. "He is all right," the man said, hesitating a little.

Tanner's hesitation coiled like a string around Ella's heart. "What are you not telling me? What's wrong?"

Tanner looked to Yana, then to Coren. Both women's faces looked as perplexed as Ella felt.

"Farda was after you to get to your brother."

Ella snorted, unable to hold it back. "Calen? Tanner, you must have hit your head harder than we thought. Why in Elyara's name would Farda be trying to get to Calen? He doesn't even know Calen exists. To him, I am Ella Fjorn, not Ella Bryer."

Tanner shook his head as though trying to clear his mind, a flash of irritation on his face. He held up his hand, drawing in another deep breath and letting it out slowly through his nostrils. "He knows precisely who you are. He knows you are Ella Bryer, he knows you come from The Glade, and he knows who your brother is."

"Even if he does, what does it matter? We are nothing."

Tanner pushed himself up further on the cot, straightening his back against the pillow behind him. "Ella, your brother is the Draleid."

"What? No…" Ella's words caught in her throat. That wasn't possible. There was no way. The laughter that left Ella's throat was more a reflex than anything else. "Calen? I think you need to get better contacts."

Silence hung in the air as Ella looked to Coren and Yana as though she expected them to burst into laughter at the ridiculous idea that her brother could be the Draleid. But neither of them did. Ella shook her head, turning her gaze back to Tanner. He returned it, unblinking. "That's just not true, Tanner. It can't be. How could it be?"

Even as she spoke, Ella's mind ran wild. Could it be true? The soldiers on the Merchant's Road had known her by name. How else would they have known? And Farda had shown up at the docks at precisely the right time. She had always thought it happenstance, but the more she thought about it, the stranger it seemed.

"Ella. There's more."

The tone in Tanner's voice pulled Ella from her thoughts. She stepped closer to Tanner's cot, her gaze never leaving his, her breath catching. "Please tell me he's all right, Tanner. For the love of the gods, please." Tanner looked away, only for a moment, but the sight sent ice flooding through Ella's veins. She gripped Tanner's forearm. "Tanner, please. Tell me."

The man shifted slightly in the cot, swallowing hard. "Honestly, I don't know. The empire is still looking for him, which is a good sign. But I truly can't be certain."

"That's good," Ella said, nodding. Her heart was galloping. She could feel her pulse pounding through her veins. *Please be all right. I can't lose anyone else.*

"Ella." Tanner's voice drifted to the back of Ella's mind.

"It's a good sign though, isn't it? They haven't found him. That has to be good."

"Ella!"

Ella almost leapt from her skin at the urgency in Tanner's voice, his hand clamping down on top of hers. All of her thoughts stopped, crashing together as she looked into the man's eyes. "What?"

"It's your parents."

"What about them? They..." Ella's breath caught in her throat as she saw the look on Tanner's face. "No." She shook her head, an involuntary laugh escaping her lips. "No. They couldn't... you're mistaken." Ella's heart twisted. Faenir whimpered as he pressed the side of his head against her leg. She tried to breathe, but her throat was so tight it felt like she was choking. An unseen force wrapped its fingers around her heart and squeezed, wrenching, twisting. "Tanner, no."

Tanner squeezed Ella's hand. "I'm so sorry."

Ella pulled her hand away from Tanner's, shaking her head. "No... they can't..." She stumbled backwards. Without another word, Ella turned and walked towards the door, Faenir following. With every step, she was certain her legs would give way beneath her. She could hear Tanner calling, but his voice faded against the wave of loss that swept through her.

CHAPTER EIGHT

AL'NASLA

Rist found himself wishing he had chosen three smaller books to stuff into his pack as he half-walked, half-ran through the palace grounds, moving as fast as he could without it looking like he was rushing, which was surprisingly difficult to do. He was already worn out from sparring with Brother Garramon, and now he could feel sweat once again slicking his brow. It seemed today was one of those days where he would constantly be chasing his own tail, running late for everything.

It didn't make matters any better when he found Neera already standing before the palace gatehouse, her black-trimmed brown robes draped over her shoulder, an overly smug grin adorning her face.

"Ah, Rist Havel decides to finally grace us with his presence." Neera gave an exaggerated bow, her dark hair hanging over her shoulders as she did. "Welcome, m'lord."

"Knock it off," Rist said, eyeing her askance as he wiped the sweat from his brow and patted down his robes, trying his best to look as presentable as possible. "Where's Sister Anila?"

"Oh relax," Neera said, laughing. "You're always so serious. She'll be here in a minute. She's speaking to one of the palace guards." Neera's expression shifted as she looked Rist over. She squeezed his hand, her eyes softening. "Are you all right?"

Rist nodded, allowing a soft smile to touch his lips. He hadn't meant to be so short with her. "Garramon gave me a letter from my parents a few days ago, and I realised on the way here that I still haven't read it."

"I can read it with you later, if you'd like?"

Before Rist had a chance to answer, he saw Sister Anila striding towards them, her blonde hair and silver-trimmed black cloak drifting behind her, a sword strapped to each of her hips. Sister Anila wasn't a particularly imposing figure, at least not in terms of size. She was no taller than Rist, she was missing her left arm up to the elbow, and only a thin layer of muscle wrapped around her bones. But what she lacked in heft, she more than made up for in ferocity. Rist had once watched her knock Tommin unconscious with an apple just to prove that anything can, and should, be perceived as a weapon. Not to mention the rumour that Neera had told him about how Anila had cut off her own left arm in the middle of a battle when she had been pinned by a fallen horse. He wasn't sure he quite believed that, but he didn't doubt that if anyone was capable of it, it was Sister Anila. "Apprentice Havel, you're late."

"Apologies, Sister Anila. I was training with Brother Garramon. We ran over time."

"I don't care," Sister Anila said, the slightest upturn of her bottom lip her only expression. "You're late."

"My apologies. I will do better next time."

"Yes. You will."

Rist let out a stifled gasp as Sister Anila sliced a thread of Air along the already-scarred flesh of his back. It wasn't common for Sister Anila to resort to that level of *'education'*. She must have been in a particularly bad mood. Rist clenched his jaw, inadvertently cutting into the soft flesh of his lip with his tooth, the coppery taste of blood touching his tongue. He focused on what Garramon had said to him that day in the courtyard. *'Because these scars built me. Each one is a reminder of the pain I endured and the pain I overcame. That is what yours are, as well. Cherish the pain. Let it bind to who you are. You will be the better for it.'*

"Thank you, Sister." Rist clenched his jaw as he spoke, his teeth grinding as he drew in a slow breath through his nose. To thank someone for causing him pain seemed counter-intuitive. But responding with anger would only have led to more pain.

Sister Anila raised an eyebrow at him, but something in her expression made Rist think she was satisfied by his reply – though he truly was terrible at reading facial expressions. It wasn't something that came naturally to him. He had worked on it, of course, spent hours studying the way people's faces moved when they were happy, sad, irritated, excited, but it was always something that required conscious effort on his part.

"Come, follow me. The drills are to begin shortly." Sister Anila didn't stand on ceremony, turning even before the last word had left her mouth.

"Thank you?" Neera whispered as she and Rist followed the Exarch.

Rist shrugged. "It worked, didn't it?"

Neera looked as though she was going to question him further but thought better of it. Instead, she simply shook her head and continued walking.

Rist smoothed down his brown robes as they approached the palace gatehouse. The last time he had seen the gatehouse up close had been when he and Neera had snuck out. Neera had suggested a return journey into the city on more than one occasion, but he had put his foot down. Or rather, he had stuck his head in his book and pretended he hadn't heard her. It's not that he didn't want to sneak out again. He did. He wanted to explore the city, to spend another night with Neera at the docks, and deep down – though he would never tell Neera – he wanted to see if he could find an Alamant who might be willing to talk to him.

Ever since that night in the city when he had seen the Alamant blowing fire in the streets, his curiosity had exploded. There were so many questions. What *was* an Alamant, really? Did each possess a similar limitation, or were they unique? Was it a general lack of power that led to becoming an Alamant, or was there more to it? Were there truly no Battlemages who had ever become Alamants? He had still not found a single book within the library that provided any tangible information on Alamants other than that they were people who were capable of touching the Spark but failed to pass the Circle's trials.

It seemed that if he were to ever get any answers to the questions that swirled around in his brain, he would have to find them himself. The true question, though, was whether to sneak out now, or to wait until they passed their Trial of Faith, whenever that might be. If they were Acolytes, they would be free to come and go as they pleased. Less risk. Rist was well aware that he tended to obsess over these kinds of things – unanswered questions – but it wasn't something he could help.

"Rist?"

"Huh?" Rist shook his head, only vaguely aware of Neera tugging at his robes. He pulled himself from his thoughts, realising they had already passed through the palace gatehouse and were only a few feet from the staircase that descended from the palace to the city below. "Sorry, I got a bit lost in my own head."

Neera frowned. "Try to stay focused, will you? As endearing as I think your constant daydreaming is, I don't think Sister Anila feels the same. And after the amount of lashes Brother Pirnil gave you the other day, I'd like to keep your back from becoming more scarred than it already is. I honestly don't understand why you just don't have the healers tend to you. Your back looks like a whipping post at this point."

"Because they are a reminder." Even as he spoke, Rist could feel some of the scabs cracking and bleeding, the blood trickling down his back where his undershirt wasn't pressed against his skin.

"A reminder? I don't think I'll ever forget."

Rist gave Neera a weak smile as they walked. When he had first seen the twisted mess of knotted flesh and scars that adorned Garramon's back, Rist had asked the same question as Neera. Even after Garramon had explained, Rist had not quite understood. But he had decided the best way to understand was to see for himself. He had been surprised at the strange motivation he had felt upon seeing the scars in the mirror. *'Cherish the pain. Let it bind to you.'* Garramon had been right. They were a reminder. A reminder that pain was simply an obstacle. And if it were an obstacle, its sole purpose was to be overcome.

As they descended the seemingly endless staircase, Rist lifted his gaze over the city. He had looked out at the city from the windows of the palace and the embassy many times, but the view from the staircase was different. It was unobstructed by walls or towers, and his range of vision wasn't limited by the size of a window. From where he stood, he could see out over all of Al'Nasla.

The city sprawled outwards from the foot of the palace steps. Rooftops and towers of grey stone spread across the landscape, split by long streets that ran the length and breadth of the city in a pattern that, now that Rist looked closely at it, was anything but random. Eighteen streets started at the foot of the steps, moving outward from the central plaza. The streets grew further apart at an equal rate as they moved towards the outer walls. The only time the streets' progress was hampered was when they reached one of the five trench-bracketed walls that encircled the city. But then, on the other side of each wall, new streets continued on the same course. Another set of streets, the number of which Rist couldn't determine, ran from the east to the west of the city, each intersecting every single one of the original eighteen streets that moved outward. It reminded him of a spider's web.

Al'Nasla couldn't match the colouring and splendour of Camylin with its red slate rooves and cylindrical towers, but in sheer size, Camylin was like a small village next to Al'Nasla. In all the time Rist had been at the embassy, he hadn't considered the number of souls that must reside within the walls of Loria's capital. Looking out over the city now, he reckoned the entire population of the villages could have fit into Al'Nasla almost a thousand times over. That guess might have been a bit north of the true figure, but he didn't think it was too far off.

By the time they reached the bottom of the steps, a cacophony of sounds filled the afternoon air, bouncing off the tightly packed buildings and flagstone streets. The calls and shouts of pedlars and hawkers, the unyielding hum of chatter, the squeaking axles of cart wheels, and, to Rist's surprise, the bleating of a particularly large goat that sat atop a stack of crates twice as tall as Rist. The crates were stacked beside a stall packed with vegetables, run by a short man with thick shoulders, a bald head, and a long moustache that dangled on either side of his mouth.

"Stay close." Sister Anila turned her head slightly as she spoke, her eyes narrowing at Rist.

"Yes, Sister." The statement hadn't required a response, but Rist's attention was too focused on the goat to care. The animal looked as though it were a king overseeing his people, a crown of horns on his head. "How did it get up there?" he whispered.

"How did what get up where?" Neera asked, looking at Rist as though he were crazy.

"The goat."

"The goat?"

"Did you not see the goat?" Rist looked back, but they had just turned a corner, and the goat was no longer in view.

"We're about to witness real Battlemages go through actual battle formations, and you're focused on a goat?"

"It was sitting on top of crates."

"Why does that make the slightest difference?"

"I was curious as to how it got to the top."

Rist jerked to a halt, almost slamming into Sister Anila, who had stopped and turned to face the two apprentices. "What in the name of The Saviour are you two chattering about? You are apprentices of the Imperial Battlemages of the Circle of Magii." Sister Anila leaned in closer. "Start acting like it."

Without waiting for a response, Sister Anila turned on her heels and continued down the long street, the implication being for Rist and Neera to follow her.

Neera let out a sigh, shaking her head, muttering as she walked. "A fucking goat…"

Rist shrugged. "I was curious."

The streets of Al'Nasla were nothing like they had been when Rist had seen them at night. They were still packed with people, still churning with discordant sounds, but the atmosphere was entirely different. The bards telling tales and singing songs, had been replaced by flower sellers, fruit merchants, fur traders, and a variety of others. The scantily clad men and women were nowhere to be seen, and, most notably for Rist, he didn't sense even the slightest sensation of the Spark, bar the general thrum in the air – which meant no Alamants.

Another difference was the smells. Rist hadn't noted any particular aromas on his last visit to the city. But now, during the day, the warm scent of fresh-baked bread drifted on the air, accented by the distinctly salty smell of cured meats and the unmistakably pungent odour of fresh fish. But above all else, it was the sweet scents of the flowers that caught his attention, reminding him of the aroma that always drifted on the air outside Verna Gritten's house – a result of her soap making. Rist had always loved walking past that house each day, particularly in the spring when traders brought Valtaran oranges into the village. Verna's orange and lily soap was quite possibly the single nicest thing Rist had ever had the pleasure of smelling. The smell filled Rist with an intense longing for home.

"Are you all right?" Neera asked as they turned another corner and passed through a wide archway set into the first city wall. "You're disappearing even more than usual."

"Me? I'm fine." Rist shook his head, giving Neera a reassuring smile. "Just thinking of home."

"This place reminds you of home? I can't image Al'Nasla is anything like your little farming village."

"I'm not from a 'little farming village'," Rist sniped before noticing the grin that was forming at the corners of Neera's mouth. "Oh, fuck off."

Neera let out a suppressed laugh, careful not to let Sister Anila hear. "You're too easy."

"You know you don't always have to try and wind me up."

"But it's so much fun. You know you'd miss it if I stopped."

Rist glared at Neera for a moment before turning his attention back to the city.

"What is it that reminds you of home?" Neera's voice was softer, gentler.

"The soap. Well, more the flowers. There isn't any soap here. At least, I don't think there is."

"Rist, come on. You're making it really difficult." Neera laughed, bumping her hip against his.

"The smell of the flowers reminds me of home. There's a soap maker there, Verna. Her orange and lily scented soap is my mam's favourite."

"That's... that's actually kind of sweet. For a farm boy."

"I'm not a farm boy. I've never worked on a farm in my life."

Neera's only reply was a wink accompanied by a smug smile. She held his gaze for a moment before turning her head and picking up her pace. "Come on, if we fall too far behind, Sister Anila will give you some new scars to remember."

Rist shook his head and followed Neera. He still found her no less irritating than he had the first day he'd met her, but it was an endearing form of irritating, if that were possible.

As they made their way through the enormous city, weaving between the throngs of people, Rist became more and more aware of the subtle shifts in people as they passed by. The halting of conversations, the whispering, the tracking eyes, the way in which people stepped aside to let them pass. At first he had simply thought himself paranoid – which was something he knew he was often guilty of and tried to push aside. But after a while, he scratched that off the list of possibilities in his mind, certain of what he was seeing. If he was being honest, Rist wasn't entirely sure how he felt about the peoples' reaction to them – was it a good thing or a bad thing? Were they scared or being respectful? After a while, he simply dropped his gaze to the street in front of him and followed wordlessly after Sister Anila. He could see a similar change in Neera. She was usually almost as bad as Dann when it came to never shutting up, but as they walked, she grew quieter and quieter.

Sister Anila seemed to notice, too.

"They are worried," the woman said, dropping back so that she walked just in front of Rist, to his left. There was a softer tone to her voice.

"Worried, Sister?"

"News travels fast, apprentice. For generations, the Lorian people have known near unwavering peace. But now there are rumblings of rebellion in the South, Urak armies are burning and raiding the villages along the foothills of Mar Dorul and the Lodhar Mountains, and refugees fill the roads across the empire. The First Army has been running drills for days now at the barracks, which has likely set rumours spinning even faster. If the sight of a Battlemage and two apprentices walking through the streets didn't elicit whispers, I would be concerned. Now, come along. We're already late."

Rist, Neera, and Sister Anila walked in silence for the next while, the whispers and sideways glances around them unceasing. It was only after they passed through the archway set into the fourth wall and into the outer rim of the city that Rist realised something: this would be the first time he had stepped outside the city walls since he had first arrived. At first, the thought struck him as strange. How could he have been there for months and never have left the city even once? This was only the second time he had even left the palace. But when he thought about it, the palace grounds themselves were around the same size as The Glade and he had only ever left The Glade a few times a year with his dad to arrange supplies for the inn.

The outer walls were cast in the same grey stone as the rest of the city and stood at least a hundred feet high, likely higher, easily thick enough for two wagons to ride along the ramparts side by side. Enormous, crenellated towers broke the monotony of the walls at clearly defined intervals, each as thick and wide as The Gilded Dragon.

"Stand back," a voice called out from up ahead, near the gatehouse that stood watch over the main passageway in and out of the city. "I said stand back!"

What had to have been at least fifty Lorian soldiers stood at the city gates, each garbed in full plate, swords strapped at their hips, red cloaks emblazoned with the black lion of Loria drifting behind them.

Standing before the soldiers and stretching back into the distance, was a line of men, women, and children. Some sat on horseback, others in carriages or the back of carts, but most were on foot. But whatever their method of travel, their faces were weary, their clothes worn and crusted with dirt and, in some cases, blood.

"Stand back and wait your turn," the same voice, likely one of the guards, called out. "You will all be processed, but you need to wait!"

"We're hungry!" A voice called back.

"We need food!"

"And water!"

"You will all be fed and watered," the guard shouted. "But if anyone tries to force their way through, there will be one less mouth to feed."

A murmur ran through the crowd at that, but the unease seemed to quieten, at least for the time being.

"Refugees have been arriving in even greater numbers over the last few days," Sister Anila said, leading Rist and Neera towards the gates.

"Why don't the guards just let them in?" Rist was aware of the ignorance of his question. There were clearly reasons as to why, but that was precisely why he had asked the question. Questions were the enemy of ignorance, and they needed to be asked.

Sister Anila frowned and gave Rist a look that let him know she thought the answer was an obvious one, which it wasn't. "Because that would lead to chaos, apprentice. Each refugee must be checked and accounted for. Otherwise, we could not cater to their needs. Without knowing their numbers and general disposition, how would we provide an adequate number of beds or enough food and water? And if we failed to do that, unrest would fester within the city. Wars are rarely won by strength of steel alone. Steel wins battles, but revolts topple kingdoms."

"I see," Rist said, giving a slight nod. That response actually answered his question perfectly, which satisfied him to no end. "Thank you, Sister."

Sister Anila inclined her head, then gestured for Rist and Neera to follow her towards the gates. As they drew closer, Rist noticed the guards were stopping people as they left the city, as well as when they entered. Though, with Sister Anila's answer in mind, he supposed that made perfect sense. To account for the number of people within the city, the guards would also need to reconcile those who left. But even from a purely logistical standpoint, Rist didn't see how their numbers would come close to being accurate with a city this large.

"Exarch." One of the guards, a tall man with a smashed-flat nose and greasy, greyish hair, gave a slight bow at the waist. He wore full plate armour, the ends of a chainmail shirt hanging just below the rim of his breastplate, his helmet held in the crook of his arm.

117

"Captain," Anila replied, giving nothing more than an almost imperceptible nod. "My apprentices and I are expected at the army camp."

"Of course, Exarch." The man bowed again, taking a step back and gesturing for them to pass.

"Thank you, Captain." Instead of walking past the man, like Rist had expected Sister Anila to do, she instead took a step closer to him, resting her hand on his pauldron. "How are things here? How are the people?"

For a moment, the captain looked surprised – he had clearly expected Sister Anila to pass him without another word – but he regained his composure, straightened his back, and tried his best to meet Sister Anila's gaze. "Scared, Exarch. Scared, hungry, and tired. And they've every right to be."

Seemingly unsatisfied with the brevity of the answer, Sister Anila continued to fix her gaze on the captain, not saying a word.

"I, ehm… Many have seen their villages burned, Exarch, their loved ones slaughtered by Uraks." An honest sadness crept into his voice. "Some have come as far as Arginwatch and the western villages along the base of Lodhar, refusing to stop until they reached Al'Nasla."

Sister Anila nodded. "What do we do with the hungry, the tired, and the scared, Captain?"

"I'm sorry, Exarch. I'm not sure what you mean?"

"What do we do with the hungry, the tired, and the scared?" Sister Anila repeated. "We feed them, we give them a place to rest, and we slay their demons. The Saviour watches over us, Captain. My brothers, sisters, and I will drive the beasts back to the depths from which they came. You feed these people, ensure the Craftsmages give them a place to stay, and we *will* slay their demons."

"It will be done, Exarch." The captain lifted his chin, determination in his voice. "May The Saviour watch over you."

"And also you."

As they made their way through the city gates, past the seemingly endless stream of refugees who eyed them with a mixture of curiosity, reverence, and caution, Rist couldn't help but stare at Sister Anila. In his time in the embassy, Rist had met quite a few mages and High Mages alike. One trait most of them shared was arrogance. It was something Rist had become accustomed to. Alongside that tended to be a complete disregard for anyone lower than them, to the point that Rist could count on one hand the number of mages with which he had held a conversation, and even the word 'conversation' was a stretch. Garramon was the exception and, to some degree, so was Sister Anila. But what Sister Anila had just said to that man showed a level of empathy he had not yet seen within The Circle.

The drawbridge creaked and groaned as Rist stepped out from under the arch of the city gates. Rist had read of Al'Nasla's dry moat. It spanned just over sixty feet – sixty-three and a half, if Rist remembered correctly. Looking out at it now, it seemed far larger. Two islands stood in the middle of the moat. The city's drawbridge connected to the first island, while a permanently fixed bridge connected the first island to the second. A third bridge, that could only be raised and lowered from the second island, was connected to the bank on the far side. It all seemed a little excessive to Rist, but he had no doubt it would be effective in the case of an attack – and what he knew about siege defence was so little it could be scrawled on a blade of grass.

Stepping close to the edge, Rist looked down into the moat, casting his gaze over the enormous trench that ringed the city. "Ninety-seven feet deep. The original trench was dug around the fledgling village of Al'Nasla in the year three hundred and thirteen After Doom, during the Uzgar War. As the city grew, the trench was filled and moved, being made wider each time."

"Is there a book in that library you haven't read?"

"Plenty. Thousands, in fact."

"It was a rhetorical question, Rist." Neera gave Rist a flat stare, the same one she always gave him when he didn't understand something that seemed perfectly obvious to her.

Rist shrugged. The mention of books caused his mind to temporarily shift to *Druids, A Magic Lost*. He would have finished it weeks ago if he'd been given some time alone, but that was a precious commodity nowadays. *Hopefully I can get to it tonight. For now, I need to focus.*

Each of the two islands that stood within the moat were slightly wider than they were long and large enough to hold twenty to thirty people at any one time. Five soldiers in red and black leathers were stationed on each island, while a further twenty held positions on the far bank, controlling the flow of refugees and visitors. Each group of soldiers nodded to Sister Anila as she, Rist, and Neera passed. Most even did the same to Rist and Neera, which surprised him. He supposed to those in the North who couldn't touch the Spark, any mage was to be respected, even apprentices. It was an interesting contrast between the North and the South. Respect versus fear. Protection versus oppression.

"That's the camp," Sister Anila said, once they had reached the far bank. She pointed to an enormous encampment that stood about a mile from the city. Rows of long, grey slate rooves peered over thirty-foot high walls. The grounds outside the camp's walls were abuzz with activity. The thunderous stamping of feet, clinking of steel and roaring of commands filled the air as groups of soldiers in full armour marched about in formation, running drills, captains and commanders shouting at the top of their lungs. Even from that distance, Rist couldn't help but be impressed by the discipline of the soldiers, who moved with an almost unnatural unity, matching each other's steps and movements to the second.

"Al'Nasla's army camp is the largest in all the continent," Sister Anila continued. "It was built to hold two armies at any one time but acts as the permanent residence of the First Army, while the city's garrison is barracked within its walls." Sister Anila turned her head, ensuring she had Rist and Neera's attention. "As of yet, we have not gone through the structure and breakdown of Lorian armies. Though, I'm sure you've read a few books on the subject, Rist."

Rist nodded, taking a few seconds to register that Sister Anila's continued stare meant she wanted him to give a deeper answer. "Each Lorian army comprises around five thousand four hundred soldiers, including four hundred cavalry, with a slight variance depending on auxiliary forces." It was only as the words left Rist's mouth he realised that meant this army camp was capable of holding over ten thousand souls at any given time. *Ten thousand. That's more than all the villages five times over.* "The cavalry is divided into four groups of one hundred, known as flights, while the infantry and archers are divided into ten blocks of four hundred, each led by a general, which is further divided into five cadres of eighty, each led by a cadre captain. The last block of one thousand infantry is led by the army commander."

As Rist finished his sentence, he drew in a deep lungful air, realising he hadn't taken a single breath while speaking. He also noticed that Neera was just staring at him, shaking her head.

"Very good." Sister Anila gave a slight upturn of her bottom lip. "And embedded within each army are twenty-eight Healers, a Consul, a Craftsmage, and one hundred Battlemages. One hundred and thirty mages in total. Today, you will meet Magnus Offa, Battlemage Commander of the First Army. It is under his tutelage that you will begin training in group combat formations. When Apprentice Battlemages are trained at the High Tower in Berona, they engage in formational training amongst groups of their peers. But we are not in the High Tower. There are only four sponsored apprentices in all the embassy, as you well know, and only you two are pledged to the Battlemage affinity. As such, you will be training directly with the Battlemages of the First Army. Exarch Magnus Offa is one of the most decorated military commanders in Lorian history. Do not squander this opportunity. Sponsored apprentices are not taken into The Circle often, and as such, very few are ever offered the level of training you receive. But let me be clear: you are expected to excel. Am I understood?"

"Yes, Sister Anila." Both Rist and Neera said in unison.

"Good. Follow me."

Sister Anila led Rist and Neera through the practice grounds, stopping every now and again to point out different infantry formations, explaining close-order and extended-order drills, and commenting on the effective uses for different weapon classes. She even recommended a book for Rist to research: *The Art of War* by Sumara Tuzan. Rist was so appreciative of her interest in his reading he neglected to mention that he had already read the book – twice.

"Battlemages are not just warriors," Sister Anila said as they rounded a group of spearmen running a close-order drill. "We are leaders of men. When the fighting starts, when steel clashes and blood soaks the ground, the soldiers will look to us for guidance. Our presence alone will save lives. And as such, we must understand war. We must understand the mechanics of combat, the tactics of battle, and the workings of the human spirit – and what breaks it."

Rist stopped dead, a low thrum resonating through his body, causing the hairs on his arms to stand on end. When someone drew on the Spark, Rist could feel it pricking at the back of his mind, but this was different. The sensation he was used to feeling was but a trickling stream compared to the ocean of power that now pulsated in the air, rippling in waves.

"You feel it." A smile rested on Sister Anila's face as she looked between Neera and Rist.

"What is it?" Neera asked, short of breath, a touch of panic in her eyes.

"It's the Spark, apprentice. In cities such as Al'Nasla, and in particular, Berona, the sensation always lingers in the air, like the burbling of a river in the back of your mind. But when enough mages in close proximity draw from the Spark at the same time, its aura seeps into the world. But it means we are close." Sister Anila continued walking, gesturing for Rist and Neera to follow.

With the Spark thrumming through the air, everything felt different, clearer. The sounds around him separated, each clanging steel boot unique, each roar and shout distinct. The air tasted crisp, like the aftermath of summer rain, and the once-gentle breeze felt almost harsh against his skin.

After a few minutes of walking past cavalry formations and groups of infantry practising the set-up and take-down of tents, the Battlemages of the First Army came into view. Even were it not for the gleaming half-plate armour and billowing black cloaks, Rist would have immediately known who they were.

They stood in two groups, side by side, opposite an arrangement of eight-foot-tall stone pillars that jutted from the ground, clearly created using the Spark.

"Dragon's Maw!" a voice bellowed.

A pulse of power rippled through the air, flowing outwards from the Battlemages. Threads of Fire and Air whipped around the formation, crackling with energy, weaving and twisting about each other. Within moments, all the threads had knotted together at the front of the formation, and a roaring pillar of fire erupted forward. The crashing waves of flame spread across the full width of the formation and rose almost eight feet off the ground.

Rist could feel the pull of the Spark in the air, calling to him, urging him to open himself. It was intoxicating. Almost subconsciously, he reached out, opening his mind, but stopped as soon as he felt a hand resting on his shoulder.

"The first time you *truly* feel it can be almost euphoric," Sister Anila said, a knowing look in her eyes.

Rist nodded, his throat suddenly dry. Beside him, Neera was still staring at the terrifying display of power, her eyes glistening in the light of the fire. Even some soldiers behind them had stopped, talking amongst themselves as they watched the Battlemages.

"This is a test of endurance," Sister Anila said, looking towards the Battlemages. "In a Group Movement such as *Dragon's Maw*, the strength of the whole relies on the weakest link in the chain. When one mage releases the Spark, the entire Movement collapses. All Battlemage companies test the endurance of their Movements periodically, so as to know their limitations."

The raging torrent of fire continued, unrelenting, for several minutes, burning just as hot and bright as it had from the start, consuming the stone pillars. Rist couldn't fathom the amount of power and discipline, it would take to maintain threads of that strength for so long. He didn't think he had ever drawn from the Spark for longer than ten or fifteen seconds at any one time. Not simply because of the strain it would put on his body, but because for every moment he held onto the Spark, he yearned to hold it for two more, which was a dangerous path to tread.

A second pulse rippled through the air, and the pillar of fire flickered from existence, the thrum of the Spark dissipating. The ground over which the flames had flowed was scorched black, every blade of grass burned to a crisp, the clay dry and brittle. The pillars of stone were painted with char but otherwise looked as sturdy as they had before.

Ahead, some Battlemages dropped to their knees, others holding their companions steady. In a sense, it was good to see their fatigue, to know they were mortal.

"Anila Uraksplitter!" A tall man with an enormous black beard stepped from the ranks of Battlemages and started towards Rist, Neera, and Sister

Anila. There wasn't so much as a touch of weariness in his gait, and not a drop of sweat slicked his brow. Rist noticed the silver trim that ran along the man's black cloak.

"Magnus Offa," Sister Anila replied, reaching out her hand.

The man batted away Sister Anila's hand without breaking stride and instead wrapped his arms around her and picked her up with the ease of a father sweeping a child into his arms.

"Magnus," Sister Anila snapped, a suppressed laugh breaking through her façade of irritation. "Put me down."

"Always so serious, Uraksplitter!" The man lowered Sister Anila to her feet, a smile beaming from ear to ear. "When did you return to the capital? Last I heard, you were in Bromis, slaying beasts single-handedly." Magnus raised his eyebrows, a playful grin twisting his lips. "Single-handedly?" He repeated, turning to Rist and Neera. "Gods, Anila, do you purposely train the sense of humour out of them?"

Sister Anila glared at Magnus for a moment before letting out a sigh. "I returned a few months ago. I'm sorry I haven't come to visit. Things have been a bit… well, you know. And I've had these two to train in swordsmanship."

"It's all right," the big man said, reaching his fingers through his thick beard to scratch his chin. One thing about the Spark's effect on aging that irritated Rist to no end was that unless a mage was particularly ancient, it was near impossible to tell how many summers they had seen. Exarch Magnus Offa might have seen forty summers or four hundred. "You could have no greater teacher, young ones," the Exarch said, resting his hand on Anila's shoulder. "I bet you wonder why she carries two swords despite only having one hand, don't you?"

"Magnus." There was no laughter breaking through Sister Anila's irritation this time.

Magnus smiled. "One time, about halfway through the first Valtaran Rebellion – so, what, ninety years ago? It doesn't matter. We were stationed with the Seventh Army at Ironcreek. It was the night after a great battle. We had taken heavy losses, but the Valtarans had lost more. Either way, Anila and I, along with a few others, were piss drunk on Valtaran wine. We'd strolled down to the creek for a bit of a wash when we were set upon by a wyvern rider. Now I don't suppose you've ever seen a wyvern, but they're vicious bastards. Imagine a dragon but the size of a war horse. They can't breathe fire, but their limbs are dense and their teeth and talons can rend steel like parchment. Anyway, the beast swoops down and rips old Harmak in half, blood and guts everywhere. Anila, being the fucking lunatic she is, leaps from a rock onto to the wyvern's back, *but—*" Magnus leaned in, dropping his voice to a whisper "—she's so piss drunk when she draws her sword, she drops it straight into the creek." The big man burst out laughing, throwing his head back and clutching his hand to his belly. Despite the clear look of annoyance on Sister Anila's face, Rist couldn't help but like the man.

"Now, mind you," Magnus continued, "she did manage to knock the rider unconscious, undo the saddle clips, and toss her from the wyvern's back. Do you know how difficult it is to kill a wyvern without a sword when you're too drunk to grasp the Spark and you've only got one arm? It's pretty fucking difficult, let me tell you. But old Uraksplitter over here held onto the beast with her legs and proceeded to beat it senseless with her shoe. Her shoe! I've never seen anything like it in all my years. Anyway, in its confusion, the creature tossed Anila to the ground and crashed into one of the rocks, then we cut it to pieces. The next day, Anila comes out of her tent with two swords strapped to her hips. I asked her why. She says 'because I'm never beating a wyvern with a shoe again as long as I live.'"

Tears of laughter rolled down Magnus's cheeks, and even Sister Anila couldn't hold back a tentative smile.

"All right," Sister Anila said, shaking her head. "That's enough of that. Magnus, the apprentices have come today to observe formational exercises and are to begin training once you have deemed their knowledge competent."

Magnus stood up straight, letting out a puff of air as he wiped the tears from the corners of his eyes. "The years have tamed you, Anila. There was a time when you would have been on the floor rolling at that story."

"I will leave you to it," Sister Anila said, ignoring Magnus's comment. "When you are finished, Magnus, could you please send the apprentices back to the embassy along with an escort?"

"Of course," Magnus replied, regaining some composure. "It's good to see you, Anila. Don't leave it so long next time."

Sister Anila gave a placating nod, then turned and made her way back in the direction they had come.

"Come on," Magnus said with a sigh. "If you're lucky, I'll tell you how she lost that arm."

CHAPTER NINE

A SHARED PAIN

Ella stood at the edge of the cliff, dust and small stones shifting beneath her bare feet, the cold wind sweeping over her skin and tussling her hair. Above her, the night sky sparkled like an ocean of diamonds, and thousands of feet below, the landscape sprawled off into the distance, almost entirely obscured by the dark of night. The only sound that touched her ears was the gentle whistle of the wind against the mountain.

Faenir lay curled up behind her, his head resting on his paws, his heart aching, the occasional low whine leaving his throat. She could *feel* his pain. It was as real and tangible as her own.

She took a long, slow breath in through her nose, letting the air swell in her chest before exhaling. She wasn't sure how long they had been there. Hours. The sun had already set by the time they had made their way from the infirmary, through Tarhelm, and onto the cliff. She had never thought any level of pain could come close to losing Rhett. She was wrong. But this was an entirely different pain.

Losing Rhett had been like fire in her veins. It had been pure pain, as though a piece of her had been ripped away, carved from her heart. This was more like a dull, unyielding ache. It smothered her, drowned her, filled her lungs with despair.

Ella's parents had always seemed as eternal to her as the sun and the moon. No matter where she went or how far she roamed, they would always be there, an anchor to home. She had not been afraid to leave The Glade because she knew her parents would always be there if she needed them, just as they always had been. To think she would never see her father's face again or hear the sweetness of her mother's voice…

Her eyes felt as though they were only moments away from shedding an ocean of tears, but not a drop fell. It wasn't that she didn't want to cry; it was more like she couldn't. There weren't enough tears in all the world to come close to the anguish that filled her bones.

Worse, she hadn't been there for them. Maybe she could have done something? Maybe she could have saved them? She hadn't even stayed to ask Tanner how it had happened. In truth, she wasn't sure she wanted to know. She didn't think she had the strength to hear it. And what would it have changed?

The sound of footsteps and shifting stones caused Faenir to lift his head, his ears pricking up, a low rumble in his throat. Ella didn't turn, instead she closed her eyes, letting the cool touch of the night's breeze wrap around her. As she stood there, she could feel Faenir's mind brushing off hers. She opened herself. Images flashed across her eyes. The mouth of the tunnel. Coren.

The footsteps drew closer, stopping beside Ella.

"I lost my parents a long time ago. We sailed from Narvona. Our ship was torn to pieces along the Lightning Coast. I was the only survivor. I was four."

Ella opened her eyes, fixing her gaze off into the night sky, shaking her head slightly as she fought back the tears that her eyes had suddenly seemed to find. "Does it ever get easier?"

"Yes," Coren answered. "And no. I can't even remember their names. My Master found me, half-dead and soaked to the bone. She said it was three weeks before I spoke a word. It's been over four hundred years, and I still feel the hole in my heart. But it is easier today than it was then."

Pulling her gaze from the sky, Ella turned to Coren. The woman was staring out into the distance. A steady stream of tears rolled down her cheek, glistening in the light of the moon. It was strange to see her so vulnerable. From the moment Ella had met her in the infirmary, Coren had seemed almost untouchable. She was a Draleid, a warrior of legend, and she held herself as such. To see her now felt almost… wrong.

Coren turned her head, her gaze meeting Ella's. "If you wish, I can arrange for you to return home. I have contacts who smuggle weapons upriver from Catagan. From there, they take a sea ship around the coast to Vaerleon. The full journey will take months as the ships stay clear of the coast to avoid Lorian patrols. But you'll get there."

"No." Ella surprised herself with the firmness of her voice, but her mind was made up. "There's nothing for me back there. I need to find Calen. Whether or not he is the Draleid, he is alone, and he needs me. He's my little brother."

"I had hoped that would be your answer."

"Will you help me find him?"

Coren gave a slight nod, smiling, her eyes still wet with tears. "If Calen is indeed the Draleid we have all heard so much about, then it is likely he is travelling with an old friend of mine – Aeson Virandr. Aeson can be difficult to track down, but we share a contact in Argona. I will reach out."

"Thank you. I can't leave him out there alone."

"Don't thank me yet. It may be months before we hear anything."

Ella nodded, turning her gaze back towards the dark-obscured landscape before her, letting the whistling of the wind fill her ears.

"I will leave you to your peace," Coren said after a few moments of silence. "Every day at sunrise, I climb to the nearest peak. When you feel ready. Join me by the eastern gate."

Again, Ella nodded.

Coren turned and made to leave but paused, resting her hand on Ella's shoulder. "More importantly, when your heart is rested, I think it would be good if you spoke with Tanner. It would mean a lot to him."

With that, Coren left, reaching down and scratching the top of Faenir's head before disappearing into the tunnel that led back towards Tarhelm.

Ella waited until the woman's footsteps had faded to a low echo before dissipating entirely, then she lowered herself to the ground, letting her feet hang over the cliff's edge. Faenir shifted, lifting himself so he could move beside her, then dropping his head into her lap. He pushed at her hand with the cold, wet tip of his snout, manoeuvring himself so Ella's arm rested over his head. Looking into Faenir's eyes, a feeling of warmth and comfort touched Ella's mind. The longer Ella stared, the more the world dulled and the more she became aware of Faenir's consciousness brushing against her own. Images drifted through the wolfpine's mind, sharp and clear but drained of colour. Memories of Vars and Freis, of her, of Calen, followed by an emotion so deep and visceral it twisted a knot in Ella's chest. It felt like a blend of love, pride, and belonging. More images of Calen followed, and Ella began to piece together what Faenir was trying to communicate: the pack. Family.

"We'll find him," Ella said, leaning down and wrapping her arms around Faenir, resting her cheek against his head. "I promise."

FARDA DREW IN A BREATH of cold morning air as he walked along the top of the hill towards where the Fourth Army had gathered. His mages had marched separately from the main force, as per his command. Centuries of war had taught him many things, one of which was that those who could not touch the Spark would always envy and fear those who could, no matter what they claimed. Armies always functioned better when the two were kept separate where possible. Otherwise, soldiers ended up dead.

As he walked, he ran his thumb along the gold coin resting in his palm, feeling every nick and groove against his skin. As much as he tried to push thoughts of Ella from his mind, it was a task easier said than done. In the centuries since he had lost Shinyara, Farda had watched thousands die. He had walked through fields of corpses, burned cities to the ground, and taken the lives of those who had many summers yet to see. In all that time, he had felt nothing. Nothing but numbness. He would have taken his own life, like many of The Broken before him, were it not for his innate stubbornness, his unwillingness to say he was not strong enough to carry on. But with Ella, something was different. She had made him *feel*. What that meant, he wasn't sure. But for the first time in a long time, his mind had tasted something other than unabating apathy. He cared for her. Felt a need to protect her like a wolf protects a cub. And yet, with all of that, he had simply handed her over to Karsen Craine. His jaw clenched at the thought of it. Farda hadn't needed another reason to despise himself, but he had conjured one anyway. He just hoped they would not break her spirit. It was her spirit he admired.

She was a weakness. Weaknesses must be burned out. Farda shook his head, snorting a laugh. Even his own thoughts weren't convincing.

Stopping for a moment, Farda squinted his left eye to lessen the glare from the earlywinter sun overhead, and cast his gaze down the sloping hill before him and onwards to Fort Harken, where an ocean of leathery skin and blackened steel besieged the enormous walls.

From atop the hill, Farda guessed the creatures numbered no more than ten thousand. Less than they had expected. Even from that distance, Farda could see the monstrous forms of Bloodmarked, standing a head above the rest of the Uraks, the runes on their skin glowing with a red light, smoke drifting into the air around them. The sight made Farda smile. There was no amount of Urak blood that could be spilt that would ever pay the debt those creatures owed for the dragon eggs they massacred at Ilnaen. And any day Farda could spill that blood was a good day.

Pulling his eyes from the horde, Farda continued to where the commander of the Fourth Army sat astride her grey-dappled horse, surveying the land with her generals.

"Justicar Kyrana, I see you have decided to join us?" Commander Talvare shifted in her saddle, her gelding snorting beneath her. She raised one eyebrow as Farda approached, her head barely turning. The woman had seen at least fifty summers, streaks of grey accenting her otherwise coal-black hair. She had reasonably broad shoulders and the lean physique of a soldier who had spent many years relying on actions over words. Farda had spoken with her multiple times over the course of the two-week-long march from Berona to Fort Harken. She was well versed in military strategy, her mind was sharp as a needle, and she had little time for talking shit. Farda respected her.

"I have, Commander Talvare. I thought it would only be polite."

The woman gave him a flat stare before turning to the general who sat on the horse beside her. General Guthrin Vandimire was a short man with oily black hair, a stubby nose, and a thick moustache. Farda had met him before. He was a coward and a sycophant.

"Fifteen, maybe sixteen thousand, commander." General Vandimire announced. His eyes narrowed as his gaze met Farda's. "The scouts report the attack began no more than an hour past. The beasts descended from the Kolmir Mountains and immediately laid siege."

"The fort's garrison numbers at approximately two thousand, twenty Battlemages amongst them, correct?"

"Correct, Commander. Though those are the official numbers, and I dare say they have likely diminished since the last count."

Commander Talvare gave no recognition that she had heard the man's answer. Instead, she continued to stare at the Urak forces, her eyes slits. "It seems the rumours of those 'monsters' were not exaggerated. You have encountered them before, Justicar Kyrana?"

"I have," Farda said, still running his thumb over the coin in his palm, feeling the raised shape of the lion against his skin. There had to be at least a hundred or so Bloodmarked. Farda had not seen one in almost four hundred years. There had been one or two after The Fall, but once the Uraks were in full retreat, the creatures had almost entirely disappeared. "They are Bloodmarked. They hold no fear, their claws can rend armour, and they are utterly ruthless. Each of them is worth a hundred of your soldiers, possibly two hundred."

"The good news keeps on coming."

"We need to send for reinforcements," one of the generals – a man who had seen maybe thirty summers, with wavy blonde hair, and a handsome face – said, his eyes widening as he looked down at the Uraks. Farda could smell the fear on him. He was the kind who would slow down during the charge to allow the others to hit the line first.

"There is no one else coming, General Tirn. The rest of the armies are spread across the continent. We're all there is, and we've already wasted too much time." Without so much as waiting for a response, the commander turned her horse to face Farda and the generals. "We march without delay. Once we are within range, we open volleys, grab the beasts' attention, draw them to us. Let's see if we can't thin their numbers a bit. General Runi, I want you and your flight leaders to take the cavalry and skirt the base of the hill. Once our infantry has engaged, I will sound the horn, and you will flank from the east, understood? The sun will be in their eyes, and we'll need every advantage we can get. Hit them hard, pull back, hit them again. In and out. Don't allow yourself to become entangled."

"Understood, commander," said a red-nosed woman with a permanently furrowed brow. She pulled on her horse's reins and rode off towards the company of cavalry that waited to the east of the main army.

"The rest of you, ready your blocks. We march at the horn."

The other generals scattered at Talvare's words, riding off towards their respective companies, readying their soldiers for what was to come.

"Justicar Kyrana. Will you be frank with me?"

Farda inclined his head. "Brutally."

Talvare smiled at that. "I have never fought an Urak force of this size. And never against these Bloodmarked. What are our chances?"

"Slim. On the field, they outnumber us two to one."

"Two to one?" Talvare raised a curious eyebrow. "Guthrin said they numbered fifteen or sixteen thousand."

"Guthrin is blind. They are ten at most. Though we had expected more. They are bigger, they are stronger, and those Bloodmarked will tear through your heavy infantry as though they are nothing."

"That doesn't change anything." Talvare turned her gaze back towards the besieged city, nodding absently. Dismounting, Talvare called over a young squire, handing the boy her horse's reins before waving him away. "We cannot sit here and let the people within those walls die."

Farda stared at the woman for a few moments. It had been a long time since he had marched into battle next to someone he respected. "When the archers have fired their first volley and we get within striking distance, hold back your soldiers. Let me and my mages go in first. We will even the odds."

The commander raised an eyebrow. "That was not the plan. The Battlemages were to provide support, striking from a distance. We are under instructions from High Command to limit mage casualties."

"Plans change. We can do more damage if we aren't wary of killing our own. Once we give you the signal, charge with everything you have."

"What's the signal?"

"You'll know when you see it."

THE THUNDEROUS BANGING OF WAR drums filled the air, each beat thrumming through Farda's body. He drew in a deep breath, letting it swell his lungs. Lightning surged through his veins. Behind him, one hundred Battlemages strode in ten columns of ten, black cloaks flapping behind them, steel breastplates shimmering in the morning sun. And behind the mages marched the full might of the Fourth Army: just over five thousand strong. The ground shook with the force of so much steel moving in unison. Glancing back, Farda could see enormous red standards painted with the black lion of Loria rippling in the wind.

Of War and Ruin

Eight hundred archers, four hundred cavalry, and over four thousand infantry. Among the infantry, half carried heavy spears, and half wielded swords with long rectangular shields. The army was built for mobility. It was built to face humans. Farda would have preferred more spears. It was best not to let Uraks get too close.

"No words of encouragement, Justicar Kyrana?" Igraine was Farda's second in command. Were it not for Karsen Craine assigning Farda to the Fourth Army, Igraine would have been next in line after the previous commander was struck ill. He was four or five inches shorter than Farda, with a muscular build and a sharp jaw. His hair was jet-black, cut short. It was difficult to tell a mage's age past a certain point, but Farda had never met the man before two weeks ago, and the eager gleam in his eye was that which only the young possessed. He must have seen no more than twenty-five or twenty-six summers.

As a Justicar, Farda often worked alone. He was only ever asked to lead a company of mages on special request – as Karsen Craine had done on this occasion. It was always strange, leading men and women he had never met into war, knowing that many of them would not live to see another sunrise.

"No."

The man continued to stare at Farda as though he believed Farda's answer was a joke.

Farda sighed, turning his gaze from Igraine, staring out at the Urak force, who were now no more than eight hundred feet away. Many of them had already turned, assessing the new threat to their rear flank. "Do everything I say, trust in the Spark, and try not to die."

Igraine nodded, as though pondering words of great wisdom. Farda almost felt sorry for the man. Almost. Igraine looked as though he was going to say something, but booming horns rose above everything else, and the Fourth Army stopped its march, the progressive halting of steel boots sounding like rolling thunder.

As Farda stared ahead at the ever-shifting swarm of leathery skin and blackened steel, his heart pounded against his ribs, blood shivering through his veins. It was simply the body's natural response. He felt no fear. If he died, he died. He would be with Shinyara once more.

"Nock."

The command rang out, bellowed by multiple captains who stretched along the line of archers that stood behind Farda and his mages. Farda kept his gaze focused ahead. Segments of the Urak force had broken away and were now charging towards the Fourth Army. That was good. Splitting their forces would weaken them.

"Draw."

131

"You have trained for this," Farda shouted, not turning his head to look at the mages who stood behind him. They had all seen battle before. They had fought rebels, had skirmishes with raiders and pirates. Some had fought Uraks. But the Fourth Army comprised mostly younger mages. Few of them had seen war on this scale. And there was no doubting it now. This was war. Ten thousand Uraks gathered in one place. And from the reports Farda had seen, there were far more than that spread throughout the continent. Fort Harken would only be the beginning. "Follow my words without question. Do not hesitate. Do not show mercy. The Uraks will not."

"Loose!"

The *whoosh* of four hundred arrows swept overhead, casting a momentary shadow on the ground beneath them. Hundreds of Uraks fell as the arrows dropped, blood spraying, bodies crashing lifeless to the ground. The charging horde engulfed their dead, sweeping over them like an endless wave.

"Loose at will!"

Arrows tore through the sky, archers loosing at varying rates of speed, creating an ever-shifting shadow on the ground below. More Uraks dropped as they charged, but for each that fell, another took its place, howling and snarling, drawing ever closer.

Four hundred feet.

"Reach out to the Spark now. Feel it, grasp it, know it."

In a heartbeat, the air thrummed with the sheer force of the Spark. Farda had almost forgotten what that had felt like. So many mages in one place, each drawing from the Spark, pulling on the Elemental Strands. It lit a bloodlust in him. He pulled heavily on threads of Fire, Air, and Spirit. The threads surrounded him and filled him, coursing through his veins, crackling over his skin.

"Forward!" Farda roared, taking a step towards the charging Uraks, then another, his stride lengthening until he was sprinting. The Uraks were only two hundred feet away now, moving like a swarm of rippling grey muscle, war cries and howls rising into the air, blackened steel glinting.

Behind them, horns rang out, battle formations taking shape. The flight of arrows had stopped.

The line of Uraks spread across hundreds of feet either side. Farda would not have blamed any of his mages who held fear in their hearts at that moment, so long as they rose above it. As they drew closer, Farda pulled heavily on the threads of Fire, Air, and Spirit.

"On my command!" he called out, his pulse surging through his veins like lightning, all sounds capitulating to the rushing blood in his head.

Out of the corner of his eye he could see his mages spreading out around him, maximising their area of effect. The Uraks would be upon them in moments. The snarling and hissing tugged at the edges of his mind, the sea of rippling grey and black charging towards them.

Farda drew in the Spark as heavily as his body would allow, a brief moment of clarity hitting him before he yelled, "Lightning Storm!"

Eldingstír. The Old Tongue echoed in his mind. Memories of a life once lived.

The air shifted, all one hundred mages drawing as heavily as they could from the Spark. Farda could see the threads of Air, Fire, and Spirit winding around them. Then, in a manoeuvre practised a thousand times, the mages executed the Movement. Threads of Air whipped around their formation, slamming into Uraks with such force that bones snapped and armour bent. The creatures howled, swiping at the wind as it tore through them like a living hurricane. The Urak lines collapsed around the Battlemages. Everywhere Farda looked, he saw great beasts hurtling through the air, screaming and howling. To his left a whip of air slammed into a Bloodmarked's knee, shattering the bone in one fell swoop.

"Second Phase!"

With the Urak lines already in disarray, the Battlemages pulled on their threads of Fire and Spirit, blending them with the threads of Air. Half a second, then a blinding flash. Arcs of chain lightning erupted from the battle formation, streaking from the outstretched hands of Farda's mages. Chunks of earth and clay were ripped from the ground and the smell of burning flesh and charred earth filled the air. The storm of death raged around Farda and his mages, lightning tearing through the air, punching through blackened steel and searing holes in leathery flesh.

The air pulsated with energy from the Spark. Farda could feel it in his bones, in his very core. A battlerush unlike any other.

By the time the Eldingstír had stopped, a clearing of over forty feet had opened between Farda's mages and the Uraks. Hundreds of the creatures lay lifeless, charred, twisted, and broken, and many more screamed and howled as they died.

There was a moment, just a single moment, where everything went silent. The Uraks howled and roared, charging over their dead, readying themselves to cut through Farda's mages like scythes through grass. Then the horns broke through the barrier of silence in Farda's head, and the Fourth Army swarmed around them, slamming into the Urak lines. The crunch of bodies was a visceral thing. Farda watched as spears ripped through leathery hides and rushing soldiers were sliced to ribbons by blackened steel. Pure chaos, as all battles were.

Farda pulled his sword from its scabbard, the mages around him following suit. The muscles in his forearm tensed, anticipating what was to come. "Stay tight. Conserve your energy. Move in pairs. Forward!"

Vibrations shook through Farda's legs as his feet slammed against the ground. The other mages fanned out around him, moving in pairs as their training dictated, threads of Air, Earth, Fire, and Spirit raging around them. Farda took a moment to appreciate the raw power that shimmered in the air, and then they collided with the Urak lines.

Two Uraks rushed towards Farda, howling as they swung their blackened blades. He caught the first strike with his sword, deflecting it sideways as he slammed threads of Air into the other beast, crushing its ribs and sending it careening into the thick of battle. Before the first Urak could recover, Farda swung his sword into reverse grip and drove it down through the creature's back. Pulling the blade free in a spray of blood, Farda swung, slicing through an Urak's jaw. Blood fountained from the beast's mangled face as the Urak collapsed to its knees, its eyes rolling to the back of its head.

Farda placed his foot on the beast's shoulder, roaring as he kicked it to the ground. The rush of battle consumed him, a fervent bloodlust gripping his mind. He would soak the soil in Urak blood.

Farda and his mages cut through the battlefield, carving their path in blood and bone. The Urak forces may have outnumbered the Fourth Army, but a hundred Battlemages was a force to be reckoned with by any measure. Everywhere they moved, bodies fell. Crushed by threads of Air and Earth, eviscerated by arcs of lightning, consumed by pillars of fire.

With a practised efficiency born of repetition, Farda's mages wielded the Spark like a weapon of the gods. Farda had never before fought with the Fourth Army, but he couldn't lie to himself – he was impressed. These mages moved together, held their line, and fought like monsters. He would be commending them in his report to the High Command once the fighting was over – if they survived.

A flash ignited somewhere to Farda's left, and an arc of purple lightning ripped through the air, tearing chunks of clay from the ground before slamming into the two mages closest to Farda – one of them being the young man who was his second, Igraine. Farda watched as the lightning tore through the mages' bodies, the force of the strike sending them crashing backwards into their companions.

Another arc of lightning erupted from the mass of Uraks ahead, claiming the lives of four more mages, their bodies crumpled in smouldering heaps.

A gap began to form before Farda, Uraks scrambling to get out of the way of whatever was coming. A man stepped forward, obsidian robes draped over his shoulders, icy-white skin pulled tight across his face. As the man moved the light of the world dimmed around him.

"It's a herald!" some soldiers called out, relief in their voices. *Fools.*

Farda tightened his grip on the hilt of his sword as the creature continued forward, the light fleeing from its touch. For whatever reason, the spirits of Efialtír's minions never inhabited Urak bodies. Elves, men, and Jotnar had been the only hosts Farda had ever known. The likelihood was that the 'Ascension', as Fane had so eloquently named it, required a link to the Spark, which left dwarves and Uraks incapable. But whatever body the spirit inhabited, it was no herald. It was a monster.

"Hold fast!" Farda roared. "Move as one!"

Almost as soon as the words had left Farda's mouth, a clutch of Bloodmarked stormed around the Fade, crashing into Farda's mages, claws rending steel and bone in single swipes, shockwaves of fire igniting the air.

"Defensive formation!" Farda reached out to the Spark, drawing his blade across his chest as he shouted, feeling the elemental strands pulsating in the darkness of his mind. He made his choice and pulled on threads of Earth, tasting the tang of iron and loam on his tongue. He pushed the threads into the ground, pulling columns of clay upward and drawing the moisture from them with threads of Fire. Within seconds, the columns of clay had formed into long, hardened spikes. He sent the spikes hurtling towards the Bloodmarked.

One of the beasts took a spike through the shoulder, then another through the neck, and one more through the eye before collapsing in a heap on the ground, its runes pulsating with a red light, pluming smoke. Two more of the beasts fell, their bodies shredded, but the rest proceeded to charge, shrugging off the attack and crashing headfirst into Farda's Battlemages, blood spraying in the wind.

Catching a Bloodmarked's swipe with threads of Air, Farda drove his sword upward, blood sluicing from the creature's neck, its runes raging with red light. He dragged his blade free, letting the Bloodmarked collapse to the ground, and turned his attention back toward the Fade just in time to see an arc of purple lightning hurtling towards him. Pulling as deeply as he could from the Spark, Farda weaved a shield of Air in front of him. The shield kept the lightning from bursting through his armour, but the blow still lifted him off his feet and sent him crashing into the back of a Bloodmarked. Hitting the beast was like slamming into a stone wall. He collided with the Bloodmarked's dense frame, then crashed to the ground, gasping for air. Not having the capacity to feel pain was one thing, but that didn't mean his muscles didn't cramp and that he couldn't feel the immense pressure that weighed down on his lungs.

Coughing up blood, he dragged himself to his feet. All around, the battle raged. His ears drummed with the clang of steel on steel, the blood-thirsty howls of the Uraks, the wails of the dying. The air smelled of dirt, blood, and fire. His Battlemages had recovered from the initial charge of the Bloodmarked and now fought tooth and nail against the immense creatures, their blades moving in whirs of steel, whips of Fire and Air tearing through the space around them. Horns bellowed in the distance – Commander Talvare's signal for the cavalry to charge.

Farda pulled his attention towards the Fade. The creature was tearing through soldiers and mages alike as though they were little more than brittle twigs, whips of Fire and Air swirling around it, arcs of purple lightning crashing to the ground, ripping through men and women, melting armour.

Drawing in a deep breath, Farda charged. He reached out to the Spark, pulling on threads of Air, wrapping them around a shield that lay abandoned on the blood-soaked ground. Pushing as much force into the threads as he could muster, he launched the shield towards the Fade, watching as it, instead, caught a Bloodmarked in the chest, tearing through the creature's stone-like hide and bursting out the other side in a plume of blood mist.

As the Bloodmarked fell, crashing to the ground in a cloud of dust, the Fade turned, its cavernous light-drinking eyes returning Farda's stare. The air rippled around the Fade as a black-fire nithrál formed in its left hand.

Every hair on Farda's body stood on end. A shiver started in his chest and rippled out through his limbs. Steel could kill him. The remnants of a soul that still clung to his body would find Shinyara once more. But if he were to die by the touch of a nithrál, what remained of his soul would be sheared from the world, left to wander alone. He would never feel the touch of Shinyara's mind again. His throat tightened.

As he reached out to the Spark, bracing himself for the first strike of the Fade's blade, Farda made a decision: if it looked as though the beast had the upper hand, he would take his own life. There was nothing in this world that would stop him from feeling Shinyara's touch again. *Nothing.*

Steeling himself and committing his mind, Farda let out a roar, swinging his blade upwards to meet the downward swipe of the Fade's nithrál. Flickers of black flame erupted from the nithrál, the antithesis of true fire, drinking light instead of providing.

Pure white-hot rage burned through Farda as he traded blows with the Fade. The battle raged around them, Bloodmarked and Battlemages tearing each other to shreds, steel and claws colliding. Farda's muscles ached, and vibrations rang through his arms from the strength of the strikes. *I will not yield.*

Drawing more deeply from the Spark, Farda pulled on threads of Earth, pushing them into the ground. He lunged forward, forced the Fade back with a torrent of steel, then dragged columns of clay from the ground, forming them into spikes, hardening them with threads of Fire. He drove the spikes through the creature's legs, then back into the ground behind it, locking it in place.

The Fade howled, its harsh screech tearing at Farda's ears as it sliced through the spikes of clay with its nithrál. But with every spike the Fade severed, two more took its place, plunging through the creature's chest and arms. Farda looked around to see that some of his Battlemages had pulled themselves from the fighting and now stood beside him, a web of threads weaving into the ground.

His chest heaving, Farda marched towards the Fade, reaching behind his breastplate, his fingers wrapping around the small red gemstone that hung on a strip of leather around his neck. He had long since told himself that he would only tap into the gemstone when he truly needed it. He needed it now.

For a moment, ice flowed through his veins. Then, as though struck by lightning, pure power surged through him, a cold fire burning his blood. The Fade's cavernous eyes widened even further. The foul creature could sense the blood Essence surging through Farda.

"Your god is calling you," Farda said as he placed his hand on the Fade's chest and looked into its light-drinking eyes.

To Farda's surprise, the Fade didn't respond. It simply stared at him, its thin, brittle lips curling into an eerie smile.

Farda pulled more Essence from the stone, letting it flow through him, flooding his veins. He channelled the Essence into the Fade, consuming the creature in an eruption of black fire that burst forth from his palm. Without a nithrál, Farda could not sever the Fade's soul from the world, but the least he could do was take pleasure in its screams as its body turned to ash.

The Fade's otherworldly shrieks echoed, reverberating in the air even after the flames dissipated and its crumpled husk of a body dropped to the ground, charred and broken.

Reluctantly, Farda released his hold on the Essence, shivering as the intoxicating power was dragged from his bones. Gritting his teeth, he tucked the gemstone back in behind his breastplate, feeling its cool touch even through his undershirt. He cast a glance around. Almost three quarters of his mages still lived, locked in combat with the Bloodmarked. The rest of the army seemed to be holding their ground, but it was almost impossible for Farda to tell. All he could do was focus on what was around him and hope that General Talvare would do her part. The sonorous bellows of command horns let him know she was certainly still trying.

Clenching his jaw, Farda charged towards the nearest Bloodmarked. He pulled in threads of Air, welling them into a knot, then hammered them into the side of the Urak's knee. The creature collapsed, bones snapping and blood spraying. The Battlemage with whom it was locked in combat took the creature's head from its body and moved to Farda's side.

"Stay close," Farda shouted to the mage, who responded with a sharp nod, wiping blood splatter from her eyes. But just as he readied himself to charge once more, four sharp horn bursts sounded, one after another, barely a second apart, piercing the din of battle. Knots twisted in Farda's stomach. Now he understood why the Fade had smiled. *Enemies from the rear.*

"The other five thousand," Farda muttered. The Uraks had lured them in. Waited for them to be caught in the claws of battle and were now marching five thousand strong right up their backsides. "Fuck." Farda cracked his neck from side to side, drawing in a deep breath. "Nothing changes," he said, grasping the other Battlemage's arm, looking her in the eyes. "If we die here, we take them with us."

"I'm with you, Justicar."

Farda nodded, then filled his lungs with air and roared. "To me!"

Farda charged into the fray where the Bloodmarked and Uraks were thickest. He swung his blade in an arc, slicing through the ribcage of an Urak, carrying the blade through and blocking the downward swipe of a blackened sword. Pushing against the momentum of the swing, Farda brought his blade back across the Urak in front of him, splitting it open across the navel. As the creature clasped a clawed hand to its gut, Farda drove his steel through its open mouth, wrenching it free, blood pouring.

"To me!" Farda roared again, this time amplifying his voice with threads of Spirit and Air. "For the empire!"

He needed to be the force the others would rally around. He needed to be a beacon. And the quickest way to light a beacon was to start a fire.

"Dragon's Maw!"

Farda opened himself to the Spark, feeling the power of the elemental strands flood through him. He pulled on threads of Fire and Air, the warmth filling his veins and the cool touch sweeping over his skin. Around him, he could sense others doing the same. With a roar, he unleashed the threads in the direction of Fort Harken, where the bulk of the Urak forces were oriented. A column of fire a few feet in diameter erupted from his hands, waves of heat rippling in all directions. Almost immediately, he felt more threads intertwining with his own, amplifying the fire, feeding it. More Battlemages fell in line beside him, lending their strength, feeding the flames. The Battlemages were followed by soldiers gripping spears and sharp steel.

"For the empire!" a voice bellowed beside Farda.

"For Loria!"

As the column of fire widened, stretching nearly twenty feet across, Farda stepped forwards, the threads of Fire igniting his veins. "Push them back! Push them towards the walls!"

The truth was that it didn't matter in which direction they pushed. With thousands of Uraks still in front of them, and another five thousand attacking from the rear, death would find them this day, and he would welcome it. He would charge willingly into death's embrace if it meant he could feel the touch of Shinyara's mind once more. The only slight flicker of hesitation in his mind was of Ella. He pushed that thought aside. She was not his concern anymore. When she had needed his protection, he had abandoned her. Cold fury surging through him, Farda drew even more deeply from the Spark, taking in as much as his body could handle, pushing it forward, feeding the fire of the Dragon's Maw. The air burned white-hot.

Farda could feel the drain sapping at him, clawing at his bones, pulling at his soul. With the amount of power he was drawing, the Spark would burn him through in a matter of minutes. He dropped to one knee, grunting as the vibration jarred his leg. But even still, he held onto the Spark. *I will not yield.* Dragging in a deep breath, Farda heaved himself upright. If this was to be his last day, he would die on his feet.

A shiver rippled through Farda, as a series of earth-shattering roars rolled through the sky like thunder. For only a moment, he allowed himself to lift his gaze. In the glaring light of the mid-day sun, four enormous shadows swept over the Kolmir Mountains, wings spread wide, and Farda's heart tightened at what, to him, was the most beautiful sight in the known world – dragons.

Farda released his hold on the Spark. Today was not his day. Looking at the weariness on the faces around him, he would not have been the first to succumb to the burn of the Spark either way. "Defensive formation!"

Reaching down, his bones aching, Farda snatched up a discarded shield and set his feet. But even as those around him formed together, Farda could see the Urak lines begin to break. But they were too late, far too late. A monstrous roar shook the air as a blue-scaled dragon dropped from the skies and unleashed a torrent of dragonfire that made a raging river look like little more than a stream The force of the blast shook the earth, tearing chunks of clay from the ground, hurling Uraks in all directions. It was a force of nature, an act of a god. The dragon soared low over the battlefield, fire carving a path of death and destruction through the Urak ranks.

Just as the blue-scaled dragon cracked its wings and rose, sending men and Uraks alike tumbling to the ground, three more of the magnificent creatures dropped from the sky, their immense frames casting shadows as large as ships. All four dragons poured raging fire down over the battle-field, weaving back and forth. Guttural howls and cries rang out as the air filled with dirt and ash.

Farda dropped to his knees, releasing his hold on the shield, a smile touching his lips.

CRUMPLED HUSKS OF BLACKENED CHAR littered the ground, broken and twisted. The taste of burnt flesh clung to the air, thick and palpable. Farda attempted to hunch down, but his right knee gave way, and he dropped to the dirt, sending wisps of ash and dust streaming into the breeze. Sweat trickled down his neck and face, carving paths through the dirt and blood that had bedded into his skin.

He pushed the charred body of an Urak onto its back, prying the sword from its grasp. The creature's blackened fingers crumbled as Farda wrapped his hand around the hilt. He cast his gaze along the blood-coated blade. Urak weapons were crude but suited the creatures well. They were dense and heavy, capable of cleaving bone and armour in single swipes. Farda gave an involuntary snarl as he looked over the blade, then turned it, lifted his hands, and buried the tip of the blackened steel into the dirt. Glowing with vibrant red light, set into the sword where the blade met the hilt, was a small, oval gemstone. An Essence vessel.

Farda was too weak to draw from the Spark, so he tapped into the gem-stone that still hung around his neck. He drew only the smallest trickle of Essence into him, then pulled the weapon apart, watching as the blade and hilt dropped to the ground with a dull clang while the gemstone floated, wrapped in Essence. Farda snatched it from the air and watched as it cast a red glow over the creases of his palm. Blood Essence. The foundation of life and creation. Held within that stone was the Essence that once gave life to the men and women that Urak had slain. It was a beautiful thing, but it was also horrid and twisted. From death, Essence could create, but it could also destroy and corrupt.

Letting out a strained sigh, Farda grimaced and pushed himself back to his feet, stuffing the gemstone into his trouser pocket. He loathed using Essence. With every drop he took in, he could feel Efialtír scratching at his mind. Others within The Circle might have seen Efialtír as The Saviour, but Farda trusted the god no more than he trusted an Urak. Any god that wished to worm their way into his mind was not a benevolent one. Whatever his beliefs, Essence was powerful, and it was better to have it and not need it, than need it and not have it.

Around him, Farda saw other Battlemages doing the same, stumbling through the dead, collecting the stones. No doubt, once the injured had been attended to, the Urak blades would be collected on wagons from Fort Harken so the stones could be harvested.

Farda's breath caught in his chest as he turned. He touched his hand against his ribs and pulled it away to see fresh blood dripping from his fingers. Not being able to feel pain had many advantages in battle. He could push through wounds that would cripple others, charge and move without impediment. But it also meant that he might not notice wounds until long after they had been inflicted. Which meant he risked succumbing to grievous injuries before he had even realised he had sustained them. And were it not for the imperial Healers and the Spark, that likely would have happened many times over across the centuries. Now that he had learned to deal with his 'affliction', the benefits outweighed the risks, but even if they hadn't, Farda had no say in the matter. Shinyara had taken his pain with her, perhaps as a parting gift.

A gust of wind swept overhead, and two shadows darkened the landscape while two more broke off, flying west after the routed Uraks. Farda drew in a deep breath as he set off towards where the dragons were setting down. He knew them by their colouring. The blue-scaled dragon was Seleraine, the soulkin of Voranur. The other, his body coated in an ocean of deep red scales, almost black along his belly, was Karakes, the soulkin of Lyina. Of the dragons still living, only Helios was larger.

If Voranur and Seleraine were here, that meant the others were likely Jormun astride Hrothmundar and Ilkya astride Eríthan. It was clear it was not Eltoar and Pellenor, as Helios would have blotted out the sun.

"Farda!"

The beginnings of a smile touched Farda's lips at the sight of Lyina striding towards him. Her bronzed skin and dark blonde hair were striking against the white plate of the Dragonguard. She crashed into him with the enthusiasm of a long-lost love, her arms pulling him in tight. "It's good to see you."

It was strange to have someone greet him so warmly. Years had come and gone since Farda had last laid eyes on Lyina or any of his kin. Even as a Rakina, his connection to other Draleid was still a tangible thing. They were not bonded by blood and bone, but by the immaterial tethers of the soul, or in his case, half a soul. Farda leaned into Lyina's embrace, savouring it. "As it is you."

"What has you down here fighting for scraps?" Lyina pulled away, clasping her hands on Farda's shoulders, eyeing him up and down. "You look like shit."

"I feel worse."

"I thought Shinyara took your pain?"

"My bones still ache and my muscles still spasm, old friend. And some wounds are not of the flesh."

Lyina's gaze softened. "Draleid n'aldryr, Rakina."

"Rakina nai dauva, Draleid."

"You will always be our brother." Lyina grabbed Farda's head and pulled it against hers with enough force that had Farda been able to feel it, he was sure his head would have throbbed.

"Till the day I return to her."

"And even then." A silent moment passed between them. "All right, enough of the sappy shit."

Farda let out a laugh, nodding. He looked past Lyina, to where Voranur approached. The elf's gait was so languid it was graceful. He glided through the field of dead, his gaze eventually lifting to meet Farda's.

"Rakina." Voranur bowed his head as he spoke, genuine respect in his voice.

"Voranur," Farda replied. "It is good to see you."

The elf bowed his head again, a half-smile gracing his youthful face for a fleeting moment. "You are lucky we came." He cast his gaze over the field of dead. He planted his foot on the side of a dead soldier, pushing the body onto its back. "The battle was lost."

"You were late."

"We were on our way from Dracaldryr," Lyina said, letting out a sigh through her nostrils.

"Tivar?"

Lyina nodded.

"How is she?"

"The same." Lyina looked to Voranur, who simply shook his head. "Fane has asked Eltoar to summon the Dragonguard so we may put an end to the wars. Eltoar agreed. But Tivar refused to come with us."

"I see. Where are Eltoar and Pellenor now?"

"Pellenor is in Berona. There are a few things there that must be seen to. Eltoar has taken Helios to Dracaldryr."

"If Tivar will listen to anyone, it will be him."

"Agreed. Once we are prepared, Jormun, Voranur, and Ilkya will fly south to deal with the uprisings. The rest of us will remain in the North to push the Uraks back. What of you?"

"I am to remain here for the time being. The Fourth Army has been tasked with protecting Fort Harken until we are relieved."

"There's not many of you left." Voranur ran his tongue over his teeth, folding his arms. It was a statement, nothing more.

"No."

"We can stay for a few days while we wait on Eltoar," Lyina said, throwing Farda a wink. "I could use a good drinking partner. Voranur only drinks Wyrm's Blood, Ilkya can't hold her liquor, and Jormun is an angry drunk."

Farda smiled, giving a slight tilt of his head. "That would be much appreciated. But before we start, I must see if Commander Talvare still walks amongst the living."

CHAPTER TEN

ECHOES OF DEEDS LONG DONE

Dracaldryr – Earlywinter, Year 3081 After Doom

Eltoar held himself close to Helios's body, the side of his head pressed against the back of the dragon's neck, his hands on Helios's black scales. Below, the light of the crescent moon glittered across the rippling ocean like a thousand shards of shattered glass.

Letting the air swell his chest, he leaned back, casting his gaze over the island of Dracladryr below them that jutted from the dark waters. Mountains covered the length and breadth of the island, their peaks capped with snow, their feet laced with rivers and forests of deep green. Thousands of eyries lay nestled into the mountainsides, enormous caverns as wide as ships. The old legends said that long before The Order was formed, long before the Jotnar and elves rode against each other in the Blodvar, thousands of years before even then, the island had been the home of the first dragons carved into existence by the Enkara, the gods. Eltoar wasn't quite sure he believed the old stories, but nonetheless, he had once spent many a night looking up at the stars from the eyries of Dracaldryr. In his time, the island had been a place where Draleid and dragons could find peace and solitude. It had been a sacred place.

Helios's wings shifted, angling downward. The familiar, almost euphoric feeling of weightlessness filled Eltoar's stomach as they plummeted. He closed his eyes, letting the wind crash over him, his legs held firm by Helios's scales. Centuries of dragonflight had trained Eltoar's muscles to ignore their natural reflex to tense. He trusted Helios, though to use the word trust felt wrong, for it didn't come close to the unwavering faith he held in his soulkin. They were not two. They were one. A single soul shared. Helios would betray Eltoar as much as the sun would betray its own light.

The dragon rolled, catching the winds that swept along the face of the mountains. *Faster.* Helios cracked his wings, then dropped, riding a current of air before rising again, stretching his wings to a point, lengthening his neck, and pulling his feet back. Eltoar leaned forward, pressing his body against Helios's warm scales. He reached out to the Spark, pulling on threads of Air, weaving them around Helios's body. He filled the space between Helios's scales, smoothing and rounding the air that encased them. Eltoar smiled as the mountains blurred to their right, the whistle of the wind almost deafening in his ears.

The world lurched as Helios folded his wings in, diving straight down, the face of the mountains flashing past, the dark ocean rising to meet them.

Eltoar drew in a deep breath, and Helios spread his wings, sweeping upward, the unseen force of the world pulling against him. Water sprayed into the air, tickling Eltoar's cheek as the dragon's clawed feet broke the surface. A momentary sadness touched Eltoar's mind when he sensed the unbridled joy that consumed Helios's heart. It wasn't a sadness born in opposition to the dragon's joy, but at the realisation that joy was too often lacking.

"Draleid n'aldryr, Helios," Eltoar whispered as he rested his forehead against the scales of the dragon's neck.

A deep rumble resonated through Helios's chest in response, followed by a flash of sorrow. Eltoar let his mind drift fully into Helios's as the dragon swept upwards, banking right, curling up and around a low peak of jagged rock. They stayed like that for some time, soaring through the open valleys of Dracaldryr, their minds wrapped together, the wind sweeping over their bodies, the low whistle filling their ears. Helios only slowed as they approached Mount Umar, the highest peak of Dracaldryr, upon which the great temple was perched.

As Helios rounded the face of a giant cliff, the valley ahead widened. A massive river bisected the valley, framed by forests of tall bushy-leafed trees, mountains rising on either side. Eltoar had seen that river many times. He had bathed in its waters, fished in its depths, and swum its length and breadth. It was the River Vahlin, which stemmed from beneath the great temple atop Mount Umar.

Helios dove, dropping so his talons left a rippling trail in the water, and his wings spread from bank to bank. Eltoar lifted his head, gazing up towards Mount Umar and the temple nestled near its peak. The great temple had existed for thousands of years – a shrine to the Enkaran Pantheon. Even from where he sat, thousands of feet below the temple itself, Eltoar could make out the enormous hundred-foot-high columns that supported the temple's stone porchway and the landing platform that jutted from the cliff face, large enough to hold ten dragons at any one time.

Helios swept through the valley, then up the face of Mount Umar before holding in the air above the platform, alighting on the cool stone, his talons clicking, dust and small rocks lifting in swirls.

A deep rumble echoed in the night, a vibration sweeping through the platform. Before them stood the hulking figure of Avandeer, the dragon to which Tivar was bound. The dragon was not a match for Helios in size, but her chest was deep, and her muscles were thick, her body still stretching almost a hundred feet from tail to snout. Scales of dull purple covered her body, growing lighter towards their edges, some as white as snow along her snout and the ridges of her eyes. The dragon lifted her head into the air, the bone-coloured horns that framed her face catching the light of the moon. Then, with another low rumble, she extended her neck, touching the side of her snout against Helios's.

Eltoar allowed a warm smile to touch his lips at the feelings of comfort and kinship that radiated from Helios's mind. The two dragons had hatched not long apart, Helios seeing only a few months more than Avandeer. Eltoar slid from his soulkin's back, pulling on threads of Air to soften his landing, his feet touching the smooth stone of the platform without so much as a sound. As he took a step forward, Avandeer pulled her neck to the side, dropping her head down and nudging Eltoar in the chest.

"I've missed you too." Eltoar rested his forehead against the tip of Avandeer's snout, his palm flat against its side. The dragon pushed into him, the warmth of her breath rolling over his skin. "She is inside?"

Avandeer nuzzled Eltoar a moment longer, then let out a short puff of air. She pushed her head against Helios and lifted herself into the air, her enormous wings spreading wide, a gust of wind swirling in her wake. Half a second and Helios followed after her. As the dragon dropped from the platform, spreading his wings in the valley below, a protective rumble resonated through his mind, images of Tivar flashing.

I won't push her. I promise. Eltoar filled his lungs with the cold night air as he turned and ascended the short staircase that led to the temple's entrance, the flickering orange-red glow of firelight from within casting shadows across the ground before him.

The great temple comprised a single enormous chamber that was six or seven times as long as it was wide, extending back into the mountain upon which it was built. Two rows of oil lanterns stood atop stone pedestals that framed the central floor of the chamber, bathing the large slabs of grey stone in firelight and flickering shadows. Behind the lanterns stood statues of each of the seven gods of the Enkaran Pantheon, stretching from the floor to the ceiling, each carved by hand millennia ago and preserved with Jotnar runes.

The statue of Achyron, The Warrior, stood by the entranceway: a young man, his face not quite human or elf. He had short hair and was encased from head to toe in plate armour, his hands clasped together on the pommel of a sword. Thirty feet further into the temple, the statue of Elyara, The Maiden, stood on the opposite side to Achyron, her long hair draped over her stone shoulders, a staff gripped in one hand, an open book in the other.

The statues continued on like that, in an alternating pattern, Hafaesir, Neron, and finally, the last statue that stood before those of Varyn and Heraya at the rear of the temple, was Efialtír, robes draped over his shoulders, a warm smile on his carved face, his hands spread wide in welcome. The depiction came from long before the god had been branded The Traitor or The Saviour. It had been carved millennia before Eltoar had taken his first breath, when Efialtír was known as The Warden, the caretaker of mind and body, the arbiter of life and death. If there was nothing else that would have told how ancient the great temple was, the inclusion of all seven gods would have been enough. It was only the presence of Efialtír's statue that had convinced Fane to leave the temple standing where he had reduced most all others to rubble.

Eltoar's footsteps echoed against the stone, amplified by the natural acoustics of the chamber, each step like the clattering of a sword. Ahead, at the far end, Tivar knelt at the feet of Varyn and Heraya, brown robes draped over her shoulders.

"I was wondering how long it would be before you came." Tivar didn't stand or turn as she spoke. She simply stayed where she was, her gaze fixed on the stone-carved faces of The Father and The Mother. "I already told Lyina and the others, I will not fight in any more of Fane's wars."

"Your brothers and sisters need you at their side." Eltoar stopped a few feet behind Tivar, his heart twisting as he looked down at his old friend. "I need you. The Urak armies are amassing in numbers we haven't seen since—"

"Since the night we slaughtered our own kind?" Tivar's voice was cold and still as she cut Eltoar short. She rose to her feet, slowly, letting out a deep sigh. "Since the night we betrayed those who trusted us most? Our brothers, our sisters." The light of the oil lamps cast dancing shadows across Tivar's face as she turned, her brown eyes gleaming. Her dark hair was pinned back behind her tapered ears, the scar that cleft her lip reaching up just beneath her nostril. "And what for, Eltoar?"

"Tivar, you know—"

"What for?" the woman roared, her voice rolling like thunder through the chamber, her fists shaking at her side. "With every passing day, my reasons make less and less sense. To break the cycle of corruption, only

147

to replace it with another? In the name of a god who now pits us against the Uraks like playthings on a board. So I need you to answer me, Eltoar. Why did we murder those whose side we should have been standing on?"

"Tivar, I..." Eltoar had asked himself the same question every day since The Fall, and much like Tivar, the answers he had given himself grew less and less convincing.

"That 'vessel' that hangs around your neck." Tivar took a step closer to Eltoar, her gaze fixing on where the gemstone hung behind Eltoar's shirt. She gave a twisted smile, shaking her head. "He manipulates us, Eltoar. Can you not see it? Can you not feel how that stone twists and turns you? How it seeps into your mind. The Order had lost its way." Tivar clapped her hands down on Eltoar's shoulders, staring deep into his eyes. "We had forgotten our purpose. We waged wars at the behest of kings and queens, and yet we stood aside when we should have held our ground. Our hubris told us we were better than those we swore to protect. Gold, fame, and bloodlust consumed us. But there were other ways. We should have tried harder, brother... we should have tried harder."

Eltoar pulled Tivar close, wrapping his arms around her, squeezing her tight, pulling her head to his chest.

Tivar's shoulders shook as she sobbed. "Nothing changed." She pulled herself away a bit, looking up at Eltoar. "You say it's different now. That's what you've said for centuries. But it's not. Fane wants us to fight. He wants us to wage war in his name, just like they did."

"It's not like that, Tivar."

"How is it not? Is that not why you have come here? To ask me to spill blood in his name?"

"There are still people who need us, Tivar. No matter what we've done in the past, we can't hide now. If we do not intervene then thousands will be lost, tens of thousands. The Uraks will not stop. You know this."

Tivar held Eltoar's gaze, tilting her head sideways, her eyes red and narrowed, the warm glow of the oil lanterns illuminating her face. She drew in a deep breath through her nostrils, quelling her sobs. "You once called those creatures allies. Asked us to trust them." She shook her head, tears rolling down her cheeks. "Then they massacred the eggs... all three hatcheries at Ilnaen, destroyed, top to bottom. Hundreds of hatchlings slaughtered before they could even draw breath."

Eltoar's heart clenched, knots twisting through his gut. A shiver rippled in his mind, spilling over from Helios, a bottomless agony consuming the dragon at the memory of the broken eggs.

"Do you know why, brother? Do you know why not a single egg has hatched since that night? Because the gods punish us. They are disgusted by what we did. By what we became. We were blinded. We followed a god of death and blood and called him The Saviour. And now the other gods punish us for our transgressions." Tivar turned her gaze to the enormous statues of Heraya and Varyn that stood before them. "At least the Uraks have no choice. They are bound to him. Their 'Lifebringer'. Without the Essence, they will wither and die. But *we* had a choice. We let Fane and those gemstones twist our minds. This darkness is on *our* shoulders. Our soulkin trusted us. And we let them die."

Eltoar opened his mouth to speak but his words caught in his throat. "There is a new Draleid, Tivar. A new hatchling."

Tivar's eyes widened, her gaze searching Eltoar's for any hint of a lie. She took a step back. "That cannot be… it cannot…"

"It is." Eltoar took a step closer, nodding. "The first hatchling in four centuries."

"Lyina never said… She didn't tell me."

"Because I asked her not to. I wanted to be the one to tell you."

"Have you seen them?" For the first time in centuries, Eltoar saw true happiness in Tivar's eyes. "What are they like? What colour are their scales?"

"I haven't seen him. Not yet. But his scales are white, as pure as the snow on the peak of this mountain."

"*Him…*" Tivar whispered. A warm smile touched her lips, tears still tumbling over her cheeks. "Bring me to him. I want to see him and meet his Draleid." Tivar took a step closer, her hands touching Eltoar's forearms, her eyes narrowing. "Eltoar…" Tivar searched Eltoar's eyes. "What are you not telling me?"

"It was Aeson Virandr who brought the egg to this continent. The Draleid flies in opposition to the empire."

"No." Tivar pushed Eltoar away, stepping backwards, all happiness evaporating. She glared at Eltoar, fury burning in her eyes. "I have fed the earth with too much blood. I will not put another one of us in the ground – not for him!"

"Tivar, please. I don't want to harm the Draleid. I only want to speak to him. I wouldn't—"

"Get out!" Tivar pushed Eltoar backwards again. "I am done, Eltoar!" Her chest trembled, tears streaming down her face, her eyes raw and red. "Anara Ilum. You remember her name?"

"I…" Eltoar stuttered, digging through his mind. "She was an apprentice, was she not?"

"She had seen no more than twenty summers when Avandeer and I chased her and Numirí here to Dracaldryr. It was eight years after Ilnaen. They had stayed hidden that entire time. When I found them, they took to the skies and fled, and I followed them. I hadn't wanted to kill her. I

149

only wanted to talk, to tell her that there was still a home for her. But as we soared through the valleys of Dracaldryr, that vessel around my neck throbbed. It was near empty. It craved Essence. We caught them in the skies, and Avandeer broke Numirí's neck."

"Tivar… I…"

"Anara survived the fall. She used threads of Air to soften her landing. But the breaking of her bond to Numirí shattered her. She begged me to kill her, Eltoar. She screamed, and she screamed. I could *hear* the pain in her voice. *Feel* it. *I* did that to her. I took her soulkin from her." Tivar shook her head side to side. "After Ilnaen, many of us died on both sides. But something about the loss in Anara's eyes broke me… It broke me, Eltoar." While she was talking, Tivar folded her arms across her chest, her hands clasping her elbows. She stared past Eltoar towards something unseen, her head twitching. After a moment, she lifted her gaze and met Eltoar's. "I *will not* put another of our kind in the ground. I will not tear another soul in half. Not on the word of that monster you call a friend. That demon you brand an emperor." Tivar's voice rose, veins bulging in her neck. "I will not!"

Eltoar reached his hand out. "Tiva—"

"I will not!"

CHAPTER ELEVEN

CITY OF THREE KINGS

Over the many centuries Therin had witnessed, he had learned quite a few things, one of which was that elven architecture held a unique beauty. That wasn't an opinion, it was a fact. Humans built from necessity: protection, control, resources. The Jotnar built for pragmatism: only what was needed, nothing more. The dwarves were masters of uniformity; smooth, angular stone – order. But the elves had always built for beauty and attunement with the world around them. To craft a city deserved the same delicate attention to detail as a painting, or a sculpture, for unlike paintings and sculptures, cities could stand the test of time. They carried the memories of generations and the aspirations of a civilisation. And above all else, if the indelible mark of a city was to be left on the world, it should be a mark that contributes to the natural beauty of things.

In the time before The Fall, Therin had spent many days at a time, weeks even, with the Craftsmages of Northern Valmíra, watching them create masterpieces the likes of which were not seen anywhere throughout the known world: statues of dragons that spanned hundreds of feet, each scale perfect; webway linked towers so intricate they appeared as fragile as glass; sweeping terraces of bone-hewn homes crafted seamlessly into the sides of mountains. Therin always thought the affinity of the Craftsmage was the most misunderstood of all who could wield the Spark. For it was not simply a natural talent in the utilisation of Earth, or Air, or Fire that forged a true Craftsmage. Nor was it raw power in the Spark. It was a deep understanding of the workings of things and the complex nature of the relationships between them. An otherworldly cognition of mechanics and intricacies that most minds could not begin to fathom. Any mage could use the Spark to destroy, but it took a special mind to create.

Which was why, as Halmír and his Highguard led Therin and the others through the streets of Aravell, past the enormous cylindrical towers of white stone, the sweeping walkways, waterfalls, aqueducts, and enormous platforms crafted from the cliffs themselves, Therin felt both an unbridled happiness and a deep, resonating sense of loss. Aravell was beautiful, but it was nothing compared to what had once been and what would likely never be again.

Beside Therin, Dann walked with his jaw slack and his eyes wide. The boy had been awestruck by Midhaven, Camylin, and Belduar. But his silence told Therin that he, too, saw the separation between what he had seen before and what was in front of him now.

"Erinian stone," Therin said as Dann ran his finger along a strip of azure stone inlaid into the low wall that framed the street down which they walked. "It draws in the sun's light, holding it, then releasing it slowly at night."

"Incredible," Dann whispered, his finger lingering on the surface of the stone. He looked around, his gaze passing over the city and the elves who stopped in the streets watching as the newcomers were escorted by the city steward and a number Highguard. "Therin, why did we go to Belduar at all? Why didn't we just come here?"

Therin let out a sigh, glancing ahead to where Aeson and Baldon strode behind Halmír, the Highguard out in front – Thalanil had taken Lyrei with him to the healers the moment they had entered the city, and Alea had gone with them to look over her sister. "There is nothing simple in this world, Dann. There are politics at play here that have been churning for millennia and have grown even worse since the fall of The Order."

Therin said nothing else. He let his words hang in the air, waiting to see how Dann would respond. The boy asked more questions than a horse had hair. Therin knew more than a few of them were asked simply to irritate him, but when Dann asked a question he truly wanted the answer to, Therin took no small pleasure in keeping that answer dangling just out of Dann's reach.

Therin could see Dann holding his breath, running his tongue across his teeth, and tapping his right hand against his hip. All three gestures on their own were nothing, but Therin had long since noticed when Dann did them together, it tended to mean he was biting his tongue.

Despite himself, Dann was beginning to grow on Therin. The boy was the physical manifestation of a headache. But there was a spark in him. An unwillingness to give up. And that was something to be admired. It was also something that was going to be needed in what was to come.

By the time Halmír led the group through the streets of Aravell, across the central bridge, along a number of walkways, up a seemingly never-ending hewn stone staircase, and out onto a circular platform that overlooked the city, the light of the setting sun was nothing but a warm glow over the mountains to the west.

Halmír stood at the mouth of the platform, three Highguard taking up positions either side of him as he gestured for Dann, Therin, Aeson, and Baldon to step out onto the platform.

"The Ephorí will be with you shortly." Halmír's gaze lingered on Therin. For a moment, Therin thought he might say something, but the elf simply curled his lips into a sad smile, then turned and left. The Highguard remained in position.

"You would think they would have more trust," Aeson said, folding his arms across his chest, frowning as he looked at the Highguard.

"Trust?" Therin laughed. "You know as well as I do, that is a commodity in short supply here."

HOURS PASSED AS THEY WAITED for Halmír to return, the moon filling the void of light left by the sun, bathing all of Aravell in its silvery touch. Therin stood at the edge of the platform, his arms folded, looking down over the city, the azure glow of the erinian stones striking against the white stone and bone-hewn buildings. The hum of chatter and footsteps drifted up from the lower levels, blending seamlessly with a constant rush of water from the aqueducts and waterfalls.

"I've never seen anything like it," Dann said, taking a place beside Therin, his hands resting on the stone wall that fenced in the platform. "Though, I seem to be saying that a lot recently."

Therin looked at Dann for a moment, then shook his head, suppressing a laugh. It was as though the young man could *feel* when Therin was most at peace and made a conscious decision to break that peace. He let out a sigh. "After The Fall, the elven Kingdoms of Lunithír, Ardurän, and Vaelen decided to build the city here in the Aravell forest. But it was a Craftsmage by the name of Líra Alunea who proposed the idea that this section be dug and hollowed, the city built within the bounds of the new basin, and the glamour constructed to keep the truth hidden. She was a visionary and one of only three elves to have ever truly mastered the Jotnar art of glamour construction."

"Where is she now?"

Therin let out a deep sigh, his throat tightening. "She died three hundred and forty-two years ago."

Dann gave Therin a weak smile, shaking his head as many do when they're not sure what to say. "I'm going to go talk to one of those guards. We've been waiting for hours."

"Dann, don't..." Therin puffed out a breath of air, watching as Dann strode off towards the Highguard.

"There's no point in trying." Aeson laughed as he took Dann's place, resting his forearms on the stone wall, looking down over the city. "Better he wastes his breath on them than us. Are you all right?" Aeson turned his head, his gaze meeting Therin's. "I know being here isn't easy."

Therin sighed softly, nodding as he leaned on the ledge of the wall beside Aeson. "I see pieces of her in everything here."

"How long has it been since you've spoken to Faelen?"

"You saw her when they found us on the way to Belduar. She has no words for me. Few here do, and I don't blame them."

Aeson gave Therin a sorrowful smile, resting his hand on Therin's shoulder for a moment. "I understand your pain. I feel Naia every day. I see her in Erik and Dahlen's faces. I hear her laugh in the wind when I'm alone. It's not all bad. It only hurts when I breathe."

"My loss is a drop to your ocean, old friend. But at least we're still here. We still have the chance to forge a better world for those we leave behind."

Therin looked towards the oldest friend he had left in the world and saw a tear glisten on Aeson's cheek. Aeson brought his hand up and grabbed the side of Therin's head, bringing their temples together, letting out a soft, broken laugh. "Na daui nai diar siel væra myia haydria, yíar'ydil."

To die by your side will be my honour, old friend.

"I denír viël ar altinua."

In this life and always.

Aeson sighed as he rested his arms back on the ledge. "When this is over, I will gladly welcome rest. Four hundred years is a long time to fight."

Therin knew the depths of sadness in Aeson's heart was something he could never truly understand. The loss of their loves was something they shared, but to lose a dragon was something entirely different.

"How long do you think they'll leave us waiting?" Aeson asked, changing the subject.

"How long is a piece of twine?" Therin smiled. "On any other day, all I would expect would be an apology from Halmír and a place to sleep for when they are ready to meet us tomorrow. But with Calen involved, I would say they Ephorí will come soon enough."

"Aruni and the boy, Valdrin? Do you know how they fare? It was here you brought them, wasn't it? The last I saw of them was when you brought Dayne and Belina to me."

"I haven't seen them in a few years. But Aruni writes to me, when she can. She still suffers from the night-terrors, still has to strap herself down. Valdrin is still quiet, but from what Aruni writes, he has become a smith of quite some reputation."

Aeson nodded softly, looking out over the erinian-lit city. "It is good to hear they are all right. I know what they mean to you."

Therin nodded slowly, allowing himself a soft smile.

No more than a half hour had passed before each of the six Highguard who stood at the mouth of the platform cracked the steel butts of their glaives against the stone. Therin straightened, drawing a deep breath to settle himself, then turned.

Halmír and Thalanil stepped onto the platform, Thalanil taking up a position to the right while Halmír stood to the left, opening his arms as six more elves strode after them.

"The Ephorí of Aravell," Halmír announced, opening his arms as the others stepped past the Highguard and out onto the platform.

The Ephorí of Aravell were second only to the rulers of the three Kingdoms that founded the city. There were six in total, a pair from each Kingdom. Traditionally, only those without the capacity to touch the Spark had been permitted to hold the position, so as to prevent stagnation. But after The Fall, it was decided that the opposite should be true, to allow the preservation and conservation of elven culture and heritage. Which was why Therin knew each of the six Ephorí by name.

Thurivîr and Ara, the Ephorí of Lunithîr, were the first to follow Thalanil and Halmír onto the platform. Both wore robes of deep crimson ornamented with vines of gold, their silvery hair tied back, an effortless grace in their gait. He had known them for centuries, but neither had spoken to him since his decision to not take sides between the elves of Lynalion and the elves of Aravell after The Fall. They didn't so much as look his direction as they took their place beside Halmír.

Dumelian and Ithilin followed, their robes the black and silver of Vaelen. Much like the others, Dumelian did not acknowledge Therin's existence, but Ithilin gave him a warm smile, the creases in her skin born from a near millennium of walking the world. Therin inclined his head.

The last of the Ephorí to step onto the platform were Baralas and Liritháin, the dark green and brown of Ardurän over their shoulders.

The Ephorí stood in pairs across the mouth of the platform.

The first to speak was Thurivîr, who drew in a noticeably long breath and stepped forward. The elf stood at a height with Therin but was more muscular with broader shoulders. His hair was black as night, his eyes a piercing blue. He had once been one of Therin's closest companions. They had spilled blood together, broken bread, and drunk until they could no longer stand. But now Thurivîr's gaze passed over Therin as though he were a shadow. "It is a pleasure to welcome you to Aravell," he said, looking out over the group gathered before him. His gaze lingered on Dann, curiosity filling his eyes. "We apologise for the delay in our coming. Halmír informed us of the situation, and there was much… *deliberation,* to be had. Rakina, diar närvarin gryr haydria til myia elwyn." *Your presence brings honour to my heart.*

155

"Ar diar, myialí," Aeson replied. *And yours, mine.*

Liritháin stepped forward, cutting across Thurivîr, ignoring the narrowed stares aimed at her by the other Ephorí. *Always with the games.* She greeted Aeson in much the same way as Thurivîr had, then turned to Baldon, bowing at the waist. "Child of Clan Fenryr. I am Liritháin Durianelle, Ardurän Ephorí of Aravell. It is an honour to find you within our walls. Varthon of clan Dvalin sends her blessings. She wishes she or her kin could have been here to welcome you, as is proper, but as you know, tonight is the night of the Caranea."

"No grievance is taken. I wish the spirits of the gods to shine on Varthon and clan Dvalin. It is a pleasure for me to lay my eyes on the home of your people. Therin Silver Fang has long been a friend of clan Fenryr, and as such, so are his kin." Baldon inclined his head, his golden eyes glimmering, a slight rumble resonating in his chest. Therin smiled at that. Baldon knew of Therin's estrangement with the elves of Aravell and the reasons behind it.

Liritháin allowed a fleeting scowl to touch her lips at the mention of Therin's name, but she simply inclined her head to Baldon.

As Liritháin's companion, Baralas, moved to begin his greetings, Aeson held his hand in the air. "Ephorí, please forgive me, but we do not have time for this. By now, I am sure you are well aware of the circumstances of our arrival. The new Draleid – of which I am sure Thalanil has spoken – is in grave danger. As is my son. I will be in the debt of whichever one of you grants us safe passage through the northern Aravell. We must reach the Svidar'Cia as quickly as possible."

Silence descended, all eyes resting on Aeson. Had it been anyone else who had spoken, Therin had no doubt the reaction from the Ephorí would have been a far louder one. But Aeson was not simply anyone. He was Rakina, and as such he was granted certain allowances. Even at that, the irritation on Liritháin's face spoke more than any words could. She cleared her throat, screwed her mouth into a tight grimace, then tilted her head. She looked back to her partner, Baralas, then to the other Ephorí, a look passing between them that made Therin's stomach uneasy. "Very well, Rakina. We have already arranged an escort."

CHAPTER TWELVE

THE PATHS NOT YET TAKEN

The sun cast a deep red glow across the world as it dipped into the western horizon, sinking into the woodland of Lynalion. The smell of burning wood incensed the air, wafting on the gentle earlywinter breeze. The wind was nothing compared to the frozen winds of Drifaien, but it still sent a rolling shiver over Calen's skin. Ahead, where the river Kilnír forked, he saw a house composed of stout logs, nestled snugly at the edge of a grove, a thick column of languid grey smoke drifting from its chimney. The house stood two storeys tall, with a small porch-covered deck that fronted the main entrance. It reminded him of the houses in The Glade – of home.

Calen shifted in the saddle, his left shoulder clicking as he rolled it back and forth, attempting to ease the stiffness that had set in. On the first day after leaving Kingspass, Vaeril had regained enough strength to see to most of Calen's, Erik's, and Tarmon's major wounds, including closing the gash along Erik's calf and relieving the residual pain in Calen's shoulder – though some aches and stiffness still remained. The elf marched to the left of Calen's horse, a weary look in his eyes and a laboured strain to his gait. Even with the toll the healing had taken on Vaeril's body, the elf had refused to trade places with Calen on the horse. The journey had taken just over two days of riding, and even Calen's body was crying out for some proper rest. He couldn't imagine how Vaeril must have felt. The only person Calen could think of who was more stubborn than the elf was himself, though he would never admit it.

As they rode closer to the house, Tarmon and Erik riding further ahead, Vaeril still trudging along at Calen's side, Calen let his mind drift into Valerys's. Every moment spent seeing through the dragon's eyes was a moment his mind didn't linger on Haem.

The warmth of the dragon's soul soothed the aches and pains that held on to Calen's mind and body. The more he let himself sink into Valerys's thoughts, the more his senses shifted and sharpened. The smell of charred wood dissipated, replaced by the crisp clean scent of cool air as Valerys swooped through the clouds overhead, so high that Calen wouldn't have known he was there were it not for their bond. Through the dragon's eyes, Calen could see so much more than the hazy glow of the setting sun. To the east and west, the woodlands of Lynalion and the Darkwood stretched for hundreds, even thousands, of miles, their mottled greens and browns disappearing into the distance in either direction. The jagged razorback peaks of Mar Dorul ran along the edges of Lynalion, dark and barren, stretching upwards like savage claws threatening to tear at the fabric of the sky.

Valerys banked left, diving through a blanket of cloud, tucking his wings in tight, dropping at an incredible speed before unfurling them once more and sweeping forward on a rushing current of air. The sensation was like lightning in Calen's veins. He could feel the gelid winds crashing against Valerys's scales, the currents of air shifting beneath his wings.

It was then, below the cloud cover to the north, that the vast emptiness of the Burnt Lands came into view. The ravaged wasteland was still hundreds of miles north, at least ten days' ride, harsh mountain peaks jutting from the ever-shifting ocean of sand and dunes. Even through Valerys's eyes, Calen couldn't see any place where the wastes ended. He knew from the maps that the Burnt Lands stretched for thousands of miles from east to west, from the foothills of Mar Dorul to the Lodhar Mountains. Captain Kiron had said the nearest point to nearest point from south to north was only about two hundred miles across, but that would bring them out at Copperstille, some thousand miles from Berona. The way Calen saw it, though, the less time they spent in the Burnt Lands, the better.

Through Valerys's eyes, Calen stared out over the vast wasteland, letting its enormity sink in. That was where he was taking his companions, his friends. That was what he was asking them to face. And not to win a war or topple an empire, but simply to find Rist. After watching Haem step through that gateway, Calen's resolve to find Rist had only strengthened. Rist was family in all but blood, and Calen would not abandon him. Not again. But what Calen did question was whether he was right in allowing Tarmon, Vaeril, and Erik to join him. He should never have asked them to risk their lives. This was not their fight. It was his and his alone. *And Dann's. I wish Dann were here.*

"I'm still not sure about this."

Calen pulled his mind back from Valerys's at the sound of Erik's voice. He turned to see Erik pulling his horse up alongside Calen's, his gaze focused on the stream of smoke that drifted from the house ahead.

"If Arkana wanted us dead, she could have killed us ten times over. She had plenty of opportunities. Why would she have let us leave the city?"

"I don't know. I just… I can't trust her."

"Then trust *me*."

Erik let out a sigh. "It's not that simple.

"It's as simple as you make it, Erik. Besides, look at Vaeril." Calen gestured towards the elf who was all but stumbling along beside Calen's horse, his stare fixed ahead, his feet moving one after another, more from sheer force of will than anything else. "He needs rest, or at least a warm meal."

Sighing through his nostrils, Erik nodded. "All right. But if there is even the slightest sign of something wrong then—"

"We'll handle it," Calen said, smiling weakly.

Tarmon had already dismounted by the time Calen, Erik, and Vaeril had reached the house. A knot twisted in Calen's stomach as the man slid his greatsword from his back, lifting a finger to his lips.

"The door is open," Tarmon whispered.

As Calen dismounted, he could feel Valerys in the back of his mind as the dragon folded its wings and plummeted through the clouds, falling like an anvil dropped from the sky.

No. You need to stay hidden.

A roar of defiance rippled through Calen's mind. Too many times Valerys had left Calen alone, and too many times he had not been able to keep his soulkin from harm. It would not happen again.

Within moments, the dragon had broken through the lowest blanket of cloud, his scales scintillating red and orange in the incandescent light of the setting sun. Unfurling his wings to their fullest, Valerys swooped overhead, stirring a gust of wind in his wake. With a crack of his wings, Valerys landed beside Calen, his lavender eyes fixed on the house that was nestled into the grove.

Calen's horse snorted at the sudden arrival of the dragon, reeling backwards. Calen didn't blame the animal. Valerys was now at least thirty feet from head to tail, his chest thicker than oak barrels. The horns that framed the dragon's face were longer than Calen's arms and just as thick. Valery's wingspan was almost twice the length of his body, his forelimbs laden with powerful muscle. The sight sent a surge of pride through Calen.

"It's all right," he said in as soothing a voice as he could muster, running his hand along his horse's muzzle. "It's all right."

The horse calmed at Calen's words, but it still shifted, stamping its feet into the ground and pulling away from the dragon. Calen continued to run his hand along the horse's muzzle as he led it over to where Tarmon had tethered his horse to a short fence that sat about ten feet from the front of the house. He tied the animal to the fence, reassuring it once more before sliding his sword from its scabbard.

"Why has nobody come out?" Erik whispered as he and Vaeril stepped up beside Calen, their swords drawn. "Valerys made enough noise to wake a village."

Tarmon turned back to them, his brow furrowed, his finger pressed to his lips. He inclined his head, gesturing for the others to follow, gripping the handle of his greatsword with both hands.

The warm glow of candlelight emanated from within the house, becoming more apparent as the sun's descent quickened its pace. Condensation clung to the insides of the windows, droplets of water rolling along the glass. Barely a sound came from within except for the crackling and snapping of burning wood.

Calen let his mind drift into Valerys's as they approached the short set of wooden steps that led to the porch-covered deck of the house. The smell of slow-cooked meat filled his dragon-sharpened nostrils. Valerys could feel the warmth that flooded the house radiating through the air in waves. But such was the warmth from the fire within that it drowned out the body heat of whoever or whatever occupied the house. Valerys took a few steps closer, his talons sinking into the ground, his neck arching, lips pulling back.

Stay back for now. Arkana said this man is a friend, but we still need to be careful.

A low growl formed in Valerys's throat at Calen's words, but the dragon held his ground, the frills on the back of his neck standing on end.

Tarmon's foot had barely touched the first step when a voice called from within, surprisingly mirthful with a slight lilt.

"Come in, come in, come in. There is no need for weapons here."

"I'm not putting my swords away," Erik whispered to Calen, both his blades gripped firmly in his fists.

Calen looked to Tarmon, then to Vaeril. Both shook their heads.

Calen nodded, tightening his grip on the handle of his sword before moving up next to Tarmon, his foot eliciting an aching creak from the wooden step. "Together."

Tarmon gave a short nod, and they moved up the steps, Vaeril and Erik following close behind. They crossed the deck in a few paces, then locked gazes once more before stepping through the door.

Long wooden floorboards ran from the front of the house to the back. The stairs leading to the second storey stood to the right of the doorway, rising to a dark-obscured landing. The living area was almost twice the size Calen had expected, as though the inside of the house was somehow larger than the outside. Two long shelves decorated the far wall, laden with thick leatherbound books that looked as though they had seen more summers than Calen could have even dreamt of. Beneath the shelves sat a mixture of heavy wooden chests and open topped boxes filled to the brim with trinkets that glistened in the firelight.

Six wooden chairs sat in the middle of the room atop an enormous bearskin rug, each turned slightly to face the roaring hearth set into the left-most wall. A thick woollen blanket was draped over the back of the nearest chair. A cookpot was suspended on a hook over the flames, and by the cookpot stood a tall, grey-haired man with long brown robes draped over his shoulders.

"Sit, sit, sit," the man said, as though speaking only to himself. He reached down to a small table that stood beside him, picking up one of six wooden bowls. "After you sit and eat, then we can talk. But like I said, there is no need for weapons. I'm sure you are all strong enough to break the bones of a frail old man without the use of a sword."

The man didn't turn to look upon the intruders as he spoke. Instead, he gripped the handle of a ladle that hung by the fire, dipped it into the cookpot, and proceeded to pour the contents into the bowl, the fire casting his shadow along the bearskin rug.

"Here," he said, turning, extending the wooden bowl out to Calen. As the man turned, Calen got a good look at his face. There was nothing particularly striking about him. He looked as though he had seen sixty or seventy summers. Deep wrinkles sat below his eyes, at the corners of his mouth, and along his forehead. His hair was almost shoulder-length, grey streaked with light brown. His eyes seemed like those of a much younger man, bright and observant. Calen wasn't quite sure what colour his irises were. They seemed to shift from a grey to a pale blue, changing with the flickering light.

"Well, come on," the man said when Calen hadn't grasped the bowl. In truth, Calen was more than a little taken aback. There he stood, in the living area of the man's house, his fingers still gripping his sword, three of his companions – one of whom was an elf – standing by his side, but the man didn't so much as bat an eyelid.

Calen hesitated before taking the bowl, still a little unsure as to what was happening.

"Good, now, take a seat while I serve your friends. And again, can you please put away that steel?" A firmness set into the man's voice as he finished his sentence, as though that would be the last time he would ask the question politely. Without waiting for Calen's reply, the man turned, picking up another wooden bowl and filling it.

It was only then that a rich, warm, comforting smell reached Calen's nostrils, and he looked down to see a full bowl of mouth-watering stew. Chunks of carrot and potatoes floated in the rich broth, next to lean piec-es of meat that looked as though it would fall apart at the slightest touch.

Calen salivated. It had been quite a while since he'd eaten something that looked even remotely as good as this.

Calen lifted his eyes from the stew to find the old man staring at him, another bowl gripped firmly in his hands. The man lifted an eyebrow, an unimpressed look painting his face.

Casting a furtive glance towards Tarmon, Calen took a deep breath and slid his sword into its scabbard. If the man wished them harm, Calen could always use the Spark, as could Vaeril.

The old man smiled. "Good. Now come, sit. I'm sure you're tired as well as hungry." He offered the bowl to Erik, who eyed the stew like it was a steaming pile of dung. The man sighed. "It's a little hot, but it's not poison. Please don't knock it from my hand. I've seen how that ends, and I don't want to ruin a perfectly good rug. Here, look." The man lifted the bowl to his lips and took a deep mouthful of the stew, swallowing. "Now, if it's poison, we'll die together. That's the best I can offer you. Take it or leave it."

His brow furrowing, Erik glanced at Calen who nodded before taking a seat. As he set himself on the wooden chair, Calen reached out to the Spark. He didn't draw from it; he just wanted to feel its energy and know it was there if he needed it. He could sense Vaeril doing the same thing.

Calen rested the stew on his lap, feeling the residual warmth from the bowl spread through his legs.

"Are you Rokka?" Calen said as the man walked towards the cookpot. There was a slight limp in his gait, barely noticeable, but enough to be distinctive.

"I am indeed, my boy," the man said while handing a bowl to Tarmon, who had already sheathed his greatsword, his eyes still watching Rokka as though the man were a wolf in sheep's clothing. "I've been waiting for you. Had this stew going since morning. I'm surprised it's not all mush to be honest. Venison, potatoes, onions, carrots, and tomato, with a sprig of rosemary from the garden out back, and a splash of Arkalen wine. I've always thought stew was appropriate for weary travellers. There's no way to make a decent one while you're on the road, at least not if you like your meat edible." The man cackled at his own joke, a phlegm-filled cough catching in his throat. He left Tarmon and Erik to take their seats while he turned back to the cookpot. "It simply takes too long. But I have all the time in the world, so what better to cook?"

"Arkana sent us here, she…" Calen's voice trailed off as the old man's words sank in. "You've been waiting for us?"

Rokka ignored Calen, filled a fourth bowl, then turned to Vaeril, his face softening as he handed it to the elf. "Det gryr haydria til myia elwyn at haryn du ocha sír myia aldryr." *It brings honour to my heart to have you eat by my fire.*

162

Vaeril stared at the man, his face expressionless. Calen wasn't sure if the elf was about to embrace Rokka or strike him down. Slowly, Vaeril sheathed his sword and took the bowl from Rokka, his gaze never dropping from the old man's.

"Here," the old man said, reaching towards Vaeril. The elf moved backwards a little, pulling away from Rokka's hand, but the man matched him, resting his palm on Vaeril's shoulder.

A tingling sensation ran down the back of Calen's neck, his eyes widening as he felt the old man reach for the Spark. *He's a mage!*

A fury rose in Valerys, a fire that Calen felt simmering in his blood as the dragon moved closer to the house, a protective urge radiating from his mind. The man drew on threads of each element, weaving them around himself in a pattern of complex spirals and motions that Calen couldn't even dream of following. It was only the shift of the expression on Vaeril's face that stopped Calen from leaping to his feet and Valerys from crashing through the wall. In only moments, Vaeril's hard stare softened, his shoulders dropping, a slight sigh escaping his mouth.

He's healing him.

"There, that should feel much better. The next time you heal, you need to remember to keep more for yourself. You elves always think you are invincible. Like perpetual children, the lot of you." Rokka shook his head, turning back towards the cookpot, leaving Vaeril standing there with a dumbfounded expression.

Calen shifted in his seat. His throat tightened, and his hand drifted to the pommel of his sword. The situation had turned in an instant. This was no frail old man standing before them. It was a mage. One capable of weaving a complex and powerful pattern of threads. Calen didn't understand the depths of how the Spark affected ageing, but if the man looked as old as he did while also being able to touch the Spark, he must have been far older than even Aeson or Therin.

"What just happened?" Erik asked, lifting himself from the chair and grasping Vaeril's shoulder. "Are you all right?"

"I'm fine," Vaeril said with a shaky nod, casting a glance towards Calen, then back towards Rokka. "He's a mage."

Erik ripped a blade from the scabbard across his back while Tarmon leapt to his feet, stepping between Rokka and Calen, pulling his short sword from the scabbard at his hip, stretching his arm out so the tip of the blade was pointed towards the old man.

"Children," the old man whispered with a laugh, once more turning back towards the cookpot, muttering to himself. "Sit back down. I have no intention of harming you. If I did, I wouldn't have wasted my stew on you. Sit, sit. Eat, eat."

Both Erik and Tarmon exchanged glances with Vaeril and Calen, who nodded.

"Are you sure you're all right?" Erik asked Vaeril, concern in his eyes.

"I am," Vaeril said, sounding as though he weren't quite sure himself. But the elf's eyes looked more awake and his movements more certain, as though the man had pulled the tiredness from his bones. Vaeril took a seat opposite Calen, resting the bowl of stew on his lap. The look on his face told Calen the elf wasn't quite sure what to make of what had just happened.

"Ahh, Elyara guide me. There are only four of you. This is a different path. My old age must be getting in the way." Rokka shook his head as he turned away from the cookpot, a bowl of stew in his hand and another empty bowl still resting on the small table at his side. The man sighed, lowering himself onto the wooden chair nearest the fire, next to Tarmon. It was only then that Calen noticed not only were there six bowls, but there were also six chairs. The man had been expecting five travellers, not four. But how had he been expecting anyone at all?

Rokka looked around, an amused expression on his face. "Have I not already proven it's not poison?" The man grasped the bowl with both hands, tipping it upwards, pouring a long draught of the stew into his mouth. His mouth still full, he gave a broad smile, a few glistening droplets escaping his mouth and rolling down his chin.

After a few moments of hesitation, Vaeril raised his bowl to his lips, Tarmon following suit. Erik looked over at Calen, shrugged, then did the same.

Calen looked down at the contents of the bowl. Thick chunks of venison, crumbly potato, onions, and carrots floated in a rich broth that smelled of his mam's winter cooking. His stomach gave a deep, belly-turning rumble. The kind that would make a wild bear jealous. But before he could contemplate tasting so much as a drop, Valerys pushed at the back of his mind. He could feel the hunger radiating from the dragon. Valerys still stood at the front of the house, his neck craned into the porchway, his head only a foot or so from the open door.

"There is a herd of deer not far from here, maybe a mile or so north," Rokka said between great slurps of his stew. "They tend to stay around the river, but they do wander."

Tarmon, Vaeril, and Erik looked at the man as though he were mad, rambling on nonsensically about deer. But Calen knew precisely what he meant. Which only raised more questions. Questions Calen would get the answers to.

Go. We are safe.

Calen could hear the rumble in Valerys's throat through the doorway. Images flashed across his mind. Blood, loss, fire. A deep sadness spilled over from Valerys, twisting knots in Calen's stomach. It was the same sadness Calen had felt in the dragon after they had been reunited outside Arisfall. Placing his bowl on the floor, Calen got to his feet and stepped out onto the porch-covered deck, ignoring the questioning stares from the others.

Valerys stood at the foot of the deck's steps, the soft moonlight glistening off his scales, his lavender eyes fixed on Calen. Valerys extended his neck forward, pressing his snout into Calen's outstretched hand, nuzzling against his palm, the softest of whimpers escaping the dragon's throat.

"We will not be separated again," Calen whispered, resting his other hand on Valerys's snout, looking out over the dragon's massive body. He still couldn't believe how large Valerys had become and how much more the dragon was still to grow. Calen remembered when Valerys had ridden at the front of his saddle, curled up tail to snout, no bigger than a small dog. They'd been through so much in their short time together. "I promise you. Myia nithír til diar. I denír viël ar altinua." *My soul to yours. In this life and always.*

Calen rested his forehead against Valerys's snout, letting their minds drift into one another's, letting the warmth of their bond quench the fires of their fear and worries. "Go," he said, running his right hand across Valerys's scales. "You need to hunt and you need to eat. We will be right here. Stay low and close to the river. When you come back, stay on the north side of the house where the grove will block you from sight."

A weak rumble of defiance rumbled through the back of Calen's mind, but he could feel Valerys's hunger. The dragon had no choice. He needed to eat. "*Go*," Calen said with a laugh, pushing at Valerys's snout. "You're too grumpy when you're hungry."

Pulling his head back, Valerys blew a gust of warm air over Calen before turning towards the forest and spreading out his leathery white wings, veins of black threading through them. With a few wingbeats, the dragon lifted himself into the air, blending with the thin layer of white clouds that painted the night sky. It only took a moment before the scent of wet deer filled Valerys's nostrils, and the dragon peeled right, diving towards the north end of the grove.

"How?" That was the only word Calen said when he stepped back into the house. Erik, Tarmon, and Vaeril looked at him as though he was just as mad as Rokka, but the old man simply smiled.

"Can someone please tell me what is going on?" Erik held out his arms, the bowl of stew still held in his right hand, bits of potato and carrot clinging to the stubble that had begun to form on his upper lip and chin.

"Sit," Rokka said, gesturing to the chair Calen had vacated. "Eat, and I will answer."

Calen stared at the man for a few moments before letting out an irritated sigh. He pulled the chair closer and planted himself on it, his gaze never leaving Rokka's. "Tell me now or—"

"*Eat*," Rokka said again, gesturing towards the bowl of stew Calen had left on the floor. "You must be gone in the morning. You have a long road ahead, and you need to eat."

A shiver ran through Calen's body. The man could simply be grasping at straws. It would not be difficult to assume that the four of them were on a long journey. But there was more than that. Other things Rokka had said since they entered the house.

By the looks on the others' faces, they were connecting the same dots. Vaeril sat in his chair, one leg folded across the other, his bowl of stew balanced in his lap. His face was as calculating as ever, but there was a curiosity in his eyes, and Calen had noticed the elf had let go of the Spark.

Tarmon leaned forward, his arms resting on his knees, an empty bowl gripped in his left hand. He wasn't looking at Rokka; he was looking at Calen, waiting on Calen's word. Erik was much the same, though he looked a little more uncertain than either Tarmon or Vaeril.

Swallowing hard, Calen reached down and picked up the bowl. The mouth-watering aroma hit him almost immediately, the warmth of the bowl spreading through his hands. He let out a sigh before tipping it towards his mouth and letting the stew pour in. It tasted as good as it looked, better even – almost exactly like his mother used to make, though she had never added rosemary.

Rokka drew in a deep breath, leaning back in his chair, casting his gaze into the burning hearthfire. "I am what most people would call a druid."

Calen choked on the stew, sitting forward, bringing his hand to his mouth to stop from spilling. "A druid? But druids died out centuries ago."

"So did most of the dragons, did they not?" Rokka laughed, still staring into the flames. Rokka's voice dropped to a sombre tone. "We are dead because that is what we wanted. If everyone thinks we are dead, nobody hunts us – much like the Jotnar. But in truth, there are few of us left. Druids don't have the long life the Spark grants to mages. Unless you're like me, touched by both sets of gods, shunned by both sets of people. A blessing or a curse, I still haven't decided. But here we are."

"How did you know we were coming?" Erik asked. "Can druids see the future?"

Rokka snorted a little. "Not all of us, no. There are many branches of druid, each with varying gifts. I am a Seerdruid. And it's not as simple as seeing the future. If it were, I would have set out five bowls and five chairs instead of wasting my time. And either way, all Seers do not see forwards. Some see backwards, others sideways. I can see the paths not yet taken.

But at any point in time, there are hundreds, if not thousands, of paths each person can walk. Each path changes the next path, and the paths of others, and so on. Millions of permutations in constant motion. When I dream or when the gods will it, I see glimpses of these paths. The most likely paths a person might walk. They are ever shifting, ever changing. Over the centuries, I have grown quite adept at judging which path is the most likely one, though evidently I am not as adept as I thought I was. The Drifaienin chose not to come then? Interesting. I had expected otherwise."

"Is he talking about Alleron?" Erik leaned forwards in his chair, his eyes wide.

"So you saw us, in your dreams?" Calen's heartbeat quickened. Ever since Valerys had lost control in the tunnels, something had changed. That night in the barn in Katta, Calen had seen things in his dreams that had felt as real as when he was awake. Skies filled with dragons, cities burning, pulsating waves of fire razing everything in their path. What was more, Valerys had seen it too. Until that point, sleep had been their one reprieve from each other's thoughts. Most of the time, it still was. When Calen was haunted by nightmares of Artim Valdock, they were his and his alone. But the other nights, when the dreams turned to things he had never seen, Valerys shared them. Until now, Calen had dismissed them as nothing more than his imagination. But what if they were more than that? Could they have been glimpses of the past? Or the future?

Rokka shifted in his chair, staring at Calen with a newfound intensity. "I did. Many times. Many different paths, each slightly diverging from the other."

"Why tell us this?" Tarmon said, breaking his silence, his eyes fixed on Rokka, a sharp edge to his voice. "If the last of the druids want people to believe they are dead, why tell four strangers who you are?"

There was a change in the air as Calen and the others realised what Tarmon was implying. Telling secrets to dead men held no risk.

"Well, I—"

"Before you answer, know that if you lie, if you in any way intend to harm the people in this room, I will gut you, mage or no."

"Believe me," Rokka said, leaning back into his chair and folding his arms across his chest, "you do not have to convince me of that. I've seen you do it four times already. I did get you once as well, I'll have you know. Though I don't like those odds."

Rokka leaned forward in his chair, keeping his arms folded, looking towards Calen. For the first time since they had entered the house, Calen saw hesitation in the old man's eyes. "Each path I see has a different feeling, a different energy, if you will. Part of being a Seer is deciphering that

167

energy and choosing which paths to walk down. Of all the paths I've seen where you arrive here, the one I wish to follow is the one in which we have this conversation. Truthfully, this can get more than a little complicated. Since we humans arrived in Epheria almost three thousand years ago, druids have been hunted. Sometimes simply from hatred of things not understood, sometimes because we were living symbols of gods that held no sway in these lands, but mostly for control. First by elves and Jotnar, then, as time passed, by our own people. I bear no loyalty to any nations, least of all this 'empire'. At this stage, the only point of my existence is to find a path where my people will not be banished to the annals of time. From what I can tell, that path involves this conversation, you leaving here before the sun rises more than two fingers above the horizon, and one more thing…" Grunting, Rokka lifted himself from his chair, making his way to the far wall. Bending over, he produced a key from his pocket, unlocked a heavy wooden chest, and rooted through its contents, muttering to himself. "You would think I'd have taken this out before you got here, but no."

"We should go," Erik whispered. "While we still can. He's insane."

"No." Calen turned to Erik, shaking his head. "Well, yes. He is a little insane. But he knew we were coming, Erik. He had food ready, chairs set. There has to be something in what he's saying."

"Does there? Can a madman not cook a pot of stew and set out chairs for imaginary friends?"

"Ah! Here it is."

Calen sat back in his chair at the sound of Rokka's voice, turning to see the man holding a flat steel disc about three inches across and no more than half a finger-width in thickness. As the man approached, Calen could see that the surface of the disc was polished to a mirror-like sheen.

"Here, take this."

Calen took the mirror disc from the old man, turning it over and back, wincing slightly as it reflected the light from the hearth. Then he saw something in his reflection that took him aback. His irises were a pale lavender, the same as Valerys's. "I…" He tried to find his words, but instead he found himself staring at the disc, examining the colour of his eyes. "What… what is this?" he said, holding out the disc. "What is it for?"

"I have absolutely no idea," Rokka said with a sigh, resting back in his chair.

"How can you have no idea?" Erik asked, his voice laced with irritation. "You can see the future. You just told him he needed it. How could you possibly have no idea what it's for?"

Rokka raised a bony finger, his eyes narrowing as he looked towards Erik, his voice taking on a sharper edge. "I do not see the future, *boy*. I see paths. And in the path I wish to follow, I give that disc to this man." Taking in a deep breath through his nostrils, Rokka lifted himself back to his feet. "On that note, it is time to rest. As I said, you must be gone from here before the sun is two fingers past the horizon. Eat more if you wish, but then rest. There are four beds already made upstairs. Room on the right. I am on the left. If you enter my room, I will stab you in the eye." Rokka turned to Calen, his eyes softening a little. "The blanket's for you." He nodded to the woollen blanket draped over Calen's chair. Reaching down, the old man rested his hand on Calen's shoulder. "Just know one thing, my boy. The path you are on will bring death beyond your wildest nightmares. I say this not to steer you from it, but to steel you for it."

Rokka sighed, his eyes lingering on Calen for a moment before he turned and made his way up the staircase by the door.

༄

TARMON STOOD IN THE DOORWAY of the old man's house, looking down at Calen, who sat on the deck staring at the sky, his feet resting on the lowest step, the woollen blanket draped over his lap. The horses, tethered to the fence in front of the house, whinnied as Tarmon stepped out onto the deck. Stretched bones clicked and muscles ached as he sat down beside Calen. "No."

Calen took a moment, his eyes lingering on the skies above, before turning, raising an eyebrow as he did.

"I've seen that face before. It's the same face you had in Straga when you told us you were going after Rist. When you expected us to let you go on your own. So I say no."

Calen laughed, a smile touching his face for only a moment. He always did that. Always pretended as though he wasn't collapsing beneath the weight of everything Aeson Virandr had heaped on his shoulders. Beneath the weight of loss. But Tarmon could see it in the way dark circles perpetually ringed his eyes, or in how his smile never seemed to last longer than a few fleeting moments. His mind seemed to constantly wander, distracted by which choice was the right one – Daymon had looked the same way after Arthur had died.

Calen rested his forearms on his knees, dropping his stare to the ground in front of the house. "I should never have let you come with me, Tarmon. I needed to come after Rist. Even if there's only the slightest of chances he is in Berona, I need to try. I can't abandon him. I just can't." Calen's voice dropped to a melancholy lament. He let out a sigh. "I know I should be going back to Durakdur. I know I should be helping Aeson build the rebellion. And I will. But I just…"

"You wouldn't be the man you are if you chose not to go after your friend. And none of us are letting you do this alone."

"It's not your fight, Tarmon. I… I can't ask you to risk your life for this."

Tarmon let out a ruminating sigh, staring off into the dark of night. "Erik is sitting inside, hunched in that wooden chair by the fire, his sleeping sack pulled up over his legs and his swords resting across his lap. He refuses to sleep in the bed because he knows you will be sleeping beside Valerys tonight, and if he is upstairs, he won't be quick enough to protect you. How he thinks he can protect you any better than a dragon, I truly am not sure, but still. The elf walked out the back door behind the staircase about five minutes after you came out here." Tarmon squinted, looking around the grove. "Which means he's probably hiding in the trees somewhere. Funny creature that he is. It's clear to me that more than his oath binds him to you, and in turn, to us all."

Calen reached back, running his fingers through the hair at the back of his head. "What's your point, Tarmon?"

"My point is," Tarmon said, meeting Calen's gaze. The purple hue that had set into the young man's eyes since Kingspass still unsettled him a little. "You may be a Draleid now, but you have no right to tell us this isn't our fight. We have stood by you, fought alongside you, bled with you, and suffered with you. We lost Falmin too, Calen. He was a good man, despite himself." Over the years, Tarmon had taught himself simply to not think of those who were gone. It was the easiest way of holding back the grief. But this wasn't the time to hold back. "We lost Korik and Lopir too. I watched my Kingsguard die in those tunnels, torn to pieces by the kerathlin. Men and women I was raised with and trained with. I watched my city burn. Your fight is our fight. I'm not sitting here because you're a Draleid. I'm sitting here because I made a choice. Because you, Vaeril, Erik, and I, we've been through things that would have broken others. We've lifted each other, carried each other, and stood by each other even when it looked like there wasn't a shred of hope. Your fight is our fight. Our fight is your fight." Tarmon looked into the night obscured grove. "This world chews us up and spits us out. It doesn't care if we live or die. It doesn't care who we love or who we hate. It is filled with misery, death, and loss. It cares little for us. But that is precisely why we must care with all our hearts, fight for the ones we love, and stand for what we believe in. Because in a world where nothing matters, what matters to us means everything. If we forget about the ones we love, everything loses meaning."

The tears that glistened in Calen's eyes took Tarmon by surprise. And in that moment, Tarmon could see the vulnerability in Calen, the true weight of both expectation and loss that hung over him. "So many are dead, Tarmon. My mam, my dad, Ella, Faenir, Ellisar, Falmin, Korik, Lopir…" With each name, Calen's voice choked more and more, his tone becoming darker, a single stream of tears beginning to flow. "The list is endless. I won't let Rist join that list. I won't let any of you."

"You don't have that control, Calen. If we die, we die. The beauty of life is in the living of it."

Calen drew a long breath in through his nostrils, nodding gently to himself. "The only thing within our control is what we choose to do with the short time we have – the things we fight for, the people we love, the things we hold dear."

A smile touched Tarmon's lips at hearing his own words spoken back to him. "Wise words," he said with a half-hearted laugh. "And that is why we go to Berona." Tarmon dropped his hand on Calen's shoulder and squeezed before lifting himself back to his feet.

"Tarmon, thank you for everything. I wouldn't be here if it weren't for you three. If you hadn't dragged me from that cell. If you hadn't – quite literally – carried me away from Arisfall."

"And I wouldn't be here if you, Valerys, and Vaeril hadn't held the imperial soldiers back in the Wind Runner courtyard or if you hadn't saved my life in the tunnels below Lodhar. Is Valerys far?"

"No. He's hunting only a mile or so north. He'll be back soon."

Tarmon nodded. "Try and get some sleep, Calen. You're going to need it."

Leaving Calen on the porch, Tarmon stepped back inside the house, the warmth of the hearthfire wrapping around his bones. Erik lay in one of the wooden chairs on the right side of the fire, snoring, his neck turned awkwardly to the side, the blanket draped across him, his swords in their scabbards on his lap.

Tarmon let out a sigh and dropped into the chair opposite Erik. He had debated going up to the bed the old man had offered. His bones and muscles would thank him for it in the morning. But despite himself, he stayed where he was, snatched his sleeping sack off the floor, and draped it over himself. His short sword and greatsword lay in their scabbards within reach on the left side of the chair. They were still too close to Kingspass to take any chances.

CHAPTER THIRTEEN

WHISPERS OF A GOD

Temple of Achyron – Earlywinter, Year 3081 After Doom

Kallinvar knelt with his hands resting on his lap, feeling the soft cloth of his trousers against his palms. The warm glow of the candles flickered, ever-shifting against the stone walls of the Soul Vault. He was alone, as he had been for some time. He wasn't sure precisely how long. Hours. He had needed the peace.

Letting out a sigh, he looked up at the alcoves set into the wall before him. One hundred alcoves for one hundred Sigils. One for each knight. The Soul Vault was where the Sigils returned if their bearers were slain. Brought back by Achyron so another might bear its gifts, and its burdens. As it stood, all but three of the alcoves were empty. All three knights had been slain at the battle of Kingspass. Irythinia, Alenor, and Verathin. Both Irythinia and Alenor had been knights of The Third, Sister-Captain Olyria's chapter.

Kallinvar knew he should have gone to see Olyria after the battle; he knew the pain she would have been in. Every knight felt the loss of a brother or sister. It surged through their Sigils, thrummed in their bodies. They were connected, one and all. But to lose a knight under your command was something different. Kallinvar wasn't sure why. Perhaps it had something to do with the bonds they created over time, or perhaps the Sigil of a captain was simply different. Kallinvar would have been more inclined to believe the former over the latter until recently.

Staring forward, his eyes traced the greenish metallic Sigil that sat in the alcove before him. Forged by Achyron himself, shaped in the symbol of the knights – a downward-facing sword set into a sunburst. The Sigils were what granted the knights their strength. They were the tether between the warrior god and his chosen. They were everything.

This particular Sigil had belonged to Verathin. Kallinvar could feel it pulsing through him. Just like he had felt the Sigil of every single knight since Verathin's death. He brought his hand to his chest, tracing his fingers over where his Sigil sat beneath his shirt, fused with his body. As he had held Verathin in his arms, he had felt a change. He had always sensed his brothers and sisters, such was their bond through Achyron, but this was different entirely. Now he could feel *everything* – their lives, their hearts, their fear. *Had you always felt this, old friend? Was this the weight you carried on your shoulders?*

In his mind's eye, Kallinvar could still see Verathin's body in his arms, bare and void of life, his soul shorn from the world. Even the thought of it caused his pulse to quicken and his jaw to clench. It wasn't right. Rage flared in Kallinvar's heart, and with it, power surged from his Sigil, setting his veins alight. Verathin had served Achyron for centuries. Hundreds upon hundreds of years. He had been Kallinvar's saviour, his guide, his master, and eventually, his friend. He had given everything. Only for his soul to be denied its deserved rest in Achyron's halls by the nithrál of a Bloodspawn Shaman. Kallinvar shook. He could still see it – the dark, flickering nithrál punching through Verathin's armour; his friend's body dropping to the ground.

Kallinvar rose to his feet, his knees feeling weak beneath him. He stepped forward, running his hand along the cool metal of Verathin's Sigil. "I will make them bleed in your name. I will make their god shake."

As he ran his fingers along the metallic surface, Kallinvar's own Sigil pulsed, sending rippling waves of energy through his body. A shiver swept over him, the hairs on arms and neck standing on end. He had felt this before, a number of times since Verathin's death. Each time he'd pushed the sensation back, holding it at bay, unwilling – or unable – to face whatever it may be. But this time, it was stronger. It burned like a signal fire, blinding his vision with a pure green light. His body shaking, Kallinvar dropped back to his knees, the shock vibrating through his legs as he hit the stone.

"Kallinvar."

A voice echoed through Kallinvar's mind, calling to him.

"Efialtír's hand grows closer to the world, my child. You must stand."

Kallinvar clasped his hands behind his head. The surge of power from his Sigil caused his body to tremble. He knew the voice to be Achyron's. Had Verathin been able to hear this too? A god's voice whispering in the depths of his mind?

"You wonder why I chose you. You doubt."

"I cannot be what he was," Kallinvar whispered, digging his fingers into the back of his head. The pressure calmed him. "I cannot be Verathin."

"You doubt," the voice repeated. *"But I do not."*

As suddenly as it had begun, the pulsing in Kallinvar's Sigil stopped, the shaking in his body ceased, and the green light that blazed in his eyes dissipated.

He knelt there, his hands clasped at the back of his head, his breaths short and rapid. Had that happened, or had he imagined it? "Please tell me I'm not going mad…"

"Grandmaster."

The word alone twisted knots in Kallinvar's heart. That title didn't belong to him. It belonged to Verathin. Taking his hands from the back of his head, Kallinvar pulled himself to his feet, doing his best to hide the tremble that had set into his hands. Ruon stood at the other side of the Soul Vault, the concern clear in her deep-green eyes. But he could not just see it, he could *feel* it. It radiated from her. *It's not right, her emotions should be her own.* The concern he could feel from Ruon vanished at the thought, as though a cord had been cut or loosened in some way. Had he done that? *Had Verathin been able to feel everything Kallinvar had felt?*

When Kallinvar didn't answer Ruon's call, she walked towards him, resting her hand on his shoulder. "Kallinvar, are you well?"

Kallinvar nodded absently, unable to meet her gaze.

She brought her hand to his chin, pulling his head towards hers so their gazes met. The softest of smiles adorned her lips. "You were my Brother-Captain. You *are* my Grandmaster. You will always be the man I am proud to fight beside. His loss burns in me as well, but for now, your knights need you. I have summoned the chapters in the war room, as you have asked. Do you know what to say?"

"I do now." Through everything, Ruon had been his keystone, the only thing that kept him standing. "Lead the way."

ARDEN STOOD NEAR THE WAR table, his arms folded, his mind wandering. No matter how many times he had seen the war table, it never failed to instil a sense of awe within him. The sheer detail in the curve of every river and the peak of every mountain.

Ildris, Daynin, Mirken, and Tarron stood beside the table, pointing at different markers on its surface and conversing over plans of action. They hadn't stopped since their arrival to the war room. Sylven and Varlin waited patiently to Arden's right. Neither woman had said a word. Which wasn't anything new for Sylven, but Varlin's tongue was usually as quick as Lyrin's. Her silence added a sense of gravity to the tension that hung in the air. Sylven, Daynin, Mirken, and Varlin hadn't been at Kingspass. They had already been on task when Verathin had sensed the convergence. It didn't take much for Arden to sense the guilt that followed them. They were no more to blame for Verathin's death than the winds of the

Lightning Coast were for a fallen tree in Valtara. But Arden understood that kind of guilt. The guilt of not being there. It didn't follow logic or reason. It simply was.

Arden looked about the war room. It was rare for him to see all the knights collected in a single place. Often less than half the knighthood were present in the temple at any one time, such was the way. The Shadow didn't stop, and it didn't sleep, so neither could they. But, in this instance, Kallinvar had recalled every knight to the temple.

As Arden glanced around the table, he met the gaze of Olyria, Sister-Captain of The Third. She had lost two knights at Kingspass: Irythinia and Alenor. He could see their loss in her eyes. Her usually fierce stare was replaced by a soft sadness. She held his gaze for a moment, then nodded, turning back to stare vacantly at the war table.

The chatter around the chamber grew louder as the minutes passed, the knights talking amongst themselves.

"Have you talked to him since Kingspass?" Lyrin stepped up beside Arden, raising an eyebrow. Last Arden had seen, Lyrin had been talking to Sister-Captain Airdaine of The Ninth.

"Hmm?"

"Brother-Capt—Grandmaster Kallinvar." Lyrin gave an awkward smile as he corrected himself. "That's going to take some getting used to. Have you spoken to him?"

Arden shook his head. He drew a deep breath, his arms still folded across his chest. Silence passed between him and Lyrin, not the comfortable kind of silence that was common with them, but a weighted one. One that held many looming questions.

"So…" The word hung in the air as it left Lyrin's mouth. "Haem. That was your name before?"

Arden's jaw clenched. When each knight took the Sigil, they were granted a new name to symbolise their rebirth. They weren't meant to talk of their past. It wasn't a rule, but it was the way. The only person he had spoken to had been Kallinvar in the Tranquil Garden after the Bloodspawn attack on The Glade. That attack had nearly broken him. Even thinking about it sent shivers sweeping over his skin. Seeing so many dead, so many he had known and loved. Ferrin Kolm, Joran Brock, Verna Gritten. Jorvil Ehrnin's boy, Aren, had seen no more than three summers by the time Arden had taken the Sigil. Arden had seen his decapitated head lying in the dirt in front of The Gilded Dragon. Seeing Erdhardt weeping over Aela's body had rent his heart. It had taken every shred of strength in his body to stop him from running to the man's side.

"It was," Arden said, not offering anything more.

"Well, who'd have guessed the Draleid was your brother? I mean, as far as coincidences go, that's something else. He rides a dragon, and you fight for a god. I…" Lyrin trailed off, letting out a sigh. "I'm sorry. You know my mouth runs faster than a horse sometimes. It's tough. All of this," he said, gesturing around the war room and the chapters of knights gathered within, "can be difficult to process on its own. To know that everything you once knew is gone is one thing, but to see it again, and to have to walk away… I can only imagine. At least my family are dead. It makes it easier, in a way. I still can't get around the idea of living for hundreds of years, though. Surely it gets boring eventually. Kallinvar is old enough to be my father's father's father's father's… father's father?"

Arden couldn't help but suppress a laugh as Lyrin's statement slowly turned into a question. Lyrin was one of the few people he had met who could bring a touch of happiness to a situation like this.

The large wooden doors at the western end of the room creaked open, and the murmur of voices that had slowly consumed the chamber ground to a halt as Kallinvar and Ruon entered, walking side by side.

Kallinvar's steps were laboured, his eyes dark-ringed and despondent. Arden had always known that nothing living, or that has ever lived, could pass through the Rift without being encased in Sentinel Armour. But he had never seen what would happen if it were attempted. He was not sure what he had expected. Something dramatic perhaps. But when Kallinvar carried Verathin's body through the Rift, it had simply vanished, every shred of Verathin's physical being broken down and claimed by the portal. Watcher Gildrick had said that is what had been done for all knights when possible. Their bodies given to the Rift, reclaimed by Achyron. When Gildrick had said it, it seemed almost poetic. But seeing Kallinvar kneeling on the stone in the Heart Chamber, his arms outstretched and empty, had been agonising.

Ruon nodded to the rest of The Second as she separated from Kallinvar and took a place to Arden's left, a weak smile on her lips as their eyes met.

"Thank you for coming, brothers and sisters," Kallinvar said as he moved to the side of the war table between Sister-Captain Olyria and Brother Holden of The Fifth. The knights standing at the head of the table had cleared a space for Kallinvar but moved back into their positions when they noticed him stop beside Olyria.

Kallinvar looked around, his gaze passing over each of the knights assembled before him. "I know it is strange," Kallinvar said, drawing in a deep breath, then exhaling through his nostrils. "There is not a knight in this room who has seen this knighthood without Verathin at its head. Not only was he the wisest of us, but he was also the best of us. Verathin knew when to tilt and when to hold back. He knew when a gentle word was more powerful than admonishment. It was he who granted many of us our Sigils, saved us, gave us a chance to fight for those we left behind instead of drifting into the void. He was our anchor. But most important-ly, he was our friend." Kallinvar turned to Olyria, resting his hand on her shoulder. "And sister, do not think I forgot those else we lost. Irythinia and Alenor. They were fine warriors and finer knights. Alenor spread much joy here. His dry humour was appreciated, and his levity was a break from the darkness. Irythinia was a beautiful soul. If I had half of her kindness, I would be four times the man I am. We all mourn with you."

Thin streams of tears rolled down Olyria's cheeks as Kallinvar spoke. She inclined her head towards Kallinvar, the smile on her lips bereft of joy.

"Before I continue, there are two matters that must be attended to." Kallinvar stepped back and made his way around the table, all eyes fol-lowing. "Sister Arlena," he said as he walked.

Sister Arlena, of The First, stood at the side of the table opposite Kallinvar, her hands resting on the war table, her eyes dark and red from crying. She lifted herself to full height. "Yes, Grandmaster?"

Kallinvar stopped before her. "You stood with Verathin for centuries. You fought by his side at The Fall. You tended his wounds. You gave him the gift of your companionship. I am proud to call you my sister-knight."

"Thank you, Grandmaster. And I am proud to call you my leader."

Kallinvar gave Arlena a half smile, nodding his head, his eyes glistening. "Kneel, Sister Arlena."

Without hesitation, Arlena dropped to one knee, her head bowed to-wards the floor.

"When you knelt, you knelt as Sister Arlena, Knight of Achyron, cho-sen soul of The Warrior." Kallinvar looked down at Arlena, drawing in a long breath. "But now as you rise, you do so as Sister-Captain Arlena, Knight of Achyron, chosen soul of The Warrior, Captain of The First."

Cheers and shouts rang out about the chamber, hands clamping, feet stomping. Arden could see fresh tears rolling down Arlena's cheeks as she rose.

"I… It is my honour, Grandmaster."

"The honour is ours, Arlena. Let it be known that you are not filling boots, you are carrying a flame."

The knights of The First, who stood around Arlena, congratulated her as Kallinvar walked back around the table. But as the cheers and chants faded, an expectant silence took hold.

All eyes followed Kallinvar as he made his way back around the ta-ble, passing where he had stood before, beside Olyria. Whispers spread through the gathered knights. "Verathin and I never discussed succession. We had lived for so long it's not something we'd thought about." Knights moved out of the way as Kallinvar walked towards Arden, Ruon, Lyrin and the other knights of The Second. "I'm sure the Watchers have their own ideas, but in this time of war, I may be Grandmaster, but The Second still need its captain." Kallinvar looked to Ruon. "Sister Ruon, kneel."

Shock spread across Ruon's face. "Kallinvar, why... you..." Ruon swallowed hard. Arden had never seen her so shaken. She dropped to one knee, bowing her head. Even as she knelt there, Arden could see the tremble in her breathing.

"Will you take this burden?" Kallinvar asked, standing over Ruon. "Will you lead The Second, as I have for centuries? Will you bear the mantle of captain?"

"It would be the greatest honour of my life," Ruon said, lifting her head.

"And knowing you has been one of the greatest honours of mine, Sister-Captain Ruon. I will continue to fight by your side, but The Second is now yours. Rise."

Another chorus of cheers and shouts thundered through the chamber as Ruon rose, shock still etched into her face. Ildris and Tarron both wrapped their arms around Ruon, Daynin, Varlin, Mirkin, Sylvin, Arden, and Lyrin all congratulating their new captain. Arden had not expected Kallinvar to name a new captain. Verathin had not granted the title to any of The First. From what he understood, it was not necessary, but some Grandmasters had seen fit to do so in the past. If it were to be anyone, Arden was happy it was Ruon.

As the cheers died down, Kallinvar pulled Ruon into a tight embrace, then rested his hands on her cheeks for a moment, before stepping back. When silence once again held sway, Kallinvar let out a soft sigh, turning towards the table, once more looking across those gathered, his gaze lingering on Arden's.

"The Blood Moon will rise within this year. The last time, we were not ready. We had grown complacent. We had thought the Shadow diminished. We were wrong. And because we were wrong, many of our brothers and sisters were sent to dine in Achyron's halls. And while we rebuilt, the Shadow grew stronger. I can feel the Taint even now. It lingers in the air. Leaches into the soil. Efialtír's hand grows closer to the world with each passing day. The traitor god feeds on the souls of the dead. Every drop of blood spilled by his servants' hands gives him strength. He seeks to carve open a path between worlds. To bring his darkness here incarnate." Kallinvar paused, gazing down at the carved stone war table. He lifted his head, looking around the table, his gaze passing slowly, as though measuring each knight. "Which is why we can no longer sit back."

A ripple of murmurs spread throughout the gathered knights and Lyrin looked to Arden, an eyebrow raised. This topic had come up before. The captains had not been able to come to a compromise. Illarin, Armites, and Valeian had all pushed for the knights to be more aggressive, but it had been Kallinvar himself, along with Verathin, who had pressed for caution.

Kallinvar raised a hand, calling for silence. The chatter ceased. "We have been too timid, too patient. We have waited for convergences and fought on our enemies' terms. No more. The time has come for the Knights of Achyron to strike at the Shadow's heart. When you want to kill a weed, you don't trim its leaves when it grows too tall, you rip it from the ground. You tear it out, root and stem. We…" Kallinvar stopped as though the words had suddenly become lost to him, floating just out of reach. He stared at the war table, muttered something to himself, then shook his head, lifting his gaze once more. "We cannot stop the Blood Moon from coming. It will rise as sure as death will one day come for us all. But what we can do is root out the Bloodspawn before death calls our names. We can hunt them, we can kill their Shamans, and we can break them."

Arden saw many of the knights nodding in agreement, looks of fervour on their faces, Illarin, Armites, and Valeian among them. But not all shared the sentiment.

"But, Bro—" Brother-Captain Darmerian of The Fourth caught himself before finishing. "But Grandmaster, if we spread ourselves too thin, we will not be able to respond to the convergences in time."

"Agreed," Brother-Captain Rivick of The Eighth said. "Was it not your own knight, Brother Arden, who in this very room argued that if we send all our knights into the field, then we will lose our greatest advantage – our mobility. That with the Rift, we can strike like lightning wherever the Shadow rears its head. I must say, I am inclined to agree. This is not a wise course of action, Grandmaster. We will be left exposed and vulnerable."

Arden swallowed hard. All eyes turned to him, expressions ranging from curiosity to irritation.

Ignoring the others, Kallinvar folded his right arm over his left, stroking his beard as he stared down at the war table. "When Arden last spoke here, I believe, Brother-Captain Rivick, your response was 'The child speaks of what he does not understand'. Am I correct?"

The colour drained from Brother-Captain Rivick's face. "Yes, Grandmaster, but—"

"So which is it, Brother-Captain. Do you agree with him, or is he a child who speaks of what he does not understand?"

"I was wrong," Rivick said, glancing towards Arden. Letting out a sigh, Rivick gave Arden an apologetic nod. "I was wrong, Grandmaster."

"Humility is a trait to be admired, not scorned, Brother-Captain. Thank you for your candour." Kallinvar unfolded his arms and reached towards the table, picking up two green counters. One for Irythinia, one for Alenor. Prior to the battle at Kingspass, Verathin had not been outside the temple and thus there was no corresponding counter to denote his position on the continent. Kallinvar stared down at the two counters in his palm before closing his fingers over them. "When we captains last stood here with Grandmaster Verathin, Brother Arden also said that the Shadow does not shy away from twisting the minds of men. That it uses our absence to its advantage and that it will get to a point where we cannot hold back the tide alone." More murmurs rose throughout the gathered knights, particularly from some of the captains, but Kallinvar continued. "We are ninety-seven, my brothers and sisters. That is our number." He tapped the two green counters on the surface of the war table. "Ninety-seven green counters for ninety-seven knights. For those of you who have not been in this room before, those of you who have not held the honour of being a Chapter Captain, each of these white counters—" Kallinvar tapped his finger against one of the hundreds of white counters dotted about the war table that sat next to small carvings used to denote allegiance "—marks a thousand soldiers. *A thousand*. In Loria alone there are over three hundred thousand soldiers, even more split between the varying armies of the Southern provinces. Hundreds of thousands of warriors willing to die to protect what they love. *Hundreds of thousands*. True, some will stand by Fane Mortem, fight for the empire they call home, but they will all invariably stand against the Shadow or fall to its will. They will make that choice with or without us. I, for one, would rather it be with."

As Arden watched Kallinvar speak, he realised what the man was doing. He was using the desire of captains like Valeian and Armites for a more aggressive stance to justify the knights reaching out. He had steered the conversation masterfully. Before the battle of Kingspass, Arden had indeed worried that taking a more aggressive stance might limit the knights' ability to react. If they pushed against the Shadow with all their strength, then they would have no knights left in the temple to react to attacks such as the one on The Glade. But after seeing what that Shaman had been able to do, after seeing the sheer devastation that Bloodspawn force had wrought on a heavily defended city like Kingspass, and after watching the life drain from Grandmaster Verathin's body, Arden's stance had begun to shift. And from the looks of many in the room, he was not alone.

If they overcommitted, they would still be left exposed, but they had no choice. They could not continue allowing the Bloodspawn to pick and choose the battlefield, stepping into the fray only when the fighting had already begun. But if they could find allies in the people of Epheria, if they could stand together against the Shadow… that might change everything.

"For too long, we have fought alone." Kallinvar leaned over the war table, rested his hands on its edge, casting his gaze over the continent of carved stone. His voice held a quiet rage. "For too long we have lost brothers and sisters because we were too proud. Because in our hubris, we believed this burden was ours to bear, and ours alone." As Kallinvar spoke, he lifted his gaze from the table, his chest rising and falling in heavy sweeps, an intensity in his eyes. A low thrum resonated from Arden's Sigil, sweeping through his body, carrying a tide of emotions in its wake. Anger, sorrow, rage. It was almost imperceptible at first, but slowly it grew until Arden was all but consumed by fervour. His jaw clenched, his lungs heaved, and cold fury swept through his veins. Around him, the other knights were the same. He could see it in their eyes as well as feel it. It was as though Kallinvar's emotions were flooding through the Sigils of every knight in the room. Kallinvar lifted his hands from the table, standing straight. He drew in a deep breath, his gaze passing across every face.

"The Shadow feeds off our division. It thrives where our pride shines. It is time, my brothers and sisters, to stand shoulder to shoulder with the warriors of Epheria. We will not let the Shadow in. We will not allow the traitor god's hand to carve a bloody path through this world." Kallinvar paused, his eyes fixing on Arden. "In the millennia past, it was not solely by our actions that the Shadow was held at bay, despite what we may like to believe. The Draleid astride their dragons were a beacon to the people of these lands. Wherever the Shadow reared its head, they stood, defiant. Wherever their fire was needed, it burned. There was a time, long ago, where we fought side by side. But four hundred years ago, when they needed us most, we stood back and waited. We allowed the Shadow to worm its way into the minds of The Order, determined not to meddle in the 'politics of the continent.'" Silence filled in the air as the chamber hung on Kallinvar's words. "We failed them then, but we will not fail them now. A new Draleid has been brought into this world. Those of you who fought at Kingspass saw how the imperial soldiers rallied around him. You saw how they fought by his side. And you saw the light of Varyn in his eyes. The empire were his enemies, and yet when they needed him, he answered their call. Whatever your opinions, you follow Achyron's creed. Do you not?"

As the question hung in the air, Ruon stepped forward, all eyes turning in her direction.

"The duty of the strong is to protect the weak!" Ruon's voice cracked as she roared at the top of her lungs, slamming her fist against her chest, her eyes fixed on Kallinvar.

Every hair on Arden's body stood on end, a shiver sweeping over his skin.

Ildris and Tarron stepped up beside Ruon, nodding to her before following her lead. "The duty of the strong is to protect the weak!" they roared in unison.

Around the chamber, the other knights and captains followed suit, a fervour rippling through the air.

"We have lost brothers, we have lost sisters, but we will never stop fighting!" Veins bulged on Kallinvar's neck as he shouted, pounding his fist off his chest.

"Pain is the path to strength!" the chamber roared back.

Arden's heart hammered against his ribs, all sounds around him capitulating to the pounding of his fist on his chest and the thrum that resonated from his Sigil.

"We will never stop!" Kallinvar roared. "The Blood Moon will rise." Kallinvar's voice dropped for a moment then rose to a shout. "But we will be there to meet it!"

HIS EYES CLOSED, HIS LEGS dangling off the edge of the plateau, and the gentle crosswind balancing out the dwindling warmth of the setting sun, Arden drew in a deep breath, his shoulders sagging as he let it out. He sat at the very edge of the great plateau just outside Ardholm's eastern wall. The plateau rose forty or fifty feet above the village – if it could still be called a village. Arden was sure it had far surpassed that title centuries ago.

He had never questioned why the platform had been constructed – he could see no practical use for it outside being a beautiful place to watch the sunset – but after the meeting in the war room, he was starting to suspect it had something to do with dragons. What other reason could there be for a city built into the side of a mountain to have an enormous plateau upon which nothing stood?

But now there were no more Draleid. Except for Calen. Even thinking of Calen's name dropped a ball of lead into Arden's stomach.

'So that's it? You're just going to leave me?' Calen's words echoed in Arden's head. He opened his eyes, a momentary sense of calm washing over him at the breath-taking sight of the setting sun's orange-red light cascading over the mountain-pierced blanket of clouds that sat just below the city. The light seeped into the normally snow-white clouds, causing them to glow with an incandescent aura. Off in the distance, the semi-circular sun, striking against a canvas of blue and white, sank into the horizon.

'They're dead, Haem. They're all dead.'

When that name had left Calen's mouth, it had been the first time in almost three years that Arden had heard it spoken aloud. He'd often had dreams or memories of his past, and in them his parents would call him by his birth name, but he'd not heard it spoken aloud. In truth, he'd never honestly thought he would see his family again, never mind hear his name. It had been something he'd had to come to terms with after taking the Sigil.

Staring out at the orange-red sky, Arden pressed his hand against the Sigil fused with his chest. Even through his shirt it was cool to the touch, as always. He kept his hand where it was at the sound of footsteps behind him – likely Lyrin, come to talk about Kallinvar's speech. A slight thrum still lingered in Arden's Sigil since that speech. Kallinvar's words had lit a fire inside many of the knights, even some who had been vehemently opposed to the idea of seeking allies not so long ago. But something had felt different about Kallinvar, as though he was a different man entirely. Kallinvar was always measured and calm. But in the chamber Arden had seen a cold fury burning in his Grandmaster's eyes, a fervour.

"I've borne the Sigil almost six hundred years. And for nearly two hundred of those, I came up here to watch the sunset almost every day I was at the temple."

Arden turned, surprised to hear Ruon's voice. He had never been able to place her accent. Ruon was one of the seventeen survivors of The Fall. Which meant Arden had always known she had seen at least four centuries. But to look at her then, he couldn't wrap his mind around the idea that her face had seen over six-hundred summers come and go; she looked as though no more than thirty had passed her by. Her hair was dark brown, and her complexion was not much different to that of any in Illyanara, though maybe a little paler than most Arden knew. Her eyes were a deep green. She was one of the finest warriors Arden had ever seen, perhaps only behind Kallinvar, Varlin, and Illarin, yet she had a kindness to her.

"What changed?" Arden asked, turning back towards the sunset as Ruon sat beside him. "Sister-Captain."

Ruon gave Arden a soft smile at the mention of her new title, then let out a sigh. "It became difficult to see the beauty in things after The Fall. Even Kallinvar spent days in the Tranquil Garden after that night, sitting in silence. To lose so many brother and sister knights… it broke pieces of me, pieces that I am still trying to put back together."

Arden had felt Irythinia, Allenor, and Verathin die. Each death had torn the breath from his chest, burning through him from his Sigil. The sorrow and loss that had filled him had been truly excruciating. He didn't

183

want to imagine the pain Ruon would have felt losing all but sixteen of her brother and sister knights. "I… I'm sorry you had to go through that."

"Pain is the path to strength, Arden."

"Pain is the path to strength," Arden repeated the phrase, unable to hide his sorrow.

Ruon shifted slightly, turning her lower lip for a moment. "You say the words, but do you understand their meaning?"

"I…" Arden hesitated. "I do. Through pain, we grow stronger. It hardens us. It tempers us. Pain prepares us for what is to come."

Ruon only gave a slight nod in response, her gaze dropping to the clouds below. "What you did in Kingspass was not easy," she said after a few moments of silence. "Few of us ever have to do such a thing. To look upon the life we sacrificed."

Arden nodded, his heart twisting, a numbness setting into his muscles. "You did the right thing, Arden."

"Did I?" Arden asked, lifting his head. "I left him, Ruon. He's my little brother. I'm meant to protect him. I'm meant to keep him safe. When he was born, I told my mam I would. I told her I'd always look after him, but he needed me, and I walked away."

No matter how hard Arden tried to block out Calen's voice, it echoed louder and louder in his mind. *'Mam, Dad, Ella, Faenir. They're all dead.'*

"You walked away because you had to, Arden."

Tears rolled down Arden's cheeks. "Did you hear what he said? They're all dead, Ruon. My dad, my mam, my sister, Faenir. Calen is alone." Arden brought his hand up and wiped the tears from his cheeks with the back of his hand. He had always imagined his family had kept on moving forward. Of course they would have mourned him, but had he not taken the Sigil, he would have died anyway, so they would have mourned him either way. At least this way, he could still protect them. He had imagined that Ella had wed, Calen had joined up with the town guard, and his mam and dad were as happy as they had always been. It had been so much easier not knowing.

A hand rested on Arden's back. "I'm sorry. My parents, too, passed after I took the Sigil, along with my three brothers, back when western Illyanara was once known as Irundir. Though I never spoke to them, I know they were within the walls when the Jinareans razed the city. The savages left none alive. Our scouts knew of the impending assault days before it happened, but as the Shadow was not involved, I had to stand and watch my homeland burn." Ruon's eyes glistened in the light of the setting sun, tears welling. "I wish I could tell you it gets easier. It doesn't. Six-hundred-and-forty-eight years have passed since that day. The pain hasn't lessened. It simply visits me less frequently."

"How do you keep going?"

"I put one foot in front of the other," Ruon said with a laugh that ached of melancholy. She let out a deep sigh. "When we take the Sigil, we pledge to forego our past lives and everything that holds us to who we were. That does not mean to forget, Arden. It means we must commit ourselves to Achyron so that we may do what must be done. You did not abandon your brother by walking away when you did, because *we* will not abandon him."

Arden nodded, pondering Ruon's words. No matter what she said, he couldn't shake the guilt from his bones. But he supposed it was something he might simply have to learn to live with.

"And what's more," Ruon said, "you are luckier than most. Your brother is a Draleid now. With the Blood Moon rising and the Shadow threatening the continent, our paths are inextricably linked. You will see him again, and you will have the chance to stand by his side."

A momentary smile touched Arden's lips at that thought. He stared down at the blanket of clouds below the plateau, watching as two Angian condors descended from a natural cavity in the side of a mountain peak about two or three hundred feet away. His Sigil granted him the eyesight to detect the distinctive black T-shaped markings on the birds' backs. He watched in silence as the creatures glided majestically along the surface of the clouds before plunging downwards through the canvas of white. "How is Kallinvar?"

"He aches," Ruon said, a tenderness in her voice. "He will recover, but when a person lives for as long as Kallinvar and Verathin have lived, you become a constant in each other's worlds. A reference point. Anchors to which the other is tethered. Without Verathin, Kallinvar is…" Ruon bit her lip, searching for the word. "Off balance. He will need us by his side, now more than ever. In saying that, I am not here just to comfort you. He has asked for you."

KALLINVAR CLOSED THE DOOR BEHIND him as he stepped into the room that had once been Verathin's study and now belonged to him. Much like Kallinvar's own study, Verathin's was illuminated by several beeswax candles that sat in stone alcoves about the room. A firm leather chair sat behind a long stone-carved desk against the back wall. Even as Kallinvar looked upon it now, he could remember his old friend sitting in the chair, stooped over scrolls and old texts, educating Kallinvar on the many things he did not know – which, despite Verathin's teachings, was still a bottomless chasm.

Again, much like Kallinvar's own study, Verathin's held little more than the desk and chair, though it was at least four times the size of Kallinvar's. Both the left and the right walls contained hundreds of open compartments carved directly into the stone; bookcases, of a sort. Each compartment was stacked full of old scrolls and texts to the point they were overflowing, scraps of parchment and lengths of ribbon sticking out from the wall. Kallinvar couldn't help but laugh, pushing the end of a worn scroll back into place. It had been Verathin who had insisted Kallinvar learn the histories of Epheria, commit them to memory as though they were his own. *'The past is the tapestry from which we learn the steps we should not take,'* Verathin had said. *'Study it, learn from it, know it. Then and only then can we hope to avoid repeating the mistakes of those who came before us. Ignore it and doom yourself to being the story the next generation learns from.'*

"You were a wise man, old friend." Kallinvar ran his finger along the bookcase, where the stone had been worn smooth from millennia of use. "Wiser than I will ever be, even if I live to see a thousand more summers."

Making his way around the desk, Kallinvar hesitated for a moment before setting himself down in Verathin's chair. It felt wrong, sitting where he sat. Just as the title of Grandmaster felt wrong before anyone else's name other than Verathin's.

"Come in, Brother Arden." It was only after he had spoken that Kallinvar realised he hadn't even waited for Arden to knock. He had sensed the pulse of Arden's Sigil long before the young man had reached the door.

Arden gave Kallinvar a strange look as he stepped into the room, and Kallinvar could feel his curiosity, but the young man asked no questions.

"Sit," Kallinvar said, gesturing to the wooden chair that sat before Verathin's – *his* – desk.

Arden nodded, lowering himself into the chair that seemed barely capable of taking the weight of his frame.

"I know Ruon has talked to you already, and she has a far better way with words than I ever will, but I wanted to speak to you myself."

"Did you know?"

The question caught Kallinvar off guard. He drummed his fingers against the desk, running his tongue along the backs of his bottom teeth. "I did," he said, meeting Arden's gaze.

"And you said nothing…"

"There would have been no solace in it, Arden. Knowing your brother was the Draleid would have changed nothing. I needed you focused."

Arden nodded absently, staring into nothing. Even if Kallinvar had not been able to read the anger and loss in the language of Arden's body, he could feel it radiating from his Sigil. Had this been how Verathin had always known what to say? It was a powerful tool, to know, without question, the emotions and sentiments of those under your command. Kallinvar felt guilt for it, yet he had not refrained from utilising it in the War Room.

Kallinvar let out a sigh, resting his palms on his desk and pushing himself to his feet. "It will take time to decide the path forward." Kallinvar leaned against the back wall of the study and folded his arms. "As eager as the knights were in the war chamber, that fervour will soon be replaced by calm, and with calm comes questions, and finding allies will not be simple. The new scattered factions who are rising will care little for what we have to say. Their only concerns will be taking and consolidating power. The nations trying to break free of the empire's hold will be single minded in their task. The elves and dwarves – the ones who remember us – have long since disavowed us."

Arden sat in silence, still looking off towards something at the corner of the study. "Why?"

"None of either race has ever been called to serve under Achyron. They believe it is proof that it is not Achyron we serve."

"And what is the truth?" Arden lifted his head, his eyes sharp.

"The dwarves are under the patronage of Hafaesir – Achyron would not take from his brother's flock. And the elves, well, their honour system does not allow them to be amongst our ranks. They do not abide by a code that binds them all, but simply one of each individual's own making, and they do this to the point of zealotry. And all this, brother, is why we must track down the Draleid. If we truly are to find allies on this continent, it will be through him. He is the common ground we share. The elves, the dwarves, the fledgling factions. He is the rallying cry."

Arden's attention piqued, his gaze meeting Kallinvar's.

"I will send Lyrin to search for answers within his network. First to Kingspass, then to Berona. We *will* find him."

"And what of me, Grandmaster?"

Kallinvar smiled, a broad grin spreading across his face. "Gather Ruon and the others. Take them to the Heart Chamber. The war against the shadow does not stop while we make plans. Now, we make the Bloodspawn bleed."

Arden lifted himself to his feet. "At once, Grandmaster."

That title would never feel right in Kallinvar's heart.

As the door closed behind Arden, Kallinvar's Sigil pulsed, a shiver sweeping through him. He clenched his jaw, his fingers twisting into fists.

"Kallinvar, my child."

Chapter Fourteen

The Path Ahead

C alen gasped, his breaths trembling as he woke. Even as he opened his eyes, he remained in almost complete darkness, Valerys's wing stretched over him like a tent canopy, trapping the warmth in, keeping the light out. A rush of panic flooded Calen's mind from Valerys's, and the dragon's wings pulled back, letting in a combination of frosty morning air and the warm glow of dawn light.

Valerys craned his neck around, nudging his snout against Calen's shoulder. The dragon's nostrils flared in panicked irritation. They had shared a dream again. Could that mean something? There had to be a connection between what Rokka had said and the dreams that Calen and Valerys shared.

This dream was new. Two armies of Draleid flew against each other. So many dragons a canopy of scale and steel blotted out the sky. On one side, elves rode astride their dragons, on the other, Jotnar – Calen recognised them from their lean muscular frames and pale bluish skin. The two armies had crashed together in the sky, raining blood and corpses over the fields below.

Calen had never seen anything like it, and he hoped he never would again. The sheer scale of death and loss pulled at his heart. He knew what it was almost immediately: the Blodvar. The great war between the elves and Jotnar. Therin had told the story many times. The war had occurred over five hundred years before humans had even set foot on Epheria, and it had raged for over two centuries. It was only the Doom at Haedr that had signalled the end of the conflict, and with it the formation of The Order. From the brink of total destruction to a new dawn.

A wave of loss flooded Calen's mind, spilling over from Valerys's at the thought of the dream. It wasn't a sense of loss for the dragons that died in the dream, but loss of what might have been.

Calen rested his forehead against Valerys's snout. He didn't say anything. He didn't have to. He simply let his mind drift into Valerys's, let every part of themselves blend. He wrapped the dragon's sorrow in warmth, pushing memories through their mind: Valerys hatching, the first time Calen had said Valerys's name, Valerys riding on Calen's saddle to the Darkwood. With those memories, he blended moments with Dann, Rist, Erik, Tarmon, and Vaeril. *We are never alone.*

With their minds melded, every sound and smell in the grove became heightened. Calen could hear frosted leaves shaking and crunching as birds flitted between the trees and squirrels scurried along the ground. He could hear the snapping of branches, the burbling of the nearby river. Even the beating hearts of the four rabbits who slept in a burrow not five feet away thumped in his ears: a mother and three kits.

One breath through his nostrils picked up lavender, pine, wet fur, and the blood of a fox almost a mile away that had been attacked during the night and was now slowly losing its fight for life.

The rush of sensation overwhelmed him, but he could feel Valerys's heartbeat slowing, his sorrow subsiding, the comfort of the bond spreading through him. "Myia nithír til diar, Valerys." *My soul to yours.*

A low rumble resonated through Valerys's throat as the dragon pressed his snout harder against Calen. Valerys couldn't articulate his thoughts like Calen could, but the warmth that radiated from Valerys's mind said more than words ever could.

"Come on," Calen said, patting the side of Valerys's jaw. "That old man said we had to be gone before the sun was more than two fingers above the horizon."

The rational part of Calen's mind told him that Rokka was simply crazy. That the old man's ramblings were a result of living alone so close to the Burnt Lands, and any sense Rokka made was simply coincidence. But something told Calen there was more to it.

The words Rokka had spoken before retiring for the night played on Calen's mind. *'The path you are on will bring death beyond your wildest dreams. I say this not to steer you from it, but to steel you for it.'* Were it not for the sadness in Rokka's eyes when he had spoken the words, Calen might have thought nothing of them. But as it were, every word had felt genuine – filled with a true sadness.

Letting out a sigh, Calen pushed off the blanket Rokka had given him – another thing that the man had seemed to foresee – and got to his feet. He strapped his sword belt around his waist, his fingertips lingering on the silk scarf he had tied through the belt's loops – the scarf he had gotten for his mother. His mother's scarf, a sword given to him by his father, and a belt gifted to him by Tharn Pimm. It didn't matter where he was in the world, those three things would always remind him of home, of everything he was fighting for, of the people he had lost.

Artim Valdock, Inquisitor Rendall, Farda Kyrana. You took everything. I will take something back. I promise you.

Just the thought of the three men set Calen in a dark mood. But as he made his way through the grove, Valerys moving beside him, a thought came to him. He swung his satchel around to his front and undid the buckles that held the flap closed. Reaching inside, he felt the cool touch of the brass-backed pendant that he had found in Vindakur along with Alvira's letter. He pulled both the pendant and the letter from the satchel before swinging it back over his shoulder.

He unfurled the letter, casting his gaze over it as the frost-crusted grass crunched beneath his footsteps.

My dearest Eluna,

I have left more. The pendant is the key.

Always remember, even in the shadow of what was lost, we can find light anew.

Your Archon, and your friend.

Alvira Serris

Calen read the letter twice before letting out a sigh and stuffing it into his satchel. *The pendant is the key.* He passed the pendant over and back in his hand, running his thumb along the intricate spiral patterns worked into its brass back, then over the cool, obsidian-cut front. White markings lay inside the black glass, depicting the symbol of The Order: a triangle, pointing upward, with three smaller triangles set at each of its edges. There had to be something he was missing. Alvira's words made no sense on their own. Could it be something that only Eluna understood?

The pendant is the key. The key to what?

The crisp morning breeze swept over Calen's face and through his hair as he emerged from the edge of the grove. He took one last look at the pendant, stuck it into his coat pocket, then swung the satchel back over his shoulder. Calen lifted his hand in the air, turning it sideways, flat against the eastern horizon over the looming woodland of Lynalion that stood a hundred or so miles away. The morning sun had only just begun to spray over the roof of the woodland, spilling orange light into the world.

"Not yet a finger over the horizon," Vaeril said, his voice carrying as he stepped out from somewhere within the grove, his green cloak – now torn and beaten – flapping lazily behind him, his sword strapped to his hip and his white-wood bow jutting over his shoulder.

Calen gave the elf a nod. Valerys had smelled Vaeril's scent the night before, no more than fifty feet from where they slept. Each person's scent was distinctive to the dragon. Once he spent long enough with someone, he could tell them apart by smell alone.

As Vaeril approached, Valerys shifted, craning his neck and lowering his head so it looked almost as though he was bowing to the elf.

"Du gryr haydria myia elwyn," Vaeril said, reciprocating Valerys's gesture with a short bow.

"I know I can't convince you to sleep inside and get some actual rest," Calen said as Vaeril stepped beside him. "But you don't have to hide."

The elf smiled. At least, it was almost a smile, more of a gentle upturn at the corners of his mouth. "Old habits die hard," the elf said. "Besides, it is easier to keep watch without your snoring distracting me."

Calen shook his head, suppressing a laugh. "Come on, the others are already waiting for us."

Calen could see Tarmon and Erik at the front of the house beside the horses, the gaunt figure of Rokka by their side, his brown robes hanging loose around his shoulders. Calen wasn't entirely sure if he trusted the man, but it wasn't as if he had any choice at this point.

"It's about time you got here," Erik said, shrugging a satchel over his shoulders. "I was about to go in there and look for you. Well, I was gonna look for him." Erik nodded towards Valerys, who stood behind Calen, his lavender eyes fixed on Erik. "He's a little easier to find."

Calen's eyes shifted from Erik, to Tarmon, to the horses, then back to Tarmon again. The horses' saddlebags all lay on the ground beside the animals, open and half emptied, while Tarmon hefted a bulging satchel over one shoulder, next to the greatsword that was strapped to his back, three more satchels at his feet.

"I figured it best we leave the horses here," Tarmon said in response to Calen's curious stare. "We don't have the food or water to attempt bringing them through the Burnt Lands with us, and they will likely die if we set them loose at its edge. Rokka has said he will take them. No sense in letting such fine animals drift into the void."

"I'll keep one," the old man said, running his brittle, liver-spotted hand along the neck of the horse Calen had ridden from Kingspass. "The others I can sell for a good price. I'll take them as payment for the satchels." Rokka frowned at Tarmon as he spoke, then pouted, turning back to the horse. "Hidranians can fetch a pretty penny around here. Whoever gave them to you must have liked you."

"They're the most expensive satchels I've ever heard of," Erik said, laughing.

"All right," Calen said. "You have a deal." He swung his own satchel around, moving his arms through the loops so that it sat on his front, then snatched up a satchel from beside Tarmon's feet and slung it around his shoulders. The satchel with the supplies was heavier. It would be easier to carry on his back. Vaeril and Erik followed suit, though their weapons made it slightly more awkward. "Rokka, thank you for your hospitality. It's been a long time since I've had a stew that reminds me of home."

"You're never going to believe this," Erik said, holding his hand in the air. He reached back to grab the satchel that hung from his shoulders but stopped. "I'm not sure which pack they are in. He baked the stew into pies. Pies, Calen! I don't know what hour of the morning you woke to get these made," Erik said, turning to Rokka. "But I don't think I can thank you enough."

Erik's beaming smile was one of pure delight. To most people, the idea of cold stew eaten from thick, crusty pies wasn't exactly a delicacy. But after surviving off mostly stale bread, cheese, and strips of meat for long enough, almost anything else sounded delicious. But to Calen in particular, this was even more so. He could still feel the weakness in his limbs, the aches and pains that plagued his muscles. It would be quite a while of good eating before he would regain the strength he had before Artim Valdock had locked him in that cell.

"Ah, there was too much for one old man. I don't like to waste." As he spoke, Rokka gave Calen a knowing look, as though he had just read Calen's mind.

"Thank you," Calen said, giving the man a weak smile. "For everything you have done."

Rokka inclined his head, the sleeves of his robes dropping over his hands.

"It's time we get moving," Calen said to Tarmon, Erik, and Vaeril, glancing towards the rising sun, its orange light spilling over the horizon.

As Calen went to turn, Rokka stepped forward, wrapping his bony fingers around Calen's forearm with a deceptive strength. "Before you go, I must tell you something that may not make sense to you now, but it will."

A strange tension hung in the air as the man gripped Calen's forearm. Both Tarmon and Vaeril had taken steps closer, their hands hovering over the pommels of their swords. Valerys edged closer, his mind pushing against Calen's, anger and fear permeating the dragon's mind. The experience in the Drifaien had set Valerys on edge. Calen tried to calm him, but Valerys ignored him. If Rokka made so much as a single motion in the wrong direction, Valerys would tear him to shreds.

Calen rested his hand on Rokka's, feeling the man's hand shake beneath his. The old man was strange, stranger than most, but there was something else in him: fear. "Tell me what you need to tell me."

Rokka nodded, easing his grip on Calen's arm. "I have lived a long time," the man said, staring absently at Calen's chest. "A very long time. And in that time, I have seen the landscape of this continent shift and change in more ways than I could explain. I've seen the birth of new mountains, rivers carved through dirt, cities rise that would put anything you've ever seen to shame. But I've also watched as dragons were torn from this world." Calen could feel Valerys's attention shift as Rokka lifted his head and gazed at the dragon. "I've watched as nations fell and rivers of blood soaked the earth and as my kind were hunted, one after another, by men, elves, and Jotnar alike, who sought to control us. But all that pales in comparison to what is coming.

"The Blood Moon is coming. It is earlier this cycle, perhaps due to thinning of the veil at Ilnaen. As the Blood Moon tarnishes the sky, the veil between this world and the world of your gods will thin even further. With each new moon, the followers of Efialtír seek to strengthen his tether between the worlds, and to this point, they have failed. But the Draleid no longer fill the sky, The Order no longer keeps the darkness at bay, and the world of men is led by those who call him The Saviour. The Blood Moon will rise as winter falls upon us once more. And this time, I fear we may not be able to hold the darkness back."

Calen's mouth went dry. Around him he could see the others had let their hands drift from their weapons, their attention focused on the old man's words.

Keeping his left hand wrapped around Calen's forearm, Rokka reached up and placed his other hand on Calen's chest. "As I said before, I do not see the future, I simply see paths – those not yet taken. In the long, winding road of time, there are anchors. People, places, and things that shape and mould the paths to be taken. You. All of you," Rokka said, his eyes fixed on Calen, before casting his gaze at Vaeril, Tarmon, Valerys, and Erik, "are one of those anchors. And I will do what I can to guide you. Last night, I had a dream in which I said these words: 'A city once lost, found it needs to be. A gem, a jewel, a trinket of sorts, but truly more a key. Not a door that it unlocks, a secret to be revealed. A trick, a mask, a painting over truth, thought forever sealed. There is a stone, a heart of blood, cast into the sea. The essence of life, drawn from birth, stolen, taken, seized. The moon of blood, of death and life, linked the two may be. For connections made will rise once more when the moon you can see.'"

"Here," he said pulling a piece of paper from his pocket and pressing into Calen's palm. "Before you ask, I already wrote it down."

Silence hung in the air, broken only by the whistling of the morning breeze. "I wish I could do more, but alas, my abilities have limits. As I said, these words may mean nothing to you now. They may seem the ramblings of a mad old fool who lives in a hut in the middle of nowhere, and perhaps they are. Even I don't know what they mean. But they *do* mean something. Now go, the sun is almost two fingers above the horizon.

CHAPTER FIFTEEN

A QUEEN, A MAN, AND A KILLER

Dahlen sat against a tall chest with his left arm crossed, propping up his right. He pressed his mouth and nose into his fist as he chewed on the knuckle of his index finger. The room in which he sat was carved from smooth stone, stacked with chests and boxes stuffed with rarities. Though, many of the things he saw would not have been considered rarities outside of Lodhar: sacks of tomatoes, squashes, peppers, oranges – any fruit or vegetables that required excessive sunlight, really; boxes of Drifaienin whiskey, Karvosi rum, Ardanian heartseed liquor, and other spirits Dahlen had never even seen; stacks upon stacks of various timber and logs. Hundreds of other goods and trinkets lay scattered about, adhering to no logical organisation that Dahlen could see. Though he supposed smugglers weren't often known for their organisational skills.

A table was cleared out in the middle of the room, a series of small maps splayed across it. Belina stood at the other side of the table, her arms folded, a frown set on her face. One of her contacts had just left, and the news the man had given was more or less what they'd expected, but it still dampened the mood.

"So, essentially, we're fucked." Belina lifted her head, her lips pursed as she shrugged at Dahlen. "I can still have us out the Southern Fold Gate by the day's end."

Dahlen gave Belina a flat stare before pushing himself off the chest and joining her at the table.

"Worth a try." She sighed, then pulled a rough drawn map of the freehold across the table. "So," she said, pointing towards the refugee quarters in Durakdur, "as we know, Daymon and the Belduarans made it to the refugee quarters and are now holed up there with Kira's soldiers blockading the entrance. And from what Tilly has just told us, both Elenya and Pulroan have reached out to Kira and are sending more dwarves. Rumours in the streets say that Hoffnar was killed by an assassin." She looked up at Dahlen. "What does all this tell us?"

"That nobody has any idea what's going on. Even the kings and queens."

"Queens," Belina corrected. "If Hoffnar is dead, that leaves only Pulroan, Kira, and Elenya. Three Queens. Which I'm all for, by the way. Women make far better rulers. But yes, nobody has a fucking clue what's happening. Which, strangely, leaves us a little less fucked."

Dahlen knew Belina was baiting him. He could safely assume she was always baiting him and be right ninety-nine percent of the time. But this time, simply out of curiosity, he decided to take the bait.

"All right, why do women make better rulers? I'm assuming it's something witty, like 'men are always thinking of their dicks.'"

"Well," Belina said with a downturn of her bottom lip, "the phrase is actually 'thinking *with* their dicks', but now that you mention it, you lot *are* fond of your dicks. No, dicks definitely get in the way, but the issue is more because men always believe they are the smartest person in the room, regardless of who else is in the room with them. Which leaves them open to being proven wrong – often."

"You just said dicks as many times as you could, didn't you?"

"Yes."

Dahlen shook his head. "And women never think they're the smartest person in the room?"

"Oh no, women think we're the smartest too, but centuries of men chasing their dicks has taught us to pretend we don't – well, not me. I'm definitely the smartest person in this room, but you're not really giving me a lot of competition. I'm also not a fan of dicks, so there's that."

Dahlen puffed out his cheeks, tilting his head back. "You're a lot, you know that?"

"I've been told. Though, funny enough, the people who tell me that are usually the ones who need me." She raised an eyebrow, a smirk on her face.

Dahlen didn't respond; he simply glared at her. The woman was infuriating beyond belief. She was also bat-shit mad – of that, he was absolutely sure. However, she was capable – more than capable. She was also the best chance he had of keeping the Belduarans alive. "All right, what's our move, then? We need to find out what is actually happening here."

"Straight to business," Belina said, standing up and folding her arms. "You really are your father's son. Not a sense of humour between you. You've got a brother, don't you? I bet he's funny. Probably took all the humour in the family. And the looks... and the smarts."

Dahlen ignored Belina. He found that was usually the best tactic for anyone who spoke too much. But unfortunately, that seemed to only spur Belina on. He looked her in the eyes and held the silence for a moment before continuing. "The first assassin that came for Daymon, before my father left, said he was sent by Elenya. The one we found in The Cloak and Dagger also said Elenya."

"I'm sensing a pattern here."

"But Daymon said it was Pulroan he made a deal with, not Elenya – Pulroan, who sent the assassins that night. Not only that, he said Pulroan had promised to help him retake Belduar once Elenya and Hoffnar were gone."

"Which also implies Pulroan's working with Kira." Belina clicked her tongue off the top of her mouth. "I'm only going to suggest one more time. What if—"

"We're *not* leaving, Belina."

"Well, technically, I can just go and leave you here. There's a nice, warm bed waiting for me in a tavern in Midhaven. A hot bath. Lamb stew. Ale. Women. You really aren't winning this competition."

Dahlen slammed his fist on the table, maps and letters lifting into the air. He drew a slow breath through his nose, clenching his jaw as he pushed his tongue against the inside of his bottom teeth. "Belina, if you want to go, then go. The people trapped in those refugee quarters only have so much food. They're likely already running out. We don't have time for your games. People are going to die."

To Dahlen's surprise, when he looked up at Belina, she was smiling. "Dayne really is going to like you." She pulled over a scrap of paper where she'd scribbled the names of the dwarven rulers earlier that day. "Look, I'm here. I don't have to be, but I am. Let's assume Hoffnar is dead." She picked up a pen from where it sat in the inkwell at the side of the table and scratched a line through Hoffnar's name. "He's no good to us. Unless you're into necrophilia – no judgement if you are." Belina paused for a moment, looking at Dahlen as though she'd expected a laugh. "That famous Virandr stare. But yes, let's assume Hoffnar is dead. Elenya has been accused by two separate assassins, and you've said that Daymon has named Pulroan and possibly Kira, though the little arsehole only actually met with Pulroan that we know of. Which leaves only Kira as the one not directly implicated. I'd also wager that, based on the way Kira attacked the Belduarans, that there was an attempt on her life as well. Which was likely blamed on Daymon."

"She was also the only one who came to Belduar's aid when the Fade attacked. If she had wanted Daymon dead, it would've been easy for her."

"Well, that settles it then. We're off to see Queen Kira."

"What?" Dahlen gave Belina an incredulous look. "It's not that simple."

"Sure it is. Well, it is for me."

"How?"

"We write her a very nicely worded letter."

Ryan Cahill

THE SOUND OF CASCADING WATER thrummed in the air, the cool touch of the resulting mist tickling Dahlen's face. He stood at the edge of a stone landing trimmed by a low wall, about an hour's walk down an enormous staircase into the seemingly bottomless chasm to which Durakdur's waterfall tumbled.

Looking out at the waterfall was an exercise in understanding just how insignificant he truly was. The raging river tumbled from the mouth of the tunnel hundreds of feet above his head, falling through the chasm with the force of a hammer, crashing somewhere unseen in the depths of the mountain. The light from the Heraya's Ward lanterns that lined the low wall of the plateau glistened through the mist produced by the crashing water, glittering and sparkling in the air like jewels.

"Beautiful things in a bloody world." Belina stood to Dahlen's left, hands clasped behind her back, head tilted upwards as she stared towards the mouth of the waterfall above. She had exchanged her long dress for a pair of padded trousers and a linen tunic tied at the collar by string. Long-healed cuts lined the dark skin of her lean-muscled arms, her breaths slow and steady.

Dahlen didn't answer her. Moments like this, when Belina's dry wit and sarcasm pulled back and she spoke from her heart, something about those moments seemed... pure, honest. He didn't like spoiling them.

Belina *had* in fact written a letter to Kira and had one of her contacts in the council chamber deliver it to the queen. Whether or not Kira would show up was the question. It had seemed almost too easy, particularly for Belina. The woman had a penchant for the dramatic and theatrical. A letter seemed too simple, too logical, but it was the pragmatic choice. If they had tried to speak to Kira on their own terms, they would have had to fight their way past her Queensguard, and that wouldn't have gone well for anyone.

Dahlen closed his eyes, savouring the sound of the crashing waves, letting his mind drift. And as he did every night before falling asleep, he pictured his mother's face in his mind. He'd been young when she died of consumption, and so most of his memories were of when she was sickly and weak. But he pushed them aside, unwilling to remember his mother as anything but the powerful woman she was. Her dark hair, falling like ocean waves. Blue eyes, flecked with spots of brown and white. Arms that held him when he needed strength. Hands that forged the swords that now lay on the floor of Daymon's chambers in the Heart. He missed her far more than he had ever admitted to Erik or their father. Erik was a few years younger than Dahlen and so had even fewer memories of their mother than he did. Dahlen had never decided whether that was a good or a bad thing. It was difficult to miss what you barely knew, but still... He would like to think that Erik remembered their mother's face.

As Dahlen's thoughts drifted, he realised there was something else he missed: his brother. In all their years, they had never been apart this long. They had always followed their father wherever he led. But they had always been together. There was nothing and no one that meant more to Dahlen than Erik. He was Dahlen's little brother. His blood. His best friend. Dahlen had made the decision to stay in Durakdur instead of going with his father to search for Erik. That had been one of the most difficult decisions he had ever made, but it still felt like the right one. Erik had his purpose. He knew who he was. Dahlen was still searching. Through the years of his father's training, through the life of blood and steel, he had always – somewhere deep down – believed that when they did finally find a dragon egg that would hatch, it would hatch for him. He knew it had been a silly notion. But children dream, and those dreams persevere.

He had given Belina a letter for his father, informing him of what had happened and ensuring him that everything was all right and to continue after Erik. With any luck it would find Aeson soon, and he would write back telling Dahlen Erik was safe and sound.

"Dahlen Virandr."

Dahlen's eyes snapped open. He glanced at Belina and they turned. The plateau upon which they stood jutted out from the rock face, a staircase on either side winding upwards towards the city. Ten Queensguard stood at each staircase in two rows of five, heavy plate on their shoulders, crimson cloaks hanging, double-bladed axes gripped in two fists. At the front of the Queensguard, on the left staircase, was Kira.

The queen was garbed in full plate, the metal almost black, golden ornamentations intricately wrought along its surface. Emblazoned across the breast of the armour was an ornate hammer, its head all swirls and spirals, four stars positioned above it in a semicircle – the symbol of Durakdur. A crimson cloak trimmed with gold hung from the queen's shoulders, and her long blonde hair flowed down over her plate, silver and gold rings laced throughout.

The dwarf took a few more steps closer to Dahlen and Belina, making no motion to reach for the axe that hung at her hip. The first line of Queensguard on the left staircase followed her. "By virtue of your father, I grant you this meeting. Aeson has been a friend to my people for generations. But let me be clear, if you show yourself to be my enemy, I will cut you down where you stand and tell Aeson where the bones are buried. Nothing comes before my duty to my people. Nothing. Am I understood?"

"Yes."

"Bit dramatic," Belina whispered.

Dahlen threw Belina an irritated glance but didn't bother to answer her.

"Your letter said you had proof of Daymon's innocence. I would see it."

A shiver swept over Dahlen, moving from his shoulders to his fingers and from his chest to his stomach, his mouth going dry. He turned to Belina, who'd pursed her lips, face twisted in a grimace.

"I had to tell her something," she whispered. "She wouldn't have met with us otherwise."

"But we don't *have* any proof."

Belina let out an awkward laugh. "Time to find some?"

"This was a waste of my time." Kira shook her head. "I truly don't want this. I had hoped our people could build an understanding with Belduar. Hoped that together we could become something greater. I tell you this so you will know I regret what needs to be done. I will allow you to leave, out of respect for your father. But if you choose to stay, you will no longer be seen as a friend to the dwarves." Kira turned, the crashing waterfall drowning out the sound of armoured boots on stone as the Queensguard parted to allow her through.

"Wait!" Dahlen reached out his hand, walking towards Kira, but four of the Queensguard darted to intercept him, their heavy armour and stout builds belying a deceptive speed he already knew was there. The guards positioned themselves between Dahlen and Kira, feet set, axes hefted to a swinging position.

Kira stopped, waiting a few moments before turning, the bluish-green flower light colouring her blonde hair. She gave a slow nod. "Speak."

"We don't have proof."

Kira let out a sigh and made to turn.

"But there *is* proof." Dahlen took Kira's silence and her raised eyebrow as a sign to continue. "Three assassins made an attempt on Daymon's life the night you attacked in the Heart."

"I didn't attack!" Kira snapped, her voice laced with a fury. Dahlen had seen her fighting in Belduar. His father had told him stories of the dwarven bersekeers of old, warriors who had honed their rage to a fine instrument of war. "Your king tried to have me killed, and I demanded he stand down. He refused. I defended my people and my home."

"That night," Dahlen said, trying his best to move past the topic as swiftly as he could, "three assassins made an attempt on Daymon's life. Ihvon killed two of them. The third is in the refugee quarters with Daymon. I had him kept alive in case he knew anything that we might need."

"And what does any of this matter?"

"If we can get inside the refugee quarters and bring the assassin to you, he can confirm what we're saying. You will have your proof that an attempt was made on Daymon's life as well as your own. Surely he would not have himself killed?"

"He might have," Kira said, her expression unchanging. "Doing so would shift the blame from him. It would be smart."

"Let us speak candidly. We both know Daymon is many things, but smart is not one of them. He lacks that kind of cunning. He is simply scrambling to survive."

That drew a fleeting smile from Kira. She gestured for the Queensguard between her and Dahlen to step out of the way, and she took their place, moving within a foot or two of Dahlen, her eyes searching his. "And why, Dahlen Virandr, do you find yourself here with this woman? Why are you not with Daymon and the others?"

"We were separated that night." Again, Dahlen avoided telling Kira of how Daymon had arrested him and attempted to frame him for the things Daymon himself had done. He wanted so badly to speak them aloud, but doing so would implicate Daymon in whatever was happening. If he was implicated, any sense of trust Kira had with the Belduaran people would vanish. "It is good we were, for it has allowed this meeting."

Kira's gaze stayed locked on Dahlen's, her stare intense. She ran her tongue across her lips, then looked to Belina. "And you. Who are you? You are not even Epherian. Narvonan, I would guess. What is your stake in all of this, and why should I trust you?"

"Straight to the point. My name is Belina Louna. And you are correct, my family is originally from Narvona. But we came here when I was very young. I'll happily tell the story over an ale or two, once this is all done. And why should you trust me? You shouldn't."

Kira raised an eyebrow at that, a curious smile on her face. "I shouldn't?"

"No."

"What are you doing?" Dahlen whispered.

"I'm not the trustworthy kind. But he is." Belina looked to Dahlen. "I've come to the conclusion Dahlen Virandr doesn't have a dubious bone in his body. In fact, I don't think he could even spell the word. Everything he's told you is true. And if he swears an oath to you, he will keep it."

Kira looked from Belina to Dahlen, then back again. "And your stake?"

"I've got nothing better to do, Your Majesty. Boredom is a great inspiration. Besides," she said, nodding towards Dahlen, "little Virandr here begged me to stay. It was quite embarrassing really."

"You say you're not honest, but that was as honest an answer as I've heard in a long time."

"I didn't say I wasn't honest, Your Majesty. I said I wasn't trustworthy."

Kira nodded, smiling. "Very well." For a long moment she just stood there, looking from Dahlen to Belina. "How do you intend to enter the refugee quarters?"

"We haven't quite figured that out yet," Dahlen admitted.

"I may have a way."

Chapter Sixteen

To Make a God Shake

A thud vibrated through Kallinvar's legs, a cloud of snow erupting into the air as he hit the ground, his Sentinel armour absorbing most of the impact. Ahead, the flames of the Drifaeinin town – Hrothfalla – blazed in the night, wisps of orange embers rising into the dark sky. A cacophony of sounds filled the night: men and beasts screaming, steel ringing, roars, shrieks, crackling fire. A tall palisade wall ringed the large town of log-composed houses, looking newly constructed – the parts that weren't shattered and charred. *The work of Bloodmarked.* Kallinvar's blood simmered at the thought of the wretched Bloodspawn, the rage within him bubbling.

He drew in a deep breath, attempting to settle his mind. He knew it was an exercise in futility. Since Verathin, Kallinvar's thoughts had not rested. He'd spent hours just sitting alone in the Tranquil Garden, watching in his mind's eye as the Shaman's Soulblade tore through his old friend's chest. He had vowed to make the traitor god shake, to make him feel the blood of his creations feed the earth, and that was precisely what Kallinvar would do.

The rest of The Second lined out to Kallinvar's right and left, the dark green of their Sentinel armour shimmering in the flames of the town, their brilliant white cloaks flapping behind them in the wind. This was as close as they had come to the whole chapter being on task together since The Fall; only Lyrin was missing. With only a hundred knights, it wasn't usually efficient to send an entire chapter of ten to deal with a single convergence. A handful of Kallinvar's knights were more than a match for a few hundred Bloodspawn. But there were exceptions. Kingspass being one of them. The concentration of the Taint in Hrothfalla hadn't felt strong enough to Kallinvar to warrant the entire chapter – though analysing convergences was another talent that was new to him – but after Verathin, he wasn't prepared to separate the others. Not yet. He couldn't lose anyone else.

"Sister-Captain?"

Ruon stepped up beside Kallinvar, snow crunching beneath her armoured boots, the eye-slits in her helmet shimmering with a green glow. "From what I saw above, we're dealing with three groups. Uraks and two human factions. Likely the residents of the town and the empire, but it was impossible to tell. Our reports tell of a civil war in Drifaien – it could all be chaos. I can take Mirken, Ildris, Arden, and Tarron to flank east, if you—"

"No."

"But Kallinvar, if we approach from two sides—"

"*No*." Kallinvar's voice dropped to a growl. He let a sigh out through his nostrils. "We do not separate. We go in together. No hammer and anvil. Just hammer."

Kallinvar couldn't see Ruon's face, but he knew the look she was giving him beneath her helm, and he wanted none of it. He stepped past Ruon towards the city, glancing at the other Knights around him. Arden, Daynin, Sylven, Ildris, and Tarron stood to his right, with Mirken and Varlin standing to Ruon's left. They were *his* knights. His brothers and sisters. They were all he had in this world – them, the knighthood, and Achyron.

I will protect them, brother. Kallinvar gritted his teeth at the thought of Verathin. *With every breath in my lungs. I won't fail again.*

"Destroy the Taint without prejudice," Kallinvar called as he marched towards the shattered wooden gates of the town, shadows of motion flickering in the flames. The sick, oily sensation of the Taint pulsed in waves. With the Sigil of the Grandmaster fused with his chest, Kallinvar felt it now more clearly than he ever had before. "There are Bloodspawn here and likely a Shaman. But there may also be imperial Battlemages drawing from vessels. Do not hesitate."

"For Achyron," came a low chorus of replies. Kallinvar could feel the slightest touch of apprehension resonate through the Sigils of Arden, Sylven, Mirken, and Varlin – the four who had borne the Sigil less than a century. Ildris, Ruon, and Tarron had been there with Kallinvar at The Fall. They had fought the traitors who had turned on The Order. They had watched as Battlemages ripped through flesh and bone in Efialtír's name. But the others had not seen that darkness. To them, the Bloodspawn *were* The Shadow. They did not yet truly understand that Efialtír's hand worked through any conduit it could find. Bloodspawn, Human, Elf, it didn't matter. This would be the first time they would truly understand the enemy that was coming. The first time they truly understood that the world was not black and white. The first time they would see the ever-shifting shades of grey that were war.

Kallinvar picked up his pace, moving into a jog, flakes of snow drifting past him, power surging through his Sigil, strength pouring into his legs.

Shrieks and screams echoed into the night, growing harsher as Kallinvar reached the shattered gates. He passed his gaze over the bodies that littered the ground before the gates and the palisade walls. Fewer than one hundred. All human. Most wearing pelts, furs, and coats of mail, the snow incarnadined around them. He noticed a few bodies bearing the black lion of Loria, no more than four or five.

A pulse of Taint rippled from beneath a face-down corpse with a black cloak.

Without breaking his stride, Kallinvar lifted his right boot and slammed it down into the dead mage's back, channelling the full force of his Sentinel armour into his leg. Bones gave way, crunching and snapping beneath the force, steam wafting from the blood that sprayed over the snow. A fierce red glow radiated from beneath the body, and Kallinvar felt another resounding crack through his boot as the mage's gemstone shattered. The glow faded, the Essence within the gemstone evaporating.

Destroy them, my child.

A shiver swept through Kallinvar at the voice that echoed in his mind: the voice of Achyron. Parts of Kallinvar told him he had gone insane for even contemplating the idea that he was hearing the voice of the warrior god. Had he lost his mind? Had grief consumed him so completely he was hearing voices?

I am with you, my child.

Kallinvar pushed the voice to the back of his mind and charged through the town's gates, summoning his Soulblade. The Sigil fused with his chest ignited in a burst of energy that seared through him like molten fire. Within moments, the green glow of his Soulblade illuminated the surrounding night.

The town's entrance plaza was in absolute chaos. Steel crashed against steel; axes, swords, and spears cleaved limbs and sliced flesh. Men in leathers, furs, and coats of mail hacked at each other, roaring feverishly, while soldiers in the red and black leathers of Loria launched themselves into the mix, seeming to hack and slash indiscriminately.

Amidst the chaos, Bloodspawn rent steel and bone, tearing through anything that moved. Two Bloodmarked occupied the plaza, their carved runes radiating a red light across the blood-dappled snow, their obsidian claws snapping bones like dried reeds.

A shriek rang out to Kallinvar's left, and two Uraks came charging, one bare-chested, the other wearing jagged plate. Both had black-steel spears gripped in their fists, their blood-red eyes glistening, teeth snapping.

Kallinvar side-stepped the first spear strike, then, feeling the power of the Sentinel armour coursing through him, brought his foot up and caught the charging Urak square on the hip. He felt bones snap as the creature howled and crashed into the Urak that ran at its side.

Before the Uraks could get to their feet, Kallinvar had cleared the distance between them. He swung his Soulblade single-handedly, shearing through the rising creature's right hand, then its neck, cleaving its monstrous head from its shoulders. Kallinvar pressed forward, marching over the beast's corpse. He slammed his gauntleted hand down on the second Urak's shoulder, holding it in place as he rammed the Soulblade through its chest. He watched as the beast's eyes widened, taking him in, then he dragged the blade from the Urak's chest, tossing the creature to the ground. Then the rest of the knights charged past him, Soulblades shimmering in the fire-lit dark of night, Sentinel armour glistening.

Arden headed straight for one of the Bloodmarked, charging towards the monstrous beast as though he had a score to settle. Daynin and Mirken hammered into a clutch of Uraks to the right of the Plaza, Ruon, Sylven, and Varlin taking up the left. Ildris and Tarron moved to Kallinvar's side.

"For Achyron, Brother," Ildris said, tilting his head. Ildris was the only knight who still referred to Kallinvar as Brother and not Grandmaster. Had it been most any of the others, Kallinvar would have taken it as a sign of disrespect. But Ildris was different. He, Tarron, and Ruon had been with Kallinvar since before The Fall. They were brothers and sisters in far more than name or title. Kin was a word that fell short of describing their bond.

"For Achyron," Kallinvar replied.

Kallinvar, Ildris, and Tarron charged across the centre of the plaza, their Soulblades slicing through leathery hide, carving through The Shadow.

A man in black and red leathers and a breastplate ornamented with the lion of Loria lunged towards Kallinvar, his blade slicing through the air. A clang rang out as the steel skittered off Kallinvar's Sentinel armour. The man's eyes widened, and he looked up at Kallinvar in momentary awe, then moved to swing his blade once more. Kallinvar struck out, feeling bone crack beneath the back of his armoured hand, the man lifting off his feet from the power of the Sentinel armour-infused strike. Kallinvar took no pleasure in taking the life of one who was not touched by the Taint, but he did what needed to be done. The battlefield was not the place to turn hearts and minds.

The rush of battle washed over Kallinvar as he and the knights carved their way through the plaza. Each motion connected seamlessly, his soul hungering for Bloodspawn flesh. He would make them pay for every drop of Verathin's blood.

All around him, the green lights of Soulblades flashed as his brothers and sisters carved through the Bloodspawn.

The longer the fighting raged, the clearer the situation Kallinvar and his knights had walked into became.

Two factions of Drifaienin tore at each other, sharp steel and heavy-rimmed shields gripped in their fists. One faction had begun to gather in clutches around the plaza, their shields marked with a depiction of what looked to be a kat painted in white. They steered clear of the knights and held back the rampaging Bloodspawn. *Defenders of the town.*

The other Drifaienin bore markings of a red wyrm on their shields, and now that Kallinvar was closer, it was clear they fought hand in hand with the Lorian soldiers. *Ruon was right. A civil war.*

Judging by the lack of Bloodspawn bodies outside the walls, it looked to Kallinvar as though the Lorians, and the Drifaienin loyal to them, had attacked the town first. The Bloodspawn must have followed them through the open gates and caught them from behind.

Kallinvar could feel the Taint oozing through the town, seeping from every crack and crevice. Its pulsing, oily tendrils snaked through the air like tree roots pushing through soil. Just the thought of the Taint made Kallinvar's mind recoil. Then he felt what he had been looking for. A source. A beating heart of festering sickness.

"Brother?" Ildris caught Kallinvar's arm as Kallinvar started off towards the sensation.

"Shaman," Kallinvar growled.

Ildris nodded, then motioned around the plaza. "I will stay here with Arden, Daynin, and Mirken. There's still more—"

"No." Kallinvar tried his best to hide his irritation and temper his fury, but it seeped through despite his efforts. "We are here to rip the Taint from this town by the roots. If we kill the Shaman, the others will break. The longer we waste, the more will die. With me, Ildris."

Ildris nodded, the green lights of his eye-slits shimmering.

"Knights, forward!" Kallinvar charged through the plaza, summoning his Soulblade once more as he did, tendrils of green light bursting from his fist, snaking around themselves, solidifying.

He swung his Soulblade, blocking the downward strike of a blackened steel blade, using the momentum to carry his Soulblade back around, carving through the torso of a second beast that was charging at him from the left. The Soulblade sheared through leathered flesh and bone, blood sluicing. The Urak howled. As the two halves of its body dropped into the dirt, Kallinvar brought his blade around towards the first creature, catching the second swing of a black steel blade. The force of the collision sent the Urak's blade rebounding. Before the creature could recover, Kallinvar wrapped his armoured hand around its throat. He squeezed, lifting the Urak off its feet, the power of the Sentinel armour coursing through him. The creature snarled and thrashed as Kallinvar brought it closer to his face. At almost seven feet tall, the beast was not used to being handled like a child's toy, but the strength of the Grandmaster flowed through Kallinvar's veins.

Images of Verathin's lifeless body flashed in his mind, fury rising in response. His training told him to hone it, to use it as his own, but at that moment, he cared little for what his mind demanded. He let the pain and loss flow through him, allowing it to burn in his heart.

"Tell your god I'm coming for his blood," Kallinvar whispered to the thrashing Urak. The beast stopped for a moment, as though it was going to speak, but Kallinvar squeezed, his jaw clenching, pulse thumping in his head. A violent *crack* sounded. The beast's head snapped left, its body going limp. Kallinvar opened his hand and let the Urak drop to the dirt, then stepped over its lifeless corpse, the green glow of his Soulblade glistening in the pools of blood that lay about the street.

As though a door had opened in his mind, memories of Verathin flooded through him. His hands shook, his mind racing. *It should have been me, old friend. It never should have been you.* Kallinvar's blood boiled as he swept through the streets, his Soulblade slicing a bloody path through Bloodspawn and Imperial mages alike. Whatever the Taint touched, he killed. *How am I meant to do this without you?* He lost himself in the rhythmic swing of his Soulblade, the burn of his grief, and the art of death.

He was only vaguely aware of the other knights moving to his left and right, cutting down any Bloodspawn that slipped past his blade. Clutches of the soldiers with white kat sigils on their shields were dotted about the streets, holding their ground, doing all they could to keep the Uraks and Lorians from the townsfolk.

Ahead, a Bloodmarked rose from where it knelt over a mass of mangled Lorian and Drifaienin corpses, soldier and civilian. Red light pierced through the smoke that drifted from the smouldering blood runes carved into the Bloodmarked's flesh. The Bloodmarked rose to almost twice Kallinvar's height, muscles tensing beneath its thick leathery hide, claws of obsidian black glinting, eyes misting with red light. The Taint radiated from the beast, rippling through the air like water from a rock dropped in a pond.

Kallinvar let out a feral roar and charged, his armoured boots pounding on the ground.

The Bloodmarked stepped away from the mass of mutilated bodies and unleashed a guttural howl. The creature slammed its rune-covered fists into the earth, a pulse of Taint erupting from its core as it sent a shockwave of rippling fire towards Kallinvar. The ground shattered beneath the Bloodmarked's strike, bodies and bits of broken wood and steel lifting into the air, dust and dirt swirling with sparks and embers as the flames ripped towards Kallinvar.

Kallinvar's first instinct was to leap out of the way, but something pushed him forwards, a voice echoing in his mind. Verathin's voice. *'We are Achyron's chosen. Our burden was never meant to be an easy one to bear.'*

Kallinvar let out a roar, his old friend's words cutting through him like a sharpened blade. He charged into the shockwave of fire and earth. Energy swept through him as Achyron's voice joined Verathin's, a power like nothing he had felt before. *Show him, my child. Show him the might of Achyron.* The voice thundered in Kallinvar's mind, the sound of the world dulling around him. As he charged, the ground cracked beneath his feet, the fire crashing into his Sentinel armour and parting around him like a raging river breaking on a boulder. He swung his Soulblade upwards, splitting through the shockwave and slicing into the leathery flesh of the Bloodmarked.

The creature reeled backwards, howling as its blood sprayed into the air. Its runes glowed with a furious red light, pluming smoke. The Bloodmarked swung a clawed hand at Kallinvar's head, but he caught the beast's wrist mid-swing, stopping its momentum dead. The ease with which Kallinvar caught the strike surprised even him, but his blood was no longer boiling, it was burning, blazing, searing. The rush of battle was taking over, thoughts of Verathin driving him forwards. He lunged, clasping his fingers around the beast's wrist while plunging his Soulblade into the Bloodmarked's chest.

The beast thrashed and howled, jagged yellow teeth snapping, its runes blazing with a crimson light, smoke billowing into the air. It slammed its clawed hand into the side of Kallinvar's helmet, knocking his head sideways, sending stars across his vision. Kallinvar glared into the creature's blood-red eyes, unleashed a visceral roar that tore at his throat, and ripped the Soulblade free from the Bloodmarked's chest. Blood sprayed as the enormous beast dropped to the ground, dust and sparks swirling into the air.

Kallinvar's pulse pounded in his ears, his breaths trembling. As he turned, he blocked the swing of a blackened spear, swiping the strike aside with his Soulblade before landing a kick in the Urak's chest with such force the snapping of bones was audible even above the crackling fires and screams that filled the night. *I will kill them all, every last one of them.*

A shout sounded to Kallinvar's right. He didn't hesitate. Wrapping both hands around the hilt of his Soulblade, he swung, roaring as he did. His blade carved through Urak flesh. Again and again, he swung, blood spraying. *It should be you here, brother.* The world around Kallinvar faded as he lost himself in the swing of his Soulblade and the spray of blood. *You were the best of us.* He roared as he cleaved an Urak's arm, swinging his Soulblade around and cleaving the beast's head. *But they took you from us.* Kallinvar's muscles burned, his throat dry from roaring as he let his heart ache. *I miss you.* Kallinvar's heart pounded like the drumming of horse hooves, his chest heaving, dragging in ragged breaths. His mind drifted, his Soulblade swung. He became death. He could not bring Verathin back, could not save his friend's soul from wandering the void. But he could carve his vengeance in blood. He could tear the Bloodspawn apart.

Kallinvar roared, swinging again and again, losing himself. A vibration jarred his arms as his Soulblade came to a halt, a burst of green light illuminating the night.

"Brother-Captain!"

The words floated in Kallinvar's mind, muddled and hazy amidst the fire of his fury. His hand shook, his lungs dragging in trembling breaths as he looked down to see a second Soulblade holding across his. A knight in full Sentinel armour stood to his right with their arm extended, green Soulblade pulsing against Kallinvar's: Arden.

"What's wrong with you, brother?" Kallinvar roared.

Arden's helmet turned to liquid metal and receded into the collar of his Sentinel armour. The young man's brow glistened with sweat, his skin flushed and red. His eyes were wide in shock as he stared at Kallinvar. "What's wrong with *me*? The duty of the strong is to *protect* the weak, Brother-Captain."

"We don't have time for this, Arden." Kallinvar looked from Arden to the two Soulblades that pulsed green light, their edges still connected. It was only then, behind the glow of the blades, that Kallinvar saw what Arden had meant. A woman stood where Kallinvar had aimed his strike, her blonde hair tied in braids, a spear gripped in her left fist, a shield emblazoned with the sigil of the white kat in her right. Two young warriors were behind her, one on his back, blood seeping from his chest, the other applying pressure to the wound. If his blade had swung through, he would have shorn the woman's soul from the world. He would have left her wandering the void for eternity, just as Verathin was. "I…" Kallinvar pulled his Soulblade back. He shook his head. "I am not your Brother-Captain any longer. Keep moving, Arden. The source of the convergence isn't far."

Arden released his Soulblade, the green light vanishing. He didn't move. He stared at Kallinvar. The sympathy in the young man's eyes twisted Kallinvar's heart. "Are you all right?"

"I said *keep moving*." Kallinvar clenched his jaw. He had no right to be angry with Arden. He wasn't – he was angry with himself. He had let his grief consume him. And in doing so, he had almost shorn the soul of an innocent.

Arden held Kallinvar's gaze for a moment, then gave a slight nod. "Yes, Grandmaster."

Arden glanced at the woman, then summoned his helmet and marched through the street towards where the Taint was resonating from, calling forth his Soulblade as he did.

Kallinvar looked at the woman who stood before him, her face streaked with blood, a gash sliced across her side. She stood defensively over the two young men, her feet wide, shield raised, spear levelled. Her mouth was twisted in a defiant grimace, but she was shaking, her hand trembling on the spear shaft. She was no enemy, she was simply protecting her own. *And I almost took her life.*

He wanted to say something, but what good would it do? No, he pushed his words down and turned to follow Arden. The best way to help these people was to kill the Shaman. This one would be different. None of his brothers and sisters would die. He would make sure of it.

As Kallinvar made to turn, a hand clasped his arm with an iron grip. He tried to yank it free to no avail. He turned back to see Ruon staring at him, her helmet gone, her dark brown hair tied at the back, her vivid green eyes, flecked with brown and gold, fixed on him.

"What *was* that, Kallinvar? What is going on in your mind?" A strange blend of anger and tenderness permeated Ruon's voice.

"Let go, Ruon. This is not the time." Kallinvar made to pull his arm away, but Ruon gripped tighter, her Sentinel armour doubling her strength. "I said let go!"

"You can speak to Arden like that, but not me."

"I am your Grandmaster!" Kallinvar growled, snatching his arm away. "It's time you treated me as such." He turned, showing Ruon his back. Something slammed into him sending him stumbling forwards. He rounded on Ruon, fury contorting his face, his hand still gripped around his Soulblade. He brought the blade up, holding the edge out towards Ruon's neck.

"Do it," Ruon said, her nose crinkling in a snarl. She leaned forward, her brow furrowed, teeth bared like a wolf, the glow of Kallinvar's Soulblade casting a green light over her skin. "To me, you will always be Kallinvar before you are the Grandmaster. You are my anchor, Kallinvar. You are what holds me here. We are one and the same. I don't care you what you say, I won't let you take Verathin's death as your own. I know you are hurting. I can see your heart bleeding each day. But you must keep control. These knights are yours now, and out here, they need you. *I* need you."

Kallinvar's chest heaved as he dragged in deep breaths. In only moments, he went from wanting to scream, to wanting to sob, to wanting to tear a hole through the world. But he pushed everything down. His teeth ground together, his hand shaking as it held the blade. Once more, Verathin's words rang in his ears. *'The duty of the strong is to protect the weak, my brother. Always remember that. No matter what happens here.'*

Kallinvar called out to his Sigil, releasing both his helmet and his Soulblade, the green light being replaced by the flickering orange-red of the burning town. He reached out his arm. "To the void and back,"

"To the void and back." Ruon repeated, clasping Kallinvar's forearm. "Not too soon, though. We've some work to do yet." Ruon gave Kallinvar a weak smile and a nod, moving to follow after the others.

Kallinvar tugged at her arm. "Thank you."

"We'll talk about it when we get back to the temple. You can't bear Verathin's loss alone, no matter how strong you are."

"Ruon, I—"

"We're talking about it, Kallinvar." Liquid metal emerged from Ruon's collar as she walked past Kallinvar, her helmet reforming, the dark green metal glinting in the firelight.

CHAPTER SEVENTEEN

OH, BROTHER, MY BROTHER

Hours after the battle in Drifaien, Kallinvar lay in the waters of Heraya's Well in the Tranquil Garden, his eyes closed, the soft sounds of birdsong and falling water rumbling in his ears as the many web-like streams of the garden fed into the pool. He drew in a deep breath, releasing it slowly. As he floated, every ache and pain faded, the Waters of Life washing them away. He still felt a slight sting in his shoulder from where a Fade's nithrál had sliced through his Sentinel armour and seared his skin. The muscles in his upper back were tight and bunched, but the tension melted away with each passing moment.

They had won the day, carved the Bloodspawn from the town, and none of his knights had died, but Kallinvar had allowed his fury and grief to cloud his mind. He had let Verathin's loss consume him. Everything had been all right – this time. But that would not always be the case. If anything had happened, it would have been on his shoulders. *I am the Grandmaster. It is always on my shoulders. I will do right by you, brother. At least, I will try.*

Footsteps broke the peaceful repetition of water and birdsong – three sets by the sound of it. Kallinvar didn't bother opening his eyes. He had expected this.

"Mind if we join?"

Kallinvar let out a sigh. "If I said yes, Ruon?"

The sound of splashing water reached Kallinvar's ears before Ruon responded. "Good point, *Grandmaster*."

Kallinvar cringed at the emphasis Ruon placed on the title. He replayed the moment in his mind where Arden had stopped him from harming the woman – stopped him from tearing an innocent soul from the world. Kallinvar knew he shouldn't have spoken to Arden as he did – as Grandmaster, he had every right to, but he shouldn't have, and he regretted it.

Two more splashes sounded. Ildris and Tarron.

"I'm not in the mood, Ruon."

"I don't care. We need to talk. You know we do."

Kallinvar drew a deep breath in through his nostrils, then let it out in a sigh, lifting himself upright, opening his eyes, and allowing his feet to touch the bottom of the pool. The water of the well shimmered, coruscating clusters of vibrant blue shifting through darker patches, glimmering as they twirled and moved in response to Kallinvar's and the other knights' bodies. Ildris, Tarron, and Ruon stood in the pool, their eyes fixed on Kallinvar.

Ildris leaned against the edge of the pool, dangling strands of moss and thin roots touching his shoulders. His skin was dark, his head shaved clean as always, his beard thick and well groomed. The man's shoulders were broad and dense, his chest like plate armour – a warrior to his bones.

Tarron stood a foot or so to Ildris's right, blond hair slicked back over his head, arms folded across his chest, his mouth curved in a half-smile that spoke only of worry.

Ruon moved through the middle of the pool, her dark hair wet and tacked to her neck and shoulders.

"We know you're hurting," Tarron said, staring at the glittering clusters of bright blue that swirled through the pool. "And we're here for you, brother. In any way you need. You know we are."

"Scars run deeper than the flesh." Ildris touched his fingers to his throat, subconsciously tracing a line left to right. It had been over six centuries since Paldrin, the Sister-Captain of The Second before Kallinvar took the mantle of Captain, had led Kallinvar and the others to the city of Ilirinth – where Aerilon now stood – to find Ildris hanging from the rafters of the armoury. The lord Ildris had been charged with protecting had been killed, along with his wife and their children. Ildris had blamed himself and taken to spirits to drown his sorrows. And when his guilt had finally consumed him, he had settled on taking his own life.

What had struck Kallinvar more than anything was how eager Ildris had been to take the Sigil. Most often when a new candidate was found, they were moments from death – the choice being to accept their fate, or to take the Sigil and live on to serve Achyron. But Ildris hadn't been close to death. Paldrin had cut the rope, and Ildris had survived. He could have refused the Sigil and continued to live, but he didn't. It was on that day that Kallinvar truly learned that wounds of the mind were as much a death sentence as wounds of the body.

"I'm all right, Ildris. I promise."

"It's not going to be that easy." Ruon moved closer to Kallinvar, the luminescent lights of the pool glistening off her skin. She tilted her head to the right, a weak smile touching her lips as she looked at him.

"Six hundred years we've fought together." Tarron pushed away from the edge of the pool, drawing level with Ruon. "Eat, fight, sleep. Each day I wake up to your ugly mug. Six hundred fucking years. That's over two hundred thousand days. That's a lot of days, Kallinvar. You're less a brother and more a limb we can't cut off. All the knights are our kin, but there are few souls in the world who have seen what we've seen and done what we've done. If it weren't for you bastards, I'd have lost my mind centuries ago. So you can push us away all you want, but we're not moving. I know your face better than I know mine – mostly because we don't have a lot of mirrors in this forsaken temple, but that's an issue I'm arguing with Watcher Ralgan about."

"What Tarron is *trying* to say," Ildris said, throwing Tarron a sideways glance, "is that lying to us is a lot harder than lying to yourself. What good is protecting each other on the battlefield if we don't protect each other off it. You let your grief take you today. Not only did it almost lead you to shearing the soul of one who had never touched the Taint, but it put your brothers and sisters in danger."

Kallinvar looked between Ildris, Tarron, and Ruon, who stared back. His throat constricted and his stomach clenched. His mind drifted to Verathin, to all the nights they had passed talking in Verathin's study, and all the drinks and meals they had shared. He thought back to the lessons learned, the knowledge passed, the hours upon hours spent sitting in silence when no words were needed. He thought back and his heart bled for his oldest friend, for the man for whom the word 'brother' had been truest of all. Despite himself, Kallinvar could feel tears burning at the corners of his eyes. He wasn't a crier, never had been. Nothing wrong with crying, it just wasn't something that came to him often. In fact, the only tears he remembered shedding had been since Verathin was taken from them. A few tears tickled his cheeks as they rolled. He didn't sob or convulse, but as he stood there in Heraya's Well, his true family around him, Kallinvar let himself cry.

"I can't be what he was, Ruon… I can't…"

"We don't need you to be what he was, Kallinvar." Ruon rested her hand on Kallinvar's shoulder, her eyes red, tears rolling. "We need *you*. We need our brother. Our Grandmaster."

"I feel lost, Ruon. Like a raft adrift at sea. He…"

"Then we'll drift on the raft with you," Tarron said, letting out a laugh, a smile curling at the corners of his lips.

"Like we said, brother, we are with you, always. Verathin granted each of us the Sigil, but *you* are our Grandmaster now, and we will follow wherever you lead."

Kallinvar brushed a tear from his left cheek, a tightness in his chest, a warmth spreading through him, battling against the cool touch of the pool's water. He took in a deep breath, then let out a sigh, smiling. "As much as this truly does mean to me, how about we put some clothes on and have a drink?" A laugh fluttered in Kallinvar's chest, growing louder and deeper, until he shook his head, his cheeks hurting. In the life they lead, happiness was fleeting. So he embraced that moment like a long-lost friend.

Ruon, Tarron, Ildris joined, doubling over as the laughter took hold. It was a whole minute before Ruon pulled herself together, a few rogue laughs still escaping her. "Come on," she said, clapping Kallinvar on the shoulder, the water swishing as she moved. "I had Lyrin pick up a bottle of Karvosi rum the last time he was in Vaerleon. I can hear it calling for us."

"You've been holding out?" Tarron gave a look of mock surprise.

"Only on you, brother. Only on you."

CHAPTER EIGHTEEN

THE EXILE

Skyfell – Earlywinter, Year 3081 After Doom

Dayne sat with his hands resting on his knees, his legs stretched out in front of him, the midday sun warm against his skin. He couldn't remember the last time he had simply sat on a shoreline and listened to the gentle breaking of the waves. It had been something he had done almost every day as a child. When he had first left home, one of the hardest things to do had been learning to sleep without the constant crashing of waves against the base of the Abaddian cliffs.

He drew in a lungful of ocean air and let it swell in his chest before he exhaled. He pushed his feet deeper into the wet sand, feeling the cool rush of water as the languid waves lapped at his skin. A little over two weeks had passed since they had retaken Skyfell. And in that time, Dayne had done nothing but sit and wait while his people bled for freedom. He didn't blame Alina for asking him to stand back until she could arrange a meeting of the council. He understood. It was a delicate situation. That didn't make it any easier.

"She's ready for you."

Dayne opened his eyes to see Mera standing at his side, gazing at the ocean, her long white dress drifting in the breeze. Even before he had left, all those years ago, it was rare he had seen her in a dress. It didn't matter. Dress, tunic, armour. She was his heart. "How is she?"

"Nervous." Mera didn't pull her gaze from the breaking waves.

Dayne nodded absently, drawing a deep breath then letting it out in a sigh. "She doesn't trust me."

"Not entirely," Mera said, sitting in the sand next to Dayne. "But she's trying. You've been gone a long time, and in that time, she has clawed and dragged her way to where she is. She brought us together. But she would be a fool to think there weren't those who would use your return to shatter everything she has built. The lost son of House Ateres. Eldest living heir of Arkin and Ilya Ateres. Your claim to lead the House is undeniable. It is yours by right."

"I don't want it. I don't deserve it."

"There are many people who don't deserve the things they want." Silence settled between them, punctuated by the waves. Mera let out a soft sigh. "I believe you. You are not the man who left Valtara twelve years ago. But you have the same heart. And I know you would do anything to protect Alina, as you always have."

"I would die for her."

"I know you would. And she knows it, too. But a lot has changed since you've been gone. There are those who look to Alina in the same way they once looked to your mother. She is strong and fierce – just like Ilya. Those who follow her would follow her to the void and back. But there are also those who seek power. Sharks waiting for the first sign of blood. That's what you are to Alina right now – blood in the water. Creating uncertainty within House Ateres could shift everything. It would leave room for another House to lead the way. Even within House Ateres itself, vipers slither, the Minor Houses seeking to gain power."

Dayne shifted, narrowing his eyes. "Who?" If he was to serve Alina, he would need to know her enemies.

"Reinan Sarr, Turik Baleer, and Hera Malik. Those three are probably the most notable. They each supported the rebellion, but that doesn't mean they support Alina."

"I know of Turik. He served my father. He was a good man."

"Good or bad, I have no doubt he would see you at the head of House Ateres over Alina. Turik has fallen on the wrong side of Alina's temper more than once, and he's not the kind of man who appreciates being led by one so young."

Dayne nodded, tapping the thumb of his right hand against each of his fingers in turn. "And Hera Malik was Veran Malik's daughter, was she not? Her mother was a thorn in my mother's side. I can only imagine Hera is the same."

Mera frowned, tilting her head sideways. "Hera would be a strong ally. She is a wyvern rider now. Many respect her. But she and Alina don't see eye to eye."

"And this Reinan Sarr? I've never heard of her House."

"House Sarr is a Minor House with a hold almost four days' ride from Skyfell. Reinan, her two sisters, and their father pledged themselves to House Ateres almost seven years ago. Her father named her as head of their House two years later, and she has garnered quite a few supporters within the vassals of House Ateres. She was fiercely loyal to Baren."

"Fuck."

"Agreed."

"All right." Dayne pulled his feet from the sand, mourning the loss of the ocean's touch as he did, then lifted himself to his feet, offering his hand to Mera, who took it without hesitation. "Let's go tell everyone I'm not dead."

THE LAST TIME DAYNE LAID eyes on the council auditorium of Skyfell was the morning before his world fell apart. It had once been his dream to stand at the centre of the auditorium, addressing an audience of free Valtarans. A dream he had hoped his mother and father would have been able to witness.

The auditorium was a massive circular structure ringed by a colonnade-supported red stone porch. Above the colonnade, the auditorium rose into a domed roof, with an oculus at the very top.

Dayne drew in a deep breath, taking in the sight.

"They're already inside," Mera said with a gentle smile. It wasn't a suggestion to hurry, simply a statement.

Dayne wasn't nervous to face the men and women within that chamber. He had seen and done things that had burned those kind of nerves from his heart. What truly set fear in his bones was letting Alina down. He nodded. "Let's go."

Six guards stood watch at the auditorium's doors, three on either side, each clutching an ash wood valyna with an ordo shield strapped to their arm. Dayne couldn't help but notice that beneath their bronzed cuirasses, they each wore the armoured skirts of a different House. Alina's doing, no doubt. The guards eyed Dayne askance at first but relaxed as they recognised Mera, waving them both through.

The main doors of the auditorium opened into a long corridor that functioned as a sort of antechamber to the central atrium. The centre of the corridor was framed by fluted columns of red stone that gave the impression that forward was the only direction to walk. But on the other side of the fluted columns, passageways and staircases branched off towards different sections of the auditorium, some leading to meeting chambers and storage rooms, others to the tiered balconies that overlooked the central atrium. Tall terracotta vases stood beside every second column, plants of vivid green dangling over their edges. At the end of the long corridor was a large set of wooden doors banded with iron.

Voices drifted down the corridor as Dayne and Mera approached the doors to the central atrium, lifted by the natural acoustics of the auditorium itself. Without reaching for the Spark, he couldn't pick out any of the words being spoken, but the number of voices let him know they wouldn't be short of an audience. He rested his palm on the rough wood of the door, the tips of his fingers meeting the cool touch of the iron bands. Mera's hand rested on his shoulder, a soft smile on her lips. She inclined her head, gesturing for him to enter.

A wall of sound poured through as Dayne pushed open the door, then in fractions of a second the cacophony faded to hushed whispers and knots twisted in Dayne's stomach. There wasn't a doubt in his mind that, despite Alina's best efforts, rumours of his return had spread.

The auditorium's central atrium was over a hundred feet in diameter. The floor was paved with large slabs of red stone, each flowing smoothly into the next. The majority of the main chamber lay within a ring of columns that supported the balconies above, with only a few feet between the outside of the columns and the atrium's wall. Above the balconies, the roof tapered into a dome decorated with tiered stone inlays. At the very centre of the dome sat the oculus, through which the light of the sun, with the aid of the candles that sat in sconces attached to the columns, illuminated the chamber.

While the balconies were empty, over a hundred people stood around the atrium, huddled in small groups, whispering, staring, the colours of various Major and Minor Houses on display.

Some Dayne recognised: Vhin, head of House Herak; and Senya, head of House Deringal. They had both been heads of their Houses when Dayne's parents were still alive. Here and there, he saw other faces that looked familiar: soldiers, politicians, nobles. The black of House Vakira, the yellow of House Thebal, and the pale blue of House Koraklon were all on display, though Dayne couldn't see the heads of House Vakira or Thebal – at least, not the ones he would recognise. But he would be surprised if the heads of each Major House – Koraklon excluded – did not show their faces now that it looked as though Alina might actually follow through on her promise of a free Valtara.

It was strange to have everything feel so familiar, and yet so different. The only thing that put him at ease was the recognition of a similar feeling in the eyes of those gathered. Some had never met him, yet others had known him since he was a child. He had changed since they last saw him, and he could see the uncertainty in their gazes.

"Come," Mera whispered as the noise in the room began to return to what it was prior to Dayne's entry. She gestured for Dayne to follow her as she made her way across the centre of the chamber to the right, where Alina stood.

Five men and four women stood by Alina's side. Of the men, his gaze immediately fell on the bright eyes and weathered face of Marlin Arkon – the steward of House Ateres. As soon as Marlin noticed Dayne, he smiled warmly and gave a slight nod. Dayne also recognised the man Mera had mentioned, Turik Baleer, standing to Marlin's right. By the lack of surprise and the broad smile on Turik's bronzed face when he met Dayne's gaze, the man had most certainly already heard of Dayne's return. For a man who must have seen more than sixty summers, Turik's white-grey hair was the only true indication of his age. Dayne didn't recognize the other three men.

Hera Malik stood to Alina's right. She had a powerful, lean frame, and the sides of her head were shaved, her raven hair twisted into a tight plait. Her fingers and hands were marked by the black ink tattoos of the wyvern riders. Dayne could understand why people looked to her. She had an aura about her – a certain confidence. He didn't recognise the other three women, but two bore the markings of wyvern riders, as well as others, which meant the third, with the blonde hair and flat nose, must have been Reinan Sarr – the woman Mera had said was fiercely loyal to Baren.

As Dayne crossed the centre of the Atrium, following behind Mera, his gaze met Alina's, and his heart stopped. He didn't think there would ever be a point when he could look upon his sister and not feel a swell of pride at the woman she had become. If Reinan Sarr had an aura of confidence, Alina was a blazing beacon. She stood in her dark leather battle armour, orange swirls enamelled along the breast plate, a sword strapped to her hip, armoured boots on her feet. The burnt orange of House Ateres was visible in her armoured skirts, and the black ink markings on her fingers, hands, and arms were on full display. She looked like she was ready for war. She looked like a *Wyndarii*.

Dayne nodded to his sister as he moved past her, taking his place beside Mera, but all he got in return was a weak smile.

"We are all here," Alina announced, raising both her palms, gesturing for the murmuring to quieten. She took a moment, casting her gaze across the room before turning her head to look at a woman in a long black tunic embroidered with spirals of white. "I had hoped we might see Tula Vakira here today."

The woman shook her head. "Tula still refuses to take sides. But it doesn't matter. She may be head of House Vakira, but the people are with you." The woman brought a closed fist to her chest. "By blade and by blood, Wyndarii. The people of Lostwren stand by the side of House Ateres. For Valtara."

Alina nodded, betraying not a hint of emotion. She turned to a man in a yellow tunic and cuirass of polished steel. "And what of Miron Thebal? Has he yet decided to join our cause?"

The man drew in a deep breath through his nose before meeting Alina's gaze. "He says he will not make the same mistake as his father before him.

He will not believe the false promises of another Ateres. He says this rebellion will be crushed, just as the last, and the one before that. All those who support it will burn in their homes. He has opened the docks at Myrefall to imperial ships and has provided shelter to Lorian survivors."

"He's a coward!" Senya, head of House Deringal, roared, her long golden plait resting over shoulder, striking against the bronzed cuirass that adorned her chest. Shouts of agreement rose around the atrium, echoing off the stone.

"We should storm Myrefall!" shouted a man in the pale blue of House Koraklon. Even seeing the blue of High Lord Loren's house sent streaks of white-hot rage through Dayne.

Dayne looked around the chamber at furious faces, each person arguing about what should be done. He looked back to Alina, who simply stood there, observing. After a few moments, Alina raised her hands once more, and the chamber quietened. She looked to the woman in the yellow tunic who had initially spoken. "Kirya, how many under House Thebal and their vassals are willing to stand by us in this fight?"

The woman shook her head. "No more than two or three thousand. Miron has poisoned them against rebellion and advised them to take no part so the empire might look upon them favourably. He tells the stories of Stormwatch. He holds the burned city as an example of what happens when you stand against the empire. He calls you a warmonger."

More shouts erupted around the chamber, and Dayne clenched his fist, his chest tightening as memories of the blazing flames burned through his mind, the screams of the dying echoing in the night. How dare this Miron use that massacre for his own gain. It was difficult for Dayne to hold his tongue. So difficult he needed to bite the side of his cheek just to snap himself back to his own mind. He could see Mera watching him out of the corner of her eye.

"Warmonger?" Alina called out, stepping into the centre of the atrium. Her gaze wasn't fixed on the woman who had spoken, but rather it moved about the gathered crowd. "Miron Thebal can call me what he wants. The words of a coward mean nothing!"

Murmurs of agreement rang about the chamber.

"For too long, the empire has stood on our necks." Dayne could see the muscles in Alina's jaws clenching. "They took my brother, Owain, when he had barely seen his first summer. Just as they did to yours, Senya. And yours, Hera. Just as they have done to every family in Valtara since the first rebellion, feeding them into their own armies. They strip us of our kin. Use them as a weapon to fuel our fear. When was the last time you saw a Valtaran who could wield the Spark? They harvest our people. Prune us like trees. They leave children to starve as they fill their ships

with our grain and our fruit. So call me a warmonger because I want war!"
The muscles in Alina's neck strained as she screamed, her fists clenched
at her sides. "I want freedom for my people! I want a world where our
children can be safe and our choices are our own. Who among you will
stand with me? This is our time. This is where we make our choices.
Who among you will fight, by blade and by blood, so that our children,
and our children's children, will not endure what we have?"

The atrium erupted. Roars and shouts resounded off the wall, steel
boots cracked against stone, fists banged against cuirasses.

"For Valtara!" Alina roared.

"For Valtara!" Dayne found himself shouting, his blood pumping in his
veins.

As the chants and shouts died down, Reinan Sarr stepped forward.
"What of the Dragonguard?"

The words brought the dying shouts crashing to a brittle silence.

Alina turned to face Reinan, glancing towards Dayne as she did.

"What of the Dragonguard, Alina Ateres?" Reinan repeated. "It was the
Dragonguard who crushed the first rebellion. It was the Dragonguard who
murdered your father and mother. And it was the Dragonguard who massacred the people at Stormwatch. How do you intend to stop them from
doing the same again? Because only a fool would follow you to the void."

Alina took a step closer to Reinan, her gaze piercing the woman. For
a moment, Dayne thought his sister might charge Reinan. Instead, she
walked past her, eyes fixed on Dayne. Alina stopped a few feet from
Dayne and Mera. "Only a fool would repeat the mistakes of the past." She
turned back towards Reinan, who stood in the centre of the gathering,
below the oculus. "The Dragonguard will not be a problem."

Reinan's stance shifted, her eyebrows raised as she studied to Alina. She
had the look of a wolf that had caught a rabbit in a trap. "Are you a seer
now, Alina Ateres? You kill off your brother and suddenly you know the
future? You expect us to simply believe your word?"

Alina's right hand clenched into a fist, her eyes narrowing.

She's baiting you. Don't rise to it. Dayne let the Spark hover just out of
reach. If it came to it, he would not hesitate.

Alina drew in a deep breath, then released it, her fingers unclenching.
"You think you can twist me, Reinan? Your infatuation with Baren is well
known. Even with him gone, you still follow him like a lost puppy. No,
I am no seer. But I have called you here for a reason. As you all are very
well aware, our war for freedom has already begun." Nods of agreement
were accompanied by the echoes of soft claps. "We have driven the empire from Skyfell and Ironcreek, along with all the lands in between. Next
we are to march on Lostwren, and Myrefall after that."

"We know this," Reinan sniped, shaking her head. "But we are still defenceless against the Dragonguard when they come for their retribution. And they *will* come."

Alina stared at Reinan, her eyes cold. "From Myrefall we take Achyron's keep. Where Consul Rinda and Loren Koraklon hide behind their walls, awaiting imperial reinforcements. Imperial reinforcements that should have arrived weeks ago. Do you know why they haven't arrived, Reinan?"

"How in the gods would I know that? What is your damned point?"

Alina smiled. Dayne couldn't help but stifle a laugh at his sister's display of arrogance. She had a penchant for the dramatic, just like their mother. "My friends, I have kept something from you." With those words, the hair on the back of Dayne's neck stood on end, his stomach twisting as Alina opened her arms, palms out. "I, unlike Reinan, do know why the imperial reinforcements are yet to arrive. But it is not my place to tell you."

Murmurs rose up around the chamber, faces twisting in confusion and irritation.

"What is the meaning of these theatrics?" a man in the black of House Vakira called out.

Alina ignored him. Instead, she turned to Dayne and reached out her hand. Every gaze in the chamber fixed on him. Whispers and mutterings spread through the gathering. His chest trembled, and his stomach turned, threatening to empty its contents. He had seen things over the last decade that would have broken other men. He had seen death, loss, torture, pain. But nothing could have prepared him for where he stood now. Drawing in a deep breath, he stepped forward, his heart beating against his ribs like a crashing wave.

He held Alina's gaze and took her hand, squeezing it. Within her eyes, he could see the fear, the worry; giving him back his name threatened to undermine everything she had built. Alina nodded to him. They had gone over this more times than Dayne could count, and yet he still felt unprepared.

He drew in a deep breath to settle himself, then exhaled through his nostrils. "War has broken out all across Epheria," Dayne said, his heart still thumping as he addressed the gathering. "Our fight for freedom is not the only one. In Illyanara, factions have risen all across the province. The keep of Arisfall was set ablaze in Drifaien. In Carvahon, imperial ships burn in the Bay of Light. In Arkalen, Yarrin has been taken by rebels calling themselves 'The Free Nation of Olmiron'. In the North itself, Uraks ravage Lorian lands. Tens of thousands flee the towns and villages at the foothills of Mar Dorul and Lodhar, seeking refuge in the cities. You want to know why the Dragonguard won't be a problem? It is because Valtara no longer fights alone. All Epheria has risen. The empire fights wars on every front, in every nation, on every scrap of land between here and Al'Nasla. The Dragonguard cannot be everywhere at once. We cannot predict everything, but if there will ever be a time to fight for a free Valtara, it is *now*."

"And who are you to tell us this?" a woman in a long linen dress in the colours of a Minor House he didn't recognise said. "Where do these reports come from?"

Dayne reached into the satchel at this side, producing a stack of broken-sealed envelopes. "These reports come from my contacts across the continent. This one," he said, handing it to the woman who had spoken, "is from Drifaien. It is written by Baird Kanar, right hand of the rebel prince Alleron Helmund. This one," he said, holding out an envelope with a multicoloured wax seal to Reinan Sarr, "Is written by Aurelian Animar of Arkalen. He leads the Free Nation of Olmiron." Dayne continued handing out the envelopes until he got to the last one. "This last letter comes from Aeson Virandr."

More shouts and murmurs rose around the atrium, but they quickly died down. It was clear that most were eager to know what was written in the letter. The theatrics had been Alina's idea. Dayne had argued against them, forcefully. But he had come very far from winning. But at that moment, he would have found it difficult to tell her she had not been right.

"What do we care for Aeson Virandr?"

"It is Aeson Virandr who has sparked these rebellions. Who has paved the way for Valtaran freedom. You have all heard the rumours of a new Draleid? They are true. There is a new Draleid. His name is Calen Bryer, and he stands against the empire."

"What good is one Draleid against nine? It matters not!" A man called out from the back of the gathering.

"Alone? None. But astride a dragon, with the wyvern riders of Valtara at his side and the free peoples of Epheria at his back, that is something different entirely. For the first time in four hundred years, there is a Draleid who stands against the empire. A Draleid who would fly wing-to-wing with our Wyndarii. This is our chance. This is when we stand and fight. By blade and by blood."

As mutterings of agreement spread through the chamber, Reinan Sarr turned to Dayne, shaking her head, holding up the letter he had given her. "These could have been written by anyone. Do you truly expect us to march to war on the words of a stranger? If we back down now, we may be given grace, but if we press and lose, they will crush us."

Dayne took a step closer to Reinan, keeping his gaze locked on hers. "I am no stranger."

"Then who are you? Because I've never seen your face here."

Dayne held Reinan's gaze for a moment before turning to Alina, who hesitated but eventually nodded, her mouth a thin line.

Dayne wrapped his fingers around the edge of his robes, the muscles in his hand clenching involuntarily. He had waited for this moment for so long. Drawing in one last deep breath, he pulled back the edge of his robes, exposing the sigil of House Ateres that had been inked over his left breast when he was just a boy. Gasps of shock spread through the chamber. Dayne saw the recognition on the faces of those who had once known him. "My name is Dayne Ateres. My father was Arkin Ateres. My mother was Ilya Ateres. With my hands bound, I watched from an imperial ship as the Dragonguard laid waste to Stormwatch. I heard the screams of dying children. I smelled the stench of burning flesh. I was there when they killed my father and my mother." Knots twisted in Dayne's chest as he relived that night. He clenched his fist around his robes, feeling tears burn at the corners of his eyes. Anger crept into his voice. "I was exiled from Valtara, told that if I ever returned, my brother and sister would be hung in the streets of Skyfell while I watched. Twelve years I have been gone. And for twelve years, I have hunted those who hurt our people. With the help of Aeson Virandr, their bodies now feed the earth. With the exception of one – Loren Koraklon. The man who is truly responsible for my parents' deaths and the deaths of all those who died that day and every day since. Twelve years I have been gone, but finally I am home." Dayne turned to Alina, bringing a closed fist across his chest. "And I am proud to stand by my sister's side as she leads our House, as she leads all Valtara to the freedom that we have yearned for. For Valtara!"

"For Valtara!"

AFTER THE INITIAL SHOCK OF Dayne's reveal, the talk had turned to politics and the logistics of war. Things of which Dayne had little experience and even less interest. He knew death. He had taken seven hundred and forty-six souls from the world. But he had never led armies. He didn't know how much grain would be needed to feed fifty thousand or how many wagons would be required to do so. He had no notions of the logistics of transporting tents, keeping morale high, or how many farriers would be needed to maintain the horses. Those things were best left to men and women better than him.

By the time Dayne, Alina, and the others set foot outside the council auditorium, the sun had sunk past the horizon, painting the sky a vivid blend of blues and oranges. He stretched out his arms, tilting his head back, feeling his bones crack and muscles ache as they attempted to purge the stiffness that had set in.

"Dayne."

Dayne turned to see Senya Deringal standing before him. He was not sure how many summers she had seen, but Senya had been the head of House Deringal when Dayne's father still lived. Now that he saw her up close, he could see the markings of time in her bronzed skin and the white and grey that streaked the golden plait running along the centre of her head, the sides shaved. But even still, in her bronzed cuirass, the green and gold armoured skirts of Deringal, and the sword strapped to her hip, she looked as fierce as she had when Dayne had last laid eyes on her. Four black rings bisected by a solid black line marked her left arm. *Blademaster.* The markings of the blade were only some of the many tattoos that laced Senya's body.

Only two of the Major Houses called Skyfell their home. House Ateres was one, and House Deringal the other. But despite their close proximity, or perhaps because of it, Senya Deringal and her husband, Larand, had been Arkin and Ilya's closest allies. They had fought side by side many a time during the infighting between the Major Houses. Senya had even helped to deliver Alina when their mother had gone into labour.

"My lady." Dayne inclined his head, bending slightly at the waist. "It is good to see you we—"

The air was knocked from Dayne's lungs as Senya pulled him into an embrace so tight he feared he might crack a rib. Even as others poured out from the auditorium, she held on, her chin digging into his shoulder. When she pulled away, her eyes were glistening and red.

"You look just like your father." She shook her head, wiping away a budding tear. "You're alive. By the grace of Achyron."

"It is good to see you, Senya. Larand, is he well? Your sons, Markan and Varsil?"

Senya shook her head, her grief evident in the quiver of her lips and the renewed shimmer in her eyes. She sucked in the sides of her cheeks, then gave the most sorrowful smile Dayne had ever laid eyes on. "The night you left… they… Stormshold."

Dayne's heart twisted in his chest, his lungs suddenly struggling to grant him breath. "Senya… I…"

"Don't," the woman said, resting her hand on Dayne's cheek. "I have mourned so much I fear there must be no more sorrow left in the world." Senya's eyes, still wet with tears, glimmered in the light of the setting sun as she looked over Dayne's face. She let out a deep sigh through her nostrils, then turned to face both Alina and Dayne, Mera and the others of House Ateres standing behind them. "I am done mourning. By Achyron and Neron, by blade and by blood, House Deringal will follow you, Alina Ateres. Freedom or a funeral pyre, I won't stop until I have one of them."

Senya reached out her arm, which Alina grasped.

"For Valtara."

Senya inclined her head. "For Valtara." She leaned a little closer, her voice dropping close to a whisper. "My Queen."

With only a short bow, Senya walked away, her retinue and vassals following, leaving Alina staring after her.

"My lady." One of the wyvern riders who had stood at Alina's side in the auditorium rested her hand on Alina's shoulder. "It is best we return to Redstone. It will be full dark soon, and even though we have the city, it is not yet safe."

Alina nodded, her eyes still following Senya.

The walk from the auditorium to Redstone was one of the strangest of Dayne's life. While Reinan Sarr and her followers sulked and scowled, a dark cloud hanging over them, and Hera Malik marched silently, Turik Baleer barely gave himself a moment to draw breath. The man was full of questions. Where had Dayne been? What had he seen? What brought him back?

Dayne couldn't lie. There was a certain warmth to Turik's enthusiasm that was almost infectious. "I came back for my family," Dayne said, glancing towards Alina as he spoke. "I came back for Valtara."

"Very right, my lord." Turik nodded his head vigorously. "May I say, it is truly an honour to have you back. When your mother granted House Baleer a place under House Ateres, I swore to her I would never falter. I swore that my line would always stand by her. To see her eldest son return brings me such joy."

"My mother had great respect for you, Turik. She said so on many occasions. I have never doubted the loyalty of House Baleer. It is good to be home."

As they turned the corner, the walls of Redstone came into view, thick and high, statues nestled into alcoves along its breadth. Lanterns hung along the top of the wall, the last of the sun's light glistening off the bronze cuirasses of the Redstone guard who stood watch on the ramparts.

"What's that noise?" one of Alina's wyvern riders asked, tilting her head.

At first, Dayne wasn't sure what the woman was talking about, but then he heard it, a high-pitched melodic sound. Strings. "It sounds like music." Dayne opened himself to the Spark. With the imperial mages no longer in the city, he was reasonably confident there would be nobody around to sense him. He pulled on the tiniest sliver of Air, letting it carry the waves of sound to his ear, following them back to their source. "It's coming from the keep."

Alina turned to Mera, then to Marlin, who shook his head, shrugging.

"Come," Alina said, picking up her pace. "Let us see what this is about."

The sound of the music grew louder the closer they got to the gates of Redstone, becoming clearer. Dayne recognised the song. "The Homecoming of Ardur Valyn."

"I recognise the melody," Alina said. "But I can't place the song."

"It tells the tale of Ardur Valyn." A warm smile spread across Marlin's face as he spoke, looking between Dayne and Alina. "He was the founder of an ancient Valtaran House, now long gone. He was also the first Valtaran to bring the Houses together under one king. Your father used to hum it to you when you were tired."

The guards standing watch at the gates straightened, tapping the butts of their valynas against the ground as the group passed them.

"What in the gods…" Dayne's voice trailed off as he walked through the gateway, his mouth hanging open. Lanterns hung from poles all about the keep's garden, some even dangling from the branches of the orange trees. Standing oil burners framed the brownish-red flagstone path that led through the centre of the garden from the gates to the main house. Everywhere Dayne looked, people garbed in white and burnt orange tunics, wooden cups in their hands, danced and sang along to the music that he now saw was coming from two bards standing to the left of the pathway, on the grass beneath one of the orange trees.

Large casks of wine were stacked by the far wall, where servants were filling cups and carving slices from a suckling pig that burned over a spit. Even before he had been exiled, Dayne couldn't remember a celebration so lavish ever being held within the grounds of the keep. In truth, he couldn't remember a celebration so lavish being held anywhere.

"What is happening here? Marlin, explain yourself." Alina turned to the Steward of House Ateres, her irritation evident in her voice. "We don't have the time, nor the resources, for something like this. You should know better."

"It is not my doing, my lady."

"By your doing or not, it ends now."

"Please, please." Turik Baleer stepped in front of the group, turning his back to the celebrations, his arms spread wide. He gestured to a man who stood by the bards, and the music stopped. After a few moments, those who had been dancing and singing noticed the procession of people gathered at the gates and stopped to pay attention. "Dayne Ateres, please forgive me for playing coy. I heard a rumour some time past that you were in fact alive and had returned to us. Naturally, I was sceptical. But once it was confirmed, I thought it only right that we celebrate what could only be considered an act of the gods." The man who had stopped the music hurried over to Turik's side, handing him a cup of wine, and just as he did, more servants carried cups towards the main group, offering them to everyone gathered.

Dayne looked to Alina, taking in the scowl that had set itself upon her face. She now held a cup of wine in her left hand, but her right hand was twisted into a fist, her thumb tucked within. She was furious.

Turik lifted his cup in the air. "To Dayne Ateres, heir of House Ateres. Your father and mother will forever be remembered by those who stood beside them, and by those they looked over. It was your mother who welcomed House Baleer into the protection of House Ateres, and I have been, and will forever be, grateful. To Dayne Ateres. The lost son has returned. Glory be to House Ateres, by blade and by blood."

"By blade and by blood," Dayne repeated, tilting his cup to Turik – as was proper. Turik's mention of him as heir didn't go over his head. Alina would not be happy.

"By blade and by blood." The words echoed through the Garden as Turik and all those gathered lifted their cups to their lips and drank deep.

"Tonight," Baleer called out, "we celebrate the return of Dayne Ateres and the freedom of Valtara!"

Cheers and shouts rang out, the music resuming once again.

"Lord Baleer." Despite Alina's outward calm, Dayne could hear the cold fury that burned in her voice. "You had no right to arrange this without my knowledge. We don't have the—"

Baleer shook his head, raising his hand for Alina to stop, which Dayne knew would only stoke her fires even more. "My most humble apologies, Lady Ateres. I simply thought, with your responsibilities as our leader, you might wish for someone lesser to take the task upon themselves to arrange the celebration of your lost brother's return. The wine and the food were both procured from seized Lorian supplies, and the two bards are my brother's sons. My wife, Lira, arranged the decoration of the gardens. Not a single coin has left the coffers." The man bowed at the waist, gesturing for Alina to join the celebrations. "Please, my lady. Enjoy the night. There will not be many more like it in the days ahead of us. Dayne, please come with me. There are many heads of Minor Houses here, some who would love nothing more than to see your face again, and others who would cherish the honour of meeting you for the first time."

Dayne looked to Alina, then back to Turik. "I'm sorry Turik, I—"

"Go," Alina said, waving her hand while shaking her head at the same time.

"Alina, please. I don't have to—"

"*Go*," Alina repeated, this time through gritted teeth.

Dayne let out a frustrated sigh. There was no winning. If he left with Turik, Alina would be furious with him for going, but if he didn't, Alina would be furious with him for going against her word. He cast a glance over towards the large casks of wine and thought to himself, 'what would

Belina do?' He could almost hear her voice in his head. *'If you're going to get in trouble either way, you may as well enjoy yourself.'*

Resigning himself for the wrath that was to come, Dayne nodded. "Lead the way, Turik."

"With pleasure, my lord."

Dayne glanced over his shoulder as he walked, seeing many of the others following in his wake. But Alina and the wyvern riders with her were like statues, their stares fixed on Dayne. Even Mera pressed her fingers into her cheek, shaking her head.

"Wine first, Turik."

ALINA BREATHED IN THE FRUITY scents of the red wine. She exhaled, then touched the wooden cup to her lips, taking a sip of the wine, letting the flavours sit on her tongue for a moment before swallowing.

She stood at the stone window ledge at the back of the study that had once belonged to her father – hers now, she supposed. Though she found it near impossible to think of it that way.

From the ledge Alina could see out over the Antigan Ocean, the light of the moon reflecting off the water, creating a distorted image as though the gods had painted haphazard strokes of shimmering white across the waves. But it wasn't the beauty of the ocean that stole Alina's attention, it was the wyverns.

The moonlight glittered off the creatures' scales as they swooped and soared across the cliffs, free falling before spreading their wings and skimming the water's surface. It was like looking out over a sky full of sparkling gems.

When they had retaken Skyfell, the wyverns had finally reclaimed the Rests that had been built into the side of the Abaddian cliffs. Thousands of Rests had been carved into the cliffs a millennium ago, but the wyverns now only numbered in their hundreds. The day would come again when every single one of those Rests was full. Alina whispered, "I promise you."

The distant sound of music and drunken celebration drifted into the study, following the creaking of the door. Alina was relieved to hear Mera's voice. "I thought I might find you here. Where are Amari and Lukira?"

"I sent them off to drink and dance," Alina said, lifting herself to her full height, taking another sip from her wine cup, still transfixed by the near-ethereal beauty of the wyverns. "As much as I'm loath to admit it, Turik is right. There are not many days like this ahead of us."

"And yet here you stand." Mera stepped beside Alina, a cup of wine in her hand. Alina glanced at the three scars that ran from Mera's forehead down over her eyes and onto her jaw – a reminder that the loyalty of a wyvern is hard won. Many wyvern riders were marked by the wyverns during their first bonding. Many died. Alina had been there the day Mera had first bonded with Audin. The wyvern was young but as fierce as any she'd ever seen. One swipe of his claw had torn through Mera's flesh. The blood had covered her face and streamed down over her chest, but besides the initial gasp of pain, Mera had pushed forward, continuing to reach out to the wyvern. Alina was almost certain it was Mera's unwillingness to give up that had touched Audin's heart. From what Alina had learned through the years, that was how wyverns bonded, by recognising their counterpoint in another. They were not tamed or broken. They chose.

"It was difficult to watch Turik and his sycophants whispering in Dayne's ear. I should have known he would find out before I told him. The man has ears everywhere. I'll give him one thing: he has balls bigger than a horse's. To arrange this under my nose? He claims it's a celebration, but it is quite clearly an attempt to win Dayne's favour. '*To Dayne Ateres,*'" she said, doing her best impression of Turik Baleer's nasally voice. She raised her cup in the air. "'*Heir of House Ateres.*' How fucking dare he, Mera? I have no idea what mother or father ever saw in the weaselly bastard."

"Bending Dayne's ear is harder than bending steel, Alina. Especially when it comes to you. There is nothing and nobody he loves more in this world."

Alina raised an eyebrow.

"Nothing and nobody."

Alina took another swig of wine, deeper this time. "I don't trust Turik as far as I can throw him."

"Neither do I."

"He's been opposed to me leading the council from the very start. But now that I lead the House too, he's gotten worse. I wouldn't mind it if he was up front, but he's a conniving shit. He plays his games in the background while we fight for something real. If Dayne had not come back, I have no doubt he would have played to have me removed and watched as House Ateres crumbled, House Baleer rising in its place."

"Most likely."

Alina turned to Mera, frowning. "You're a woman of few words, Mera. But even for you, you're not saying much."

Mera sipped her wine. "Alina, there will always be people who try to sink their claws into you when you climb higher than them. That is an eternal truth. But no matter how hard they try, they will never *be* you.

You are Alina Ateres. You have fought and clawed your way to get here. The head of House Ateres belongs to you. Dayne might be the eldest, but it is yours by right. You need to trust him."

Alina leaned forwards, resting her arms on the stone ledge, cool against her skin. "We stood here that night. Do you remember?"

"We watched the wyverns, just as we do now."

The smile that touched Alina's lips was one born of both happiness and a deep sadness. "I convinced Dayne to let me stay up and watch the sunset – and the wyverns."

"You were pretty adamant. He never could say no to you."

"I trusted him then, Mera. And he left me. He left me and Baren alone."

"That's not fair, Alina. You know as well as I do he had no choice."

"Did he not?" Alina asked, turning her head to Mera. "He could have fought."

"And died."

"Some things are worth dying for." A few moments of silence passed, and Alina looked to Mera. "What?"

Mera shook her head, letting out a sigh that oozed of irritation. "I'm trying not to slap you."

"Excuse me?" Alina lifted herself to a standing position, stumbling slightly sideways as she did. The wine seemed to be affecting her more than she had realised.

Mera turned to her, and for the first time Alina saw true anger in the woman's eyes. She had seen Mera angry, more times than she could count, but she had never been on the receiving end. "Do you even care what he's been through? He watched them kill your parents. They made him watch as they burned the people of Stormwatch alive. He left to save your life. And he has spent twelve years dragging himself back here. Have you seen the way he looks at his hands when he thinks nobody is watching? Like they're covered in blood. Dying for someone is easy. Killing for someone is far harder. And Dayne would do both for you without a thought."

Mera stopped and took a breath. Her chest trembled, and her right fist was clenched at her side.

"I'm sorry, Mera... I didn't mean to..."

Mera shook her head. "Don't waste apologies on me. Dayne would die for you. And every soul under the gods knows he will carve rivers of blood through this world to keep you safe. He deserves more than this."

With that, Mera emptied the contents of her cup, slammed it on the table, and left.

As the door closed behind Mera, Alina launched her cup across the room, hearing an audible *crack as* it split against the wall.

Chapter Nineteen

Svidar'Cia

The rushing wind crashed against Valerys's scales, sweeping over him as he sliced through the air, banking left and right, soaring along the currents as he used the cloud cover to obscure himself from the eyes of anyone who might look up from the ground – just as Calen had instructed. The slightest adjustment of his wings, and Valerys rose at such speed Calen could feel the force that pulled against him, even from thousands of feet below. He could feel the warmth of the dragon's heart, the sheer power of his body. Their heart. Their body.

In the distance Valerys caught sight of the ocean of sand, dunes, and jagged cliffs. Broken ruins of what had likely once been cities and towns dotted the landscape, only the tips of towers and highest points of walls breaking through. Judging by the distance and the pace they were setting, they would reach the true edge of The Burnt Lands by noon. Before Calen could think of the wasteland to which they were marching, Valerys cast his gaze downward, his eyes adjusting to the cliff below, bringing the craggy rock into focus. Small patches of heat dotted the side of the cliff, moving only rarely. He folded his wings and dropped into a dive, plummeting like a ball of lead dropped from a tower. As he fell, he caught a strong, musky odour. To Calen, it was nothing more than the stench of piss-soaked dirt. But images flashed across the dragon's mind: long, gnarled horns, striated like the trunk of an old tree. Fur matted with dirt and shit. Hooves as black as jet, thick and worn.

Shifting, Valerys drifted right, waiting, the taste of blood already in his mind. In one smooth motion, he unfurled his wings, catching the wind in a movement so fierce Calen felt as though his own body would pull apart even though he walked safely on the ground below. The dragon swerved so his belly was parallel to the cliff face, so close Calen feared the rocks might tear him open. The wind whistled, crashing and breaking against Valerys's body, his right wing pointing towards the sky, his left pointing towards the solid ground thousands of feet below. Valerys was so close now he could hear the heartbeat of his prey. He pulled his wings back, momentarily halting his forward momentum, hanging as though suspended sideways, then snatched an enormous mountain goat from its perch on the cliff face, his talons sinking into the goat's flesh like fingers into soft clay, warm blood spilling. The animal bleated and thrashed as Valerys angled his wings once more and swept away from the cliff face.

In the back of his mind, Calen could hear a distant voice.

"Calen?" Erik let out a sigh. "You're gone again, aren't you?"

Slowly, Calen's mind drifted from Valerys's. He could still feel the beat of the dragon's heart, the thrum of his wings, the hunger in his belly, every flare of emotion that ignited in his mind. But he no longer saw through Valerys's eyes, and he could feel the separation between them once more, the point where Calen stopped and Valerys began. Ever since being freed from the cell in Drifaien, ever since having those manacles removed, the collision of their minds had caused something to shift in the bond between them. It was as though two raging rivers had been held back and allowed to build, only for them to come crashing together once more, creating a force twice what they had been before.

"What do you think?" Erik continued, though Calen hadn't heard what his friend had been saying.

Calen raised an eyebrow, throwing Erik an apologetic look.

"The old man's riddle. *'A city once lost, found it needs to be'*. It has to be either Vindakur or Ilnaen. Unless there happens to be a whole host of other cities lost to time that we don't know about, which is actually a distinct possibility, but it's always better to focus on what you know with these things."

Since leaving Rokka, they had marched for ten days. Each night they made camp far later than they should have and broke it before the sun had yet crested the horizon. It wasn't as though they were hurrying towards a ticking clock, but every minute they weren't moving was another minute Rist was alone, and Calen had allowed himself to wait far too long already. Every day as they marched, Erik spent his time attempting to tease out the meaning of Rokka's riddle to the point that it was almost as maddening for everyone else as it was for Erik.

"Ilnaen?" Vaeril chimed in, a curious look on his face. "Ilnaen is not lost. It resides in the Svidar'Cia – The Burnt Lands."

"True." Erik shrugged, his lips twisting in a pout. "But what does lost *mean*?"

"What do you mean 'what does it mean?' It means lost. Location unknown."

Erik smiled as though he had been waiting for Calen to say just that. "Does it though? When Dahlen and I were children, our father used to test us with puzzles and riddles. Dahlen was always better at it than I was. But my father always used to say that there's more than one way to skin a kat. Lost might not mean lost by location, but it could mean lost as in lost in battle. Lost in a sense of morality, in a sense of understanding. So many options."

"Very good," Vaeril said. "I would never have looked at it that way."

Somehow, Vaeril had managed to make his words sound as though he were disappointed with himself rather than impressed with Erik, which amused Calen to no end.

"Thank you... I think." Erik laughed, shaking his head. "Anyway, the 'The moon of blood, of death and life', has to be the Blood Moon, as we've already agreed, but the 'There is a stone, a heart of blood, cast into the sea,' that one's stumping me."

"I think it's all stumping you," interrupted Tarmon, dropping back to join the conversation, nudging Erik with his shoulder. "You've been at this for days, and so far the only thing you're certain of is that the moon is a moon. I'm not sure that counts as progress."

"I'll figure it out... eventually."

Calen let the conversation fade to the back of his thoughts. Over the past few days, he had noticed the lands around them changing. Despite the season, the morning sun grew warmer with each passing day, and the farther they walked from Kingspass and the closer they drew to the Burnt Lands, the more arid the world around them became. Slowly, plants and grass began to dwindle, thinning with each mile, and the ground grew ever more cracked and broken. Large, barren furrows carved through the dirt where rivulets and streams had once flowed but were now baked and devoid of moisture. It had been over two days since he had last seen a tree with leaves. Four since he had seen a blade of grass. The animals had grown scarce as well. The only other living creatures Calen had seen in the last day or so, besides Valerys, were lizards and small kat-like animals with dusty brown fur and black rings around their legs – and the mountain goats that Valerys was so fond of.

"My people tell legends of this place." Vaeril moved to Calen's side, his green cloak drifting behind him. "Nobody truly knows how Fane created such destruction. Every bralgír has their stories, every scholar their theories, but none of them truly *know*. Anyone who had been close enough to witness what happened died in the flames. But it is said that whatever he did that night shredded the veil between our world and the world of the gods, and through it, Efialtír's corruption seeped into these lands."

"Even that is still a theory, no? A story." Tarmon raised an eyebrow, sweat glistening on his brow and along the bridge of his nose.

236

Vaeril pulled his mouth into a half-frown. "Over the centuries, many of my people have journeyed into the Svidar'Cia in search of what was lost. In the hopes they might find something of use in the ruins of Ilnaen and other cities destroyed that night. Not one of them has ever returned."

Calen let out a sigh, chewing on the edge of his lip. Had he gone mad, trying to cross the Burnt Lands? That was a question he asked himself every morning as they rose.

"Calen." Vaeril said the name as though he had to force himself to not say 'Draleid'. "May I ask you a personal question?"

"You don't have to ask permission, Vaeril."

"Amongst my people, it is courtesy that when asking a question that one believes might cause distress of the heart, they ask permission first."

Fingers of anxiety wrapped around Calen's heart. Whatever questions Vaeril thought might need permission to be asked were not questions Calen was looking forward to answering, but he nodded.

"Are you well?"

Those three words cut into Calen like a sharpened blade. Even before he could speak, he could feel the tears at the back of his throat, threatening at the corners of his eyes. How had three simple words hit so hard? Without asking, Calen knew the truth of Vaeril's question: Haem. Calen hadn't spoken much, if at all, of Haem since they left Kingspass. It was easier to push the thoughts into the darkest caverns of his mind. Dwelling would only cause him more pain. It would only slow him down. Haem had left him, but Rist needed him. Every minute he gave to Haem was one he took from Rist.

"No," Calen whispered. If it had been Erik or Tarmon, he might have lied. Lying was easier. But for some reason, lying to Vaeril seemed wrong. Erik had been following his father's path when he and Calen had met. Tarmon had simply had the misfortune of being trapped with them all in the tunnels. But Vaeril had sworn an oath to Calen before they had even exchanged a word. He had bound himself to Calen's path. He had made that choice. The elf had given Calen so much when he had known so little. He had left his home, his people, his world. And in that time, he had stood by Calen through everything. Even now, he marched by Calen's side towards the Burnt Lands, unflinching. No, he wouldn't lie to Vaeril. "Do you have siblings, Vaeril? Family?"

The elf nodded, a touch of melancholy in his smile. "Three sisters... My brother, Heraya harbour his soul, was taken by the Aldithmar over a decade ago. My father was lost trying to search for him."

"I'm sorry..."

Vaeril shook his head. "It was a long time ago."

"Does it get easier?"

237

"It does not." The elf smiled as he spoke, but it was not a smile born of happiness. "I don't think losing the ones you love ever gets easier. It is the only pain your body truly remembers. When you think back on a broken leg, you do not weep from the agony. But when you remember you will never look upon your father's face again, it cuts as fresh as the first day. What does get easier is carrying on. The weights on our shoulders rarely get lighter, but we can get stronger."

Calen nodded, returning Vaeril's sorrow-touched smile. He could feel Valerys's mind as the dragon's sadness melded with his own. The dragon soared through the air, his hunger now satiated, never allowing himself to drift too far from Calen and the others. Calen would have given anything to be up there with him, feeling the warmth of Valerys's scales beneath him, the rush of the wind as it swept over their body, but the wound the Fade had inflicted in the dragon's side still ached. It had healed well since Kingspass, but he still wasn't strong enough to take Calen on his back, not with the distance they still had yet to cover. Even then, Calen could feel the wound throbbing from the strain Valerys had put it under when snaring that goat.

As the day passed and the sun rose higher, its heat rising to the point that sweat tacked Calen's shirt to his chest, the already sparse remnants of withered trees faded, the only plant life being patches of dry brittle bush that looked as though they might snap into pieces at the hint of a breeze. Where the cracks in the dried ground had once been small and thread-thin, they now spread out like a spider's web, some over a foot wide and three times as long. It looked as though segments of the ground had shrunk and curled in on themselves, like shards of shattered ceramic.

The air smelled of nothing but dirt, dust, and heat. It was so devoid of moisture Calen could already feel his lips drying, his breaths catching in the back of his throat. Ahead, a ridge rose a few hundred feet, stretching into the distance, casting shadows over the cracked ground, its continuity broken only by a few narrow gaps created by fissures in the rock that led upwards through the ridge.

A shadow swept across the ground, moving from east to west, followed by a gust of wind that swept spirals of dust into the air. With a crack of his wings, Valerys alighted on a patch of shattered clay beside Calen, the brittle ground beneath him breaking and snapping under his weight. A low rumble resonated from Valerys's chest as the dragon leaned his head down, and Calen rested a palm on his snout.

"The waste starts just over the ridge and stretches as far as the eye can see," Calen said, images of what Valerys had seen shifting through his mind. Sand, dunes, cliffs, rubble, and more sand.

"I think we could have guessed that." Erik folded his arms, tilting his head towards the enormous ridge that stretched across the landscape before them.

Despite the sadness that still clung to him from thinking of Haem, Calen couldn't help but laugh. He shook his head and made to walk towards the nearest passage through the ridge that looked easily passable but stopped at the touch of Tarmon's hand against his chest.

"We have no idea what we might find out there," the big man said, glancing towards the ridge that guarded the heart of the Burnt Lands. "We've come too far to jump headfirst into this without some idea of what we are going to do."

Calen nodded. Tarmon was right, of course. Just as he always was when it came to the need for a level head and a path forward. "Kiron said it was about two hundred miles from nearest point to nearest point."

"If we walk in a straight line," Tarmon added. "And there's no chance of doing that. And we have no idea how accurate the map was."

"Hope for the best, prepare for the worst." Erik brushed crusted dirt from his trouser leg, pulling his waterskin from his pack. "That's what my father always says."

"Aeson Virandr is a wise man." Tarmon folded his arms, scratching at the stubble on his chin. "We could be out there for two weeks, possibly three, possibly longer. We should travel in pairs at all times. If you need to take a piss. In pairs. If you need to scout ahead. In pairs. If you need to—"

"In pairs," Erik cut in. "We get it. Everything in pairs."

"Erik with Vaeril. Me with Calen," Tarmon said, scowling at Erik. "If you or I get separated, we have no way of lighting a signal. With their magic, Calen and Vaeril do."

Vaeril looked at Tarmon, then back to Calen. The uncertainty on his face was evident.

"We're staying together," Calen said, meeting Vaeril's gaze. "But Tarmon's right. If for any reason we get separated or something happens out there, we need to do everything we can to make sure Tarmon and Erik aren't left on their own."

The elf nodded, though still looked unsure.

"Vaeril, water will be scarce. Each day, we'll need you to draw water from the ground just as you did in the tunnels." Tarmon rolled his tongue across his teeth, glancing back at the ridge. "Each day we march as far as we can, even if it aches and burns. We take rotating guard shifts, two at a time. This place is our enemy. It wants us dead. The quicker we pass through, the better, understood?"

"Understood."

A thin layer of sand coated the ground near to the ridge, like dust on an unused table. But the closer they drew, the thicker the sand became until it had completely covered the shattered ground beneath, Calen's feet dragging with each step. Up close, the gap resembled a narrow valley, walls of dusty brown rising either side, a path of sand and sharp rock leading upwards towards the top of the ridge.

Tarmon marched ahead as they half-walked, half-climbed their way through the narrow path, his greatsword strapped to his back, his shortsword at his hip. The man still wore the core of his steel plate Kingsguard armour – the breastplate, vambraces, greaves, boots, and a shirt of mail – though it no longer held its mirror-like sheen, and his purple cloak was long since tattered and lost. A narrow hole, about an inch wide, was still visible in the plate, just a few inches above Tarmon's hip on the left side of his back, where the arrow had pierced him in Belduar.

As they neared the top of the path, Calen drew in a deep breath, attempting to settle the nerves that had begun to fester within him. This was their point of no return. He had brought them here, and he would die before he let anything happen to them. He had lost too many already.

"By the gods…"

Calen looked up to see that Tarmon had reached the end of the path and now stood atop the ridge, staring out at the heart of the Burnt Lands. A quick look passed between Calen, Erik, and Vaeril, and they all picked up their pace.

A gust of wind swept over Calen as he stepped onto the ridge, the sun beating at his skin with renewed vigour.

By the gods.

An ocean of sand, dunes, and cliffs was splayed out before him. Seeing it through Valerys's eyes had somehow dulled the sheer immensity of it. The sand went on for eternity, glittering in the light of the sun. It swept as far as the eye could see in every direction, rising and falling like ocean waves, broken only by jagged rocks and cliffs of brown stone.

"It's actually kind of… beautiful." Erik ran the back of his hand across his brow, flicking sweat down into the sand at his feet. "From here, anyway. I don't think I'll have the same opinion once we're in there."

A *thunk* to Calen's left drew his attention. He turned to see Tarmon's satchels, swords, sword belt, and scabbards lying in the sand while the man undid the buckles and straps of his armour, stripping it and dumping it in the sand.

"What are you doing?" Calen asked as Tarmon undid the last of the straps on his breastplate and let it fall into the sand with a subdued *thud*.

"I'll die of heatstroke if I try and cross this place in that armour," he said, reaching down and stripping his greaves and pulling his feet out of his armoured boots so he now just stood in a sweat-soaked linen shirt, thin linen trousers and a pair of socks.

"Why didn't you get rid of it at Rokka's cabin?" Erik asked.

"Might have needed it between there and here." Tarmon lifted one of the satchels, rooting around inside and producing two long, brown hooded cloaks, one of which he handed to Calen, and a pair of ankle-covering boots, slipping his feet into the boots and tossing the cloak around his shoulders. "It will help keep the heat off your skin."

Calen nodded, swinging the cloak around his shoulders and tying it tight.

"You might need it out there," Erik said, nodding towards the seemingly endless sea of sand.

"I'd rather be taken by a sword than the sun." Tarmon fastened his sword belt back around his waist and strapped his greatsword into place across his back before lifting the satchels up once more. "Prepare for the demon you know, instead of fearing the one you don't." He took one last longing look at his armour, then started off into the endless sand. "Come on, we can't waste sunlight. According to the maps, Copperstille is to the north-east." He stuck out his hand, tracing the path the sun had followed through the sky. "Which is somewhere in this direction."

"*Somewhere in this direction?*" Erik asked as they followed Tarmon.

"Most definitely." Tarmon glanced at Calen with a wry smile. "It's a feeling."

Calen could see Erik was about to throw his arms up in protest, but he stopped when Tarmon turned his hand over and opened it, revealing a small brass compass with a black and red needle.

"Courtesy of our new friend, Rokka," Tarmon said with a victorious grin.

Erik glared at Tarmon, shaking his head. "I preferred you when you didn't make jokes."

CALEN'S FEET DRAGGED, SINKING WITH each step. The sand pulled at him, sapping the energy from his bones. He'd never felt anything like it. He'd walked along the coast at Milltown and near the edge of Ölm, but it had been nothing like this, nothing even close.

The blazing sun was only halfway through its downward arc, which meant they could only have been marching for four or five hours at most, but Calen's body ached as though he'd been wading through knee-high water for days. Beneath his cloak and leather armour, his shirt clung to his body, saturated. Sweat slicked his forehead, pooling in his eyebrows before dripping. The air he dragged into his lungs tasted dry and harsh on his tongue, as though it had been baked in a clay oven. "It shouldn't be this hot in earlywinter."

"No," Tarmon said, heaving in deep breaths, his feet sinking into the sand, his massive frame lumbering. "It shouldn't."

"This place is not natural," Vaeril said. The elf was the only one among them who hadn't got so much as a bead of sweat on his brow.

"Therin told stories in The Gilded Dragon of how Fane created the Burnt Lands when he destroyed Ilnaen." It felt strange to think back to a time when rushing to The Gilded Dragon to hear Therin's stories had been a regular occurrence. Back to a time when his mam and dad would join them, Ella too, and Haem when he wasn't on duty. The thought of it wrenched Calen's heart. He pushed it to the back of his mind, pressing it down, tucking it away with all the other things he couldn't afford to feel.

Vaeril nodded, sadness etched into his face. "One of the stories our bralgír tell is that with the Blood Moon at its fullest and the veil between the worlds thin, Fane fuelled his Blood Magic with the souls of all who died that night, leaving the remnants of who they once were to taint these lands. There is no other way he could have wrought such horror."

"May The Mother harbour their souls," Tarmon whispered.

The only sounds that followed were the crunching of sand and the whistling of the wind. They carried on like that for hours, trudging across the ocean of sand and rock, the sun beating down over their backs. No matter which direction Calen looked, all he could see was clear blue sky, the rolling dunes stretching into eternity. Overhead, Valerys soared, using the air currents to carry him a mile or two away before circling back. Even through the dragon's eyes, Calen could see nothing but sand, dunes, and rock stretching off to the edges of the world. It had been that way since they had entered the Burnt Lands. Calen hadn't told the others. It had to be a trick of the mind, something created by the dark magic that created this place. He was sure of it – mostly. Before they had entered, Valerys had been able to see the mountains of Mar Dorul and Lodhar in the distance. *Mountains don't just disappear. There's no need to panic the others.* He was quickly beginning to understand why so many had perished trying to cross the Burnt Lands.

As the sun dipped into the western horizon, its light slowly fading, the heat that had battered them all day began to dissipate. At first, it was a relief; the air became easier to breathe, and each step was less laboured. But then the warmth continued to drain as though it were being forcibly pulled from the air. By the time the moon had supplanted the sun and the sky had turned a dark, star-speckled blue, Calen's breath plumed out in front of him, and his jaws chattered. He shivered, the sweat on his skin and in his clothes turning cold.

Much like the snow in Drifaien, the sand seemed to hold the light, creating a perpetual twilight that held true darkness at bay.

"We need to find somewhere to shelter," Tarmon called out, pulling his cloak tighter around himself, the icy wind picking up. "If it gets any colder, we'll freeze out here – not to mention we don't know what else might be roaming these dunes."

"Agreed," Calen said. "If we find somewhere enclosed, then we can use the heat of Valerys's body to keep us warm."

After a few more minutes of marching, Erik extended a hand towards a rock formation that protruded through the sand, his breath misting in the air. "Over there."

Looking closer, Calen could just about see a dark patch near the base of the rock formation that looked as though it might have been a cave.

Tarmon nodded, dipping his head to avoid a gust of sand that swept up into the air.

The rock formation rose about fifty feet from the sand and was easily as wide and thick as three houses joined together. At its base, a large flat plateau fronted an opening wide enough for three or four people to pass through at a time and only about a foot or so taller than Calen. As they drew closer to the plateau, however, Calen caught sight of something that caused him to stop in his tracks, his muscles tensing: a host of bodies lay splayed across the rock and half-buried in sand at its front.

Calen opened himself to the Spark, its warmth driving the cold from his body. He felt Vaeril do the same. To his left, Tarmon and Erik slid their swords into their hands.

"They're long dead," Erik called as he knelt at the base of the plateau, where one of the bodies lay, its legs buried in the sand, its head and back resting against the rock. "How long, I couldn't say. Months, maybe. I've never seen a body like this. It's like it was dried out or cured. It's not rotting like I'd expect. It doesn't even smell bad. One thing is for sure, something stripped most of the flesh clean after the body was cold. There are teeth marks in the bone and bloodstains everywhere."

Calen's stomach turned even before he laid eyes on the corpse over which Erik stood. The phrase 'it's not rotting like I'd expect' didn't sit well with his constitution. The acidic taste of vomit threatened the back of his throat, but he pushed it back down. A rusted coat of mail was draped over the body's shoulders, a battered shield half-buried in the sand beside it. Most of the flesh had been stripped, exposing large patches of sun-bleached bone through the armour. The small areas of skin that remained around the face and left arm looked just as Erik had described: brittle as over-dried strips of meat, ready to crack and shatter at the slightest touch.

Looking around, Calen guessed there had to be at least fifty bodies scattered around the plateau and buried in the sand. Some were missing limbs, others had rusted swords and knives still entangled in their bones.

"There was a battle here," Tarmon said, stepping onto the plateau, using his foot to turn over the body of a man with a small hand axe embedded in his ribs. "And both sides lost."

"Their armour…" Vaeril strode through the centre of the plateau, his gaze sweeping across the bodies.

"What about it?" Erik rose to his feet, following the others onto the plateau.

"Look closer."

"Enough games, Vaeril. What is it?" Erik snapped, his patience uncharacteristically short.

What's he so mad about?

"It's all the same." A hint of irritation crept into Vaeril's voice.

Calen looked to Vaeril, raising an eyebrow and tilting his head, asking the question without words: Are you all right?

Vaeril let out a heavy sigh, then glanced towards Erik before nodding.

The elf rarely let his anger or irritation show. Calen nodded, then grimaced as he knelt beside a corpse whose flesh had mostly been picked clean. His gaze passed over the corpse's empty eye sockets, speckled with patches of dried skin and stained with blood, before looking at the image of a roaring lion on the soldier's breastplate – the same image that each of the others wore. "They all bear the black lion of Loria."

A warning flashed through Calen's mind from Valerys. Instinctively, he reached for the Spark, pulling his sword from its scabbard and tossing his satchels onto the plateau.

"What is it?" Tarmon dropped his satchels, sliding his greatsword from the scabbard across his back.

A rhythmic pulsing sound filled the air, like that of a stone skimmed across a frozen lake, high pitched and shrill. It rose and fell, shifting and moving around them.

Vaeril dropped his satchels and shrugged his bow from his back, opening himself to the Spark. Erik did the same, drawing his swords.

Calen reached out to Valerys. *Show me.* He let their minds drift together, their consciousnesses blending. Panic spilled from Valerys, twisting to fury, his wings hammering against the air. He wasn't far, less than a mile. Calen tried to see through the dragon's eyes, but all that lay before him was sand and dunes. Then something moved in the dunes, and Valerys banked left, pressure building within. Pure fury pulsed through Calen's veins, sweeping the air from his lungs, causing his jaw to clench as Valerys unleashed a torrent of dragonfire.

The dim twilight receded as Calen saw Valerys through his own eyes, bursting from a dark cloud above, his fire sweeping over the dunes below him, an icy rage consuming him.

"Calen?" Erik stepped beside Calen, looking out over the sand to where Valerys swooped low, soaring towards them.

"Something's coming."

"No shit."

Calen slowed his breathing, feeling Valerys's fury burning in his veins, igniting the strength in his bones. *Draleid n'aldryr.* Calen let go, giving over completely to the bond. Energy rippled through him, his and Valerys's thoughts colliding. A visceral roar tore through the night as Valerys unleashed another torrent of dragonfire, lifting clouds of sand into the air, setting brittle bushes and shrubs alight. Calen gripped his sword with both hands, the deep purple glow of his eyes shimmering off the steel, washing his hands with a weak, purplish hue.

Through Valerys's eyes, Calen saw shapes flitting across the dunes, dark and as quick as anything he'd ever seen, illuminated by the fires Valerys had started.

A high-pitched shriek erupted to Calen's left, and he spun, swinging his sword as he did. The blade tore through flesh, biting into something hard. Calen felt the crunch of bone, the blade holding for a moment, then sliding through, warm liquid splattering on his face – blood. He looked down to see the body of a kat-like creature, split across the middle. It looked about half the size of a wolfpine, but its body was slender, wiry slabs of muscles, dense bone, and a coat of charcoal-black fur.

Whoosh.

Calen didn't see the arrow, but he heard the thud as its target dropped, the momentum carrying the creature across the stone. Hisses and roars rose around them, claws clicking. Calen turned to see Erik and Tarmon moving across the plateau, their blades shimmering in the twilight, blood spraying.

Something pounded into Calen's legs, and he went crashing down, gasping for air as his back collided with stone and the wind was knocked from his lungs. Pressure on his chest. A pair of gleaming eyes looking down at him. Calen shifted and drove his sword upwards. The creature shrieked as the blade plunged into its neck, warm blood spilling over Calen's hand and face. Reaching for the Spark, he pulled on thick threads of Air and slammed them into the creature's belly, sending it careening into the air and sliding free of his blade.

Calen heaved himself to his feet, raking his blade across another creature's side as he did. They were everywhere, snapping and snarling. A clutch of them bounded onto the plateau, teeth bared, eyes gleaming, black fur blending with the night. They held a few feet from Calen and Vaeril, watching, waiting. Up close, Calen could see they each had a third set of limbs that protruded from the sides of their deep chests, tucked tight to the body between their front legs. The limbs were much smaller than the others and held three hinge-like joints, the ends tapering into long black scythe-like talons. "What in the name of the gods are they?"

Before Vaeril could answer, the creatures lunged, springing off their hind legs, their front legs spreading, their scythe-like limbs extending outward. Vaeril dropped one of them with an arrow to the eye, but a second crashed into him. Calen made to pull on threads of Fire, stopping at the sound of the stone-shaking roar that rippled through the night.

Valerys crashed down, snatching one of the creatures in his talons and slamming it into the stone. Kicking back his right leg while his talons were still embedded in the creature's torso, Valerys ripped the howling beast in half, blood and gore spraying, intestines spilling onto the stone, steam wafting. A bloodlust ignited in the dragon, rippling through him, spilling into Calen. The dragon spun, the spearhead tip of his tail hacking into the skull of the beast that stood over Vaeril. The creature's body went limp then dropped over the elf as Valerys heaved his tail free from its skull like an axe springing from a tree, blood sluicing. The dragon swung his neck around, snatching one of the creatures in his jaws before slamming it down with such force cracks spread through the stone beneath it.

Calen reached down and heaved Vaeril to his feet. But as the elf said his thanks, the words drowned in the back of Calen's mind. The only sound Calen could hear was the thump of his and Valerys's heart, the pulsing of the blood in their veins, the slow drag of the heavy breaths leaving the dragon's nostrils. Pure power radiated from Valerys's mind, primal and raw. The dragon's rage was a tangible thing. These creatures would never threaten his family, would never harm his soulkin. He would not allow it. Valerys's head kicked back.

"Erik, Tarmon, get down!" Calen grabbed Vaeril and dragged him to the ground as Valerys craned his head over them, unleashing a river of dragonfire that illuminated the night like a blazing sun. Valerys's lavender eyes gleamed in the light of the flames, shadows dancing across his horn-ridge face, his white scales painted an orange-red hue.

His heart pounding, Calen rose to his feet, pulling on threads of Fire and Spirit. One of the creatures leapt from the shadows, scythe-like limbs bared, razor teeth glistening. Calen pulled on threads of Air, catching the creature mid-flight, Valerys's bloodlust searing through his soul. One twist and the beast's neck snapped. Calen let it drop to the floor. He funnelled his threads of Fire and Spirit into Valerys, feeling the dragon's rush as his flames grew brighter and burned hotter.

In the light of the flames, Calen saw Tarmon and Erik in the sand by the edge of the plateau, their eyes fixed on Valerys's fire, their swords gripped in their fists. A long gash ran along Erik's left arm, and Tarmon had a cut above his eye. Around them, the creatures that hadn't been caught in the flames fled into the night, hobbling, hissing, and shrieking.

Calen knew he should release his threads, let the Spark dissipate, but the power was intoxicating. He could feel Valerys in his mind, pushing him on, urging him to take more, pull deeper, let the flames burn brighter. A desperate urge to protect roared at the back of his mind, blending with fury, beating back flashes of loneliness, an unwillingness to let any harm come to the bond. Calen slowed his breathing, trying to pull himself back. He rested his hand on the scales of Valerys's chest, just below where his wing sprouted.

"It's all right." Calen released his threads of Fire, drawing solely on Spirit, weaving them into Valerys's mind, just as he had done in the tunnels below the mountain. "We're safe, Valerys. Du vyin alura anis." *You can rest now.*

A tentative calm washed over the dragon at Calen's words, and Calen could feel Valerys begin to let go of his fire, his heart slowing, his fury ebbing.

Once Calen had reached out to the Spark, he had almost forgotten the chill that had descended over the wasteland as night fell, but as he slowly released the threads of Spirit he'd weaved, the cold crept back in, sending a shiver through him.

As the flames of Valerys's dragonfire died out and faded, the ground was covered in crumpled husks, charred fur and skin still glowing bright orange, snapping and crackling, sparks drifting on the breeze. The smell of burnt fur and boiled blood hung heavy in the gelid air. Once, that putrid smell would have turned Calen's stomach, but now, with Valerys's mind entwined with his, it was a war drum, a feverish calling. He pushed it back, squeezing his fingers around the hilt of his blade, surprised at the strength it took. His own breaths vibrated in his ears. He drew in a deep lungful of air, then let it out slowly, running his free hand across Valerys's scales. "It's all right."

The words were more for him than Valerys.

"Draleid." Vaeril's hand clapped down on Calen's shoulder, his eyes searching Calen's, then checking over him.

"I'm fine, Vaeril. But you're not." Calen reached out his hand, pushing Vaeril's cloak aside to show a long slice through the left breast of the elf's leather armour, blood seeping through.

"It's nothing," the elf said, looking at the wound as though it were nothing more than a scrape. "It will need stitches and some brimlock sap."

"They're ugly bastards." Erik grimaced as he stepped onto the plateau, kicking one of the creatures onto its back with his foot.

"Takes one to know one." Tarmon wiped the blood from across his brow, looking down at the creature, then back over towards Calen and Vaeril, his gaze resting on Valerys for a moment. "Everyone all right?"

Erik glared at Tarmon, shaking his head as he dropped to one knee beside the creature.

"We're fine," Calen said. "Nothing a few stitches can't fix, aye Vaeril?"

Vaeril inclined his head, his attempted smile interrupted by a twinge of pain.

Calen leaned over Erik, who was examining the body of the creature. Up close, Calen could see it wasn't actually covered in fur, at least not any kind of fur he recognised. It was more akin to a blackish-grey leather that looked as though it had been cut short and stretched over the creature's bones and muscles. Its head was similar to a kat's, but where its ears should have been were deep recesses that sank into a compact skull. The muscles on its neck and shoulders were thick and bunched, while its tail was long, sleek, and muscular, tapering off to a point. Its hind legs were long and dense with striated muscle, while its front legs were slightly shorter and more similar to arms. Both pairs of legs ended in obsidian black claws that looked as sharp as any blade. The scythe-like talons on the creature's third limbs were as long as daggers, curved and smooth as glass.

"What in the gods…" Erik emphasised every word as he pulled back the creature's top lip, exposing a powerful set of jaws set with thick, razor-sharp teeth, a pair of large fangs on both the bottom and top rows. He ran his finger along the scythe-like talons of its third limbs, resting his hand along the gaping wounds in the creature's side where Valerys's teeth had punctured.

Calen shifted, allowing Valerys's head to extend past him and crane over the dead animal. The dragon watched with interest, the cold light of the moon causing his lavender eyes to glimmer. A feeling of confusion drifted through the dragon's mind, blending with anger, guilt. It took Calen a few moments to realise the cause of the dragon's emotions: Valerys hadn't seen the creatures coming until they had almost been upon them. He hadn't been able to sense their heat or pick up their scent in the wind. It had been a stroke of luck that the dragon had glimpsed the shifting shadows as they stalked the group.

"It is an N'aka," Vaeril said, looking down over the creature. "From time to time they stray from the Svidar'Cia in search of food. They stalk the outer woods of the northern Aravell. Those of my people who were alive before The Fall say the N'aka only first appeared after Fane created the Svidar'Cia. Many believe they are twisted forms of creatures that once were. They are scavengers mostly, but in packs this size they can be deadly. We've likely given them cause to steer clear, particularly with Valerys by our side, but I would still be surprised if they abandon us entirely. There are likely far more of them out there, and I would think there is significantly more meat on our bones than their usual prey."

"At least we know they can bleed," Tarmon said, wiping the N'aka blood from his greatsword with a cloth. "I'm happy to face anything that isn't a Fade. If it bleeds, I can kill it. Is the meat edible?" There was no humour in Tarmon's voice. "They look like they're mostly skin and bone, but we need to conserve as much of our cured food as we can. There's no telling how accurate Captain Kiron's map actually was."

"You want to eat that thing?" Erik stared at Tarmon, eyes wide.

"Meat is meat." Tarmon shrugged, looking to Vaeril for an answer.

Vaeril shrugged. "I don't know anyone who has tried."

Valerys leaned forward and snatched the creature into his jaws. Its limp body dangled while blood dripped onto the stone. Jerking his head upwards, Valerys shifted the creature in his mouth, then clamped his jaws down and ripped his head to the side, tearing the N'aka in half. Calen winced at the crunches and snaps of bone. The other half of the creature's body hit the stone with a wet slap, entrails spilling out, blood splattering.

"Beautiful." Erik covered his mouth with the back of his hand. "Now he decides to share food."

"What does he think?" Tarmon asked, a smile touching his lips.

"He'll live." A rapacious hunger radiated from Valerys as the dragon choked down his meal of skin, bone, and tendon.

"Suddenly, I'm not very hungry." Erik stared at Valerys, open-jawed.

"Valerys has found some smaller creatures that roam the dunes. They don't have much meat, but they'll keep him going if he can catch enough. For now—" a lump caught in Calen's throat as he looked down at the N'aka's sloppy remains, the taste of vomit hitting his throat at the idea of eating it "—Vaeril, can you cook that? Once we eat, we can sleep for as long as we can spare, then keep moving at first light."

Calen turned to Erik. "Can you keep an eye out in case any more of these N'aka come looking again?"

Erik inclined his head and turned to look over the ocean of sand that still held a surprising visibility, even in the night.

"What are you going to do?" Tarmon asked.

"I'm going to check deeper inside the cave," Calen said, reaching out to the Spark, pulling on threads of Fire, Air, and Spirit, weaving them together until an orb of bright white light coalesced before him. "Make sure there's nothing waiting for us in there. I've made that mistake before."

Tarmon pulled his short sword free of its scabbard. "In pairs."

CHAPTER TWENTY

THE PATHS ONCE WALKED

Calen brought his hand to his eyes as the blazing light of the fires that burned around him cast shadows all about the village, the pearlescent moon hanging in the sky above. The smell of smoke and ash drifted on the air, thick at the back of his throat. Everywhere he looked, people ran about carrying buckets of water, screaming and shouting into the night. The noise rang in his ears, growing sharper and then dulling, as though his head was half submerged in water. He knew the voices and recognised the faces. Tach Edwin, Ferrin Kolm, Verna Gritten, Mara Styr… he was in The Glade. Panic set in. He tried to focus, settle his mind.

The last thing he remembered was leaning back against Valerys's scales as Erik and Vaeril took first watch. That's when he realised he couldn't sense Valerys. Couldn't feel the touch of the dragon's mind intermingled with his own. He'd fallen asleep. This was one of those dreams, the ones that felt real, so vivid.

A blood-chilling scream ripped through the night, sending shivers down Calen's spine, his heart thumping against his ribs; just as it had that night. *This is the night the Uraks set fire to the village… the night that Haem and the rest of the guard drove them back into Ölm Forest. The night that… No. No, I don't want to see this again.* Calen trembled, his hands shaking at his side. *Please, no.*

"Calen? What are you doing out here? It's not safe. You need to get back to the forge with the others. Dad will be looking for you." Another shiver rippled through Calen's body. He remembered those words as well. They were etched in the corners of his mind.

Calen turned to see Haem standing in front of him, a head taller with thick, broad shoulders. Streams of sweat carved paths through the dirt, blood, and ash that marred his face and matted his hair. He wore the deep blue of the town guard, covered by a leather cuirass with greaves and vambraces to match. He held his sword in his right hand; blood coated the length of its blade. He looked exactly as he had that night. Calen's heart twisted in on itself. *Haem…*

Haem rested his hand on Calen's shoulder. He had blue eyes – like Vars. "Calen, you need to go help Dad, okay? You can't come with me. Go to the Forge. Dad and Tharn Pimm are there with the others. You'll help them keep Ella and Mam safe, won't you?" A soft smile touched Haem's lips as he nodded his reassurance. "They need you over there."

"Haem, we need to go. *Now.*" Rhett Fjorn appeared by Haem's side, his sword gripped firmly in his fist, his face and armour tarnished with splatters of blood and dirt.

"Give me a moment." Haem clasped his other hand down on Calen's shoulder, holding his gaze. "I have to go. I'll be back before the morning. You'll look after Ella and Faenir for me, won't you? They're tough, but she gets scared too."

Calen could hear himself answering, saying exactly what he had said that night. "I'll keep them all safe. I promise."

But Calen knew now how hollow those words were. He hadn't kept Ella and Faenir safe. He had let them die. Just as he had let his mam and dad die. The empire had come to the Glade looking for him that day. Images of Inquisitor Rendall's blade plunging into Vars's chest flitted across Calen's mind. Farda Kyrana setting the house ablaze. His mother's screams. They had all died because of him.

Calen wanted to scream at Haem. He wanted to beg him not to go, but he couldn't. He had never been able to do anything in these dreams, only watch. The boy who stood amongst the burning buildings wasn't Calen. It was an echo of the past. Instead, he dropped to his knees, tears streaming down his now ash-coated face, as Haem and Rhett disappeared into the flames and flickering shadows. All around him, the village burned, and the screams and shouts of the villagers filled his ears. He should have argued that night. He should have gone with Haem. He was old enough to fight. He could have done something. He *should* have done something.

The world tilted and everything shifted, sending Calen's head into a spin. The houses, the flames, the people. Everything became a blur, like unconnected brush strokes of colour on a black canvas. Then, as quickly as it had started, it settled.

Dark streaks of green and brown surrounded him, a cold light shining from above. He was in a forest. Ölm Forest – he wasn't sure how he knew, but he could feel it. Nothing around him was solid. Everything seemed thrust into a constant state of motion, shifting and changing, slightly out of focus. It reminded him of being drunk on Lasch Havel's mead after a night in The Gilded Dragon. That feeling where nothing was quite as it should be, yet he still knew what it was.

The ringing of steel shrieked through the woods. Howling, clashing, colliding, and then everything shifted once more. All around him, Uraks and town guard crashed together. Massive creatures, laden with dense muscles and thick leathery skin, with weapons of blackened steel. Hazy streaks of red light trailed with every swing of the Uraks' blackened blades, matching the pulsating glow that radiated from their eyes. The ringing of steel sounded in Calen's ears. The crunching and snapping of bone, the screams of the dying, the howls of the fighting. *This can't be real... I was never here. I didn't see this. Please... don't show me this...*

"Keep pushing them back!" Haem's voice echoed through the night. Calen watched as his brother carved a blood-soaked path through the monstrosities, his sword shimmering in the light of the moon that drifted through the forest canopy. He was a force of nature. Everywhere he moved, Uraks fell, the town guard gathering around him. "Drive them back to the Ridge!"

Calen's heart thumped in his ears, swallowing all other sounds. Again, everything shifted.

"It's a trap!" Rhett Fjorn's voice rang out, echoing endlessly. Red lights flickered, leaving streaks in the night as the Uraks descended on the town guard, blackened steel slicing through leather and skin, blood spraying. Rhett and Haem stood beside Durin and Almin Netly, Fritz's brothers, the rest of the town guard gathered about them. The Uraks crashed into the guard like a raging river. Calen watched as Almin's head was taken from his shoulders, and Durin's left leg was cleaved at the knee. It was a massacre. *They never stood a chance.*

"Fall back!" Haem's voice rang out. "Fall back!"

The guards tried to flee, but the Uraks cut them down as they ran, carving through them as though they were only playthings.

"Haem, we need to go!" Rhett called.

Calen's vision blurred and flashed. He looked to see his brother standing over the prone body of Durin Netly, his sword sweeping in glittering arcs of steel. Haem deflected a blackened blade to his left, then drove his sword up through the creature's chin, sliding it back out in a spray of blood. Two more of the beasts fell to Haem's blade before a black spear tip sliced his thigh, and he let out a howl. He drove his blade through the creature's chest, collapsing backwards as the spear tip was wrenched free by the dying Urak's grip.

"Haem!" Rhett's scream was so loud it sounded as though his throat might bleed. He charged towards Haem, his blade slicing through Uraks as he moved. A blackened steel blade plunged into his shoulder, another sliced at the meat of his thigh. He kept pushing. An arrow caught him in the calf, and he dropped to one knee, almost immediately dragging himself back to his feet and taking an Urak's head from its body. Rhett was within touching distance of Haem when a black spear burst through

Haem's gut, blood spilling from the wound and out through his fingers. Haem dropped to his knees, swallowed by the mass of leathery skin.

"No!" Rhett charged but was sent careening into the base of a tree as a monstrously large Urak swiped his legs from under him. Rhett turned as he fell, moving to strike out with his blade, but the Urak slammed its foot down on Rhett's arm, the violent sound of snapping bones ringing clear in the night. Rhett's scream chilled Calen's blood.

The enormous Urak twisted its leathery fingers through Rhett's hair, hauling him to his feet. In its other hand, it raised a blackened steel sword, a glowing red gemstone set into its blade, pulsating with hazy red light. As the creature drew back its arm, Rhett's hand moved in a flash of steel. The beast howled, dropping its sword and clawing at its eye, where a steel pommelled knife now protruded. With a guttural roar, the creature launched Rhett backwards into the woods, sending him tumbling through the foliage. *Rhett never left Haem. He went back for him.* At that moment, Calen swore he could feel his heart bleed, tears burning his eyes. Vars had treated Rhett like a gutless coward. He had said things that could never be taken back. And Rhett had never once said anything in return. He had let Calen's dad unleash every drop of his pain and fury, while never arguing. But in the end, Rhett hadn't left Haem to die. He had been willing to give his life for his friend, without the slightest hesitation. He should have been treated like a hero. He should have been treated like a son.

Once more, the world around Calen shifted. Vibrant greens and reds flashing past Calen's eyes, everything blurring, a weightlessness setting in his stomach.

When everything settled, he was still standing in the forest, but the fighting was over. Corpses littered the ground, Uraks and humans alike, limbs severed, shattered bones breaking through skin. Blood mixed with the clay and dirt on the ground, pooling in hollows. There were no cries or moans, no calling out and wailing in pain. Only death. When Calen focused, the world became clearer, sharper, and he could see the faces of the dead. Almin and Durin Netly lay beside each other, crumpled in heaps. Lara Birwick was pinned to a tree by a spear through the right side of her chest, her gut sliced open, intestines piled on the ground before her, steam wafting. Juran Styr, Lina's older brother, was cleaved in half at the navel, his body splayed over a flat rock. Everywhere he looked, he saw the faces of those he knew. Faces he never thought he would see again. Men and women who had marched into Ölm forest that night and never returned.

A spluttering sound drew Calen's attention, and once more, the world shifted. He now stood amongst the bodies, only a foot from Almin and

Durin. Another cough and a splutter. Calen turned to see Haem lying on his back, his fingers clasped tight to the wound in his gut, blood spilling through the cracks. Calen ran to Haem, crashing to the ground at his side.

"It's all right," Calen said, resting his hand atop Haem's, touching his left to his brother's cheek. Even though part of him knew this wasn't real, his heart pulled against him. "Please. Please, Haem, don't leave me."

But despite Calen's sobs, Haem didn't so much as turn. He lay there, his hand to his gut, spluttering, lifting his head to look at the wound. With a groan, Haem let his head collapse back down onto the bloodied earth. Calen could see him trying to speak, but every time he opened his mouth, blood splattered up over his lip.

"He is alive?"

"Yes, Brother-Captain. Though he is not long for this world."

Calen spun around, falling backwards on his arse at the sight of four warriors covered head to toe in smooth green plate. White capes hung from their shoulders, and the slits in their helms shimmered with green light. *They're the warriors who had saved us at Kingspass, the ones who Haem fought beside.*

The warrior at the front knelt beside Haem, ignoring Calen as though he weren't even there.

Words passed between Haem and the warrior, muffled to Calen's ears, then once more becoming clear.

The green-plated warrior leaned over Haem. "If we save you, are you willing to forgo your past life and everything that holds you to the person you are now? Are you willing to bear the Sigil of Achyron? To follow his creed and serve The Warrior until the day you are taken from this world?… Let it be known that if you take the Sigil of Achyron and betray his creed, the life will be stripped from your bones in the most painful way that you could imagine. It is not an easy cross to bear. Will you accept it?"

Calen watched as Haem choked, blood sprinkling from his mouth. "Yes."

Once more, the words became muffled, and time seemed to flicker. The man now held a strange piece of metal in his hand. It was the same greenish hue as the armour he wore, and it was wrought in the shape of a downward-facing sword set into a sunburst – the same symbol the warriors bore on the breast of their armour. He held the metallic symbol over Haem's chest, then pressed down. Smoke plumed into the air, and Haem screamed.

Calen tried to move, to leap towards his brother, but his body wouldn't respond. He was frozen in place. Everything shifted. The forest dissolved to an empty blackness, the echoes of Haem's screams reverberating in Calen's mind.

They saved him.

CALEN DRAGGED IN A RAGGED breath of scorching air, the sun blazing in the sky above. Sand crunched under his feet as he climbed towards the top of the dune where Vaeril already stood, his green cloak flapping in the wind. Calen's legs felt as though they had been hollowed out and filled with lead, each step taking the effort of two. His muscles ached and burned, begging him to rest, and he could feel the blisters forming on his heels and the sides of his feet, the scratching of his boots against dried skin. The sand sank and pulled with each step, actively leaching the energy from his body.

They had spent at least a week marching as quickly as their bodies would allow, stopping only to catch their breath, drink, eat and sleep. Each day took more from them than the last, wearing them out, breaking them down, their tempers growing shorter. Since the N'aka had first attacked, more of the beasts had continued to stalk them. By day, the N'aka kept their distance, trailing a few miles from the group, prowling in the dunes. As Valerys soared, he had seen them in packs of three or four, watching, waiting. Every time the dragon swooped, they scattered into the dunes. By night, they came closer, their eyes glimmering in the perpetual half-light, a pulsating noise reverberating from their throats, like the sound a stone makes when it's skimmed across a lake. They never attacked. They waited.

As the group marched, Calen had spent almost every waking moment reliving the dream he'd had of The Glade. Of Haem. Going over and over it in his mind. Could it possibly have been real, or was he simply losing himself? Could it have been like the dreams Rokka spoke of? But of the past instead of the future. Calen cursed himself. He should have asked the old man when he'd had the chance. It didn't matter either way. Calen wasn't a druid. He wasn't even sure Rokka was. *I'm going mad.*

He stopped for a moment, giving his legs much needed respite as he pulled his waterskin from the satchel strapped to his back, sighing in relief as the cool liquid touched his cracked lips. Replacing the waterskin, he called out to Vaeril. "Anything?"

The elf stood in silence, staring at whatever lay on the other side of the dune. In the past few days, the heat and exhaustion had gotten to them all. Tarmon and Erik's tempers had frayed on more than one occasion, and Vaeril had grown increasingly silent and withdrawn.

"Vaeril," Calen called out again, resting his hand on the elf's shoulder. "Is there anything…"

Calen's words caught in his throat as he looked over the other side of the dune. Shattered towers and broken walls of tarnished whitish stone pierced through the blanket of sand, the rotting corpse of a once great city. The longer Calen looked, the more he saw. The crumbled remains of homes, temples, and markets. Streets flooded with sand and rock. The ruined husk of what must have once been the keep.

As Calen looked out over the ruins of the city, everything shifted, just as it had in his dreams. His vision flickered, sharpening then dulling, tinting with a bluish hue.

"By the gods." Erik stepped up beside Calen, Tarmon at his side. "Calen, what's wrong with you?"

Erik's voice dulled, becoming muffled in the back of Calen's mind. Calen closed his eyes, shaking his head, burying his fingers into his scalp, a low ringing noise resounding in his ears. *Stop it. Stop it.*

As though responding to his thoughts, the ringing noise halted, yielding to silence. Calen opened his eyes, light and sound crashing over him.

He no longer stood at the top of the dune. Grass and earth lay beneath his feet, tall trees of vivid green spreading out on either side of him, the smell of fresh baked bread drifting on the breeze. Before him, the sun sprayed down over a city easily as large as Midhaven, ringed by enormous walls of white stone broken by flat-topped towers adorned with rippling banners of red emblazoned with a golden stag.

The trill of birdsong rang through the air, accompanied by the chatter and noise of a bustling city. Axles squeaked, children laughed, feet slapped against stone, hawkers and pedlars hollered, their voices blending into a cacophony of shouts.

Calen took a step forward, his jaw agape. *What in the name of Elyara is happening?* He looked out at the city, watching as flocks of birds swerved between the rising towers and streams of people marched through the enormous gates. It felt as real as his vivid dreams. Real enough to touch. But he wasn't asleep? How could this be a dream? A strange blend of worry and awe rushed through Calen's mind, spilling over from Valerys's. He could feel the air breaking on the dragon's scales as Valerys dove through the clouds above, watching the world through Calen's eyes.

But just as Valerys broke through the bank of clouds, the world shifted once more, flickering. Bone-chilling screams echoed, a shiver sweeping over Calen's skin. The feeling of awe that permeated the air twisted, warping into something more akin to pure horror, chilling Calen's blood, his throat tightening, his heart seizing. A wall of deep red, almost black, fire swept over the land, moving like a wave, hundreds of feet into the air, stretching as far as Calen's eyes could see. His vision went black, then flashed with images. Waves of sound battered his mind: screams, shrieks, howls. The dark fire crashing into the walls, sweeping over the city, unyielding, unrelenting. Elves screamed and shrieked as their flesh was burned from their bones, their souls stripped from their bodies. Calen dropped to his knees, the sheer abject grief clutching him in its grasp as thousands of lives were scoured from the world. Tears streamed down his face, an unabating ache clutching his chest. A sickly, oily sensation swept through the air, probing at the corners of Calen's mind, pushing, scratching, grabbing. Then it was gone.

Calen's vision flickered once more, and he was kneeling in the sand at the top of the dune he had been standing on, the ruins splayed out across the landscape before him, the fire gone. His shoulders convulsed; his gaze fixed on the city.

"Calen!" Erik dropped to the sand beside him, his hands clasping on Calen's shoulders, fingers wrapping around his cloak. "What's wrong?"

Calen could feel the tears still streaking down his face. In the back of his mind, he could still see the images of the fire. The death. The destruction. "I… saw something…"

"What do you mean? What did you see?" Erik pulled at Calen's head, trying to look into his eyes, but Calen just stared past him towards the city.

Valerys dropped from the sky, his white scales tarnished with a brownish hue, his shadow momentarily blocking out the sun as he spread his wings, cracking them against the air, sweeping clouds of sand into the spirals. A deep pain and sadness seeped from the dragon's mind into Calen's. Their shared soul ached. So many lives gone, snuffed out in an instant.

"I saw what happened here…" Calen's thoughts were jumbled in his head. Lingering remnants of the vision flickering through his mind. "That night… the night The Order fell… The fire from Therin's stories. It killed everyone…" Calen gripped Erik's forearm, bringing his left leg up, and heaved himself back to his feet along with Erik.

"Calen, for fuck's sake, you're not making any damn sense." Erik's fingers tightened around Calen's cloak, the irritation that had made its home in Erik's voice over the past few days returning. "How could you have seen it? That was centuries ago."

Calen rounded on Erik, tears still in his eyes. The emotions that swirled within him took over. "I watched them die, Erik." The screams echoed in Calen's mind. The shrieks as fire burned flesh and rent souls. "I…" Calen shook his head. "I can't explain it. But I saw it."

"Let go of him." Tarmon grabbed Erik's forearm, yanking his hands off Calen's cloak.

"Don't touch me," Erik snarled, squaring off against the Lord Captain, who was over a head taller than he was.

A deafening roar erupted from Valerys as the dragon leaned his head forward, a deep rumble resonating from his throat. Valerys broadened his chest, his wing spreading, lips pulling back in a snarl, exposing rows of alabaster teeth. Both Tarmon and Erik took a step back.

Calen stepped between Erik and Tarmon, placing Valerys at his back. "This place is getting to us all." Calen took a moment, battling the sorrow that lingered from the vision. He gritted his teeth. "The heat, the lack of sleep, the exhaustion, those gods damned creatures stalking us day and night. *Take a breath.* This place wants us dead. Don't make its job easier." He pulled his waterskin from his pack, tossing it to Erik. "Drink. We'll rest for a minute and go around."

"It's quicker if we go through." Erik gripped Calen's waterskin, the muscles in his hand tightening, his jaw clenching, his eyes fixed on Calen.

"Erik, I don't want to go through. Horrible things happened here." Memories flitted across Calen's eyes. Flesh peeling from bones, skin bubbling. "Unspeakable things."

"Why is that your decision to make?" Erik stepped closer to Calen. The tip of his nose was red and burned, a blister forming at the side of his nostril. His lips were cracked and broken, dried from the sun. Their moods had all been short as the Burnt Lands took their toll, but Erik's had been shortest. "This place is almost as bad as those damn tunnels. It doesn't end. And those *things* don't stop. They're just waiting for one of us to weaken. Waiting for this place to wear us down. I'm not spending another minute more here than I have to. This isn't where I die."

"Easy, Erik," Tarmon said, resting his hand on Erik's shoulder, grunting as he shifted the weight of his satchel. "We have seen our way through worse than this. If there are things in that city Calen fears, then we can go around. We can take an hour less sleep, make up the time."

"Get your damn hand off me," Erik snapped, swiping Tarmon's hand away, his tone changing from irritated to enraged in an instant. He turned, attempting to meet Tarmon's gaze, but the Lord Captain stood a head taller. "You're always there, aren't you? Standing behind Calen like a lapdog, brooding, waiting to do whatever he says. It's pathetic." Erik shoved Tarmon in the chest, catching the bigger man off guard, sending him stumbling backwards a step or two.

"You're one to talk." Tarmon cracked his neck side to side, dropping his satchels into the sand. "That's all you do," Tarmon said, pushing Erik back. "Talk, talk, talk. But every time your back's against the wall, you crumble. You're weak," he said, hitting his closed fist against his chest. "In here—" he tapped two fingers against his temple "—and in here. I need to stand behind Calen, as does Vaeril, because if it were only you at his back, he'd be dead already. You'd have died in those tunnels, shaking and weeping. Broken."

"You're going to protect him like you protected your king, are you?" Erik's voice dripped with malice. It was as though he were another person entirely. "Because that turned out so well."

"Watch your fucking tongue, boy." Tarmon's hand dropped to the pommel of his short sword. "Your father's name won't protect you out here!"

"Both of you, stand down!" Calen stepped between Erik and Tarmon, pushing them in the opposite directions. "What is wrong with you?"

Realisation flashed across Erik's eyes, a look of shock on his face, then it was gone. He glared at Tarmon, his jaw clenched. "I just want to get out of this place. We can go around, but we better make up the time."

Without another word, Erik stormed off, making his way down the side of the dune, the sand tumbling beneath his feet.

"Tarmon, I…" Even as Calen was speaking, Tarmon snatched up his satchels and walked past him, following after Erik, his fists clenched at his side, a cold look in his eyes. Vaeril followed after Tarmon without a word, only giving Calen a passing glance.

A low rumble resonated from Valerys's chest as the dragon lowered his head, his gaze moving between the others and the ruined city.

"I don't know," Calen said in answer to an unspoken question. Something was wrong with their family, something deeper than exhaustion and hunger. The Burnt Lands was getting inside their heads.

Valerys's head snapped to the left, and a jolt of awareness rippled through Calen. Calen let himself see through Valerys's eyes. Not so far away, only fifty or sixty feet from Erik, dark shapes prowled through the dunes, hiding amongst rock formations and patches of brittle thorny bushes, moving slowly and steadily – N'aka. It was as though the creatures could sense weakness.

"Fly low," Calen said, resting his hand against the ridge of horns that framed Valerys's jawline. "Make sure they see you."

A rumble of agreement touched the back of Calen's mind and Valerys lifted into the air. Calen would have much rather climbed onto the dragon's back and felt the cool touch of the wind against his cheeks, but Valerys was still weak from Kingspass, and something told Calen he would be needed on the ground. Had he not been there just then, Tarmon and Erik would likely have bled each other into the sand.

Letting out a long sigh, Calen set off down the side of the dune after the others.

"Here," Aeson called, rising to his feet and letting out a sigh as he cast his gaze across the ridge before him that marked the borders of the Burnt Lands, the sun unnaturally warm overhead. Sweat slicked his brow and dripped from the tip of nose.

Dann, Therin, and Baldon were spread out around him, while Thalanil and his elves searched even further along the ridge. They had spent hours looking for signs that Calen, Erik, and the others might have already entered the Burnt Lands. With each hour that passed, Aeson had grown more hopeful that they had beaten them to the pass. But now a sinking feeling took hold of his gut.

Therin and Dann were by his side in a matter of seconds, the latter on his knees, his fingers touching the claw marks indented in the dried clay.

"They've already entered."

Aeson nodded, his jaw clenching.

"What are we waiting for?" Dann asked, rising to his feet as the elves gathered around them, green cloaks flapping in the hot wind. "We finally know for sure that they have come this way."

Aeson didn't answer the question. He stared down at the claw mark, then up towards the ridge, grimacing as the sun's glare caught his eyes.

"We had hoped to cut them off before they got here. We can't follow them through," Therin said. "To enter the Burnt Lands is to forfeit your life. There is no crossing."

"What are you saying?" Dann took a step closer to Therin, but the elf turned his gaze to the ground. "Therin. What the fuck are you saying?"

"He's saying they're already dead." As soon as the words left Aeson's lips, his heart twisted and his gut turned. *Erik.*

"No." Dann shook his head, that same steel in his eyes that Aeson had seen in the tunnels. His gaze locked on Therin's. "No."

Dann turned and made to walk off towards the ridge, but Therin caught him, clasping his hand on Dann's shoulder. "Dann, going in there is a death sentence."

"And staying here is Calen's death sentence. He'd go after me, Therin. Don't tell me he wouldn't."

"What's done is done, Dann. He's already gone through. That can't be changed. Calen might be alive – they all might be. They might find a way to the other side. All we can do is hope. But if we go in there, we *will* die. There is no rescuing him."

"I'm going in," Aeson said, his voice firm.

Therin's brow furrowed in confusion. "Aeson, you know as well as any that you can't. We've tried before. We barely made it out alive. The Svidar'Cia warps your mind."

"My son is in there, Therin. I promised Naia."

"And what happens to Dahlen when you die in there?"

"I—"

"And what about the rebellion you've built? You hold fury at Calen for chasing after Rist when he should be here, yet you do the same thing."

"It's different!" Aeson roared, stepping closer to Therin, his fist clenched at his side. He hadn't felt his anger begin to rise.

"There is more at stake here than one man's life. That is what you said. It was true when you said it, and it's true now."

Aeson's blood boiled in his veins. He clenched his fist so tight his arm shook. No matter what decision he made, he'd be abandoning one of his sons. What kind of choice was that? What kind of cruel god would force that upon him after how much he had already lost?

Therin cupped Aeson's cheek. "We need to use our heads. Going in after them won't help anyone. If you walk in there, Dahlen will be left alone. Naia would never want that."

"So we abandon them?" The fury in Dann's voice mimicked that which burned in Aeson's veins.

"No, we trust them." The elf turned to Baldon, who stood a few feet away, his fur-covered head tilted in curiosity, his fangs glistening white. "Baldon, can you communicate with the Angan of Clan Fenryr on the other side, see if they can watch the edge of the Burnt Lands?"

"For the son of the Chainbreaker, my clan would cross into the void itself," the Angan said, bowing his head. "It will take some time, though. No son or daughter of Fenryr resides within your 'Burnt Lands', for fear of the madness. I will have to thread a thought chord around its edges and await a response."

"Please."

"It will be done, Silver Fang." Baldon inclined his head, then folded his legs where he stood, dropping himself to the ground, his golden eyes closing.

Aeson's breath trembled as he looked down at the Angan, then to Therin, then to Dann, whose face was carved fury. Aeson wanted to roar, he wanted to drag in threads of Earth and shake the ground. But instead, he simply stood there, staring down at Baldon.

Please. Please don't take him from me, too.

CHAPTER TWENTY-ONE

ON THE BRINK

"I t smells like shit." Belina stood with her arms folded, her head just shy of touching the roof of the freshly Spark-carved, cylindrical tunnel they stood in.

"There's no shit, Belina. You just watched Ariveer carve it with the Spark. It hasn't been used for sewage yet."

"Well then, I can smell the shit that will be here in the future. So, this is Kira's big plan? Finish connecting the sewage system for the refugee quarters and have us march through it? She's a cunning bitch, making us walk through shit. You've got to admire her."

"There's no shit." When Kira had first suggested the plan, Dahlen had argued with her about the fact the Belduarans had gone that long without a functioning sewage system when all she'd had to do was commission a Craftsmage to finish the work. It was then he'd discovered the blame for the sewage system not being completed could not be entirely laid at the dwarves' feet. Daymon and his nobles had not been able to come to an agreement with the dwarves as to the compensation they would receive when the Belduaran people had finally been able to resettle themselves. Dahlen could have understood if the dwarves had been trying to extort the Belduarans, but according to Kira, all the dwarves had wanted was a supply of fresh, above-ground grown fruit and vegetables, to which Daymon had responded by breaking off negotiations. Kira could have been lying or simply stretching the truth, but honestly, it sounded like something Daymon would have done.

A few feet ahead of Dahlen, Ariveer, the Alamant Craftsmage who Kira had commissioned to carve the tunnel into the refugee quarters, had stopped and turned to Belina and Dahlen. He was an elf, dark hair falling over tapered ears. "All right, we're at the edge now. One more push and we're through. Once you pass through, I'll close the opening behind you so nobody will discover your passage. I will wait here for six hours. When you come back, tap something metal against the rock. After six hours, you'll be on your own."

"All right, thank you, Ariveer."

The elf nodded. "Are you ready?"

"Wait, no." Belina scratched at her chin. "How will we know when six hours have passed? We won't exactly be stopping to check the clocks on the walls, and there's no way I can count for that long. I've the attention span of a drunk fish."

Ariveer gave Belina a strange look. "My apologies. This is for you." The elf reached into the pocket of his trousers and produced a small golden sphere attached to a long chain, about the size of Dahlen's palm. It looked like a closed metallic seashell with spirals and patterns carved into its surface.

"What is it?" Dahlen asked as he took the object from Ariveer, surprised at its deceptive weight.

"May I?"

Dahlen nodded, and the elf reached out and pressed his finger against something on the object's side, eliciting a sharp click as it opened to reveal an interior that looked like a smaller version of a clock, the numbers one through twelve etched into its surface, moving around the edge of the circle in evenly spaced intervals. A golden clock hand was fixed at the centre.

"It's a timekeeper," the elf said, gesturing towards the clock hand and around at the etched numbers. "It's a clock, but it fits in your pocket. A recent dwarven invention. Compressing everything into such a small space means it's not particularly accurate, but it gets the job done. It's already wound and synchronised to my own timekeeper."

Dahlen looked at the timekeeper, then closed it and hung the chain over his neck, tucking it beneath his shirt. He'd left his leather armour in the smuggler's den and instead wore a linen shirt and padded trousers along with a sword, that Belina had acquired for him, strapped to his hip. The refugee quarters were likely teeming with people, which meant blending in would be their best chance. "All right. We're ready."

Ariveer nodded and turned back to the wall of stone that closed off the end of the tunnel.

"Oleg first," Dahlen said to Belina as Ariveer began to carve a small passage through the rock and into the section of the sewage system that had already been constructed. "He'll be able to tell us where they're keeping the assassin. We get him, we get out. No detours."

"It's a straight-forward plan, Dahlen. I don't think we need a recap."

Dahlen nodded, letting out a sigh. He'd said it aloud more for himself rather than Belina. His experience at The Cloak and Dagger in Azmar had only cemented that subterfuge was not his strong suit. Steel and blood. They were his currency. What he'd trained for. What he knew. Fighting, at the very least, was quick. There was no time to worry and fret, to let anxiety sink in. All this sneaking around set his heart hammering and twisted an unabating knot in his stomach. "Remember," he said, looking Belina in the eye, "no killing."

"So you keep saying, but that's going to make this a lot more difficult."

"*No killing, Belina.* The Belduarans are on our side. They're good people."

"Not even a little maiming?"

Dahlen narrowed his eyes, turning to watch as Ariveer stood before them, his hand twisting and turning, fingers moving, the stone before him melting into liquid, pulling back into the tunnel and melding smooth with the already-carved stone. No light came through from the other side, but Dahlen could feel the emerging breeze touch his skin. He coughed and gagged, a putrid odour filling his nostrils and catching in his throat. "Fuck." He retched, putting his hand to his stomach, trying to hold back the vomit. "What in the gods is that smell?"

Belina held her shirt up over her mouth and nose. "I told you I could smell shit."

Ariveer turned back to them, pinching his nose between his finger and thumb. "I made the opening above the waste on the other side. If you climb up and stay to the right, you should avoid falling into the pool."

"The pool?"

"Without adequate waste drainage, the sewage on the other side has been funnelling into the holding pool, building up. Just stay to the right."

"Fantastic."

ONCE DAHLEN AND BELINA HAD climbed through the opening, Ariveer had closed it behind them, and they'd made their way up through the main tunnel, then climbed out into a service corridor. Dahlen now stood at the edge of an open stone doorway, looking out over one of the sweeping walkways that bridged the divide between the two sides of the enormous cavern that was the refugee quarters.

Men, women, and children hobbled along the walkway, their clothes tattered and dirty, weakness born of hunger obvious in their lethargic motions. The clamour of footfalls and shouts filled the air, rising from the main street and the lower levels. Dahlen had no doubt the stench in the cavern would have turned his stomach had they not spent the previous half hour walking alongside a river of human excrement.

Dahlen and Belina stepped out onto the walkway, pushing through the crowd and making their way to the stone ledge that framed its edge. He rested his arms on the ledge and looked over the refugee quarters. Rows upon rows of doors and walkways were set into the wall on the other side of the gargantuan cavern, sets of staircases connecting each level to the next, rising hundreds of feet from the ground below to the ceiling above. Innumerable walkways spanned the gap between the two sides of the cavern, an intricate spider's web of stone.

A few hundred feet below, the main street of the refugee quarters was crammed with people like grains of sand shifting past each other, shouts, footfall, and chatter echoing through the chamber.

Dahlen looked towards the entrance to the refugee quarters that led out towards Durakdur. A low wall had been erected at the top of the stone staircase that descended into the main street. It was difficult to see anything at that distance, but the bluish-green light of the flower lanterns glimmered off the steel plate of the soldiers who were lined across the entrance, standing ready.

"Before the attacks, Daymon assigned Oleg a small room to act as his office not far from here," Dahlen said to Belina, still looking out over the shifting mass of people on the street below. He pointed up towards a walkway that ran along the opposite wall. "It's on the other side, three levels up, marked with the symbol of Belduar on the door."

"Let's get going, then." Belina looked about her, a worry on her face Dahlen wasn't used to seeing. Her gaze fell on a young man walking past, his eyes sunken, face gaunt. "Hunger is a horrific way to go."

"You know, empathy suits you," Dahlen said as he pushed himself away from the ledge and started off through the crowd, Belina following.

Belina frowned, giving a shrug. "Too much of it can get you killed. Selective empathy. That's a survivor's method right there." Belina pushed past two men who were arguing over what looked to be a piece of hard, mouldy bread. "How have they gone through the food so quickly?"

"There isn't much food stored here. Logistically, the dwarves can only provide enough for a few days at a time. Feeding tens of thousands of people is no easy task, and the balance of farming and consumption in these mountains is delicate. They've sacrificed a lot to help us." Dahlen thought back to when he had first entered the refugee quarters with Ihvon to help distribute rations and how he had gone back many times again to help. There had been something warming about helping people without spilling blood.

Belina nodded, using her hands to steer her way through the crowd as Dahlen led her across the bridge to the other side of the chamber. A few people gave Dahlen a second look as though recognising him, but none of them said anything, for which he was grateful. The last thing he needed was to draw any attention to himself.

"So, are you going to tell me why you neglected to tell Kira about Daymon's involvement in everything with Pulroan?"

Dahlen frowned, stepping off the bridge and turning left towards the nearest staircase that led to the next level up, wading through the river of refugees. "I considered it. But telling her would've implicated Daymon in whatever is happening here. And although I'd like little more than to see Daymon dangle from a noose, it would be the Belduaran people who would suffer. They would be not only without a leader, but without a home, and the dwarves surely would not continue to shelter a people whose leader had made an attempt on their own. I thought it better to keep that information close for now. If we somehow find a way out the other side of all this, I'm sure I'll find a way to use it."

"You know, you're not half as stupid as you look."

"I think that's actually the nicest thing you've said to me."

Belina shrugged, pouting in agreement. "It might be the nicest thing I've said to anyone."

"That's eh… yeah. That's a little sad."

Dahlen led Belina up a series of three staircases and along a walkway until they finally came to a metal door with an etching of a crossed axe and sword in front of a lonely mountain.

As he rested his hand on the cold door handle, Dahlen saw Belina tap her fingers against the pommel of one of the many knives strapped to the belt at her hip. He frowned at her.

"I know, I know. No killing." She gestured for Dahlen to open the door.

The office looked as Dahlen had remembered it when he'd visited with Ihvon, except where previously it had been neat and meticulously arranged, it was now a mess. Lanterns of Heraya's Ward were strewn about the room haphazardly, some hanging from the ceiling, some resting atop stacks of papers Oleg had brought from his permanent embassy in the Heart a few weeks back, and others sat on the floor or atop the emissary's desk.

Nothing adorned the smooth stone walls, and the room itself was relatively sparse. A few items of clothing lay in heaps on the stone, and sheets of parchment were scattered about the place. Archways were set into the far wall and the wall that stood on the left side of the room, one leading to a small study and the other leading to a tiny rectangular area with a single straw-filled mattress.

"Anthea, is that you? We need to find a way to get through to Daymon. According to these numbers, we'll be out of food in a matter of days. What did Captain Harnet say? Does she think there's a way to reach the Queen?" Dahlen couldn't help but smile as Oleg Marylin stepped through the archway set into the wall on the left side of the room, scratching at his unkempt beard with one hand, an open ledger held out with the other, a pair of reading glasses resting on the bridge of his nose. The man stood there in silence for a moment, turning the page of the ledger, his eyes flitting across the words written within. "Anthea? Has someone stolen your tongue?"

The man continued to read through the ledger, anxiously scratching at his beard. He tried to turn the page again but found it stuck to the page behind it. He frowned, licking his finger, then swiping the page across.

Dahlen let another moment or two pass before he spoke. "Oleg, it's me."

The man jumped at the sound of Dahlen's voice, scrambling to grab hold of the ledger as it fell from his grasp. "Sweet mother of my mother's mother! My lord, what are you doing here?" Oleg tossed the ledger on the desk beside the door, scurried past Dahlen, and stuck his head out onto the walkway, looking frantically from side to side. "Did anyone see you?" The emissary pulled the door closed, sliding a bolt across it, then pressed his back against the metal, drawing in laboured breaths, resting a hand on his belly, sliding the other one across his hairless head. "I thought you were dead. We all did. I'd heard Daymon had you arrested, but then when you disappeared after the attack in the Heart, we assumed you'd been killed."

"As you can see, Oleg. I'm still very much alive. And I'm going to need your help if we're going to get out of this. But before that, how is Ihvon? Has he recovered?"

The man nodded slowly. "Yes, my lord. But... the king... Once he learns you're alive..."

"Oleg, I have some things to tell you about your king, but they are to stay between us, for now."

"Oh!" The man's eyebrows shot up, and he lifted a finger into the air. "One moment. Stay right there."

"Oleg we don't have time for this." Dahlen puffed out his cheeks in exasperation, running his hand through his hair as Oleg disappeared back through the archway.

"He's kind of cute," Belina said with a downturn of her lip. "In a 'jittery uncle who can't remember where his shoes are' kind of way."

Dahlen stifled a laugh at that.

"Here," Oleg said, stumbling over a book on the floor as he stepped back through the archway carrying a long bundle of cloth. "You can thank Lumeera. She had them carried from the Heart. When you disappeared, she gave them to me for safekeeping."

Oleg folded back the cloth, revealing a glint of steel beneath.

"My swords..." Dahlen reached out, running his fingers across the steel. "Oleg..." He shook his head, a smile spreading across his face. "I owe both you and Lumeera a debt that I can't articulate. Thank you. I don't have my scabbards with me. Can you do me one more favour and have them left by the sewage holding pool?"

"Do I want to know?"

DAHLEN STOOD ON A CROWDED walkway on the upper levels of the refugee quarters, leaning against a tall stone pillar, his gaze fixed on a metal door that stood at the top of a narrow stone staircase, two guards in polished plate and purple cloaks standing on either side.

"This is where they're keeping him?" Belina stood beside him, running her thumb along the blade of a throwing knife that fit in the palm of her hand. The woman carried more weapons than Dahlen could count.

"The refugee quarters weren't made with prisoners in mind. If Oleg says the assassin is being held here, this is where he is." He pulled the timekeeper from beneath his shirt, clicking open the latch. "Two hours before we need to be back."

"Plenty of time. As long as your anxious little friend comes through on his word."

"Oleg is a good man."

"I hear that a lot," Belina said, shrugging. "What is a 'good man'? What defines 'good'? What I've noticed is those who describe *themselves* as good men are often far from it. And those whom *others* describe as good men tend to have a nasty habit of dying young."

Dahlen frowned, closing over the timekeeper and sliding it back under his shirt. He looked through the crowd, searching for any signs of the distraction Oleg was to arrange. "A good man is a man who does what they know to be right."

Belina gave Dahlen an amused look, slipping her finger into the ring that sat at the end of the throwing knife, spinning it. "You live in a world of black and white, Dahlen. Though I'm sure you'll soon see the grey."

Dahlen made to argue, but a man's voice roared, rising above the chatter and footfall. "We want food!" the man called out. "We *need* food!"

Other voices cried out in agreement, the atmosphere of the crowd turning on a pinhead. Dahlen could feel the tension shift in the air.

"A true king feeds his people!"

More and more people stopped, their chants rising in fervour.

"A true king fills his people's bellies instead of his own! He doesn't allow his people to be penned in a cage with disease and hunger taking us one by one!"

Dahlen looked towards the two Kingsguard who stood either side of the metal doorway that guarded the building where the assassin was being kept. Both of them had taken a step down the stone stairs, trying to get a better look at what was causing the crowd to gather and chant.

Dahlen saw the glint of armour throughout the crowd, caught by the bluish-green flowerlight of the lanterns. *It's working.*

"I haven't eaten in three days!" a woman cried.

"My little girl is coughing up blood! We can't stay here!"

Another shift rippled through the crowd, an anger bubbling, a rage festering. The change was so sudden, Dahlen almost couldn't believe it. Shouts and cries rang out, men and women roaring at the top of their lungs.

"They've taken the bait," Belina whispered.

Dahlen looked towards the doorway and saw the two guards no longer stood watch. He cast a worried glance towards the baying crowd. He had wanted Oleg to create a distraction, not start a riot.

"Come on." Belina grabbed Dahlen by the arm and heaved him forward, dragging him through the crowd. "These kinds of things are like wild-fires. You've got to let them burn themselves out."

Belina and Dahlen pushed their way through the crowd, ascending the steps to the metal door set into the wall of the cavern, Dahlen casting one last look over his shoulder before they stepped inside.

The entranceway of the building was nothing more than a short, barren corridor, devoid of any signs of life. None of the Belduarans had been in any way eager to turn this place into a home. The corridor was narrow, maybe five or six feet across, just enough to swing a sword. Four flower lanterns sat on flat sconces set into the walls, alternating, two on each side, a metal door directly across from each lantern. At the corridor's end, it branched off left and right.

"Oleg said they're holding the man down the end of the corridor on the left, and that there's usually only two or three of the Kingsguard stationed in here at any one time. Daymon can't spare the numbers."

"Well, best get to it, then. No time to lose." Belina set off down the corridor, her steps as light as feathers. "Follow my lead," she whispered, giving Dahlen a wink.

"Belina."

Belina kept walking, picking up her pace.

"Belina," Dahlen hissed, keeping his voice as low as possible. He had been on the other end of one of Belina's plans before, in The Cloak and Dagger, and it was not an experience he was looking forward to repeating. "Belina…" He reached out and grabbed a hold of her shirt, tugging.

Belina stopped, wrapping her fingers around his wrist. "Your mother was a whore and your father is an arsehole. You're a combination of both."

"What?" Dahlen squeezed his hand around the fabric of her shirt. He knew she was playing with him, he just wasn't sure how. "Belina, why would you…"

Belina tugged at Dahlen's wrist, the side of her linen shirt ripping, exposing dark skin. Then she pulled a throwing knife from her belt and sliced a thin gash across the top of her forearm. She rubbing her fingers in the blood and spread it across her face, sliding the knife back into place. Before Dahlen had any idea what was happening, she shoved him backwards and dashed around the corner.

"Belina!" Dahlen called in a hushed voice, chasing her. "What are you…" Dahlen let his words trail off. Three guards in burnished plate stood before a metal door at the end of the corridor, purple cloaks knotted at their shoulders. Belina broke into a full run, and her plan finally clicked into place in Dahlen's mind. "No, Belina, don't you dare!"

"Please!" Belina called out, faking a stumble, her voice rising twice as high as he'd ever heard it. She sounded like a damsel from the bards' stories, her shirt ripped, blood spread across her face. She glanced back, winking. "Help me! He's trying to kill me!"

"Fuck it, Belina. Why do you always use me as bait?" Dahlen ripped his sword from its scabbard, setting his feet as the three Kingsguard pulled their swords free and moved towards Belina. He didn't want to kill any of the guards, but he was pretty sure they wouldn't share the same sentiment when it came to him.

Belina threw herself to the ground, flailing theatrically. It was like watching a bard act out a drama.

The three Kingsguard put themselves between Dahlen and Belina, each of them holding sharp steel in their fists.

"Put the weapon down, and we can end this before it begins," one of them said, shifting his feet into a wide base. "You're outnumbered."

Behind the guards, Belina got to her feet and palmed a knife with each hand.

"Belina, no killing!"

The look of confusion on the Kingsguards' faces was trumped only by the almost comical frown that spread across Belina's. She narrowed her eyes before letting out a sigh. As the guard nearest to her turned to see what was happening, Belina drove one of her knives in between the plates of his armour at the elbow, leaving it lodged, forcing him to release his grip on his sword. As the man howled, Belina grabbed him by the helmet and pulled him back. She used her second knife to slice through the leather strap that held the helmet in place before slamming the pommel repeatedly into the side of his head before tossing him to the ground.

The other two guards turned away from Dahlen, moving on Belina together. They swung their swords as wide as the corridor would allow in an attempt to cleave her in half, but the woman dropped low, sweeping their feet out from under them with a deceptively powerful kick. One guard stumbled backwards and tripped, his momentum and the weight of his armour throwing him off balance, crashing to the ground. The other just about managed to keep his footing, catching himself on the wall.

Dahlen slid his sword back into his scabbard as he ran, leaping for the still-standing Kingsguard. He thew his full weight forward as he charged the guard to the ground. The force of the impact dragged the air from Dahlen's lungs, the guard's full plate making him feel as though he had tackled a stone wall. The pair scrambled as they hit the ground. A knee collided with Dahlen's stomach, and it was all he could do not to vomit. He spun himself up, landing on the guard's chest, knees on either side of her body, hands clasped around her throat. Dahlen squeezed, then pulled, lifting the guard's helmeted head off the ground, then slamming it back down into the stone until her body went limp. His chest heaving, Dahlen dropped down beside the guard, sweat dripping from his brow, lungs burning. He could see the slow rise and fall of the woman's chest beside him. It was infinitely harder to *not* kill, but he'd fought beside these men and women. He'd bled with them. They were not his enemies.

A cry rang out, and Dahlen looked up to see Belina roll past the last guard, who had gotten back to his feet, and bury a knife in the back of his calf as she came to the end of the roll. She slid a second knife from her boot and rammed it into the man's other calf, dropping onto her back and kicking him in the back of the knee. The man cried out, tumbling forwards, hands reaching backwards, attempting to grasp the two knives that were now lodged in his calves. As the man fell, Belina rolled backward, tucking her knees close to her chest, then launched herself to a standing position in a feat of acrobatics Dahlen was absolutely certain he would never attempt.

Belina took a step forward, then kicked the howling man in the face, snapping his head back and knocking him unconscious.

"Fuck!" Belina lifted her foot, grasping it with both hands, hopping on her other leg. "Shit, that hurt." Belina grimaced, lowering her foot to the ground and letting out a sigh.

"Really?" Dahlen said as Belina helped him to his feet, still moaning about her foot.

"What?"

"*Help me! He's trying to kill me!*" Dahlen did his best impression of Belina, raising his voice higher than hers for dramatic effect.

"Oh, get over it. You're so dramatic."

"*I'm* dramatic?"

"*No killing!*" Belina said in a mocking tone, contorting her face and spreading her palms.

Dahlen shook his head, looking down at the guards, one with a knife protruding from the gap in his armour at his right elbow, another with two knives jutting from the backs of his calves. "Did you really have to do that?"

"You're right, I shouldn't have."

"Really?" Dahlen couldn't hide the surprise on his face. Even if Belina agreed with him, her admitting it was rarer than an eclipse.

"Really. I should have just asked nicely and shown them my tits." A grin spread across Belina's face. "I'm sure that would have worked. Everyone loves tits. I—"

"Belina."

"What?"

"Stop saying tits. I get it. Please, stop."

The grin on the woman's face grew even broader, and she gave Dahlen a wink, pulling her knives from where they were lodged in the unconscious men, kicking one in the head as the pain shocked him awake.

"Let's just get this over with." Dahlen turned the door handle and pushed.

CHAPTER TWENTY-TWO

FRIENDS CLOSE, ENEMIES CLOSER

Dahlen's heart caught in his throat as he stepped through the doorway. Standing there, in the middle of the sparse stone room, one hand pressed to his side, the other wrapped in a bandage and grasping the hilt of a sword, was Ihvon. Behind him, another man – the assassin – lay in a crumpled heap, hands bound by a rope that was knotted to a bolt that had been driven into the floor. "Dahlen... You're alive."

The last time Dahlen had seen Ihvon, the man had been lying unconscious on a stretcher in the Heart of Durakdur, Kira's dwarves and the Kingsguard carving chunks from each other around him. Dahlen's first instinct was to go to Ihvon, to check that his friend was all right. It felt strange to think of Ihvon as a friend – they hadn't known each other for long – but that's exactly what Ihvon was: a friend. And friends weren't something Dahlen had many of. But he could see something in Ihvon's face, a hesitancy, and so he stayed in the doorway, his muscles tensing. "As are you." A moment passed, and Dahlen took a step forward. "It's good to see you on your feet."

Ihvon moved back, ensuring he stood between Dahlen and the prisoner. He lifted his sword, grimacing, the wound from the knife the assassin had driven into his ribs still plaguing him. Ihvon inclined his head towards the corridor behind Dahlen, where the three Kingsguard lay unconscious. "As much as the sentiment is returned, it appears you do not come as a friend. What are you doing, Dahlen?"

"They are all alive. I swear it."

Ihvon looked to Belina, raising an eyebrow. "She doesn't do 'alive.'"

"Because it's you, Ihvon. Full honesty – I stabbed two of them but only in the leg and the elbow. They'll live. But judging by the hand he was holding his sword with, I think one of them might have difficulty with, eh..." Belina closed her hand into a fist and moved it up and down. "You know." Both Dahlen and Ihvon stared at Belina, but she just shrugged – as she always did. "I said full honesty."

Ihvon turned back to Dahlen, shaking his head, a hardness setting into his eyes. "What is this, Dahlen?"

"I've come for him." Dahlen gestured towards the assassin, who lay in a heap behind Ihvon. "Kira needs proof an attempt was made on Daymon's life the same night one was made on hers. He is the only proof we have."

"I can't let you take him. This man tried to kill Daymon. He cannot go free. Daymon would never—"

"Daymon is the reason we're here, Ihvon!" Dahlen could do nothing to stop his voice from rising, anger seeping into his words. Ihvon was one of the wisest men Dahlen had ever met, but when it came to Daymon, the man was as blind as a bat. "He made a deal with Pulroan. He knew those assassins were coming. He let everything happen. He's been playing you all along, Ihvon. He's been playing us all."

"I know." Ihvon let out a heavy sigh, lowering his sword.

"You know?"

"Well, I didn't know for sure he'd made a deal with Pulroan, but I had suspected. He's met with her far too many times, and each time he would either make an excuse or start an argument so he could dismiss me. I've known Daymon since the moment he drew his first breath. I know when he's lying. And I know he tried to have you arrested to cover something up. He's been acting strangely for a while now. He kept pushing to confront the dwarves, kept calling for action, even when it made no sense. Even now, he wants the assassin to hang. He's anxious, paranoid. He's not himself, Dahlen."

"I don't give two shits about Daymon. There's no excuse for what he's done. I'm here to keep these people from starving to death. If I can bring proof to Kira that an attempt was made on Daymon's life, she might back off."

"You can't trust dwarves, Dahlen. They're oath-breakers. She'll stab you in the back first chance she gets."

"Don't tell me who I can and can't trust. She's been more honest with me than either you or Daymon. She doesn't want bloodshed, Ihvon. Not with Belduar. But Daymon has forced her hand. And it wasn't her who had a knife stuck in your side."

"It doesn't matter." Ihvon let out a grunt as he shifted his stance, his long-broken nose wrinkling. "If Daymon made a deal with Pulroan, he's as culpable as she is. The dwarves will take his head from his shoulders and leave our people to rot here. I can't let that happen." Ihvon bit his lip, looking back at the man who lay behind him. "I can't, Dahlen. I can't put Daymon's head on a block."

"Why do you protect him? He's a coward. He'd sell the skin off your back if he thought it would save his."

"He's a boy!" The fury in Ihvon's voice took Dahlen off guard. "He's a child, Dahlen. He wasn't ready for this. He's drowning, swallowing water, just trying to stay afloat. I caused this. I can't just let him fall."

"You caused this? Ihvon, you had nothing to do with this. You've stood by him at every turn. Even now, after his actions almost killed you." Dahlen drew in a breath, holding it for a moment before releasing it. "I haven't told Kira what Daymon has done." Dahlen could see the surprise on Ihvon's face. The man lowered his blade slightly. With Ihvon's injuries, Dahlen was sure he could simply get the better of him and leave with what they'd come for – particularly with Belina's aid – but that wasn't how he wanted to do things. "I told you. I'm here to make sure the Belduarans are safe. I couldn't give a fuck if Daymon hangs from a bridge, but right now, keeping the blame from his head keeps these people safe."

Ihvon started to speak, but a flash of recognition crossed his face, and he stopped. Before Dahlen could say anything else, Belina stepped across him. "I've had enough with you two measuring dicks. Despite wanting to stab that rat-faced little prick you call a king, Ihvon, what Dahlen is trying to do will likely be the only way that snot-nosed shit gets out of this alive. And, if it matters to you, so will all the others inside this stone-entombed animal pen. You're better than this."

"Belina, you know I love these people. I—"

"Save it, Ihvon. We've known each other a long time and I know that face. You're stubborn as a mountain on a good day, and that face tells me it's a bad day. Keep all your fancy words of honour and duty and all the other shit you spout. Dahlen could have left. In fact, I asked him to. But he stayed. Despite the fact that your turd-hearted dickweed of a king tried to pin him with the blame for his own incompetence, Dahlen stayed. Now, there is clearly something else going on within that thick skull of yours. But if you believe any of the crap you spout about looking after the people of Belduar, you will let us take that man to Kira. And if you don't, I will drop you on that senile old arse of yours and stick a knife through the hand you pleasure yourself with. Then, we will take him anyway." Belina shrugged. "And while we're sharing here today, you call dwarves oathbreakers yet serve a king who is more concerned about saving his own skin than the starvation and sickness of those he is sworn to protect. I've only spoken with Kira once, but it is clear she has more integrity in her little toe than that rat-bastard has in his entire body. And another thing—"

"Belina." Dahlen rested his hand on Belina's shoulder, and to his surprise she actually stopped, her breaths slow and trembling as she met his gaze. Dahlen inclined his head, giving her a soft smile. He turned to Ihvon, stepping past the man's blade. "Your duty is to the men and women out there who are starving and sick. It's to the children who might never feel the sun's light again or grow old enough to know what it is to feel the warmth of another. You owe *them*. Not him. They are here because of what *he* has done, and I won't let them pay with their lives. I won't!" Dahlen shook, clenching his jaw to stop it from trembling. He held Ihvon's gaze, trying his best to control his breathing. He hadn't felt the anger rising. He slowed his breathing. "If you don't let us take that man, Daymon and everyone else here will die of hunger and disease. It will be slow and painful. Even if you don't care for the people, which I don't believe for a second, us walking out of here with that man is the only way Daymon has a chance of living."

Ihvon stared back at Dahlen, his eyes dark and ringed with purple. Slowly, Ihvon let his sword fall to his side, nodding. "Take him. Bring him to Kira. I will do what I can to reason with Daymon. He has a good heart. He's just lost."

~⊚~

AFTER BELINA AND DAHLEN LEFT with the assassin, Ihvon pressed his back against the stone wall, sliding to the ground. He ran his hands across his smooth head; once it had been full of thick, black hair.

He had caused this. All of it. Had he not been weak, the Fade would never have gotten into Belduar. Arthur would still be sitting on his throne. Daymon would be unburdened, learning the tenets of rule from a man far more qualified than Ihvon. Belduar would still be standing, its people – *his* people – would not be trapped beneath a mountain of stone, beholden to the whims of warring dwarves, and starving.

Ihvon swallowed hard, running his fingers over the mess of twisted flesh that had once been his ear. He let out a long breath. He had taken that injury the day the Depth Stalkers had taken Alyana and Khris from him. Khris's screams still plagued Ihvon's nightmares, echoing into the waking world, scratching at him day and night.

Nobody understood. Not Arthur, not Aeson. They had always told him the dwarves were not to blame for what had happened. That if they had gone back, they all would've died. Ihvon would've died. But that was just the point. The dwarves had taken that from him. They had kept him from dying with his family. They had forced him to live without the warm touch of Alyana's lips, without the curious questions of Khris's mind.

That anger was what the Fade had twisted, and as a result, Ihvon had caused the death of his closest friend, a man he'd known his entire life, a man who had trusted him implicitly. Now that friend's son held the weight of an entire people on his shoulders. And Daymon was crumbling.

Once again, nobody understood. Ihvon had taken Daymon's father from him. He had caused all this pain. And now, no matter what road they walked down, Ihvon would not allow Daymon to stand alone. He would not.

KIRA SAT ON HER THRONE atop the dais in the council chamber. She had been there for an hour or so, one leg crossed over the other, her chin resting on the knuckles of her right hand. Even though her armour had been crafted to fit her perfectly, it still scratched and itched. Wearing it to battle was one thing, but wearing it every moment she was awake was tiring. The steel weighed her down, making the burden on her shoulders a physical thing. But she wore it because it was her duty to do so. She was at war. Whether the word had been said aloud or not, that was the truth of it. She was at war. And despite appearances, it was not a war with humans, with the people of Belduar. It was a war among her own kind. She would never ask her warriors to raise an axe against their own unless she was willing to do so herself.

Whether or not Daymon had played any part in what happened, she had no doubt the man was not the mastermind behind it all. He didn't have the intelligence for it, and what wits he did have were spent feeding the ego of the petulant child within him. His only true motivation was to be like his father – that much was clear. In a way, Kira pitied him. Arthur Bryne had been a strong ruler, and he had been a man she respected. To live in that shadow was no easy task. But just because she pitied him, didn't mean she wouldn't crush him if needed. No, if Daymon was anything, he was a puppet dancing on the strings of another.

Elenya, Hoffnar, and Pulroan. At least one had betrayed them all. Kira let out a sombre laugh, sitting back in her chair, looking about the chamber, her gaze passing over the statues of the gods and the empty thrones atop the dais around her. The Freehold had been formed almost a millennium ago, after centuries of war between the kingdoms. It had not been perfect, but it had lasted. It had persevered. And through that perseverance, the stone of the mountain had been deprived of dwarven blood, and each kingdom had thrived. But it appeared that time of peace was now gone.

She'd heard from the rumours of those who had been travelling that night that Hoffnar no longer drew breath. Kira had not believed it at first.

Surely it could not have been true. In the days after, Kira had tried to send scouts to Volkur, and to Azmar and Ozryn, but all three had closed their Wind Tunnels, as she had. As the days passed and emissaries arrived from Elenya and Pulroan, no word came from Hoffnar, and Volkur's Wind Tunnels remained closed. Either all those eligible were vying for the throne, carving chunks of flesh from each other in the hopes of grasping power, or Hoffnar was responsible for the attacks and had closed off his Kingdom in preparation for war.

Both Pulroan and Elenya had assured Kira of their innocence and offered aid in containing the Belduarans in Durakdur, which she had accepted on the condition that Elenya and Pulroan themselves come to Durakdur. Her advisors had warned her against doing so. But if either or both of Elenya and Pulroan were responsible for the attacks, it was best to have them close. They could not wage war surrounded by Kira's armies.

Kira lifted herself to her feet, turning to the statue of Hafaesir behind her throne. The Smith, the patron god of all dwarves. Their creator. Kira held strong faith in the gods, but she was not like some zealots who used their twisted beliefs in preordained fate to justify their deeds. Her fate was her own, her path carved through the force of her own will. She had not inherited the crown, like the kings and queens of men and elves. She had earned it, chosen by her people as the one to lead, as was the dwarven way. Still, she couldn't help but ask the question: "Why?" She moved her gaze from the hammer in Hafaesir's hand, to the thick plate that covered his arms and chest, to the knotted beard laced with rings that fell from his face. "We are your people. Why do you not step in when we threaten to spill our own blood?"

She had not expected a response. The gods did not wait around, listening to the whispers of mortals. Kira let out a sigh, running her hand through her ring-laden hair.

A booming clang echoed through the short corridor outside the chamber, followed by footsteps and shouts. Kira turned to face the double doors that marked the chamber's entrance.

"Stop. You can't just—"

The doors to the council chamber burst open, Dahlen Virandr and his companion striding through, tossing a cloaked man to the floor.

∽⬮∾

"HERE IS YOUR PROOF." DAHLEN looked up at the queen, who stood on the raised semi-circular dais in the centre of the chamber, the statues of the gods and the banners of the kingdoms arrayed behind her. She wore the same steel plate she had worn at their meeting by the waterfall. A pair of long hand axes hung from the weapons belt strapped to her hips, and a large double-bladed battleaxe rested against the side of her throne. *She's ready for war.*

Kira's Queensguard took up positions around Dahlen and Belina, two on each side, axes hefted in their grips, crimson cloaks touching the stone floor. Unable to stop Dahlen and Belina from entering without coming to blows, they had settled with surrounding them – a compromise Dahlen was more than happy with.

Kira stayed silent as she descended from the dais, eyes fixed on the man who knelt on the ground before them. The clink of her boots on stone reverberated through the chamber, each one clear and unchallenged by any other sound, bar the thumping of Dahlen's heart.

Kira stopped before the assassin and pulled the man's hood from his head to reveal a face that had been beaten black and blue, a nose so shattered it could have been made of glass, and an eye so bloody and broken Dahlen was sure it would never be of use again. Dahlen grimaced at the sight of the man's mangled face. The last he'd seen of the assassin, the man's nose had been shattered by Ihvon, but the new damage had been freshly dealt.

"You treat your prisoners well, then." The queen placed her hand beneath the man's chin, lifting it so he met her gaze, not a hint of sarcasm in her voice. "If he had been my prisoner, I would have taken his hands, then there would be no need for these bonds. To leave an assassin with his hands is to wait for a blade in your back."

"I like her," Belina whispered, folding her arms, her lips forming into an impressed pout. "What?" She gave Dahlen a look of innocence in response to his glare. "Tell me a single word she said that wasn't true."

Kira let the man's chin drop. "You have my thanks. My questioners will glean the truth from him. Then we will act accordingly. If he confirms what you have told me, I will grant Daymon an audience."

"Give me five minutes alone in a room with him." Belina tilted her head to the side, staring at the assassin. "He'll talk. I can guarantee it."

"Belina! That—"

A spluttering cough interrupted Dahlen, the assassin dragging in a ragged breath. He lifted his head to Kira. "If you permit, I will tell you what you want to know."

"And why would you do that?" Kira asked, dropping to one knee before the assassin, meeting his gaze.

The man coughed again, splattering the ground with blood, droplets marring the surface of Kira's pristine armour. "I've seen too many summers to be stupid enough to endure torture in the name of gold. A reputation can be rebuilt. A body cannot. Ask me your questions, and I will answer. After, set me free, and you will never see me again. You won't find a fairer trade."

"And how do I know you will be truthful?"

"How do you ever know? Are answers extracted through pain and mutilation guaranteed to be more truthful than those openly given?" Dahlen couldn't help but be impressed by the man's composure. Had that been him kneeling before the dwarven queen of Durakdur with the threat of torture and death looming over him, he did not think he would be so calm. "How would you ever know if what I say is truthful? If anything, I would be more likely to spew lies to questions of which I did not have the answers, simply to end the pain. Ask me your questions, and I will answer honestly. Then let me go. Honesty for honesty."

Kira rose, turning back towards the dais. "Who hired you?"

"I do not know. My instructions are left for me in a chest in The Cloak and Dagger in Azmar, along with half the coin. The other half is left once the task is completed."

Kira didn't look back at the man. "How did you get into the Freehold?"

"We have always been here, in one form or another. But I came, along with others, on your Wind Runners during the evacuation."

Belina stepped past Dahlen and dropped to her haunches beside the man. "The Hand will hunt you."

"I know." The man grimaced. "Just as they hunted you, Belina Louna. But you hunted them back. You are legend."

Belina patted the man on the cheek. "But you are not me. They will hunt you, and they *will* kill you."

"Better die with a blade in my hand than strapped to a bench while being tortured."

"Truth." Belina rose to her feet, moving back to Dahlen's side. "May Heraya embrace you."

Kira looked from the assassin to Belina, then back again, curiosity in her eyes. "Did you make an attempt on the life of King Daymon of Belduar?"

"I did. Our instructions were to kill the King and his advisor, Ihvon Arnell."

"And myself? Queen Elenya? Pulroan? Hoffnar?"

"I do not know. We are broken into groups, with each group only ever informed of their own tasks to prevent a situation such as this from rippling. But I was told to say it was Elenya who sent me."

Kira nodded. "Thank you. Your honesty has been appreciated." Kira pulled a hand axe from the loop of her belt and placed it into the man's bound hands. Dahlen was confused at first, but then the man gave a slow nod, bowing his head. In a flash, Kira pulled her second hand axe free and swung the blade into the side of the man's head with a wet crack. The steel was wedged so tight only a thin stream of blood trickled around it. The assassin twitched, reaching his hand up to feel the blade of the axe. He dropped to his side, rolling onto his back, still twitching. He stayed like that until his lungs stopped drawing breath and his eyes rolled to the back of his head, the life fleeing from his body.

"What was that?" Dahlen roared, taking a step closer to Kira as her Queensguard held him back. "He told you what you wanted to know. You gave him your word!"

Kira put her foot on the man's chest and heaved her axe free, blood spraying in a single spurt. "He was a hired assassin. One of a number who attempted to kill Daymon and all the rulers of the Freehold. What if there is no orchestrator? What if the empire is trying to set us against each other? Either way, he was not a man who could be set free. Deep down, he knew that. He died with a blade in his hand, just as he wished."

Belina rested her hand on Dahlen's shoulder. "I don't like it either, but it is a better death than he would've received from the Hand. They don't tolerate betrayal."

"You gave him your word." The words left Dahlen's throat in a growl as he leaned against the Queensguard.

Kira wiped the blood from her axe with a cloth she'd pulled from her belt, then slipped it back into the loop at her hip, picking up her second axe from the floor and doing the same. She gestured for her Queensguard to step aside, then moved so she was only a few inches from Dahlen. For someone who stood almost a foot shorter than Dahlen, in her plate armour, axes hanging from her belt, blood speckling her otherwise pale skin, and a cold ferocity in her eyes, Kira cut a strikingly intimidating figure. "My people are on the verge of war, Dahlen Virandr. Do you understand what that means? War? It means their lives hang in the balance of every decision I make. The empire slaughtered the dwarves of Kolmir and Helmund. They burned the dwarves of the Rolling Mountains alive in dragonfire. My entire species constantly teeters on the edge of existence. The dwarves of the Lodhar Freehold, the dwarves of Aonar, and the dwarves of the Jade Mountain in Arkalen are all that remains of our once proud people. If you for a second think that I would weigh their lives as equal to that of a cut-throat who sought my blood, you are a terrible judge of character. I am not Daymon. I care little for my own life compared to that of my people. I will do anything to keep them safe." She looked back down at the assassin's lifeless body, letting out a sigh. "I do not like Daymon Bryne. He is a shadow of what his father was, and what's worse, he has but a sliver of Arthur's compassion. But I do not seek war with Belduar, nor do I wish the senseless loss of life. There is already enough blood to be spilt. You may go to him and tell him I wish to talk of peace. If he agrees, I will meet him here. Mirlak will take a regiment of my guard with you." Kira gestured towards one of the Queensguard, who stood to her right.

Dahlen looked to Belina, who nodded. He bit the corner of his lip. "No."

"No?"

"The Belduarans in the refugee quarters are starving. You know this. While you and Daymon trade words, they will continue to starve. Give me food to bring to them, and I will deliver your message to Daymon."

Dahlen knew he had nothing to bargain with. Kira could have left the Belduarans to starve, and there was nothing he could have done about it. But from what she had just said of her own people, he didn't think her the type to leave people to starve – despite the coldness with which she had killed the assassin.

Kira tapped her fingers along the head of the axe that hung at her right hip, her tongue running across cracked lips. "I will arrange for wagons of grain, fruit, beans, and roots. When they are ready, you will leave with them and deliver my message."

"You have my thanks, Your Majesty." Dahlen inclined his head. He wasn't always sure how to behave around royalty, and he was certain he often got it wrong, but he tried. Another thought niggled at the back of his mind. "Your Majesty. There are more Belduarans beyond Durakdur. There are those in the other cities. What word do you have of them?"

A weak smile touched Kira's face. "Both Elenya and Pulroan assure me the Belduarans in their cities are well. I cannot imagine they are much better off than those here, but they are alive. As for those in Volkur, I do not know. The Wind Tunnels to Volkur have been closed since the attacks and I have heard nothing from Hoffnar. They may still draw breath, but I would not hold out hope. If the assassins in Volkur did indeed succeed in killing Hoffnar, there will undoubtedly be those among the Volkurans who blame the humans. It is better to hope for the best but prepare for the worst. For now, my commander, Mirlak, will bring you somewhere you can eat, drink, and wash. Forgive me for saying so, but you smell like shit."

Belina burst out laughing. "I told you!"

～∞～

KIRA FOLDED HER ARMS ACROSS her chest as Mirlak escorted Belina and Dahlen from the chamber. She had not laid eyes on Belina before this day, but despite the woman's outwardly lax demeanour, it was clear she was a warrior of some skill. And if the words that had passed between her and the assassin held truth, she had not only once been a member of the Hand but had also broken free – a feat Kira did not believe was an easy one.

But it was not Belina that held Kira's attention. Dahlen Virandr was a human of integrity – a quality few of them possessed. He was, by all measure, his father's son. The young man had no stake in this, and if he'd wanted to, Kira was sure he and Belina could have found a way to leave Lodhar with little effort. But he had stayed, and the woman had decided to stay with him. Both of those things said more than words ever could. A man who not only chose to weigh his life against the lives of those for whom he bore no oath, and a man who could convince a woman like that to do the same.

If Dahlen Virandr had been king of Belduar instead of Daymon Bryne, this all would have been very different.

CHAPTER TWENTY-THREE

THE DARKNESS TWISTS

The elemental strands pulsated in the back of Calen's mind, twisting and turning in on each other, radiating power. They were one, and they were many, a blend of colours, emotions, and sensations. Since he had first touched the Spark, the distinction of the strands had grown sharper and clearer. The colours were barely noticeable, faint and faded, only visible when Calen truly searched for them. Water pulsed with a sky-blue hue, Fire burned a muted red, Earth transitioned between a faded green and a sand-brown, Air was near translucent, perceptible only by its occupation of space, while Spirit held a faint white. The strand of Fire called to Calen. No, 'called' was too unsubstantial a word – it roared and howled, yearning to be set free. Calen pushed it away. It was not Fire he needed.

Reaching out, Calen touched the strand of Spirit with his mind, just as Vaeril had instructed. He drew threads from it, letting them seep into his body and sink into his blood. Then he felt it – the ward of Spirit Vaeril was attempting to construct. In a fraction of a second, Calen's grasp on the Spark flickered and vanished, his body feeling empty, the Spark's warmth gone. "Gods dammit!"

"You need to focus," Vaeril said, his tone curt. "Protecting against a ward is reactive. If you set your guard too early, your attacker can account for its presence. Too late and... same outcome." The elf let out a tired sigh, pulling the hood of his cloak so it shaded more of his pale face from the blazing sun. Slowly, Calen felt the familiar sensation of the Spark begin to return as Vaeril lowered the ward he had erected around Calen. "That's enough. We are wasting our energy when it is already in short supply."

"But surely there is a way to—"

"I said it's enough!" Vaeril stopped, leaning towards Calen, his face shrouded in shadow. For a moment Calen thought he saw a faint reddish glow emanating from the elf's eyes, but then it was gone. Vaeril's chest was trembling, and his teeth were grinding. The elf shook his head as though trying to calm something within himself. "I'm tired, Calen. That's enough."

"É dir mære?" *Are you well?*

Vaeril held Calen's gaze for a moment, then let out an irritated sigh and stormed off, his cloak billowing in the wind, sand whipping into the air.

Days had passed since Erik and Tarmon had come moments from tearing each other apart. But since then, neither Erik nor Tarmon had spoken more than a few words, and Vaeril hadn't been much better.

Overhead, Valerys drifted on the currents of air, saving as much of his energy as possible. With each passing day Calen had hoped beyond hope that, through the dragon's eyes, he would be able to see mountains or cities appear on the horizon, but instead each morning all he saw was sand, rock, and the bones of the dead. Not two days past, they had come across the broken skeletons of dragons jutting through the ocean of sand, weathered and bleached by the sun. The agony had nearly consumed Valerys. Were it not for the looming possibility of meeting the same fate, they would be mourning still.

As Calen looked through Valerys's eyes and saw nothing but the endless wastes, he prayed to all the gods that he had not led his friends to die in this dark place. He had never been a true believer in the gods. He had been raised with their names on his lips and their virtues in his ears, and he had hoped for their existence, but he had never held the unwavering faith that some did. Since finding Valerys, that had changed. The luminescent plants that gave light to the dwarven cities were surely a gift from Heraya, her light granting the gift of life in the darkest of places. The Portal Heart in Vindakur had carried them across the continent in the blink of an eye, from the Lodhar Mountains to Drifaien. If that had not been the work of a god – of Hafaesir – then Calen was not sure what was.

HOURS PASSED AS THEY TREKKED across the sand, over rock formations and dunes, through graveyards of bone and rusted steel, the sun slowly sinking beyond the horizon. The further they walked through the vast wasteland, the more remains they found. Men, horses, dragons – some isolated and alone, others in mass graves spread across the sand. The sight of bleached bone and rusted steel had become so frequent the group no longer stopped to see what might have happened.

As the light of the setting sun sprayed a warm glow over the eastern horizon, Valerys alighted beside Calen. The dragon's massive wings lifted clouds of sand into the air, his scales glowing with an incandescent orange-red hue. Valerys had made a habit of landing whenever the sun began to set. The N'aka kept a greater distance from the group whenever Valerys was on the ground, and as they were still some five miles from the rock formation to the north-east that they had spotted earlier, the sun would be long set by the time they reached it.

"Come here." Calen patted his hand on the scales of Valerys's jaw, touching his forehead against the dragon's snout. He could feel the tiredness that ached through the dragon's body. Food had been harder to come by for Valerys than Calen had hoped. The N'aka had proven incredibly difficult to hunt, and the other creatures Valerys had found had been small, chitinous things and lizards no bigger than rabbits. If they didn't find a way through soon… *We will find a way.* Calen moved towards Valerys's side, dipping under his wing. "Let me take a look." He brushed his hand over the long scar that ran across Valerys's side where the Fade had struck him with lightning. Vaeril had attempted to heal the wound many times, but he had said it was 'resistant'. Whatever magic the Fade had used left wounds deeper than the physical. It was just like the scar that twisted the flesh on Dann's shoulder. Still, it *was* healing, just slowly. The scar was hardening, fusing like scales. Whether it would ever heal fully, Calen wasn't sure, but as long as it ceased to cause Valerys pain, he would be happy.

Warmth touched his mind, a reassuring pressure from Valerys, insisting he would be fine. The feeling was followed by a second, a longing. Images of blue skies and clouds filled Calen's mind, the sensation of wind brushing against his scales.

Calen rested his hand on the scar. Since feeling Valerys's scales beneath him when the dragon had taken him from Arisfall, Calen had felt a deep yearning – the same yearning that pushed at him now from Valerys's mind. He wanted to fly, to truly be as one. "Once you're healed."

An irritated rumble resonated both in the dragon's throat and his thoughts, defiant, insistent.

"You might feel all right, but you're not. You're tired, and you're hungry, and we have no telling how many days are ahead of us." *Or weeks.* "Besides, we can't leave the others down here alone, not with the N'aka stalking us."

Calen had expected Valerys to push back again, but instead he felt an acquiescence in the dragon as Valerys shifted, craning his neck around and nuzzling his snout into Calen's chest. A protective feeling radiated from Valerys's mind.

"Calen, move!" Erik called out from up ahead, turning, his arms spread out wide, his breath misting as the temperature began to drop. "We don't have the time for that shit. We need to get to shelter!"

"Come on," Calen whispered to Valerys, letting his hand soak up the warmth of Valerys's scales for just another moment. *Myia nithír til diar. I denír viël ar altinua. My soul to yours. In this life and always.*

A low rumble resonated from the dragon's throat, a touch of pride in the back of his mind as he followed Calen up the gradual hill of sand before them towards where Vaeril, Erik, and Tarmon waited.

"I'm not a performing dog," Vaeril snapped at Erik as Calen approached. The elf let out something akin to a hiss, then stormed past Erik.

Erik reached out and grabbed Vaeril's shoulder, pulling. "I just want—"

Vaeril turned and shoved Erik in one fluid motion, the force of the shove sending him tumbling backwards into the sand. "You humans always want something. And if you want it, you take it. No matter how much blood needs to be spilled. Your kind are the reason we hide in the trees. Your greed, your hunger."

Erik scrambled to his feet, clawing at the sand, shock turning to fury. He rammed his palms into Vaeril's chest, but the elf stayed firm and leaned his neck forwards. Vaeril and Erik stood there, foreheads squared, eyes full of fire.

"Will you two stop acting like children? We need to keep moving or we'll be like sitting ducks out here, ripe for the hunt."

"I just wanted some fucking water," Erik growled, his eyes not leaving Vaeril's, his teeth grinding, an unnatural edge to his voice.

"Here." Calen pulled his waterskin from his pack, hearing the dregs sloshing around at the bottom. "Finish this. I'll search for water deposits once we reach shelter. Vaeril has been showing me how. We're all tired, Erik. But we can't be far from Copperstille now."

Erik shifted, something flashing across his face. He pulled his head away from Vaeril's, turning towards Calen, the light of the new moon glinting in his eyes. "What did you say?"

"I said you can have my water. I'll draw more from the ground once we've reached the rocks."

"No." Erik shook his head, moving towards Calen, his eyes cold and piercing, an unsettling calm sweeping over him. "Not that." Erik grasped the collar of Calen's cloak, twisting it in his fists. "'*We can't be far from Copperstille now.*' How do you not know? Valerys can see the edge of the Burnt Lands, *can't he?*"

A ripple of anxiety swept through Calen. He still hadn't told them that the horizon had shifted, even for Valerys, since they had entered the Burnt Lands. He had hoped it wouldn't come up, that they would reach the edge of the waste within the time that Captain Kiron had suggested, but it had been far longer. A rumble deepened to a low growl, reverberating in Valerys's throat as the dragon loomed over Calen. The dragon's lip pulled back in a snarl, baring his teeth. Family or not, nothing and nobody would harm the bond.

"Erik, let go."

"Answer me." Cold fury shook Erik's voice.

"I will answer," Calen said, trying his best to keep his voice calm. He could feel the fire burning through Valerys. No matter how strong their bond, after everything that had happened, Calen would be powerless to stop Valerys from striking Erik down. "But *let go*."

Erik glanced towards Valerys, whose scale covered jaws now hovered over Calen's head, his eyes glaring down at Erik, warm breath wafting. "I can put a blade in you before he even blinks."

"Put a blade in me? Erik, listen to yourself! What's wrong with you?"

"Answer his question." Calen glanced to his right to see Tarmon standing beside them, his hand resting over the pommel of his sword.

"All right." Calen reached up and put his hands on top of Erik's fists, pushing them down. He felt a resistance, but eventually Erik relented and let go of Calen, though the cold look in his eyes remained. Vaeril stood to Calen's right, his eyes shifting between Erik and Calen, his expression unreadable. The hairs on Calen's arms stood on end – part from worry and part from the fast-descending chill of the cold night air. He drew a deep breath through his nostrils, attempting to calm himself, then exhaled, his breath misting in front of him. "I don't know how far the edge is. As soon as we entered the Burnt Lands, the horizon changed. The mountains vanished. All Valerys can see in any direction is sand and rocks. But I'm absolutely sure if—"

"Why didn't you tell us?" Tarmon's voice was low and gruff as he took a step closer to Erik and Calen.

"Because we still have the compass, and we know the Burnt Lands end. There *is* another side, whether we can see it or not. I didn't think there was a need to worry. But I should have told you. I should have."

"Of course." Erik gave a deep, rumbling laugh, pulling back from Calen. He turned towards the vast emptiness of never-ending wasteland. "You must think you're so important now, don't you?" Erik turned back, holding Calen's gaze, that deep laugh still rumbling in his chest. "You must think you're so *special*. The Draleid." He dipped his shoulders into a mocking bow, venom dripping from his voice. "But you're the biggest joke of all. One hope, one spark to ignite the fires of rebellion. That's what my father said. That's what we trained to become, Dahlen and I. Then you come along. The son of a blacksmith who fancied himself a hero." Erik stepped closer to Calen, their eyes level. "What kind of cruel trick are the gods playing on us? You let your family die. You went back there after my father told you not to. Your pride and your ego were unmatched even then. You *needed* to be there, needed to absolve yourself. And because of that, they all died. You let Ellisar die as well. Korik. Lopir. Falmin. And now you risk our lives. You drag us across this gods forsaken wasteland to try and save the friend you left behind. You allow us to walk through this ocean of sand to our deaths, not even deeming us worthy to know that you can't see the other side? How fucking dare you. Rist is dead, Calen. You left him to die, and now you lead us to the same fate." Erik squared up to Calen, so close Calen could feel the warmth of his breath. "I should gut you right now and leave you here as carrion."

Calen clenched his fist, pushing Erik's words to the back of his mind. *Something is wrong. Something is very, very wrong.* "Erik, listen to—"

Erik rammed his hands into Calen's chest, his eyes cold with fury. "We needed a symbol, but all we got was a coward who thinks of nobody but himself. We should be with my father, fighting, bleeding. There are people out there who need us. We should be making a difference. We should be—" Erik made to step closer to Calen again, but the edge of Vaeril's curved sword now rested against his neck. "The dog bares his teeth."

"Move any closer to the Draleid, and I'll slit your throat. You have been warned."

Erik pressed his neck against Vaeril's blade, a thin stream of blood trickling. "Let's see how fast you are, *elf*."

Calen opened himself to the Spark. He felt Valerys pull their minds together as the dragon moved his wings across Calen. Fear and fury pulsed from the dragon's heart. Something was wrong with his family. He could feel it in his bones. If any of them tried to harm his soulkin, he would rip them from the world. As Valerys lowered his head to the ground, a deep rumble resonating from his body, threads of Spirit twisted around Calen, winding and weaving, knotting together with thin threads of Air. The threads packed on top of each other, the force of their power pushing outward until Calen could no longer contain it. A shockwave erupted through Calen's body, and the threads of Air and Spirit erupted outwards, like a rock dropped in a lake. The force of the blast sent Erik, Tarmon, and Vaeril crashing backwards into the sand.

"Stay down!" Calen shouted. "Listen to me. Something is wrong! You're not thinking straight!"

Erik was the first to rise, one of his swords gripped in his fist. He made to lunge towards Calen, but Valerys reared onto his hind legs and slammed Erik to the ground with his forelimb, unleashing a visceral roar that resonated through Calen's bones.

"Stay down!" Calen roared, his heart hammering against his ribs, beating them as though they were an anvil. Out of the corner of his eyes, he saw Vaeril and Tarmon rising to their knees, but neither of them stood any higher.

"You're right." Vaeril clutched the side of his head as he spoke. "Something *is* wrong. I can feel it clawing at me." The elf's fingers clenched into a fist at the side of his head. Even as he spoke, his chest rose and fell in heavy sweeps, the effort of his restraint evident. "The thoughts in my head... they're not my own." Vaeril lifted his head. His irises were tarnished with a dull red hue.

A chirping pulse sounded behind Calen, mimicked by a second, and then a third, more and more rising spreading around them.

The sand shifted to Calen's left, eyes gleaming as an N'aka erupted from a sandbank, hurtling towards Calen. Before Calen could even draw his sword, Valerys pulled himself from Erik and spun, his spearhead tail slicing into the N'aka's skull in mid-air with a wet slap. The creature's body flopped over itself, dangling, blood flowing, the tip of Valerys's tail embedded in its skull.

More shapes shifted around them, only part-obscured in the perpetual twilight, scavengers sensing weakness in their prey.

Valerys snapped his tail outwards, sending the limp body of the N'aka hurtling away. Then all hell broke loose.

Calen slid his sword from its scabbard, sweeping it across his body, cleaving the jaw of an N'aka that had come upon him with impossible speed. All around, he saw glints of steel and flashes of obsidian claws.

Valerys lunged forwards, cracking his wings against the air for extra lift. He smashed into two N'aka who were lunging towards Calen, his talons rending their flesh. A swipe of his tail split one of the beasts along the side, shattered bones, blood, and entrails spilling into the sand, steam wafting in the cold air. But even as the dragon tore through the creatures, more spilled from the darkness. Three N'aka leapt onto Valerys's back, the scythe-like talons of the third limbs slicing into his scales. A cry sounded to Calen's left. He spun to see Tarmon on his back, two of the creatures tearing at him, his sword in the sand a few feet away.

Vaeril stood a few feet from Tarmon, sweeping his blade in an even stroke, slicing through leathered hide, opening chests, severing limbs. The elf moved fluidly, but Calen could see the exhaustion that gripped him, blood streaming from a nasty cut on the side of his head.

Where's Erik?

A warning flashed from Valerys's mind, and Calen swept his swords upwards, a metallic clang sounding as his blade collided with one of Erik's. Erik swept his second sword low, aiming for Calen's gut. It was only by sheer luck that Calen stepped backwards fast enough to avoid his intestines being spilled out into the sand.

"You did this!" Erik roared, lunging forward. His eyes had turned to a near-black, his irises a vibrant red.

Calen moved backwards, frantically trying to block Erik's swings. There was no world where Calen could stand toe-to-toe with Erik. He dropped into Crouching Bear, letting the forms of the fellensír – the lonely mountain – flow through him. Vibrations jarred his arms as he caught Erik's ferocious strikes, turning them away as best as he could. Searing pain burned through his left quad, then across his forearm, steel slicing through flesh.

"Erik, stop!"

Erik lunged forward, feinting high then striking low, his blade slicing through the flesh of Calen's left calf. Calen dropped to one knee, the strength in his left leg momentarily giving way.

"Erik!"

A flash movement and Tarmon was charging, crashing into Erik with a dropped shoulder. Erik tumbled backwards into the sand, colliding with two N'aka who had been charging towards him.

Calen looked to Tarmon, who stood before him, chest heaving, eyes blackened with red irises just as Erik's had been, greatsword gripped firmly in his fists. Tarmon held Calen's gaze, and Calen could see the conflict warring within the man: his jaw twitched, clenching and unclenching; his hand shook; veins bulged in his head and neck, straining.

With an almighty roar, Tarmon turned away, cleaving an N'aka in half as it leapt through the air, its body slopping to the ground.

I need to do something, and I need to do it now. I can't let this happen. Not like this.

Calen opened himself to the Spark, feeling the cool touch of Air, the rough grate of Earth, and the calming touch of Spirit as he pulled the threads into him. Something thrummed in the back of his mind: Fire, calling to him.

Calen reached out to Valerys, feeling the dragon's consciousness roar in fury, blazing like a raging inferno. He let their minds slide together, let Valerys's strength become his, Valerys's power fill his bones. *Draleid n'aldryr.* The words in his mind ignited a surge that swept through him. The power of the Spark flooded his veins, rippling, pulsing, yearning to be free. It was all Calen could do to hold the power at bay, to contain it, to harness it. His body trembling, he separated the threads into three cores, one consisting of Spirit, Air, and Fire; the second, Fire and Earth; the last simply Spirit.

I need to protect them. Protect my family.

"Close your eyes!" He roared, screaming so loudly his throat felt as though it would crack and bleed. Closing his own eyes, Calen pushed the threads of Fire, Air, and Spirit together, forming a baldír, flooding it with more power than he had ever pushed into a baldír before. Even through his eyelids, he could see the flash of bright light. Pulsing shrieks tore through the night as the baldírlight burned the N'akas' eyes.

Calen reached out with thin threads of Spirit, weaving them like tendrils through the air, searching for the N'aka around him, surprised to find almost a hundred of the creatures. Once his threads of Spirit were tethered to the N'aka, Calen pushed threads of Earth into the sand below him, feeling the ground ripple in waves. He could feel the N'aka fleeing, scrambling from the blinding light of the baldír. Part of him wanted to let them go, to let them run. But that part of him paled in comparison to the burning, furious rage that surged through the soul he shared with Valerys. The rage of a dragon was a thing like no other. And so Calen let go. He answered the call of the Fire, letting it burn through him.

He pushed that energy into the threads of Fire and Earth, lifting the sand, moulding it into spikes, heating it with the rage of a dragon's heart. With his eyes still closed, Calen let out a scream that tore at his chest, hearing Valerys's roar match his own.

Valerys's rage consumed him, power burning through his veins, energy crackling over his skin like lightning erupting outwards.

TARMON LAY TREMBLING IN THE SAND, his right hand grasped around the hilt of his greatsword, his left hand clasped over his closed eyes, his lungs burning, blood seeping from the plethora of cuts that laced his body. His mind was chaos. Voices whispered at the edges of his consciousness. Whatever Calen had done had pushed them back, but they were still there, calling to him, clawing at his mind. *What's happening?*

The blinding light began to dissipate through the gaps in his fingers, pulling away. Slowly, he took his hand from his face and peeled one eye open, flinching as the fading baldírlight burned.

What in the name of Varyn and all the gods…

All around, N'aka hung suspended in the air, their bodies pierced by spikes of glass that seemed to almost glow, illumined by the light of the moon overhead. There had to be nearly a hundred of the creatures hanging lifeless, their crimson blood streaming down the long glass spikes, dripping and pooling in the sand.

Erik and Vaeril lay on their backs, their hands over the faces.

At the centre of all the death stood Calen and Valerys. The ground beneath Calen's feet had turned to glass, glittering in the purple light that misted from his eyes, drifting both outwards and upwards, just as at Kingspass. He stood with his feet shoulder width apart, his curved sword gripped tight in his right fist, his chest heaving as he dragged in long breaths. Valerys rose behind Calen, towering, his black-veined wings spread wide, his white scales gleaming in the moonlight despite the blend of sand and crimson blood that coated his body, dripping from his tail and jaws. Just as Calen's, the dragon's eyes misted with a purple light, scanning the battlefield, watching for signs of movement, a deep rumble resonating from his chest.

The pair looked as though they had been sent by the gods.

His chest heaving, his arms trembling, Calen dropped to his knees, letting out a gasp as he hit something solid where he had expected sand. He looked down to see he knelt on what appeared to be glass, illuminated by the purple glow from his eyes. The glass spread outward, with him at its centre. It rose at random points, jutting upwards into flicks and spikes. All about him, N'aka hung dead, their bodies perforated by glass, limbs hanging loose, blood flowing in thin streams held back by the glass.

He felt Valerys's mind wrapped around his own, cradling it. He didn't have to look to know the dragon stood over him, wings spread wide, rage still smouldering in his heart.

Calen let his arms droop to his side, his fingers still loosely gripped around the hilt of his father's sword. Though his bones were weary, Calen's veins burned with energy. It rippled through him. At any other time, drawing so much from the Spark would have knocked him to the point of passing out. *How is this possible? Did I do this?* He tried to release his hold on the Spark to find he had already let it go, and yet he could still feel the same warmth. The glass beneath his feet shimmered, reflecting the purple light that glowed from his eyes. But more than that, he saw a second source of light in the glass – another pair of eyes.

Calen heaved himself to his feet, at the same turning towards Valerys, who was standing behind him. The dragon was beautiful. Twice as large as a bear, wings even larger, dense muscle rippling beneath his blood-splattered scales. A glowing purple mist drifted from the dragon's eyes, like steam rising from frozen steel. The power that Calen felt was the bond. There was nothing to explain it, but he knew. The energy thrummed through both him and Valerys, yet it seemed to come from somewhere unseen, a core that was both separate and together. Calen could feel it in his mind as he could the elemental strands of the Spark. What he felt now was something entirely different to anything he had felt before. This was balance – a harmony of two souls.

"Calen."

Calen turned at the sound of Tarmon's voice. Energy crackled through him, lightning in his veins. He clenched his fingers around the hilt of his sword. Valerys leaned his head forward, blood dripping from his jaws.

The big man shook his head, stumbling forwards. His left hand clasped to a wound over his right breast. He limped, favouring his left leg. Blood and dust marred his face, streaked by sweat. "My mind is my own. Whatever you did pushed the voices back."

Whatever I did? What did I do? The memory was hazy. A blinding light, power surging. At the last minute, he had pushed threads of Spirit outwards to amplify the Fire and Earth… Had that done something?

"But I'm not sure for how long." Tarmon stumbled and Calen stepped forwards to catch him. Somehow, the hulking man felt light in Calen's grip. "I can still hear the voices scratching at the back of my mind, pushing to get back in."

"It's all right," Calen whispered, lowering Tarmon to a patch of sand where the glass hadn't spread. "The others…"

Both Erik and Vaeril were slowly rising to their feet. The left side of the elf's face was coated in blood, his blond hair matted to the side of his head with thick globs of dark red. He sheathed his sword as he rose, casting his eyes at the suspended bodies of the N'aka.

Erik didn't so much as glance at the bodies hanging from the glass spikes. He stared at Calen wordlessly. As though only just realising he still held both his swords, Erik slid them into the scabbards on his back.

"Tarmon is right," Vaeril said, groaning as he touched his hand to the side of his head. "I can hear it too… It's like whispers, echoing faintly. But they're growing stronger. I hadn't noticed them before. They're like a slow-acting poison."

As Calen stood there, the pieces slowly began to slip into place in his mind. "It isn't the N'aka that kill whatever enters the Burnt Lands. It isn't the N'aka, and it isn't the heat, or the endlessness. It's themselves."

Both Tarmon and Vaeril looked at Calen as though he were mad.

"I… don't… follow." A grunt broke up each word that left Tarmon's mouth. The man clasped the wound in his chest, his muscles tensing and slackening as he forced himself to stay standing.

Erik finally spoke. "The soldiers on the plateau. They were all Lorian. But their wounds weren't all caused by claw and talon… They were made by steel. They killed each other… The N'aka just picked at the scraps."

Calen nodded sombrely. The realisation was a dark one.

Vaeril's head tilted upwards, an acknowledgement in his eyes. "They were on the same side. Of course."

"You need to go." Erik stepped towards Calen, a look of hesitancy in his eyes – and guilt. "Take Valerys and fly. Whatever is causing these voices doesn't seem to affect you. If… if you stay, we'll…." Erik looked at his blood-covered hands, then back up towards Calen. "I won't let that happen, Calen. I refuse." Erik let out a gasp, clasping both his hands to the sides of his head. He stopped, shaking his head and settling himself. "No," he whispered, swallowing hard. He pulled his hands away from his head. "I can feel it, like a weight pressing down on me, whispering. You need to go *now*."

"I'm not leaving you."

"Calen, I—"

"I'm not leaving you!" The anger in Calen's voice was part his own, part Valerys's. He hadn't noticed his hand clenching into a fist or the deepening of his breaths. "There has to be a way."

"No one has found a way through in four hundred years."

"Nothing has ever been done, until the day it is," Tarmon grunted, leaning on a thick spike of glass that jutted upwards from the sand. "And there hasn't been a Draleid in four hundred years either. Likely no-one else has ever had this chance inside this deathscape. We need to use it. What did you do, Calen?"

"I'm not sure…" Calen trailed off, trying to think. "Something took over… The bond. The bond between me and Valerys. I tethered threads of Spirit to the N'aka—" A realisation struck "—and to you! I tethered threads of Spirit to the three of you to make sure you weren't struck. Then I pushed threads outwards in a wave… I…" Black spots filled Calen's memory. The bond had taken over. "I'm not entirely sure what I did…"

Erik and Tarmon's faces dropped, a darkness looming over them. But Vaeril barely even reacted. He had seemed deep in contemplation since Calen had mentioned Spirit. "Vaeril, is there anything you can…"

He felt Vaeril reach for the Spark, pulling on threads of Spirit. The threads drifted on the air, weaving around Vaeril's body like ribbons attached to strings before encasing him from head to toe, each thread wrapping around the next in a dedicated pattern, spinning a latticed web. A ward of Spirit. The elf let out a sudden gasp, dropping forward onto his hands. Calen moved towards him, but Vaeril held up an open palm.

"I'm all right."

Whatever the elf had tried hadn't worked.

Vaeril drew in a series of deep breaths, steadying himself, then once more pulled on threads of Spirit, drawing them into himself, weaving them around and through his body. The threads expanded, layering over each other, constantly in motion, shifting, whirling. After a few moments, a visible shiver ran through Vaeril, and his shoulders drooped, his head hanging back, a relieved smile on his lips. The elf rose to his feet, a weary look in his eyes.

Calen rested his hand on Vaeril's shoulder. "Did it work?"

The elf nodded. "I think so. The voices aren't completely gone, but they're holding in the back of my mind, and they aren't pushing any closer." The elf stopped for a moment, taking a breath. "You feel nothing? Hear nothing? No whispering voices or oily sensations snaking through your thoughts?"

Calen shook his head. "Nothing."

"Your bond with Valerys must protect you. That has to be it. If you hadn't been here, we would've slit each other's throats. It goes a long way towards explaining why nobody has ever left this place. Can you follow what I'm doing?"

"I think so." Calen nodded hesitantly. If he focused, he could see the elf's threads of Spirit weaving through his body, see the patterns as Vaeril had been teaching him.

"The darkness is a tangible thing," Vaeril said. "As soon as you try to push it away, it will push back. Don't try to attack it, deflect it. If you try to push against it, it will drain you faster than you can blink. Don't be a wall, be a rock in a river. It's not as complex as a true ward of Spirit. You're not blocking me from the Spark, you're deflecting the darkness. Redirecting it. When you're ready, lay your threads over mine. Use them as a guide. Mimic them. Then I will let go of my own."

Calen nodded. He felt Valerys's hesitancy, his lavender eyes focused on Calen. Drawing in a deep breath, Calen reached out to the Spark. He could feel it pulsing in his mind, the elemental strands twisting and turning. Carefully, he pulled on threads of Spirit, just as Vaeril had done.

"Good, push them through me and around me. Wrap them around my core. Keep them in constant motion – that's the hardest part."

Calen drew in another breath, then did as Vaeril instructed, pushing the threads through the elf's body and wrapping them around, never allowing them to stay still, keeping them in constant motion, tracing them over the threads Vaeril had already laid. A force pushed back, hard and fast, like a wall of steel closing in around Calen.

"Don't fight it," the elf said, looking into Calen's eyes. "Redirect it."

"I'm trying," Calen said through gritted teeth. He tried to steady his breathing, to focus. The energy that had thrummed through him was slowly fading. He could feel it evaporating as Valerys's rage calmed.

"Good," the elf said as Calen's threads began to move over his own. "That's it. Let it break over you, wash around you."

After a few moments, Calen felt the force pushing against him lessen. It didn't vanish entirely, but it faded to the edges of his consciousness. He felt Vaeril release his own threads.

"Very good," Vaeril said, panting, reaching out and resting his hand on Calen's shoulder. The elf's eyes were dark and sunken, like someone who had just woken up from the night after drinking their bodyweight in ale.

It took a while for Vaeril to catch his breath before he was able to cast shields around Tarmon's and Erik's minds. But when he did, the relief was visible on their faces. The elf folded his arms across his chest, then let out a sigh. "A ward like this one doesn't take much energy to maintain, but with this darkness pushing against it, neither of us will be able to hold in place for longer than half a day. Even at that, it's near impossible to be sure."

Coils of dread twisted in Calen's stomach.

"What, so that's just it?" Erik said. "Come nightfall, we kill each other?"

"No." Vaeril moved his tongue across his teeth, pondering. He let out a sigh. "We have two choices. Either Calen and I can alternate, one resting while the other shields the whole group, or we work together and segment our shielding."

"How long can you hold the shields if you alternate?" Tarmon asked, wiping the blood from his greatsword with a cloth from his pack and sheathing the blade.

"If I gave you a number, I'd be telling you a lie. But far less than if we split the burden."

"That's not the real problem though," Calen said, his mouth a grim line as he looked to Vaeril.

Realisation set into Tarmon's face. "You're going to have to sleep sometime."

"And if I sleep and something happens to Vaeril…"

"We kill each other." Erik stared at two N'aka who had been skewered by a single spike of glass that stood almost six feet in length and was almost half a foot across.

"Then, we have one option." Tarmon folded his arms. "We move forward to shelter, we bind mine, Erik, and Vaeril's hands and feet, and strap the weapons to Valerys. Calen can rest while Valerys watches over us, and our feet and hands will be bound. When we wake, Calen can shield Vaeril, untie him, then move to myself and Erik."

Vaeril turned his lip down in a satisfied pout. "And I'll be too drained at night to draw from the Spark so I won't be a danger that way."

"So we make ourselves bait for the N'aka?" Erik puffed out his cheeks and shook his head. "Fantastic."

"Doing it this way will ensure we cover the most ground possible during the day. And I say the quicker we leave this place, the better." Tarmon rested his palm on one of the bloodied glass spikes. "Besides, I think the N'aka might look for easier prey now."

THAT NIGHT, AS CALEN SAT beneath the cover of an arched rock, his back against the side of a sleeping Valerys, his breath misting in the air, he felt something. A low resounding beat, slow and rhythmic. It wasn't a sound or a vibration; it didn't ripple through the air. It was a pulse. The beating heart of the waste, calling to him. *Thump.* He could feel it in his bones. The pull was so strong it took everything Calen had to stay where he was. Behind him, in the full cover of the rock, the others lay sleeping, hands and feet bound.

'What kind of cruel trick do the gods play on us? You let your family die… You let Ellisar die as well. Korik. Lopir. Falmin. And now you risk our lives. You drag us across this gods forsaken wasteland to try and save the friend you left behind.' Erik's words echoed in Calen's mind. Whether Erik had meant them or not, they still held truth. His family had died because he had brought the empire to The Glade. That had been his doing. There was no way around it. Ellisar, Korik, Lopir, Falmin. In one way or another, they had all died because of Calen. No matter the path forward, more would die. Hundreds. Thousands. The thought threatened to consume him. It gnawed at his mind. He hadn't asked for this, yet here he was.

I cannot bring back those who are gone. But I can fight for those who are left.

He tightened his fingers around the hilt of his sword, which sat on his lap. Subconsciously, he traced the fingers of his left hand along the intricate spiral patterns of the blade his father given him while he held his gaze on the ever-shifting sand of the dunes.

Thump.

Calen drew in a deep breath, casting his gaze towards the star-framed horizon. He knew what called him. He had seen it in his dreams. Ilnaen. The heart of all the darkness that had destroyed this place.

Thump.

WIND CRASHED AGAINST CALEN as he tore through the sky. Above him, a pinkish-red moon hung low, illuminating charcoal clouds. Below him, a city burned. Flames raging, white stone tarnished with black soot.

What is this place?

Power surged through him as his wings beat against the sky, shimmering an emerald green in the eerie moonlight. Dread and panic consumed his heart. Every fibre of his being cried out, desperate to reach wherever he was going.

It's another dream.

Ahead, an enormous tower rose from the city, so tall it scraped the clouds. A white stone chamber stood at the tower's top, connected by a stone walkway to a building that looked to be a larger version of the Belduaran keep. But he wasn't concerned about the walkway or the keep. What he wanted was in the top of that tower.

No, not what he wanted – what he *needed*.

Reaching deep inside, he unleashed a roar so primal, so visceral it shook his bones. Then, a familiar feeling coursed through Calen. Pressure building. Something he had come to know so well. But this was *different*. Raw power. It burned through him like a river of lightning, surging through his veins, through his soul. Then, when the power built to a point that he could no longer hold it within, he opened his jaws and unleashed a torrent of dragonfire on the outer wall of the tower, crashing against the stone. The wall of the tower exploded inwards under the force of the blast, consuming the inner chamber in a cloud of stone and dust.

Following the path of his flames, Calen cracked his wings against the air, burying the claws at the end of his forelimbs into the stone on either side of the newly created opening, anchoring himself with his talons.

There, standing beneath him, her blue níthral radiating light across the white stone, was who he had come for: his soulkin. His beating heart. Everything that was anything in the world. Alvira.

Two hooded figures stood before Alvira, rippling black fire blades in their hands. *Fades.* Once more, lightning rippled through Calen's body, the pressure building, burning. Those creatures needed to die. He could not let them harm Alvira. That could never happen. He would not let it happen. Just as the pressure built to a head, Calen opened his jaws, and a raging river of dragonfire poured forth. The creatures howled and screamed as their dark souls were ripped from the shells of flesh they had stolen.

Within the chamber was another. A traitor. A murderer of both Draleid and dragon. Eltoar.

An earth-shattering roar tore through the sky, giving Calen only a moment's warning before Helios, the black-scaled dragon that was bound to Eltoar crashed into his side with such immense force it ripped him free of the tower, his talons raking long furrows through the stone.

Vyldrar! Alvira's words thundered through Calen's mind. Grief. Sorrow.

He clawed and snapped at the other dragon as they plummeted. He needed to break free. He couldn't leave Alvira alone. She needed him. He roared as Helios's talons raked along his side, and he shrieked as Helios tore at his neck.

He needed to protect Alvira. But he could see the void. Hear it calling to him. Fear gripped Calen's mind. Not fear for his own life, but for Alvira's. Fear of leaving her alone in the world. He thrashed, raking his talons down Helios's side, ripping away scale and flesh, bathing him in dragonfire. But it wasn't enough. Helios had always been his better. Always been larger, stronger. But he had once been a friend. Even then, he could feel the regret, the sadness, radiating from Helios's mind.

Every part of him howled in pain as the bigger dragon ripped at him with its claws and tore at him with its teeth. Helios's jaws clamped around his neck. He pulled his mind as far from Alvira's as he could – he didn't want her to feel him die.

Calen closed his eyes.

CALEN GASPED AS HE JOLTED upright, a chill sweeping through him. His heart pounded, his chest trembled, and his body dripped with a cold sweat. He reached out for Valerys, aching to feel the warmth of the dragon's mind. He turned, his body shaking, the night's chill evaporating as he laid his hand on the scales of Valerys's side, and he felt the dragon's mind touch his.

Concern radiated from Valerys at the feeling of Calen's panic. The dragon, who had stayed awake to guard the group while Calen slept, brought his head around, a deep rumble resonating from his chest.

Calen got to his knees, resting his forehead against Valerys's snout, running his palms along the ridges of horns that framed the dragon's face as he tried to process what he had just seen. Every hair on his body still stood on end, pure, unbridled grief ripping at his heart, tearing strips from him. That had been Alvira Serris, the Archon of the Draleid, and the dragon to which she had been bound, Vyldrar. Calen knew without having to question. He had seen through Vyldrar's eyes, felt his heart. Even as the more logical half of his brain told him it had only been a dream, he knew it had been real. No dream could have felt like that. No dream could have held such pain. He had felt Vyldrar's fear as he died, his loss, his heartache. Even when Vyldrar had died, his only thought had been of Alvira. Calen lifted his head, looking into the shimmering lavender of Valerys's eyes, black slits running through their centre.

"My soul to yours."

A deep rumble reverberated in Valerys's throat as the dragon pushed his head against Calen's hands. Valerys couldn't speak, not in the way Calen could, but the pure warmth that spilled over from the dragon's mind said more than words ever could.

Soulkin.

CHAPTER TWENTY-FOUR

FAITH

Rist sat on a bench in the gardens outside the embassy kitchens, a large oak tree hanging over him, blocking out the glaring light of the sun. He held a deep wooden bowl filled with beef stew in his left hand and a spoon in the other.

Mages of all affinities sat around the garden, chatting and eating their lunch in the midday sun. They were mostly of middling rank, their colours proudly displayed in their robes and cloaks, but some wore garments touched with silver, marking them as High Mages.

Rist drew in a deep breath, closing his eyes for a moment, the low hum of chatter setting a baseline in the back of his mind. The gardens beside the kitchens were his favourite place to eat lunch for precisely this reason. At times he preferred the silence of the library or his quarters, but there were just days when the background hum of life set his mind at ease.

If I'm quick eating this stew, I can get some reading in before I meet Garramon.

Rist had reached that point in *Druids, a Magic Lost* where he spent every moment he wasn't reading thinking about reading. He was about halfway finished – while also being a fifth of the way through *The Forging of an Empire*, which was incidentally turning out to be exactly the sort of read he had been looking for. He was starting to see what Garramon had meant when he said the writing in *Druids, a Magic Lost* became little more than babble and lost all structure after a while. Though it seemed there was more to it than that. Duran Linold was throwing around wild claims to do with Druids and the Varsund War, old gods, and the altering weather patterns. The strangest things were mentions of the Varsund War, which happened over a thousand years after Duran Linold had written the book. All the while, the writing style had begun to slowly change from a factual recording to more of an informal journal. On the surface, Rist could see why anyone would brush it off as babble. Duran's words certainly wandered, but the man's observations were still astute – even in the wanderings.

Stop letting your own mind wander. Eat.

Rist dipped his spoon into the stew, salivating as he lifted it back out, seeing a hunk of beef dripping with oil-glistened sauce. The muscles in his stomach threatened to spasm as he brought the spoon to his mouth – not from hunger, but from overuse. Sister Anila had asked Brother Magnus to let Rist and Neera observe formational exercises and allow them to join in once he had deemed their knowledge competent. Instead, he had let them watch once and then tossed them into the mix. It hadn't only been formational exercises in relation to the Spark that he had tossed them into. No, he had included them in combat formations, close-order and extended-order drills, stamina and endurance training, and even the 'fine art of latrine digging', as Magnus had insisted it be called – in its entirety, every time it was mentioned.

A pair of hands clapped down on Rist's shoulders, and he let out an aching groan, his hand jerking, the hunk of beef and spoonful of stew falling to the ground.

"It goes *in* your mouth, Rist." Tommin dropped himself down on the bench beside Rist, his smile as broad and unrelenting as ever.

"Tommin, you're a bastard."

"Now, now, no need for foul language. I'll have Neera wash that mouth out with soap." Tommin winked. "So this is where you ran off to after Brother Pirnil's lecture. Speaking of bastards, he cut me deep today. I'm going to have to get one of the other healers to look at it."

Sighing, Rist lowered his bowl of stew down to his lap. "Tommin, he asked why you were late and you said, 'Wouldn't you like to know?' What did you think was going to happen?"

"I was telling a joke, clearly."

"Have you met Brother Pirnil? He doesn't joke."

"I can't let you be the one taking all the lashings. You give him reasons to strip the skin on your back so often I'm beginning to think you enjoy it." Tommin winked again, letting out a laugh. "Anyway, how's the stew?"

Tommin reached over and grabbed Rist's spoon, dipping it into the stew, then lobbing it into his mouth.

"I wouldn't know." Rist glared at Tommin, snatching the spoon back from him. "I haven't tried it yet."

"Ish good," Tommin managed to say, his mouth still half full of stew. Tommin reminded Rist a bit of Dann – he was a bit nicer, far less coordinated, and he probably had no idea how to skin a kat, but he had that same natural cheekiness to him.

Rist grunted, shaking his head and lifting the bowl of soup from his lap, licking his lips as he dunked his spoon back into the stew.

"How're you feeling?"

Rist leapt forward as Neera stuck her hands between his arms and tickled his ribs. He tried desperately to keep his grip on the wooden bowl of stew but watched in agony as it slipped from his fingers and *clacked* against the ground, the stew spilling out into the well-maintained grass. "Fuck!"

As soon as the word left his mouth, Rist's body tightened. All around him, mages turned and stared at his outburst, more than a few eyebrows raised. They all knew who he was. They knew each apprentice. There were only four apprentices in the entire embassy, after all. The entire city, for that matter. But it was not simply them knowing him that was the problem, it was them knowing that Garramon was his sponsor. *'Need I remind you that your insubordination to other mages reflects on my ability as a sponsor?'* Rist flinched as Garramon's words floated in his mind. Garramon, unlike Brother Pirnil, was not quick to inflict direct physical pain, but he most definitely had other methods of admonishment.

Rist looked down at the spilled stew in the grass, chunks of beef and potato staring back at him, steam wafting. His stomach rumbled, and he let out a sigh. He turned to Neera, noticing Lena standing beside her, blonde hair draped down over her green-trimmed brown robe.

Neera must have seen the frustration on Rist's face because she actually apologised, which was about as rare a thing as a blue moon.

"It's all right," Rist said with a sigh, dropping down to pick up his bowl and spoon from the ground. "I wasn't hungry anyway."

"I don't know," Neera said, wrapping her fingers around Rist's bicep. "You're going to need it to fill these arms out. I've never seen a skinny Battlemage."

Rist jerked his arm away from Neera, his jaw clenching reflexively.

"Rist, I didn't mean it like that."

"Yeah." Rist snatched up his pack, suppressing a groan as his muscles spasmed – the effects of so much training with Brother Magnus and Sister Anila. "I know. I just need to go. Brother Garramon asked me to meet him after I'd had lunch, and he doesn't like waiting."

Neera reached out, touching Rist's hand, but he pulled it away, giving her a weak smile and nodding to both Lena and Tommin as he walked off towards the main embassy. Lena had an awkward look on her face as though she had just watched a grown man kick a puppy, but Tommin looked as clueless as ever, beaming from ear to ear as he waved after Rist, looking shocked as Lena slapped him in the back of the head.

Rist's heart pounded against his ribs as he made his way through the embassy, his eyes fixed on the gilded black carpet that ran the length of every floor. He focused on the elaborate patterns of red and gold woven into the black fabric, not allowing his mind to fixate on Neera's words. He knew she had not meant it the way it had come out. At least, he didn't think she did. But that had not taken any of the sting from her words. He didn't want to be skinny, or frail, or small, or whatever other way people chose to describe him. He'd never asked for it. He would have given most anything to be as strong as Calen, or any of the other men in the villages, but it just hadn't been something he was gifted with.

Rist clenched his fist as he walked, his eyes tracing over an elaborate depiction of a pride of red and gold lions worked into the carpet. He had tried to put on weight, tried to eat more, but it had never stuck. Perhaps it had been because back home his diet had always been limited to whatever food they could afford at the time. The food in the embassy was like nothing he had ever seen. Braised beef with carrots, potatoes and thicky gravy; roast chicken stuffed with breading and salted bacon pork; duck slow cooked in its own rendered fat; baked rabbit served with layered potatoes, all soaked in a sauce made from wine. Whatever Rist wanted, the kitchen provided. On one hand, it brought him a deep comfort to know that he wouldn't be going hungry any time soon, but on the other hand, it felt wrong that so much food was at his fingertips here while some people back in the villages could go weeks on just grains, tubers, and whatever they could hunt. And often the portion sizes he received in the embassy were the same as would be split between two or three back home. It was the way of things. Some people just had more than others. But just because it was the way of things didn't mean it was right.

Over the past month or so, Rist had spent nearly every spare moment training. Be it honing the Spark with Brother Garramon, training in the sword with Sister Anila, battle formations with Brother Magnus, or the many, many hours of sword forms. Strength and muscle had not been gifted to him, but it would not be kept from him either. *Nothing worth having is ever easy, son. And nothing that's easy is ever worth having.* Rist could almost hear his father's voice speaking the words.

"Rist."

Rist looked up to see Brother Garramon standing before him, silver-trimmed black cloak draped over his shoulders and a curious look in his eye. Rist inclined his head. "Brother Garramon, please excuse me, I was lost in my thoughts."

"Not much different than usual then," Garramon said, giving Rist a soft smile that had once been as rare as Neera's apologies but seemed to be slowly growing more frequent. "Come, I wasn't expecting you so soon. I thought you'd still be eating. But now is as good a time as any. I was on my way to arrange one last thing."

Rist followed Garramon through the corridors of the embassy and out into the palace gardens, squinting at the glaring sun overhead, nestled snugly in blue skies.

"Brother, what are we doing?"

Garramon simply smiled again and nodded towards the doors of the library that lay across the garden, its many storeys rising high, its slate grey roof cresting over the palace walls. Naturally, Garramon's response – or lack thereof – served only to ignite a plethora of new questions, but Rist held them at bay. If Garramon had wanted to give answers, he would have. That was something Rist genuinely appreciated about his sponsor: he was straightforward. There were no games or twists or turns. If Garramon wanted to tell you something, he told you.

Once they had entered the library, Garramon spoke to one of the librarians, who looked at Rist with a narrowed gaze – likely because he knew Rist hadn't returned a number of his books to their shelves – then scuttled off to gather whatever Garramon had asked him for.

"Come," Garramon said, gesturing for Rist to follow him. "We are going to the top floor."

Rist hesitated. He had never been on the top floor. The library was an enormous building, longer than it was wide, with its two ends curved. It rose five storeys, each storey crammed with seemingly never-ending bookshelves, benches, tables, and small nooks. Candles sat on tables, the wicks only lit when someone was reading, while glass-encased oil lanterns stood on sconces fixed into the walls at evenly spaced intervals along the bookshelves. Despite the fact that having the flames so close to all those books set knots of anxiety in Rist's stomach, he did have to admit that the warm ambient glow combined with the earthy scent of ancient pages added an extra depth to the beauty of the library itself.

If Rist was being honest with himself, he had likely spent more time within the library's walls than he had his own quarters in the last while, but he had still never been to the top floor. The top floor was usually reserved for those who had been granted their full colours. The moment of hesitation faded away quickly, Rist's curiosity more than piqued.

Rist followed Garramon up the staircase on the opposite side of the long hall, then further up through the storeys, all the while admiring the sheer volume of knowledge contained within the great building. There were few thoughts that excited him more than being given a week alone in one of the reading nooks, any book he wished at his fingertips – something he thought best to never tell Neera. He didn't suppose he would ever be given that opportunity, but it was a worthy dream to have.

When they reached the top of the staircase, Rist was surprised to see it wasn't guarded whatsoever. The only sign that it was even restricted was a red velvet rope that hung between the two posts. Rist shook his head, letting out a low laugh. He had always thought the top floor would be guarded, but he had never actually looked for himself. He had been told it was off limits until he received his colours, and so he had simply left it alone. For the same reason he had never left the bounds of the palace until that night with Neera, he had never actually considered even attempting a journey to the top floor. It was off limits. Rules were rules, and breaking them would inevitably lead to an awkward situation – which even the thought of caused his stomach to turn in anxiety – and likely a completely avoidable reprimand.

"Are you well?"

Rist lifted his head to see Garramon standing on the landing of the top floor, the red velvet rope unhooked from the post and now in his hand.

"Hmm?"

"Are you well, apprentice?"

"Apologies, Brother." Rist made his way up the last few steps and onto the landing, Garramon re-hooking the rope behind him. "I was just…"

"Lost in your own thoughts again?" Rist nodded, and Garramon shook his head. "You're going to have to learn to control that lest it happen at a more inconvenient time."

"Why isn't the top floor guarded?"

"Guarded?" Garramon laughed. "There is nothing up here to guard, apprentice. The restriction is simply so that those who have been granted their colours have a place to sit in peace. A benefit of achievement, if you will. No," Garramon said, before Rist could even ask another question, "we do not keep restricted books on this level, or anywhere, for that matter." Garramon gave Rist a knowing look. The man seemed to know Rist a lot more than Rist had given him credit for. "Emperor Mortem believes that no knowledge should be restricted, for that is simply an obstacle to advancement. Now, come."

"If no knowledge should be restricted, then why can't I find any material on the trials or Alamants?" Rist had meant to keep that question to himself, but it had somehow slipped out, as most of his questions tended to. He braced himself for Garramon's answer while following the man along the balcony of the top floor that overlooked the rest of the library.

Garramon didn't turn. "Reading materials on Alamants are scarce, not restricted." Garramon turned a corner around a bookshelf. "It is simply a topic not many have pursued. I would recommend *The Weak Are Many, the Strong Few* by Gorgamel Alteer or *The Weakest Link* by Brinna Sonoen – though, as you can likely gather from the titles, neither are exactly unbiased accounts. With regards to trials of Faith and Will, materials are not restricted, they simply do not exist, for reasons that I hope are now clear to you. Had you known what to expect in the Trial of Will, it would not have been the same test."

"I suppose that makes sense." Rist frowned. Garramon's answer did indeed make sense, but it still wasn't one Rist was happy with.

"Here." Garramon stopped at a doorway covered over by a red velvet curtain, oil lamps fixed to the walls on either side, the glass that encased them blackened by smoke. He pulled back the curtain and gestured for Rist to enter.

"Oh, by Elyara." Rist got about two steps past the curtain before he stopped, staring around the room with awe. To anyone else, the word 'awe' might have been a touch dramatic, but for him, it was perfect. The room was about half the size of Rist's quarters, illuminated by glass-encased oil lanterns fixed to the walls. The wall on the right was obscured by a bookcase of dark, striated wood, every shelf full edge to edge with heavy leatherbound books. An L-shaped couch was pressed against the left corner of the room, upholstered with red velvet and golden tacks. The walls behind the couch were adorned with vivid tapestries woven with threads of various shades of red, black, gold, and white. A long table stood before the couch, crafted from the same dark wood as the bookshelf, thick and sturdy-looking. Four stacks of books sat on the table, each consisting of at least ten separate volumes.

Rist picked up the top book of the nearest stack, running his finger across the debossed title on its front – *Lifeblood, the Blood of Life.*

"Take a seat."

Rist set the book back atop the stack, then sat himself down on the couch as Garramon closed over the curtain behind him. His eyes lingered on Rist for a moment before he walked to the other side of the table and lowered himself onto the couch, moving a stack of books to the edge. He reached into his pocket, producing a small, black wooden box, placing it on the table, his hand hovering over its top for just a moment before he pushed it towards Rist. "Within this box is your Trial of Faith."

Rist's mouth grew suddenly dry, every drop of moisture fleeing. He swallowed reflexively, a hurricane of butterflies twisting in his chest. "I… al-already?"

Rist wanted to progress. He wanted to be raised to Acolyte, to earn the colours of the Battlemages, to feel the touch of the black robes draped over his shoulders. It was what he was training for. But simply hearing the words 'Trial of Faith' sent Rist's mind back to the horrors of the Trial of Will. A shiver ran through him, his breaths catching in his chest.

Memories flitted through his mind. Neera's dead body, her skin and lips pale and blue. The people of The Glade, broken and twisted, butchered. Tharn Pimm's body pinned to the wall of Iwan Swett's butcher by a blackened blade. The faceless man dragging his blade across Rist's mother's throat.

Calen.

'You should have been by my side.' Calen's words echoed.

'You've become a monster.' Rist's own voice was familiar yet foreign.

'I had to become one to defeat one.'

Rist drew a deep breath, settling himself, his chest trembling. He examined the box without touching it. It was small enough to fit in his palm and comprised two sections of black-stained hardwood joined together by a golden hinge at the back. But curiously, there was no clasp set at its front, no way to open it without breaking it. "What is it?"

Rist felt Garramon reaching for the Spark, drawing in thin threads of Air. The man funnelled the threads into the front of the box, moving them in a clockwise pattern. An audible *click* emanated from within, and Rist's heart stopped, his breath holding, his eyes staring. With the aid of a thread from Garramon, the lid of the box opened, and a deep crimson glow radiated from within.

Rist stared for a moment, his eyes wide, his mouth ajar. A small red gemstone, no bigger than a grape, sat within, nestled snugly on a bed of purple satin. The stone glowed with a crimson light that pulsated and moved. "I've seen one of these before."

The words took Garramon by surprise, his eyebrows raising. "Where?"

"In Ölm forest." Rist reached out, letting his hand hover just above the gemstone, the crimson light washing over his skin. "Set into the blade of an Urak's axe."

"Hmm." A deep rumble resonated from Garramon's throat, and he shifted in his seat.

"What is it?" Rist turned his attention from the gemstone, meeting Garramon's gaze. "Brother," he added hastily when he realised his tone had been rather curt.

"It is an Essence vessel. The gemstone has the very particular ability to bind Essence to its structure – the red glow you see is the light of the Essence."

Rist looked at the glowing gemstone. When he had first seen the gemstone in the Urak's axe in Ölm Forest, it had been translucent, but at some point a red glow had begun to radiate from it. Given that the axe was used to kill the wolfpine and take the Urak's head from its body, it didn't take a genius to connect the two threads. The question was one he wasn't sure he wanted to know the answer to. "Brother Garramon, what is Essence?"

"The day you shy away from asking questions is the day I will be truly concerned. Essence is the life force of all living things. It flows within you and me both at this very moment. But it cannot be used until it is free from its physical constraints."

"Until someone dies for it."

Garramon's mouth twisted, but he gave a short nod. "It's not as simple as that, but yes."

"It's Blood Magic." Rist pulled his hand away from the gemstone, suddenly feeling as though he would need to scrub the taint of its glow from his skin.

"That is a name for it, yes. But it is a name used by those who do not understand *what* it is."

Rist stared at the pulsating gemstone, his chest tightening.

"Let *me* ask *you* a question, Rist. When is it noble to kill?"

"I…" The question caught him off guard. Was it a trick? "It's never *noble* to kill."

"Not even in defence of the defenceless? What if you come across a man, a rapist, a murderer? And you find him in the motion of committing his next unspeakable act. And the only way to stop him is to kill him. What then? Is that noble?"

Rist ran his tongue across his now increasingly dry lips. "I… I'm not sure."

"When armies go to war. Hundreds die. Thousands. Tens of thousands. Blood spilled only to feed the soil – bodies returned to earth. Those who are victorious return home, hailed as heroes, champions of their people. But to those whose loved ones were slaughtered, they are murderers – despicable people who should be cast into the void. It's not so black and white, is it, this world we live in?"

Garramon's question was a rhetorical one, but Rist shook his head anyway. He wasn't feigning interest. Discussion of morality was a truly fascinating thing – at least as far as Rist was concerned. But with Garramon's words repeating in his head, Rist realized he hadn't asked the truly pertinent question. "Brother, you said my Trial of Faith was within the box. What *is* the trial?"

Garramon ran his tongue across his teeth, the fingers of his right hand tapping against the dense wood of the table. "The Trial of Faith is for any who wish to be granted Acolyteship of the Imperial Battlemages. It is to tap into a vessel and draw on the Essence within. It is to show faith in your Brothers and Sisters and in Efialtír himself. To trust in them."

The blood in Rist's veins turned to ice, his breath catching in his lungs. "You… you can't ask that of me. To be given my colours, I must open myself to Blood Magic? Brother, surely you see how wrong that is."

"You must be willing to challenge your preconceptions, apprentice. Do you believe every story you are told?"

"Of course not." Rist's voice was shaky, his throat and mouth dry. *Blood Magic? What in the gods is happening?*

"Then why do you hold so unshakingly to the poisonous words whispered in your ear as a child? To call Essence Blood Magic is the same as a hero branded a villain. The ability to harness and wield Essence is Efialtír's gift to us. I know in the South you call him The Traitor, for his refusal to abide the laws of the other gods in the time long past, but he truly *is* The Saviour, my apprentice. Through the gift of Essence, Efialtír allows something to come from death. He allows the act of creation to be born from destruction. With the wielding of Essence, no death is in vain." Garramon let out a sigh, then gave Rist a weak smile. "If I have learned anything of you, it is that you take nothing and nobody for their word. You question. You poke and prod. You yearn not simply for answers, but for understanding. You refuse to follow. These are not just qualities of a good man, apprentice, they are qualities of a leader, and they are qualities I admire. That is the reason I brought you here and not to some ceremonial chamber or the rickety chair in my study. These books before you are the deepest, most complete accounts of the wielding of Essence. They are the most objective texts I know of. There will still be bias within their pages, but I trust you to see through that. You are not limited to these texts. I have asked Gault, the librarian, to provide you with any other texts you wish." Garramon pulled himself to his feet, his eyes briefly gazing at the gemstone. "You have one week to make your decision. Have faith in me and The Circle and draw from the vessel, or refuse. The choice is yours, and I am convinced you will see the correct path."

Rist's stomach was doing somersaults, threatening to empty itself onto the table before him. "Brother?"

Garramon stopped with his hand on the edge of the curtain. He didn't turn. "Yes, apprentice?"

"What will happen if I refuse?"

"You already know the answer to that, Rist." Garramon pulled back the curtain, stepped through, then closed it, not waiting for Rist to ask another question.

The Spark will be burned from my body, and I will be cast from The Circle. It wasn't much of a choice, but at least it was a choice.

CHAPTER TWENTY-FIVE

WATER TO BLOOD, BLOOD TO BONE

How are you feeling?" Ella closed the infirmary door behind her, giving Tanner a weak smile. With the exception of Tanner, Ella, and one new occupant who lay sleeping in the bed at the back of the room, the infirmary was empty.

"I've been better," Tanner replied, wincing as he pushed himself upright in bed. "But Coren does a good job of easing the pain."

Ella moved to the side of the bed, resting her hand atop Tanner's. "I'm sorry I didn't come to see you sooner. I didn't know what to say."

Tanner shook his head. "It's all right."

"No. It's not. You risked your life to find the truth. You realise if anything had happened to you, Yana would have killed me in my sleep?"

Tanner spluttered. "Don't make me laugh." He clasped his hand to his stomach, choking laughs escaping his throat. "It hurts when I laugh. Yana would never have killed you. She's not as fierce as she looks."

Ella raised an eyebrow but didn't say a word.

"All right," Tanner acquiesced. "She might have killed you."

"She most definitely would have killed me. Tanner, why?"

"Why what? Why did I stay?" Tanner drew a deep breath, grunting in pain. "I don't have any children, Ella. The gods never saw fit to grant me that gift. Rhett was the closest thing I ever had. With my brother moving south, I never got to see them much, but I would have done anything for them. And from the moment I met you, I could see the same love in you. And the way Rhett spoke about you in his letters." Tanner rested his hand on Ella's, smiling as he shook his head. "He loved you so fiercely. I couldn't protect him, but I can protect you."

It was only the tickling sensation on Ella's cheek that let her know she was crying. She sniffled, shaking her head. "That's not something you have to do."

"Oh, I'm well aware. Something tells me you have no problem looking after yourself, especially with that shadow you call a wolfpine." Faenir grumbled at the mention of him, not bothering to lift his head from where he lay curled up by the door. "If you do nothing else in this world, you protect your family, Ella Fjorn. And let me tell you, whether you swore the oaths or not, you are my family now."

AN INTERCONNECTED SERIES OF TUNNELS, just like the one Ella currently walked down, linked all the chambers, alcoves, and caverns of Tarhelm. Ella ran her hand along the smooth stone of the tunnel as she made her way from the living quarters to the southern gate. The tunnel wall held none of the usual roughness of hewn rock. It was as flat and unwrinkled as polished steel. Yana had explained to her that the entire outpost had been carved using the same magic that Farda, Coren, and Farwen wielded. But knowing it was one thing, and understanding was something entirely different.

Every fifty or so feet, beams of light sliced through the dimness of the tunnel, particles of dust and powdered rock floating in the illuminated air. The main chambers utilised lanterns and torches. Some of the larger caverns even had openings in the rock ceiling to maximise natural light. But in the tunnels, it wasn't practical to keep lanterns burning, so long circular passages, no more than half a foot in diameter, were utilised to funnel light from the outside. Yana had called them 'light vents'.

Ella stopped at the nearest vent, squinting as she stared within. The light that now drifted through was dawnlight. The sun had not yet risen above the horizon.

"Come on," she said, scratching the top of Faenir's head, picking up her pace.

The tunnel opened into a small chamber no more than twenty feet wide and half that across. Four guards in various leathers and steel breastplates, leaned against the walls and sat about on upturned crates.

Standing near the entrance to another tunnel on the other side of the chamber was Coren. The woman was garbed neck to toe in plate armour, a helm with a thin slit for eyes resting in the crook of her arm. It had been almost two weeks since Coren's offer for Ella to join her at dawn, but if the woman was surprised to see Ella, she showed no signs of it. "Good." Coren offered a slight upturn of her lips. She nodded towards a bench that sat to the left side of the tunnel entrance. "Put that on."

Ella looked down at the bench, her gaze falling on a folded shirt of mail and a heavy-looking set of steel plate armour that was laid out meticulously: a breastplate, helm, pauldrons, a pair of greaves and bracers, heavy gloves and boots, and every other piece of armour Ella had ever seen. "Why?"

"Just put it on."

Ella stared back at Coren for a moment, but eventually acquiesced. Whatever the woman had planned that required a full plate armour, Ella wasn't sure she wanted to know. But if she was going to have any hope of keeping Calen safe, she needed to learn whatever Coren had to teach.

Ella let out a sigh and picked up the coat of mail by the shoulders, letting the links unfurl with a series of clinks and jingles. She slipped her arms through, hefting the mail over her shoulders, letting it slide down over her torso. She looked down at the set of steel plates and armour laid out on the bench. "All of it?"

"All of it."

THE SUN WAS BARELY VISIBLE over the Veloran Ocean in the east as Ella stepped from the tunnel out onto the mountainside, the armour clinking as she walked, weighing her down, sweat already forming on her brow and the small of her back. Donning the mail and armour had given her a new appreciation for those that did it on a regular basis, and not simply for the weight of it or the awkward movement, but for how claustrophobic it felt. She was an insect encased in a carapace, her body unable to breathe.

Coren and Faenir stepped out of the tunnel behind her. Faenir brushed his side against Ella's hip, attempting to alleviate the anxiety that she had only just noticed was setting in.

The tunnel to the eastern gate led out into a small basin dotted with trees and bushes, through which a rivulet flowed. The Firnin Mountains rose around them, sweeping out and upwards, winding peaks of sandy-brown rock and twisted-limbed trees, the occasional patches of green dotted about. The squawks of early birds and the whistle of the mountain wind filled the air, accented by the burbling of the rivulet.

"Please, in the name of Heraya, tell me we're not climbing to there." Ella pointed towards a jagged peak that jutted up towards the sky to the east, looking as though it was only vaguely connected to the mountain they now stood on.

Coren laughed, shaking her head. "Not yet. You would most definitely die if we attempted that. Today we climb to that peak." Coren pointed towards a nearer peak that still looked as though it reached a few thousand feet higher than where they were currently standing. "There's a copse of fir trees at the top, and the view is spectacular."

Ella rolled her head, trying to relieve some of the tension that had already begun to set into her neck and shoulders. She puffed out her cheeks. "How is this going to help me?"

Coren smiled and started walking. "Try to keep up."

Within minutes of trekking up the side of the mountain, Ella's legs were on fire. Her lungs heaved, every breath vibrating in the helmet

Coren had insisted she wear. Ella had always considered herself to be physically fit. She had always spent her days being active, working in the forge with her dad or helping her mam tend to the wounded and gather herbs and plants. But she supposed trekking up the side of mountains in full plate armour was a slightly different thing.

Faenir, however, loved every second. The wolfpine loped ahead, flitting between the sparse trees and shrubs, leaping between ledges of rock, his fur ruffling in the wind. Ella couldn't help but smile at the sense of freedom that touched the wolfpine's mind – that was something she was still getting used to: the ability to sense Faenir's emotions, to *feel* his thoughts. If she focused hard enough, she thought she could even smell through his nose. Everything became sharper and clearer: the freshness of the wind, the distinct scent of pine needles, the damp of moss.

Minutes became hours as they climbed, and the burn in Ella's muscles turned to unceasing agony. Her legs refused to obey her commands, her stride more a hobble than anything else. Her lungs heaved, dragging in ragged breaths. Sweat saturated the shirt and thin trousers she wore beneath her armour. Ella lifted her head, seeing Faenir padding along beside her, a low whine emanating from his throat, Coren walking a few feet ahead, only partially visible in the glare of the sun, which seemed to burn hotter in the North than it did in the South.

Ella let out a gasp as her armoured foot caught a rock and she stumbled. She held herself upright for a moment, but then her legs spasmed, and she dropped to the ground, the vibration jarring her arms as her palms slammed against the rock. Her stomach turned, and her mouth began to salivate in the way it always did right before she needed to vomit. The familiar acidic taste hit the back of her throat, and Ella emptied the sparse contents of her stomach out onto the ground in front of her, vomit spilling through the opening in her helmet.

She pulled off the helmet and tossed it to the side as she knelt, drawing in short breaths, the taste and stench of vomit clinging to her throat, her lungs and muscles burning.

"We can turn back if you need to."

Ella lifted her head to see Coren standing in front of her, staring down, arms folded across her chest, an emotionless expression on her face.

"Why do I have to wear this?" Ella coughed as she lifted her hands and pulled herself upright on her knees, her breaths heavy and laboured.

"How tall are you?" Coren asked, turning to face Ella, the light of the rising sun glinting off her metal helmet.

"How tall am I? What does that have to do with anything?" Ella let out a sigh as Coren stared at her. "I don't know, five and a half feet?"

"And how much do you weigh? I'd wager two thirds what most men weigh. Maybe half."

"What's your point?" Ella asked, shifting irritably.

"In a battle line, none of that matters," Coren said, moving so she stood in front of Ella, her dark eyes glinting through the slits in her helm. "If you're slightly smaller or weaker, your brothers and sisters will protect your flank. Strength is not in the individual, it is in the unit. But you don't have the training, the discipline, or the time to fight that way. If you are going to stay here, you are going to have to contribute. When you're standing face to face with a man in plate armour, head and shoulders above you, a fury in his heart – what will you do then? You have Faenir to protect you, but what if he needs you to protect him?"

"I would never let anything happen to him." To Ella's own surprise, a snarl caught in her throat, and her fingers clenched into a tight fist. Out of the corner of her eye she could see Faenir had turned to face her and Coren, the hackles on his back raised.

Coren took another step closer to Ella. "I cannot teach you to become a sword master in the time we have. That takes years – decades, even. Nor can I load you with slabs of muscle. But I can teach you to never stop. I can train you to push through the pain, to carry the weight on your shoulders. You need to be willing to fight harder than anyone who stands in your way. You need to be able to demand your body keep moving when your legs are burning, your lungs are heaving, and every fibre of your being is screaming at you to stop. That is what it takes."

Behind Coren, Ella could hear a deep growl resonating in Faenir's throat. The wolfpine took a few tentative steps closer. Ella drew in a deep breath and curled her hands into fists, her fingers dragging over the dirt and dust that coated the rock, then hauled herself to her feet, ignoring the pain. Without so much as a word, Ella picked up her helmet and strode past Coren, clenching her jaw with every step. The peak didn't look far. If she could keep at a solid pace, she could make it in less than half an hour. If she took it slowly, her body would hurt less, but the pain would last longer. It would be better to just push through. "Try to keep up."

ELLA COLLAPSED TO HER KNEES as she reached the summit of the peak, tossing her helmet to the ground a few feet away, spluttering as she dragged in lungfuls of air. Even as she knelt there, her legs shook, screaming in pain. She let herself drop down onto her back, her armour clinking against the stone, the warmth of the sun on her face beating away the bitter chill of the wind.

Her hair was matted to her face and head by sweat. Every piece of exposed skin was cold as ice, whipped and bitten by the wind, though her body as a whole was on fire. Her muscles seared with pain, and the heat of her body baked within the armour she wore. When Coren had said she climbed the nearest peak every morning, this was not what Ella had envisaged. She swallowed, trying to add some moisture to her dry lips.

A shadow moved over Ella's field of vision, blocking out the light of the sun. Ella squinted, letting her eyes adjust, but before they did, a wet tongue dragged across her face, accompanied by an uncomfortably warm breath. Ella let out a laugh, scratching the side of Faenir's enormous head. "Get off me, you lummox."

The wolfpine whined and licked Ella's cheek once more before prodding her in the side of the head with his wet nose and plodding off to drop himself somewhere in the sun.

Footsteps passed, a shadow momentarily blocking the sun. "Water?"

Ella grunted, lifting herself to an upright position and turning to see Coren perched on a rock near the edge of the peak, looking as though she had barely broken a sweat, which irritated Ella to no end. But irritated or not, at that moment, Ella would have sold her own soul for a drink of water. Gritting her teeth, Ella pushed the pain to the back of her mind and pulled herself to her feet, stumbling slightly as she did.

Ella snatched the waterskin from Coren's outstretched hand, glaring at the woman, who smiled back smugly. She dropped down near the edge of the peak, letting out an unashamed groan as the cold liquid touched her lips. The waterskin was over half empty when she finally pulled it away from her mouth, dropping her forearms onto her knees, trying her best to slow her deep, laboured breaths. The acrid taste of vomit still clung to the back of her throat from earlier. She had never gotten sick from physical exertion before. It wasn't a particularly delightful feeling.

"It's beautiful, isn't it?"

Ella narrowed her eyes as she lifted her gaze to Coren's, but before she said anything, she realised what Coren was talking about. From where they sat at the summit, they could see everything for miles around the Firnin Mountains. Rolling hills; squared-off sections of farmland in varying stages of yellow, brown, and green; rivers carving their path through the earth.

"Over there," Coren said, pointing towards a swath of dark green woodland, "is the Elkenwood, the town at its edge being Merchant's Reach. The city of Elkenrim lies just out of view to the east." Coren moved her hand left, pointing towards an enormous mountain range that dwarfed the Firnin Mountains. "Those are the Kolmir Mountains, and the fortress at their feet is Fort Harken, the empire's military chokepoint between here and Al'Nasla."

"That's where Farda went." Ella felt something pushing at her elbow. She looked down to see Faenir's snout poking under her elbow. After a second, the wolfpine's whole head came through, and he rested his chin on Ella's lap, his eyes gazing out over the landscape below.

Coren let out a soft sigh, turning to meet Ella's gaze. "Who do you think Farda is?"

"I know he's a mage," Ella snapped. She hadn't meant to react so irritably, but she was sick of being treated like some wayward child, and the pitiful smile that spread across Coren's face only served to further fuel the fire of Ella's irritation. "And he's already told me he's a Justicar for the empire." *Whatever that truly means.*

Coren turned back to the landscape that spread out below, letting a breath out through her nostrils. "Farda is more than a mage. I'm assuming Yana or Tanner told you what I am? What Farwen is?"

Ella nodded, her heart twisting at the thought of how Yana had said Farwen described the loss of her dragon. *Like every piece of her was broken at once, with no way of putting it back together.* Ella pulled her elbow in tighter around Faenir's neck and head, scratching at the side of his fur-covered cheek with her fingers.

"Farda is not a mage. He is a Rakina, like me, and like Farwen. It is a word in the Old Tongue that means 'One who is broken', or 'One who survived'."

Ella's words caught in her throat, and she shook her head. "What... what are you saying?"

"Farda was once a Draleid – one of the finest of his time, and a close friend of Alvira Serris, our leader. When I was only a child, my master, Kollna, used to tell me stories of Alvira, Farda, and Eltoar Daethana. She used to hold Farda up as an example of what a warrior should be. Not in how they should fight, but in how they should carry themselves, in how they should treat those they protect. But a year or so before The Fall, Farda changed. He drew into himself, grew reclusive, grew cold. I had only met him a handful of times, but even I could feel it."

"I..." A thousand questions peeled through Ella's mind, yet she could barely form even a single sentence. Her heart palpitated, and her breath caught in her throat. If Farda had been alive at The Fall, he had seen at least four hundred summers. "What... what happened?"

Coren shook her head. "I truly do not know. But he was not the same man. My master went to see him on many occasions and always came back troubled. In the years since The Fall... whatever he was, and whatever you think he is, he is not that person. His heart is cold and black, and his hands are covered in blood."

"And there is no blood on your hands?"

Coren held Ella's gaze for a few moments, the right corner of her mouth lifting slightly before she turned away once more, letting silence descend.

"Farwen believes you have druidic blood in your veins."

Ella didn't answer. She simply continued staring off into the distance, her fingers methodically scratching under Faenir's jaw. The wolfpine responded with a satisfied grumble.

"I'm inclined to agree with her, though we both may be wrong. We met a man almost two hundred years ago, a few miles north of the Aonan Wood. He travelled with a hawk twice as large as any I or Farwen had ever lain eyes on – much like Faenir. His name was Galveer, and I believe the hawk went by Kurak. Farwen and I were exhausted and starved after fleeing from Imperial Inquisitors in Aeling. When we stumbled into his camp, he didn't so much as bat an eyelid. It was as though he had already seen us coming. He offered us to share in his food and the warmth of his fire – which was no small thing. In the wilds, kindness is not often rewarded. We'd been running for so long. We were so tired."

"What does any of this have to do with me being a druid?"

Coren stared at Ella for a moment but didn't answer the question directly. "Galveer noticed Farwen holding her hands beside the flames, fingers growing raw and red, unflinching." Coren's voice trembled a little. She sniffled, pressing her tongue against her top teeth. "She started doing that after she lost Syndril. Particularly in those first two centuries. Anyway, he asked us outright if we were Rakina. To which we answered by drawing our swords."

"What happened?" The words slipped out despite Ella's best efforts to hold on to her irritation at Coren for not giving her a straight answer.

"He didn't even flinch. Neither did the hawk. He told us what he was, but more than that, he told us of a man like us, who had survived The Fall and was building strength against the empire."

"Coren, I'm sorry, but I still don't see how any of this pertains to me."

"Apologies," Coren said. "When it comes to stories, I tend to ramble. We travelled with Galveer for weeks as he brought us to Aeson. Along the journey, he told us of some of the things he could do, of how he and Kurak were connected. That was how Farwen recognised what you are. Everything about you and Faenir is the same. The way you move together, the way he acts around you. When we asked Galveer about Kurak, he told us that some druids inadvertently bond with specific animals. When that bond is created, the animal grows larger, stronger, more intelligent. Their thoughts and feelings bleed into the druid, and the same happens the other way around. It is clear that Faenir is a recipient of these qualities."

Ella looked at the wolfpine who still sat with his chin resting on her lap, his golden eyes looking up at her as though he were proclaiming his innocence for whatever crime Ella thought he might be guilty of. Even then, she could feel the touch of his mind, distant but present, and she knew without a semblance of doubt that Farwen had been right. Ella was a druid.

Turning so her legs draped over the edge of the cliff, Ella let out a heavy breath and lifted the waterskin back to her lips, only for a low grumble to sound beside her. She looked down to see Faenir staring back at her, his head only just lifted off his paws, his tongue hanging from his mouth as he panted.

Ella narrowed her eyes. "You're not even tired."

Faenir grumbled again, the noise sharpening to a whine at the end while he turned his head.

"Oh, fine. You only ever want it because I have it. You know it, and I know it." Ella let out a puff of air, shaking her head. "Open your mouth."

Ella proceeded to tip the waterskin sideways, letting the water pour out in a thin stream. Faenir tilted his head, lapping at the stream as it fell, most of it splashing off his face, wasted. Ella couldn't help but laugh, scratching the top of Faenir's head with her gauntleted hand.

"Here."

Ella turned, wincing as Coren's armour reflected the sun into her eyes. As Ella's eyes adjusted, Coren handed her something.

"What is it?" Ella looked down to see she now held a small leatherbound book, tied closed with a leather strip.

"It's a journal," Coren said, reaching into her satchel once more to produce a pen and a small inkwell, then handed them to Ella.

"I'm not really the journalling type," Ella said, giving Coren an apologetic smile.

"If you are a druid, we should see what you can do. And seeing as there's nobody here to teach you, we're going to have to stumble through this. I figured it would be helpful to log the process as we go, see what you can really do. It's what Master Kollna used to have me do when I was learning to weave threads of the Spark."

"That makes sense." Ella pulled off her glove, then opened the leather strip and thumbed through the thin pages of the journal, feeling the coarse touch of the paper beneath her fingertips. "Where do we even start?"

"With him." Coren nodded at Faenir. The wolfpine let out a rumble and lifted his head, tilting it to the side, his ears pricking.

"What about him?"

"Galveer was able to push his mind into the minds of animals, see through their eyes, move their limbs. He called it 'Shifting'. I don't know how he did it or if it's a common thing druids can do, but I figure if you have a special bond with Faenir, it must be easier to do it with him than any other animal."

"Shifting?" Ella looked at Faenir, who stared back, his golden eyes gleaming. As she held the wolfpine's gaze, she became vaguely aware of the beating of his heart, thumping just slightly off rhythm with hers, slower. Sounds around her grew sharper, more distinct; the wind was like waves slamming against the cliff, but amidst it Ella could pick out the clattering of bare branches, the chirping of birds, the slow, slightly weary drag of Coren's breaths.

Ella slowed her breathing, keeping her eyes focused on Faenir. The fresh scent of cool air suffused her, followed by salt and sweat, a tinge of loam, fresh cracked bark. In the peace of it, her mind drifted to Rhett. The smell of his clothes, the earthy scent of leather and metallic tinge of polished steel that always clung to him after his patrol duties, and the sharp smell of peppermint from the soap he bought from Verna Gritten that only ever seemed to linger for an hour after he bathed before being overcome by the leather and steel. The thought twisted Ella's heart, images of Rhett's smiling face lingering in her memory. *He always smiled with his eyes.* A wave of anger flooded through Ella, her teeth grinding, her fingers curling inwards, a primal fury rippling in her veins. More images of Rhett, the spear bursting through his gut. The blood. So much blood. Ella's own voice echoed. *'Don't you dare leave me!'*

The memory was so vivid she swore she could feel his hand resting on her cheek. She looked down to see Faenir still staring back at her, but now his lips were pulled back in a snarl, his nose crinkled, his teeth bared, the hackles on his back raised. A deep guttural growl rumbled in his throat. It was his anger she was feeling. His and hers together, feeding each other. But more than anger radiated from Faenir's mind. Regret. Loss. Guilt. *Why guilt?* Hundreds of images flashed across Ella's eyes like strikes of lightning. Images of Ella and Rhett, of them leaving The Glade, sleeping beneath the stars, outside Pirn, Camylin, in the wagon, on the merchants road. *You were with us the whole time? Watching over us…*

Another pang of guilt, and Faenir whimpered. Images of him looking down from somewhere, a ridge maybe? Lorian soldiers, the wagon. Dust swirling as Faenir's paws ate the ground. Blood.

Tears welled at the corners of Ella's eyes, and she reached out, resting her hand against the coarse grey fur at the side of Faenir's face, shaking her head. "It's not your fault… It's not."

Another whimper left Faenir's throat. Guilt. Loss.

Ella leaned forwards, wrapping her arms around Faenir's massive neck, his fur prickling her skin. She squeezed, feeling him push into her. Faenir's emotions tangled with her own, pushing and pulling. Sadness, anger, grief. Ella pulled away, placing her hands on either side of his face, her fingers scratching into his fur, tears burning her eyes. "You saved me. *You* saved me. It isn't your fault. It's theirs. And we will rip them apart."

"Ella?" A hand rested on Ella's shoulder, and she turned to see Coren staring at her, eyes wide.

Ella only then realised her chest was rising and falling in heavy sweeps, her hands shaking at the sides of Faenir's head. Her lips twisted in a wolf-like snarl. "I'm all right," Ella said between trembling breaths, her blood still hot, her jaw clenching.

"Did it work?"

Ella shook her head. "I don't think that was Shifting. That felt like something else entirely." Ella settled herself, slowing her breathing. She looked back at Faenir, his anger still simmering within her. "I've made my decision."

Coren raised an eyebrow.

"I want to fight."

Chapter Twenty-Six

To Know Your Place

Kallinvar stood over the war table, his palms resting on its cool stone edge. He felt as though he spent the majority of his time standing in the war room now, planning, moving pieces on a board. It didn't feel right. It wasn't him. His place was on the field of battle. Even before Verathin had given him the Sigil. He'd entered the Amendel guard as soon as they'd let him in, and that's where he'd stayed until Amendel fell, and Verathin had saved Kallinvar from falling with it.

He'd tried his best to go with the rest of The Second when he could, but without him in the temple, the others couldn't utilise the Rift; they were hamstrung. He let out a sigh, lifting his head towards the two captains who stood before him: Darmerian, Brother-Captain of The Fifth, and Airdaine, Sister-Captain of The Ninth. He'd barely spoken a word since they'd entered the chamber.

Kallinvar turned his gaze back to the table before he spoke, not having the strength to look Darmerian in the eyes. He looked over the carved stone map, stopping at the ridged mountains that rose a few inches – Wolfpine Ridge. "Darmerian, Watcher Gildrick tells me The Fifth have done well looking over Illyanara. I am sorry about Sister Urilin. She was a brave soul." Kallinvar clenched his jaw as he spoke. Urilin had been slain by four Bloodmarked in a town an hour south-east of Camylin. When Kallinvar had extended Darmerian's watch from the west of Illyanara across the whole province, the Brother-Captain had warned Kallinvar that Bloodspawn numbers were growing too large in the region. But all Kallinvar had done was ask him to hold strong. They didn't have the numbers, and the Uraks had learned – they were spreading themselves out, using their hordes to their advantage.

"That she was, Grandmaster. She will be missed."

Kallinvar wished he had words that would grant Darmerian some peace. But he didn't. He knew all too well what it was like for a captain to lose a knight under their command. He knew the visceral, heart-rending pain, like a hot knife carving into his flesh. Even then, Kallinvar could feel Urilin's loss echoing through his Sigil. He was finding that as the Grandmaster, not only could he *feel* the emotions of his knights, but their loss resonated within him as well, lingering far longer than it ever had before. And yet, he knew his pain was nothing next to Darmerian's.

And I caused it. I sent them there. I should have given more.

Yes, Kallinvar wished he had the words, but words had never been his strength. Words of battle were one thing. Setting courage in hearts and fire in veins, *that* he could do. But talk of the heart, talk of pain, that was as alien to him as the ever-elusive notion of peace. And so he simply gave Darmerian a sorrowful smile and nodded. "What of the factions you approached? What do they say?"

"There is a faction based here." Darmerian leaned forwards, pointing a finger towards the foothills of the Baylomon Mountains, by the coast. "They call themselves the Red Suns. They're gathering strength, organising. And they've fortified a town along the coast, maybe six or seven thousand fighters. They're not truly a force yet, more a rabble, but they're on the right path."

"And what did they *say*, Darmerian?" Kallinvar tried his best to keep the frustration from his voice.

Darmerian scrunched his mouth, biting the side of his bottom lip. He let out a sigh. "They said they will pledge themselves to our cause."

Kallinvar raised his eyebrows, stepping back, surprised.

"They will pledge themselves to our cause," Darmerian repeated, "if we support their leader in his claim as the King of Illyanara."

"Fuck…" Kallinvar leaned on the table, shaking his head. It had been the same across the continent. Just as Kallinvar had predicted. The rebellions that were breaking out had been devastating for the empire. That, combined with the resurgent attacks of the Bloodspawn and the chaos caused by the new Draleid, had spread the Lorians thin. Even with dragons, a continent was not an easy thing to control, and the empire no longer had many dragons. Unfortunately, the side effect of a crumbling empire was that all the small lords and would-be kings and queens were carving each other apart in the pursuit of dropped power. "Any others?"

"There's a faction that controls a large section of land south of Fearsall. They are constantly at odds with the Red Suns, and they fly the banner of old Amendel." Darmerian gave Kallinvar a look as he said that – the banner of old Amendel. Kallinvar's home.

In his mind's eye, Kallinvar could see the red banner rippling in the air, a white gryphon emblazoned across the front. Much like the druids, the Jotnar, and many others of times long past, the gryphons were gone now, slaughtered to the last when the Illyanaran army took Amendel's capital. Kallinvar shook the thoughts away. "And what did *they* say?"

"Actually, their leader, a woman by the name of Aryana Torval, said she would be willing to meet with you."

"Good. I'll make it happen. Others?"

Darmerian went on to point out spots on the war table where smaller factions had begun to gather strength across Illyanara, Kallinvar marking the locations with small blue markers. No fewer than fifteen, though some numbering less than a thousand. When Darmerian finished, Airdaine did the same, though none of the factions she had encountered in Varsund had extended the same offer as this Aryana Torval, who flew the banner of old Amendel.

Once Kallinvar had dismissed Airdaine and Darmerian, he had less than a minute or so to breathe before another knock sounded at the door. Kallinvar reached through his Sigil, but felt no response on the other side of the door, which meant his new guest wasn't a knight. He let out a subdued sigh. "Come in."

The door creaked open, and a storm of footsteps followed. Kallinvar lifted his head to see Watcher Gildrick entering the war room, white-trimmed dark green robes flowing behind him. Another watcher strode along at his side, a dark-haired woman with bronzed skin and a sharp face; she looked young, no more than twenty summers. Two priests of Achyron shepherded a number of porters carrying trays of food, some cups, and jugs of wine and water into the room, their green cloaks missing the white trimming that marked Gildrick and the woman as watchers.

"What is all this, Gildrick?"

"You've been in here for twelve hours, Kallinvar. The sun has risen and set without you seeing its light. The Sigil might grant you great strength, but you need to eat, drink, and sleep just like the rest of us. And seeing as I can't force you to sleep, I may as well feed you."

Kallinvar made to protest, but Gildrick raised a greying eyebrow, an unyielding expression on his face. Kallinvar couldn't help but stifle a laugh at that, thinking of how he had once given the same look to Gildrick when the Watcher had seen no more than fourteen summers.

The porters set out foldable tables beside the war table, laying down trays of steaming hot meats, thick slices of cheese, a block of butter, and a beautiful loaf of ash bread – a staple bread of Amendel, leavened with pearl ash.

"As appreciative as I am, Gildrick, I couldn't eat all this if I had an entire day and an empty stomach."

"Which is why we shall be helping you." As the two priests shuffled the porters out of the room, closing the doors behind them, Gildrick reached over and filled three cups with wine.

"We?" Kallinvar looked from Gildrick to the young watcher at his side who gave Kallinvar an awkward, if enthusiastic, smile.

"This," Gildrick said, handing Kallinvar a cup of wine then gesturing towards the young woman as he handed over her cup, "is Watcher Tallia. She is my new charge and will be shadowing me from now on. I know you had called for me earlier, but I was tied up in arranging a few things for the festival tonight. I apologize for my lateness, but I thought it was better to be late than to not show at all, and I also thought it a good learning experience for Tallia."

"Your apology's not necessary." Kallinvar took a sip of wine as he cut a slice of ash bread, slathered it with butter, stacked meat and cheese on top, then devoured it in two mouthfuls. In truth, he had spent so long in the war room and talked to so many knights and watchers alike, the hours had blurred together, and Kallinvar had entirely forgotten he had asked Gildrick to come at all. But the questions he had for the Watcher were important ones.

"First lesson, Tallia, is Grandmaster Kallinvar has the table manners of a hog." Gildrick frowned at Kallinvar before gesturing for Tallia to take her choice of food.

It was etiquette within the temple and amongst the people of Ardholm that the lowest of rank or station should eat first. It had always been that way. Verathin had told Kallinvar that it fostered trust and understanding. The knights might be Achyron's champions, but every person within the temple and the bounds of Ardholm had their part to play. It was a tradition that Kallinvar had fallen afoul of many times since taking over the title of Grandmaster. He was not used to being the highest of rank in any room, and he had taken many of his meals alone recently. He gave Gildrick an apologetic look, then washed down the bread, meat, and cheese with another mouthful of wine. Until just that moment, he hadn't realised he was starving.

Shaking his head at Kallinvar, Gildrick gestured to Tallia, and the young woman handed him a dark leather satchel from which he produced a stack of journals that he set on a foldable table to his left. "When we spoke this morning, you asked about Verathin. I took the liberty of breaking these free from the vault in the Watcher library."

"What are they?" Kallinvar asked, swallowing another mouthful of wine as he narrowed his eyes at the stack of journals.

"They are chronicles of the Grandmasters, taken by the Watchers. There are some still in the vault that date back to the very first Watchers, but they are nearly illegible at this stage." Gildrick tapped his finger against the leather of the top journal. "Most of the important information has been transcribed into these over the years."

"And these contain—"

"Everything," Gildrick said, finishing Kallinvar's sentence. "From thoughts and feelings to tactics and advice. But most importantly, what I think you're looking for – detailed accounts on the gifts granted to the Grandmaster."

"It's like you can read my mind, Gildrick."

"Well, I've known you all my life. If I didn't have some idea what you were thinking, I wouldn't be a very good Watcher."

Kallinvar smiled, looking at the grey touching Gildrick's temples, the marks of time on his face. In his centuries, Kallinvar had known many Watchers, priests, cooks, and porters. He had seen them all grow from children, watched them mature, then wither, their bodies caving to the incessant abrasion of time. It was one of the many burdens of the immortality granted to the knights. To live forever was a notion chased by many dreamers, but it was, in many ways, a poisoned chalice. Life had meaning because it had an end. Without the end, each day was just a blur in a vast ocean. Kallinvar had seen nations rise and fall, rivers carve paths through the world, and landscapes change in their entirety. But if he was honest with himself, the hardest part was growing to care for someone while knowing you would be there to lay them in the ground when they died. He had seen many knights struggle with the notion. Some, though few, had taken their own lives, unable to come to terms with their new reality.

When Kallinvar was young and his elder sister had died on a hunt, their mother had told him that time heals all wounds. What she had said was true to a point, but only within the bounds of a single lifespan. When a lifespan was extended, the meaning was inverted. Time no longer healed all wounds, it created them as the permanency of loss became ever more present. For a knight to truly accept who they were, they needed to embrace their new purpose, their new meaning: to protect the world from The Shadow.

Kallinvar bit the side of his lip, realising he'd been staring at Gildrick for longer than he intended. He gave another smile, then let out a puff of air and walked around to the other side of the war table, surveying the land. Counters of numerous colours were scattered around the carved stone map. Stacked white counters sat beside carvings, denoting the allegiance and relative size of armies in their thousands. Black counters marked wherever a major Bloodspawn attack had occurred, while red counters marked wherever the knights had not arrived in time to stop those attacks. From the start, the red counters had been far more numerous than the black, but now there were at least two red for every black. There weren't enough knights.

Green counters marked positions of knights outside the temple – eighty-six at that moment. Kallinvar could feel each one of them. Their life force pulsed through him, resonating in his Sigil, an unseen tether connecting them. It had overwhelmed him at first, but looking at the war table helped him visualise things, helped his mind reconcile the new sensations. Where each counter sat on the war table, Kallinvar could see the knight to whom it belonged. Brother Ormin and Brother Lumikes of The Sixth were investigating a smaller convergence near the Aonan Wood. Sister-Captain Olyria and two of her knights, Turilin and Galvar, were at a town near Yarrin in Arkalen. Sister-Captain Arlena of The First was with Jurea and Helka near the Darkwood to see if there was any truth to the rumours of elves within. He'd sent Brother-Captain Armites and four of his knights to Lynalion, but in truth, he held out little hope of the elves there entertaining any form of alliance. Many of the other counters were scattered around the war table – knights sent to intercept convergences, to watch over vulnerable areas, or to engage in ambassadorial missions to strong factions.

"Was there something in particular you wanted to ask, Kallinvar?" Gildrick raised an eyebrow, and Kallinvar realised he had been silent for almost four or five minutes.

"Many things," Kallinvar muttered, folding his arms across his chest. "Aside from these notebooks, did Verathin ever talk to you about his gifts?"

Gildrick pouted and tilted his head. "Not really. From time to time, yes, or when I asked. But Verathin served as Grandmaster for over eight centuries. He'd asked all his questions a long time before I was brought into the world." Gildrick narrowed his eyes. "What is it?"

"Nothing." *Except that I'm hearing the voice of a god in my head.* It had been a while since Achyron had spoken, but Kallinvar could feel him there at the edges of his mind. It was both anxiety-inducing and awe-inspiring. Had Verathin heard The Warrior too? Had the other Grandmasters? Kallinvar would have asked Gildrick outright if it hadn't sounded so insane. No, now that Gildrick had brought Kallinvar the journals, Kallinvar would search those first. If the answer was written within those pages, then Kallinvar would not have to ask the question aloud. "Tell me," Kallinvar said, stroking his chin. "It is likely in the journals, but you might be able to save me some time. The convergences."

"Ah, yes. How are you finding them?"

"Stomach-churning." Kallinvar gave an uneasy smile, thinking back to the last time he had sensed a convergence. "It's like the world around me dims, and all the sounds blend into a discordant wave that crashes over me. But more than that, they take too long to decipher. I can feel the Taint pulsing, pounding, hammering in my head." Kallinvar glanced towards the young Watcher, Tallia, becoming aware how openly he was speaking in front of someone he knew little of. "I can't focus on it. I can't narrow in. Entire villages have been lost by the time I've organised my thoughts, Gildrick."

"I see." Gildrick stepped towards the war table, his left hand clasping his right elbow, his right hand scratching at the stubble on his face. "Verathin did tell me, when I was young, that he used this table to map out the Taint."

Kallinvar raised an eyebrow.

Gildrick ran his tongue across his teeth, tilting his head sideways. "He said that aside from the convergences, there was also a base level of the Taint that he could feel across different areas. And the same as you, the feelings and sensations were overwhelming. Instead of trying to unravel the…" Gildrick clicked his tongue off the roof of his mouth as he pondered, snatching at the right word. "… ball of twine in your mind, if you will."

"I'm not sure that's a fantastic analogy, Gildrick, but continue."

"Instead of trying to unravel the ball of twine in your mind, use it to thread a tapestry and lay it over the map."

Kallinvar did his best to suppress a laugh. "Is there a less poetic way to say that?"

Gildrick let out an unimpressed sigh. He looked to Kallinvar, then to Tallia, and back to Kallinvar. "It can be hard to build something without a framework. Instead of trying to focus on the convergence in your mind, where it's muddled with everything else, lay it over the war table. Lay it over a map of Epheria. Use the map as your framework. Feel the Taint through the map. Verathin had said it always helped, particularly when he was learning."

Kallinvar frowned. It was easy for Gildrick to say, but it wasn't so easy to do. Still, it was worth a try. His head had been throbbing constantly since he had received the Sigil of the Grandmaster, particularly when any convergences occurred. Perhaps this was the solution.

Tracing his finger along the carved stone, Kallinvar walked around the war table, taking it in, examining it in its entirety before stopping back where he'd started. He looked down at the green counters, focusing on the single counter at Kingspass: Lyrin. Kallinvar had sent him to reach out to his network in Kingspass and the surrounding areas to see if he could uncover any information on where the Draleid had been headed. He would likely be signalling Kallinvar soon to send him on to Berona.

Looking down at the green counter, Kallinvar could feel Lyrin's Sigil pulsating. As he focused, he matched his connection with Lyrin in his mind to the counter on the war table, overlaying them. And almost immediately, it clicked. Where Lyrin's counter sat on the table, Kallinvar could feel the thrum of Lyrin's Sigil, an almost imperceptible green glow radiating from the counter. The glow must have been in his mind, for it didn't touch the surface of the stone, but he could see it, nonetheless.

"Is it working?" Kallinvar could hear the earnest curiosity in Gildrick's voice.

AFTER AN HOUR OR SO of questions, Gildrick and Tallia left Kallinvar to examine this newfound layering of his mind over the map on the war table – they'd also left the food and the wine.

Kallinvar slathered a layer of butter over a thick slice of ash bread, carefully layering slices of cheese and ham roasted in a jacket of redcurrant jam. When he'd placed the last piece of cheese, he dropped a big dollop of honey on top and smeared it around the mountain of meat and cheese, then took half of it into his mouth in a single bite, sighing through his nostrils in satisfaction.

As he chewed, he looked down over the war table. It had taken the better part of the hour with Gildrick to truly layer the sensations of the Taint and the pulses of his knight's Sigils over the stone-carved map, but once he had pieced it together and visualised it on the map, he'd felt a weight lift off his shoulders. Beside the counters that marked Brother Ormin and Brother Lumikes, Kallinvar could physically see a dim red glow where he'd sensed the convergence of the Taint. The glow wasn't truly there. It was his mind's visualisation of the convergence. But just being able to see it like that made it so much easier to comprehend. He would have to properly thank Gildrick.

Kallinvar took another bite of bread, cheese, ham, and honey, washing it down with a long draught of wine, then looked back over the table. Everywhere he had sensed convergences, big and small, he could now see glowing patches of red, their size commensurate to the strength of the convergence. In other places, he could see dim layers of red stretching over large patches of land: Mar Dorul, Kolmir, areas of Wolfpine Ridge, and many other sections of the map where Bloodspawn dwelled. But more than anywhere, the Burnt Lands glowed so ferociously the light was opaque, a blanket of red. Nowhere else on the map held anywhere near that level of the Taint.

Kallinvar scratched his chin, taking another drink of wine. He'd been to the Burnt Lands a number of times since The Fall, his Sigil protecting him from the madness that dwelled within. The Taint was so thick there that breathing the air was like drinking oil, and yet, he'd not found nearly enough Bloodspawn to justify even a fraction of that Taint. A handful here or there, pillaging broken cities, but nothing that would explain why the Taint was so thick, and why it spread through nearly all the Burnt Lands. *There has to be an explanation.*

As Kallinvar refilled his cup, already feeling the warmth of the wine spreading through him, he touched his hand against his chest, feeling a pulse ripple through his Sigil. He let out a sigh, a soft smile touching his lips. It seemed he wasn't going to get any more than a half-hour's worth of solitude. But for Ruon, he would allow it.

The war room door creaked open. "I thought I might find you here."

Kallinvar filled a second cup with wine and handed it to Ruon. "I just needed to look it over again."

"You've been looking it over for hours, Kallinvar. You need to sleep or at least take a break."

Kallinvar gave Ruon a half-hearted smile, meeting her green-eyed stare for a moment before looking back down at the table and pointing to a spot just north of Cardend, where two green counters lay. "Sister Oryn and Sister Vendire are fighting here, right now." A red glow pulsed beside the counters. "The more I look, the more I think I should have sent another with them."

"Kallinvar." Ruon placed her full cup of wine down on a foldable table left by the porters, then rested her hand on Kallinvar's shoulder. "You *need* to sleep."

"Brother Maklas died two days ago because I sent him and Sister Yirsa to investigate a convergence near the Marin Mountains. I hadn't sensed the true power of the convergence. They were swarmed by Bloodmarked and a Shaman. Sister Yirsa barely got out with her life. Maklas died because I wasn't good enough, Ruon. And he hasn't been the only one."

"And his loss is felt, but he was a knight, Kallinvar. He was one of Achyron's champions. He knew the risks. We all do. This is what we are made for. Don't take his death away from him by claiming it for yourself."

"Words, Ruon. Those are all just words. I should have sent more knights. I made a bad decision, and Maklas suffered for it."

"And you will make more bad decisions. So will I. That's the way of things. We pick ourselves up, we learn, and we do better the next time."

"That's what I'm doing now – learning."

"Learning works better with sleep." Ruon sliced a piece of ash bread and spread a thick glob of honey across it, letting out a soft laugh. "Gildrick never forgets, does he? When he found out I was born in Valean, he somehow sourced seeds from a gileam tree and had them planted in the gardens. Three years later it bore fruit, and ever since he brings me gileam whenever he comes to see me. I hadn't eaten gileam in over five centuries until he found those seeds."

Kallinvar smiled at that. Ruon was right, Gildrick embodied every-thing that it was to be a Watcher. He truly cared for the knights. Not just their bodies, but their minds and their souls. Over seven hundred years, Kallinvar had never met someone as selfless as the Watcher. The day Heraya would take Gildrick into her arms was a day Kallinvar dreaded. "He has a good soul."

Ruon nodded, moving around the other side of the war table, taking stock of the land. "If you won't sleep, will you at least come with me to the festival in the village? I've heard there's a young woman who has quite a singing voice. I could do with hearing someone sing."

Kallinvar folded his arms and stared at the table. The Earlywinter festi-val was celebrated in Ardholm at dawn of each new year, marking both the passing of another year and the birth of a new one. In Kallinvar's first few centuries as a Knight, he had attended the festival many times. But as the years moved on, one hundred turning to two, then three, then four, it all started to lose meaning. The people of Ardholm lived longer lives than humans born elsewhere in Epheria. Some even lived to see almost two hundred summers, though that was rare. But even then, that was nothing when compared to the near eight hundred summers Kallinvar had seen. What was the passing of another year to someone who might live to see two thousand? And yet, this time, as Ruon stood across from him, Kallinvar found himself nodding. He let out a sigh. "All right. A song or two might not be a bad idea."

"Good. Some of the others are already out there. But Varlin and Ildris are in their quarters. We can get them on the way."

Kallinvar grunted an agreement, thinking. "How is Arden? I've not spoken to him since Kingspass."

Ruon gave Kallinvar a lopsided smile, drawing in a slow breath through her nose, then letting it out in a sigh. "He's struggling. It hasn't affected him in the field. If anything, he's been a force of nature every time I've gone with him. But when we get back, he's silent. And with Lyrin gone on task, he spends most of his time alone. He's trying, Kallinvar, but seeing his brother has affected him deeply."

"Hmm." Kallinvar scratched at his beard. "As it would any of us. If the Draleid accepts our help, I will need to decide which of us to assign as his guards. My mind battles my heart. I'm not sure if Arden is ready to face that."

"We never know we're ready until we're in the thick of it."

"True enough. Come," Kallinvar said, finishing the last of the wine in his cup. "Let's go hear this young woman sing."

ARDEN LIFTED HIS ELBOWS FROM his knees and pulled himself into an upright position, taking a long draught from his tankard of ale. He'd never liked ale; the aftertaste was too bitter. Having grown up on the sweetness of Lasch Havel's mead, that bitterness was even more evident. But the innkeeper at The Salted Sparrow, Erkin Turnbat, had insisted Arden try his new batch of ale – as he did any time Arden wandered through Ardholm. He was a nice man, and Arden found it very difficult to say no to him.

Arden sat on one of several wooden benches that surrounded the many firepits burning across Ardholm. It seemed that every soul within Ardholm and the temple of Achyron had poured out into the streets to celebrate the earlywinter festival. Priests and watchers stood about in their green robes, sipping cups of wine and laughing with the village elders, watching over the children who were dancing and singing along to the music being played by some of the older children on lutes and drums. Arden recognised porters and chambermaids from the temple, though the smiles on their faces were far wider than he'd ever seen them before.

Above, the star-speckled sky glimmered, bathing Ardholm in silvery moonlight.

A sorrowful smile spread across Arden's lips as he looked over the festival, the people dancing, singing, drinking. It reminded him of the Moon Market in the villages back home. He hadn't minded it the previous years – if anything it had been a nice reminder – but after seeing Calen, everything felt different. He couldn't stop replaying the conversation in his mind. Calen's words echoing.

'Where were you? I needed you… I need you.'

Arden shuddered at the words, taking another mouthful of ale. The logical part of his brain told him there was nothing he could have done differently, even if he'd wanted to. Had he not taken the Sigil, he would've died that day in the forest, and then there would have been nothing he could have done to look after Calen and his family. At least this way, he could still do something. He could push back the Shadow. He could fight. And now that Calen was a Draleid, maybe, just maybe, Arden might have the chance to make up for the time they'd lost.

'Mam, Dad, Ella, Faenir. They're all dead!'

Arden downed the last of the ale and got to his feet, the warmth of the fire kissing his skin. Some of the children ran to him, raising their fists to their foreheads as a sign of respect. They tugged at him and pulled at him, asking him to join them in their dancing. He was about to acquiesce when he looked up to see four figures walking down the steps from the temple, mostly shrouded in shadow, only the touch of cold moonlight giving them shape. But Arden didn't need to see their faces to know them. Kallinvar, Ruon, Ildris, and Varlin had still been inside the temple.

"Another time," Arden said, ruffling the hair of a small boy who tugged at his shirtsleeves. The boy frowned but let go, the look on his face saying that he was less than impressed. Arden gave a nod to the priests who stood nearby and then set off back towards The Salted Sparrow. He might not have enjoyed the taste of ale, but the desire to be black-drunk pulled at him, and the more ale he drank, the better it would begin to taste.

'Haem…' Calen's voice resounded in Arden's ears as though his brother had been standing right beside him. Prickles crept over Arden's skin. He closed his eyes for a moment and drew in a breath, holding it in his chest. That name – Haem – was his, it belonged to him, and yet it didn't. He hadn't heard that name uttered aloud in over two years. It was a remnant of who he used to be. *Am I still that person?* Arden let his breath out slowly, pursing his lips slightly and focusing on the air leaving his mouth. *I'd still die to protect Calen. I'd still give my life for his in a heartbeat.*

"Brother Arden?"

Arden opened his eyes, turning. Watcher Gildrick stood behind Arden, the warm light of the many firepits dancing across his face, his white-trimmed green robes draped over his shoulders, a mug in each hand, steam wafting.

"Watcher Gildrick." Arden pushed his earlier thoughts from his mind, trying his best to muster a half-smile. "Enjoying the festival?"

"I am indeed. Though it feels a little strange to be celebrating while the world is at war, don't you think?"

Arden let out a soft breath through his nose, nodding.

"Here." Gildrick handed one of the mugs to Arden.

He took the mug in his right hand, then cupped both hands beneath it, feeling the warmth spread through his palms. The earthy smell filled his nostrils immediately. He stared down at the hot tea for a moment, then looked at Gildrick. "Arlen Root tea…"

Gildrick smiled, taking a sip from his mug. "It tastes like shit."

Both Arden and Gildrick burst out laughing.

"It really does," Arden said, still laughing. "It was my mam's favourite."

A comfortable silence descended between the two men. The tea warmed their hands as music played and children sang.

"Sit with me a while, will you?" Gildrick asked, inclining his head towards the bench where Arden had been sitting. "I've heard Yara Ilmire will be performing here soon. She's young but I have it on good authority she's the best bard in Ardholm."

Arden scrunched his mouth. In truth, all he wanted to do was be alone. And before Gildrick had appeared, that had been precisely his plan. But

Gildrick just had a way about him. Arden looked down at the mug of dark liquid in his hands and took a sip, breathing in through his nostrils as he did. The warmth spread through his mouth and throat. He looked up at Gildrick. "It really does taste like shit."

CHAPTER TWENTY-SEVEN

SHIELD OF MY FATHER

Dayne stood at the window ledge as the morning sun rose, its light spraying over the Rolling Mountains. That was the only downside to his old chambers: they didn't look out over the ocean. But even at that, a lightness filled Dayne's heart as he gazed over the dawn-lit city of Skyfell. Over twelve years, he had clawed and dragged his way through dirt, and blood, and death. But now he was finally home.

Dayne shook his head, rubbing his fingers into the creases of his eyes, wiping away the beginnings of tears, a smile spreading across his face.

"Do you not sleep?" Mera's arms wrapped around his chest from behind, her skin warm. He could feel her cheek pressing against his back, her hair tickling his skin.

Dayne pulled his elbows in, clasping Mera's arms against his body, resting his hand over hers. He ran his thumb over the black ink tattoos on her fingers that marked her as a wyvern rider. "Not much, not in a long time. And not again until Loren Koraklon is cold on the ground, and we are free."

Even the thought of the man who now called himself 'High Lord Loren' made Dayne's teeth grind. The man who had betrayed Dayne's family on the night the empire burned the people of Stormwatch alive.

Mera squeezed Dayne tighter, forcing the air from his lungs. "It's too early for talk of death."

"Mera, let go." Dayne laughed, feigning an attempt to break free.

"Only if you can make me," Mera said with a laugh, shimmying across his back to avoid his grasp.

Dayne turned, lifting Mera into the air, her legs wrapping around his waist, her eyes fixed on his. He traced her face with his gaze, her bronzed skin, the three scars that ran from her forehead to her jaw, her ocean eyes, her smile, the dimple in the left cheek. Was this what it felt like to be happy? He never wanted to lose this feeling. Something in his heart twisted, a pang of worry chilling his veins.

"Dayne, what's wrong?" Mera pulled her legs away and dropped her feet to the floor, reaching up and resting her hand on his cheek.

Dayne tilted his head, pressing his cheek into her palm. Just her touch brought a smile to his lips. He drew in a deep breath, then cupped her face in his hands. "Leaving you here all those years ago was the hardest thing I've ever done." Dayne's voice trembled. "I stood there, Mera. Right outside the door. I never *wanted* to go. I never wanted to leave you, or Alina, or Baren. I had no choice, Mera. I had no choice..."

"I know." Mera pulled Dayne's head down and kissed his forehead. "What's done cannot be undone. Time only moves forward, and therefore, so can we. We are here, now, and we have a long bloody road to walk. But we'll do it together."

"I love you." Dayne shook his head as he spoke. "I've never stopped loving you."

"You're a lot sappier than you used to be. Have you grown soft?" Mera laughed, holding Dayne's gaze, then let out a sigh, pushing her nose against his. "I love you too." She ducked from Dayne's grasp, the soft morning light touching her bare skin as she pulled a shirt over her head and began dressing herself in her leathers.

"Patrol?" Dayne asked, pulling the strap of her breastplate around and doing up the buckle.

Mera nodded, patting the buckle Dayne had just closed, double-checking his work. "Some imperial ships have been sighted along the coast. Alina wants us to stay visible so they keep their distance. Are you meeting Marlin to break the fast?"

Dayne shook his head, letting out a rueful sigh. "Alina asked me to meet her just after sunrise."

"Ah."

"Why, ah?" Dayne pulled on a linen tunic and trousers, slipping his feet into sandals.

"No." Mera shook her head, pulling her sword belt around her hips and fastening it tight. "I'm not doing this anymore, Dayne. I'm not going to stand in the middle between you two. She is my leader and my friend. You are my heart."

Dayne snatched up the dress Mera had worn the night before and tossed it at her as he walked to the door, laughing as it caught in the air and draped itself over her face.

"You'll regret that," he heard her call as he stepped from the room and out into the corridors of Redstone.

Dayne was only a few feet from the closed door when he realised he was still grinning from ear to ear. But soon his smile faded. His happiness didn't vanish, it didn't wither and die, but it became more subdued. For twelve years, he had carved rivers of blood through Epheria. He had hunted and killed. He had done things he had never thought he would do. And he had done it all for one reason: to come home. Yet now, here he was, walking the corridors of Redstone, Mera in his heart, Alina leading the House, Baren alive, and still he couldn't hold the happiness in his mind. There was too much still to do, too much blood yet to spill. The one thing he had not anticipated about happiness was that once he had it, he would be terrified of ever losing it. Maybe that was his penance for leaving: to never truly know the meaning of peace.

As he walked, Dayne brushed his hand along the reddish stone of the fluted columns that lined the corridors, his fingers slipping into the grooves, the stone smooth against his skin. Morning light drifted through the arched windows set into walls on the right side, carving through the dim corridor, painting bright arches of light on the walls opposite, dust suspended in its beams. The smell of burning oil still lingered in the air from the night before, the gentle citrus aroma of the orange trees in the garden and the city's orchards carrying on the wind.

The familiarity of it all brought Dayne's memories to the fore: charging through the corridors, Alina clinging to his back like a crazed monkey, Baren running beside them, their mother chasing, their father feigning disapproval while he and Marlin laughed. Those days were long gone. But Dayne was still happy to have those memories. Life in Valtara had not been easy. The empire had ensured that. But there had always been love within these walls – something Dayne had allowed himself to forget as the years wore away at him.

The corridor opened to the landing that fronted Alina's study – which had once belonged to their father – and acted as an internal balcony overlooking the entrance hall of Redstone. An ornately carved stone bannister framed the edges of the balcony, dropping on either side into the two sets of stone staircases that led to the ground floor.

Two Redstone guards stood on either side of the stained wooden doors, garbed in bronzed cuirasses and burnt orange armoured skirts, ordo shields strapped to their backs, thick shafted ash wood valynas gripped in their fists. But of everything, it was the bronzed steel of the guards' armoured boots that Dayne settled on; war was here.

Dayne rested his hand on the bannister opposite the doors and looked over the entrance hall where porters, servants, and maids dashed about preparing for the day. Redstone guards stood in pairs about the hall, backs straight, spears gripped in fists.

His gaze lingering for only a moment, Dayne turned towards Alina's study.

"My lord Ateres," the guard on the left said, inclining her head, her bright green eyes visible through the almond shaped slits in her helmet. She had four black ink rings on her right arm, two on her left. *Almost a spearmaster, proficient in the blade.* "Lady Alina waits for you inside."

Dayne nodded, his mind recoiling at the title. "Thank you."

As the guard motioned to open the door, Dayne reached out his hand, signalling for her to wait.

"Is all well, my lord?"

"What is your name?"

"My name?"

"You do have one, don't you?" Dayne allowed himself a smile and lifted a curious brow.

"I... yes. Tarine, my lord."

"My name is Dayne, Tarine. It is a pleasure to meet you. What is your House?"

The woman paused, glancing towards the other guard. "Tarine of House Valanis, my lord."

"Tarine of House Valanis." Dayne let the name percolate, pulling memories from the shelves in his mind. "House Valanis has served under House Ateres for many a century. It is a proud name. Your father stood alongside mine. May we honour both of their memories by doing the same."

Tarine stood a little straighter, clapping her arms down by her side and giving a deep bow of her head. "By blade and by blood, Lord Ateres."

"By blade and by blood, Tarine of House Valanis." Dayne turned to the other guard. "And your name?"

"Benin of House Andeer, my lord." The young man nodded, bowing slightly at the waist.

"Another fine House." Dayne looked over the two guards, memorizing their eyes. They each looked as though they had seen no more than twenty-five summers. "It is a pleasure to meet you both." Dayne moved forward, stepping past Tarine to open the doors himself.

Stepping into the study was like moving back through time. The three soft couches that Dayne's father had always kept in the centre of the room – that Baren had removed – were now back in place. The old Valtaran weapons that had hung on the eastern wall were gone, paintings and small tapestries of vivid colour taking their place.

"Good, you're here." Alina leaned back against the front of her desk that sat on the opposite side of the couches before the large open window, her orange and white robes held with a bronze clasp wrought into the shape of the wyvern of House Ateres. Marlin Arkon stood beside her, his white flecked hair tied back, orange robes over his shoulders.

"I see you've redecorated. I…" Dayne's voice trailed off as he looked to the western side of the room, where the bookcases lined the wall. Suspended on wooden stands, polished and pristine, were two sets of armour that he would have recognised anywhere in the world. "How…" The moisture fled from Dayne's mouth, his lips going dry, a lump forming in his throat. He looked to Alina, then moved towards the armour, reaching out his hand, his fingers brushing against the hardened leather of what he knew was his mother's cuirass. The leatherwork had been restitched, the surface polished, but it was most definitely hers. It held the same marks and nicks. The spiral patterns of orange and white worked into the dark leather were identical. The sigil of House Ateres along the chest.

A shiver swept through Dayne's body, memories of Sylvan Anura – the Dragonguard – taking Ilya Ateres' head from her shoulders while she knelt on the deck of that boat, her eyes locked with Dayne's. He pushed back the memory, swallowing hard, fighting the tremble in his hand. "Alina… how is this possible? How did you find them?"

Dayne moved his hand to the second set of armour, feeling the cool touch of hardened steel as he set his hand on his father's cuirass. Matching greaves and vambraces were set on a small stool before the cuirass, armoured skirts of white and orange held on branching arms at the middle. A bronzed Valtaran helmet sat at the top of the stand, a crest of white horsehair running from the front to the back. A polished ordo shield sat at the base of the stand, resting against the armoured skirts, the wyvern of House Ateres emblazoned across its front.

Dayne's pulse was a deafening, pounding thump in his head as he traced his hand along the cuirass, his fingers resting on a ridge in the centre of the chest where the steel had been fused back together. The tremble in his hand won out. His breaths grew rapid, and his skin turned cold as he remembered his father screaming at Dayne to run, his cries cut short as Sylvan Anura's blade punched through his sternum.

"They brought the bodies back, Dayne." Dayne didn't turn, but he knew by the sound of Alina's voice that she stood behind him. "They dragged them through the streets like dead animals and strung them up in the main plaza. Loren forced me and Baren to sit day after day and look at them dangling. 'The price of rebellion,' he said. I see mother's headless body every time I close my eyes. I'm not sure if I really remember her face. They left them there for days, the birds pecking at them. They would have left them longer had Marlin and Savrin not cut them down. Even then, Loren tore the city apart looking for them."

Dayne reluctantly pulled his hand from the chest of his father's cuirass and turned to Alina. Her lips were trembling, her eyes raw and red, and for a brief moment she wasn't the fierce warrior, the wyvern rider, the leader. She was simply his little sister. Dayne wrapped his arms around Alina and pulled her close. Feeling her sob against his chest ignited a blend of fury and sorrow in his veins. Dayne held Alina until the tremble in her shoulders stopped. He leaned back, clasping his hands at the sides of her arms, looking her dead in her bloodshot eyes. "We will strip the flesh from Loren Koraklon's bones, we will drive a blade through his heart, and we will leave him as carrion for the birds. By blade and by blood, I promise you."

Alina wiped the tears from her face, a cold look setting into her eyes. "Do you remember what I said? Valtara will either be free, or it will burn. I meant those words. This is the end. The end of chains or the end of breaths. You told me you would stand by my side until your lungs took their last breath, until your heart ceased to beat. You asked me to let you be my sword." Alina turned, a cold fire burning in her eyes. "Well, I'm asking you now. Will you be my sword, brother?"

"I am yours." Dayne clenched his fist and brought it to his chest. Killing was something he had never enjoyed doing, but he had grown to understand the necessity of it. And killing on a battlefield, in the name of Valtara's freedom, was a different thing to killing for coin or for revenge.

Alina nodded. "Good." She clenched her jaw and stepped past Dayne, resting her hand on the bronzed steel cuirass that their father had once worn. Her palm pressed against steel, Alina clenched her fingers into a fist. "I've spoken to Marlin." Alina glanced towards Marlin, who stood silently by the desk, his arms folded. "And I've decided I want you to reform the Andurii. I want you to stand where our father stood."

Dayne's breath caught in his chest. Anywhere Alina sent him, he would fight. Anything she needed of him, he would do. But this… The Andurii had been the finest warriors of House Ateres. The tip of the spear, the beating heart of the Ateres army, blademasters and spearmasters both. In his lifetime, Arkin Ateres had been their leader. Dayne was not fit to lace the boots of an Andurii warrior, never mind wear the armour or hold the shield. It would be like lighting a candle and calling himself a dragon. "Alina…"

"No." Alina shook her head, her lips twisting downward. "You told me you would do anything for Valtara's freedom. Don't you dare tell me you won't do this."

"It wouldn't be right." Dayne held out his arms, showing the two black rings on each. "I haven't earned that. I haven't fought in a shield wall in over twelve years. I'm no spearmaster, nor blademaster."

"But you fight like one." Alina pushed at Dayne's chest, causing him to stumble backwards. "You have the heart of the Andurii beating in that chest! Our father's heart. His blood, *our* blood. I need this, Dayne. The wolves are circling. They smell weakness. We need to show them that House Ateres is stronger than it has ever been, or this rebellion will die without ever truly taking its first breaths. The Andurii are more than a wall of shields and spears. They are a symbol, a rallying cry. Where the white crests of the Andurii march, our people will follow. I can rule the skies, Dayne. Like our mother did. But if we are going to succeed where others have failed, I need you to carry the wyvern of House Ateres on your shield. I need you to inspire. You are Dayne Ateres. Son of Arkin and Ilya Ateres. You are finally home. Now I need you to fight for it. I need you to sweat, and bleed, and be willing to die for this House and the people in it. If the empire wants Valtara, they will have to pry it from our cold, dead hands. Words are cheap. Show me who you are."

Alina's chest rose and fell in heavy sweeps, her jaw set, her stare fixed on Dayne, fury burning in her eyes.

Dayne drew in a deep breath, then looked to Marlin, who hadn't said a word since Dayne had entered the study. He stared at Dayne for a moment, then moved closer. "Your father once told me that battles are won with steel and skill, but they are lost in hearts and minds. The Andurii are a symbol, Dayne. Of House Ateres. Of Valtara. Of hope. Alina is right. If the people of Valtara see the white crests of the Andurii, see the wyverns on their shields, the cloaks on their shoulders, they will spin legends. Since you were a boy, you've had a fire in you. Where you led, others followed. I can get you steel, and I can find you warriors to wield it. But only you can light the fire in their hearts, make them believe. You watched your parents die. You watched Stormwatch burn. You feel that anger in your bones. I know you do, because so do I. Take it and use it. Don't let it all be for nothing."

Dayne ran his tongue across his teeth, a knot twisting in his chest. He turned back towards his father's armour, running his fingers across the fused ridge on the sternum. "How long do I have?"

"We are currently gathering supplies and mustering, cutting the empire from Skyfell and Ironcreek by the root. We march for Lostwren in three days' time."

"That's not nearly enough time, Alina. I cannot train three hundred men to fight together in three days. All I will be doing is preparing them to die."

"I think you misunderstand me, brother. Marlin and I have talked at length with the commanders and have selected the finest warriors House Ateres has to offer. The best of us. All I am asking from you is to stand at their head. To show the strength of House Ateres."

Dayne's gaze moved between Marlin and Alina, and then down to the ordo shield that lay resting against the stand – his father's shield. He reached down, brushing the steel with his fingertips, then slid his arm through the central strap, wrapping his fingers around the grip near the shield's rim. He hefted the shield, feeling its weight, casting his gaze over the sigil of House Ateres emblazoned across the front. He didn't deserve to hold it. But if that is what his sister needed of him, then that is what he would do. "I will need to meet them."

Both Marlin and Alina smiled, and Marlin inclined his head. "They are already waiting for you, my lord. I can take you to them right now."

Dayne couldn't help but suppress a laugh as he looked between Alina and Marlin. They had already known what his answer would be. He drew in a deep breath and let it out in a puff of air. "Lead the way, Marlin." Dayne turned to speak to Alina. To tell her he would not let her down. But she held up her hand, shaking her head.

"Actions. Not words."

Dayne nodded, allowing himself a smile. "She would be proud, Alina. They both would. I am." Dayne rested his father's shield back against the wooden stand, treating it as though it were as fragile as a pane of glass. "Marlin?"

"Yes, my lord." Another smile touched Marlin's lips as he said the words 'my lord', clearly taking a sense of satisfaction from the uncomfortable look on Dayne's face. "Follow me."

⌘

AFTER DAYNE AND MARLIN LEFT, Alina allowed herself to crumple, sitting against the back of the leather couch, leaning forward, her elbows pressing into her quads, her hands clasped around the back of her head. She took in a long, trembling breath and let it sit in her chest, slowing the pounding of her heart. When she could hold it no longer, she let it out in a sigh, pressed her fingers into her scalp, then rose to her feet.

Telling Dayne what Loren had done to their parents' bodies had taken a toll on her she hadn't expected. As had hearing Marlin describe the horrible things that Dayne had seen the night that everything fell. Alina wanted to hate Dayne for leaving. No matter what Mera said… no matter what anyone said. He had been her big brother. He should have been there for her and Baren when they needed him, when their parents' bodies were dragged through the streets and strung up in the plaza. He just should have been there.

When they were younger, Alina had seen Dayne as nothing short of a hero. He had always been so strong and confident, so sure of himself. Now he seemed to question every word that touched his lips. Scars laced his body, and something cold had found a home in his eyes. He was no longer the young man she had always looked up to. He was something else entirely.

Alina wanted to hate him, but she couldn't. Even with everything that was different, Mera was right. He still had the same heart, that same aura that surrounded him. He was a leader of men, whether he knew it or not. Most important of all, he was her brother.

Alina rested her hand on the leather cuirass that had once belonged to her mother. The cuirass Ilya Ateres had worn the day she died. "I'm trying…"

CHAPTER TWENTY-EIGHT

SHOW THEM WHO YOU ARE

She hasn't changed in the slightest," Dayne said as he followed Marlin through the corridors of Redstone, smiling as he thought of Alina. More than a few whispers passed between servants and porters at the sight of Dayne, some stopping to incline their heads, some smiling, some frowning. After the meeting of the council and the celebration Turik had arranged, news of Dayne's return had spread through the city of Skyfell like wildfire. It wasn't long before he noticed that, although many were glad of his return, there were some who laid blame at his feet. Blame for what happened, blame for leaving, blame for everything since then. He didn't begrudge them that. His feet had been the place he had laid his own guilt all those years. What was a little more?

"No," Marlin answered, laughing and shaking his head. The light drifting through the arched windows cast shifting shadows across his wrinkled face. Dayne wasn't sure how many summers Marlin had seen. More than forty, perhaps fewer than fifty. His skin was leathered by the sun, his hair flecked with grey and white, but his hawk-like eyes still gleamed bright blue, and his body still held the physique of a warrior. "She hasn't. She's still the same ball of fire she's always been."

"Thank you for looking after her all this time."

"Looking after her?" This time Marlin's laugh reached his belly. "Alina doesn't need looking after. She needs holding back. She would charge into a dragon's open jaws in the hope she could carve it apart from the inside out. You see this?" Marlin pulled back the neck of his robes, gesturing to a nasty-looking scar that ran from his collarbone down onto his back. "She gave me that while we were sparring when she was fifteen. I learned something about Alina that day."

"And was that?"

"If you think you have her beat, you've already lost."

Dayne let out a sigh, pride swelling in his chest. "It's right that she leads the House. She was born for it."

"Aye, she was. She's like your mother that way. She's a force of nature."

The smile that touched Dayne's lips was born of both warmth and melancholy. His mother had been the fiercest woman he'd ever known. Even her love had burned in him like a fire. She was a warrior, a mother, a leader. She was all. And Dayne could see her in every breath Alina took. Which only made it hurt all the more that Baren had allowed the empire to take Alina's firstborn – his nephew. In his heart, Dayne knew that blame wasn't fair. The empire took the firstborn of all Valtaran families. An exception would not have been made for Alina, just as one hadn't been made when their mother had given birth to Owain. But something inside just wouldn't allow him to let it go.

Marlin stopped, resting his hand on Dayne's arm. As Dayne looked at the Steward of House Ateres, the man who had been like a second father to him his whole life, he realised that since he had returned, they had barely spoken. "Dayne, I know it's hard, being back, everything being so different to what it was, not knowing where you stand. I can see it in you. But trust me, having you here lights a fire in her. She's always been tough as steel, always willing to bleed for what needs to be done, but since you've returned, there's something in her that wasn't there before. She walks as though the world isn't quite so heavy anymore. This is your home, my boy. I want to make sure you know that." Marlin turned his head for a moment, a tear glistening on his cheek.

"I…" Marlin drew a breath and steadied himself. "Some things are so hard to say you have to say them there and then lest you lose the courage. Dayne, when we got separated that night, I had no idea it would be the last time I'd see you for twelve years." Marlin choked out a laugh that held no happiness to it. He bit the side of his lip, then looked Dayne in the eyes. "I'm sorry. Your father was one of the best men I ever knew. He treated me like a brother, and he cared for you all with a rare love. Your mother… well, what words could be used to sum up a woman as fierce and devoted as Ilya Ateres?" One or two people lingered in the corridor to see what was going on, but Dayne paid them no heed. "They didn't deserve to die that way, and you should never have had to see it. I should have been there. I should have protected you."

"If you had been there, nobody would have been left to watch over Alina and Baren. Nobody to guide them. Nobody to keep them safe."

"Fine job I did of that."

"Baren made his choices, just like we all must." Tears threatened him as he looked at Marlin. The man had always been a bastion of stoicism. Dayne and Baren had joked that Marlin was a statue brought to life. "If you had been there, you wouldn't be here now. And I need you here now."

Marlin nodded, snorting as though he were clearing his nose. "Come on. We don't have time to waste standing here like whimpering children."

"I think you were the only one whimpering," Dayne said, giving Marlin a wry smile.

Marlin led Dayne down through keep and past the dining halls, then out into the practice yard that lay at the eastern edge of Redstone's grounds next to the housing for the main garrison.

Even before they stepped out into the yard, the methodical sounds of marching feet and clanging wood and steel filled the air, shouts and commands ringing out, echoing through the corridors of stone. Dayne tried to settle himself, tried to still his rapidly beating heart. Aside from the fact that he only bore two markings of spear and blade, making him quite clearly not of Andurii standard, he was more than aware that many of the men and women in that yard likely held the same sentiment towards him as some of the servants and porters in the keep.

"Respect is earned." Marlin clamped his hand on Dayne's shoulder.

Dayne looked at Marlin in confusion.

"Respect is earned," he repeated. "It doesn't matter what anyone thinks of you. Show them who you are. If you show those men and women that you are willing to bleed for them, they will bleed for you too, my boy. I promise you that."

Dayne nodded, clenching his jaw.

The practice yard of Redstone was enormous. It stretched a few hundred feet wide and long, ringed by a low wooden fence, the ground flattened and covered in sand. Over five hundred years ago, Dayne's ancestors had expanded it to allow space for both the Redstone guards and the Andurii. Dayne's father had once told him that the decision to train the Andurii next to the Redstone guards had been made to inspire the guards, to show them the strength of the House, to show them what they could become.

A pathway ringed the yard, framed by orange trees that were evenly spaced along the edge of the keep, leading around it and off to other sections of the grounds.

Across the yard, men and women marched in close order drills, valynas and ordo shields gripped in their fists. Some were bare chested, some in light linen tunics and trousers. There were at least three hundred gathered, broken into groups of fifty, moving in blocks of ten across and five deep. The rhythmic pounding of feet sent a low tremor through the ground. The clang of steel as shield walls were engaged was beautiful to Dayne's ears. Dayne's heart swelled with pride at the discipline and precision with which the soldiers carried out the manoeuvres. After the night his father's rebellion had been crushed before it even began, Dayne lost all hope of laying eyes on a sight like this again.

"Continue close order. Five beats, then realign," a man in a leather cuirass shouted as he saw Dayne and Marlin approach the entrance to the yard.

"AH-OOH," came the reply, voices in perfect unison.

The drumming of spear on shield rang out. *Dum, dum, dum, dum, dum.* On the fifth beat, the formations shifted, the second rows separating, the first rows drawing back through the ranks, the new first row closing order. Dayne had once practised the same drill. It was a formational shift used during longer battles to allow those at the front to rest. It was a movement that could only be performed at certain points during a battle and required nearly perfect synchronisation and discipline to ensure the enemy couldn't take advantage of the shift in rank.

As Dayne and Marlin reached the entrance to the yard, four men and a woman approached, each wearing cuirasses of bronzed steel in different styles but all bearing the burnt orange and white of House Ateres on their skirts.

"Steward." The man who had noticed Dayne and Marlin approach stepped forward, reaching out his hand to Marlin and grasping his forearm.

"You have done well, Dinekes. You all have. They look as fine as any warriors I've seen in this yard."

"My thanks, Steward Arkon." The man turned toward Dayne, and it was in that moment that Dayne recognised him. Dinekes Ilyon. He had been a member of the Redstone Guard when Dayne's father had still been alive. He had fought by Dayne's side during the attack on Redstone. The man had held three markings of the spear and two of the sword then, but now Dayne saw four rings of black ink on each of Dinekes's arms, each set bisected by a single line. Dinekes made to speak, but Dayne got there first.

"Dinekes. I cannot begin to say how happy I am to see your face."

A shocked look crossed Dinekes's face, but he quickly concealed it, bowing his head. "My lord Ateres." Dinekes clenched his hand into a fist and held it across his chest. "It is an honour to stand beside you again. When I first heard rumours of your return, I thought them impossible. By blade and by blood, I am yours, my lord. To the pits of the void and back."

The hairs on the back of Dayne's neck pricked, his stomach suddenly lighter. So little had he expected Dinekes's words that he could actually feel tears threaten his eyes. He pushed them back. *Collect yourself, now is not the time.* Instead, Dayne reached out and grasped Dinekes's forearm, clasping his fingers tight. "The honour is mine. I am yours, by blade and by blood. I belong to all Valtara, to its freedom."

For a moment, Dinekes just stared at Dayne, slack-jawed, then his lips curled to a smile, and he nodded. "This is Odys, Ileeri, Barak, and Jorath. We are the five captains assigned to you by High Commander Arenen."

Odys, Ileeri, Barak, and Jorath greeted Dayne and Marlin. None showed Dayne the same outward level of respect as Dinekes had, but neither were they disrespectful. It was more than Dayne felt he deserved.

"None of them know why they are here?" Marlin asked Dinekes as they entered the practice yard. Dayne noticed more than a few soldiers breaking step as they turned to look at him, exchanging whispers.

"They do not. Lady Alina felt it better those words come from her brother's mouth. For now, all they know is that we are readying to march for war, and they have been chosen to form a new regiment under Lord Ateres's command."

Marlin nodded. "Good. Carry on. Have them run through close order and extended order as well as single sparring."

"Not all bear the full markings," Dayne said as he cast his gaze over the soldiers, noticing that many of the soldiers gathered did not bear the final vertical mark of master on either forearm – some only bore three rings on one of their arms. In Dayne's father's day, all Andurii bore the full markings of the master on both arms.

Marlin's gaze was locked on a pair of soldiers sparring with staff and shield. "True spearmasters and blademasters are in short supply. We never recovered after that night, Dayne. But Andurii are not trained, they are forged. True, we want the finest warriors the House has to offer, but that isn't enough. We aren't here today to observe their skill. We are here to observe their hearts. For some hearts grow stronger in the fire, while others break. That is the difference. The Andurii never break, they never back down, and they are always willing to die for the person standing to their left. It is far easier to teach a man to wield a spear than it is to teach them to bleed for another. That is a trait that must be learned by oneself."

Until that moment, Dayne had forgotten that Marlin had once been an Andurii before Arkin Ateres had asked him to step aside in order to become the Steward of the House. "Marlin, are there any others? Any more Andurii who survived?"

Marlin simply gave Dayne a weak smile, then gestured for Dayne to follow as he strode towards a weapons rack at the edge of the yard. Just as Dayne caught up with Marlin, the man turned, tossing him a valyna.

Dayne snatched the spear from the air, drawing a breath as he did. He savoured the familiar smooth touch of the ash wood beneath his fingertips. Instinctively, he moved the spear about him, feeling its weight, gauging its balance. It felt like home. How many hours had he spent practising his forms when he was younger? Too many to count. It had been years since he had last held a spear and moved through the forms, but it felt as though it had only been moments. He turned, twirling the wooden shaft, feeling the weight of the valyna's spiked butt swinging like a pendulum. He brought the tip around, moving from Crouching Wolf, into Patient Tiger, the butt of the valyna whipping up sand as he brought it around himself along the ground. Dayne had moved through ten joining forms before he realised how carried away he had become. He swept the spear through the end of Swooping Crane, then drove the butt into the ground. Some of the soldiers around him stared openly, and the captains watched with curious gazes.

"It's good to see that look on your face," Marlin said as he handed Dayne a large, circular ordo shield, rough etchings carved along its rim. "I used to love watching you practice your forms. There are few I've seen who move so naturally with the spear."

Marlin turned and grasped a valyna of his own, hefting an ordo shield onto his arm. He tilted his head towards the ranks of soldiers who had stopped staring and returned to their tasks. "They have heard you are Dayne Ateres, risen from the dead. It will do some good to show them how alive you are."

Dayne tightened and loosened his grip on the valyna in his right hand. He tensed his left forearm, feeling the muscle rub against the leather strap of the ordo, his fingers gripping the handle near the edge of the shield.

Marlin stepped close enough that only Dayne could hear the words that passed his lips. "Those rings on your arms mean nothing." Marlin looked down at the two rings of black ink that marked Dayne's forearms. "Show them who you are." Marlin turned to the five captains who were overseeing the drills and sparring. "Each of you, arm yourselves. If we fight together, we practice together."

Each of the five captains nodded in acquiescence and snatched up spears and shields.

Knots twisted in Dayne's chest as he and Marlin joined the ranks of the nearest group, stepping into the front line. Most of the soldiers gave Dayne a tentative bow as he stepped into rank, but even as they did, he could see them assessing him, weighing him, measuring him. Dayne had purposely taken the position at the front right of the group. The front right was the most vulnerable position in a Valtaran shield wall, and it was also the position his father had always taken. Within the shield wall, each shield overlapped with the shield on the left, creating an unbroken link of warrior protecting warrior. But all positions on the right side of the shield wall held no such protection, particularly on the front line. As such, the most experienced warriors usually took their place on the right side, with the first among those taking position in the front line. Dayne knew the quickest way to show these warriors he was willing to bleed for them was simply to bleed for them. As he set his feet, Alina's voice sounded in his mind. *Actions, not words.*

Marlin, who stood directly beside Dayne, nudged Dayne's elbow. "They're waiting on you, commander."

Dayne drew in a lungful of air, then let it out slowly. He called out the command to begin and fell into the motion of the drill, feeling rusty as he switched his spear into an overhand grip, hefting his shield into position. A dull vibration jarred his arm as Marlin's shield, and all other shields along the row, were pulled into position, a singular metallic *clack* as the shields snapped together.

Hours passed as they worked through the drills methodically, the sun rising higher, sweat slicking Dayne's body, his muscles burning from a level of prolonged use he hadn't experienced in years. Roars and shouts of commands echoed off the stone walls, always answered by the clang of steel or the chants of 'Ah-ooh'.

Each and every one of the gathered soldiers was exceptional. Each held the spear and shield as though they were born gripping them in their fists. At first, Dayne felt slow and clunky, out of place. But after a while, muscle memory took over, until the motions were as effortless as breathing. Thousands of hours of practice reigniting in his veins. Twelve years of killing and spilt blood making his mind sharp and his muscles resilient.

That is one thing I have that none of them truly do. They have not seen the things I've seen. The empire has had a collar around their necks since the day I left. They do not know death like I do. When they wash their hands, the water still runs clear. The souls Dayne had sent to dine in Achyron's halls weighed heavy on his shoulders. He remembered every face, every voice, every breath that was someone's last. But at that moment, the blood on his hands gave him a sense of calm. He may not have the markings on his arms, but the weight that bore down on his soul told him he had earned his place.

After a few hours, they broke for water and food. Porters from the kitchens brought out trays of bread, cheese, slow-roasted pork, and fresh fruit – all likely 'commandeered' from the imperial supplies. There was little talk as they ate. Over the years, Dayne found that was always the way – unless the food was bad, then there was a lot of talk. Once the food was gone and the water jugs empty, the porters cleared everything away, and then everyone got back to their feet, a few aches and groans arising due to sore muscles.

"You're feeling it, aren't you?" Marlin said as he snatched up his spear, squeezing Dayne's shoulder. "The fire in your veins."

"It's good to be home." Dayne hefted his shield onto his arm and made to grab his spear, but something hit against his shoulder, knocking him off balance. He fell sideways, his shield hitting the ground, the leather strap forcing his arm to twist awkwardly. He caught himself with his right hand, the sand burning against his palm. When he looked up, he saw a man that looked as though he had seen no more summers than Dayne, with short dusty brown hair, a scraggly beard, and a cold look in his eyes. He was tall and lean, his chest bare above linen trousers and leather boots.

"Apologies, *my lord.*"

Dayne curled his fingers into a fist, grains of sand coarse against his skin. He clenched his jaw, biting the inside of his cheek as the man walked on, joining a clutch of soldiers who stood on the opposite side of the yard. He spat a mixture of saliva and blood – freshly drawn by his own teeth – into the sand, then lifted himself to his feet.

"Use it." Marlin gripped Dayne's arm, his fingers squeezing tight. "It's single sparring next. Show them who you are."

Dayne nodded, not taking his eyes off the man who had knocked him. He had seen soldiers test each other before, push them to see what they were made of. But something in the man's voice had felt more than that.

Spears were traded for quarterstaffs as the soldiers broke into groups for single sparring. It would do nobody any good to be wounded by the tip of a spear. Quarterstaffs could still do considerable damage in the right hands but were both a far safer sparring tool and a fairly good spear replacement. As a child, Dayne had taken many a black eye and bruised cheek from Marlin's quarterstaff during sparring. Once Marlin had actually struck him so hard he'd broken Dayne's nose. A slight bump still remained where Marlin had struck.

"Today, single sparring will work a bit differently to usual." Marlin said as the group of fifty or so soldiers they had run drills with gathered around. Across the yard, Dayne could see the other captains giving similar instructions to the other groups. Marlin must have briefed them prior to Dayne agreeing to reform the Andurii. "I select one of you, then that person selects their opponent. The victor will then select a new combatant, who will in turn select their opponent. Understood?"

Nods and murmurs of agreement answered. Marlin pointed towards a tall, lean woman, hair streaked with grey, her face all planes and angles. Dayne thought he recognised her from the Redstone guard when his father had still been the head of the House.

"Let's see who she picks," Marlin whispered, folding his arms across his chest as he took his place next to Dayne.

The woman cast her eyes around the group, then pointed towards a man who stood a head and a half taller than she, with shoulders that looked as if they could carry a horse and a gnarled knot of twisted flesh along his right arm where he had likely been burned. The man nodded, hefting his shield and cracking his neck.

They circled each other like wolves, eyes locked, shields held high. The behemoth of a man was the first to strike, lunging with an underhand stab of his staff towards the woman's knee that easily could have broken a bone.

The woman slammed her shield down against the staff, knocking it into the sand. She stabbed towards the man's head with her own staff, only to see the blow deflected by his shield rim. After the first blows were struck, the two danced around each other, nipping and biting, creating openings, then striking like flashes of lightning. Despite the man's size, they were so evenly matched that Dayne thought the victor would be the one who tired slowest. The man easily weighed twice the woman, but she was a master at creating angles and leverage. She didn't block his blows directly; she changed their direction and slid past them, using the man's own momentum against him. They both bore the full markings of blademasters, but where the man bore four rings of black ink on his right forearm, the woman bore full markings: four black rings and a bisecting black line. Though their rank only differed by a single marking, that difference was plain to see in the way she moved and the quickness of her mind.

Just as Dayne was admiring the fluidity of the woman's footwork, the larger man took a feigned opening and struck, only to find himself on the receiving end of a wooden quarterstaff to the nose. The man crashed like a boulder, blood dappling the sand. Cheers rose, but the woman didn't acknowledge the applause. Instead, she moved her quarterstaff into her left hand, clutching it with the same fingers she held the handle of the shield with, then reached down and helped the man to his feet. They touched foreheads and grasped forearms, exchanging a few words.

"Your names?" Dayne asked, inclining his head.

"Urica," the woman replied, bowing deeply at her waist.

"Of House Gordur?" Dayne was certain now that he recognised her.

"Yes, my lord. And may I say, praise Achyron for returning you to us."

Dayne smiled at Urica, inclining his head, then turned to the man, raising an eyebrow.

"Rexin of House Malik, my lord. By blade and by blood, I am yours."

"Kin of Hera Malik?"

"Aye, my lord. I am her younger brother, by the light of a single summer."

Dayne nodded. "Your blade is welcome, Rexin Malik."

Urica selected the next combatant, and she and Rexin stepped from the centre of the circle.

"That is the heart we are looking for," Marlin said, staring after Urica and Rexin as the next warriors circled each other, two men, one lithe and built of wiry muscle, the other short with a knotted grey-black beard and a cleft lip.

Dayne glanced towards Rexin and Urica. "They are going to pains to declare their loyalty to me. Is there something I should know, Marlin?"

"Nothing you don't already see. Many here remember you for your valour and your name. Some fought beside you at the Battle of Redstone, saw you storm the walls with no more than a spear, a shield, and two guards at your back, and others fought beside your father. They are simply ensuring their allegiance is known. There are some who see your return as a threat to Alina's position and others who still blame House Ateres for the massacre that occurred that night at the hands of the Dragonguard."

"If they blame House Ateres, why are they here?"

"Because they still fight for Valtara. This rebellion is more than just House Ateres, as you are well aware."

A chorus of cheers drew Dayne's attention towards the sparring. The lithe man lay on his back, the end of the bearded man's quarterstaff against his neck. Both men gave their names at Marlin's request and made similar declarations of loyalty towards Dayne.

The sparring continued in much the same way for the better part of an hour, with many of the warriors addressing Dayne after their fights had ended, though some of them said nothing, which, when laid against the outward displays of loyalty by the others, said everything.

"Alina risks a lot by granting me this honour," Dayne whispered to Marlin as a younger man took one of the more one-sided beatings of the day at the hands of a densely-muscled woman with tight-braided hair and a silver arm ring around her left bicep.

"She wants you by her side, Dayne. That and, in truth, having you lead the Andurii and gaining some measure of success would make her and House Ateres as a whole look stronger. She leads the rebellion now, but at the slightest sign of weakness, people will come for her head." Marlin turned and acknowledged the woman with the arm ring as she stood over her defeated opponent, turning back to Dayne as new combatants were chosen. He let out a deep sigh. "The poison of man, Dayne, is not being able to see past our own greed, even when we stand to gain for doing so."

"Dayne Ateres!" The voice rose clear above everything else, firm and deep.

Around them, the group parted, their heads turning towards the source of the voice. Dayne wasn't even the slightest bit surprised when the man who had knocked him over earlier strode into view, his chest still bare, a thick-shafted quarterstaff in his right fist, a bronzed steel ordo hefted on his left arm. In truth, Dayne had expected the challenge from the moment he had seen the look in the man's eyes, but he hadn't expected it to be quite so dramatic.

Dayne shifted his shield, sliding his arm fully through the leather strap, tightening his fingers around the handle near its rim.

"I challenge you."

"And I accept." The smile and the slight bow at the waist that Dayne gave the man only seemed to irritate him further, which suited Dayne perfectly. If the man was angry, he would be easier to fight.

"Not with this." The man's lip curled in distaste as he looked at his quarterstaff, which was stained with blood at both ends. He tossed it to the ground. "To first blood with the spear."

Dayne hesitated a moment, then turned to Marlin, expecting the man to advise against such a dangerous challenge, but instead he found Marlin handing him a spear.

"Do not hesitate. Do not contemplate mercy." Marlin's words resonated in Dayne's mind. They were the same words Marlin had spoken to Dayne the night the empire had attacked the city.

Dayne took the spear from Marlin, letting the air swell in his chest before exhaling. He nodded, then turned to the man who had issued the challenge. "To first blood."

The man grunted, rolling his shoulders and spitting into the sand.

"I would know the name of the man who wants to see my blood."

"Thorken is my name. Thorken of House Ulthir. Now a house of one. My family were in Stormwatch the night the Dragonguard set it aflame."

The circle around Dayne and Thorken grew larger as the other groups in the yard gathered, abandoning their sparring to witness the duel. Thorken's theatrics began to form sense in Dayne's mind. The man had called Dayne out so publicly to humiliate House Ateres in front of its finest warriors. Dayne tightened his grip on the spear's shaft, his knuckles going pale. He took no pleasure in causing pain, particularly to one of his own, but Marlin was right. Dayne needed to make an example here. "I will give you one opportunity to back down with your honour intact, Thorken of House Ulthir."

Thorken stepped into the now ever-expanding circle, sand shifting beneath his weight, his muscles glistening with sweat in the light of the midday sun. "Words of a coward. I will make you whimper before I make you bleed."

Dayne let out a sigh, rolling his shoulders and stepping forwards. Now he had no choice. "First blood."

Thorken shifted off his back foot, powering forwards, his spear in underhand grip, his shield across his body. Dayne tensed the muscles in his left arm, firming his grip on his shield, dropping his foot back to brace himself.

Thorken's shield crashed into Dayne's with the force of a battering ram, sending a jarring ripple through Dayne's arm and shoulder. Only instinct told him to snap his head to the right, the sharp sound of steel slicing through the air beside his left ear. Thorken had switched his spear into overhand as their shields collided, stabbing with a blow that easily would have sent Dayne to dine in Achyron's halls.

The markings of the spearmaster on Thorken's right arm had not been cheaply earned. The man moved with the speed of a wolf, his spear snapping like a viper, testing Dayne.

Thorken pulled back, circling, then charged once more, feinting with a drop of his shield and striking his spear forward, missing Dayne's throat by a hair's breadth as Dayne swung his neck backwards, too slow to bring his shield up. He wasn't used to holding one. It already hung heavy in his grip. Dayne brought his spear across, swatting away Thorken's, only for his head to nearly be taken from his shoulders by the rim of Thorken's shield.

Time and time again, Thorken charged like a man possessed, and each time, his strikes were intended to be killing blows. Dayne felt the atmosphere around them shift, the eagerness switching to apprehension.

But no fear touched Dayne's heart. He had fought warriors like Thorken a hundred times. Each one of them lay cold in the ground.

Spears and shields collided again and again, the vibrations dulling Dayne's shoulder to a numb ache. With every failed strike, Dayne could see the fury burning hotter in Thorken's eyes, the frustration building. More than that, with every failed strike, Dayne learned. He watched the patterns, the movement of Thorken's feet, the repetition in his strikes.

Feint, feint, strike. Feint, strike, strike. Feint, strike, feint, strike. In his anger, Thorken was methodical, drilled to precision, perfect in his execution, his body reverting to years of training. And that was where his weakness lay.

The muscles in Dayne's left arm and shoulder burned, screaming at him, demanding he drop the shield. He drew in a ragged breath and ignored the pain, burying it deep down where its screams were nothing more than whimpers.

Thorken swung his shield as though it bore a sharpened blade on its rim, forcing Dayne to step backwards. As Dayne was exposed, Thorken struck towards his head. Dayne deflected the blow with his shield.

Feint, feint, strike.

With Dayne's shield lifted, Thorken jabbed his spear, aiming to slice through the artery that pulsed in Dayne's inner thigh. Dayne swung his left leg around, the spear slicing past, its tip lodging in the sand. With Thorken's arm extended, Dayne struck out with his spear, slicing the tip of the blade along the top of the man's forearm, drawing a thin stream of blood.

Roars erupted, spears banging against shields.

"It is done," Dayne said, his words battling against the cacophony of voices.

The muscles in Thorken's jaw twitched, and he glared at Dayne, pulling the tip of his spear from the sand. *Those aren't the eyes of a man who has accepted defeat.*

Thorken roared and lunged forward, thrusting his spear towards Dayne's chest. Dayne tucked his left arm into his body, twisting at the hip to bring his shield up as quickly as he could. The clang of steel on steel resonated in Dayne's ears as Thorken's spear tip bounced off Dayne's shield, dulled slightly by the wooden underlayer of the ordo.

So be it. In that one moment, everything changed. Now Dayne was free. He no longer felt the need to pull his strikes, to cause as little harm as needed in the name of drawing blood.

Do not hesitate.

Dayne pushed off his back foot, ramming his shield against Thorken's. The aggressive strike caught the man off guard, and he stumbled backwards, raising his shield. As he did, Dayne switched his spear into overhand grip in one fluid motion and thrust down, slicing the blade through the tendon at the back of Thorken's right heel. He felt the steel severing skin and tendon like paper. The man howled, his leg buckling beneath him. Dayne let go of his spear, leaving the tip buried in the sand behind Thorken.

Thorken flailed as he stumbled backwards over the spear, blood pouring from the deep gash in his heel, staining the sand. He tried to catch himself, tried to stay on his feet, his face contorting in pain.

Do not contemplate mercy.

Dayne swung his left arm as though throwing a hook, his fist clenching around the handle of his ordo. A vibration jarred his arm as the rim of his shield slammed into Thorken's chest, the distinct sound of bones snapping. The man released his grip on his spear as he fell, blood spraying from his mouth as he hit the ground, deep, rasping, spluttering noises dragging from his throat.

Silence consumed the shouts and cheers that had resounded off the stone walls that surrounded the practice yard, pierced only by Thorken's blood-wet coughs and gasps.

Dayne stood over the man and lowered the tip of his spear to Thorken's throat. He looked in Thorken's eyes. The anger was gone, supplanted by icy fear. Dayne took a moment, drawing in a deep, unobstructed breath, then turned to the man who stood closest to him. "He has a severed tendon, broken ribs, and a punctured lung. Get a healer."

The man, no more than thirty summers, with a knotted blond beard and shaved head, stared at Dayne, dumbstruck.

"*Now!*"

Dayne dropped to one knee beside Thorken, leaning close so only he could hear. "I am sorry for what happened to your family. My heart bleeds with yours, just as my parents dine in Achyron's halls beside yours. When you recover, if you choose to follow me, I will give you the chance to carve your vengeance from Lorian flesh. I promise you. But if you ever disrespect my House again, and in turn my sister, I will bleed you slow. I will strip the flesh from your bones and hang you from the Skytower for the birds to feast on. Nod if you understand."

Thorken coughed and spluttered, blood splattering from his mouth, dappling his lips and chin. The man's eyes still held cold fear, but he nodded, if only just.

Dayne rose to his feet as two healers broke through the crowd and dropped down beside Thorken. One of them must have been an Alamant, for Dayne could feel them drawing from the Spark, pulling on thin threads of each elemental strand. If the Alamant knew what they were doing, Thorken's recovery would be less than a quarter the normal time.

Dayne turned, searching the crowd for Marlin and found the man's bright eyes staring back at him. Marlin nodded to Dayne, and Dayne nodded back. *Show them who you are.* As the healers worked on Thorken, murmurs rose amongst the gathered soldiers.

Dayne shifted, sand crunching under his feet. The murmurs slowly faded into the wind as he stood there in silence, shuffling feet and clinking steel audible as the soldiers waited for him to speak. Dayne had seen his father do the same thing many times, and when Dayne had asked Marlin why Arkin Ateres had stood in silence for so long, Marlin had answered, *'There is nothing that makes men sweat more than silence where there should be none.'*

The wind whipped over the walls of the keep, whistling through the courtyard and lifting up wisps of sand. "I did not come here today to put Valtarans in the ground." Dayne's voice rang clear and true, all eyes focusing on him. Over three hundred souls. "The empire has done enough of that already. I came here because I was told you were the best House Ateres had to offer. The greatest warriors beneath the banner of the wyvern. I came here to see if you had the heart to stand by my side, to bleed for this nation, to call yourselves Andurii."

Dayne felt the air change at the mention of the word 'Andurii'. Whispers rippled through the soldiers ringed about him, faces twisted in uncertainty and doubt. The Andurii were warriors of legend. For a man or woman to count themselves among the ranks of the Andurii was to leave an indelible mark on the history of Valtara. Dayne let his words sink in, let the whispers die down.

"We have three days before the joint armies of the rebellion march for Lostwren, where Imperial forces have surrounded the city, attempting to pressure Tula Vakira to openly re-declare House Vakira's allegiance to the Lorian Empire. In three days, I will leave this city, and those who walk beside me will call themselves Andurii. But that title isn't something that is given, it is something that is earned, and we will earn it in blood. I will die for you if Achyron demands it, for no man or woman is greater than Valtara. But if you are not willing to die for me and those around you, then leave now."

Feet shuffled and murmurs spread as those gathered waited for Dayne to continue.

Dayne's arm burned from the weight of the ordo shield strapped to it, but he didn't release his grip. He would not show weakness of any kind.

"I meant what I said." Dayne's voice cut through the whispers. "If you leave now, you leave with your honour intact. If you stay and hesitate, and your brother or sister dies because of it, I will kill you myself."

Silence hung heavy in the air, thick and palpable. Feet shuffled and slowly some began to move. A man stepped from the ring of people and looked him in the eye. He was tall with a flat nose and short black hair, his chest bare, ordo and valyna in his hands. He was no older than Alina. "You talk of honour, yet when your people needed you, you ran. My mother was an Andurii. She fought beside your father. She died in the gardens of Redstone. You are not fit to stand where she stood. You are not fit to lick her ashes."

The man spat into the sand, threw down his spear and shield, then left, the crowd parting before him.

Dayne stood and watched as more did the same. One by one, they stepped forward, spitting into the sand, then leaving. Just short of sixty. Fewer than Dayne had expected, but more than he had hoped.

"Good," Dayne called out once the last of them had left. The group of soldiers that stood around him now was far smaller, but he was happier for it. He found Dinekes and the other captains, then gave them a nod.

"Form up!" Dinekes roared, his voice carving through the silence. "Wall to wall combat formations!"

In contrast to the silence, the drum of scrambling feet was like rolling thunder, a low vibration thrumming through the sand. Dayne made his way over to Marlin, who stood with his eyes fixed on Dayne, his arms folded across his chest.

"You spoke well. You're definitely your father's son."

Dayne clenched his jaw, suppressing a grunt from the now searing pain in his left arm. He released his grip on the ordo's handle, letting the shield drop into the sand with a muted thud, then snatched up a waterskin and took a deep draught. He wasn't thirsty, he just needed an excuse to drop the shield. "We'll need to replace the numbers we've lost."

"I have a few in mind." Marlin kept his arms folded across his chest, his gaze flitting between the shield walls that had formed across the sparring yard. He looked down at Dayne's shield, then up to Dayne. "Pick up that shield. You've a long way to carry it yet."

As the orange-red glow of the setting sun sprayed over the walls of Redstone, Dayne dropped into the sand, his muscles burning and aching, his body saturated with sweat. Aside from Marlin, the captains, and a few stragglers, the practice yards were empty. He had asked the captains to send the soldiers off for evening meal. War was one of the few excuses a Valtaran citizen had for missing evening meal with their family, but once they marched through the gates of Skyfell, there was no telling how many, if any, of Dayne's newly formed Andurii would ever lay eyes on their families again. It seemed only right he grant them these last three meals.

One by one, the captains bowed their heads and made their leave. Dayne reciprocated the gestures as he sat in the sand, his lungs heaving. He no longer cared to hide his exhaustion.

"Today was a good day," Marlin said, extending his hand.

Dayne let his head drop back, dangling, then puffed out a breath of air, shook his head, and took Marlin's hand, his muscles screaming as he heaved himself to his feet. "It was a start."

Marlin nodded absently. "I'm going to go scrape this sweat off before we eat. Care to join?"

Dayne shook his head. "I'm going to check on Thorken's wounds, then I need to speak to Alina. I will see you at evening meal."

Marlin gave Dayne a knowing smile, then inclined his head, clapping his hand on Dayne's shoulder. "Like I said, you're definitely your father's son. Also, we must arrange for you to receive your markings of the spear, now that you've beaten a spearmaster in single combat."

Dayne raised a curious eyebrow, but Marlin only smiled at him and walked on, leaving Dayne standing there, the gentle wind turning his sweat cold. It took a few moments for Dayne to think back and realise: Thorken was a spearmaster. There were two ways to gain the markings of the spear or sword: to be granted them through the passage of trials, or to earn them in war and be awarded the ink by a commanding officer. But regardless of how the first four rings were earned, the final marking of master could only be attained by besting one who had already achieved the rank, in single combat, ensuring the next generation would always be, at the least, equal to the last. Defeating a master in honest combat at any stage would grant a person the rank for themselves, no matter their current rank, but it was uncommon – no, it was unheard of.

"Excuse me, my lord."

Dayne turned at the voice and found himself looking into the eyes of a young man who had seen maybe twenty-three or twenty-four summers, four black rings on each arm. He was young to have achieved such a rank, yet no younger than Alina. The young man wore a long, belted tunic with a sword and two knives at his hip. His eyes were a dark brown while his shoulder-length hair was black as night. Dayne had seen him sparring during the day – he was a fine warrior. "Yes?"

"I wanted to return this, my lord." The young man pulled one of the knives from his belt, gripped it by the blade, and offered the handle to Dayne. "And to let you know that it saved my life."

Dayne took the knife, staring at it for a moment. He looked back at the young man, then to the knife. It was a heavy knife with a forward-curving, single-edged blade for thrusting and cutting. He'd had one just like it before… Dayne looked back at the young man, his eyes narrowing. "Iloen? Iloen Akaida?"

The young man nodded, the light of the setting sun spraying across the sky at his back.

Iloen let out a grunt as Dayne forgot all levels of etiquette and pulled him into a tight embrace. Iloen had been a boy of no more than twelve summers the last time Dayne had laid eyes on him. He had been a kitchen porter along with his mother, Sora. His father had been in the Redstone guard. Dayne had nearly killed the boy when Iloen snuck up on him during the attack on Redstone, and Dayne had sent him into hiding with that knife.

Iloen laughed as Dayne pulled back and looked him over.

"You've grown into a fine young man. Your mother and father?"

Iloen shook his head. "Just me."

Dayne nodded, a deep sadness setting in. He handed the knife back to Iloen. "This is yours. Not mine."

"My lord, I can't. I—"

"No." Dayne pushed the knife into Iloen's hands, folding the young man's fingers around the hilt. "Repay me for it by driving the blade through the ribs of any man who seeks to send me to Achyron's halls."

Iloen's back stiffened, and he stood straighter. "By blade and by blood, Andurios."

Dayne's words caught in his throat at the mention of the title that had once been his father's: Andurios – first of the Andurii.

AFTER LEAVING THE PRACTICE YARD, Dayne had gone to check on Thorken in the infirmary. The man had been unconscious, but the Alamant healer had assured Dayne he would make a full recovery within a few days – the graces of having a healer who could touch the Spark.

Part of him wanted nothing to do with Thorken. The man had tried to kill him under the pretence of a duel to first blood, after all. But Dayne saw a lot of himself in Thorken. He had seen a few less summers than Dayne, which meant he had likely been around Baren's age when the empire had stormed Skyfell and burned the people of Stormwatch alive. Less than eighteen summers and his entire family had been taken from him.

Dayne had spent twelve years burning his revenge through Epheria, hunting those who had taken his world from him. He could forgive Thorken one attempt on his life.

After visiting the infirmary, Dayne made his way to Alina's study and found it empty. He closed the door behind him, breathing in the blend of aromas that reminded him of the past. The distinct scent of leather from the couches, the aroma of old books, the sweet, barely noticeable tinge of citrus. As he crossed the room, Dayne looked towards the two sets of armour that stood before the bookcases, a soft smile touching his lips at the sight of the white-crested helmet and bronzed cuirass that had once been his father's.

Two large pieces of fabric were draped over the heavy wooden desk that sat before the long open window at the back of the study, one a deep orange, the other a brilliant white.

Dayne picked up the white banner, the smooth waxy touch of silk beneath his fingertips. He held the banner out in front of him and let it unfurl, its folds smoothing as it dropped to the floor, creasing against the stone.

The banner was rectangular in shape and too big to open fully. But even with the bottom of the banner folding against the floor, the curled wyvern of House Ateres was clear across its centre in deep burnt orange. Dayne had never seen a banner bearing the sigil of House Ateres – the empire had expressly forbidden the flying of House banners after the first Valtaran Rebellion. The sight of it caused a fluttering in his chest.

After a few moments of staring at the banner, Dayne draped it over the desk, casting his eyes across the sigil of House Ateres once more before turning towards the second bundle of fabric. He unfurled the orange fabric to find a second banner that held a sigil of two black wyverns coiled around each other, a white spear between them. The symbol of the first rebellion, the symbol that had once been intended to be the new emblem of a free, unified Valtara.

Beating wings drummed in the air, and the silk banner rippled, a gust of wind sweeping through the long stone window ledge opposite the desk.

The pale light of the moon that had drifted in through the window vanished, a shadow sweeping across the room, splitting in the light of the waning oil lanterns that hung from the walls. Dayne looked away from the banner to see the gleaming scales of Alina's wyvern, Rynvar. The wyvern was at least one and a half times the size of Mera's wyvern, Audin. His scales, rather poetically, were a deep, vivid orange trimmed with black. The wyvern's talons grasped the stone window ledge, the muscles in his legs rippling beneath its scales, his forelimbs clasped to the outside wall. Rynvar craned his thick neck through the window, his eyes fixed on Dayne. Black slits bisected irises of a blue so rich and vibrant they seemed almost unnatural. Rynvar's lip curled slightly, bone white teeth glistening in the dim firelight.

"What do you think?" Dayne heard Alina's voice and the metallic clang of buckles being undone before he saw his sister slide from the saddle on the wyvern's back onto the window ledge. She touched her head against Rynvar's jaw, eliciting a sound not dissimilar to a purr from the deadly creature.

The wyvern dropped backwards from the ledge, disappearing from view as Alina climbed down into the room. Her dark leather armour, enamelled with orange swirls, was the mirror image of Rynvar's scales.

"Your face?"

Alina touched her fingers to a patch of blood that marred her right cheek and jaw, shaking her head. "It's not my blood. We found an imperial regiment holding out near the coast." Alina moved behind the desk, her blue eyes meeting his for only a moment, a soft smile on her face. She reached out, gesturing for Dayne to hand her the banner that he still gripped in his hands. "Well, what do you think?" she repeated, taking the banner into her hands and holding it out in front of herself. "I plan on flying them both as our armies march. A free Valtara."

"It's perfect."

Alina held the banner in her grasp, her eyes alight as she looked it over. All Dayne could see was their mother: the angle of her cheekbones, the creases of her smile, the strength in her shoulders. The two of them truly could have been twins. He could hear his mother's voice echoing in his memories. The words she whispered to him only moments before she died. *'You, your brothers, and your sister are the best things I ever did with my life. Look after each other, Dayne.'*

"What are you staring at?" Alina narrowed her eyes at Dayne as she folded the banner back up and set it down on the desk. She raised an eyebrow before shaking her head. "How did today go?"

"Well."

"Good," Alina said. "I will send word to the armourers. The armour and weapons have already been crafted for the most part, but they will need to be measured to fit. You and your Andurii—" it was strange to hear that "—report to the armourers after first light tomorrow for measurements. With a bit of luck, any adjustments that need to be made can be done before we leave for Lostwren."

"About that." Dayne moved over towards the bronzed armour that had belonged to his father, touching his fingers against the fused ridge that sat in the middle of the chest. Aside from the ridge where the sword had come through, a number of other dints and nicks marred the surface of the cuirass and helm, and a long shallow groove sliced into the face of the ordo shield.

"Of course." Alina stepped out from behind the desk, and Dayne could see tears welling in her eyes, her dark leather armour gleaming in the lamplight. "He would have wanted you to wear it."

Dayne allowed his hand to linger on the fused ridge in the centre of the cuirass before turning to Alina. "I meant what I said, Alina. By blade and by blood, I am yours. No matter what rumours are whispered or lies are spread. I might be the eldest child of House Ateres, but you are its rightful leader, and I am proud to stand by your side. I spent twelve years hunting the people who killed our parents, the people who broke our world. Most are dead now. Others wish they were. Loren Koraklon is the last of them. I *will* be your sword. And I will see his blood feed the earth."

"Actio—"

"Actions, not words. I know, I know." Dayne pulled Alina close, wrapping his arms around her – something he wished he had been able to do more of over the years. "But sometimes words are important too, little monkey."

"Ugh!" Dayne grunted as Alina's fist connected with his ribs. "What was that for?"

"I'm not a child anymore, Dayne." She pulled away from his embrace, but the slightest hint of a smile rested on her face. "Come on, we should head for evening meal. If we're much later, Marlin will hit you a lot harder than that."

Dayne let out a laugh. "After you." *Little monkey.*

CHAPTER TWENTY-NINE

THE L WORD

The sun rose. They walked. Feet throbbed, lungs burned, muscles ached. The sun set. They stopped. Calen and Vaeril released the shields. They bound Tarmon and Erik's hands and legs, then Calen bound Vaeril's. Calen and Valerys alternated watch. They tried not to freeze.

That was how each day passed. Eight by Calen's count. Each worse than the last. Blisters formed on blisters. Skin burned, turning a pinkish red. Exhaustion racked them all. At least in the tunnels, Vaeril had been able to heal the small things as they went. But here, after hours of walking in the heat and the sand, holding wards in place over Tarmon and Erik, the elf barely had the strength to stand.

With each day, the pulsing thump that had called to Calen that night slowly faded, as though the source grew farther away. And each night, Calen was pulled into those living dreams. Never before had they come so frequently. Never so many back-to-back. Perhaps it was this place? It seemed to affect nearly everything else; to assume it could alter his dreams wasn't a particularly big stretch. It was definitely easier to believe than the idea that he truly *was* seeing into the past. But the dreams had started long before he set foot in the Burnt Lands – right after Valerys lost control in the tunnels. Could that have changed something?

Calen let out a sigh, shaking his head. Sweat dripped from his brow and formed a glistening coat across his skin, his lips cracked and dry. He looked up, watching as Valerys flew low, scales glinting in the sun.

"Are you two all right?" Tarmon stood on a patch of flat rock up ahead, sand blowing across his feet, his cloak billowing, Vaeril at his side.

Calen pulled his waterskin from his pack and nodded, taking a mouthful of the warm water. He was as well as he could be. His muscles ached from trekking across the sand, and they burned from the constant use of the Spark. Holding the shield around Vaeril's mind for hours on end, sometimes having to hold a second shield over Tarmon or Erik to take some strain off Vaeril, was taking its toll.

"I'm sorry."

Calen froze at the sound of Erik's voice behind him. He swallowed a mouthful of water, running his tongue over his lips to soothe the pain from the cracks, then replaced the waterskin into the pack. "It's all right, Erik."

"No," Erik said as Calen turned to meet his gaze. "It's not."

Erik and Calen had hardly spoken since the night the darkness had overcome Erik and the others. *'We needed a symbol, but all we got was a coward who thinks of nobody but himself.'* His eyes were even darker and more sunken now than they had been then. He had cleaned the N'aka blood from his face and hands with water Vaeril had dragged up from under the sand, but it still stained his clothes, and it had only taken a day or so for dirt to accumulate on his face and in his hair.

"I already told you," Calen said, wanting the conversation to end. "I know you didn't mean—"

"I did."

Calen just stared back at Erik. That wasn't what he had expected the man to say. *'You let your family die.'*

"I mean… not all of it. Those voices got inside my head, twisted me. It was like a building pressure, a boiling in my blood. It took the tiniest thoughts and set them ablaze. You didn't kill your parents, the empire did. Rendall and Farda did. Ellisar died doing what he thought was right. Korik and Lopir died trying to get home – which was where you were trying to bring them. I'd be lying to you if I told you I didn't have doubts about what we're doing. If I told you I was *sure* trying to cross this place just to save one man was a good decision, and if we're going to die in here, I don't want to be lying to you."

Even with the Spark running through his veins, Calen's blood felt cold. His throat tightened to the point it was hard to swallow. *I didn't want this. I didn't want any of this.* "Erik…"

Erik took a step closer. "I don't know if this was a good decision. But I'm here. I didn't know if it was a good decision from the start, but I came anyway, and I always will. Look, we don't need to cut our hearts open right here in the sand, but I just wanted to say I'm sorry. I…"

Erik's words faded to a dull hum as Valerys's mind collided with Calen's. An icy ripple swept over the dragon's body. Panic set in, burning bright. His and Valerys's both. Through the dragon's eyes, Calen saw nothing. The only sensation on his scales was the touch of ice. Unbridled fear followed. Calen's chest tightened, coils of dread twisting in his stomach. Calen spun around, frantically scanning the sky for any signs of his soulkin. Nothing.

A chill swept over him, every hair standing on end. Then Valerys was gone. Completely gone. Calen couldn't feel him, not his mind or his heart… or his soul. "No… no, no, no."

Valerys? Valerys? Please… please don't leave me alone.

Calen turned and ran. He ran towards the last place he had felt the touch of Valerys's mind. The muscles in his legs screamed at him, burning and aching at the same time, but he ignored them. Pain was inconsequential. Erik called his name, his words whispers caught in a storm. Nothing mattered but Valerys. Calen's heart hammered, his mind a tempest.

"Valerys!" Calen's throat scratched and felt as though it tore. His lungs stretched. "Valerys!"

What in the gods had happened? He had been there, and then he was just gone. "Valer—"

Calen slammed into something unseen, knocking the wind from his lungs as the world ignited in a brilliant white light. The same wave of ice crashed over him that he had felt from Valerys. Seconds passed, hours, minutes… it was impossible to tell.

Warmth flooded him, his knees hitting the ground, vibrations jarring his bones. His hands crashed down onto brittle clay as a thousand thoughts and emotions crashed into his mind, overwhelming him. Loss, desperation, happiness, warmth, relief. *Valerys!* He was whole again.

The bright light that had consumed the world faded, and in its place, stood Valerys. The dragon was completely unharmed, white scales shimmering, lavender eyes staring back at Calen. Valerys spread his wings and craned his neck down, pushing the flat of his head into Calen's chest, an all-encompassing relief flowing between them.

Calen clasped his hands on either side of Valerys's snout, resting his head against Valerys's. Calen closed his eyes, the tears of joy that rolled down his cheeks mingling with those of loss that had previously carved the path. "I thought I'd lost you."

A deep rumble resonated from Valerys's throat, echoing in the back of Calen's mind. Warmth flooded over from Valerys. Calen leaned forward, letting Valerys take his weight. He squeezed his hands against the horns that framed Valerys's jaw, once more whispering, "I thought I'd lost you…"

Two thumps sounded to Calen's left, followed by a third to his right. He kept his eyes closed, slowing his trembling breaths.

"By the Waters of Life… How is this possible?" There was more shock than awe in Tarmon's voice.

It was only then Calen realised he hadn't seen anything except Valerys. Nothing else had mattered. He pressed his head even more firmly against Valerys's. "I denír viël ar altinua." *In this life and always.*

"I never thought I'd be happy to see a Lorian banner."

Lorian Banner? Calen drew in one last deep breath, then opened his eyes and looked past Valerys. They stood on a wide cliff ledge composed of cracked clay and brown stone. Plains of broken earth sprawled two or three hundred feet below, patches of grass and trees sprouting in the distance. A huge square tower rose a few miles to their left, its stones a greyish black, its flat top ringed by crenelated battlements. The Dead Tower? Surely it cannot be… Calen turned his gaze further north.

In the distance, an enormous lake spread for miles, its calm surface glistening in the light of the sun that blazed overhead. *Lake Berona.*

Walls of white stone rose on the far side of the lake, sweeping for miles left and right, hugging the edge of the water. Massive rectangular towers with flat, open tops large enough for a dragon to land rose from the walls. Enormous banners hung from every second tower, rippling in the wind, their crimson colouring striking against the snow-white stone. The banners were too far away for Calen to make out any details, but the red and black could have been nothing but Lorian.

A number of buildings rose above the others within the city that was easily twice the size of Camylin. An enormous keep sat in the city's centre towered, upon a rise in the land. It was ringed by multiple walls and towers that were at least half again the size of the walls that surrounded the city. A city within a city. No, a fortress within a city.

Further to the northeast, a tower rose three times as high as any other in the city. It was so tall Calen couldn't fathom how it could have been constructed by mortal hands. A web of walkways and sweeping arches extended outwards from the towers' lower storeys, connecting it to the surrounding buildings. There wasn't a doubt in Calen's mind that was the tower they had come for. The High Tower, home of the Circle of Magii.

They made it. They had crossed the Burnt Lands.

"How have we come so close to Berona?" Vaeril asked, looking towards the city, then turning back to look behind himself.

Calen turned as well. Behind them, large patches of brown rock sat amidst an endless sea of sand.

Tarmon pulled out the compass Rokka had given them, shaking it in his hand, then checking the face. "It points true. Berona just a touch northwest of the Dead Tower. But we should have come out at least a week's travel from Berona, near Copperstille."

"Whatever darkness holds the Svidar'Cia clearly twists more than minds," Vaeril said, looking down at the compass. "At least, for once, it appears luck was on our side."

"Don't say it." Erik reached back and ran his hands through his sand-crusted hair, dropping to his haunches. "Never say the L word, Vaeril. As soon as you say it, you lose it." Erik let out a sigh. "Just promise me we don't have to do that again."

"We have to do it again," Tarmon said frankly, raising one eyebrow and shaking his head. "We have to get Rist, and then we have to cross again. You already knew this."

"I know, I know. Just let me enjoy the moment."

Calen gave a weak smile, trying his best to enjoy the newfound luck with the others, but all he could do was stare into the distance at the enormous city of white stone, crimson and black banners rippling in the wind, the High Tower rising above everything else.

We're coming for you, Rist.

CHAPTER THIRTY

THE SAVIOUR

Rist sat with his back against the trunk of an oak tree in one of the many gardens of the embassy – a spot that had quickly become one of his favourites. His legs were folded, his notebook open in his lap, a pen and inkwell at hand, and his parents' most recent letter beside him.

Neera sat to Rist's left, her head resting on his shoulder, her arms folded across her chest. It was something they had taken to doing quite often – sitting in the gardens talking, relaxing between their lessons and practice. Though since Garramon had revealed the Trial of Faith, Rist found it difficult to focus on anything else.

"Rist?" The touch of irritation in Neera's voice let Rist know she had asked a question, and he had not answered. Rist had never been good at reading people. Not like Calen or Dann, or anyone else, for that matter. It had gotten him in trouble on more occasions than he could count – was someone joking? Were they serious? Sarcastic? Annoyed? Rist had never understood how everyone else seemed to know these things almost instinctively. Of course, if someone was smiling, he knew they were happy. Then again, that wasn't always true either. But with Neera, he could tell. Not at first, but slowly he had learned. It was like reading a book. She had different tones of voice for the things he did wrong. If her nose didn't crinkle when she smiled, then it wasn't a *real* smile, and if she didn't snort when she laughed, the laughter was simply placative. If she was like a book, she was his favourite book.

"Rist?" she repeated, her tone once again changing, a smile touching her lips as she pulled away and glared at him, her nose crinkling. She was annoyed, but happy for some reason.

Rist realised he had been staring at her. Staring into those dark eyes. "Sorry, I was lost in thought. What did you say?"

Neera pursed her lips, shaking her head. "It's all that empty space in there," she said, her smile widening. "Easy to get lost with so much room. I asked what they're like – your parents."

Rist looked down at the notebook in his lap.

Mam and Dad,

I'm sorry it's been so long since I last wrote, things have been

Rist reread over the unfinished line – the only line. They'd been there for just short of an hour, and that was all Rist had been able to write. He'd tried, but his mind kept drifting to the vessel that sat in the box in the pocket of his robes that lay in a heap beside him. The Essence Vessel. The trial. Rist had barely slept in the three days since Garramon had opened that box. He spent every spare moment in that room – which Garramon had kept reserved for him – reading through every page of every book, his appetite for understanding growing more rapacious with each page. Even when training with the First Army, or practising the sword with Sister Anila, it was all he thought about. His 'daydreaming', as Brother Pirnil had called it, had earned him more than a few new scars, courtesy of the Scholar.

"Rist?" Neera's voice was back to the initial irritation. Her eyes were narrowed. She was examining him in the way that she did. "If you don't start answering me, I'm going to pull pages from your favourite books. I swear to Efialtír. I'll start with the one about druids."

"You're a monster," Rist said with a smile.

"I wasn't joking. I'll pull out the most important pages from each section so that when you read the conclusions, they won't make any sense." Neera raised her eyebrow, tilting her head slightly.

"Message received." Rist folded over the notebook, setting it beside the letter from his parents, then clasped his hands at his knees and stared up through the thick branches of the oak tree. "My dad is a firm man. He works hard – too hard most of the time. But he's a good dad. He's always been there for me. He'd do anything for me and mam. Mam's a handful. Possibly the single happiest woman in all the villages, though. She's always going, like a ball of energy. I miss her… a lot."

Rist felt tears form at the corners of his eyes. Talking about his parents only made him feel guiltier about taking so long to respond to their letters. Garramon had only given him one recently, but they had sent another a few weeks before. He'd just had so much going on. So little time.

"They sound lovely." Neera smiled, the slightest of crinkles forming on her nose. After a moment though, the smile faded, and she stared off at the grass.

She hadn't spoken of home. Not once. But Rist also hadn't asked. He always forgot. He asked a lot of questions. Well, he didn't think he did, but everyone always told him he did. As far as he was concerned, he asked the appropriate number of questions. But he knew he often didn't ask questions about emotional things. Not because he didn't care – he did, deeply – but because his mind fixated on the questions that were the most pressing. "What are your parents like?"

"Mine?" Neera let out a sigh, running her fingers through her black hair. "They were great, actually. My mother was the guard captain in our village, just east of Holm. Fiercest woman I ever knew. She taught me how to hold a sword as soon as I was strong enough to pick one up." Neera's eyes glistened as she talked of her mother, the shell of sarcasm and wit that usually surrounded her disappearing. "My father, Heraya bless his soul, was about as strong as a malnourished chicken. He was actually kind of like you." Neera gave an exaggerated shiver, shrugging. Rist glared at her. "I suppose you're stronger than a malnourished chicken. I've seen you training, eating extra meals. Anyway, when I said he was like you, I meant that he was gentle and kind. He adored books and tinkering with small gadgets. But ultimately he was an academic. He studied the formation of metal alloys, particularly alloys formed with the iron ore mined from Mar Dorul."

Neera's use of the past tense didn't evade Rist. "How did they die?"

Even as he asked the question, he could hear Calen's voice in the back of his mind, admonishing him for his lack of sensitivity. Again, lack of sensitivity wasn't his intention. Asking the obvious question was simply the best way to get the right answer.

Neera drew back for a moment, her brow furrowing. "You really have no idea how to just ask a normal question, do you? It's not that hard, all you have to do…" Neera's voice trailed off as she looked at Rist, her expression softening. She let out a sigh. "Sorry… It was a year or so before I came here. Uraks attacked our village in the night. More than we'd ever seen at any one time. My mother tried to protect us, but… There were too many. She died on her feet, just like she'd have wanted. My father tried. He picked up her sword and stood over me. I can still see his blood spilling over the floor. That was when I touched the Spark for the first time. The Inquisitors hadn't been to our village since I was very young, and when they had come, I was with my mother and father at the mine. But when the attack ended, and the soldiers arrived, Sister Ardal was with them. Once she'd seen what I could do, she dragged me here. Didn't even give me a chance to bury them. Not even to say goodbye." Rist reached over to wipe the tears from Neera's face, but she swatted his hand away, sniffling. "Happy now?"

"Why would your tears make me happy?"

"I didn't mean…" Neera let out a sigh, wiping the sleeve of her black-striped robes across her face. "Just shut up." Neera leaned back in, resting her head against Rist's shoulder once more.

They sat there for a while, not speaking, just watching as people walked past. Rist had thought to rest his hand on Neera's, but from everything he was learning, this was not the right time. If Neera wanted his hand, she'd take it. He didn't mind sitting there in silence, though. It was actually quite nice, and it gave him time to think about the trial.

After a while, Neera left to do extra studies with Sister Ardal. Once he was alone, Rist packed his things into his satchel and set off for the library.

Gault, the librarian Garramon had asked to look after Rist, nodded as Rist entered. The man looked as though he had seen the better part of sixty summers – over twenty thousand sunrises. His hair was thinning and grey, mostly white, while his skin bore deep furrows – from years of throwing dirty looks, no doubt. Despite time's obvious wear, Gault moved like a man half his age, spry and full of life. To Rist's surprise, the man had actually been quite pleasant with him over the past few days. "Not today, Gault. I have all the materials I need. Though, if there was a spare cup of Arlen Root tea, I'd be forever grateful."

A wrinkled smile crossed Gault's face, and he nodded, his voice cracked and hushed. "I'm sure I can find some, apprentice Havel."

Rist smiled as the man scuttled away. The first day after Garramon had left Rist in the room upstairs, Rist had wandered down to see Gault and ask if he had any accounts of Blood Magic or Essence that originated in the South prior to the Liberation. But as he had asked the question, the earthy smell of Arlen Root tea wafted under his nose. That smell hadn't touched his nostrils since the last time he'd visited Calen's home. Freis had always had a fondness for Arlen Root tea. For some reason, Gault's hardness had softened when Rist explained the tea reminded him of home.

Rist made his way through the library and up the stairs, breathing in the smell of the books, that earthy, almost vanilla-like scent of time-incensed paper. It was one of his favourite smells in the entire world. As usual, he took his time, sauntering from floor to floor, lingering at bookshelves that stretched the length and breadth of the walls, admiring the craftsmanship of the bindings and the leather work. By the time he had reached his study room on the top floor, his heart was full.

He pulled open the red curtain that hid the interior of the room and stepped inside, closing the curtain behind him before dropping himself onto the couch and promptly opening *Blood Magic, A Curse and a Gift*, by Holdir Arthrang of Drifaien. This particular book had proven to be the most balanced opinion Rist had found amongst all the materials he had gathered.

The only sadness Rist had found amongst having all these books to read was that he still had not gotten any further in *Druid, a Magic Lost* – or any of the other books he had smuggled out of the library. So many books to read, so little time to read them; that always seemed to be the case.

Rist was only three pages in when he heard the curtain slide over. The earthy smell of Arlen Root tea wafted in the air. He was coming towards the end of the page, so he didn't lift his gaze. Instead, he simply smiled. "Thank you, Gault. I really do appreciate it."

"I'll be sure to let Gault know."

Rist's back stiffened. He'd not heard that voice before. Without lifting his gaze, he moved to fold the corner of the page, then remembered the smack Gault had given him the first day for doing so. *Three hundred and fifty-two.* He hadn't brought a bookmark with him. His memory would have to suffice. It often did. With the page memorized, and the awkwardness hanging thick in the air, Rist set the book on the table and turned to look at the stranger.

It was a man, no taller than six feet, his hair short and black. By the look of him, he'd seen no more than forty summers. His robes were black as night, but where Exarchs of the Battlemages wore black robes trimmed with silver, and Primarch Touran wore black robes trimmed with gold, this man's robes were trimmed with a deep red. His eyes, physically, were no stranger than Rist's, but it wasn't their appearance that made them different, it was their intensity; the man looked as though he was staring into Rist's soul. Every hair on Rist's body stood on end, and his chest tightened.

He knew this man. He'd never seen him. But he knew him. Rist leapt to his feet as gracefully as he could manage, meeting the man's inescapable stare. He bowed his head, unsure as to what the proper etiquette was. "Emperor Mortem, my deepest apologies, I—"

"Sit down, apprentice. There's no need for apologies." Fane Mortem placed the mug of Arlen Root tea down in front of Rist, then took a seat on the other side of the L-shaped couch. The more Rist looked at him, the more he saw. The emperor may not have been as tall as Haem Bryer or as grisly as Exarch Magnus, but he had an aura about him, a confidence in the way he moved, an effortless grace. Not for a second did Rist doubt that the man sitting across from him had the power to break mountains and tear open the sky. The emperor ran his fingers along the spines of the books stacked closest to him. "Garramon said you were hesitant."

Garramon talks to Fane about me? "I'm not hesitant, Emperor. I..." Was this one of those times where Rist shouldn't say what he was thinking? Most likely. But it didn't seem like this was a man to lie to. "I simply wish to learn. Where I come from, Efialtír is The Traitor. Blood Magic is the work of dark spirits. This is not a decision to be taken lightly."

To Rist's surprise, the emperor raised an eyebrow, amused, his lips twisting into a smile. "You're not afraid to speak your mind. That's something I can appreciate." Fane picked up the book at the top of the stack and thumbed through it. "Knowledge is a powerful thing, apprentice. That is an age-old adage that many people spout, but few have taken the time to truly contemplate. In my younger days, I spent countless hours in the great library of Ilnaen in the pursuit of knowledge – the pursuit of bettering myself. I see that in you. How many of these have you read?"

"All but this one," Rist said, lifting *Blood Magic, A Curse and a Gift* in the air.

Fane let out a suppressed laugh. "Impressive. The vessel, do you have it?"

The mention of the Essence vessel twisted a knot in Rist's stomach, but, even still, he reached into the pocket of his robes and produced the small black wooden box, setting it on the table.

Without a word, Fane picked it up. A ripple of energy swept outwards from the emperor as he reached out to the Spark and pulled in threads of Air, weaving them through the locking mechanism of the box. Rist had never felt anything like it. When others opened themselves to the Spark, Rist could sense it, a tingle at the back of his neck, a subtle disruption in the normality of things. But when Fane opened himself to the Spark, it was like a drum had been beaten, a rippling wave of power moving through the air. The box popped open, emitting a soft red glow over the emperor's face.

"Do you know why Garramon sponsored you?" Fane didn't lift his gaze from the grape-sized gemstone that sat within the box. When Rist didn't answer, Fane continued. "You have the potential to be one of the most powerful mages we have found in centuries. Have you noticed the thrum in the air of this city? The low vibration that fades to the back of your mind?"

"I… yes." Rist had sensed it from the moment he had arrived, but he hadn't been sure what exactly it was. He had dismissed it at first. Then, over time, he had forgotten about it entirely. "At least, I think I have."

"That thrum is the centralised power that resonates in the fabric of this world when so many who draw from the Spark are in the same place. Few cities remain that truly hold it. Here, Berona, and Easterlock, perhaps Arginwatch, though it's been a few hundred years since I've visited. Most of us cannot emit that energy alone, not unless we open ourselves to the Spark. That is why when we send our Inquisitors to search for gifted children, they must teach the children the basic principles of touching the

Spark. There are a select few whose power is so raw it bleeds through. To the untrained eye, it's nothing. A wave of heat rippling off steel. But to those who know what they are looking for, it is a sign of true strength. You are here, Rist Havel, because when we found you, Brother Garramon was insistent that you had the power to become a hero of legend – a champion of the empire. And having met you now, I'm inclined to agree."

Rist shuffled uncomfortably. This was the emperor of the Lorian Empire. Fane Mortem. Rist had heard story after story about how the man who sat before him had betrayed his own. How he had orchestrated the fall of The Order and the scouring of the elves and Jotnar from the main body of Epheria. Everything Rist had ever been told painted Fane Mortem as a monster. Yet here he was, simply a man. A man who radiated more power than Rist would ever have believed possible, but a man nonetheless.

Fane glanced towards Rist and set the box on the table. "Doubts are good, apprentice. Doubts fuel the thirst for knowledge. And I'm sure you have been told tales of my misdeeds, horror stories of how Efialtír is the father of all darkness." Rist tensed. Was the man reading his mind? "If I've learned one thing that I can pass on, it is that the truth is nothing more than the amalgamation of lies." Fane reached down and plucked the gemstone from the box, holding it in the palm of his hands, the red glow washing over his skin. "Uraks are mindless beasts, are they not?"

Rist sat forward, perplexed by the question. "I would say yes, but something tells me I would be wrong."

Fane smiled. "Very wrong indeed. Do you know what is within this stone?"

"According to what I've read, it is Life Essence. But as to what that actually is, every book seems to disagree."

"Books tend to do that," Fane said with a laugh. For a man said to have caused the deaths of hundreds of thousands, he laughed a lot. "Life Essence is the force that grants all existence. It flows in all living things. Some refer to it as the soul, but that is not true. Essence and the soul are two entirely different things. If a body is a raging fire, then the soul is the wood that burns. It grants shape and structure, uniqueness. Essence is the air that grants life to the fire. You said that Efialtír is known as The Traitor where you are from." Rist tensed at that. "Well, he was also named The Traitor when I was a child. Do you know why?"

Rist wished he knew, but of all the things he had taken an interest in growing up, the gods weren't one of them. Neither was magic. Rist had always preferred to learn about the tangible world. He believed in what he could see and feel. Time was a precious thing, and he preferred not to dedicate his to chasing half-truths spouted about gods he would never see. Though the last few months had changed that outlook considerably. He shook his head.

Fane nodded. "Apologies if I digress, but I often find without the background, a painting lacks substance. Did you know humans were not born in Epheria? We migrated here thousands of years ago from Terroncia. I've always found that fascinating. We brought our own gods with us – Kaygan, Dvalin, Bjorna, Vethnir, and Fenryr. The druidic gods. Physical beings of great power – or so the legends say. After a few centuries, our people adapted to the ways of these lands, and the old gods faded while new gods took hold.

"As the legends go, the gods of Epheria were a higher form of god, the Enkara in the Old Tongue. It was said that the Enkara made a pact that once life was given to the creatures of this world, they would leave their physical forms, bequeathing this plane of existence to their creations. But as seems to be the natural order of things, after a time, wars broke out. The elves, Jotnar, dwarves, dragons, and all the other races – many of whom no longer draw breath – destroyed each other over land, wealth, power. The dragons were Varyn's own creation. His guardians. But within them brewed a rage like no other, a fury that burned in their hearts. And so it was said that Varyn created the bond as a way to temper that fury. The calmer natures of the elves and Jotnar would balance the rage within the dragons. Hafaesir feared for the safety of his creations: the dwarves. And so he refused to allow a tether between the dwarves and the dragons. He struck a bargain with Heraya, and between them, they provided the dwarves with the means to live within the mountains where they would be safe from the winged creatures."

Rist leaned forwards, resting his elbows on the table. Calen had always been the one enraptured by stories of old, but now Rist understood – stories were simply books told aloud. They weren't as objective or reliable, but still. The difference here was that Rist wasn't reading a second-hand account of events cobbled together by a disgruntled historian. This was Fane Mortem. He had seen centuries. He had witnessed the fall of The Order – void, he had caused it. Fane stared at Rist as he talked.

"Of course, binding dragons to the other races did nothing. They still warred, still slaughtered each other in their hundreds, thousands. Varyn had created the dragons, Hafaesir the dwarves. Elyara and Achyron created the elves together. Heraya filled the lands with flora and fauna. Neron built the oceans and filled them. But it was Efialtír who cut a sliver of his own heart to grant life to all existence. Which was why, when the creations of the Enkara slaughtered each other and fed the soil with their blood, Efialtír was distraught, inconsolable. He had loved the denizens of this world with every fibre of his being. He had given them his heart, and they were wasting it.

"And so, one day, when the flames raged across the lands, the rivers ran red, and the earth refused to grow for the salt that had been sown, Efialtír broke his pact with the other gods. He descended from the realm of the Enkara, taking physical form in this world. And, carving another sliver from his heart, he created a tether between the two realms. Through this tether, the Essence spilled so the loss of each life could be recycled; from death could come life anew. It was for this he was cast aside from the Enkara, branded as The Traitor. A god who wished only to save his creations from their own destruction, exiled for breaking an oath that would have left the world in ruins." Fane stared into the gemstone, the red glow casting shadows across his face.

Rist sat in silence for a few moments, processing everything Fane had just told him. It was a fascinating tale, truly. But with little more than words to hold it afloat, Rist could give it no more credence than the tales Therin wove in The Gilded Dragon.

Just as Rist was about to speak, the curtain opened again, and Gault stepped through, bowing so low he almost folded his rickety body in half. In his left hand, the man held a small wooden box, no more than a foot long and a few inches wide, which he laid on the table before Fane. "As requested, Lord Emperor. Light of The Saviour upon you."

"And upon you, Gault. You have my thanks."

A smile as wide as a canyon beamed across Gault's face as he stepped backwards from the room, staying bowed the entire time.

"He's a lovely man," Fane said as he pulled the box closer. "If a little formal. Now, before you say anything, Garramon already told me you wouldn't believe me on merit. Do you?"

"No," Rist said, honestly. He narrowed his eyes at the box, wondering what was inside. "It is a fascinating story, but it is still only a story."

"Well said. You are even more like me than I had anticipated. Before I show you something that isn't simply a story, did you know that Efialtír has even more names? That he is not simply The Traitor or The Saviour?"

Rist raised an eyebrow, curious, and shook his head.

"Like all the gods, Efialtír has had many names over the years, changing with the world and the eyes through which he was seen. The Lyonin referred to him as The Blood God. The early men knew him as the Harbinger of Shadow. The old Arcanians knew him as The God Who Walks in The Light of The Moon – a little long winded, but beautiful in its own way. The Uraks, however, have a different name for him: Lifebringer. Which, after quite a tangent, brings me back to my original point – Uraks are not mindless beasts, as much as I'd wish them to be."

"Over four centuries ago, I was a Battlemage of The Order. My true calling would likely have been as a Scholar, but my prowess in combat was deemed 'wasted' on that path. Even so, I constantly pursued knowledge. My appetite for it – much like yours – was rapacious. But The Order believed that knowledge should be controlled. Anything they did not agree with or understand, they buried. So after searching and searching, I travelled to Mar Dorul, where the Naiwell Woods touched the foot of the mountains. It was there an Urak Shaman awaited me as though he had always known I would come. He did not attack me or strike me down. He welcomed me and brought me to their hold."

"Why? Why would any Urak do such a thing?"

"Our peoples had been at war for thousands of years – he wanted me to understand why. He wanted me to listen to Efialtír and see the work of The Lifebringer. It was within the walls of that mountain that I saw the true power of Essence. The Shaman explained to me that thousands of years ago, the Uraks were struck with a disease like no other. Hundreds, thousands of their children were stillborn. Their hearts beat in the womb but eventually gave out. The disease spread slowly at first, but after a time, a decade had passed since an Urak child had been born."

Despite himself, Rist found a knot twisting in his heart. The beasts he had seen were savage and cruel. Monsters by every definition of the word. But even so, he felt their loss viscerally. His own mother, Elia, had lost four children to stillbirth after Rist. The losses had almost broken her. To lose a child that way was not something he would wish on anyone. "The Essence?"

Fane nodded. "In their hour of need, with the Blood Moon high in the sky, Efialtír whispered in the ears of each of their monarchs from Mar Dorul, to Kolmir, to Aonar. He could not watch more of his children suffer. Once more, he offered the world a gift. The gift of life from death. He showed the Uraks where to find gemstones capable of storing Essence and how to use them. Through Essence, he allowed them to save their kind, and thus children were born."

"Efialtír can bring life back to the dead?"

"Not quite. That is a gift he has never bestowed. But through Essence, each child is cured of the disease symptoms in the womb. However, the disease itself persists, lying dormant until it is carried to the next generation. But through Essence, each generation can give their children the gift of life."

"And the Uraks are also tethered to Efialtír," Rist whispered, nodding. "They are chained to him, beholden to his gift."

"They are. Without Essence, the children remain still at birth. Though chained is a rather harsh term."

"Even so," Rist said, contemplating everything Fane had said, and thinking of what he'd read over the past few days, "to fill the vessels with Essence and save the lives of their children, they must first take life." Slowly, it was all coming together. "That is why they fight. That is why they are so savage. For every life they take, they can save one of their own children."

"Precisely." Fane sat back, placing the gemstone back into the box.

"But… It's not right… Why would a god push the Uraks to commit such atrocities… to kill…"

"Your thought process is exactly as mine was when I first learned the truth, but it is ultimately flawed. You consider everything in isolation, when in reality not a single concept or idea exists in such a state. The world itself is an uncountable myriad of moving pieces, each influencing each other at any given time." Fane must have seen the look of confusion on Rist's face. He folded his arms across his chest and pressed himself back into the couch. "Do you remember the Varsund war in the South?"

"I wasn't born when the Varsund war broke out."

"But you know of it? You've heard of the tens of thousands that died? Of how the River Almellon ran red with blood? How corpses littered the streets of Oberwall?"

Rist nodded, unsure where Fane was going with this.

"The Varsund war was only one of many such wars. Wars that claimed the lives of thousands upon thousands, and for what? So a king could have a little more land? We kill each other by the hundreds every day – humans, elves, dwarves. Is our cause for killing any more noble than the Uraks, who seek only to give life to their children? Like I said, all truths are nothing more than the amalgamation of lies. Stories twisted and changed by the teller to suit a narrative of their choosing."

"Could the same not be said of this tale now?" As soon as the words left Rist's mouth, he regretted them. Not for a lack of sensitivity, but because upon immediate reflection it didn't seem like a wise thing to say to a man who could crush him into the ground with the stroke of a hand.

"It could," Fane said with the upturn of his lip. "But what do I have to gain in making you sympathetic towards the Uraks? I bear no love for those creatures. I simply think it best to understand. Understanding is everything. But instead, let me show you."

Rist furrowed his brow, watching as Fane slid the top off the wooden box, then dipped his hand inside, pulled out something obscured by his grasp, and set it on the table. He moved his hand away to reveal the body of a small bird.

The creature was no more than a few inches long. Its body was short and stubby, its bill long and black. The tiny, scale-like feathers of its body were a shimmering sea-blue, the hue changing with the flickering candlelight, while the feathers that lined its head were a blend of pink, orange, and red, glistening with the metallic qualities of steel or silver. The creature's chest rose and fell in long, slow sweeps, shuddering with each exhale.

"It's dying," Rist said, leaning closer, his gaze moving over the creature. Rist noticed that one of its wings was broken, feathers ruffled and plucked, blood dappling its metallic colouring.

"It is." Fane's gaze moved from Rist to the small creature. "Healing with the Spark has limits – a mage's power, but also their knowledge and understanding of anatomy. A powerful mage would stand no chance at stopping infection without the knowledge to do so. And a knowledgeable mage could not bring a man back from the brink of death if they were not powerful enough to do so, lest they give their own life in the trying."

Fane looked down at the glowing red gemstone that sat in the black box Garramon had given Rist, then pulled back the sleeve of his right arm to reveal a golden bracelet that held six glowing gemstones, each half the size of the stone in the box. His hand hovered over the dying bird. "Essence is not Blood Magic, Rist. It is Life Magic. Both the Spark and Essence require a pool of power to work. The Spark takes its strength from the user, draining them; it has very hard limits. Essence, on the other hand, takes its strength from the life of the world and passes it on, completing the circle, wasting nothing. Acts of unfathomable power can be performed when enough Essence is gathered in one place. Of course, just as the Spark can be used for destructive means, so too can Essence. It can conjure waves of fire, bolts of lightning. It can bring down walls, crush stone. But it can also take death and use it to breathe life. This hummingbird was attacked by a hawk in the palace gardens this afternoon while I was eating. As you can see, it stood little chance. One of the guards decided to use the hawk as target practice, and stuck it with an arrow, but not before the hummingbird was gravely injured. This vessel here—" Fane tapped the pulsating red gemstone that sat at the top of the bracelet "—contains the Essence of that hawk, which I captured as it was passing from this world. And so, death breathes life anew."

With Fane's words, the gemstone at the top of the bracelet glowed, its light washing over the emperor's face and hand. Moments passed, and Rist could feel and sense nothing. He wasn't sure what he had expected, a sensation similar to the Spark, perhaps? Is *this what I've been told to call 'Blood Magic'? This feels like...* "What in the gods..."

The small bird twitched. Its long bill darted side to side. Its breaths, once drawn out and ragged, grew sharper, its lungs filling. The bird chirped, more life pouring into its body. With a jarring snap, the broken wing pulled back into place, and the hummingbird lifted from the table, its shimmering blue wings moving in a blur, faster than anything Rist had ever seen.

The creature hovered above the table, the low hum resonating from its wings clearly the origin of its name.

Rist reached out a hand, but the creature flitted away, moving near Fane's shoulder, chirping. Even the Healers in the embassy could do nothing like this with the Spark – not with such little effort. Despite the bird's size, it would have taken quite some energy to fix its wounds and bring it back from the brink of death. From what Rist understood about healing, along with the medical understanding required to tend the specific wound being healed, the energy taken from the healer was twice what was given to the patient, and the closer the patient was to death, the more energy they required. Rist looked from the hovering bird to Fane, who sat with his arms crossed, a satisfied look on his face.

"How is this possible?"

"Not only is it possible, but with the remaining five gemstones on this bracelet, I could do it five more times without tiring. Do you see now? Do you see how the truth you were raised on is no more or less true than the truth you resist? The only truth in this world is the truth you believe."

Rist stared at the bird, watching it zip back and forth, its wings a blur of motion. He nodded slowly. Rist turned his gaze from the bird back to Fane. He was under no illusions that most apprentices – sponsored or no – ever received a personal visit from the emperor of Loria to convince them to proceed with their Trial of Faith. "Emperor Mortem?"

"Yes, apprentice?" The emperor looked up towards the hummingbird, holding out his hand. Much to Rist's surprise, the bird came to him almost immediately, alighting on his extended finger.

"Is it truly still a trial of 'faith' if you have explained so much to me?"

The emperor laughed. "You ask the right questions, apprentice Havel." Fane drew in a breath then rose to his feet. He pulled on a thread of Air, using it to open the red curtain, then extended his arm. The hummingbird hesitated for only a moment before flitting through the opening. As the emperor made to leave, he turned. "The journey is yours, apprentice. All I have done is provide you with the tools you will need to walk the path. Every step you take will require faith. This is simply the first."

The emperor stepped from the room, his red-trimmed cloak drifting behind him.

Rist let the tension seep from his body, his shoulders drooping as he leaned into the soft leather of the couch. Had that truly been Emperor Fane Mortem? The man who struck down The Order, chased the elves into Lynalion, and drove the dwarves back into the mountains. The man who was feared from one end of the continent to the other. Rist knew it was. From the second Fane had stepped into the room, it had been clear who he was. But he had been nothing like what Rist had expected. Nothing at all.

From the stories Rist had been told as a child, he'd expected a broad-chested behemoth with dark eyes that drank in the light of souls. He'd expected Fane to be ruthless, primal. But the man had been none of those things. He had been thoughtful, inquisitive, and open. He had radiated power and authority, but not through thick armour and sharp steel, or righteous anger and fury, but through the simple surety of who he was.

Rist sighed, then reached forward and pulled the wooden box with the red gemstone closer, the light pulsating. He bit the corner of his lip, then closed the lid.

Chapter Thirty-One

Honour

The roar of the waterfall drowned out the squeaking axles, clip-clopping hooves, and armoured boots on stone as Dahlen and Belina marched across one of the many walkways that bridged the courtyards and platforms of Durakdur, a stream of food-bearing wagons trailing behind them.

The wagons were drawn by creatures that looked similar to ponies. Ihvon had called them virtuks. But where ponies had coats of short hair, these animals had a thick, white hide of leathery skin. Articulated sections of grey, armour-like carapace grew from their skin, covering their backs, sides, and shoulders, along with a section that formed around their heads and necks like helms. And where ponies had soft muzzles, virtuks had hard carapace-covered beaks. He'd seen them many times before when the dwarves had brought food rations into the refugee quarters. They didn't look like creatures he would want to get on the wrong side of. Ihvon had explained to him that the virtuks were traditionally war mounts of the old dwarven kingdoms, but in times of peace they had been transitioned into beasts of burden to keep their numbers viable.

Fifty of Kira's Queensguard marched alongside the column of wagons. Ten at the front, ten at the back, and the other thirty spread throughout.

"It is good to see you alive and well, Virandr."

Dahlen had been pleasantly surprised to find that both Yoring and Almer – two dwarves he had fought alongside at the battle of Belduar – had been selected as part of his escort. In the midst of the chaos, familiar faces were a welcome sight.

"As it is you, Yoring. How is your knee?"

"Aye, it creaks and groans," the dwarf said, the gold and silver rings knotted in his beard shimmering in the flowerlight of the lanterns. "But it does its job."

"He still uses it as an excuse when he's too lazy to spar." Almer nudged Yoring in the shoulder, causing the dwarf to stumble a little. "But truly, we are thankful to Heraya for sparing you, Dahlen. May your fires never be extinguished and your blade never dull. When the queen gave the order to attack the Belduaran lines, I thought of you."

"Aye," Yoring agreed. "Had you not helped Almer carry me to the Wind Runner in Belduar, we would both be char and ash now, returned to Hafaesir's forge."

Dahlen gave the dwarves a soft smile, his memories turning to the Heart, the bolts that ripped through the Kingsguard, tearing limbs, rending steel, spraying blood. The memories clenched his heart in a fist, pulling around his lungs, tightening, blending with the smell of burnt leather and flesh from Belduar. *I am the son of Naia and Aeson Virandr. I am strong of mind.* Images flashed of the healer who had carried Ihvon's stretcher, broken bone protruding from the stump of his shoulder where the bolt had torn his arm free. Screams. *I am the son of Naia and Aeson Virandr. I am strong of mind.* His father's voice rang in his head. *Give your mind a task.* Dahlen focused on his breathing, slowly in through his nose, releasing through his mouth. *Slow everything.*

His focus was only broken by the unfamiliar concern in Belina's voice. "It does get easier."

A shiver rippled through Dahlen as the haze lifted from his mind. He tried to collect his thoughts and ask Belina what she meant, but all that came out was a muddled, "Hmm?"

"The scars and wounds of our past. Dealing with them gets easier. When we see and feel traumatic things, they cling to us like thorns."

"I'm fine." Dahlen let out a sigh, running his hand through his hair. He pushed the pads of his fingers against his scalp. "Leave it be, Belina. There are more important things to deal with."

"You men are all the same. You carry pain and shame yourself for feeling it until it breaks you. It's not weak to hurt. It's human."

Dahlen frowned at Belina but didn't answer. This was not the time to deal with demons in his head. First, they needed to deal with the demons who plagued the tangible world.

The column of wagons and Queensguard marched across the walkways and platforms, drawing eyes from all around. Whispers spread from every platform and courtyard as market-goers halted, and armourers and blacksmiths stopped mid-swing. Above, dwarves looked out over the low walls that lined the web of bridges and paths, gawking at the procession.

The closer they drew to the enormous waterfall that was the jewel of the mountain chasm within which Durakdur had been built, the louder the crashing water became. The thunderous roar consumed all other sounds, hammering like a chorus of drums beating harder and harder against the rocks.

Ahead, an enormous platform connected the city to the refugee quarters via a broad walkway that passed no more than fifty feet from the waterfall. Dahlen had stood on the platform many times since entering the mountain city, just as he had walked across that walkway. But where before the platform had been mostly empty, it now played host to hundreds of armoured dwarves, some astride virtuks, sharp steel gripped in their fists.

Had Kira not already warned him, he would have been caught by surprise at the sight of the green and silver banners of Azmar and the white and black of Ozryn. Several of each stood amidst the ranks of dwarves, joined by the crimson and gold of Durakdur. But despite Kira's warning that Pulroan and Elenya had sent soldiers to join her own, Dahlen had not expected their strength of presence.

Alongside the armoured dwarves, Dahlen also noticed a number of the mobile Bolt Throwers sitting atop raised metal platforms that were fitted with cogs and wheels.

"Hold!" a voice called as Dahlen and the column of wagons reached the platform the dwarven soldiers stood upon.

Dahlen found himself pleasantly surprised by the sight of another familiar face as Nimara, the dwarven warrior who had escorted Dahlen's father through the tunnels in search of Calen and Erik, stepped forward to where Dahlen's walkway met the platform, a number of armoured dwarves marching beside her.

The hammer of Durakdur was emblazoned across the dwarves' breastplates, four stars arranged around the head.

"May your fires never be extinguished and your blade never dull, Dahlen Virandr." The dwarf's long blonde braid, laden with gold and silver rings, trailed over the shoulder of her thick plate. A half-smile adorned her face as she inclined her head.

Dahlen repeated the greeting, as did Mirlak – the Queensguard Kira had placed in charge of the column.

"By order of the Queen, we are to pass through the blockade," Mirlak said, his crimson cloak trailing just short of the stone.

"Of course." Nimara gave a slight nod, her respect for the Queensguard evident. "And the wagons?"

"They are to pass through as well."

"At once."

"What is this?" More dwarves approached, cloaks of green and silver draped over their shoulders – Pulroan's Queensguard. One marched ahead of the others – the captain, most likely. A broad-chested dwarf with ashen grey skin and a thick beard of knotted black, laden with enough rings of gold and silver to rival Nimara's. "What are these wagons?"

Mirlak stepped forwards, an immediate tension setting into the air. "By order of Queen Kira of Durakdur, we are to pass through the blockade and meet with the Belduaran king."

The captain of the Azmaran Queensguard looked past Mirlak, paying as much heed to the dwarf's words as Dahlen would have paid to a child's. "And what are these wagons carrying? Is that food? Is your queen mad?" The dwarf came a step closer to Mirlak, and the atmosphere shifted. The other Queensguard who'd marched at the front of the column along with Mirlak moved to their leader's side, Yoring and Almer included.

"You will step aside." The tone in Mirlak's voice left no room for negotiation.

The other dwarf didn't back down. "If we let food through, this siege will be extended by weeks. We cannot allow it."

"It is not your place to allow it or forbid it."

"My queen—"

"Your queen has no say here." Mirlak dropped his hand to the axe hanging at his hip, the rest of his guard doing the same. Nimara gave a quick gesture with her hand, and the dwarves under her command moved to surround the Azmaran Queensguard. Dahlen could see movement buzzing all about the platform, dwarves from each of the three kingdoms trying to see what was happening. "This is Durakdur. Not Azmar. You are here by allowance of Queen Kira, out of respect for Queen Pulroan. But while you are here, you will do as you are told. Stand aside."

The leader of the Azmaran Queensguard glared at Mirlak, his jaw visibly clenching. The tension was so thick, Dahlen could feel it in the air before the dwarf turned to one of his companions and whispered something. The other dwarf grunted a nod then marched off towards a bridge that stood on the opposite side of the enormous platform.

"Queen Pulroan will hear of this." The captain stepped aside, gesturing for the other Azmaran dwarves to do the same.

"I'm sure she will." Mirlak gave the captain a nod, raising his hand as he walked past, gesturing for the wagons to continue. "Carry on through."

"That was tense," Belina said, once again taking joy in pointing out the obvious.

"It has been since the attacks," Mirlak replied, gazing at the dwarves from Azmar and Ozryn who were gathered around the platform. Now that they were up close, Dahlen could see that the dwarves of the other kingdoms held themselves distinctly separate. There was no mingling. He was beginning to understand what Kira meant when she had placed such an emphasis on the word 'war'. To him, conflict between humans was not only normal, it was expected. Whether it was over food, land, love, power, or simply for the sake of itself, conflict was the fulcrum of humanity's existence. But outside the world of men, his understanding had always been more limited. Dwarves were dwarves. Elves were elves.

His own ignorance had never been more apparent to him than at that moment. Kira was on the precipice of watching her own kind tear each other apart.

As they marched across the platform, wagons in tow, the other Durakduran soldiers nodded to them and straightened their backs.

"What *is* the situation here, Captain Nimara?" Mirlak asked, stopping before he stepped onto the walkway that connected the platform to the refugee quarters.

"At the entrance to the city, Commander? Or between our own?" Nimara held a knowing look in her eyes.

"Both, Captain."

"There has been little trouble with the Belduaran refugees. They seem well aware of their position, but if the food were to run out, I suspect they would do as all dying animals do. The situation with the forces from Ozyrn and Azmar is quite different. I understand why our queen has accepted their aid, but it puts us in a precarious position. The forces of Ozryn have remained reasonably civil, barring a few tense exchanges, but the Azmaran forces have been as tightly wound as a boar's tail – they also arrived with larger numbers than we had expected."

Mirlak nodded, his eyes narrowing as he looked at the crowded platform around him. "Keep a careful watch, Captain. And send word to the queen that we may need reinforcements here."

"Commander?"

"If you fear the darkness, Captain, bring a light. Preparation is nine-tenths of victory."

"Yes, Commander. It will be done."

"See that it is."

As the Queensguard and the column of wagons started to move across the walkway, Nimara grasped Dahlen's arm. "May your fires never be extinguished, Dahlen Virandr."

"And may your blade never dull, Nimara…" Dahlen searched his mind for Nimara's full name but realised he had never asked it, nor had he been told.

"Nimara Kol." The dwarf gave Dahlen a broad smile, the rings in her hair sparkling. His throat tightened as though he was looking down the shaft of an arrow. She was quite beautiful, but more than that, she had a confidence about her, a strength. "Aeson Virandr spoke often of you as we searched those tunnels. You and your brother. And now Queen Kira entrusts you with this task. I hope Hafaesir watches over you, for the man that holds the faith of both a queen and a Rakina is a man I might like to share a tankard of ale with."

Before Dahlen could answer, Nimara had inclined her head and set off back across the platform to carry out Mirlak's instructions. He just stood there for a moment, dumbstruck.

Belina elbowed Dahlen in the ribs, a twisted grin spreading across her face from ear to ear. "She likes you."

"Fuck off, Belina."

"No, I'm jealous. *That* is a *woman*. What I wouldn't give for five hours alone with her."

"Five hours?"

"That reaction right there is why she'd be happier with me." Belina gave Dahlen a wink and set off across the walkway, the sound of her laugh following her.

A semi-circular landing jutted from the end of the walkway, connecting to the rock face into which the passageway to the refugee quarters was set. The last time Dahlen had been here, the passageway had been guarded by ten Lorian Kingsguard and a pair of Kira's Queensguard. Now though, what had to be at least two hundred dwarves in full plate occupied the landing. The cloaks of Azmar, Ozryn, and Durakdur were all present. Each queen had sent segments of their own guard.

Nearly a hundred dwarves in crimson cloaks stood facing the passageway, heavy shields planted against the stone before them, thick-shafted spears resting atop the shields. Roughly fifty dwarves in cloaks of green and silver stood to the right of the landing, while half that number in black-trimmed white cloaks guarded the left.

The wagons had halted in the centre of the landing, just before the line of crimson-cloaked Queensguard. Mirlak spoke to one of the dwarves who stepped forward to greet them, then turned to Dahlen. "Now it is your turn."

"My turn?"

"The Belduaran forces blockade the other side. If we are to enter, we will need them to stand down." Mirlak gestured towards the passageway set into the rockface. The dwarves who formed the shield wall across the opening had parted, allowing Dahlen to see the light glinting off steel at the passageway's other end. "They wouldn't spit on me if I was on fire. But for you, they might listen."

Dahlen wasn't so sure. Daymon would just as soon see him hanged. But that depended on what Ihvon had said to the king. Not that Daymon heeded advice either way. But they'd come this far. Dahlen nodded. "All right."

Dahlen drew a lungful of air, then let it out in a short breath, an anxious shiver prickling his skin as he moved past the line of dwarves, Mirlak moving with him.

"You're not leaving me standing there with a bunch of short-tempered dwarves," Belina said, catching up with Dahlen just as he reached the entrance to the passageway. "Besides, your father will kill me if anything happens to you."

Dahlen made to argue but stopped himself. It wasn't worth the effort. The woman was stubborn as a rock. "Fine. Just don't say anything."

"Seen but not heard. My speciality."

Were the situation not so tense, Dahlen might have laughed at that. Instead, he simply gave Belina a short nod and stepped into the passageway. He could hear each beat of his heart hammering in his head. His breath trembled as he exhaled.

Now he was within the bounds of the tunnel, Dahlen could see a line of Kingsguard holding teardrop shaped shields across the opening at the other end, the bluish-green flowerlight reflecting off the burnished steel.

"You're going to have to actually say something," Belina whispered, leaning in. "You know, with your mouth."

"Belina."

"Seen but not heard," Belina whispered again, her voice fading.

Dahlen sucked his cheeks in, biting at the soft flesh, then let out a short breath. "I am Dahlen Virandr," he shouted, his voice rising only just above the thunderous waterfall behind him, reverberating down the smooth-carved stone passageway. "I have come with a peace offering of food from Queen Kira of Durakdur. No more blood needs be spilled. She wishes to talk to King Daymon."

The echoes of Dahlen's voice rang out, then faded. He heard shuffling feet and hushed whispers. Seconds turned to minutes.

"I don't think they heard you," Belina whispered. "Maybe a bit louder?"

"Belina, shut your..." A gap formed in the line of Kingsguard at the other end of the passageway, and two figures stepped through, their faces shrouded in shadow against the backdrop of flowerlight.

Dahlen's eyes adjusted, and he made out the faces of Lumeera Arian and Oleg Marylin – the new Lord Captain of the Kingsguard, and the emissary to the Freehold.

"It is good to see you alive, Lord Virandr." Lumeera stood a good twenty feet from Dahlen, but her voice carried through the stone passage, the sound of crashing water filling the air around them. The woman stood with her hand resting on the pommel of the sword at her hip, her purple cloak rippling in the backflow of air that swept through the city from the Wind Tunnels.

"As it is you, Lumeera. I would speak to Daymon. I bring food and a message from Queen Kira."

"He has been expecting you," the woman called back. *So Ihvon did tell him I was alive.* "You and the food may enter, but the queen's guards must stay."

"I cannot allow that," Mirlak bellowed, shifting his feet. "Dahlen Virandr and Belina Louna are envoys of the queen, and as such are under the protection of the Queensguard."

"They come alone or they do not come at all."

"We accompany them," Mirlak called back, holding his breath for a moment. "Or you starve."

Dahlen glanced at the commander of the Queensguard, but Mirlak's gaze was fixed on the other end of the tunnel.

Whispers passed between Lumeera and Oleg, tension in their voices.

"Ten of your guard may accompany them. No more," Lumeera called out.

"A good offer," Dahlen whispered to Mirlak.

"Twenty," Mirlak shouted, before turning to Dahlen, whispering, "If things take a turn in there, we'll be glad of every axe."

"Fifteen."

"We take twenty or you starve, Belduaran. Your choice."

"Why are you even negotiating?" Belina whispered to Mirlak. "It's not as if they have anything to negotiate with. You have food, they're starving."

"If we wish to talk with their king in good faith, that is the way we must start. I do not want to see them starve. It was not long ago I fought beside them in the courtyards of Belduar."

"Twenty." Without another word, Lumeera and Oleg turned and walked back towards the refugee quarters, the gap in the Kingsguard's line remaining after they'd passed through.

Mirlak gathered nineteen of his guard, Yoring and Almer among them, and signalled for the wagons to start moving as he, Belina, and Dahlen made their way through the passageway to the other side.

The familiar wave of heat washed over Dahlen as he stepped from the passageway and onto the top of the stone staircase that descended into the refugee quarters, the stench of sewage and sweat clinging to the back of his throat.

Rows of Kingsguard in burnished steel plate, purple cloaks resting on their shoulders, filled the landing at the top of the staircase and down the stairs, leaving an unbroken line through the centre where Oleg and Lumeera were now walking. Dahlen stopped for a moment, looking out over the cavernous chamber that was the refugee quarters of Durakdur.

For the first time since he had come to this place with Ihvon, the enormous central street that stretched off into the distance, was all but empty. Tents were pitched here and there, likely where the soldiers and new arrivals had been sleeping, and some refugees walked about, but for the most part it was barren. Above, thousands and thousands of eyes stared down as people flocked to the parapets of the many walkways of the upper levels. Somehow, even with this many people all gathered in one place, Dahlen could barely hear a whisper. The only sounds were slaps of feet on stone, the squeaking of wagon axles, and the clip of virtuk hooves.

"By Hafaesir." Mirlak covered his mouth and nose with his hand. "What is that smell?"

"Shit, soup, and sweat," Dahlen said, repeating the words Ihvon had said the first time Dahlen had visited the refugee quarters. "When you squeeze forty thousand souls into a cavern with little ventilation, the damp from the waterfall, and no sewage system, this is what happens. Take away their food, and that last scent clinging to your nose is death. Aside from the soldiers, many of the people here are old or sick, some with young families that couldn't travel to the other kingdoms."

Mirlak took his hand from his nose and looked up at the many people who lined the rising walkways. "I am sorry. I didn't know. May Heraya watch over them."

Dahlen gave Mirlak a weak smile then set off down the staircase after Oleg and Lumeera.

"What about the wagons?" Belina asked, looking back at virtuk-drawn wagons of food.

"The mages will flatten the stairs," Dahlen said, without looking back. "Only takes a few moments."

"Did nobody think of this glaring design flaw? I mean, it's clearly not conducive to getting wagons in and out."

"It's not a design flaw." Mirlak, Yoring, Almer, and the other Queensguard around them were listening. Dahlen could see the tilt of their heads. "It's about control. Many of Belduar's mages were killed in attacks on the city. Having stairs instead of ramps kept the dwarves in control of the food."

None of the dwarves spoke, but Dahlen saw the looks on their faces as they descended the stairs, Belduaran Kingsguard standing on either side, backs stiff, shields held high. In that situation, Dahlen would have expected to see fear or anxiety, or even animosity – they were walking into the belly of the beast, surrounded by enemies – but instead, all he saw was shame.

"Dahlen Virandr, risen from the dead." Daymon's voice echoed through the enormous cavern, amplified two-fold by the emptiness. Daymon stood at the bottom of the staircase, dressed neck to toe in gold-trimmed plate as though he was marching to war. Ihvon stood on Daymon's left, Lumeera and Oleg on the right. Along with several Kingsguard, a number of others that Dahlen vaguely recognised were gathered around the man: nobles and advisors. From his memory, some were decent, but just as many were little more than sycophants trying to worm their way into Daymon's graces now that his father was gone.

"Daymon." Regardless of the circumstances, Dahlen still couldn't bring himself to call Daymon a king. The title burned like acid on his tongue. "I come on behalf of Queen Kira. I am here to talk of peace, should you be willing."

"Is this her attempting to insult me once more?" Daymon took a step forward, the Kingsguard moving in line. "She will not even come herself? And what if I don't wish to talk of peace? What then, Dahlen Virandr?"

"Then you will allow your people to starve." If Dahlen had heard no whispers before, they now filled the cavern, blustering like a gale. Daymon's demeanour shifted in an instant, the bravado evaporating from his face as he looked up at the walkways above.

"Come, then, and we will see what the dwarf queen has to say."

"She wishes to embarrass me in front of my people!" Daymon roared, veins bulging in his forehead and temple, spittle flying. His face was red, fists clenched. He had brought Dahlen, Belina, and Mirlak to a large rectangular room on the second floor of the cavern – a room which, judging by the marks on the floor, had once slept at least ten people.

Ihvon, Oleg, and Lumeera stood to Daymon's left, on the opposite side of the room, while some of the other nobles stood against the walls, offering *tssks* and grunts when appropriate. Dahlen counted sixteen Kingsguard, all with their hands resting on the pommels of their swords.

"She wishes to *feed* your people, Daymon!" Dahlen was doing all he could to remain calm and level, but Daymon's idiocy was making that a challenge.

"I'm no fool. She attacked us, took our food, and now holds it ransom. She wishes to show my people that she can care for them where I cannot. No. I will not have it!"

"Daymon, please. Think of—"

"I am your king!" Daymon roared, cutting Ihvon off mid-sentence, his hands trembling. "Would you have me bow before her too? Have me spit on my father's legacy?"

"She took you in, Daymon. When the dragons laid waste to your city, she took you in." Dahlen tried to cut the tension in the room. "The dwarves carved a refuge for you in their home. They gave you food, shelter, water. They asked for nothing in return. Is that not enough to show their intention?"

"Their intention? They sent an assassin after me. They fired bolts through my men. They herded us into this pen of their making, and now they lord over us, letting us starve, then offering us food so that we are beholden to them."

You know damn well who sent that assassin. Dahlen ground his teeth. Holding his temper was no easy task when faced with a man who lied as easily as he drew breath. It would have been simple to call Daymon out before his nobles and Kingsguard. To tell the whole room of his deal with Pulroan. But it would still be his word against Daymon's, and Dahlen would likely end up with his hands bound again or hanging from a noose. Not only that, but even if the others believed him, it would serve no purpose. The tension between the dwarves and the people of Belduar was already at a height – revealing that Belduar's king was involved in a plot with Pulroan would only lead to more blood.

"Making peace doesn't show weakness," Dahlen said. "It shows strength. It shows that you put your people's needs before your pride." Silence filled the air, all eyes moving from Dahlen to Daymon. "Kira wishes to end this. She offers you food, peace, respite. Too much blood has been spilled already, Daymon. All she wants in return is that you come to her aid if she calls."

"She wants my fealty." Daymon's lip trembled as he spoke the words, his jaw tensing, veins throbbing. "She spits on my father's legacy. We should carve our way out. Show them the power of Belduar."

Something snapped inside Dahlen.

"It is you who spits on your father's legacy!" The Kingsguards stepped from the walls as Dahlen drew closer to Daymon, matching the man's stare. "Arthur was wise, caring, and strong. He put his people first. Not himself. He was everything you are not." Dahlen jabbed his finger against Daymon's breastplate. To his surprise the Kingsguard didn't move to stop him. They just watched, ready if the situation escalated further. "Do you care so little for these men and women at your side that you would have them die for your pride and your pride alone? You would have them starve just to make a point? You would have them bleed so you would not seem weak? You're a fucking coward!"

"Get out!" Daymon roared, his face inches from Dahlen's, his eyes bloodshot, his hands shaking. "All of you, out!"

CHAPTER THIRTY-TWO

AN OATH FULFILLED

Dahlen tilted his head back and ran his hands through his sweat-soaked hair as he, Belina, and Mirlak made their way down the stairs from the second level to the main street of the refugee quarters. He blew out a puff of air, shaking his head. He rested his hands on his hips and looked over the street.

The line of Kingsguard had reformed across the entrance, a few hundred holding position at the top of the landing and down the stairs. Nearby, men and women who had escaped from the Heart sat amidst a cluster of tents, flower lanterns scattered around them. The wagons that had carried the food were arranged in the middle of the street, the virtuks, their riders, and the rest of the Queensguard who had been granted entrance to the refugee quarters, standing beside them.

A few stragglers roamed around or sat on steps, eating raw carrots and celery and taking bites of a small brown-skinned fruit called jaka that the dwarves were fond of, but for the most part, the enormous street was empty. The refugees must have gathered their food and taken it straight back to their chambers. "Gods damn it."

"That went spectacularly." Belina pouted. "I particularly liked the part where you called him a coward. Who would have thought that might upset him? Such a child."

"Not now, Belina."

"Yes, now." Belina grasped Dahlen's arm and turned him towards her. He couldn't remember a time when her voice had taken on such a serious tone. "That man-child is a snot-nosed prick. But you lost your temper. If these people starve, it's on you as much as it is him."

"It damn well isn't!"

Belina tilted her head to the side, raising her eyebrows in much the way Dahlen's mother had done when he'd been a child and he had said something they'd both known was untrue.

Dahlen shook his head, clenching his jaw, the muscles bunching in his neck. He drew in long breaths, trying to settle himself.

Belina moved her head so their gazes met. "Twice I've seen you argue with him, and both times you've lost your temper. You said what you wanted because it made you feel strong. You knew what would happen when you called him out in the Heart, and again you knew what would happen this time."

"How could I have?"

"How could you not? Did you really think calling him a coward would make him change his mind? You're better than that." Belina jabbed her finger at Dahlen's chest, where his heart was. "In here. But you need to use this." She slapped him across the side of the head.

"Aagh, what was that for?" Dahlen rubbed where Belina had slapped him, frowning.

"You need to learn when to say what you want to say, when to say what you *need* to say, and when to shut your mouth. There's a time and place for each. You were just as much a child in there as he was. The only hope of him meeting with Kira now is if he feels shamed enough by what the people in that room saw. Sometimes you impress, and other times... well, let's just say you're a fucking idiot."

"It's done now." Dahlen bit at his lip. "I guess we wait."

"Mmm."

"How did it go?" Yoring called out, removing his helm as Dahlen, Belina, and Mirlak approached.

"As well as trying to take a shit in a kerathlin nest," Mirlak replied, letting out a heavy sigh.

"That bad?" Almer asked.

"Worse." Dahlen dropped to the ground beside one of the wagons, leaning back against the wheel. Belina sat beside him, folding her legs beneath herself.

"What now then?"

"We wait." Mirlak raised his eyebrow, glancing around at the group of Kingsguard who had taken up positions nearby, watching. "The queen said we had twenty-four hours. If we must sleep here, that is what we will do."

The twenty Queensguard and the virtuk riders gathered around, waiting. Most of the Queensguard stayed standing, ready and alert as though the whole place might come tumbling at any moment. Yoring and Almer sat across from Dahlen, laying their helms and battle axes on the ground, their hand axes still hanging from their belts.

After a while, some of the Belduarans who had been eating on the steps meandered over, one or two children asking if they could pet the virtuks. To Dahlen's surprise, the dwarves that had ridden the virtuks were more than happy to let the children rub their hands along the virtuks' carapace-covered snouts. Though, it was more the children's parents Dahlen was surprised by. One bite from those hardened beaks and a child would lose their hand.

"How can he sit in that room debating?" Dahlen whispered to Belina as he looked at the refugees who had begun to gather around the dwarves, more and more seeming to appear from nowhere. Some were old and frail, others missing limbs, while some carried their children on their shoulders. Each of them looked tired and hungry, eyes sunken, skin pulled tight. "These people need him. They need food, safety. They need to get out of these mountains. Humans weren't made for this. It should be an easy choice."

"There is a reason honour is a dangerous thing," Belina said, leaning her elbows down against the knees of her folded legs. "Honour and religion." She let out a short sigh at the curious expression on Dahlen's face. "Both honour and religion are things mortals use to justify atrocious deeds. To absolve themselves of the guilt they have so deservedly gained. They are more dangerous than any blade or any dragon. If a god tells a man to murder a child, they will oblige. It wasn't their choice – it was the word of a god. That man is not a murderer – he is a conduit of divine will."

"What of honour?"

"Honour is no different. It is why I asked you what you considered a good man to be. For some, a good man is no different from a man with honour. But that couldn't be further from the truth. Honour is entirely dependent on the wielder of that honour. What one person might deem honourable, another may not. It is honourable to stand by your oaths, is it not?"

"Always." Almer cut in before Dahlen could answer, the dwarf turning to face Belina.

"Always? What if the person to whom you are oath sworn commands you to cut the throat of an innocent dwarf?"

"My queen would never."

"But what if she did?"

"I…"

"What would be the honourable path? To obey your oath, or to spare the innocent?" More of the dwarves, and some of the gathered Belduarans, shuffled closer, listening intently to what Belina had to say. Dahlen often forgot the woman was a bard. Her lute was still tucked away in the smuggler's den in the Heart, but even without it, the way she spoke was captivating. She was like a woman split in two. One half was sarcastic, flippant, and at times downright crude. Whereas the other was thoughtful and poignant, her words captivating. He had never met anyone quite like her. "Being honourable is not what makes someone a 'good man'. Being a good man – or woman—" Belina narrowed her eyes looking around theatrically, playing to the gathering crowd "—is about grasping the concept of what is right and wrong but also understanding which right takes precedence and turns the other into a wrong. It is right to hold true to your oaths, but that right becomes a wrong when the oath to which you are bound calls for you to do something that is wrong."

A few scattered claps sounded amongst those gathered and Dahlen looked around to realise not only had people come from their makeshift homes on the ground floor to see who their new guests were, but others had come out onto the walkways above, carrying flower lanterns.

"Belina?"

Belina raised an eyebrow at Dahlen.

"Can you sing without your lute?"

The woman contorted her face into a look of mock insult. "Can I sing without my lute? How dare you, Dahlen Virandr. The lute is simply accompaniment. I am the talent."

Dahlen inclined his head, gesturing towards those who had come out to the walkways and who had gathered on the street.

Belina looked up, lip turning out as though impressed, then gave a soft nod, understanding. "Has anyone heard the ballad of the Breaker of Chains?"

Some of the dwarves shook their heads, whispers spreading through the still-building crowd.

Belina gave a soft smile, straightening her back and drawing in a deep breath. And as Belina started to sing, a shiver ran down Dahlen's back, his skin prickling, hair rising. Her voice was soft and melodic, tumbling over itself, rising and falling. It was beautiful.

> *There was a man, of humble lands*
> *Who rode to war, at honours call*
> *And in that war, the blood did feed*
> *The lands, the trees, and growing seeds*
>
> *There were people, as old as the seas*
> *As old as the mountains as rooted as trees*
> *And though the war, was not their own*
> *Chains drew them in and chains made them bleed*
>
> *Tired and weary, the man did become*
> *Through fire and blood, the man he did roam*
> *Till a killer made their home in his bones*
> *A dealer of death who longed to go home*

And on one faithful winter's eve,
The man met the people as old as the seas
As old as the mountains as rooted as trees

And on one faithful winter's eve
The man's faith was shaken, his hands they were stained
And so this man set on his path
The path to become the breaker of chains

Dahlen found himself sitting forwards, captivated by the melody of Belina's voice. This song was entirely different from the song he had heard her sing in the inn; it was more personal, more raw. His emotions swirled as Belina's voice rose and fell, delicate and intricate, an ornamented tapestry of words.

More people had gathered around, descending from the upper levels, flower lanterns in hand. Even some of the Kingsguard who stood at the stairs had turned, listening intently.

Dahlen looked up to see hundreds, if not thousands, of bluish-green lights resting on the parapets of the walkways that rose towards the ceiling, the cavern looking like a star-speckled sky.

In the enormous cavern, Belina's voice carried, echoing off the stone. Out of the corner of his eye, Dahlen spotted a man he knew to be a mage. The same one who had stood behind Daymon during his coronation speech and amplified the new king's voice.

When honour called, for deeds him to do
The man turned his back, the man he refused
For the killer he was, the same man remained
Till the day he became the breaker of chains.

For when hope is lost, and stars lose their glow
It's the heart of the man to which you most hold
And these are the words as old as the seas
As old as the mountains as rooted as trees.

Though the words stopped, Belina kept singing the same beautiful melody, and as Dahlen listened he could hear others around them joining in, some humming, some singing in full voice. When it seemed as though the crowd had learned the melody, Belina started singing again.

It was there, as he sat on the ground of the refugee quarters of Durakdur beneath the mountains of Lodhar, Dahlen witnessed a moment of beauty amidst all the bloodshed. And so, he let himself feel it, and he hummed.

For when hope is lost, and stars lose their glow
It's the heart of the man to which you most hold
And these are the words as old as the seas
As old as the mountains as rooted as trees.

And so I tell you a truth, as old as the seas
As old as the mountains as rooted as trees
For this world to live and love to reign,
We all must become the breakers of chains.

When the words stopped and the lingering echoes of the melody faded, silence fell over the cavern. Hundreds of feet high, thousands of feet long. Tens of thousands of souls. Not a single sound. That silence lingered, holding for a long moment before a chorus of claps and chants erupted, rising to the point that even the low drum of the waterfall outside was swallowed whole. Looking up, Dahlen saw thousands of people lining the walkways of the upper levels, hands clapping, lanterns glowing like fireflies.

"That was beautiful," Dahlen said to Belina, though he could barely hear his own voice over the cheering.

"I know," she replied, giving Dahlen a wink.

Dahlen laughed, shaking his head. "You had to ruin it, didn't you?"

Belina shrugged, a smile touching her lips before her expression changed as she looked at something behind him.

"What is it?" Dahlen followed Belina's gaze to the entrance at the top of the stairs. The Belduaran Kingsguard were moving about, shields raised, swords levelled, roaring commands that were drowned out by the refugees who were still cheering and shouting.

Yoring and Almer leapt to their feet, the Durakduran Queensguard hefting their battle axes from their shoulders as they looked up at the commotion by the entrance.

Dahlen rose, slipping his swords from the scabbards across his back just in time to hear a blood-chilling scream pierce the cavern as an enormous bolt ripped through the lines of Kingsguard at the entrance. Men and women in full plate crashed down the stairs, armoured bodies bouncing off the steps. But the scream hadn't come from the soldiers. It had come from a woman no more than ten feet from Dahlen. She screamed as she stood over the mutilated body of an elderly man whose arm had been ripped free by the enormous bolt.

Dahlen's gaze lingered on the old man for a moment. Blood spurting from the joint of the man' shoulder as he lay dying. Sound dulled as though someone had cupped their hands over Dahlen's ears. His heartbeat sent tremors along his bones. Images flashed of both battles of Belduar. Dragons, fire, blood, bone. Dahlen clenched his jaw and pushed the thoughts down. As he did, the world around him came back into focus. All the chanting and cheering had stopped, and the shouts of the Kingsguard at the entrance echoed through the cavern.

"What's happening, Mirlak?" Dahlen did his best to pull the accusation from his voice, but some of it no doubt lingered. There was little chance it was anything but dwarves coming through the passageway. If Kira had betrayed them, there would be no getting out of this. "Kira said she would give us time."

"By Hafaesir, I do not know. I swear to you." The dwarf looked at Dahlen, his gaze unflinching. "My queen would not go back on her word. Whatever comes through, we're by your side, Lord Virandr."

"No," Dahlen looked from the dwarves to Belina, then over to the Belduaran Kingsguard at the entrance to the cavern. A group of guards had stayed at the top of the stairs, holding a line of shields across the entrance, but the rest – a hundred or so – had fallen back to the main street, forming a defensive line, abandoning the stairs, readying themselves for whatever came through. "You stay here. Defend the people if anyone breaks through, but stay back. If it is dwarves who come through, the Kingsguard will not see the colour of cloaks. They'll just spill blood."

"Aye." Mirlak nodded. "Wise words. Nothing will get past us."

Shouts and cries rang out from the entrance and Dahlen looked up to see armoured dwarves riding virtuks, crashing through the Belduaran lines. The virtuks kicked and thrashed as they charged, beaks snapping, powerful hooves sending men and women careening backwards, tumbling down the staircase. The dwarves sitting astride the creatures swung their double-bladed axes side to side, cleaving through helms and armour. Cloaks of green and silver billowed behind the riders as they charged.

It was Pulroan, then. She's come to take Daymon.

"Hold yourselves back," Dahlen said to Mirlak. "Daymon already doesn't trust Kira. It won't take much for him to think you're part of this."

Mirlak gave Dahlen a gruff nod. "But if it looks like the tide is turning the wrong way, we'll not be leaving you to die."

"Much appreciated, Mirlak." Dahlen gave the dwarf as much of a smile as he could muster. He looked to Belina. She nodded, pulling her short sword free and slipping a knife from her weapons belt.

The virtuk riders had crashed through the Kingsguard who stood across the cavern's entrance, more dwarves surging through the passage behind them. The riders charged down the stairs, slamming into those Kingsguard who had pulled back to form a line across the street. The

Kingsguard were holding their ground, staying tight, blocking with shields, hacking and slashing with sharp steel. But the virtuk riders carved through them, the stout armoured beasts charging like battering rams, axes swinging from their backs like pendulums of death.

A virtuk crashed through the line of Kingsguard, swinging its carapace-covered head side to side, clamping its beak down on the hand of a Kingsguard that struck at it. The virtuk's rider hefted their axe and cleaved the arm at the elbow, the Kingsguard screaming as he staggered backwards.

And then Dahlen charged, Belina at his side.

"Take their legs," Belina called out as she rushed past Dahlen, knife and sword glinting in the flowerlight. She drew her sword across her body, then hacked into the virtuk's leg, steel slicing through the creature's knee in a spray of blood. The virtuk collapsed, taken by surprise at the sudden loss of a limb. As the creature and its rider stumbled and fell, Belina, without missing a beat, threw her left hand back and drove her knife into the rider's eye as the dwarf turned their head towards her. In the same motion, she ripped the knife free, charging towards the next Virtuk.

Daymon stood by the window, hands clasped behind his back as he looked out over the main street. He drew in a slow breath, grinding his teeth, watching as his people gathered to listen to that woman with Dahlen Virandr – Belina Louna – sing her song. Hundreds had stepped into the streets. Thousands lined the many walkways of the quarter, the light of the bluish-green lanterns sparkling all around. *I fucking hate those damn flowers.*

Ihvon stood silent to Daymon's left, arms folded, staring out at the scene. Not a word had passed between them since Daymon ordered the Kingsguard and nobles from the room after Dahlen left.

"Say it, Ihvon."

Out of the corner of his eye, Daymon could see Ihvon turning his head. "Say what, *my king?*"

Daymon bit down on the inside of his lip at Ihvon's emphasis on the words 'my king'. Before his father's death, trust had been something he had given freely. But that first attempt on his life the night they fled to Durakdur had shaken him. Despite all of Pulroan's machinations, when the woman had come to him with her offer of aid in retaking Belduar, she'd insisted she had not been responsible for the attempt. And Daymon believed her. But that only made everything worse. If Pulroan hadn't been responsible then there was someone else out there trying to kill him. Which meant there were few people left whom Daymon could truly trust, and Ihvon was one of them. Daymon let out a soft sigh, dropping his gaze. "My father's not coming back, is he?"

The question was rhetorical on the surface. Of course Arthur wasn't coming back. Daymon's father was dead. But in the back of Daymon's mind, a piece of him had kept clinging to the idea that maybe this had all been some horrible nightmare.

"No, my king, he is not." Ihvon kept his gaze fixed on the street outside. Ihvon had always understood him – Ihvon and Tarmon. But Daymon had finally come to terms with the fact that Tarmon had never made it out of Belduar. *I should never have let him stay at the Wind Tunnels.*

"I'm sorry, Ihvon." Daymon pressed his fingers into the creases of his eyes, trying to relieve some of the exhaustion that had set in. "For everything. None of this would have happened if my father were still wearing the crown."

Ihvon let out a heavy breath. "You need to stop idolising him, Daymon. Your father was a good man, but he was not without fault. There is nothing to be gained by comparing yourself to him. You are your own man. And we would likely be in the exact same position regardless of whose head the crown sat upon. There is little your father could have done against dragonfire, just as there was little you could have done."

Daymon lifted his gaze back out towards the street. The sound of the woman's singing echoed through the stone cavern. Even more people had gathered now, singing the melody over the woman's words. It was actually quite soothing. A moment of peace within the madness. "What do you think I should do, Ihvon?"

"Do you want honesty?"

"You are the king's advisor. It is time I learned to take your advice. Or, at the least, let you give it."

Daymon thought he saw a smile gracing Ihvon's face, though it was difficult to tell through the man's thick beard. "You should talk to Kira. I'm no lover of dwarves, you know this. Still, of them all, she is the one who came to our aid when we needed it most. Not once, but twice. As loath as I am to admit it, in our darkest hours, she showed us who she is. If there is one of them I would put my faith in, it is her. Besides, that is the burden of leading. You do whatever you must to protect your people. And right now, your people are starving, sick, and they want to go home. They want to see the sun." Ihvon rested his hand on Daymon's shoulder, turning him from the singing outside. "The reality, Daymon, is that if we don't get out of here, if you don't put food in their bellies, you will lose the people. The only reason you haven't lost them already is the threat of the dwarves. If word gets out that you have turned Kira's peace talks away, despite the hunger here, there will be a revolt."

"But I am their king."

"In their eyes, a king who cannot feed his subjects is no king at all." Ihvon held Daymon's gaze. "Your father is not here. But if he was, the first thing he would tell you is that even a king who is loved by all will lose the support of his people once their bellies are empty. Humans are a fickle species. We are only ever three meals away from chaos. What little rations we have left will soon be gone, Daymon. My advice would be stop thinking of yourself as their king and start thinking of them as your people. Set your pride aside. Talk to Kira. Do what needs to be done to feed your people and to bring them back to the light of the sun."

Daymon turned back to the window, letting Ihvon's words percolate. The woman had stopped singing, and thunderous applause was reverberating through the cavern. "You're right." It felt as though hands were clamped around his throat, and his mouth was dry. "I've spent every waking moment and every restless night in fear that I wouldn't be the king my father was. I've done so much wrong." Daymon shook his head, a half-smile touching his lips as he laughed at his own stupidity. "I was walking in his shadow, demanding to be called king. But I had forgotten what made him such a great king to begin with. He was loved, Ihvon."

"He was. By many but not by all. Nobody is loved by everyone, Daymon."

Daymon nodded. He wiped away a tear that was forming at the corner of his right eye. His father had spent Daymon's entire life leading by example, showing him how a king *should* act. But the moment Arthur died, Daymon allowed all of that to slip to the back of his mind. He had allowed himself to be ruled by fear of failure. He'd made one bad decision after the next. But not anymore. "I will speak with her."

"I will inform Dahlen Virandr of your decision, my king."

"I lied to you, Ihvon. It wasn't Dahlen Virandr who made an attempt on my life."

"I know."

"You know?"

Ihvon gave a slow nod.

"And you're still here? Why?"

Ihvon let a sigh out through his nose, scrunching his mouth. "I made an oath to your father. I told him I would watch over you no matter what happened. That I would see you honour his name. That is an oath I intend to keep. We all do things we regret, Daymon. We all make poor choices. We cannot change the past, all we can do is ensure the future is better."

Daymon made to respond to Ihvon, but as he did, he noticed the Kingsguard he'd placed at the entrance of the quarter shifting about. He could see some of them gesturing wildly, shouting and roaring, but the applause at the woman's singing drowned all other sound. He leaned closer to the glass, narrowing his eyes. In the streets below Dahlen Virandr pulled his blades from his back, Kira's Queensguard joining him.

A shriek rose above the dwindling applause, and Daymon watched in horror as an enormous bolt tore through his Kingsguard and hammered into one of his citizens below, blood and bone spraying in a cloud.

"We're under attack!" Ihvon called out from behind Daymon. "Lumeera!"

DAHLEN DRAGGED HIS BLADE FREE from a dwarf's throat, blood spewing from the open wound. He twisted, reaching his left blade across his right shoulder, plunging the tip into the eye of a dwarf that was coming up behind him, crimson spilling down the steel. Dahlen yanked his sword free as the dwarf dropped like a stone.

He took in his surroundings, lungs burning, his hair tacked to his forehead with sweat. The Kingsguard had held well, as he'd expected from warriors of their ilk. Even when the virtuk riders had hammered into their lines, they had rallied and pushed back. But when Pulroan's dwarves had wheeled two bolt throwers through the passageway, the Kingsguard had been forced to break rank. Bravery and discipline aside, standing in close formation awaiting bolts built to take down dragons would have been idiocy at its finest. And so around him, the Kingsguard and the dwarves of Azmar hacked at each other with axe and sword, rending armour and cleaving bone.

The dwarves were trying their damnedest to push through and into the refugee quarters beyond, but the Kingsguard gave little ground.

Dahlen leaned backwards, catching sight of a dwarven axe swinging towards him in a wide arc. The blade missed his torso by a hair's breadth, and he brought his blade across, taking the axe wielder's head from their shoulders. Blood sprayed in spurts as the body collapsed.

A blur at the edge of his vision and he swung again. The blows from the dwarven axes were too heavy to take head-on with his shorter swords, which meant he needed to move on instinct alone. Steel crashed against steel, and then a knife was pressed against Dahlen's throat.

"Good to see you're still alive," Belina said with a nod. The blood splattered across her face made her look unhinged, as though she were a smiling maiden of death. "Down." Belina grabbed Dahlen by the shoulder and pulled him past her, lunging forwards with her knife. She drove the blade to the hilt through the slits of a dwarf's helm, then yanked it free and stabbed it into the dwarf's neck.

Dahlen stumbled but caught himself, sidestepping the swing of a blood-slick axe, before taking the wielder's hands at the wrists and sweeping his blade across the dwarf's face. He felt the clang as his sword hit the dwarf's helm and the bite of skin and bone as he opened up a deep gash through the dwarf's mouth, snapping teeth and slicing flesh. The dwarf reeled backwards howling in agony.

Dahlen turned, but something hammered into him, lifting him off his feet, sending him crashing to the ground. The air fled from his lungs as he hit the stone. A dull buzz droned in his head, and he gasped and choked, trying desperately to drag the air back, to fill his lungs.

Belina's blood-smeared face appeared above him, and then her hands were wrapping around the arm loops in his leather armour, heaving him to his feet. "Get up."

Still dazed, Dahlen looked to where he had been standing and saw two Kingsguard impaled through the chest by an enormous bolt, their heavy plate granting them as much protection as paper. He gave Belina a short nod of thanks. Then roars rang out from behind, and he turned to see burnished steel and purple cloaks. Daymon and Ihvon were charging down the stairs behind them, at the head of more Kingsguard.

"For the king!"

"Looks like he's found his stones," Belina said, wiping blood from her eyes. "I still think he's a rat-faced prick."

Dahlen steadied himself, uneasy from hitting the ground. He looked to Daymon and the charging Kingsguard, but then something pricked at the back of his neck – an inkling. Around him, the Azmaran dwarves were disengaging, turning towards Daymon. The surviving virtuk riders shouted and roared, alerting the others to the king's presence. Then they were charging. In his elaborate plate, Daymon stood out like a rose among thorns.

Screams and cries rang out as a bolt crashed into the charging Kingsguard, followed by another. Dahlen watched as one of the few remaining Belduaran mages deflected one of the bolts, stopping it from hitting Daymon only for a second bolt to rip through the mage's chest. Blood sprayed as bolts burst through armour and shattered bone, but Daymon kept charging, sword raised. "For Belduar!"

And then Daymon and the Kingsguard were smashing into the chaos.

Of War and Ruin

IHVON BROUGHT HIS SWORD DOWN into the neck of a dwarf as he, Daymon, and the Kingsguard crashed into the melee. Rings of mail broke and split, blood sluicing as steel carved through flesh and hacked into bone. He pulled his sword free, then smashed the pommel down into the face of an un-helmed dwarf, feeling the crunch of bone.

His bones ached and creaked under the weight of his armour, tired from years of wear and tear. But even still, the steel of his plate felt like the embrace of a long lost friend, his sword a tender lover. He held no love for court politics, fancy clothes, and half-truths. He understood it well enough, but if it were oil, he was water – they simply did not mix. Fighting was simpler, more honest, more visceral. A part of him hated that he enjoyed it, but it was who he was.

Ihvon turned away the downward swing of an axe, catching it on his angled blade. He slid the steel of his sword along the axe's haft, slicing through fingers and hacking into the dwarf's neck, splitting rings of mail. The dwarf fell, and Ihvon moved to Daymon's back, protecting the king from the rear.

Everything was chaos. Dwarves bearing the markings and cloaks of Azmar were pouring through the passage into the quarter, some swinging battle axes like crazed beasts, mouths frothing, war cries echoing from their lips, while others rode astride those virtuks, long axes swinging and slicing. Some of the Kingsguard who had been guarding the entrance were still standing, but the stairs were littered with bodies and blood-stained purple cloaks.

That old bitch Pulroan has decided to cut her losses, then. She must have come to ensure Daymon is never able to tell the others of their dealings. But where are the others? Ihvon saw no black and white cloaks of Ozryn or crimson cloaks of Durakdur amidst the fighting. And in the mass of bodies, he couldn't even see the Queensguard who had come with Dahlen. *Something to worry about later.*

Ahead, Ihvon spotted Dahlen Virandr wheeling through the mass of bodies, his path marked by screams and sprays of blood. Belina fought at his side, striking like a snake, steel slicing. Alone, they were both warriors fit for bards' tales, but together, they were a force of nature. The Kingsguard who had held the street were rallying around the two, forming near the centre of the fighting. Were it another day, at another time, Ihvon had no doubt the Kingsguard would have ripped these oath-breaking dwarves apart. But the Kingsguard were weary and hungry, worn down by the months below ground, the fighting, and the lack of food. The Kingsguard numbered less than six hundred now – and many of them injured. They had lost over a thousand in the retreat through the city, most dying in the streets to dwarven steel and bolts, others succumbing to their wounds after.

More of Daymon's Kingsguard poured from the tents that had been pitched in the middle of the street, wearing nothing but shirts and trousers, blades gripped in their fists. They were those who had been resting when the dwarves attacked.

"Protect the king!" Lumeera Arian stood to Daymon's left, shield hefted. Daymon had assigned her to the position as Lord Captain of the Kingsguard out of necessity. She had been in the right place at the right time. But as chance would have it, she was a fine fit for the role. She was strong, sharp, and loyal.

Daymon plunged his sword between the neck and shoulder of a dwarf, ripping it free in a spray of blood. He charged like a bull through the fighting, pushing towards where Dahlen and the other Kingsguard had gathered. "Forward!"

"Daymon, no!" Ihvon cursed Daymon as the king charged forwards. The dwarves were already spreading around them, filling the gaps as Kingsguard fell. He grabbed Daymon by the pauldron and pulled him back. "There's too many. If we charge the centre they'll surround us."

Lumeera and a clutch of the Kingsguard fell in around Daymon and Ihvon, shields raised.

"I've stood aside too long, Ihvon. I won't be that king anymore. And I'll be damned if I let anyone think Dahlen Virandr has more courage than I do."

"Courage is no good if you're dead!"

"At least if I die, I'll die fighting for Belduar. Just like he would have. If we don't get to them, they're dead. I'm not leaving my guard to die like animals."

Ihvon gritted his teeth but nodded, grasping the back of Daymon's helm. The only way they were getting out of this alive was by a miracle, and he could hardly deny Daymon the chance to fight side by side with his guard. The chance to defend Belduar one last time. "Stay close to me. Your guard will fight tooth and nail by your side, but if you fall they will fall with you. We make an opening and let our warriors pull back to us. Let's teach these bastards what Belduaran steel feels like."

Daymon gave Ihvon a nod, and then they were cutting their way through the dwarves to Dahlen, Belina, and the Kingsguard at their centre. Heavy axes crashed into helms and breastplates, Kingsguard falling in droves, but they gave as good as they got, swords carving through dwarven flesh, stabbing down into cave-dwelling hearts.

Dahlen Virandr appeared at Ihvon's side as they broke through to the centre, twin swords gripped in his hands, face streaked with blood, a number of gashes along the front of his leather armour. He turned, catching the swing of a dwarven axe with the strong of his blade before driving the tip of his second sword into the dwarf's groin, where the armour was weak, blood spurting as an artery was severed. "It's good to see you, old man. I hope you have a plan."

"Stay alive as long as we can."

"Same as mine, then."

"If we can pull back to the walkways, we can narrow the field, kill the advantage of their numbers."

"As good a plan as any – if we can get there."

"Like I said, stay alive as long as we can."

A howl erupted behind Ihvon and he turned to see a knife plunge into the eye of an axe-swinging dwarf. The knife slid through the opening in the dwarf's helm and sank to the hilt, the dwarf dropping like a sack of stones, axe bouncing off the ground.

"Are you two just going to stand around?" Belina dropped to one knee, yanking the knife free before flipping it and launching it into the thick of dwarves.

"Fall back to walkways!" Ihvon roared. He turned to Lumeera and gave her a nod.

"Shields up! Protect the retreat! Protect the king!" At Lumeera's words, the Kingsguard who had cut through the dwarven ranks snapped their shields into place, holding a path open for the retreat. Ihvon knew no other group of warriors disciplined enough to pull off such a manoeuvre in the thick of a battle; pride swelled in his heart. As they pulled back through the path of shields, the Kingsguard on either side fell together, forming a line, but then a whistling sound ripped through the air, and a bolt slammed into the Kingsguard lines.

A man fell to the ground, shrieking and howling, his arm a mess of shattered bone and torn flesh. Another collapsed, hands clasped around his knee where his leg had been pulverised and ripped free. A second bolt crashed down, and more Kingsguard fell.

A series of roars erupted to the left, coils of dread twisting in Ihvon's stomach. *They've gotten around us.* He turned, raising his sword, only stopping when he saw the crimson-cloaked Queensguard of Durakdur hammering into the flank of the dwarves from Azmar, faces red as they unleashed guttural war cries, axes cleaving and rending. They were like warriors possessed, veins bulging, eyes wild.

"Now is our chance!" Daymon roared. "Forward! Forward! For Belduar!"

Ihvon turned at the sound of Daymon's voice, frantic. "No! We need to pull back! Daymon, there are too many!"

But it was too late, Daymon had charged, Lumeera and the other Kingsguard moving at their king's side. Ihvon's heart clenched, panic flooding his veins as he rushed after Daymon. He caught the gaze of

Dahlen Virandr and saw the young man curse as he turned on his heels, blades moving in a whir of steel.

A dwarf crashed into Ihvon's side, knocking him off balance. He staggered, turning as the dwarf rammed the head of their double-sided axe into his chest. The blow knocked the wind from Ihvon's lungs, searing pain igniting along his sides as the axe's twin points pierced his plate, pushing into his flesh. He threw his arm forward, driving his blade into the dwarf's open mouth. The dwarf's lips bulged and split at the corners, sliced open by the steel, teeth snapping, blood pouring, and then their eyes rolled to the back of their head, and Ihvon dragged the blade free.

Ihvon let out a howl as the dwarf fell, their weight pulling on the axe that was still lodged in his plate, its bladed points tearing upwards through the flesh of his belly. He wrapped his free hand around the top of the axe haft, drew in a deep breath, then ripped it free, letting the weapon clang against the ground. He clenched his jaw, driving the pain down, and charged after Daymon.

Everywhere Ihvon looked, steel shimmered and blood sprayed, the bluish-green light of the lanterns giving the world an ethereal glow as dwarves and men left the mortal plane. Axes and swords swung, the crush of bodies pressing down. He saw Daymon ahead and carved his way towards the young king, calling out. "Daymon! We need to fall back!"

Daymon drove his blade down through a dwarf's throat, ripping it free with a spray of blood. He turned, hacking the blade down into a dwarf who had been moving for Lumeera's side, then turned to Ihvon, a look of fervour on his face. He raised his sword in the air and roared, "For Belduar! For Arthur!"

Shouts and cries echoed Daymon's, his words driving renewed strength into those around him. Since the first assassination attempt, Daymon had spent too long worrying only of himself. But now, Ihvon burned with pride as he watched Daymon fight for his people, as he heard the young king called his father's name.

But as quickly as it came, that pride turned to abject horror as an axe blade cleaved Daymon's raised arm at the elbow. Even after the axe had hacked through the steel and bone, sliding out the other side, the look of fervour on Daymon's face remained, his arm holding in the air. And then Daymon's eyes widened, blood spurting from the severed limb. The king pulled his arm down in front of him, staring at the empty space where his hand had once been, sword clattering to the ground.

Ihvon hacked and slashed at everything around him, muscles burning as he dragged his way through the mass of bodies, steel slicing into flesh, bouncing off plate, cutting into coats of mail. He looked up to see Dahlen Virandr and Lumeera both turning to Daymon, realising what had happened. But before any of them could do a single thing, Daymon lifted his gaze, his eyes locking with Ihvon's and then another axe slammed into his side, carving through the plate as though it were made of clay, slicing into his flesh and bone. Shock touched Daymon's face, followed by pain.

Ihvon watched as Dahlen drove his blade through the neck of the dwarf who held the axe, while Lumeera slew two more who were charging Daymon from the rear.

Daymon dropped to his knees, half the axe blade still buried in his side, blood pumping from the stump of his right arm where the axe had cut through just above the elbow.

Ihvon cut down the last dwarf that stood between him and Daymon, pushing past, dropping to the ground beside the boy he had helped raise. The boy he had sworn to protect. The boy who was now a man, and a king, but would always be a boy in Ihvon's eyes.

"Daymon!" Ihvon grabbed the sides of Daymon's helm. He lifted the man's head and looked into his eyes. "Look at me. Daymon."

Daymon's eyes were glassy, his breathing slow and laboured. Each breath was a drawn out rasp, blood coating his lips. "…Ihvon…" Daymon swallowed, his head lolling to the side.

"You're not alone, Daymon. I'm here." Ihvon watched the life drain from the boy whose shoulders should not yet have been burdened with the weight they had been forced to carry – the boy he had failed. Every muscle in Ihvon's body clenched as he pulled Daymon closer, tears burning at the corners of his eyes. He squeezed, Daymon's armoured body pressed against his, his fingers still wrapped around the hilt of his sword.

Ihvon's heart tightened, as though it had been wrapped in chains as weightlessness settled in his stomach. He rocked back and forth, holding Daymon's lifeless body, heedless of the madness around him. Then, he lowered Daymon to the ground, resting his hand on the king's cheek. "I'm sorry, my boy. I'm so sorry."

Ihvon's chest trembled as he pulled himself to his feet, cold tears carving through the blood that marred his face. Around him, Dahlen, Belina, Lumeera, and the other Kingsguard fought tooth and nail, their wounds collecting, lethargy dragging at their movements. Slowly, cold fury spread from Ihvon's heart, chilling his blood, sweeping through his chest and out through his arms and legs.

So this is it. This is where I die. He clenched his jaw, his fist tightening around his sword's hilt. *I will take as many of you with me as the gods allow.*

Ihvon unleashed a guttural roar, his body shaking. He swung his sword down into the neck of a dwarf, mail rings breaking, blood flowing as the steel cut into flesh and bone. He dragged his sword free in a spray of crimson, caught the swing of an axe, then raked his blade across the wielder's face, opening their mouth and nose, shattering teeth. Leaning his left shoulder back, he drove the blade to the hilt into the dwarf's blood-filled mouth, bursting through the neck on the other side. He let go of the hilt and grabbed the axe from the collapsing dwarf's lifeless hands, and roared. Rage flowed through him, shaking his bones. His lungs burned, and he felt his neck veins bulging as he unleashed his war cry. "For Daymon!"

Ihvon screamed in fury as he carved through the dwarves, cleaving limbs and splitting skulls with the weight of the axe. He swung and swung, letting his rage take over, a primal bloodlust filling him. Something slammed against his right leg, followed by a dull pain that pressed at the edges of his mind. He looked down to see a wide gash in the armour covering his thigh, blood pouring from the wound. He gritted his teeth and carried on killing, the rush of battle holding his pain at bay.

He felt the crush of bones breaking as the pommel of an axe crashed into his cheek. He didn't remember losing his helm. His face throbbing, Ihvon turned and rammed the head of his axe into his attacker's face, the twin points of the blades slicing into the dwarf's eye and cheek, knocking them to the ground and taking the axe with them.

As Ihvon turned, what felt like a battering ram crashed into his chest and stole the air from his lungs. He tried to breathe, but all he could manage was a spluttering cough, the iron tang of blood filling his mouth. He looked down to see a twin bladed axe buried in his chest. It had sliced through his plate, carving into his ribs, filling his lungs with blood. Pain blended with a strange sense of calm.

He looked to the dwarf who held the axe, the blade lodged firmly in Ihvon's plate. The dwarf stared back at him, a brief moment of recognition between the two, then Ihvon closed his fist and rammed it down into the dwarf's forearm, breaking his grip on the axe's haft. A look of shock crossed the dwarf's face as Ihvon grabbed him by the neck loop of his armour and dragged his face onto the axe's second blade that jutted from Ihvon's chest. A surge of pain twisted as the dwarf's face slammed down on the blade, steel ripping through flesh, teeth, and bone. He pushed the dwarf away, dropping to his knees, his vision blurring, the light fading in his eyes.

Ihvon drew in a rasping, blood-filled breath, then collapsed, the world growing dark around him as he lay on the cold stone beneath the mountains of Lodhar. At the very least, he would finally be with Alyana and Khris once more.

DAHLEN'S BREATH CAUGHT IN HIS chest as he watched Ihvon fall, blood pouring over the man's lips, seeping from around the axe blade in his chest. Dahlen wanted to go to him, to be there, but Ihvon was too far away. In seconds, the man was lost from Dahlen's sight, swallowed by the battle. He'd had seen Daymon fall only moments before. No matter their differences, he took no pleasure in seeing Daymon's death and even less in seeing Ihvon's anguish as he held the young man in his arms.

Belina and Lumeera stood at Dahlen's side, hacking, slashing, and stabbing, doing all they could to stay alive. The Kingsguard had gathered around them, shields raised, clinging to life by the tips of their swords. Daymon and Ihvon's deaths had rocked them, had stolen the fire in their hearts. Now they fought for nothing more than their own lives.

Through the mass of Azmaran dwarves, Dahlen saw the crimson cloaks of Durakdur's Queensguard, Yoring, Almer, and Mirlak among them. But there were simply too many Azmarans.

Kingsguard fell around him, bellies opened, throats slit, limbs severed.

Dahlen stabbed out with his left blade, driving it down through the neck of a dwarf before stepping back tight to Belina, lungs heaving, muscles aching and burning. The dwarves' heavy plate meant he had to be precise with his strikes. Each swing or stab needed to be a killing or maiming blow, otherwise his blades would simply skitter off the steel harmlessly.

He caught Belina's gaze. Blood marred the woman's dark skin, numerous slices and cuts marked in crimson through her shirt. It was the first time he had truly seen her mirthless.

A horn bellowed, low and sonorous followed by another, and then the thundering of hooves filled the cavern. Cries rang out, dwarves shifting all around. A host of virtuk riders cut through the Azmarans like a raging river, axes swinging, blood spraying. The ground shook beneath Dahlen's feet, a tremor rising through him. He looked about frantically, trying to understand what was happening. A virtuk charged past him, sending him stumbling backwards. That was when he saw crimson cloaks billowing behind several of the virtuk riders, here and there a splattering of black and white.

Elenya and Kira.

More horns bellowed, and then Kira's voice rose above everything, amplified by a mage. "Dwarves of Azmar, lay down your weapons, or return to Heraya's embrace!"

Dahlen's heart pounded, chest heaving as he looked about him, praying to any god that would listen. *Please, let them surrender.* He gripped both swords tight, trying to slow his breathing, the aches and pains of his body slowly coming to the fore as he stood still.

Ryan Cahill

The clang of steel on stone sounded, ringing through the cavern. Then more followed as the dwarves of Azmar dropped their weapons.

Chapter Thirty-Three

A Path of Your Own Making

Tense silence hung in the air of the council chamber. Dahlen sat on a short wooden bench that rested against the wall – the same bench Daymon had sat on when Dahlen had first laid eyes on the chamber after the battle of Belduar. His entire body ached and groaned, muscles knotting and burning. Blood was caked into his hair, and he could feel it clinging to his skin, mingled with dried sweat and dirt. All he wanted was to bathe and sleep, and yet he feared the nightmares he knew would plague him once he closed his eyes. The nightmares that touched him even then, clawing up from the pit of his stomach: the blood, the death, Ihvon's body, the look on Daymon's face as the axe carved through his arm.

Dahlen drew in a deep breath, running his hand through his blood-matted hair, shaking the thoughts from his head. Nightmares could wait for him in his sleep. He was sick of dealing with them while he was awake. He turned to Belina, who sat next to him. "Are you all right?"

She was leaning forwards, her arms rested on her knees, her short hair dangling over her face. She drew in a long breath, then lifted herself upright, turning to Dahlen. Her lip was split, dried blood marked a gash that ran from the back of her jaw to her chin, and much like Dahlen, her face was marred by a mix of grime, blood, and sweat. She nodded, her usual snark and charm nowhere to be seen. She gave Dahlen a weak smile, despondency in her eyes. "I've known Ihvon a very long time. A *very* long time. He always did right by me. Even when I didn't do right by him." She shook her head and Dahlen could see a tear glistening on her cheek. It felt wrong to see her like this. "The last place he would have wanted to die is down here. At least he is with Alyana and Khris now, stuffing his face in Achyron's halls, complaining about the smell of dwarves." She let out a soft, choking laugh, then drew another deep breath through her nose, exhaling slowly, the brief moment of levity fading. "That was really fucking close."

Dahlen nodded, unable to muster any words that would matter. Ihvon was dead. So was Daymon. All the anger and irritation Dahlen had held towards the young king had vanished in an instant when he saw Daymon take that axe. The pettiness and squabbling meant nothing. Death had a way of stripping back things to their essential parts, and, in essence, Daymon had been nothing more than a lost young man desperately trying to cling to his father's legacy and failing. That was something Dahlen could relate to.

He lifted his gaze to where Kira and Elenya sat on their thrones atop the raised semi-circular dais, a sombre mood hanging over them as they sat in silence, both still garbed in full plate. Queensguard with cloaks of both the crimson of Durakdur and the black and white of Ozryn filled the chamber, surrounding the dais and forming a line from the thrones to the entrance, Yoring, and Almer among them.

On the other side of the chamber Lumeera Arian stood with Oleg Marylin and a number of the Belduaran nobles Dahlen recognised from his meeting with Daymon. After Kira and Elenya had cleared the Azmaran dwarves from the refugee quarters and discovered Daymon's body, they had escorted all those who might be considered for succession to the council chamber in the Heart. Oleg and Lumeera had been brought along due to their stations, while Mirlak had told Dahlen and Belina that Kira had requested their presence specifically. The queen, however, hadn't spoken to them since they'd arrived.

Dahlen shifted at the sound of armoured boots echoing from the corridor outside the chamber, pausing as the doors creaked open. Dahlen and Belina rose to their feet, the entire chamber turning to watch as an escort of Kira's Queensguard, Mirlak at the front, led a dwarf in sharp-cut plate through the doors, a green and silver cloak draped over her shoulders. They led her through the chamber, dropping her to her knees at the foot of the dais, chains clinking around her wrists.

Dahlen pushed his way towards the dais, low whispers and the sounds of shuffling feet rippling through those gathered.

"The Commander of Azmar's Queensguard was slain in the fighting, my queen," Mirlak said, looking up towards Kira on her throne. "This one claims to be the highest ranking left alive."

Dahlen looked at the dwarf who knelt at the foot of the dais. She was young. Her face was marred by blood and bore a few fresh wounds. The rings in her hair were mostly bronze, one or two silver, and no gold.

Kira lifted herself from her throne, a number of her Queensguard moving closer as she stepped down from the dais, eyes fixed on the kneeling dwarf. "Your name?"

Wearily, the dwarf lifted her head. "Almat."

Mirlak gripped the back of the kneeling dwarf's neck. "You will address the queen as Your Majesty."

"Your Majesty." Almat fell forwards as Mirlak let go of her neck.

"Where is your queen, Almat? First, she orders a cowardly attack on the guards of both Durakdur and Ozryn, turning on her own kind. Then she launches a full assault on the Belduaran refugees, and now she has fled?" Kira moved so she stood over Almat, muscles tensing in her jaw. "You will answer in her stead. Do not make me ask twice."

Almat looked up at Kira. It seemed as though she was going to speak, but then Kira's gauntleted hand smashed into her cheek. Almat fell to the side, catching herself with one hand, spitting blood onto the stone.

"If you do not give me the answers I seek, I will take your head from your shoulders and show it to the next dwarf I drag in here. You have spilled the blood of your kin on this day. You have started a war that could break our people. Do not think I will find mercy for you. Heraya will not save you from Hafaesir's wrath."

Almat pulled herself upright, wiping the blood from her mouth, chains clinking. "Queen Pulroan is dead, Your Majesty."

The look of pure shock on Kira's face was mirrored in the murmurs that spread through the chamber.

Behind Kira, Elenya stood from her throne, fire-red hair curling over her armour, eyes narrowed. She pulled a short hand axe from a loop on her belt. "I spoke to Pulroan only hours ago. If you are lying, I will skin you alive with my own blade."

"By Hafaesir, I swear to you, Your Majesties. We were guarding the refugee quarters, as commanded, when Queen Kira's guard arrived with the humans and the wagons. Our captain sent word to Queen Pulroan that the Belduarans were receiving aid. But when the messenger returned, he did so with the remainder of our queen's guard and all the forces we had brought with us through the Wind Tunnels. Queen Pulroan was murdered as she bathed. Our commander caught the assassin in the midst of the act, and in his haste to escape, the assassin dropped his knife." Almat grunted, shifting her knees and straightening her back. "The blade bore the sigil of Belduar on its crossguard. King Daymon of Belduar ordered the death of our queen. We didn't wish conflict with Durakdur or Ozryn, but honour demanded we exact vengeance."

"This is all you have?" Kira asked, tilting her head. "You spilled the blood of your kin, started a war between the kingdoms of the Freehold, and attacked the refugees of a nation under our guard because you found a dagger? Do you have this dagger?"

"I… no, Your Majesty. It was our commander who found it, may Heraya embrace him."

"And you did not think to bring any of this to us?"

"Honour demanded we—"

"Honour demanded you kill your own kind?" Elenya roared, stepping closer to Kira, veins bulging in her neck. "That is not honour, it's pride."

Tense silence filled the chamber as Kira looked down at the kneeling dwarf, her breath visibly swelling in her chest. "Take her," Kira said to Mirlak, releasing the air from her lungs. "Confine her with the others. If this is true and Pulroan is dead, there is much that will need to be discussed."

"It will be done, my queen." Mirlak bowed his head, dragging Almat to her feet by her hair and passing her to a Queensguard who stood at his side. Mirlak moved to the side as the rest of the prisoner's escort marched her from the chamber, the doors closing heavily behind them.

"Well," Belina whispered. "That's not good."

The tension in the chamber was palpable. Both Kira and Elenya's expressions were unreadable, while Dahlen could see the Belduaran nobles whispering to each other. There were six of them in total. Four men and two women, all looking as though they had seen at least forty summers. Dahlen had spent enough time around Daymon's court to know most of them were snakes in fine clothing but hadn't bothered to learn much more about them.

"Is it true?" Kira's voice echoed through the chamber, quieting all whispers. The Queensguard who stood between her and the Belduarans shifted, moving out of the way so as to create an open space.

None of the Belduaran nobles uttered so much as a whisper, fear evident in the language of their bodies. Dahlen couldn't blame them. They stood in a closed chamber, surrounded by dwarves in heavy plate with sharp axes hanging from their backs. Not only that, both Kira and Elenya looked as fierce as lions in their sharp-cut plate, ring-laden hair tied in braids – and Elenya still held a tight grip on her hand axe, her knuckles pale.

"No." Oleg Marylin stepped forwards, leaving the group of whispering nobles behind him. Of them all, Oleg was the last voice Dahlen had expected to hear. The man was usually quiet and reserved. Conflict had been something he'd regularly shied away from. He often seemed lost in his own head. The man scratched nervously at his unkempt beard, his feet shuffling. "Your Majesty," he added, hastily. "It is not true."

"And do you have any proof that it is not?" Elenya stepped down from the dais, standing beside Kira, her eyebrows raised.

"Forgive me, Queen of Ozryn." Oleg swallowed hard, settling himself with a long breath. "But the burden of proof does not lie with the accused. It lies with the accuser. If I were to accuse you right now of the same deed, would I need to prove your guilt or would you need to prove your innocence?"

Belina leaned close to Dahlen, whispering. "That little man has the stones of a bull. The face of a hog, but the stones of a bull. I like him."

A tense moment passed where Dahlen was worried Elenya might strike Oleg down for simply suggesting she might have had a part to play in what had transpired, but then, surprisingly, she smiled. "You speak truth, Oleg. But still, the queen of Azmar is dead and your king stands accused of her murder, after already being accused of others. That is not promising."

"It sounds more convenient than anything else, Your Majesty." The words that left Oleg's lips were surprisingly strong and confident with a hint of snark, the usual chirpiness gone from his demeanour.

Dahlen had never seen him like this. The man had pulled a cloth from his trouser pocket and now clenched it between his fingers. It was only then Dahlen realised Oleg's hands had been covered in blood and dirt, which now marred the cloth. He had forgotten the man had insisted on carrying Daymon's body back to the young king's sleeping chamber before leaving the refugee quarters.

"I'm sorry, Your Majesties." Oleg twisted the cloth in his fingers, his gaze lingering on the floor for a moment before lifting to meet the attention of the two warrior queens. "Many of the men and women I've known for years are now dead. They lie in their own blood waiting to be burned, returned to ashes. My people are scattered about the kingdoms of your Freehold, starving and without a home. And now, my king, a young man who I watched grow from a babe, lies dead, alone, no mother or father to weep over him. I do not believe he arranged for the killing of Queen Pulroan. I do not see how it would be possible, given that we were confined to the refugee quarters. What's more, it is a little too convenient that the assassin would drop a blade marked with the sigil of Belduar. I'm no assassin, but I don't believe one worth their salt would make a mistake like that. Please, for the sakes of all our people, can we find a way to move past this?"

"Well, I am an assassin," Belina whispered to Dahlen. "And I can safely say there's plenty of idiots out there who'd do just that… but he's right."

Kira stared at Oleg for a long moment, then turned her gaze to the nobles. "Do any of you have anything to say of this? You who believe yourselves worthy of the crown."

Silence. A few of the nobles shuffled, uncertainty plain on their faces, but none spoke.

"There is a way," Kira said, glancing towards Elenya. "Once word of Pulroan's death circulates throughout the Freehold, and Daymon Bryne's name is spread as the one who gave the word, the dwarves of Azmar *will* want more blood – no matter how convenient the proof. But if the people of Belduar were to be under my protection and that of Queen Elenya, the Azmarans would not have the strength to move against you."

The air in the chamber shifted, the weight of Kira's words setting in.

"I fucking knew I liked her," Belina whispered, folding her arms, puffing out her bottom lip appraisingly as she stared at Kira.

"What are you saying?" One of the nobles – a tall, stringy man with a long face, white-grey hair, and wrinkled tunic of deep purple – asked, taking a step towards Kira. Judging by the tone in his voice, Dahlen was reasonably sure the man knew precisely what Kira was saying.

Kira's steps echoed as she walked through the opening of Queensguard, stopping before the tall man and tilting her head sideways as she stared up at him. Now they stood beside each other, Dahlen could see Kira was at least a foot and a half shorter but somehow seemed the far more imposing figure. She said nothing as she stared at the man. "And what is your name?"

"I… ehm…" The man collected himself, straightening his back. "My name is Lord Geor Darna, son of Ulder Darna, son of…"

The man's words trailed to a stuttering halt as Kira held her hand up. "I don't need the name of every man who came before you. Their deeds are their own. You cannot live off them." Kira turned, walking back to the foot of the dais, where Elenya stood, then turned to face the nobles, Oleg, and Lumeera. "What I am saying, *Lord Geor Darna*," Kira continued, "is Elenya and I will continue to feed and house the people of Belduar while you gather yourselves. We will reach out to Azmar and negotiate the release of your people in the refugee quarters there before the rumours begin to spread. After that, we will aid you in the reconstruction of your city. Reports say that the empire has abandoned the ruins due to the wars breaking out across the continent."

"You have our humblest of thanks, Your Majesty." Geor bowed so deeply that even Dahlen was a little embarrassed by it.

Kira simply looked at the man, waited for him to stand straight, then continued. "In exchange, the city of Belduar will become a vassal of the Lodhar Freehold."

Gasps of shock broke out through the nobles, and Lumeera's face dropped. Oleg's expression didn't change. It was clear he had been expecting something along these lines.

"Unacceptable!" a woman with her dark hair tied into a plait roared. "The Kingdom of Belduar has stood for thousands of years!"

"And now the city has fallen, and its king is dead!" Kira snapped, her demeanour changing in an instant. "My people came to your aid and died for your freedom. It is by the grace of our generosity that you still draw breath, that you have food and water to fill your bellies. If we had not brought you here from Belduar you would be nothing but char and ash." Kira took a step closer to the nobles as she spoke, each one of them shifting backwards. "And in that time, you haven't shown even a trace of gratitude. Your presence has brought nothing but blood and death. You can go," she said, throwing her arms in the air. "Take your people and march through the Southern Fold Gate. Trek along the mountain passes. Rebuild your city with your bare hands." Kira narrowed her eyes, the rings knotted throughout her blonde hair glistening in the bluish-green of the flower lanterns that hung about the chamber. She stood at least a foot shorter than any of the nobles, and yet before them she was a giant. "Watch as your people starve and wither. Over a hundred thousand Belduaran souls reside within the Freehold. You have no fields. No crops. No medicine to treat the sick. You have no wagons or horses. You have precious little of anything. Your people will be dead, dying, or fled within a fortnight. Each of you covets the crown, yet none of you understand what it is to care for a kingdom."

The Belduaran nobles stared at Kira, their expressions shifting from indignation to disbelief and back again.

Behind Kira, Elenya spoke. "As a vassal of the Freehold, the dwarves of Azmar would be unable to move against you. Belduar would be given the time to gather and care for its people. You would be provided food and water and would be granted access to the Freehold's Craftsmages to assist in the reconstruction of the city. And a Keeper of the Mountain would be appointed to act as the city's leader."

"We would need time to think on it," Oleg said to looks of scorn from the nobles, who clearly saw him as having little right to speak in these discussions.

"The time for thinking has passed, Oleg," Kira said. "This decision is to be made here and now. The future of Belduar is to be decided within the walls of this chamber."

"You're not giving us much of a choice," one of the nobles said. He looked to have seen at least fifty summers, his jaw square, his shoulders broad enough to have been a warrior's.

"We are giving you more of a choice than you deserve."

"We could take what we need at the blade of an axe," Elenya added, lifting her own axe slightly as though for emphasis. "But that is not what we want."

The broad-shouldered man stared at Kira and Elenya for a moment, then gave a gruff nod and turned back to the other nobles, murmurs spreading through the group as they discussed in hushed whispers. Voices rose and fell. Dahlen couldn't make out the words being exchanged, but tempers were clearly fraying. One man with white speckled hair jabbed his finger into Geor Darna's chest, then turned and stormed from the chamber, another man following him, leaving only Geor Darna, the square-shouldered man, and the two women.

Silence held after echoes of the closing door faded, then the broad-shoul-dered man turned back to Kira and Elenya, sucking in his cheeks, his eyes tracing along the ground. He drew in a long breath, then released it as he lifted his gaze. "We agree. We will need time to decide who will bear the mantle you propose. This Keeper of the Mountain. But we will swear fealty to the Freehold in exchange for everything you have offered."

"You misunderstand," Kira said, shaking her head. "*We* will choose the Keeper. Not you."

"Absolutely not!" the woman with the dark plait said, folding her arms across her chest.

"We will not allow that." Geor Darna added, his voice firm.

"This is not a request," Kira said. "It is a condition. If Belduar is to become a vassal of the Freehold, then the first Keeper will be chosen by the Freehold. In the future, you will be allowed to make the decision for yourselves, but we are at a delicate point in our history. The fate of our two peoples hangs in the balance. In his short time, Daymon Bryne's arrogance and unwillingness to compromise fractured our long-standing friendship. We will not allow that to happen again. And so our decision is made."

The silence that filled the chamber, hanging on Kira's words, was so complete Dahlen was sure he would have been able to hear a feather brushing against the ground.

Kira's gaze passed over the gathered nobles, unflinching. She turned back to Elenya, who nodded, then drew in a deep breath and spoke. "Oleg Marylin." All heads turned to the emissary, eyebrows raised, gazes flitting. None looked more shocked than Oleg himself. "You have served as the Belduaran emissary to the Dwarven Freehold of Durakdur for many years. You understand our culture and our people, just as you do that of Belduar. You are wise, measured, and kind. It is our belief that with you as Keeper of the Mountain, the relationship between our two peoples can flourish. What say you? Will you help us mend this bridge? Will you help us rebuild what has been broken?"

"You cannot be serious?" Geor Darna scoffed. "He is not of noble blood. He is an emissary, nothing more!"

"Hear, hear," the dark-haired noble said.

"You humans place too much stock in blood," Elenya said with a sigh. "There is no such thing as noble blood. Blood is blood. Nobility is in the doing of things. In that, Oleg has shown far more nobility than any of you." Elenya turned back to Oleg, who still looked as though he had just woken up from the most shocking dream of his life. "Well then, what say you, Oleg Marylin?"

Oleg looked down at the floor, the blood-stained cloth clenched between the fingers of both his hands. Around him, the Belduaran nobles were bickering, doing their best to hold back their contempt. The man shuffled his feet, lost in thought, then lifted his head, his gaze moving from Kira to Elenya. "The bodies of my king and my friends lie cold, awaiting their return to ash. If you help us take the bodies through the Southern Fold Gate and arrange proper pyres so that they may return to ash under the light of the sun, then I will accept. But not until that is done." He shook his head. "Not until they rest."

The nobles descended into silence as Kira stared back at Oleg. "It will be done, Oleg. Even in this, you show why you are the wisest choice. The sun will set within a few hours. I will arrange the Craftsmages to construct the pyres. Mirlak, arrange the virtuk wagons." Kira nodded towards Mirlak, who nodded back and made for the chamber's entrance, taking a handful of the Queensguard with him. "Come. Much has been lost this day. Let us see that the dead are sent into Heraya's embrace with the dignity they deserve."

HOURS LATER, WITH THE LIGHT of the setting sun spraying over the mountain peaks, Dahlen stood in the open basin that fronted the Southern Fold Gate. The warmth of the funeral pyres washed over his dirt and blood crusted skin, the light of the flames dancing across the faces of those gathered. It was only as he stood there he realised he'd not stopped shifting the bodies onto the carts long enough to even splash his face with water.

The basin was packed to overflowing with Belduaran nobles, Kingsguard, Durakduran and Ozyrnian Queensguard, and a spattering of other faces Dahlen didn't recognise. It would not have been possible to allow the entirety of the Belduaran people to witness the returning to ashes, but Oleg had said a ceremony would be performed once Belduar was rebuilt.

Dahlen stared into the fire, his chest tight as a clenched fist. Even there, as he felt the touch of the sun's light for the first time in months, he couldn't bring himself to find more than a sliver of happiness. In the heart of the flames, he could still see Daymon and Ihvon's cloth-wrapped bodies amongst the hundreds of others. The familiar sensation of tears threatened his eyes, his gaze unwavering.

He'd held no love for Daymon, but in a strange sort of way, he'd found a kind of kinship between them. They were both two young men, trailing in their fathers' shadows, trying to find their place in the world. Dahlen understood that pressure. The pressure to be something more, to be something special.

In travelling the continent with Erik and their father, Dahlen had not come across many people he had ever truly considered a friend. Growing attached to a person only meant it would be more difficult when he would eventually have to leave them or lose them. But in Ihvon, Dahlen had found a true friendship. The kind that simply was. The kind that needed few words and fewer explanations. Dahlen not only respected Ihvon, he had genuinely enjoyed the man's company. As the sparks rose into the dusk sky, Dahlen found himself thinking back to when the pair had sparred in the Heart's training yard – to when Ihvon had left Dahlen flat on his arse.

'Nine times out of ten, you win that fight.' A soft smile touched Dahlen's face as he thought of the words Ihvon had spoken when he had beaten Dahlen in the practice yard. "I guess we'll never know, my friend. I guess we'll never know…"

A few minutes passed in relative silence, the snap and crackle of the fire, the sniffle of tears, and the shuffling of feet the only sounds. Before the pyres had been lit, Oleg had spoken a few words to those gathered. A soft lament for the men and women lost. Even the nobles had barely uttered a word since then.

"You were my first choice."

Dahlen raised an eyebrow, turning his head to see Kira standing beside him. She had finally removed her plate armour and now wore a leather cuirass that flowed down into silken skirts, her muscled arms on display. The crown atop Kira's head and the rings in her blonde hair glinted in the firelight.

"You were my first choice," Kira repeated, answering Dahlen's raised eyebrow. "Oleg will make a fine Keeper. But you were my first choice."

"I'm not even Belduaran."

"No," Kira said plainly. "You're not. But the men and women of Belduar respect you. I see where I have no eyes, and I hear where I have no ears, Dahlen Virandr. Even so, had I chosen you, they would have had no choice in the matter."

"Then why didn't you?" Dahlen kept his gaze on the flames, drawing in a sharp breath as the fire truly caught on the cloth that garbed Ihvon, burning brighter.

"Because I see this is not yet your place. Where will you go? To your father?"

Dahlen nodded, feeling a steady stream of tears rolling over his cheek. "I will go to Argona. Our contact there should know where my father is. Or at the very least, he will be able to reach my father. I'll stay to see that Oleg is settled, then I will make my way."

"Will your companion be travelling with you?" Kira nodded towards Belina who stood a few feet to Dahlen's right, the light of the flames casting shifting shadows across her dark, blood-stained skin. He'd never seen the woman so sombre. It felt wrong. Like seeing water flow upwards.

"I'm not sure. That's like trying to predict which way the wind will blow."

Out of the corner of his eye, Dahlen saw Kira nodding. "Let me know what you require for your journey, and I will see you have it. Your father has been a friend to the dwarves of the Lodhar Freehold for hundreds of years, but you have now earned that in your own right, Dahlen Virandr. You are a friend here."

Dahlen pulled his eyes from the funeral pyres for a moment, meeting Kira's gaze. He allowed a half-smile to form on his lips, then dipped his head ever so slightly. "May your fire never be extinguished and your blade never dull, Queen Kira."

Chapter Thirty-Four

Onwards

The clinking of the buckles that held Alina firmly in her saddle on Rynvar's back barely pierced the rushing wind in her ears. With her hands gripped firmly around the handles at the front of the saddle, she looked down over the landscape below.

The city of Lostwren lay upon the flat plains of grass and rock that sprawled outwards in all directions. The city's sandy brown walls rose thirty feet or so, topped with crenelated battlements and intersected by square towers that rose another fifteen or twenty feet again. A mix of Lorian soldiers and warriors of House Vakira stood atop the walls, though there were far more Vakirans than Lorians.

Further into the city, the rooves of orange slate and the tiered seating of the semi-circular amphitheatre, for which Lostwren was famous, glowed in the light of the afternoon sun.

Alina raised her right fist, signalling the Wyndarii that rode with her to bank left. To her right Mera, Amari, and Lukira all gave the signal of acknowledgement.

"Circle back," Alina said to Rynvar, pressing her face to the deep orange scales at the side of the wyvern's neck so he could feel the vibrations of her voice. Rynvar gave a rumble of acknowledgement, then caught the wind and banked left with such speed Alina would have been ripped from the saddle were it not for the straps that connected it to a belt that wrapped around her waist.

As the wyvern circled back, Mera, Amari, Lukira, and near a hundred more Wyndarii following suit, Alina cast her gaze over her forces that had already surrounded the city.

The bulk of the warriors of her own House – House Ateres – fronted the main gates of the city, rippling banners of orange and white held high, the wyvern of House Ateres and the sigil of a free Valtara emblazoned across them. The forces of House Ateres numbered just over seven thousand. She could have mustered more, but they did not yet have the infrastructure to feed that many mouths on an expedition like this; they would have to rely on the strength of their spears, the fear of the wyverns, and the loyalty of the Valtaran people. Even from high above on her saddle, Alina saw the white plumes of Dayne's Andurii at the front of the Ateres lines and the shifting mass of Turik Baleer's cavalry.

To the left and right of the Ateres forces, spread around the city, Alina saw the colours of all the Major Houses. The green and gold of Deringal, Senya likely standing at the front; the red of House Herak; the yellow of House Thebal; and even the black of House Vakira and the pale blue of House Koraklon. If she squinted, she could make out some of the banners that belonged to Minor Houses – banners that, along with those of the Major Houses, hadn't been displayed in decades due to Lorian laws. Men and women of all the Houses had flocked to Alina's call, picking up their spears and shields in the name of a free Valtara. It was a powerful notion, a noble one. She would need to make use of it before the weariness of war took over.

With Senya Deringal and Vhin Herak openly supporting Alina, the warriors of their houses made up the bulk of the remaining numbers. If they could take Lostwren with little bloodshed, they would be able to add the might of all the banners that flew under House Vakira to their cause.

Alina didn't consider that to be too difficult a task. From the reports, the majority of Valtarans who fell under the banner of House Vakira supported Alina's rebellion. It was only Tula Vakira's desire to sit and wait that kept the people of Lostwren from the fray – that and the Lorian forces that now occupied the city. Alina had hoped to reach Lostwren before the imperial forces pushed Tula to re-declare House Vakira's allegiance to the empire, but she had quite clearly been too late. Even with that, the Vakiran forces within the city still looked to outnumber the Lorians. Alina was quietly confident that once her forces were in place, the white crests of the Andurii visible from the walls, the banners of a free Valtara rippling in the air, and the skies full of wyverns, they could convince the Vakiran forces to turn on the Lorians from within, and major bloodshed would be avoided. Where it was possible, she would prefer Valtarans not kill Valtarans.

A quick surrender would make all the difference.

Alina leaned forwards, pressing her body against Rynvar's, her right hand gripped around the saddle's handle, her left pressed against the wyvern's neck. As the wyvern circled back once more, dipping towards the white plumes of Dayne's Andurii, Alina couldn't hold back the smile that spread across her face or the pride that swelled in her chest. Not only were the banners of all six Major Houses rippling in the wind next to one another, for the first time in Alina's entire life, but ahead of her, near filling the skies, were over three hundred of her Wyndarii and their wyverns.

She had left a number to defend Skyfell and several more detachments to patrol the newly secured regions, but the bulk of her Wyndarii had travelled with her to Lostwren, scales of all colours glinting in the warm sunlight. The wyvern riders of Valtara were born again. And they would see Valtara free.

Mera sat astride Audin to Alina's right, her hands moving frantically through various signals before she pointed to the east. The signals Mera had made set Alina's hairs on end: Urgent. Friend. Attack.

Alina turned her gaze towards where Mera was pointing in time to see fifty wyverns drop from the sky towards the city walls. The wyverns dove at immense speeds, unleashing shrieks and roars as they did. There wasn't a doubt in Alina's mind that it was Hera Malik leading the charge. The wagon of a woman had already spent many nights arguing with Alina's plan to force a surrender, and now it looked as though she had decided to go behind Alina's back and take the option away from her. No matter the outcome here, Alina would have to make an example of Hera.

Alina watched for a few moments as the wyverns descended on the walls, shredding through the Lorian and Vakiran warriors alike in a blur of tooth and talon.

A blinding flash erupted from somewhere along the walls, followed by high-pitched screeches, and Alina watched as two wyverns fell from the sky, plumes of dark grey smoke trailing behind them as they slammed into the ground in clouds of dust. More flashes, then arcs of blue and purple lightning were ripping through the sky, crashing into wyverns. A hail of arrows followed the lightning; more wyverns fell.

"Gods damn it!" Alina signalled to Mera, Amari, and Lukira, who passed the attack message on to the other Wyndarii captains. They couldn't leave their sisters to die. *Elyara curse you, Hera.*

"Attack!" Alina shouted, loud enough so Rynvar could hear her over the wind. There was a moment's calm, and then the wyvern lurched forwards, his body rippling like a wave as he gathered momentum, then dropped into a dive.

To Alina's left, Mera and Audin matched Rynvar's descent, the wyvern's deep red scales glistening, Mera reaching for one of the three javelins strapped to the right side of her saddle. On her right, Amari and Lukira rode astride Syndil and Urin. The two brown-scaled wyverns were half Rynvar's size, but they were quick and ferocious. Past Alina's wing-sisters, she could see the rest of her Wyndarii diving towards the walls, their wyverns unleashing blood-chilling shrieks.

The air tore past Alina's face as Rynvar angled deeper into his dive, the bitter chill nipping at her exposed skin, causing her eyes to water. She reached down, her fingers brushing the spruce wood shafts of the three javelins strapped to the right side of her saddle. Without taking her eyes off the walls below, she undid the clasp of the first javelin, yanking the weapon free from its resting place, seeing her wing-sisters do the same out of the corners of her eyes.

Alina drew in a long breath, settling herself, then picked her target: a thick-chested man bearing the black lion of Loria on his breastplate.

By blade and by blood, I will find freedom, or I will die in the trying. Alina rolled her right shoulder, stretching out the muscles. She tightened her grip around the shaft of the javelin, the softer spruce wood feeling as light as a feather in comparison to the dense ash wood of a valyna.

Alina gripped the left handle of her saddle, the wind whipping past her as she leaned backwards, angling her body to throw the javelin. One of the first things a newly blooded wyvern rider learned was never to throw their javelin across the body of their wyvern. At the speeds wyverns moved, all it took was the slightest shift in balance to send sharp steel through the body of the creature that protected your life. When Alina had first bonded with Rynvar, there had been nobody to teach her, but luckily she had taken a keen interest in wyverns since she had been a young girl and had read every book on the creatures that had ever been stored within Redstone's library.

She waited for the thick-chested man to come within range, the beating of Rynvar's wings thumping in her ears. As the man lifted his sword and made to slice through the neck of a Wyndarii who had fallen from her wyvern and onto the ramparts, Alina pulled her arm back, the muscles in her shoulder and back bunching, then launched the javelin across Rynvar's flank.

The wyvern was lifting again, pulling away from the walls by the time Alina saw the javelin hammer into the man's chest with a heavy slap, knocking him backwards and sending him plummeting from the far side of the walls.

A rain of javelins followed Alina's, Lorian and Vakiran soldiers dropping like flies as the weapons found their marks. The wyverns roared and shrieked as they swept over the city, their riders unleashing piercing war cries.

As much as Alina wanted to join the shouts and cries, she could not. For although the fire of battle burned in her veins, she could also see the lifeless bodies of women and wyverns strewn about the ramparts and the ground below on either side of the wall. She could even see some of the Wyndarii who had survived their falls, fighting tooth and nail on the ramparts. She lifted her right arm and gave the signal for another javelin pass.

Twice more, Alina and her Wyndarii rained death on the Lorian and Vakiran soldiers who manned the walls, shredding them with javelins.

She regretted the loss of each Vakiran life, but Hera Malik had forced the situation; she had given the Vakirans no choice but to stand with the Lorians and defend the walls. And if Alina had to choose between the lives of Vakiran soldiers she had never met and her Wyndarii, there wasn't a choice to be had.

Bolts of lightning from Lorian mages and hails of arrows claimed the lives of several more wyverns and their riders.

As Rynvar circled back around for the fourth time, Alina took stock of the situation. They needed a plan. A battle of attrition was not the fight Alina wanted this day. And they would not take the city by simply harassing the walls – besides, she was out of javelins.

A quick glance showed her that Dayne and the other commanders had brought their ground forces closer to the city walls, likely confused as to what in the void was happening. *Gods damn you, Hera, for forcing my hand.* Alina hadn't seen Hera and her wyvern Yarsil amongst the dead or fighting on the walls – the woman must have avoided the sting of steel and lightning. But as she looked down, Alina could see a cluster of Wyndarii had formed atop the walls, not far from the gatehouse.

"Two birds, one stone," she whispered. Alina leaned in to Rynvar, pressing her head against his scales. "Draw up close to Mera."

Without a moment's hesitation, the wyvern angled his wings, caught the air, and glided next to Audin, Mera's wyvern.

"I'm going to land on the walls!" Alina roared at Mera, trying to raise her voice above the rushing wind.

"Are you mad?" Mera called back.

Alina smiled at that. Being called mad usually meant she was thinking along the right lines. She pointed down to where the surviving Wyndarii had formed near the gatehouse. "I'm not leaving them. If we can take the gatehouse, we can open the gates and let Dayne and the others in." Alina jerked backwards as a gust of wind caught Rynvar, almost sending him crashing into Audin. "The longer the fighting goes on, the more we lose. We need to end it. Me, you, Amari, and Lukira. The rest can support."

Mera hesitated for a moment, then nodded, pulling back to issue orders to the others. As Rynvar circled towards the walls, Alina patted at her weapons belt, feeling the hilts of the short swords strapped at either of her hips and the knives slotted into the leather strap across her lower back. She felt the weight of the small, circular dardik shield on her back. It always felt strange going to battle without a valyna gripped in her right fist and the handle of her ordo shield strapped to her arm. But the ordo and the valyna were too heavy for Wyndarii to carry; they would weigh the wyverns down too much.

After a few moments, Audin, Syndil, and Urin drew level with Rynvar. Alina gave the hand signal: attack.

She urged Rynvar down and gripped onto the handles of her saddle with all her strength as the wyvern plummeted, twisting left and right to avoid arcs of lightning and hails of arrows. "Mage," Alina shouted to Rynvar. "Kill."

Alina heard the ringing of steel as arrowheads caught Rynvar's scales at an angle and skittered away. Then Rynvar crashed down, vibrations jarring Alina's arms and shoulders as the wyvern dropped onto a Lorian mage in a spray of blood and bone, talons rending steel like paper.

As Rynvar ripped open the man's throat, Alina slipped a knife from her back, turned, and launched it through the eye of a Lorian soldier who was charging towards Rynvar from the back. She reached down, undoing the buckles that held her in place, pulling them free with practised ease, then slid from the wyvern's back, her feet finding stone with a *thud*.

"Go!" Alina roared, slapping her hand down against Rynvar's scales so hard it went numb from the sting. He was a stubborn beast and was always reluctant to leave her alone – which was a trait Alina actually appreciated, but staying on the walls would only turn him into an easy target.

The wyvern roared in response, whipping his tail and knocking several Lorians off the ramparts before snatching two soldiers in his talons and leaping into the air, blood and gore spraying as flesh tore and bone shattered. Roars rippled through the air as Audin, Syndil, and Urin followed after Rynvar and Mera, Amari, and Lukira drew close to Alina.

Alina shrugged her dardik shield from her back and slid a short sword from its scabbard at her hip, and then she was charging towards the cornered Wyndarii, towards the gatehouse. "For Valtara!"

"Forward!" Dayne roared at the top of his lungs, thrusting his spear into the air. Around him shouts and war cries rang out, men and women eager for the first taste of true battle. *If only they knew, they wouldn't be so eager.*

Marlin's hand clamped down on Dayne's shoulder, and the man leaned in close. "My lord, we cannot simply charge. Alina's plan was to force their surrender. The gates are closed, and we've not erected any siege equipment yet. We'll be at their mercy."

"You saw her land, Marlin. Alina is on those walls. We can't leave her there. We charge." Dayne shrugged off Marlin's hand and turned towards the walls, readying to break into a run.

Marlin lowered his voice, leaning closer. "Don't be stupid, Dayne. The lives of these men and women are in your hands now. You've been away a long time, but you're not just making decisions for yourself anymore."

Dayne narrowed his gaze at Marlin, then grunted, turning towards the Andurii. "My sister, your chosen leader, fights on the walls of Lostwren," he called out, bellowing so loud his lungs burned. "Will you leave her to fight alone? Will the Andurii leave her to fight alone?"

"HA-OOH!" came the response, a chorus of spears clattering off shields.

The majority of the main force couldn't hear a word Dayne shouted, but once the Andurii started to charge, the rest would follow. That was the reputation Alina wanted him to build, and he would build it.

"What about the gates, Dayne?" Marlin grabbed the back of Dayne's helmet, locking their gazes. "Heroics are one thing, but we'd need a battering ram to break them down, and we've not yet built one."

Dayne pulled Marlin's head against his, their helmets clinking. "I am the battering ram."

With that, Dayne turned and broke into a sprint, hearing the thundering of feet charging behind him. He had not yet told the Andurii, or anyone outside of his family, that he could command the Spark. He had hoped to be able to keep that a secret for a while longer – Valtarans had a tempestuous relationship with mages – but he was going to have to tell them eventually. Today might as well be that day.

As Dayne charged towards the forty-foot walls of sandy stone, he opened himself to the Spark, feeling its warmth flood him. He let his consciousness drift across the pulsating elemental strands, his mind lingering on the cool touch of Air and the calming sensation of Spirit. Through his years with Belina, Dayne taught himself to use the Spark subtly, to make the slightest of shifts and adjustments to give himself an edge. But training with Aeson had taught him not only to refine that ability but also to harness the raw power within himself. There was going to be nothing subtle about what he was about to do.

Blood pumping, heart pounding, Dayne's feet ate the ground.

"Shields!" he roared, lifting his shield and angling it as a shadow rose from the walls above, a hail of arrows momentarily blocking out the light. The slightest of glances back over his shoulder showed him that the Andurii had not charged as a single unit. A clutch of warriors had set off at Dayne's back without hesitation, but others had lingered, leaving them off the pace. In truth, he didn't blame them. One of his first commands as their Andurios was to order them to charge towards a closed gate. He was more surprised that any of them at all had chosen to follow him so blindly.

Dayne pushed his shield further away from his body, making the angle steeper. Already, his arm burned from the weight of it, but the Spark flooding his veins pushed the pain to the edges of his mind. A number of *thunks* sounded as arrows smacked against the front of his shield, the angle and concave shape of the ordo sending them skittering away. But then a burst of splinters sprayed, and Dayne turned his gaze to see a steel arrowhead jutting through the wood. There was a second spray of splinters and another arrow came through the shield, the edge of its head slicing through the skin of Dayne's forearm. He hissed, gritted his teeth, and pressed on.

A glance over his shield rim told Dayne they were almost at the gates. Dayne pulled deeply on the Spark, drawing in thick threads of Air and Spirit, weaving them round each other, letting the Spirit augment the Air. He allowed the threads to swell, pushing energy into them. There were more precise ways to open the gates with the Spark. But all of them took time and patience, neither of which Dayne had. Alina's plan had been to turn the Vakirans within the city against the imperial forces. That was still doable, but only if the odds were stacked on their side. They needed to get inside the walls.

He saw threads of Fire, Air, and Spirit whirling through the air above, bolts of lightning ripping across the sky. From his gauge, there were only four mages – and judging by the focus of their threads, they were too focused on the wyverns to contemplate reinforcing the gate. The empire wasn't used to facing mages on the battlefield. They were accustomed to having complete superiority when it came to the Spark. That made them complacent; it made them vulnerable.

He drew in a long breath, the sounds around him capitulating to the thrum of the Spark in his blood, the world crystallising for a brief moment, then unleashed the thick threads of Air and Spirit slamming them into the centre of the wooden gates. A thunderous boom sounded, clouds of stone dust pluming from where the gate was fixed to the wall, but the gate remained closed.

More arrows skittered off Dayne's raised shield, one piercing through the bottom in a spray of wood. Some of his Andurii had caught up with him; they were more used to carrying the weight of the heavy ordo, valyna, and armour. They pulled alongside him, leaving enough space so as not to provide an easy target.

They were only thirty paces from the gates.

Once more, Dayne slammed thick threads of Air and Spirit into the re-inforced wood, and once more, the gates creaked and stone dust plumed, but they remained standing.

"Is there a plan, Andurios?" one of the Andurii, a woman named Tarine Valanis who had previously been one of Alina's Redstone guard, roared. As she shouted, an arrow burst through her shield in a spray of splinters and stopped shy of plunging into her eye.

"Keep the shield further from your face!" Dayne called back. The woman had four markings of the spear on her arm, but she had never seen true war. She had never had to protect herself from a hail of arrows. "We go through!"

Tarine gave Dayne a sharp nod, shifting her shield further from her face, glancing towards the arrowhead that now protruded from the inside of the rim.

They were only ten paces from the gates.

Dayne clenched his jaw and pulled from the Spark one last time, feeling the warmth of it burn in his veins. Through his threads of Spirit and Air, he could feel the subtle vibrations of the gate's drawbar snapping, the wood weakening, the metal twisting. With a roar, he unleashed another torrent of Air and Spirit, and the gate burst inwards, hinges snapping, wood splintering. The iron-braced gates lifted through the air and slammed into the Lorian and Vakiran soldiers who had been waiting on the other side. Screams and cries rang out as the men and women were crushed beneath the weight of the structure that had once protected them.

"Forward!" Dayne roared, a chorus of cries answering him, more and more Andurii pulling level with him.

Dayne charged through the gates, ramming into the soldiers on the other side. Their lines had been broken by the crashing gates, and Dayne slipped into the cracks. He swung his left arm forward, ramming the rim of his shield into a man's nose, hearing the snap of bone accompany the spray of blood. As the man fell backwards, Dayne thrust his valyna forwards and into the belly of another Lorian before sweeping it to the side, creating space. He moved like a man possessed, taking advantage of the disarray the gates had created. Blood sprayed wherever he sliced, and bone snapped under the weight of his shield. He whipped threads of Air around himself, knocking the soldiers back, keeping them at the distance he needed.

As Dayne carved through the Lorians, the Andurii crashed in beside him, spears striking out like vipers, wyvern-emblazoned shields glistening in the sun.

A hand clamped down on Dayne's shoulder, pulling him back, and he heard Marlin's voice. "You're Andurii now. We fight together. We fight as one. Call it."

Dayne clenched his jaw, quelling the fire in his veins. For twelve years, blood and steel was all he had known. That hadn't changed, but now he wore the wyvern of House Ateres, and he fought beside men and women who shared the same cause. By blade and by blood, they would break the chains from around their people's neck. He cast a glance towards the walls where he saw wyverns swooping and slicing through Lorians and Vakirans alike, a clutch of Wyndarii fighting near the gatehouse. He needed to get up there, but he couldn't leave his Andurii alone. He had to find a way to turn the battle quickly. "Shield wall!"

Feet shifted, ordo shields snapping together as the Andurii reacted to the call. It felt strange for Dayne to be fighting in a formation again, foreign and yet soothingly familiar. Marlin stood to his left, Tarine and the young Iloen to his right.

"Let's show them what Valtaran steel tastes like," Dinekes Ilyon, one of the new Andurii captains, said from behind Dayne. The Andurii captains lined the right side of the shield wall, with Dayne at the front. It may have been many years since he'd last fought in a shield wall, but most of it had been like muscle memory. He still wasn't skilled enough with the spear and shield to truly operate at the front right of the shield wall, but his ability with the Spark filled the gaps in his skill. The one thing that would take time for him to get used to again was the weight of the shield in his left hand, the burn in his shoulder.

With the shield wall formed, the Andurii pushed forwards, slow and steady, step after step, dirt grinding beneath their feet. Spears bit into flesh and shields forced the Lorians and Vakirans backwards. Alone, the Vakirans might have been capable of standing against the steady shield march, but with their forces scattered amongst the less organised Lorian soldiers, they couldn't forge themselves into a coherent shield wall. And so they died like lambs under the unceasing march of the Andurii shield wall. The men and women around Dayne had not been Andurii long. They hadn't yet earned the reputation of the legendary warriors who had come before them, but each of them were chosen for their skill, strength, and resolve. They were the finest warriors House Ateres had to offer. Many were blademasters or spearmasters; some were both. And there were no warriors in Epheria more legendary than the blade and spearmasters of Valtara – had the empire not possessed the strength of dragonfire, history would have been different.

As the Andurii pushed through the yard that fronted the gates of Lostwren, and more of the free Valtaran forces charged through the gates and reinforced their flanks, the city's defenders fed the ground with blood and began to break.

A tingling sensation ignited in the back of Dayne's mind, and before he could react, threads of Earth and Spirit struck out towards the Andurii on the left side of the wall. Screams and cries rang out as the greaves that guarded the shins of those Andurii collapsed inwards, snapping bones.

As the Andurii from the other rows moved forwards to fill the gaps left by their injured companions, Dayne followed the threads back to where he saw a Lorian Battlemage riding astride a black war horse, the power of the Spark radiating from them.

"Take my place," Dayne roared to Dinekes, who stood behind him. Dayne heard Marlin shouting at him, but he ignored the man, leaping out of the shield wall. He swung his shield forwards, slamming the rim into the throat of an unsuspecting Lorian soldier, crushing his windpipe, then swung it back, smashing a man's jaw.

Dayne pulled in threads of Air, feeling their cool touch over his skin. He clenched his fist around the shaft of his spear, threw his shoulder back, then launched the spear through the air with every ounce of strength in his body. As the spear sliced through the air towards the Battlemage astride the black war horse, Dayne corrected its course with threads of Air and sliced through the Battlemage's own threads with Spirit.

The spear caught the mage in the chest like a battering ram hitting a gate, Dayne's threads of Air pushing it forward with inhuman power. The spear punched through the mage's sternum and lifted them from the saddle of their horse, sending them careening backwards.

Dayne fell back towards the Andurii line. He snatched up a dropped spear, falling in beside Marlin, Dinekes moving back to the second row. Around them, the rest of the Valtaran forces were carving through the Lorian and Vakiran forces alike. At least two of the Lorian Battlemages were now dead, and Dayne couldn't sense any more threads around them.

"That was idiotic," Marlin growled as Dayne fell in beside him.

"That mage needed to die. He's dead now."

Marlin grunted in response.

"We need to get to Alina. We're winning here, but she—"

A sharp roar ripped through the air, and Dayne turned to see Alina's wyvern, Rynvar, drop from the sky, drawing level with the walls. Then Alina was leaping from the ramparts, the orange spirals on her armour giving her away. For a few moments, Dayne's heart clenched as Alina hung in the air. Then with the ease of someone mounting a horse, Alina landed on the saddle, barely flinching as she slammed down, her free hand gripping onto the saddle's handle. As Alina and Rynvar descended towards the fighting in the yard, more wyverns followed, roaring and shrieking, their riders calling out war cries. The sight and sound alone caused the Lorian and Vakiran soldiers to hesitate, their gazes turning to the skies.

Javelins rained down from the descending Wyndarii, Lorian soldiers dropping in sprays of blood. The wyverns followed the javelins, crashing down on top of the waiting Lorians, talons tearing through armour, teeth ripping limbs.

Rynvar, orange scales reflecting the sun's light with an incandescent glow, dropped down atop three Lorians. Two of the soldiers were crushed beneath the wyvern's weight, blood spraying as talons sliced deep. The third soldier stumbled backwards, blood spraying from the stump of their neck, their head firmly caught in Rynvar's jaws.

As more of the wyverns crashed down, ripping apart the already wavering Lorian forces, Alina looked to Dayne, then began to call out. "Warriors of House Vakira. We are not your enemy!"

It took Dayne a moment to understand why Alina had looked to him, but then it clicked into place, and he pulled on the Spark, weaving threads of Air and Spirit into his sister's voice, amplifying it so it resounded through the yard. "We fight for a free Valtara! Fight beside us rather than against us! Any who turn their spears on the Lorians will be granted a place in a free Valtara, as our brothers and sisters!"

Tension hung in the air, the snarls and pulsing chirps of the wyverns breaking the silence that had descended. Then, slowly, men and women in the black of Vakira, ordo shields on their arms, black, swirling tattoos at the sides of their head, turned their spears towards the Lorain soldiers they had previously fought beside.

ALINA RESTED HER HAND ON the orange scales of Rynvar's snout, her thumb tracing the black edges. "Rest easy. You did well."

The wyvern leaned his head into Alina's hand. Soft clicking reverberated from his throat, followed by a low rumble. Alina smiled, tracing her fingers along a groove that had been cut into the scales at the side of Rynvar's snout, less than half a finger's width deep. Wyvern scales were strong, but they weren't impenetrable. She drew in a deep breath, wiped the sweat from her brow, and looked around the courtyard that fronted Lostwren's main gates.

All around, Lorian soldiers were being bound with rope and chains. Healers were tending to the wounded, strapping bandages around wounds, splinting damaged limbs, and trying to ease the pain of those who would not survive their injuries – unlike the Lorians, the Valtarans did not have access to healers who could use the Spark. Alina saw the bodies of at least ten wyverns lying about the yard. Some lay in pools of their own blood, their bodies sliced open by arrows and spears. Smoke still drifted from knotted wounds of melted scales where the Lorian mages' lightning had knocked the creatures from the sky. She did not doubt they had lost at least a score more wyverns across the city.

"Alina."

Alina turned to see Dayne walking towards her, the white-crested helmet of the Andurii nestled in the crook of his right arm, his shield strapped to his left.

Dayne dropped his shield, a cloud of dust rising as it hit the ground with a clang. He reached out and grasped Alina's forearm, pulling her closer and planting a kiss on her forehead. He pulled away, streaks of blood marring the weak smile that spread across his face. "The city is yours. With the exception of a few, every Vakiran soldier we've come across has pledged allegiance to the cause. Tula Vakira and her personal guard are still holed up in the keep, but I don't think their decision will be any different."

Alina stared at her brother wordlessly for a moment, her gaze tracing his face, her mind replaying his words. Her heart still beat faster every time she saw him. He was alive. Such a small, simple, fact. But it still felt strange to her. Her brother was alive. And not only was he alive, he stood before her wearing their father's armour, leading the Andurii, fighting for a free Valtara. All she wanted to do was embrace him and sob – to cry the tears for everything that had happened, the tears they should have shed together across the years – but everything was so much more complicated now. Aside from Alina's anger at Dayne for leaving in the first place, he was also a clear obstacle to her leadership. He was the rightful heir to House Ateres. He was the eldest and there were many who would rather see him as the head of the House.

"Alina?" Dayne reached out, eyes narrowing as he looked her over. "Are you hurt? Rest. I'll fetch a healer."

"I'm fine," Alina snapped, slapping Dayne's probing hand away. "I'm not your child, Dayne. There are many with far graver wounds than myself. Your Andurii, did they take many losses?"

"Forty-three. More than I'd like," he said, scratching at a patch of dried blood on his cheek. "But less than I'd feared when charging through those gates. What happened, Alina? The wyverns attacking wasn't part of the plan."

"Hera Malik." The name left Alina's lips with a growl. A deep rumble resonated from behind Alina, and she turned to see Rynvar looking towards the sky, veins of ice running through his blue eyes. Following the wyvern's gaze, she saw several dark shadows descending towards the yard with the sun at their backs. "Speak of Efialtír, and he shall appear."

Five wyverns dropped into the courtyard, alighting on the stone, their wingbeats drumming up clouds of dust. Alina recognised the dull yellow scales of Hera Malik's wyvern, Yarsil. She strode towards them, Dayne and Rynvar following as Hera and the other Wyndarii slid from the backs of their wyverns.

"What a battle!" Hera called out to Alina, gazing about the yard and raising both her arms in the air. "Onwards to Myrefall!"

Alina's fingers curled into fists as she marched towards Hera, her heart thumping, jaw clenching. She swung her right fist and cracked Hera in the cheek.

The woman stumbled, touching her hand to where Alina's fist had broken the skin and drawn blood. "How dare—"

Alina slammed her fist into the bridge of Hera's nose, feeling a crunch beneath the weight of the strike, blood spraying down over Hera's mouth and chin.

As Hera fell backwards, her wyvern, Yarsil, unleashed a roar and leapt towards Alina, jaws opening, eyes burning with a cold fury. The wyvern spread his wings, reaching its neck out, but before he got within a foot of Alina, Rynvar crashed into him, jaws closing around his neck. Rynvar lifted the smaller wyvern off the ground, then slammed Yarsil down, pinning him against the stone.

"Let him go!" Hera roared. She pulled her sword from the scabbard at her hip and lunged, blade driving towards Alina's chest.

Alina twisted, allowing the blade to slide past her, then slammed her hand down on the flat of the extended blade and swung her elbow into Hera's nose as the woman's momentum carried her forwards. Alina extended her foot and sent Hera sprawling to the ground, blood streaming from her nose. "You risked the lives of every warrior under our banner." Alina kept her voice level and calm as she stepped over Hera, who lay on the stone, propped up on her elbows, blood still pouring from her nostrils. "You disobeyed direct orders. You were reckless, idiotic, and selfish."

"We won!"

"Tell that to our dead." The sound of shuffling feet caused Alina to glance up and see the Wyndarii and wyvern loyal to Hera standing a few feet away, weapons drawn. It took a moment for Alina to understand why they were not charging. Then she saw Dayne standing to the left, shield in one hand, sword in the other, shards of shattered stone floating in the air around him.

Shrieks, rhythmic chirps, and roars signalled the return of Mera, Amari, Lukira, and the other Wyndarii Alina had sent to scout the rest of the city.

Alina slid her sword from the scabbard at her hip and lowered it to Hera's neck, tilting the blade at an angle so as to lift Hera's chin. "Today, you caused the deaths of over twenty of your wing-sisters, along with their wyverns. You caused the deaths of hundreds of Vakiran warriors – *Valtaran* warriors. You're responsible for every man, woman, and wyvern that died here today. What say you, Hera of House Malik?"

In spite of herself, Alina couldn't help but be impressed by the way Hera held Alina's gaze despite the steel at her neck. The woman stared back at Alina, swallowing hard in the silence between them. "I say I will take whatever is due. Death was not my intention, but it is what my actions have caused." She drew in a short breath. "Forgive me."

Alina hadn't expected that. She lifted her gaze from Hera and looked at the gathered crowd around them. The entire courtyard had ceased in its actions. Hera's Wyndarii and their wyverns still stood ready to pounce on Alina, only Dayne's presence stopping them, shards of broken stone swirling around him. Mera, Amari, and Lukira had dismounted and now stood only a few feet away, swords drawn. Many others – warriors, healers, and citizens alike – had stopped in their tracks, watching, waiting.

Fuck. Hera wasn't stupid. Anything Alina did now would spread through the camp like wildfire.

Alina ran her tongue along the inside of her bottom teeth, staring down at Hera, who, to her credit, had not moved her neck from Alina's blade. Hera gave a slight flinch at the sound of Yarsil whining, Rynvar still pinning the wyvern's neck to the ground. Alina exhaled slowly, then pulled the blade away from Hera's neck. "You will personally build the pyres for the dead. You, and those who followed you, will burn the bodies so they may see rest." Alina reached out her hand and pulled Hera to her feet, staring into the woman's eyes. "I know we don't see eye-to-eye, Hera. But we both want the same thing. We both want a free Valtara. This city could have been taken without bloodshed. The Vakirans are as Valtaran as you and I. They are our people. There will be plenty of blood to come."

Hera nodded, her gaze wavering for the first time. "It will be done... Thank you."

Alina leaned in closer, dropping her voice to a near-whisper. "By blade and by blood, if you ever again challenge my leadership the way you did today, I will take your head and stand it on a spear before the gates of Redstone." Alina held her stare on Hera's, unblinking. She wanted the woman to understand. She would fix the head on the spear herself.

"I will not." Hera's gaze flitted from Alina to her wyvern, Yarsil, who had grown increasingly still under Rynvar's weight. "Please, let him go."

Alina nodded. "Rynvar. Release."

The wyvern released his grip on Yarsil's throat but hovered over him a moment, a deep growl resonating in his throat – a warning.

Yarsil pulled himself to his feet, balancing with his forelimbs, shaking his head and neck like a dog would do when wet. Blood trickled over his scales where Rynvar had bitten his neck.

As Hera moved to comfort Yarsil, Alina turned to Dayne, who had allowed the shards of stone to drop to the ground.

"She is not the forgetting type," he said, gesturing towards Hera. He looked wearier than before, his eyes sunken, his legs unsteady. She had only ever seen Dayne use his magic a handful of times when she was younger, and even then, she barely remembered it, but she did remember seeing him grow weary after. But she had never seen him use it like he had this day: smashing in the gates of Lostwren, ripping through the ranks of Lorians and Vakirans alike, whirling shards of stone around himself as though he were in a hailstorm. Her brother had become far stronger than she had given him credit for. "You should have taken her head."

"Once, you told me not a single life you'd taken had brought you any happiness. Now you tell me I should have killed one of my own?"

"Her death wouldn't have brought you happiness, but it would have brought you safety. She's a Wyndarii, she has strength. You don't leave someone like that waiting around."

"I want to destroy the empire, Dayne. Not replace it." Alina stared into her brother's eyes, finding nothing but weariness staring back at her. "Have your Andurii march through the streets. Let the white crests and the sigil of House Ateres be seen. Once the city is secure and the Lorians contained, you have my permission to refill your ranks with warriors of your choosing, as is custom. We march onwards to Myrefall at dawn's light."

Chapter Thirty-Five

The Pain in Waiting

Aeson stood atop a low ridge, arms folded, looking down over the small camp they'd been living in for over three weeks. It was nestled in beside a patch of dead trees and a high rock formation, with a deep furrow in the dried earth near the northern edge that had once been a river. Three weeks and they'd heard nothing from Baldon's kin on the other side of the Burnt Lands. Nothing to tell Aeson if Erik and Calen were alive or dead.

Every morning he woke in a cold sweat, despite the sweltering heat that radiated from the Burnt Lands. Nightmares plagued him; twisted dreams of dark things. Each night he watched his sons die. Erik in the wasteland, driven mad by Efialtír's touch, torn to shreds by Valerys. Dahlen at the tip of a Lorian blade or sent to Achyron's halls by the poison of the Hand whilst he slept.

Over the past four centuries Aeson had made as many enemies as he had friends. If he were to die chasing Erik into the Burnt Lands, Dahlen would be left alone to face the seeds Aeson had sown. And the likelihood was that he would die if he attempted to do so. There would come a point where Aeson simply wouldn't be able to wait for Erik any longer.

Naia, my love. Please guide me. Be my compass.

Aeson closed his eyes as the warm, sand-dusted breeze swept over his skin. He pictured Naia's face in his mind. Her eyes, brown with flecks of green and gold. Those eyes had held more love than Aeson had felt in hundreds of years. They saw him, saw everything he had forgotten about who he was and who he needed to be. That nose, the way it crinkled when she smiled. Those lips that scrunched together when she knew he was up to something. Images turned to sensations as Aeson remembered the soft touch of Naia's cheek against his fingers, the feeling of her hair as he ran his fingers through it. But more than anything else, he remembered how they would stay awake until the early hours just talking. He would have listened to the sweet sound of her voice until the rivers dried, mountains crumbled, and the wheels of time stopped turning. She'd always been more clever than Aeson could have ever hoped to be, always quicker to comprehend, always first to see the way forward. What's more, every word Naia spoke made sense. She *understood* the world, and talking about it brought her so much joy. Often times she would have persuaded him to her point of view within five minutes, but he would allow her to argue for hours just to see the passion in her eyes.

A soft smile touched his lips. Aeson opened his eyes as a tear rolled down his cheek. He could have filled an ocean with tears and never spent long enough mourning the death of his heart. The death of his heart after the sundering of his soul. Naia and Lyara. All he had left tethering him to the mortal plane was Erik, Dahlen, and the visceral need to carve apart the people who shattered his world.

Aeson cast one more look over the Burnt Lands. From where he stood, he could see over the ridge that marked the beginning of the arid waste-land, an ocean of sand broken by patches of rock and ruined cities obliter-ated by Fane Mortem's Blood Magic, reduced to remnants of a time long past. Aeson had tried to enter the waste only once before, almost four hundred years ago. He and Therin had taken a group to search Ilnaen, to see if there was anything in the ruins of the city that might give them hope. They had made it no more than a few miles in when a mage by the name of Goran Freck stumbled and smashed his head on a rock. The group made the decision to rest in a cave while Goran's wounds were tended – they'd spent weeks in the saddle trekking through Lorian lands from Highpass to Copperstille, and none of them had argued against the opportunity to get a few days' rest.

Now that he looked back, he could see the signs of the madness setting in: the tempers flaring where there had been no need, the sideways stares, the bubbling anger. By the fourth day, Goran himself, a man that Aeson considered a close friend, had slit the throats of three men while they slept, muttering of betrayal and slithering snakes as he did so. Aeson held Goran while he died, after driving a knife through the man's heart. He could remember it now, the whispers in his mind, the oily sensation that crept through his body – the blood on his hands.

Fifteen souls had entered the wasteland. Only three left alive: him, Therin, and Halya Dreken. Even that had only been possible due to Therin holding onto his mind a little longer than the others. Had they made it any further into the Burnt Lands, there wouldn't have been a hope of them finding their way back out. Aeson wasn't sure what kind of magic had created the illusion on the edge of the Burnt Lands that made them seem endless, but by the time they'd stepped through and knelt on solid ground, the whispers in Aeson's head had come far closer to convincing him to take his own life than he'd ever admit.

Aeson drew in a breath, the warm, dry air filling his lungs, then exhaled slowly, allowing his memories to fade. He made his way down the side of the ridge upon which he had been standing, his fingers aching from the climb. He would simply have jumped and softened his landing with threads of Air, but his ability to touch the Spark had been even more unreliable recently than it had been before. By the time he'd made it to the bottom, his fingers and palms were coated with a mix of wet and dry blood where the rockface had reopened the cuts he had earned climbing up each of the previous days. He didn't mind the stinging; pain was a reminder he was still alive.

"See anything new today?" Therin asked, a mocking tone in his voice. Elves weren't known for their sense of humour – at least, not among humans – and Therin, even after centuries, was still not much different. But the elf had a dry sarcastic wit that only became apparent after some time.

"Aye," Aeson said, taking his place beside Therin, looking over the small camp. Four tents stood at the base of the rock formation, hidden from the view of anyone who might be passing by – though Aeson didn't think that would be an issue this close to the Burnt Lands. Four elven rangers had stayed with them under orders from Thalanil, but the rest had returned. At present, all four of the rangers sat on rocks or on the ground, laughing hysterically at Dann who sat in the dirt with his legs crossed, all his attention focused on something in his hands. Baldon, the Angan, was perched atop a flat rock, his long, fur-covered legs folded, his eyes closed. "I saw an elf with a sense of humour."

Therin smiled. "Rare, those are."

"Have you heard anything of Alea and Lyrei?"

Therin shook his head, pressing the fingers of his right hand into his cheeks then dragging them down. "They will have been punished for failing in their oath to protect Calen. But with the storm that is coming, I imagine the elders will be lenient."

Aeson let out a grunt. Elves were obsessive in their adherence to honour. So much so that it often bordered stupidity.

"What of Lyrei?" Therin asked.

"What of her?"

Therin raised an unimpressed eyebrow.

"It is up to her to complete her Holmdúr, Therin. She stepped over a line."

The elf gave a tut. "You *both* stepped over a line, Aeson."

"When we return to Aravell, I will speak to her." As silence settled between them, Aeson folded his arms, turning his attention back to Dann and the elves. He couldn't remember the last time he'd seen four elves

444

erupting with such genuine laughter. "What's Dann doing now? He's not trying that trick with his thumb again, is he?"

Therin shook his head, letting out a deep laugh. "Come on, it's better to show you."

Aeson followed Therin over to the centre of the small camp where Dann and the elves sat. He squinted as he moved closer, trying to see what Dann held in his hands. "Is he… is he whittling?"

Therin nodded. "That's not what's funny."

"You're all just jealous," Dann said, shrugging, as he worked a small knife into the block of wood in his hand. That drew another round of laughter.

"What's he doing?" Aeson whispered to Therin.

"He's trying to develop his valúr." Therin smiled, a touch of laughter in his voice, but Aeson could also see a sliver of pride in Therin's face. Therin didn't take to many people, and when he did, he was often still withdrawn, but Aeson saw a connection growing between Therin and Dann as they'd travelled. In truth, Aeson understood why Therin had taken a liking to the young man. Dann was the living embodiment of a pain in the arse, but Aeson admired his heart and his loyalty.

"And why, in the name of all the gods, is he trying to do that? And now, of all times?"

"Is there a better time than while we sit on our hands waiting?" Therin raised an eyebrow, and Aeson shrugged, acquiescing. "When we feel helpless, we often turn to things that are within our control, something to grasp on to, something to ground us."

Aeson nodded, softening. "Is he any good?"

Therin choked on his laughter. "I've never seen anyone as terrible in my life, and I've lived a very long time." He reached into the pocket of his robes and produced a small piece of carved wood that seemed to have no discernible shape whatsoever.

Aeson took the piece of wood, turning it over in his hands. Up close it did look somewhat like a face, but the features were squashed and mis-shapen, one eye almost twice as large as the other and what looked to be something resembling a nose but instead seemed more like a smashed apple. "What *is* it?"

Therin let out a sigh, his mouth drawing up in a thin line. "It's meant to be me."

"You've looked better."

"He's doing you now."

"He's *what?*" Aeson looked across at Dann who lifted his head and met Aeson's gaze, holding up the partly-carved wooden block in his hands, igniting a chorus of laughter from the elves gathered around him.

"Elyara, give me patience. I'm going to string him up by his ankles."

"He finds light in the darkest of places," Therin said, his expression sombre as he looked at Dann, who had turned back to carving the wood. "It's a special quality. He jokes and he laughs, but he's lost, Aeson. He's seen no more than twenty summers. He's thousands of miles from his home, and those closest to him are beyond his saving. Give him a break. He's trying."

∽

As NIGHT SET IN, DANN lay with his head resting on his satchel, which he'd placed atop a low, flat rock, his blanket draped over his legs. As unnatural as the heat was during the day, at night the air was as cold as any he'd known in The Glade.

The others sat around him, gathered by the fire. Languin, Thrain, and Alyra sat to Dann's left, huddled together playing a game with strange twelve-sided dice, while the other elven ranger that had been left with them, Ilwin, stood watch atop the nearby ridge in case any travellers stumbled upon them or the others returned from the Burnt Lands.

Therin and Aeson sat at the other side of the fire, engaged in deep conversation, the light of the flames dancing across their faces. Normally Dann's curiosity would have been scratching at him to hear what they were talking about, but at that moment he didn't care. It didn't matter if they were talking of war, rebellion, betrayal, or their favourite type of cheese. None of it made a difference. All that mattered was Calen and Rist.

Dann wasn't sure how he was *meant* to feel: sad, angry, alone. When Rist was taken back in Camylin all those months ago, Dann had been certain they would find him again. Everything Aeson had said made sense. If Rist could indeed use magic, or 'touch the Spark', as the others had called it, surely the empire wouldn't have killed him. Rist *was* alive. He just knew it. But Dann had always thought that he and Calen would go together, because that was what they did – they stayed together. Since they were little, the three of them had been inseparable. Calen had been the heart, Rist had been the brain, and Dann had been the idiot they looked out for. They were his brothers, the only ones he'd ever had. But now, not only was he alone, he was helpless. All he could do was sit around and wait.

He lifted himself into a sitting position and reached into his pocket, pulling out the block of wood he had been carving, rolling it around in his hands. His valúr.

Of War and Ruin

'It is elven custom that any elf who wishes to hold an instrument designed to take life must also learn to create.' Therin's words when Dann had found him sketching.

Dann ran his thumb over the rough wood, the firelight causing shadows to flicker across the wooden features. He remembered sitting in the back of the cart almost a year ago, his hands covered in blood – the blood of the first man he'd ever killed. Dann remembered seeing Calen on the ground, a man stood over him gripping a double-bladed axe. He remembered lunging forwards. He remembered the bite of the steel as his sword plunged into the man's neck, the crunch of bone, the release as the blade burst out the other side. Dann closed his eyes for a moment, his fingers tightening around the carving in his hand, the memories flitting through his mind.

His hands trembled, a lump forming in his throat. His mouth felt dry as cotton, his palms clammy. He opened his eyes, looking down, seeing blood covering his fingers, staining his palms, dripping from the carving. His heart beat so viciously he could hear it thumping in his ears. Clenching his fist around the carving one last time, he tossed it into the fire, watching as the flames swallowed it whole, a few sparks rising into the night.

He looked down. No blood marred his hands, at least not physically. *I can't clean that stain by carving a piece of wood.* Dann's breath trembled as he drew in slowly and exhaled. *It was shit anyway.*

"You humans are strange creatures, Dann Sureheart." Dann hadn't heard Baldon approach. The Angan stepped from the dark of night, the firelight glimmering in his amber eyes, then gracefully set himself on the ground beside Dann, folding his long, willowy legs beneath him. No matter how much time Dann spent around Baldon, he still couldn't get used to the Angan's appearance. He was *almost* human, except he wasn't. His body was covered in a thick grey fur, as rough as a wolfpine's. The nails at the end of his fingers and toes were more akin to claws than anything else. The fur on his face was shorter than the rest of his body. His brow was thick and harsh, his eyes a golden amber that glimmered in the night. His nose was the only part of his face besides his lips devoid of hair. It was black and leathery, like a wolf's, flatter than a human's, wider, with curled nostrils and a narrow groove that ran down through his lip.

Dann raised his eyebrows in surprise. He hadn't spoken much with Baldon. The Angan didn't speak much with anyone. *Yeah, we're the strange ones.* "Sureheart?"

Baldon pouted, fixing Dann with an intense stare, golden eyes glinting. "It is the name you have earned. As Therin Eiltris is Silverfang, Aeson Virandr is Broken One, you are Sureheart."

447

Dann nodded, pretending any of what Baldon had said made sense. He would have pressed the question further if he'd thought Baldon would have given him a straight answer. But from the little Dann could tell of the Angan, he spoke more riddles than Therin.

The fire crackled and popped, spitting embers into the night, joining the song of insects and the whistle of the wind. Dann couldn't help himself. He shifted to his right so that he faced Baldon, curiosity getting the better of him. "Why are we strange?"

"You spend hours carving your thoughts into the wood. Then you cast the wood into the fire, burning time you cannot get back." Baldon lingered on each word, his voice harsh. The Angan always spoke that way, as though he didn't trust his tongue to produce the correct sounds.

"It was shit," Dann said with a shrug.

Baldon drew in a deep breath, staring towards the fire, the light reflecting in his eyes. "To master a craft, one must first fail in every way possible."

"Where I come from, we have a saying that's pretty similar. 'Before you can run, you must first learn to walk.'"

The Angan licked his lips, pondering. "They are not similar."

"Yes, they are." Dann spread his arms in protest, staring at the creature, suppressing the laugh in his chest. Mocking Aeson was fun, irritating Therin was even more so, but Baldon was different. There was an honesty about him, a simplicity.

"No," Baldon insisted. "They are not."

"All right, then. Out with it."

Baldon's face scrunched in uncertainty. "Out with what?"

Dann sighed, running his hand through his hair in exasperation. "It's a turn of phrase. It means tell me what you're trying to say."

"Ahh…" Baldon's top lip curled, revealing a row of sharp canine-like teeth, his tongue flicking against their tips. "*Out with it.* Yes. I understand." He turned so he was facing Dann, his clawed hands resting on his knees. "'Before you can run, you must learn to walk' does not hold the same meaning because the concept of failure is not present, nor is it part of the intent. Walking is simply a precursor to running. It implies there are a series of steps that must be completed in a particular order and that success is not the hopeful outcome but rather the inevitable one."

"How is that *really* any different from what you said?"

"Because, Sureheart, mastering a craft does not require a series of steps that must be completed in a particular order. It requires perseverance and determination in the face of failure. The fear of failure is a concept that you humans have adopted more than any species on the mortal plane. I have seen it through generations. Often, with humankind, it is the *fear* of failure that prevents advancement, more so than failure itself. You spent hours carving your thoughts. Your first attempt was horribly poor."

"Ouch. Way to pull the punches, Baldon."

The Angan curled his lip in what might have been a smile but could also have been a sign that he was hungry. It was impossible to tell. "Your first attempt was horribly poor," he repeated. "Your second was less so. Among my kind we hold our failures close, so as to learn from them. We take pride in them because failing means you tried. You can only ever succeed if you allow yourself to fail."

"Well… that was actually quite insightful. You know you should talk more. You're actually better conversation than those two." Dann nodded towards Aeson and Therin who still sat on the other side of the fire, though they now sat in silence.

"What is rare is special."

"We're going to have to agree to disagree there, Baldon. Mead is pretty special, as is wine… as are spirits. I would prefer they never be rare."

Baldon's face twisted in what Dann could only assume was confusion. "I know of mead and wine. They are the liquids your kind consume to forget the sorrows that plague you. But spirits are the physical manifestation of the plane hereafter, such as those that attacked us in the Aravell. They are very different things, though you speak of all three as the same."

"I mean the spirits you drink, Baldon. Not the spirits that nearly killed us. And hold on, you don't only get drunk to forget. It's fun."

"You drink spirits?" What passed for Baldon's eyebrows rose, a look of shock on his face.

Dann let out a sigh, digging his fingers into his cheek in exasperation. Before Dann could try and explain, Baldon let out a gasp, jerking backwards, his spine straightening, his pupils expanding so the usual amber colour of his eyes was barely a sliver, then the Angan's eyelids snapped shut, and he sat there in silence, rigid.

The sounds of footsteps and shuffling bodies signalled that Baldon's sudden change had not gone unnoticed. Aeson and Therin were standing over Dann within moments, their eyes fixed on Baldon, the elves watching intently.

"What's going on?" Dann asked. "What is—"

"Shhh," Aeson hissed. "For once in your life, shut up, Dann."

"Well," Dann muttered, "that was a bit harsh." Dann's irritation vanished when Baldon's eyes snapped open once more, glowing gold.

"The son of the Chainbreaker has emerged from the Burnt Lands."

Chapter Thirty-Six

Berona

"So many." Calen couldn't believe his eyes as he, Erik, Vaeril, and Tarmon approached the unbroken river of refugees that led from the gates of Berona, past the lake, and stretched onwards into the distance. The sheer number of souls simply did not seem possible – they easily would have filled all the villages back home ten times over.

Calen had initially been worried they would stick out like sore thumbs at the city gates, their clothes, skin, and hair matted with blood and crusted with sand and dirt. But as he looked at the people before him, he realised that wasn't going to be an issue. Some rode on weary horses, others sat on the backs of wagons that looked as though they had been dragged through the void, splintered and bloodstained. But most travelled on foot, traipsing mindlessly forwards, their stares blank, their clothes torn, their shoulders drooped. Calen had heard the Urak attacks in the North had been ferocious, but he had never imagined anything of this scale. Never in his wildest dreams. There had to have been thousands of people trudging towards Berona, a city that was likely already filled to the point of overflow. How many homes and towns had been destroyed? Hundreds at the least. How many had been killed? Thousands. *This is what war truly looks like.*

As he took in the corpse-like march of those seeking shelter, Calen remembered Tarmon's words at Kingspass. *'Tonight, those men and women are not empire soldiers. They are just people. People who don't want to die. And they need us. They need you. They need a Draleid.'*

Calen had thought he'd understood then, but it was only now that it truly made sense. Now, as he saw people no different from his own, people who were likely farmers, blacksmiths, hunters, tanners, innkeepers. Soldiers died in war, but it was these people who suffered.

"There has to be thousands of them," Erik whispered as they joined the procession. A rickety wagon, pulled by a horse that looked like it hadn't eaten in days, rolled along beside them, axles squeaking from lack of oiling, uneven wheels thumping against rocks that had been kicked onto the paved road. "And this isn't even the main entrance. The main gates are at the northern face of the city."

Someone let out a harsh chesty cough to Calen's left. "Where you coming from, m'boy?"

Calen turned to see an old man hobbling beside him. At least sixty summers lined his face, his cloak was charred and stained with blood, torn to the point of being almost unusable. A raw wound ran along the man's forearm, only partially scabbed, angry red flesh around it. *Infected.* Redness like that and swelling, along with increased warmth from the area, had been the first things Calen's mam had taught him to look for in a wound. Followed by oozing and sharp pain. *In severe cases, Calen, if left untreated, even a small infection can lead to nausea, fever, shock, and in many cases, death.* The thought of his mam sent a twinge of panic through Calen. He clapped his hand against his hip, where the silk scarf he had bought her all those moons ago still hung, looped through the belt that held the sword his father had given him. The panic was followed by guilt, at the soft waxy touch of the scarf beneath his fingertips, slightly tarnished by dirt and sand. He had almost forgotten it was there. It was the only thing he had left of his mam, and she'd never even held it.

"We are coming from Copperstille," Tarmon chimed in when Calen didn't respond. "And you? You look like you've travelled quite a distance."

"That I have," said the old man with a cough, phlegm catching in the back of his throat. "All the way from Ravensgate..." The old man stared into the distance, his eyes glazing over.

"Ravensgate? That's a long way to travel alone."

"I wasn't alone at the start..." The man shook his head, and Calen noticed his hand shaking at his side. "We ran from Ravensgate to Bromis, but they kept coming. I lost my son and his wife in there. My grandson took an arrow to the neck going through the pass... But they let me live. Why did they let me live?"

The man's hand continued to shake, his head twitching sporadically. Something in his memories must have triggered him. Calen understood that all too well; he could still taste the ash on his tongue from the walls of Belduar, still hear the crackling and popping of charred skin, the stench of voided bowels.

Calen rested his hand on the man's, squeezing gently. The old man's hand stopped shaking, and his eyes regained their focus. "You're here now. It would take a hundred thousand Uraks to break through Berona's walls."

"Uraks?" The man shook his head back and forth, back and forth, more a spasm than a motion. "No, no, no. Not Uraks. *Elves.*"

451

Calen spun his head around at the mention of the word 'elves', his eyes meeting Vaeril's who had a panicked look on his face. Vaeril had insisted on coming with them into Berona, despite the fact that he himself acknowledged the stupidity of it. He walked with the hood of his cloak pulled tight over his head, his hair tied in a way that covered his ears, but if any guard stopped them and took a closer look it would be plain to see he was an elf. Like Dann, Vaeril was as stubborn as a rock once he'd made up his mind – particularly when it came to his honour and his oath.

"Elves?" Erik raised a suspicious eyebrow, glancing at Calen and the others. "Surely you mean Uraks?"

"I meant what I said," the old man snapped, his timid demeanour flipping in an instant, teeth grinding and nostrils flaring. "Thousands of them." The man's eyes grew glassy again. "They cut us down like livestock. The fire… the dragons… I can still hear the screams." The old man stared at Calen, his eyes piercing. "Nowhere is safe. Nowhere. They're coming."

The old man stumbled sideways, knocking into a woman who then fell to her knees. The woman's husband started shouting, and then they were swallowed by the swarm of people. Calen wanted to go back to help, but he quickly realised there was nothing he could do. One old man in a sea of refugees. He turned, looking to Vaeril.

"I don't know." The elf grasped at his chin, a worried look in his eyes. "It could…" He lowered his voice. "The elves of Lynalion might have declared war. It *is* possible. I just never thought the day would come."

"Hold on," Erik said, a smile mixing with an expression of incredulity. "That man was clearly insane. We would have heard if the elves of Lynalion had declared war."

"We've been in the Burnt Lands for weeks, Erik – I've lost track of how many. Anything could have happened in that time." As Calen spoke, he felt Valerys's blood pumping as the dragon swooped and snatched a thick-furred goat from the side of a cliff some fifty or so miles away. Even as the dragon tore into the goat's flesh, anxiety flooded into his mind, worry and fear. Before they had set foot in the Burnt Lands, Valerys had understood what would happen when they reached the other side. He understood he couldn't come with them into Berona. Rist was as much Valerys's family as Erik, Dann, or Tarmon, and Valerys would do anything for his family. But that didn't mean the dragon didn't burn with both rage and panic at the thought of letting Calen be so far away. Valerys had insisted on staying closer to the city, but the risk was too great. If anyone spotted him, word would spread like wildfire. And they were in Loria now. The Dragonguard could be anywhere. *Three days. If we can't find him in three days, we'll leave, I promise.*

A deep rumble resonated in the back of Calen's mind. Reluctant acceptance.

"I'll ask around when we get inside," Erik said. "If anything like that has happened, Ingvat will know. But the old man was mumbling about dragons. I honestly think he's been broken by the Urak attacks. I've seen it before. The mind is a fragile thing."

Calen nodded, glancing behind him to see if he could spot the old man. As the column of weary refugees marched towards the western gate of Berona, Calen couldn't help but feel his heart bleed at their broken souls. At first, the massive procession had reminded him of the road into Camylin, packed with so many people. But this was nothing like the road to Camylin. There was no joy, no wonder, no bubbling excitement or anticipation.

These people were exhausted, mentally and physically. Calen saw it in their empty stares, their despondent expressions, the lethargic shuffle of their feet. Even those on horseback had drooped shoulders, their fingers barely holding the reins, the horses starved and moving with a listless gait. Not a stitch of clothing was untorn or free of dirt, and only the lucky few travellers were not marred by bloodstains.

Passing through the gates had been far easier than Calen had anticipated. Over a hundred Lorian soldiers and guards had stood watch over the enormous arch of white stone, hollering and shouting commands at the refugees as they flooded into the city. But there were simply not enough of them to deal with the flow of people.

"They're going to close the gates soon," Tarmon whispered, looking around as they passed beneath the archway, shuffling shoulder to shoulder with those who walked beside them. "The city will overflow if they keep them open like this. They've lost control of the influx."

"What does it matter?" Calen asked. "These people need the protection of Berona's walls. Surely they wouldn't turn anyone away?"

"It's not as simple as that," Tarmon said with a weak smile. "There is more to consider."

"What more is there to consider than ensuring the people are safe?"

"Capacity, food, squalor. A city is only built to be able to provide for a certain number of people. Try and cram too many in and the sewage systems will overflow, disease will spread, food will grow short. And that is when things are normal. But now, with the Uraks attacking, they need to consider potential siege situations. Sieges are rarely ended by the attackers scaling the walls. It's starvation that kills. Starvation and disease. Letting too many in can be as a much a death sentence as turning them away. Sometimes it can be worse."

"Worse?"

"Have you ever seen someone starve to death? It's slow, creeps on you. Pulls the meat from your bones to feed your heart. You can see the pain in a person's eyes." Tarmon looked at the expressions on Calen and Erik's face, reading the unspoken question – when had Tarmon seen this? "My father. Belduar has been cut off from outside trade for a long time. Longer than I've been alive, and our relations with the dwarves have been tempestuous. When I had seen no more than five summers, our crops were struck by blight. It wouldn't have been so bad had we not relied so heavily on tubers. Not all the crops died but enough that thousands starved. My father had been splitting his rations between me, my sister, and my mother. We didn't realise what he was doing until it was too late."

"I'm sorry, Tarmon." A knot formed in Calen's throat. He had no doubt that Vars would have done the same thing in that situation. That was the kind of man he was. Calen hadn't thought about it before, but he was happy that, at the least, his dad's death had been quick. The sight of it was burned into Calen's mind – Inquisitor Rendall's sword sliding through Vars's chest, Vars's body dropping, lifeless to the ground. The sound of his mother's screams still haunted him. He would never forget that day.

The numbness.

'Wake up! Wake up!'

The emptiness.

'Please, please, for the love of the gods, wake up! Dad…'

The rage.

Tarmon rested his hand on Calen's back as they pushed through the throngs of people, the streets even more packed than the road outside. "Death is the only thing we are assured of in life. It's not how we die that matters, it's how we live."

It HAD TAKEN HOURS to find an inn that had any space, and even at that the only room available in The Black Horse was essentially a broom closet with three beds wedged in. Truthfully, calling them beds was generous. They were cots with rotten wood and rusted bolts, rammed so close together there wasn't space for a sheet of paper between them. Likely all the rooms in every inn in the city looked exactly the same. With this many people seeking refuge within Berona's walls, every innkeeper would be fitting as many beds in as many rooms as possible.

Calen tossed his satchel on the middle bed, behind which was the room's solitary window, wooden framed and arched with a large crack running from the left side to the bottom. Had they been anywhere else, the draft would have left a chill in the air, but Berona seemed to hold on to some of the unnatural heat that consumed the Burnt Lands. The morning held a gelid touch, but that had soon evaporated once the sun had risen clear into the sky. Calen didn't even want to know what the place was like during summer.

He dropped himself on the thin, rigid 'mattress', sure he heard a snapping sound beneath him. Tarmon and Erik were tossing a coin for the last bed, loser having to sleep in the sliver of space between the end of the beds and the door.

"Crowns." A broad smile spread across Tarmon's face, stretching into a grin.

"Ugh. Fuck the gods. Gimme that." Erik snatched the silver coin out of Tarmon's hand and stuffed it into his own pocket. "We're running low on coin as it is. We're tossing again tomorrow night."

"If you get scared, you're welcome to share the bed with me." Tarmon's grin grew wider as he tried not to laugh.

"How could anyone share a bed with you? You barely fit on it yourself. I pity your mother having to give birth to you. I bet you came out with a full beard and shoulders as wide as a wagon."

"I'll keep you warm," Tarmon said with a wink, still keeping a straight face.

"I'd rather cuddle up to a wyrm."

Tarmon's eyebrows shot up, and he bit his lip, looking over to Calen, then back to Erik.

"Oh, fuck off, you know what I meant! I'm going to reach out to Ingvat. She can put us in touch with Father's contacts in The Circle. Can one of you see if there's anything decent for supper downstairs? I'm sick to death of eating that leather N'aka meat and salted strips of beef. Also, I'd murder a priest for a bar of soap and a hot bath."

"Sure," Tarmon said, his lips turned down as he tried to contain himself. "What's your preference? Sausage?"

Erik narrowed his eyes at Tarmon. "You be careful, it's been a long time since I've felt the warmth of a woman." A smile crept across Erik's face as he stepped from the room, and both Tarmon and Calen burst out in a fit of laughter.

Vaeril, who sat cross-legged on the bed at the far left of the room, pulled a whetstone and a small leather container of oil from his satchel and began to sharpen his blade. He lifted his head as Calen and Tarmon's laughter subsided, looked between both men, raising an eyebrow and shaking his head as he turned back to his blade. The elf's reaction only caused Calen and Tarmon to break out in more laughter.

It felt good to laugh. Calen didn't laugh as much as he used to. Then again, it was usually Dann who made him laugh. He felt a pang of guilt at the thought of Dann alone, but tried his best to push it aside. As soon as he found Rist, they would go back to Dann together. The plan had already been set. Find Rist, cut straight back through the Burnt Lands, then Vaeril would lead them through the Darkwood to the elves, and they would make their way to Durakdur from there. It all seemed a lot easier when it was laid out nice and simply like that. But Calen was well aware that not a single one of those tasks would be simple. And even once all that was done… there would be a war to face. Aeson's war.

'Why do you put yourself through this for people who only seek to control you?' The words Artim Valdock had spoken when Calen was locked in that cell. *'The men and women you protect would see this continent burn, so long as they have their revenge. And they would use you as a puppet to achieve this. They are not your allies or your kin. They are your puppet masters.'*

They were words Calen had spent many a night thinking on. He had tried to dismiss them, to let them wash over him. But no matter how hard he thought on it, he could not help but find truth in the words.

"Calen?"

Tarmon's voice pulled Calen from his thoughts. "Huh?"

"I'm going to go scrub my body until it's raw. I suggest you do the same. You smell like shit." Tarmon turned to Vaeril. "I'll have a serving girl bring you up a bucket and a cloth. The place is too packed for you to take a bath."

Vaeril nodded, expressionless as he continued to run the whetstone over his blade.

Calen pulled himself up from the edge of the bed, the blisters on his feet stinging, his muscles aching. "We won't be long, Vaeril."

Calen hated the idea of leaving Vaeril on his own after what they had all just been through, but they couldn't risk bringing him down to the baths. The towns and villages in the South were one thing. But if someone recognised that Vaeril was an elf, he would likely be killed on the spot in Berona. From what Erik had said, any bad blood between elves and humans in the South was nothing compared to the sheer hatred that festered in the North.

"Take as long as you need, *Calen*." A smile touched Vaeril's lips as he emphasised Calen's name, showing the conscious effort he was using to not say Draleid. "The Lord Captain is right, you do smell like shit."

AN HOUR LATER, THE SKY dark overhead, Calen let out a sigh of relief as he stood in one of Berona's many dark alleyways, rain drumming against him, saturating his cloak, tacking his hair to his head. He tilted his head back and smiled as each cold drop brought its own tiny fragment of happiness. The water Vaeril had been able to drag up through the sand in the Burnt Lands had only been just enough to keep them all from dying of thirst. That, combined with the scorching heat and sand – which he had developed a new hatred for – had given Calen an appreciation of rain.

Tarmon and Vaeril both stood to Calen's left, hoods pulled up, the Lord Captain leaning against the white stone wall of the alley, his hand resting on the pommel of the short sword at his hip. Erik and Aeson's contact, Ingvat, stood a foot or so to the right, discussing something as they stood out of the rain under a roofed walkway.

When Erik had said his contact's name was Ingvat, Calen's mind had conjured the image of a large burly man with a thick beard and bushy eyebrows. As it turned out, Ingvat was a small woman with long blonde hair and a nose that had been broken more than once. Her gentle smile would have been more at home on the face of a comforting mother than a smuggler working to overthrow the empire. She wore a dark cloak over a leather vest and sturdy-looking trousers, a short sword strapped on her right hip.

"Are you sure they're coming?" Erik frowned, looking to Ingvat.

"They're coming. Have some patience, Erik." Ingvat leaned back against a column that propped up the roof of the walkway. A broad smile crossed her face as she looked Erik from head to toe.

"What?"

"The last time I saw you, you were no taller than I am, and you couldn't grow a beard to save your life. Your mother would be happy with how tall you are. She always said she wished her boys would grow taller than their father."

Erik let a sigh out through his nose, giving a soft smile. He didn't speak of his mother much. Calen remembered him saying she had died from consumption when he was young, but that was all he had said. Calen had only seen one man die of the disease before, and Freis hadn't let him get close in case it spread, but from what he saw and what his mother had told him, he knew it was a horrible way to die. First the lungs went, leading to coughs so harsh they cracked ribs. Then parts of the skin blackened, growing cold to the touch. The disease then consumed the fat and muscle, leaving the victim withered and stick thin, a taut bag of bones. His mother had said the whole process could take weeks, and there was no cure. Just the thought of it broke Calen's heart. Nobody deserved a death like that.

Amidst the constant drumming rain, Calen heard footsteps, splashes as feet slapped against wet stone. A tension snapped into place as everyone's head turned the direction from which the footsteps sounded, down the shadow-shrouded alleyway where the only light was the glimmering of the pale moon in the puddles that welled in the cracks of the paved stone.

Since Calen had entered the city, he had felt the Spark thrum in the air, not overtly, but enough that he was constantly aware of it. It clung to the air like the aftermath of a storm, like a mist of latent energy. He didn't want to imagine how many mages would need to be gathered in one city to cause that effect. But at that moment, he felt something more. That low thrum was disrupted by the more tangible sensation of someone very close pulling threads into their body.

A quick glance in Vaeril's direction let Calen know he wasn't imagining it as the elf pulled his sword from his scabbard. Calen did the same while opening himself to the Spark, preparing to pull on threads of Spirit, as Vaeril had shown him – he wouldn't be warded the way Artim Valdock had warded him, not again. The others were slightly slower to react as they couldn't sense the threads, but they knew Calen and Vaeril well enough to follow suit, the rasping of steel echoing against the stone.

"Swords away," came a calm, level voice, barely audible above the hammering rain. It was the voice of a man, gruff and harsh.

"Let go of the Spark," Calen answered, his fingers tensing around the hilt of his sword, his jaw clenching.

"The end of my watch is signalled by smoke. My life is measured not in years, but in hours. The thicker I am, the longer I live."

"You are a candle." The irritation in Erik's voice was evident as he stepped out from the protection of the covered walkway, turning back towards Ingvat. "You know who I am – this is a waste of time."

"*She* knows who you are—" A tall, heavy-set woman with harsh eyes stepped from the shadows, a long black cloak draped over shoulders, vibrant yellow robes peeking through from beneath. Her skin was tanned, her accent difficult to place. If Calen were to be pushed for an answer he would think it was a blend of Arkalen and Drifaienin. High pitched with a slight lilt. "—but *we* cannot take any chances."

A man followed behind the woman, slightly shorter than she was, with a thick black moustache and a shaved head. Both his cloak and the robes beneath it were black as night. A knot twisted in Calen's stomach, and he tightened his grip on the pommel of his sword. *A Battlemage.* "Meeting you out in the open with little planning is already a risk too far if you ask me." The man moved out of the shadows, his eyes fixed on Erik. "This one must be Aeson's son. He has the same arrogance."

"You'll find I have a lot of his qualities." Erik took a step from beneath the walkway, the steel of his swords glinting in the faint moonlight that reached down through the towering buildings

"Easy. They're on our side. Put your weapons away." Ingvat stepped after Erik, resting her hand on his shoulder.

Erik looked back at Ingvat, over towards the newcomers, then back again, before finally sliding his swords back into the scabbards on his back, Tarmon and Vaeril were slower to follow suit.

"I count Aeson a friend," the Battlemage said, inclining a head. Calen could feel the man release the Spark. "Look, it's not safe to stay out here too long, the Beronan Guard patrol the streets throughout the night, and I dare say we are an odd group – two mages, an elf, an Alamant, a known smuggler, a man clearly bred from Jotnar stock, and the son of one of the most wanted men in the empire. It's best we make this quick. You can call me Black, this is Gold. Our real names are of no consequence. Ingvat says you're looking for someone by the name of Rist Havel?"

Calen's heart skipped a beat, and he took a step closer to the man. "Yes. Have you seen him? Have you heard of him?"

"Who's the Alamant?" The man narrowed his eyes, moving closer to Calen, looking him up and down. "I've not seen eyes like that before."

Calen turned his gaze towards the ground, suddenly very conscious that his eyes now held the same lavender hue as Valerys's. Therin had told him of Alamants; those who could touch the Spark but had either broken free of the Circle or were cast out.

"He's a friend." Erik's voice was firm, a finality in his tone. "Like you said, it's best we make this quick. Rist Havel, have you heard the name?"

The moment held in Calen's mind as though encased in ice, the drum of the rain filling his ears. *Please. If any of you gods are listening, please.*

Black shook his head, a genuine look of disappointment on his face. "No apprentices or initiates by that name have been registered in the High Tower. Not in the last few years, at least."

Calen's heart sank. He was a fool for ever believing it might be that simple. "Are you sure? Are you *absolutely* sure?"

"Quite sure," the tall woman, Gold, said, her voice soft, her eyes softer. "I oversee initiate registration within the tower. There have been no initiates by that name. I'm sorry."

"He could have gone by a different name." Calen's heart was beating frantically. He hadn't come all this way simply to give in. "When he was taken, he might have given a false name."

"Even if that were the case, there would be no way of knowing. There are currently over four thousand initiates, apprentices, and acolytes housed within the High Tower. A proverbial needle in a haystack, if you will. I'm sorry, but in this endeavour, we cannot help you."

"That can't be it." Calen stepped towards the woman, close enough to see the flecks of brown in her green irises. "I want to see for myself. I *need* to see for myself."

The woman held Calen's gaze, seeming unperturbed by the desperation in his voice. "You will not find anything in that book that I haven't already told you. I am not lying. Already, I risk my life in what I do."

"Then take me inside. Let me look for him."

"Now?"

"Right now. Please."

"And what would you do?" The Battlemage raised an eyebrow and suppressed a laugh. "Sneak into every room and look over the initiates while they slept? There are forty-three floors in the High Tower. Hundreds of rooms, up to twelve initiates and apprentices in each. I haven't heard a more ridiculous plan in my life. The tower guard wouldn't even ask questions. They would have your throat slit before you got to the second floor. Skulking around the High Tower at night simply isn't an option. It will only end with you dead and our heads on the block. I'm sorry, but you and this Rist Havel simply aren't worth the trouble."

Fifty miles away, Valerys sat in the open mouth of a large cave set into the side of a cliff. Calen could feel the beating of the dragon's heart, the slow rise and fall of his chest, the air expanding in his lungs. But more than that, Valerys's rage burned in Calen, seeping through the back of his mind, boiling his blood. They had not come this far to walk away now. Rist was Calen's family, and by that measure, he was Valerys's too. Calen's jaw clenched, his hand shaking. "We lost good people, waded through a sea of Urak blood, and dragged ourselves across hundreds of miles of the Burnt Lands to be here now. We are not leaving without seeing inside that tower. Now either you help us, or I will carve my way in."

"What in the gods?" The man's eyes held something Calen never thought he would see in the eyes of a Battlemage: fear. "What *are* you?"

Vaeril rested his hand on Calen's shoulder, his fingers squeezing firmly. He whispered, "Your eyes."

What? My eyes? It was only then Calen saw the soft glow of the purple light reflecting off the Battlemage's rain-wet face, shimmering in the pools of water on the ground, and colouring the white walls of the alleyway. Still, Calen didn't back away. Valerys's anger still burned in him, their minds still fully entwined.

Gold moved to stand beside Calen, a smile spreading across her face as she met his gaze. "They call you the Warden of Varyn. That's a powerful title for one so young. Though, seeing you now, I have to say it fits."

"What?" Calen had no idea what the woman was talking about, but he dropped his hand to the pommel of his sword, which he had re-sheathed.

Gold tilted her head, a look of disbelief on her face. "It truly is you. Stories reached the city some weeks back. Stories of how a horde of Uraks swarmed Kingspass. Of how Bloodmarked laid waste to everything in their path. Then a white dragon descended from the sky, and a man with glowing purple eyes appeared. And that warriors fell from the sky, encased in armour of dark green, white capes at their backs, swords of pure green light – the Knights of Achyron no doubt."

Vaeril stepped between Calen and the two mages, his eyes locked with Gold's, his sword half drawn, threads of Spirit and Air weaving around him. Tarmon and Erik had also shifted, moving closer, their stares cold.

"Put your cocks away." Gold rolled her eyes. She turned to Erik. "I see your father has given you his trust issues along with his arrogance." The woman reached out her hand, her fingers long and dainty. "It is a pleasure, Draleid. Had I known nothing of you, I would still be glad to finally meet you. But tales of your deeds at Kingspass are already fast-growing legends – they are a welcome counter to the lies being spread by the empire. 'A Draleid sent by Varyn himself'. While I certainly wouldn't go that far, to know you are the kind of man who protects those who cannot protect themselves, even if they lie on the other side of a war, that is an admirable quality."

"What lies do they spread?" The way the woman spoke of the empire, Calen could have sworn she wasn't a mage at all. Therin had told him of the colours associated with each of the affinities within the Circle. The yellow robes beneath her cloak indicated that she was a Craftsmage. Why did she stand by the empire if she wanted it toppled?

"The kind you spread when you're worried," Gold answered, her lips curling into a smile. "You were right to conceal your identity. You were just very bad at doing so. But don't fear. I have lived enough centuries to be sure of the mistakes I've made and to be resolute in my path to setting them right. Now, we're going off topic. I believe I may have the answer to where you will find this Rist Havel."

"Why didn't you say?"

"Because until this moment, I didn't know who you were and therefore didn't know the significance of the information I hold. There is an Inquisitor by the name of Rendall Malkas—"

"Rendall…" The name left Calen's mouth in a growl. His own anger was fed by the rage that roared through Valerys's mind at the thought of the man who had killed their father. The man they in turn would kill. "Where is he?"

"Calen." Erik's voice was soft as he rested his hand on Calen's shoulder, but Calen shrugged him off, only barely managing to contain the fury inside.

"Ah, so you know him. Well, Rendall recently took on a sponsored initiate, which means their name would not have been recorded in the Tower's registry. But I pride myself in knowing the secrets of this city and it happens that this new initiate is a young man who hails from the villages of western Illyanara. A village known as The Glade."

Calen's eyes widened at the mention of his home. It had to be Rist. There was no other possibility.

"I had a feeling that might stir something in you."

A hint of suspicion curled in the back of Calen's mind. "Why would you think that name means anything to me?"

"Oh, come now, give me the respect of not playing games. I may be a Craftsmage, but my business for Aeson is in information. Rumours spread, news filters down, soldiers talk. After a while, enough pieces can be put together, if you know what you're doing."

Calen held Gold's gaze, drawing in a deep breath, then exhaling slowly, the rain cold against his skin. "Are you certain this initiate is Rist?"

"He might well be. But then again, he might not. Never take a possibility for a certainty, Draleid. No matter how likely." The woman gave a slow nod, pursing her lips. "What is this Rist Havel to you?"

"A brother," Calen said without missing a beat.

"And what would you risk to find him?"

"Anything."

"The Inquisition headquarters in Berona are stationed in the city dungeons. The dungeons are over a hundred feet below ground in the northern section of the city, are labyrinthine in their design, and have only a single access point. Many of the Inquisitors have been sent the length and breadth of the continent to hunt down those who seek to instigate rebellion and solidify the empire's hold on the High Lords in the South. This leaves the Inquisition in Berona quite poorly stocked. But there will be a number of Praetorians left to guard the prisoners, along with a handful of Inquisitors. Rendall has been gone from the city for the past week, but he's not left the Inquisition headquarters for more than an hour at a time since he returned."

"He's here?" Something awakened within Calen. An anger so deep it didn't rage or swell, it burned white-hot.

"He is."

"Take me there."

"Fail to prepare and prepare to fail. No, tonight is not the night. I can arrange robes and armour for you all, a map of the labyrinth, and potentially the number of the interrogation rooms Rendall has most recently been using. But I can do none of that if we go tonight. I will gather those things and meet you in The Ugly Duckling, just north of the Lukar Bridge, once the sun sets and the streets begin to empty."

"Am I the only one who thinks this is insanity?" Erik said. "Break into a dungeon in the heart of the empire, with only one exit that is designed specifically to keep people trapped."

"If it was you in there, I'd go. What is the point in trying to save everyone if I can't save the people who matter the most to me? I'm going whether you come or not."

Erik simply gave a short nod. "I never said I'm not coming with you – I'm just pointing out the insanity of it all."

"We will need a count of how many Praetorians and Inquisitors remain within the city." Tarmon looked to Gold. "Can you do this?"

The woman pulled at the edges of her cloak, covering over the sliver of yellow that had been visible. There was a smile on her face and a glint in her eye as she looked at Tarmon. "I like a man who gets straight to the point." Her smile widened. "I believe I can. My contacts within the Inquisition are few, but they are reliable."

"How are we getting in?"

"You're going to walk straight through the front door."

CHAPTER THIRTY-SEVEN

ONE LAST REQUEST

Dahlen checked the contents of his satchel one last time before closing the flap, fixing the buckle into place, and lifting it up beside his swords, which lay in their scabbards on the desk at the back wall of the room Kira had arranged for him.

He checked over the scabbards, ensured the leather straps were in good condition, and examined the sword blades before strapping the weapons to his back.

Once they were both secured, he rested his hands on the satchel, hesitating a moment. It felt strange to be leaving after so long. Strange to be leaving the people of Belduar, whom he had developed an affection for, and also to be leaving the dwarves, many of whom he had grown to consider friends.

Ever since he was young, Dahlen had followed in his father's footsteps. He had dreamt of being the missing piece to Aeson's puzzle – of being the Draleid his father was searching for. That dream had been all-consuming. It had defined him. And when Valerys had hatched and bonded with Calen, that dream was shattered like a pane of glass. Dahlen was lost. Like a ship cut adrift at sea with no sails or oars. Although he had told his father that staying behind in Durakdur was because Ihvon and Daymon needed him, the truth was that he had needed them. Staying in Durakdur and investigating the assassinations with Ihvon had given Dahlen a chance to carve out something in this life that was his alone. And yet, strangely, it was that freedom that had convinced him his place truly was at his father's side. Not walking in Aeson's shadow, but standing at his side, fighting for the very same people he now called friends. Fighting to protect the people Ihvon and so many others had died for. There was a fire in him now, and he would see it burn.

"Your bootlace is undone."

Dahlen almost leapt from his skin at the sound of Belina's voice. The damn woman moved like a ghost. "I'm not falling for that again."

"Suit yourself," Belina said. Dahlen could hear the shrug in her voice. "You're the one who'll end up face first on the stone when you trip."

Dahlen sucked his cheeks inward, biting down, then shook his head, let out a sigh. "I hate you."

"You love me." Belina clicked her tongue off the roof of her mouth as she stepped further into the room. "Everybody loves me." The upturn of Belina's bottom lip played in Dahlen's mind; he didn't even have to see it to know it was there. "It's a fact."

Dahlen's looked down at his two perfectly laced boots, then shook his head and slung his satchel over his back, facing Belina. Despite how irritating she was, Dahlen was happy to see some of her usual snark had returned. "Are you ready?"

"Ready is a state of being," she said, angling her chin upwards as though she was a queen. "But yes, my lute and pack are waiting by the Southern Fold gate under guard by three very eager, young Belduaran men."

Dahlen rolled his eyes, laughing. Belina had already informed him that her intention was to travel south, to Valtara, but she would journey with him just past Midhaven until the road forked.

Footsteps echoing in the corridor outside the room were followed by the sight of Oleg Marylin and Lumeera Arian standing in the doorway.

"Dahlen, Belina. Good, good," Oleg shuffled into the room, moving awkwardly in the tight fighting doublet of purple and gold. "I had been hoping to catch you before you left for the gate."

"Oh Keeper of the Mountain. It is such an honour." Belina crossed one arm over her belly and stretched the other out behind her, bowing so deeply she almost folded herself in half. Dahlen couldn't help but stifle a laugh. Belina had been exaggerating her mannerism towards Oleg ever since Kira and Elenya had affirmed his new position after the funeral pyres. "How may we be of assistance, *my lord*. Might we caress the noble backside?"

The glare Oleg gave Belina would have turned a river to ice, but beside him Lumeera was smiling from ear to ear.

"What can I do for you, Oleg? Or, Lord Keeper." Dahlen gave Oleg a bow, though a far less mocking one than Belina.

"Stop that, the both of you." Oleg frowned, pulling at his doublet, shifting it to what was most likely a more comfortable position. "This thing chafes everywhere."

Oleg glanced at Lumeera, who nodded back, and they both took a few steps further into the room.

"What is it, Oleg?" Panic ignited in Dahlen's stomach at the serious look on Oleg and Lumeera's faces.

"Nothing like that," Oleg said, raising his open palms. "Don't worry. I have come to ask one more thing of you both."

"Well?" Dahlen asked after a few moments had elapsed.

Oleg raised an eyebrow, a smile spreading from ear to ear. He looked from Dahlen to Belina, then back again. "Are you going to speak that way to the Lord Keeper of the Mountain?"

Everyone in the room burst out laughing. Had it been anyone else who'd spoken, there would have been nothing funny about the sentence, but because it was Oleg, Dahlen couldn't hold back his laughter.

"You know what?" Belina asked, choking down a laugh.

"What?" Oleg asked.

"You've clearly been watching me closely because your delivery was excellent."

Oleg puffed out his cheeks, shaking his head as he wiped tears of laughter away with the sleeve of his doublet. He drew in a few deep breaths, settling himself. "Lumeera and I have come here to ask something of you."

"We know... *Lord Keeper.*" Belina let out a laugh. "Sorry, I couldn't help myself. Please, continue."

Oleg threw Belina a glare, then shook his head, resting his hand on his belly, where the buttons on the tight doublet were bulging. "With everything that has happened, and everything that is yet to pass, there are some Belduarans who wish to leave for lands where the dwarves hold no sway. Some who want to start anew. I was hoping that since you are both travelling already, you would be willing to join their escort. Kira has informed me that the reports coming in are that between Uraks, bandits, and imperial soldiers, the roads across Illyanara are perilous for travellers. The people trust you both, they feel safe around you."

"And the more sharp steel we have, the better."

Dahlen looked to Belina, who, predictably, shrugged, then turned back to Oleg. "And you're just going to let them go?"

"It is not my place to allow or not allow. I am no king. They are people of Belduar, and they will remain so no matter where they go. But it is my task now to protect them. And so that is what I intend to do. It may well be that we all follow them in time. But for now, I want to see what this new relationship with the Freehold will bring. I fully believe we can restore Belduar to what it once was."

"And who is their escort?" Belina asked, raising a curious eyebrow.

"A number of my guard will make up the escort," Lumeera said. It was only then Dahlen noticed the lack of a purple cloak at her shoulders. "Without a king, there is no Kingsguard. But that does not mean we will not continue to defend Belduar and its people. I will remain here, along with the bulk of the surviving guard, to ensure Oleg's safety, but a number have volunteered for the journey. They are set to journey to the old villages west of Ölm Forest. The cities are already rammed with refugees, and the word is that many have begun to gather in the western most village, just along the coast. Our hope is to find not only refuge there, but a place to contribute."

Belina puffed out her bottom lip, tilting her head sideways. "If you'll provide the coin for me to take a ship across the sea from Salme to Skyfell, I'll—"

"Done," Oleg said, cutting Belina's sentence short.

"And wine. I want wine. Oh, and cheese. And maybe some of those spongey cakes the dwarves love."

Oleg shook his head, laughing. "I'll see what I can do." The man looked to Dahlen.

"I cannot, Oleg." Dahlen let out a sigh. "I must go to Arem in Argona. I've been away from everything for too long. I need to find my father, and Calen, and Erik. I have a place in the fight to come."

Oleg ran his tongue across his teeth, looking at the ground. "This *is* the fight, Dahlen," he said, lifting his gaze to meet Dahlen's. "What are we fighting for if not people?"

"It's not that simple, Oleg."

"Is it not?" Lumeera asked. "I've fought beside you a number of times now, Dahlen Virandr. And it has always been clear to me why you fight. You fight to protect. Everything you do is in defence of others."

Oleg gave Lumeera a soft smile, then looked at Dahlen. "These people are scared. They've lost their homes, their kin, and their king. Everything they've known is broken. I wish they would stay, but I cannot say I don't understand their desire to leave. I would not ask this of you, but I cannot spare many guards to escort them. The nobles are still not happy with my appointment, and the Hand are likely still lurking."

Dahlen made to speak, but before he could, Oleg spoke again.

"If you would accept, I can send a hawk to your contact in Argona, telling them where you have gone, and they can then in turn relay your father's location to you there. The journey to Argona is much the same as to the western villages, but a hawk flies far faster than a horse gallops. By the time you reach the villages, there will likely be a message already waiting for you. You lose little to no time, you help get these people to a safe place, and you find where your father is. We all get what we want."

Dahlen turned to Belina, but the woman raised her hands. "Don't look at me. You can tag along, but you're not getting any of my cheese."

Dahlen shook his head, looking back at Oleg, who stood with his hands clasped behind his back, beads of sweat forming on his brow. Oleg was still the same strange, slightly awkward man Dahlen knew as the Belduaran emissary to the Freehold, but he was most certainly taking to his new role with aplomb. Dahlen looked towards the ceiling, puffed out his cheeks, then released a sigh. "All right. But you must send the hawk today. I'll need one letter addressed to Arem himself, explaining what is to be done, and then a second letter to be forwarded on to my father so he knows everything that has happened here and that I am well."

"It will be done." Oleg's smile stretched from ear to ear.

"All right," Dahlen said, double checking his satchel's straps. "Gather them, and let's get moving."

Oleg's smile grew even wider. "They're already waiting for you."

DAHLEN STOPPED IN HIS TRACKS as Oleg and Lumeera led him and Belina through the stone doorway and out into the enormous chamber that fronted the Southern Fold Gate. "You said a *few* people, Oleg."

What had to be nearly two hundred men and women – even some children – were moving about the chamber, stuffing packs, checking straps, and readying themselves.

"Well, I never actually said how many," Oleg said with a shrug. "There are one hundred and sixty-seven in total, with twenty-three former Kingsguard as escorts. Kira and Elenya have provided enough rations for two weeks – salted goat, hard cheese, crusty bread – along with enough gold and silver to ensure a safe journey. A gesture of goodwill on their part."

"All right." Dahlen looked over the people gathered, his gaze softening. What Oleg said had been true, by the time they reached the western villages, a hawk would easily have travelled to Arem in Argona, and the reply would likely be awaiting Dahlen. If he could ensure these people found a new place to settle in that time, there was no reason he shouldn't.

Dahlen grasped Oleg's forearm. "It's been an honour, Oleg. Be careful. There are still too many things unanswered here – too many things at play."

"I'm in good hands," Oleg said, looking towards Lumeera, who inclined her head.

"I have no doubt of that, but there are knives in the shadows here still. Whoever killed Pulroan still lurks. Have you heard anything of Volkur and Azmar?"

"There is a moot today in Azmar to decide Pulroan's successor. Though, it is common for dwarven succession talks to stretch on for weeks, even months in some cases. As for Volkur, the Wind Tunnels still remain shut since the night of the assassination attempts. But that also, is not uncommon. There have been many occasions where a kingdom has shut itself off from outside influence when choosing a new king or queen. The question is what Kira and Elenya will now do."

"What do you mean?"

"They are in a position of strength," Oleg said, pushing out his bottom lip. "Consolidating the other two kingdoms into their own before new rulers are selected is a viable option. Though it will not come without resistance."

Dahlen nodded slowly, taking in what Oleg had said. He squeezed the man's forearm. "Take care of yourself, Oleg. And you too, Lumeera." Dahlen released his grip on Oleg's forearm and grasped Lumeera's instead. "The Kingsguard may be no more, but you were a fine Lord Captain."

"Even though I put you in bonds?" Lumeera's lips pulled into a smirk.

Dahlen let out a short laugh, nodding. "Even still," he said. "Though, I'm not quite sure I forgive you."

"Dahlen Virandr," a voice called from behind Dahlen. "You didn't think you'd get away from me that easily, did you?"

He turned to find himself looking down at the smiling face of Nimara – the dwarven captain who had been at the entrance to the refugee quarters before the attack and had also helped Dahlen's father search for Calen and Erik. She wore a breastplate of thick steel, her muscled arms bare, her long blonde braid draped over her right shoulder. "Nimara Kol. May your fire never be extinguished and your blade never dull. What are you doing here?"

Nimara repeated the greeting, her gaze never leaving Dahlen's. "Queen Kira asked for volunteers to travel with the Belduarans, to act as escorts and envoys for when we reach the western villages." Nimara gestured behind her to where twenty dwarves were securing their packs and checking their weapons. To Dahlen's surprise, and delight, he noticed Yoring and Almer among them. "Our people have spent too long beneath this mountain, and I for one wish to see more in my life than stones and glowing flowers. Besides, you still owe me that tankard of ale."

Dahlen could feel the heat of his cheeks reddening as Nimara gave him a wink. "I'm sure that can be arranged."

"Oh, it better be, Virandr," Nimara said as she turned and started back off towards the other dwarves. "We'll be ready to leave when you are."

Something sharp poked Dahlen in the ribs, and he looked to see Belina elbowing him. "If you don't take her up on that drink, I will. And once I work my magic, you won't stand a chance." Belina puffed out her cheeks. "What. A. Woman." Belina drew in a long breath through her nostrils as she stared after Nimara, then shook her head. "Right, it's about time we started off. I've wasted enough time playing mother to all you helpless children, and I can guarantee Dayne has gotten himself into a waist-high pile of shit that he'll need me to drag him out of. Off to the villages, then to Valtara. Now, Oleg. I was promised wine, cheese, and cake."

CHAPTER THIRTY-EIGHT

BLOOD FOR BLOOD

Rendall drew in a deep lungful of sweltering, shit-and-vomit-tinged air. Sweat slicked his brow, and his shirtsleeves were rolled up to his elbows, his red robes folded and laid neatly on the long wooden table at the side of the interrogation room, his sword and weapons belt on top. The dim light of the candles set into the alcoves about the room cast flickering shadows across the stone. He tilted his head back, rolling his neck from side to side, releasing the aches and stiffness in a series of cracks.

A small, leather-wrapped journal; a pen; an inkwell; and an open canvas wrap were sat across the top of the table by his side, while a red leather satchel lay at his feet. Reaching down, Rendall touched his finger against the cold steel of one of the many knives that rested in sewn-in pockets of the wrap. Many of the other Inquisitors preferred to use brutal contraptions such as racks, wooden horses, thumb screws, or spiked iron collars. But not Rendall. There was nothing personal in those implements, nothing… intimate. Rendall did not consider himself an honourable man. He would be a fool if he did. There were only two types of honourable men: those who sought to blame a higher cause for the atrocities they committed, and idiots. No, Rendall was not an honourable man. But he did believe in respect, and if he was going to break someone's soul, he owed them the respect to do it with his own hands. This *elf* barely counted as 'someone', but at the same time its resilience had impressed him – irritated him, but impressed him.

Rendall lifted the leather-wrapped book, opening the strap that held it closed. He flicked through the blood-marred pages, coming to the most recent entries.

Day 9

Sensory Deprivation: Nine days in total darkness and absence of sound.

Physical method: Skin peeled along the entirety of right arm. Salt rubbed into wounds.

Results: Prisoner did not speak. Prisoner did not scream.

Day 23

Two days since previous interrogation.

Sensory Deprivation: Twenty-three days in total darkness and absence of sound, with the exception of seven visits for interrogation (previously documented).

Physical method: Forced water inhalation. Right hand placed in boiling water. Skin peeling of upper back, left calf, and left cheek.

Results: Prisoner did not speak. Prisoner did not scream.

Note: Prisoner shows beyond average resistance to interrogation methods. New tack to be taken. Increased duration of sensory deprivation to be used. Fourteen days without break.

Day 37

Fourteen days since previous interrogation.

Sensory Deprivation: Thirty-seven days in total darkness and absence of sound, with the exception of eight visits for interrogation (previously documented).

Physical Method: Forced consumption of Dreamviper venom. Continued hallucinations for approximately eleven hours. Prisoner showed extreme discomfort, exhibited fear response: shaking, shivering, and grunting.

Results: Prisoner did not speak. Prisoner did not scream.

Rendall sighed, tapping his finger on the paper. He closed the notebook and set it back down on the table. Even then, the only sounds Rendall heard were the clinking of chains, the slight pop and crackle of candles, and the low grunts of the elf as it hung in the centre of the room, a manacle clamped around its right wrist and a glob of metal fused to the stump of its left hand, both chained to the panels on the ceiling. Its ankles were chained to the two panels on the floor, pulled tight so it had little room to wriggle. A thick blend of blood and sweat coated the elf's body, streams of crimson running from freshly peeled patches of skin to drip onto the stone floor.

Rendall's apprentice stood to the elf's left, sliding a sharp paring knife along the creature's ribs, peeling flesh away cleanly. He wasn't usually one to admit it, but the young man was coming along well – Rendall might even have said he was a natural. The first few days he had choked and gagged simply from the air in the room. The sight of peeling flesh had caused him to empty the contents of his stomach more than once. But after a few weeks, he took to it like a duck to water. Rendall would make an Inquisitor of him yet.

"You know, despite what you might think, I don't enjoy torturing you." *I do enjoy the challenge though.*

Rendall's voice echoed against the walls of the square room. He looked into its eyes. He had let it keep both its eyes to enhance the effect of the light deprivation, but seeing how little progress they had made, that would have to change. Despite the admiration Rendall was developing for the creature, he could not afford to take any longer in extracting information. News had already swept across the continent of what the Draleid had done at Kingspass, and it didn't take a Scholar to know that the burning of Arisfall was the boy's doing as well. The Grand Inquisitor had already let Rendall know that his failure to provide anything useful from the elf was reflecting poorly on the Inquisition.

In that analogy, Rendall was a mirror. And in the Inquisition, any mirror that reflected poorly was shattered. Rendall had no intention of being shattered. "You will not survive this. You know that, and so do I. I simply cannot make that happen. But what I can do is make you a promise. If you tell me everything you know of the Draleid, I will end your life quickly. The pain will be gone. The darkness will dissipate. The emptiness in your soul will fill. If you do not tell me, I will take your eyes and leave this room. I will never come back. I have wasted too much time on you already. But I will ensure you are kept here hanging just as you are. You will be fed and watered every day. I will ensure that your miserable life is as long, painful, and hopeless as it can possibly be."

CALEN'S BREATHS TREMBLED AS HE ran his hands over the red robes that sat on his shoulders and fell over his chest and legs, stopping just shy of his ankles. The rainfall had continued from the night before, each drop drumming against the hood of the borrowed robes, cold as it trickled down his face. He could hear Gold and Black talking but paid no heed to their words. He clenched his jaw, memories taking shape in his mind. Rendall's cold eyes. The long red cloak knotted at his shoulders. The steel breastplate that bore the Black Lion of Loria. Rendall Malkas. At last Calen had learned the man's full name. The full name of the man who had not only killed his father, but was the cause of everything.

Rendall Malkas. Farda Kyrana. Artim Valdock.

Calen's anger bubbled, sifting through the inferno that was Valerys's fury. Miles away, the dragon's chest resonated with a deep rumble that threatened to turn to a roar. Calen felt the rock of the cliffside part beneath Valerys's talons, the heat resonating from his body. The dragon wanted to burn Berona to the ground. He wanted to hear Rendall's screams, hear his skin crackling. It was all Calen could do to hold Valerys back.

He will die by my hands. I will look into his eyes as I pull the life from him. Once again, Calen remembered that death could not be beautiful. He knew killing Rendall would bring him no peace. His father would not be returned from Heraya's embrace. Neither would Ella, or their mother, or Faenir, or any of those killed when Rendall brought his men to The Glade that day. They were gone. No, Rendall's death would not bring peace, and it would not bring back those Calen loved. But Calen didn't want anything to come of Rendall's death. What he wanted was simple. He wanted Rendall to die knowing that it was Calen who held the blade, that the lives the man had taken had come to take his.

"Calen? Are you listening?" Tarmon's hand rested on Calen's shoulder, the man's eyes fixed on his. Tarmon was garbed head to toe in the red plate of the Inquisition Praetorians. It was strange to see the Lord Captain of the Belduaran Kingsguard in the armour of the enemy. The man was already a titan, a head taller than most others, shoulders carved from stone. But in the gleaming red plate, Tarmon looked like death itself had taken physical form and come to claim the souls of the living.

Calen nodded, his mind still replaying scenes from that day. Rendall's sword driving through Vars's chest, the look in Vars's eyes, Freis's screams. *'No, no, no…'* The memories burned in him, wrapping his soul in flames, hardening his heart. *I will kill you today.*

Erik and Vaeril stood beside Tarmon. Erik was also garbed in the red plate of the Praetorians, while Vaeril stood with his hands before him, manacles around his wrists, his hair matted to his head by the rain, ready to play the prisoner.

Gold nodded to Black, then turned towards everyone gathered in the alley around the corner to the entrance of the Inquisition headquarters. She looked at Calen. "One last time, repeat the plan to me."

"Once we get to the main entrance, the guards and the clerk are inside the doors. We know Rendall and his apprentice are currently within the Headquarters, and from what your contact has told us, they are likely in the interrogation halls as we speak. I will pose as Inquisitor Halsen, an Inquisitor originally hailing from Argona, only recently raised to full Inquisitor. My Praetorians—" Calen gestured to Erik and Tarmon "—and I have just captured an elf who was found poisoning the water supply of Dunmarken, a town forty miles north of Berona."

"Do we really need all this back story?" Erik asked, rolling his eyes.

"Better to have it and not need it, than need it and not have it," Gold replied. "Now remember, as I was unable to get the number of the interrogation room Rendall is currently using, you will need to find it. It is not uncommon for Inquisitors to trade prisoners and other pieces of information between them. You have promised Rendall this elf in exchange for information on the movements of rebels near Elkenrim. That should be enough for them to give you the number of the interrogation room he is currently using. Once you're inside, any Praetorians guarding the corridors will likely leave you alone. They don't often question the movements of Inquisitors. According to my sources, there are no more than twenty Praetorians currently set to guard the dungeons. Nobody ever tries to break in, and without a map, anyone who breaks out is usually dead for a week or so before their rotting bodies are found. Do you have the map?"

Calen patted the pocket of his new robes, feeling the folded map within.

"Good. Now if your friend is in there, and assuming he is fit to move, I have divided another set of armour between these two packs." Gold handed a large bulging pack to both Erik and Tarmon, which they each slung onto their backs. "If he puts that on, there shouldn't be any questions getting out. Where are you to meet us once you're out?"

"At the back of the Raven's Ruin fletchery," Tarmon said with a nod.

Gold had shown them the fletchery on their way to the Inquisition headquarters. Aeson's network had built an underground passage out of the city beneath the fletchery, much like the passage Calen and the others had used beneath Oliver's Apothecary in Camylin. Regardless of whether they were able to leave through the city's gates, using the underground passage was simply cleaner.

"All right, we best get moving to make sure everything is in place. I wish you luck." Gold gave Calen a slight bow. "Whatever happens, it was truly an honour to meet you."

Black nodded to the group, following Gold down the dark, rain-pummelled alley, disappearing into the shadows.

Calen drew in a deep breath. The others were looking to him: Erik and Tarmon in their ruby red plate, Vaeril with streaks of rain running down his face, manacles clasped at his wrists.

"I know this has been said already, but thank you. I cannot explain what this means to me, to have you here by my side. To bring Rist back." *And to kill Rendall.*

Erik lifted the visor of his red helmet, a look in his eyes that said more than any words ever could. "If we can't protect the ones we love, we're no good to anyone. I wasn't sure if coming here was the smart choice, and it likely wasn't. What we're about to do certainly isn't. But it's the *right* choice. Where you go, we go."

"I can't believe I'm saying this." Tarmon lifted his own visor, turning up his lip at Erik's words. "But young Virandr here took the words right out of my mouth. Let's get this done."

Calen turned to Vaeril, resting one hand on the saturated shoulder of the elf's cloak, the other hand checking his manacles. "Are you sure you are all right?"

Vaeril gave a sombre nod. "They are unlocked, and the key is in my pocket either way. I am with you Draleid... Calen. I am with you." Vaeril turned to Tarmon, who carried Vaeril's white wood bow, sword, and pack. "Try not to lose those."

"I'll do my best, master elf."

The entrance to the Inquisition headquarters was a large rectangular structure of dark, almost black, stone that rose twenty or so feet from the ground, stark next to the smooth white stone buildings around it. It held no windows of any kind, and the door was built from sturdy oak banded with Iron. Long red banners with a black trim, bearing the Black Lion of Loria, rippled in the breeze on either side of the doorway, their ends splitting into two points.

Calen filled his lungs with rain-damp air. He let the air sit in his chest, settling himself. Two emotions warred within him: fear and anger. Fear that Rist might not be in the cell and that Calen might still not be strong enough to fight Rendall. Anger at everything that twisted man had done. As his hand began to shake at his side, a warmth flooded over him from Valerys. The dragon shared Calen's fears and stoked the fires of his fury, but at the same time, Valerys gave him a sense of calm. Valerys might not have been standing by Calen's side, but he was with him. They were one.

The rain hammering down against his robes, Calen walked towards the door of the Inquisition headquarters, Tarmon and Erik following him with Vaeril marching in between them.

The heavy, iron-barred door creaked as it opened, the sound echoing down the long corridor on the other side. The corridor was rectangular in shape, crafted from the same near-black stone as the outside of the structure. Thick candles sat atop sconces along the walls, each candle alternating sides – beeswax, judging by the bright, warm glow. The air was thick and heavy, tinged by an unpleasant odour that Calen couldn't quite place.

The corridor stretched on for thirty or so feet, the sound of Erik and Tarmon's armoured boots echoing against the stone. A small rectangular room sat at the corridor's end, no larger than the kitchen of Calen's home.

Two Praetorian guards stood on the opposite side of the room, on either side of an arched stone doorway that fronted a stairwell leading down into the ground.

A man in red plate sat at a sturdy wooden desk on the left side of the room, his helmet placed atop a chest behind him. Stacks of paper, a pen, an inkwell, and a large beeswax candle sat on the desk, the candle's flame bathing the man's face in a warm light. He looked as though he had seen no more than thirty summers, with long black hair tied at the back; sharp, angular cheekbones; and skin as fair as any Calen had seen. He sat scribbling away in an open ledger, *tssking* at something on the pages within. At the sound of the footsteps, he lifted his head, looking as though he were about to admonish whoever was interrupting his work, but all irritation vanished as he set his eyes on Calen. He sat up straighter. "Welcome, Inquisitor. Light of The Saviour illumine you."

Calen's mind scrambled for the appropriate response. They had gone through the plan meticulously, but somehow a simple greeting had slipped through the cracks. After what felt like a full minute but was in fact only a second or two, Calen settled on precisely what he thought an Inquisitor might do. He frowned and grunted, which only seemed to make the man sit straighter.

"Inquisitor Rendall Malkas, he is here?" Calen kept his eyes locked on the man's, doing all he could to exude an air of authority that he did not naturally possess.

"I emm…"

"You emm?" Calen frowned.

"My apologies, Inquisitor, I've not seen you here before, and you look so young, I—"

Calen opened himself to the Spark and pulled on thin threads of Air – he could already feel the Spark being used somewhere below, far enough away that it barely registered, but he *could* feel it. He pressed the thread of Air against the man's throat, just enough for him to feel it – just what he figured an Inquisitor would do when questioned.

476

The look of helplessness on the man's face didn't make Calen feel powerful, though; it made him feel like a monster. And at that moment, he understood why Dahlen had reacted the way he did when Calen had used the Spark during their sparring. Against the Spark, Dahlen was helpless, just as Calen had been when Rendall had killed Vars. Just as helpless as the Praetorian was now. The thought of it sent a shiver through Calen's spine; it repulsed him. He released his hold on the Spark.

The man swallowed hard, reflexively touching his fingers against his throat.

"Inquisitor Rendall Malkas?" Calen repeated.

"Yes, he is here," the man stuttered. "You have business with him, Inquisitor…?"

"Inquisitor Halsen." Calen nodded towards Vaeril. "I've an elf for him. Found this wretch attempting to poison the water in Dunmarken."

"Another elf?" The man narrowed his eyes at Vaeril, his lip curling in disgust. "Horrible creatures altogether." He held his stare on Vaeril for a long moment before nodding slowly. "Yes, yes. Inquisitor Malkas is currently performing interrogation in room one-four-seven. Room one-four-nine is available, Inquisitor." The man opened up a broad cabinet that hung on the wall behind, picking out an iron key and handing it to Calen, inclining his head in deference.

Calen took the key and slid it into the pocket of his robes. *Another elf?*

As the man lifted his head, his eyes met Calen's, his brow furrowing. Calen had no doubt the man had just noticed the strange purple hue of Calen's irises. He looked as though he was about to say something but remembered the threads of Air against his neck earlier and thought better of it. "Will you be requiring an additional escort? I can have Lars or Ulrika accompany you." The man gestured towards the two guards who stood at the entrance to the stairwell

"That will not be necessary." Calen gestured for Erik and Tarmon to follow him as he moved towards the stairwell.

"Umm… Inquisitor, the log?"

Calen froze. *Act like you know what you're doing.* He took a moment to let himself think, steadied his nerves then turned, letting out an irritated sigh. "I have more important things to be doing." He put on the firmest voice he could muster, lifting his chin.

"I'm sorry, Inquisitor. But everyone must sign in. You know this. Inquisition rules." The man's voice trembled. Even here in the heart of Loria, garbed in the red plate of the Inquisition Praetorians, a man was still just a man. A man doing what he was told. A man who knew the power of a mage.

Calen held out his hand, trying to look as unimpressed as he could. "Quickly now. Stop wasting my time."

The man gulped, dipping a pen in the inkwell, then handing it to Calen while sliding a ledger across the desk. Calen took the pen and signed his false name in the ledger, noticing Rendall's entry just above his and an empty space for the exit signature.

Inquisitor Rendall Malkas and apprentice. Interrogation Room 147.

Calen's gaze lingered on the name, letting it sink in. *Rendall is here.* Up until that point it had been a hope. But now it was confirmed. The man who killed Calen's dad was in the dungeons.

Calen pushed the ledger back across the desk, handing the pen to the Praetorian clerk on the other side, then turned and made for the stairwell, a fire smouldering in his heart.

⟗

RENDALL STOOD WITH HIS ARMS folded, his head tilted to the side as he watched his apprentice peel the sharp blade along the elf's inner thigh. The elf twitched and grunted, the muscles in his jaw spasming, his chest rising and falling in ragged breaths. Rendall had never encountered a living creature with this level of resolve. Nothing and no one – elves, humans, Jotnar, and dwarves alike – had ever endured the sheer quantity of pain Rendall had inflicted on this elf. Months in almost full sensory deprivation. It was quite extraordinary. He had seen others attempt to do as much, but their minds had scrambled, and they had been left as pale shells of what they had once been. But even before him now, the elf's unwillingness to break was as clear as it had been on the first day.

Rendall happily would have spent months longer testing the resilience of the elf's mind. He would have cherished the opportunity to break it down to its constituent parts, to examine it, to comprehend what truly gave rise to the creature's fortitude. It wasn't a species-based quality. He was sure of that. He had broken a number of elves in his time. This one was unique.

"Slower," Rendall said, clicking his tongue off the roof of his mouth, frowning at his apprentice. "The goal isn't to remove as much skin as possible, it is to prolong the pain, to peel back the layers of hope. You must understand this fundamental thing."

"Yes, master." The young man nodded, drawing in a deep breath as he continued his work. At first, he had been cocksure and brazen. Rendall had broken that out of him – not all of it, just enough to eliminate undeserved hubris. A man must be broken down before he could be built back up; that was something Rendall believed with his whole heart. This apprentice would make a good Inquisitor. He was still a little skittish when it came to carrying out the hands-on work, but he took it in his stride. He was willing to do what needed to be done.

Rendall stepped closer, clutching the elf's sweat-soaked hair between his fingers and lifting its head back. The creature didn't open its eyes. The muscles in its jaws twitched and spasmed, while its breaths, though ragged and weary, were slow and steady, almost meditative. *Truly fascinating.*

It was unfortunate this would be the last day of interrogation. But Rendall knew when to cut his losses. Still, it was good practice for his apprentice. Best to put these last hours to good use. He pulled his fingers from the elf's hair, letting its head drop, hanging loose.

He dropped his hand into his trouser pocket as he walked back towards the table with foldable wheels that held his notebook. His fingers brushed against something smooth and cold. A smile touched his lips. It was the flat rock that his daughter, Ara, had found on the coast that morning and insisted he take it for 'protection'. Which was of course ridiculous, but he humoured her. When the mind of a child was so easy to please, it made little sense not to do so. She had also managed to find an almost identical stone to give to Forina as well, Efialtír bless her tiny heart.

Rendall moved the stone between his fingers, hesitating when he sensed something, a tingle as though someone had drawn from the Spark, faint, but noticeable. Within the Inquisition headquarters, and particularly down in the interrogation halls, the thrum of the Spark that vibrated through the city was non-existent. There weren't many Inquisitors still within Berona's walls that night, and he had expected most of them would be busy drinking their coin away. Perhaps it was Markova or Yerrick. Those two were partial to interrogation after a few drinks. Either way, it wasn't his concern. Another hour or so and he'd leave the elf to wither away. Or perhaps he would go back on his word and allow the creature a quick death. Rendall was sadistic, he knew that, but he wasn't a monster.

꒰꒱

THE AIR IN THE DUNGEON'S corridors was far cooler than that of the city, the blazing heat above kept out by the stone walls and the soil that surrounded them. But even so, the unpleasant odour that Calen had smelled in the antechamber had grown even more pungent as he descended into the dungeon itself.

Calen held the map in front of him as they moved as swiftly as they could through the maze of corridors. Even with the map, it was no easy task. The stairwell dropped fifty or sixty feet into the ground, likely more. According to the map, the Beronan dungeons were a sprawling network of tunnels and chambers that dug even deeper into the ground and spread out for quite some distance. It was difficult to tell on paper, but it looked as though the corridors overlapped each other, rising above and sinking below like the weaves of a wicker basket or spider's web.

The western section of the dungeons contained kitchens and living quarters, with many vents rising to the surface, each marked by a small black circle with a line through it. Below the living quarters were offices or studies of some kind, while the northern section held bathing rooms and privies that drained into the River Horka.

What Calen was interested in was the eastern section that contained an even more convoluted mess of corridors: the interrogation halls. The clink of Tarmon and Erik's armoured boots reverberated off the stone, drumming in the tight corridor. Every corridor and chamber looked as though it had been hewn straight from the rock, smooth to the point of seeming polished. Just like the tunnel that had taken them into the back of Belduar, the Beronan dungeons must have been cut using the Spark.

Many of the corridors were lit with thick, slow-burning beeswax candles set in sconces that cast a bright light over the stone, but many others were shrouded in darkness, the sconces empty or candles extinguished. That made sense. It was likely the candles were only lit as they were needed, otherwise at least a score of attendants would be required to maintain the candles day and night.

As they moved through the network of tunnels towards the eastern section of the dungeons that held the interrogation halls, Calen couldn't help but feel a slight pang of panic as memories of the tunnels below the Lodhar Mountains flashed in his mind, the endless walking, the kerathlin, Valerys's panic. These corridors were not much different. They twisted and wound unceasingly, some ending in stairwells that sank further into the earth, only to rise on the other side. The deeper they travelled, the more Calen was aware that without the map, there was no chance they would be able to find their way back out.

As they walked, the sensation of someone drawing from the Spark grew stronger. It wasn't constant. It only tingled every few minutes as though whoever was drawing from the Spark was doing so in bursts.

After a while, the heavy wooden doors set into stone on either side of the corridors had begun to bear numbers.

"Even the numbers are jumbled," Vaeril whispered as he touched his hands against a set of steel numbers nailed to the wooden door on his left, his hands now free of the manacles. Two-two-three. "Every door in the last section started with five. The one before started with nine. All of these doors start with two."

Calen looked at the map, running his finger along the corridor network connecting interrogation room two-two three with the number of the room the clerk had given him: one-four-seven. "It's this way."

Just as Calen was about to set off down the corridor, the creaking of a door echoed.

"What's that elf doing walking free?" A woman garbed in red robes stepped from one of the interrogation rooms about ten feet ahead on the right. She looked no more than forty summers. Her speech was slurred, and her robes were dishevelled. Blood marred her gaunt, sun-darkened face. She had clearly spent the earlier part of that night drowning her sorrows in ale. She stumbled, shaking her head as though trying to loose the dizziness that held her in its grasp, then narrowed her eyes at Calen. Her body tensed, a moment of lucidity crossing her face. "You're no Inquisitor. How did you get in here, and where did you get that map?" The woman pulled a sword from a scabbard beneath her cloak, stepping towards Calen. Vaeril, Erik, and Tarmon moved to intercept her.

She opened herself to the Spark, and Calen darted forwards, pulling his sword free from beneath his cloak, already closer than the others. The Inquisitor made to swing for his head, but he brought his blade up, the clang of steel ringing in his ears. She stumbled backwards, and Calen slammed the coin pommel down into her face, teeth snapping, blood pouring out over her lips and chin. As she hit the floor, Calen felt her draw in threads of Spirit and Fire.

Calen was quicker though, Valerys's rage burning through him. He dove after her, driving his blade through her gut until he felt the steel crack against the stone beneath her, jarring his arm. The woman let go of the Spark, blood spluttering from her lips and pouring from the wound in her gut, streaming out around Calen's sword.

Calen's hands were trembling on the hilt, his jaw clenching, teeth grinding. Valerys's anger suffused him, and he let it in. He twisted the handle of the sword and pulled it free as the Inquisitor's chest stopped drawing breath. Guilt twisted in his chest as he rose to his feet and looked down at the lifeless body before him, blood pooling on the stone. Anger quickly devoured his guilt – that woman had just been torturing someone.

Calen moved to the door the woman had come through, resting his fingers on the handle.

"We need to do something with the body," Tarmon said from behind him. "Not much we can do about the blood, but if someone finds the body here, they will raise the alarm immediately."

Calen pushed open the door, a wave of heat hitting him like a brick wall. The stench of shit, vomit, and blood, caused him to gag. He took a moment, holding the back of his hand to his mouth, then lifted his head to look around the room. Flickering candles illuminated small alcoves in the walls.

For a moment, the anger that had flooded Calen's veins vanished, a shiver rippling over his skin, coils of dread twisting in his stomach. The body of a young man lay strapped to a long wooden table, iron clasps around his wrists, ankles and neck. Long, razor-thin cuts laced his naked body, blood smearing his skin, dripping down his side and pooling on the floor. Fingers were missing on both hands, and smoke rose from where eyes had once been, now twisted messes of scarred and burned flesh. Calen was relieved that the young man no longer drew breath, for the pain he must have endured would have been otherworldly. *How could someone do this to a living thing? How could anyone inflict this kind of torture?*

Calen's hands trembled, the fingers of his sword hand clenching around the leather-wrapped hilt. "May Heraya harbour your soul," he whispered through gritted teeth.

"Can we put the body in here…" Erik's voice trailed off and he audibly gagged as he looked into the interrogation room. He turned his head away, closing his eyes. "What in the gods?" He hocked phlegm from his throat and spat it on the stone, looking as though he were going to vomit. "These Inquisitors aren't even human."

"Leave the body where it is," Calen said as he turned from the room, glaring at the corpse of the dead Inquisitor, his lip curling, all guilt burned from him. "She doesn't deserve to share a room with him. If they come, they come."

Calen opened himself fully to Valerys as he stalked down the cold stone corridor towards interrogation room one-four-seven. He let their minds drift together. Let their hearts beat as one. Even separated by miles, they were one. Energy rippled through Calen, crackling. In his mind's eye he saw Rist lying on that table, mutilated, broken, dead. Every second he wasted, increased the odds of that outcome. He would not waste a second more.

A SHIVER RAN DOWN RENDALL'S spine, and he turned away from his apprentice, who was cleaning the knives and instruments before packing them into the cloth wrap. His gaze fell on the door. Someone else had drawn from the Spark. Someone close.

Something was wrong. He could feel it in his bones.

Rendall strode across the room to where his sword and belt lay atop his robes. He lifted the belt and fastened it around his hip, sliding his robes around his shoulders. "Hurry up, just toss them into the satchel."

"But master, there's blood all over them. They'll rust if I don't—"

"You think I don't know what blood will do to steel?" Rendall grabbed the young man by the throat, turning his head so their gazes met. "Toss them into the satchel, *now*. And if you ever question me again, I will take your tongue. You don't need it."

Of course, that was an idle threat. The young man would be of a little use without his tongue. An Inquisitor who couldn't ask questions was less than useless. But he didn't need to know that. He simply needed to obey.

The sensation of someone drawing from the Spark ignited in the back of Rendall's mind once more, except closer, much closer. He saw threads of Air whirling, and then the door was lifting from its hinges, iron snapping, bolts flying free from the rock. The door hurtled across the room, slamming into the wall on the far side in a metallic thud, stone dust spraying, light from the corridor carving into the dimly lit interrogation room.

A man stepped through the doorway, a curved elven blade in his right hand and the red robes of an Inquisitor draped over his shoulders, though it was clear he was no Inquisitor. His eyes pulsated with an ethereal purple light that misted outwards like steam wafting from the surface of a frozen lake, fury carved in the lines of his face.

Rendall pulled on threads of Spirit, weaving them around the man, warding from the Spark. But the intruder drove a spike of Spirit through the ward before it formed and sent a whip of Air crashing into Rendall's chest. Rendall's feet lifted, and he was careening through the air. He wrapped himself in threads of Air, but pain still twisted up his spine as he crashed against the wall, his fingers barely managing to keep their grip on his sword hilt. He dropped to one knee, shaking his head, then pulled heavily from the Spark, letting it flood through him as he rose to his feet.

And now, you die.

Cold fury blazed in Calen's veins as Rendall rose to his feet. In his mind, he could hear Valerys roar, the dragon's rage burning within him, consuming everything. Two bodies, one soul. The man who had brought the empire to their village stood before them. The man who had killed their dad.

A figure hung from chains in the centre of the room, head drooped, hair tangled and knotted, blood streaming from a myriad of cuts. In the dim light, Calen couldn't make out who it was.

A young man in brown robes stood beside a rickety table between the prisoner and Rendall. He pulled a gleaming knife from a cloth wrap atop the table and lunged towards Calen. *It's not Rist…*

Calen waved his hand and sent a whip of Air snapping at the young man's legs, knocking them from under him, his head hitting the ground with a crack. He didn't move. Calen fixed his gaze on Rendall, power surging through him, the Spark hot in his veins. *Finally.*

Rendall sent a whip of Fire at Calen, but Calen turned it away with threads of Air, walking forwards as the flames flickered from existence. Calen dropped into Striking Dragon, wrapping both hands around the hilt of his father's sword. Then they crashed together.

The forms of the svidarya flowed through Calen like a raging river, steel crashing against steel as Rendall blocked strike after strike, the vibrations jarring Calen's arms. All the while, Valerys's rage seared Calen's muscles, energy crackling across his skin.

Rendall slammed a thread of Air into Calen's gut, sending him stumbling backwards. The Inquisitor followed after him, his blade moving in a blur of steel. A metallic clang rang out as Calen caught the blow, his blade sliding along the Inquisitor's, snagging at the crossguard. Calen remembered Aeson's teachings. *Each part of the sword is a weapon, forget that at your peril.* As Calen's blade hit Rendall's crossguard, he angled his blade straight ahead, then pushed off his back leg.

The manoeuvre caught the Inquisitor off guard, steel slicing across his cheek, drawing blood, but as the man leaned away from the blade, Calen flicked his wrists back and threw all his strength into his arms and shoulders, ramming the coin pommel into Rendall's jaw. He crashed into the wall behind him, blood pouring from his mouth, dripping over his lips and down his chin.

Calen heard Tarmon, Erik, and Vaeril scrambling into the room, armoured boots pounding against stone. He ignored them, lunging towards Rendall. The Inquisitor had recovered and turned Calen's blade aside with a quick flick of his wrist. Then pain exploded on the side of Calen's head, stars flitting across his eyes as Rendall's fist connected. He staggered backwards, the Inquisitor closing in, his fist dappled with blood. They exchanged another flurry of blows, and Rendall's steel sliced through Calen's robes, burning across his shoulder, then raked across Calen's forearm, causing him to lose his grip on his sword.

Tarmon and Erik charged Rendall, but the Inquisitor hammered them with a thread of Air, knocking them into Vaeril.

"Who in The Saviour's name do you think you are?" Rendall growled, stepping towards Calen. The man slammed threads of Air down on Calen's shoulders, driving him to his knees. As he stood over Calen, Rendall paused, his eyes narrowing, recognition flashing across his face. "It's you."

Calen looked up at the Inquisitor, taking in the man's face, the light of Calen's eyes casting a purple glow across Rendall's skin. Rendall's feet shifted, the rippling movement of his body signalling an impending swing of his blade. Time crystallized, Calen's vision narrowing until he saw only Rendall. Energy overtook him, Valerys pushing his strength into the bond, roaring, his talons gouging furrows in the rock of the cliffside upon which he was perched. Only rage burned within him.

Calen let the Spark surge through him, just as he had in the Burnt Lands. He drew in thick threads of Air, shaping them into a sphere and slamming them into Rendall's chest. The Inquisitor careened through the air. Even with the threads of Air Rendall wrapped around himself, cracks still spread through the stone as he crashed into the wall.

Calen rose to his feet as the Inquisitor dropped to his knees.

"You killed my dad." Calen's voice didn't tremble; it was clear and true.

Drawing in ragged breaths, Rendall lifted his head, his black hair saturated with sweat, blood dripping from his lips and streaking his face. A choking laugh escaped his throat. "If I'd known what you'd become, I'd have killed you too." He spat blood onto the floor. "Better late than never."

A red glow radiated across the stone as Rendall pulled a sharp-cut, pulsating gemstone from the pocket of his robes. It was the same as the one Artim Valdock had used in Drifaien. The one that allowed him to use magic that Calen couldn't see: Blood Magic. Calen's upper lip curled reflexively.

A blur of movement came from Calen's left, and Vaeril launched himself towards Rendall, blade glinting in the mix of red and purple light. Memories flashed through Calen's mind. The Fade taking Ellissar's head. Artim Valdock snapping Lopir's neck. Ice spears punching through Falmin's chest. He would not let it happen again. Calen lunged forwards, roaring as he did, using threads of Air to pull his sword from the ground, wrapping his fingers around the hilt as he moved.

The Spark thrummed in the air around Vaeril and Rendall, threads of Fire, Air, and Spirit whirling and twisting, steel crashing against steel as the elf struck again and again.

Calen moved into Charging Boar, his blade clattering against Rendall's. From the corner of his eye, Calen saw Erik and Tarmon moving towards them, but the room was too small to make use of their numbers. Rendall pivoted, turning away a swipe of Vaeril's blade, a plume of black fire erupting from his hand, the red gemstone glowing in his fist. The elf threw himself to the ground, his sword clattering as the black fire roared over him.

Calen lifted his leg, pushing threads of Earth into his bones, wrapping his foot in threads of Air. He unleashed a guttural roar, hearing Valerys's thunder in his mind. The Spark burned within him, searing his veins, but the pain only pushed him onwards. Using all his might, he hammered the flat of his foot into Rendall's chest, pushing with threads of Air.

A violent snap of bones filled the room as Calen's foot connected, sending the Inquisitor once more slamming backwards into the wall, the cracks spreading further. Rendall dropped to his knees, his sword still clasped in his right hand, the gemstone glowing in his left. He let out a spluttering cough, sprinkling blood over his lips.

The gemstone began to glow ferociously, but Calen snapped at the Inquisitor's arm with threads of Air, knocking the gemstone free and pulling it into his own grasp. He could feel the stone calling to him, pushing at the edges of his mind, oily and twisted. Calen pulled on threads of each elemental strand, feeling their power radiate through him, then channelled them into the stone, crushing it, breaking it, snapping it. He squeezed his fist as hard as he could, and a burst of red light flashed from his palm, slivers of bright crimson piercing the gaps in his fingers. The light died, and the stone shattered, broken fragments dropping to the floor.

Rendall let out a howl, throwing himself to his feet. He swung his blade at Calen's head, his movements desperate. Calen met the swing with the strong of his sword, knocking Rendall's arm back. Turning the blade, Calen swept his sword across Rendall's chest, slicing through the Inquisitor's robes and the shirt that lay beneath, carving a bloody gash into the flesh. Calen drew his sword arm back and grabbed the man by the shoulder. He pulled Rendall towards him and drove his sword into the man's chest. He felt blade bite into flesh and grate against bone, a thump signalling that the crossguard had hammered into Rendall's sternum.

Calen shook as he pulled his head back, looking into the eyes of the man who had killed his dad. "He was unarmed..." Calen stared into Rendall's eyes, his voice cracking, hands shaking, chest trembling.

Rendall made to speak, but he coughed and spluttered, blood coating his lips and dribbling down his chin.

Calen pulled his sword free, and the man dropped to the ground, landing on his knees, then falling onto his side, blood pouring out onto the stone.

Calen released his hold on the Spark, feeling the drain spread through him, dragging the energy from his bones. He dropped to his knees beside Rendall's lifeless body, voices a dull drone around him. He drew in slow breaths of dense, hot air, blood and sweat tacky on his skin.

Vars was still dead.

Calen looked at the intricate spirals that ornamented his blade – the blade Vars had given him. Blood coated the steel, Rendall's blood. As Calen knelt there, weary in both body and mind, the voices of Erik, Tarmon, and Vaeril swirling around him, only one thought filled his head: *Rist.*

CHAPTER THIRTY-NINE

LOST AND FOUND

re you all right?" Erik grasped Calen's forearm and helped him
to his feet, red plate armour glimmering in the dim candlelight.
He looked down at Rendall's lifeless body, his lip curling, then
back to Calen, looking into his eyes, checking him over.

Calen nodded, struggling to align his thoughts. "Rist…" Calen turned
towards where the man had hung suspended from chains. What if Gold
had gotten it wrong? What if Rist wasn't the apprentice? What if he was
the prisoner?

The prisoner was now on the ground, Vaeril and Tarmon standing
over him. He was naked and unconscious, blood streaking from a myriad
of cuts that laced his brittle malnourished body, some long and thin, some
broad as though the flesh had been peeled away. His dark hair covered his
face, falling over his chest, knotted and tangled with clumps of dirt and
blood. "Is he… is…"

"It's not Rist."

Erik's words cut straight to Calen's heart, stealing the air from his lungs.
Weightlessness set in his stomach as though he was falling. They couldn't
have come all this way for nothing. They couldn't have. Calen's heart
thumped erratically. Warmth flooded through from Valerys, the dragon
doing all he could to ease Calen's pain, to settle his mind. He stumbled
closer to where Tarmon and Vaeril leaned over the body, looking to Erik
and then back again. "No… it has to be. Erik, it has to be."

Calen dropped to his knees beside Tarmon, letting out a suppressed
grunt as the vibration jarred his legs, knocking some of the air from his
lungs. *It has to be Rist.*

"Draleid."

Calen looked to Vaeril, who knelt on the other side of the man, blood
covering his hands and face. Vaeril had a look in his eyes that Calen
couldn't place, his eyes wide in disbelief. "Draleid… it's Gaeleron."

"Gaeleron? But…" Calen stared back at Vaeril, then at the unconscious
prisoner on the floor. Since escaping Belduar, and stepping through the

Portal Heart into Drifaien, Calen had tried not to think about who had made it down the Wind Tunnels – the thoughts would have consumed him, and there was nothing he could have done to help. He had just told himself that the others had made it. Aeson, Dahlen, Ihvon, Alea, Lyrei, Gaeleron.

Vaeril leaned forward and brushed the prisoner's matted hair from his face, pulling it back behind a tapered elven ear. Knots twisted in Calen's stomach. The elf's skin looked so taut and brittle Calen thought it might shatter at a touch. The bones of his face protruded like the teeth of a serrated knife. Calen stared until the pieces began to slot together. The shape of his eyes, the line of his brow, the thin scar that ran horizontal along the elf's right cheek. But even as he knew it was Gaeleron, he still couldn't believe it. The elf looked as though he stood on the edge of the void. "He's been here all this time…" Calen swallowed hard, as he looked down over Gaeleron's scarred and beaten body. The elf's chest rose and fell softly, rasping breaths escaping his mouth. Gaeleron had treated Calen stiffly when they had first met, but the elf had sworn the oath to protect him. He had been proud, and strong. It was he who had first taught Calen the forms of the svidarya. To see him like this… "Vaeril, will he live?"

Vaeril turned away, and Calen saw a stream of tears carve through the blood and dirt on the elf's face. Calen had never seen Vaeril cry. He'd rarely seen the elf show more than a hint of emotion. Seeing him cry was like a hammer to the chest. Vaeril drew a sharp breath through his nose, wiping away tears with his sleeve, leaving blood smears in their place. "Whatever they were doing to him, they kept healing him afterwards." Vaeril ran his hand across Gaeleron's right arm. "The scars here are where they waited too long, and the tissue didn't knit properly."

"Why in the name of Varyn would they do that?" Erik stood over the others, looking down at Gaeleron, his eyes wide, mouth ajar.

"To keep him alive. To spend longer torturing him." The muscles in Vaeril's jaw twitched, his hand clenching into a fist. Vaeril picked up Gaeleron's left arm. The elf had lost his left hand at the first battle of Belduar, but that had been a clean cut. Now the flesh at the end of the limb was knotted and twisted, scarred as though it had been set aflame. "They fused the manacle to his arm. I removed it and healed what I could. If we can get him somewhere safe, I can do more. But we need to leave. Someone *will* come."

Calen nodded, his heart thumping against ribs, his emotions wavering between guilt, anger, and sadness. Gaeleron had been here all this time. Months and months, he had been tortured and starved. If it were not for Calen the elf wouldn't even have been at Belduar. *No, not now. He needs you now.*

"Calen Bryer?" a voice croaked.

Calen stiffened. His head shot up, his breath catching in his chest. He knew that voice. It was drier and harsher than he remembered, but he knew it. It just couldn't be possible that he would hear it here. Slowly, Calen pushed himself to his feet, swallowing hard. He ran his tongue over his cracked lips and turned.

Standing before him, brown robes draped over his shoulders, part-dried blood, from where Calen had smashed his head off the stone, smeared over his forehead and eyes, was Fritz Netly.

Fritz Netly of The Glade.

"It *is* you," Fritz said, looking at Calen, wincing as he touched his forehead. The young man seemed different. His eyes still held the same cold, calculating look they always had, but there was an uncertainty there now, a crack in his arrogance. "It's you," Fritz repeated, but the meaning was different. "You're the Draleid... He never told me why they wanted you, but..." Fritz stopped, realising he had said too much.

Calen's mouth went dry, his fingers tightening around the hilt of his sword, his breaths growing short. He looked from Fritz to Rendall's corpse to Gaeleron, who lay unconscious behind him. Calen's blood began to simmer. Valerys's mind drifted into his own, rage spilling over. The dragon wanted Fritz dead, his blood coating the floor.

"Were you part of this?" Calen gestured towards Gaeleron. His voice more growl than words.

"Those are the robes of a Circle apprentice." Erik took a step closer to Calen and Fritz, his tone flat.

"I didn't... I mean..." Fritz stuttered, his eyes flashing from Gaeleron to Calen to Erik. He was no longer the young man Calen remembered. He still looked like a snivelling, conniving bastard, but there was a meekness to him now. "You need to under—"

"Were you a part of this?" Calen shouted, his lungs burning, his throat scratching, Valerys roaring in his mind. He hadn't realised he crossed the distance between himself and Fritz before grabbing the man's robes and slamming him against the wall.

Fritz nodded, his eyes darting around, unable to meet Calen's gaze. "I didn't have a choice. I swear it."

"You swear it?" Calen brought his blade to Fritz's throat. "Your word means less than nothing. Do you think I don't remember? You sent an arrow through Rist's leg. You forced us to walk deeper into Ölm. He could have died, and you would have drunk to his memory, pretending it was all an accident." Calen pressed the blade harder against Fritz's neck, drawing forth a trickle of blood. "Swear all you want, nobody is listening. How are you even here? What did you do to worm your way north?"

"Calen, please."

Rage flooded Calen's veins, burning so brightly his hands trembled and his mind spun. Valerys urged him forward, the dragon's fury calling for Fritz to suffer for what he had done to Gaeleron. Calen roared, "What did you do?"

"What… your eyes?" Fritz's voice quivered, purple light reflecting off his face, gleaming in his eyes.

Calen raised his chin, pushing his blade that little bit harder, drawing more blood.

A hand gauntleted in red plate rested on Calen's forearm. It didn't pull Calen's blade away, it simply rested. Tarmon's voice was soft in Calen's ear. "This is not the way."

"You saw what he did to Gaeleron," Calen hissed through gritted teeth, his eyes still fixed on Fritz's. "I know him, Tarmon. He's just like Rendall."

"He is unarmed and afraid."

"He would drive this blade into my throat if it was the other way around."

"But you are not him." Tarmon's words were simple, but they pushed through Calen's rage, causing his resolve to falter. "You do it this way and it *will* haunt you."

Calen glanced at Tarmon, their eyes meeting. He turned back to Fritz, then nodded, gritting his teeth, pulling his blade back ever so slightly, blood trickling over the steel. "Was Rist ever here?"

"Rist?" Genuine surprise permeated Fritz's voice. He pushed his head back against the wall, trying his best to create as much distance between his neck and the blade's edges as he could. "Why… why would he be here? I haven't seen him, I swe—I haven't seen him."

"They took Rist." Calen leaned forward, leveraging the blade against Fritz's neck. "You better give me more than that."

"I don't… I can't…" Fritz looked down at his dead master. Tears streamed from his eyes, but Calen had a feeling they were more for himself than tears at the loss of Rendall's life. A look of recognition flashed across Fritz's face. "There is something. Master Malkas, he spent time in the room across the corridor. He never let me in…" Calen saw the wheels turning in Fritz's mind. "It *could* be Rist."

Erik stepped past Tarmon, lifting his visor, leaning in closer to Calen and Fritz. "You better not be lying, or I'll bleed you right here."

"I'm not!" Fritz said, with a touch more irritation than Calen thought he'd intended. "I'm not," he repeated, softer. "I don't know if it's him. But there *is* someone in there. Someone he didn't want me to see. It's the only reason I can think of."

Calen turned to Tarmon.

The big man nodded. "This place is fairly empty. It should be a while before someone realises we're here." He looked at Fritz. "If you're trying something, I'll kill you myself."

Fritz shook his head, wincing as the steel brushed his neck.

"Vaeril, how is he?" Calen looked at where Vaeril knelt beside Gaeleron, threads of each elemental strand whirling around them both, weaving into Gaeleron's body in twisting patterns and multitudes of combinations. Now that Calen had seen Vaeril heal a number of times, he could follow the threads, but he still had no idea what they were doing. The Spark required comprehension as much as any craft or skill Calen had ever seen, and healing with it seemed to require the same knowledge as a skilled surgeon or city healer. The understanding of precisely how to clean, care for, and heal a wound was vital.

"I'll need a few more minutes, Draleid. All I can do is make it safer for him to be moved."

A lump formed in Calen's throat as he looked down at the crumpled heap that was Gaeleron. He drew in a deep breath through his nostrils, trying to calm his building fury. His fingers tensed around the handle of his sword, the blade still pressed to Fritz's neck. He turned to look the man in his beady eyes. "Take us to the room."

Fritz nodded, the relief clear on his face. "You'll... you'll have to take the sword away."

Calen drew in another long breath, his fingers tightening and loosening on the hilt in quick succession. He pulled the sword away, wiping the blood on his red robes before sliding it back into the scabbard at his hip. "Take us."

"I just need to—" he gestured towards Rendall's body. Calen went to pull his sword free again, but Tarmon was quicker. The Lord Captain grabbed Fritz by the shoulder, his sword lying crossways against the man's stomach. "The key, the key," Fritz said, raising his hands with his palms out. "It's in his robes."

Tarmon inclined his head towards the body, letting out a short grunt.

Fritz scampered towards Rendall's body, kneeling beside it, his brown robes dipping into the pool of blood that had seeped from the corpse. He rummaged through the dead man's robes, producing a thick, iron key.

Fritz led Calen and Tarmon into the corridor, leaving Erik to watch over Vaeril and Gaeleron. The heat of the interrogation room had drifted to the back of Calen's mind, but as he stepped into the corridor, the cool air brushed over his skin. Another pang of guilt ignited in his chest. *Gaeleron's been breathing that air this entire time. Every waking moment must have been agony.*

"It's this one," Fritz said, crossing the corridor and stopping before a thick wooden door identical to the one they had just come from, except this one had the numbers one, four, and eight nailed to it. He fumbled with the key, slotting it into the hole and turning until a *click* sounded.

"Let me repeat myself," Tarmon said as Fritz rested his fingers on the handle of the door. "If you are in any way leading us into something here, I *will* kill you. And it won't be slow."

Fritz nodded, swallowing hard, then opened the door.

The air was just as dense, hot, and foul as it had been in the other room, the stench of sweat, vomit, and voided bowels thick like tendrils snaking down the back of Calen's throat. Except for the wedge of light that carved its way in from the candles in the corridor, the room was shrouded in darkness. Calen heard the sounds of clinking chains, shuffling, and low whimpers.

"Tarmon, can you pass me a candle?"

Calen could have cast a baldír, but he felt the drain sapping at him. He'd pulled deeply from the Spark when fighting Rendall, and he couldn't risk weakening himself any further in case he needed to fight again – which was, unfortunately, likely.

Tarmon pulled a thick beeswax candle that looked as though it had only recently been lit from its sconce and handed it to Calen. With the candle held out in front of him, Calen stepped into the interrogation room.

"In the name of the gods…"

The light from the candle washed over the stone of the square room, casting shadows about the walls and floor. A bare-chested man, bones stretched his skin, hair grey and brittle, sat with his back to the far wall, his head buried in his knees which were pulled to his chest. He wore a pair of ragged trousers covered in a vast array of multicoloured stains, some dark and red, others light yellow and brown. The man rocked back and forth, muttering to himself, chains around his ankles clinking.

It was only when Calen took another step into the room that he saw the other figure lying on their side, curled up with their arms wrapped around their knees, head shaking erratically from side to side. They wore a tattered dress that looked as though it had once been pure white, em-broidered with flowers, but now it was a brownish grey, blood staining patches that had been sliced and cut.

Calen turned to Fritz, fury redoubling. Fritz had always been an arse-hole – always. But even for him, this was darker than Calen could have ever imagined. "What do they do to people here?"

"I… I don't know. I've never been in this room before."

"But you knew." Calen had to stop himself from dropping his hand to the hilt of his sword. He clenched his jaw and made his way to the man who sat against the far wall. The light of the candle cast shadows into deep recesses of the man's body, where the fat and muscle had wasted away and the skin pulled in tight around the bones. All of a sudden, Calen's time in Artim Valdock's cell felt like nothing. At least, it was nothing compared to this.

"It's all right," Calen said, reaching out to the man, trying to keep his voice as calm and level as possible. The man didn't respond. He didn't even turn his head. He simply continued to rock back and forth, muttering.

Calen leaned in closer.

"Can't... remember... Why can't I? His face..." The man's voice was hoarse and broken as though his throat hadn't been touched by water in days.

Calen dropped to one knee beside the prisoner. The man didn't look like Rist, but then again, how could anybody look like themselves when their body had been broken this badly. "Rist?"

The man twitched at the mention of Rist's name, and Calen's heart jumped. The tiniest spark of hope ignited within him.

"Rist? Is that you? Are you all right?"

The man stopped rocking, his muttering fading. "No..." The man shook his head, his shoulder length grey hair tossing side to side, his gaze still fixed between his knees. "It's not you. It's not. It can't be. He did it again. More things that aren't real." Terror crept into the man's voice, his breaths becoming erratic. "You're not real. You're not real."

What have they done to you?

"I'm real, Rist. I'm here." The man took a sharp breath as Calen rested a hand on his arm. He clasped his hand on Calen's and lifted his head, staring into Calen's eyes. Calen's heart ached as he met the man's wild gaze, dark eyes set in sunken hollows, face gaunt, a thick scar running down over his left eye and disappearing into a blackish-grey, bedraggled beard. *It's not him.* The sense of loss that swept over Calen wasn't something he could articulate. It left a hollow in his chest and an ache deep inside that flitted back and forth between pain and numbness. *All this way.* He had dragged Vaeril, Tarmon, and Erik all this way, and they still hadn't found Rist. A flicker of warmth burned in him at the thought of Gaeleron. They had found Gaeleron. That meant something.

"Calen?" the prisoner croaked.

A knot twisted then unravelled in Calen's stomach, sending a shiver through him. *Did he just say my name?*

"It's not real," the man muttered. He began to shake his head back and forth again, then stopped, lifting his gaze to Calen's once more, a moment of lucidity coming upon him. His eyes widened. "Are you real?"

Calen nodded and took in the man's face again, looking over every mark, every dotted freckle, settling again on the eyes. Tears rolled down the prisoner's brittle cheeks, touching his cracked, blood-marred lips.

"Is my son here?"

The hairs on Calen's arms and neck stood on end. He looked closer. The man's cheeks were sunken, bones stretching his skin like tent poles. His beard was so wild and knotted it covered most of his face, his hair grey and tangled. Calen's eyes settled on the thick scar that ran over the man's left eye, starting an inch above the brow, avoiding the lid, and continuing down his cheek before disappearing into his beard. *No. It can't be.* Calen had been told the story of that scar many times. Of how it had been an accident – two children sparring with steel swords when they should have used wood. Calen's heart began to beat so loud he could hear it drumming in his head. *Thump.* A low whistle drowned out all other noise. *Thump.* Calen leaned forwards and wrapped his arms around the man, careful not to pull too tight on his fragile frame. Tears streamed down Calen's face. He had no control over them, they simply flowed and flowed, snot dripping from his nose.

"Lasch."

As soon as Calen said Lasch Havel's name, Rist's dad broke into sobs, his shoulders convulsing. Lasch Havel had always been hard as iron. Never cold or rough, but it was well known he was not a man whose bad side was a good place to be. He cared deeply for those he loved and bore absolutely no horseshit from anyone else. He had never been anything other than kind to Calen. Whatever Rendall had done to break Lasch's spirit so completely made Calen want to kill the man again. "It's all right. I'm here. I'm going to take you out of here."

It took a few moments for Lasch's sobbing to die down, but he continued to shake, the moment of lucidity he had experienced fading. As Lasch pulled away, Calen had a realization. He lifted himself to his feet and dropped beside the woman in the battered floral dress, pulling at her shoulder gently. "Elia, Elia."

She shook and rocked, just like Lasch, lying on her side, keeping her face buried against her knees. Elia had always been slight of frame, but now she looked so small and frail, she was almost like a child. It seemed only days since she was pinching Calen's cheek before The Proving, her shrill voice rising above all others.

"Elia, it's Calen. I've come to get you out of this place."

The woman continued to rock as though she had no control over the motion, but she lifted her head from her knees. Her face was emaciated and fragile, her skin parchment-thin and pale as bone, her eyes bloodshot. Where once she had commanded a broad, loving smile, her lips were now thin and frail, devoid of all joy. "Calen? Are you really here?" Tears glistened in the candlelight as they rolled from Elia's eyes, streaming down her face, pooling in the crease of her nose, and dripping onto the floor. "It *is* you..." Still rocking slightly, Elia reached up and touched the backs of her fingers against Calen's cheek. He leaned into her touch. "Don't cry, Calen. It's all right. It will all be all right."

Elia's words caused Calen's tears to redouble, flowing freely as he pulled Elia into a soft embrace. Here she was lying tortured and starved on a dungeon floor, and *she* was comforting *him*.

"I'm getting you out of here," Calen whispered, not because he felt the need for silence, but because Elia seemed so brittle that words might break her.

Calen rose to his feet and turned to see Fritz staring down at Elia.

"Is that Lasch and Elia Hav—"

Calen grabbed Fritz by the throat and slammed him against the wall of the interrogation room. He could already see the purple glow of his eyes against the stone wall as unbridled fury swept through him. Even in the back of his mind, Valerys didn't roar or snarl, he didn't carve furrows in the rock. Cold rage held the dragon – held them both.

Gurgling sounds escaped Fritz's throat. Calen squeezed tighter, pushing the man up the wall. "They are your people," Calen growled, his throat scratching. "Yours! They raised you – The Glade raised you!"

Calen's mind flashed to the dream he'd had – or was it a vision of the past? It was near impossible to tell – of Haem standing over the prone body of Durin Netly, Fritz's brother, his blade shimmering in the moonlight, Uraks charging from all sides. Calen loosened his grip on Fritz's neck. "You look after your own, Fritz."

Calen wanted to choke the life from Fritz. He wanted to make him suffer for the suffering he had allowed to happen. But instead, he tossed him to the stone, Tarmon's words echoing. *'You are not him.'*

Fritz choked and spluttered as he hit the ground, pulling his hands to his neck, shuffling backwards into the shadow-touched corners of the interrogation room.

"We need to get them out of here," Calen said to Tarmon.

"Can they walk?"

"I don't think so. At least, not fast enough."

"We'll never sneak them out past the guards upstairs. We could put Gaeleron in the armour, but he'd barely be able to hold himself upright, and that would still leave us with these two."

"We're going to have to fight our way out then. I'm not leaving them."

"I never suggested that," Tarmon said, resting a hand on Calen's shoulder. "We'll get them out of here. I can carry him." Tarmon gestured towards Lasch, who still sat huddled against the far wall.

With that decided, Calen opened himself to the Spark and pulled on threads of Earth, channelling them into the manacles around Elia and Lasch's ankles. As he had with the walls in Belduar, he pushed the threads through the manacles, feeling for the weakest points, crushing them. A second or two passed, then the manacles snapped open, breaking into pieces as they hit the floor.

Calen dropped to one knee beside Elia, laying the candle on the ground and sliding a hand under her back, the other beneath her knees. "I've got you. It's all right. It's all right." Elia pulled away at first, but then curled into Calen's chest like a child overtired from a long day. She weighed almost nothing. Elia had helped raise him – both her and Lasch. She had been Freis's closest friend since long before Calen was born. She had cradled him, fed him, and treated him as though he was her own son. To see her like this broke parts of Calen's heart that had only barely stopped bleeding. He shifted her in his arms, trying to make her more comfortable, moving her arm around his neck for support.

Tarmon had Lasch over his shoulder. Even withered and malnourished, Lasch was still quite a bit heavier than Elia.

Calen nodded towards the door, then stopped. "Fritz, you're coming too."

Fritz was barely visible in the flickering candlelight, his face bathed in shadow. He still had one hand clasped to his neck.

"Stay if you want, but you won't live long once the Inquisition realise you did nothing to stop us." The last thing Calen wanted was the conniving bastard with them, but he knew leaving Fritz behind was as good as killing him. And Calen wasn't ready to be that person. He hoped he never would be. A moment passed before Fritz heaved himself to his feet, stepping from the shadows, blood trickling down his neck from where Calen's blade had cut into him earlier.

With Elia in his arms, Calen stepped from the interrogation room and moved back across the corridor to where Vaeril and Erik were helping Gaeleron to his feet. The elf was now awake, but his head hung, knotted hair dangling, arms wrapped around Erik and Vaeril's shoulders. Rendall's bloodied robes were draped around him.

"He can walk as long as we aid him," Vaeril said in response to the question Calen hadn't asked.

Calen nodded. Gaeleron looked like he was half a moment from passing out, but Calen wasn't about to argue. "Once we get back to the entrance, we'll have to deal with the guards and move quickly from there."

"What about him?" Erik nodded towards Fritz, who still stood in the hallway, blood-stained robes pulled tight.

Calen let out a sigh. "He's coming with us."

"Are you sure that's a good idea?"

"No. I'm not."

Tarmon shifted Lasch on his shoulder, looking over at Fritz. "If he tries anything, we kill him." The words weren't spoken to Fritz, but they were most definitely intended for his ears.

Leaving the interrogation room, Calen pulled the map from the pocket of his robes, shuffling Elia to one side as the group moved as quickly as they could down the dungeon corridors. Gaeleron's legs seemed to move more of their own volition than any conscious thought from the elf. Calen didn't even want to try and contemplate what kind of pain Gaeleron had been through since Belduar. So many questions floated in his mind: Had Gaeleron been captured after the battle of Belduar? Or had he made it to Durakdur and the dwarven city had fallen? Were there more down here? No, Fritz would have said it. He would have said anything to save his life. The only thing about Fritz that Calen trusted was his desire to look after his own skin. *Keep moving. Save who you can. Focus on what's in front of you.*

He pulled the map open awkwardly with one hand. "Fuck."

"What's wrong?" Erik called from behind.

"The map's covered in blood. I can barely read it. I think it's a left ahead."

"Are you sure?"

"As sure as I can be."

Calen turned the corner, stopping in his tracks.

"Why are you stopping?" Tarmon asked, looking at Calen as he turned the corner after him. Then he saw why.

A man stood in the middle of the corridor. He was tall and gangly, with dark skin and wiry muscle, his head shaved clean, a short beard covering the lower half of his face. The man wore loose-fitting linen trousers tucked into leather boots, an unbuttoned black shirt over his shoulders, and a sword strapped to his hip. His shoulders were half as broad as Tarmon's, and he was no taller than Calen, but there was something about the way he held himself that made Calen uneasy.

"You need to turn around," the man said, folding his arms, a look on his face that was more akin to an impatient father than a Lorian soldier.

"We can't do that."

Erik and Vaeril turned the corner behind Calen, Fritz beside them. Calen heard muttering and then the rasp of swords being drawn.

"You're outnumbered," Erik said, stepping up beside Calen, his gaze fixed on the stranger, a sword gripped in each fist. "Step aside. There's been enough blood tonight."

The man gave a half-hearted smile as though Erik had said something that was equally sad and amusing. "You count differently than I do." His gaze passed over Calen and the others, his tongue rolling over his lips. Finally, he gave a shrug. "I didn't come here to shed blood."

"Then step aside." Calen sounded far more confident than he actually was.

"We don't have the time for this," Erik whispered in his ear.

"You're right, we don't," the man answered, taking a step closer. *How had he heard?*

"I'm ending this." Erik strode forwards, his swords glinting in the candlelight. But as he moved, Calen felt the man before them draw from the Spark, pulling threads of Air into himself.

Calen lay Elia on the ground and leapt towards Erik, opening himself to the Spark. He sent a thread of Spirit shearing through the man's thread of Air, as Vaeril had shown him. The stranger simply raised an eyebrow, giving a downturn of his lip, then drew the sword from his hip and braced himself for Erik's charge. Within seconds the corridor was filled with the sounds of clanging steel.

The man turned away Erik's strikes as though they were nothing, whirling around him, feet moving in a flash. Calen lunged, driving his blade towards the man's stomach, but the stranger spun on his heels, cracking his pommel on the back of Calen's head. Calen stumbled, dropping to one knee, his head spinning, spots of colour flecking his vision. He pushed himself to his feet.

The stranger twirled between Erik, Tarmon, Vaeril, and Calen as though sword fighting was simply a dance, steel glimmering, feet moving in a blur. A thread of Air crashed into Vaeril, knocking the elf on his back, threads of Spirit wrapping around him, moving in a latticed pattern, closing him off from the Spark. Calen tried to slice a spike of Spirit through the man's ward but caught a pommel to the face, followed by something hard to the gut.

As Calen doubled over, he felt Valerys in the back of his mind, pushing him, urging him on. This wasn't like when he faced Rendall. Valerys was scared – terrified. The man who stood before them was far stronger than Rendall – far stronger than anyone Calen had encountered. Calen let the dragon's mind wrap around his, let the rage in. Energy surged through him, and he hurled himself towards their attacker, threads of Fire, Air, and Spirit spiralling around him.

The man sidestepped a stab from Erik, then sliced his blade along Erik's cheek, leaving a thin trail of blood. He could easily have taken Erik's life then and there. Why had he not?

He's toying with us.

Calen struck out with whips of Fire and Air, letting the svidarya flow through him, moving from Howling Wolf, to Eagle's Claw, into Raging Sea. But the man countered every strike without breaking a sweat.

A wave of energy rippled outwards from the man, threads of Spirit and Air spiralling. Calen had never felt a strength like it. Not in Aeson. Not in Therin. Power radiated from him like the light of the sun, blinding to anyone who could see the Spark. Then something was slamming into Calen, hammering against his chest, throwing him backwards, dragging him to his knees. Around him, he could see the same was happening to Erik and Tarmon, with Vaeril still pinned down and warded.

"As amusing as that was, no more games," the man said, moving so he stood in front of Calen, paying no heed to the others. "If I let you go, will you talk to me?"

Calen grunted, struggling against the bonds that held him down, a strange blending of Air and Spirit that felt as strong as mountain roots. His teeth grinding, Valerys's rage still blazing through him, Calen nodded. "Very well."

Just like that, the threads holding him in place vanished, and Calen fell forward, taken aback by how quickly the man had followed through. He lifted himself to his feet. "Who are you, and what do you want?"

The man studied Calen. "Interesting." He leaned closer. "I've not seen a Draleid develop eyes like that before."

Calen froze. How in the gods did this man know who he was?

"The way you move. The way the rage flows through you. The way the others fight around you. No," the man said, shaking his head. "I can't read your mind, but when you live to see as many centuries as I have, you learn things."

The man's relaxed demeanour unsettled Calen. He was acting as though they hadn't spent the last few minutes trying to tear each other apart.

"You've been betrayed. One of your contacts within the city has informed the Inquisition of your presence here. Luckily, the affinities of The Circle don't work well together – too much bickering. So they haven't passed on the information. They would prefer to take you in themselves. That gives us time. If you trust me, I can show you a different way out of the city."

"I… what…" Calen couldn't get his thoughts straight. Who in the void was this man, and how did he know so much? "Who are you?"

"If I wanted you dead," the man said, ignoring Calen's question, "you'd be dead. If you listen to the air, you will hear armoured boots. One hundred and twelve Praetorians, ten Inquisitors. Many still drunk, others called in from patrol." The man opened his arms outwards as though he had just presented the most logical argument in the known world.

Calen looked at the others. Vaeril was pinned to the ground, encased in a ward of Spirit. Tarmon and Erik were on their knees, threads of Spirit-reinforced Air holding them in place. Gaeleron sat slouched against the stone wall, drawing in ragged breaths. Elia and Lasch were huddled together, shielding their eyes from the light of the candles. Fritz knelt a few feet away, just staring.

He pulled on threads of Air and Spirit, letting them flow through him, then he pushed them out, feeling the vibrations, the currents of air, as he had done in the tunnels below Lodhar – the drift, Falmin had said the Wind Runners Guild called it. The crash of steel on stone thundered in Calen's ears, and he pulled back the threads, thinning them, letting the sound dull. Armour. Weapons. Footsteps. He couldn't tell how many, but they *were* coming.

"I do not trust The Circle, and I trust the Inquisition even less. As a result, I constructed a small tunnel that leads from here into the storeroom of an empty house within the city. That tunnel is concealed by a touch glamour." The man pulled out a flat disk-shaped rock, smooth as glass. Hues of purple and pink reflected the light, thin veins of white crawling through the rock's opalescent surface "This is the key that unlocks the glamour." To Calen's surprise, the man held out the opalescent purple rock and dropped it into Calen's hand. "You don't trust me. Which is wise. But not conducive to escaping this place. Take the key and go."

"How do I use it?"

"Aeson has truly neglected your education, hasn't he?"

"You know Aeson?"

The man held up his hand. "Know him? Yes. Respect him? Yes. Though I do not believe he would consider me a friend. Either way, funnel thin threads of Spirit into either end of the key, then bring them together at the centre. As you do, picture a lock in your mind. The key will lead you to the tunnel. Once you find the glamour, weave six threads through the key and into the glamour, then open the lock in your mind. Do you understand?"

"Yes, I think so." Calen looked at the polished rock in his hand, the various hues of purple and pink shimmering as he turned it. "Why?"

"You look after your own." A knowing smile curled the man's lips, a touch of sadness creasing at the corners of his mouth.

"You…"

"My name is Pellenor Dambren. I was once a Draleid, many lifetimes ago. I made choices I'm not proud of. I did the wrong things for the right reasons, and I've had many years to think."

"You're a Dragonguard." Calen's hand instinctively fell to the hilt of his sword, the Spark blazing through him.

"You'd be dead before you moved an inch."

Calen didn't move, but he kept his hand resting on the pommel of his sword, the Spark still flooding through him.

"Yes," Pellenor said with a sigh. "I am one of the Dragonguard. I was set to watch over Inquisitor Malkas, to see what plans he was hatching. And then I found you."

Pellenor took a step closer to Calen.

Calen dropped his hand from the pommel to the hilt, pulling on threads of Fire, but before he could do anything, a tear streaked down Pellenor's face. The man wasn't sobbing, or convulsing, or even showing much emotion whatsoever, but the tear glistened in the candlelight as it rolled down his cheek, and in that moment, Calen saw something true within the man. A grief, a loss that had consumed him.

"Before you came, we thought we were the last. We thought the gods had punished us for what we did. That they had taken the life from dragons in response to our betrayal. And then your soulkin hatched, and everything changed. We're not hunting you, Calen. We've been trying to find you, to protect you. You are the last hope for the survival of our kind." Before Calen could think to react, Pellenor pulled him into an embrace, his arms wrapping around Calen's back. Then the man whispered, "I know you can't trust us, and there are some of us you shouldn't trust. We've left dark history in our wake. I am not here to drag you in chains towards the destiny of our choosing. There is a temple atop the highest peak of Dracaldryr. When you are ready, light the beacon on the temple's roof. We will come. But first, you need to get out of these dungeons."

Calen made to speak, but Pellenor pulled away, glancing towards the others who were still pinned in position.

"There's no time. Take the key and go."

"Why are you doing all this?"

"Because it's what I should have done four hundred years ago. I can't change the things I've done, time doesn't move backwards. But it is never, nor will it ever be, too late to see the mistakes I've made. You go, I'll buy you some time. Draleid n'aldryr, Calen Bryer."

"Rakina nai dauva," Calen responded, the words leaving his lips of their own volition.

Pellenor nodded, then turned and walked back down the corridor in the opposite direction. The threads of Air holding the others evaporated.

Erik, Tarmon, and Vaeril hauled themselves to their feet, panting and shaking off invisible chains.

"Who in Varyn's name was that?" Erik held his two blades in his fists, staring down the corridor where Pellenor had disappeared into the shadows.

"You didn't hear what he said?"

Erik shook his head.

"He created a ward of silence," Vaeril said, stepping up beside Calen, checking him over for injuries.

A ward of silence? How had Calen not noticed?

"Who was he?" Erik repeated.

"He just said he was a friend." Calen hated lying. He owed Erik and the others more than lies, but this was different. While Calen was locked in the cell in Arisfall, Artim Valdock had said many things, but one in particular clung to Calen's thoughts. *'The men and women you protect would see this continent burn, so long as they have their revenge. And they would use you as a puppet to achieve this. They are not your allies or your kin. They are your puppet masters. The Dragonguard are your only true kin.'* At the time, Calen had understood the man was trying to get inside his head. Though, there were many truths in his words. But now, seeing Pellenor, hearing the sadness in his voice… it was something Calen needed to think on himself – him and Valerys. Even then, in the back of his mind, Valerys had gone quiet. All the dragon wanted now was for Calen to get out of Berona. "He gave me a key." Calen held out the opalescent stone.

"Calen, that's a rock."

"It's a glamour key," Vaeril corrected, leaning forwards to get a better look. "Like your father used in Belduar."

"We don't have much time. He said one of our contacts has betrayed us and told the Inquisition of our presence here."

"How can we trust him?"

"Erik, trust *me*. We need to go."

Erik ran his tongue along the top row of his teeth, then nodded. "Lead the way."

Once they had gathered the injured and Calen had Elia curled in his arms once more, he did what Pellenor had instructed. He opened himself to the Spark and pulled on threads of Spirit, weaving them into either end of the key, which he had placed in his pocket. He joined the threads at the centre of the key, and tried to picture a lock in his mind – which was harder than he thought it would be. It was like that time Dann had asked him if he breathed in or out when drawing back a bow string. 'In' was the answer he had come to eventually, but as soon as Dann had asked the question the answer had been nowhere to be found.

Breathe. Think.

Calen took a moment. He thought of home, back in The Glade. He imagined himself approaching the front door, but couldn't picture the lock. He went to his room, to the small chest his father had given him that sat below his bed. Vars had given it to him along with his practice sword.

Now that he looked back, there had been little sense to it. What was the point in keeping a wooden practice sword in a locked chest? He supposed it made the sword feel special. Calen pictured the chest's lock. It was brass and rectangular, floral ornamentation along the edge, the keyhole at its centre. The bottom two thirds of the lock were fixed to the chest itself, while the top third was fitted to the lid.

As the lock began to take shape in his mind, the key-stone in his pocket gave off a pulse that sent a low vibration through the Inquisitor robes he wore. The pulse lowered to a thrum, and as Calen lifted his head, he saw a faint purple line of mist extending from where the stone sat in his pocket, outwards, back the way they had come, around the corner.

"Can you see that?" Calen glanced to the others then back at the line of purple mist.

"See what?" Erik asked.

"Follow me."

Calen followed the line of purple mist, moving as quickly as his Spark-drained legs would carry him with Elia draped in his arms. His heart thudded. His breaths were short and ragged, each one burning in his lungs. As they ran, they passed through corridors lit by no more than a single candle and others shrouded in total darkness, but the line of mist remained. Lefts, followed by rights, followed by lefts. Staircases and in-tersections. Calen's head spun with the number of twists and turns. *Gold didn't lie – this place truly is a labyrinth.*

With each step, they moved deeper into the network of corridors that made up the dungeons. The map in his pocket was so bloodstained it was unreadable. He was leading some of his closest companions on the words of a man he had only just met – a man who admitted to being a Dragonguard. He glanced back. Erik and Vaeril had their arms around Gaeleron, half helping, half carrying him along the corridor. Tarmon ran with Lasch over his shoulder, holding the man in place with his right hand, his left hand hovering near the pommel of his short sword. To Calen's surprise, Fritz was still with them, keeping pace, carrying nothing but his own desire to live. Calen had expected Fritz to skulk off at the first chance he got, but clearly Fritz had considered his chances of living to be better served by leaving than staying.

Then, abruptly, the purple line stopped, disappearing into a wall that marked another corner.

"What's wrong?" Tarmon asked, breathing heavily, sweat dripping from his nose, Lasch draped over his shoulder. "Why've we stopped?"

"This is where it ends..." Calen reached out and touched the wall. It was solid, though it felt *different*. He wasn't sure what that difference was, just that it was different.

"Calen, what do you mean, 'this is where it ends?'" Erik asked. "We're in the middle of fucking nowhere here."

"This is where the trail ends. It leads here." Calen kept his hand pressed against the wall where the line of mist stopped.

"This is the glamour? Well, open it, then. Unless you're feeling a little rusty and need some more sword practice. We can always turn around and fight our way out." Erik shrugged with his free shoulder, giving a half-smile. It was good to see him joking again.

Calen hefted Elia in his arms. Opening himself to the Spark, he did just as Pellenor had instructed, funnelling six threads of Spirit into the keystone and then onwards through the wall. He pictured the lock again, then opened it, hearing a *click* echo in his mind.

As though it had never been there in the first place, the wall where Calen had held his hand was now gone. Vanished. In its place was a gaping hole that stretched a few feet across and rose about an inch over Calen's head. Through the hole was complete darkness.

"Do you trust that man?" Erik asked, looking into the shadow-shrouded hole.

"No."

"Not that it matters. We don't have many options. Tarmon, you're going to have to crouch."

AFTER ABOUT FIFTEEN MINUTES OF trudging up through the long tunnel by baldírlight, Calen emerged into a room that was no bigger than his own room back in The Glade. A few barren shelves stood against the far wall, and a stack of empty baskets sat beside a wooden door that likely led out into the house Pellenor had spoken of.

With a sigh of relief, Calen lay Elia down beside the baskets, brushing a few strands of her brittle, greying hair to the side. Just the sight of her gaunt face, purple-ringed eyes, and cracked lips set a fury in Calen. Elia had always been one of the most kind-hearted people Calen had ever known. At times he had found her unrelenting cheeriness to be irritating, but as he looked at her now, he would have done anything to give that back to her. *This* was what they were fighting for. *This* was why Calen would never stop.

"I thought your contacts said there was only one way in or out of this place?" Tarmon said to Erik as he hauled himself out of the long tunnel, laying Lasch down beside Elia. He removed his red plate helmet, letting out a sigh of exhaustion as he wiped sweat from his brow.

"Well, they were hardly going to know about this, were they?" Erik stepped through the tunnel after Tarmon, helping Gaeleron through, Vaeril and Fritz following after.

Once they were all through, Calen rose to his feet and leaned back against the door, running his hands through his sweat-slicked hair. He leaned his head back, releasing a long breath. "We need to get to the Raven's Ruin."

"What if the Inquisition are already there?" Tarmon asked.

Calen looked to Erik. "Are there any other passages out of the city?"

"Erik shook his head. "Not that I know of. There used to be one under the locksmith's on the eastern edge of the city, but the empire collapsed it over two years ago."

"Then we don't have a choice. We can't stay here, and we need to get the others out of the city." Calen could feel Valerys scratching at the back of his mind. *Come, but stay above the clouds. We can't risk anyone seeing you unless we need you.* As soon as the words touched Calen's mind, Valerys cracked his wings and lifted himself into the air, rain pouring from dark thunderclouds and crashing against his scales. "Erik, can you lead the way?"

Erik nodded. "I don't have a clue where we are, but once we get outside I'll have a better idea."

Calen dropped to his haunches beside Elia, allowed himself one last exhausted sigh, and lifted her into his arms once more. He turned to Fritz. "Help Erik carry Gaeleron."

"What about the elf?"

Calen glared at Fritz. "Vaeril needs his hands free in case we run into any Inquisitors. Now shut up and pull your weight, or I'll leave you here to be put on the other side of those interrogation rooms."

Fritz looked as though he was going to argue but then thought better of it and gave a curt nod, taking Vaeril's place beside Gaeleron.

Pale moonlight drifted through the dirt-coated windows of the house beyond the storeroom, which was devoid of any signs of life, empty except for a table, some chairs, and a hearth fire that had clearly never seen the touch of a flame. A trail of layered footsteps marked a path through the dust that coated the floor, leading from the storeroom to the front door of the house. The drum of rainfall beat against the roof, a crack of thunder rolling through the sky.

Erik moved over towards one of the windows, brushing some dirt aside and peering out. "We're not far."

"All right. Let's go, then. Lead the way."

The slapping sounds of feet on wet stone echoed as they made their way through the streets of Berona, the rain pummelling them, skies of dark clouds overhead rumbling with thunder. Except for the odd drunk who gave them sideways glances and refugees sleeping beneath archways and tunnels, the streets were empty. Once or twice they pulled into a side alley as a patrol of city guard passed, but it was quite clear no alarm had been raised, no search called. Pellenor had not lied, the Inquisition hadn't spread news of Calen's presence. They must have wanted him for themselves.

"Up here." They stepped into a narrow back alley, and Erik gestured towards a two-storey building with a sloping orange slate roof, wedged in between two larger buildings. "The door's already ajar," he whispered as they reached the small wooden door set into the back of the fletchery, pulling both his swords from the scabbards across his back.

Calen shifted Elia in his arms, looking down at the woman who was still curled up like a babe born too early, weak and frail. Her head twitched, always to the left, her eyes darting about beneath closed lids. He whispered, "We're almost there."

As Erik leaned his shoulder against the door, pushing it open slowly, Calen opened himself to the Spark. He didn't pull on any threads but kept the strands within arm's reach, floating, pulsating in his mind if he should need them. Now that he was back up in the city, he could feel the thrum of power resonating in the air – that should keep him masked from any mages as long as he doesn't pull on any threads. He felt Valerys's wings beating against the air, carrying him towards Berona faster than any horse or ship could dream of. The dragon soared through the clouds, staying out of sight from any who roamed the lands below.

"It could very well be a trap," Vaeril said, as Erik and Fritz drew up beside him, Gaeleron propped up between them.

"Oh, it's definitely a trap." Erik shrugged. "But there's no other way out of this city with two elves, Calen, and the rest of us looking like we've had a swim in a bloodbath. Besides, we've spent so long in tunnels and wastelands, fighting Fades and madness. I've missed being able to kill the things trying to kill me."

"Hear, hear," Tarmon whispered back, short sword gripped in his free hand, Lasch still lumped over his shoulder.

The bottom storey of the fletchery was lit only by the cold light of the moon that drifted in through the windows set in the far wall that faced out onto the main street. But even in the dim light, the red gleam of Praetorian armour was clear to see. Bodies lay all around the room, upturned buckets of goose and turkey feathers tacked to pools of blood, arrow heads and strips of wood scattered about the place. "We're too late…"

"No." Vaeril dropped to his haunches, looking about the dead. "They're all imperials. Eleven Praetorians and an Inquisitor." Vaeril inclined his head towards a crumpled mess of a woman in the corner of the room lying in a pool of blood and feathers, red robes draped over her shoulders, her left arm severed at the shoulder.

"You're damn right they are."

Calen snapped his head around to the left, towards the arched doorway that sat in the building's dividing wall. Vaeril rose to his feet, dropping into Rising Dawn. Erik ducked out from Gaeleron's arm, drawing his blades, leaving Fritz to take the injured elf's weight. Tarmon raised his guard, readying to drop Lasch if needs be.

A man stood in the doorway, a suit of smooth overlapping green plate covering his body. He had no helm, and he looked as though he had seen five or six more summers than Calen. His brown hair reached his shoulders, and he bore a smile that seemed out of place with the death in the room. A sigil in the shape of a downward facing sword set into a sunburst was emblazoned across the breast of the armour in brilliant white. Calen had seen that strange armour and that sigil only once before: on the warriors at Kingspass.

The man raised his armoured hands. "Easy now. I think there's already enough blood on this floor for one night. I pity the one who has to clean this place."

"He's with us," Gold said, stepping through the archway and past the warrior. "Come we need to get out of here, now. We've been betrayed. Tarka – who you know as Black – was working for the Inquisition the whole time. Seven years he's been with us. Seven years and I didn't see it."

"We can lament later, Surin," the warrior said to Gold. "For now, we need to get the Draleid and the others out of the city. There's more inquisition on their way here now, and I reckon they won't be too happy when they get here."

Surin nodded, a melancholy smile on her face. She inclined her head towards the archway. "Come. The passage out is this way. When Tarka betrayed us, he disclosed the information of our network within the city. Those we could rescue have already escaped."

Calen gestured for the others to follow Surin. Once Fritz and Erik had helped Gaeleron through, Calen stopped in front of the man in the green armour.

"The name's Lyrin. It's good to finally meet you. You're shorter than I thought you'd be."

"You're one of them." Calen shifted Elia in his arms, his eyes fixed on Lyrin, his breath catching in his chest.

"A Knight of Achyron, yes. Like Arden. Or I suppose Haem. Still feels strange to call him that though. Speaking of which, if I let any of these Taint-wielding bastards touch a hair on your head, he'll not be too happy. So we should probably get moving."

Hearing his brother's name spoken aloud twisted a knot in Calen's chest. *Why do they call him Arden?* Calen pushed the thoughts to the back of mind, where he locked them away with all the others. He nodded, then stepped past Lyrin into the other room where Surin was waiting for him by a trapdoor in the floorboards.

She gestured for Calen to step down into the passageway, nodding towards Elia, who was still curled in Calen's arms. "You'll need your hands to get at least part of the way down. I'll pass her down to you."

Calen turned to Lyrin. He heard armoured feet slapping against wet stone outside. A pulsating red glow shimmered in the dark, refracting off the glass window panes. "Are you coming?"

A smile crept across Lyrin's face. "You go. I've just got a little more redecorating to do. I'll be right after you."

Chapter Forty

True Colours

You're sure?" Garramon sat behind his desk, his right leg folded over his left, fingers stroking his chin. He looked down at the small black wooden box Rist placed on the desk.

"I'm sure, Brother." Garramon had given Rist a week to decide, and even after Emperor Mortem's visit, Rist had waited, and studied. The day before, Sister Ardal had given Neera the same trial – her own essence vessel. Neera had told Rist immediately, which twisted a pang of guilt within him because he had kept the vessel a secret as Garramon had asked. It had made sense at the time. Telling Neera about it would have unfairly led to his own bias creeping into her mind when it came time to make her own decision – and yet, something still felt wrong about lying to her. Well, not lying, but omitting. But despite the differences in the definitions of the words, it still felt the same. And she had neither lied nor omitted anything to him. "I have taken my time and weighed the information. Though I would be lying if I told you the emperor's visit hadn't played a big part. I'm ready to move forward."

"Fane?" Garramon's face twisted in a look of surprise that he quickly tried to hide.

Rist raised an eyebrow. "Yes… Brother?" For a split second Rist worried he'd said something he shouldn't. "Did you not know?"

Garramon frowned, then shrugged. "I was aware he wished to speak to you, but I wasn't aware he had already done so. Either way, it does not matter. This choice must be your own."

"It is." Rist shifted in the wooden seat, leaning forwards, his heartbeat slowly rising in his chest, thumping the blood through his veins. He would be lying if he'd said he wasn't nervous. But nerves were a good thing, they told him he was still thinking clearly. "I'm ready."

Garramon gave a slow sombre nod. Rist wasn't sure how he'd expected the man to react. Garramon wasn't a particularly emotional man, at least not outwardly, but Rist had expected something… *more*. After a few moments of silence, Garramon lifted himself from his chair and walked around to where Rist sat, resting his hand on Rist's shoulder. "Today, when you feel the touch of Essence in your blood, you will cease to be an apprentice, and you will rise to become an acolyte of the Imperial Battlemages." Garramon looked down at Rist, their stares meeting, the slightest hint of a smile touching the man's face. "I have never before seen someone rise so quickly and so effortlessly. And I do not use the word 'effortlessly' to diminish the sheer determination and dedication with which you've trained, but simply to emphasise the level of your potential. Yes, this rapid progression is, in part, due to the circumstances we find ourselves in, threatened by war on all sides, but I feel it is important to stress that you are, in no uncertain terms, exceptional. Your swordsmanship needs work – a lot of work – and as a whole, you are still rough and unrefined, but your only obstacle is time. Your..." Garramon paused for a moment, pondering. "Your 'friend', Neera, will likely rise to acolyte shortly, but she will never touch the heights you will one day reach. The same stands for the others – Tommin and Lena. All of this, Rist, is a long-winded way of saying I'm proud of you. I often tell you how your insubordination and tardiness reflects on me as a sponsor, but I do not tell you often enough how proud I am of your dedication."

Rist stared back at Garramon, dumbfounded. That was, quite simply, the nicest thing anyone had ever said to him. Calen and Dann had always looked out for Rist, protected him. His mother and father had always loved him and had supported him in all he attempted. But he was protected because he was weak and frail, because he was a 'bookworm', because he was just that little bit different. But here in the Circle, where Garramon had found Rist weak, he hadn't protected him, he had given him the means to strengthen himself. He had pushed Rist and believed in him. When Garramon had seen Rist's tendencies towards books and study, he hadn't derided him or mocked him but found him more books and even pretended not to notice when Rist snuck tomes from the library – he understood, or at least, he made every effort to do so. When it came to Rist, where everyone else saw weakness, Garramon saw strength. Where everyone else saw a peculiarity, Garramon saw a uniqueness to be fostered. Every step Rist had taken along this new path, Garramon had been there by his side, not protecting him, but pushing him forward. "Thank you, Brother Garramon."

The man nodded, his expression returning to its usual stoniness. He gestured towards the desk.

Rist drew in a deep breath then stood, staring at the wooden box, knowing what lay within.

"Essence is the power, Rist. You are simply the conduit. Reach out with your mind, touch the vessel with your consciousness. It is known as 'tapping' into the vessel, like tapping a spring for water or a tree for sap."

Rist opened himself to the Spark. He felt the elemental strands twisting and turning in the emptiness of his mind, radiating power, pulsating their distinctive light. He savoured the feeling for the moment, letting the Spark fill him. Then he pulled on a thin thread of Air, weaving it through the wooden box, pushing and pulling at the internal locking mechanism. *Click.*

The lid popped open, and there, sitting on a bed of purple satin, emitting a red glow, sat the grape-sized gemstone that had been the focus of his thoughts.

"Essence is not like the Spark. You consume it from the moment you tap the vessel. It burns like firewood. It strengthens you, nourishes your body, makes you faster, stronger. What is within that vessel is only a taste."

Rist's hand hovered above the stone. Garramon's voice faded into the background, dulling at the edges of Rist's mind. The only sounds that touched Rist's ears were the slow, methodical breaths that filled his lungs and the thumping of his heart. He could feel the sweat beginning to form on the palm of his hand, his cheeks warming. *Nerves are good.* This was not a small step. In his mind, stories and tales battled. Legends of good versus evil. Black versus white. That was how stories were told. But what was white in Illyanara was black in Loria, and so the other way around. It all meshed into grey. The truth was grey – an amalgamation of both sides. *All truths are nothing more than the amalgamation of lies.*

Rist played his conversation with Fane over in his mind. He watched the power of Essence bring life back to the broken hummingbird. *'And so, death breathes life anew.'* And with that, he came to his decision: Essence, regardless of where it was sourced, was not good or evil, just as the Spark was not good or evil, for nothing is inherently evil. Good and evil are in the doing of things. It is not Essence or the Spark that makes a man evil. What matters is what a person does with the power they are given. And Rist would use this power to do good. He knew it in his heart.

Rist slowed his breathing and did as Garramon had instructed. He focused on the small, glowing gemstone that sat before him, watching its red light pulse, the edges of his vision dulling. In truth, he wasn't sure what he was actually meant to do. Telling someone to reach out with their mind was one thing, knowing how to actually do it was another thing entirely. *Patience. Breathe.*

Time was measured only by the thumping of his heart. He pushed out with his mind, imagining his consciousness touching the cool surface of the gemstone, imagining it pushing through – tapping in.

Frustration welled when nothing happened, but then his vision faded to black, and panic took hold. A ripple of ice washed over his skin, his blood going cold. Then all feeling left him, touch, smell, sound. He was floating in a void.

After a few moments of nothingness, the world snapped back into focus. Sound crashed against him in waves. Light scorched at his eyes. Scents and smells flooded his nostrils, from the leather of Garramon's chair, to the earthy aroma of the books on the shelf, to the sharp scent of fresh-cut grass from the gardens. More than that, Rist felt power. Power unlike anything he had ever felt in his entire life. It coursed through his veins, his muscles feeling as though they had been carved from stone.

Before him, the gemstone sat in the box, resting atop the purple silk, its crimson light vivid and bright. With each breath, Rist felt as though he would suck the air from the room.

"Incredible, isn't it?" Garramon's voice was crisp and clear, resounding in Rist's ears as though amplified by a score of horns. The Exarch stepped in front of Rist, looking into his eyes. "Efialtír's gift. A feeling like no other. Now, I know it is difficult, but you must let go. Do not waste the Essence within the vessel. It is not easily obtained."

As Garramon's words echoed in Rist's mind, he realised something: someone had died to give him this power, and he could feel his body burning it, wasting it. He pulled his mind back, gasping as the essence fled his body. The power drained, his senses dulled, and the world around him lost its new-found sharpness. A twinge of sadness tweaked within him at the loss of strength, but he pushed it aside.

Rist looked down at the gemstone, his chest heaving, beads of sweat forming on his hands and brow. The light of the gemstone already looked weaker, dimmer. The strength it had given him had been intoxicating. Like lightning searing his veins, demanding to be unleashed. Rist may have decided that Essence was not evil, but at that moment, he also made the decision to use it sparingly and only when he truly needed it. He could see how addictive that power could be.

It is not easily obtained. Every drop of Essence was drawn from the taking of a life, and so it must be cherished and respected. That was a vow Rist would not break. Not for anything or anyone.

Simply feeling the power of the Essence, then having it dragged from him, had taken more out of Rist than he had anticipated.

He tried to steady his breathing as he looked up to see a soft smile on Garramon's face. The man reached behind his desk, opened a drawer, and produced a folded bundle of black, a touch of brown visible along the edges. Garramon placed the bundle on the desk, then moved to Rist, pulling Rist's black-striped brown robes from his shoulders – the robes of a second tier apprentice. "Rist Havel. Your strength of will was tested, pushed to its limits and tempered in the Well of Arnen. Your faith in those around you was pressed and tried. The true tests of a person's strength are not physical, but mental. In this, you have shown yourself strong beyond measure." Garramon unfurled the bundle, revealing robes of jet black trimmed with brown – the robes of a Battlemage acolyte. He slipped the right sleeve over Rist's arm, pulling the robes over Rist's shoulders until Rist himself slid his left arm into the other sleeve and shrugged the robes into place. *Black.* Pride swelled in Rist's chest. He was still not a fully-fledged Battlemage, but he had finally earned his colours.

"Let me see you." Garramon stood back, clasping his hands on Rist's shoulders. "You wear it well."

"Thank you, Brother Garramon."

"It's just Brother now, Acolyte. Or Garramon, whichever you prefer."

"Thank you, Brother."

Garramon inclined his head, smiling. He moved back behind his desk and produced another, smaller, black bundle, along with a smooth, double-edged dagger with a gold crossguard, a black leather handle, and a hollow golden ring for a pommel. "This," Garramon said, touching the other bundle, "is your cloak. Tomorrow morning I will bring you to the armourer, and we will have a breastplate fitted and arrange any other armour that should fit your combat style. When you are to march to battle you will replace the robes with your cloak."

"To battle?"

Garramon nodded, biting his bottom lip as he looked down over the robes. "For an acolyte to become a Battlemage, like a blade, you must be tempered and tested. By the week's end we will, both of us, be marching with the First Army to meet with the Fourth Army at Fort Harken, and then onwards to connect with the Second Army at Steeple. There is trouble along the eastern coast, and Supreme Commander Taya Tambrel has called for a joint response."

Rist didn't move, certain a dumbstruck expression occupied his face. Battle? Already? He was to go to war? Rist had always known this would happen. There was no depth of naivety that could leave someone unaware that a man with the title of Battlemage would one day have to walk towards battle – he just hadn't thought that day would be soon. *Neera… Tommin, Lena.*

As though reading Rist's thoughts, Garramon spoke. "It is likely Neera, Tommin, and Lena will join us with the First Army. Each of them should become acolytes before we march." Garramon picked up the dagger and moved back around the desk to where Rist stood, plucking the dim gemstone from the box as he did. "That fear in your heart, don't fight it, embrace it. Fear is good. It keeps you sharp. Just make sure you never let it rule you." Garramon lowered his head, raising an eyebrow as he met Rist's gaze.

Rist nodded. He felt the sensation of Garramon reaching out to Spark. The mage drew in threads of Fire and Earth, funnelling them into the hollow circular pommel of the dagger, heating the metal, drawing it out, expanding it. After a moment, Garramon placed the Essence vessel into the hollow, which had been expanded to accommodate the gemstone, then pulled the metal tighter around the stone, moulding it with Fire and Earth, fixing it in place. Once it was done and the heat was pulled from the metal using threads of Fire, Garramon handed the dagger to Rist.

"What's this for?" Rist asked, turning the dagger over in his hands, admiring the craftsmanship of the carved lion heads that roared on either side of the crossguard.

"An integral part of being raised to the rank of Battlemage involves one last step. You have opened yourself to Essence, but to truly be counted amongst the ranks of this affinity, you must give as well as take. A vessel does not *have* to be fused with a weapon in order to draw in Essence, but in this particular case, it is important that the deed is purposeful, and so this dagger must be used. When we do march to battle, Rist, you will be given the chance to take the final step on the first stage of this journey. You must refill what you have taken from the vessel."

"You want me to…" Rist looked back down at the dagger – its smooth, steel blade; its ornate, golden crossguard; the tough, black leather. His gaze stopped at the dimly glowing gemstone set into the pommel. Suddenly the weapon took on a new meaning.

"I want you to take something from death. We are marching to war, Rist. Thousands will die. Tens of thousands before this is over. At the very least, we can take something from all that death."

Chapter Forty-one

Where Loyalties Lie

Silence consumed the Andurii command tent when Dayne pulled back the canvas flap and stepped in from the night. Small foldable tables held thick candles that washed the tent in a warm light, casting shadows like the sun through trees.

Marlin and the five other Andurii captains – Dinekes, Odys, Ileeri, Barak, and Jorath – stood around a central table that held a rough drawn map of Valtara. They still wore their bloodied armour from earlier in the day, stitches holding wounds closed, skin bruised yellow and black. They had come into conflict with Lorian forces four times since leaving Lostwren for Myrefall, securing five towns along the way and bolstering their numbers by two thousand. The Andurii had been at the heart of each battle, and they had earned their victories with blood and sweat.

The captains looked up from the map, eyes fixed on Dayne, backs straightening as they greeted him with a stiff, "Lord Ateres."

"At ease," Dayne said, wiping the sweat and dirt from his brow with his right hand, before tossing a waterskin across the table to Marlin. He undid a second waterskin at his belt and tossed it to Ileeri, who snatched it out of the air with effortless grace, pulled the stopper from the top, and brought it to her lips.

"Wine, my lord?"

"You've earned it." Dayne mustered as broad a smile as he could, but all he wanted was his cot. His body groaned from the fighting, his soul pulled at him from such prolonged use of the Spark, and his left arm burned so brightly from holding the ordo shield for so long it felt as though it might fall off. "I've had casks dispersed through the company. It's Lorian, so it probably tastes like shit, but it's better than water for curing aches and pains. Maybe it will even give you a good night's sleep."

Ileeri let out a laugh, followed by a heavy sigh as though releasing a weight from her shoulders. She closed her eyes and drank a mouthful, then passed the skin to Odys, who stood beside her. "You have my thanks, my lord."

"And you have mine, Ileeri. You all do. You have fought like champions since donning the armour. The Andurii name is once again spreading throughout Valtara." Dayne turned to Marlin, raising his hand at the offer of the wine. "What news from the scouts?"

"Myrefall is well fortified. We can't get an exact number on the garrison. But last reports placed over ten thousand warriors under the banners of House Thebal. It is likely Miron has called most of those banners back to Myrefall, to keep his seat secure. Over the last week, many Lorian ships have docked in Myrefall's harbours. Meaning, all in all, there is no way to tell the numbers we face." Marlin took another swig of wine, then leaned on the table, trailing his hand across the map. "The lands from Myrefall to Achyron's Keep are heavily patrolled by a mixture of Thebalan, Koraklon, and Lorian forces. Even with the warriors of House Koraklon who have declared for your sister, High Lord Loren still holds sway over some thirty thousand. And from the reports, those Lorian reinforcements have finally arrived. Taking Myrefall and Achyron's Keep will be no easy task."

Dayne nodded, folding his arms. "What of dragons? Have there been any sightings?"

A few eyebrows raised at that.

"I thought you had said the dragons would be too distracted to be a problem, my lord?" Barak was a broad chested man with a head as bald as a polished stone and a clean-shaven face. He was a few summers Dayne's senior and bore full markings of both the spear and the sword, along with a number of other Valtaran tattoos that coiled about his shoulders and legs.

"I cannot see the future, Barak. And one should always hope for a calm sea but prepare for a storm that shifts the oceans. There are rebellions breaking out across the continent, true. But the more ground we gain, the more noise we make, the more blood we spill, the more likely it is that the empire might deem us worthy of the Dragonguard."

"Fair words." Barak nodded, looking down at the map, a touch of worry creeping onto his face. The same concerned look spread across the other captains, but none of them spoke.

"None in Valtara," Marlin said, answering Dayne's question. "But there have been sightings in western Illyanara, along with Drifaien. It may not be long before they turn their gaze to us."

"I will speak to Alina." He had asked Alina to reach out to Aeson multiple times, but she was as stubborn as an angry mule. With the number of wyverns under her command, a single Dragonguard would not turn the tide of this war. But a single Dragonguard at the head of an army of fifty thousand or more, supported by companies of Battlemages was a different prospect entirely. And that was assuming the presence of only one Dragonguard. The wars across the continent had bought them time, but it had not bought them certainty. If they reached out to Aeson, Dayne had no doubt in his mind the man would send aid. Dayne let out a sigh. *You'll have to listen eventually, sister. Just don't let it be too late.*

Dayne lifted his hand and scratched at his stubbled chin. There was a question he'd been avoiding that needed asking. "I need you all to be honest with me."

The tone in Dayne's voice shifted the air in the room, and each of the captains looked to him, a wariness in their gazes.

"We have not spoken it aloud." Dayne let out a sigh, his gaze passing across each of the captains. "But it is now known that I hold the power to wield the Spark – that I am a mage."

Marlin, Ileeri, and Dinekes, held Dayne's gaze as the words hung in the air. Jorath, Barak, and Odys shifted uneasily, their stares finding vacant spots to study.

"I would know if this revelation has compromised me in your eyes and in the eyes of our people. The power to touch the Spark was not something I chose. It was something I was born with. A gift from Achyron, so I may better protect Valtara. I would—"

"No," Barak said, cutting Dayne short, lifting his head to meet Dayne's stare. "It is strange to us, my lord. For many years, we have only known pain from those who wield your power. But you are Dayne Ateres. Andurios. You are returned to us from the dead. Not only that, but we have seen you on the field of battle. You are a tempest. And I for one, am proud to stand behind you. By blade and by blood, you have my oath, Andurios."

"And mine." Ileeri pulled fist across her chest. "Your great, great, great grandfather allowed my House to fly the banner of House Ateres. We were nothing. We *had* nothing, but he took us in. Now, over a hundred years later, here I stand. You are a symbol, my lord. A symbol that the tide is turning. A symbol that Loria no longer holds dominance over magic. No, you are not compromised in our eyes, nor in the eyes of our people. You are hope." Even as Ileeri's eyes glistened, Dayne could see the anger in the way her jaw tensed and her breaths deepened. "Too many years, they've taken everything from us. Our pride. Our food. Our children—" Ileera swallowed, her words wavering "—By blade and by blood, we are yours. You are my Andurios, and I will follow you to the pits of the void."

"By blade and by blood," the other captains chorused.

CHAPTER FORTY-TWO

CHASING RUMOURS

Good. Deflect the blow, don't take the weight of it," Coren called, her voice muffled by the drumming in Ella's ears as she shuffled her feet, trying her best to turn Tanner's blows away, which, even with him still recovering from his injuries, was no easy feat.

Ella still wasn't used to the full suit of armour Coren insisted she wear when they did their morning treks to the peak. It was heavy and barely allowed for any movement. It felt like moving inside an oven. Sweat slicked Ella's body, soaking through the shirt and trousers she wore beneath the armour, coating her brow and stinging her eyes. She was in better condition than she'd been the first few times Coren had brought Tanner up with them to spar, but not by much.

Tanner moved in, swinging his blunted practice blade to Ella's left. The force of his swing shook her arms, but she held tight. Then in a blur of motion, he twisted his wrist and forced Ella's sword down, her wrists giving way. Ella heard Tanner's heavy breaths as his sword rested against the mail that covered her neck.

Faenir snarled, rising to a position somewhere between sitting and standing, his nose crinkling, hackles rising. Ella shook her head, and Faenir sat down, rolling onto his side, tongue hanging out as though nothing had happened.

"You're getting better every day," Tanner said, pulling the sword away from her neck and removing his helmet. Sweat rolled down Tanner's brow, dripping off the edge of his nose. A broad smile adorned his face, soft wrinkles creasing at the corners. Ella knew she would never get over the fact Tanner smiled with his eyes. *Just like Rhett.* Those creases at the corners of his eyes were all Ella needed to believe Tanner was Rhett's family.

"You just took my head off," Ella said, before removing her helmet and throwing her head back, blowing out a puff of air as the cold wind tickled her face. Above them, the sun blazed, bathing them in a heat that felt entirely unnatural to Ella for this time of year.

"I didn't say you were good. I just said you were better," Tanner said with a laugh, taking a waterskin from Coren, who also handed one to Ella. He sat on a rock beside Faenir, throwing the wolfpine a cursory glance. "You said your father trained you when you were younger?"

Ella nodded, taking a swig from the waterskin. "He used to train Calen and me in sword forms. I stopped practising as much when I got older, but I still kept it up."

Tanner nodded and rolled his head, eliciting cracks from his neck. "I never met your father. But my brother told me stories about him. Vars Bryer. Said he was a good man. One of the best with a sword he'd ever seen. Said he fought in the Varsund War."

Ella gave Tanner a weak smile, staring absently at a piece of cracked earth near the man's feet. She knew he was only trying to make her feel at home, but as she was, any thoughts of her parents cut straight at her heart. The wound was still fresh, and she had a feeling it always would be.

As though sensing Ella's discomfort, Faenir let out a rumble and stood. The wolfpine padded over to Ella, nuzzling the side of his face against her shoulder.

"He's gotten bigger," Coren said matter-of-factly, examining Faenir.

"A lot bigger." Tanner took another mouthful of water, then tilted his head to look at Faenir.

Ella took a step back from Faenir, much to the wolfpine's irritation. He *was* bigger. So much so that Ella couldn't believe she hadn't noticed. His chest had deepened, his shoulders and neck were wider, the muscles on his legs looked denser, and the crown of his head now rose over Ella's shoulders. *When did that happen?* Ella reached out and rested the palm of her hand against Faenir's right cheek, the coarse outer fur prickling her skin. The wolfpine let out a low whine and leaned his head into Ella's hand.

"Just as Galveer said." Coren folded her arms, a satisfied smile on her face.

Tanner raised a curious eyebrow, and Ella repeated what Coren had told her about the druid, Galveer, and his hawk, Kurak. About how some druids could bond with specific animals and how those animals in turn would become larger, stronger, and smarter.

"Makes sense," Tanner said with a shrug.

"Does it?"

"No." Tanner let out a deep laugh, spluttering as he choked on a mouthful of water. "But after the things I've seen, you learn to accept what doesn't make sense. I mean, I've seen dragons, and Coren here is a four-hundred-year-old elf."

"Fair point," Ella turned her bottom lip in a pout. "You don't look a day over three hundred though."

"Thank you." Ella could tell Coren was trying her best to keep a straight face but a chuckle crept through, curling the corners of her mouth into a smile. "Come, it's best we make our way back down. Juro and the scouts will have returned by now."

THEY FOUND FARWEN AT THE centre of Tarhelm's main plaza talking to two men. Ella recognised one of them – Juro, head of the Tarhelm scouts. He was a lithe man with a narrow jaw. His face was sharp and angular, and his dark, greasy hair hung just short of his shoulders. If Ella had run into him while travelling she would've hidden in a bush, but he seemed a decent man from the few interactions she'd had with him.

She didn't recognise the other man, though. He stood a head taller than Juro, with a flat nose, short black hair, and a thick beard that looked as though it had been carved with a chisel. He held himself like a warrior, back straight and shoulders square. He wore dark leather armour with a brown cloak.

"What news?" Coren asked as they drew closer.

Juro and the other man turned, casting a glance over Ella, Coren, Faenir, and Tanner. They both took a step backwards at the sight of Faenir but composed themselves quickly and nodded their welcomes before giving a slight bow to Coren.

"Juro's scouts have caught wind that the Lorian First Army has left Al'Nasla and is approaching Fort Harken. They'll be there in a few days. They've also got news that the Second Army has left Arginwatch and is heading towards Steeple."

Coren nodded, her face twisting into an unreadable expression. "Do we know where the First Army are headed after Fort Harken?"

"My scouts' guess is the Fourth Army is joining them and they're moving on to Steeple together," Juro said.

"Guess? We need more than guesses, Juro."

The man shrugged. "Guesses are all we have, Coren. The soldiers haven't been told much, only to march. The Lorians are keeping tight-lipped on this one."

"The letters," Ella blurted, then stopped as the others stared at her.

"What letters?" the flat-nosed man asked, his eyes narrowing.

Ella watched as the look of curiosity on Coren's face slowly shifted to understanding. "The communications we've been intercepting from the eastern cities."

"What of them?" Farwen asked.

Ella looked around the group. Each of them was staring at her expectantly. All of a sudden she wasn't sure if she should have said anything, but then she felt Faenir brush against her shoulder, a soft rumble in his chest. *Fuck it.* "They were all talking about attacks on the eastern cities. Of armies raiding. But one in particular was sent by a commander near Gildor – Giana… something?"

"Giana Karta?" Juro suggested, his hand cupping his chin, fingers pressing into his cheeks in thought.

"Yes! That's her. She sent the letter to her brother."

"Olivan," Juro chimed in.

Ella nodded.

"Can you please get to the point?" Flat Nose said with a sigh.

Faenir took a step forward, moving past Ella, and turned his head towards the man, nose crinkled, teeth bared and dripping with saliva. The rumble that previously held in the wolfpine's chest rose into his throat, sharpening to a growl. Faenir's hackles rose, the hairs on Ella's arms rising with them.

Flat Nose met Faenir's gaze, turning out his bottom lip. "Please, continue."

Ella glared at him. "Giana Karta wrote her brother, who was stationed in Arginwatch, asking for aid. She said they'd lost contact with Easterlock and Ravensgate and that their scouts had disappeared. She also said that there were stories of armies sweeping across the east, razing everything."

"Stories are no better than guesses, Ella," Coren said. "But either way. If we intercepted that letter, then it never reached Arginwatch as intended."

"It didn't, *but* Giana said she also sent letters to both Berona and Al'Nasla and who knows where else. If any of them got through, that could be exactly why the armies are moving *and* where they are going. But even if the letters never arrived, surely there would have been survivors from the attacks. Some of them must have reached this side of the pass."

"The empire wouldn't move three entire armies for stories." Tanner frowned. "What Ella says adds up. If the empire are mobilising three armies at the same time, and they are all meeting at Steeple, then that means whatever whispers are coming out of the east are more than just stories. And, from memory, there were six armies stationed on the eastern side of the pass. Three around Easterlock, one at Ravensgate, one at Gildor – Giana and the Sixth Army – and one at Khergan. Before I left Berona, the Twelfth Army was to be moved from Khergan and sent to watch over Berona's western border with the Lodhar Mountains. That would make Olivan's Second Army at Arginwatch the closest. The pieces fit. It looks like one of her letters got through."

"Agreed," Coren said, her brow furrowed. "Farwen?"

"A group of Juro's scouts didn't report back. They were stationed a few days ride from here, southwest of Elkenrim. Juro, Varik, and I can go see what happened to them, then while we're there, we'll move on to the main road past Elkenrim and wait for the Lorian armies. We'll follow them, see what we find, cause some havoc along the way."

"Sounds like a plan. Take twenty with you. Whoever you like and Ella."

Ella froze, a lump forming in her throat. "Me?"

Coren nodded. "There's only so many times I can drag you up and down that hill. And we don't have the years to train you slowly. Go with Farwen and the others. Use your head. Watch and learn. You'll learn more in the field than you ever will swinging a blunt sword."

"But… I…" Part of Ella wanted to go. She was quickly growing sick of waiting around, repeating the same tasks every day. One of the reasons she'd wanted to leave The Glade was to break free of the monotony. But this felt a little like running before she learned how to walk. And what if Coren heard back from Calen while Ella was gone?

"If Ella is going then I'm going with her." Tanner's expression was flat, his arms still folded. He met Coren with a cold stare that said he expected her to argue.

"No." Coren shook her head. "You still need to recover."

"I'm going. It wasn't a request."

"Tanner you shouldn't…" Ella let her words fade away as the man gave her a flat stare, a hardness in his eyes.

"Don't be an idiot, Tanner. You know you still have healing yet to do. I'm not a true healer. I can only do so much at a time. Besides, Yana will slit my throat when I sleep if I let you go like this."

"Let me go?" Tanner scoffed, raised an eyebrow. "I've given everything for this cause. I will go where I damn well please." He turned to Juro. "When are you heading out?"

Juro looked like a half-drunk teenager caught taking a piss in the middle of the street by his own mother. He gulped, glancing at Coren, then back to Tanner. "We…" Juro swallowed hard as Tanner shifted, his teeth visibly grinding. "We'll be leaving within the hour, I'd say."

"Come get me when you're saddling the horses. I'll deal with Yana." Tanner turned and stalked off towards the tunnel that led to the living quarters.

Ella stared after him, unsure of what to do or say. She'd be lying if she said she didn't want him to come. Tanner was one of the only people Ella actually trusted – Tanner and Yana. Farwen and Coren had treated her well, but Ella just couldn't bring herself to trust them entirely. There were a few others within Tarhelm who she'd spent time with. Juro had been kind to her, she supposed. And Ardle and Keela, two of Juro's scouts had made the point of joining Ella while she ate on one of her first nights, and they'd joined her every night since – when they weren't out on an assignment. But still, she didn't truly *trust* any of them. Only Tanner and

Yana. But Tanner was in no shape to leave Tarhelm. Sure, he was able to best Ella in sparring, but that wasn't exactly an impressive feat.

Coren folded her arms and glared at Tanner's back as the man stepped into the tunnel on the other side of the chamber. If looks could kill, Tanner would have been lying in a pool of his own blood. Coren sucked her cheeks in, then let them out, turning to Ella. "Get your things ready. Some clothes, your sword, and your journal. Juro will sort you out with a blanket roll and general supplies. I'll come see you before you go."

With that, Coren turned and stormed off in the opposite direction to Tanner.

The rest stood in silence, men and women moving through the plaza around them, going about their daily tasks. In the heat of the argument Ella had forgotten they weren't alone.

"Well." Varik pursed his lips. "I guess I'll see you all at the northern gate in an hour."

When Varik left, Farwen turned to Ella, her usual serious expression on her face. "I'll come for you once I've everything arranged. Make sure you're ready."

Juro reached up and ran his hands through his greasy hair, his fingers carving thick furrows. He leaned his head back and let out a sigh. "Why am I always in the middle of these things?" The question was more posed to the world itself than to Ella. He looked across the chamber, then shook his head as though resigning himself to fate. "I'm going to get some rum. Something tells me I'm going to need it."

ELLA SAT ON THE COOL stone floor of her chambers, Faenir splayed out in front her, his enormous head resting in her lap. A continuous rumble emanated from the wolfpine's throat as she scratched behind his left ear and under his chin. She still couldn't get over how big he'd gotten. He was more like a horse than a wolfpine. A horse with claws, razor-sharp teeth, and a diet that consisted purely of meat – which was a terrifying thought.

The longer Ella looked at Faenir, the more she felt his mind bleeding into hers. The lingering smell of smoke from the candle she had snuffed out grew sharper, mixing with the handful of lavender Ella had found just outside the eastern gate and now kept by her bedside. Judging by the sense of calm that washed over Faenir, the smell of lavender meant the same thing to him as it did to her – home. As Ella breathed in the smell, she could see herself standing outside her home in The Glade, her mam tending the garden, the vibrant purple of the lavender petals sticking out amongst the green.

"I can't believe they're gone," Ella whispered as she scratched Faenir. As soon as the words left her mouth, Faenir's head shot up, his ears pricked, eyes of molten amber fixed on hers. He let out a high-pitched whine and nuzzled his snout into Ella's hand. Loss, sympathy, kinships – all three bristled at the edge of Ella's consciousness, followed by images of Ella holding Faenir when he was only a pup, a feeling of comfort as he fell asleep in her arms. Memories followed the images, Freis feeding Faenir raw cuts of deer or rabbit before she cooked, even when food was scarce. Vars coming home from The Gilded Dragon after more than his fair share of meads and rolling around with Faenir on the kitchen floor.

Ella wrapped her arms around Faenir's thick neck and pulled the wolf-pine close. He didn't shuffle or pull away, instead, he leaned in, letting out a low whimper. Ella tangled her fingers in Faenir's fur, pulling him tighter. Still, she didn't cry. She wanted to. She really and truly wanted to. Coils of grief twisted in her chest at the thought of her parents, her stomach twisting, but the tears didn't come. This had happened a number of times since Tanner had told Ella about her parents. The grief seemed to come in waves for both her and Faenir. One moment she was fine, having come home after spending the day practising and shadowing Coren, then a memory would slip into her mind and grief would consume her. Then, just as quickly as it had come, it would vanish. But no matter what, she couldn't find the tears to cry.

"I know you miss them too," Ella said, pressing her cheek against Faenir's before placing a kiss on the top of his furry head and standing, much to the wolfpine's dismay. Ella ruffled the top of Faenir's head, letting out a short laugh. "Sometimes you're like a puppy pretending to be a wolfpine, you know that?"

Faenir let out a whine, resting his head on his paws, his ears flattening.

"You're not helping your case." Ella gave Faenir a weak smile then set about double checking her pack. What did a person bring on a scouting mission? She'd packed an extra shirt and trousers, some smallclothes, a tin of brimlock sap, her coin purse – not that she thought she'd be needing it – and some other bits and pieces, including the journal Coren had given her.

Ella reached inside the pack and pulled out the journal, flicking through the pages. She'd tried 'Shifting' with Faenir every day since the first attempt, but it had never worked the way Coren had described. From what Coren had said, Ella should have been able to truly push herself inside Faenir's mind – see through his eyes, move his limbs. But that hadn't happened. She'd been able to feel his emotions, see images of what he saw, watch flashes of memory, but it hadn't felt anything like what Coren had said. *Maybe I just don't have that gift? Or maybe I'm not a druid at all.*

Ella stuffed the journal back into the bag and moved over to the chest by her bed where she'd stored everything she'd brought with her from home. She pulled out the long, brown, hooded cloak that lay folded at the top of the chest, then made to close the lid when her eyes fell on a cream dress with a maroon floral pattern worked into it. She hadn't worn that dress since Pirn – Rhett's eyes had always lit up when he'd seen her in it. Ella's jaw clenched reflexively, another touch of anger and guilt brushing against her mind from Faenir as the wolfpine felt her sadness.

A knock sounded at the door, and Coren stepped through, not waiting for Ella to answer. "Farwen and the others will be ready to go soon. I'll take you to them."

Ella's gaze lingered on the cream floral dress. She smiled, letting out a sigh as she closed the lid of the chest, turning to Coren.

The woman wore a sleeveless dark blue tunic, her black hair tied back with a string, and a stack of leathers in her hands that rose to her chin, a helmet at the top. "I brought you these," Coren said, smiling at Faenir as she crossed the room, laying the leathers on Ella's bed.

Ella ran her gaze across the pieces of armour, assessing the craftsmanship by force of habit – something her dad had drilled into her. The cuirass was made of boiled leather, connected by straps to articulated spaulders. A pair of vambraces lay next to a set of greaves, tassets, and a leather helmet.

The leatherwork looked top notch; definitely something even Tharn Pimm would be proud of. "Thank you," Ella said, tugging at the straps. "I'm not sure what to say."

Coren shrugged. "Well, I need you to protect yourself out there, and as good a training tool as that plate armour is, I don't think you'd last too long lugging it around in a fight. We can look at having some smaller segments of plate made for you when you get back, but for now this will let you move with a lot more freedom while still keeping you protected."

"I…" Ella ran her finger along the metal rim of the helmet.

"Come on. I'll help you put it on, then we need to get you to the northern gate. Best not keep them waiting."

"ARE YOU FUCKING STUPID?" YANA stood, the knuckles of her closed fists leaning on the wooden counter that sat in the middle of her and Tanner's quarters. Her coal-black hair fell in soft curls, a sleeveless tunic showing the lean muscles of her arms. She glared at Tanner with a fury that burned holes through him. *But by the gods you're beautiful.* "Absolutely not. Not a hope. Efialtír will grow daisies on his head before I let you walk out of here in this state."

Tanner smiled, motioning to move closer.

"If you take another fucking step, I'll cut your balls off and feed them to the pigs." Yana held up a hand, a finger pointed at Tanner in warning. "And wipe that damn smile off your face. You're not cuddling your way out of this one you handsome oaf. Where is she? I'll just kill the bitch and be done with it. Then you'll have no honour to go protecting."

Tanner let out a sigh, unable to keep himself from smiling. Yana's anger didn't scare him. She was fierce. That was part of why he loved her. In fact, he adored when she was angry. That burning look in her eyes, the way she stood, the way she clenched her jaw. She looked invincible. "It's not about honour, Yana. You know that."

Yana raised an eyebrow and let out a mocking laugh. "It's *always* about honour with you. All men are the same." Tanner reached forward, but Yana slapped his hands away. "Don't fucking touch me, Tanner. I'm not joking. I will *not* let you march out of here to throw your neck on the line for some stray girl you hardly know."

Tanner stepped closer, but Yana pushed him in the chest. He smiled again. She was half his size, but by the gods did she have strength in those arms. "My heart—"

"Don't you dare." Yana tilted her head to the side, her lip curling.

"Rhett is dead, Yana." Tanner let the sadness touch his smile. "My nephew is dead. I'm the one who asked them to go through Gisa. I put them on the merchant road. That girl out there is to him what you are to me. She is family, and I will not let her be alone here. I won't do it. I'm not going with her to protect my honour – I'm going with her because she needs me."

Yana stood there, motionless, staring at Tanner with an unreadable expression. Then she turned and stormed off towards the other side of the room.

"Yana, please." Tanner threw his arms out. "What are you doing?"

She snatched up a satchel from the ground, dropped it on a table, and undid the buckle. She didn't even turn her head as she began stuffing it with supplies: bandages, a tin of brimlock sap, needle and thread. "I'm coming with you, you fucking idiot."

Tanner let out a laugh and rushed across the room, wrapping his arms around Yana from the side. He pulled her in tight, resting the side of his head on the top of hers. "You are the fire in my heart."

Yana shuffled in Tanner's embrace, continuing to pack the satchel. "I'll fucking set you on fire if you don't let go of me."

Tanner laughed and brushed Yana's cheek with his hand, yelping when she bit his finger – not hard, but harder than he would have liked.

She tilted her head. "I warned you."

Tanner ignored her, touching his forehead against hers. "I would say I would die for you, but dying for you would do you no good. Yana

Aleera, I will love you every second of every minute I draw breath. I will love you with my whole heart and nothing less." Tanner lifted Yana's chin and she kissed him.

After a moment, Yana pulled away shaking her head. "You really do talk too much, you know that? Now go and pack before I change my mind."

Tanner placed a kiss on Yana's forehead and turned to fetch his satchel from the bed chambers. By the time he'd reached the doorway, Yana called to him. He raised a questioning eyebrow.

"I love you too. Idiot."

⌒⊚

FARDA LET OUT A SIGH, his breath misting out in front of him and rising towards the night sky where the crescent moon sat, cold and pale. Dirt crunched beneath his boots as he walked through the Fourth Army's camp that sat atop the hill near the main gates of Fort Harken. The *clink-ing* sound of his coin rang out methodically as he flicked it into the air again and again, casting his gaze over the camp.

Tents and campfires were spread about the landscape, sparks and embers spitting into the night. The only sounds were those of the crackling fires, buzzing insects, whinnying horses, and the occasional hum of subdued chatter.

He passed a group of soldiers sitting around a fire, barely a word passing between them as they stared absently into the flames while chewing on slices of pork and bread sent from the fort.

The camp had been sombre since the battle only two weeks past. They'd lost a third of their number that day. Almost two thousand souls claimed by the Uraks before Lyina and the others had appeared. Just over three hundred injured, half of who would never fight again. If Lyina hadn't arrived, those numbers would have been far greater.

Farda truly was happy to set his eyes on Lyina and Karakes again. It had even been good to see Jormun, Voranur, and Ilkya, though their demeanours were far darker than Lyina's. Each Draleid who had sided with Eltoar and followed Fane had dealt with the centuries differently. Each faced their own struggles in coming to terms with what had happened that night in Ilnaen and in the years that followed.

Where Lyina had clung to her kin, searching for solace in the hearts of those she cared for, Jormun, Voranur, and Ilkya had leaned into the darkness, letting it drown them. Of the three, Voranur was closest to the person he once was, but still even he had grown cold and apathetic to the lives of others.

Eltoar had thrown himself into the preservation of the Draleid, all but consumed by trying to understand why the eggs had stopped hatching. He'd spent many years scouring Epheria, gathering every dragon egg he could find, doing all within his power to find a Draleid who could form a bond. But when days turned to weeks, turned to years, turned to a century, it became clear that the laws of probability had failed him; if the eggs were going to hatch, they would have done so.

After Aeson had killed Shinyara, Farda himself had contemplated taking his own life many a time just to be with her again, just to feel the touch of her mind. Sheer stubbornness was the only thing that had swayed his decision, that and a nagging feeling that there was still more for him to do – still *something* he was needed for before he could finally rest. Six hundred years was a long time. He would welcome the rest when it finally came.

Turning the corner around a red and cream canvas tent, he stifled a laugh at the thought of his title: Justicar. On paper it was a title of some renown. Justicar of the Imperial Battlemages. Mighty warriors, free from the tethers of The Circle to enact the emperor's will across the land as they saw fit. In truth, Justicar was simply the title given to a Dragonguard who had lost their soulkin and still retained the ability to fight. It was a meaningless platitude. Farda was nothing more than half a soul floating on the whims of fate.

Clink.

The coin rang as it flicked through the air, landing with a thud in Farda's open palm. He looked down, seeing a crown staring back at him from the surface of the tarnished gold coin. "Not yet, then."

As Farda continued to stroll through the camp, two figures emerged from behind a tent to his left, their faces obscured by shadow.

"Still not sleeping?" Commander Talvare said as she approached Farda, the warm glow of a nearby fire illuminating her weary face, the streaks of grey in her hair shimmering as they caught the light. General Guthrin Vandimire stood at her right, almost a head shorter than the commander, his beady eyes glaring at Farda, his thick moustache twitching. Three generals had fallen in the battle at Fort Harken; Farda had been upset to hear one of them wasn't Guthrin. *Weasel of a man.*

Two soldiers in steel breastplates and black and red leathers stood on either side of Guthrin and Talvare, their backs straightening as they recognised Farda.

"Not in a few hundred years," Farda said with a half-smile. "And you?"

"I'm a grandmother. We never sleep. Don't have the hours to waste. Better spent checking these idiots aren't sleeping on watch. You and your Battlemages are ready to leave when the First Army arrives?"

Farda nodded. He'd lost thirty-seven mages in the battle, along with four Healers. "We'll be ready when we're needed, Commander Talvare, rest assured. I'll not keep you from your checks. Sleep well with the few hours you can spare." Farda flicked his coin as he moved off, snatching it out of the air and flicking it again.

"What in The Saviour's name are you doing with that coin?" Guthrin asked as Farda passed him. "I always see you playing with it like a child with a toy."

Farda stopped, clicking his tongue off the roof of his mouth. *Clink.* The coin dropped into his open palm. Crowns. *Not today, then.* Farda turned to Guthrin, putting in the most inauthentic smile he could muster. "It's for deciding whether you live or die."

Taking a moment to savour the look of pure horror on Guthrin's face and the sound of Talvare's laughter, Farda turned and continued on his way, flicking the coin into the air.

After a while, he found himself approaching the tent he'd always known he was walking towards: the Dragonguard command tent. It was set at the top of a slight rise, near the western edge of the camp. It stretched around fifty feet by fifty feet, its canopy as white as snow, ornamented with gold, a black flame emblazoned on each side. At the tent's peak, a rectangular flag that bore both the black lion of Loria and the flame of the Dragonguard flapped languidly in the breeze.

As Farda approached the tent, a shape shifted to his right, shadows bending, light reflecting off a mass of flowing scales that Farda had mistaken for a shadowed hill. The longer Farda looked, the clearer the tint of crimson at the edges of the scales became. A low rumble resonated from the shape, deep and powerful. The dragon lifted its enormous head from where it had been lying on the ground, its shifting ocean of black scales glinting in the moonlight. Eyelids pulled back, and Farda found himself staring into dark red, smouldering eyes bisected by black slits.

"Helios…"

Not bothering to lift himself to his full height, Helios extended his neck, moving his enormous head closer to Farda, horns as long as Farda's legs framing his face and jaws, scars cleaving through scales where centuries of battle had left their mark. In the darkness it was near impossible to see Helios's full size, but even before the fall of The Order, Helios had been the largest of all Epherian dragons. According to the historians, there were only three or four dragons in all recorded history that were said to have grown larger than Eltoar's soulkin. Helios was hundreds of feet from head to tail, his wings spreading twice that again. And even then as Farda stood before him, the dragon's chin scraped the ground at Farda's feet, the crest of his snout rising far above Farda's

531

head. He could have walked into the dragon's mouth without bowing his head. Helios's rumble rose into his throat, mouth opening to show rows of snow-white teeth as long as swords, warm breath smelling of blood and ash.

Farda placed his hand on the tip of the dragon's snout. "Det er aldin na vëna dir, yíar'ydil. Du vier mæra mielír val dun dier del går." *It is good to see you, old friend. You look more powerful with each day that passes.*

Helios pressed back against Farda's hand, giving a rumble of recognition before returning his head to where it had previously lain. It was then Farda noticed the glint of more scales beside Helios, a shape two-thirds the size of the great black dragon, scales deep red. Karakes didn't lift his head, which lay still across Helios's tail.

Farda took a moment, letting his eyes adjust to the darkness without the campfires to dull his night vision. He looked over the two dragons, and warmth wrapped around his melancholy heart. For as beautiful as the two magnificent creatures were, they were not Shinyara. They were not the fire of his heart, the best half of his soul. She was gone, waiting for him.

He could have stood there for hours watching over the dragons. Centuries ago he would not have gone a day without gazing upon skies filled with the beautiful creatures, but now it had been years since he'd laid eyes on a dragon that still drew breath. He could have spent more time with Eltoar, Lyina, and Pellenor; they would have welcomed it. But he had not been able to bring himself to face his own loss each and every day.

"Farda!"

Farda looked up to see Eltoar Daethana striding towards him from the command tent. The elf wore a black tunic with a pair of baggy trousers, his snow-white hair drifting behind him. Even dressed as he was, Eltoar looked every bit the warrior of old, his shoulders broad, his chest built like plate armour, his gait strong and confident. After four hundred years, he still very much looked like the First Sword of the Draleid.

A crack of light pierced through the tent's canopy behind Eltoar as Lyina emerged, dressed much the same as her commander, dark blonde hair tied up, lips curled in a smile. She nodded to Farda as she approached.

"Brother." Eltoar wrapped his arms around Farda, pulling him into an embrace that verged on breaking bones. He pulled back, then clasped his hands around Farda's head, pulling their foreheads together.

Farda placed his hands on top of Eltoar's. "It's good to see you, Eltoar. I wasn't aware you were here. Lyina told me you had gone to Dracaldryr to speak with Tivar."

Eltoar recoiled at that, pulling his hands away, his gaze turning to the ground momentarily. "I arrived a few hours gone. Lyina told me you were here. I was waiting until the morning to come find you. But I should have remembered you sleep as little as I do."

Farda gave Eltoar a weak smile. "Tivar?"

"She remains at the temple."

Farda nodded. That was what he'd expected. He hadn't seen Tivar in decades. Lyina and Karakes had flown him to the temple to speak with her some forty years ago, but she'd been so consumed in sorrow she'd barely spoken a word to him.

In the silence, Lyina stepped past Eltoar and hugged Farda, kissing him on the cheek.

"What is your plan, then?" Farda asked, looking to Eltoar.

"We will move east with the Fourth Army once the First Army arrives. Pellenor will join us shortly. What have you been told?"

Farda pouted, shrugging. "Not enough. All we know is that we've lost contact with the eastern cities, but survivors have been reported, only a handful, elderly and children. They've shown up in Berona, Steeple, and Elkenrim, telling of great armies, some whispering of elves and dragons. Is it possible? Do you know more, brother?"

Eltoar nodded, a sombre look on his face. "After Dracaldryr, I flew to the eastern cities. Fane had sent scouts, but none reported back. Then, as you say, survivors began to appear."

Farda looked to Lyina, who stood with her arms folded, her eyes fixed on the ground. "What did you find?"

"Death." Eltoar sighed. "Easterlock, Ravensgate, Gildor, and Bromis. All gone. Nothing but charred husks, walls broken and shattered, fields burned. The handful of survivors that reached Steeple and beyond were the only ones." Eltoar lifted his gaze to meet Farda's "Mounds of bodies as high as the city walls were stacked outside the gates, burned to nothing but bones and ash."

"There's hundreds of thousands of souls across those cities, they can't all be—"

"Gone," Eltoar said, finishing Farda's sentence. "Whatever happened along the eastern coast, it wasn't an attack, it was an extermination."

"Who? The Karvosi? The Ardanians?"

"I'm not sure." Eltoar seemed as displeased with that answer as Farda was. "I flew along the coast to track the army, but about fifty miles north of Bromis a dense fog-covered the lands for miles in all directions. It lifted a few hundred feet off the ground, like the clouds had fallen to the earth. I've never seen anything like it."

"The children and the elderly," Farda said, contemplating. "Could it be possible?"

Farda could see in Eltoar's eyes that he understood. It could not be a coincidence that the only survivors were those either too young or too old to fight. The elves' code of honour would have demanded they be left alive.

"I've come to the same conclusion. And if we're right, and the elves of Lynalion have finally left the shelter of the woodland, then we will need far more than the three armies. And if more of our kin survived…"

"If they have, they won't see us as kin anymore. They'll see us as demons."

CHAPTER FORTY-THREE

TRUST ME

Kallinvar descended the staircase into the sparring chamber, the sounds of ringing steel, shifting feet, and grunting resounding off the stone walls. Ruon and Varlin walked at his side, not a word passing between them.

As he stepped into the sparring chamber, Kallinvar cast his gaze over the sand-filled pits, of which there were ten – one for each chapter. With so many knights on task across Epheria, the pits were nearly empty.

Brother Gardan, Brother Vodrin, and Sister Firya occupied the sparring pit that belonged to The Eighth. They were arranged in a straight line a few feet apart, their blades in hand as they moved methodically through their sword forms, sweat glistening on their skin.

Sister-Captain Emalia was in the centre of The Tenth's pit, her palms flat down in the sand, eyes closed, arms tucked tight to her ribs, her muscles slick with sweat as she held her body parallel to the ground. Verathin had found Emalia almost two centuries before The Fall, holding herself up on her spear, blood pouring onto the stone of Faldara's throne room, bodies splayed about her. When the Aldurites stormed Faldara and forced their way into the keep, Emalia had killed thirty-four Aldurite soldiers in defence of her king, and then, as she bled out onto the floor, her king had fled, thanking her for her sacrifice. There were few souls in the world Kallinvar held more respect for.

As he turned his head left, Kallinvar found what he was looking for. Arden and Tarron were sparring in The Second's pit, the colliding swords ringing sharp through the chamber. The two knights came to a stop as Kallinvar, Ruon, and Varlin approached.

"Grandmaster," they chorused, drawing heavy breaths, sweat slicking their brows.

Kallinvar inclined his head. "Brother Arden, Brother Tarron." Kallinvar drew in a deep breath, turning to face Arden. "Lyrin has found the Draleid."

Arden stepped forward, his mouth opening, eyes widening a little. "He's found Calen?"

Kallinvar looked back to Ruon, who frowned. She had counselled against what Kallinvar was about to do, and she was more often correct than not. But in this, Kallinvar trusted his own judgement. It was he who had given Arden the Sigil, he who had seen into the man's soul. "He has. They are in Berona now."

Arden stood straighter, lifting his chin. "I understand, Grandmaster."

Kallinvar raised an eyebrow in surprise. "What is it you understand, brother?"

"That I cannot be with you when you go to him. Achyron must come first." Arden sheathed his sword and dipped his head.

"Yes, Achyron *must* come first. And with that in mind, brother, I would ask you to join Sister-Captain Ruon, Brother Ildris, Sister Varlin, and Brother Lyrin in forming the Draleid's honour guard, should he choose to accept it."

Arden lifted his gaze, meeting Kallinvar's. The look of shock on the young man's face was plain. His lips began to move, but it took a few seconds before words followed. "I…" Arden stared at the ground, drew in a breath, then dropped to one knee, bringing his fist to his chest. "Thank you, Grandmaster. I will do as Achyron needs."

Kallinvar stepped forwards, grasping Arden's forearm and lifting him to his feet, pulling him close. "I need you to protect him with your life, Arden. The Blood Moon will rise before we see winter, and he is the rallying cry. We will not survive the coming shadow without him."

Arden's stare was hard, his jaw set. He squeezed on Kallinvar's forearm. "I would give every drop of my blood for him."

THE MOON HUNG IN THE night sky like a chalk etching, pale and cold, its glow the only light as Calen took Erik's hand and pulled himself from the hatch at the end of the tunnel. In the hour or so they'd spent fleeing through the tunnel from Berona, the rain had stopped, but the sodden ground still slushed beneath his feet as he steadied himself, resting his hand on Erik's shoulder. "Thank you. The others?"

Looking around, Calen could see they had emerged at the edge of a pine forest. All about, men and women leaned against trees; sat on rocks, stumps, or down in the waterlogged grass. They were a motley array of characters. Some wore the black and red leathers of Lorian soldiers, others were garbed in silks and linens that spoke of wealth, while some looked as though they'd spent more than a few nights living on the streets. Calen even spotted three who wore the black plate and red cloaks he'd seen adorning the Beronan Guard. To his right, he saw Surin – or Gold as he'd known her – talking to Erik's contact, Ingvat, and a few others. Surin's vibrant yellow robes stood in stark contrast to the dark and gloomy night.

Erik nodded to Calen's left, over towards a patch of grass and trees where Vaeril and Tarmon stood, watching over the others. Lasch Havel sat with his back against a tree trunk, his eyes closed. Elia lay in the wet grass, her head rested on Lasch's lap, his hand trembling as he stroked her hair. Beside them Gaeleron sat atop a flat rock, Rendall's crimson cloak draped over his shoulders, his head hanging low, eyes fixed on the dirt. A blend of warmth, sorrow, and disgust twisted in Calen, burning, smouldering.

Calen's mind turned to Fritz, who was standing near Tarmon, leaning against a tree, his brown robes pulled tight, gazing around at the others that had escaped the city with them. Calen's chest trembled, and his fingers clenched into a fist. Even just the sight of Fritz standing anywhere near Gaeleron, Lasch, and Elia lit a fire in Calen. He felt Valerys readying himself to break through the clouds above, fury surging through him. He drew in a deep breath, trying his best to settle himself. *I am not him. I am not him.*

Erik grasped Calen's arm, his fingers closing around Calen's bicep, tugging so that Calen looked him in the eye. "He's not worth the air he drags into those wretched lungs. But right now, the others need you more than they need your blade. I'll keep an eye on him."

Calen nodded, grasping Erik's forearm. "Thank you."

"Don't mention it. He has a very punchable face." Erik gave Calen a half-hearted smile.

"No, Erik. *Thank you.*" Calen's throat tightened as his thoughts shifted to Rist. "We made a deal, and I'll do as I promised. We didn't find Rist, and there's nothing pointing towards him ever having been here. We can go back."

Erik sighed. "We'll find him. If he's out there, we *will* find him. This is us. Your family is our family. And we've found some of our family today." Erik nodded over towards Gaeleron, Elia, and Lasch. "Come on."

Calen and Erik made their way over to the others, and Calen dropped to one knee in the sodden grass before Gaeleron.

The elf lifted his head, his blood-and-dirt-matted hair clinging to the side of his face. The elf's lungs rasped as he drew in a breath, his broken body shivering. Gaeleron's eyes were two sunken wells ringed in purple, his cheekbones threatening to pierce through his brittle skin. He choked and coughed, spluttering as he tried to speak.

Calen caught Gaeleron as the elf jerked forwards from the coughing. "It's all right. We've got you. It's all right."

"Draleid…" Gaeleron's voice was harsh and rough.

"I'm here. So is Vaeril, and Erik." Calen didn't mention Tarmon. Gaeleron had only met the Lord Captain briefly. There would be time for introductions later. "We're taking you across the Burnt Lands. We're going to Aravell."

Gaeleron nodded weakly, as though Calen's words had barely even touched his ears. "I didn't break…" The elf shook his head. "I didn't break."

Calen clenched his fist and tears stung his eyes, but he held them back. "I know you didn't. I know. Det er aldin na vëna dir, myia yíar. Du é varno anis." *It is good to see you, my friend. You are safe now.*

Gaeleron's eyes became more lucid as Calen spoke the Old Tongue. "Du gryr haydria til myia elwyn, Draleid." *You bring honour to my heart, Draleid.*

As Gaeleron spoke, tears streamed down his cheeks, his eyes glistening. The sight of the proud warrior reduced to skin and bone broke Calen's heart.

"Ír, det er dir vol gryrr haydria til myiar." *No, it is you who brings honour to mine.*

Gaeleron grimaced as he tried to smile, but before he could speak, gasps and whispers rose around the copse, soon turning to shouts.

"Dragon! Dragon!"

Calen returned Gaeleron's smile and squeezed the elf's shoulder gently before rising to his feet and turning to meet Valerys as the dragon plummeted from the sky. From below, Valerys's white scales and black-veined wings blended with the clouds and the dark night. As those around him scattered, some hiding behind rocks and trees, others pulling swords from scabbards, Calen stepped out into the grass, allowing his and Valerys's minds to drift together.

Loose blades of grass, droplets of water, and small flecks of earth whipped up into the air as Valerys levelled himself with a powerful crack of his wings. The earth shook beneath Calen's feet as the dragon landed, pale lavender eyes glistening.

Pain and sadness radiated from the dragon, images of Gaeleron, Elia, and Lasch flashing between his and Calen's minds.

"It's all right." Calen reached his hands up, resting them on either side of Valerys's snout, pulling the dragon's head down to his. Valerys's warm breath swept over Calen, a rumble resonating in his chest. Valery's pupils, sitting amidst the seas of iridescent lavender that were his eyes, had pulled so narrow and thin, they were almost black lines.

Calen drew in a breath, feeling his and Valerys's hearts beat as one. "From here on out, we will not be separated. I promise you. Myia nithír til diar. Ayar elwyn, ayar nithír." *My soul to yours. One heart, one soul.*

Valerys let out a rumble of agreement, nudging Calen backwards with his snout, a warmth spreading from his mind.

Whispers and murmurs sounded behind Calen as those who had run and hidden began to emerge, realising Valerys was not one of the Dragonguard.

Calen patted the scales of Valerys's snout, then turned to find Surin walking towards him, a few others following tentatively behind her, all eyes fixed on Valerys.

"By the gods," Surin whispered to the wind, resting her open palm across her heart as she walked. "It is true…" Surin stared at Valerys , a look of wonder on her face, before she shook her head and turned to Calen. "Where will you go?"

Vaeril, Erik, and Tarmon made their way over, each nodding to Valerys, who rumbled a greeting in return.

Calen wasn't sure how far he could trust Surin. He barely knew her. He had already talked to Vaeril and the others, and they had agreed they would go to the Aravell to seek refuge while they attempted to make contact with Aeson and Dann and all those in Durakdur. "We will cross the Burnt Lands and find a safe place to rest."

Surin nodded, looking back towards those who had gathered around her. She took a step closer to Calen. "If you'll have us, we'd come with you. There's no place for us in Berona, and Tarka knows every safe haven for four hundred miles. We'd all be in the Inquisition dungeons within a week."

Calen wasn't sure what to say. He looked around as those gathered moved closer. How in the gods would they be able to get them all through the Burnt Lands alive?

"I can connect you with other groups, here in Loria. They will take you in," Erik said, stepping up beside Calen. "There is one west of Berona, in the Firnin Mountains. I guarantee Tarka doesn't know of its existence. Coren likes to keep them separated."

Before Surin could speak, Aeson's contact, Ingvat, moved to her side, dark cloak hanging loose around her shoulders. "We'd never make it to the Firnin Mountains. Aside from the imperial patrols and the Inquisition, Uraks roam these lands like wolves now. Many of the towns and villages near Greenhills and around the base of the mountains have been razed, the people slaughtered." She turned to Calen. "We'd come with you, please. The reason we're here is because we believe in Aeson's cause. We are willing to fight." Ingvat looked over Calen's head, towards Valerys, who loomed behind Calen, scales glistening in the moonlight, lavender eyes watching. "If you'd have us, we'd follow you, Draleid."

"You don't even know me."

"You fought at Belduar," Ingvat said, turning to those around her, their murmurs rising. "You fought at Kingspass, even though the empire was hunting you. Even though you owed them nothing, you fought. The official story was that you fled, and the mages routed the Uraks. But the truth spreads like a wildfire. You have a name now, across the North. Did you know that? Those who saw you fight at Kingspass call you the Warden of Varyn. The man who fights alongside a dragon. The man whose eyes mist with the light of The Father." Ingvat fixed Calen with an intense stare. "It seems you make a habit of laying your life down for people you don't know. And if that were not enough, you crossed the Burnt Lands to find one of your own."

Surin stepped forwards. "We do not know you, Draleid. But we know your deeds. And we know Aeson Virandr. Besides, to turn us away would mean sentencing us to death. The Inquisition do not take kindly to traitors. We would share the same fate your companions were doomed to." Surin glanced towards Gaeleron, Elia, and Lasch, who were still over by the trees. "You crossed the Burnt Lands once. It can be done again."

"It's not that simple," Calen said, looking around at those gathered. There had to be nearly fifty of them. He and Vaeril had barely managed to shield three. There was no way they could shield fifty.

"How many mages are amongst your number?" Vaeril looked to Calen. The same thought must have crossed their minds.

"There are seven, including me. Two Scholars, a Battlemage, two Craftsmages, a Consul, and a Healer."

"That's not enough," Calen whispered to Vaeril. "We could barely shield ourselves. Seven of them could shield ten – eleven at most."

Vaeril pressed his fingers into his cheeks as he thought. "It's not a linear calculation, but if we halve the length of time we shield, then bind them and sleep, we could double the amount we can protect. We'll move slower, but we can take more… theoretically."

"It's still not enough." Calen ran his hands through his hair, shaking his head. "It's not enough, Vaeril."

"Better to save some than none," Tarmon said.

Calen let out a sigh, holding his hands at the back of his head. He'd lost so many. The Glade, Belduar, the tunnels, Drifaien… As Calen stared at the ground, thinking, Valerys shifted, eliciting gasps from those gathered. The dragon craned his neck over Calen so his head rested a few feet off the ground, his eyes level with Surin's. The woman's hair and robes rippled from Valerys's breath. To Calen's surprise, she met Valerys's gaze, unmoving.

Warmth washed over Calen, a protective instinct. Images of those they had lost drifted through Valerys's mind: Falmin, Ellisar, Korik, Lopir,

Vars, Freis, Ella, Faenir… Each time, they were helpless. Each time they had been forced to stand by and watch as those they cared for were taken from the world. But they were no longer helpless. And they would no longer stand and watch. Valerys turned his head, his lavender gaze meeting Calen's.

Draleid n'aldryr. Calen nodded, energy rippling through him from the bond. He looked to Surin and the others. "We will take you with us."

"Thank you," Surin said,

"Crossing the Burnt Lands will not be an easy journey. Some of you will die."

The woman's face hardened. "All of us will die if we stay. We've been fighting this fight for years now. We know the risks."

Calen nodded. "You said you had a Healer with you?"

"I will have him tend to your wounded," Surin said, already knowing the intent of Calen's question. "Though he can only tend to the wounds of the body. Those of the mind they must overcome on their own."

"They won't be on their own."

Surin inclined her head. "I will have Sander tend them."

"What did I miss?" Calen turned to see Lyrin emerging from the hatch that led back to Raven's Ruin. The man's dark green plate gleamed in the light of the moon, marred by bloodstains along the breast and arms, spatters on his legs. Lyrin shrugged. "It doesn't matter. The others will be here in a moment. I collapsed the tunnel at the fletchery, so we have some time, but we should get moving as soon as we can."

"The others?" Erik turned, raising an eyebrow at Lyrin.

"The other knights." Lyrin didn't look at Erik as he spoke. Instead, he strode past him, Tarmon, and Vaeril, moving towards Calen and Valerys. The man lifted his right hand, the green plate gauntlet turning to liquid metal and receding back into the cuff that stopped at his wrist. In the same motion, Lyrin wiped the sweat from his brow, looking past Calen and up at Valerys, a smile spreading across his face. "He's incredible…"

Valerys lowered his head towards the knight, and Lyrin raised his hand. "I eh… I wouldn't do that if I were you," Erik said with a shrug.

Valerys's lips pulled back, a low rumble resonating in the dragon's chest. A puff of air from Valerys's nostrils swept across Lyrin's face and through his hair.

The man immediately brought his hand to his head, smoothing out his ruffled hair before throwing a glare at the dragon, which quickly turned to a smile. He bent one knee and gave a slight bow at the waist. "It's a pleasure to make your acquaintance."

Valerys answered with a rumble of recognition turning away from the knight, no longer interested.

"I don't know what your parents were feeding you," Lyrin said, turning to face Calen. "But I want to find out. You end up a Draleid, and Arden's the size of a mountain."

A knot formed in Calen's throat at the mention of Haem. He swallowed hard. He wanted to ask Lyrin about Haem, but the knight put his hand over the Sigil on his breastplate, his expression changing.

"They're coming."

A bright green orb burst into life a few feet to Lyrin's left, hovering in the air. The orb pulsated, wisps of light drifting into the dark of night, causing the pools of water in the grass to shimmer. Then, without warning, the orb flattened into a disk, spreading itself over twenty feet in diameter, its centre turning black as tar, rippling like water while the edges glowed with green light.

Silence hung in the air, broken only by the murmurs and the squelching of feet in the muddy grass as people shifted uneasily, faces illuminated by the green glow. Valerys lowered his neck, a deep growl resonating in his chest. The dragon's lips pulled back, nostrils flaring, his white scales painted in a green hue.

Vaeril, Erik, and Tarmon stepped closer to the green ringed pool of black that hung in the air, the tension clear in their movements. Calen felt Vaeril pulling on threads of Spirit and Fire. Steel rang as swords were pulled from scabbards and knives drawn. Threads of Air and Earth whirled around a man who wore the black robes of a Battlemage, a long-shafted axe in each hand.

Those who were not warriors stepped behind the others, fear evident in their glistening eyes.

The surface of the rippling pool pulsed, and Calen tensed. The black liquid bulged as though something was pushing through from the other side. The surface tension held for a moment before an armour-clad figure stepped through and out into the copse.

They wore the same smooth, green plate as Lyrin, golden trim running along its edges and outlining the white sigil emblazoned on the breastplate. A brilliant white cloak knotted at the pauldrons flowed over his shoulders.

The warrior stepped forwards, his armoured boot depressing into the sodden ground. In Kingspass, Calen hadn't looked closely at the armour the knights wore. But as the warrior stepped closer, Calen could see that, just like Lyrin's, the armour flowed over the man's body as though it had been poured into place, filling all weak points, moving smoothly with each motion. The warrior's helmet seemed as though it were a part of the rest of the armour, flowing up from the collar, over the neck, and forming tightly around the head, slits of green light for vision. There was no smith in the known world who could create armour like that.

Of War and Ruin

The hovering well of black pulsed and bulged again, four more figures stepping through, one after the other, the black liquid sliding over them and returning to its rippling state. Their armour was identical to Lyrin's. Only the first warrior who stepped through bore the golden markings. *Their leader.* Calen's memory fell into place. The warrior who stood before them must have been the one who held the body of his companion in the central plaza of Kingspass after the battle – the one the other knights had called 'Grandmaster'.

Once the other three knights were through, a tremor ran through the gateway of black and green, and it collapsed inwards, the air around it shimmering as it vanished.

The Grandmaster took a step toward Calen, the other knights moving around him. Just as Haem's had at Kingspass, the Grandmaster's helmet turned to liquid, receding into the collar of his armour. Gasps and murmurs spread through the gathered crowd. Calen felt the Spark thrumming in the Air as each of the mages pulled threads into themselves, preparing for the worst.

Calen would have been in shock had he not already seen this unnatural armour at Kingspass. Even then, he couldn't help but think back to before everything changed. Seeing warriors like these would have shaken him to his core a summer ago, but now they were simply something else in a world that was constantly revealing itself.

The grandmaster's hair was short and black, speckled with grey, a beard covering the lower half of his face. His face held the weight of about thirty summers, but Calen had a feeling the man was far older than that. A number of thin, long-healed scars marred his face, and his eyes were a deep blue. He fixed his stare on Calen. As he reached out his hand, the metal along his right arm turned to molten steel, tumbling across his newly-exposed skin, melding with the main body of the armour. "Calen Bryer, it is an honour to finally meet you. My name is Kallinvar, Grandmaster of the Knights of Achyron."

✑

His arm outstretched towards the young Draleid, Kallinvar's words echoed in the night, followed by silence and an owl hooting in a nearby tree.

Kallinvar hadn't gotten a good look at the man in Kingspass. He was tall, though still a head shorter than Arden. His shoulders were broad, and his frame was solid, but Kallinvar still saw the lingering effects of imprisonment and malnutrition in his face. The sword at his hip was of elven design – late First Age by the look of it, made long before even Kallinvar's time. *Curious.* An autumn-red scarf was looped through the young man's sword belt, vines of gold and cream sprawled across it.

As Kallinvar took the measure of the young man, his gaze fell on those that stood around him.

The dragon to which the Draleid was bound loomed over the young man, its gaze fixed on Kallinvar and his knights, a persistent rumble in its chest. The dragon was even larger than it had been at Kingspass. From head to tail it was almost forty feet, wings capable of spreading twice that size when fully open. It had been so long since he'd seen a dragon this close, he'd forgotten what devastatingly beautiful creatures they were. Power radiated from the creature, ridges of horns the length of Kallinvar's forearm running along his jaw and framing his face, dense muscle rippling beneath thick scales, teeth as long as daggers. The sheer presence of the creature was indomitable. He'd forgotten how fast they grew. From memory, many reached as large as fifty or sixty feet from head to tail by the time they'd seen two summers, though this particular dragon looked as though it would reach that size even sooner.

Two humans and an elf – the same three who had fought with him at Kingspass – stood at the Draleid's side. The taller of the men looked as though he had been chiseled straight from a mountain. He stood a measure for Arden in height, his shoulders broader, legs like tree trunks, his experience evident in his measured breaths and level stare. A long greatsword hung over his back, a short sword strapped at his hip, a clearly commandeered set of Praetorian plate adorning his shoulders.

Twin swords peeked over the shoulders of the second man, who was smaller in both height and stature than the first. He held himself like someone who was well acquainted with blood and steel.

Whereas the two men stood to the Draleid's left, close and ready to step across him, the elf was like his shadow. As Kallinvar had stepped through the Rift, he'd seen the elf move to position in front of the Draleid, hand drifting to the pommel of the sword at his hip.

The body language of the three warriors showed they were willing to die for the people they stood beside. The elf in particular would allow his body to be drained of blood quicker than he would allow a drop to be taken from the Draleid – of that, Kallinvar was sure.

Kallinvar had always believed you could learn the most important things about a person's character by studying those around them. And in those short moments, Kallinvar had learned several things, but chief among them being the Draleid inspired fierce loyalty. The kind of loyalty that could never be bought or earned through fear.

The Draleid stared at Kallinvar for a long moment, as though weighing the cost of the words he would choose. The heavy weight on shoulders so young was clear in every breath that Calen Bryer took. The young man let out a long-held breath, then clasped Kallinvar's extended forearm. "The honour is mine, Grandmaster Kallinvar."

The words held some truth, yet Kallinvar felt there was more to them – a question yet unasked. Either way the tension visibly drained from those around them. A quick glance told him that the those gathered had not expected to be where they stood at that particular moment; they were dirty and restless, bags stuffed and bulging. It was clear they had fled the city with little notice and in a state of panic. Through the Sigil, Lyrin had not been able to communicate the situation. They had agreed that he would reach through the Sigil once if he wished to return to the temple and twice if he had found the Draleid, but one look had told Kallinvar all he needed to know.

"You saved us at Kingspass." The Draleid locked eyes with Kallinvar. In his centuries, Kallinvar had seen eyes of many colours, from the shimmering green of the Bjorna Angan, to the crimson of the Bloodspawn, and the molten gold that touched the bloodlines of elves. But he had never before seen eyes such as the Draleid's: pale lavender, specked with spots of vivid purple and white. What's more, in Kingspass the young man's eyes had glowed with a bright light, mist drifting into the air as he moved. *The light of Varyn.* Just as the Soulblades of every knight shimmered in Achyron's green, in the old scriptures the colour purple had always represented Varyn, The Father, protector of all things, creator of dragons. It could have been a coincidence; the dragon's eyes held the same hue. Though Kallinvar had never before seen a Draleid inherit the eye colour of the dragon to which they were bound, and Kallinvar didn't believe in coincidences. Whatever the reason, there was significance in it. Of that, he was sure.

"We did what needed to be done," Kallinvar said. *And we paid dearly for it.* A lump formed in Kallinvar's throat at the thought of Verathin, Allenor, and Irythinia.

"Had you not come, we would no longer be drawing breath." A look of understanding crossed the young man's face. "Thank you."

Kallinvar gave the Draleid a half-hearted smile, inclining his head. "We have been searching for you since that night, Calen Bryer."

The Draleid's eyes narrowed, mud squelching as he shifted. "Searching for me? Why? Who even are you?"

"We are the Knights of Achyron." Kallinvar moved a step closer to the Draleid. "We fight in the name of the warrior god himself. There is much we must discuss. But for now, what is important is that you know we stand by your side. We have come here to offer you our aid." Kallinvar gestured for Ruon, Ildris, Varlin, and Arden to step forward. "There is a war coming, Draleid. A war that will eclipse anything and everything you've ever known, and I believe you have a part to play. I promise we will talk on this once you are safe, but for now I ask that you accept these knights as your honour guard. I assume your plan is to cross the Burnt Lands once more. My knights will make that task a much less arduous one. And they will stand by you in the war to come."

"*Why*?" A glint of pulsing light shimmered in the Draleid's eyes, his demeanour shifting. Behind him the dragon bared its teeth, frills on its back rising.

"Because I failed the Draleid once, and I won't do it again." Kallinvar allowed his anger at his failings to fuel him. "The same darkness that struck four hundred years ago is coming once more, but this time we are weaker, and it is stronger. It is behind you that the people of this continent will stand."

The Draleid shook his head, his gaze fixed on the ground. The smile that spread across his face held no mirth, and the rumble in the dragon's chest grew deeper. "You're just like him – Aeson Virandr. You don't care about me. All any of you care about is controlling me, using me, twisting me." As the Draleid lifted his head, his eyes glowed with purple light, mist rising in wisps. "What did you do to my brother?"

The question was one Kallinvar had expected. "Arden—"

"His name is Haem!" The Draleid's eyes pulsed, the air changing around him, thrumming with energy. Kallinvar could not touch the Spark, but the centuries had taught him to perceive the markings of its influence on the world. The dragon spread his wings and stretched out his neck, baring his razor-sharp teeth. The dragon and the Draleid were mirror images of each other, fury seeping from them. "His name is Haem, and he is my brother. You took him from us – from me."

The Draleid made to move closer to Kallinvar, but a bright green light burst into life, and Ruon stood at Kallinvar's side, Soulblade gripped in her fist, levelled at the Draleid.

"Take another step," she said, her helmet receding into her armour, her cold stare fixed on the Draleid. The dragon snapped its head down, rows of razor-sharp teeth inches from Ruon's head, eyes smouldering. Along with the dragon, the elf had drawn his sword and now held it level with Ruon's cheek. Ruon didn't flinch. "See who dies first. You may be a Draleid, but you are speaking to the Grandmaster of the Knights of Achyron. You *will* show him the respect he shows you. For it is a respect you have, as of yet, done nothing to earn."

CALEN'S HEART HAMMERED. HIS HANDS trembled. Valerys's rage blended with his own, amplifying it, thrumming through them both. His jaw twitched, teeth clamping as he tried to calm himself. Each breath felt like a hurricane in his lungs. The emotions had come like a flash flood, sweeping through him without warning. Ever since seeing Haem in Kingspass, Calen had pushed everything down, buried it in the depths of his mind where he kept all other memories of his family. There had been no time to grieve. No time to sit, and weep, and mourn. He had always had to keep moving, keep fighting. Everyone had either wanted to kill him, control him, or look to him for answers. *But Haem is alive.*

"You do not have to accept our help, Calen." The Grandmaster – Kallinvar – said, his voice level and calm despite the tension. "But the last time the Blood Moon rose, we stood divided and Efialtír broke us all. The Order fell, the empire rose, and my knighthood was brought to the edge of oblivion. I do not seek to control you, or to use you, or to place strings around your limbs. I seek to stand by your side when the Shadow comes. I seek to learn from the mistakes of the past."

"Why should I trust you?"

"Don't." One of the knights stepped forwards, moving to Kallinvar's side. A tingle swept across Calen's skin, hair pricking. A fist clenched his heart. The knight's helm rippled, turning to molten steel and crawling back over his skin and hair, melding with the armour's collar. Haem took another step closer to Calen, meeting his gaze. "Trust me."

Chapter Forty-Four

Blood and Oaths

Calen drew in a slow breath, wind howling like thunder in his ears. The warmth of Valerys's scales against his palms was in enmity with the icy chill that swept over him like a crashing wave. His body shifted with a crack of Valerys's wings, lifting higher, pushing through a thick bank of clouds, before diving. They were one. Eyes, ears, heart, and body. The world was clearer, sharper. Their heart thumped, slow and rhythmic. Their body narrowed, slicing through the air.

The first time they had flown together had been after Tarmon and the others had rescued Calen from Arisfall, and Calen had not been entirely conscious. It was a feeling like no other. A closeness of body and soul that felt intrinsic to life. As they tore through the cloud-laden sky, Calen came some way closer to understanding the nature of the bond between them. They were two halves, blended at all points, one incomplete without the other. Together, they were something entirely different than what they had each been before.

Calen leaned back, spreading his arms wide, filling his lungs with ice-cold air. There, dropping through the night, Valerys below him, he felt no fear in his heart, no anxiety or burdens. This was where he was meant to be. This was where he belonged. Even as the dragon spread his wings and banked hard left, Calen barely shifted where he sat at the nape of Valerys's neck. He felt the binding between them, the intrinsic magic that held Calen in place and moulded the dragon's scales to his presence.

Power radiated from Valerys as he broke through the clouds and into the open sky, muscles rippling. Calen could still remember the vulnerable, frail creature that emerged from the egg in the forest outside Camylin. The creature that had spent more time asleep than awake and only woke to be fed. The memory caused him to smile from ear to ear. It was nearly impossible to reconcile that small creature with the dragon beneath him now. Shoulders three times as wide as a horse, wings that could spread past five carts side-by-side, jaws that could rip an Urak in half, fire that could melt steel.

Below, through Valerys's eyes, Calen could see the camp they'd set up for the night, feel the warmth radiating from the bodies. No fires had been lit so as not to betray their position to any Lorians who might have been following them from the city, but Calen could see the threads of Fire being used to cook two deer and some fish that had been skewered on spits. After Calen had agreed to taking the five knights with them, the group, along with the Lorian rebels, had set off for the Burnt Lands. From what Calen could see from Valerys's back, there was nobody following them, but it was better to be safe than sorry. They'd walked through the remainder of the night and the next day, stopping only an hour or so ago to set up camp, eat, and rest.

Calen had spent most of the time on dragonback. Partly to make up for the lost time not spent flying with Valerys while the dragon was injured, and partly because the idea of talking to Haem sent anxiety coiling through him. All he wanted was to pull Haem into an embrace and not let go. For over two years Calen had mourned his brother's death. He'd wept, grieved, lost his temper, drank his sorrows, and finally had begun to come to terms with the loss, only to then find his brother still drew breath but had decided to let his family believe he was dead.

Calen let out a sigh, shaking his head, as Valerys spread his wings to their fullest and soared over the camp, eliciting a series of gasps and cheers from those below. Calen smiled at that, his mood lifting.

Valerys alighted on a clear patch of earth on the far side of the camp below a rising rock face, whipping up swirls of dust and dirt with his wings. Calen slid from the dragon's back, softening his landing with thin threads of Air. If it had been up to him, they would have flown for hours, sweeping through the barren valleys that bordered the Burnt Lands and soaring across the cloud-filled night sky. But they had spent too long away from the group as it was, and, in a way, he felt indebted to these people. If he hadn't come to Berona to find Rist, they would still be sleeping in their warm beds, still going about their normal lives. They had fled their homes because that Battlemage, Black – or Tarka, as Sulin had called him – had betrayed them, but it had been Calen's arrival that had triggered that betrayal.

Warmth touched the back of Calen's mind, and he looked up to see Valerys staring out over the camp, head lifted high, shoulders pushed back, a deep rumble resonating in his chest. The dragon's lavender eyes glistened as he gazed over the gathered men and women. A sense of pride filled Calen, spilling over from Valerys, the instinct to protect, to defend. *Our people. Our family.*

Calen rested his hand on the scales of Valerys's chest, resting his fingers for a moment on the beginning of the long scar of fused scales that ran along the dragon's side from the Fade's lightning. "Our family is getting bigger."

An urge to roar rippled in Valerys's mind, a primal instinct to tell the world that these people were now under his protection. But the dragon held back. They were halfway between Berona and the Burnt Lands, the Beronan Lake at their back. They couldn't risk giving their position away.

A warning from Valerys flashed in Calen's mind, giving him a moment's notice before he heard Haem's voice.

"Calen."

Calen's throat felt as though it had been pulled tight with rope, his chest seizing. Every drop of moisture in his mouth evaporated. He didn't turn. He stood frozen with his hand resting on Valerys's chest.

"Please, Calen."

Calen tried to stop his stomach from somersaulting. He straightened his back, lifted his chin, and turned. He let his anger rise; Haem deserved it. "What do you want me to say, Haem? Or should I call you Arden? You walked away when—"

The wind was knocked from Calen's lungs as Haem crashed into him, wrapping him in an embrace so tight Calen thought his bones might break.

"I love you, I've missed you, and I'm here."

Calen had managed to keep his composure until he felt the cold wetness of Haem's tears against his neck. That broke him. He leaned into Haem's embrace, squeezing back, his fingers twisting in the linen of Haem's shirt. Tears streamed down Calen's cheeks, mixing with snot. A dam broke, everything he had been holding back pouring forth. He wept for his mam and for his dad. He wept for Ella and Faenir and all those he hadn't been strong enough to save. And he wept for the brother that had come back to him. Calen shuddered, his stomach lurching, twisting into knots, his body jerking with the strength of the tears, and Haem just held him.

"I'm here, little brother. I'm here."

They stayed like that, tears streaming down both of their faces, arms holding tight. Finally, a warm breath blew over him, sweeping his hair off his face, followed by the scaled snout that nudged his side.

Reluctantly, Calen pulled away from Haem, wiping the tears and snot from his face with his sleeve.

Haem looked from Calen to Valerys, who loomed over them, fore-limbs grinding into the ground, shoulders rising at least twice Haem's height, muscular neck stretching even higher, white scales gleaming. Valerys stared down at Haem before lowering his head so their gazes met. A feeling of deep interconnected intimacy drifted from Valerys's mind to Calen's. This was the brother the dragon had never met. The kin taken from him before birth. The kin that had now been returned.

Valerys leaned forwards, tilting his head so the flat of his snout pressed against Haem's shoulder, nudging him. A low rumble sounded in the dragon's chest, more purr than anything else.

"Rest your hands on the sides of his snout," Calen said to Haem, wiping the fresh tears from his cheeks.

Haem did as Calen asked, hesitating only for a moment. "Does it have a name?"

"*His* name is Valerys. It means *Ice* in the Old Tongue."

"Valerys," Haem whispered, running his fingers along one of the long horns that framed Valerys's jaw. He then swept them across the dragon's scales, feeling at a groove that had been scratched into a scale just above Valerys's lip. "It's as if he knows me."

"You are family," Calen said, his eyes locked on Haem. "He knows you as I do. He is me, and I am him."

Haem reached out one hand and rested his palm against Calen's cheek, brushing a tear away with his thumb. "You've grown, little brother."

"I've had no choice," Calen said, wishing he had put less sting in the words. With a low rumble, Valerys pulled away from Haem and dropped to the ground, curling up, his tail meeting his snout, enclosing Calen and Haem in a ring of his body. Calen lowered himself to the ground, resting his back against Valerys's side. "I'm sorry, I didn't mean it like that."

Haem sat at Calen's side, pulling his knees towards his chest. "I'm sorry I wasn't there. I would have given my life to be. I would have given anything to take that pain from you."

"I watched them die." Calen stared at the ground, a tear streaking down the bridge of his nose and dripping from the tip. Haem was the only one who could ever truly understand. The only one who could comprehend the pain.

"I'm sorry, Calen." Haem's voice trembled. Calen looked up to see tears streaming from his brother's eyes. Haem had sucked in his cheeks, biting down on the insides as he stared off into the distance.

"It's my fault." Calen shook his head. "I'm the reason they're dead. The empire came looking for me. I killed a soldier in Milltown. I—"

"It's not your fault." Haem cut Calen off. "Don't you dare hold that weight on your shoulders. I won't let you."

Calen drew in a breath, then let it out through his nostrils. "I killed the man who killed dad... drove my sword through his chest in Berona." Calen's words lingered in the air, followed by a short silence. "Why didn't you come back?" He could feel the tears welling in his eyes again, but he pushed them down, his stomach twisting. "Why did you let us think you were dead? If you'd been there... if you..."

"I *was* dead, Calen. Or at least I was dying when Kallinvar and the others found me in Ölm Forest. We chased the Uraks from The Glade and pushed them towards Wolfpine Ridge, but it was a trap. They surrounded us. I watched everyone die. I was bleeding out from a gut wound, and Kallinvar offered me a chance to keep fighting." Haem pulled back his shirt revealing a metallic green tattoo in the same shape as the symbol the Knights of Achyron wore on their armour: a downward facing sword set into a sunburst.

Calen's mind drifted to that dream he'd had in the Burnt Lands – the dream of Haem in Ölm Forest. Had it truly been real? "What is it?"

"It's the Sigil of Achyron. It's what saved me."

"Did it hurt?"

"Like you wouldn't believe," Haem said with a short laugh. Calen's heart clenched. Haem's smile was something he'd never thought he'd see again. "If I had said no, I would have died there and then, in a pool of my own blood, surrounded by everyone I'd grown up with. Saying yes meant that in some way I could still protect you. It meant hope. But I couldn't come back. Taking the Sigil means swearing your life to Achyron. It's an oath of the soul, and to betray that oath means to have your soul burned from you. I couldn't come back until it was what Achyron required of me. I'm here now, and I'm not letting you fight this fight alone." Haem leaned over, touching the side of his forehead against Calen's. "I promise."

They sat in easy silence.

"You passed The Proving then?" Haem gave Calen a half smile, a prideful look in his eyes.

Calen nodded. "Despite Fritz Netly's best efforts."

Haem looked over Valerys's tail, his eyes narrowing. "Did I see that little shit here, with the others?"

"It's a long story."

"We have a lot to catch up on. And a lot of time."

❧

TARMON SAT ON THE TRUNK of a fallen tree near the edge of the camp, the tip of his greatsword resting on a folded cloth, the flat of the blade against his inner thigh. He ran a lightly oiled whetstone along the edge of the blade methodically, his hands moving through the motions born of repetition.

Across the way, Valerys was curled up from head to tail, Calen and his brother sitting on the ground, resting against the dragon's side. They'd been there for hours now, talking, laughing, crying. At first, after what had happened at Kingspass, Tarmon had been worried. Calen had a temper. A righteous temper, but a temper nonetheless, and Valerys's was no better. The pair of them fuelled each other.

But the unease had drained from him when he'd seen the two embrace. Calen might have been a Draleid, but he was still only a young lad with the weight of the world on his shoulders. More than any of them, Calen had needed a bit of happiness. Especially after they'd not found Rist in Berona.

"What will you do?"

Tarmon looked to his right at the sound of Vaeril's voice, the elf dropping to the ground and folding his legs beneath him, the light of the moon bright against his white-blonde hair. "What will I do with what?"

"In a few weeks we will be in Aravell. There, we will reach out to Aeson Virandr, and the rebellion will truly begin. What will you do?"

"Still not sure what you mean."

Vaeril drew in a breath, looking over at Calen. The elf was a strange one, but Tarmon had come not only to respect him, but to admire him and to consider him a friend. There wasn't a doubt in Tarmon's mind that Vaeril would give his life not only for Calen, but for any of them. "You are Lord Captain of the Belduaran Kingsguard."

"Ah." Tarmon frowned. He understood what the elf was asking. At first, when the Wind Runner had crashed in the tunnels below Lodhar, Tarmon's only thoughts had been to get back to his king, to get back to Daymon. The young man had a good heart, but he had been consumed by the loss of his father. He needed guidance.

But the more time Tarmon spent with Calen and the others, those thoughts drifted increasingly towards the back of his mind. It was not a simple question. Belduar was his home, but the city was gone now, charred and burned, destroyed by the empire. His parents were long taken into Heraya's embrace, and both his brother and sister had been killed in the Fade's attack on the city.

Erik, Calen, Vaeril, even Valerys – they were his family now. They'd fought, bled, suffered, and lost together. Honour tugged him towards Daymon and Belduar, but his heart tethered him here. He let out a sigh, sitting up straight, pulling the whetstone away from his blade. "I'm not sure."

Vaeril nodded, standing and slinging his bow across his back. The elf was likely going off on one of his patrols. Regardless of whether Vaeril had been assigned first watch, he often took it anyway. The elf rarely slept, and even if he did, it was with one eye open and a hand on his bow. He took a few steps, then turned back to Tarmon. "We are Vandasera, you and I. Erik and Calen too."

Tarmon raised an eyebrow.

"It is a word of the Old Tongue. It means to be bound not by words but by honour and a singular purpose. An understanding of what is right. Vandasera. Oathsworn."

⤫

SHADOWS CRISSCROSSED THE GROUND, CAST by the cold light of the moon breaking through the trees that lined the eastern edge of the camp. Erik slid his knife from the sheath at his hip. He flipped it into a reverse grip, his thumb resting against the pommel, fingers wrapped tight around the hilt.

He weaved through the foliage, his steps light and purposeful. He drew his breaths in through his nose, releasing through his mouth, slow and careful. Ahead of him, a shadowy figure stalked through the thicket, the hood of their dark cloak pulled up over their head, bow held firmly in their left hand.

Erik had been just about ready to wake Tarmon to replace him on watch when he'd heard rustling in the trees, a branch snapping. At first he'd thought it a fox or a kat, but then a heavier snap sounded – too heavy for either animal and too sure footed for anything larger.

Ahead of him, the figure moved from tree to tree, moving like someone who understood how to move silently in a forest but hadn't spent enough years putting theory into practice. They stood too high, moved too quickly, and left signs of their passage everywhere. Erik picked up his pace, moving when the stranger moved, using their noise to hide his own.

After a few minutes, he could see where they were going. They were working their way towards the rock face that dropped from the ridgeline at the far end of the camp. *Where Calen and Valerys are sleeping.*

Looking through the trees, Erik saw shapes moving around the camp – the others who had been set on watch. But if this archer could get a clear shot from the woods, it wouldn't matter how many eyes watched the night.

As Erik drew closer, he drew his breath in slower, holding it for longer. He crouched as he moved, lowering his centre of gravity. He was close enough now he could make out the brown colouring of the archer's cloak, illuminated by the sporadic rays of interspersed moonlight.

He glanced ahead. They were only twenty feet from the trees nearest to where Calen was sleeping. With his eyes adjusted to the dim light, Erik could just about make out the rise and fall of his friend's chest against the gleaming white of Valerys's scales; the dragon's scales seemed to almost draw in the moonlight, harnessing it. Calen slept in a half-seated position with his head resting against Valerys's side, a blanket drawn up over him. To Calen's right, another figure sat on the ground, legs crossed, sword resting across their lap. Erik had no doubt it was Calen's brother. Erik hadn't gotten much of a chance to speak to the man, but he seemed decent enough. He and the other knights had been on watch all night, most of them still wearing that strange green armour.

A few more paces and the archer was slowing, scanning for the right spot. The figure slipped an arrow from a quiver on their back.

Snap.

"Fuck." By the time Erik had felt the resistance of the branch buried beneath the foliage, it had been too late, he'd already placed his weight on it. It was only by instinct that he threw his shoulder back, praying to Achyron and Elyara both that he'd picked the correct shoulder. A *whoosh* tore through the air, soaring past his left side, followed by a *thunk* as the arrow lodged into a tree.

The lack of pain was Erik's second assurance the arrow had indeed missed him. He lunged, twisting to his left as the archer swung their bow in an arc, glancing off the side of Erik's head. Erik brought his knife across his chest, then stabbed down into the back of the archer's elbow, skin parting, tendon snapping away from bone. The archer let out a horrendous shriek, reeling backwards as Erik yanked the knife free, stepping forwards.

The archer pulled a knife from somewhere beneath their cloak, the steel glinting, left arm hanging limp. They swung the knife in frantic swipes, slashing at Erik.

Erik waited. As they slashed their blade across Erik's path, Erik stepped forwards, clamped his hand around the back of the archer's wrist, holding their knife hand in place, then rammed his own knife blade down through their forearm, twisting. He could feel the vibration as the blade grated against bone, blood spilling out through the wound. He must have missed the artery, as the blood was spilling as opposed to spurting. The archer stumbled backwards, one arm hanging limp by their side, tendon severed at the elbow, blood streaming from the other.

Erik lunged, grabbing the stranger by the throat and slamming them back against a tree trunk, head bouncing off hard wood. Reaching up with his knife hand, Erik pulled the stranger's hood down.

"You fucking rat." Erik found himself staring at the shocked face of the Inquisition apprentice they had taken from Berona. The one who hailed from Calen's home village – Fritz, Erik was sure his name was. The man's face was narrow and slender, a hooked nose at its centre, sharp weaselly eyes either side.

"I'm... sorry... I..." Fritz tried to choke words past Erik's iron grip, but Erik only squeezed tighter, pushing him harder against the bark.

"What are you sorry about?" Erik said, shaking his head in disbelief. "I'm actually curious." He loosened his grip on the man's neck. "Come on, speak."

"I'm sorry," Fritz said, his voice hoarse, breaths ragged. "I didn't... I'm not..."

"You're sorry for getting caught. You thought killing Calen with an arrow while he slept would, what, win you favour with the empire? Grant you fame?" Erik stared into the man's beady eyes. "Calen let you live after what you did to Gaeleron, after what you allowed to happen to that man and woman. I don't know why, but he did. I'm not Calen. And I won't risk his life for yours."

Shock touched Fritz's eyes before Erik flipped his knife and drove it up through the bottom of the man's chin, pushing until he felt the hilt click against bone. Fritz jerked for a moment, blood spluttering from his mouth, eyes gaping, then Erik twisted the blade and dragged it free, letting Fritz slump to the ground, still twitching.

Erik dropped to his haunches, wiped the blood from his knife on Fritz's robes, then slid the knife into its sheath. He looked at the dead man as he rose to his feet, lip curling in contempt. He had to die. Erik had known men like him. He was a weasel, a rat, and he would have done anything to get ahead or save his own skin. Leaving him alive would have put Calen and all the others at risk.

Erik snatched up the bow and pulled the quiver from Fritz's back. No doubt the man had stolen it from one of the fleeing rebels.

Erik turned to leave and found himself staring straight at Vaeril. The elf was close, white-wood bow gripped in his left hand, arrow already nocked. He slipped the arrow back into his quiver and nodded, moving to leave Erik where he stood.

Things had been frosty between Erik and Vaeril since the Burnt Lands. At least, they had seemed so to Erik. It was hard to tell with Vaeril. "Vaeril, wait."

Vaeril stopped, turning, lifting an eyebrow, the moonlight pale against his skin.

"The things I said, in the Burnt Lands—"

"Are already forgotten." The elf slung his bow over his shoulder and disappeared in the dark, blending with the woodland.

CHAPTER FORTY-FIVE

THE WOLF WITHIN

Rain drummed against the hood of Ella's cloak, soaking through, weighing it down, the cold seeping into her skin. The bay mare Farwen had arranged for her, Bell, neighed, her hooves sloshing in the mud. Faenir loped along beside Bell, his back barely lower than the horse's, his fur flattened to his body under the weight of the rain.

Tanner and Yana rode to Ella's left, at the edge of the trees. Yana had shown up with Tanner at the northern gate, a storm raging in her eyes. Even Farwen didn't ask any questions when the woman insisted on joining the party, which Ella figured was a good idea. Farwen may have been a centuries old elf, but Yana had the ferocity of a wild bear. The flat-nosed soldier Varik and two of the other scouts rode ahead, their shapes only just visible in the night.

Ardle and Keela, the two of Juro's scouts Ella knew from Tarhelm, along with two scouts Ella had never met before, rode on Ella's right, hoods drawn.

Farwen and Juro had taken the rest of the scouts to search deeper into the woodlands that framed the main road in search of any signs of Juro's missing scouts. According to Farwen, Juro had sent a group of five scouts about sixty miles southwest of Elkenrim, to keep watch on a Lorian outpost that had begun to report an increase in activity over the past few weeks. But the scouts hadn't reported back.

Ella dipped her head and tugged at the rim of her hood, trying her best to keep the frigid touch of the rain off her skin and out of her eyes. Her cloak was already soaked through, and she could feel the cold in her bones, but the least she could do was provide herself with some relief.

The rain continued to fall as they skirted the edge of the woodland, keeping off the main road. It hammered down relentlessly, pools of water forming, small streams trickling down the slope towards the road. With each step, Bell's hooves sunk deeper into the mud. The mare whinnied, her ears flattening against her head.

"It's all right," Ella whispered, running her hand along the horse's saturated neck. With her words, she could feel the horse's anxiety at the sodden earth fade. Bell's distressed whinny softened to a warm neigh, her muscles relaxing and ears standing up.

"How are you feeling?" Keela asked, drawing her own mare closer, her orange eyebrows striking against her dark complexion.

"How am I feeling?" Ella lifted her gaze from Bell to Keela. "Cold. Wet."

"She meant about being out on assignment," Ardle said with a laugh. "This is your first time coming out with us, but I get the feeling you already knew precisely what she meant."

"Sorry," Ella said, shaking her head. She hadn't meant to be so curt. But her patience had begun to fray ever since Tanner had told her about Calen. It had been weeks since Coren had reached out to her contact – Aeson Virandr, she'd said his name was. Still, they'd heard nothing back. Coren had said it could take some time, and with everything going on across Epheria, Ella was sure it would take even longer. But sitting around and waiting while she knew Calen was out there being hunted clawed at her from the inside out. "A little nervous, in truth."

"So was I." Keela smiled at Ella. "I worked my family's fields before I joined. It takes a while to get used to the shift."

"What made you join?" Ella pulled Bell's reins a little tighter, shifting in the saddle. The people of the South had many reasons to despise the Lorian Empire, but she'd never considered that anyone in the North could feel the same way.

Keela hesitated, looking forward into the night. "Soldiers killed my father in a drunken bar fight. Stabbed him in the neck with broken glass. My mother died from the Blackrot three years before. That left me and my two brothers on our own. When I reported what had happened, the local lord just sent me away and told me to be happy I still had a farm. Two days later the soldiers set the fields alight, then salted the ground and beat me and my brothers until our faces were so swollen we couldn't speak. As it turns out, the lord told the soldiers that I'd reported them, and they came to teach me a lesson. We were near starving when Yana found us begging in the streets of Berona. She offered us food and warm beds. We took them. Then she told us we could leave if we wanted, but that we were welcome to stay. That was four years ago."

"What's your story then?" asked one of the scouts Ella hadn't met before, barely waiting for Keela to finish. "You show up outta nowhere with a wolf the size of a horse and suddenly you're best pals with the commanders? Don't think I haven't seen Commander Valmar taking you out the eastern gate each morning."

"Leave her be, Laran." Ardle threw the woman a glare, frowning.

"Oh, you've your eye on her then, Ardle? I should've guessed."

"Shut up, both of you," said the other scout Ella hadn't seen before. He was older than the others with sun-bronzed skin, hair more grey than black, and the bottom half of his face covered in a thick, meticulously kept beard. He reminded Ella of her dad. "Looks like they found something."

Ella looked up to see Juro emerging from the edge of the forest on his black gelding, rain dripping down his cloak.

ELLA WELCOMED THE BRIEF RESPITE from the rainfall provided by the canopy above as she and the others followed Juro through the forest to where they found Farwen and the rest of the scouts standing over the remnants of what had once been a campsite.

A saturated pile of ash and half-burned wood lay at the centre, packs and blanket rolls strewn about, damp and torn. Three mangled bodies lay in the mud, armour rent like dry parchment, limbs strewn about. Maggots and other insects crawled over swollen, bloated flesh. The putrid fetor of damp, rotting flesh assaulted Ella's senses.

Her stomach turned at the sight, but she forced herself to keep looking. *Push through it.* The taste of vomit touched the back of her tongue, acidic and sharp. She swallowed, forcing it back down.

"You get used to it," a woman with braided grey hair and a leathered skin said.

"May Heraya embrace them." Keela held her hand to her heart as she looked down over the rotting corpses.

"Two more bodies by the edge of the camp," Farwen said as Juro dismounted.

Juro shook his head, folding his arms, droplets of rain dripping from his hair down over his face. "They were good people. Strong. Loyal."

"At least we've no doubt as to who is responsible. Fuckin' filthy beasts." Varik sat on the back of his horse, taking in the gore and bloodshed.

Juro frowned at Varik, then dropped to his haunches beside one of the rotting corpses, his hand resting on a gold torc wrapped around the arm. "Alder. He'd seen no more than nineteen summers."

Ella hadn't noticed Yana slide from her saddle. The woman rested her hand on Juro's shoulder, a tenderness in her that Ella had rarely seen. "We will bury them before we move on."

Farwen looked as though she was going to protest, but she nodded as she met Yana's glare. The elf looked at the gathered warriors. "We bury the bodies, then we move on."

AN HOUR OR SO PASSED as they rode through the forest, hooves slapping against mud, rain drumming against the canopy and forming deep puddles wherever the moonlight pierced. Soaked to the bone, Ella's thighs had begun to chafe, which was not a good sign considering they still had days' of riding before they reached Steeple.

She let out a grunt as she shifted in her saddle, trying to relieve the ache that had set into her lower back. She'd ridden horses a fair amount when she was younger, but not in the last few years. It seemed her mind remembered the basics, but her body didn't.

The sound of mud sucking hooves drew closer to Ella's left, and she turned to see Yana pulling her horse up beside Ella's. Yana's hood was pulled over her head, droplets coalescing at its peak before dripping down onto the saddle. Ella's eyes had adjusted enough to the night to see the scowl carved into Yana's face, the smouldering anger in her eyes. They rode side by side for a while, neither of them speaking.

"If anything happens to him," Yana said, not looking at Ella. "*Anything.* I'll—"

"You'll kill me, I know. You've told me before." Ella let out a sigh. "I didn't ask him to come with me, Yana."

"You're smarter than that." Yana pulled gently on her horse's reins, her expression softening. She looked away as if contemplating something for a moment, then offered Ella a half smile.

"What?"

Yana shook her head. "Nothing. Just… try not to get yourself killed, or he'll throw himself on the blade trying to chase after you."

"I'll do my best," Ella said, letting out a short laugh. "I'm a big advocate of not dying."

"Good." Yana's smile warmed. "Not dying would be appreciated."

The woman pulled on her reins and said something to her horse, who slowed, moving back to where Tanner rode a few feet behind them.

Tanner raised an eyebrow as Yana dropped in beside him, water trickling down her face, her horse letting out a soft neigh.

"What are you staring at?" Yana scowled in the way she did when she knew Tanner's answer was going to be something sweet or emotional. Yana had the biggest and warmest heart Tanner had ever known, but if he ever told anyone that, he was absolutely certain she would never speak to him again. She had a reputation for being a hard woman, a reputation she liked, so she tended to hide behind that scowl.

"Nothing," Tanner lied, his eyes following the droplets of rain as they rolled down her soft skin and over her lips. There was no situation where she wasn't the most beautiful woman he'd ever laid eyes on. None. But again, that was something better implied than stated. Yana was quicker in the mind than he was – by a large distance. She always knew what he was thinking just by his eyes or the look on his face. She just liked to pretend she didn't.

"Hmm." Yana narrowed her eyes as though a child had just told her they would behave if left to their own devices.

"What did you say to Ella?"

"I told her if anything happens to you I'll kill her."

Tanner laughed, wiping the water from his eyes. "You like her."

Yana frowned but didn't answer, instead looking off into the depths of the forest. She signalled her horse to move and pulled away from Tanner, drawing up beside Farwen, who rode ahead.

Tanner stared after her, allowing a soft smile to rest on his lips. They had tried for children – many times. Two had been born still. Three lost in the womb. They'd blamed themselves for a long time. One night – a few days after their second still birth – Farwen had found both Tanner and Yana weeping in one of Tarhelm's alcoves that looked out over the plains between the Firnin Mountains and Fort Harken. Until that night, only Coren and Alari, the infirmerer, had known the depths of Tanner and Yana's struggles. But when they told Farwen, the elf said something that had stuck with both Tanner and Yana until this very day.

'My people believe that what is grown in the womb is simply a vessel. It is our gift to the soul that will one day become our child. When our children are born still, we believe the soul has chosen to wait for a different vessel, one that aligns with their hearts. In some cases, we cannot build the vessels our children need. But that does not mean there is not a soul out there that needs our love. It is said that life is a gift from the gods, but love is what gives life meaning.'

Ella wasn't a child, but she was someone who needed love.

ELLA LOOKED BACK TO SEE Tanner and Yana talking, Tanner laughing, Yana frowning.

She couldn't help but smile. Looking at Yana and Tanner, she saw everything she'd ever wanted with Rhett. A love that was true. A love that pushed through anger and irritation. A love that permeated everything. When Ella was younger, she'd always thought that when she found the right man, every moment would be like dancing on the edge of the world. But when she'd met Rhett, she'd understood that love was about finding a soul that resonated with her own. It was about wanting to give without ever needing to take. Looking at Tanner and Yana, she understood that even more. They were opposites in almost every way. He was calm and stoic, his words few, his smile tender. She was brash and fiery, her tongue sharp and her wits sharper. And yet, they were everything the other needed. They were, as Farwen had said, Ayar Elwyn. *One Heart.*

As Yana rode away from Tanner to join Farwen, Ella shook her head, trying to push Rhett from her mind. Now was not the time. She dropped her hand to her hip, pushing her cloak aside, her fingers resting on the triangular pommel of the sword Farwen had given her. She wasn't used to carrying a blade. She could feel the weight of it dragging at her left side, swinging as she moved. Even then, she felt the need to double check it was there. Seeing the bodies at the campsite had set a fear in her. Memories of the Uraks at Farrenmill. Their blood-red eyes, leathery skin, jagged yellow teeth, obsidian-black claws. In the back of her mind, she could still see the beasts tearing through the Lorian soldiers like scythes through grass. Blood spraying over the dirt. Bones snapping, cracking, breaking.

Snap.

Ella jerked, tensing, wet leather squeaking as her left hand tightened around the reins. To Ella's right, Faenir's ears pricked. The wolfpine stopped for a moment, sniffing at the air. The smell of rain flooded Ella's nostrils, far more crisp and clear than her own senses were capable of perceiving. The fresh, earthy scent filled her, so strong it left an almost metallic taste on her tongue. Faenir's senses were her own.

She shook her head looking about the group. There were twenty-four of them in total. Ella counted amongst the twenty Coren had told Farwen to take with her. Along with Tanner, Farwen, Juro, and Varick. Each of them rode on horseback through the dark, damp forest, rain drumming, hooves squelching in the mud. Most marched onwards, unperturbed. But a few looked as nervous as Ella, their faces pale, their hands gripping their reins so tightly Ella could see the veins bulging through their skin.

More scents drifted to Ella, breaking through the scattering of fresh rainfall, augmented by Faenir's senses: blood and wet fur – the festering carcass of a deer not far away; the deep, earthy smell of loam; the sharp tang of mushrooms with blue caps and yellow spots, images crossing Faenir's mind.

"You all right?"

Ella nearly jumped out of her skin at Ardle's words. She'd been so lost in the smells she hadn't heard him, Keela, and one of the other scouts approach. The other scout looked close to Calen's age. Her skin was pale as ice, her blonde hair matted to her face. It must have been her first excursion as well, as Ella could see the anxiety in her eyes. Ella frowned at Ardle. "Do you make a habit of sneaking up on people?"

"Well, I'm a scout. It's kind of what I'm trained for."

"Fair point," Ella said. She looked back over at Faenir, whose ears were still pricked, nose sniffing in the air. Wariness radiated from the wolfpine, a sense that something wasn't as it should be.

"Can he smell something?" the blonde-haired scout asked, leaning forwards, her eyes focused on Faenir, concern in her voice.

Ella frowned. "He's not sure. It's hard for him to tell in the rainfall. It breaks the scents, scatters them. But there's something…"

"What? You can tell all that?"

Ella turned to see the blonde woman staring at her – Ardle and Keela too. She'd forgotten that her link with Faenir wasn't widely known. It was only really Farwen, Coren, Tanner, and Yana who had any idea. And in truth, Ella wasn't exactly eager to go telling people she thought she might be a druid. They'd look at her as though she'd lost her mind – she looked at herself as though she were losing her mind.

Ella made to answer the woman, but then something changed in the air, the wind shifting, carrying the scent of blood and the sound of heavy feet slapping against mud. The hackles on Faenir's back rose. A deep growl resonated in the wolfpine's throat. Farwen stared at Faenir then shifted her gaze to Ella.

Faenir's snout crinkled, and his lips pulled into a snarl. The wolfpine snapped at the air, his snarl turning into something savage as he charged into the dark of the forest. Images touched Ella's mind, the change in the air taking shape: dense, muscled bodies and blood-red eyes. She howled at the top of her lungs.

"Uraks!"

No sooner had Ella shouted than an Urak leapt from the darkness, unleashing a visceral war cry, blackened steel blade swinging. The beast's call was cut short as Faenir leapt and slammed into it in mid-air like a battering ram, dropping it to the ground. A savage snarl rang out, tearing and snapping as Faenir ripped out the Urak's throat. The iron tang of blood touched Ella's tongue, and she shivered, her body recoiling at the sensation.

The forest erupted into chaos, leathery shapes bursting from the dark, howling. The clashing of swords rang out, shouts and screams rising, the drum of rainfall hammering in the background.

Something *whooshed* past Ella, followed by a blood-chilling scream. She turned to see the blonde-haired scout shrieking, her eyes fixed on Ardle who sat upright on his mount, a black arrow shaft with white fletching protruding from his left eye. Ardle's arms dangled by his side, his head lolling backwards as his horse snorted and stomped before bolting. Ardle slipped from the saddle, landing in the mud with a wet slap, the horse vanishing into the night.

A roar sounded to Ella's left, and Bell reared, snorting and squealing. The mare's feet must have caught in the mud, for seconds later Ella was falling, her heart hammering, blood thumping, a feeling of weightlessness filling her. As Ella fell, she saw a blackened blade sink into the neck of the blonde-scout, blood spraying.

Ella twisted as she fell, slamming into the ground face-first, the mud sucking around her, pushing into her nose and her open mouth. Spots of light flickered in the darkness covering her eyes. Ringing. Panic turned her blood to ice. She clambered to her knees, frantically wiping the mud from her eyes, sounds returning. Through her hazy vision she saw Bell floundering on the ground, muscular body twisting and turning, trying desperately to lift herself to her feet. A black spear crashed through the mare's head, killing her instantly.

Blood-red eyes fixed on Ella, set into grey skin latticed with old scars. Ella pushed back, her arse slamming against the mud, her hand reaching for the sword at her hip. Her fingers slipped around the mud-covered hilt, and she pulled the blade free. The Urak lifted its spear and struck down.

Ella spun in the mud, the spear tip missing her by inches, burying into the ground. As the Urak pulled at the spear shaft, Ella dragged strength from the pit of her stomach and threw herself to her feet, swinging the blade with her right hand. It skittered against the spear shaft, then she felt a brief touch of resistance as the sword bit into bone, before the steel sliced through the Urak's fingers.

Blood pumped from its disfigured hand, and the beast roared, catching Ella in the face with a swipe of its arm. Pain exploded in Ella's nose, stars flitting across her eyes, then she was crashing into the ground once more. Her head was ringing, vision blurring. She scrambled to her feet in time to see Faenir crash into the Urak's chest, tearing chunks of flesh free as they fell to the sodden ground. Faenir clawed at the monstrous beast, his claws gouging furrows of blood through its leathery skin. He wrapped his jaws around the creature's neck, then thrashed his head side to side until the Urak's neck snapped.

Faenir stood over the creature, his chest heaving, a snarl resonating in his throat, blood coating his muzzle and dripping into the mud. The wolfpine's head dropped low, hackles raising as he backed towards Ella, snapping and snarling.

Ella's hand shook, and she clutched the hilt of her sword. Around her, the men and women she'd travelled with fought for their lives, steel crashing, mud squelching, blood spraying. In the middle of it all, Farwen moved like a woman possessed, the path of her blade marked only by the trail of blood it left in its wake.

Ella watched as the elf drove her blade up through an Urak's jaw, heaving it free as she spun, cleaving another Urak's arm at the elbow before bringing the blade back and driving it through the beast's head. Farwen clasped her fingers into a fist, and Ella watched in horror as the steel breastplate of one Urak and the vambraces of another crumpled in on themselves, bones snapping like twigs, blood spurting. The creatures howled, their bodies breaking beneath the force of their own armour. Another twirl of Farwen's blade and she sliced open the belly of a wolf-like creature that looked almost as large as Faenir, its back coated in stone-like scales. The creature shrieked and thrashed as its intestines slid free, slopping into the mud.

Again, Farwen motioned with her hand, and tree roots burst from the ground, twisting around themselves, forming pointed spikes that impaled a number of the leather-skinned beasts, pinning them to trees.

"Ella!"

Ella turned to see Keela stumbling towards her, her hand clasped to her stomach, blood pouring through her fingers. The sight brought images of Rhett to the fore. The tip of the spear bursting through his gut, blood pouring through his fingers like a burst dam – the fear in his voice. '*Ella?*'

"Ella?"

Ella trembled as Keela's voice mirrored Rhett's, pulling her from her thoughts. The woman reached out, her mouth opening in a wordless scream as a blackened blade sliced through air and cleaved her arm at the elbow before swinging back and hacking into the bridge of her nose.

The Urak heaved its blade free like ripping an axe from a tree, blood spurting from the wound. Keela collapsed into the mud.

The edges of Ella's consciousness dimmed. The sounds of battle faded until all she heard was the beating of her heart, each thud filling her with ice. The cold flooded her veins, rivers of ice carving paths through her body. With the ice came a fury like nothing she'd ever felt. Something clawed at her from within. Something feral. Something untamed. A howl rippled through her mind, her hair rising like hackles across her skin. Beside her, Faenir lowered his head, his amber eyes fixed on the Urak, his face twisted in a snarl, his fur weighed down by rainfall, stained crimson by blood.

The Urak unleashed a guttural howl and charged, swinging its black-ened blade in a sweeping arc.

Ella and Faenir lunged together, their minds connected by an unseen cord. The wolfpine dove beneath the swing of the Urak's blade, his powerful legs launching him ahead of Ella. Faenir slammed into the Urak's legs, tearing at the beast's leathery flesh, carving through muscles and gouging bone. When Faenir last protected Ella from the Uraks in

Farrenmill, he had been half the size of the monstrous creatures. Now, his shoulders were as broad as the beast's, his muscles just as dense. The Urak collapsed, howling and thrashing, letting go of its sword as it swiped frantically at Faenir with its clawed hands.

Ella's blood burned in her veins as she charged. The howl of a wolf rippled in her mind, drowning out all other sounds. Her nose throbbed from where the Urak had caught her. A blur of motion flashed to her left, and another of the beasts charged, a glowing gemstone set into its spear. The Urak roared and thrust its spear forward. Reflexively, Ella sliced her blade, redirecting the spear tip as Farwen had taught her. The Urak stumbled at its shifted momentum. Her back foot sinking into the mud, Ella swept her sword back up along the shaft of the staggering Urak's spear. The blade smashed into the creature's jaw, carving through its chin, smashing through teeth and bone, and bursting out the other side. As it reared back, Ella plunged her sword into its gut, driving it to the hilt. Something hammered into her side, sending her spiralling to the ground.

As she slammed down into the mud, the burning feeling that had been clawing at Ella's mind – the howling wolf – flared into life, her skin itching, her fingers curling. She dug her hands into the mud, dragging herself to her feet, lunging at the Urak that had crashed into her. She caught a glint of steel shimmering in the mud, and she snatched the short sword as she moved, narrowly avoiding the swinging claw of the Urak.

Growling, Ella threw herself forwards and rammed the sword into the Urak's side. She pulled the blade free in a spray of blood, then drove it back in. A bloodlust filled her, a feral fury, clouding her mind with a red mist, raging. A wolf howled within her. Again and again she drove the blade into the Urak's torso, steel grating against bone and carving through flesh. The beast stumbled backwards, its lifeblood leaking from its ravaged side. Ella leapt onto its chest. She clawed her free hand into the beast's shoulder, felt her nails break skin followed by the warm touch of blood. The Urak fell and Ella drove her blade down into its chest in a series of frenzied stabs before letting go entirely and instead clawing at its face, her nails tearing strips of flesh.

The Urak hit the ground, mud and dirt spraying the air. Ella slashed, her claws rending. The red mist consumed her, each moment blurring into the next. She lost all sense of time. Her jaws clamped around something, blood filling her mouth, and then she was heaving herself to her feet, running to where Faenir ripped at the Urak that had killed Keela. She leapt onto the creature's back, snapping and snarling, her arms wrapped around its neck, her teeth ripping flesh.

Faenir ripped a chunk from the Urak's calf, and the beast fell backwards.

The air punched from Ella's lungs as she hit the ground, the Urak crashing on top of her. The creature thrashed, raking its clawed hand along the side of Ella's head, carving lines of searing pain into her skin. With the pain, a howl ignited in her blood, echoing in her mind. Ella answered with a howl of her own, finally feeling the wolf within her, understanding it, knowing it. The wolf wanted to protect her, to keep her safe, but she needed to set it free, and so she did. Her nails lengthened, hardening to claws, and she could feel her teeth changing and sharpening. The red mist filled her mind, and the wolf howled within her once more.

She opened her jaws and sank her teeth into the Urak's neck, thrashing her head side to side, tearing open the flesh, blood spilling over her face. As she did, she sank her claws into the far side of the beast's head, raking flesh.

The red mist dulled her mind, the world blurring as she ripped and tore at the Urak. She was herself, and she was not.

She drew in heavy, laboured breaths as the creature lay dead on top of her, blood coating her clawed hands. Then the weight was lifting from her chest, Faenir dragging the body off her. Ella pulled herself upright, kneeling in the mud, her chest heaving, lungs burning. A shout rang in her ears, far sharper and clearer than anything she'd heard before. Yana. Ella threw herself to her feet, yanking a sword from an Urak's body as she ran.

Yana, Tanner, Juro, and two others stood together, swords moving in a blur as they held three Uraks at bay. Two bodies lay before them, one missing a leg, the other in a pool of mud and intestines.

One of the men fell, a blackened sword driving through his neck, the gemstone in its blade pulsating with a red light.

Ella clenched her fist around the hilt of her sword, the wolf within her howling, snarling in her blood. Faenir bounded past her, leaping at the nearest Urak, jaws wrapping around its arm, ripping and tearing as he dragged the creature to the ground.

Ella swung her blade as she reached the others, hacking into the leg of the Urak closest to her. She let go as it lodged into the Urak's bone, blood spilling around it. The Urak roared in pain, turning to catch Ella across the face with the pommel of its sword. Bone crunched, skin splitting, pain bursting. Ella's knee pounded into the sopping mud, her own blood mixing with that already in her mouth.

She looked up to see Tanner's blade slicing through the Urak's throat, a second blade driving into its chest. The Urak howled, ignoring the weapons lodged in its body, and rammed its blackened blade through the belly of a man with a shaved head and a knotted brown beard.

'But I can teach you to never stop.' Coren's words resonated in Ella's head. *'I can train you to push through the pain, to carry the weight on your shoulders.'*

Ella unleashed a primal howl, the wolf burning in her blood. *'You need to be willing to fight harder than anyone who stands in your way.'* She reached up and wrapped her hand around the hilt of the blade she'd left buried in the creature's leg. With a heave, she rose to her feet and pulled the blade free, the momentum forcing her to step backwards. She plunged the steel into the Urak's chest, heaving it free, driving it back in, snarling, roaring. She lost herself in a frenzy of blood and steel, her throat raw, her muscles burning.

She dragged the blade free one last time, and the Urak staggered backwards, catching itself before it fell, its body shredded, leaking blood. It raised its blackened blade, choking breaths escaping its throat.

Before Ella could move to finish the creature off, a blur of grey flashed past her, and Faenir leapt, closing his massive jaws around the Urak's head. He hauled it backwards, slamming it into the mud. The Urak shook feebly, trying to break free, but Faenir let out a savage snarl, spittle and blood spraying as he crunched into the Urak's skull. The wolfpine thrashed his head side to side, rending flesh and cracking bone until the Urak's arms fell, lifeless, by its sides. Moments passed before Faenir released the creature's head, and still, the wolfpine stood over its body, blood dripping from his jaws, bits of flesh sticking from his teeth. A vicious growl resonated in his throat as though he was daring the beast to come back to life.

Ella staggered forwards, the call of the wolf fading as pain pushed through. She dropped into the mud, the cold seeping into her bones from her saturated clothes. Her nose throbbed and felt as though it had been stuffed with wads of cloth, while the side of her head burned where the Urak had clawed her. Glancing around, she saw Farwen and the last of the scouts had slain whatever Uraks were left.

Yana dropped to one knee in front of Ella, a hand clasping on her shoulder, the other tenderly probing the gashes at the side of her head. She met Ella's gaze, blood flowed from a deep slice along her right cheek. "Are you all right?"

"I've been better." Ella coughed as she spoke, blood catching in her throat. She released her grip on her sword, letting it splat into the mud.

"You've broken your nose." Yana narrowed her eyes as she examined Ella's nose. She ran her tongue across her top teeth, pushing out her lip. Yana leaned forwards, cupping her hands against the sides of Ella's face, resting her thumbs on either side of Ella's nose, just below her eyes.

"What are you doing?" Ella swallowed. She knew what was coming. She'd seen her mother do it a handful of times. But her mother had stuffed Alpaisea leaves up the nostrils to numb the pain.

"You're a stupid little girl," Yana said, tutting, shaking her head. "You've no place out here."

Ella clenched her fist, leaning forward, feeling the anger begin to rise within her. "What did you ju—Aagh!"

Yana clasped Ella's face tight, wedging her hands against Ella's nose and pushing hard from the left.

Crack.

Ella howled, trying to pull away. Blood spilled into her mouth, but Yana didn't let go. She pushed again with her thumbs, and Ella felt a grinding crunch, more blood dripping, then a *click*. Yana let her go, and Ella fell backwards into the mud. She clasped her hands to her nose, recoiling in pain at her own touch. Her nose felt as though it had been hit with an axe, then stuffed with rags. Even thinking about drawing a breath through her nostrils sent pain shooting through her. "What the fuck did you do that for?"

Yana knelt in the mud, picking at something in her teeth with her tongue as she stared at Ella. She shrugged. "Could've left it the way it was. Averaged out that pretty face." She laughed, dragging Ella to her feet as she rose. She leaned in, clapping Ella on the cheek gently. "There is no god in this world that could explain what you did here. But you did good."

"Yana. What am I?" The question caused Ella's stomach to churn. That red mist, that feeling of bloodlust, still touched the edges of her mind, sending shivers through her. She looked down at her hands. Her nails had shortened and returned to normal, but her skin was red with blood. A quick probe with her tongue told her that her teeth were no longer sharp fangs.

"You're a druid," Farwen said, appearing over Yana's shoulder, blood splattered across her face – none of it her own. "If we were not certain before, we are now."

CHAPTER FORTY-SIX

IT IS SWEET AND PROPER

The unabating drum of footsteps and horse hooves blended with the incessant chatter of earnest soldiers, the clinking jingle of mail, and the snorting and groaning of the pack animals who towed the endless line of supply wagons. The sounds had become nothing more than background noise to Rist after the second day's march. He held one hand on Trusil's reins, the other on the double-edged dagger Garramon had given him, gold crossguard glinting in the waning sun, a faint red glow emanating from the gemstone set into the pommel. He rocked slightly, still getting used to the movements of the bay gelding beneath him. His thighs chafed, and his stomach muscles burned. Trusil had been one of many gifts Garramon had bestowed upon Rist after he passed the Trial of Faith. In some ways the trial had been far simpler than the Trial of Will, but in others it had been far more challenging. As he rubbed his thumb across the semi-translucent gemstone set into the pommel of the dagger, he knew the last step would be the hardest: to take a life.

He was marching to war. *To war...* The thought was almost incomprehensible to him. How had he, of all people, ended up here? He wasn't Calen or Dann. Had either of them ended up in this position he would have found it easier to understand. But him? No, Rist was far more inclined to sitting by a warm fire with a good book and a tankard of mead. Yet, he felt something deep within him – a nervous energy, an excitement. He was not the boy he had once been. His muscles were thicker, more accustomed to use. As he held the dagger in his palm, he saw the callouses he'd earned from hours upon hours of sword work. But more than that, he felt the low thrum that rippled through the air as the mages of the First Army sat astride their horses around him, marching in a loose formation within the enormous column of soldiers that stretched towards the horizon both ahead and behind.

He was still Rist Havel, still himself, but he was also more. He was an acolyte of the Imperial Battlemages. And he was certain of one thing:

despite how sorely he missed Calen and Dann, and his mam and dad, *this* was where he was meant to be. He finally had a purpose, and he was amongst those who understood him. Other mages. For the first time, Rist felt as though he truly belonged.

Garramon, Anila, and Magnus rode ahead, their long black cloaks draped over their horses' backs. Magnus's booming laughter echoed through the low valley where they marched, the mountains of Kolmir rising on their right, the Elkenwood smothering the land in brown and green to their left. Since meeting Exarch Magnus Offa, Rist had quickly taken to the man. There was a warmth about him, an honesty. He reminded Rist of the people back home.

To the right of Garramon, Anila, and Magnus, was a large retinue of a hundred riders garbed in black steel plate, roaring lion-head pauldrons on each shoulder, enormous warhorses as dark as jet that Rist knew immediately as Varsundi Blackthorns. The riders were the Blackwatch, the personal guard of the Supreme Commander of the Lorian Armies, Taya Tambrel. Rist had been introduced to the woman, along with Commander Marken Kort – commander of the First Army – the day before they had set out for Fort Harken.

Supreme Commander Tambrel was one of the tallest women Rist had ever met, taller even than Calen. Her shoulders were dense with muscle, her eyes piercing. Her long, silvery hair was tied in a single braid. Even in their short meeting, Rist could see why she bore the title of Supreme Commander. In a room with Garramon, Anila, Magnus, and a number of other high-profile warriors and commanders, Taya had talked rings around all of them. She was curt and to the point, her wit sharper than any blade.

"It suits you, you know." Neera, who was riding to Rist's left, gave him an appraising look. "You still look terrified on the horse, but the armour suits you, at least."

Rist frowned at that, patting Trusil on the neck. He tucked in his chin, looking down at the steel breastplate that Garramon had arranged for him and that now adorned his chest, the roaring lion emblazoned across its front in black. The breastplate wasn't the only thing Garramon had arranged. A pair of ornate steel vambraces that had once been Garramon's now adorned Rist's forearms. A pair of matching steel greaves protected his shins, sturdy black leather boots covered his feet, and a fine steel long-sword hung from his hip.

Rist slid the dagger back into its sheath and rested his hand on the lion-head pommel of the sword Garramon had given him – an Imperial Battlemage's sword. The pommel had been carved from the tusks of a Truscan Boar. The creatures were native to the eastern cities, and from the paintings Rist had seen in *Devastating Creatures: Claw, Tooth, And Fang,* they stood at a height with an eighteen-hand horse, thick chested, covered in dark brown fur, and tusks thicker than Rist's legs – though that wasn't saying much.

"I didn't get a sword," Tommin said, a touch of sadness in his voice, white robes trimmed with a strip of brown hanging over his shoulders. Tommin rode beside Neera atop a dun gelding two or three hands shorter than Rist's mount. "I got a knife – a small one."

"You're a Healer, Tommin," Lena said with a shrug. "I've seen you with a sword. We'll be safer if you don't have one."

"I'm sorry, by the way," Rist whispered, leaning closer to Neera as Tommin and Lena exchanged insults.

Neera raised a curious eyebrow.

"For not telling you when Garramon started my Trial of Faith. You told me straight away and…" Rist stopped, seeing Neera tilt her head back, giving him the look that meant she thought he was being stupid. "What?"

She let out a sigh. "You're one of the most intelligent people I know." She narrowed her eyes, looking at Tommin and Lena. "I know that might not be saying much, but you are. Yet somehow you're also an idiot. You didn't tell me, Rist, because that's who you are. Not because you wanted to lie to me, or you didn't want me to know. You were told not to, just as I was, but unlike me, you follow rules to the point of insanity. The only time I've seen you break a rule of your own volition is when you sneak books from the library. And even that says something. Did you truly not think I knew?"

"I… wait, what?"

"Considering you have such a love for books, I'm surprised you don't realise how much of an open one you are. Your whole demeanour has changed in the last week. You spend hours on end in the library, yet when I go there I can't find you. And when we're all together, you're off in your head, thinking…" Neera scrunched her lips, contemplating. "And also you mumble in your sleep." She smiled, her nose crinkling. "I told you because I wanted to share it. You didn't tell me because you didn't want to influence my decision. It's all right. I have no doubt you weighed the rules against the impact your decision might have on my decision and came to the logical conclusion that it was best not to tell me."

Rist's head hurt, an aching thump pulsing as he tried to follow what Neera was saying. "So… you're *not* mad at me?"

"I didn't say that."

Rist shook his head, muttering. "Equal parts confusing, irritating, and completely unavoidable…"

Neera narrowed her eyes. "What did you say?"

"Nothing, just something my father says."

By the look on Neera's face, she was about half a second away from telling Rist precisely where he could shove his father's sayings when an earth-shaking roar echoed through the valley with the force of a raging river. Trusil jerked to a stop, snorting and tugging at his reins. All about, horses did the same – with the exception of the Varsundi Blackthorns who barely even reacted. Murmurs spread through the column.

"Is it—"

A second monstrous roar, even louder than the first, drowned out Tommin's words. Rist clapped his hands to his ears as the avalanche of sound reverberated through the valley. Horses stamped, donkeys brayed, and soldiers shouted as two enormous figures swept around the Kolmir Mountains, soaring through the valley, blotting out the light of the setting sun, their shadows blanketing the ground.

"The Dragonguard!" Shouts rang out, echoing, cheering.

Rist stared at the sky, mouth ajar. Never in his wildest dreams had he imagined creatures so large. Both dragons were bigger than any ship he'd ever seen, with wings spreading twice as wide as the dragons were long. But even at that, one was clearly larger than the other, covered in an ocean of black scales, its chest as deep as a house, neck thick like the trunks of multiple trees strapped together. The other dragon had scales of a deep red that gleamed as they reflected the fading light.

The dragons soared through the valley, their wings spread, moving with an effortless grace that should not have been possible for creatures their size.

"That one's Helios," Magnus called as he pulled back to the acolytes, Garramon and Anila staring after him. Even through his thick black beard, the smile on Magnus's face was clear. He pointed towards the enormous black dragon, who flew in front of its companion, drawing closer at a frightening speed. "The dragon bound to Eltoar Daethana. High Commander of the Dragonguard. That elf is a legend among legends. The finest warrior I've ever seen. Even in the old days, Eltoar was First Sword of the Draleid." The two dragons ripped through the sky overhead, a ferocious gust of wind following in their wake, whipping up dried leaves and dirt. Rist's cloak billowed, his hair blowing back. Magnus raised his voice, bellowing. "Efialtír bless whichever army stands in their way!"

LESS THAN AN HOUR AFTER seeing the dragons, Rist's section of the column emerged from the Kolmir Valley and out onto the open plains that lay before Fort Harken. The Fort was hemmed in against the mountains by enormous stone walls twice as thick as any Rist had laid eyes on, including those at Al'Nasla. A number of towers and high buildings rose above the walls, each with flat tops rimmed with battlements. The keep loomed at the back of the fort, rising almost seven storeys and built from stone with a black hue.

Trampled farmland and the husks of burnt-out buildings sprawled outwards from the foot of the walls – a field of ash, blood, char, and death. The Uraks had likely burned everything outside the wall when they'd attacked.

Past the fort, set on the top of a rise, was a war camp, red banners bearing the black lion of Loria fluttering in the breeze. The camp sprawled in all directions, a sea of canvas tents. The now-familiar noises of a war camp drifted on the breeze: the clamouring of runners and porters, the hammering of steel and iron, the whinnying of horses, the calls and shouts of soldiers.

Despite the war camp's sprawling size, it was still smaller than it would have been before the battle that had taken place here only a few weeks before. Garramon had told Rist the Fourth Army had lost almost a third of its strength.

Ahead, Garramon turned his horse and rode towards Rist, Neera, Tommin, and Lena. "Rist, Neera, come with me, Magnus, and Anila. Lena, Brother Halmak is looking for you. He would have you join him before heading to the command tent."

"What about me?" Tommin asked, raising his brows hopefully.

Garramon frowned but didn't get a chance to answer as Sister Danwar approached on a skewbald, fiery hair falling in long curls, white robes rippling behind her. "The command tent is no place for a Healer, Acolyte. That is where soldiers go to arrange death." She threw a glance at Garramon. "We will go to the triage tent. The last battle left many wounded, and they require as many Healers as can be mustered."

"Yes, Sister Danwar." Tommin pulled away on his dun, joining Sister Danwar as they rode off with the other Healers. They separated from the main column headed towards the western edge of the Fourth Army's war camp.

"Damn Healers," Magnus scoffed, rolling his head around, eliciting a series of violent cracks. "Bunch of self-righteous pricks."

"They do quite literally save lives, Magnus," Sister Anila said, her lips twisting somewhere between a smile and a frown. Her horse's reins were looped around the stump of her left arm, resting in the crook of her elbow, which she pulled tight to her chest.

"They do," Magnus said with an irritated shrug. "But they don't have to be so fucking smug about it."

"Come." Garramon stared up the column, searching for something. "Let us find Supreme Commander Tambrel and Commander Kort. We are to meet with the Fourth Army's command while our forces rest and resupply."

⌛

HORNS BELLOWED OUTSIDE AS FARDA stood with his left arm crossed, propping up his right. He ran his thumb over the gold coin, feeling the familiar nicks and grooves, the rise and fall of the embossed crown, worn over time. He was in the command tent of the Fourth Army, standing before a long wooden table with a map of Epheria tacked down into the wood. A number of thick, slow-burning candles were perched atop the table and set about the tent, supplementing the fast-dying light of the sun that drifted through the tent's opening.

Commander Talvare leaned against the other side of the table, her palms pressed against the wood, her gaze fixed on the map. Her surviving generals were arrayed around her. "Two weeks forced march to Steeple."

"We could shed some of the convoy, Commander," Guthrin Vandamire suggested, plucking at the corner of his moustache, his oily hair shimmering in the candlelight.

"An excellent idea, General." Farda flicked the coin in the air and was disappointed when he saw the crown staring back at him. "We will move faster with fewer wagons. Food and supplies be damned. If we get hungry, we'll eat the horses."

Commander Talvare lifted her gaze from the table, strands of greyblack hair falling down over her sweat-touched face. She gave Farda a wry smile.

"I was only trying to make a suggestion, Justicar Kyrana."

"Make an intelligent one next time, I implore you."

"Are you going to let him speak to me like this?" Guthrin snorted, throwing out his hands at Talvare.

Talvare frowned, glancing from Guthrin to Farda and back again. "Let him? He is a Justicar of the Imperial Battlemages. Did you not see him on the battlefield, General Vandamire? Or were you too far back to see the front? Justicar Kyrana was right, your suggestion was idiotic. Get out of my sight before I have you flogged."

"Commander, I—"

"Did I speak too quietly for you, Guthrin? Did I stutter? *Get out of my sight.*"

575

Guthrin looked around for support, but the other generals averted their gazes. Only Farda met the man's stare, and he purposely smiled as broadly as he possibly could. There were few pleasures in life, and many of them were small and fleeting. But seeing the look on that dimwit's face before he stormed from the command tent was a moment Farda would savour.

"I despise that man." Talvare stared after Guthrin for a moment before turning her gaze back to the map on the table.

"And yet he is a general in your army."

"Not by choice. Some appointments are out of our control. It doesn't matter. I will ensure he rides in the vanguard for the battles to come. That will either temper him or deal with him. Either way, he'll be less of a pain in my arse."

"Commander." A man no more than twenty summers stepped into the tent and bowed. By the sweat on his brow and his heaving breaths, he'd likely run from the far end of the camp to deliver his message.

"Yes? I'm assuming there was more to your message than simply my title?"

"Yes, Commander Talvare. Apologies." The young man swallowed hard, standing up straight. "The commanders of the First Army approach. They are making their way through the camp now."

"Send them through, soldier."

"Yes, Commander."

The messenger was gone from the tent no more than a short while when two towering warriors in jet-black plate stepped through the tent's entrance, pauldrons shaped in the likeness of roaring lion-heads, long-swords at their hips, shields strapped to their backs – Blackwatch. The soldiers moved to either side of the entrance, statues of black plate.

Supreme Commander Taya Tambrel followed the warriors through the entrance, her silver hair tied back in a braid, red-trimmed black plate clinking as she moved. She scanned the tent as she entered, assessing, judging. Across the centuries, Farda had seen many men and women take the title of Supreme Commander. But none of them had compared to Taya Tambrel. She was cold, curt, and harsh. But she was also straight-forward, no-nonsense, and fantastically good at what she did.

As Talvare welcomed the Supreme Commander, Farda watched over the rest of the new entrants. Commander Marken Kort of the First Army was next through the doors, chin lifted so high Farda thought he might scrape it off the tent's roof.

The man's generals were next, ten in all, some Farda recognised, some he didn't. Brother Halmak of the Consuls followed, a blonde young acolyte at his heels.

"Farda Kyrana, of all the tents in all the lands, you're standing in this one. C'mere you old dog." Magnus Offa was not one for etiquette or standing on ceremony, which was something Farda appreciated. The hulking giant of a man stepped through the entrance and pulled Farda into a bone-crushing embrace, clapping him on the back and lifting him off his feet. "It's good to see your angry face, little man."

Only Magnus could call Farda 'little man'.

"It's good to see you, too, Magnus. Now, put me down."

"You're just as grumpy as you've always been. Good to see you haven't changed. Look who I've brought with me." Magnus turned back towards the tent's entrance, bowing and spreading his arms in a theatrical fashion.

"Anila..." Farda took a step forwards as Anila entered the tent, silver-trimmed black cloak flowing behind her, steel breastplate glistening, a sword strapped to each hip. Her golden hair tumbled over her shoulders, streaked with silvery-white. Farda saw her look of surprise – watched it twist into a scowl.

"Good old Uraksplitter herself," Magnus bellowed, clapping Farda on the back.

"Farda." Anila inclined her head.

Before Shinyara died, Anila and Farda had been close. Lovers and friends both. But ever since, Farda grew distant, apathetic. He hadn't spoken to Anila in almost two hundred years. In all that time, he hadn't seen the wrong in his isolation, but whatever Ella had awoken in him, he could see it now, and it twisted in his chest. Farda pulled Anila close.

"What in the fuck are you doing?" Anila pushed him away, an incredulous look on her face, her stoic façade cracking.

"Saying hello to an old friend." Farda nodded, a soft smile touching his lips. Even as Anila continued to frown at him, Exarch Garramon entered the tent, two acolytes at his side.

The first of the acolytes was a young woman with raven-dark hair and shrewd eyes. She walked with a confidence usually reserved for those who had seen many more summers, her shoulders pushed back, chest out.

The other was a young man whom Farda couldn't help but feel he recognised.

Farda could feel the power radiating from him. It was nothing compared to that which came from Magnus, Garramon, or Anila, but for one so young, it was impressive, more than impressive – it was curious.

"Farda, it's good to see you." Garramon grasped Farda's forearm, inclining his head. "From what I've heard, the fight we are marching towards will not be a simple one. My reports also tell me there are a number of Justicars who march with the Second Army."

"Garramon. It's been a few years. You've sponsored?"

"Aye." Garramon gestured towards the young woman. "This is Acolyte Neera Halar, she is not my charge. But her Sponsor, Sister Ardal, is of the Consuls. She does not march with us, Neera travels with me." Garrmon laid his hand on the young man's shoulder. "This is Acolyte Rist Havel. Rist, this Farda Kyrana, Justicar of the Imperial Battlemages."

CHAPTER FORTY-SEVEN

THE ENEMY OF THE ENEMY IS NOT MY FRIEND

Ella pressed her back against the large rock, slowing her breathing, tightening her grip on the short sword she'd picked up during the Urak attack a week or so before. She looked to her left, seeing one of the scouts, Suka, pressed up against another rock, their gazes meeting. The sun had set an hour or so ago, the slightest glow of its lingering light illuminating the hillside.

A few feet away, crouched in a low ditch, Faenir's eyes gleamed, his ears pricked. Images of three men touched Ella's mind, the glow of a torch, the smell of leather, dirt, and pickled fish. Since the Urak attack, since hearing the call of the wolf in her blood, Faenir's thoughts had seeped into hers, mixing, blending.

Ella still wasn't sure how to feel about it. In a way, it felt more natural than anything ever had. But she could still taste Urak blood, still feel flesh tearing beneath her teeth. She could barely remember anything from when she lost control and the wolf had taken over, but she remembered enough to make her skin crawl.

She heard the crunch of dirt and the low drag of breaths. The warmth of torchlight cast an orange glow across the ground, scattering shadows.

"Looks clear to me," a man said.

"If it meant you could head back early and fill your belly with that filthy pickled fish, it would always look clear to you, Jon."

"Can't fight on an empty belly."

"We've still got this whole section to clear, arsehole. Then you can eat."

Ella pulled in a breath, holding it, readying herself. *I will not lose control. I will not.* The footsteps drew closer, scents growing stronger in Faenir's nostrils.

Suka looked at Ella, nodding. The Fourth and First armies had passed Elkenrim only two days ago. Almost seven thousand soldiers by Juro's reckoning and three dragons – the third dragon joining them the night before. *Dragons…* The creatures were enormous, casting shadows so large Ella had no doubt they could shroud the entire Glade in darkness. Ella could have spent hours just watching the creatures fly. There was a devastating beauty about them.

Since the armies had come into view, Ella and the others had been stalking them from the hills, killing off the scouts that strayed from the main column. Tanner had insisted on staying with Ella when they separated to take out the scouts, but Farwen hadn't allowed it.

'A bird doesn't learn to fly by staying under its mother's wing,' the elf had said. Instead, Ella had been paired with Suka. The woman was a few years Ella's senior, a Lorian native from a village north-east of Highpass. She was a little brash but was quick on her feet and had seen more than her fair share of scraps.

Ella nodded.

"What's that?" one of the men said, the crunching of footsteps stopping. A low growl hummed in the air. In the ever-dimming dark, the men couldn't see Faenir as the wolfpine crouched in the ditch. Faenir smelled fear – the scent caused the wolf within Ella to claw at the back of her mind.

"Fancy a warm meal now?" Ella remembered the voice from earlier – Jon.

"Quit your whining. You can take point."

"Me? Can you not hear that? It's probably a fucking bear or a wolf. I'm not stumbling on one of those bastards in this dark. I like my arms firmly attached to my body, thank you."

"Jon, if you don't move, I'll hack your arms off myself."

"Look, Bern, If there's one thing I know—"

"You know nothing, Jon. Move."

The man grumbled, but the sound of footsteps resumed. Across the way, Suka bent her knees, sliding a knife from her belt. Faenir went silent, but Ella felt his muscles tensing, lips pulling back.

Ella's heartbeat quickened, breaths growing shorter. She didn't want to kill, but the wolf in her blood howled, itching to get out. Even as she held it back, she could feel its pull and taste the bloodlust. *No!* The wolf howled in defiance. *I'll do it. But I won't ever hunger for it.*

Dirt crunched next to Ella, a man stepping past her.

"What the fuck?"

A glance showed Ella that Suka had already stepped from behind her rock, driving her knife into the throat of the man closest to her, blood spilling into the dirt as the body dropped. Two remained: the one closest to Ella, and the third man, who had seen Suka kill his companion.

Ella lunged forwards, stabbing out with her short sword, finding resistance in the form of studded leather. The man roared as the blade sliced through the leather and sank into the soft flesh beneath. The wolf howled in Ella's blood, tasting the iron tang in the air as Ella ripped the sword from the man's side.

He screamed, clutching a hand to his side, but collected himself and lunged, cracking his fist into the bridge of Ella's nose.

Blinding pain followed a crunch, a ringing in Ella's ears. She stumbled backwards, the man following after her. Another fist slammed up into her chin, and she was falling, head spinning, the ground rising to meet her.

'You need to be willing to fight harder than anyone who stands in your way.' Coren's words rang in Ella's ears.

Her vision blurry, Ella rolled as she hit the ground, a thud following as the man's sword sank into the earth where she had landed. Her heart pounding, she slammed her foot against the flat of the man's blade, knocking it out from under him. With his weight pressed down onto the pommel, he stumbled forwards, and Ella jabbed her blade into his chest. The man coughed, spluttering, but reached down to grab Ella by the throat. She placed the palm of her left hand against the pommel of her short sword and pushed forwards, ramming the blade further into the man's chest, down to the hilt.

He jerked, collapsing. Ella twisted, angling him so he fell to her left and crashed into the dirt. Her right hand still wrapped around the hilt of her sword, Ella shoved herself to her feet and climbed on top of the man, ripping the sword free. She drove the blade back down, blood splattering. Again and again she tore the blade free before driving it back down. Red mist tainted her vision, the call of a wolf howling in ears, snapping and snarling.

By the time Ella forced herself to stop, sweat dripped from her brow, her breaths shuddering, chest trembling. Her hands shook as they held the hilt of the sword, blood coating the steel, dripping from the tip. Steam wafted from the butchered corpse below her, and her stomach turned at the sight of the man's mutilated chest. It looked as though he'd been savaged by a... wolf. *What... what am I?*

"He's dead," Suka said, resting her hand on Ella's back as she dropped to her haunches. "Not sure I've ever seen someone *quite* as dead. I'm glad you're on our side. Don't worry, the killing itself gets easier. The guilt doesn't. If it does... well, we'll cross that bridge when we come to it."

Ella looked back down over the corpse, her throat tightening at the sight of the shredded leather and flesh. She forced the vomit down as it touched the back of her throat. A low grumble sounded to her left. Faenir

581

stood over the body of the third Lorian scout, blood dripping from his muzzle, his amber eyes locked on Ella.

After dragging the bodies into the ditch Faenir had been lying in and covering them with branches and foliage, Suka, Ella, and Faenir, made their way along the hillside to where they were to meet the others.

Farwen, Juro, Varik, Tanner, Yana, and the other nine remaining scouts who had left with them from Tarhelm were already there.

"Much trouble?" Farwen asked, looking Ella up and down. Blood and dirt covered Ella's hands, chest, and face, and her nose throbbed.

"Three scouts. Dealt with them handy enough." Tula nodded to Ella and winked.

"Good. We'll keep them on their toes."

Ella moved to the edge of the hill. A river of flickering torches filled the valley bellow, stretching for miles. Amidst the glow of torchlight, Ella could make out canvas tents of red and cream, soldiers dashing about, rippling banners emblazoned with the black lion of Loria.

"They're moving faster than we'd expected," Juro said, studying the valley.

"We should wait for them to pass through, then we can cut off the supply train and torch it." Varik shrugged, his pursed lips visible through his thick beard. "The wagons won't be able to keep this pace. There'll be distance between them before Steeple. Let's see how they do without blankets, food, medical supplies… Not too well I'd wager."

"No." Farwen folded her arms, the silvery light of the moon catching the three scars that ran from her jaw, down her neck, and into the folds of her cloak. "We will follow them, harass them a bit, but we won't fully engage."

"And why in the gods not? How often do we see two imperial armies pooling together? Potentially a third. Not bloody often. With a handful of us, we can take out all their supplies at once. Elyara would name us idiots for not taking the opportunity to cause so much chaos."

"Yes, it would be chaos." Farwen tucked a strand of mixed white and brown hair back over her tapered ear, eyes still searching the valley below. "But that would slow them too much."

"Isn't that the whole idea?" Varik looked at Farwen as though she were mad.

"You want to use them," Tanner said, a broad smile spreading across his face.

"Am I missing something?" Varik frowned, looking to the others.

"Whoever the empire are marching against are not our friends either," Ella said, Farwen's words starting to make sense to her. "And if they have indeed taken the eastern cities, then they have not only swept aside six imperial armies but the garrisons of each of those cities as well. Instead of kicking the empire's feet out from under them now, it would be smarter to follow them, observe them, and learn what this threat is. Then, with any luck, they will destroy each other, and we can pick apart the pieces. Instead of taking out one enemy, we take out two."

"Work smart, not hard," Juro said, giving Varik a wink.

CHAPTER FORTY-EIGHT

THE CALM BEFORE

The sun had almost disappeared behind the mountains to the west when Rist dropped to his haunches, his fingers wrapped around the lion head pommel of his new sword, sweat dripping from his brow. He slowed his breathing. He and Sister Anila had been moving through the sword forms ever since they'd set up camp. Anila had been off kilter since they'd joined with the Fourth Army almost two weeks ago. It seemed sword forms settled her. Rist hadn't minded. He was glad to have a partner – even if Anila had been more abrasive than sand.

"You're dropping your left shoulder on form two, movement four, just as you transition into movement five," Anila said, pulling Rist back to a standing position. "It leads you to putting too much weight on your front foot, which makes you slow to pivot. Straighten your back, bring yourself into balance."

"Yes, Sister. Thank you." As an acolyte, Rist could refer to other mages by their first names, and he did – except with Sister Anila. For some reason, it felt strange to even think about doing so.

Anila nodded, taking a second to look about them.

The mages always pitched their tents at the edge of the main army's camp, which suited Rist just fine, fewer eyes watching as he practised. A few feet away, Neera, Tommin, and Lena sat in the dirt by a campfire, their tents at their backs. Around them, the other mages of the First Army stood about talking and chatting, some sipping wine and spirits from mugs. As far as Rist was concerned, taking up prime space on the wagons for casks of wine and spirits was a waste, but he seemed to be alone in that opinion. They were less than half a day's march from Steeple, and according to their scouts, a dense layer of fog was encroaching on the city from the east, stretching for miles in all directions. Garramon brought Rist to the command tent each night, where the generals and commanders discussed the battle ahead of them. They still weren't aware of who or what they were marching against. The rumours Rist had heard had stretched from Karvosi invaders, to Ardanians, to elves that had come back to claim the lands of their ancestors, all the way to Achyron himself.

Whoever, or whatever it was, they would be standing face to face within a day. But as far as Rist was concerned, it didn't matter. There was nothing in the mortal world that could stand against the Dragonguard. Since joining with the Fourth Army at Fort Harken, Rist had forced himself to wake with the sun so he could watch the creatures spread their wings in the morning sky. He had never seen such effortless power. Each dragon was easily over a hundred feet from head to tail, likely more. Helios was even bigger still.

"Acolyte."

Rist shook his head, feeling as though he'd come out of a hazy dream. Anila was staring at him, her brow furrowed, eyes questioning. "Sorry, Sister I was—"

"Lost in your thoughts." Anila let out an exasperated sigh. "That's a common theme with you. Make sure it doesn't happen in the heat of battle, lest your thoughts be permanently separated from your body."

"She's saying your head will be cut off!" Rist turned to see Magnus strolling into the mages' camp with an iron banded cask thrown over his shoulder, his voice booming over the low hum of activity. Garramon walked alongside the big man, his hands clasped behind his back, an amused look on his face. Magnus stopped beside the campfire that Neera and the others had built, dropping the cask down onto the dry grass.

"Thank you for clarifying, Magnus." Sarcasm dripped from Anila's words as she rolled her eyes and let out another sigh as if the world was nothing but an irritation to her.

"Any time, Uraksplitter." Magnus gave Anila a wink, gesturing to Tommin. "Throw us those bags, will you, lad? Need something to prop this cask on."

Tommin looked from Magnus to the two large bags that rested near his own feet. "They're the spare blankets, Exarch."

"I didn't ask what they were, lad, I asked you to throw them to me. You'll have no need of blankets after a few cups of this." Magnus patted the top of the cask, shaking his other hand at the two bags.

"I'm not sure Sister Danwar would—"

"Oh, piss off, lad. Throw me the bags before I use your back instead."

Tommin straightened reflexively, then stood and brought the bags to Magnus, who laid them one in front of the other.

"I 'requisitioned' this from the infantry," he said, tilting the cask on its rim, inspecting it. He puffed out his bottom lip in a seemingly satisfied pout, then stuck his hand into his robes and produced a handmade wooden spigot. "It's a good thing I keep one of these beauties on me at all times."

"At all times?" Neera gave Magnus an incredulous look.

"In case of emergencies." Magnus pulled a soft wooden bung from the top of the cask, tossing it to the ground and replacing it with the spigot. He slotted the spigot into the hole, then slammed it down with a thin thread of Air. His use of the Spark for something so insignificant was something Rist had noticed more and more as he'd travelled with the Battlemages of the First Army. Whereas he had only ever used the Spark when necessary, they used it as effortlessly and thoughtlessly as they used their hands and fingers.

In a feat of strength that Rist was sure he would have no chance of replicating, Magnus heaved the cask up and dropped it on its side atop the bags. He called for Tommin to fetch him a cup, to which Tommin responded like a puppy desperate to please.

It wasn't long before they were sitting around the fire, sipping away at their second – or fourth, in Magnus's case – cup of wine, the last rays of the setting sun lingering along the horizon. Rist had not tasted wine until he arrived at the embassy in Al'Nasla. He hadn't been sure he liked it at first, but it had grown on him. The wine that he now swirled in his cup though was better than any he'd tasted in all his time at the embassy. It was sweet and full, its aftertaste melting into his mouth.

"Not quite the same as what we get in the embassy," Garramon said with a short laugh, nodding towards Rist's mug. The man sat to Rist's right, knees pulled to his chest, firelight flickering across his face. "It's a tradition," he said, lifting his cup to his nose and drawing in a whiff. "The finest wine in the North is made just a few days ride southwest of Catagan, on the other side of the Kolmir Mountains in a small region known as Etrus. The weather there is ideal for growing grapes. The heat of the Burnt Lands is balanced out, the soil is perfect, and it rains just enough. Each year, half the casks are brought to Al'Nasla. From that, half again are taken for the emperor who distributes them as he needs – most ending up in his own cellar. The other half are given to the armies to carry with them whenever they march."

"Why?"

Garramon gave a slight shrug, tilting his cup outwards. "On the eve of battle, the least you can give those willing to lay down their lives is a good cup of wine." He laughed as he spoke, shaking his head. Although Garramon had grown warmer towards Rist since they'd first met, Rist had never seen the man laugh like he did then. It was likely the wine more than anything, but whatever it was, it was nice. "Honestly, Fane has always loved wine. It was his idea. A simple gesture, but an appreciated one."

Rist took a mouthful from his cup, savouring the fruity flavours on his tongue. It was strange to hear the emperor of Loria referred to simply as

'Fane'. So many bards' stories in the villages had been spun of 'the dread emperor Fane Mortem', or 'Fane Mortem, the mighty hero', depending on which bard was telling the tale. Descriptions of Fane tended to vary wildly, but the one thing that always stayed the same was the power the emperor possessed. Even after meeting the man himself and seeing that Fane Mortem was truly a living, breathing human and not a demi-god, Rist had still been awed by the aura of power that radiated from him. So to hear Garramon mention him as though he was nothing more than a childhood friend was like hearing a dragon described as a lizard.

"All right," Magnus said, wine sloshing in his cup as he heaved himself to his feet. He looked around at those gathered about the fire. As they had begun drinking, more of the First Army's mages had joined them, grabbing cups of wine and sitting beside the fire. "As is tradition… *hic*… apologies, drank my wine too fast." Magnus held his breath for a moment that let out an enormous belch, followed by a sigh of relief. "Much better. Now, as is tradition, who'd like to hear a story?"

Cheers and claps rose around the crowd. More mages drew closer and settled on the grass.

Magnus gave a mock bow, holding his arms out wide, droplets of wine dripping from his thick, black beard. "How about I tell the tale of how the legendary Anila Uraksplitter lost her arm?"

More claps and cheers. Rist looked over towards Anila, who sat beside two Battlemages Rist knew as Talik and Mura. If looks could kill, then the glare on Anila's face would have skinned Magnus alive. "You can tell it, Magnus," Anila said. "But if you do, the next story you'll be telling is of how the great Magnus Offa had his balls cut off in the night."

Roaring laughter erupted, mages clapping and stamping their feet. Magnus laughed as hard as anyone. Anila smiled as she shook her head.

"Well, seeing as I'm rather fond of my balls, I think we'll steer clear of that particular tale." Still laughing, Magnus raised his cup towards Anila, inclining his head, to which she responded in kind. "How about, instead, I tell you of the time I rode the legendary Sea Snake along the Lightning Coast?"

Rist looked to Garramon. "Did that actually happen?"

"No," Garramon said with a laugh, giving a shrug. "But it's a good story. And all good stories hold a little truth."

∽

FARDA STOOD BETWEEN TWO PITCHED tents, his arms folded, his head tilted to the side. He pinched his top lip with his bottom teeth, thinking.

Ahead, in a small clearing surrounded by tents, mages of the First Army had gathered around a campfire while Magnus Offa told his story of the time he rode the Sea Snake from the cliffs of Khergan to the edge of the Lightning Coast. Farda had heard the story many times, though it had been centuries. In reality, Magnus had eaten enough hallucinogenic mushrooms to kill a horse and had leapt off a low cliff near Khergan while clinging to the felled trunk of a small tree. The man was lucky he hadn't died. They'd found him almost a week later, after he'd been washed ashore at Bromis. As far as Farda was concerned, in this particular instance, the truth was far funnier than the lie, but as long as Magnus was the one telling the story, the truth would seldom be told.

Magnus had invited Farda to sit and drink by their fire, but even if Farda had enjoyed the company of people, he owed it to the mages of the Fourth Army to drink with them that night. If they were going to fight at his side, the least he could do was share a drink by theirs.

Even so, Farda had not been able to stop himself from passing by Magnus's camp on the way. There was something scratching at the back of his mind, a puzzle that needed working out – the young man that Garramon had sponsored. Farda could see him now, sitting in the grass beside the other acolyte that was travelling with Garramon, a mug of wine gripped in his hand. Not only was something about the man's face irritatingly familiar, but his name had also rung a bell in Farda's head. *Rist Havel. Why is that name so familiar?*

Farda spent a few long moments looking at the young man, trying to place him. He knew the answer to his riddle was floating just out of reach in his mind.

Without even realising he'd removed it from his trouser pocket, Farda felt the familiar touch of the coin in his palm. Magnus was at the part of the story where he'd used seaweed to create reins for the Sea Snake. The only true part of the story involving seaweed was that when Magnus had washed ashore, he'd been almost covered in seaweed. Letting out a sigh, Farda slid his coin back into his trouser pocket, turned, and made his way to the other side of the camp, where his own mages had pitched their tents.

"So all it takes is war to see you again, you crusty bastard?"

Farda stopped, trying to place the voice, then turned to see two women and a man strolling towards him, the light of the moon and the campfires illuminating their faces.

"Hala, I'd heard you were travelling with the Second Army from Arginwatch." Farda reached out and grasped Hala's forearm as she extended it. It had only been ten or twenty years since Farda had last seen her. Not a particularly long time. He still found it strange to look upon her since her soulkin, Dalyianír, was taken from the world. Farda had been fortunate – if he dared use that word – that the things Shinyara had taken with her had not been physical. She had taken his pain, his empathy, his ability to care. But when Dalyianír was slain over the Bay of Light only two or three decades after The Fall, the colour in Hala's hair had drained to snow white. Even her brows and the hair on her arms. Along with that, Hala's fingers on her left hand had curled up into a perpetual fist, hardened like stone. Other things had been lost too. Things below the surface. But the woman never lost her heart or her humour.

"I see you've been busy trying to track us down then," the other woman, Gunild, said, her head twitching as it had since she'd lost Borallis. She gave Farda a smile that held more than a drop of pity.

"I've been—"

"Busy gallivanting, I suppose." The last of the three, Ilyain, offered a hand to Farda. If it wasn't difficult enough to be an elf without a dragon in an empire dominated by humans, the gods had decided to strip Ilyain of his sight when Voraxes was torn from him.

Farda drew in a long breath, letting out a sigh as he grasped Ilyain's forearm. "Something like that."

Farda looked over each of the three that stood before him. Just like him, they were Justicars – the name Fane had bestowed upon those who had become Rakina since the days of The Fall. Farda despised the title. At least to be Rakina meant something. *One who survived.* Justicar was simply a title given so soldiers knew what to call those who were no longer Dragonguard. It had been meant as a sign of respect – a reminder that they still had a place within the empire. But Farda had always seen it as an insult – a reminder of everything he had lost and everything he had turned his back on.

"You're on the way to drink?" Hala said.

Farda was unable to decide whether it was a question or a statement. He treated it as a question. "I am."

"Well then, lead the way."

Farda raised a curious eyebrow. "Will you not be drinking with the Second Army? You arrived with them."

"You drink with those you are willing to die beside," Ilyain said, turning his head in the direction of Farda's voice. "We marched with those of the Second Army. But if it's all the same to you, in the morning, if we're to die, we'd rather do it with our own kind."

FROM WHERE ELTOAR STOOD UPON one of the few plateaus amidst the jagged peaks of Mar Dorul, he could see for miles in either direction, the chill of the sharp wind cutting against his face. Thousands of feet below, the city of Steeple sat atop the River Halda – the middle of the three rivers known as The Three Sisters. Two walls encircled the city, lanterns burning along the ramparts and in the windows of homes. Beyond the protection of the walls, more homes, farms, and markets sprawled outward, the dim glow of candles in windows.

West of Steeple, the campfires of the Lorian armies spread far and wide, the landscape looking as though it was a mirror of the star speckled sky cast in an orange hue. To the east, however, through Helios's eyes as the dragon soared overhead, his presence only visible where he blotted out the stars, Eltoar could see a thick layer of fog rolling across the land, tendrils of grey slithering outwards like snakes.

"What do you think?" Beside Eltoar, Lyina stroked a long braid of her blonde hair, staring at the rolling fog, her white plate glowing as it reflected the light of the moon.

Eltoar folded his arms, his foot tapping against the dust-covered rock. His gaze didn't shift from the west. "I think many are going to die tomorrow."

Lyina let out a sigh but carried on. She'd always done that, always tried to push through Eltoar's dark moods. "I've never seen anything like this fog." Lyina took a step closer to the edge of the plateau, and Eltoar could feel her pulling on threads of Fire and Spirit, weaving them through her eyes, granting herself Moonsight. "It's as though it's alive. You said it spread for miles when you were north of Bromis?"

Eltoar nodded. His meeting with Tivar had left a sour taste on his tongue, and he'd not had much desire for conversation since.

"It would take thousands of mages to hold something like that in place over such a distance. And even then, I'm not sure how feasible it would truly be." Lyina let the silence hang in the air between them, waiting for Eltoar to contribute, then turned. Eltoar had expected her face to be all scorn and irritation, but instead he found soft eyes and a look of empathy. "Tivar will come around, Eltoar. She will."

Eltoar shook his head. "No, she won't."

I will not put another of our kind in the ground. I will not tear another soul in half. Eltoar had not been able to push Tivar's words from his mind.

"Pellenor said he believed the new Draleid would go to the temple and light the beacon. It could take days, months, years. But Pellenor is almost never wrong with these things. If I was this new Draleid, I would want to know the past. I would want to speak to the only true kin I have. When he goes to the temple, he will see Tivar, and she will see the light of hope in what he can bring." Lyina leaned forwards, drawing Eltoar's gaze. "We will make it right."

"Can it ever be right, Lyina? It is Aeson Virandr who teaches him. Aeson will never forgive what we did. Never. And neither will the others. Even if this new dragon brings new life, can the past ever truly be reconciled?"

"There is always hope, my friend. And it is towards hope we will stride, come of it what may."

Eltoar gave Lyina a soft sigh, then looked back out over the land before him. Moonlight glinted off the rushing water of the Three Sisters. "Tivar said something that I can't get out of my head. She said the dragon eggs have not hatched because the gods are punishing us for what we did."

"Perhaps," Lyina said, folding her arms and looking out over the camp-fires of the Lorian armies. "But if that is truly what has happened, then they are no gods worth following."

Wing beats sounded, a gust of wind sweeping Eltoar's hair forwards. The sandy-scaled body of Meranta soared overhead, wings spread wide as the dragon turned towards the plateau, dropping lower, icy blue eyes glimmering in the moonlight. Meranta was the smallest of the three dragons there at the Three Sisters. But even then, she was only a few handspans shorter than Karakes from head to tail, while being consider-ably slimmer in build.

The plateau was far too small for Meranta to land, so instead, the dragon cracked her wings, holding in the air as Pellenor slid from her back and dropped the twenty feet to the plateau, softening his landing with threads of Air. Wisps of dirt and dust were swept up and caught by the wind as Pellenor landed gracefully, his knees and back slightly bent, something gripped in his fist. Pellenor straightened his body as Meranta lifted higher into the night sky, moving to join Helios and Karakes as the three dragons spiralled around each other, playing as children would.

"Anything from the other side?" Lyina asked.

"This should put the debate to rest," Pellenor said, tossing whatever he had been holding at Eltoar and Lyina's feet. "Scouts. Five of them near the source of the River Girdil."

Eltoar nodded. At his feet lay the helmeted head of an elf, blood still dripping from its severed neck.

Chapter Forty-Nine

A Burden Shared

Calen pulled down the hood of his cloak, the warmth of the day's sun fading. He winced as he watched the sun sink into the western horizon, his breath already misting. He didn't think he would ever get used to the way the temperature in the Burnt Lands went from scorching to freezing in such a short span of time.

He took a waterskin from his pack, unplugged the stopper, and poured a trickle into his mouth - just enough to wet his cracking lips and moisten his dry tongue.

"We're settled in for the night."

Calen turned to see Ingvat – Aeson's contact who Erik had first reached out to – standing beside him, her dark cloak about her shoulders. She tugged on the long, blonde braid that dropped down past her chest. "Surin and one of other Craftsmages – Holbrok – used their magic to forge the rocks together, creating a nook for the injured. It should help keep them warm."

"How are they?" The night before, some of the rebels who had joined them had fallen behind, drained from the heat, tired due to the lack of food. By the time Valerys had heard the screams, the N'aka had already claimed three lives and injured four more.

"Vaeril says two might live, but there is little he or Kiko can do for the other two. They are too close to death to be healed."

Calen nodded softly, chewing at the inside of his cheek.

"It was our choice," Ingvat said, tilting her head so she could meet Calen's gaze. "You told us some of us would die, and we accepted the risk."

Calen let out a sigh through his nostrils, pressing his fingers into the back of his neck as he looked out over the twilight glow of the setting sun. More dead because they followed him. More blood spilled.

Ingvat moved so she stood in front of Calen, blocking his view, an un-yielding glare on her face. The woman was old enough to be his mother, and in some ways, she reminded him of just that. "Don't give me that sulking, brooding look. The others might look to you like some kind of god, but I know what you are. You're just a man, Calen Bryer. A man with a dragon, but a man, nonetheless. Beneath it all you are nothing more than flesh and bone. You can't carry the weight for every drop of blood spilled around you because if you do, you will drown. War is coming, and most of us have been committed to it since before you were nursing at your mother's tit. We knew the risk. We've always known the risk. The consequences are ours to bear. We must mourn the dead, and we must move on."

Calen stared back at Ingvat, his throat tightening. If only it was that simple, if only he could just move on.

The woman let out a sigh and rested her hand on Calen's shoulder as she made to return to the others. "Your task is to lead. I don't envy you. But our task is to *choose* to follow. *Choose*." She emphasised the word. "Take away their choice and you take away who they are. Use their loss, let it fuel you, but understand it was their choice, not yours. They died for what they believed in. Many aren't so lucky."

Ingvat's expression softened, and she squeezed Calen's shoulder before setting off to where some of the others were setting up spits to cook the tasteless N'aka meat.

Calen drew in a long breath, tilted his head back, and exhaled. He reached down to where his sword hung from his hip and took hold of the silk scarf knotted between the loops of his belt: his mother's scarf. He had only noticed recently that he had taken to rubbing his thumb and forefinger across the waxy material whenever his mind pulled him to darker places. "I miss you…"

He'd found grief to be a strange creature. It wasn't all-consuming and unyielding. It came in flashes and waves, as though Calen's mind only periodically remembered he would never again hear his mother's voice. He would give almost anything just to see her one more time, just to have her force a mug of Arlen Root tea into his hands. He closed his eyes, clenched his fist around the scarf, and shook his head, trying to loose the thoughts.

The cold of the falling night creeping across his skin, Calen let out a slow sigh, opened his eyes, and followed Ingvat to where the others were camped within the rock formation.

Haem, Tarmon, Erik, and some of those who had fled from Berona – those who had been part of the Beronan guard – stood watch around the perimeter of the camp, extra blankets draped around their shoulders in preparation for the frigid night. They would move in closer soon, but after the recent N'aka attack, they decided to set camp a little earlier and double the watch with a wider perimeter.

Erik puffed out his cheeks as Calen passed. He could see the weariness in his friend's eyes. Erik had told Calen what had happened with Fritz before they'd entered the Burnt Lands. Calen had been surprised at the pang of sadness he'd felt at the news. Fritz had always been an arsehole, but what he'd done in the dungeons of Berona was far beyond that; it was twisted and cruel. And yet, Fritz had still been a reminder of home, a fragment of a past forever gone.

"I'll take over soon." Calen rested his hand on Erik's shoulder, giving him a sympathetic smile.

He made his way through the camp, checking on the men and women who lay about, before moving to the back where Vaeril knelt with the Healer who had come with them from Berona.

Kiko was a young-looking woman who hailed from Arkalen, though when it came to mages, trying to gauge how many summers they had seen was like trying to guess how many blades of grass were in a field. She was small, with short black hair straight as needles. She had 'kind eyes', which was something Calen's mam always used to say. And despite the situation they currently found themselves in, she was relentlessly positive. She was always the first to wake in the morning and always laughing at things that weren't even particularly funny. She was – again, as his mam used to say – a 'breath of fresh air'.

Kiko and Vaeril knelt on the rock beside Lasch, Elia, and Gaeleron, who sat amongst the injured. They had trekked through the Burnt Lands for eleven days and nights without stopping, and in that time Gaeleron had regained a semblance of his former self. He was not able to hold full conversations, but he was speaking, and he was also walking without aid – thanks, in no small part, to Vaeril and Kiko's healing.

Elia and Lasch, however, had barely spoken a word between them. It was almost as though they had gotten even worse since leaving Berona. They *had* spoken, here and there, in broken sentences. But mostly they retreated into themselves, whispering, answering questions that had never been asked and asking questions that made no sense. Elia was doing better than Lasch. On a few occasions, when talking with either Calen or Haem, she had seemed to regain her senses. But those moments were fleeting, and she often fell back to wrapping her arms around herself, her head twitching to the left.

Vaeril and Kiko had tried to help them, but as Vaeril had explained, healing with the Spark was not as simple as waving his hand. The Spark's ability to heal was more a powerful amplifier of knowledge than a magical cure for ailments and injuries. One could not heal a wound without the understanding of how to do so. And in that, wounds of the mind were near impossible to heal with the Spark alone, because it was difficult to understand something you could neither see nor feel.

"Little change," Vaeril said to Calen, pulling a waterskin away from Lasch's lips. The elf stared at the broken man for a few moments before rising to his feet. "They grow stronger with each day, though not by much. The progress is there, which is what matters. They need food and rest, far more than they are getting in the Svidar'Cia. Elia still refuses water more often than not."

Calen knelt before Elia, leaning his neck so as to meet her gaze. Her face was still gaunt, cheekbones threatening to pierce paper skin, eyes still sunken and dark-ringed. She was frail, broken. Calen gestured for Vaeril to hand him the waterskin, and he lifted it to Elia's lips. "Elia, it's me, Calen. Please, you need to drink. I can't keep you safe if you don't drink."

Elia's gaze darted back and forth between the sand-dusted rock and Calen, streaks of red painting the whites of her eyes, dried blood crusted on her cracked lips. Her fingers trembling, she took the waterskin from Calen as though she feared it might bite her.

Calen gave her a soft smile, gently resting his hand on the back of hers, urging her to raise the skin to her lips. "It's all right, just drink. I'm here. I won't let anything hurt you. I promise." Calen pulled the waterskin away and touched it to his own lips, taking a sip, then handing it back to Elia. Seeing her like this, so weak and broken, cut into his heart in a way that left a physical ache in his chest.

Elia's head twitched, and her tongue moved across her cracked lips, eyes darting from Calen to the waterskin. After a few moments, she lifted the skin to her mouth and took a short sip, followed by a longer one, and finally she lifted the skin up and drank with a rapacious thirst. She coughed and spluttered, choking on the water, pulling the waterskin away. Once the coughing stopped, she pulled the skin back to her lips and drank with abandon. When she finished, Elia panted like a tired animal, exhaling through her nose and dragging air back in through her mouth. "It tastes right…"

Calen's jaw clenched as he took the skin from Elia and handed it to Vaeril. That was the third time he had helped Elia drink the water. Each time she had treated it as though it were poison. He hadn't understood at first, but then he'd remembered Lasch's words in the interrogation room. *'It's not you. It's not. It can't be. He did it again. More things that aren't real.'*

It hadn't taken Calen long to realise that Rendall had been feeding them poison that broke and twisted their minds. Of all the lives Calen had taken, Rendall's was the only one for which he held no regret. It had brought him no happiness. But neither had it brought him even the slightest trace of guilt. That was a man he would have killed twice, and if he could go back, he would do it slower.

Calen rubbed his thumb across Elia's blanket-covered shoulder, feeling little more than bone. "I'll get you back home, Elia. I'll get you both home. Just stay strong."

Elia's eyes gleamed, the light of the fire behind Calen shining in them. She stared at Calen as though looking at a ghost, her mouth ajar. "You've always been a good boy, always. I said that to my Rist. I said, 'You stick with him'." Elia's head twitched as she nodded to herself. "And Dann too. He's a troublemaker that one, but he's got a good heart. He does." Tears rolled down Elia's sand-crusted cheeks. "My Rist is lucky to have you both. He's a good boy too… always a good boy… I miss him…" Elia stared at the ground for a moment, then looked at Calen. "Where's Freis? She told me she'd…" Elia's words faded, her head twitching. She dropped the waterskin, tucked her hands under her armpits, and leaned back against the wall as though she'd not been speaking at all.

Calen's throat constricted, tears threatening to fall. Elia did that sometimes, talked about Fries and Vars as though they were still alive. Each time was like a dagger to Calen's heart. He reached to his hip and once again rubbed the scarf between his fingers. Gently, he picked up the waterskin and stood.

Vaeril gave him a weak smile, taking the waterskin back. "*Väet.*" Time. "*Du haryn myia vrai.*" You have my thanks.

Calen moved to where Gaeleron sat with his back against the rock wall, staring into the flames of a nearby campfire. The elf still wore Rendall's red cloak – at least in death the man finally did something worthwhile in keeping Gaeleron warm. Some of the fleeing rebels had brought spare clothes, which meant Gaeleron now wore a pair of linen trousers, a loose cotton shirt, and a pair of sturdy boots that were a size too small. The elf also held a blanket over the robes.

"How are you feeling?" Calen asked as he dropped to his haunches beside Gaeleron. Calen felt like an idiot for asking the question. He knew the answer all too well; he still had scars of his own from when Artim Valdock held him in that cell. Scars he feared might never heal.

Gaeleron turned his gaze from the fire. His skin still looked as brittle and attenuated as it had when they'd found him, cheekbones protruding, eyes sunken. The flesh at the end of his left arm, where his lost hand should have been, had healed quite a bit since they'd left Berona – with Vaeril's help. Where it had been red and raw, twisted and blistered, it had regained a natural colour, the flesh smoothing. Long, thin scars ran down the length of the elf's neck, disappearing beneath the folds of the red robes. Calen looked at the scars and remembered Vaeril's words when explaining why Rendall would have healed him after torture. *'To keep him alive. To spend longer torturing him.'*

The elf grimaced as he pushed himself back against the wall. "I have seen better days." He coughed, something catching in his chest, but palmed Calen away when he tried to help. "I am all right. I do not need the mothering of a human who carries an elven blade."

"Well, you're definitely getting better." Calen let out a soft laugh, the edges of his mouth curling into a half-smile. "I'll go and see if Ruon has some food for you."

As Calen made to stand, Gaeleron reached out and grabbed his forearm. The elf's grip was weak as a child's. "Thank you, Draleid. I know you did not come looking for *me*, but you also did not know I was lost. You brought me from that place, and I will forever be thankful." The elf stared into Calen's eyes. "You have changed in the time since we last spoke – you have grown. When I am stronger, I will test how you flow through svidarya."

What Calen believed was meant to pass for a smile touched the elf's lips, followed by a wince.

"I look forward to it."

Calen moved about helping one of the knights, Varlin, and three rebels – a man named Jin and two women, Loura and Ohna – pass out the food that Ruon and some of the others had been cooking. Calling it food was stretching the definition of the word to its breaking point, but it was edible. The bulk of it was roasted N'aka meat, which was tough, chewy, tasteless, and dry as sand. There was also the legs of some reptiles they had found, and the spotted eggs of large birds that nested in a rocky crevice nearby. Surin had created a cavity in the ground with the Spark and filled it with water from underground, which she'd boiled to cook the eggs.

With more people, they had been able to hunt better and find a slightly wider variety of foods. And thanks to the presence of the knights, the madness that tainted the Burnt Lands seemed to hold back. Which was something they had only discovered a few days previously, when Vaeril had collapsed after pulling from the Spark for too long and trying to shield too many at once.

Calen groaned as he sat on a flat rock beside the fire where Ruon was still roasting N'aka meat – just the smell of the flesh turned Calen's stomach.

"Here." The woman ripped a hunk of N'aka meat off the spit Surin had forged and skewered it with a sharpened twig. She looked as though she had seen no more than thirty summers, but Haem had told Calen that she had seen over six hundred. Whereas a connection to the Spark slowed the ageing of living things, whatever magic coursed within the veins of the knights seemed to freeze it entirely. "When you start feeding others, it's easy to forget to feed yourself."

"I didn't forget." Calen took the meat from Ruon, scrunching his nose as he sniffed it. "I was just building up the courage."

Ruon laughed, turning the meat on the spit before tearing a strip off with her teeth from a skewer in her free hand. Calen looked at the woman, catching a glimmer of the metallic green tattoo that marked her chest, the top of which was visible through the split at the collar of her tunic. Since he had accepted Grandmaster Kallinvar's offer of an honour guard and they had set off for the Burnt Lands, Calen hadn't spent much time talking with the knights, except Haem – for which Calen felt little guilt; he could spend an entire lifetime talking to Haem and never make up for the time they'd missed. Haem had answered many of Calen's questions, such as who the knights were and how they were able to do what they were able to do – though Haem's only answer for the latter was that their abilities were a gift from the warrior god.

A thousand more questions still burned within Calen, but the foremost of those couldn't be answered solely by speaking with Haem: who were the knights – the people themselves – and what did they *truly* want? Who were these men and women, so valuable that Achyron himself chose to hold their souls back from entering his halls?

"It hurt, if that's what you're wondering." Ruon pulled back the collar of her tunic to show more of the metallic tattoo, running her finger across it.

"What *is* it?" Calen couldn't help but lean a bit closer, watching how the light of the fire reflected off the tattoo's surface as it would polished steel.

"It is a gift, from Achyron himself."

He let out a sigh through his nostrils. "That's what Haem said."

"It must be difficult." Ruon stared into Calen's eyes. He hadn't realised how vibrant the green in her irises was, flecked with spots of gold.

"What?"

"Seeing him." Ruon nodded towards where Haem stood, his smooth metallic armour now covering all but his head, his hand resting on the pommel of the sword at his hip. "Hearing us call him by a different name. It must be difficult."

Calen looked into the flames of the cookfire, pressing his tongue against the point of his canine tooth. "Why do you call him Arden?"

"It is part of taking the Sigil," Ruon said in a matter-of-fact, tone. "To be given the Sigil of Achyron is to be snatched from the jaws of death and offered a chance at life once more. But as you well know, everything has a price. Arden was told that price before he accepted, as we all were. And he chose to pay it, so that he would have the chance to continue protecting you – at least, in some capacity. Taking a new name is a symbol of... a rebirth, of sorts."

"Does anyone ever say no? You ask dying people if they want to live. Surely some say yes, simply to escape death."

"You would be surprised. Like I said, the price is clear, and some are simply not willing to pay it. Some have seen their share of this world. Some are tired. And, in a few cases, the captain or Grandmaster granting the Sigil decides the candidate is not worthy. Sometimes for precisely the reason you gave. Because making that decision solely out of self-preservation is a sure mark the wrong candidate has been chosen." Ruon turned the spit and stared into the flames for a moment. "It does not happen often, a knight having to look upon the life they sacrificed and then also getting the chance to step back into it in some form. He cares for you, deeply. You are all that tethers him here. You are why he said yes."

Calen nodded, staring into the flickering flames, watching as they popped and crackled, sparks rising into the night.

Ruon shifted in place. "How are the others? Have any of them shown signs of the madness?"

Calen shook his head. "We wouldn't have made it across if you were not with us. That much was clear when Vaeril collapsed. We wouldn't have been able to shield them all."

"I was aware that my brothers and sisters and I were immune to the madness of the Taint here, but I was not aware that would extend to those around us. We have not had the ability, nor the cause to test such a thing. I can feel it even now." Ruon lifted her gaze, staring out over the vast, sand-covered wasteland. "The Taint permeates every crack and crevice of this desolate land. It oozes through the air like a sickly oil, staining everything it touches, pulsing like a beating heart. The sensation scratches at me, makes my skin itch. But where we walk, it pulls back like a shadow fleeing the light of the waking sun."

As Ruon spoke, Calen felt a familiar sensation rippling through his mind. He rested the skewer Ruon had given him on the flat rock – half the N'aka meat untouched – and rose to his feet. "Thank you," he said, inclining his head. "For looking after him."

As Calen turned away from the fire, he watched Valerys drop from the sky, wings spread, the broken carcass of an N'aka in his jaws. Valerys had grown more adept at hunting the creatures since they had re-entered the wasteland.

Valerys dropped the broken body of the six-limbed beast into the sand, blood dripping, then reached his neck out, a low rumble resonating from his chest. Calen stepped forwards, ignoring the carcass, and rested his palms against the dragon's snout, laying his cheek flat against Valerys's scales.

The dragon tilted his head, leaning into Calen, a wave of comfort flooding through the bond as a low whine escaped his throat. Images of Haem flashed across Calen's mind, from when they were young, images that were his own but that Valerys shared. Those were followed by memories of Vars, Freis, Ella, and Faenir, the meaning of which was obvious: pack, clan, family.

Calen drew in a lungful of air, lifting his head momentarily before resting his forehead against Valerys's scales. "Come on," he said, exhaling. "Let's do one last circle."

⁓◦

ARDEN TILTED HIS HEAD BACK, twisting his face in irritation as the cold wind whipped sand across his face. He rested his hand on the pommel of the sword at his hip, watching as Calen moved about the makeshift camp. His brother stopped and checked on each and every one of the fifty so or rebels who had come with them into the Burnt Lands before moving on to where Lasch and Elia Havel sat with the healers.

Seeing Lasch and Elia had twisted something in Arden's gut. They were good people by every measure of the word. Kind, caring, honest. Growing up, Arden hadn't been as close with them as Calen was. Rist and Calen, along with Dann, had always been inseparable, but the Havel's didn't have a son Arden's age. He was closer with the Fjorns and the Netlys – Durin and Almin would have been ashamed of what Fritz became. But Haem had watched how Lasch had treated Calen like a second son and how Elia had fawned over him, her frantic positivity almost contagious.

Would things have been different if he had been there? Would Lasch and Elia have suffered the way they had? Would his mam and dad be alive? He knew the thoughts were poisonous and pointless. If he had said no to Kallinvar's offer, he would have died in Ölm Forest and everything would have played out the same. But that didn't stop his thoughts from drifting that direction.

"I'd wager he's not the boy you remember?"

Arden turned his head towards the voice to see Tarmon Hoard standing a few feet away, arms folded across his chest. According to Calen the man had once been Lord Captain of the legendary Belduaran Kingsguard. Arden didn't have to stretch his imagination too far to see it. Tarmon was one of few who matched Arden for height, and he was broader in the shoulders, his arms thicker. More than the physical though, he had an aura about him, a stoicism that extended past the quiet brooding type Arden had known in the town guard of The Glade.

Tarmon Hoard watched and observed. He spoke rarely, but when he did, Arden had noticed the man's opinion was rarely wrong. It reminded him of something his father had told him after Arden had gotten into a shouting match with Joran Brock shortly after they'd both joined the town guard. *'The power of words is in the choosing of them, my son. Not just in the choosing of which words to speak, but in choosing when not to speak at all. The man who speaks rarely but wisely is heeded far more often than the man who can't hold his tongue.'*

"No, he's not the same boy I remember." Arden looked back at Calen, who had just finished handing out skewers of that horrid N'aka meat and boiled eggs, and now sat with Ruon. "He's grown, more than he should have had to."

"He's seen a lot in a short time. Been through a lot."

Arden nodded sombrely, trying his best to push the thoughts of Ella and his parents from his head. To know Calen went through that loss alone clawed at his insides. What he would have given for his parents to see Calen now, to see the man he had become having barely witnessed twenty summers. "Thank you, for being there for him when he needed it." Arden turned to meet Tarmon Hoard's gaze. "Thank you for being what I couldn't."

CHAPTER FIFTY

FAMILY TIES

Alina undid the buckles on her belt, grimacing as the stitches in her side pulled and threatened to tear. Beneath her, Rynvar gave a series of soft clicks, then a rumble as he leaned his head down and tilted his wing, bringing Alina as close to the ground as he could.

She let out a grunt as her feet touched the soft grass. Beside her Amari, Lukira, and Mera slid from their wyverns' backs and joined her.

"I won't be long," Alina whispered to Rynvar, running her hand along the black-trimmed orange scales of his snout and looking into the sapphire blue of his eyes. She drew in a sharp breath and squared her shoulders, clenching the muscles in her jaw to hold back the pain from where the Lorian spear had sliced through her leathers.

"It's still bleeding."

Alina looked down to see a line of blood seeping through her tunic. "Fuck... The stitches must have opened. I'll have Diara restitch it. It doesn't matter – better they see that I bled too." She inclined her head towards where the Andurii had built their campfires on a flat-topped hill, tents pitched at the top and bottom.

As Alina and her wing-sisters neared the top of the hill, four figures rose around the fire, the light of the flames illuminating their faces: Marlin, Dinekes, Ileeri, and Barak – the Andurii captains, though Odys and Jorath were missing.

Seeing the captains stand, the other Andurii who sat around the fires did the same, realising it was Alina who approached. She saw more familiar faces amongst them: Tarine Valanis, who had once guarded her study in Redstone; Iloen Akaida, whom she had known since she was a child; Juna and Thuram, whom she had assigned to watch over Dayne when he'd first arrived in Stormshold. They straightened their backs, open hands pressed against their chests. "By blade and by blood," they chorused.

"By blade and by blood," Alina repeated, stepping into the firelight. "Please, sit. Rest."

Tentatively, many of the Andurii settled back into the positions they had been sitting in, groaning from the wounds sustained that day as they did. The four captains remained standing.

"You're bleeding." Marlin took a step towards Alina, but she waved him away, frowning.

"That's what happens when someone cuts you. You should know." Alina raised her eyebrows and nodded at the bandages that were wrapped around Marlin's arms and over his shoulder. "Where are the others?"

The looks on the captains' faces answered that question, and Alina felt a flash of worry for Dayne until she reminded herself she had seen him after the fighting at the River Artis.

"Odys and Jorath dine in Achyron's halls. Odys died in the ambush, Jorath near the end."

Alina closed her eyes for a moment, nodding slowly. "I'm sorry."

"Do not be." Marlin shook his head. "I would have given the same call, as would any of us."

Earlier that day, they had been crossing the River Artis towards Myrefall when they were ambushed by Thebalan and Lorian forces. The Lorian mages had collapsed the bridges after only a fraction of Alina's forces had crossed. Dayne's Andurii, along with Senya Deringal's forces and Turik Baleer's cavalry had been trapped on the far side. Thebalan and Lorian warriors fell upon them, emerging from the woodlands to the west, Varsundi Blackthorn riders leading the charge. When Alina had ordered the rest of the force to cross the river, the Lorian mages froze the water solid. All who had tried to cross were frozen in place – those who survived would never walk again. The blood and shattered limbs was a sight that would haunt Alina's nightmares until the day she died.

Alina looked over the faces of the Andurii captains before her. She and Marlin had selected them carefully. They were masters of the spear and blade from Houses that had supported House Ateres for generations, and each of them had sworn loyalty to Alina. Odys and Jorath had done the same. Alina had always known there would be blood and death on this path to freedom. It's all she'd ever known. She'd seen her parents' bodies swinging in the plaza, seen Kal's cold body lifeless on the ground – her love, dead. The empire had only ever shown her blood and death. Though that didn't make the weight of it any easier to bear. "Where is Dayne? I need to speak with him."

THE COLD LIGHT OF THE moon washed down over the fields of corn, wheat, and barley as Dayne's horse walked along the dirt path that led to the old farmhouse. Wooden fences on either side marked the edges of the fields.

The dirt crunched beneath the horse's hooves, breaking the nocturnal chorus of chirps and clicks of the kiakas – winged insects about the size of Dayne's thumb – that were synonymous with the Valtaran countryside.

Dayne's family had owned the farm near Myrefall for over three hundred years, but they'd always rented the land around the house to a local farming family – House Url. Dayne's father had brought Dayne, Alina, and Baren to the farm many times when they were younger, mostly to escape the constant chaos of Skyfell. They would often play in the fields and swim in the ocean. Some nights they would even share evening meal with House Url. Daemon Url had protested at first. "A House like yours shouldn't be sharing evening meal with a House like mine," he would say.

Arkin Ateres had pretended to be insulted, before laughing and telling Daemon off for even suggesting such a thing.

This farm was a happy place with few complications, which was a rare treasure.

"Easy boy." Dayne slipped from the saddle as the horse drew close to the farmhouse. He tethered the animal to the edge of the fence and ran his hand along its muzzle, patting its cheek. "I won't be long."

The farmhouse was built almost entirely from Thrakian oak except for the roof shingles, which were made from Lakala wood. Dayne's father had once told him that the natural resins in Lakala wood helped protect from moisture. The house stood only a single story high but stretched almost a hundred feet long and just over thirty feet wide. A wooden deck extended from the front, with three steps leading to the main door.

Three Thrakian oaks stood tall amidst the patchy grass of the grounds that surrounded the house, sentinels of generations passed. In Dayne's memory the grass had always been lush and green, but rainfall had been scarce recently.

Dayne made his way up the steps, avoiding the second; it had always creaked.

He touched the door, slowly as though he was afraid the wood might burst into flames. The front door was the newest part of the house, new enough to be almost smooth. Dayne's brother, Baren, had smashed the old, rotted one off its hinges when he had seen no more than fifteen summers. He'd been chasing Dayne through the house, but when Dayne had leapt through the front door and slammed it behind him, the iron latch had fallen and locked into place. He'd known the door had needed replacing, but when Baren burst through and sent the door careening down the steps in a cloud of splinters, he'd realised just how rotted it truly was. Their mother and father had just laughed, deep, bellyaching laughs.

They ate their evening meal on the deck that night: pork stuffed with cheese – made from a blend of sheep and goat's milk – garlic, and sun-dried tomatoes, all glazed in a tangy sauce. It was one of the memories that had stayed crystal clear amidst a sea of blurred images and half-truths.

He touched his fingers against the door, taking one more look at the deck and the old chairs his mother and father had once sat in, before pushing forwards and stepping inside.

Within seconds he knew Baren had been there no more than three weeks past but was now gone. The sweet, citrusy smell of paoen flowers mingled with the distinct aroma of thyme hung in the air. The flowers sat in a terracotta vase on the short table at the far side of the room, sagged and colourless. Those flowers grew in the garden out back, and Baren had always loved their smell. He had also always been meticulous about their care once picked. The flowers would have lasted almost two weeks with his attention, and about another seven sunrises to get to their current state. The wooden floors had been swept, and the central table, along with the countertops, had been wiped down, but a layer of dust had resettled on both.

"You were supposed to wait for me." Dayne shook his head. He slipped a round-backed knife – the one Therin had given him all those years ago – from his belt and flipped it into reverse grip before stepping further into the room that acted both as the antechamber and the kitchen. Years with Belina had drilled into him to keep a knife handy even when he thought he wouldn't need one. *'Knives are your friends, Dayne. Unless they're in my hands and you've pissed me off.'*

Dayne held back the reflexive smile that crept onto his face as he imagined Belina saying the words. He stepped across the room, avoiding the creaky floorboards by force of habit. A sheet of paper lay on the table at the centre of the room, folded in half.

Dayne reached out to the Spark, giving an involuntary groan of relief as warmth flooded his body, stilling the aches and pains in his joints, calming the burning where steel had sliced his flesh earlier that day. He pulled on threads of Air and Spirit, allowing the cool touch to tickle his skin before he weaved the threads together and pushed them through the house. He let the threads drift on the air and snake across the floor, feeling for subtle vibrations: heartbeats, shifting feet, held breaths. After he pushed the threads through every room, he let go of the Spark but kept the knife in his right hand, Belina's voice again sounding in his head, *'Put it down and I'll put it in you.'*

Dayne lifted the letter from where it sat on the table, folding back the top half with his thumb.

Brother,

What do I say? What can truly be said that would ever make better the things I've done? All these years I told myself I was doing what you would have done – what needed to be done to hold the House together. But as I sit here, waiting, I realise that all I did was tear the House apart.

Loren Koraklon had Mother and Father's bodies strung up in the plaza. For days they forced Alina and me to sit there and watch as they swung in the breeze. They didn't even use rope. They used meat hooks. They treated them like livestock, humiliated them. I'm not writing this so you will pity me. I'm writing this so that you know I understand that I was wrong.

I watched that, and I told Alina to bite her tongue. I told her we needed to fall in line for the sake of the House. I wanted to protect her, but I made her watch our mother's headless body swing. I told myself I was doing what you would have done, but I know you never would have done that.

I can't change it. I can't make it right. There are so many things I can't make right, but I'm not going to sit here and stew in my own self-loathing.

Alina's boy, did she ever tell you what she named him? I don't suppose she did. I've already taken so much from her, I won't take that. Ask her. When Loren demanded her child be taken, as all other firstborns were, a woman called Helaena Lakaris was the one who took him, along with the others.

I can't change the past, Dayne, but I wanted you to know I've not turned my back on my family. It just took you to remind me what family truly is. I'm going north. I know a smuggler who operates out of Myrefall. He can get me to Antiquar. I'll find him, Dayne, our nephew. I'll find him, or I'll die in the trying. I'll send reports to old Girda who runs The Orange Tree just outside Skyfell. If something does happen, at the least you can finish what I've started.

One more thing, brother. In Redstone you told me you haven't forgiven me, just as I have not forgiven you. I don't ask for your forgiveness. But I wanted you to know you were wrong. I do forgive you. You came back.

Look after her,

Always your shadow, forever your brother,

Baren

A tear fell from Dayne's cheek, landing on the page with a *splat*, the moisture turning the paper translucent. He just stood there for a few moments, his body tense, then, still gripping the letter, he wrapped the fingers of his left hand around the table's edge and roared, hurling the table through the air, threads of Spirit and Air whipping around him. The table crashed into a support post and snapped in half, splinters spraying. He stood in the middle of the room, shaking, his fingers squeezing around the handle of the knife in his right hand.

He drew in ragged breaths, his jaw clenching so tight he thought his teeth might snap. His family had been torn to shreds. And it had all started that night just over twelve years gone. That one night had changed his entire life. The empire had taken *everything*. Loren Koraklon had taken everything. Dayne knew three names from the boat where his parents died: Sylvan Anura, Harsted Arnim, and Loren Koraklon.

Harsted was nothing but char and ash; Dayne saw to that. Sylvan Anura only wished that was her fate. There had been many others along the way. Eight hundred and twenty-six in total between that day and now. But Loren Koraklon... Dayne would rip that man's heart from his chest.

The sound of wingbeats echoed outside, thumping over the kiakas' chorus. Dayne glanced to where the table lay in two pieces, splinters littering the floor, then shook his head. If the world was ever in a place where he would have cause to bring happiness back to this farmhouse, he would replace the table. Until that day, it would stay broken, just like everything else.

Dayne took a moment before going back outside, knowing what was awaiting him. He slid the round-backed knife into its sheath on his belt, then stepped out into the warm Valtaran night air.

"What are you doing here, Dayne?"

Alina stood about six paces back from the bottom step of the deck. She still wore her leather skirts and sturdy riding boots, but her cuirass was replaced by a simple cream linen tunic marred by a blood streak along the left side. Behind her, Rynvar stood with his winged forelimbs pressed into the ground, his neck extended over Alina's right shoulder. The wyvern was almost big enough to be a small dragon, his neck thick with muscle, body twice the size of most other wyverns.

Rynvar stared at Dayne, lips pulling back in a snarl, blue eyes fixed on him.

"It's been a long time," Dayne said, avoiding the second step as he descended from the deck to the ground. "And today has been a hard day. We have happy memories here."

Alina let out a laugh that was tinted in no small part with anger. "Have you ever noticed how you do that? Is it on purpose?"

"Do what?" Dayne narrowed his eyes at Alina.

"How you lie without lying? It *has* been a long time. It *has* been a hard day. We *do* have happy memories here. None of those things are lies. But they're not why you're here."

"Not today, Alina." Dayne made to step past his sister.

"I know Baren is alive. You know I know that Baren is alive. So let's not play games. Just like you did now, you never actually told me you would kill him that day. I knew you wouldn't. Maybe that's partly why I left you to it." She turned her head, letting out a long sigh through her nostrils. "Why is he alive, Dayne?"

Alina stared into Dayne's eyes with an intensity that caused his chest to tighten.

"Because he is family, Alina. And there's not much of that left."

Alina's voice became cold and level. "He had Kal killed. Baren had Kal's throat slit and left him to die like a pig."

"Alina, he—"

"He killed the only man I've ever loved, Dayne!" Alina's scream was so harsh her voice cracked, fire burning in her eyes, tears welling. "The only man I've ever loved... The only man besides Marlin who showed me any kindness after our father died and you left. Baren had him bled like an animal."

Dayne turned away, unable to look into Alina's grief-stricken eyes. "He did it to save you, Alina."

Alina sniffled as the laughter left her throat, snot and tears standing in the way of pure rage. "Is that what he told you?" She ran her tongue across her teeth and wiped snot away with her closed fist. Dayne couldn't help but notice both her hands were clenched, thumbs stuck into the fist – what she'd always done as a child when she was angry. "He told me that too. Told me he did it to stop Loren from flogging me in the plaza. Can I ask you a question, Dayne?"

Alina didn't wait for a response.

"If it was Mera, would that answer satisfy you? If I bled Mera dry and left her to die alone on a cold floor, would those words have been enough?" Alina's voice dropped to a sombre lament. "Kal laughed. All the time..." Her voice trembled, her words catching in her throat as tears rolled down her cheeks. "He was always laughing. He was the light of my life and the father of my child... the same child Baren took from me. You can stand there and say he did it to protect me, but would you have done the same? Or would you have come to me? Would you have treated me like a sister, like an equal? We could have come up with a plan... We could have done something... anything." Alina sniffed, wiping the tears away with a closed fist. She let out a cough and shook her head, straightening her back, changing the conversation. "I came looking for you, to see how you were after today. You lost Odys and Jorath. Along with fifteen more. The captains are still taking count of losses, and there are many still in triage. We lost over a thousand today... and it happened on my command. We should have scouted more. I should have had wyverns covering the sky days in advance. I should have been more prepared. I'm sorry."

"Men and women will die under your command every day until this war is over, Alina. You've led us to victory after victory. We've taken all the lands from Skyfell to Ironcreek to Myrefall in a matter of months. You've made the right call every step of the way. The truth of war is that no matter how much you win, you always lose." Dayne let the sound of the kiakas break the tension, their rhythmic chirping and clicking filling the air. "The garrison at Myrefall is near ten thousand strong. Lorian ships fortify their port and keep them stocked to withstand a siege. Ten thousand or so more patrol the open lands between the city and Achyron's Keep. Loren Koraklon's banners have swollen to near thirty-five thousand on last count, and the Lorian reinforcements arrived weeks back."

"Why are you telling me everything the scouts told me this morning?"

"Because it's time you considered what I've said. It's time we send a hawk to Aeson."

Alina's stance shifted, her chin rising a bit higher, her shoulders rolling back. "I've told you. This is *our* fight. This is *our* land. I'm happy to use his war as a distraction, but I will not go crawling on my knees to the man who promised our parents the world and abandoned them when they needed him. We are Valtarans. Our blood traces back for thousands of years. The blademasters of Valtara are legend. We *will* drive the empire from our home. And we don't need Aeson Virandr to do it."

"At what cost, Alina? How much Valtaran blood must feed the soil before Valtara is free?"

"As much as it takes!" Alina roared. Her chest heaved, her breaths trembling. She steadied herself. "I will not send our people to die needlessly. But there are some things worth bleeding for, some things worth dying for. If Loren has thirty-five thousand, then we will wait, and we will raise the banners of every House, Major and Minor, from the southern coasts to the Abaddian cliffs. They will stand for a free Valtara, and we will raise an army that will make the ground shake."

Dayne couldn't help but admire the flames that burned in Alina's heart. There *were* some things worth bleeding for, worth dying for. And Alina was one of those things. As was Mera. He had said much the same thing to Aeson Virandr about six years ago. "Alina, I am your sword. Wherever you send me, I will go. Whatever battle, I will fight it. Whatever price, I will pay it. But we need to use our heads as well as our hearts. The new Draleid stands by Aeson's side. A dragon is worth ten thousand men."

"What have dragons ever done for us, Dayne? Dragons took everything from us. Dragonfire burned Stormwatch. Dragonfire killed every rebellion before this. It is dragonfire that put the Lorian boot on our necks."

"And it is steel that took our father's life and our mother's head." Dayne's voice rose higher than he had intended, his blood flush with anger – not at Alina but at life and the cost of living, at everything that had been taken. "Would you have us fight with sticks because of what steel has done?"

Alina glared at Dayne, and he could see the cold fury in her eyes. She turned and walked back towards Rynvar, the wyvern dipping his neck to allow her to mount him. "Be ready in the morning," Alina said, her voice devoid of emotion. "We march for Myrefall at dawn's light. I will have High Commander Arnen select a hundred of his best. You can bolster the Andurii ranks with whomever you choose. Be ready to bleed. Valtara demands it."

Alina whispered something to Rynvar, and the wyvern let out a series of clicks followed by a roar as he stepped forwards, cracked his wings against the air, and took flight.

Dayne stood and watched as the orange-scaled wyvern vanished into the clouds above, the beating of his wings lingering on the air.

CHAPTER FIFTY-ONE

THE THREE SISTERS

Rist stood atop a rise of earth and clay that had been forged into an observation tower by the three Craftsmages of the gathered Lorian armies. The tower had been constructed to give a better vantage point overlooking the would-be battlefield. It wasn't a complex structure by any means, but it was effective in its simplicity – something Rist was sure Andelar Touran would approve of. The tower rose as high as a two-storey house, steps of clay leading to a flattened landing at the top. Rist, Garramon, and all the commanders and generals of the First, Fourth, and Second armies stood upon the landing, gathered around a Spark-forged podium of stone and clay that held a scale reconstruction of the area around the city of Steeple. Rist had only been permitted to attend because Garramon was his sponsor, and even then he had drawn a few looks from the gathered generals.

News that elven scouts had been found skirting the River Gurdil at night had spread through the camp like wildfire that morning. The commanders and generals had been at the tower since just after the sun had risen, arguing over tactics, manoeuvres, logistics, and positioning. The talks had held Rist's interest for a while, but eventually it had descended into a repetition of the same points, along with far too many 'what-ifs'.

With the voices of the arguing commanders floating to the back of his mind, Rist turned from the clay map and looked over the landscape ahead. The Three Sisters – River Halda, River Gurdil, and River Dalwin – carved through the plains of grassland that spread for miles, joining together some distance in the north. The tower had been built with the River Dalwin at its back, the rivers Halda and Gurdil splitting the lands at its front.

Rist drew in a deep breath and held it for a few moments, trying to settle himself as he gazed out at the fourteen thousand Lorian soldiers who were spread across the grasslands below the tower, stretching to the banks of the river Halda, the city of Steeple off to the right.

He had never seen as many souls gathered in one place as they were now. Of course, he'd been in Camylin and Al'Nasla, where many times that number resided. But he had never actually laid eyes on what fourteen thousand people truly looked like, steel glinting in the light of the blazing morning sun, movements rippling across the ranks like waves. With so many in one place, even the most subtle sounds – the shuffling of feet, the rubbing of steel plate and leather – could be heard far and wide.

Several more towers of clay and stone, constructed by the Craftsmages, rose throughout the ranks of soldiers, regiments of archers perched at their tops.

There had once been a time where Rist had seen the town guard of The Glade as the mightiest of warriors. In their steel breastplates and tabards of regal blue, swords strapped to their hips. It was only the guard that could stand against raiders, Uraks, and brigands. They were the strongest of the strong and the noblest of the noble. Rist still saw those men and women as strong, noble warriors, but looking out over the combined might of the First, Fourth, and Second armies of the Lorian Empire, he understood just how naïve he had been in thinking the town guard could ever have stood against this kind of power. Though, if there was one thing he'd learned during his time in Loria, it was that the empire wasn't the enemy. The Uraks didn't care what flag they waved, they would kill them all the same. The North and the South would be stronger together.

Looking past the River Halda, across a wide plain of grass, and then to the River Gurdil, Rist could see the thick wall of grey fog spreading for miles left and right, rising over a hundred feet. The fog had reached the banks of the River Gurdil the night before and then had simply stopped, as though waiting. Rist had already decided there was nothing natural about the fog. It was a construct – of that he was sure. But of what, he still hadn't worked out. There was nothing in his memory from *A Study of Control* or *The Spark: A Study of Infinite Possibilities* that seemed to fit. Nor could he pull from any of the other seventeen manuscripts he had read that pertained to the use of the Spark. He flicked through the pages of the books in his mind, searching for something, anything that might fit. He tilted his head to the side, narrowing his eyes, trying to see deeper into the fog. *What if it isn't the Spark? What if it's something else entirely? A Skydruid?*

"You can feel it in your bones, can't you?" Magnus stepped up beside Rist, scratching at his beard while looking out at the Lorian forces. Every time Rist set eyes on Magnus, the man seemed taller and broader. "The air changes before a battle. Your mind grows restless, your blood turns wild." Magnus let out a long, ponderous sigh. "Elves… I can't say I've ever looked forward to having to face them on the field of battle again."

Rist looked to the man, then back out across the landscape. "Are they much different from us?"

Magnus shrugged. "Outside of living to see twice our natural summers, they're skin, bone, and blood. So in that sense, no. Take their heads, pierce their hearts. They'll die just like we do. But it's not *what* they are, more *who* they are. Even before the liberation, they were relentless, single-minded, and brutal. If the legends are to be believed, when humans first arrived in Epheria, it was only the grace of the Jotnar that stopped the elves from slaughtering us to the last." A smile curled on Magnus's lips as he shook his head. "I'd bet they fucking regret that now. They will want blood and vengeance. Their honour will demand it."

"The commander of the Dragonguard is an elf, is he not?"

"Touchy subject, lad. Eltoar is a Draleid. I know we don't use the word anymore, but it's more than a title. It's a species. He's as much an elf as a dragon is a snake. In the old times, when one was bonded to a dragon, they were considered to have become something… different. He is an elf, but he is not. He will take no pleasure in this battle, but nor will he shy away from it. Ah," Magnus said, raising an eyebrow and inclining his head towards something in the distance. "Speak of The Saviour and he shall appear."

A rumbling cheer rose from the gathered soldiers below, and Rist looked up to see the gargantuan shapes of three dragons dropping from the sky, blotting out the light of the sun, wings spread like the embracing arms of Heraya herself, colossal shadows sailing over the armies below. The dragons swept over the Lorian forces to raucous applause, then climbed, soaring over the tower upon which Rist and the others stood.

Rist tilted his head back and watched as the gargantuan, black-scaled body of Helios tore through the sky above him, unleashing a monstrous roar that only drew further chants and shouts from the soldiers below.

"They're always so fucking dramatic." Magnus shook his head as the other two dragons, Karakes and Meranta, soared after Helios, sweeping in a wide arc, then turning back to alight on the grass near the base of the tower. "I'm surprised they don't attach tassels to the dragons' tails – make more of a show and dance about it. Come." Magnus turned back towards the others. "Let's see what news they bring."

The Supreme Commander, Taya Tambrel, dipped her head as the three Dragonguard reached the top of the clay steps, their dragons resting on the grass below. "Commander Daethana. Lyina, Pellenor."

Rist had seen the Dragonguard from a distance, but he had not seen them up close. They each wore suits of stunning white plate armour that seemed both impossibly light and incredibly strong. Golden ornamentation decorated the edges of the armour with a level of detail that would have looked more at home on a painting or tapestry, and a flickering black flame was emblazoned on the centre of each breastplate.

Tense silence held in the air at the top of the tower as the three Dragonguard removed their helmets. Rist swallowed, his mouth growing dry. The three warriors radiated an unerring sense of power and calm, their presence alone shifting the atmosphere in an instant. There was no arguing or bickering, only silence and, in some cases, reverence.

Commanders and generals stepped aside, allowing the Dragonguard to take their place beside the clay map.

"What news do you bring, Eltoar?"

"Nothing we don't already know, Commander Tambrel." Eltoar extended a finger towards the map. "The fog spreads from here to here. Stretching back for about five miles."

"Do we just sit and wait then?" Olivan Karta, the commander of the Second Army, said, incredulous. Rist had only met the man a handful of times. He'd seemed decent but also brash and impatient, a certain anxiety about him. More than a few heads turned at his words, but Rist's gaze focused on the two Dragonguard either side of Eltoar.

An amused smirk spread across the face of the Dragonguard to Eltoar's left, who Rist figured must have been Lyina Altair, judging by the fact she was the only woman amongst the three. While the Dragonguard at Eltoar's right shoulder, Pellenor Dambren, simply raised a curious eyebrow, glancing towards Lyina.

"You seem eager…" Eltoar shook his head, waving his hand as though searching for a name.

"Olivan Karta, Commander. I am the leader of the Second Army. And I *am* eager. My sister's forces were stationed just north of Gildor. We've had no contact in weeks. Months."

Eltoar stared at Olivan, his gaze unwavering. "In your eagerness, what would you have us do, Commander Karta?"

Olivan returned Eltoar's stare for a moment before dropping his gaze.

Eltoar drew in several long breaths, extending the tense silence. Rist couldn't get over the way in which Eltoar used the absence of words to smother Olivan with his authority. Eventually, Eltoar turned his gaze from Olivan and looked out at the River Halda and River Gurdil. "The true warrior forces the enemy to move and is never moved by them, Commander Karta."

Rist recognised the words immediately. They were from *The Art of War* by Sumara Tuzan.

"The elves have come along the eastern coast, razing everything in their path." Eltoar glanced at Olivan, sympathy touching his face. "They are here for a reason, and they will not simply stop where they are. They will leave the cover of that veil, or we will fight within it. Our position is strong, and it would be unwise to abandon it. The elves have come this far. Their honour demands they fight. Patience is half the sword. When the battle does commence, my wing and I will not be able to charge headfirst into the fray. The elves have had centuries to prepare for this. They will come ready to face dragons. We will need your mages to focus on engaging their counterparts and eliminating any projectile-based weaponry."

"Are we absolutely certain it's the elves?" Marken Kort, commander of the First Army, said, puffing out his chest and folding his arms.

"I can fetch you their heads, if you'd like?" Lyina gave an upturn of her lip, opening her arms. "They're a little bloody. But if our word isn't good enough, I can surely go and fetch them for you, Commander. It's no trouble at all."

Before Marken could respond, a cacophony of sound rose up behind Rist, emanating from the gathered soldiers at the foot of the tower. Whispers blended with shouts and clanging steel. As Rist turned to face the landscape of the Three Sisters, his jaw slackened, eyes widening, his skin prickling. He took a step closer to the edge of the landing.

Past the Lorian forces, past the banks of the River Halda, and past the banks of the River Gurdil, the fog was dissipating, tendrils of grey snaking outwards across the water and grass, thinning and fading.

At the edges of his vision, Rist saw Magnus, Garramon, and the Justicar, Farda Kyrana, standing beside him, others shuffling, trying to get a better look. As the fog thinned, more than a few gasps came from the generals and commanders around Rist, and a lump formed in his chest.

An ocean of gold and red lay on the other side of the River Gurdil stretching back and over a rise in the land. Sunlight glinted off polished steel, red cloths and tabards striking against ornately carved golden armour. Enormous crimson banners rippled in the wind, the sigil of a golden stag emblazoned across their front. Rist could not even begin to determine the size of the elven host. But what was clear was they numbered at least twice that of the combined Lorian forces. *Thirty thousand at the very least…*

"Eltoar," Magnus called out. "I think we're going to need those dragons."

⟳

THE MEETING OF OPPOSING COMMANDERS before a battle was an old elven tradition, from long before even the Blodvar. It was a way of determining whether a battle could be avoided and if not, it was a sign of respect. It was not a custom that Farda had seen observed in a long time, but when they had seen the elven party separating from their forces and moving towards the river Dalwin, Supreme Commander Tambrel had ordered Farda, Magnus, and Commander Talvare to ride out with her and meet them. The other commanders – Marken Kort, Olivan Karta, and the mage commander of the Second, Urla Rint – had stayed behind with the armies. Taya had invited Eltoar and the others but they had refused, which Farda had expected.

And so that was where Farda now stood, in the open grass between the River Halda and the River Gurdil, the sun resting in the sky, his gaze fixed on the approaching elves.

"I still say we should have brought horses," Magnus whispered to Farda.

"I don't think that would have gone down too well with the elves," Farda answered back.

Magnus snorted. "They've just burned four cities to the ground and slaughtered hundreds of thousands. Do you really think us not riding horses is going to cause them to say 'Oh, this has all been a terrible misunderstanding, we'll turn around now'? This is all a waste of time if you ask me."

Taya threw Magnus a scowl, her red-trimmed black plate glistening in the light of the sun overhead. "We are trying to avoid bloodshed here."

"Apologies, Supreme Commander." Magnus gave Taya the most dramatic bow Farda had ever seen, then turned back to Farda, whispering, "Tell me you've never fought elves without telling me you've never fought elves."

Farda smiled at that but didn't respond. Instead, he tapped his fingers against the coin in his trouser pocket, contemplating. As the elves drew closer, Farda's chest tightened, memories bubbling to the surface. Memories of Ilnaen, of blood and fire. Memories of the years afterwards, of the wars and death. Memories of Shinyara. He settled himself with a long breath, still tapping the coin in his pocket.

The elves came to a stop about ten feet from Farda and the others, each garbed in flowing gold plate and coats of shimmering mail, teardrop-shaped shields strapped to their backs. One elf stood at the front, a crimson cloak embroidered with threads of gold knotted at her shoulders, a long-shafted battleaxe protruding above her shield. Farda recognised her immediately. *Princess Vandrien of Lunithír.*

Magnus leaned in and let out a puff of air. "Well, that's not good."

Before The Fall, Princess Vandrien was one of the most renowned mages in all Epheria. At that point, she had seen no more than a hundred summers and yet was already a living legend. Vandrien was not somebody Farda had expected to lay eyes on ever again. In truth, he had hoped she'd died in the chaos. Her presence here changed everything.

Silence held between the two groups, the steel of armies glinting at their backs, wind rustling in their ears.

Supreme Commander Tambrel glanced towards Farda and the others, then spoke, her stare fixing on Vandrien. "I am Supreme Commander Taya Tambrel of the Lorian Empire. There has not been war between our peoples in centuries, and now you come from your trees, burn cities, and slaughter thousands. Today will be your reckoning. You will pay in blood for what you have done. But first, I would know your name so I can tell my emperor who died here today."

Magnus whispered to Farda, his mouth scrunching. "Very diplomatic... I thought she wanted to *avoid* bloodshed. Do you think we should tell her who she's talking to?"

Farda gave Magnus a sideways glance but didn't answer.

Vandrien stepped forwards, the two elves closest to her matching her step. She looked over those gathered, strands of her white-blonde hair visible beneath her helmet, her gaze holding on Farda for a fraction of a second longer than the others. He was Rakina. She knew him, and she knew that he had been part of everything that had happened. "En aldin går til dauva, Taya Tambrel. Laël Vandrien Lunithír, Aldryr un evalien, Inarí un Numillíon."

Taya looked back at Farda.

Farda pressed his tongue against his teeth, drawing in a long breath and looking from Vandrien to Taya. "She says her name is Vandrien Lunithír, Fire of the elves, and queen of Numillíon – Lynalion. She says it's a good day to die."

Judging by the scowl on Taya's face, she was not impressed.

"Speak plainly." Taya's voice dropped to a growl as she turned to Vandrien. "I know you speak the Common Tongue. Why are you here?"

The slightest of smiles touched Vandrien's lips. "It is custom among my people to speak before we kill each other. I have come to offer you the rite of Alvadrû – combat sacrifice. You and I. When I win, your forces will kneel and be taken as prisoners, but they will not be harmed."

"And if I win?"

"You will not win."

Farda reached into his pocket while Magnus stifled a laugh at his side. He pulled the coin free, ran his thumb over the lion marking, then flicked it into the air. *Clink.* A simple question. Does he take the Alvadrû or not? If he wins, mass bloodshed is avoided. If he loses, he is with Shinyara once more. Magnus looked at him out of the corner of his eye. The coin hit his palm. *Crowns.* He nodded, exhaling through his nose, then placed the coin back in his pocket. *Not today, then.*

"If I will not win," Taya said, a tremble of anger seeping into her voice, "then why would I accept this Alvadrû?"

"To save the lives of your warriors." The pure calm on Vandrien's face was unnerving, even to Farda. "Do you accept?"

Taya's hand dropped to the pommel of the sword at her hip, fingers tapping against the steel. The mere fact that she was even contemplating it spoke volumes about who she was. But Farda hoped the woman declined. Taya was a fine warrior, and much like Commander Talvare, she was direct and honest. Farda admired her and would rather not see her blood splattered across the grass. He might have stood a slim chance against Vandrien, but Taya was a lamb staring down a lion.

"No." Taya shook her head. "I will not allow this battle to be decided on the stroke of a single sword."

Vandrien inclined her head ever so slightly. "Dauva alaith."

Without waiting for a response, Vandrien turned and started back towards the bank of the River Gurdil, where her forces awaited, the shimmering gold of their armour sweeping across the landscape. Without Eltoar, Lyina, and Pellenor, the battle would already be lost ten times over. But with them, they stood a chance.

"What did she say?" Taya asked, turning to Farda.

Farda let out a sigh. "Die well."

RIST WATCHED AS TAYA TAMBREL and the other commanders turned and marched back towards the armies. Horns sounded, and soldiers rushed into formation as the commanders separated and made their way towards their respective forces.

"It didn't go well then?" Garramon called out to Magnus as the Exarch pushed his way through the soldiers of the First Army, reaching the mages.

"About as well as setting fire to your own shit," Magnus said with a shrug. "It's Princess Vandrien, Garramon. Well, *Queen* Vandrien now. And she's not here to play nice."

Rist had never heard the name, but the look of uncertainty on Garramon and Anila's faces told him all he needed to know.

"At the moment, there's no way of knowing how many mages are on their side, but I think it's safe to say they won't be short in that area. Taya wants us to hold back at first. Gauge what kind of strength they have. Once Taya gives the signal, or the elven mages show themselves, we're to split into five groups of twenty. Two groups will stay back and provide support for the dragons when they're airborne. The other three will cut into the elven lines from the flanks, force them inwards where the dragonfire can do the most damage. The other armies will do the same. Our priority is countering the elven mages. We can't let them focus on the Dragonguard. I'll get Hadlbrak and Torim to lead the support groups. Uraksplitter, Garramon, would you do me the honour of leading the other forward regiments? There's few among us who've faced elves before. Your experience could be the difference."

"It would be my honour, Brother," Garramon said, inclining his head.

"And mine." Anila mimicked Garramon's gesture.

"How kind of you to give me a hand, Uraksplitter." Magnus raised his eyebrows, looking from Rist to Neera – who stood at Rist's side – then back to Anila.

"I'm going to kill you in your sleep if we live through this, Magnus."

"If you want into my bedchambers, Uraksplitter, all you need do is ask."

More horns signalled for the armies to take their final position.

"I'm going to cut your stones off." Anila patted her hand on the pommel of the sword that hung at her right hip.

"Oh, talk filthy to me, Uraksplitter."

Rist felt something graze his hand, and he turned to see Neera staring at him, her gloved hand touching his. She was garbed just as he was: a coat of mail, a lion-emblazoned breastplate, vambraces, greaves, leather boots, and a brown-trimmed black cloak draped over her shoulders. Her dark hair was tied back with a piece of twine, and she gripped her helmet in her right hand.

"Are you scared?"

Rist nodded. He was terrified. Even more than he'd been during The Proving. More than when they'd found the bear in the cave, more than when Fritz had put the arrow through him, and more than when the Uraks had attacked. Calen and Dann had been by his side then. He'd still been scared, but having them there had made it somehow more bearable. Now though, he stood on a grassy field, thousands of miles from the place he called home, wearing the black cloak of an Imperial Battlemage, staring down an army of elves, and he found himself asking the question: what in the gods was he doing here?

Rist stared back at Neera, hearing Magnus and Anila arguing behind them, knowing that Garramon was simply giving the pair his patented unapproving look. The North wasn't his home, and the empire was far from loved in the villages. But, in the Circle, Rist had found something that had always evaded him – a sense of understanding, a sense of belonging. No, this wasn't his home. But he had no way of getting back to the villages, and the Circle had begun to teach him of who he was and who he wanted to become. The Spark was a part of him now, and he a part of it. Besides, something told him that these elves, just like the Uraks, wouldn't stop in the North. And so, even though he was a hair's breadth away from soiling himself, he was certain this was where he needed to be.

Rist closed his fingers around Neera's, squeezing. He had been so single-minded in his studying and practising over the past while that he had spent very little time by her side. And yet, Neera was a large part of Rist feeling like he belonged. She was even more sarcastic than Dann, equal parts infuriating and confusing, and she pushed Rist outside of more comfort zones than he'd even known he'd possessed. But she was also caring, and witty, and strong. She accepted Rist for who he was and asked no apologies of him. "We'll get through it," Rist said, resting his other hand on Neera's cheek and leaning in to kiss her.

"Agh!" Rist let out a grunt as a sharp pain twisted in his wrist.

"You're not kissing me here," Neera said, incredulous. "We're on a battlefield, you goat."

Rist pulled his hand away, shaking it as he tried to relieve the pain. "Sorry. Damn, that hurt." He rubbed his right hand over where Neera had twisted the joint on his left wrist. "I just thought—"

"No." Neera cut across. "After. I'll feel your warmth after. You keep me alive, and I'll keep you alive. Deal?"

"Aren't you two fucking adorable?" Magnus craned his head past Garramon, a broad smile pushing through his thick, black beard. "Uraksplitter, this could be us. See what you're missing?"

"Enough, Magnus." Garramon looked to Magnus, then nodded to where the elven forces had begun to march.

The smile vanished from Magnus's face.

The low rise upon which Rist and the other mages stood allowed them to see just over the heads of the soldiers positioned in front of them.

Sunlight glinted in a rippling wave across the ocean of golden armour as the elven forces marched, their numbers covering every blade of grass. The sound of so many armoured boots filled the air, drowning out the burbling of the Three Sisters, the murmurs of the Lorian soldiers, and even the whispering of the wind. The elves moved with such precision, if Rist had closed his eyes he would have thought their footsteps were the beating of a drum, methodical and hammer-strong.

As they reached the bank of the River Gurdil, the advancing elves ground to a halt. The metallic clang of thousands of boots and steel plates coming to a stop resounded across the field in a singular *snap*. And then a thrum resonated through Rist, the hairs on his arms and neck pricking, the sensation of the Spark pulsing through the air in waves of immense power. The feeling was so intense Rist's breaths trembled, and his hands shook.

Innumerable threads of Fire, Earth, and Water erupted from within the ranks of elves and plunged into the river. Within seconds, the flowing water before the elves, was gone, lifting towards the sky in clouds of wafting steam. Then the ground shook, and the riverbed rose, its banks sinking inwards until it was nothing more than a gentle slope in the ground, dead fish and dried reeds laying in the dirt.

As Rist watched, he was reminded of the opening paragraph in *The Spark: a study of infinite possibilities.*

The Spark is power incarnate. The power to create, the power to destroy, the power to bend, fold, and manipulate the world itself. Before the ships of men arrived on Epherian shores, the elves and Jotnar shaped the lands to their will. They carved rivers, dragged mountains from the ground, and sung forests into existence. The Spark's only limit is the scope of our own understanding and the bounds of our own inability to see the world beyond what we can touch.

"Well," Magnus said. "I guess it's the Two Sisters now."

For the first time, Magnus didn't laugh at his own joke. In fact, his expression didn't change at all.

A moment passed, then the elves were marching across the ground that had once been the River Gurdil, the drum of their footsteps echoing.

Rist squeezed Neera's hand one more time, then pulled away, resting his palm on the lion-head pommel of the sword at his hip.

Horns bellowed, three sharp bursts followed by two longer bursts, and then the Lorian armies were moving into their final positions before the elves crossed the River Halda. Rist's heart was beating like a hammer.

As they moved, Garramon turned to Rist. "Feel the fear, Rist. Acknowledge its existence, but never let it control you. Today is the day you earn your colours."

Chapter Fifty-Two

Dragonbound by Fire

The clang of steel and the screams of the dying consumed everything, crashing like a waterfall in Rist's ears. He clenched his jaw, trying to ease the tremble in his hands. Ahead, the spears and swords of the First Army fought shield to shield against the elves, with the Fourth and Second armies spreading out to the left along the elven lines while Rist stood a hundred or so paces back with the other mages of the First Army, waiting, as instructed.

This wasn't what Rist had thought battle would be like. The bards had woven tales of mighty warriors charging against each other, battlerush overcoming them as they carried out feats of heroism and valour. But that couldn't be farther from the truth.

This wasn't heroic or valorous. This was slow, grinding, and dark. Ahead, bodies crunched, and shields smashed together. There were no heroes swinging their swords in arcs of triumph. There were only men and women screaming and howling as steel sliced through flesh, severed limbs, and soaked the trodden grass in blood. Those that fell were trampled, those that stood were crushed. All the while Rist waited and watched, the sounds of crunching bone and blood-chilling screams etching themselves into his mind.

If he had been forced to charge head-first into battle, he wouldn't have had the time to contemplate his own mortality. But no, each clang of steel was like a ticking clock. Each scream, a reminder. Blood and death was coming, it just had to carve its way through the soldiers in front of him first. The thought of it turned his blood cold. "Can't we do anything? We can't just let them die."

Garramon looked to Rist, then out towards the front line, moving his tongue slowly over his lips. "There is a plan, Rist. Battles are often not won in the fighting, but in the planning."

Rist swallowed hard. *The Art of War*, by Sumara Tuzan had often told of that very same concept. *First you win, then you fight. For if you fight before winning, you will be defeated.* It was a touch convoluted, but the sentiment remained the same. "Wasn't it you who told me that commitment to a broken plan is often the reason commanders send men to their deaths?" Rist asked, his tone sharper than he had intended. "That refusal to adapt is fatal?"

A rare smile crept onto Garramon's face, and he shook his head. "I need to be careful about how much I teach you," he said, casting a glance ahead towards the fighting, then looking back to Rist. "Refusal to adapt is fatal, yes. But changing the plan not because it is broken but because your nerve doesn't hold is equally so."

"It's the way of war, lad." Magnus turned to Rist, a hard look on his face. "We all have our parts to play. If we charge forward now, we'll break our own formations, pull them out of position. We need to have patience. Their mages will show themselves, and when they do we'll crack them open. I admire your will to fight, but don't be so eager to die. You'll get your chance. There's one thing about plans and battle lines – they're all well and good until someone uses the Spark. Our only advantage is the Dragonguard. We need to hold strong."

In the distance, behind Magnus, farther along the lines, Rist could see Taya Tambrel and her Blackwatch sitting astride their enormous mounts, their black plate glistening in the sunlight, hails of arrows soaring over their heads from the towers erected by the Craftsmages. She was shouting and roaring commands, the details of which Rist couldn't hear.

Magnus looked over the mages of the First Army, then across to the other blocks of swordsmen and spearmen, a pensive look in his eyes. Beside him, Garramon and Anila did the same, as did a number of the Battlemages around them.

"Brace!" Magnus called out, threads of Air and Spirit whipping around him, the other mages following suit, their threads weaving together into a Spark-wrought shield spread across the mages and the soldiers around them.

With so many mages gathered in one place, Rist had barely felt the shift in the air, the tingling sensation running along his skin. Just as Magnus had shown him, he pulled on the threads he needed and bound them to the shield of Spirit and Air the other mages had formed.

A blinding flash and then a web of interwoven arcs of blue lightning erupted from amongst the elven ranks. The lightning ripped through the soldiers at the front, slamming into the shield, tearing up chunks of earth and clay, and smashing into the archery tower that stood only twenty or so feet to Rist's left. The ground beneath Rist's feet shook as chunks of clay and stone crashed into the Lorian ranks, soldiers screaming as they were crushed and buried alive.

More bolts of lightning flashed, more towers falling, more archers thrown from their perches wreathed in flames.

Rist's breath caught in his throat, panic setting into his veins. He called to Neera, but his voice was drowned out by more screams and then the soldiers ahead of him were hurtling through the air, crashing against each other and slamming off the ground as threads of Air swept through the Lorian ranks, tearing them asunder. Rist could see threads of Fire and Spirit joining the threads of Air, weaving around them, and he recognised the movement. *An inverted Lightning Storm.* It was a variation of one of the five primary Spark formation movements Magnus had taught Rist and Neera.

"Hadlbrak, Torin – support. Garramon, Uraksplitter – counter!" Magnus roared, thrusting his sword into the air. The man charged towards the wide opening created by the first phase of the Lightning Storm, other Battlemages moving with him, threads of Spirit, Fire, and Air weaving around them.

Rist felt a hand grabbing at his cloak and he looked up to see Garramon staring into his eyes. "Feel the fear, use it." The man's voice was sharp, the muscles in his jaw tensing, and then he pushed Rist forwards, Neera and Anila charging beside them.

The blend of panic and power that coursed through Rist's veins numbed him to the vibrations of each step drumming his legs. The feeling of so many mages drawing heavily from the Spark was like lightning surging through him, igniting his blood. Sounds drummed and thrashed in his ears, his senses dulling to the euphoria of the Spark. Then he drew in a short breath, his training flooding his mind, Magnus's voice echoing.

"Counter!"

Rist's senses burst to life as he pulled on threads of Fire, Spirit, and Air. Beside him he felt the others doing the same, and then their threads were slicing through those of the elves, severing the Lightning Storm before it could grow any more fierce.

Threads of Fire and Air swirled around the Battlemages, augmented by threads of Spirit.

"Stay beside me!" Garramon called out, not turning his head.

Rist met Neera's gaze for a moment. A pang of worry flashing through him. What if she died? What if this was the last time he ever saw the light in her eyes?

Something heavy crashed into Rist's stomach, knocking the air from his lungs and sending him careening the ground. He gasped, squeezing his fingers tight, the resistance telling him he still held onto the hilt of his sword. The ground sloshed beneath him, the grass trodden and soaked in blood. An elf stood over him, golden armour shimmering, crimson tabard blowing in the wind. The elf pulled its spear back, then crumpled as a sword crashed into its face, teeth snapping, mouth peeling open.

Rist's breaths trembled as he lay in the blood-soaked mud, feet stamping around him, the bodies of humans and elves trampled where they lay, then Neera was hauling him to his feet, blood dripping from the length of her sword. "Are you hurt?"

Rist shook his head, unable to form words. A glint of steel flashed to his left, and he spun, bringing his sword up just in time to turn a blow from an elven spear. The elf drew the spear back and made to run it through Rist's gut. In a panic, Rist swung his sword, but the elf swatted it away and jabbed forwards. Before the blade could slide through below Rist's breastplate, he wrapped it in threads of Air, angling it to his left, then pushed threads of Earth into the elf's plate and squeezed, his pulse pounding in his head, fear clenching his heart.

The elf's breastplate held for a moment, then collapsed inwards in a vicious cracking and snapping of bones, blood spraying. A look of shock crossed the elf's face, and then they dropped to the ground.

Rist stood in the chaos, his eyes fixed on the crumpled elf, his drumming heart swallowing the sound of the fighting around him. He lifted his gaze. The elves' Lightning Storms had shattered the Lorian front lines. Everywhere Rist looked, elven spears, swords, and axes carved through Lorian leather, blood soaking the ground. He froze, unable to process the carnage, his hands shaking.

"Form up!" Garramon's voice pushed through the drumming of Rist's heart, and a hand grabbed the collar of Rist's cloak, dragging him back into place. "Dragon's Maw!"

FARDA'S BLADE RASPED AS HE dragged it free from an elven breastplate. He leaned forwards, pushing the elf to the ground, then plunged his sword into the neck of another. His mages held a tight formation around him as they pushed their way through the elven flanks. A little over sixty of them had survived from the battle at Fort Harken, and he counted no more than four or five lost here.

Taya Tambrel's plan was working so far. The elves had done as anticipated and barged through the centre of the Lorian lines, believing their strength to be far superior. And with that, the Lorian mages had crashed through the openings and spread along the flanks, funnelling the elves inwards. *Elven arrogance.*

Horns blew, sharp and short. Five bursts. The horns were answered by a series of earth-shaking roars.

Time for the next step. Hopefully Magnus and the others are in position. Farda opened himself to the Spark, drawing heavily on threads of Earth and Spirit. "Fissure!"

⚮

Eltoar held his breath as every muscle in Helios's body tensed as the dragon lunged upwards, cracking his wings against the air, his body snaking side to side to gain leverage, muscles rippling. A moment later and they were lifting higher, the wind crashing against Eltoar's face from the west.

Over Helios's left wing, the deep red scales of Karakes glistened in the warm sun, Lyina mounted at the nape of her soulkin's neck. Pellenor and Meranta flew to Eltoar's right, wings spread wide, riding the currents of air as they banked left, turning towards the battlefield.

"It worked," Lyina called, her voice funnelled on threads of Air.

Eltoar looked down over the mass of crashing bodies. From atop Helios's back, the separation of elves and men was clear. On the western side, below the foot of the observation tower, the black and red of Loria flowed across the grasslands, smashing into a field of glittering gold armour. At the centre, the black and gold were a chaotic mess. The lines had broken, and the elves were pushing through, emboldened by the bloodshed. That had always been a weakness of elves, one they shared with many of the great predators. If they smelled blood, they were relentless in pursuit of the kill, their arrogance blinding them to their weakness.

As Helios, Karakes, and Meranta swept south, along the edge of the battlefield, Eltoar pulled his and Helios's minds together, seeing through the dragon's eyes. Below, he could see the Lorian Battlemages charging along the elven flanks, funnelling the elves inwards. Then he felt a pulse of the Spark ripple and watched as the Battlemages on either side performed the Fissure movement.

Rumbling cracks sounded as threads of Earth and Spirit burrowed into the ground below, deep fissures ripping through the earth. The fissures spread about ten feet wide, tearing through the elven forces, ripping through rock and clay. From dragonback, Eltoar watched as elves stumbled backwards, some falling, bones breaking. Within moments, the fissures had spread from both flanks and joined in the middle, creating a physical divide in the battlefield and slicing the substantially larger elven forces in half.

On one side, the elves who had pushed forward were now caught between the advancing Lorian forces and a ten foot wide trench of shattered rock, cut off from the main body of their host. On the other side, the remainder of the elven forces were trying desperately to traverse the trench, but it was deep and wide, and the Lorian Mages were preventing the elven mages from closing it.

Eltoar tore his eyes from the battlefield and drew in a deep lungful of air, pressing his forehead against the scales of Helios's neck. There was a time when he would have called these elves his kin. That had changed when he became a Draleid, and it had changed even more with the fall of The Order and the wars that followed. Even if he had still considered them his people, they would not consider him theirs, and there was not a doubt in his mind they would take his head from his shoulders the first chance they could. But none of that meant he would take any pleasure in what was to come. "Må Heraya tuil du ia'sine ael," he whispered. *May Heraya take you into her arms.* Eltoar lifted his head, the icy wind slicing through the slits in his helm, Helios's body shifting beneath him. He let out a resigned sigh, then pulled on threads of Air, channelling his voice to Lyina and Pellenor's ears. "Endryía."

Engage.

With that, the three dragons dropped towards the battlefield, swooping down the cliff face. Eltoar rested his hands on the sides of Helios's neck, their hearts beating as one, their lungs swelling with cool air. The ground rushed towards them, their gaze fixed on the shimmering gold of the elven ranks caught behind the trench. Through Helios's eyes, he could see the realisation setting in on the elves' faces as they looked to the sky. Even as the dragons drew closer, some of the mages were still trying to close the fissures, the Lorian Battlemages holding them back. "Du vyin alura anis. Haydria cianor val diar dauva."

You can rest now. Honour comes with your death.

There was fire in Eltoar's soul as Helios filled his lungs, the pressure building within him, hands clenching, jaw tightening. Then, as one, both Eltoar and Helios let the air free from their lungs. A raging column of dragonfire crashed down into the elven ranks. The force of it tore chunks of earth and clay free. Those who weren't turned to ash and dust were lifted into the air as the mightiest dragon the known world had ever seen cast his fire upon them.

Two more streams of dragonfire poured forth from Karakes and Meranta on either side of Eltoar, and all three dragons angled their wings, sweeping across the battlefield, raking their fire through a sea of shimmering gold. The sheer force from the manoeuvre pressed against Eltoar's body, shaking his bones, but he held on, feeling the rage and bloodlust that seeped from Helios.

A ripple of the Spark pricked in the back of his mind, and arcs of lightning surged upwards from the elven ranks. All three dragons ceased their fire, wheeling and spinning, the lightning sweeping past them. And as more arcs rose, Eltoar felt the Lorian Battlemages doing their part, slicing through the elven threads with the Spark.

"Again," Eltoar whispered, a rumble of acknowledgement from Helios touching the back of his mind. The dragon lifted higher into the air, Karakes rising to his left, Meranta to his right. As they reached the edge of the battlefield, the dragons carried on to where the two remaining rivers joined into the River Caldír, then banked to the right, holding formation as they did, centuries of attunement to one another allowing them to move in perfect synchronisation. The three dragons were three parts of a singular whole.

As they came back around, the damage they had wrought came into view. Streaks of char as wide as two wagons were lined with raging fires as flesh, wood, and earth burned, melted pools of armour clinging to bone.

Eltoar took a brief moment to feel guilt and sorrow, then set the feelings ablaze. The elves still outnumbered the Lorians by a wide margin. "Endryía!"

At the command, the dragons plummeted once more, spreading their wings at the bottom of the dive and unleashing torrents of earth-shaking dragonfire. They were the harbingers of death, the augury of Heraya's embrace.

As flames poured from Helios's jaws, Eltoar opened himself to the Spark and pulled on threads of Spirit and Fire, funnelling them into his soulkin pushing even more power into the dragon's fire. The elves would not break and rout, but if he could cause enough damage to make a tactical retreat a viable option, they might take it.

As the dragons carved paths of fire through the elves, Eltoar looked to where the Lorian forces had closed around the elves who had been trapped by the trench. Cutting off the escape route meant those elves would fight to the death and take as many souls with them as they could. It wasn't an ideal plan, but it was the only one that would give them a chance. The division of the elven forces allowed for limited collateral damage from the dragonfire.

Eltoar jerked forwards as Helios cracked his wings and changed direction to avoid a spear thrown with threads of Air. More spears ripped through the sky as though they had been launched from dwarven Bolt Throwers, but whips of Air and Fire from the Lorian Battlemages tore them out of the air. Even if the mages had not been providing support, hitting a dragon with a spear in full flight was akin to trying to catch the wind. It happened, but it was rare.

As Helios, Karakes, and Meranta reached the far side of the battlefield and swept upwards, a monstrous roar shook the air, and Eltoar's blood turned cold.

Eltoar didn't need to look to Lyina and Pellenor to know they felt the same trepidation. That was a dragon's roar; there was no mistaking it. Seconds passed, the three dragons soaring towards the mountains of Mar Dorul, and then an enormous figure burst from within the cover of the jagged peaks, black as a shadow against the light of the blazing sun, wings spread wide.

"Eltoar?" Threads of Air carried Lyina's voice to Eltoar's ears.

Before Eltoar could even begin to gather his thoughts, another shadow-clad shape, this one even larger than the last, rose from within the mountains, sweeping upwards into the sky.

It cannot be.

Then a third shape emerged, and a fourth, and a fifth... and a sixth.

Chapter Fifty-Three

Broken by Death

It cannot be.

Eltoar's heart clenched as the six winged shapes rose higher, scales glittering in the sunlight. A fist tightened around his lungs, his pulse racing like a galloping horse. He pressed his hands against Helios's scales, the dragon's emotions swirling and crashing in his mind. Loss, anger, awe, shame, confusion. Had more dragons hatched or had these Draleid and their dragons stayed hidden in Lynalion all these centuries? Who were they? Memories of times long past flooded his mind. Faces of the Draleid he had once known. Hundreds of faces – thousands. But those memories were soon replaced by images of blood and fire, by the screams of the dying, and the sight of Ilnaen burning. Guilt was something Eltoar had grown accustomed to, but now, as he watched the dragons soar through the air, wings spread wide, the feeling washed over him in waves.

"Eltoar!"

Lyina's voice echoed in his head, but he ignored her, instead watching as the dragons shifted and plummeted towards the battlefield, ignoring the Dragonguard, thunderous roars rippling through the skies.

Eltoar turned to his right, seeing Pellenor sitting astride Meranta, eyes fixed on the shapes above. He could see the same sense of guilt and loss on Pellenor's face as he felt in his own heart.

"Eltoar!"

As the other dragons dropped low towards the battling armies, Helios, Karakes, and Meranta swept up the side of the cliffs, catching a current of air, then banking left. The entire time, Eltoar didn't take his gaze from the six elven dragons. None of them were even nearly as large as Helios, but each was at the least a measure for Meranta, and two were as large as Karakes.

"Eltoar!" Lyina called once more, anger seeping into her voice. "We need to do something!"

As Lyina's words touched Eltoar's ears, the six dragons dropped low, sweeping over the elven forces, casting dark shadows across the mass of shimmering gold. Eltoar could hear each beat of his heart pounding in his ears. He watched as the dragons spread out. He watched as they approached the fissure that split the battlefield. And he watched as they unleashed rivers of dragonfire down over the Lorian armies. The roar of dragons blended with the screams and shouts that echoed across the plains as the dragonfire carved paths of death and destruction through the Lorian ranks.

All the while, Eltoar just watched. His mind told him to fight. These dragons and Draleid were not his friends. Even if they may once have been, that was true no longer; he had assured that with his own choices. And yet with the hatching of the white dragon and the emergence of the new Draleid, things had shifted within him; there was hope for their kind once more.

"Eltoar, what are you doing?" It was Pellenor who called out this time.

Eltoar made to speak, but no words left his lips. Memories continued to rush through his mind. Tivar's words in the temple at Dracaldryr repeating themselves. *'I will not put another of our kind in the ground. I will not tear another soul in half.'*

"The soldiers are lambs to the slaughter down there, Eltoar," Lyina shouted.

Eltoar turned to Lyina, his body rocking as Helios hammered his wings against the air, holding in place. Eltoar whispered, more to himself than in answer to the others. "They're our kin…"

"I can't just let them die!" Pellenor called out.

Eltoar's throat tightened as he turned to look at Pellenor.

Pellenor shook his head. "I can't." A sombre tone crept into Pellenor's voice. "What are we if we just let them die?"

Before Eltoar could respond, Meranta shifted, cracking her wings against the air, and then she was diving, plummeting towards the battlefield.

Rist crashed to the ground, his knee sinking into the soft earth, panic slithering through his veins. Without a thought, he swung his blade as he turned, the clang of steel reverberating through his arms as the elven spear slammed down. He may have blocked the strike, but the force of it, combined with his precarious position, sent him tumbling backwards, his elbows digging into the blood-sodden earth.

Around him, men and women screamed and howled, the incandescent light of dragonfire blazing.

The elf followed after him, jabbing downwards with his spear, but Rist turned the weapon sideways with a thread of Air, then kicked at the elf's feet, knocking them off balance. Another thread of Air to the elf's chest and they stumbled, crashing to the ground. The elf made to rise, but an obsidian hoof slammed down on their chest as one of the Blackwatch trampled them, charging onwards.

His heart thumping, Rist dragged himself to his feet, heaving in deep lungsful of air. Everything was chaos. When the dragons had appeared above the mountains, the soldiers had cheered. They had thought more of the Dragonguard had come to turn the tide. But when the dragons soared over the elven forces, and drew closer, a wave of panic had rippled through the Lorian armies. Then the fire came, and Rist lost everyone.

Around him, elves and Lorian soldiers hacked and slashed, all semblance of rank broken. As he stepped backwards, still dazed, the ground squelched beneath his feet. He searched the faces of the trampled dead, praying to Heraya that he wouldn't see Neera among them. Even the thought twisted his heart.

Breathe.

Rist clenched his fists around the hilt of his sword, slowing his breaths. But nothing stopped his hands from shaking or his chest from shivering. To his left, he watched as two elves hacked a man to pieces, steel slicing through flesh, a spear plunging into his throat, a sword taking his arm. They were savage, brutal – efficient.

Panicked, Rist turned to see an elf striding through the madness, red cloak billowing, golden armour gleaming. Threads of Fire, Air, Earth, and Spirit whirled about the elf. Whips of Air struck out, snapping necks and breaking bones while a column of fire poured forth from the elf's hand.

Rist stepped backwards, his heel sinking into the blood-sodden mud, then stopped, clenching his jaw. He wanted to be brave, to be strong, but even as he took a step forwards towards the elven mage, his hands shook, and his legs felt as though they had been filled with lead. This was nothing like the practice yard.

A flash of motion to his right, and Anila and Farda Kyrana, along with a clutch of Battlemages, burst from a mass of bodies, threads whirling around them.

Anila charged the elven mage, moving like a wolfpine, low and fast, one sword hung at her hip, the other gripped firmly in her fist. She twisted, narrowly avoiding an arc of lightning, then burst forwards, steel raised.

Farda sliced through the elven mage's threads, cutting them short before they could touch Anila.

Anila reached the elven mage, their swords clashing. As steel crashed against steel, Anila twisted her sword and drove it down through the elf's foot, pinning them to the ground. The elf howled, but even as their screams rang out, Anila shifted past them, slid her second sword from her belt, and took the elf's head from their shoulders.

Rist watched as more elven mages poured through the chaos on the other side, crashing into the Battlemages that had come with Anila and Farda. The concentration of the Spark in that one area set a thrum in the air that Rist could feel in his bones.

As Rist readied himself to charge, he caught movement out of the corner of his eye and twisted at the waist, just in time for steel to slice through the flesh of his left forearm, above the vambrace. At first, he barely felt anything, then the wound burned as though he had been cut with fire. He let out a howl as he stumbled backwards, his right hand still gripped around the hilt of his sword.

The elf who had attacked him pushed the advantage, lunging with their curved blade, intent on emptying Rist's innards onto the mud.

Rist tripped over something, his feet slipping. Panic permeated everything: it snaked into his mind, trembled in his hands, wrapped around his heart, and hardened in his legs. He kept himself upright by sheer force of will, his eyes flitting back and forth as men and elves ripped each other apart. He swung his blade up frantically, trying to take the encroaching elf off guard, but the elf was too quick and blocked his swing with ease, knocking Rist's blade from his hands before swinging for his head.

Rist threw himself backwards to avoid the elven steel but felt its sting as the blade sliced him from chin to lip, the coppery taste of blood filling his mouth. Rist's back foot slid on the muddy earth, and he dropped to one knee, dread turning his veins to ice. He lifted his gaze to see the elf closing him down, curved sword raised above their head, arcing through the air.

His heart drumming in his ears, he reached out to the Spark and let his instincts take control. He pulled on threads of Water and Earth, pushing them into the ground beneath the elf's feet. He dragged the moisture from the sodden earth, pooling it one place, softening the mud even more, then pulled with threads of Earth, sucking the elf downwards. A moment of confusion touched the elf's face. Where they had expected to find solid ground, their lead foot sank into mud. Fear pushing him forward, Rist lunged, almost collapsing as his back foot slid on the mud. He threw himself forward, ramming his shoulder into the elf's chest.

The pair crashed into the blood-soaked earth, the elf howling, their trapped legs giving off a terrible snapping sound. Rist scrambled atop the elf, straddling them. His first thought was to strike down with his sword, but he no longer held it in his grasp. A sharp pain exploded in the side of his head, and Rist reached down, almost blind with the stars blurring across his vision. He wrapped his fingers around the elf's throat, squeezing. *Don't let go. Don't let go.* Another punch slammed into his ribs, knocking the wind from his lungs. He squeezed tighter, the elf thrashing beneath him, his knees sliding on the wet earth. As he squeezed and squeezed, the elf's helmet slipped from their head, and Rist found himself staring back at a face that looked no older than his. Her golden hair was tied tight, and her soft features were free of dirt and blood.

The elf stared back at him. Rist loosened his fingers, a feeling of revulsion crawling over his skin at what he was doing. And in that moment, the elf shifted, and a piercing pain erupted in Rist's upper back. The shock alone caused Rist to jerk backwards. He drew in short breaths, his head spinning. Then the pain redoubled as whatever the elf had stabbed into his back was pulled free.

Panic consuming him, Rist remembered the dagger Garramon had given him. He reached his hand to his hip, fingers fumbling, and pulled the dagger free. The hilt in his grasp, he grabbed the elf's forearm, slamming it down into the sodden earth, seeing the glint of steel in the elf's hand. With the elf's arm pinned, Rist slammed the dagger into the pit of her elbow, feeling the blade scrape against bone as it drove the whole way through. He twisted the hilt – as he had read to do in *Killing,* by Taran Kovak – slicing through the arteries and veins. In a frantic rush, he yanked the dagger free, blood pumping from the wound, then plunged it into the elf's neck.

The elf's eyes widened, her mouth gaping as she clasped her free hand to her neck. Rist twisted the dagger, pushing it deeper with all his strength. The elf thrashed beneath him, her mouth filling with blood, her eyes bulging. After a moment, the thrashing stopped and the elf's body went limp.

Rist felt a pull from the pendant around his neck. He could *feel* the Essence leaving the elf's body. He hesitated, fear and uncertainty burning within. But Fane's words rang in his mind. '*Through this tether, the Essence spilled so that the loss of each life could be recycled; from death could come life anew.*' Rist opened his mind, and for a fleeting moment his entire body went cold, pain vanishing, air fleeing his lungs. The gemstone set into the pommel of the dagger glowed furiously with a bright red light.

Rist heaved the dagger free, stumbling backwards as he hauled himself to his feet, slipping in the mud. His breaths shivered as he stared at the dagger, at the black leather handle, at the roaring lion heads carved into the crossguard, and finally at the glowing red gemstone set into the circular pommel. His hands shook as he continued to stumble aimlessly backwards.

He looked back to the elf, lifeless on the ground, a shard of bone protruding from her left shin where her legs had been trapped in the earth.

A series of roars erupted in the sky, and Rist lifted his gaze to see the dragons circling back, wings spread wide, casting dark shadows. He stopped in his tracks, unable to move, his body frozen. He stood and watched as pillars of fire spewed forth from the dragons' jaws, sweeping across the battlefield towards him.

He wanted to move, but his body didn't respond to his commands.

The dragonfire drew closer, the force of the immense power seeming to shake the air itself, the smell of burning flesh and charred earth drowning out Rist's senses.

He trembled, his throat tightening. As the dragons drew even closer, their flames raking across the battlefield, Rist's feet finally responded, and he stumbled backwards, tripping over something but holding himself upright. He looked down to see the eyes of a dead man staring back at him. Fear squeezed his lungs and clenched his heart as he lifted his gaze. The dragonfire was close enough for him to feel its heat, to feel its fury.

"Rist!"

Something crashed into Rist lifting him off his feet, and then he slammed into the earth, his head spinning, stars flitting across his eyes. Rist snapped his eyes shut as howls and cries rang out, the earth shook, and the light of the dragonfire burned like the sun.

"Stay down!" Whoever had tackled Rist to the ground now lay on top of him, their body splayed across him as the dragonfire swept around them.

After a few moments, the earth ceased its shaking, and the sound of cascading flames yielded to the aching moans and wails of those still alive. A fist gripped Rist's cloak and dragged him forwards, a hand resting on his cheek, prying his eye open.

"Rist, look at me. Are you hurt?"

Rist's vision was blurry. His eyes strained, but he kept them open as a hand patted at his sides, arms, and shoulders, searching him for wounds. As his vision focused, he found Garramon kneeling over him. The man's face was streaked with blood and cracked dirt. Rist saw worry in his eyes. Rist coughed as he tried to speak, his throat dry and cracked. "I'm all right."

Garramon nodded, letting out a long breath. He met Rist's gaze, his expression hardening. "Never freeze like that again. Ever. There is no quicker way to find Heraya's embrace." Garramon shifted backwards onto his haunches, then reached out and grasped Rist's arm, pulling both of them upright.

Streaks of blackened earth raked the ground around them, fires burning, bodies of elves and men alike charred and crackling, armour melted.

Between streaks of burnt earth, men and elves were lifting themselves back to their feet, readying themselves for the fight to continue. Rist turned towards where the fissure had split the battlefield, seeing a mass of golden armour shimmering in the sunlight, marching forwards. The elves had closed the fissure.

An air-shaking roar erupted overhead, and Rist looked up to see two dragons crashing together with the force of colliding stars. Fire streaked and jaws snapped, talons raking scales and raining blood.

∽

COLD FINGERS WRAPPED AROUND ELTOAR's heart as he watched Meranta crash into one of the smaller elven dragons, one with vivid green scales and wings of pale blue. It had been centuries since he had seen dragon fight dragon, and watching it now filled him with a sense of dread. He drew in a deep breath, a tremble setting into his hands, Tivar's words once more ringing in his ears. *'I have fed the earth with too much blood. I will not put another one of us in the ground.'*

Eltoar shook his head. The past was the past. No matter how long he lingered there, it would not change. He needed to deal with the present, with what was in front of him. And right now, Pellenor wouldn't even last minutes without Eltoar and Lyina. Eltoar set his jaw. He would defend his own, no matter the cost. A deep rumble resonated through Helios, a primal fire dulled by a resigned sadness. "Endryía." *Engage.*

Helios's body shifted, wings angling, and then the dragon dove towards Meranta and the others. The great dragon unleashed a monstrous roar that rippled across the sky, sending dull vibrations resonating through Eltoar's bones. In his periphery, he could see Lyina and Karakes matching them on their left, red scales shimmering. "Engage, but don't kill." he called out, threads of Air carrying his voice. "Not unless you have to. They are our kin. We just need to distract them long enough to cover the retreat."

If more of our kind have survived…

"They will not spare us the same grace, Eltoar." Lyina said nothing more, and Eltoar didn't respond. They both understood. If these Draleid and dragons were truly survivors of The Fall, then they would bear no love for the Dragonguard. They were the last vestiges of a dying race, but in Eltoar's heart, he feared he had shed too much blood for their kind to ever truly be whole again. For now, all he could do was hope.

Wind whipped past Eltoar's face, crashing over Helios's scales, their minds drifting together, their hearts beating as one. In life, they were two halves of a whole, two souls merged, each body an extension of the other.

A dragon with scales of muted yellow ripped through a cloud to Eltoar's left, jaws opening, the flickers of fire forming in their mouth. But before the dragonfire could be set free, Karakes crashed into the creature's side, dark talons tearing through yellow scales, jaws wrapping around the smaller dragon's neck. Karakes opened his jaws and bathed the dragon with fire, flames washing over yellow scales. As the dragons hurtled through the air, a deep sorrow flooded Eltoar and Helios's joint mind. To be fighting kin once more was not something they had ever hoped for. They pushed the sorrow aside, focusing forwards. They would try to find a peace. They had to try.

THE HORNS OF RETREAT BELLOWED in Farda's ears. Around him, men and women fled for their lives, staggering through the charred fields of the dead. Cries and wails rang out, the last breaths of the dying – the sounds Farda recognized as the true song of war.

Farda stood amidst the chaos, but he cared not for what was happening on the ground; his concern was in the skies. He watched as the dragons tore strips from each other, plumes of fire streaking across the sky. Had the elven dragons been hiding in the woodland of Lynalion all this time? Or had they been hatched? The answer to that question could change everything. Though Farda thought it unlikely the dragons had been hatched, simply by the way they moved in the air. These dragons knew war; they had lived it. More likely they had stayed hidden in Lynalion, waiting until the empire was at its weakest, until the Dragonguard's numbers had dwindled.

"We need to go." Ilyain's voice rang in Farda's ears as his fellow Rakina rested his hand on his shoulder. "The battle is lost, my friend. Eltoar and the others are fighting to buy us time. We would do well not to squander it. The elves are licking their wounds now, but if we linger they will sweep forwards."

Even without his sight, Ilyain saw more than most.

Farda clenched his jaw, glancing back at Ilyain's unerring stare before turning towards the sky once more. Even with Helios, there was little chance Eltoar, Pellenor, and Lyina would be capable of prevailing against six fully grown dragons without suffering themselves. "Gunild? Hala?"

"Gunild no longer walks the mortal plane. She flies with Borallis once more."

Farda turned at the sound of Hala's voice. The woman's white hair was tarnished with a mixture of wet and dry blood, her cloak in tatters. The sight of his old friend released a knot of tension in Farda's muscles, but the words she spoke pulled at his core. Gunild was dead. Another of his kin, gone. His heart ached, and even that brief moment of sorrow set his hairs on end. It had been centuries since he'd felt an emotion like that. Centuries since Shinyara had stripped him of that ability when she left the mortal plane. Only since finding Ella had even the slightest sliver of the ability to care returned to him.

"Draleid n'aldryr," he whispered, almost to himself, resting his hand over his heart, his throat tightening.

"Rakina nai dauva," Ilyain and Hala answered, resting their hands over their hearts.

Farda tapped his fingers against the coin in his pocket, looking from Ilyain to Hala, then out towards the dragonfire-raked battlefield. "We cover the retreat," he said, letting out a short breath. "The elves have taken heavy losses themselves, but we know what happens when they smell blood." Before turning, Farda cast his gaze towards the sky once more, to where Helios, Karakes, and Meranta swirled around the elven dragons, jaws snapping, talons raking. *May the gods watch over you, my friends. Draleid n'aldryr, Rakina nai dauva.*

ELTOAR CAST A GLANCE DOWN towards the battlefield. The Lorian forces were in full retreat now, streaks of charred earth and lingering fire marking where the elven dragons had ripped their ranks asunder. But the elves had also taken grave losses and looked to be consolidating. All Eltoar and his Dragonguard needed to do was give the Lorian forces the chance to regroup into a stronger position while they fell back. Without the dragons overhead, the elves likely wouldn't sweep forwards. Elven battle tactics were aggressive, but they still valued life.

Eltoar pulled his gaze back towards the sky and a drew in a deep breath, pressing his hands into the scales of Helios's neck. Ahead, Meranta and the green-scaled dragon snapped at each other, talons raking, plumes of fire streaking through the skies. A number of bloody tears marred Meranta's sandy wings, but a gaping wound ran the length of the green dragon's side, blood trailing in the wind. Two more dragons circled, a smaller dragon with a deep blue colouring, and a golden-scaled dragon as large as Karakes, with wings of pale cream. The two circling dragons snapped at Meranta, but mostly held back for she was entangled with the smaller green dragon. He looked past the two circling dragons, his eyes fixed on Green Scales. *Pull them apart.*

Helios let out a bone-shaking roar that earned the attention of the two circling dragons, who scattered, unwanting to face Helios head on. He cracked his enormous wings, shifting in the air as his legs swept forwards. Helios crashed into the green dragon's side, one talon wrapping around the creature's neck, the other breaking through the scales on their ribs and anchoring into flesh.

With another roar, Helios cracked his wings and heaved the dragon free from Meranta, snatching it like an eagle would a hare. The smaller dragon thrashed and snapped, dragonfire pouring from its jaws, but Helios simply spread his wings, catching the air current and using the momentum to launch the green dragon through the sky. The smaller dragon tumbled through the air in a tangle of wings, streaks of blood whipping in their wake.

Before Eltoar had a chance to do anything, the two circling dragons swept forward. Both the golden-scaled dragon and the smaller blue dragon missed Helios by only a few handspans as they swooped in from either side, jaws snapping shut. Despite Helios's size, he was quick in the air, several lifetimes worth of warfare honing his senses sharper than any blade. As Helios banked left, angling his body for another sharp turn, Eltoar pulled on threads of Air and amplified his voice through the skies. "Brothers, sisters. Enough of our kind dine in Achyron's halls. There are few of us left. Let us not make that number even smaller."

No response came. All Eltoar heard was the crashing wind as Helios tore through the air, the golden dragon and the blue dragon close behind. Above, he saw Karakes's red scales shimmering as the dragon weaved between the other three elven dragons, Lyina's threads of Air and Spirit whipping back and forth, slicing through threads cast by the other Draleid.

Eltoar glanced back in time to see two columns of dragonfire searing towards them. "Rise!"

The force of Helios's sharp upwards turn pressed Eltoar against the dragon's scales. Were it not for the power that moulded Helios's scales to Eltoar's presence, he would have been thrown hurtling backwards.

"We need to disengage!" Pellenor's voice rang in Eltoar's ears as Meranta drew up alongside Helios, the pair of dragons breaking in and out of the clouds. Blood streaked from a number of wounds along Meranta's side and back, and a long gash was ripped through her right wing.

"Agreed. Lyina and Karakes," Eltoar called back. He didn't wait for a response. Without a word, Helios cracked his mighty wings against the air and turned back on himself, making towards where Karakes was attempting to break free from the three elven dragons. If not for Karakes's size and ferocity, the other dragons would have torn him to shreds already. But as it was, he was just about holding his own.

As Helios and Meranta drew closer, soaring in a tight formation, both dragons roared – a warning they would not have given if they had desired to kill. One of the smaller dragons, with vibrant purple scales, broke away, spiralling down, but the other two redoubled their efforts to rip Karakes from the sky.

Helios focused in on the larger of the two: a deep-chested dragon with crimson scales and a long neck. Pressure built deep within Helios, sending energy rippling through the bond. Then, Helios unleashed a torrent of orange-red dragonfire. As the crimson-scaled dragon twisted and turned, desperately trying to avoid the touch of Helios's raging flames, Helios crashed into the creature's side, wrapping his jaws around the dragon's long neck. Using his momentum, Helios bit down and hauled the red scaled dragon through the air, pulling them away from the fighting. As the dragon thrashed, Helios tore strips through their right wing, ripping the membrane apart in sprays of blood – a wound that could be recovered from, with the aid of Healers, but one that would take them out of this fight.

Helios released the shrieking dragon from his grasp and let it spiral towards the ground. Eltoar turned his head to see Karakes and Meranta snapping at the smaller dragon with scales black as jet. He looked about, trying to locate the remaining elven dragons. Counting the dragon whose wing Helios had just shredded, there should have been four more. But thick clouds had begun to fill the sky, and visibility was low. This was the ideal point to fall back. They had given the armies ample time to retreat and regroup.

"Fall back!" Eltoar called out, using threads of Air to funnel his voice to Lyina and Pellenor. Without hesitation, Karakes and Meranta disengaged from the black dragon and doubled back towards Eltoar.

An arc of lightning ripped through the air, missing Meranta by the breadth of a hair. A flash of gold followed the lightning, streaking across the sky, and then the large elven dragon was crashing into Meranta's flank, ripping and tearing with tooth and talon. The golden dragon was larger than Meranta, larger even than Karakes, and more powerful by a distance. Eltoar's screams had barely left his throat by the time the creature had ripped Meranta's left wing clean from her body. The dragon's shrieks and wails twisted Eltoar's heart.

Two more streaks flashed through the sky, and two of the elven dragons collided with Karakes, preventing him and Lyina from going to Meranta's aid.

The roar that left Helios's throat shook the air, and a rage seared the bond, rippling from Helios to Eltoar, consuming them both, burning in their veins, pushing back the agony. A dragon's rage was a powerful thing. But if left unchecked, it could cause devastation the likes of which many could only imagine. The Draleid was the balance. Eltoar was the ice to Helios's fire. But now, as Helios tore through the skies towards Meranta and the golden dragon, Eltoar leaned into that rage, opened his heart to the fire.

With each passing moment, he felt pieces of his already broken heart shatter. A beat of Helios's wings, and he watched as the golden dragon ripped open Meranta's chest. A thump of his heart, and his body clenched at the sight of the beast's jaws locking around Meranta's throat, ripping and tearing, blood pluming into the air as the dragons spiralled downwards.

"No…" Eltoar couldn't hear his own words over the roaring of the wind and the roaring of dragons, but the pain in his heart was a physical, tangible thing. Meranta and Pellenor were his kin. No, they were more than kin; they were fragments of his soul, remnants of who he had once been. And as he watched them fall from the sky, Helios's rage consumed him. "Rip them from the sky."

Helios answered with a thunderous roar before crashing into the golden dragon with the force of a falling mountain. His strength burned in Eltoar's veins, and Eltoar pushed their minds even deeper together, rage and fury flooding every corner of their soul. They were fire and fury. They were death and deliverance.

He roared at the top of his lungs as Helios opened his jaws and clamped them around the golden dragon's body. So vast was their size difference that Helios's bite near tore the creature in half, his teeth ripping through the Draleid's torso as they sat at the nape of their soulkin's neck.

The bond ignited, Eltoar could feel bones break and scales shatter as Helios bit down with all his strength. The dragon thrashed his head from side to side, ripping the golden dragon's chest to pieces and tearing the Draleid in two at the same time. Helios pulled his talons forwards and sank them into the golden dragon's back. At the same time, he wrapped his jaws around their neck. Then, in one smooth motion, he ripped the dragon's neck from their body, blood spraying in the wind. With both the dragon and the Draleid torn from the world, Helios let their bodies fall and unleashed a roar that was equal parts fury and sorrow, the pain of seeing Pellenor and Meranta fall still burning within.

Shrieks and roars answered, and the remaining elven dragons fell on Helios with a fury. Jaws snapped and talons raked as the five dragons tore at Helios and Eltoar, arcs of lightning ripping through the air, whips of Fire cracking, threads of Air attempting to pull Eltoar free from his soulkin's back. But for every wound Helios took, he gave twice over. Eltoar rocked from side to side, jerking forwards and back as his soulkin twisted through the air. He weaved threads of Spirit, Fire, and Air around them, redirecting rivers of dragonfire while slicing through the other Draleid's threads. His heart was cold fury. They had taken Pellenor and Meranta from this world, and in doing so they had shorn the word mercy from Eltoar's mind. He roared, sending an arc of lightning crashing into the chest of the purple-scaled dragon, and then the iron tang of blood touched his lips as Helios tore into the tail of the smaller green dragon.

The blue elven dragon hammered into Helios's side, talons tearing. But as quickly as the dragon had attacked, it was ripped free by Karakes who burst through a bank of clouds, anguish seeping through his roar. Karakes collided with the blue dragon, thrashing and clawing.

Helios bit down harder on the green dragon's tail and swung them through the air like a plaything, ripping the tail free and launching them upwards. As the green dragon flailed and flapped, their wings fighting against the force of the upward motion, Karakes circled back, cracked his wings, opened his jaws, and tore the creature in half, ripping into its flesh, tearing its wings asunder.

As the broken remnants of the green dragon fell to the earth, the three remaining elven dragons wheeled away, their shrieks piercing the sound of the crashing wind.

Eltoar's heart thumped against his ribs so hard he feared they might break. His body shook from head to toe. He tried to swallow, but his throat was dry as sand. In his mind's eye, he watched the golden dragon tear Meranta to pieces. The thought snatched the air from Eltoar's lungs, and Helios unleashed an agony-wrought roar. With the roar, the fury that had burned in Eltoar's veins subsided, replaced by complete and utter sorrow. The grief that gripped him was such a physical thing that he collapsed against Helios's scales, his heart aching, eyes burning.

Weightlessness set into Eltoar's stomach, and he jerked backwards as Helios folded his wings and plummeted towards the ground with aban-don. Through the dragon's eyes, Eltoar could see a blood-soaked crater in the earth below, at the western edge of the battlefield, near the River Dalwin, where Meranta had crashed down. Lyina and Karakes were al-ready below them, Karakes's red wings spreading wide as he alighted on a clear patch of earth.

Eltoar slid from Helios's back before the dragon touched the ground. Dust and dirt spiraled into the air as his feet touched down, knees bend-ing, threads of Air and Earth preventing his legs from snapping with the impact. He drew a long, rasping breath into his lungs, then lifted himself to his full height, his chest tightening as his gaze fell on Lyina, who knelt by the crater, wailing, shoulders convulsing, her helmet lying on the ground beside her.

She turned at the sound of Eltoar's footsteps, her eyes raw and red, tear-carved paths running through the blood on her face. Karakes stood over the crater, soft whimpers escaping his chest as he touched his snout against Meranta's broken body.

It was only when Eltoar drew closer he saw that Lyina held Pellenor's head against her lap, his body splayed out on the ground before her. Lyina looked as though she was trying to speak, but all that escaped her throat were sobs and whimpers.

Eltoar dropped to the ground beside her, his gauntleted hand resting against her cheek. He could feel the tears streaming from his eyes, but he made no motion to stay them. He reached out and rested his palm on Pellenor's lifeless body. "I am sorry, my friend. I am so sorry…"

CHAPTER FIFTY-FOUR

FAMILY BY CHOICE

Dann wiped the sweat from his brow and drew a long breath in through his nostrils, holding it in his chest, allowing it to swell and grow before exhaling it in a single, "donkeyballs." He shook his head, looking down at the small wooden carving in his hand. He'd been working on this particular carving since before the sun had risen that morning. And now, as the sun sat just above the western horizon, what was supposed to be a carving of a kat resting atop a thick branch instead looked like a dead, beaten cow that had collapsed on a barn door – and even that was being generous. He shrugged, puffing out his cheeks in exasperation. If he told Therin he had always been intending to carve a cow, maybe the elf might be impressed. But he could already hear Therin's voice in his head. *'A valúr is not for the admiration of others, Dann. It is to understand creation so that we may better appreciate the loss that comes with destruction. Blah, blah, blah…'*

It was only when Dann saw Therin shifting where he sat – a few feet to Dann's right – that Dann realised he had said the inside part out loud.

The elf stared back at Dann, an eyebrow raised, a tin of charcoal sticks resting precariously on his knee and a small sketchbook in his hand.

Dann pursed his lips and gave Therin an acknowledging nod, holding eye contact until Therin frowned, shook his head, and went back to working away on his sketchbook. The elf's hand moved across the page with a level of unconscious thought that Dann could never have replicated in his wildest dreams. Sketching seemed as effortless to Therin as breathing.

Dann let out a sigh, leaning forwards so his forearms rested on his knees, shifting his arse in an attempt to relieve some of the natural irritation that came with sitting atop the dried out husk of a fallen tree. He tossed his lump of mutilated wood from one hand to the other, then stood, patting the small shavings from his trousers. He made his way across the camp towards where Drunir stood with Aeson and Therin's horses, tethered to a post, drinking from a heavy wooden barrel. The heat that came with being so close to the Burnt Lands meant that the three horses had spent so much time with their muzzles plunged in water, Dann was beginning think they had given up and decided to become fish – a decision he envied.

As he made his way to Drunir, the dried and cracked earth snapping beneath his boots, Dann cast his gaze across the rest of the camp. It had been weeks since Baldon had brought news that Calen had not only emerged on the other side of the Burnt Lands but had also re-entered with a large party at his back. In the wake of that news, more elves had been sent from Aravell to stand watch along the edges of the Burnt Lands in case Calen and the others emerged from somewhere other than where they had first entered. Most were currently performing that task, but some still lingered around the camp, cooking food over spits, sharpening steel, resting, and, in general, looking more regal in their flowing green cloaks than any living thing had a right to.

For Dann, having so many elves around only served to highlight Alea and Lyrei's absence. The pair had not returned after Lyrei had been taken to the healers in Aravell. When Dann had asked the other elves how Lyrei was recovering, most had simply ignored the question, while others had given nothing more than short answers saying that she was well. He had thought to ask Therin, but he already knew the answer would be heavily skewed towards some babble about honour, as it almost always was. When they did finally return to Aravell, he would make a point of finding Alea and Lyrei himself.

A snort from Drunir pulled Dann's attention away from the elves and back towards the horse. He couldn't help but smile as the horse lifted his head from the barrel and shook it side to side, whinnying, water dripping from his muzzle. "Come here, you."

He patted Drunir on the cheek, the horse's hair soft against his fingers, then touched his forehead against Drunir's muzzle. "How are you feeling? You can't still be thirsty. You've drunk your body weight today."

The horse snorted, leaning his head against Dann's. There was something about Drunir that gave Dann a sense of calm he'd never truly experienced before – a peacefulness. Letting out a short laugh, he scratched at Drunir's cheek with his left hand, while extending his right hand along the horse's neck and shoulders, checking him over. "You really are a handsome bastard, aren't you?"

Drunir snorted, and Dann continued to stroke the horse's neck and muzzle while looking towards the edge of the camp, near the tents, where Aeson and Baldon stood alongside the newcomers who had arrived only a couple of days before – two of which, Dann had already met: Asius and Senas.

The two giants stood either side of Aeson, half again taller than he was, making him look as though he were nothing more than a child at their side. Dann had forgotten quite how massive the pair were. He'd also forgotten their skin was blue. Which, in hindsight, should have been a difficult thing to forget. But given everything that happened since meeting the giants in Ölm Forest, he figured he'd cut himself some slack. Though in truth, their skin was more a pale icy blue than it was the deep blue of the oceans or the sky – he wasn't sure if that made a difference, but it made him feel better to think it did.

The other newcomers were more Angan. There were five in total – and Baldon, who made six. One of the Angan was from Baldon's clan, Fenryr. Aneera was her name. The other four looked as though they were from a different species entirely. Therin had said they were part of a clan called Dvalin. They stood a measure for Baldon and Aneera in height, they had faces and fur, and when in their human-like shape, they walked on two legs – but that was about all the similarity they shared. Fur as white as snow covered their bodies, and their faces were soft and broad. Their eyes were like those of deer: reddish brown with a black pupil in the shape of an oval that ran laterally. Coal-black antlers veined with gold grew from the front of their heads, folding backwards and rising just slightly. Their legs were double hinged, like a goat's or a deer's, which meant they walked awkwardly on two feet, which were actually hooves. Now that he looked more closely, he was sure that the enormous white stag ridden by the elven captain that night in the Darkwood during the Urak attack had been one of these creatures in their more animal form. *Shapeshifting wolves and stags… how in Elyara's name did I get here?*

Apparently Aneera and Asius had helped Calen escape from the High Lord in Drifaien. Even the thought of that twisted in Dann's chest a little. He let out a sigh through his nose, resting his forehead against Drunir's neck. Dann, Calen, and Rist had been friends since as long as Dann could remember. Brothers, more than friends. He couldn't think of a time in his life he had not been able to turn to Calen and Rist. They were the only people who put up with his endless questions, his inability to ever make the right decision, the fact he somehow always ended up in the wrong place at the wrong time, and his tendency to rub people in every wrong way imaginable. They had always been there for him – always. And what had he done to repay them? Nothing but let them down when they needed him. It was he who had gotten so drunk he couldn't fight back that night Fritz and the others jumped him and Calen. It was he who had led Rist and Calen to the bear's den in Ölm. It was always him. Ever since they were young, it had always been Dann who had gotten them all in trouble.

And then he had allowed Aeson and the others to convince him to leave Rist with Dahlen in Camylin. Now Rist was gone, and if Dann was being honest with himself, he knew that Rist was likely dead. And all this time, since Belduar had fallen, Calen had been on his own: lost, running, and imprisoned. And now all Dann could do was stand around like a spare thumb, waiting, useless, hoping that Calen would come charging over the ridge that fronted the Burnt Lands. He'd never felt so helpless in his entire life. He was a fuckup – he knew that. He always had been, and likely always would be. But he had always worked damn hard to make sure he would be able to help those around him when they needed him. How many hours had he spent learning the bow? Learning to hunt and track, to cook and forage? Thousands.

Dann shook his head, allowing himself a weak half-smile as Drunir snorted again, nuzzling him. "I'm all right," he said, scratching at Drunir's neck, much to the horse's contentment. He pushed the thoughts to the back of his mind. "I'll *be* all right."

Sighing must have been the only thing his body knew how to do that day, for once again Dann found himself tilting his head back and letting out a long drawn-out sigh, the blazing sun warm against his cheeks.

"How is he?"

Dann turned to see Therin walking towards him, green cloak trailing just above the dusty ground. The elf lifted a waterskin to his lips, drinking deep before handing it to Dann.

"Still has a better sense of humour than you, if that's what you're asking." Dann laughed as he took the waterskin from Therin, smiling to let the elf know he was only joking. Though, he wasn't joking entirely; for a horse, Drunir had a surprisingly good sense of humour.

"And he's still better looking than you," Therin said, cupping his hand at the side of Drunir's left cheek. Drunir snorted, shaking his head side to side.

Dann pulled the opening of the waterskin from his mouth, narrowing his eyes at Drunir. "Traitor."

Drunir shifted – not at Dann's words, but at something else. The horse stepped backwards, snorting loudly, bracing his neck upwards, eyes widening and nostrils flaring. It was the first time Dann had seen Drunir truly startled. The other horses followed suit, stamping and snorting, attempting to pull free from their tethers.

"Whoa, boy. Easy," Dann reached out a hand, but Drunir shook his head taking another step back. "*Easy*," Dann repeated. "What in the gods has gotten into you?"

Drunir snorted again but seemed to calm a little, allowing Dann's hand to rest on his cheek, but the other horses continued as they were. Dann turned to Therin but saw the elf was staring in the direction of the setting sun. He made to speak only to notice that Aeson and the others had moved and were looking at the sky in the same direction as Therin. The elves who had stayed in the camp had also all stopped what they were doing.

Therin reached to his hip, wrapping his fingers around the hilt of his sword, which set a knot in Dann's stomach. He'd left his own sword, along with his bow and arrows, in his tent – something he now vowed he would never do again.

"Therin, what is it?" As Dann spoke, he heard what the others must already have: the beating of wings.

"A dragon."

Dann didn't have to be told to know Therin was using the Spark. The elf always tended to have a look of singular focus on his face every time he did.

Dann swallowed hard, stepping closer to Drunir, running his hand along the horse's muzzle. Then he saw it. A dark shape rose from behind a cracked hill to the west, sweeping towards the sky, the sun at its back casting it in shadow. The dragon twisted, turning in the air and diving, spreading its wings as it drew closer to the ground. It was coming straight for them.

"Therin?" Dann's pulse quickened, his chest tightening. Drunir shuffled beside him, snorting.

"It might be Calen and Valerys." Therin didn't take his eyes from the dragon.

"That? That thing up there might be Valerys?" Dann stared at Therin with a look of incredulity, then turned back towards the sky. The last time Dann had laid eyes on Valerys, the dragon had been no bigger than a small horse – a fire-breathing, scale-covered horse with wings, razor-sharp teeth, and a proclivity for killing things, but a horse, none-theless. The dragon that soared towards them was massive; not that Dann knew what constituted massive when it came to dragons.

The dragon soared across the sky, wings spread wide, the glow of the sun still making it difficult to determine anything other than the creature's shape.

"*Therin…?*" Dann shifted back another step. The closer the creature drew, the larger it became.

A smile spread across Therin's face, and the elf shook his head, bringing his hand away from the hilt of his sword.

It took Dann a few moments to see what Therin had seen, but as the dragon shifted in the air, the sun caught its scales at just the right angle to reveal a colouring of pure white fading to black. "… Valerys."

The dragon dropped low, then rose and swept overhead, disappearing over the ridge at Dann's back, spirals of dust whipping into the air in its wake. All eyes in the camp followed Valerys's flight, and silence descended. Seconds passed where the only thing Dann could hear was the beating of his own heart. Then another wingbeat sounded.

Thump.

A gust of wind swept overhead as Valerys came back into view, wings angled as he circled around the camp. The dragon cracked his wings once more, then dropped to the ground only twenty or so paces from Dann, brittle earth snapping beneath his weight, dust spiralling.

If Dann hadn't been sure the dragon was Valerys up to that point, he was certain once the dragon turned towards him, pale lavender eyes regarding him with curiosity. "It is you…"

Dann took a few steps forwards, doing nothing to hide his awe. The dragon had to have been at least forty feet from head to tail, with a wingspan over twice that. He was easily three times larger than last Dann had laid eyes on him. His chest deeper and broader, his neck thicker. The horns that framed his face were as long as Dann's feet, and about half as wide as his forearm.

Valerys let out a low rumble, lowering his head towards Dann and pulling back his lips to reveal rows of sharp teeth as big as knives. Even the dragon's head was now wider than Dann's shoulders. Valerys looked as though he could tear a horse in half with a single bite. Somehow the dragon managed to look more ferocious and feral than Dann remembered, while at the same time developing a sense of violent grace and beauty that all large predators seemed to possess.

This was not the small creature that had crawled from the egg all that time ago. This was a creature of immense power, strange nobility, and deep intelligence. This was a dragon of old. A dragon of legend.

Before Dann could get any closer, shouts rang out, some of the elves pointing in the direction Valerys had come.

"Calen." Dann's heart stopped.

Valerys lifted his head at the sound of Calen's name, turning his neck towards the setting sun. There, in the distance, cresting a small hill, were the shapes of people.

Dann hadn't realised he was running before he heard the sound of the dry earth cracking beneath his feet. He'd dropped Therin's waterskin. His pulse drummed in his ears. His lungs burned.

As he drew closer, the figures had crested the top of the hill and were now coming down the other side. There had to be at least fifty of them. Had they all crossed the Burnt Lands? How? For the first time in his life, Dann pushed the questions to the back of his mind. He just kept running.

"Calen?"

Those in the group had already been staring at Dann as he ran at them, but as his voice echoed out, the group stopped entirely. A voice called back, "Dann?"

A moment passed, and then a man stepped to the front of the group, a hooded cloak draped around his shoulders and up over his head. Then he was running, his hood blowing back.

Dann crashed into Calen with all the caution of a blind bull, the collision knocking the air from his lungs. He wrapped his arms around his friend, squeezing as hard as he could, feeling Calen do the same. "I thought I'd lost you."

Calen pulled Dann in tighter, held the embrace, then pulled away. The face that Dann looked upon was familiar yet different. It was leaner, tarnished by exposure to the elements and more than a few thin, new scars. But more than that, there was something different in Calen's stare – it was harder, colder. Then, as Dann held Calen's gaze, he realised something else was different: Calen's eyes had changed colour.

The corners of Calen's mouth pulled upwards into a weak smile, then fell back to a thin line, sadness touching his face. "I tried, Dann."

"You tried what?" Dann shook his head a little, his hands clasped on Calen's shoulders. He knew he looked at Calen as though he were looking at a ghost, but there was nothing he could do to help it.

"When I got free, I went looking for him." Calen looked at his feet, then back up, his eyes pleading. "I'm sorry I didn't come to you first. I knew Aeson never would have let me leave if I did. It was my only chance to try and find him. I needed to try."

"Rist…" Every muscle in Dann's body tightened, and he held his breath. He pulled his gaze from Calen and frantically searched the faces of those who stood at his friend's back. He saw two of the elves who had been set to watch the Burnt Lands, as well as Vaeril and Erik, along with another man he recognised but couldn't put a name to. They looked a bit worse for wear, but they were alive. That was what mattered. More than a handful of those gathered looked as though they'd just crawled free from the void, hooded cloaks drawn up over their heads. "Is he…"

Calen shook his head before Dann could finish the sentence. "He wasn't there." Calen looked down again. "He wasn't in Berona. He wasn't…" Calen's words caught in his throat, and Dann could see a tear glistening as it rolled down his friend's cheek.

Dann's heart sank as the sliver of hope was snatched from him, but he grasped Calen's head and brought their foreheads together. "It's all right. You're here. Now. We *will* find him, Calen. I know we will."

Aeson's voice sounded over Dann's left shoulder. "Erik, my boy!"

Dann pulled his gaze from Calen to see Aeson stride past him and pull Erik into a tight embrace, wrapping his arms around his son.

"*Det er aldin na vëna du.*" Dann turned to see Therin standing to his right. Asius and Senas stood about a foot behind the elf, their hands clasped at their backs. A warm smile rested on Therin's face, and he looked at Calen as a father might.

"It is good to see you too, Therin." Calen brushed the heel of his palm across his face.

"Come here, my boy." Therin leaned forwards and embraced Calen, clasping his hand at the back of Calen's neck. "You're a sight for sore eyes."

"Why don't you ever hug me like that?" Dann raised an eyebrow.

"Because you're already too needy," Therin answered with a wry smile.

Calen pulled away from Therin, a laugh catching in his throat, turning to a cough. "It feels like nothing's changed."

"Not entirely true," Therin said, nodding towards Dann. "He's more irritating now than he was before, if you can believe it."

"I can believe it."

"Easy now," Dann said, clapping Calen on the back.

As they stood there, at the edge of the Burnt Lands, the soft glow of the setting sun spraying over the hills and mountains to the west, Dann waited and watched as Asius, Senas, and the elves who had remained at the camp greeted Calen and the others. It was all he could do to stop a silly grin from spreading across his face. Calen was here. He was safe. He was alive. There was a time when none of those things had seemed a possibility.

"How could you have been so selfish?"

The sound of Aeson's voice caused Dann to clench his jaw involuntarily. Silence filled the air, the sound of chatter and shuffling feet fading as those gathered turned to look at Aeson. The man stood only a few feet from Calen, Erik at his side, his face twisted into a hard stare.

"He wasn't—"

"I'll deal with you later," Aeson snapped, cutting off Erik. The man fixed his gaze on Calen's. "How could you traipse across the continent while knowing how many lives hung in the balance? Knowing how much had been sacrificed, how many lives given, so that Valerys's egg could be brought here. You owe a debt—"

"I owe *nothing*." Calen words were more a growl than anything else. He stepped closer to Aeson, meeting the man's gaze with an iron stare. Wingbeats sounded, and Valerys dropped to the ground behind Dann, his neck stretched out over Calen, teeth bared, a deep rumble resonating from his chest. The dragon postured in much the way a wolf would when watching over a cub. Calen shook his head. "I'm not doing this."

"Yes you are." Dann saw the muscles twitching in Aeson's jaw. "You're not a child anymore, Calen. You're a Draleid. That means something. There are people relying on you now. People who need you. Not only was crossing the Burnt Lands stupid and selfish, you put Erik's life in danger, and Tarmon's, and Vaeril's. All for what? To find one man?" Aeson shook his head, scoffing. "The arrogance of youth."

Aeson stared at Calen, who remained silent, staring back. Out of the corner of his eye, Dann noticed some of those who had come with Calen, Vaeril included, stepping closer, a tension in their movements.

"Are you done?" Calen asked, breaking the silence. When Aeson didn't answer, Calen moved closer, their faces only inches apart. The rumble in Valerys's chest grew louder, and the dragon's neck dropped lower, hovering above Dann's head. "You came to my home." Calen paused, exhaling through his nostrils. His voice was level, but Dann knew the anger that simmered below the false calm – he could feel it. "You brought the empire to my doorstep. My parents and my sister are dead. Do you even care? Were they anything to you?" Calen pursed his lips in disgust. "No, they weren't. They were just another necessary casualty in your war – in your *quest*." As Calen spoke, a purple glow began to emanate from his eyes, light misting in wisps. The only reason Dann didn't think he was hallucinating was the look on Therin's face. "You would see all Epheria burn so long as Fane and the Dragonguard lay dead. But you don't understand, this world doesn't care about you or me, or revenge. We are nothing. So yes, when I saw a chance to find Rist, I took it. I went after one man because if we forget about the ones we love, everything loses meaning. You might have forgotten that, but I haven't. I am not your puppet, and I never will be. I'll fight this war, but not for you. For them."

The low whistle of the wind was the only sound that broke the silence, spirals of dust sweeping into the air.

After a few long moments, Aeson stepped back. "There's food and water at the camp," he called, his stare holding on Calen for a second before moving about the newcomers. "Eat, drink, and rest. This large a number will draw attention, but there is no sense travelling in the dark. We will leave for Aravell at dawn."

Without another word, Aeson turned and strode towards the camp. But even with Aeson gone, the tension still hung thick in the air. Calen hadn't moved, his jaw was clenched, his body tense. Valerys still stood behind Dann, looming over the gathering. Even Erik had not walked after his father and instead kept his gaze focused on Calen. After a moment, Calen gave Erik a nod, and the man called out to the others, ushering them onwards to the camp.

Calen let out a long breath as he turned to Dann, his anger still evident in the language of his body. He gave Dann a half-hearted smile.

"The eyes are new." Dann shrugged, giving Calen a pout that slowly turned to a smile.

A genuine happiness touched Calen's short laugh, and he pulled Dann into an embrace so tight it risked popping a lung.

"If you leave without me again, I swear to the gods."

"I won't." Calen pulled tighter. "I promise."

"He didn't stop moaning for even a day," Therin chimed in.

Dann was about to snap back at Therin, when he heard a voice that seemed strangely familiar.

"Dann Pimm. You look taller since the last time I saw you."

Every hair on Dann's body stood on end as he looked over Calen's shoulder at the source of the voice. "You're dead…"

Haem Bryer pulled the hood of his cloak down, smiling softly. He looked almost identical to the last time Dann had seen him – the night he died. He was still a mountain of a man, legs built from tree trunks, shoulders as broad as an ox, and a surety in the way he held himself, but most of all, he looked very much alive.

"So I've heard."

"How?" Dann looked from Haem to Calen. He could tell by Calen's expression that it was still a topic that held more than a touch of sensitivity – not that that ever bothered him.

"It's a… It's a long story. Why don't I tell you over some food?" Haem smiled at Dann, the smile weakening a touch as he looked towards Calen.

"You know what?" Dann stared at Haem, his mind still feeling as though his eyes were playing a trick. "Fuck it. It's not like I've understood anything that's happened in the last year anyway. Come on, let's get you some food, and you can explain how you've returned from the dead." Dann let out a laugh of disbelief, shaking his head. That wasn't a sentence he had ever expected to say.

As Dann turned to lead Calen and the others back towards the camp, he saw Baldon and the other Angan – Aneera – walking towards them, their long, willowy legs carrying them with a strange grace. Dann didn't think he would ever get used to the shapeshifters; to the way they looked 'almost human'.

As the two Angan drew closer, their gazes fixed on Calen. Vaeril, Haem, Erik, and the other man whom Dann vaguely recognised tensed, a deep growl rumbling in Valerys's throat as the dragon turned his head towards Aneera and Baldon. Before Dann could say anything, the two Angan both dropped to one knee before Calen.

"Son of the Chainbreaker."

CHAPTER FIFTY-FIVE

STRINGS AND CHAINS

alen drew in a breath of heavy, loam-tinged air, letting his gaze drift across the forest. The last time he had been in the Darkwood he had barely been able to see more than a foot in front of himself. But now, as the group marched through the dense wood towards the elven city of Aravell, rows of baldír were lined on either side, white light pushing back the ever-pressing dark.

The rebels who had fled with Calen across the Burnt Lands walked behind him in a column, along with Gaeleron, Lasch, Elia, and Haem and the warriors who had come with him. Dann was back at the tail end of the group, walking with Elia and Lasch, as he had done since the moment he had recognised them. The pair were finally able to walk unaided, but the journey across the Burnt Lands had done them no favours.

Aeson, Senas, and some of the elves walked at the front of the column of people, leading the way. Aeson hadn't spoken to Calen since their confrontation, which suited Calen just fine; he could still feel his anger simmering beneath the surface. All the man had done since the moment they had met was attempt to tie Calen with strings and march him around like a puppet. Not anymore. Calen would not allow it. Like Aeson had said, there were people who needed him now. But he would be no use to them if he was nothing more than a head on a stick spouting the words of another man.

"How are you feeling?" Therin asked, handing Calen a waterskin. The elf hadn't left Calen's side since the moment they'd been reunited. Neither had the two wolflike creatures who now walked to Therin's right, their long languid gait seeming so effortless it was almost graceful.

"I've been better." Calen gave Therin a weak smile as he accepted the waterskin, taking a deep mouthful before handing it to Erik, who walked at his left. Calen nodded towards the two creatures. They hadn't spoken since they'd knelt before Calen and called him 'Son of the Chainbreaker'. They had simply risen to their feet and stood about like statues. "What *are* they, Therin?"

"They are Angan of Clan Fenryr," Vaeril chimed in from behind, a sort of reverence in his voice. "Shapeshifters. Children of old gods." Vaeril nodded towards one of the four enormous white stags that walked at the edges of the group, black, gold-veined antlers snaking upwards. "And they are Angan of Clan Dvalin. They are bound to my people by promises made when we first decided to settle within Aravell. It is their presence here that provides us safe passage."

"That it is." Therin gave Vaeril a soft look, like that of a father who had just been given the sweetest of compliments. It had been so long since Calen had seen Therin, or any of the other elves from Aravell, besides Vaeril, that he had almost forgotten the way in which most of the Aravell elves had treated Therin. It had only ever been Vaeril, and sometimes Alea, who had offered Therin so much as a smile.

Therin turned his head slightly to look at the two Angan, then looked back at Calen. "There is much I need to tell you. Much you do not know. I had asked Baldon and Aneera not to say more than they did, so that I may explain things to you as they are."

"When, Therin? There are always so many things I'm not being told. And every time I ask, I'm told to wait. I'm done with waiting, Therin. You once told me that the day we stop learning is the day we are consumed by what we do not know. The list of things I don't know seems to get longer by the day. You do me no favours by adding to that list."

"Tonight." Therin nodded, more to himself than to Calen. "Tonight I will tell you everything."

HOURS PASSED AS THEY MARCHED through dense, dark woodland, the light from the many baldír casting shadows as they moved.

Occasionally, Calen thought he saw figures staring at them from the depths of the shadows, eyes of smoking white mist. He had thought them tricks of the mind until Vaeril had explained that they were the Aldithmar – the spirits that inhabited the Darkwood. The same spirits that had taken Vaeril's brother. It was these creatures that the Angan of Clan Dvalin held at bay.

The how and why of it were questions Calen simply had not had the energy to ask. All he wanted to do was reach this elven city – Aravell. For months, upon months, upon months, all he had done was run and fight. He was tired. He would ask questions later.

A warmth touched his mind, easing some of his aches and pains, dulling the burn of the blisters that had formed, burst, and reformed on his feet since leaving Berona. Valerys had grown too large to navigate the forest and so instead soared above the dense canopy, staying low, riding the strong currents of air that swept in from the coast. *It's all right.* Calen drew in a slow breath, settling himself, and, in turn, helping to settle Valerys's own worry. *Therin said it's not much further.*

A rumble of disagreement sounded at the back of Calen's mind, and he let himself drift into Valerys, relief washing over him. Through the dragon's eyes, he saw an ocean of dark green that spread hundreds of miles in all directions. The seemingly endless canopy broke only sporadically where wide rivers carved their way through the land or mountain peaks rose to scratch at the sky full of dark clouds. No rain fell, but claps of thunder rippled through the air, flashes of light illuminating patches of sky.

It took a moment for Calen to understand what Valerys was trying to show him: there seemed no end in sight. "Therin, I thought you said it wasn't much further?"

Therin raised an eyebrow at Dann, who had joined them an hour previous.

The smile that spread across Dann's face at that moment worried Calen far more than any smile should. "Just wait for it."

Calen narrowed his eyes, then shook his head. Nothing that put that wide a grin on Dann's face could be something Calen would enjoy. Still, whatever it was, he didn't care. Dann could pull whatever tricks he wanted, Calen was just happy to see him. Seeing Dann brought all of Tarmon's words into perspective for Calen. *This* was what he was fighting for. For Dann, Rist, Elia, Lasch. For his family, those he had lost and those who had come back to him.

Calen turned his head as he walked, a smile touching his lips as he saw Haem walking next to Tarmon. The two of them were so large the elf walking beside them looked like a child. Haem was a little taller, but Tarmon was broader in the shoulders.

He's alive… The word 'happy' barely scratched the surface of the emotions Calen felt when he looked at Haem. And yet, Calen had spent two years coming to terms with the idea that Haem was dead – with the notion that he would never again lay eyes on his brother. Haem had explained to him what had happened. He had explained *why* he had not come back, but that alone wasn't enough to drive the loss from Calen's heart, nor the anger that lingered. He couldn't stop himself from thinking what if Haem had been there the day Rendall and Farda had killed their entire family? They might all still be alive. And Calen might not have been so alone all this time.

Once more, warmth flooded over from Valerys.

Not alone. Not entirely.

Calen pulled a deep lungful of air in through his nostrils. He knew thinking like that was a dark path to walk down, but still, his mind pulled towards it.

The thought of his parents pulled Calen's attention to Elia and Lasch, who walked beside Aeson's contacts from Berona, Ingvat and Surin.

Calen still hadn't told Elia and Lasch about Rist, about how he was taken. He had tried, but their minds were still not what they used to be. Parts of them had returned, slowly, as they crossed the Burnt Lands, but only in flashes. His heart ached just looking at them. After reaching the camp at the edge of the Burnt Lands, Calen, Dann, and Haem had taken it upon themselves to bathe Lasch and Elia, to clean the dirt and dust that had crusted into their skin. Calen had expected them to fight and argue, but all they did was curl up and shiver like frightened animals. The sight had caused both Calen and Dann to break down. It was only Haem's steady hand that had kept them going.

Calen bit down gently on the inside of his cheek, let out a sigh, then looked towards the head of the group. He stopped dead in his tracks and dropped his hand to his sword, pulling it free from its scabbard, while at the same time opening himself to the Spark. Aeson and the others who were leading were gone – vanished into thin air.

Barely a second passed before Tarmon and Erik were at his side, weapons drawn, eyes searching the forest around them. Haem and the other knights were right behind them, metallic green liquid flowing over their bodies, melding with their clothes, forming their armour.

The silence in the forest was broken by a deep, bellyaching laugh that echoed and rippled on the wind. Dann dropped to his haunches, covering his mouth with his hands, his shoulders convulsing with laughter.

Erik and Tarmon turned to Calen, confusion in their eyes.

Dann tilted his head back, let out a heavy sigh, then stood. "I've literally been waiting for that to happen for about two miles." He started forwards, the light from the baldír either side of him duplicating his shadow. He stepped over a thick, gnarled root, raised an eyebrow, then walked forwards and disappeared.

"It's like the Burnt Lands," Erik said, eyes narrowing. "An illusion."

Calen moved forwards, voices calling him, and then he was blinded by white light that caused him to snap his eyes shut and raise his forearm across his face. He took another step forwards, feeling solid ground beneath his feet. He peeled his eyes open a little bit at a time, the light dulling. He pulled his arm away from his face and let his eyes adjust. "How..."

What stood before him should not have been possible. The Darkwood was gone, and the sky above was dark and etched with grey-black clouds, pale moonlight breaking through in thin strands. A courtyard of smooth white stone spread in all directions, laced like the leaves of a tree with veins of azure stone that radiated a beautiful, soft light. The courtyard was filled with rows upon rows of elves armoured in pristine silver plate that flowed over their bodies like water, shimmering in the light of the glowing stones. Each elf grasped long-shafted spears with curved blades. Green cloaks were draped over their shoulders, flapping in the gentle breeze. A clear pathway stretched from where Calen stood – Dann at his side now – through the ranks of elves, and onwards, towards an enormous set of whitish gates that looked as though they had been grown rather than built. The same azure stone meandered through the bone-like material of the gates, bathing the courtyard in its strange light. White walls extended on either side of the gate, connecting to massive cliffs that rose hundreds of feet, framing the courtyard. No city, or painting, or work of art Calen had ever seen could have come close to comparing to the sight before his eyes.

Footsteps sounded as more people followed Calen and Dann through the invisible barrier. Calen turned to see Erik and Tarmon stepping through, hands covering their eyes, Vaeril and Therin following close after. It was only then that Calen realised the Darkwood was not gone; it still lay behind them, but it rose steeply, as though they had been walking down the side of a mountain the entire time.

Even as Calen pondered the thousand questions that flitted through his mind, horns bellowed. The gates of hewn bone began to open, and a procession marched through from the other side.

"We didn't get a welcome like this." Dann folded his arms and squinted, looking out over the courtyard. Even though the sun had long set, the light from the moon along with the soft glow of the azure stones glittered and reflected off the polished silver elven armour, lighting the courtyard in much the way the sand in the Burnt Lands had cast the waste in a perpetual twilight.

As the gates on the other side of the courtyard continued to open and the procession advanced, flickers of orange-red torchlight mingled with the white that radiated from baldír orbs. The steady drum of footsteps filled the air.

A surge of elation swept through Calen's mind, giving him no more than a moment's notice before an air-shaking roar thundered overhead, crashing against the cliffs and resounding through the open courtyard.

The drum of feet slammed to a halt, and a wave of gasps and whispers rippled across the gathered elves. Even some of those who had come with Calen – rebels from Berona, along with the elves who had guided them through the Darkwood – stopped and stared towards the sky as Valerys burst through the invisible barrier overhead, wings spread wide, jaws open.

The dragon unleashed a second roar, his scales shimmering in the light of the glowing azure stones, the black veins of his wings stark against the white membrane as the moon shone down from above. Calen took that moment to truly appreciate the power and wonder of Valerys.

Valerys was still only a fraction the size of those that had laid waste to Belduar, but he was a far cry from the vulnerable creature that had crawled from that egg almost a year ago near Camylin. And as Calen saw the looks of awe on the faces of the closest elves, a smile spread across his face. The dragon swept across the cliff face and over the procession of elves. He cracked his wings against the air and alighted beside Calen, his talons clicking against the stone as the resulting gust of wind blew Calen's hair off his face.

"They didn't welcome you like this," Erik said, turning to Dann as Valerys lowered his head and nuzzled the tip of his snout into Calen's outstretched hand, "because you didn't bring a dragon."

"The Ephorí of Aravell," Therin said, nodding towards the procession marching towards them. "Before we go any further, Calen. I need you to listen to me."

Calen turned to Therin but didn't speak.

"Nothing here means what you think it means. A smile, a frown, a kind word, an admonishment. When we first brought you through the Darkwood, we brought you to Belduar and not to Aravell. We did that for a reason. These are my people, and I love them dearly. But there are things at play here that have been brewing for centuries. Each of the Ephorí clutches at power and will do anything to find an advantage over the others. The Triarchy are no different. Each one of them will seek to use you for their personal gain."

"That is not much different to what I already know," Calen said, looking towards Aeson, who now stood a few feet away with Asius, Senas, and two of the Dvalin Angan by his side.

"It is *very* different. Aeson has his flaws, many of them, but no matter what you feel, he fights for a wider cause than simply his own interests. He has lost almost everything to this war, and still, he fights. There are those among my people who would stand by your side in the void itself, but there are those who would use you as little more than a ladder to climb higher."

A hand touched Calen's shoulder.

"I'll be right there with you." Haem gave Calen a weak smile.

Calen slid his sword back into its scabbard and rested his hand atop Haem's, inclining his head. He turned back towards the procession. As the elves drew closer, Calen saw seven figures marching at their head, two in robes of red and gold, two in robes of black and silver, two in robes of dark green and brown. And on the far right, strode what looked to be an Angan of Clan Dvalin, the veins of gold in their black antlers shining in the moonlight. Many of the elves who followed the leaders wore similar colours, lanterns and banners held high.

"The Angan is Varthon, Matriarch of Clan Dvalin. Dvalin are close to Fenryr. With Baldon and Aneera at your side, you should find a friend in Varthon," Therin said, leaning close. "The two in black and silver are Dumelian and Ithilin of the Kingdom of Vaelen. Even by mage standards, Ithilin has seen a vast number of summers. She is wise beyond her years and tempers much of Dumelian's brazenness." The elf gestured to the pair of elves in the middle. "Thurivîr and Ara, the Ephorí of Lunithír, wear the crimson and gold. I have known them for many centuries. Lunithír was the largest of the five elven kingdoms before The Fall, and that pride and arrogance is still present in everything they do – use it against them. The last two are Baralas and Liritháin of Ardurän. They are both sharp as steel, and having been reared in Ardurän, they were forged in the fires of politicking and mind games. They are like vipers, sweet as honey and deadly as Nightfire."

"Therin, it sounds like you're preparing me for war."

Therin's sombre expression didn't shift. "We're already at war, Calen."

"I see you're in one of those sunshine and rainbows moods you're famous for." Dann raised an eyebrow at Therin.

"Therin Eiltris speaks the truth, Calen." Calen hadn't noticed Vaeril moving closer. The elf's gaze was fixed on Therin. "As a Ranger, I pledged to serve all Aravell, but by birthright I am of Vaelen descent. The political rivalry between the kingdoms extends back to long before we made our home in Aravell. It has only worsened since."

Before Calen could answer, the horns sounded again, this time sharp and short. He turned to face the procession that now stood no more than twenty feet from Calen and the others, the six Ephorí and Varthon at the front.

As the sounds of the horns echoed off the cliffs and slowly faded, silence descended, the whistle of the wind and the flapping of cloaks and banners the only sounds.

One of the Ephorí stepped forwards – Thurivîr, judging by his crimson and gold robes. He stood over six feet tall, hair as black as jet with broad shoulders.

"Welcome," Thurivîr called out, his voice so subtly amplified by threads of Air and Spirit that Calen had barely felt the elf draw in the Spark. "To—"

The ground shook and quivered as Valerys stood to his full height, leaned on his winged forelimbs, extended his neck, and unleashed a roar so primal and visceral Calen felt it ripple through his entire body. Valerys's roar echoed through the courtyard of white stone as spittle flew from the dragon's mouth. It was a rage that burned through their shared soul. It was pride and power. It was a message, a pronouncement.

"There will be no strings or chains," Calen whispered, his voice drowned out by the seemingly never-ending roar of the dragon at his side.

As the sound slowly subsided, the lingering echoes fading, the dragon held his pose, looming over the gathered elves, his nostrils flaring, white scales tinged with azure light. The silence that followed was short lived, whispers spreading through the gathered crowd.

Calen saw the Ephorí exchanging glances, and then Thurivîr came forwards, his steps a little less certain than they had been. "Welcome to Aravell." The elf cast his gaze across the gathering, his stare resting on Calen and Valerys. "I am Thurivîr of Lunithír, Ephorí of Aravell. It is our great pleasure to welcome you, Calen Bryer, Draleid, soulkin of Valerys. And we also welcome your companions with open arms. Were it up to me, we would have held a more ceremonial welcome."

Out of the corner of his eye, Calen caught Dann raising an eyebrow, his mouth twisting as he stifled a laugh. The sight brought a smile to Calen's lips, along with the realisation of just how much he had truly missed Dann. Missed his laughter and his energy, his positivity, his candour. Dann was many things, and growing up he had always somehow managed to find trouble wherever he went, but of everything Dann had always been open, honest, and genuine. He was a light that Calen had sorely missed. Allowing his gaze to linger on his friend for another moment, Calen looked back to Thurivîr, who seemed to have noticed Calen's lapse in attention and was thoroughly unimpressed. *Good.*

"As it stands," Thurivîr continued. "Given the situation in the North and your presence here, the Triarchy have requested an immediate council. Please, Draleid, follow me."

ONCE THEY HAD ENTERED THE city, an elf by the name of Halmír had escorted the fleeing rebels to a hall in which they could eat and drink, while Gaeleron, Lasch, and Elia were taken to the Healers to see what could be done. Calen had asked two of the Knights of Achyron to go with the rebels and watch over them. Which left the remainder of the group following Thurivîr and the other Ephorí through the streets of Aravell, elven guards in smooth silver plate flanking them on either side.

It had seemed to Calen that each city he had laid eyes on since leaving The Glade held more splendour than the last, as though they were in perpetual competition. But when it came to sheer beauty, nothing was on the same plane of existence as Aravell. It was all Calen could do to not openly stop and stare as he walked in front of Valerys, who himself covered barely a third of the street's breadth.

The entire city resided within an enormous system of valleys that carved their way through the land, somehow hidden by whatever magic had created the barrier. And even to call it a city felt crass. It wasn't a city. It was a canvas, an oil painting of white stone through a valley of lush green, illuminated by moonlight and the soft azure glow of what Calen now knew were called erinian stones. Cylindrical towers, enormous bridges, archways, and gargantuan platforms swept across the valley, flowing through the landscape itself, weaving through rock, over and under waterfalls, and blending seamlessly with the natural flow of things.

Horns bellowed a song Calen didn't recognise as the group walked. Elves flooded the streets, walkways, and platforms that ran above and parallel to the one Calen and the others walked along. They leaned on parapets of smooth white stone, stretching out their necks, their gazes fixed on the procession, fixed on Valerys.

Ahead, the Ephorí stopped and now stood before a truly gargantuan structure of bone-white that rose from the ground like the roots of a tree shooting upwards, spiralling around each other and stretching out into walls that looked as though they were wings, reaching hundreds of feet into the air. Veins of erinian stone ran through the wing-like walls in delicate patterns, their soft glow making the structure look more like a work of art than a building. As Calen moved his gaze across the vast structure, he could see alcoves holding great statues and arched windows hewn into the outer walls. There was surely nothing in all Epheria that could compare to such a thing.

From where the Ephorí stood at the end of the long street, a staircase ascended towards an arched doorway.

Thurivîr turned back to Calen and the others, but when it looked as though he were about to speak, one of the Ephorí in dark green and brown robes, stepped across him, bowing slightly as he looked to Calen.

"Forgive me, Draleid. Our introductions were quick and sorely lacking at the gates." The elf raised his eyebrows and cast a glance at Thurivîr, whose stare remained cold and stony. "I am Baralas Thrain, Ardurän Ephorí of Aravell. It is my greatest pleasure to make your acquaintance."

"Alaith anar, Baralas. Din atuya gryr haydria til myia elwyn." *Well met, Baralas. Your welcome brings honour to my heart.*

The elf's back straightened, confusion twisting his features. "Du talier il Enkaran?" *You speak the Old Tongue?*

"You would do well to hold your tongue, Baralas." Ara, the second Ephorí of Lunithír shook her head. "You insult the Draleid with your ignorance." She gave a deep bow towards Calen, her crimson and gold robes falling in folds about her arms. "Haydria cianor val din närvarin, Draleid." *Honour comes with your presence, Draleid.*

"Enough." The Ephori Therin had named as Ithilin glared at both Baralas and Ara, creases streaking her time-touched face. "We will have time for your sycophantic bickering later."

Calen had to fight the urge to smile as the older elf put the others in their place.

Ithilin, inclined her head only slightly. "What Thurivîr had intended to tell you is there is a platform near the top of the Mythníril." She gestured towards the enormous white building that stood before them. "Your soulkin may wait there undisturbed. Nourishment will be provided."

Calen nodded to Ithilin before turning to Valerys. The dragon lowered his head, pale lavender eyes staring back at Calen. His nostrils flared, and he nudged the tip of his snout into Calen's outstretched hand. The dragon lifted his head, extending his neck over Calen. He took a step forwards, forcing armoured elves to step out of the way of his winged forelimbs. A tension held thick in the air as Valerys slowly lowered his head, lips pulling back to show alabaster teeth, his lavender eyes fixed on the six Ephorí. The dragon held himself like that for a few moments, a deep rumble resonating in his chest, then spread his wings wide, causing elves on the walkways above to jump back from the parapets. Valerys lifted into the air, scales glimmering in the light of the erinian stone, and then he was rising upwards sweeping across the city, circling the massive structure of Mythníril, the murmurs of the gathered crowds sounding after him.

As Valerys disappeared from view, a protective wave rippled through Calen's mind, and he was under absolutely no illusions that if even the slightest hint of fear were to touch Calen's heart, Valerys would burn the whole city to the ground.

"Well," Dann whispered, leaning closer to Calen. "You've gotten better at speaking elf."

Aeson pressed his tongue against the roof of his mouth, his eyes fixed on Calen while the others watched Valerys.

Much had changed since the night Belduar fell, more than Aeson had realised. Valerys had grown more quickly than almost any dragon Aeson had known. Most would have been little more than half Valerys's size at this stage. Perhaps the dragon's size could be attributed to the dragon's Valacian heritage, or perhaps he was simply inclined towards rapid growth. Either way, it meant Valerys had become a far greater asset than Aeson could ever have hoped at this stage – though it also meant Calen was equally as dangerous as he was necessary.

The boy was no longer a boy; that much was clear. Calen carried himself like a man who had seen twice his years, and his eyes held a weight Aeson had only ever seen in those who knew death intimately. There was danger in that. Aeson had spent too long, sacrificed too much. Calen would have to be steered with great care. He had a good heart, but he was yet young, and despite what he might himself believe, he still had a lot to learn.

As Thurivîr ushered them up the staircase towards Mythníril, Aeson's gaze rested on Erik. *My son.*

Having at least one of his sons back within arm's reach lightened Aeson's heart a little. Though the letter Aeson had received from Dahlen not long past had not carried favourable news, it had at the least assured Aeson of his son's safety. The dwarves and Belduar were important for what was to come, and as much as he would have wished to ride to his son's aid, he was beginning to understand that he needed to trust in Dahlen to make the right decisions, to be his own man. It was what Naia would have done.

Aeson let a smile touch his lips as Erik passed him, Calen, Vaeril, and Tarmon Hoard at his side, and made his way up the stairs towards Mythníril. Erik and Dahlen were everything. They were all he had left, all that pushed him forwards, and all that allowed him to open his eyes each morning. He would see Eltoar Daethana die. He would see the empire fall. And he would see a better world for his sons to grow old in.

Chapter Fifty-Six

Before the Fire Comes the Spark

Despite his prior declaration of urgency, as Thurivîr and the other Ephorí led the group through the wide hallways of Mythníril, the elf paused every twenty or so feet to give brief lectures on the many statues, tapestries, and works of art that decorated the walls. Calen also noticed that each time they stopped, they did so only before something that bore significance to the Kingdom of Lunithír.

The main hallway of the great structure of Mythníril was over twenty feet wide and hewn from stone as white as fresh snow. Large latticed openings in the ceiling allowed the light of the moon to drift in, augmenting the soft glow of the lanterns that sat in bronze sconces along the walls. Many doors of ornamented bronze lined the long hallway, likely branching off to the numerous chambers and halls of the great building, but the Ephorí walked past each of them, leading the group forwards and up multiple sets of stairs, walking for as long as it would have taken Calen to cross from one side of The Glade to the other and back again, until they finally came to a set of bronze doors so large Calen thought they must have been built for Jotnar.

The thought gave him pause, and he turned to see Asius and Senas standing beside one of the Knights of Achyron – Sister-Captain Ruon. Calen had not gotten much of a chance to speak to Asius or Senas since emerging from the Burnt Lands – so much had happened all at once – but once they had been given the chance to rest, he would make a point of seeking the Jotnar out to thank him for what he did in Drifaien.

The great bronze doors opened to reveal a vast chamber that spread in a semicircle. The floor was a single enormous slab of white stone that would have been impossible to create without the Spark. Arched windows were set along the far wall, overlooking the valley beyond – walkways, platforms, and bridges sweeping back and forth through the bounds of nature, illuminated by veins of erinian stone. It was only when Calen looked closer he saw that between each arch stood a column

Spark-carved from white stone into the likeness of a tree. The columns rose higher and higher, branches spreading out and joining together to support the ceiling above, as though they walked beneath the canopy of a stone forest.

An oculus lay at the very centre of the ceiling, allowing the light of the moon to pour through, illuminating a white stone table in the middle of the chamber. The table was at least twenty feet long and fifteen feet wide, the soft azure glow of erinian stone radiating from its surface.

Three elves stood about the table, delicate crowns of black and gold winding about their heads, each garbed in robes the colours of their king-doms: crimson and gold for Lunithír, black and silver for Vaelen, green and brown for Ardurän.

With the doors fully open, the elven warriors in silver plate who had escorted Calen and the others through the city marched in and lined themselves along the outer rim of the chamber, the butts of their curved-bladed spears resting on the stone.

There was a beat of silence as the doors closed, and the three elven rulers looked over the new entrants to their chambers. The Ephorí moved to stand between the group and the elven rulers who stood about the table.

Thurivîr stepped forwards and bowed deeply. "Galdra Lunithír, son of Arynil and Luvien Lunithír, King of the Lunithíri, Protector of Aravell."

Marked by his crimson and gold robes, King Galdra was tall and lithe, his jaw and face narrow, his eyes sharp as a hawk's. His silver-white hair was short, falling only to his tapered ears, his eyes the same molten gold as Alea and Lyrei's.

Ithilin and Baralas each stepped forwards and introduced the rulers of their respective kingdoms: Queen Uthrían of Ardurän and King Silmiryn of Vaelen.

Queen Uthrían was a match for Calen in height, with sun-touched skin and long black hair that flowed over robes of green and brown. King Silmiryn was shorter and stockier than Galdra, with hair of pure white and robes of black and silver. His eyes stayed fixed on Calen as Ithilin introduced him.

Each of the three rulers made their way around the table and stood in a line before the Ephorí.

Aeson stepped forwards. "Queen Uthrían, King Galdra, and King Silmiryn, det er aldin na vëna du. Ata mur vået harys veinier sidiel vir sidir talien."

Calen wasn't sure precisely what Aeson's words meant, but he believed it was somewhere along the lines of 'It is good to see you. It has been too long since we last spoke'. He had continued his lessons in the Old

Tongue with Vaeril after being separated from Therin, but there was still much he had yet to learn.

"Vir é haydrir al din närvarin, Rakina." They said at once. *We are honoured by your presence, Rakina.*

Aeson gave a deep bow, holding it for a moment before returning to his full height. "Please accept my apology that I could not have come when we first passed through Aravell or again when we rushed to the Svidar'Cia. And also, please accept my thanks for providing us not only with safe passage through the wood, but with more eyes so that we could better watch for the Draleid's return. On that note, before we begin, allow me to introduce to you the reason we are standing here today. The fruit of centuries of labour. The spark we have been looking for to light the fire. The first free Draleid in four centuries, Calen Bryer, soulkin of Valerys."

Seeing the expectant looks on the faces around him, Calen stepped out of the group, swallowing hard. For some reason, this particular moment was more nerve wracking than staring down one of those Urak Bloodmarked. Each of these people before him wielded immense power, Aeson included. And each of them wanted to tie strings around him and hold him up as a banner for war.

But as the nerves shivered through him, the touch of Valerys's mind brought calm. He could feel the dragon's wings beating, heart thumping, and he let out a short sigh. "Du haryn myia vrai, Inari un Aravell." *You have my thanks, rulers of Aravell.* Therin had told Calen that 'Inari' could be used for both kings and queens, he just hoped he had used it correctly. "Din atuya gryrr haydria til il Ileid." *Your welcome brings honour to the bond.*

Calen's breaths trembled as he stood there. He prayed to Elyara that he remembered the greeting as Therin had thought it.

"Your command of the Old Tongue is quite remarkable, Draleid." King Galdra pouted. "For one so new to it. Det er du vol gryrr haydria til Aravell. Du, ar Valerys." *It is you who brings honour to Aravell. You, and Valerys.*

King Silmiryn mimicked King Galdra's greeting, a broad smile spreading across his face as he did.

"Haydria t'il Ileid," Queen Uthrían corrected, holding her stare on Calen. She stepped forwards, her long black hair drifting back in the slight breeze. She looked as though she had seen no more than thirty summers, but Calen was under no illusions she hadn't seen more than ten times that number. The Queen moved so she was standing directly before Calen, her gaze never leaving his. Her eyes were as dark as her hair, seeming to have no separation between iris and pupil.

She reached out and grasped Calen's forearm, pulling him in closer, and Calen could feel himself subconsciously reaching for the Spark.

As Uthrían's fingers wrapped around Calen's forearm, ringing sounded in his ears, his vision shifting and blurring. Light flashed across his eyes, blue then white. Memories crashed into him, not his own. Images in motion, flashing and flickering. He was in a large chamber, banners of dark green emblazoned with the symbol of a white star. Children were running towards him – elven children. Elves dashed around in a panic, screaming and shouting. Then the walls erupted inwards, stone hurtling, blood spraying.

A flash of light and Calen was standing atop a hill, looking over a battlefield. Everywhere he looked, dragons soared through the skies, crashing into each other with abandon and unleashing rivers of dragonfire down atop the soldiers below. A voice screamed, seeming to come from all around, echoing, "Myia'nari! Myia'nari!" *My queen! My queen!*

The world flickered. Calen still stood atop the hill, but now the battlefield was more fire than earth. A dragon was hurtling towards him, scales of vivid yellow, flames pouring from their maw. An enormous dragon the colour of emeralds dropped from the dark clouds and caught the yellow dragon in their jaws, tearing it from the sky, blood trailing in the wind.

Again, the world shifted and an elven warrior in pristine white plate stood before Calen, the symbol of The Order marked in black across the breast. Calen knew this elf, loved him. A lover… no, a son. "Myia'nari. Il vyara… myia'kara… é dauva. Il raethír er veinier."

My queen, the princes… my brothers… are dead. The battle is lost.

The world shifted, and Calen now knelt on the floor of the great hall, panting, Queen Uthrían's fingers still wrapped around his forearm. Trying his best to slow his breathing, Calen stared into the queen's dark eyes, and he knew without a shadow of a doubt what he had seen: the death of her world, of her sons.

The queen stared back at him, her expression unreadable. Had she relived that moment with him? Did she know what he had seen?

As Calen's senses returned, he felt the thrum of the Spark resonating through the room, vibrating in the air. He felt it from King Galdra and King Silmiryn, but he could also feel it from multiple places behind him.

He grunted, lifting himself to his feet. How long had he been taken by the vision? *Was it a vision? Is that what they are?*

A shape moved to Calen's left, and Vaeril now stood at his side, helping him to his feet, eyes fixed on Queen Uthrían. Calen could feel the Spark flowing through the elf.

The queen, however, seemed unperturbed. She moved her gaze from Calen to Vaeril. "You are a ranger of Aravell, are you not? Yet you dare grasp the Spark in my presence?"

Vaeril dipped his head. "I am Vandesera, Inari. Sworn to protect Calen Bryer, first by honour, then by heart."

Uthrían gave an upturn of her bottom lip, then turned her attention back to Calen, her black eyes searching his. She held their gaze for a moment, then released her grip on Calen's forearm and turned back towards the table that held the centre of the room. "Come, we must decide the path forward."

Aeson, Therin, Asius, and Senas all glanced towards Calen as they made their way to the table in the centre of the room, more than simple curiosity in their eyes. Therin's gaze in particular lingered longer than the others.

Calen swallowed hard, his heart still pounding like a hammer on an anvil, his breaths still trembling. Only Erik, Tarmon, and Vaeril had seen him taken by a vision of the past before.

"Are you all right?" Tarmon gripped Calen's arm, looking him over. "Was it...?"

Calen nodded, his throat feeling tight. Here he was in a room full of people who wanted to control him, and the first thing he had done was show them a weakness.

Another hand rested on Calen's shoulder, pulling firm.

"Lift your head and stand tall." Calen turned to see Haem giving him a nod. "It is by our own will that we pick ourselves up when we fall." Haem held Calen's gaze for a moment, recognition passing unspoken between them – their father's words. "You are Calen Bryer, Draleid. Don't let them make you feel less." The corners of Haem's mouth turned into a soft smile. "They would be proud. That much I can tell you for certain."

Calen drew in a deep breath, then let it out slowly, returning Haem's smile. Looking at his brother's face still felt strange. He turned to Vaeril, thanking him, then started off towards the table, Erik, Tarmon, Vaeril, Dann, and the knights walking behind him.

"It's a map," Dann whispered as they approached the white stone table. "Of all the known world. There's Narvona, and Ardan."

Calen looked casting his gaze over the map carved into the white stone table. The mountains rose, and valleys fell, looking as they did from Dragonback, while thin strips of erinian stone were used to mark the rivers and lakes. The names of each region were carved delicately in the Old Tongue, inlaid with more erinian stone, emitting a soft glow.

"Let us speak plainly." King Galdra stood with his arms folded, the gold in his robes shimmering from the light of the erinian stones. "You have come here because there is nowhere else you are safe. And we welcome you with open arms. Rakina." Galdra turned to look at Aeson. "You have long been a friend to our people. Since before Fane Mortem's rise and the fall of The Order. You have spent centuries instigating rebellions across the continent since then, trying, and failing. In those centuries we have helped where we could but have remained within the bounds of Aravell lest we incur the same fate as those before us. But now, everything has changed. A dragon egg has hatched." Galdra extended a hand towards Calen. "For the first time in four hundred years. We do not yet know the extent of this new discovery. Whether this means we have found a new dawn and more eggs will begin to hatch, or whether this is simply an anomaly. You travelled to Valacia to find the egg in the hopes the Valacian eggs might be different to our own. Perhaps that plays a part but we cannot act on what we do not know for certain. For now, we have instructed the Dracârdare to keep warm the eggs we have, and we will soon begin to test for the Calling. But whatever comes from it, we now have a full Draleid who stands against the empire."

King Galdra looked to King Silmiryn, and a silence held for a moment or two before the black-robed king spoke. "The Blood Moon is fast approaching, so say our scholars who study the old texts and the stars. We thought we would have another year perhaps, but it appears the cycle grows shorter. And with the Blood Moon, the Uraks have brought devastation to Epheria." The king looked at the table, moving his hand from Mar Dorul across the main body of Loria. "Their hordes sweep across the land, harvesting Essence, while the armies of the empire scatter to keep hold of the territories they once seized from us. They are more than simply a nuisance. With each passing day, their strength grows. Our reports also tell us that the seeds you have sown across the years, Rakina, are beginning to bear fruit. The southern provinces are rebelling, factions are rising. After all this time, we believe it is finally the moment you have been searching for. But there is much that must be discussed. We cannot walk into this blindly."

Queen Uthrían sighed. "What my kin are trying to say is that they have finally pulled their tails from between their legs and agreed with me." Uthrían leaned across the table, laying her hand flat against a stone depiction of the Antigan Ocean. "The elves of Aravell will fight with you. We are tired of waiting and watching. Sick of being penned in like livestock. When word spread of a new Draleid and a newborn dragon with scales as white as the purest snow, a fire ignited in our people. Then our traders along the edges of the wood heard news of a great battle at the Lorian city of Kingspass. Of a dragon whose roar shook the earth and a Draleid whose eyes misted with a purple light – the Warden of Varyn. That is some title to earn amongst those who should be your enemies. And beside this Warden of Varyn, warriors fell from the sky wielding blades of green light – nithráls. And upon their breasts they bore a sigil not seen by my people in hundreds of years. The Knights of Achyron and a Draleid – both thought long dead." Uthrían looked to Haem, Ruon, and Varlin; the three knights who had entered the chamber. "We found your brothers and sisters roaming the edges of our wood not so long ago, Sister Ruon." The look on Queen Uthrían's face led Calen to believe that she and Ruon had met more than once before. "We left them to deal with the Aldithmar until they fled through your portal. There has long been fractures between my people and your knighthood. But I would speak with Verathin. After we are done here. He owes me that much. Now is not the time to stand divided."

"Grandmaster Verathin was slain at the battle of Kingspass." Ruon did not look away from the queen, but Calen heard the loss in her voice. "His soul was shorn by an Urak Shaman, lost to wander the void. Grandmaster Kallinvar stands in his place."

Uthrían nodded, swallowing. "Verathin will be missed. I will pray to Heraya that she finds his soul in the void." Uthrían slowly turned her gaze towards Calen, her fingers curling on the stone table. "My people are fond of twisting words over words and layering meanings, but as Thurivîr said, today we talk plainly. Rakina Aeson brought you here. I know what he wants. He is a man of singular desire. But what of you?" A tremble crept into her voice. "We stand here, brandishing you like a battle standard, but will you fight with us, Draleid? If we commit to standing, will you *bleed* with us? In the name of what was lost, for what is, and what may yet be?"

In that moment, Calen knew that Uthrían *did* know what he had seen in his vision, and her words stirred a fire inside him. In the back of his mind he could feel Valerys, and then a roar echoed through the valley beyond.

"Calen is committed, Your Majesty." Aeson didn't look to Calen as he spoke. "He has lost much to the empire and to the grip of Efialtír. He and Valerys are proven in battle. Their mettle tested. Their training is far from complete, but with my brothers and sisters here, we can ensure that is provided."

Calen clenched his jaw, anger churning in his gut. He could feel the strings pulling at him as Aeson swore Calen's commitment. He made to speak, but King Silmiryn spoke first, leaning over the table, his silver hair shimmering in the azure light of the erinian stone set within. "The Draleid is a start, but we will need more than that. Who else has pledged to your cause?"

Aeson looked from Silmiryn to Uthrían, then across to Therin, Asius, and Senas.

"My people are pledged to Aeson Virandr's cause." Asius's deep voice echoed through the room. "We are few in number, but we will fight till our last."

"Asius, son of Thalm." Queen Uthrían gave Asius a deeper bow than Calen ever would have expected from someone of royalty. "And Senas, daughter of Iliria. My apologies, I should have greeted you sooner. Our peoples were once the gravest of enemies, but since the Blodvar and the Doom at Haedr, we have stood together, trusted in each other. It is a great honour to continue that bond."

Both Asius and Senas responded with slow tilts of their heads.

"Forgive me, Asius, son of Thalm, Senas, daughter of Iliria," King Galdra said. "I, too, have been negligent in my duties. And now I must ask your forgiveness once more. What *is* your number? How many Jotnar are left to stand?"

"All is forgiven, Galdra, son of Arynil. Even in our years, this life is too fleeting to hold grievances." Asius drew in a long breath. "For hundreds of years, my people were hunted, survivors driven into the wind. After Aeson suspected that Calen might have heard the Calling, Senas, Larion, and I delivered messages to those loyal to our cause. Afterwards we roamed the continent in search of our kin. Even now, Larion still searches. After the battle at Belduar, I sought out Baldon and others of clan Fenryr." Asius gestured to Baldon and Aneera, who stood silently to his left. "With their aid, we have located almost one hundred of my kin who are willing to fight." Asius looked to Calen a smile touching his usually stony face. "We are few, but we pledge our lives to this cause. As I said in Belduar, I say again now, Calen Bryer, son of Vars Bryer. It is with honour that I stand beside the Draleid once more."

Calen had not spent long with Asius, but he had felt a connection with him, something different. Somehow, he felt as though Asius understood him. But what cut into Calen's heart was knowing how few of the Jotnar still drew breath. But once again, as Calen made to speak, Aeson got there first.

"We are honoured to have you, old friend." Aeson leaned forwards, resting his hand on a patch of carved stone that represented Karvos. He reached across and pointed towards the west. "Along with the Jotnar, Dayne Ateres has returned to Valtara. His sister now heads a rebellion that, from my last reports, has already taken back Skyfell, Ironcreek, and the lands surrounding. Dayne and the Valtarans, and their wyverns, will be a powerful ally."

"Wyverns?" A look of genuine shock touched Thurivîr's face, disappearing within moments when King Galdra glared at him. Calen wasn't sure if the Ephorí had spoken out of turn or if Galdra was irritated by his open shock. Either way, the same question rang in Calen's mind. He had heard stories of wyverns and the fabled wyvern riders of Valtara. But from all he knew, the wyverns had died out nearly a decade ago, victims of a vicious disease.

"Yes." Aeson glanced up from the table for only a moment. "I don't know the particulars, but it seems news of the wyverns' demise is much exaggerated."

Aeson continued to point across the map, naming allies who had pledged to their cause: lords, ladies, warriors, courtiers, and in some cases entire factions. Despite Calen's anger, he couldn't help but be in awe at the depth and complexity of the network Aeson had established. But he supposed four hundred years was a long time. One name in particular, however, drew Calen's attention.

"Alleron Helmund, along with another, Baird Kanar, lead a rebellion against High Lord Lothal Helmund in Drifaien. So far, their efforts have borne fruit and almost half the province bears their banner. Within six months, we will have fortified positions across the Southern lands and, with luck, in the North too. There are still many unknowns – rogue factions and claimants to power who are taking this opportunity to carve something of their own. No plan survives the planning, and the hearts of mortals are fickle things. Even in Valtara, Dayne is pledged to us heart and soul, but it is his sister, Alina, who leads the rebellion. She will need convincing. We will need to reach out to each of these prospective allies and secure their allegiances once more. I believe that once they see Calen and Valerys, once they have something tangible to stand behind, they will swear to us."

"And how might we reach out to so many?" King Silmiryn folded his arms across his chest, scratching at his chin. "Riders and hawks would not be reliable, not to such a large number across so many miles. Not with the war that ravages the lands."

"No." Aeson pouted, shaking his head. "And riders would not be enough. We need the people to *see* Calen. We cannot just tell them there is a symbol to rally behind. We must show them. I suggest we utilise the Angan of Clan Fenryr to communicate with those who would join us. Send word that we gather *here*. If some need to be convinced, we can travel. But if we bring them to us, we can cover more ground in less time. If we select carefully, we can build a strong network, and then the legend of the new Draleid will grow itself."

"It is a wise plan," King Galdra said, surveying the table with his hawk-like gaze. "We would need to be careful not to fully reveal our presence and intent, but it is a prudent course of action. We build while the empire crumbles."

A low growl reverberated through the stone hall, and it took Calen a few moments to understand where it was coming from: Baldon.

The Fenryr Angan stood with his gangly, fur-covered arms folded, his golden eyes gleaming and his lips curling back, exposing sharp teeth.

"You forget yourself, Broken One. We are not hounds to be ordered." The Angan's words left his throat in what Calen could only describe as a snarl. His voice was strange, like nothing Calen had ever heard. "We carry great respect for both The Bound and The Broken, but *do not* think to treat us as pieces in your game of war – your kind have used us enough for that." Baldon's gaze passed from Calen to Therin – who Calen was only now realising had not spoken even a single word. "Our vow to the Chainbreaker and his line is our bond." The growl that emanated from Baldon's throat grew deeper. "We care little for your war or your gods. We are here in the name of Therin Silver Fang and the son of the Chainbreaker. Both of whom have received little respect at this table." Baldon's eyes narrowed as they passed from Therin to the elven rulers and Ephorí.

Beside Baldon, Aneera stirred, raising her clawed hand and resting it on Baldon's shoulder. A soft rumble resonated from her throat. "We will do as the Broken One asks. But only if it is he who asks it of us." Aneera dropped her hand from Baldon's shoulder and rested it against her stomach, inclining her head towards Calen. "Your father wished this day would never come, but we swore that when it did, we would care for you and stand by your side as he stood by ours. Our vow was not one made in debt but in deep respect. My people weep for the death of the Chainbreaker. May the spirits curse he who held the blade."

Calen looked back at Aneera, his mouth dry and chest tight. Who was his dad to these creatures? He wanted to ask the question there and then, but it was neither the place nor the time. Therin had said he would tell Calen everything that night, and Calen would make sure he kept to his word. "The man who killed my dad is dead. I spilled his blood myself." Calen's words caught in his throat, tears threatening him at the memory of the day Rendall had pulled Vars from the world. But he held back the tears, holding the loss deep inside. He clenched his jaw, swallowing. "Though he will never have suffered enough…"

Calen lifted his gaze to Aeson and Therin staring at him. He had not told them of how he had killed Rendall.

"A blood debt has been paid," Aneera said with a nod.

Calen sucked in his cheeks, looking to Aeson. He couldn't help the anger that simmered in the pit of his stomach, fanned by Valerys's flames in the back of his mind. He knew that, at least in part, it was not a rational anger. Despite everything, Aeson had done all he had said he would. And not only that, he had kept Dann safe this entire time. Even still, that didn't stop what Calen was about to say from grating at him. "You would do me a great honour, Baldon, Aneera, if you were to aid our cause by communicating with Aeson's contacts in my name." Once again, Calen's throat tightened at the thought of his dad, but he pushed them back, turning to Haem, who stood a few feet to Calen's left. The Angan clearly did not yet know that Haem was also Vars Bryer's son, but Calen didn't think Haem cared. The look in his eyes was not dejection or irritation but one of deep sorrow, of loss, and of regret. He gave Calen the slightest of nods, a glimmer in his eye. Calen looked back to Baldon and Aneera. "I don't know what my dad did to earn your trust so completely, but I know I will do everything I can to honour him and to honour whatever passed between you."

With the sound of Calen's words fading, a sharp-toothed smile spread across Baldon's face, and he inclined his head. "Tell us where to go, and it will be done. The Angan of Clan Fenryr are by your side. I will say this, son of the Chainbreaker – you have his heart and his way with words."

Suddenly, simply by virtue of Baldon's words, it became infinitely harder for Calen to hold back his tears. But he did, because he needed to. Instead, he simply nodded his thanks and looked to Aeson. "You have your messengers."

Aeson stood there for a moment, looking back at Calen, his expression unreadable. He ran his tongue across his lips, nodding softly. He looked towards the elven rulers. "Are my brothers and sisters prepared?"

Brothers and sisters? Calen looked to Therin, who glanced back, offering only a weak smile.

"They are, Rakina." Sadness crept into Queen Uthrían's voice. "They await you both in Alura."

"Du haryn myia vrai, myia'narí." *You have my thanks, my queen.* Aeson looked to Calen, and where Calen had expected to see anger or irritation from the way Baldon had spoken to him, instead Aeson's stare was soft, a gentle sympathy in his eyes. "Calen, I'm going to need you to come with me. It is time for you to learn who you are."

CHAPTER FIFTY-SEVEN

WAR IS NOT BEAUTIFUL

Rist stumbled through the makeshift camp, the taste of blood and dirt coating his tongue. The stitches in his chin and lip pulled, fresh blood trickling. He swallowed, trying to add some moisture to his mouth and throat. The result was a heaving cough that pulled the stitches even tighter.

It was somewhere around midday. The elves had stopped pursuing about the same time the day before, but the armies had kept marching in an attempt to put more distance between them.

"Don't break those stitches," Sister Anila said as she checked over her handiwork. Rist's chin and lip weren't the only parts of his body that had been stitched back together. Anila had sewn the flesh on his arm, chest, leg, and back. The triage tents were overloaded, and the Healers were so overworked that bodies were being tossed in ditches, some of them still groaning. Thankfully, Rist's wounds hadn't been dire enough to require true healing.

Shouts and calls rang out, accompanied by squeaking wheels, horses snorting and whinnying, and the constant drum of footfall. Not a single person passed Rist that didn't look as though they had just crawled from beneath a mound of bodies.

"There're only three more triage tents." Garramon glanced back at Rist and Anila with a disapproving look. "If they're not there, they're dead."

The words cut Rist as though they were sharp steel. When the camp had been set, Garramon had settled the mages of the First Army, counting the dead, feeding and watering the living. None of them had seen Magnus since the battle. For the past few hours, Garramon, Anila, and Rist had been searching through the triage tents for any sign of Magnus and also of Neera. Rist had been separated from her during the fighting. He'd called her name and searched for the past two nights since the battle, but everything had been chaos; the armies had spread out over miles, the injured and dying being wheeled on carts like sacks of grain.

At the far end of the camp, the hulking shapes of two dragons loomed. Helios, the black-scaled mount of Eltoar Daethana was so large he could easily have been a hill of onyx. Rist had seen both dragons fly over the past two days, their bodies scored with more marks and wounds than he could count. The Healers had been tending to them day and night. The third dragon, Meranta, had been slain at the battle of the Three Sisters. Rist hadn't considered that dragons could die. It hadn't even been a possibility in his mind. What in the known world could kill a dragon? Well, it turned out the answer was another dragon.

That was something that had shaken the Lorian soldiers to their core. Not only was one of the Dragonguard dead, but the elves had dragons. He'd heard soldiers whispering about it as they marched. Each kept their voices hushed to avoid being overheard, but everywhere Rist turned, they were all whispering the same things. Fear consumed them.

"There." Garramon sidestepped a man wheeling a wooden barrow of severed limbs, blood pouring into the dirt. He nodded towards a white tent twenty feet away.

Rist couldn't pull his gaze from the barrow. His stomach turned, and in no more than a few moments, he was emptying its contents into the dirt, heaving and coughing, his wounds flaring with pain as though he was being sliced open all over again. Vomit clung to the back of his throat, reddish-orange tinged saliva hanging in strings.

A hand grasped Rist's shoulder and pulled him up right.

"Pull it together," Sister Anila said. Rist had expected her expression to be cold and unyielding, but instead he saw sympathy in her eyes, the usual harsh line of her mouth twisting into an almost pitiful smile. "You've seen worse in every triage tent so far." Anila's expression softened even further. "And we don't have enough food for you to keep puking it up. Come on, there's only three more."

The first of the three remaining triage tents was the worst Rist had seen. He saw gut wounds, severed limbs, men and women with holes the size of fists in their chests. The screaming scratched at his ears, clawing to get inside his mind. And the smell caused him to gag – just like it had in all the other tents. As it turned out, most people emptied their bowels when they were close to death, and the smell of shit in the triage tents had mixed with the iron and acid tang of vomit and set about battling the sharp antiseptic scent of brimlock sap and burning flesh from the cauterised wounds. Even with the Spark, the Healers were being pushed far past their capabilities. Rist knew little of healing, but he did know that whatever a Healer gave, they lost twice over in return; the more severe an injury, the more Healers it would take to mend, the more likely it was a Healer would take their own life in the process.

When they hadn't found any sign of Magnus or Neera in the first tent, they moved on to the second, which was situated near a burbling brook that flowed through the northern edge of the camp.

Much like the other tents, when Rist stepped through the pinned-open flaps of the second last triage tent, his senses were assaulted. Wails, groans, and shrieks filled his ears. The stench of death plugged his nostrils. A wave of heat rolled over his skin.

He looked about, his head scattered by the chaos. Men and women were crammed together, lying on the ground or standing against poles, barely enough space for the Healers, garbed in white robes, to move around. The lucky, or unlucky, had cots. But those were mostly for the soldiers who could no longer walk. A man lay unconscious – at least Rist hoped he was unconscious – on a cot to the left of the entrance, bloodied bandages covering two stumps of leg that had been cut from the knee down. Rist turned away, a fist closing around his stomach.

"Garramon, Uraksplitter, Acolyte Havel! About time. I'm just about done."

Rist lifted his head to see Magnus Offa standing shirtless with has arms spread wide. Two Healers moved around him, one wearing the full white of the Healer affinity, the other with a brown stripe trimming the edges – an acolyte.

Magnus's beard was burned to cinders on the right side, the eyebrow on the same side completely missing. His arm from his shoulder down to his elbow was covered in burn scars that looked as though they had been sustained a decade ago but had clearly been inflicted during the battle – the power of Spark healing. A plethora of cuts and bruises covered the man's body, so many he looked as though he'd been shredded by a wolfpine then dragged behind a moving cart. But despite it all, Magnus was smiling.

Anila gave a sigh of relief. "We thought you were dead."

"Oh they tried," he said, with a broad, toothy grin. With the right side of Magnus's beard burnt away, for the first time since Rist had met the man, he could actually see Magnus's mouth – well, half of it. It felt odd, as though he was looking upon a stranger. "Oh you better believe they tried. One elven bitch came close, but I ran her through with a snapped spear shaft. Uraksplitter, you should have seen her face when I held her into the dragonfire like a rabbit on a skewer—Agh!" The man slapped away one of the Healers' hands. "Heal it, but don't stick your finger in."

"Where've you been? It's been two days since the fighting."

"I got pinned beneath a horse. Bastard knocked me senseless. By the time I'd come to and had enough energy to knock the thing off me, the elves were already giving chase. I've spent the last two days catching up, killing as many of the pointy-eared fuckers as I could along the way. One of 'em stuck me like a pig last night, and I just about crawled back here." Magnus pointed down to a mass of knotted flesh just under his rib cage, about an inch in diameter. "Achyron almost had me as a drinking partner. He would have, if it weren't for an over-eager Healer acolyte who burned herself out trying to save me." Magnus's tone grew sombre towards the end of his words, the usual mirth evaporating from his voice. He nodded towards the Healer who stood beside him, working over a deep gash in his shoulder. "Heraya embrace her. She was too young to have taken my place."

The Healer, a tall broad-shouldered woman with short dark hair and a hooked nose, held Magnus's gaze, then inclined her head, a brittle smile touching her lips. She went back to work on his wounds.

Magnus grimaced as the woman pulled at him, looking him over. "How are my mages?" Magnus, held his breath for a moment "How many casualties?"

Garramon stared at Magnus. Rist understood why the man was hesitating. If he had to give the news, he wasn't sure he'd be able to find the words no matter how hard he looked.

Magnus's voice turned to a growl. "For the love of the gods, tell me, you bastard."

"Eighty-two dead."

Magnus's face dropped, his jaw slackening, eyes losing their lustre.

"Eighty-two dead," Garramon repeated. "Nine wounded. Three of those won't make the night. They were hit by dragonfire. One of the elven dragons crashed down into our ranks during the retreat. Yoric, Allana, Urka, Theo, Dremaine, Kalder, Luna, Tomas, and Pula – each of them barely have a scratch, but they're shook."

Magnus swallowed. His lips looked as though they had been about to form words twice, but nothing came. Seeing Magnus like this cut into Rist's heart more than anything else he had seen since the battle. Magnus was always full of laughter and levity, he had seemed impervious to the darkness of the world, but now Rist could see his heart bleed. The man nodded to himself, biting at his lip. "I'll go to them."

"Finish here first. You're no good to anyone when you look like a walking corpse."

"Mmm," Magnus grunted. A flicker of life touched his face, and he looked at Rist. "Your woman is here. Though, don't tell her I called her that. She's a fiery one."

"Neera?" Rist did nothing to hold back the urgency in his voice. "She's here? Where? Is she all right?"

"Behind me to the left, by the tent pole with the strip of white cloth hanging from it. Aye, she's alive, lad. She'll live, she'll walk again, and she'll hold a blade. Many aren't as lucky."

Rist looked to Garramon, but the man was already gesturing away. "Go."

Rist pushed his way through the triage tent, grimacing with each step as his new wounds burned in objection, his many stitches pulling tight. "Neera?"

A few soldiers looked at him with curious glances, the Healers glaring as he got in their way.

"Neera?" he called again, ignoring the stares. He stepped over two men on the ground he was reasonably sure were dead, then carefully avoided the legs of a woman who's right arm had been cleaved just above the wrist. There had to have been hundreds of soldiers in this tent alone, and only a handful of Healers between them. The acrid stench of vomit still clung to the back of his throat, his stomach threatening to empty once more. The bards had left this part out of the stories: what happens *after* thousands of men with sharp steel go to war. They never weaved tales about what happened after, never sang songs about the woman who returned home with no legs or the man whose body was covered in blisters and scars. No, those would not make for fine drinking songs.

Rist shuffled his way around a plump Healer with shoulders as broad as an ox, and then he saw it: a tent pole with a strip of white cloth snagged on a splinter of wood.

"Neera?" He pushed his way forward, more forceful now. *Please be all right.*

"Rist?" The voice that answered was weak, but Rist would have known it anywhere.

He shoved past a skinny man with greasy black hair and no shirt, blood still streaming from a wound along his back. Then he saw her.

Neera lay in a cot, her head propped on an old leather satchel and a folded blanket. A brown woollen blanket was draped over her legs, two feet sticking out the end, socks but no boots. Above the waist, she was bare, but bloodied bandages covered her from the navel to just below her throat, wrapping over her right shoulder. Her dark hair was tacked to her forehead with sweat, and stitches held a gash that ran diagonally across her left cheek, over her eye, and through her brow, stopping about an inch from her hairline. "Rist?"

Rist dropped to his knees, ignoring the pain that jolted through him from the impact. He rested his hand on Neera's arm, wrapping his fingers around her bicep gently. "What happened? We got separated and... I couldn't find you. I thought..."

"I thought the same." Neera grunted as she shifted herself to a more upright position, resting her hand on Rist's. "Are you hurt?"

"Are you asking me if *I'm* hurt?" Neera winced, and Rist squeezed her arm a bit tighter. "I'm fine. Nothing some rest and time won't fix."

She lifted her arm and traced her thumb from Rist's lip down over his chin, over the stitches where the elven spear had sliced through the flesh. It stung, but he didn't move. "What was it you said about scars?"

"Each one is a reminder," Rist said, touching his hand to Neera's cheek, rubbing his thumb back and forth.

"Of the pain we endured and the pain we overcame." Neera nodded weakly. "I remember." She squeezed her hand on Rist's, pulling herself even further upright, her dark eyes giving him a mournful look. "Well, I'm going to have a few reminders." Neera looked down towards her bandages.

"It's all right. You'll heal. The Healers here are the best in all the empire."

It was only then as Neera looked at her bandages that Rist realised what she meant. With the bandages tied tight, it was difficult to see, but the curve of her chest was flatter on the right side, and now that he was paying more attention, he noticed the bucket on the ground was full of discarded, blood-soaked bandages. He'd been so focused on her limbs and her breathing, he hadn't thought to look for anything else. "What happened?"

"I took a spear to the chest towards the end of the fighting. It cut deep. The elf was going to finish me. The Justicars were covering the retreat. They took its head from its shoulders. The one with the scar over his eye – Kyrana. I can't remember his first name. He held the bleeding back with the Spark and carried me. When we got to the forward camp, it was almost deserted. They'd already begun falling back to safer ground. The Healers told him there was nothing they could do. But he—" Neera lurched forwards, coughing, blood splattering across her bandages. She waved Rist away when he tried to settle her. "He grabbed one of them by the throat and said if I died he died. The Healer did what he could. There was a lot of blood and he was already drained from helping those who had gotten back sooner. He closed the wounds, kept me alive. I was lucky."

Rist didn't know what to say. He wasn't good with words. All that mattered was that she was still here. He cupped her cheek and planted a kiss on her forehead more tenderly than he ever had before. She didn't swat him away or make a jibe. She reached her hand under his arm and pulled him closer. Only a few seconds passed, then Neera pulled back.

"I'm really happy you're alive," Rist said.

Neera laughed, shaking her head, another cough breaking through. "I'm happy you're alive too."

"How long will you be cot-ridden?"

"They'll have me up by the end of the day," Neera said with a half-hearted shrug. "They need the cot. Have they said where we're moving to?"

Rist shook his head. "Garramon says there's a meeting tonight, now the elves have fallen back and aren't pursuing anymore. Have you seen Tommin or Lena?"

"Lena came through earlier with Brother Halmak. I saw her but I didn't speak to her." Neera gasped as she finished speaking.

"What is it?" Rist scooped his hand behind Neera's back, trying to support her. "I'll get a Healer."

"No, I'm fine." Neera pulled Rist's head back, stroking at his ear with her thumb and forefinger. "I just twisted wrong. I saw Tommin yesterday, but I've not seen him today. Sister Danwar is running around somewhere, so he can't be far."

"I'll get you some water. If you want, Garramon and I can help you back to the tents after you've rested a bit. Or I can come back and help later. Are you well enough?"

Neera nodded. "Someone else needs this cot more than I do, and I'm not bleeding much anymore. The Altwied Blood helps – it eases the pain. Come on, help me up, we'll get water on the way."

"Now?"

"*Now*." Neera let out a short gasp as she grabbed hold of Rist's shoulder and started to heave herself to her feet.

"You're stubborn as a mule," he groaned, wrapping his arms around her and pulling her upwards.

"At least I don't look like one." Neera's face caught between a grimace and a smile. "What?" she asked when he glared back at her. "All right. You're my hero, Rist Havel. So brave and strong. Now do as heroes do and carry me back to the tents."

Rist stared at Neera, weighing up his chances of success if he tried to carry her. On a normal day, his odds might have been seven in ten. It wasn't that she was heavy, but more that he wasn't particularly strong. But on this day, he was even weaker than usual, and his body ached.

"Rist?" Neera narrowed her eyes, looking at Rist as though he had just said the most idiotic thing in the world – but he hadn't even spoken. "Rist, I was joking." She tilted her head to the side. "Please don't try to carry me. We both know that won't end well."

"Oh. Is it wrong that I'm happy you said that?"

Neera pulled a face that was halfway between a smile and one of those looks she gave him when she thought he'd done something stupid. "Just help me back to the tents. The smell in here will kill me faster than anything else."

Rist pulled Neera up the rest of the way and gathered the bits of armour, her cloak and sword included, that were strewn around the cot.

The Healers must have discarded them in a hurry when trying to save her. Neera wrapped her arm around his right shoulder, wincing as she lifted it, and he hefted her belongings under his left armpit, holding them tight. It almost would have been easier to just carry her.

They were making their way back through the triage tent, stumbling like a three legged donkey, when Neera spotted Sister Danwar, orange hair tied in a knot of curls at the back of her head, stark against the white of the Healer's robes.

"Sister Danwar?" Neera called.

The woman stood over a bucket that sat on a low folding table, scrubbing her hands in the water within. She didn't turn or answer.

"Sister Danwar?" Neera repeated as she and Rist crossed the tent towards her.

Rist saw Sister Danwar's head turn a fraction, her ear twitching. She'd heard Neera's call. The woman lifted her hands to her temples. They were stained crimson from the fingertips right down to the back of her palms.

Neera called louder, though they were only a few paces away. "Sister Danwar?"

"What?" Sister Danwar slapped the side of the water bucket, knocking it from the table, spilling its contents into the dirt and soaking a man who lay on a cot. The woman turned, her eyes afire. Her usually pristine white robes were covered in blood. Stains of crimson and pink blended with patches of char. Her face was no different, dried and congealed blood stuck in every wrinkle and crease, skin stained. The woman's hands were bleeding, skin worn away from scrubbing and washing, the tips of her fingers wrinkled like dried fruit. "Oh… It's you."

Rist looked back again at the man Sister Danwar had accidentally soaked in the bloody water. His eyes were closed, and he wasn't breathing.

Dark circles creased Sister Danwar's eyes, dried blood caked at the edges. She looked as though she hadn't slept since the battle. The woman let out a groan and placed the fallen bucket back on the table. Facing away from Rist and Neera, she let out a sigh, then turned back, swallowing. "Are you all right?" The woman touched at the sides of Neera's bandages, giving a sympathetic turn of her mouth. "When were the bandages last changed? There's still bleeding."

"Only hours ago," Neera assured her. "The Healer seeing to me was exhausted, she didn't have the energy to close everything with the Spark. She told me she'd take the stitches out in the next few days and heal it fully."

"Come closer." Sister Danwar reached out, pulling Neera towards her.

"No, honestly, I'm—"

"When I say come closer, Acolyte, you do as you are told. You're not a Battlemage yet."

Rist felt Neera tense, her back straightening. He kept his arm around her as she moved towards Sister Danwar.

The woman rested her hand on Neera's shoulder and weaved a tapestry of threads through her. All five elements. Rist had watched Healers work before. Most of them, like regular healers or surgeons needed a direct line of sight to a wound to see what they were doing. But the most skilled, like Sister Danwar, seemed to be able to *feel* the injuries with threads of the Spark as though they were seeing them with their own eyes.

"There," Sister Danwar said, the drain clearly sapping her strength as she staggered backwards a step. She had pushed herself to the edge of what her body could handle. "Keep the bandages on for now." Sister Danwar swallowed hard, drawing in a slow breath to steady herself. "The wounds are closed, but the bandages remind you not to over exert. Take them off before you sleep. The stitches are loose between the bandages and the skin. Now go, there's more needs doing here."

"Sister, I know Tommin will likely be needed through the night," Rist said as the woman turned away. "But if he could join us to break the fast tomorrow, it would be appreciated."

Sister Danwar stood still for a moment, and when she turned she looked at Rist in a way that turned his blood cold. "Tommin is dead."

A shiver spread outward from Rist's chest, and Neera gasped beside him.

"Dead? But he wasn't fighting," Neera said. "I only saw him yesterday…"

Some of the Healers travelled with the armies into battle, but those Healers – known as Bloodhounds – were few and far between. Most stayed behind the lines in the forward camps to heal the wounded after the battles. Rist realised he had been staring at Sister Danwar without saying a word. "How?"

Sister Danwar let out a sigh, shaking her head. As cold as the woman could be from time to time, Rist could see much of Calen's mother – Freis – in her. They were both Healers. Freis didn't have the Spark to help her, but she had a heart like few others. Rist could see that same heart in Sister Danwar, but at that moment he could feel it breaking. "Last night," she said. "I left him alone to see to one of those who had survived the dragonfire. The man wouldn't have lived to see the sun rise today, but Tommin needed practice, and the man deserved to die in as little pain as possible. I'm not sure what happened but when I turned, the man was screaming, and the hilt of a knife was jutting from Tommin's neck. I couldn't save him."

"No…" Neera trembled as she spoke. "No, that's… He couldn't have… He wasn't fighting." Tears welled in Neera's eyes as she looked at Rist. "He wasn't fighting, Rist. That's not fair…"

Sister Danwar sighed. "War isn't fair, Neera." That was the first time Rist had heard Sister Danwar call one of the Acolytes by their first name. "It is bloody and it is horrific and it is everything that is wrong with this world. He died quickly. He was lucky."

FARDA STOOD IN THE COMMAND tent with his arms folded. He could feel the dirt and sweat crusted together on his face, and his joints ached; the aches had gotten worse with time.

Nobody had spoken in minutes. All the surviving commanders and generals, along with Eltoar Daethana, Garramon, and Anila, stood about, blood still crusted in their clothes, exhaustion carved into their faces. Most still wore their armour, or at least pieces of it.

Of the commanders, only Marken Kort of the First Army had been slain in battle, along with the mage commander of the Second Army. Judging by how few bodies occupied the tent, the generals had fared far worse. Commander Talvare had lost three generals at the battle at Fort Harken, but the commanders of the First Army and the Second Army had brought full compliments with them to The Three Sisters. That should have made twenty-seven in total, but only fourteen stood in the tent. And, much to Farda's irritation, that oily-haired shitweasel of a man, Guthrin Vandimire was one of the survivors.

Supreme Commander Taya Tambrel leaned over a folding table in the middle of the room, her palms pressed flat against the wood. What remained of her silver hair dangled over her left shoulder, the right side of her head shaved, stitches holding together a long, angry wound that ran from her eye, slicing off the top of her ear, and stretched to the back of her head. The woman had refused the Healers, having a surgeon simply stitch her up and send her on her way. Farda had respected that. Most commanders would have taken the best care for themselves; Taya did not.

Sweat dripped from the end of her hair onto the wood. The table held no map; they didn't need one. Their only decision was forward or back.

"There is no sense in it, Supreme Commander." A gangly general said, breaking the too-long silence. He looked to have seen his sixtieth summer, which, as far as Farda was concerned, was an achievement in itself for most soldiers who couldn't touch the Spark.

Taya lifted her head, looking at the man.

"No sense in it?" Magnus Offa scoffed. "There are sixty thousand souls crammed into Steeple. At least. You know what those pointy-eared bastards did to the cities on the eastern coast. Not going back means we are as good as killing every man and woman of fighting strength within the city. And even then, even with their honour, the helpless are always casualties of war. You should take your sword off and leave. Only someone willing to use a sword should carry one."

"Say that again," the old man growled, moving towards Magnus. He was reasonably tall with squared shoulders and muscled arms, but Magnus would tear him in half without even needing to touch the Spark.

Taya slammed her fist on the table. "They've killed enough of us. We don't need to kill any more for them." She ran her hand through her hair, folding it back over her head. With her breastplate removed, Taya stood in a sweat-soaked woollen tunic that clung to her muscled shoulders and arms, sleeves rolled up to her elbows. She gave a heavy sigh. "What do you propose we do, Magnus?" Taya pulled herself into an upright position, opening her arms. "I don't like the idea of ceding ground. And I despise the idea of leaving those in Steeple to fend for themselves. But we haven't begun to count our losses. We've spent the last two days moving away from Steeple and the Three Sisters, trying to keep ahead of the elves, trying to regroup. And now that we can finally tend our wounded, you would have us go back and fight?"

"We took losses, Commander." Olivan Karta, commander of the Second Army, extended a pleading hand. "That is true, but the elves took more. They are hurting like we are. If we push back now, catch them unawares, we can break them. I know we can. Steeple's garrison will add another three thousand to our number."

Farda couldn't help but laugh.

"What are you laughing at, *Justicar?*" The man emphasised the word as though it were an insult. Farda raised an amused eyebrow, but out of the corner of his eye he saw Eltoar shift from where he leaned against a tent pole, a dangerous look about him. Eltoar hadn't spoken since he'd entered the tent, and Lyina hadn't come with him. Pellenor and Meranta's loss had shaken them both to their core, and a darkness hung over Eltoar's head.

"I'm laughing at you." Farda frowned. "What did you say, 'break them'? Before two days ago, had you ever fought elves, Commander? And I don't mean the ones you shackle and collar and force to toil in Dead Rock's Hold. I'm sure you've beaten enough of those. No, free elves. Had you?"

The man hesitated. Farda could see uncertainty mixing with anger. "No. But—"

"You can't break elves, Commander. Not in battle. Through torture, maybe. Days of endless pain. You can break any mind that way, if you have the required lack of empathy. But in battle, the elves do not rout. They would sooner take their own lives. It seems, Commander Karta, you have forgotten the first rule of war."

"And what is that, *Justicar?*"

"Know your enemy better than you know yourself," Commander Talvare said, looking to Farda. Her grey-streaked black hair was matted with blood and her left arm was wrapped in bloodied bandages, but she still looked as though she could beat half the men in the room to a bloody pulp. "It also appears, Commander Karta, that you're not very good with numbers. Before the battle, our forces were in the region of fourteen thousand, the elves must have had over thirty. By my count – which admittedly, is rough – we've lost at least half our number. Seven thousand dead. Now you say the elves took heavier losses than us. Even if they took double, that would still leave them with more warriors than we started the battle with. They still outnumber us two to one. They have more mages, and…" Talvare looked to Eltoar and went silent.

Olivan followed her gaze. "What? The dragons? We killed two of their beasts, and we only lost one. We've still got two left. I'd take those odds."

"Would you?" Eltoar pushed himself away from the tent pole, the tent's lanterns casting shadows across his angular face. He still wore his white plate, the black flame of the Dragonguard across its chest, blood and dirt marring its usually pristine surface.

"I would." Olivan seemed to be the only one in the room who hadn't grasped the change in atmosphere.

"How many lives, I wonder?" Eltoar drew within a foot of Olivan, tilting his head to get a better look at the young commander. Though, to Farda, most people were young. This man couldn't have seen more than thirty-five summers. Young for a commander, but then again, war wasn't a profession where many people lived to see their later years – without the Spark of course.

"How many lives what?"

"How many lives you'd be willing to throw away for your pride."

"This has nothing to do with my pride." Olivan took a step closer to Eltoar, straightening his back. The naivety of youth. He didn't seem to understand he was a pup accepting the challenge of a dragon.

Eltoar moved so he stood less than an inch from Olivan. The Dragonguard commander was a head taller, shoulders broader by a distance. "Magnus spoke of the people within the walls of the city. His thoughts were for their lives. But you, you reek of arrogance and pride. You are a child playing war games. How did you rise to this position?

Family, no doubt. You didn't earn it. That much is clear." Eltoar shook his head, glancing towards Taya. "We should make for Elkenrim. The elves have taken heavy losses, and they will regroup and solidify their position. They have reached a point where pursuit is no longer a requirement of honour. Despite the size of their force, that was but a fraction of their power. A test, if you will. We need to fall back and send hawks. Fane must know of the developments here."

Eltoar turned to leave, making it only a few steps before Olivan's voice cut through the room.

"Spoken like a coward."

Eltoar stopped.

Well. That was fucking stupid.

Eltoar turned. He looked at Olivan, his eyes cold, then marched back towards the commander, stopping so close they likely could have smelled each other's breath. "Say it again."

"I…" The man gulped, having to tilt his neck to meet Eltoar's gaze. Farda felt a fleeting touch of admiration for Olivan as the man found a semblance of courage deep within his gut. "You are a coward."

A flash of motion and Eltoar's hand stretched out, fingers wrapping around Olivan Karta's throat. The man choked and coughed, slamming his hands down on Eltoar's. But Eltoar's grip was iron. Farda felt him reach for the Spark, threads of Earth weaving through his bones.

With one hand wrapped around Olivan's throat, Eltoar lifted the man off his feet. A few gasps sounded, but none of the tent's other occupants were stupid enough to do anything. Even Taya Tambrel just stared, her mouth open.

"You dare call me a coward?" Eltoar stared up at the man. Olivan's face had gone red, and his legs were kicking. "I have lived to see more men die than you've seen blades of grass. My kin and I gave you this empire. We died for it. The 'beast' that we lost. Do you even know her name?"

It looked as though Olivan were trying to speak, but the man couldn't get any words out. His face was red as a tomato now, eyes straining, veins bulging.

Farda pulled his coin from his pocket, running his thumb over the nicks and grooves.

"Her name was Meranta. She died so that you and the rest of the soldiers could escape. Her soulkin was Pellenor. He was quiet and contemplative." Olivan thrashed and gurgled as Eltoar spoke. But Eltoar carried on as though he were speaking last words over Pellenor's funeral pyre. "He was kind. He rode to war when it was required of him, but he never sought it out. Despite all his power, he never thirsted for battle. He was no coward. I notice, Commander Karta, your hair is clean, as are your hands and your face."

Much to Farda's surprise, Eltoar released his grip on Olivan Karta's throat.

Olivan dropped to his knees, dragging in ragged breaths, his hands clasping his throat. Fear turned to fury, raging in his eyes. He made to speak, but Eltoar reached back and wrapped his fingers in the man's hair, pulling tight.

"Pellenor and Meranta died so that these armies could fall back safely. They didn't die so a wretch like you could send more men and women to their deaths so you could be part of some bard's tale."

"Get your filthy fucking hands off me!" Olivan roared, his voice hoarse and raspy.

Eltoar twisted his fingers more, pulling the man's hair harder, leveraging his head back and forcing him to stretch out his back. "You are nothing but a mark on time. You don't deserve the gift they gave."

In one smooth motion, Eltoar pulled a knife from his belt with his free hand, then drove it into Olivan's exposed neck. The man's eyes bulged, his hands clasping the hilt of the blade, blood pouring down over his chest. But Eltoar twisted the knife, then jerked it. Olivan went limp, blood flowing freely. Eltoar released the man's hair and let him drop to the ground with a *thud*. He looked at the knife, his nose crinkling, a touch of disgust on his face, then he tossed the weapon onto Olivan's body.

Farda continued to run his thumb over the gold coin in his hand, tracing the shape of the crown. The silence in the tent was so thick it was a palpable thing. Each of the generals and commanders were either staring at Eltoar or Olivan Karta's lifeless body.

His head still angled down at the man, Eltoar's eyes flicked up, looking towards Taya. "We fall back to Elkenrim as soon as the injured can move. Have the messengers send hawks. I'd go myself, but you would be lambs to the slaughter if the elves attacked." He glanced back at Olivan. "That man wasn't fit to wear the lion." He looked around the room. "Few of you know war like what is coming. Pride no longer has a place. We are not prepared for this. But it is coming nonetheless. And when it comes, you do not want men like him at your side." He let his words fade before shaking his head. "Don't send him off with the others, dump him in a ditch. It's what he would have done with your bodies if nobody was looking."

As Eltoar turned and left, he stopped beside Farda. "We would like you with us tonight, Brother. Ilyain and Hala too."

Farda inclined his head. "Laël val du, Akar."

I am with you, Brother.

CHAPTER FIFTY-EIGHT

SOWING CHAOS

Ella stayed low, keeping her breaths steady as she crept through the grass. She moved from cover to cover, tree trunk to boulder, Faenir at her heels. Despite his bulk, the wolfpine moved like a shadow, his steps eliciting not so much as rustle.

Ahead, the torches of the Lorian camp flickered in the night, clustered together at the foot of the hill, backed by a forest on the other side.

Suka moved to Ella's right, along with two of the other scouts: Arlon and Ferol. Both Arlon and Ferol were twins near Ella's age. They were tall and gangly, but where Arlon had grown a scraggy beard, Ferol was clean shaven, his hair long and slicked with oil where Arlon's was tight cropped.

Varik and Juro shifted through the night to Ella's left alongside two more scouts, Jaks and Ligin. They moved as though the shadows bent around them.

The night was as dark as any Ella remembered, the moon blanketed over by black clouds. And yet, Ella could see better than she should have been able to, though the world's colour seemed faded, shades of grey rather than greens and browns.

She stopped for a moment, resting her hand on the trunk of a tall tree, closing her eyes as she steadied her breathing. Everything over the last few weeks had happened so fast. The red mist clouding her thoughts, the wolf calling in the back of her mind, the coppery tang of blood on her tongue. She would have been dead twice over had the wolf not howled in her blood. But it terrified her to her core. The lack of control, the savagery, the bloodlust. She had felt it. The wolf pulled at her even then, clawing to get out, hungering for control. *No. I will not.*

"Slow and steady," Suka whispered. Ella could hear her breathing, drawing deep, slow inhales, then exhaling through her nostrils.

Ella matched her breathing, nodding.

"It gets to us all sometimes." Suka held her hand on Ella's back. "Death is an ugly business."

Ella looked back at the woman. She wanted to tell her that it wasn't what they were about to do that set the anxiety in her bones. But how did she tell someone she was terrified of losing her mind? How did she tell someone she was afraid that if she lost control for even a moment, she might become a monster? Instead, she settled with a soft, "Thank you."

"All right," Juro whispered as he, Varik, and the others came closer, looking down the hill towards the Lorian camp. "Tanner, Yana, and the others should be in position near the supply wagons. The Lorians still have their hackles up, so when Farwen draws their attention, most of them should clear from the camp, but keep your wits about you, there will still be plenty of sharp steel down there."

Those gathered responded with a nod, their breaths misting. They had all witnessed the battle a couple of days gone. They'd watched it from atop a hill to the east of where the Three Sisters met. What they'd seen had shaken each of them – Farwen most of all. The elves had left Lynalion and were waging war. Not only that, but they had dragons. A year ago Ella had never even seen the Dragonguard. All she had heard were stories, tales to keep the South in line. But now, not only had she seen dragons with her own eyes, she had watched them die, watched them tear each other to shreds. The sight had set a fear in her that had caused her hands to shake.

After the battle, Ella and the others had stayed parallel to the imperial army, matching their movements from afar as the elves harried them, nipping at their heels. When the elves pulled back and consolidated and the Lorian army had made camp near the bottom of a gently sloping hill, Farwen decided the time to strike was now. While the Lorians were watching for what was behind them, they were blind to what was coming from the other side.

Ella and those with her were tasked with slipping into the camp once Farwen had dragged most of the soldiers away, while Tanner, Yana, and the others were creeping along the northern edge, ready to destroy the supply wagons. Get in. Set fire. Get out. While all this was happening, they had sent two of the scouts back to Tarhelm on horses to report on what had happened and what was coming.

"We need to move closer," Varik whispered, looking over the trunk of a fallen tree towards the camp. "Once the alarm is sounded, we don't want to waste a second."

"Agreed." Juro gestured towards one of the twins. "Arlon, torches."

Arlon hefted a large sack from his shoulders, long rag-covered sticks jutting from the top. Before the battle, Juro had procured a small barrel of rendered fat from a travelling merchant on his way to Holm, which had been used to soak the rags for the torches.

Ella took her torch from Juro, the wood rough against her fingers.

Slowly and steadily they made their way further down the hill, drawing lower to the ground as the trees thinned and their only cover was long grass, bushes, and the black of night. They stopped at the edges of the camp's torchlight, hunkering down behind a rise in the land.

Juro peeked over the crest of the rise. "Looks like they were in such a rush they didn't space the tents out, and the wind's blowing north-east. Perfect night for a fire." He dropped back down, resting on his haunches. "We move on my mark. Not a second sooner, not a second later. Ella, Suka, and Jaks with me. Ligin and the twins with Varik."

"We know the plan, Juro." Varik spoke in a hushed whisper, his voice calm and level.

Juro glanced at Ella.

"Wait for Farwen to cause a panic," Ella said. "Move on your mark. Stay together, stay low. Don't get ambitious, let the fire do its job. Get in and get out."

"And don't hesitate," Varik added. "You hesitate, you die."

"And make sure to drop the torch," Arlon added, scratching at his long beard.

"Drop the torch?" Ferol gave his brother a curious look.

"Well, if you don't drop the torch, then the empire will see you running away." Arlon shrugged.

"Fair point, brother. You've got the brains, I've got the looks."

Ella moved her gaze from Ferol to Arlon and back, eyes narrowing.

"What?" Ferol asked

"You're twins," she said. "You look exactly the same."

A brief moment passed, and both Arlon and Ferol gave Ella a look as though she had just said the most nonsensical thing they had ever heard.

Horns bellowed, cries and shouts burst from the camp, echoing in the night, carrying on the wind.

"As amusing as whatever this—" Juro gestured towards Ella, Arlon, and Ferol "—is, I think that might be our cue."

The shouts grew louder and widespread, until eventually Ella heard the words, "Elves, to the east!"

She risked a glance over the crest of the rise. Soldiers were running about carrying torches, mail shirts clinking, feet crunching into the dirt. A loud neigh rang in the air, and a group of horses charged past the outer rim of the camp, black as ravens, larger than any horses Ella had ever seen. Their riders were garbed in black plate that matched the horses, and curved blades hung at their hips.

"Blackthorns," Varik whispered.

Ella's heart pounded as she watched the Lorian soldiers stumble from their tents, strapping armour on as they did, running to answer the calls and shouts. She felt the wolf clawing at the back of her mind while at the same time Faenir nudged against her hip, trying to calm her. He was so large now his head would have been at her shoulder if he was standing at full height. Whatever she was, druid, or something else entirely, she wanted it gone. But if it was gone, then so was her newfound connection with Faenir. That was when it had all started: when Faenir had found her after Rhett.

"Slow and steady," Suka whispered, resting her hand on Ella's leg. "You control it, it doesn't control you."

Ella's heart stopped for just a second, her mind becoming crystal clear. "What did you say?"

"It doesn't take a genius like Arlon to see you're battling something." Suka squeezed Ella's leg. "And we all saw you in the forest and then again the other night with the scouts. Whatever beast is pulling at you, you are its master."

Juro's voice sounded before Ella could say anything more. "Move, now. Ella, Suka, Jaks, with me."

THE LIGHT OF THE TORCHES sent shadows flitting about the camp, ever-changing as the soldiers scrambled to and fro, dragging themselves from their tents, some of them fresh from sleep, some of them drunk on wine. They clambered into armour, strapping weapons belts around their waists.

Farda stood with his arms crossed, watching.

"What's happening?" Ilyain asked, tilting his head sideways to hear what he couldn't see. Chaos always made it harder for him to hear. Farda felt the man reaching out with threads of Air and Spirit, attempting to decipher the cacophony of noise.

"It seems we're under attack," Hala mused with a downturn of her bottom lip.

"What's happened?" Farda called out to a group of soldiers who were charging past. None of them answered, they were too focused on buttoning their leathers and strapping their weapons on. If the elves truly were attacking, everyone in this camp would be slaughtered. "Fucking idiots."

Farda reached out to the Spark and pulled on threads of Air. He snatched one of the soldiers around the neck, pulling them off their feet and dragging them across the dirt towards him. The other soldiers stopped in their tracks, gasping as they watched their companion grasp at the invisible tether around his neck.

Farda walked towards the man, pulling him across the dirt with the threads as he did. He reached down, grabbed a fistful of the man's shirt and hauled him to his feet. "When I call you, you answer. Understood?"

The man looked about as shocked as Farda would have expected, his face red as a slapped arse, his clothes now covered in dirt and dust. He drew in trembling breaths, eyes wide. "Yes..." A realisation dawned on the man's face. "Justicar Kyrana."

Farda loosened his grip a little, but still kept his hold on the soldier's shirt. "What has happened? Why was the alarm sounded?"

"The ehmm... the..." The soldier shook his head, swallowing hard, sweat glistening on his brow. "The elves, Justicar."

"What about the fucking elves?"

"They've been sighted. Scouts were attacked. To the southeast."

Farda nodded, pressing his tongue against the roof of his mouth. He released the man from his grip, pushing him backwards. "Go, don't keep your commander waiting."

The man staggered backwards, his eyes fixed on Farda. After a moment, he turned and rejoined his companions, looking back over his shoulder as they carried on.

"What news?" Hala raised an eyebrow, brushing white hair from her face.

Farda pulled his coin from his pocket, tracing his thumb around the edges. "The elves have attacked some scouts and are on their way here."

"They left scouts alive to report this?"

"Apparently." Farda flicked his coin in the air.

"Something is off." Ilyain's head was tilted to the side, his tapered ears listening.

A roar ripped through the night, and Farda looked up to see the gargantuan shape of Helios soaring overhead. The dragon's scales were so black the only way Farda could follow his movements was by watching where stars and clouds disappeared. *No Karakes and Lyina. They are still in mourning then.*

The coin thumped in Farda's hand. He looked down. "You're right. Something *is* off."

⚬

ELLA MOVED THROUGH THE CAMP as swiftly as she could without causing a racket. She stayed low, one hand wrapped around the shaft of her un-lit torch, the other resting on the short sword that hung at her left hip. Juro and Suka moved ahead of her, Jaks behind.

Now that most of the soldiers had gone, Ella was intensely aware of the sound of crunching dirt as she moved, the flapping of tent canvases in the wind, and the sound of her own breathing. Even her heartbeat felt as though it were as loud as a drum. She could feel Faenir's anxiety even from where he stood, near the camp's western edge. The wolfpine hated being apart, hated leaving Ella under anyone's protection but his own. But a wolfpine the size of a small horse wasn't exactly conducive to sneaking around. She would have tried to calm him with her own stillness, but she wasn't calm herself. She was scared, anxious, and a touch excited. They were inside a Lorian camp, and she was under no illusions that the Lorians would kill her where she stood if they found her.

The cream canopies of the Lorian tents flapped in the wind, banners and flags casting shadows in the torchlight, dark clouds covering the moon overhead. Ella's heart drummed louder.

"Back," Suka hissed, pressing Ella against a tent canvas. Ahead, Juro crouched behind a wagon.

A group of six Lorian soldiers emerged along a trodden dirt path between two tents ten or so feet ahead, moving towards the eastern edge of the camp.

"Move," Juro whispered as the soldiers jogged off into the distance.

They moved through the camp until they reached a spot where many of the tents were crammed together, the paths between them barely wide enough for someone to walk sideways.

"Here." Juro stopped beside a stack of crates. He dropped to his haunches and ran his hand across his weapons belt, his hand resting on the pommels of each knife that adorned his leather before resting on his sword. He nodded to himself, then looked to Ella, Suka, and Jaks. "We need to spread out a bit, make it hard to fight the fires. Light your torches off one of theirs. Stay low. Don't fuck around – wait till the fire catches, then move. Set two or three aflame, no more. They're close together and the wind is strong, the flames will feed themselves. Once you're done, get back here and then out the same way we've come in."

"What if there's a problem?"

"Problem? If anything goes wrong, run for your fucking life." Juro looked at each of them, eyes finally resting on Ella. "They're in the middle of nowhere here. Elkenrim is three days ride. The elves are between them and Steeple. They're hurting. If we can hit them hard here, it'll make all the difference. These are the chances we wait for. The few against the many. Now." Juro hefted his torch. "Try not to fuck it up."

Juro inclined his head towards them, then darted across the dirt, raising his torch and lighting it off a Lorian torch staked into the ground before vanishing around a tent. Jaks followed him.

"Don't go far," Suka said, gripping Ella's arm. She nodded over her right shoulder. "I'll go that way. You move a few tents ahead, then come straight back here."

Once Suka vanished between the canopies, Ella was alone. Farwen's words once again rang in her ears. *'A bird doesn't learn to fly by staying under its mother's wing.'*

She settled herself with a breath, then made her way towards the dirt path the soldiers had emerged from. Where did she even start? How was she to know a good place to start a fire? *Anywhere. Just start a gods damned fire and get out of this place.*

Ella drew in a short breath, exhaling sharply. She tightened her fingers around the shaft of her torch and darted across the dirt path to where a standing torch was lodged in the ground, flame burning bright. Her own torch burst into flames after only a few moments of being held in the fire. She stopped and looked over her shoulder, constantly searching for any signs that a Lorian soldier had seen her. *They're gone, for now. Most of them, anyway. Just get it done and get out.*

Ella's throat suddenly felt dry as cotton. There was something different about this. Killing someone who was trying to snuff the life from her was one thing. It was still dark and horrible and it made her feel like dirt. But this... She wasn't naïve; she knew people would die here. Men and women still sleeping, some in drunken stupors, some staying behind to guard. The flames would claim them. Death was death, but this just felt... it just felt different. But then as she stood there, Rhett's face floated from her memories, blood spilling from his mouth, the tip of the spear jutting from his stomach, her name on his lips. Her own screams.

'Don't you dare leave me! Rhett Fjorn, do not leave me alone!'

Something shifted in her. The wolf howled in her blood, sensing her weakness, snapping, lips curled back, fangs bared. She could feel Faenir too, only just, his emotions dull at the back of her mind. He snarled, memories of Rhett pulling at him. The edges of her vision tinged red. Her hands tensed around the torch, and she could feel her muscles bunching in her back. *I am in control.*

She was in control, but the only problem was she wanted the wolf, she needed its strength, so she let it bleed it into her. Her mind was set. These people would have lit her on fire and walked away as she screamed. They took her Rhett from her, they took her love. *My Ayar Elwyn. My One Heart.* She would not let them take any more.

Ella dropped to her haunches and touched the torch against the canopy, watching as the material caught fire, losing herself in the flames for just a moment. As the flames flickered and blew in the wind, spreading, she turned to the tent behind her and did the same thing. The days had been dry, so the canopy caught fire in seconds. She moved forwards through the tents, touching the torch off their bases until the flames could feed themselves. Juro had said to burn only two or three and let the flames catch, but something had taken her: an anger, a fear, a fury. Even the thought of it set her jaw clenching, a snarl forming in her throat.

A harsh voice called her back to herself.

"You, stop!"

Ella froze. She turned, the torch gripped in her hand, to see a man charging towards her in nothing more than his small clothes and loose tunic, a sword gripped in his fists. Ella made to reach for her sword, but then Farwen came rushing from between two tents and hammered into the Lorian with her shoulder.

He crashed to the ground, scrambling to get back up, but Farwen leapt on top of him, lifting her blade, then driving it down through his chest. He coughed and spluttered, blood sprinkling from his mouth. Farwen twisted the blade in a sharp jerk. The man convulsed, then went limp. She rose to her feet, stepping on the man's chest and ripping the blade free in the same motion. "What in the gods are you doing?"

"I…" Ella looked to the torch in her hands and then over the tents around her. The night was ablaze. She hadn't even counted, she had just burned. "I wanted to make sure…"

"Farwen, Ella?" Juro emerged from the darkness of a path between two tents, his voice a hushed whisper. "What are you doing? We need to get out of here."

Farwen looked to Ella, matching her stare.

"Let's go." Ella glanced down at her torch one last time then tossed it into the rising flames of a nearby tent.

Screams rang out as people awoke shrouded in fire and burning canvas. A glance over her shoulder showed Ella nothing but flames and sparks. Juro had been right. The weather had been so dry, the tents so close together, and the wind so strong, that the flames had spread as though burning through a field of wheat in high summer.

Part of Ella roared in triumph, her heart pounding. But that part paled in comparison to the guilt at the sound of the screams and shrieks that filled the night. She had caused those screams. She had burned those people alive. Regardless of the rationalisation, that was a cold, hard fact. And it was something she was going to have to learn to live with, because she knew it would never leave her.

A thunderclap sounded, and sharp pain lanced her in a wave from head to toe. Then she was hurtling through the air. She tensed, closing her eyes, wind whipping around her. She crashed into something with a *snap*. Fabric closed around her, and the wind was knocked from her lungs as she hit the ground.

Ella gasped, dragging in air, her head spinning, ears ringing. Pain burned up her back and across her left shoulder. In her mind she could feel feet hammering against the ground. *Faenir.* She tried to lift herself but fell, her hand catching something. She was going to get sick; she could feel it in her gut. Vomit rose, but she choked it back down, gritting her teeth.

She grunted, peeling open her eyes to see a dizzying haze. The touch of dry canvas beneath her hands let Ella know she had been thrown into a tent. The snapping must have been a pole; that would explain the pain in her back. She shook her head, the haze that blurred her vision lifting. She could taste blood. Her own. The slowly emerging throb in her mouth told her she had bitten her tongue.

Flames blazed, sweeping back and forth in the shifting winds, consuming everything they touched. Ella grunted, leveraging the corner of what must have been a crate on the inside of the tent. But when she finally hauled herself to her feet and her vision cleared, her heart seized, and a shiver swept over her skin.

Juro hung in the air, impaled on the shaft of a snapped tent pole, legs and arms dangling, blood pooling in the dirt beneath him. Ella stumbled forwards, her balance deserting her. The sound of clashing swords pulled her attention to the right.

Farwen moved in a flash of steel, exchanging blows with perhaps the only two people, bar Coren, who Ella had ever seen move like the elf. One had hair as white as snow, a sword gripped in her fist. The other was dark skinned, with a shaven head and a curved blade – an elf. *What is another elf doing here?*

The three danced around each other, each predators stalking their prey, steel probing for weaknesses and slicing.

Ella reached down to her hip, relief filling her when she felt the pommel of her short sword. She pulled the weapon free and charged. Farwen wouldn't have left her; she wasn't leaving Farwen.

As Ella charged forwards, two Lorians stumbled from a tent that was already half aflame. One wore a tunic and leather trousers while the other was shirtless in a pair of string-drawn linens. Both looked as though they had just had a rude awakening from a drunken stupor; both held sharp steel in their fists. They looked to Farwen and the two strangers, then over to Ella. A flash of grey burst from the dark and crashed into the shirtless soldier, knocking him back into the tent. The man's companion turned to the tent, blood-chilling shrieks rising from within. A second later, Faenir leapt from the tent's depths, crashing into the remaining soldier's chest, tearing and ripping. The wolfpine clamped his jaws around the man's throat and ripped a chunk of flesh free with a spray of blood.

Ella continued her charge, her gaze locked on the dark-skinned elf. She threw herself forwards, swinging her sword towards his head. The elf threw her half a glance, then swung his hand as though he were swatting a fly. Ella could sense a slight shift in the air, then something unseen cracked into her left side, sending her sprawling to the ground. She leapt to her feet only for the invisible force to hammer her back down again, sending a burst of pain jolting up her lower back. *He's a mage.*

The wolf howled in her head, a burning sensation spilling through her veins. She clenched her jaw, the wolf snapping and snarling – waiting.

A glance told Ella that Farwen was holding her own against the white-haired woman, but blood now leaked from a gash on her arm and a slice across her left leg.

All right. Ella drew in a trembling breath, acquiescing to the wolf in her blood. *Be free.*

An all-consuming howl answered from within. Her fingers curled, tightening around the hilt of her sword. She felt her fingernails growing thicker and sharper, scratching at the dirt. The red mist fogged Ella's vision, a strength igniting within her. She leapt to her feet and lunged towards the elf, Faenir beside her, a vicious growl in his throat. Just as the other times the wolf had flooded her veins, an unseen tether pulled taut between her and Faenir. They moved as one.

Ella's hackles raised, and she sensed another shift in the air – the elf's magic. She swerved sideways, Faenir bounding to the left. An invisible wave passed her, its path marked by the whipping of dust from the ground. Ella snarled, not stopping, then launched herself at the elf. She swung her blade, but the elf met it with ease, knocking her off balance. He extended his hand, wrapping his fingers around her throat and lifting her off her feet.

Faenir snarled and lunged, leaping straight for the elf's throat, but Ella felt that same ripple in the air, and the elf's magic slammed into the wolfpine, knocking him backwards through the side of a tent. Ella swung her sword, but something unseen, something she couldn't sense, caught her arm midway through the swing, freezing it as though she was trapped in ice.

The elf stared into Ella's eyes, giving a downturn of his bottom lip. A red glow emanated from beneath his breastplate. "A druid…"

Ella's sword hand tensed, that same unseen force peeling her fingers back against their will, her hand shaking violently. She felt the short sword fall from her grip, heard it hit the ground. The whole time, the elf's hand remained clamped around her throat. She wanted to kick and growl and roar, the wolf within her thrashing to break free, but something held her firm, like a thousand threads of twine wrapped tight.

A fury flared in her mind, and Faenir burst from within the tent he had been thrown through, hackles raised, saliva dripping from his snapping jaws. The wolfpine bent his legs and launched himself at the elf. Dread shivered across Ella's skin, and she watched as Faenir was caught by the same invisible force that held her in place. The wolfpine snapped and snarled, mouth frothing and spittle flying. The red glow beneath the elf's breastplate intensified, and Faenir's snarling turned to pleading whimpers, his body twisting. The whimpers turned to shrieks.

"Let him go!" Ella roared, her voice muffled by the fingers around her throat. The wolf in her blood howled and howled, thrashing and raging. She screamed as she pulled at her invisible bonds, trying desperately to break free.

As she screamed, the red mist poured over her mind, covering her eyes, drowning her senses, consuming her. Then, in an instant, everything was black, dark, and empty. She could still feel the elf's fingers around her throat, her lungs fighting to drag in air, but he was gone from her vision, as was the entire camp, and Faenir. Panic flared as she lifted her hands; where there should have been skin and nail, instead her fingers, hands, and arms were wrought with a shimmering white light as though she were some kind of spirit. She looked down at her legs and torso to see the same white light. What was more, she wasn't standing on anything, she was floating, weightless, in an endless sea of black. She looked around, but everything was dark, no sounds or smells drifted on the air. *What is happening? Where am I? Where is Faenir?*

She touched her fingers to her throat, where she could still feel the elf's grip tightening. The sensation was distant, as though her body was separate from her mind. *Is this the void? Am I dying?*

Frantically, Ella looked around, still seeing nothing but blackness. *I can't die... I can't. I can't leave Calen alone.* As Ella's hands began to shake, something changed in the dark. Small spheres of light came to life, spreading through the blackness like stars in the sky. There were hundreds, thousands of them. They burst into life all around her. She could feel things radiating from them: thoughts, emotions, consciousness.

Without anything more than a thought, Ella's ethereal body drifted upwards towards two small spheres of light close to her. She was unsure as to what she was doing or what she might find, but she couldn't just wait for the elf to choke the life from her physical body. As she drifted upwards, more glowing spheres emerged, becoming clearer. Ella reached out her hand as the two small spheres she'd been pushing towards whipped past her. As they drew closer, they took shape – two small birds, wings flapping, bodies wrought in an ethereal light. More of the spheres took shape around her: birds, rats, mice, lizards, donkeys, horses. She couldn't see any people, or even Faenir, but she could feel the wolfpine faintly in the back of her mind. Each of the spheres were living things, or maybe their minds or souls; Ella was sure of it – she could *feel* it.

I'm not dead then. At least, not yet.

Her physical body felt so far away, yet the pressure of the elf's grip still set a burning in her lungs. *I need to do something – anything.* Ella pushed her mind further, seeing small spheres of glowing light almost everywhere she looked. In the distance, two spheres as big as houses materialised, one almost twice the size of the other. She reached out, desperate. Whatever was happening, there had to be something she could do to save herself. Gently, she tried to brush her mind against the smaller of the spheres, but dread filled her as she drew closer and the spheres took shape, spreading. Enormous wings, bodies laden with muscles and scales, jaws framed by horns longer than Ella's body, eyes that, even in the misty white glow, shifted and shimmered like molten steel.

Dragons. As the realisation flooded Ella, the dragon roared, its ethereal shape turning to look at her as the sound rippled through the darkness.

It can feel me.

Ella pulled her mind away, scrambling, panic pounding through her, a fear the likes of which she'd never known piercing her heart. And then she brushed against a smaller sphere that took the shape of an owl, its spirit-like wings leaving a trail of white mist behind it. Ella pushed herself into the owl. The darkness burned with a flash of bright light, and then the world returned, and Ella could see more than simply endless black. But she wasn't looking through her own eyes. She was in the air, swooping downwards towards the camp, fires blazing in the night. Everything was sharper and clearer, but the world lacked colour; it was all blacks, greys, and whites. It was the single strangest sensation she had ever felt. She was free, light as the wind, soaring. But she was also close to death, those fingers tightening around her throat, her feet dangling. Her mind was in the owl, but her body was in the camp below, fading. Was this what Farwen had spoken of when she had said the druid, Galveer, could push his mind into that of animals? Was this Shifting? Whether it was or not, she needed to do something; she needed to save herself.

Without thinking, Ella plummeted towards the camp, the owl's natural instincts guiding her. She could feel the pulse of her own true body, feel her heartbeat fading. She honed in on it.

Everything was bright as day, the light of the flames almost blinding, but the owl's eyes were far more powerful than her own. Within moments, she saw what she was looking for – she saw herself. Farwen and the white-haired warrior were still exchanging blows behind the dark-skinned elf, steel flashing in the firelight.

Seeing her own body held up in the air, the life being choked from her by the elf, filled Ella with an unsettling kind of fear. How long had her mind been in that strange place? What happened if she died while her mind was in this creature's? Where would she go? She didn't have time to contemplate it.

She unleashed a high-pitched shriek and dove towards the elf who held her. Ella crashed straight into the elf's face, talons slicing through skin like soft clay, blood sluicing. A rush of relief sparked in her as air flooded the lungs of her true body, a dull feeling of pain as it hit the ground. But that rush was soon cut short as the same unseen force that held Faenir in place pressed against the owl's body, wrapping around it, crushing it. Ella squawked and screeched, flapping her wings, trying desperately to get away as the pressure crushed her fragile ribs, tiny bones snapping.

A realisation set in: *I'm going to die.* She didn't know how to pull her mind from the creature, had no way of escaping. She was helpless. Pure undiluted fear turned her soul to ice as the elf's magic pulled tighter.

Snap.

Ella opened her eyes, screaming, shrieking, pushing backwards in the dirt. Tears were in freefall down her cheeks, her chest convulsing. Her throat felt as though it had been crushed by a rock. She wrapped her arms around her chest, shivering, the sound of snapping bones filling her ears. She had died. She'd felt the world close in around her, felt the pain of bones snapping, saw the light fade as the owl was crushed. She sobbed and convulsed, until a dark shape stood over her.

Something crashed into Ella's face, slamming her head backwards against the hard-packed ground. A thin, sharp noise rang in ears, her stomach turning, the pain almost blinding.

"Ilyain." A dark form took shape over Ella. Her vision blurred. "Why is she alive?"

"She's a druid." That voice was the elf's. She recognised it. "Farwen?"

"I let her go." The second figure moved, white hair coming into focus as Ella's vision cleared.

A second blow struck Ella in the face, and then everything went dark.

CHAPTER FIFTY-NINE

MAKE WHOLE WHAT IS HALF

The enormous bridge of white stone upon which Calen walked extended over a chasm that stretched for what must have been at least two hundred feet. Erinian stone lined the low parapet of the bridge, the soft azure glow augmented by the incandescent firelight of the lanterns set at evenly spaced intervals. Above, the sun and the moon shared the sky, their natural light dimmed by dark clouds. On either side of the bridge, rivers fed waterfalls that flowed over the edge of cliffs, cascading into the depths of the chasm, the crashing roar of water filling the air. The forests atop the cliffs were thick and lush, as dense as the densest parts of the Darkwood Calen knew.

Valerys let out a puff of air, and Calen felt the awe radiating from the dragon walking behind him and Aeson, talons clicking off stone. The bridge was so large that even Valerys could walk along it without his winged forelimbs touching the parapet on either side, the warm light of the lanterns and soft glow of the erinian stone accenting his white scales.

"Where are we going?" Calen asked. After meeting with the triarchy, Aeson had taken Calen from Mythníril immediately. He had refused to let anyone come with them, which had elicited a number of hot tempered words. In the end, Calen had agreed to go, much to Dann's chagrin, simply to stop the arguing. Also, Aeson had agreed they would be back by nightfall. It was the easiest option.

Aeson didn't turn. He continued walking at the same measured pace, his eyes fixed ahead. "You will see soon enough."

"No, Aeson." Calen stopped. "All you have done is tell me as little as you possibly could at any given time. You string me along, promising me answers that you almost never give. Since meeting you, I've lost almost everyone I've ever cared for. My mam, my dad, Ella, Faenir, Rist. I'm not following you blindly anymore. You tell me now, or I'm not taking another step."

Aeson turned. Valerys moved forwards, extending his neck, a deep rumble resonating in his throat as Aeson came closer to Calen, but to Calen's surprise, Aeson didn't round on him with anger. His eyes were soft, his expression mournful. "I am sorry." The words took Calen completely off guard. "You were right. What you said by the Burnt Lands. I would give anything to see the empire fall. To see Fane and the Dragonguard lifeless on the ground." He drew in a deep breath, biting his lip and shaking his head. "You have experienced loss, Calen. Deep, foundation-shaking loss. I do not deny that. But you have only begun to feel a shred of the things that have been taken from me. The empire took half my soul, they took my world, my kin. They took everything I knew and destroyed it. I don't speak of Lyara often, mostly because the thought of her burns like fire, but also because there are few who could understand what it is to lose a dragon. But you can. Lyara was taken from me by a Draleid who betrayed us, Sylvan Anura, and the dragon to which she was bound, Aramel. The fear Lyara felt in the moments before she died is burned into my soul like a brand. She was terrified, Calen. Not for herself, but for me. She was terrified of leaving me alone in this world. There is a reason why the word Rakina means both 'one who is broken' and 'one who survived'. I am alive, but I am limping. I will never be whole again. It takes all my strength simply to rise each morning. I would set this world on fire for her. I would burn it to the ground and sleep in the ashes. But I will settle for tearing the empire to pieces and building a world that is better for those who come after me. For Erik, and Dahlen, and you. Because that is the man I once was, and it is the man I strive to be again. So please, for the love of the gods, stop fighting me. I am trying."

A stray tear ran down Aeson's cheek, his eyes glistening, breaths trembling. Calen didn't know what to say, and to his surprise, he found tears welling in his eyes. He reached out to Valerys, letting their minds merge. Aeson's words had given him a deep, visceral need to feel their shared soul, to feel Valerys's presence. Sorrow bled from Valerys and into Calen. He could feel the dragon's fear at the thought of leaving him alone in the world.

Calen turned and reached up his hand. Valerys nuzzled the tip of his snout into Calen's palm. Calen remembered a time when he could carry Valerys on one arm – a time when Valerys could curl up at the front of a horse's saddle. But as the dragon stood before him now, those times would scarcely be believable. Valerys's head alone was larger than Calen's torso, his muscles dense, chest deep, and wings capable of spreading twice as wide as Valerys was long. The horns that framed his face had once been no longer than Calen's thumb, and now some were the length of his arm. The dragon looked back at Calen with those pale lavender eyes and let out a puff of warm air.

"Draleid n'aldryr, Valerys. Myia nithír til diar." Calen leaned forwards and touched his forehead to Valerys's snout, then turned back to Aeson. "All right."

Aeson swallowed hard, his gaze holding Calen's. "I—"

"I said all right, Aeson. And…" Calen looked at the stone floor of the bridge, then lifted his head. "I don't have words that could give back what you've lost, but I… I understand what you're fighting for."

Aeson gave Calen a smile so weak it could barely hold itself together, then inclined his head and turned, continuing across the bridge.

As they walked, the bridge sloped downwards, connecting to a white stone landing on the other side that was built onto a cliff's edge. From the landing, they followed a path framed by tall broad-leafed trees that Calen didn't recognise. The branches connected overhead in a perfect arch, so perfect he was certain the Spark had been used to form them into the shape. And so tall were the trees that even Valerys could stand at full height without grazing the branches.

Aeson stopped where the path led through a Spark-carved archway in a sheer rock face that disappeared upwards past the trees' canopy. Through the arch, Calen could see only skies and more rock. Words were carved into the stone above the archway.

"Draleid n'aldryr, Rakina nai dauva. Ikin vir vänta. Ikin vir alura. Marai viël alanín til ata ilynír abur er kerta." Calen whispered the words, trying his best to find the right pronunciations. He could make out the first section; he knew it well. *Dragonbound by fire, Broken by death*. But he didn't recognise many of the other words in the rest of the script.

"Dragonbound by fire, Broken by death. Here we wait. Here we rest. Until we are called to make whole what is half." Aeson turned to Calen, his eyes searching. "Your Old Tongue has improved – you speak it well." He drew in a long, almost pensive, breath, then exhaled slowly. "Come, it is past time."

"Past time for what, Aeson?"

"You will see." Without another word Aeson walked through the archway, stepping onto the platform on the other side.

Valerys craned his neck over Calen's head as Calen read the words above the archway once more. "Until we are called to make whole what is half."

Something about the words resonated in Calen, and he thought he knew what he would find on the other side of the archway. He took a tentative step forwards, held for a moment, then followed Aeson through. Valerys followed, ducking his head to fit.

On the other side of the archway, the rock face rose, spreading hundreds of feet in a circle and sloping downwards toward a central courtyard. What looked like homes hewn from the same bone-like material as the city gates were nestled into the rock face. The buildings blended into the mountainside, flowing naturally as though they had been grown from the rock rather than built. Platforms fronted each of the buildings, pathways of cultivated grass leading down towards the enormous courtyard in the centre.

The courtyard itself was massive. It must have been almost three hundred feet in diameter. It was broken into sections divided by a system of bridges and small streams that were fed by cascades that flowed from around the homes built into the rock, following the paths to the centre. A large circular platform of white stone occupied the middle of the courtyard, a small thicket of trees at its centre, while lanterns stood on pedestals all about its perimeter.

It was on this platform that figures stood, staring at Calen, Aeson, and Valerys.

Aeson waited a moment, allowing Calen the chance to take it all in, then gave him a soft smile and started down the sloping path that connected their platform to the courtyard.

As they drew closer to the bottom of the path, three of the figures moved forwards from the larger group. One was a man, as tall as Haem and as broad as Tarmon, with dark hair that fell past his chest and down to his waist. The second was a Jotnar, her pale, whitish-blue skin shimmering in the lanternlight. She stood half again taller than the man, her hair red as blood. The third was a woman, small in stature with hair as blonde as straw. She sat in a chair crafted from a blend of steel and the same bone-like material as the homes that lined the rock face. Two wheels were fixed to the sides of the chair, slanted outwards at a slight angle. The centre of the wheels were covered by plates of bone white, while the rim was a deep grey-black.

Another twenty or so humans, elves, and Jotnar stood behind the three, watching.

The Jotnar with blood red hair stepped forwards, inclining her head. "Aeson Virandr, son of Torun Virandr, it pleases me greatly to lay eyes on you once more. It has been too long, my brother."

"Thacia, daughter of Ulin, the years have been long, and I am sorry."

"Forgiveness is easily given, considering the circumstances of your return."

The sound of wingbeats reverberated through the circular basin, and the Jotnar glanced upwards – as did all those gathered. Within moments a gust of wind swept over Calen, blowing his hair forwards, and Valerys alighted on the stone behind him, wings spread wide, neck stretched forwards. Their minds drifted together, seeing as one, feeling as one. Curiosity and a caution filled them both.

The Jotnar, Thacia, moved closer, the man and the woman in the wheelchair, moving with her. She looked up at Valerys, her head moving with his, staring into his eyes. A smile curled her lips. She dropped her gaze to Calen, her eyes a dark brown, almost black. "I never truly believed this moment would come – none of us did – yet, I hoped. But now that we are here, I am unable to find the words to adequately capture what I wish to say." The only Jotnar Calen had ever met were Asius, Senas, and Larion. And even with the three of them combined, he had not seen half the emotion that swelled in Thacia's eyes. "I am Thacia, daughter of Ulin, soulkin to Myrax, Broken by death. I would know your names, so that I may call you my kin."

Calen's hair stood on end at the Jotnar's words, and he found himself struggling to draw breath, the air catching in his throat. When he'd read the inscription above the archway, he had hoped to find more Rakina. But at the same time, he had not. Because if more Rakina still lived, that meant there were more souls like Aeson's, shorn in half, tortured, alone. "I…" Calen looked over the others who stood behind the Jotnar. Were they all Rakina? "I am Calen Bryer, son of Vars Bryer and Freis Bryer. My soulkin is Valerys, son of Valacia."

Whispers spread throughout those gathered, and Calen was sure he heard Valerys's name repeated.

"It is true, then." Thacia held her gaze on Valerys as she spoke. "You did travel to the Icelands, my brother?"

"I did." Aeson lifted his head to look at Valerys, a smile spreading across his face.

"Valerys," Thacia repeated, another smile touching her lips at the name. "*Ice*. It is a name well chosen. A Valacian dragon. Never in my days did I believe I would see such a thing. Not in the before, or now." She tilted her head sideways. "Alaith anar, Valerys. Din närvarin er atuya sin'vala, mentat ar altinua." *Well met, Valerys. Your presence is welcome here, now and always.*

The dragon lowered his head over Calen's shoulder, his snout dipping in what was almost a bow, a recognition of Thacia and what she had lost in Myrax. She was Rakina – one who survived.

When Valerys had lifted his head, Thacia reached out to Calen. "You and Valerys are a sight for the sorest of eyes, brother. There are no words in this tongue or any other that could convey the happiness in my heart."

Calen took the Jotnar's massive forearm, his fingers wrapping around the bluish skin. He had no idea what to say, but there was something comfortable in the silence between them.

After a few moments, Thacia released her grasp and gestured towards the woman who sat in the wheelchair. "Calen, Valerys, may I introduce you to Chora Sarn, daughter of Ekara Sarn, soulkin to Daiseer, Broken by death."

"Oh." Chora Sarn looked almost bemused. "We're doing me now, are we? I thought we were just going to stare longingly into each other's eyes until we grew hungry." She shifted her hand on the left wheel of the chair, pulling it backwards, reorienting herself so she faced Calen. "Apologies about Thacia here. It's said that once you become a Draleid, you cease to be anything else, but I don't think anyone told her. She practically oozes Jotnar. It's good to meet you, Calen." Chora had to tilt her neck back to look up at Valerys. "It's good to meet you, too," she called out in an exaggerated manner. "But if you could come a bit closer, that would be appreciated. This chair doesn't exactly make me taller."

Valerys gave a low rumble and once more craned his neck down, stretching his snout towards Chora. The woman was far less formal than Thacia had been. She reached out and rested her hand on Valerys's scales. She closed her eyes and drew in a breath, holding it for a moment before exhaling and opening her eyes once more. "You're beautiful," she whispered to Valerys as she looked up into his lavender eyes. "Not as beautiful as my Daiseer was, but beautiful, nonetheless." Valerys acted more like a pup than a dragon before Chora, turning his snout as she patted his scales. "A Valacian dragon…" She shook her head. "Never in my days." She turned to Calen. "Have your eyes always been that colour?" Chora's eyes narrowed, her gaze shifting from Calen to Valerys and back again. "Judging by your expression I'd say that's a no. Well, that's new. You've piqued my curiosity now, Calen Bryer. Now, I'm told I talk too much – I disagree, but that's beside the point – so I will pass you on to Harken." Chora gestured towards the tall man with the hair to his waist, but then glanced at Aeson. "Oh, also, it's good to see you too, Virandr. You've lost weight. You never were good for eating enough, even as a youth."

"It's good to see you too, Chora." The smile that touched Aeson's lips was a genuine one, the likes of which Calen hadn't often seen from the man. "I see Daiseer still hasn't taken your tongue."

"Not for lack of trying." Chora spread her arms out wide, gesturing to her chair. "Bastard went for the legs. He was always a greedy one. No doubt he'll come back for more one day."

"If we're quite done, it's an honour to meet you both, Calen and Valerys." The tall man whom Chora had gestured to bowed at the waist, once for Calen and once for Valerys. "I am Harken Holdark, soulkin of Thorandír, Broken by death. I am sure this must be beyond overwhelming for you both. And I can see in your eyes that you have lost much on your journey here. But you are amongst your own kind now. We are kin. Come, let me introduce you."

Harken, Thacia, and Chora proceeded to introduce Calen to each of the Rakina who had gathered in the central courtyard. Most were elves or humans, but besides Thacia there were two more Jotnar – Aelmar and Moras. Calen tried to remember each of their names, but there were too many. *Rakina... The Broken...* Even the thought felt strange. Until saying the inscription above the archway, Calen had not imagined there would be others besides Aeson. Why had Aeson not brought him here sooner?

"Come," Chora said, her chair shifting back and forth, threads of Air turning the wheels. "We can stand here all day, but I'm getting hungry and there's still something I believe you will want to see. There will be plenty of time to talk later."

"Chora speaks the truth," Thacia said with a nod. "Come, walk with us."

"Ahem." Chora raised an eyebrow, but after a moment she shook her head, let out an exaggerated sigh and moved towards the other side of the courtyard, using threads of Air to turn the wheels of her chair.

Harken stared after Chora, puffing out his cheeks, but Aeson just laughed, following her.

"My arms get tired," Chora said after a moment, glancing at Calen as he moved beside her. "The threads of Air, I mean. I know you're wondering, but you're the polite kind, I see that in you. I'll beat it out of you. I can use my hands to move the wheels, but my arms get tired. Using the Spark is easier."

"What happened?" As soon as the words had left Calen's mouth, he wanted to drag them back in. "I'm sorry, it's not my place."

"Sorry?" Chora chortled, a cough catching in her throat. "Ah the young. You'll learn. When Daiseer died, I lost many things. The feeling in my legs being one of them. I'm sure Aeson already told you that when the bond is broken, those who survive – for lack of a better word – *lose* things. Some lose something physical, like the ability to use my legs. Others lose things that nobody can see, like Harken's sense of humour."

The tall man glared at Chora, rolling his eyes.

Chora placed her hands on the wheels of her chair, adding her strength to the threads of Air to push her over the small bridge before them. Ahead was a pathway through the rock, like a small valley.

"Some lose a single thing," Chora continued, "Others lose... a lot more. Most lose the will to live. Even those of us who have survived have to fight that battle each day."

Calen looked around at the Rakina who walked with them. There were almost thirty, including Aeson. "How is this possible?" He looked to Aeson. "And why haven't you told me?"

"Don't worry, Virandr. I can answer that." Chora spun her chair, stopping the procession. She let out a sigh, running her tongue across her lips. "How do I put this?" She clicked her tongue off the roof of her mouth. "This is all there is. This is the last of us. Twenty-nine, including Aeson, and Coren and Farwen – who are in the North. If there are more, they have remained hidden even from us. There were once thousands of our kind. We filled the sky. But when dragons go to battle against one another, the sky bleeds. After Ilnaen fell, and the wars that followed, the elves established this place and erected the glamour. They had no choice but to be careful with whom they reached out to. You must remember this was at a time where our own brothers and sisters drove knives into our backs and hunted us like animals. So, carefully, methodically, and with the utmost caution, the elves of Aravell sought us out in the hopes of preserving the Draleid. At first, we continued to fight. Many of us were still Bound, and we refused to lay down and die. But as the years wore on, our numbers dwindled, our soulkin were slain… It became difficult to keep going."

She spread arms wide, gesturing to the Rakina. "This is a lot for anyone. Virandr, here is unique. You see, most of us, deep down, we're just waiting to die. That's the hard truth of it. I can't speak for everyone, but I know it is revenge and hate that drives me. It is a fire in the pit of my stomach that refuses to let Daiseer's death mean nothing. I think that might be the difference between those who die and those who become Rakina after the bond is broken. It's not about strength or weakness. It's about purpose. Some want nothing more than to be with their soulkin, the half-soul they have left yearns for it. To be bonded is their purpose. While others, like me, find their purpose in the physical plane. But of us all, there are three who hold to a purpose more strongly than any. Aeson Virandr," Chora gestured towards Aeson, giving an almost mocking bow at the waist. "And two others who were young at the time of The Fall, Coren Valmar and Farwen Ethylion. Whatever it is in their hearts that drives them, after a while, they refused to remain here. For them, I imagine, all we do is remind them of what they've lost. It has been a very, very long time, even by our standards, since I last laid eyes on Aeson Virandr. And I suspect, the only reason he is here is for you." Chora looked up at Aeson. "Did I get all that? I've grown forgetful in my old age."

"I'm sorry it's been so long, Chora." Aeson looked to the other Rakina. "All of you…"

"Oh, not you as well. Apologies are a waste of time, Aeson. I've told you this ever since you were young. Apologise by getting drunk with us tonight, not by giving us platitudes. Now, come, we've wasted enough time already."

As Chora and the others set off towards the path that split the rock ahead, Calen couldn't help but notice the despondency in the way each of them moved – a certain lethargy that showed no care for the next step they would take. What had each of them lost? Most of the physical losses were obvious: one elf had milky eyes, one woman didn't have a single strand of hair anywhere Calen could see, while another's left arm hung limp by his side. But the losses he couldn't see were the ones that cut the deepest – those of the mind and the soul.

The closest Calen had come to understanding what being Rakina felt like was when Valerys burst through the barrier that surrounded the Burnt Lands and when Artim Valdock placed those rune-marked shackles around Calen's wrists. He had still been able to sense Valerys in the back of his mind, but even then the sense of grief and loss had almost consumed him. He remembered leaning into Artim Valdock's grip as the High Mage closed his hand around Calen's throat, all sense of self-preservation gone. His jaw clenched reflexively, and he had to resist the urge to fold his arms across his chest and tuck hands under his pits. That position had given him some form of comfort while in the cell.

In response to the memory, a protective feeling washed over Calen, a rumble resonating in Valerys's throat. The dragon leaned down, letting out a puff of warm air as he nudged Calen with the side of his white-scaled snout.

But then, as that feeling of warmth drifted through the bond, a roar thundered in the distance, echoing down the pathway ahead and filling the courtyard.

A rush swept over Valerys, his eyes widening, neck jerking up. Their minds crashed like twin thunderstorms, bleeding into one another. The sensation was so powerful it was almost overwhelming.

Valerys lifted his head, cocking it to the side, lavender eyes staring ahead. The dragon's heart was galloping. A second roar erupted, and Valerys leapt into the air, wings carrying him high, a surge of excitement rippling through him. He cracked his wings and soared overhead, sweeping past Chora and the others before gliding towards the pathway.

Calen broke into a run after him, throwing etiquette to the wind. The elation that Valerys felt now coursed through Calen's veins. *Dragons. There's more dragons. Valerys isn't alone.*

He pushed past Aeson, Harken, and a slender woman whose name he had learned was Ah-aela, and charged towards the pathway ahead.

"Calen, wait!" Aeson called.

But Calen didn't stop. His feet pounded against the stone as he ran after Valerys, who soared overhead. If finding the shattered dragon eggs in Vindakur had brought Valerys agony and grief, the sound of that roar was like lightning in his veins. Calen had never felt the dragon's heart – their heart – beat so ferociously. Walls of rock rose on either side as Calen entered the pathway, which consisted of a single long slab of Spark-hewn white stone. The path was deceptively wide, almost a hundred feet from side to side. The open sky above was painted with the light of the setting sun that filtered through a scattering of dark clouds. Valerys unleashed a roar that shook Calen's bones – an answer to the one they had heard. The dragon's wings stretched almost from wall to wall, black veins streaming through white, muscles rippling with each wingbeat. The path was short, and Calen saw it opening ahead into a mountain glade.

Valerys's wingbeats drifted through the passage, amplified by the rising walls of rock on either side. He was already swooping down when Calen reached the end of the path and stepped out into the glade.

Calen stopped at the mouth of the passage. He looked about, eyes wide as he heaved deep breaths, his lungs burning. What he had thought was a glade was, in fact, a plateau that stretched for hundreds of feet in a horse-shoe shape, dotted with trees and bushes. A small stream ran diagonally across the plateau, then tumbled off the edge of a sheer drop. Much like the area they had just been, the plateau was nestled into an enormous basin of steep rocky cliffs, with more plateaus extending all about it. At the far side of the basin, the cliffs gave way to a long valley that stretched off into the distance.

But it was not the wonders of the basin carved from the Spark that took Calen's breath away. It was the dragons. "Elyara guide me…"

Two lay in the clearing of the plateau, one beneath an enormous tree and another by the stream. Each was easily three times Valerys's size, with horns as long and thick as Calen's legs and wings that looked like the sails of a ship. The dragon beneath the tree had scales of dark yellow accented with hints of green, while the one by the stream was pure black with wings of dark blue. Long scars of fused scales ran along their bodies like markings in old stone.

Around the basin Calen saw three more dragons curled up on other plateaus. One was a muted shade of pinkish-white with wings red as blood. The second was so grey it blended with the stone. The third was blue as the ocean, scales trimmed with white.

A roar thundered through the cavern, and Calen lifted his gaze towards the sky. The dragon dropping from the upper levels of the basin was enormous, larger again than either of the two who lay curled up on the first plateau. Its scales shimmered even in the fading light, glowing an emerald green. Calen realised he had seen this dragon before when Queen Uthrían's fingers had wrapped around his forearm. '*Myia'nari. Il vyara… myia'kara… é dauva. Il raethír er veinier.*'

The elf's words echoed in Calen's mind like a lingering shadow. *My queen, the princes… my brothers… are dead. The battle is lost.*

Both Valerys and the massive green dragon circled around the basin, eyes fixed on one another, and for a moment fear clutched at Calen's heart. If that dragon decided to attack Valerys, it would tear him to shreds in a heartbeat. They circled, drawing closer, coiling around each other.

The green dragon roared, the monstrous sound reverberating off the rock that surrounded them, and Valerys swerved away, dropping towards the plateau.

Calen could feel the fear in Valerys's heart as he plummeted towards the plateau, cracking his wings and alighting on the grass, leaves and snapped twigs spiralling in the air. As soon as Valerys touched the ground, he extended his neck and gave an air shaking roar to match that of the other dragon.

Calen broke into a run, his heart fluttering and pounding at the same time. He tried to reach his mind out to Valerys's, but the storm of emotions that crashed through the dragon was indecipherable. Fear, rage, grief. "Valerys!"

Calen glanced towards the sky. The green dragon was plummeting, falling like a stone dropped from a tower. Except this creature *was* the tower. As it landed, it unfolded its terrifyingly large wings, sending a gust of air sweeping across the plateau and knocking Calen off his feet. Calen reached out to the Spark, pulling from it like it was the Waters of Life. He launched himself to his feet, but a hand clamped down on his shoulders. He spun, whipping threads of Air around him, refusing to let anyone stop him from going to Valerys's aid.

Then the Spark was gone, his threads sliced. The Jotnar, Thacia, stood before him, a sympathetic smile on her face. Threads of Spirit wound about the Jotnar, connecting between her and Calen, encasing him in a ward of Spirit. She took a step towards him. "Calm, brother." Thacia extended an open palm. "Ithrax is blind. She uses her roars to map the world around her."

Calen gulped, adding moisture to his dry throat. Being warded made his skin itch. It brought back memories of Drifaien – of being helpless while Artim Valdock drove spears of ice through Falmin's chest and snapped Lopir's neck.

He pushed away the thoughts and turned. The green dragon, Ithrax, now stood beside Valerys, making the white dragon look like nothing more than a child at her side. Ithrax was easily four times Valerys's size. As Calen watched, he felt the threads of Spirit dissipate, and then Thacia and the others were beside him, each of the Rakina watching as Ithrax stood over Valerys.

"That dragon is the soulkin of Queen Uthrían's son, isn't she?"

"How could you possibly know that?" One of the Rakina said, a skeptical look on his beard-covered face.

"Yes—" Harken curled a length of his hair in his fist, looking at Calen with a strange curiosity "—how do you know that?"

"I just… I just do."

"You are correct." Chora studied Calen, giving him a look he knew meant she would be asking more questions. "Ithrax is the soulkin of Prince Athír Ardurän. Athír died at the Battle of the Golden Fields, shortly after the city of Varien fell to the empire. We won that battle solely because Ithrax tore four Lorian dragons to pieces and savaged the Lorian army – all without her fire. Her misery was our salvation. We are forever grateful and forever guilty, for she saved us, but we couldn't save her."

A feeling of pure sorrow seeped from Valerys into Calen, and he looked over to see Ithrax and Valerys nestling their heads together, Valerys's dwarfed by that of the green dragon.

"If you are here and you have dragons – dragons of legend, dragons that could turn the tide of any war – why are you hiding? Why am I important at all?"

"I will always envy the simplicity of a young mind." Chora's smile spoke nothing of happiness, only regret and loss. "Ithrax is blind and lost her fire when Athír died. Sardakes—" Chora pointed towards the black dragon who lay by the stream "—moves only to eat and drink. He cannot fly – that ability was taken from him when he lost Faraline. The others are all Broken in their own way, each without their fire. Dragons, Heraya bless their souls, suffer greatly when their soulkin are taken from them. The breaking of the bond is far more severe for a dragon. It is much rarer for a dragon to become Rakina than it is their Draleid. Most lose their minds, bereft." Chora drew in a long, pensive breath through her nose and let it out in a sigh. "It is said that in the making of the world, Varyn crafted the dragons as sworn protectors, his guardians on the mortal plane. Creatures of untold power, born solely to enforce the will of The Father. Through the bond, the Draleid gain much. We gain a connection to the Spark and, as such, extended life. We gain power and strength. And of course, the companionship of dragons. But do you know what the dragons gain?"

That particular question was one Calen had indeed asked himself.

"Dragons are fire and flame. They are fury incarnate. After the wars of creation, Varyn himself, in his wisdom, realised that kind of power was too great and that the dragons were wrought of too much rage to wield their flames with true consideration. And so, he took it from them. He took their fire, and he created the bond. The Draleid would gain access to the Spark, long life, and strength to wield as guardians in Varyn's name.

In return, the dragons would be re-gifted their fire, their fury and rage tempered by the blending of souls. Through the bond they gained compassion, understanding, sorrow, happiness, grief, love. So when a Draleid is killed and the bond is broken, most dragons lose all semblance of who and what they are except for rage and fury. Their loss consumes them, and in turn, they consume. These dragons are all that is left. Six. From thousands, only six survived the breaking of the bond and lived to this day. And now, with the exception of Ithrax, each have as little active desire to live as moss on rocks. Their hearts are broken just as their souls are. And that, Calen Bryer, is why we *hide*. We fought for years, centuries in some cases, but eventually, it wore us down. We are The Broken, each of us only fragments, where you are whole." Chora gestured to Valerys, who was now nudging the black-scaled dragon, his heart aching. "That is why you are important. Because you are the future of our race, and through your bond, you wield a power that we do not."

"Calen." Aeson's voice was little more than a whisper, but it still held the same firm tone Calen was used to.

Tears welled in Calen's eyes as he looked at Valerys, watching as the dragon leaned his head down and nudged the black-scaled dragon who lay by the stream, urging his kin to stand. Calen reached out, wrapping Valerys's mind in his own, trying all he could to bathe his soulkin in warmth, just as Valerys had done for him so many times. With each nudge that Valerys gave to the unmoving black dragon, Calen's heart broke a little more. It wasn't simply the sense of loss that rent Valerys, it was the feeling of hope that first roar had given him. The hope that had been ripped away. "Myia nithír til diar, Valerys. I denír viël ar altinua. Aiar væra svid nur dar aiar haryn narda. La vandír denír til du." *My soul to yours, Valerys. In this life and always. They will burn for what they have done. I pledge this to you.*

Calen's hand fell to his hip, brushing the silk scarf that hung there before wrapping his fingers around the pommel of his sword – his mam and dad, with him always. The empire had taken them from him, just as they had taken Ella, Faenir, Korik, Lopir, Ellissar, Falmin, Heldin, Alwen – the list was endless. And in that time, all Calen had done was run. From The Glade to Belduar, from Belduar to Drifaien, from Drifaien to Berona. And it was here, standing in the elven city of Aravell that he made a decision: he would run no more. Drawing a deep breath, he turned to look at Aeson.

The man stood with the other Rakina at his back, Chora and Harken to his left, Thacia, the Jotnar standing by Calen's side.

"Chora told you why I hesitated to bring you here, but she didn't tell you why I finally decided to do so." He took a step forward, his eyes searching Calen's. "Whether you like it or not. War is here. It is being fought right now. You've seen what the empire will do to keep its hold. What it did in your home. What it did to Gaeleron, to Lasch and Elia Havel. Before Belduar fell, I had contemplated bringing you here. But I wasn't sure you were ready."

"Ready for what?"

"Ready to understand what it is to be Broken. Ready to contemplate the reality of what your death would do to Valerys and what his would do to you." Aeson took another step forwards so he was only inches from Calen. "You understand now, don't you? You understand why I fight. You understand why I would burn the empire to the ground for what they took. Not just from me, but from all The Broken. I saw it in your eyes near the Burnt Lands. I saw the fire. This is where it begins, Calen. This is where you learn what it is to be a Draleid. While the Angan send out our call, and while we choose those who will stand at our side, we will train you in the old ways. Teach you everything you should have learned if Fane and the empire hadn't taken that opportunity from you."

"What of the others?" Calen's hands trembled, his jaw clenching. The sorrow that radiated from Valerys bubbled and burned, twisting into a rage at the thought of everything that had been taken.

"Whoever has travelled with you," Chora Sarn said, throwing a glance at Aeson who looked as though he were about to protest, "is welcome here. You are our kin. And to put it plainly, Calen, you are our hope. It is to you that people flock. To the man astride the snow-white dragon. People seek out symbols, that is simply the way of things. And you are unequivocally the greatest symbol of rebellion we have had in four hundred years. And you will need good people around you. All will be welcome to stay here, in Alura. I will send for Craftsmages to hew quarters from the stone. It will be done by tonight. And with that, go, bring your companions here, for tonight we will drink, we will eat, and we will celebrate. There's been precious little to celebrate of late."

"Hmm." The tall, long-haired Rakina, Harken, raised an eyebrow.

"Say it, Harken." Chora folded her arms, rolling her eyes.

"The Triarchy will not appreciate us having a celebration before they arrange one for Calen themselves."

"Each of them are likely beating seven shades of shit out of each other for the chance to parade him around," A small Rakina with fair skin and long, dark hair said, shaking her head. Her name was Lira, if Calen remembered correctly. She was no bigger than Elia Havel but held herself like a man twice her size. "While they bicker, we can drink."

"Let them be angry," Chora said with another roll of her eyes. "They're always angry. We'll invite them. The first dragon in four hundred years has hatched. I'm having a drink."

Of War and Ruin

CHAPTER SIXTY

TALES AND TRUTHS

Calen sat on a smooth spark-wrought bench of white stone, a fire pit blazing before him. Dann, Vaeril, Erik, Tarmon, and the two Fenryr Angan – Aneera and Baldon – sat in a circle around the fire. Night had descended, and Chora and the other Rakina had arranged a celebration in the central courtyard of Alura, their home within Aravell.

Chatter and footsteps filled the air as rebels, Rakina, elven dignitaries, and people of note – who Calen had been methodically introduced to – talked and drank wine. Even Queen Uthrían had shown her face, along with Ithilin, one of the Ephorí of Vaelen, and Varthon with some of her Dvalin Angan. Just as Harken had suggested, the other elven rulers and Ephorí had apparently not been too pleased with Chora for arranging celebrations before they did.

Lanterns and fire pits were lit all about the courtyard, their incandescent light blending with the soft glow of inlaid erinian stone and the pale wash of the moon.

"It's not that bad." Dann looked from Calen to Vaeril. The elf held a small block of wood that had been carved into something that vaguely resembled a human face. "It's not! Baldon says I've come a long way. He wants me to do his likeness next. Tell them."

Baldon, who sat with his fur-covered legs crossed, gave Dann a curious look, golden eyes shimmering. "It is true, Sureheart's craft has come far. His first attempt was horribly poor. This is markedly more proficient, though still poor."

"Sureheart?" Calen whispered, more to himself than anyone else.

Dann took a draught of his wine, then shook his head, not hearing Calen. "We're really going to have to work on your compliments, Baldon."

"It wasn't a compliment," the Angan said with a shrug. "It was a statement of fact. Your rate of improvement is no more than normal. But it *is* improvement. Mastery is not something you achieve based on the speed at which you improve, but due to your ability to persevere in the face of failure. It is repetition, dedication, and consistency. We have discussed this."

Dann puffed out a sigh then laughed. "I take back what I said before, Baldon. You shouldn't talk more. You were right, what's rare is special."

Calen wasn't sure what kind of response he had expected from the Angan, but he was surprised when Baldon's lips curled into what looked to be a smile, sharp white teeth showing.

Beside Calen, Vaeril turned the block of carved wood in his hand. The elf gave a downturn of his lip. "The pursuit of a valúr is not a small thing, Dann. You bring honour to your name. I am impressed."

Vaeril made to hand the carving back to Dann, but Erik gestured for Vaeril to pass it to him. "What is a valúr?" He asked as he looked the wood over. "I've not heard that word before."

"Amongst my people—" Vaeril turned towards Erik, taking a sip of wine from his cup "—it is taught that to possess the ability to destroy you must first understand what it is to create. Any who wish to be trained in the bow, sword, the Spark, any weapon, must first take on a valúr – the pursuit of creation."

Erik gave a half smile as he looked over the carving. "That is a sentiment that many would do well to learn."

Across from Vaeril, Tarmon leaned forwards, resting his elbows on his knees, wine sloshing in his cup. The big man was already on his fifth cup, and Calen had never seen him in such good spirits. "I have a question," he said, resting his chin on his fist. "Does Aeson Virandr know you carved a likeness of him? Because I've never known the man to take kindly to mockery."

"It's not mockery I… Fuck off!"

Dann, Tarmon, Erik, Calen, and even Vaeril burst out laughing. Dann leaned over and knocked his cup of wine off Tarmon's, shaking his head. The pair had been getting on well, and seeing it brought made Calen smile. He had felt his friend's absence each and every day, but it was only upon seeing him again that Calen understood what it was Dann had always given him: hope. Dann wasn't as chirpy as Elia Havel had always been – and hopefully would be again – but he had a way about him that reminded Calen that despite everything he had lost, there was still so much left.

"I'm just saying," Tarmon said, spilling some of the wine from his cup and taking the carving from Erik. "He looks like he fell out of a tree and hit every branch on the way down."

A hand rested on Calen's shoulder as Erik and the others burst out laughing.

"Mind if we sit?" Haem stood over Calen. Lyrin and Varlin, two of the Knights of Achyron, were at his side.

Calen just stared back at Haem for a moment, looking over his brother's face. He didn't think there would ever come a time where even just the sound of Haem's voice wouldn't be like music in his ears. "Never."

Calen slid over on the bench, gesturing for the others to sit. Haem sat beside Calen, Lyrin on his right, while Varlin moved around and took a place on the ground beside Baldon and Aneera.

Varlin's skin had a coppery hue to it, and four circles of black ink bisected by a black line adorned both her forearms. Her head was shaved tight on either side, her blonde hair tied into a plait. She was Valtaran, or at least she once had been. Calen wasn't sure as to the correct order of things when someone was taken into the knighthood.

"What is it we're talking about?" Lyrin asked, leaning forwards to look at the carving in Tarmon's hand. "What in Achyron's name is that?"

"Not you too." Dann tilted his head back and let out a sigh. "It's a process, all right. I'm still learning. You can only ever succeed if you allow yourself to fail."

Lyrin took the carving from Tarmon. "Well, you've definitely got the last part right."

Dann snatched the carving from Lyrin, setting it down on the bench beside him. "Well, if I spend as much time carving as you do combing your hair, I'm sure I'll be a sculptor by the end of the week."

Both Haem and Varlin erupted in laughter, while Lyrin glared back at Dann.

The two began trading insults, Tarmon, Vaeril, and Erik joining in. Baldon and Aneera sat in silence, watching, while Varlin stared into the flames, running her finger along the black line tattoo on her right forearm.

"How are you feeling?" Haem asked, leaning closer.

"Tired." Calen took a sip from his wine cup. "I don't remember the last time I wasn't tired."

"Me neither." Haem gave Calen a weak smile, swishing the wine about in his cup. "Calen, I know we've talked, but I just wanted to say I'm proud of you. I'm not sure I could have done what you've done."

Calen nodded, looking into the fire. "Can I ask you a question?"

"Always."

"When you fought the Uraks in the forest that night... the night you... The night you died." Calen swallowed, a knot catching in his throat. He couldn't lift his gaze from the fire. "Do you remember what happened to Rhett?"

Silence passed between them, and Calen regretted asking the question, though he'd wanted to ask it for days. If what Haem remembered aligned with what Calen saw in his dream, well, that would go a long way towards being sure that what he saw was more than a simple dream.

"He tried to save me," Haem said after a few moments. "He was calling to me. He took an arrow, but he just kept cutting through the beasts. Everyone always told me how great a swordsman I was – Dad loved it. But that was only because Rhett never bothered to show off. I was never as good as he was. He was almost to me, but then…" Haem touched his hand to his stomach, fingers pressing against the linen shirt. "They were all dead when Kallinvar gifted me the Sigil. Every one of them."

Calen turned from the flames and looked at his brother, his pulse quickening. "Haem, Rhett didn't die that day."

The colour drained from Haem's face, his eyes growing wide. "What do you mean?"

"He didn't die that day," Calen repeated. "He was the only one who lived. When he got back, his arm was broken, he was covered in blood, and he was half dead."

"Rhett's alive?"

"I hope so." While travelling through the Burnt Lands, Haem had told Calen of the Urak attack on The Glade. Of seeing Erdhardt holding Aela's body in his arms. Of Ferrin Kolm, Marlo Egon, Joran Brock… There had been more, and likely more again that Haem hadn't found. Calen had no idea who from The Glade still lived. He still hadn't told Dann; there hadn't been a chance. He tried not to think on it. "He and Ella were courting."

A broad smile swept across Haem's face, and he laughed. "He finally plucked up the courage, then? He'd been pining after her for a whole summer. How were they?"

Calen could feel the tears wetting his eyes. "They were good. In love. He treated her like she was the moon and the stars, and she was herself with him – you know, annoying."

Haem laughed, drinking a mouthful of wine. "That's what sisters are for…" He sighed, staring at the flames in the fire pit. The silence that passed between them was sombre – Ella was gone.

Calen lifted his cup to his mouth and downed its contents, letting out a long sigh. He shifted in his seat, then heaved himself upwards. "I need more wine. Another?"

Haem shook his head. "I've had enough, I think. I know we're among friends, but we still need to stay alert."

Calen stared at Haem, allowing himself just another moment.

"What?" Haem looked back at Calen, then down at his shirt. "Have I spilled the wine?"

"No," Calen said with a laugh, his chest tightening. "I just never thought I'd see your face again." He drew in a breath through his nose, shaking his head to try and stop the tears he knew were forming. "I'll be back in a minute."

Calen made his way to where one of many casks of wine was propped up on a stand, a tap jutting from its end. He passed Asius and Senas, stopping to talk for a few minutes, then saw Surin, Ingvat, and a few of their rebels, smiles on their faces, cups of wine in their hands. As he walked, he admired the courtyard itself: the white stone, the tall trees at its centre, the lanterns that blazed atop the pedestals, the streams and bridges that ran around its perimeter. And beyond the courtyard, to where the homes of bone-white were nestled along the rock face. A hundred or so feet up, at the end of a long grass-covered path, was a plateau four times as large as any of the others, backing into a massive alcove that had been carved into the rock with the Spark. The plateau had been created that evening by elven Craftsmages, and upon it sat eight of the Spark-wrought homes, rising multiple storeys.

In The Glade it had taken weeks or even months to build homes, but the Craftsmages had done it in hours. Calen had watched in wonder as they weaved threads of all the elements through the rock, carts of white stone, a material that looked like antlers, and various powders and liquids. Not a single piece of timber was used.

Chora had ensured enough rooms had been constructed to accommodate Calen and all the others, including those who had come with them from Berona – Surin, Ingvat, Kiko, Loura, and the other rebels. There had been one or two disapproving faces amongst the Rakina, and Aeson in particular, but Chora had waved them away. Calen understood; this was their place of rest, their sanctuary. He had tried to express his appreciation to Chora, but his words hadn't felt enough.

He held his gaze on the plateau as he opened the tap and filled his cup. Could this be home? At least for now? It was peaceful, and seeing the others smile and laugh lightened Calen's heart. The Rakina had named it Alura – *Rest*. The name seemed fitting, but Calen didn't think he would find much rest, not with what was to come. It was then, as he closed the tap on the cask of wine, that Erik's words from the hall in Belduar rang in his mind. *'We have to allow ourselves the small things.'*

"How's the wine?" Calen hadn't heard Aeson approach.

"I'd never had wine before leaving The Glade." Calen still held anger in his heart for Aeson. No matter what the man had lost, he was still trying to make Calen his puppet. But Calen was doing his best to understand, to find a middle ground. "It's not Lasch Havel's mead, but it's not bad."

A sympathetic smile touched Aeson's lips. "I'm sorry for what happened to them." He shook his head. "There are some people in this world, hard as it is to believe, who thrive on the pain of others."

Calen nodded. "He's dead now. He can't hurt them anymore."

"They're resting?"

"They are, Gaeleron too. One of Sulin's people – Loura – is watching over them. She said she didn't have much of a taste for drinking and loud noises."

Aeson folded his arms and turned, looking out over those gathered in the courtyard. "They're not Sulin's people, Calen. They're yours – ours. They've not come here on their way to somewhere else. They came here to follow you."

Two men and a woman – whom Calen recognised as the Healer, Kiko – passed by, raising their cups to Calen and Aeson. "Draleid."

Both Calen and Aeson raised their cups in return, and Aeson smiled as though his point had just been proven.

Calen sighed, taking a sip of wine and crossing his arms.

"Both the Havels and Gaeleron will recover, Calen. There is nowhere on the continent that would be better for their recovery. They will get the best of care here, and the elven Healers are masters in the treatment of the mind. There are some who dedicate their entire lives to better understanding the things we can't see."

Calen nodded absently. He knew Aeson was right, but he just couldn't get the images of Elia and Lasch in the interrogation room out of his head. Their brittle skin and sunken eyes, the sight of their ribs poking through, the fear in them. It was not something he wanted to think on. "Aeson?"

"Hmm?"

"What did you lose?"

Aeson turned to face Calen, an uncertain look on his face. "What do you mean?"

Calen wasn't sure how to ask the question or if it was even a question that should be asked. But Aeson owed him that much. "When Lyara died, what did you lose?"

Aeson stared back at Calen for a long moment. His smile, when it came, was weak. He turned to look at a group of Rakina who stood around one of the fire pits. "To be Rakina is a strange thing. No loss is the same. Each two souls blend differently, it seems." Aeson pointed towards the tall, broad-shouldered man with hair down to his waist who had greeted them when they arrived in Alura. "Harken looks as though he's lost nothing, doesn't he? Next to Chora, who will never walk again, or Dynan – over there in the red tunic – whose fingers curled inwards and hardened like stone. But Harken's loss was... cruel. When Taravin died, he took Harken's memories. Not all of them, but those of his family, of his little girl and wife. Other memories as well. Things as small as how to tie knots and as vital as how to speak. It took Harken years to learn to talk again – the adult mind isn't as absorbent as a child's. He also cannot touch the Spark or see colour." Aeson took a long drink of his wine. "It's a strange thing. The only commonality is a loss of the will to live. Those here have all fought against that pull, some more than others. Finding a purpose helps." Aeson re-crossed his arms and pressed the wine cup against his shoulder, tapping his fingers on the rim of the cup. Aeson stared into the crowd, his jaw clenched, eyes glistening. He stood like that for a few quiet minutes, and Calen saw the pain the question has caused Aeson. He wished he could take it back. Aeson could be a harsh man, and single minded, but Calen was beginning to understand him – to understand why he was the way he was.

"My connection with the Spark is tenuous. Sometimes I can feel it, sometimes I can't." He looked at his feet. "I can't feel the middle toe on my left foot, believe it or not." He laughed, shaking his head. "Naia always found that funny." Aeson's expression shifted at his own mention of his dead wife. Calen remembered Erik telling him she died of consumption when Erik was young. "I lost things I can't put my finger on. Contentment," he said with a shrug. "The will to exist. I came close to taking my own life many times. My mind sometimes feels like an endless ocean, and I'm just swallowing water, drowning."

"How do you even…" Calen's voice trailed off. He couldn't begin to contemplate how a person pushed past such a thing.

"I make a choice to live every day. It's not easy. Some days it feels like the hardest thing in the world. The only thing that kept me going was the need to ensure her death wasn't in vain and to make sure those who destroyed my world felt her pain. When I found Naia, it was as though she filled the gaps in me, eased the pain. Her contentment was mine, and when she passed into Heraya's arms, it broke me all over again." Aeson looked towards where Erik, Haem, and the others were still drinking and talking. "Erik has her eyes and her sweetness. He's kind, like she was. Dahlen has her fire and her mind, the way she looked at things, the way she protected others. They're what keep me going now. I want to see the empire crumble, but it's Erik and Dahlen I'm fighting for."

In less than a day, Aeson had been more honest with Calen than he had been throughout the entirety of the time they had known each other. He had no doubt this particular moment was aided by the wine, but he appreciated it no less. He thought back to that cell in Drifaien, that emptiness the rune-marked manacles had created, and in the back of his mind he could feel Valerys's warmth. The dragon was in the eyrie with the others, curled up between Ithrax and the pink-scaled dragon – Thurial. Both joy and sorrow radiated from Valerys; he had found more of his kin, but they were broken, Rakina, little more than shells of what they had once been.

"I'm sorry." Calen looked at the ground, then lifted his gaze to meet Aeson's. "For going after Rist. I mean, I'd make the same choice again if I had to." He allowed himself a sombre laugh. "I'll always try to help the ones I love, but I could have done it differently. I was just… I was scared if I went back you wouldn't have let me go, and I needed to go."

To Calen's surprise, Aeson smiled. "You're probably right, I wouldn't have. You would have made a fine Draleid, Calen, even before."

The sound of clapping and cheering echoed through the courtyard, and Calen looked towards a fire pit near the yard's centre where Therin had risen to his feet and was now bowing theatrically.

"All right, all right." Therin raised his hands in the air, gesturing for quiet. "Settle down." He waved his hands at Calen and Aeson, and then to the others scattered about the yard. "Gather round, gather round." He lifted his cup to his mouth and drained it, holding it out. "If I'm going to tell stories, someone better keep me supplied with wine."

To Calen's surprise, it was Dann who leapt to his feet and grabbed Therin's cup, giving the elf a mocking bow and making his way towards the wine cask behind Calen and Aeson.

"He's drunk," Dann said, a gleeful smile on his face. "I've never seen him drunk. He might not answer the question 'can elves grow beards', but I can make him answer the question 'do elves vomit when they're drunk'."

Dann skipped off towards the wine cask, a devious glint in his eye that Calen had missed.

"He's always asking the important questions," Calen said with a laugh, taking a mouthful of his wine.

"I came dangerously close to cutting out his tongue."

"Have you seen the carving?"

"Don't talk about the carving. Please, for the love of the gods, don't talk about the carving." Aeson puffed out his cheeks and shook his head. "Let's go hear some of Therin's stories."

Calen almost spat out his wine with laughter as Aeson continued to shake his head, taking a seat by the fire before Therin, the others gathering around.

Haem approached, throwing his arm around Calen's shoulder. "I never thought I'd hear one of Therin's stories again. It takes me back to the Dragon."

Calen savoured the feeling of his brother's arm around his shoulders and the sound of Haem's voice. It brought him back to being in The

Gilded Dragon too. He lowered himself to the ground, finding a place between Haem and Tarmon – who had just taken a seat on the stone. Of course, he had managed to sit between the two largest men in the courtyard, besides Harken, who stood with his arms folded on the right side of the fire.

Therin moved so he stood in front of the fire, grabbing the cup of wine from Dann.

"Shift over." Dann didn't wait for a response as he dropped down between Haem and Calen, shuffling himself into the narrow gap. Once he'd wedged himself firmly in place, he gave both Calen and Haem a big, shit-eating grin, then took a mouthful of wine. "Just like old times."

"You haven't changed in the slightest, Dann Pimm."

"I'd say the same to you, but you were dead, and now you're not. That's a pretty big change." Dann stared at Haem, then his eyes widened, and he waved his hand frantically. "It's a change I'm happy about!"

Haem let out a sigh. "Shut up, Dann."

"You know, I think you're going to get on with Aeson." Dann turned to Calen. "What's that smile for?"

"Just happy to be back, Dann." Calen took a sip of his wine. "Just happy to be back."

"All right, quiet down." Therin stumbled slightly, much to Dann's amusement. "Who here has heard the tale of The Huntress and The Exile?"

AN HOUR OR SO PASSED with Therin weaving story after story. One of Surin's people, a lithe young woman by the name Indira, emboldened by wine, had taken over the task a few stories ago with the encouragement of her companions. And, much to everyone's delight, she was a better story weaver than most Calen had heard in The Glade – not quite as good at Therin, but still fantastic.

"Brilliant." Therin stood, using Aeson's shoulder for leverage. "Another cheer for Indira."

Claps and whistles rose, but Therin frowned. "You can do better than that!"

The applause grew louder, and Calen looked around, knowing his smile stretched from ear to ear. There were over a hundred souls gathered in the courtyard – elves, Rakina, Angan, rebels – and each of them were hanging on every word Therin said. The last time he had felt any kind of comfort like this had been back in Belduar when Arthur had arranged a feast for their arrival. The thought soured in Calen's mind. He would never see Arthur again. Another good soul taken by the empire. Some of Arthur's last words pulled to the front of Calen's mind. *'I'm not here talking to you because you are a Draleid. I'm here talking to you because I believe in who you are.'*

Calen's chest tightened at the words. He pulled out of his own head only when the fire pits about the courtyard snapped and crackled, pluming sparks into the air.

"Now, are there any tales anyone wishes to hear?" Therin called. "The Demise of Durin Longfang? The Death of Amendel? The Ghosts of Ilragorn?"

A number of voices shouted, calling out names of tales and stories, some of which Calen had heard, some he hadn't. He wasn't sure if it was the wine, but something stirred within him, and he straightened his back, leaning forwards. "Tell us the tale of the Chainbreaker."

Calen had spoken louder than he had intended, and the voices quietened, eyes turning to him. He hadn't expected such a sudden reaction.

The smile on Therin's face quickly faded, and he stared at Calen, sobering. "Later," he said, dropping his voice to a more sombre tone. His eyes flashed to Haem for a moment. "Now is not the time."

"No." Calen shook his head. "I would like to hear it told like this, Therin. I don't want to know his past, I want to hear his story." Therin hadn't told Calen the Chainbreaker was Vars, but it hadn't taken much working out when Baldon and Aneera had called him the son of the Chainbreaker. "Please."

Therin drew in a long breath, twisting his tongue in his mouth, then acquiesced. "All right."

Dann leaned in, elbowing Calen in the ribs. "Finally. I've been trying to get him to tell this story for months."

Both Calen and Haem glared at Dann, but Dann was completely oblivious. He took a long draught of his wine, then shuffled himself into a more comfortable position, ready for the story.

"This story," Therin said, staring off into the distance, "is different from the others. For I am not just the teller of this tale, I am its observer, and to tell it, I must go back to the year three-zero-five-four After Doom. The Varsund War had been raging for four years, and fires blazed from Gilsa to Midhaven." Therin swept his left hand through the air, his right still firmly gripping his wine cup. Now that Calen could touch the Spark, he could see the threads of Air and Fire that Therin wielded to blow a gust across the courtyard and send flames flickering into the night. Being able to see the threads should have taken away some of the wonder, but somehow it did no such thing. "The cities of Torebon, Haling, Kald, Hewe, and Aylia were all under Varsundi control, the Arthyn Plain was a mass grave, the Dornang River ran crimson, and Carvahon had all but conceded victory, leaving Illyanara to fight alone against the might of High Lord Rayce Garrin and the Varsundi armies."

Therin took a draught of his wine, allowing the silence to settle.

"The Varsundi were relentless. Not only was Rayce Garrin one of the greatest tacticians seen since before The Fall, he also had three of the finest warriors Varsund had ever produced in his close circle. The fierce and famed general, Durin Longfang, named after the enormous greatsword he wielded, had never lost a battle. Taran Shadesmire was widely considered by some to be the greatest swordsman in all Epheria. And it is said that Halya Starn could cave in the heads of two men with one swing of her mace. Not only that, but Varsund's cavalry, the legendary Varsundi Blackthorns, dominated every battlefield they trod on. Over the course of those first four years of the war, the number of major battles in which Illyanara emerged victorious could be counted on one hand of a four-fingered man.

"It wasn't until the summer of that year, when the Illyanarans, led by the emerging general Burdock Folkwin, defeated Halya Starn and her forces at the Battle of the Shallow Trench, that the tide began to turn." The light of the surrounding fire pits glistened in Therin's eyes, his silver hair coruscating. "With Folkwin at their head, the Illyanaran armies went almost a year without tasting a major defeat, and in that time, they pushed the Varsundi back across the Marin Mountains. However, in the winter of the year three-zero-five-five After Doom, calamity struck when Burdock Folkwin and some twenty thousand Illyanarans suffered the single largest defeat the war had seen when they were slaughtered at the Battle of the Blood River. It is said the River Almellon ran red for three days and the bodies were piled so high they looked like hills in the night. It was in the aftermath of this vicious defeat that I stumbled upon a company of Illyanaran swordsmen, led by a young captain named Vars Bryer who had survived the battle – barely."

Therin straightened and raised his arm, and Calen could see the threads of Fire, Spirit, and Air, weaving around him, drawing in the light. "It was there, in the dead of night, beneath the canopy of the Elmwood to the west of Haling and the River Almellon, I told Vars and his surviving companions the reason they had lost the Battle of the Blood River so crushingly. The reason the Varsundi armies had known they were coming. The reason twenty thousand souls were sent to dine in Achyron's halls." Therin stopped, watching as all gathered hung on his words, the fire pits crackling in the night. "Rayce Garrin and the Varsundi had captured a god."

Gasps broke out, particularly from the rebels who had come from Berona. The elves and many of the Rakina barely flinched. And out of the corner of his eye, Calen saw Baldon and Aneera bow their heads, placing the palms of their right hands over their foreheads.

"Many of you know the Enkaran pantheon, the elder gods – Varyn, Heraya, Elyara, Achyron, Neron, Hafaesir, and the dread Efialtír." Hisses and boos rang out, the crowd playing to Therin's theatrics. "But when the humans came to our shores in the year three hundred After Doom, they brought with them their own gods, lesser gods, gods of flesh and bone – Fenryr, the wolf god." Therin threw his hands in the air, weaving threads Fire, Air, and Spirit. The flames of the pit erupted upwards into the night, taking the form of a howling wolf. "Dvalin, the stag." Therin gestured towards Varthon and some of her Dvalin Angan, the fire behind him forming into a charging stag. "Vethnir, the hawk. Bjorna, the bear. Kaygan, the kat." With each god, Therin wrought their forms from flame, letting them fade into the night. "It is said that each was as big as a dragon but could shift their forms to mimic ours. With their gods came the druids, and…" Therin looked to Baldon and Aneera. "The Angan."

All eyes turned to Baldon, Aneera, and the Dvalin Angan, whispers filling the courtyard.

"Since before the elder gods breathed life into the elves, the dragons, and all others we know in Epheria, the lesser gods have roamed the known world. And in that time, the Angan, formed in the images of their patron gods, have protected and served faithfully. In the summer of that year, Rayce Garrin captured the wolf god, Fenryr. And in doing so, he forced all Angan of the Clan Fenryr to do his bidding. Against their will, they were forced to slaughter and murder, acting as both monstrosities on the battlefield and assassins in the dark. But most importantly, their ability to communicate across vast distances instantaneously gave the Varsundi an advantage unlike any other. And so I gave those Illyanaran warriors a choice. Come with me, help me to free the wolf god, and, in doing so, aid their nation far more than they ever could on the field of battle, or go and take their chances trying to return home.

"Only four chose to stay, and among them was their captain, Vars Bryer. For the next three years, we moved across Illyanara, Varsund, and Carvahon, seeking answers and aiding the Illyanaran armies wherever we could. It was we who sunk the Varsundi fleet in the Bay of Light, emptied the coffers at the gold mine of Aonar, caused the cascade at Torebon, and lit the great fires of Ballmar. But one by one, those who pledged themselves to the cause lost their lives, until only Vars and I remained."

Therin emptied his cup of wine, gesturing for Dann to pass over his own – which he did with a beaming smile, enraptured by the tale. The elf took a mouthful, then dropped to his haunches, holding his gaze on Calen and Haem. "And let me tell you, I would call Vars Bryer as much a brother as a friend. He was wise, thoughtful, caring, and passionate. But he was also quick to anger and protected his own with a ferocity I have rarely ever seen. Vars was not a mage. He was not a Draleid or a being of mystical power. He was simply a man, but he was a man whose legend untold was a crime unto itself. His name should have been sung across Illyanara. He should be spoken of in wonder and awe like the great blademasters of old. For it was Vars Bryer who slew Durin Longfang in single combat and broke the siege of Argona. It was Vars Bryer who defeated Taran Shadesmire at the battle for Vaerleon. And it was Vars Bryer who ended the Varsund War."

The hairs on Calen's arms stood on end, his skin prickling. There was so much he didn't know about his dad. So much he wished he had been told. He lifted his right hand and wiped away tears that had begun to fall, at the same time feeling Haem's arm wrap around his shoulder.

Haem didn't speak, but he pulled Calen in tight, his hand squeezing, and Calen saw tears glistening on the side of his brother's face.

"Many credit the breaking of the siege of Argona and the death of Durin Longfang as the turning point in the war. The truth? It was not the blood that spilled from Longfang's veins that turned the war, it was the words that left his lips. For Durin was a good and honourable man, and it was he, after three years of searching, who told us where the wolf god was chained – beneath the city of Varsund itself. The heart of the enemy."

More gasps spread about the courtyard, and even Dann sat in silence, staring at Therin.

"And so, with the siege broken and the location of the wolf god now known, Vars marched through the streets of Argona and demanded a council with High Lord Castor Kai himself. And when that council was granted, Vars demanded that Illyanara march on the capital of Varsund come the dawn of the next day. When Castor Kai laughed in his face, Vars tossed down the bloody greatsword of Durin Longfang, and Castor Kai's tone changed. We talked, the three of us, along with Castor Kai's most trusted generals, deep into the night, and at dawn we rode for Varsund with fifty thousand swords at our backs. More joined as we marched across the plains, and past the Marin Mountains, and by the time the first siege tower was raised, near seventy thousand souls stood before the walls of Varsund.

"But while the armies battled on the walls, Vars and I found our way inside the city. For though the Angan were bound to serve the Varsundi for fear of their god's safety, one by the name of Baldon Stormseeker, who sits before you now—" Therin gestured towards Baldon, bowing at the waist "—saw there would be no end to the torture unless something was done. It was Baldon who first told me of Fenryr's capture, and it was Baldon who secreted us into the city during the siege. And there, deep in the dungeons of Varsund, beneath the keep itself, we found the wolf god, chained and beaten, a rune-marked collar around his neck, streams of blood flowing from where starglass had sliced his flesh. Fenryr was guarded by Varsundi soldiers, a clutch of Blood Mages, and Rayce Garrin himself. Never before have I seen a man's blade move like that of Vars Bryer's in that dungeon. And when Rayce Garrin's head hit the stone, Vars pulled the collar from Fenryr's neck, broke the chains from his arms and legs, and carried him to where the moon's light could touch his skin."

Therin let out a long sigh, drank from his cup, and looked at the moon. "But when Vars, Baldon, Fenryr, and I crept from the city, fire raging all around us, we were set upon near the edge of Lake Vasund by men and women bearing the six stars of Illyanara. Castor Kai had sent his son, Dorian Kai, to claim Fenryr for Illyanara. Dorian thanked Vars and me for delivering the wolf god but demanded we hand him over. Vars refused to allow chains to once more be placed around Fenryr's neck. And so we fought beneath the moon's light, Fenryr too weak to stand and the energy sapped from my bones by the Spark. But Vars was a man possessed. He fought like a god among men, Baldon at his side, and he fed the soil with the blood of those sent for him. And from that day forth, the Angan of Clan Fenryr pledged to always answer Vars' call or the call of his blood. For he had freed their god, Fenryr, and in doing so he had freed them – freed them of the blood and murder they had been forced into. He had become the Chainbreaker."

CALEN PRESSED HIS TONGUE AGAINST the sharp edge of his tooth, staring into the smouldering fire. He drew a breath through his nose, the scent of burning wood tinging the air. The crackling of the fire was the lonely sound that filled the courtyard. Many had stayed and drank for hours after Therin had told the story of the Chainbreaker – of Calen's dad. But one by one, they had left, until only Calen, Dann, and Haem remained.

Dann sat on the ground to Calen's right, leaning back against the white stone bench upon which Calen sat. Haem was on Calen's right, leaning towards the fire, his arms rested atop his legs.

Calen still wasn't sure how to feel or what to think. Hearing Therin tell his dad's story as though Vars was a hero of old was something Calen would never forget as long as he lived. But at the same time, it had filled Calen with a longing that could never be sated. He would never see his dad again.

Dann sighed and sipped his wine. "I still can't believe your dad is the one who killed Durin Longfang." He shook his head, staring at the fire. "I still remember Therin telling us the story of the siege of Argona."

Dann looked back at Calen, and Calen gave him a weak smile. The silence that followed was broken only by the sound of footsteps.

"You're still here?" Therin appeared from behind Calen, stopping by the fire. The elf lifted his hands, turning his palms towards the flames. He looked towards Calen and Haem. "I've lived for hundreds of years, and I only knew your father for a small portion of that time, but I count him among the closest friends I've ever known." All the early theatrics were gone now, and Calen could hear the loss in Therin's voice. "He was a singularly unique soul, and he loved you both, your sister, and your mother with everything he had." The fire crackled and popped as Therin nodded to himself. "I miss him dearly."

Haem shuffled beside Calen, the firelight glowing softly against his face. "Therin, all those years you came to The Glade, and all those years you acted as though you were nothing more than a travelling bard. Why? Why did you both keep it all a secret? Why did our dad never tell us?"

The question was one that had floated in Calen's mind for hours.

Therin's cloak blew back in the gentle night breeze. He looked towards the dark, cloud-filled sky, then gave Haem a weak smile. "A few months before the attack on Varsund, your father returned to The Glade. And then, just after the siege of Argona was broken, he received word from your mother – she was with child."

"Me?"

Therin nodded, his gaze lingering on Haem. "Children change your perspective on things. But also, by the end of the war your father had made an enemy of both Castor Kai, and Rayce Garrin's heir, Korim Garrin, who is now the Varsundi High Lord. Both wanted his head. His only saving grace was that after the Battle of the Blood River, the Vars Bryer who had joined the Illyanaran army was presumed dead. Castor Kai knew him only as Cassian Tal – a name you might recognise."

Calen sat up straight, narrowing his eyes at Therin.

"Wait." Dann shifted in place, pushing himself back up against the stone bench. "Vars is Cassian Tal, *the* Cassian Tal?"

Cassian Tal was a legend. Every bard who passed through The Glade weaved tales of the greatest swordsman Illyanara had ever seen. The name of the man who killed Durin Longfang had never been known, but most storytellers had credited the deed to Cassian Tal. So many stories had been sung in Tal's name that it was long believed he was never truly a man but instead a fabrication, for no man could have achieved so many feats.

Therin nodded.

Dann puffed out his cheeks, then took a mouthful of wine. "Is he Achyron, too? Maybe he's Alvira Serris?"

Therin chuckled, looking back at the fire. "War is strange. Vars and his soldiers were among the few who survived the Blood River. There was always the chance they wouldn't be seen as heroes but as deserters. How else does one survive such a slaughter? So it was decided that the four who joined me would take up new names. Castor Kai and all others knew him only as Cassian Tal." Therin looked to Haem. "So, in answer to your question, after freeing Fenryr, your father made the choice to put family over all else. His first—" Therin gestured at Haem "—would draw his breath before the end of that year, and Vars refused to let you or your mother pay for the choices he made. I visited as often as I could, every year, sometimes twice a year. He asked that in the open we never acknowledge our past so as no links could be drawn between us. From time to time, we would meet near Pirn. He would bring a cask of Lasch's mead, and we'd talk and drink until the sun rose. But those times were few and far between."

Therin pulled his hands away from the fire and sat on the ground before Calen, Haem, and Dann. "About five summers ago, a man we once knew visited The Glade. He was not a man to be trusted. And so the Angan laid a cub at your father's feet. A cub blessed by Fenryr himself, gifted to watch over your family."

"Faenir?" Calen narrowed his gaze. "No, my dad found Faenir in Ölm Forest. His mother had died giving birth, as had the other cubs."

"There's truth in every lie. Vars did find Faenir in Ölm Forest, but he did not find the wolfpine nestled against the body of his dead mother. He found him in Baldon's arms. Baldon almost had to force your father to take Faenir."

"Even for your kind, the Chainbreaker was a stubborn man."

Calen turned to see Baldon standing behind him, eyes gleaming in the night. The Angan bowed deeply, then made his way around the bench. He lowered himself to the ground beside Therin, folding his fur-covered legs beneath him. He looked from Haem to Calen. "Your father risked everything to help my people. He did so with no promise of reward. He had a special heart, and I mourn him. But I also find happiness in seeing that he passed his heart on so that it may beat within his children. You honour him in your actions and in your words. You are the sons of the Chainbreaker."

Chapter Sixty-One

The Past is Now

Aeson stood at the edge of the Eyrie's main plateau, the wind cool against his face. His legs were unsteady from the wine, but he kept his eyes closed, drawing in long breaths through his nose.

"I will take him each day for lessons in flying and creating fluidity of the bond." Chora Sarn's voice cut through the sweet silence. "From what I can tell, he's had little time on dragonback, something that must be rectified immediately. Therin, if you and Thacia could take charge of his Spark instructions, that would be appreciated."

"Consider it done, Chora," Therin answered.

Aeson opened his eyes and turned back to the group – all twenty-six of the Rakina who resided in Alura, along with Therin, Asius, and Senas. After the celebrations, Chora had called for a meeting to discuss the path forward. Even though there was no 'leader' per say, Chora was the eldest among them, and she had been one of Alvira's top commanders before The Fall. "I will continue his teaching in the blade, but I would appreciate it if you would join me, Harken, and also you, Atara."

"Gladly." Harken stood with his back against a tree, his arms folded, the end of Sardakes's black tail curled around his legs.

"What is the point?" Atara Anthalin was an elf of the now lost kingdom of Caelduin. She was one of the greatest blade masters Aeson had ever known. She suffered greatly when her soulkin, Seynarí was taken from her. "What is the point in any of this, Aeson? All we are doing is setting this man on a path of pain. Will you look him in the eyes when Eltoar Daethana slays his soulkin? Will you whisper your apologies when Helios rips Valerys apart like a plaything?"

"Atara is right," one of the others, Willam, said. He sat on a flat stone, his legs folded, his eyes fixed on Aeson. "We all know that no matter how much time we spend training this man, he will never be able to face even a single Dragonguard, never mind all of them. It is a fact, Valerys is too small. Even Meranta or Eríthan are twice his size. And Eltoar and the others have trained in the Spark and the blade for centuries. Do you expect Calen to best them? Eltoar, the one who slew Alvira Serris? The one who bested you, Aeson? What we should be focusing on is the egg and how it hatched. Creation over destruction. Longevity over revenge. It came from Valacia, perhaps that is the route we should follow."

Aeson nodded slowly, thoughts of that night in Ilnaen flooding his mind, images of Alvira approaching him on the bridge to the Tower of Faith. Not a day passed when he did not wonder what might have been different if he had not trusted Eltoar that night. Would Alivira still be alive? He shook the thoughts from his head. "The elves have already instructed the Dracârdare to keep the eggs warm and will begin testing for the Calling come dawn's light. On that, they have asked for one of us to oversee the process – I suggested Ferdinan, but as this is of such great importance, I would ask for more volunteers." Aeson looked at a short, flame-haired man with dark eyes, who nodded. Aeson turned back to Willam. "Simply procuring a single egg from Valacia almost cost me my life and the lives of my sons. We lost over a hundred companions, and I'm still not sure how we made it out alive. That is a path for the future, maybe, but not for now. You do not give Calen enough credit, Willam, or you, Atara. He wields a blade well, far better than I did when I had seen his summers. His father taught him well." Aeson glanced towards Therin, giving his old friend a weak smile. Therin had never told Aeson of Vars Bryer, but he supposed it all made sense now. "And his advancement in the Spark is unmatched. I have never known another soul to learn so quickly."

"A benefit of being bonded to a Valacian dragon, perhaps?" Chora suggested, scratching her chin. "It has always been said that Valacian dragons hold a strong connection to the heart of the Spark. Perhaps the stories are, for once, not embellished." She turned to look towards Therin. "You knew his father. Is there druidic blood in his veins perhaps? A closer bond with the dragon than is normal? I've not seen it before, but that doesn't mean it is impossible."

"Not that I know of. But—"

"It does not matter," Atara snapped, shaking her head. "The others will rip him apart as though he was a child. They will tear Valerys to pieces, and the blood will be on our hands. They won, Aeson." Atara took a step closer to Aeson, the others watching her in silence. "The war is over. The Order is no more. You have been chasing a fallacy for centuries, and you will not find your answer in more blood. I know you blame yourself for Alvira, but sending this young man to his death will absolve you of nothing."

Aeson cleared the distance between himself and Atara in a matter of moments, his blade in his hand before he'd even realised he was moving, the edge pressed to Atara's neck. "Say that again."

"Do it." Atara leaned forwards, pressing her neck against the blade's edge, drawing blood. She looked tired, her eyes sunken. "Do it, Aeson."

"Enough!" Chora's cheeks were flushed with anger. "Those of you who want no part in this, leave now. None of us will begrudge you, and it shows no weakness. You have all suffered more pain than any soul was ever meant to know. You have earned your rest. But in the same vein, *we* will fight. And I will not have you spilling doubts into Calen's mind or fighting against everything we wish to do. You are our brothers and sisters until the day our souls leave this world, and even thereafter. Show us the respect we show you."

Aeson gritted his teeth and pulled his blade away from Atara's throat, sliding it into the scabbard across his back. He looked into the woman's eyes. "Forgive me, Atara. My losses pull at my soul recently. I've not been holding my temper well."

"No," Atara said, shaking her head. "Forgive *me*. I will help train the young Draleid. I still do not believe there is a point, but Seynarí would be ashamed of me if I did not try. I owe her a reason for not joining her."

Aeson cupped his hand at the back of Atara's head and pulled their foreheads together. "We are of the same cloth, you and I. When we die, we will do so in flame and fury. Whatever path we choose, dying quietly in a place like this was never in our stars. I will make you believe."

"Please do, brother. I would welcome it."

Aeson gave Atara a soft smile, pulling his head away. As he did, he saw a number of the Rakina had left without a word, and a few now stood separate.

"I've lost enough," a tall elf by the name of Malkir said, giving a slight bow at the waist. "I am ashamed to say it, but my fight is over. Draleid n'aldryr, myia'ydilar. La maeri du aldryr ar orimyn."

Dragonbound by fire, my friends. I wish you fire and fury.

More Rakina left, each saying their piece, until, aside from Aeson, only Chora, Thacia, Harken, and seven others remained. Ten in total. Ten of twenty-six. Aeson had hoped for more.

Atara remained, as did Willam, surprisingly. Aelmar and Moras – two Jotnar – still sat beneath the canopy of one of the trees. Numeni, Dernin, and Lira all stood together on Aeson's right, nodding to him as his gaze met theirs."

"Thank you." Aeson looked at those who remained.

"There will be time for thank yous when this is all over," Chora said, turning her chair to face Aeson. "For now, there is much…" Chora's voice faded, her eyes narrowing at something behind Aeson. "I believe we have company."

Aeson turned to see a small green sphere floating behind him. A moment passed, and the sphere spread, flattening into a disk, its centre growing dark as obsidian. The disk rippled like liquid, and then a shape stepped through, armoured in smooth, flowing green armour, the sigil of a downward sword set into a sunburst emblazoned across the breastplate.

"Aeson Virandr." The figure's helm rippled, then turned to liquid, flowing backwards into the collar of the armour, revealing the face of a man with dark hair and a thick, dark beard. "It has been far too long."

"Kallinvar. You look as though time has forgotten your face."

"The sky is calling the ocean blue, my friend."

Kallinvar stepped towards Aeson and they pulled each other into a tight embrace. The man's armour was cold even through the cover of Aeson's shirt. It was a strange thing; Aeson hadn't seen Kallinvar since the night Ilnaen fell. And before then, he'd never even met the man. Yet somehow it felt as though he were embracing one of his oldest friends – a kindred soul.

After a few moments, they pulled apart, and Aeson took a step back. "I take it one of your brothers or sisters travelling with Calen told you of this place?"

"Sister-Captain Ruon. She contacted me through the Sigil as soon as you arrived here. She has told me that three elven rulers reside here, those of Lunithír, Vaelen, and Ardurän, and that they wish to meet with me. I will do so in the morning, but I thought it best I speak to you first. I wanted to let you know the Knights of Achyron are behind you." Kallinvar looked past Aeson to those gathered. "We failed you, the night Ilnaen fell and the years after. We should have been there sooner. We should have stood by your side. We didn't, and both of our people suffered for it. We are here now, and we wish to rectify that mistake. We will stand and fight at your side. We will support Calen in the battles to come."

Snapping twigs and rustling grass sounded as Chora wheeled herself closer to Kallinvar. The man loomed over her like a giant, his dark green armour making him seem even larger than he truly was.

Chora looked up at the man, her gaze unwavering. "You did not fail us, Kallinvar. We failed ourselves. Just because you were not able to stop us from breaking doesn't mean you hold the blame for it happening. I am sorry for your loss. That night and more recently. Verathin was a unique soul. He was kind, measured, learned, and thoughtful. His loss is felt keenly, though I could not think of a better soul to stand in his place."

Kallinvar looked down at Chora, his chest swelling as he drew in a deep lungful of air. "You honour me, Chora Sarn. Beyond words. Verathin's is a soul that can never be replaced. He was not only my Grandmaster, but a mentor and a friend. It appears we have each of us lost things that can never be replaced. As I said, I have come here to tell you the Knights of Achyron will not stand back again. We will fight with you at every turn, and we hope you will do the same. The Blood Moon will taint our skies in a matter of months. I believe this is when Fane Mortem will attempt to tear the veil between worlds. And I would have us stand together as best we can when that day comes, as well as in the battles that will follow."

CHAPTER SIXTY-TWO

THE STORM, IT WAITS

Kallinvar stood at the edge of the plateau, the light of the sun spraying through grey clouds, the rain cold against his face. His shirt and trousers clung to him, saturated. He could have summoned his Sentinel armour, but there were times when he just needed to breathe.

He looked out over the elven city that wove through the valley, twists of bone white snaking in and out of the rock, the sun glinting off the famed erinian stone, the crashing of waterfalls unceasing. He'd missed sights like this. For centuries, all he'd seen was Ardholm, the temple, and battle. Even before The Fall, the knights had remained in seclusion more often than not. They had not been granted a second chance at life to spend their time absorbing the wonders of the world, they had been granted a chance so as to preserve the wonders for others.

"Grandmaster."

Kallinvar allowed his gaze to linger on the beauty of the city before turning to see Ruon, Lyrin, Varlin, Ildris, and Arden stepping onto the white platform. Each knight was garbed neck to toe in their Sentinel armour, the Sigil of Achyron emblazoned in white across the chest. "Brothers, sisters. I take it the journey across the Burnt Lands was relatively without incident then?"

"We lost some," Ruon said, sadness flickering in her eyes. "But most survived. The Taint has consumed the wasteland. It clings in the air like a fog, seeps into the sand. It has been so long since I've set foot within the bounds of the Burnt Lands, I'd almost forgotten. But it's worse than it was, thicker, heavier."

"What does that mean?" Arden asked, looking from Ruon to Kallinvar. The young knight hadn't been there at The Fall. He'd not truly experienced what it was to wade through a world weighed down by the Taint.

"It means that as the Blood Moon grows closer, the veil between worlds grows thinner. I'd already felt it before you crossed. There are other plac- es where the veil is thin, but nothing like the Burnt Lands. The entire waste is covered in the Taint." Kallinvar looked over the parapet at the city. "I spoke with the elven rulers. They, too, are wary of what is coming. And even they, with all their games and politics, understand what is at stake. They have agreed to allow us to attend council alongside them, the Ephorí, and Aeson Virandr's rebels – including the Draleid." Kallinvar said, resting his hand on Ruon's shoulder. "It seems that escorting the Draleid here and finding this place has taken more steps in securing allies than any of our other efforts. Messages have also been sent to the leaders of prominent factions and those who have a distaste for the empire, inviting them to talk. I will join talks when possible, but in my stead, Sister-Captain Ruon, I trust in you."

"Understood, Grandmaster." Ruon inclined her head in a way that was too respectful for Kallinvar; it was not something he was used to.

"Kallinvar, my child. Hear me."

Kallinvar closed his eyes for a moment, drawing in a slow breath.

"Are you all right, Kallinvar?"

Ruon's voice cut through the noise in his head. "Fine." He opened his eyes, meeting her gold-flecked green stare.

"How long are we to stay here, Grandmaster?" Varlin inclined her head as she spoke.

"As long as you are needed, Sister Varlin. Is there a problem?"

Varlin looked up, the light catching the black ink tattoos on her neck and arms. "I just… I don't like being out of the fight, Grandmaster." She looked at the others – Ildris, Ruon, Lyrin, Arden. "Our brothers and sisters are out there, holding back the Shadow, fighting… dying. And we're here, watching over the Draleid like mother hens – drinking and growing fat. It doesn't feel right."

"I, too, feel uneasy, Brother," Ildris said, his gaze fixed on the stone of the platform. "I will go wherever you send me, wherever Achyron demands. I will do what is needed of me. But…"

"I understand." Kallinvar drew in a long breath. "And I know that what I'm asking of you is not easy. For any of you." He passed his gaze over each of the knights. "But when you took the Sigil, you knew that nothing would be easy. You know why it is important to ensure the Draleid is safe, even here. Nobody thought Ilnaen could fall until it fell. Nobody thought The Order could be destroyed until it was. The moment we believe we are safe, fat, and happy is the moment a knife will open our throats. Protect the Draleid. Stay vigilant. Gildrick and the other Watchers predict the Blood Moon will tarnish the sky in a matter of months. They say this cycle is shorter than the last, and the moon will rise sooner. I feel it. The Bloodspawn activity is growing. Their attacks are more frequent, their numbers larger. The Bloodmarked are becoming more resilient, Fades more numerous. The veil is thinning. The storm is coming. That much I promise."

Kallinvar pushed open the door to Verathin's study, the wood cracking against the stone. He cursed, shaking his head as he closed the door more gently behind him.

"The veil is thinning, my child. You must be ready. You must listen to me. It is not simply the storm we must fear but what comes after."

"Get out of my head." Kallinvar pressed the fingers of his right hand into his temple, passing the many open compartments on the right wall, scrolls and old texts poking out.

He dropped into Verathin's chair. The desk was covered in the time-worn journals of the old Grandmasters. Kallinvar had read through almost every one of them. He'd not found even a single instance of a Grandmaster hearing Achyron's voice – which troubled him greatly. What if this wasn't Achyron? What if this was all some trick?

"Kallinvar."

"Get out of my head," Kallinvar repeated.

"Kallinvar."

"I said get out!" Kallinvar swept his hand across the desk sending journals, scrolls, and stacks of parchment crashing to the ground. He stood, shaking, his breaths deep and ragged, his jaw clenched, fury burning within him.

Hear me!

Burning energy radiated from Kallinvar's Sigil, pulsing through him, and with it came a blinding green light. He fell to his knees, closing his eyes and pressing his fists against his head. Slowly he peeled open his eyes.

"What in Achyron's name…" Verathin's study was gone, and Kallinvar knelt on a plateau that sat at the edge of an enormous cliff, waters of luminescent blue swirling about him, cascading off the edge. Before him, enormous islands floated in the sky, their tops covered in canopies of lush green. Gargantuan buildings rose through the canopies, looking as though they had been wrought from the same metal as his Sentinel armour. Rivers and streams of luminescent water flowed off the edges of the islands, crashing down hundreds of feet to the lands below.

A shriek pierced the sky, and Kallinvar stumbled backwards as three birds as large as horses swept upwards past the cliff, their feathers shimmering in a mix of metallic purples and blues.

"Welcome, my child."

Kallinvar's Sigil pulsed, ripples of energy sweeping through him, the hairs on the back of his neck standing on end. He swallowed, his lips dry. Kallinvar drew in a breath, pushed it out slowly, and looked back.

A figure wrought entirely from shimmering green light stood before him. It was easily twice his height, its body thick and broad.

"Who are you?"

"You know who I am." The voice came from the figure, but at the same time it echoed in Kallinvar's mind. The green light dimmed, revealing a man who stood at least twelve feet tall, encased from neck to toe in smooth green plate. The pauldrons were wrought into the shape of burning suns, the metal rising and twisting like flickering flames, while the breastplate pushed together in the centre forming the shape of a downward facing sword.

The man looked young. Thirty summers, no more. His hair was dark as night, his eyes a glowing, almost incandescent green from corner to corner.

"Achyron..." Kallinvar dropped to one knee, bowing his head and pulling his hand across his chest. He clenched his fingers into a fist so tight they trembled. "Forgive me, I have lacked faith."

"My child, rise. Your faith is unwavering."

Kallinvar's heart hammered against his ribs, pounded in his head. But even so, he rose, looking upon the warrior god himself. "This cannot be real..." He looked to Achyron and past him to where more islands floated in the sky. "It cannot."

"This is very real, my child, and the hour is urgent, we have little time. Efialtír grows stronger with each day as more Essence of life flows through the veil and lesser gods flock to his side. That is why I have spoken to you. That is why I am risking everything by pulling your soul here. You must hear me, and you must be ready."

"I am yours, Achyron." Kallinvar inclined his head. He felt the urge to kneel once more but fought it.

"The Alignment – what you call the Blood Moon – is almost upon us. It will paint your skies red within the passing of three moons. You must be ready, Kallinvar. The Urithnilim – the Fades – are but minions. With the tears already made in the veil, this Alignment will allow far greater forces to cross and take physical shape in your world. I..." Achyron turned his head towards the sky, eyes narrowing. He stepped forwards, looming over Kallinvar like a mountain. "I must send your soul back. The others are searching for me. I cannot step between the worlds, lest I break ancient oaths that I am already bending. But know this – as the veils thins, and the Alignment approaches, Efialtír is not the only one whose sway on this world grows. I will do what I can. What I have brought you here to tell you is that the alignment *will* happen, my child. It is inevitable. You cannot stop Efialtír's harbinger from widening the tear in the veil. Too much has been set in motion. But you must meet him when he does.

You must limit the crossing and close the tear. Then prepare the world for the war to come." The god's eyes pulsated with green light as he looked down on Kallinvar. "The Alignment is only the beginning – only a single step in the Great Deceiver's plan. Do not doubt, my child. This was always meant for you. You are my chosen."

"Pain is the path to strength." Kallinvar bowed his head.

As Kallinvar went to speak, his Sigil pulsed, and a sharp noise pierced his ears while blinding green light obscured his vision. It felt as though his body was being pulled in a hundred directions, dragging, tearing, ripping.

"Kallinvar?" Watcher Gildrick's voice echoed in Kallinvar's ears. "Kallinvar, what happened? Watcher Ilmire, get a healer! *Now!*"

Hands rested either side of Kallinvar's face, and he opened his eyes to see he was kneeling on the floor of Verathin's study, parchment, scrolls, and journals scattered around him. Watcher Gildrick knelt before him, hands clasped at the sides of Kallinvar's face, eyes fixed on Kallinvar's own.

"What happened? Kallinvar, answer me. Are you all right?"

"I saw him, Gildrick."

"Saw who? Look at me, Kallinvar. Saw who?"

"Achyron. I saw the warrior god."

Chapter Sixty-Three

Choices and Fate

Rist's breath misted before him as he walked, the morning sun cutting through the thin clouds overhead. Earlywinter had long made way for spring, and summer was fast approaching, but the morning air still held a slight chill.

He looked at Neera, who walked to his right, giving her a soft smile. Most of her wounds had healed or scabbed over, but he could still see the bandages poking through her shirt around the right side of her chest and shoulder. She'd not talked about it, but he hadn't seen the crinkles of her nose or heard her snort with laughter since that day in the triage tent.

"What do you want?"

"Nothing." Rist tried not to sound defensive, but he was pretty sure he failed.

"Then why are you looking at me like that?"

"Looking at you like what?"

"Like a puppy who's found its mother."

"Ahh," Magnus boomed, turning from where he walked in front of them, fresh scars marring his arms and neck. Even though the right side of Magnus's beard had been burned to nothing during the battle at The Three Sisters, the man had decided to keep the left side covered in thick black hair. It was more than a little disconcerting to look at and somehow made Magnus seem even more unhinged. "Young love. Like I said, Uraksplitter, that could be us if you just give it a chance."

"With a beard like that, Magnus, the only thing you'll be bedding is a blind wolf."

"Ain't nothing wrong with a little danger, Uraksplitter."

Anila gave Magnus a cold stare, then shook her head.

"So, Garramon. They've not been able to get a word out of the girl?"

Garramon shook his head but didn't speak. He hadn't spoken since Taya Tambrel had sent for him to come to the tent where they were keeping the girl they had captured during the fires the other night. Rist didn't know much except that after the alarm was raised to warn of an elven attack, a group of rebels had untethered the horses and set fire to the wagons and tents. Many of the sick and injured had died in the flames, left behind and unable to crawl from the blazing tents. Hundreds had lost their lives.

Rist wasn't sure how he felt about that word: rebels. He'd heard of the fighting in the South – some of it in Illyanara, though mostly in the east. He'd heard of the factions rising across the province, each warring against one another, but all raising their banners in opposition to the Lorians. Even the High Lord, Castor Kai, had not re-affirmed his allegiance, which was not being taken well in the North. Rist reckoned that if the Uraks hadn't been attacking so savagely, and now the elves, more soldiers would have been sent south. But that word echoed in Rist's mind. *Rebels*. Would that be what the people of The Glade would be called if they rose up? Nothing more than rebels. The thought set his skin crawling.

"She must be strong as an ox," Magnus said. "There's no Inquisitors here, but there's some who would be more than happy to cause pain to another. I'd like to meet the girl with balls of steel. But I suppose that's why Taya sent for you, Arbiter."

Garramon stopped in his tracks.

"I didn't mean anything by it, Brother." Magnus frowned, showing his open palms. "We both know it's true. She didn't ask for Exarch Garramon, she asked for the Arbiter."

Garramon drew in a long breath through his nose, his eyes fixed on Magnus. Magnus towered over Garramon, his shoulders half again as broad, his neck thick and muscled, his hands as large as shovels. And yet, somehow it was the look in Garramon's eyes that set Rist on edge.

"Let's get this over with." Garramon turned and walked off towards the centre of the camp – or what was left of it after the charred tents had been removed. The Craftsmages had been able to weave replacements from the supplies that survived but only enough to force the soldiers to sleep double, like birds packed into a nest.

Six guards stood watch over the front of the tent, four in the black and red of Loria, steel breastplates strapped across their chests, and two in the black plate of Taya Tambrel's Blackwatch. The two Blackwatch guards stood almost a head taller than the other, helmets and pauldrons wrought in the shape of roaring lion heads.

"She's waiting for you," one of the Blackwatch said, dipping his head only slightly as Garramon approached.

Garramon nodded in answer, stepping past the guards and into the tent, Rist and the others following after.

The tent was square and twice as large as the one Rist, Neera, Garramon, Anila, and ten other mages of the First Army shared. Taya Tambrel, along with a short, squat man with bandages wrapped around his left forearm and another who Rist recognised immediately as Eltoar Daethana, stood to the right, beside a long wooden table. The captive stood at the back, her hands bound by shackles chained to a post.

"What in Efialtír's name is that beast?"

At the sound of Magnus's voice, a hulking shape lifted to its feet on the left side of the tent, a deep growl resonating in its throat. It was a wolfpine – Rist would have recognised it anywhere – but it was far larger than any wolfpine Rist had ever laid eyes on. Its fur was matted with blood and dried dirt, patches missing where scars had been raked through flesh. There was something familiar about it – something that niggled in the back of his mind. The wolfpine snarled and snapped its jaws, howling. An iron collar wrapped around its neck chained it in place, but with each creak of iron, Rist became more and more uncertain as to whether the chain would hold.

"Ehm… are we sure that chain will hold?" Magnus asked, scratching at the bearded side of his chin.

"No." Taya Tambrel turned to acknowledge the tent's new entrants. "It broke free already and killed four men. If it weren't for the commander," Taya said, gesturing towards Eltoar, "it would have been much worse than it was. I've had Craftsmages forge thicker chains and double them up. Hopefully that'll hold the beast." Taya reached out her hand and clasped Garramon's forearm. "Exarch Garramon, it's good you're here."

"Why not kill it?" The coldness in Magnus's voice surprised Rist. The man was usually so full of laughter, but cold moments like that reminded Rist that Magnus was far more than just a joke teller.

"Because the Justicars believe she is a druid and the wolf some kind of… bonded animal."

Eltoar Daethana lifted his gaze from whatever he was reading at the long table. Standing without his plate armour, in a simple white tunic and black trousers, Rist could see just how broad shouldered and muscled the commander of the Dragonguard truly was. Somehow, Eltoar seemed even more intimidating without his armour. His snow-white hair was tied up, and a sword with a black dragonhead pommel hung at his hip. "Ilyain has encountered druids before," Eltoar said with a shrug. "If he says this is a druid, she is a druid. Besides, you have seen her eyes and teeth."

"You questioned her?" Garramon looked past Taya and Eltoar, to the squat man at the end of the table who wore a brown leather apron, an unfurled wrap of sharp steel tools laid out before him.

"Aye, it was me, Exarch. The name's Lerol Holts, of the Blackwatch." The man wiped his hands with a cloth, then stepped clear of the table, stuffing the cloth in one of the apron's pockets. "She's a feisty bitch – bites more than the wolf." The man lifted his bandaged arm. "Here, see for yourself."

The man reached his hand towards the captive woman, yanking it back as she came alive, thrashing, pulling at her chains, jaws snapping shut.

"Down, bitch." Lerol drove his fist hard into the woman's jaw, blood spraying across the dirt and grass upon which the tent had been pitched. She lunged forwards, her chains clinking as they caught behind her, and Lerol slammed his fist into her jaw once more, which sent her back a pace or two but didn't knock her down. She stood there, breathing heavy, sweat and blood dripping from her hair.

"What has she said?" Rist could tell by the curl at the edge of Garramon's lips that he was dissatisfied with Lerol's methods. It was the same look he'd given Rist on a number of occasions; Rist had made sure to memorise it.

"Nothing." The man made a guttural hocking noise, then spat a lump of phlegm into the dirt. "She's more feral than the wolf. Be better to see if it'll talk."

"You might not be wrong." Eltoar looked to Garramon.

"You want me to talk to the wolf?" Lerol asked, perplexed.

Rist could see Garramon's jaw clenching. "If she is a druid," he said, letting out a sigh, "then she will bear a deeper connection to the animal than is natural. We've seen it before, only the once. A man and his hawk. He was being questioned by the Inquisition. Not a word left his lips for six days."

"What happened on the seventh day?" Magnus asked.

"On the seventh day, the Inquisitor in charge of questioning ripped off the hawk's wings, and the man broke down into incoherent babbling."

"Did he talk?"

"No." Garramon shook his head. "He broke free of his bonds and tore the Inquisitor's arms off. We only even heard of the account through the account of the Inquisitor's apprentice."

"Well," the squat man, Lerol, said. "Perhaps we don't kill the wolf, just hurt it until she talks."

The woman's head twitched, lifting to look towards Lerol. "If you touch a hair on his head, I'll rip out your throat."

The voice was a more growl than anything else, but something about it sounded familiar. He leaned his head down, trying to see the woman's face, but it was covered by sweat-soaked hair.

"Well," Lerol said. "Looks like we have a plan then. That's the first thing she's said since she was dragged in here."

"I meant it." The woman jerked her head, flicking her hair to the side so she could see. "I will rip your throat out. I…"

Her voice trailed off, her stare turning to Rist. It was all Rist could do to stifle the gasp that rose in his throat. The woman's face was covered in dried blood, marked where the sweat had streaked through, and her nose was recently broken – judging by the fresh swelling – but he had absolutely no doubt who it was chained to the post.

Ella… What in the gods are you doing here?

Rist saw the recognition in her eyes, and he knew she was likely asking the same question: what was Rist doing amongst the Lorian armies? The pair of them were in places the other never would have imagined them being, but Rist had even more reason to be surprised: Ella was dead. She had died in the fire that had killed Freis. Unless she hadn't been sleeping there that night… Unless she had already been gone. The only place Rist could have imagined her being was with Rhett Fjorn. Her and Rhett's relationship was The Glade's worst-kept secret. A hundred more possibilities flitted across Rist's mind, but in the end he decided one thing: it didn't matter how, it only mattered that she was alive. And if that was Ella, was the wolfpine… *Faenir? It can't be. Can it?*

Ella turned her head back towards Lerol, a growl rising in her throat.

What happened to you?

Out of the corner of his eye, Rist saw Garramon looking at him with a narrowed gaze. The man didn't say anything, but he didn't have to. It was clear he'd seen Ella's hesitation when she saw Rist. Had he seen the recognition? Would it matter if he had? All of a sudden Rist felt alone in a foreign place. Simply being from The Glade made him vulnerable in this situation, and that was something he'd not had to face.

Garramon's gaze shifted to something behind Rist, and he heard the sound of dirt crunching beneath boots.

Rist turned to see Farda Kyrana, the Justicar who was leading the Battlemages of the Fourth Army and the man who had carried Neera from the battlefield at The Three Sisters – the man who had saved her life. He was as tall as Calen with shoulders even broader. A scar ran across his right eye. His dark hair fell down near his jaw, and a beard covered the lower half of his face.

"You called?" The man slowed as he entered the tent, looking about, taking stock of the tent's occupants.

"Yes, Justicar Kyrana, thank you for coming." Taya moved away from the table and grabbed Farda's forearm. "We are due to move out by sunrise a day from now," she said, turning towards Ella. "We already have the elves at our back, but I would prefer to know we don't have a horde of rebels waiting at our front. Questioning has been slow, despite Lerol's best efforts, and I assure you he is quite adept at this particular skillset. I have asked Exarch Garramon to aid in the interrogation, but your fellow

749

Justicar, Ilyain Altair, says that you have experience with druids. He himself refused to aid."

"I do. Though not as much as Ilyain himself." Farda stepped further into the tent, passing Rist. His face was almost unreadable, except for his eyes, which widened as though he'd just seen a ghost. It was then that Rist realised Ella had lifted her head and was staring at the Justicar, an intensity in her gaze.

"Oh, I see she likes *you* already." Lerol let out a throaty laugh, coughing up another ball of phlegm.

Farda ignored the man. He pulled a small gold coin from his trouser pocket, running his thumb across its surface as he stared at Ella.

"Lions or crowns to see who goes first?" Lerol pulled a cloth from his pocket and rubbed Ella's blood from his fist. "The real question is do you start on the girl or the wolf?"

"It's a wolf*pine*." Farda didn't move his gaze from Ella as he spoke. A moment passed, and then he flicked the coin into the air.

FARDA SAT ON A STACK of crates at the southern edge of the camp, where the mages had set up. He'd been in that same position ever since leaving the interrogation tent. He'd refused to aid and simply left instead. There'd be questions – from Eltoar, from Taya – but he cared little.

He flicked the coin into the air with a clink that rang out in the night, piercing the din of insects, then let it drop into his palm without bothering to look at the result.

Soldiers had passed by every quarter-hour or so, swords at their belts, eyes wide and alert. There had been no more drunken wallowing since the night of the attack – the rebels really had chosen their timing perfectly.

Farda let out a heavy sigh, repeatedly flicking the coin. He had not expected to see Ella in that tent. He had always hoped she'd found a way to escape Berona, but he'd never have expected she'd join with the northern rebels – he didn't even want to know the odds of that. If he were to put his money on it, he would have guessed Tanner Fjorn was responsible. Farda had not previously seen any reason to connect the man to the rebels, but Tanner certainly had the constitution for it. He was a man Farda respected, the kind of man who would fight for something.

On top of it all, she was a druid now. How in the name of all the gods had that happened? It was clearly in her blood. What that meant for the Draleid, Farda was unsure, but he cared little for what happened with the Draleid anymore.

The question was, what did he do now? He flicked the coin again. *Clink.* Farda held his palm outstretched, but the metallic ringing stopped dead and the coin never landed in his palm.

"She is gone, Brother." Ilyain stood beside Farda, his hand closed in a fist, the coin within. Only the faintest scar marred his face from where the owl had clawed him. The Healers had done a good job. He stared off into the distance, his sightless eyes staring at nothing in particular. The elf might never have been blinded, for all it impeded him. Even then, Farda could not feel any threads of the Spark augmenting Ilyain's perception. "You need to stop punishing yourself."

"You know I can't do that." Farda looked up at the cold moon etched into the night sky, pale white clouds dispersing its light. He held out his hand, and Ilyain dropped the coin onto his palm.

"No," Ilyain agreed. "But whatever it is you're debating now, trust yourself again. Do not let the fates decide. What is the point in living on with half a soul if we do not follow our hearts? They're all we have left."

Farda turned to look at Ilyain, who still stared off into nothingness.

"Don't look at me like that." The elf raised his eyebrows, his lips curling at the edges.

Farda could do nothing but laugh. He bit his lip and shook his head, letting out a puff of air.

"Whatever it is, Hala and I are with you."

"You say that without knowing?"

Ilyain shrugged. "We've both recently decided there's little point in the knowing of things. We'd rather trust in the knowing of people."

"And what brought about this thinking?" Farda asked. "There's something that's changed in you, old friend."

"A bad decision, followed by centuries of contemplation, followed by a sign from the gods. As I told you before the battle – if we're to die, we'd rather do it with our own kind."

Farda nodded softly. He looked at the coin in his palm and flicked it into the air. "I don't think you're going to like what my heart is telling me to do."

The coin landed.

"It's the druid, isn't it?"

"What makes you say that?"

"You've been in the same spot since you got back from the tent." Ilyain blew out a puff of air. "I don't think she's going to like me very much. I wasn't particularly gentle with her."

Farda closed his fingers around the coin. He squeezed tighter until he could feel the pressure of the metal pushing against the bones of his hand. He let out a long breath, then slid the coin back into his pocket.

"I'll go wake Hala."

FARDA RAN HIS THUMB OVER and back across the coin as he approached the interrogation tent. The two Blackwatch guards who had been posted there earlier were now gone, but four new soldiers in the black and red of Loria stood watch.

The soldiers' backs straightened as Farda approached – they knew him. *Good.*

"Justicar." The nearest soldier on the left of the tent's entrance nodded. "Supreme Commander Tambrel is no longer here, Sir. She has retired for the night."

"And she's left you standing out here?" Farda allowed a smile to creep across his lips.

The man laughed but shuffled his shoulders, standing straighter. "Happy to do it, sir. That wench in there killed good men and women."

"That she did," Farda said with a nod. "I was in earlier, assisting Exarch Garramon with the questioning. I have a few more 'questions' to ask of our new guest."

The guard gave Farda a grin. "Ask all the 'questions' you want, Justicar. She deserves all the 'questions' she can get."

"I'll see to it…?"

"Pardem, sir. Tal Pardem."

"I'll see to it, Tal Pardem." Farda stepped past the guards and through the tent's entrance, allowing the smile to fade from his face. *Insufferable twit.*

"Ah, Justicar Kyrana. What a pleasant surprise."

Farda snapped his gaze upwards, finding himself staring at the smiling face of Commander Talvare. Two of the commander's generals stood to her left – General Hanat and General Fulker, both younger women with dark hair – while Guthrin Vandimire stood by her right, his oily black hair glistening in the light of the freshly lit lanterns that hung from posts about the tent.

"Commander Talvare." Farda gave a quick nod. He didn't bother to acknowledge Guthrin. The man wasn't worth the energy it wasted for Farda to move his neck. "What brings you here at this hour?"

"I've never seen a druid before. When Supreme Commander Tambrel told me we had one in chains, I had to come and see for myself. I have to say, she and the wolf are rather impressive." Talvare turned back towards Ella, who knelt on the ground with the chains lifting her arms into the air. "Though she seems so young for one who has caused so much chaos." Talvare looked at Farda, eyes narrowing. "I could ask the same of you, Justicar Kyrana. What has *you* here at this hour?"

"There's a few more questions I'd like to ask her."

"And you come back now?" Guthrin's voice oozed with disapproval, his beady eyes fixed on Farda. "At this hour?"

"There is an art to interrogation, Guthrin." Farda stepped towards the table at the right side of the room, where Lerol had left his interrogation instruments. He reached over to the leather wrap that rested on the table, pulled at the strings and unfurled it. The polished steel implements glinted in the lantern-light. "You see, the key is to never let them sleep."

Farda picked up a particularly gruesome-looking tool shaped like a shears but with sharp teeth instead of cutting edges. He had no idea what the thing was called or what it was used for, but by the looks of it, it could only have been used to tear pieces of flesh from someone. He turned to Guthrin, snapping the jaws of the toothed-shears closed. "You break them slowly. You never stop. Stopping lets them rebuild."

He placed the shears back on the table and picked up a small, scythe-like tool that looked as though it would have been more at home in a surgeon's hands. "Now, if you would excuse me, there are questions to be asked and answers to be gleaned. I wouldn't think you'd have the constitution for it, Guthrin."

"Come." Talvare looked back at Ella, who knelt on the ground. She gestured to Guthrin and the other two generals. "I have no fear of blood, but I've had my fill of it for now."

For a moment, Farda saw the man's resolve waver, but then a surprising hardness set into his eyes. "You said you wanted to see a druid, Commander. Better an awake one than a sleeping one. We should stay, at least for a while. Let us hear her speak."

Talvare let out a long sigh, looking from Farda to Guthrin, rolling her eyes. "All right."

Footsteps sounded behind Farda, and he turned to see Garramon's young acolyte, Rist Havel walking into the tent, his eyes wide when he took in the tent's occupants. *What in the gods is he doing here?*

"And who the fuck are you?" Guthrin rolled his eyes. "I think you're lost. How did you get past the guards?"

"Because he's an acolyte of the Battlemages, Guthrin." Talvare shook her head. "Your powers of observation are too often lacking." Talvare fixed her gaze on the young man. "I am Commander Talvare of the Fourth Army. What is your name and why you here?"

"I'm Acolyte Rist Havel," the young man said. There was an awkwardness to him. He held his arms tight to his body, his fingers fidgeting, and he looked as though all he wanted to do was run from the tent, but he also met Talvare's gaze without hesitation. "I've met you before, Commander Talvare." Rist bowed deeply at the waist. "And also you,

General Vandimire, General Hanat, General Fulker, Justicar Kyrana. It was an honour."

The young man had a remarkable memory for names. Farda looked from Rist to Guthrin, whose face now bore a self-important grin. *Flattery will get you everywhere, Rist Havel.*

"And what, in the emperor's name, are you doing here?" Guthrin pulled at the end of his moustache, glaring at Rist.

"Exarch Garramon is my Sponsor. He's asked me to check on the druid. I'm to give her water." The young acolyte pulled a waterskin from a satchel that hung at his side.

Well. He's clearly lying. But why?

"Have at it then, boy. Then make yourself scarce."

The situation was getting more out of control by the minute. There were too many variables.

"Farda?"

The gruff voice caused Farda to clench his jaws.

"Kyrana, is she calling you by name?"

Fuck. Farda turned away from the young acolyte and looked from Guthrin to Ella. Out of the corner of his eye, he saw the wolfpine, Faenir, shift, heard a slight jingle of his chains.

"Farda... please, help me."

Guthrin dropped his hand to the pommel of his sword, widening his stance. "Why would she think you would help her, Kyrana? Something you wish to confess?"

"Stop being such an idiot, Guthrin. Keep your dick in its sheath. It's not like you know how to use it." Talvare looked to Farda. "Farda, what *is* going on?"

Farda looked from Talvare, to Rist Havel, to Guthrin, accepting that this wasn't going to happen the easy way. He drew in a breath, then gave a sharp whistle.

"What in the void was that?" Guthrin didn't move his hand from the pommel of his sword. He took a step closer to Farda, eyes narrowing. "I've always thought you were..."

They had all heard it: the sound of four bodies hitting the ground outside the tent.

Guthrin ripped his sword from his scabbard, holding it like a child would a stick. How the man had ever attained his position as general was beyond Farda. Though from what Talvare had told him before, it likely had something to do with his bloodline. Whatever it was, incompetence always tended to float upwards. The other two generals shifted their stances and dropped their hands to their sword pommels but didn't draw steel.

"Farda." The tone in Commander Talvare's voice changed, growing softer. Her hands stayed away from her sword. "Whatever you are about to do, don't. It's not too late."

"In the void it's not too late." Guthrin extended his sword. "Lay your weapon down and come peacefully or—"

"Or what?" Farda asked, cutting across the man. "Or you'll skewer yourself on my sword?" Farda sighed. The young acolyte, Rist, hadn't moved. He stood with his feet glued to the ground. Anyone else might have thought he was scared, but that was not the case; he was watching. "I'm taking the druid, and I'm leaving. I don't want to kill you – well, I'll happily kill *you*," he said, gesturing to Guthrin. "But Ayura—" he found himself using Commander Talvare's first name "—I would rather not have this go down that path. Drop your weapons belt to the ground and stand by the table. You too," he said, nodding to the other two generals.

"Use your head, Farda. None of this makes sense." Talvare's voice remained level as she spoke, but Farda also noticed she didn't reach to undo her weapons belt.

Guthrin stepped forwards, sword raised. "I'll make sure they take your head for this, Kyrana. Boy." He gestured towards Rist. "You're a Battlemage. Make sure he doesn't try anything."

Rist raised a curious eyebrow but didn't reach for the Spark, nor did he answer Guthrin.

Farda pulled the coin from his pocket, holding it in front of Guthrin. "Do you remember what I said this coin was for, Guthrin? I don't suppose you do. I don't suppose you remember much beyond how to eat, sleep, shit, and be a fucking idiot." With the words leaving his lips, Farda realised he hadn't appreciated just quite how much he despised the weasel of a man. "I said this coin is for deciding whether you live or die."

Guthrin's eyes narrowed at the coin, and Farda could see the man swallow, see the tremble of his sword. It would have been easy to use the Spark, but doing so would alert every mage in the camp. He looked to the acolyte. "Think quickly, or this will be you."

He flicked the coin in the air.

The beginnings of a war cry left Guthrin's throat as he lunged forwards, but it was cut short as Farda side stepped and swung the blade of the scythe-like torture implement into the soft flesh at the side of Guthrin's neck. Blood spilled over the steel as Farda yanked the man closer, using the small scythe like a hook. Guthrin dropped his sword to the ground, reaching his hands up to clasp at the steel in his neck.

Farda snatched the coin from the air, not bothering to look. He pulled harder on the small scythe, dragging Guthrin closer. The man choked and spluttered, blood pouring from his neck and mouth like a fountain. "You did well to live this long."

With the coin still held in his free hand, Farda gripped Guthrin's shirt. He held the man in place as he ripped the scythe forward, tearing it through Guthrin's throat and pulling it free. He released his grip, letting Guthrin fall, limp, blood pouring freely.

Farda stood over Guthrin, drawing in a slow breath. He threw the small scythe to the ground. "Step aside, Ayura. I don't want to kill you."

He was telling the truth. Of all the commanders Farda had met in his time, Ayura Talvare and Taya Tambrel were up there with those who truly held his respect.

Talvare looked down at Guthrin's body, her gaze holding for a few moments before she looked back at Farda. Her stare was hard as steel. He could see the fear in her, but she dominated it. *Yet another reason to respect you.* "I can't do that, Farda."

"Don't be stupid. Leave now. Nobody will ever know you or your generals were here. I killed the guards, found Guthrin here, and killed him too. Then I took the druid and left." He looked at Rist. "Does that sound right to you?"

Farda saw the glint of acknowledgement in the young man's eyes. "It does, Justicar."

"Good. You see, Talvare, you live, your generals live, the acolyte lives, and I go on my merry way. We all win."

"Not Guthrin."

"Guthrin was a prick."

"Fair assessment." Talvare swallowed hard, drew in a long breath, and slid her sword from its scabbard. "I can't let you take her, Farda. If she has information about a rebel attack, I need to know."

"Step out of the way, Ayura."

"No."

Farda gritted his teeth. They didn't have much time. Ilyain and Hala were watching the entrance, but they still needed to get out as quickly as they could and put as much distance between them and the camp as possible. "Don't make me do this, Ayura."

"I'm not making you do anything. This is your choice, Farda. If you're going to kill me to get to her, then take accountability for it. Don't hide behind me or that coin." Talvare shifted her stance, moving into Raging Wind. Unlike Guthrin, Talvare knew how to handle a blade.

"So be it. For what it's worth, this does not make me happy."

"Nothing could ever make you happy, Justicar Kyrana."

With that, Talvare lunged, immediately taking the offensive. General Hanat and General Fulker drew their swords and moved by Talvare's side.

Farda pulled his blade from its scabbard, turning away Talvare's swing. She moved like a woman of half her years and hit with the force of a wild bull. But still, Farda knew the inevitability of what was to come.

Hanat struck at Farda's head, but he dropped, swinging his blade and opening her belly. As Farda came up, Fulker stabbed at his torso. He twisted, the blade sliding past his chest. She overextended. He placed the flat of his hand on her back and pushed as he drove his sword through her neck from the other direction.

He yanked the blade free in time to deflect a swing from Talvare. She came at him three more times, her swings measured, her stance wide. She almost caught him with a stab to the chest, but Farda twisted, meeting her blade with his, then turning it to the side before bringing his own steel back around and slicing through the skin and bone of her left forearm. Talvare let out a scream as the steel cleaved through bone. Farda kicked at the inside of her knee, feeling a crunch. She fell to her good knee, howling, and Farda plunged his blade into her throat.

Talvare looked up at him, her eyes wide, blood sprinkling her lip.

Farda pulled the blade free, kneeling beside Talvare and catching the back of her head before she fell backwards.

"I'm sorry," he whispered as he lay her down gently. She tried to speak, but blood filled her throat and mouth. "I truly am."

Farda knelt, his hand resting on Talvare's cheek, until he saw her last breath fill her lungs. And even then, he knelt for a moment longer. He couldn't remember the last time he regretted taking a life. With a long, remorseful sigh, he rose to his feet, drawing in a deep breath. He turned to the acolyte, readying himself. There was only so far he was willing to trust a stranger. "You—"

"I came to free her too."

"You what?" Farda stared at the young man, doing nothing to hide the look of confusion he knew adorned his face.

"I came to free Ella too."

"How… do you know her name?"

"How do *you* know her name?"

Farda made to answer but stopped himself. "You're not the one asking the questions here."

"I grew up with her," the acolyte said. Farda wouldn't have been inclined to believe him, but then the pieces he had been missing slipped into place. He knew why the young man had looked so familiar when he had accompanied Garramon to the command tent that day outside Fort Harken. *Rist Havel – the Innkeeper's son. The one who escaped with Calen Bryer. What are the odds?* Farda had heard little on the Draleid after he had gone to intercept Ella at Gisa, and the Fade had attacked Belduar.

Did Garramon know who he had in his possession? Even as Farda asked himself the question, he knew the answer: of course Garramon knew. The Arbiter was not a man who made mistakes easily.

Farda stared at the young man for a moment longer, then grabbed a rag from the table to his right and wiped the blood from his sword.

"All right. I don't have time for a hundred questions." He slid his sword back into its scabbard. "What was your plan? Charge in here and then what?"

Rist looked back, an expression on his face as though Farda had asked a ridiculous question. "Open her shackles and set her free."

"And how were you planning to do that?" Farda himself had settled on using the Spark being the simplest available way. It would alert the others, but it was the quickest way.

The young man narrowed his eyes as though Farda had just asked him a trick question. He reached into his pocket and produced a set of small iron keys on an iron ring. "I stole the keys from the interrogator, Lerol, while we were here earlier. How were you planning to do it?"

Farda pursed his lips. Had he thought acquiring the keys would have been that simple, that is precisely what he would have done.

"Farda…" Ella's voice was harsh and dry. Her head still hung forwards, hair dangling. Dried blood covered her hands, wrists, and arms from where the manacles had sliced into her skin.

Farda snatched the key from Rist, then moved to Ella, unlocking the manacles and catching her as she collapsed into his arms. He pushed back her sweat-slicked hair, patting the side of her cheek. "Ella, Ella. Stay awake."

He peeled open her drooping right eyelid. Her eyes were glazed, almost vacant.

"Faenir," she mumbled, "Free him…"

Farda lay Ella on the ground, then turned to where Faenir had been collared to find the wolfpine standing at full height, glaring at him with amber eyes. The creature truly had grown enormous since Farda had last laid eyes on him. The crown of his head easily stood a match for Farda's chest, and his shoulders were dense and broad, muscle rippling. There was now absolutely no doubt in Farda's mind that Ella was a druid.

"Easy." Farda reached out an open palm, speaking in as calm a tone as he could. He glanced back at Rist. "Make sure she's all right. Give her some water." He heard the sound of shuffling feet as he turned back to meet the wolfpine's gaze.

A deep growl resonated in Faenir's throat, and the wolfpine's lips drew back in a snarl, saliva dripping from his long fangs.

"I'm pretty sure you don't like me," Farda whispered, taking another step closer to the wolfpine. "But if you promise not to eat me, I'll unlock that collar."

Negotiating with the animal seemed like a waste of time, but from Farda's experience with druids – which, admittedly wasn't too deep a well – any animal that bonded with an Aldruid grew keener of mind, and he could see that in Faenir.

The wolfpine's growl deepened, but then he stretched one grey paw forwards and bowed his head for Farda to unlock the collar. As Farda inserted the key and turned it, eliciting a click, a snarl sounded behind him.

The wolfpine's collar fell with a thud, and Farda turned to see Ella on top of Rist, her face contorted in rage, her eyes shimmering a molten gold, her teeth and fingernails longer and sharper than they had any right to be. The only reason the acolyte wasn't torn to the shreds was the barrier of Air he had hastily placed between them, holding Ella above him.

"How could you?" Ella snarled, her voice trembling with rage. "How could you fight for them?"

"Ella?" Farda placed his hand on Ella's shoulder.

"Don't touch me!" Ella drew in trembling breaths as she stared at Farda, her amber eyes gleaming in the firelight.

Faenir moved beside Farda, a slight whimper emanating from his throat as he looked at Ella.

"Ella, we need to go. Now. Other mages will have felt him touch the Spark."

Ella turned her glare from Farda back to Rist. To his credit, the young acolyte seemed more startled than scared, and the shield of Air he had constructed was solid.

"Ella, I'm sorry. I had no idea it was you. As soon as I did, I took the keys, I—"

"How could you?" Ella repeated, her lip curling back, exposing two pairs of elongated fangs – one at the top, one at the bottom. "You're meant to be his closest friend. How could you turn on him, Rist? How could you fight for them?"

"Turn on him? Turn on who?"

Farda rested his hand on Ella's shoulder. She snapped her head around, nose crinkling, eyes shimmering gold. "What?"

"We need to go, Ella. We don't have time for this."

Ella shook her head, looking from Rist to Farda, exhaustion clear in every motion. The burst of energy she had used to charge at Rist was fading, her eyes dropping. She staggered backwards off Rist, looking down at him. "I thought more of you. I thought you'd be with him. Your parents would be ashamed."

Ella stumbled, and Farda reached forward and caught her, wrapping his arm around the small of her back. She groaned as the pain from her wounds finally pushed through her adrenaline.

Within a second, the wolfpine was at his side, lips pulled back, razor-sharp teeth exposed.

"I'm trying to *help* her. You're getting in the way." Farda reached his right hand under the backs of Ella's knees and stood to his full height, lifting her and cradling her like a child.

The wolfpine backed away, his growl interspersed with low whines.

Footsteps sounded at the entrance to the tent, and Ilyain called in. "Farda, we must go. There's activity. Whoever used the Spark has alerted them."

Farda nodded, shifting Ella in his arms. He looked down at Rist, who still lay on the floor. "Tell them I killed Talvare and the others and that you got lucky. Understood?"

"Understood," the young man answered, his voice wavering as he looked up at Ella. "Where are you taking her?"

"That's a question you know I won't answer. And you don't seem like a stupid man. Mind your tongue."

"Mind my tongue?"

Farda lifted his boot and slammed it down into the acolyte's face, throwing his weight behind it. The young man's head bounced off the ground, and his nose split, spraying blood over his face. A quick glance told Farda Rist was still breathing.

"Ilyain, let's get Hala and go."

CHAPTER SIXTY-FOUR

THE SCARS OF TIME

Calen focused his breathing, exhaling slowly as he moved from Charging Boar into Patient Wind, sweeping through into Striking Dragon, keeping his eyes closed.

Sweat streaked down his face, stinging at his eyes and dripping off his chin. His muscles burned, but he had no intention of stopping. Moving through the sword forms felt like home, like The Glade was wrapped around him. He could hear his dad's voice. *Focus, Calen. Concentration won't keep you alive, but lack of it will kill you. Keep your balance. Balance beats speed. Speed beats strength.*

It had been so long since he'd felt the calm that came with the forms, the peace. He'd not found the time to go through the forms since before Kingspass. He hadn't realised how much he'd missed it until now.

"Into Rising Dawn," Aeson said, his voice nothing more than a dull whisper at the edges of Calen's mind.

Calen moved into Rising Dawn, letting his muscle memory take over. They had been there for hours, since before the sun had crested the mountains, while the courtyard was lit only with the residual glow of the erinian stone inlaid into the ground. Aeson and two of the other Rakina – Harken and an elf named Atara – had begun taking Calen through the forms and sword movements each morning since the celebration. Erik, Vaeril, Dann, Tarmon, and Haem had joined them while many of the Rakina and the rebels sat about the courtyard, some watching, some not. The other Knights of Achyron stood about in their full suits of Sentinel armour as though standing guard in the middle of a viper's nest.

The day after the celebration, Baldon and Aneera had reached out to the others of Clan Fenryr, passing on the message that was to be relayed. An Angan envoy was to be sent to each of the major leaders across the continent that might be sympathetic to their cause – identified by Aeson – along with those to whom Aeson had long been allied. Each would be invited to enter the Darkwood, to come and meet Calen personally. If there was a hint of deception, they would be left for the forest to claim, for the Aldithmar – the spirits. But if they came in good faith, they would be led through the wood by Dvalin Angan and rangers. It wasn't a plan without risk, but the Rakina, the Triarchy, and the elven Ephorí had all agreed it was the safest and most efficient method – they had even let Calen feel as though he actually had a say in the matter.

Calen, though, had gotten his first taste of what the politicking between the rulers was truly like when King Galdra had suggested no meetings should be arranged with any outside forces until a suit of armour had been made for Calen. He had insisted that if Calen was to be taken seriously as a new Draleid, he would have to look the part. But it was when King Silmiryn had suggested one of his smiths craft the armour that the debate truly began. Silmiryn, Galdra, and Uthrían had argued for hours on end, wired barbs hidden beneath overly pleasant words. It wasn't until Therin suggested an alternative armourer who bore no allegiance to any of the three kingdoms that the arguing stopped. Even then it had taken an unnatural amount of time for the three rulers to agree.

But they still insisted nothing be done until the armour was ready and Calen had been taught how to present himself. That had started a whole new argument between Aeson and Galdra, which, to Calen's surprise, Aeson eventually conceded.

Even then, as Calen moved through the forms from Crouching Bear into Howling Wolf, Calen cared little for the games and arguments. All he could think of was that he would eventually have to come face to face with the High Lord of Illyanara, Castor Kai. The thought filled him with cold fury. Castor Kai had betrayed Vars and tried to get him to chain a god, and now Aeson and the others expected Calen to put a smile on his face and convince the man to throw his strength behind their cause.

Calen focused. He would deal with that when it came. And while the Angan were passing on messages and decisions were being made, Calen would train, as he had done each day since the night Therin had told Vars's story. While Aeson, Harken, and Atara had been training him in the sword, Therin and Thacia – the blood-haired Jotnar – had been instructing him in the Spark. Chora was to guide him on the art of riding dragonback as well, but as of yet that hadn't started.

There was something comforting about the familiarity of it all, the regiment and repetition. It reminded him not only of practicing the sword with his dad but of the weeks spent travelling with Rist, Dann and the others – the last time Rist, Calen, and Dann had all been together.

"Eye of the Storm into Charging Boar, then back to Patient Wind."

Calen did as instructed, his eyes still closed. Aeson's voice melted into the back of his mind. The motions within the fellensír movement were more precise than the svidarya, more controlled and rhythmic. Where svidarya swept like fire, moving with the changing winds of battle, fellensír was like water, shifting and flowing, steady and unbroken.

"Break."

Calen drew in short breaths. In through his nose, out through his mouth, settling himself before slowly opening his eyes. He winced, the sun glaring. Aeson, Erik, Harken, Atara, Vaeril, Dann, and Haem stood around him, evenly spaced, sweat glistening on all their faces bar Vaeril's. Tarmon had dropped to his haunches, his sword resting on the ground in front of him. The man tilted his head back and puffed out his cheeks, looking towards the sky.

"You all right there, big man?" Erik smiled. "Need me to fetch you some water?"

"I'll strangle you while you sleep," Tarmon said, dropping back onto his arse.

"Is that a promise or a threat?" Erik gave Tarmon a wink then slapped him playfully on the back of the head. He grabbed some waterskins that rested by one of the white stone benches, tossing one to Tarmon. "You're always trying to get into my bed."

"You'd be so lucky. Little shit." Tarmon snatched the waterskin out of the air, pulling the stopper free and taking a mouthful of water. "It's just all these forms. Hours and hours. The same thing again and again. Give me a greatsword any day, and point me in the direction you need me."

"Spoken like a true human battering ram," Erik said with a laugh.

"You'll get better." Vaeril slid his sword into his weapons belt, which sat by a bench to his left.

"See," Erik said with a pout. "Even Vaeril thinks you'll get better. And he's not great with compliments."

"I was talking about you," the elf said, snatching the waterskin from Erik.

Erik said nothing but glared at Vaeril, his lips curling into a subtle smile.

Calen took a waterskin from Dann, looking around the courtyard as the cold water granted his cracked lips some relief. Some Rakina sat on benches, talking or watching the sword forms, while others were sprawled on the grass at the yard's centre, shaded by the thicket of trees. Thacia and Chora were deep in conversation a few feet away. Thacia, standing over twice Calen's height, towered over the woman in the wheelchair, but somehow Chora still seemed to be the one in control. Only ten of the Rakina had agreed to participate in Calen's training. The idea that some of them might not have wanted to fight the empire wasn't something he'd contemplated. But once he'd thought about it, he understood. There was only so long someone could fight.

"You still need to raise your guard," a familiar voice croaked.

Calen turned to see Gaeleron walking across one of the many stone bridges that connected to Alura's central courtyard, his dark hair tied back, a walking stick in his right hand. His left arm was draped around Therin's shoulder as he walked. A mixture of joy, guilt, and sorrow filled Calen, who had to force himself to hold his gaze on Gaeleron. The elf had once been broad-shouldered and layered with dense muscle, his movements smooth and graceful. But now he was more skin than muscle, and his gait was slow and unsteady as he leaned on both Therin and the walking stick for support. The elf had been given an endless supply of food since arriving in Aravell, as had Lasch and Elia, but Calen knew what it was like after being starved for so long. It had taken him days to be able to eat properly after being freed from Drifaien, and even with that his appetite had always been larger than most.

"Alea, Lyrei," Dann whispered.

And sure enough, walking behind Gaeleron and Therin, their heads lowered, their hands clasped before their stomachs, were Alea and Lyrei. Something about the way the twins walked, as though towards a funeral pyre, pulled at the back of Calen's mind. He'd not seen either of them since arriving back in Aravell. Both he and Dann had asked after them multiple times, but Therin had simply told them that Alea and Lyrei would return when they were ready. Which seemed more than a little ominous to Calen, but elves had strange traditions.

Calen slid his sword into his scabbard and walked towards the group, looking from Gaeleron to Therin. "Should he be out of bed?"

"Yes, I should." Gaeleron pulled his arm from around Therin's neck, leaning heavily on his walking stick. "And don't talk about me as if I'm not here." The elf grimaced, leaning down harder on his stick. "The Healers say I need to build back my strength, among other things. Therin was helping me." Gaeleron looked at Therin, a soft smile touching his face. It was the first time Calen had seen any of the elves, bar Vaeril, show Therin anything other than derision.

"I was merely heading in the same direction." Therin gave Calen a nod of acknowledgement.

"He's been by my bedside each day. The others, too." A moment passed where Therin and Gaeleron held each other's gaze. Gaeleron turned back towards Calen. "Vaeril has been teaching you fellensír?"

"He has. How can you tell?"

"Because Vaeril was never strong in fellensír."

"*You'll get better*," Calen heard Erik say behind him, mimicking Vaeril's voice as well as he could, then laughing with Tarmon.

"When I am stronger, I will correct the mistakes he has drilled into you, and we will start on the valathír – the Frozen Soul."

"We don't need a swordsman, we need a Draleid." Chora Sarn's voice rang out across the courtyard, and Calen looked to his left to see her wheeling her way towards him, Thacia striding at her side. They stopped beside Calen and the others, giving their greetings. "While I don't doubt Calen's swordsmanship needs improving."

"Harsh," Calen heard Dann whisper from behind him.

Chora leaned over in her chair, making a point of staring at Dann until the silence became uncomfortable. "While I don't doubt Calen's swordsmanship needs improving," she repeated, "it is not on the ground, in the crunch of bone and steel, that we will need him most. It is in the air, on dragonback. He needs more time flying and more time strengthening the bond between him and Valerys."

Even as Chora spoke, Calen could feel Valerys in the back of his mind. The dragon had spent much of his time in the eyrie with the other dragons. Valerys discovering he was no longer alone should have brought a warmth to his and Calen's shared heart, but instead, the emotion that now hung over Valerys was grief. The other dragons were despondent and listless. And no matter what Valerys did, only Ithrax, the enormous green dragon who had been bound to Prince Athír Ardurän, paid him any heed and, on occasion, flew with him.

"There is time in the day to both fly and spar," Harken said, folding his arms across his broad chest. "And he must also learn to control the Spark."

"What about sleep?" Calen suggested. "Sleep is good."

"You can sleep when you're dead." Atara stepped forwards so she stood at Calen's side. She was only an inch or so shorter than he was, with silvery hair tied into a ponytail. "Which will be sooner rather than later if you don't train. Helios is five times Valerys's size and Eltoar Daethana is one of the single greatest blademasters to have ever graced Epheria. Jormun and Hrothmundar are merciless – souls bred for killing. Each and every one of the Dragonguard have honed their skills for centuries. You do not have time to sleep, lest you wish to see your own blood feed the earth."

"Well," Dann whispered on Calen's other side, "that was cheery. Maybe we should take her off the motivational speeches though."

Atara glanced at Dann, then looked back to Calen. "I speak only the truth."

Nobody spoke as Calen looked back at Atara. This was not the first time Atara had reminded him of the likelihood of his death. She seemed to find at least one opportunity a day.

"Draleid." Calen turned to see Alea and Lyrei stepping towards him, their heads still bowed.

"Alea, Lyrei. It's so good to see you both. How are you feeling?"

Neither elf responded, but to Calen's surprise, they both dropped to one knee, each resting one hand atop their standing knee, the other across their chest.

"We have come to ask your forgiveness, Draleid." Alea lifted her head, her golden eyes shimmering. She was crying. Calen couldn't think of another time he'd seen an elf cry.

"What's wrong? Forgiveness for what?"

"Forgiveness for failing you and for failing our oath." Lyrei didn't lift her head as she spoke. "We wish to swear again, to bring honour back to our hearts. We wish to protect you and Valerys, as we promised."

Alea looked to Lyrei for a moment, then back to Calen. "As punishment, our oaths were stripped. Our honour shorn. We would take our oaths again and regain our honour. If you would have us."

Calen's words caught in his throat. He looked around at the others, finding all eyes focused on him. He turned his gaze to Therin for help, but the elf simply looked back at him with a blank stare, his mouth a thin line.

Calen let his gaze flit between Alea and Lyrei. "On one condition."

"Whatever it is, we accept."

He drew in a short breath, then reached down, holding his hands out to Alea and Lyrei. Alea looked at him tentatively, while Lyrei kept her head bowed. "Nakar myia lär ar anwê."

Take my hands and rise.

Lyrei lifted her gaze. The last time he had seen them both, his command of the Old Tongue had not been as strong. Calen gestured once more for them to take his hands, which they did. Gently, he pulled them to their feet. He bit at his lip, weighing up what he was about to say. It was something he'd been considering for quite a while, but he wasn't sure how it would be taken. He gestured towards Vaeril, Erik, and Tarmon, who walked over. Once Erik, Tarmon, and all four of the surviving elves who had sworn oaths to him stood together, he spoke. "Vaeril, Gaeleron, Alea, Lyrei. Your oaths have brought me great honour. Elissar gave his life to protect mine, and there is no way I could ever repay him for that. But now I tell you that you are each free of the oaths you swore. Your honour is intact, and you owe me nothing."

Gaeleron and Vaeril remained still and silent, their gaze fixed on Calen. But Alea and Lyrei began to protest. Calen raised his hand and they ceased.

"Each of you—" He looked from the elves to Tarmon and Erik "—have risked your lives for me more times than I am comfortable with." He slid his sword into his scabbard and dropped to one knee. "I will allow you to swear an oath to me, if you allow me to do the same."

"This is a bit dramatic, Calen. Even for you." Erik smiled broadly, shaking his head. "But I like it." He lowered himself to one knee in front of Calen.

Tarmon followed close behind, grunting as his knee hit the stone. He nodded to Calen. Tarmon always was a man of few words.

Calen looked back up to Vaeril, Gaeleron, Alea, and Lyrei. The elves' oath to him had always been something that made him uncomfortable. It had always scratched at the back of his mind. His life was not worth more than theirs – it simply wasn't. But from Therin's teachings, he'd learned that if he was to deny their oaths, it would bring harm to their honour in a way he never wished to do. This was the only balance he'd been satisfied with.

Vaeril was the first to kneel. He inclined his head towards, Calen, smiling softly.

Calen lifted his gaze to Alea, Lyrei, and Gaeleron. "You do not have to swear an oath, but if you insist, then so do I. Your lives are as important to me as mine is to you. To deny me this would do great harm to my honour."

Both Alea and Lyrei knelt, nodding.

"I would, Draleid." Gaeleron leaned on his walking stick, looking down. "But if I kneel I'm not sure I could rise again." A smile touched his lips. "I will stand. Repeat after me." He drew in a short breath, grimacing as he shifted his weight. "I hereby swear oath."

"I hereby swear oath," Calen and the others repeated.

Dann dropped down beside Calen, resting his hand on one knee.

"What are you doing?"

"I felt left out," Dann said with a shrug. He looked up to Gaeleron. "Carry on."

"I'm not swearing oath to him," Erik said, nodding at Dann. He let the words hang for a moment, then nodded to Gaeleron, smiling.

"I hereby swear oath," Gaeleron repeated, "by witness of those here and the six who watch over us, to protect those before me with all my strength. To bleed for them, to fight by their side, and if needs be, to die by it."

Calen, Erik, Vaeril, Dann, Alea, Tarmon, and Lyrei all repeated the oath.

"It is with honour that your oath has been witnessed by those here and by the six who watch over us," Therin said, moving closer. Therin reached out his hand and helped Calen to his feet. The elf had an unreadable expression on his face. "Calen, come with me. We are to meet Valdrin shortly."

LESS THAN AN HOUR LATER, Calen and Therin walked in silence across the bridge that connected Alura to the sprawling city of Aravell. Ruon had insisted that Haem come with them.

Calen cast his gaze about the smooth white buildings, walkways, and bridges that swept through the valley and blended seamlessly with the nature around them. He traced his finger across the surface of erinian stone inlaid into the parapet of the bridge they walked across, its soft azure glow now gone as it absorbed the light of the sun.

"You have learned much of our ways and our culture, and I believe I have Vaeril to thank for that as much as I do myself." Therin stared over the edge of the bridge as he spoke. "What you did was clever. I am aware you were not comfortable with the oaths sworn to you, but had you simply removed them, Gaeleron and Vaeril might have accepted it, Alea and Lyrei I'm not so sure. Gaeleron endured pain that would break most souls, and Vaeril has protected you selflessly. They would both have been free of their oaths with the understanding their honour was intact. But Alea and Lyrei believe they have failed you. Their oath was stripped from them as a punishment. They came to you looking for redemption. What you did was clever, but to swear an oath like that to someone is no small thing among elves, Calen. "

"It's not a small thing to me either, Therin." Calen glanced at the elf, letting out a sigh. "I don't want people standing beside me simply because of *what* I am. I want them to stand there because of *who* I am. If they are willing to bleed for me, then I am willing to bleed for them."

Therin gave Calen a weak smile, letting out a sigh. "You are your father's son." He turned to look at Haem, who walked a few feet behind them. "You both are. He would be proud beyond measure." Therin looked down at Calen's hip, smiling once more. "I gave your father that sword after he saved my life in Ballmar. The blade you carry at your hip was forged in the late First Age, over a thousand years ago. It was given to me by my father, and his mother before him, and before that it belonged to an elven Draleid by the name of Mythara. It has seen more war and bloodshed than you could begin to imagine. And in your father's hands, it was the blade that slew Durin Longfang, Taran Shadesmire, Rayce Garrin, and many other names you have heard in the bards' tales."

Calen dropped his hand to the coin-shaped pommel of the sword his father had given him.

"That was Dad's?" Haem asked, looking down at Calen's sword. It was then Calen realised that Haem likely had nothing to remember their parents by.

"It was. He gave it to me after The Proving." Calen gripped the pommel tighter, then stopped. He reached down and undid his sword belt. "It should be yours," he said, offering the sword, scabbard, and belt to Haem.

Haem smiled but shook his head, pushing the gift back. "If he had meant it for me, I would have been wearing it that night in Ölm Forest.

No, that's yours, Calen. Besides," he said, patting the sword at his hip. "I already have mine."

Calen didn't doubt the sincerity of Haem's words, but he saw his brother's gaze linger on the sword as Calen strapped his belt back on.

Elves stopped and watched as Therin, Calen, and Haem walked through the streets of white stone. Many of them bowed their heads, greeting Calen with, "Draleid."

Therin led them through the city, across walkways, up stairs, and over long bridges, until they approached a long pathway of grass that led upwards towards a plateau upon which stood two large white buildings and an enormous, broad-leafed tree. The building on the left of the plateau had two storeys, its outside covered in green vines that bloomed purple flowers. The building on the right was smaller and backed against a river that emerged from the mountainside, crashing its way down the cliff. A large white wheel was connected to the back of the building, dipping into the river, turning as the water flowed.

A warm smile spread across Therin's face, his stare fixed on something at the top of the path. Calen looked to see an elf emerging from the building on the left. She wore a long green dress that held tight around her waist, then flowed outwards. Her blonde hair tumbled over her shoulders. Her wrists were scarred and raw, fresh scabs ringing her flesh as though she had recently been held in shackles.

She pulled Therin into a tight embrace, wrapping her arms around him and squeezing, her head nestling into the crook of his neck. Calen had never seen an elf so emotional before. "It's been too long, Therin."

"I'm sorry, my child." Therin pulled the elf in tighter, drawing in a long breath. "There have been others who've needed my help, just as you once did."

"Just as I always will."

Therin held her close then pulled away, smiling. "Calen, Haem—Arden – whatever you prefer."

"Arden, please." It felt strange for Calen to hear the name leave Haem's lips.

"Well then, Calen, Arden. This is Aruni."

"Du gryr haydria til myia elwyn, Aruni. Laël Calen Bryer." *You bring honour to my heart, Aruni. I am Calen Bryer.*

"The Draleid." Aruni held Calen's gaze, and as she did, he saw her irises were black, ringed with a pale red. He'd never seen anything like it. "You speak the Old Tongue well," she said, inclining her head. "Let er du vol gryrr haydria til myialí, Draleid." *It is you who brings honour to mine, Draleid.*

"I don't speak the Old Tongue," Haem said, inclining his head towards Aruni. "So I can't show off like he can, but it is a pleasure to meet you. I am Arden of the Knights of Achyron."

"The pleasure is mine, Arden."

Therin looked towards the building on the right, which Calen assumed was the forge. "Valdrin?"

Aruni nodded. "He's inside. Though, he's working. You know how he gets when he's working."

"I do." Therin let out a soft laugh. "Still, best to let him know we're here."

Aruni led Therin, Calen, and Arden to the front of the white-stone forge, but as soon as he pushed open the door, a voice called out from within.

"No."

"Valdrin, it's me," Therin called back.

Calen had never thought he'd miss the forge. He'd always loved the time spent there with his dad and Haem, but smithing had never been something that pulled at his heart. But now as he looked through the sliver of open door to see the burning orange glow against the walls, feel the familiar heat on his skin, and smell the metallic tinge in the air, a melancholy-touched nostalgia swept over him.

"And I'm me," Valdrin called back. "But still, no. I'm working."

"I know you are, Valdrin, but we had arranged this time already. If you could—"

"No."

Therin drew in a long breath and let it out in an irritated sigh, shaking his head. He closed the door over.

"Come," Aruni said with a laugh. "You know what he's like. I'll make some tea, and you can tell me stories while we wait."

The sun moved from the east to the west as Calen, Haem, Therin, and Aruni sat in the grass-covered clearing between the house and the forge. After a while, Valerys had flown from the Eyrie, eliciting calls and shouts from within the city as his white scales shimmered in the light of the sun. The dragon now sat curled up on the grass, with Calen sitting back against his long tail.

On any other occasion Calen might have been irritated at the idea of being made to sit and wait like a child, but not now, for the hours spent sitting on that grass would forever be a memory Calen would look back on to keep warm. Sitting with Haem, listening to Therin tell stories to Aruni while the sound of crashing water and chirping birds filled the background, the soft glow of erinian stone slowly emerging as more clouds passed overhead. Never in his wildest dreams would he have imagined himself there. In the chaos that consumed his life, these moments of peace were a rare thing. And Calen found himself thinking on the words Falmin had spoken when they were trapped in tunnels below the Lodhar Mountains: *'There is nothing more important in the darkness than a ray of light.'*

The thought brought a smile to Calen's lips. He missed Falmin dearly. The man had a way of seeing through the darkness of the world. Calen's thoughts turned to his memory of Falmin trudging through the snow in Drifaien, using the Spark to funnel more and more snow into Korik and Lopir's paths, and tossing snowballs at the back of Tarmon's head.

Calen pulled his mind back before he got lost in memories, as he had a tendency of doing. He looked over at Aruni, who was listening intently to Therin telling a story of how he found Dann starting his valúr – which she found beyond hilarious. As he looked closer he saw scars rising from the neck of her dress that hadn't been visible while she was standing. He could only see the faint ends of the scars, but the flesh seemed to be almost black in colour, standing in enmity against her pale complexion. The scars were different to the ones on her wrists, of that Calen was sure. And even now as he looked at the elf's wrists, he could see the fresh scabs had cracked, blood trickling.

"Oh, I'm sorry," Aruni said in a fluster, her gaze flashing from Calen to her wrists. She pulled a cloth from a pocket in her dress and dabbed at the blood.

A flood of guilt washed through Calen. "No, I didn't mean to stare."

"It's all right," Therin said calmly. He reached over and gently pulled Aruni's hands together, resting his on top. Calen felt Therin pull from the Spark, threads of each elemental strand weaving about him, pulling together in several separate combinations and funelling into his and Aruni's hands. After a moment, he pulled his hands away. Dried blood still remained, but the scabs had fallen off, new skin now in their place.

"Thank you." Aruni's voice grew even softer than it had been before.

"The night terrors haven't eased then, I take it?"

Aruni shook her head, rubbing the trembling fingers of her right hand against the old scars on her left wrist. "They still scare Valdrin. He's grown so much, but they bring him back to that place…"

Therin rested his hands over Aruni's once more, giving her a soft smile.

"Come," a voice called from within the forge behind them.

As they stood, Calen moved around to Valerys's head. The dragon's left eyelid opened, revealing one pale lavender eye that watched Calen intensely. Valerys lifted his head, pressing the tip of his snout into Calen's chest.

"I'll be back shortly." Calen rested his palms on either side of Valerys's snout, rubbing his fingertips over the smooth scales. "And we can fly back to the Eyrie. I'll stay there with you tonight."

A low rumble emanated from Valerys's throat, and the dragon let out a warm puff of air that caused Calen's shirt to ripple, then lowered his head back onto the grass.

Therin paused with his hand on the door, drew in a short breath, then pushed.

Both Calen and Haem gasped as they entered. The workshop was enormous, easily four times larger than their dad's had been. A forge built from white stone occupied the right-hand wall, two enormous bellows working in tandem to feed the blazing heat. A number of benches, grinding wheels, and anvils were set about the floor while the entire left wall was covered in tools: ball-peen hammers, straight-peen hammers, flatters, lump hammers, sledgehammers, a vast variety of chisels and tongs, punch and drifts, fullers, swages… The list went on and on. Calen's dad would have thought he was dreaming if he'd seen it all.

"Therin." An elf emerged from the back of the workshop, his gaze fixed on Therin. He was tall and lean, his hair short and black. His face was coated in dirt and grime, and he wore a pair of leather trousers and a thick leather apron over a short-sleeved cotton shirt. It was often difficult for Calen to tell the age of an elf, but this particular one appeared even younger than Calen.

"Valdrin, you look even stronger than the last time I saw you."

"I am stronger," the elf said matter-of-factly.

Both Valdrin and Therin leaned forwards, pressing their foreheads together and resting their right thumbs on the other's temple. There was something in the moment that felt warm to Calen, gentle.

Therin gestured to Calen and Haem. "This is—"

"The Draleid," Valdrin said before Therin could finish his sentence. The elf moved towards Calen, a strange intensity in his gaze. He turned his head sideways, and studied Calen. "I've watched you train these past few days. You are shorter up close – shorter than expected."

"I'm taller than you are."

"I'm not sure what my height has to do with your height." Valdrin passed a glance over Haem, a curiosity adorning his face at the green Sentinel armour. "Interesting," he said before turning his focus back to Calen.

The elf circled Calen, whispering to himself. He grabbed Calen's left arm, lifting it and bending over to look up at Calen's armpit and side.

"I…" Calen tried to protest, or at least to speak, but Valdrin just kept circling.

"Impressive," Valdrin said, stepping back and holding his hand to his chin as he looked Calen over.

"Ehm... thank you?"

Valdrin looked up at Calen, confused. "Oh, not you. Me."

"You?"

"Yes, me. Therin, could you take a look at his ears? I don't think they're working."

Calen turned to see a broad smile on Therin's face, and by the time he turned back to Valdrin the elf was already walking away.

"Follow me," the elf called over his shoulder as he walked towards an archway set into a wall that divided the workshop.

Therin's smile spread wider, and he gestured for Calen and the others to follow Valdrin.

"He's a little..." Calen searched for the word.

"He's himself," Therin said. "Unapologetically so. There is no net in his brain that filters the words before they touch his lips, and he sees things as they are. Come."

Calen, Haem, and Aruni followed Therin, stepping through the archway at the end of the room.

Suits and segments of armour stood all about the room, mounted on stands and hooks. They seemed more works of art than armour. Elaborate ornamentation decorated each one, while some helmets were wrought in the depiction of animal heads – stags, hawks, wolves. One suit looked as though the steel had been grown like roots rather than forged and hammered into shape. Swords, axes, spears, and all manner of weapons hung on the walls behind the armour, blades curved and delicate, veins of gold wrought through the handles.

"All the gold in the villages couldn't pay for a fraction of this armour," Haem whispered, just loud enough for Calen to hear.

"No gold could buy it," Valdrin said, turning to look at Haem.

"What do you mean?"

"They're not for sale," the elf responded plainly. Valdrin turned back towards the armour he'd been standing beside. It wasn't a full suit, just chest and back plates suspended on a stand, with pauldrons at the shoulders, but the beauty of it took Calen's breath away.

The breastplate was sleek and smooth, slightly raised at the centre of the chest to turn away stabbing blows, with four articulated panels that guarded the stomach area. The pauldrons were a touch ostentatious for Calen's taste – wrought into the shape of roaring dragon heads – but he couldn't deny the almost otherworldly craftsmanship that had gone into them.

"I've gotten most of your measurements right," Valdrin said as he moved around the armour, turning his head this way and that, glancing back and forth between Calen and the armour without ever meeting Calen's gaze.

"But I think I need to go a bit wider on the shoulders and chest." He looked back at Calen. "Yes."

"What are you talking about?" Calen moved closer to the armour, looking it over.

Valdrin looked at him as though he had three heads. "Your armour. What else would I be talking about? This is just the base, and aesthetically it will be changed, but I believe I have the shape right. I've been watching you practice, seeing how you move, how you fight. It should suit you."

"Wait… no. You couldn't have crafted this from seeing me practice. I've only been here a matter of days – something like this would take months. Even with all the tools you have here." Calen ran his hand across the tiny scales that had been etched into the pauldrons. "Even the detailing alone."

"Valdrin is one of few elven smiths who forges and shapes with the Spark as an aid," Therin said, moving beside Calen, examining the breastplate. "And of them all, I dare say he is the most gifted still drawing breath. He is also the only practitioner of rune-smithing – courtesy of Thacia's teaching."

An uncomfortable look flashed across Aruni's face at the mention of rune-smithing, but it was gone as quickly as it had appeared.

"It's incredible," Haem said from behind Calen.

"It's a template." Valdrin knocked three times on the back plate, as though checking it were indeed made of steel.

"A template?"

Once more, Valdrin looked at Calen with a curious gaze. "Yes, a template." He walked over to Haem, touching the breastplate of Haem's Sentinel armour.

Haem looked to Therin, then back at Valdrin, his eyes asking what he should do. Therin simply smiled and shrugged.

"This is Sentinel armour, isn't it? You're a Knight of Achyron."

"It is, and I am." Haem raised his eyebrows as he looked down at the elf, who continued to touch different segments of Haem's armour.

"In one of Scholar Harthyr's books, it said the armour can move like a liquid and that you can control it with your own will. Is that true, or is it another one of those half-truths historians are so fond of?"

"I'm not entirely sure how it functions, but yes, it can—"

"Show me." The elf stood back, looking at Haem expectantly.

Haem looked back at the elf, more than a touch of hesitation in his expression. But he held out his hand, and Calen watched as the green gauntlet turned to liquid metal and receded, pulling back over Haem's fingers and rolling over his knuckles until his entire hand was free.

"Fascinating." Valdrin snatched Haem's hand, pursing his lips appraisingly. The elf let go of Haem's hand, then moved back to the armour. "I will make you a full suit," he said, looking at Calen but never meeting his gaze. "It will take about two months, I think. Maybe three." He looked towards the roof, as though counting something on the ceiling. "I would like to observe you more. Not just while sparring, but while you are flying too." Valdrin's eyebrows shot up. "May I meet the dragon?"

CHAPTER SIXTY-FIVE

WEBS UPON WEBS

Aeson stood with his arms folded at the edge of the cliff. The wind slapped his face with rain that felt like sheets of ice, his cloak billowing out to the right. Overhead dark clouds dispersed the sun's light, painting the world in a grey hue. Before him lay a system of tight valleys coated in dark forest. He had only visited Aravell a few times across the centuries, but each time the scope of what the elves had created, along with the power of the glamour that concealed it, left him awestruck.

Líra, the elf who had led the entire endeavour, had always been exceptional, but Aravell was without a doubt her masterpiece.

"Here he comes." Chora sat in her chair to Aeson's left, her face and hair dripping, the hood of her cloak blown back onto her shoulders. Her eyes were keener than his.

The young elf, Valdrin, who Therin had rescued all those years ago from the empire, stood beside Chora. He had insisted on coming to watch Calen fly and now stood in nothing more than a soaked linen tunic and trousers with his hands clasped behind his back. He was a peculiar one, but he had been through a lot.

A few moments passed, and then Aeson saw a white flash in the distance. Valerys tore through the valleys, moving at speeds Lyara had only achieved after she'd seen her tenth summer. The dragon rose and fell, catching wind currents as he wove in between the jutting cliff faces, disappearing then reappearing from Aeson's vision.

Beside Aeson, Chora weaved threads of Fire and Water through the air. Sections of rain coalesced, forming spheres of ice as threads of Fire pulled the heat from them. And then the spheres were careening through the air towards Valerys and Calen as they rounded a cliff face.

The dragon spun, dropping low, spheres of ice crashing against the rock behind him. Valerys rose above the next wave of projectiles, rolling in the air as he did, holding himself in an upside down position. Aeson couldn't help but be impressed, not just by Valerys's agility and reactions, but by how Calen managed to hold his position. Even with the intrinsic magic that moulded a dragon's scales to their Draleid and held them in place, holding on during manoeuvres like that at those kinds of speeds was no easy feat.

Chora launched more spheres of ice, each of which Valerys avoided. Threads of Fire and Water swirled in the air, forming the rain into a thick sheet of ice before Valerys. The dragon unleashed a pillar of fire, wrapping his wings around himself, making himself as small as possible as he flew through the melted hole at the centre of the sheet. Valerys dropped for a moment, then unfurled his wings, catching the air currents and sweeping upwards.

Chora formed the rain into another sheet, to which Valerys reacted by performing the same manoeuvre, but this time Chora formed a second sheet of ice as soon as the dragon's fire ceased. Valerys flew through the gap in the first sheet only to crash through the second, unleashing a roar that echoed through the valley. As the dragon hurtled forwards, attempting to regain control of his flight, Chora launched another wave of ice spheres.

Aeson felt Calen pull from the Spark as a streams of fire poured from the young man's hand. Then, the fire cut off sharply.

"Two in the chest." Chora folded her arms and sat back in her chair as Valerys swept past them, wings spread wide, a gust of air following in his wake. "Still, impressive. Their bond is unlike anything I've seen in ones so young," Chora remarked without turning her gaze from the valleys ahead. "Perhaps the Valacian dragons truly do have a deeper connection to the Spark. Or perhaps there is something more. I've heard the Lorians who travelled with Calen across the Burnt Lands refer to him as the Warden of Varyn. They say he swept through the battle of Kingspass, his eyes misting with a purple light. Now, that is something I'd like to see."

"Purple light," Valdrin whispered to himself.

"You know how stories spread." Aeson ran his tongue across his teeth, looking out into the distance as Valerys soared back through the valleys.

"It is not true? His eyes do not glow?"

Aeson grunted. He had seen the purple light in Calen's eyes when they had argued outside the Burnt Lands. "All I'm saying is tales grow with the telling."

"If I didn't know you better, young Virandr, I'd think you were jealous."

Aeson laughed, turning to see Chora staring back at him, her smile stretching from ear to ear. She was the only one who still referred to him as 'young Virandr' – it was nice. "Jealous?"

Chora smiled again, raising a knowing eyebrow, then her expression grew more sombre. "What do you think of him, Aeson? Do you truly think he can do what needs to be done?"

Aeson let out a heavy sigh. "Not on his own."

A gust of wind swept across the cliff as Valerys soared past, banking left and right before dropping and disappearing around a cliff edge.

"He is gifted. That much is clear. But even if he had decades, which he does not, seven of the nine living Dragonguard remain in Epheria. Even Eltoar and Helios would not be able to fight those odds alone."

"True enough." Chora sat in silence for a moment. "But he is not alone."

"No." After Calen had sworn the oath with Gaeleron, Vaeril, Alea, Lyrei, Erik, Tarmon, and Dann, Gaeleron had made his way to the courtyard each day to observe Calen's forms and sparring. Vaeril, Alea, and Lyrei had remained tight to the young man's side. Vaeril in particular seemed to have a close bond with Calen. Erik and Tarmon Hoard – a man Aeson knew as an impeccable judge of character – were as close to Calen as brothers now, though with what they'd been through that didn't surprise Aeson. What was unexpected though, was how Sulin, Ingvat and the others from Berona looked to Calen. For all the arguments between them, Aeson had to admit the young man had a heart that people gravitated towards.

In Aeson's experience, there were two things that caused people to follow: fear or devotion. Fealty could be won through fear in a heartbeat. Fear was powerful, and it led people towards truly atrocious acts in the name of self-preservation. But it was fleeting – as soon as something came along that inspired greater fear, everything changed. Devotion, on the other hand, was hard earned, through actions and deeds. Whereas adversity often eroded fear, it only strengthened devotion. Fear could win battles and wars, it could sweep armies aside. But devotion was what held nations together. The empire built everything on fear and anger. As far as Aeson was concerned, a little bit of both was needed.

"Aeson?" The call was broken by the wind and the rain. He turned to find Ingvat standing at the top of the downward path, her long cloak flapping in the gale that swept over the cliff, her hair and skin saturated. The woman approached as he turned. "Therin sent me to call on you. Some of the Angan have returned, and letters have arrived from Argona."

THE WIND BLEW SO fiercely Aeson stumbled sideways as he stopped before one of the myriad of bridges that swept across the city of Aravell. And while the wind howled, the rain beat down like hammer strikes against his hair and face.

"Just over there!" Ingvat called, pointing towards a plateau set into the rock about fifty feet up on the other side of the bridge. She was close to him, but she had to shout to raise her voice above the roaring wind.

Aeson nodded his acknowledgement. "Ingvat," he called as she turned to make her leave. "Thank you for keeping him safe."

Ingvat shook her head, shaking droplets of rain free. "Your son is just as you are. He can handle himself."

"That he can." Aeson moved closer to Ingvat, resting his hand on her shoulder and leaning in closer so they wouldn't have to shout. "How many came with you from Berona? I should have come to you sooner, but there's just not been a spare moment."

"Forty-two survived the journey." Ingvat pulled at her hood, using it to shelter her voice from the wind.

"How many can fight? Mages?"

"All can hold themselves well. A Battlemage, a Healer, a Consul, and two Craftsmages – Sulin included. We lost two Scholars in the wasteland."

Aeson nodded again. "It's time we start making something of them. I'll need a breakdown of each and every one of them. What do you think of him?"

"Calen?" Ingvat asked, raising a saturated eyebrow. "I followed him across the Burnt Lands, Aeson. You know the answer to that question."

"True enough." Aeson patted Ingvat's shoulder and watched as she walked down a winding path of smooth white stone before he set off across the bridge. He made his way across, then up towards the plateau. A white pergola covered the plateau, the wind *whooshing* as it hammered rain against the structure's roof in sweeping sheets. Beneath the shelter of the pergola, Therin stood by a large stone table, Baldon, Aneera, and two more Fenryr Angan at his side. Even before Aeson drew close, he could feel the ward of silence that shrouded the plateau.

As Aeson stepped through that boundary of the ward, the pounding of the rain and howling of the wind vanished in an instant, giving way to silence. "You know we could have just done this somewhere indoors?"

Therin looked up from the other side of the table, his silvery hair dripping as it hung around his shoulders. "I don't visit Aravell often. I do not like to waste my time hemmed within the confines of four walls. It gives me warmth to look upon the things she created."

Aeson gave his old friend a nod of acknowledgment, allowing a smile to touch his lips. He understood. There were few things in this world that reminded Aeson of Naia – Erik, Dahlen, and the swords she had forged for all three of them. For Therin, there was only Faelen and the city of Aravell to remind him of Líra, which seemed bittersweet considering he so rarely got to look upon either of them, and Faelen refused to speak to him.

A map of Epheria was splayed out across the table, held down by four smooth stones. Beside the map was a leather sack, a small leatherbound notebook, a pen, and inkwell.

"What news?" Aeson looked to Baldon and Aneera.

Baldon stared back with those golden eyes, then looked to Therin.

"We have word from Baird in Drifaien," Therin said, tapping Drifaien on the map. "Those loyal to Alleron have taken Longforge, Helmund's Basin, and Whiterun. He's confident if they can take Arisfall, the rest of the region will swear fealty. Alleron needs no meeting – he swears his loyalty to Calen."

"Calen makes quite the impression."

"Indeed," Therin looked up from the map, smiling.

"Others?"

"Aryana Torval in Illyanara, who flies the white gryphon banner, has agreed to meet. She would be a strong alternative to Castor Kai – who has also agreed to meet Calen, though as we've discussed, that should wait. We've also received word from many other factions across Illyanara, Arkalen, and Drifaien. The larger factions are waiting for an audience, but those with smaller numbers are moving this way. There are rumblings of a great battle near Steeple, but the details are not yet known. It's all hearsay at the moment. Though there's talk of elves – and dragons."

"Dragons?"

"Like I said, hearsay. The Dragonguard were there, so it's more probable that stories have gotten muddled. But if the elves of Lynalion have left the woodland, the landscape is about to change. And if they were ever to do it, now would be the time. The empire is weak, only seven of the Dragonguard remain, and the South is in chaos."

"Indeed," Aeson scratched at his beard. He hoped the rumours were not true. Another player in the game would only complicate matters. But they would cross that bridge if they came to it. "What of Valtara, Varsund, and Carvahon?"

"Even with our connections, it takes time," Baldon said, leaning forwards, his words slow and thoughtful as though he was remembering how his tongue should form the sounds. "None of our kind are yet near the lands you call Valtara or Varsund."

"There has been word from our people in the north of Carvahon. Gandry reports he's gathered some two thousand in the mountains near Dalery and marches them towards Aravell in groups of one hundred as we speak. And Hodin says that if Calen so much as flies over Ballmar, the city will open its gates."

"What was the last we heard about High Lord Kalas?"

"As always, he's refusing to take a side. He allowed imperial fleets to be torched in the bay, but I don't believe he'll openly declare for us unless he believes he has no choice."

Aeson nodded, folding his arms and stroking the side of his cheek with his index finger as he looked over the map. "Ingvat said letters arrived from Arem in Argona?"

"Yes." Therin reached into the leather sack and produced a thick stack of envelopes, placing them on the table before Aeson. The first stack was followed by a second, then a third.

Aeson let out a sigh, sifting through the letters, pushing aside those he believed could wait while opening those that looked urgent. One was from a contact who kept watch over the gold mines in Aonar, another from a smuggler in Antiquar, another from the captain of the city guard in Catagan. His heart thumped as he eyes fell on two envelopes strung together, the top sealed in crimson wax and the hammer sigil of Durakdur.

"Everything all right?" Therin asked, looking up from the map.

"It's from Durakdur." The last letter he had received from Durakdur had been from Dahlen, telling him of what had happened between Belduar and the Dwarven Freehold. But that had not been pressed with any particular Sigil. Realising he'd grown silent, Aeson lifted his head and gestured towards the other letters. "Could you help me with those?"

Therin held Aeson's gaze for a moment, then nodded and proceeded to pull a stack of letters towards him.

Aeson cracked the wax seal on the top envelope, then pulled out the letter, unfolding it.

Father,

That first word breathed life back into Aeson's veins.

I'm not sure how to say this – Daymon Bryne and Ihvon Arnell are dead. Tensions rose to a head within the Freehold, and the Azmaran forces attacked the Belduarans – Daymon and Ihvon died in the fighting. Queen Kira and Queen Elenya came to our aid, and the Azmarans were put to the question. There is still more afoot within the Freehold, webs within webs, I'm sure of it.

After the fighting, Kira and Elenya forced Belduar into a vassalship in exchange for food, water, safety, and aid in retaking the city itself. Oleg Marylin was selected as 'Keeper of the Mountain' – a new title devised by the dwarves. As it stands, Pulroan is dead, Hoffnar is dead, and Kira and Elenya hold power over the Freehold. There is a moot currently being held in Volkur, and one soon to follow in Azmar. Though, from the whispers I'm hearing, it is likely that Kira and Elenya may consolidate power. They have both reiterated their support for our cause, as has Oleg.

Oleg has asked me, along with Belina, to aid in the escort of some two hundred Belduarans to safety in the western villages. I have accepted – our destination is Salme. Forward any reply there. Once the Belduarans are settled and I have received your location, I will come.

D

Aeson read the letter over twice. A lot had changed beneath the mountains of Lodhar. One of the Fenryr Angan was already on their way to the Freehold. Once there, communication with Kira and Elenya would be easier. Whether the Freehold had two rulers or four did not matter, so long as they were aligned to the cause. Both Kira and Elenya were brash and quick to anger, but it was Kira who came to Belduar's aid the night of the Fade's attack.

Aeson let out a sigh as his eyes settled back on the start of the letter – *Daymon Bryne and Ihvon Arnell are dead.* Ihvon and Aeson had butted heads on many occasions, but Ihvon had been one of the few people in the world who Aeson had truly called friend. That list was growing ever shorter with the passing years. To read of his death felt like nothing more than a dream. The man was carved from stone, and his blood was made from fire – there was a time Aeson believed that nothing on the mortal plane could kill Ihvon Arnell. That time, he supposed, was gone. *I'll drink for you, old friend. At least you're finally with Alyana and Khris again. Enjoy Achyron's halls. I will see you there when he calls me.*

Aeson's gaze settled on the name of young Daymon Bryne. The boy had not been ready. The only solace in his death was that Arthur had not had to be the one to light the pyre. Arthur – another friend no longer walking the mortal plane. Aeson whispered, "Living has its price."

Aeson folded the letter and slipped it back in its envelope. He cracked the seal on the second envelope.

Old Man Virandr,

I've tried to kill you seven times, but you're a stubborn bastard. I bet you still haven't forgiven me despite everything I've done since then – you do love a grudge. Well, when Dahlen said he was sending you a letter, I asked Oleg to tag this one along as well because, by my reckoning, I've stopped your son from dying three times now. What does that mean? That means four more times and we're even. And at the rate everyone with your last name finds trouble, you'll be owing me pretty soon.

I'll be travelling with him on my way to Dayne. Who knows, maybe he'll do something stupid again.

Your favourite,

Belina

p.s. Ihvon died the way he would have wanted – with sharp steel in his hand. I took some ashes from the pyre. I'll spread them over the ocean. He always liked to watch the sun rise over the water.

Aeson couldn't help but allow himself a smile as he folded the letter. Belina had a way about her. There were few people on the continent more dangerous and even fewer with larger hearts. He looked up to see Therin had walked towards the edge of the pergola, rain splattering against his back as he read a letter. "What's that?" he asked, slipping Belina's letter back into its envelope. "Dahlen's all right, but... Therin?"

The elf continued to read, ignoring Aeson.

"Therin? What is it?"

Therin lifted his head, looking back at the letter, then back to Aeson. "It's from Coren."

"And?" Aeson did nothing to temper the impatience in his voice.

Therin drew in another long breath, reading over the words again. "It's Calen's sister, Ella. She's alive."

"Alive? Where is she?"

"I'm not sure how long ago this letter was sent, but she was in Tarhelm with Coren. Tanner brought her in. He can't go back to Berona." The shock on Therin's face slowly spread to a smile. "We need to tell Calen."

Aeson reached out and grasped Therin's shoulder. His mind was racing, and his heart sank at the word that was about to leave his lips. "No."

Therin shrugged off Aeson's grasp, stepping backwards. The look on the elf's face was as though Aeson had just suggested killing a child. "What do you mean no, Aeson? We *need* to tell him. His sister is alive. Ella is alive. He needs this."

"And what will he do when you tell him?" Aeson held Therin's gaze, eyes wide. "What will he do, Therin? He'll mount Valerys and set off across the Burnt Lands, straight back into Fane's grasp. You know he will. He won't stop for a second's thought. He's done it before, but now Valerys is large and healthy enough to carry him. He'll be like a beacon to the Dragonguard."

"Then we tell him he can't go." Therin shook his head, incredulous.

"Listen to yourself." Aeson swallowed hard, adding moisture to his dry throat. He stepped back and drew in a long breath. "You're being naïve if you believe you can tell Calen his sister is alive and alone in the mountains in Loria, and you think he won't ignore every word that leaves our lips afterwards. Ella is safe. She is with Coren, and Farwen, and Tanner. They will look after her and when the time is right, we will send for her. It's better to bring her here than let him go there. This is about more than just his pain, Therin. It's about more than yours and more than mine – more than any one of ours." Aeson grasped both of Therin's shoulder, looking into the elf's eyes. "Do you think I want to be saying this? Do you think I don't know how monstrous I sound? Of course I don't want to keep this from Calen, but what choice do we have? If we tell him, he will go. He proved that with Rist. That is who he is, and that's something I would never change about him. But if he takes that dragon and flies to Tarhelm, he *will* be ripped from the sky, and all of this will have been for nothing. I've sacrificed more for this cause than most people could even begin to comprehend, and if this is the choice I need to make, then I will make it. If he hates me, he hates me. It doesn't matter. Sometimes we have to make the hard decisions, whether we like them or not. We can't just make the ones that let us feel good about ourselves."

Therin stared at the letter.

"I need you to promise me you won't tell him, Therin."

The elf looked up; Aeson could see the struggle in his eyes.

"I need you to promise me. We tell him, and one or more of them *will* die. We don't, and they may live. Your conscience or their lives. On your honour, Therin."

Therin shoved Aeson away with anger that Aeson had rarely seen from the elf. His jaw was clenched, his brow furrowed. Therin out a roar. "Gods damn you!"

Baldon, Aneera, and the other Angan looked over.

Therin shoved the letter against Aeson's chest. "He deserves to know, Aeson!"

Aeson held his ground. "You can be the one to light the pyre then, Therin."

"I hate these games, Aeson. I hate them."

"I know." Aeson moved closer to his old friend and rested his hand on Therin's shoulder.

Therin shook his head, the muscles in his jaw clenched. The elf let out a long sigh, his shoulders drooping. "On my honour."

CHAPTER SIXTY-SIX

BY BLADE AND BY BLOOD

No."

Alina shook her head, fists curled against the table, sweat slicking her brow from the humid heat trapped within the tent. All her commanders, generals, and allies were piled in, crammed like fish in a net, inuding Aldon Thebal – who had taken over as Head of House Thebal after Dayne had slain Miron at the battle for Myrefall – and Rinek Larka, who acted as the voice for all those who had been banners for House Koraklon but had answered Alina's call.

They were preparing for their assault on Achyron's Keep. The keep was four days march, and Loren Koraklon held a force of over forty thousand strong along with another fifteen thousand Lorians and a contingent of Battlemages, so said the scouts. They'd been debating for hours

But all of that had been put on hold when the creature, who now stood at the other end of the table, had announced himself at the camp's edge. It looked as though it were part human, part wolf. Its body was coated in thick white fur, covered by loose strips and patches of fabric. Its limbs were long and muscular, dark claws protruding from its feet and hands, while its face seemed almost human, barring its flat wolf-like nose, long ears, and golden eyes. It had called itself an Angan.

Silence filled the tent, all eyes on Alina.

"Tell Aeson and this 'son of the Chainbreaker' that Valtara is busy dealing with Valtara. We will not stand against them, but we do not have the time to aid them in their war, nor we do we need their aid here."

The Angan stared back, its golden eyes gleaming in the light that drifted through the tent's thin canopy. "Very well, Alina of House Ateres. I will send the message, though I will remain here, as instructed, should you change your mind."

"We will not change our minds."

The creature inclined its head, a flicker of its lip showing sharp teeth, then turned and strode from the tent.

The ensuing silence was then broken by Turik Baleer. "Alina, surely we should talk about this."

"About what, Lord Baleer?"

"There's over fifty thousand warriors defending Achyron's Keep and likely more prowling the lands around, waiting to flank us. We lost thousands taking Myrefall, and Lorian loyalists are raiding our supply lines daily. Not to mention a contingent of Lorian Battlemages now resides within the walls of Achyron's Keep. Now is not the time for pride. We should agree to meet. Even in the time it takes to arrange the meeting, more of our forces will arrive."

"Turik speaks sense." Rinek Larka met Alina's gaze and didn't shy away. She liked him, he spoke his mind, and he was Valtaran through and through. But in that moment, she wanted to slit his throat.

"Were you in Skyfell, Rinek, the last time we relied on Aeson Virandr? The last time dragons flew over Valtara?"

"No." He shook his head, knowing full well that Alina already knew the answer. "I was on the farm near the Hot Gates."

Alina gave a half smile. "Good. Then you weren't there when Aeson left us to die. You weren't there when the dragons ripped our wyverns from the sky, or when they turned Stormwatch into a furnace and burned everyone alive."

"We cannot let the past cloud our judgement," Ola Yarek, a Wyndarii commander, said. She was older than Alina by the light of at least ten summers, hair dark as coal.

"No," Alina said, pouting and shaking her head. "You're right, we can't. But neither can we fail to learn from it. Failure to learn and adapt means death." Alina looked down at the table, pressing her fists against the wood. "We have come so far... How many years have we been preparing for this, Senya?"

Alina lifted her head, looking to Senya Deringal who stood at the right side of the table.

"Seven at least."

"And what have we sacrificed to get here?"

"Everything."

"Everything," Alina repeated, nodding. "And we are finally here." She stood at full height, looking about the room. "We stand on the edge of a precipice. A free Valtara is before us and all we need do is grasp it. But if we take one wrong step, if we hesitate, if we doubt, we will fall, and this will not be a fall we will stand back up from. Would you put that in the hands of Aeson Virandr? Would you really claw and drag your way here, through blood and dirt, through death and despair, only to hand your fate to another?"

"No." Mera stepped beside Alina, chin raised. "I am a Wyndarii of Valtara. I will bleed for my people, and I will die for them. Our fate is our own."

"Our fate is our own," Alina heard someone repeat from the left side of the table.

"Our fate is our own," Vhin Herak said, nodding.

Tula Vakira, Tyr Arnen, and Sara Herak mirrored the words, as did many others at the table. Alina noted the faces and names of those who remained silent. As long as they remained so, she was happy, but things were rarely that simple.

Among the silent was Dayne. Though, that didn't surprise her. She was actually happy he remained silent this time. All they had done was argue on this topic since the farm. His voice would only have added weight to Turik Baleer's.

Knocking silenced the chatter as Senya Deringal tapped the pommel of a knife against the table. "If I may?"

Alina inclined her head. Senya had always spoken in her favour.

"Before this campaign began, I told you that I wouldn't stop until I had freedom or a funeral pyre. Nothing has changed. I pledged that House Deringal would follow you. Nothing has changed. Now I stand here with my fellow free Valtarans, steel at our hips, Lorian blood at our backs, and Loren Koraklon cowering behind the walls of Achyron's Keep. Once we crush him and take hold of the Hot Gates, no army will enter Valtara by land. And I, for one, wish to take that step as a unified nation, not a rabble of arguing Houses." Senya paused. "One Valtara under one Queen."

Alina's heart stopped, and her breath caught in her chest.

"A queen who bleeds for Valtara, a queen who would sacrifice everything so her people could know the taste of freedom, a queen who knows the cost of living. One queen, whose name is Alina Ateres."

Murmurs spread across those gathered.

"I propose that before we march on Achyron's Keep, we crown Alina Ateres as Queen of a free Valtara, so that we fight this last battle as one. One army, one nation, under one queen. There are none here who have given more, none who would *continue* to give more. Alina Ateres, Queen of Valtara. All in favour, say 'Aye'."

Senya looked to Alina, inclining her head, then spun the knife in her hand and drove the blade into the hard wood of the table. "Aye."

"Aye," Vhin Herak called out.

"I've been waiting a long time for this." Marlin Arkon stepped forwards, the white crested helmet of the Andurii in the crook of his arm. "By blade and by blood, my Queen. Aye."

More followed, slamming their hands on the table or driving their blades into the wood, each calling out 'Aye', until their voices filled the tent.

"It is settled." Senya Deringal stepped forwards. "Before the sun sets, Alina Ateres will be crowned Queen of Valtara."

A FEW HOURS LATER, WITH the warm light of the evening sun tinting the sky orange, Alina stood at the top of a small hill, trembling.

Ahead of her, tens of thousands of Valtarans spread from the foot of the hill back to the first line of tents that made up the camp, the bronzed steel of their cuirasses glinting in the sunlight. A singular empty strip stretched through the centre of those gathered, from the hill back to the camp – a path for the procession.

The heads of all the Major Houses and their families stood to her right, Dayne included – they hadn't spoken since the tent. Part of her wished they had, part of her was happy they hadn't. They'd been arguing a lot since the farm at Myrefall. To the left, the heads of many of the Minor Houses loyal to House Ateres stood facing those of the Major Houses. Past them, Mera, Amari, Lukira, and fifteen of the other Wyndarii closest to Alina formed an honorguard towards the gathered crowd, their wyverns standing behind them, scales glistening. Above, wyverns filled the sky, roars and screeches echoing; the sight of it took her breath away.

"How do you feel?" Marlin Arkon stood behind Alina, garbed in white and burnt orange robes – the colours of House Ateres. The steward of House Ateres, soon to be the Queen's Archilius – the title historically given to the chief advisor of Valtaran rulers. There was no man more deserving.

"Like I'm going to die if my heart doesn't stop racing," Alina whispered. *Is this actually happening?*

"I remember the day you were born," Marlin whispered, leaning closer. "You were a fighter even then, almost took Senya's eye out as she delivered you. You know how I always tell you I got the scar beneath my chin from falling off a horse in battle with House Vakira? Well, now that you're going to be queen, I may as well tell you I got it when you were three and you hit me with a stick."

Despite herself, Alina laughed, keeping her head facing forwards. Marlin had been a father to her when her own was taken from the world. Through everything. Through the darkest of days and the stormiest of nights, he had been her constant, her anchor, and, at times, her compass. She hadn't told him that enough.

"When I eventually share a toast with your father and mother in Achyron's halls, I'll tell them of this day. The day their daughter became queen of a free Valtara. Your father will cry. He was always the crier."

Etiquette be damned. Alina turned to see tears streaming down Marlin's face, his eyes red.

"Turn back around you fool," he said, letting a laugh slip through as Alina turned back to face the crowd. "They're happy tears. This was everything they fought for, everything they died for. They would be so proud of you they wouldn't know what to do with themselves... I'm so proud of you."

Alina reached back and grasped Marlin's hand. She could feel a tear rolling down her cheek but rubbed it away with her shoulder.

A roar erupted from the camp, forcing all other sounds to capitulate. Then Alina watched as Rynvar rose from the tents, lifting into the air, wings spreading wide, orange scales scintillating in the sun. The wyvern swept across the gathered crowd, who had fallen into silence. Drums filled the air, rhythmic and deep, followed by horns. Marlin squeezed Alina's hand, then let go.

Alina settled herself, slowing her breathing as Senya Deringal walked from the camp, through the centreline that divided the gathered crowd, banners of each of the Major Houses billowing in the wind behind her and banners of the Minor Houses behind them. Of all the banners, however, it was the two at the front, behind Senya as she walked, that truly swelled the pride in Alina's chest. One was white as snow, the wyvern of House Ateres at its centre in a vivid orange. The other was orange, two black wyverns coiled around each other, a white spear between them: the banner of a unified Valtara.

Alina stood straighter, lifting her chin.

As Senya drew closer, a procession of attendants and bannermen following in her wake, Rynvar curled his wings and dropped from the sky, alighting on the top of the hill behind Alina, a gust of wind blowing her long robes forwards. She was not dressed like a queen, of that she was sure. She wore no silk or jewels, no gold. A strand of white ribbon tied up her hair, and linen robes of burnt orange adorned her shoulders. Alina Ateres had not marched to a coronation, she had marched to war, and war was no place for silks or jewels.

The drums and horns slowed, giving one final burst before stopping as Senya Deringal reached Alina. The woman took a few steps forward, four attendants moving with her. She looked to Alina, inclining her head and smiling. Senya turned back towards the crowd, nodding to Dayne, and then as she spoke, her words resounded across the open fields as though they had been shouted within the walls of a stone temple. "Warriors of Valtara," Senya called out, "we are four days march from Achyron's Keep. Four days' march from destiny."

Cheers rang out, feet stamping. Senya raised a hand, and the silence returned.

"A free Valtara," she continued, her voice booming like claps of thunder. "Stripped of chains and bonds. We will take it by blade and by blood. We will carve it in the annals of time. And there is one who has dragged us here, one who has manifested our destiny by sheer force of will. She pulled the wyverns back from the brink of extinction. She took a rabble and forged it into a rebellion. She showed the Lorian Empire why it should once again fear Valtaran steel. Alina of House Ateres, First of the Wyndarii, Rider of Rynvar."

As though responding to Senya's words, Rynvar unleashed a monstrous roar, his wings spreading out behind Alina. The gathered crowd of warriors cheered and chanted, feet stamping.

Senya looked to one of the attendants who Alina now noticed held what looked to be a small pillow draped in blue fabric. Atop the fabric sat a gold circlet woven with twists and spirals, a shimmering orange sunstone set at the front. A crown. Senya must have had the thing made before they'd even marched.

The sight of the crown only served to set Alina's pulse racing even quicker. All of a sudden she found herself wondering what to do with her hands. Where did she put her hands? It seemed a simple question to answer, and yet no answer came to her, so she settled on clasping them together across her stomach, squeezing tight to stop the trembling.

Senya took another step closer, the attendant following after her. "Alina Ateres," her voice boomed, amplified by Dayne's magic. "I ask you not to kneel like those who came before you. Our people have knelt for too long." Senya lifted the crown from the fabric, fingers gently clasping it on either side. "I ask you to stand tall and proud."

Alina's heartbeat grew so loud it sounded like a war drum in her head, pounding. For a brief moment she looked out over the crowd, bronzed armour glinting in the warm light of the sun, the skies tinted orange, filled with wyverns. Then she looked back to Senya and saw a soft smile on the older woman's face.

"Do you swear, Alina Ateres, to defend Valtara above all else."

"I do, with all my heart."

"Do you swear to charge into the fires that may come, to fight when the world tells you to flee?"

"By blade and by blood."

"Do you swear to give your heart and your soul?"

"I swear."

Senya drew in a deep breath, then lifted the crown.

"Dayne Ateres is the true heir!" The voice wasn't augmented by magic, but it echoed, sounding like thunder in Alina's ears.

Senya stopped, as did Alina's heart. Alina's gut twisted, her muscles tightening. Senya lowered her arms and turned, revealing that Turik Baleer had stepped from where he had stood with the heads of the other Minor Houses.

Alina saw Senya begin to speak, but she grabbed the elder woman's arm, squeezing. Senya looked back. Alina shook her head, jaw clenched. She saw the rage in Senya's eyes as plainly as she felt it in herself, but she held back, turning her gaze to Turik. The man had always been a snake, but now he was out in the open for all to see, and with any luck, he would draw the other snakes out too. *Opportunity is always there, you just have to see it.*

"I'll take his head from his shoulders," Marlin growled, moving to step past Alina.

Alina held her hand back, stopping Marlin. She nodded towards some of the others who stood amongst the Major and Minor Houses. It was clear to see who was truly shocked and who was not. "Moths to a flame, Marlin."

Mera, Amari, and Lukira looked to Alina from where they stood, just past Turik. She gave them a sharp shake of her head. Behind her, Rynvar's growl rumbled in his throat.

Turik looked at Alina, a flicker of a smile touching his face.

You crusty bastard of a man.

"Dayne Ateres is the eldest child of Arkin and Ilya Iteres," Turik bellowed, the veins in his neck bulging as he roared. His voice didn't carry far enough for the soldiers in the fields to hear – except for those near the front – but they knew something was happening. Alina could see the shifting glint of sunlight off armour, hear the rising murmur. "The head of House Ateres is his by birthright if nothing else!"

Alina looked at those to her left and right, searching for signs, scanning faces.

"But more than birthright, upon return from his exile, Dayne Ateres has led us from victory to victory while Alina claimed the spoils. The Andurii stood at the front of every battle line. They swung their blades wherever the fighting was thickest. When Alina's wyverns started the battle at Lostwren, Dayne charged the walls with nothing but a spear and a shield. When Alina ordered us to cross the river Artis, it was Dayne Ateres and his Andurii who held back the Lorians and saved both my and Senya Deringal's lives." Turik stared at Senya, shaking his head. "And again, it was Dayne who charged the keep at Myrefall, Dayne who took the head of Miron Thebal. If I laid his claim at your feet, by birthright alone it should be enough. But he has earned your loyalty, earned your fealty!"

A few cheers rang out from the ranks of the soldiers who gathered in the open field, the sound of steel clanging off steel. A number of the nobles shifted.

"King Dayne of House Ateres, Andurios, Champion of Valtara! King Dayne!"

The anger and wrath that had coursed through Alina's veins turned to ice when more voices began to chant back to Turik's call. "King Dayne!"

Rynvar shifted behind Alina, dropping lower to the ground, his head hovering over hers. More and more voices rang out. Some of those who represented the Minor Houses joined the chorus, as did some of the military captains. But none who belonged to the Major Houses chanted, though that meant nothing – they were likely keeping their loyalties close.

The chanting came to an abrupt stop, a few gasps rising in those gathered near the top of the hill as Dayne stepped from his position.

DAYNE'S HEART POUNDED AS HE walked towards Turik. He could feel his throat tightening. He glanced at Alina, seeing the shock on her face. To his left and right the nobles of the Minor and Major Houses stared at him, mouths agape. Dayne studied them, taking notes in his head of their expressions. He drew in a breath and focused on Turik.

"You are the rightful king," Turik called out as Dayne approached. "Alina is the leader of the Wyndarii, but she is no queen. That crown belongs on your head. It is your birthright."

Turik's words rang out, echoing. The man gave him a nod, a knowing smile touching his lips.

Dayne rested his palm on the pommel of his sword as he walked past Turik, stopping about fifteen feet short of Alina.

Wings beat in the sky above, the shrieks and roars of wyverns echoing as not a word passed between the thousands of souls who stood watching, waiting. Dayne glanced over his shoulder towards Alina's Wyndarii. The tension in them was clear as day, their gazes fixed on Dayne. Amari and Lukira in particular looked as though they were ready to cut him down where he stood. Of them all, only Mera stood calm and stoic, Audin looming over her. Mera was the only one who knew what was about to happen, the only one he'd told. She nodded.

Dayne nodded back, then took another step closer to Alina. He pulled his sword from his scabbard, the rasp cutting through the tension-thick air.

As soon as he did, the atmosphere shifted to panic. Senya Deringal stepped between him and Alina. Marlin pushed past Dayne's sister, fire in his eyes as he glared at Dayne. Part of Dayne thought maybe he should have told Marlin, but he couldn't have risked it.

Dayne drew in a breath, then exhaled slowly as he turned away from Alina to face Turik. The longer Dayne held the older man's gaze, the more Turik's expression changed, and confusion filled his eyes. Dayne pointed the tip of his blade at Turik. "Find a sword, Turik."

Turik's face contorted. "What? My King, we have talked about this. What are you doing? I—"

"I am not your king," Dayne snapped, his calm broken. For months, ever since that night Turik had arranged the celebration without telling Alina, Dayne had allowed the man to whisper in his ear. For months he had watched as Turik manoeuvred his way through the political land-scape, making subtle suggestions, vague promises, and planting seeds of uncertainty about Alina's ability to lead. Dayne had wanted to cut him down each and every day, but if his years with Belina had taught him anything, it had been patience. He could hear her even then. *'Why kill one when you can use them as bait to kill many. Not two birds with one stone, Dayne. Fifteen birds with one boulder. Hard and fast.'* Turik had allies, those who shared his thoughts and opinions. If this display didn't draw them out, the next part might scare them off.

"You are a poison, Turik, an infection." Dayne turned to one of the guards who stood at the edges of the Minor Houses – a young man no more than twenty summers, two black rings on each arm. "Give him your sword."

The guard looked at Dayne, uncertain. He swallowed, his gaze flitting from Turik to Dayne, then to Alina. Dayne shook his head. "Fine." He squeezed his fingers around the hilt of his own sword, then tossed the blade through the air. A cloud of dust rose as the sword landed in the dirt before Turik's feet with a clang.

"Pick it up."

"My King, let us talk about this in a civil manner. There appears to be a deep misunderstanding." The sound of Turik's slithering voice scratched at Dayne's ears. "I meant no—"

"There is no misunderstanding," Dayne growled. "You meant every word you said, Lord Baleer. You questioned my sister's decisions. You questioned her right to rule. By blade and by blood, I am her sword. You seem to have forgotten the ways of our people, Lord Baleer. Family is the blood that runs in your veins. They are the beating of your heart. I am sure Alina could kill you with her own hands for your treason, but today of all days – the day she is crowned queen of a free Valtara – her hands deserve to be free of blood." *And mine will never be clean.* "My father had great respect for you, gods' know why. Which is why, out of respect for him, instead of stringing you up for your treason, I offer you the old ways of our people. I offer you the Athima tis Aleas – the Blood of Truth."

Alina took a step forwards. Her gaze was fixed on Dayne, and the thumb of her right hand tucked into a fist told him she was angry, but the worry in her eyes was genuine.

"And if I refuse?" Turik stood tall, his stare never leaving Dayne's. The man had seen his sixtieth summer, but his body was still lean muscled, and he moved like a man half his age. Turik also held four markings of the blade. He was no lamb.

"I will take your head," Dayne said plainly. "Under the laws of Athima tis Aleas, whoever's blood feeds the earth, their opponent holds the weight of truth and shall not be reprimanded. The dead will be offered all burial rights. If you wish, you may nominate a champion in your stead."

"I volunteer!" A young man burst from the ranks of the Minor Houses, the falcon of House Baleer on his tunic. Dayne recognised him as Turik's son, Rogal. He stood a head taller than Turik, his muscles lean and dense, though he had seen less than half his father's summers, and he bore only three markings of the blade.

"You will stand aside," Turik growled at his son. "You will not dishonour me."

"Father," Rogal leaned in closer, "please."

A pang of sympathy twisted in Dayne's chest as he listened to Rogal plead with his father. Dayne would have done the same if it were him. In his years, Dayne had killed many fathers. He'd killed mothers, sons, daughters. Everyone was something to someone. But killing a father in front of their son was something that cut deep into Dayne. *I will do what must be done.*

Rogal Baleer looked from his father to Dayne, fear radiating from him in waves. Dayne may have only bore two black rings on his left arm compared to Turik's four – just one marking short of a blademaster – but Turik had seen his sixtieth summer, and Dayne knew that word of his skill had spread through the camp from battle to battle. Dayne's markings were earned in blood.

"I wanted you as my king." For some reason, Turik's words stung more than Dayne would have expected. There was sincerity in them, as though Turik had truly believed Dayne would have betrayed Alina. That alone told Dayne the man had no idea who Dayne was. Turik leaned down and picked up the sword Dayne had tossed at his feet. "And for that you would kill me?"

"You wanted my favour, Turik, because you lacked my sister's. You wanted power, nothing more." Dayne rolled his shoulders, eliciting a cascade of cracks. "We are days from achieving the first free Valtara in hundreds of years, but that wasn't enough for you." Dayne bit at the corner of his lip. "No, Lord Baleer, I would not kill you for wanting me as king. I would kill you for risking everything we have bled for. For stoking the fires of a civil war while we are on the brink of freedom. I would kill you for standing against Alina. Enough talk. Begin."

Dayne's blood went cold in his veins as he moved towards Turik. His instincts told him to open himself to the Spark; one thread of air and the man's neck would snap. Dayne pushed his instincts away. The Spark had no place in Athima tis Aleas, and even if it did, even Turik Baleer deserved the honour of knowing how and why he died.

As Dayne drew closer to Turik, the older man lifted his blade, raising it into Soaring Falcon. Dayne kept walking forwards. With no blade in his hands, proximity was his friend; he needed to limit Turik's reach advantage. Turik lunged, slashing at Dayne, but Dayne leapt backwards, avoiding the sharp bite of steel and shifting around to Turik's right. A quick glance told him those gathered had begun to move closer, those at the back trying to watch unimpeded.

Three more times Turik swung. Three more times Dayne evaded, shifting his feet, watching for the subtle tells in Turik's movements. On the fourth attempt, Dayne allowed Turik to get closer, his blade slicing through the front of Dayne's robes. *Eager for the kill.*

Dayne had found there were times when anger was a weapon to be wielded, and times when it needed to be buried deep down. Turik needed to bury his, but he brandished it with every strike.

Dayne and Turik circled, Dayne controlling his breaths; in through his nose out through his mouth. His muscles twitched, readying themselves. *Fear exists only to highlight courage.*

Dayne stepped close. Too close. So close he may as well have painted a target on his gut. And, like an enraged hunter, Turik stabbed at the centre.

Dayne waited, watching the steel shimmer as it cut through the air. Then, at the last moment, when Turik had no opportunity to shift his angles, Dayne twisted, leaning backwards. Turik's blade sliced through Dayne's robes and scored his stomach. Dayne bit down the burning pain and slammed the heel of his palm against the flat of the blade, before driving his hand forwards and ramming his palm into Turik's nose. Blood sprayed, bone and cartilage crunching. As Turik stumbled backwards, Dayne brought his hand down and grasped the hilt of the sword, squeezing his fingers. As he ripped the blade free from Turik's grasp, Dayne

pushed the man backwards with his left hand. With the sword held in reverse grip, Dayne swung it through the air, the steel slicing open Turik's
throat, blood pouring like wine overflowing its cup. Dayne brought the
sword through its full arc before resting his left hand on the pommel and
driving the blade through Turik's throat. He pushed the blade through to
the hilt, the steel bursting out the other side. Turik hung there, choking
and spluttering on his own blood, held upright by the strength of Dayne's
arm. Dayne wrenched the sword free in a spray of blood, and Turik
dropped to his knees, clasping at his throat as the crimson river flowed.

Sweat slicked Dayne's brow, and his chest heaved as he stood over
Turik Baleer's lifeless body. About him, all those of the Major and Minor
Houses watched in silence. Even the screeching and roaring of the
wyverns above had ceased.

Dayne slowed his breathing, looking down at the blood that pooled
around Turik's body. He took no pleasure in the man's death. "By blade
and by blood, may Heraya embrace you, Turik Baleer."

He wiped the sword clean on his robes, then slid it back into place
in the scabbard at his hip. As he lifted his gaze, he saw hundreds of eyes
fixed on him. Some held sorrow, others anger, but most looked stunned.
Dayne found his gaze meeting Rogal Baleer's. Tears streaked the young
man's cheeks, his eyes red. Shame and guilt were two emotions Dayne
considered old companions; they visited him then as he watched the son
weep for his father. He also felt a touch of admiration at the strength
Rogal showed in not dropping to his father's side. The laws of the Athima
tis Aleas were clear: the blood of the slain – the Blood of Truth – must be
left to flow undisturbed.

Dayne looked at Turik Baleer's body once more before turning and
walking towards Alina. He stopped beside Senya Deringal and held out
his hand without a word.

"By blade and by blood." The woman inclined her head, then placed the
sunstone crown into Dayne's hand.

Dayne nodded back, then continued on to Alina. And there, at the top
of the hill, with the banner of a free Valtara flapping in the breeze behind
him, Dayne knelt and held the crown high, staring into Alina's eyes. "By
blade and blood, I am yours, my Queen."

CHAPTER SIXTY-SEVEN

A PATH AND A PURPOSE

Sparks drifted from the fire as a log collapsed. Farda didn't flinch. He wasn't looking at the fire. He was looking to his right, where Ella sat with her back against a rock, her legs pulled to her chest, her gaze lost in the flames. Faenir was curled up at her side, his head resting on his paws, his eyes focused upwards, never leaving Ella.

She hadn't spoken since they'd fled the camp. Not in days. At night she shook and trembled, the wolfpine sitting by her side like a tireless sentinel. By the light of day she walked, ate, drank, and then waited for the sun to set. Farda didn't like it. Something was very wrong.

To Farda's left, Hala got to her feet, dirt crunching under her boots. In the light of the fire, the woman's white hair stood in even starker contrast to the dark of night. She stared at Ella for a moment, then let out a sigh. "I'm going to join Ilyain on watch. He's blind, after all. Come to think of it, calling it watch is a little insensitive – only took me a few hundred years to realise that. Better late than never." She leaned down to Farda as she passed, dropping her voice to a whisper. "Try and get her to talk. This is all a little pointless if we don't know where we're going. If she doesn't, I vote south. Vaerleon or Land's End. Somewhere far away from this madness. Perhaps even Karvos – they make good rum." Hala stood back to her full height, then walked to Ella, holding out a waterskin and shaking it, the water sloshing within. "You need to drink more, whether you speak or not."

Ella didn't turn her gaze from the fire, but Faenir was on his feet in a matter of seconds, hackles raised, lips pulling back, a vicious growl resonating in his throat, the light of the fire causing his eyes to gleam an unnatural white.

Hala rolled her eyes, tossing the waterskin on the ground beside Ella and walking off. "Fucking wolves…"

"Wolfpine," Farda whispered, watching as the night swallowed Hala. Faenir gave a final grunt and dropped himself back down beside Ella, his head resting on his paws.

"You're going to have to speak eventually." Farda picked up a twig and snapped it into pieces, tossing the bits into the fire one by one. "Otherwise we'll be roaming for the rest of our lives."

Silence passed between them save for the crackling of the fire, then Ella's gaze shifted, and she was staring at him, her eyes flickering amber. "Did you know?"

"Know what? About the acolyte? Rist Havel?"

Ella just stared. There was something changed in her, something altered in her foundations. She had always been sharp, always quick with her wit, and she'd always possessed a spirit unlike any he'd known. But now she was... colder, both strong and brittle, like paper-thin steel.

"No," Farda said, honestly. "I had no idea."

"All you do is lie."

Farda raised an eyebrow.

"You knew who I was the entire time. From the moment I met you in Gisa. The only reason you got Shirea and me on that ship was because you knew who I was and who Calen was. What was your plan, capture me, use me as bait?"

There was an apathy in Ella's voice, a sense of distance that unsettled Farda.

"Yes." He nodded, biting the insides of his cheeks as he looked into the fire. There was no sense in lying to her. She already knew, that much was clear, and her mind was quicker than his.

"You could have taken me at any point from Gisa to Berona. Why didn't you?"

"I told myself it would be easier if you walked on your own two feet, less of a struggle." Farda shook his head. "But in truth, I don't know why."

"Did you kill Shirea?"

Farda nodded. He heard Ella drawing in a long breath. He'd expected her to charge at him, claw at his face, try to run him through with his own sword, but as he lifted his gaze, he saw she was just sitting there staring into the flames.

"You left me to be taken in Berona," she said, never looking at him. "That much I worked out a long time ago. Those men came for me too quickly for it to have been coincidence. You were sent to take me. You killed Shirea. You left me for dead in Berona." Ella met Farda's gaze, the first sign of emotion touching her face in the tremble of her lip. "Why are we here? Why did you break me free? What games are you playing, Farda? I'm too tired for games."

Farda pulled his gaze from Ella's and studied the dry earth at his feet. He tapped his hand against his pocket, feeling the click of his nail against the coin. He hesitated for a moment, then pulled the coin from his pocket, the dulled metal glinting in the firelight.

"Not that fucking coin." Ella shook her head, a growl creeping into her voice.

Farda held the coin in his left palm, tracing his fingers over its time-worn surface. "Ilyain and Hala told me you were with Farwen. She's alive by the way – Hala has known Farwen since Farwen was a child. She let her go."

That caught Ella's attention, a flicker of relief in her eyes.

"If Farwen was there, I'm assuming Coren isn't far either. Those two have been inseparable for a long time." Farda flicked the coin, letting it drop into his palm. Lions. He swallowed hard. "Two hundred and forty-nine years ago, my dragon, Shinyara, died."

Ella lifted her gaze, but judging by the lack of surprise on her face, Farda figured Coren had already told her that part.

He drew in another breath, his throat tightening, a tremble setting into his hands. "The day she died…" He stopped. Across the centuries, if there was one thing that re-tethered Farda's emotions to his heart, even for a moment, it was Shinyara. His light. His soul. He clenched his jaw. "The day she died, I had a choice to make. Another Draleid, Aeson Virandr, along with his companions, had killed three of my kin, ripped them apart while they slept. It was dark, stormclouds blanketed the sky and lightning tore through the air. There were two of us to their four. We had two dragons, they had three. Shinyara didn't want to pursue them. There were too many, and the storm was too bad. She was scared. For me and for her. Linare and Teranaine didn't want to go, either. 'Enough blood had been spilled that night,' Linare said."

Ella was staring at him now, as was Faenir.

"But I couldn't let it go." Rage bubbled in him at the memories of his three brothers and their soulkin lying broken across the ground, flashes of lightning illuminating their savaged remains. "I stood on the cliff where we had landed, the rain battering me, so heavy it may as well have been a waterfall. And I pulled this coin from my pocket." He stared down at the battered coin, flicking it over and back. Crowns. Lions. "I said to Linare, 'If it lands on crowns, we turn back, but if it lands on lions, we follow them, we rip them from the air, and break them against the cliff.' I was so arrogant back then. She agreed. I flipped the coin. It landed on crowns."

Farda lifted his gaze towards the cloud-covered sky of black. "I stuffed the coin into my pocket and refused to turn back. I mounted Shinyara and rode after them. Teranaine and Linare were struck by lightning trying to keep up. Linare died instantly and Teranaine cried out as she fell. Within moments, the Draleid we were chasing fell upon Shinyara and me.

We sent two to dine in Achyron's halls, but they had already torn strips through Shinyara's wings. We ripped the last pair, Halder and Toring, from the world as we fell, and then we crashed on the cliff. I should have turned back, and because I didn't, Shinyara died that night. Aeson Virandr drove his blades through her skull and tossed me from the cliff into the waters of the Lightning Coast. By some miracle of the gods or a twisted joke, I washed up on the shore near Bromis the next morning. I wish I'd died – part of me did. In the Old Tongue, they call us Rakina. It means 'one who is broken'. But when a dragon dies, you're not broken. No…" Farda shook his head, his hand closing around the coin. "You're shattered. Your soul is shredded and splintered, its many fragments thrown to the wind. You are nothing, you are nobody. All you feel is empty, and cold, and wrong. That's why I trust the coin. That's why I let fate decide. Partly because everything lost meaning after Shinyara died, but partly because the one time I didn't listen to fate, I lost the only thing left in this world that I cherished. And with her she took my pain, my love, and my happiness…"

Farda stared at the coin in his palm, his finger tracing its time-worn edge. Tears trickled down his cheeks. It had been so long since he had cried, he'd forgotten what it felt like. "You want to know why I came back for you?" Farda let out a short laugh. "In truth, I'm not entirely sure myself. But for the first time… Ella?"

Hearing shifting and tossing, the crunching of dirt, Farda lifted his gaze to see Ella lying on her back, convulsing, her hands twisted towards her chest. He leapt to his feet, but Faenir bounded towards him, head lowered, hackles raised, nose crinkled in a snarl. He was more a bear than a wolfpine.

"Get out of the way, you stupid animal!" Farda took a step towards Ella, who still lay convulsing on the ground, but Faenir snapped his jaws, his amber eyes cold and savage. "What are you doing? Let me help her!"

Faenir stared back at Farda. The creature's eyes gleamed with under-standing, but he didn't move. The wolfpine backed across Ella, standing over her convulsing body, snapping and snarling at Farda.

Farda looked down at Ella. She was spasming, her head jerking side to side. He met Faenir's amber gaze. "Let me help her, or I will go through you."

Faenir lowered his head and arched his back even more, saliva dripping from the his jaws.

"Fucking wolfpine." Farda dove forwards, reaching out to the Spark and pulling on threads of Earth and Spirit. He raised his right arm as Faenir lunged. The wolfpine's jaws closed around Farda's forearm. He felt pressure but not the pain. Faenir thrashed his head left and right, trying to rip Farda's limb to pieces, but Farda bound the threads of Earth and Spirit and pushed them into the skin and bone of his arm, thickening them, hardening them. He could only strengthen them so much though, and it wouldn't be long before the creature snapped straight through.

Farda dropped to his knees beside Ella, pushing his arm back at Faenir, trying to keep the wolfpine at bay, the pressure building and building.

"Ella!" He grabbed at her head with his free hand, his shoulder jerking back as Faenir pulled at him. Ella's eyes were closed, rolling back and forth behind the lids.

"Farda?" Hala dropped from atop the ridge behind Ella, shock and urgency in her voice. She ripped her sword from its scabbard, charging forwards as Ilyain following her.

"No!" Farda called out. He felt a snap in his arm. "Stay back!"

"Farda, we—"

"No!" He shook Ella, grabbing the back of her head. "Ella! Ella!" Farda could feel the warm blood trickling down his arm, feel the Spark draining from him as the threads of Earth and Air woven into his skin and bone gave way. Then, it stopped. The pressure lifted.

His chest heaving, Farda turned to see the wolfpine had let go and now stood looking back at Farda, his snarl gone, his hackles lowered, the fur around his muzzle wet with blood. Farda's arm was a mess of punctures and bite marks, blood still pouring, but for the most part, it was intact. The threads of Earth and Spirit had prevented the wolfpine from simply tearing it clean off. He would deal with it after.

He turned his attention back to Ella. The spasms and convulsions had stopped. Farda cupped his hand around Ella's cheek and pulled her head towards him. "Ella? Ella, open your eyes."

Hala dropped to the ground beside Farda. She glanced warily at Faenir, who, barring the blood that dripped from his muzzle, now looked as placid as a pup. She grabbed at Farda's arm, looking over the damage. "What the fuck were you thinking?"

Farda glanced back at Hala but only grunted.

"Farda?" Ella croaked.

"Ella." Farda looked down to see Ella's eyes were open, her irises shifting like molten gold. "Talk to me." He patted at her cheek as her eyelids drooped. "Stay awake. Talk to me."

In the back of his mind he felt Hala weaving threads through his arm. She wasn't a Healer, but she knew enough to keep him from dying of blood loss. A crunch let him know she'd fixed his broken bone.

Ella groaned, blood trickling from her lips from where she must have bit down while convulsing. Her eyes were fully open now. She shook her head, pushing herself upright so her back rested against the rock behind her.

"It's not pretty, but it'll do." Hala let out a sigh, patting Farda's forearm and dropping onto her backside. She glared at Faenir. "I would have just killed the beast."

Farda glanced at his arm to see it was now a mess of pink and white scars, blood staining his skin. It looked exactly as it should have – as though he'd been savaged by a massive wolfpine and somehow survived. He thanked the gods Shinyara had taken his pain.

"I heard something," Ella muttered, becoming more lucid. She brought her left hand to the side of her head, pressing her fingers into her temple. "It was like a… a high pitched noise that stabbed through my head."

Farda opened and closed his hand, testing his fingers still worked, eliciting stiff pops and cracks. *Good, I like that hand.* He looked back at Ella. "Are you all right?"

Ella nodded, wincing. "It was like someone was pushing their thoughts into my mind. Images, words, feelings… I saw my brother." Ella looked at Farda, and her eyes widened, then narrowed.

"You can trust me, Ella. I promise."

"Trust you?" Ella shifted where she sat, pushing herself back against the rock, the fingers of her left hand still pressing into her temple. "All you've done is lie. Every word that leaves your lips is a lie. You are the last person I can trust."

Farda leaned a little closer. "What I told you about Shinyara. The only other people who know what happened that night are Aeson Virandr, Hala, and Ilyain. Almost two hundred and fifty years and I've now only told three people."

"You're with the empire."

"I walked away from the empire the moment I carried you from that camp, the moment I killed a woman I respected to break you free."

"I never asked you do to that."

"Well it's done."

Ella looked from Farda, to Faenir, then at the mess of scars that was Farda's arm. Her eyes softened. "I saw Calen and a dragon – a white one. It wasn't even half the size of the ones the Dragonguard rode. They were in a forest and a city built from stone as white as the dragon's scales." She grimaced, rolling her neck, pressing her fingers harder against her temple. "It's like a nail has been pulled from my head."

"What else did you see?" Ilyain moved so he stood behind Farda, his arms clasped behind his back.

"How's your face?" Ella growled, her lip pulling back to expose teeth that looked to sharpen as she spoke, four fangs lengthening.

"I'm sure it looks as pretty as yours does right now," Ilyain said without missing a beat. He dropped to one knee beside Farda, looking in Ella's general direction, though Farda knew his eyes saw nothing. "I only attacked you because you were attacking us. Now, if you're done, I believe I may know what you experienced."

Ella's lip trembled, her eyes still flickering molten gold, but her teeth returned to normal, fangs shortening. "Go on."

"There are creatures called Angan – shapeshifters, guardians and servants of the druidic gods. They have the ability to communicate with each other across great distances using only their minds. Aldruids – such as you – can tap into these communications, but only if they are sent by Angan of the same clan as their patron god."

"Their patron god?"

"The Angan and druids of old worshipped five gods wrought in flesh. In this case, given the wolf, I believe you to be a daughter of Fenryr."

"And how do you know all this?"

Ilyain paused for a moment. Farda knew how hard it was for Ilyain to talk of Andras.

"My love – my Ayar Elwyn – Andras, was an Aldruid of Bjorna, though he spent his life hiding it. The details aren't important, but Andras often experienced what you just did, though over time he learned to control himself when it happened. What did you hear, see, feel? The Angan communicate in images, emotions, and feelings as well as words."

Ella's stare flitted between Ilyain, Farda, and Hala. "No." She pressed her hands against the rock behind her and pushed herself to her feet, stumbling sideways, Faenir moving to her side. "I'm not telling you anything. I'm not."

She took a step forwards but stumbled, and Farda caught her by the shoulder. "Where do you think you're going?"

"Get your hands off me." Ella swatted Farda's hand away, staggering backwards before stabilising herself.

"We can help you find him, Ella."

"Help me? You've been trying to find him from the start. Was this all part of your plan? How fucked up are you? I'm not leading you to him!"

"Imperial scouts are combing through every square inch of land from here to Fort Harken. They're not just looking for you, they're looking for us." Farda slapped his chest and gestured to Hala and Ilyain. "We risked our lives to get you out of there. And if you try and go out there on your own, they will have you strung up by the time the sun sets tomorrow. Then you will know what true torture is." Farda grabbed Ella by the shoulders, ignoring the growls from Faenir. "Look into my eyes." Farda's heart was beating harder than he'd it felt in centuries. She was just so gods damned stubborn. "I don't know what it is you've done to me, but when you're near, I don't feel so fucking broken. That's why I came back. That's why I'm here. And if the last thing I do is get you back to your brother, then at least I'll have done something decent in the last four hundred years that would explain why I'm still alive while Shinyara is dead. There has to be a fucking reason I'm still here. Now let me help you."

Farda's hands shook as he held Ella's shoulders. He could kill her for making him feel like this – for making him feel anything at all. Shinyara had taken that from him; it belonged to her. Ella had no right to give it back to him. He let go of Ella's shoulders, turning away, meeting Hala's gaze for a fleeting moment. The pity in her eyes only served to further drive the rage in his cold icy heart.

"The message was meant for someone else." Ella's voice cut through the silence. Farda didn't turn. He stayed staring at the ground, the light from the fire flickering. His hands still shook. "I don't understand everything, but there's a gathering… I think. Or, an invitation. The images were of a forest that spread into the distance. Dark thunderclouds overhead. Lightning. It felt… *wrong*. As though it was a place of sanctuary but also of great fear, as though something was watching… I don't know, that's all I could understand."

"It's enough." Farda lifted his gaze to see Hala walking towards him.

"The Darkwood," Ilyain said. "We've known for a long time that elves had taken refuge there. Aeson has many friends amongst the elves, and the Aldithmar claim the wood as their own. It would make sense that he would go there."

"With the emergence of the Lynalion elves, we can't take a ship from the Lightning Coast – not that I'd want to." Hala scrunched her mouth, contemplating. "And the Burnt Lands is all but impassable. If we go northwest we can take a riverboat from Catagan to the coast. Gisa will likely be under lockdown, but we could sail past the Bay of Light. Maybe dock at Kingspass or Falstide. It will take a bit longer, but we won't run into any patrols. Between the three of us, we are owed enough favours for a hundred lifetimes."

Farda straightened his back, clenching his jaw and letting out a long breath through his nostrils, settling himself. He cupped his hands to his face and rubbed away the grime and tears. "Neither of you need come," he said to Hala and Ilyain. "This journey does not end happily. You know that."

"We've lived too long anyway," Hala said. "Our endings were never meant to be happy."

Ilyain's hand rested on his shoulder. "Like we've said – if we're to die, we'd rather do it with our own kind. I've lived too long to die fighting for something I don't care about anymore. Besides, I would very much like to lay eyes on this new Draleid. If Aeson allows it before taking our heads. It's about time we faced our past."

"I can't just go." Ella stepped forwards, stumbling a little, her legs still weak. She looked at Farda for a long moment, her gaze feeling as though it was boring into his skull. "Coren and the others. I need to let them know I'm all right."

"We go now, or we don't go at all, Ella. Coren will want us dead on sight. Our history is… complicated."

Faenir padded over to Ella, brushing his muzzle against her shoulder. He let out a low whine, his ears folding back against his head, his eyes seeming as though they were asking a question.

Ella scratched at the wolfpine's cheek. "All right," she whispered to Faenir. After a moment she looked to Farda, her eyes having returned to their natural green. "How long will it take?"

"Before we get into that," Hala said, stepping closer. "We came back to tell you we have company."

Tanner slid his sword from its scabbard as quietly as the steel would allow, wiping the sweat from his brow as he did. Ahead, he could see the flames of the campfire flickering against the walls of the alcove nestled into the rock.

Farwen moved to his left, Yana to his right, both of them with swords in hand.

"Remember," Farwen whispered, "one or more of them can touch the Spark. We need to rush them, take them quick."

Tanner nodded, knowing Farwen wasn't looking at him. He tightened his grip around his sword, the muscles in his forearm squeezing. When he'd heard Ella had been taken back at the imperial camp, the air had fled his lungs. If it hadn't been for Farwen assuring him they would get her back, he would have gone after her there and then. Yana had been worse; he'd had to hold her down.

"I didn't let you go just to have to kill you again, young one." The voice echoed in the night, bouncing off the rock.

Tanner stopped in his tracks, Farwen and Yana doing the same.

Farwen looked about, her eyes tracing the low ridge line that ran towards the alcove ahead, stopping as though she'd seen something – though how she had seen anything in the pitch black he had no idea.

"We've come for the girl, Hala. We don't want a fight," Farwen called.

A figure stepped from the all-consuming dark, dropping from the low ridge to the ground. A woman stepped forwards, her hair white as snow, the fingers of her left hand curled into a fist. "That's good, young one. Because I won't let you live twice."

"Where is she?" The words left Yana's mouth in a growl as she took a step closer to the white-haired woman. Tanner reached out to pull her back, but she was already moving closer.

"Feisty." The woman smiled, looking at Yana as though amused. She didn't move an inch, but Tanner saw Farwen tense, and then Yana's sword was ripped from her hand by something unseen, clattering against the stone.

"Not that I think you could do anything worthwhile with it," the white haired woman said. "But I'm not a fan of sharp steel in my face. Call it a preference. Turn around, Farwen. Dylain was a friend, I do not wish to cause his soul any more pain."

"Don't you say his name." The raw anger in Farwen's voice was something Tanner had rarely seen from the elf. She had spoken of Dylain before – her old master at the time of The Fall – but his memory had always brought sadness, not anger. "Don't you dare *ever* say his name. Don't even think it."

"I knew him better than you, young one."

"You let him die."

"Two sides to every coin. Isn't that right, Farda?"

As if appearing from nowhere, Farda Kyrana stepped from the shadows to the left, one hand resting on the pommel of his sword. "Tanner Fjorn." Farda laughed. "Of all the people I thought I'd meet out here in these hills, you were not one of them. You got sick of the keep in Berona then?"

"You're the one who fled the Lorian camp. Change of heart yourself?"

"Interesting choice of words." The twist in Farda's lip was barely visible, illuminated only by the pale moonlight. "Is that Yana? Yana Veradis? There really were a lot of you rebels in Berona, weren't there? Leave now, and we can all walk away."

"We're not leaving without Ella." Yana stared at Farda, her voice firm. When she was like this, there was no turning her around.

"Well you're not leaving with her. Of that, I can assure you."

"Tanner?"

The hairs on Tanner's arms stood on end at the sound of Ella's voice. "Ella? Are you all right?"

Shadows flickered from within the alcove ahead, and two figures emerged, followed by a third that walked on four legs – Faenir.

Tanner walked forward, moving towards Ella, only to hear the rasp of steel and find the tip of Farda's blade pressed against his chest. Farda shook his head.

As Ella drew closer, Tanner could see she was limping, her hand resting on Faenir's back for balance. Her clothes were bloodstained, and a number of cuts and bruises marred her face and neck. The figure that walked beside her was an elf with dark hair and skin.

"Farda, put down the sword." Ella sounded weak, but there was a firmness in her voice.

Farda looked to her, eyes narrowing slightly, but kept his blade where it was.

Ella stopped a few feet away, a grimace twisting her face. She looked from Tanner, to Yana, to Farwen. "The others?"

"Juro is dead." Farwen answered. "As are Jaks and Ligin. Arlon, Ferol, Varik, and Suka all made it out safe. They're on their way back."

Ella nodded sombrely. "I'm not going back."

"What?" The word had left Tanner's mouth before his mind had filtered it. "Ella, what are you talking about?"

"I know where Calen is, Tanner. Farda is taking me."

"You can't trust him, Ella." The press of steel against leather reminded Tanner that Farda still held his blade against Tanner's chest. Both men stared into each other's eyes. "He wants you to lead him to Calen. That's all he's wanted from the beginning."

Ella and Farda exchanged a glance. "There's more to it, Tanner. Thank you, for everything you've done, but I can't go back. Please, just go. You've already done so much for me. Calen is the only family I have left, and he's alone. He would never leave me, and I'm not leaving him."

"And I'm not leaving you." Yana slid her sword into her scabbard, moving closer to Ella. "We're coming with you."

"We're what?" Tanner could do nothing to hold the shock from his voice.

"We're going with her." Yana said plainly. "I'm not leaving her on her own with these people."

"These people have names," the white-haired woman said with a shrug.

"Yana…" Ella looked from Yana to Farda, then back. "Yana, it's all right. You've already—"

"No." Yana shook her head. "You're not about to rationalise us away. I can't speak for Farwen, but I can damn well speak for that big idiot." Yana gestured to Tanner. "We're going with you. Your brother is the Draleid. If you're going to find him, I'm sure we'll find plenty of rebellion there too. We're not letting you go alone. It's not happening. So either you let us come with you, or I carry you back over my shoulder."

Yana was not the kind of person to grow fond of someone, and Tanner had seen the way she acted around Ella: like a mother wolf watching over her cub. So, he stared at the woman he loved, his heart almost breaking at the way her voice trembled.

"We're coming with you, Ella. For Rhett. It's not a discussion." Tanner clenched his jaw as he waited for the response. He would soon see if Ella was as 'free' as Farda was claiming.

"All right." Ella limped forwards and opened her arms to Yana.

Yana pulled Ella into a hug, rubbing her back, and Tanner could hear her whisper, "You stupid, stupid girl."

Ella's laughter brought a smile to his face. He raised his eyebrows to Farda, who pulled the sword from Tanner's chest.

"Who'd have seen this coming?" Farda pursed his lips in amusement, sliding his sword into its scabbard. "Tanner Fjorn, High Captain of the Beronan Guard – a rebel. And now here we are. Fascinating how the world works."

Tanner grunted at Farda, turning to see Farwen approaching.

"I cannot go with you," Farwen said, grasping Tanner's forearm. "There is too much for me to do here. I must tell Coren everything that has happened." She leaned in close, lowering her voice. "You will always have a home in Tarhelm. When you reach your destination, send correspondence to Hilka, and be careful, Tanner. No matter what, don't drop your guard."

"I won't, I promise. Stay safe, Farwen. With what we witnessed at The Three Sisters, the North is a very different place."

Farwen nodded and squeezed Tanner's forearm, then walked to Farda, her stare cold. "If you—" She looked at the others, the elf and white-haired woman "If *any* of you bring even the slightest of harm to these people, I will personally hunt you down. I will make it my sole purpose."

"Draleid n'aldryr, Farwen. If we see each other again, maybe we will once more fight on the same side," the white-haired woman said as Farwen made to leave.

Farwen stopped. She looked back at the white-haired woman. "Forgiveness doesn't come that easily, Hala. Not for the things you've done."

"Farwen." Ella hobbled over to Farwen and pulled her into a hug. The elf took a moment to look shocked, then returned Ella's embrace. "Thank you, for everything. Please, tell Coren the same and that I will be back."

Farwen pulled away from Ella and nodded. "It will be done. It was a pleasure, Ella Fjorn. You would have made a fine Draleid. May the gods watch over you."

With that, Farwen turned and disappeared into the night.

CHAPTER SIXTY-EIGHT

HOME IS CARRIED WHEREVER YOU GO

Dann let out a grunt as he hauled himself up the stairs, the muscles in his arms and back spasming. He'd been practicing the sword with Calen every day. He didn't give half a shit about the sword, and he despised waking up before the sun, but since they'd arrived in Aravell, Calen had been pulled left and right by anyone who could get their hands on him. Practicing the sword was the only way Dann could truly guarantee he'd get to spend any time with Calen. And now that he'd sworn that oath, he kind of had to show his face.

Not to mention, along with the sword, he had spent his afternoons practicing the bow with Alea and Lyrei. Lyrei had even begun speaking again after Aeson had paid her a visit. They'd not talked for long, but once he'd left it was like she'd gone back to being her old self.

All in all, Dann was absolutely fucking exhausted. But he was the happiest he'd been in quite some time. And he made sure to hold on to that happiness as he pushed open the door at the top of the stairs.

The room was three times as large as his own back in The Glade. Two beds sat against the far wall, both with a small side table. Between the side tables, Loura, one of the rebels who had come with Calen across the Burnt Lands, sat in a chair with her legs crossed, a book bound in green leather held in her hands. She looked up as he entered, raising a finger to her lips as she placed the book on the table beside her and got to her feet.

"They're sleeping," she whispered, resting her hand on Dann's shoulder and ushering him towards the archway set into the wall on the left side of the door he had just come through.

The moonlight sprayed down as they stepped out onto the balcony. The earlier wind and rain had stopped, and the air held a warmth in it that spoke of the beginnings of summer.

"How are they?" Dann asked, turning to Loura. The woman had seen only a summer or so more than he. Her hair hung past her shoulders, and she always wore it down. Elia, Rist's mam, had been suffering with night terrors since they'd arrived in Aravell, and Loura, along with some others, had volunteered to watch her through the nights. Dann often visited when he knew she was there.

"Good." Loura looked back into the room. "They ate even more today than yesterday. They were asking for you and the Draleid – I mean, Calen."

Dann laughed. "He gets a bit touchy when you call him 'the Draleid'. He's like that. I'd make sure everyone calls me 'the Draleid'."

Loura smiled, the light of the moon glinting in her eyes.

"Thank you," Dann said, resting a hand on the white-stone balustrade and looking back in at Elia and Lasch who lay asleep in their beds. "For caring for them."

Loura shook her head. "It's the least I can do. Calen brought us here from Berona. I hated it there – always looking over my shoulder, always wondering if someone would come for me, each day feeding into the next. Besides, I like the quiet. It lets me read."

"What did you do, in Berona?"

The warmth wilted from Loura's face, and she placed her right hand over her left. "I was a whisperer. I…" She glanced at Dann, hesitating. "I was a courtesan. Many of my clients held high positions in the Circle, some in the Beronan nobility. Many liked to talk when we lay. I would feed those whispers to Sulin, and she to Ingvat."

Before all of this, Dann had never been to a city, but he knew what a courtesan was. He understood why sitting by Lasch and Elia's bedside and reading was a welcome respite. "You're here now."

Loura nodded, a joyless smile on her face.

"Drunir's outside." Dann leaned out over the balustrade and whistled. The response was an excited neigh that echoed in the night.

"You better be brushing him." The joy returned to Loura's smile, and she laughed. She jabbed a finger into Dann's chest. "Or I swear…"

"I'm brushing him, I'm brushing him. It's a two way street. I brush him, he brushes me. Then we both sing a song, or well, I sing a song, and he has to listen, because he's a horse."

"You're an idiot," Loura said, laughing.

"At your service." Dann gave a mocking bow. "Go, he likes you more than me. Then maybe go get some sleep. I'll stay here until the next person comes."

Loura looked at Dann for a moment, her gaze softening, then she nodded. "You better not just sit here drinking wine again."

Dann lifted his hands. "Under Elyara's eyes, I swear. Who's taking over from you?"

"Good." Loura narrowed eyes as though trying to find something in Dann's gaze. "Ingvat will be here in a few hours to see through the night."

"Ugh." Dann tossed his back. "Anyone but Ingvat. She makes you feel guilty just by looking at you."

"That she does… but only if you're actually guilty of something." Loura smiled knowingly, then stepped back into the room, checking on Elia and Lasch before making her way to the door, giving Dann a smile before she closed it behind her.

"Just you and me," Dann whispered, looking over Elia and Lasch.

Two wooden chairs sat against the wall to the left of the balcony arch. He grabbed one, pulling it towards himself and shrugging his satchel from his back. He dropped the satchel into his lap as he lowered himself into the chair.

Dann undid the satchel's buckles, opening the top flap and pulling out a stoppered ceramic jug of mead he'd managed to find in the city. He lay the satchel on the ground, hearing the clink as two more jugs knocked against each other.

"She said no wine," he whispered to himself, smiling. The sound of Drunir nickering drifted through the window.

Dann pulled the stopper from the top of the jug, holding his nose over the mouth, taking a deep sniff. He covered his mouth as he coughed, the sharp scent of spirits hitting the back of his throat. "Well, it's not going to be as good as yours," he whispered to the sleeping Lasch.

He held his nose further away, getting the slightest tinge of honey.

"One for me." Dann lifted the jug to his lips and took a mouthful, feeling the burn as the mead slid down his throat. It was nowhere near as sweet as Lasch's mead – more of a spirit than a wine. But it would do. "One for you." Dann lifted the jug in the air, gesturing towards Lasch. "Well, two for me, I suppose." He took another deep mouthful, letting out a sharp hiss after he swallowed.

"How are they?"

Dann turned to see Calen standing in the doorway. His friend looked as though he'd spent the last few nights getting beaten to a pulp for fun. Calen's eyes were ringed with purple, his hair was saturated from the rain, a fresh cut – still trickling a thin stream of blood – adorned his right cheek, and his shoulders drooped.

"Sleeping." Dann pulled himself to his feet, his muscles arguing with him. He gestured for Calen to take his chair as he pulled the second chair over and dropped into it. "I take it the flying is going well?"

Calen puffed out his cheeks in response, hobbling across the room, undoing his sword belt as he did and resting it on the ground. He let out a long, heavy sigh as he sank back into the wood. After a moment, he looked to Dann and down to the jug in his hand. "What's that?"

"Mine."

"Dann."

"There's more in the satchel." Dann nodded to the satchel that sat on the ground beside Calen's chair.

Calen reached down and pulled out one of the ceramic mead jugs, looking it over with scepticism.

"It's mead… Well, it's what passes for mead here. Tastes more like…" Dann stopped and watched as Came pulled the stopper from the top of the jug and took a long, thirsty mouthful of the mead. "It's pretty strong, you probably shouldn't…" Dann pursed his lips as Calen continued to drink. "All right, what do I know?"

Called pulled the jug from his lips and let out a long sigh, followed by a heavy breath. "It tastes like piss."

"Honeyed piss," Dann corrected, holding up one finger. "It's an important distinction. Because if it didn't have that hint of honey, I'd really be wondering."

Calen sat forward, leaning his elbows on his legs as he choked on his laughter, trying to stay quiet for Elia and Lasch. He took a few slow breaths, then lifted his head, looking over the man and woman who lay in the two beds. "They're here because of me, Dann."

"Don't think like that."

"It's true. I started all this when I brought Erik's mantle out after him in The Two Barges."

"No, I'm pretty sure you started all this when you decided to step between imperial soldiers and Aeson, but, you know, semantics."

That drew a short smile from Calen, but he just took another breath and another swig from the jug. It felt strange for Dann to see Calen this way. Dann had changed since leaving The Glade, he knew that, but not as much as Calen had. Calen had always had a spring in his step, always seen a bit of sunlight on the dark days. That was still there, somewhere below the surface, but it was covered by a weight that pressed down on his shoulders.

"That's who you are, Calen. You're the guy who gives back the mantle. I'm the guy who's drunk, wondering where you've gone. And Rist is the guy who's so busy reading his books he never realised there was a mantle in the first place. Did you ever think that if it was me or Rist who had picked up that mantle, we probably wouldn't even be here? It's funny how that works."

"Do you listen to yourself sometimes?"

"On occasion." Dann pursed his lips. "When the mood strikes. How about we keep drinking this mead while we watch over this little role-reversal here." Dann gestured towards Lasch and Elia. "Then, when Ingvat comes to take over and explains to us why we shouldn't be drinking ourselves silly, we go, pick up the rest I've stashed under my bed and take my horse to meet your dragon."

༄

THE VIBRATIONS OF TRUSIL'S STEPS jarred Rist's back, slow and steady, methodical. The horse was tired; Rist didn't blame him. They'd been marching for days with little rest since they'd received a response from High Command that the First Army – what was left of it – was to head to Berona to receive new orders. The Second and Fourth Armies had stayed behind at Elkenrim, waiting to receive reinforcements, and the Dragonguard had stayed with them. With the elves from Lynalion and their dragons now occupying all the land east of Steeple, there hadn't been much of a choice.

Around him, what remained of the First Army trudged, rather than marched, across the grass-covered plains, lethargy in every step. The First Army had fared better than the others, which left them with a little over two and half thousand still alive. Barely a soul spoke, and not a shred of joy was shared between them. Even the horses and pack animals – the ones they had managed to track down after Ella and the rebels had set them free – were sombre.

Now that Rist had seen war, he understood even less about the bards' tales. Nothing heroic or noble had come from the battle at The Three Sisters. Only death and darkness. Rist dropped one hand to his side, fingers brushing the gemstone set into the pommel of the dagger Garramon had given him. Without looking, he knew it glowed with red light. He could feel the Essence within. Half of his mind wanted to tap into it, to feel that sense of calm and power. But the other half recoiled, knowing what had been done to acquire the Essence. Every night when Rist closed his eyes, he saw the elf's face – the shock, the realisation. Every night he watched her die, feeling her life Essence pull into the gemstone. He clenched his fingers into a fist and lifted his hand back to Trussil's reins.

"Do you want to talk about it?" Neera rode to Rist's left. She hadn't spoken in a while.

"About what?" Rist wasn't trying to be coy. He truly struggled to pick any one of the dark things that had happened recently.

"The druid – the girl."

Rist sighed, shaking his head.

After Farda and the other Justicars had set Ella free and left him unconscious on the ground, he'd woken to Garramon, Magnus, Anila, and some of the other mages storming into the interrogation tent. They questioned him, and he told them the truth, mostly. He hadn't told them he'd hoped to set Ella free. Instead, he'd said that Garramon had sent him to give her water – which, of course, he hadn't, but to Rist's relief, the man corroborated his story. Everything else Rist had told them was the truth: he'd found Commander Talvare, General Vandimire, General Fulker, General Hanat, and Farda already in the tent. Farda had killed the others and taken Ella, leaving along with the other Justicars. That had been enough of a scandal most of them had forgotten about Rist entirely – he'd simply been in the wrong place at the wrong time.

But when Garramon had brought Rist back to the mage camp, he'd questioned Rist further. Garramon had asked Rist to leave the tent before Ella had been questioned, but from what Rist had heard, she hadn't spoken a word. But Rist knew Garramon had realised she was from The Glade just by the look she'd shared with Rist. And so Rist decided to tell him the truth, to tell him that he'd gone to set her free. He knew Garramon would have pieced it together, and it would work in his favour if he was honest with the man. He could trust Garramon.

At first, Garramon had reacted calmly. He'd told Rist not to tell anyone what had really happened, and he'd even thanked him for his honesty. But the man's calm demeanour had changed when Rist had told him Ella's name. Why Ella's name had mattered so much, Rist didn't know. It didn't make any sense, but then again, none of it did. Ella was alive. Not only was she alive, she was burning Lorian army camps with the rebellion. And on the side of even less sense: she was a druid. Rist had spent every night since reading *Druids, a Magic Lost* by candle light, focusing entirely on the sections to do with Aldruids. Everything about her had lined up with what Duran Linold had claimed about Aldruids – even down to what he'd heard about her apparently using an owl to attack the Justicar. It all felt like something from a bards' tale. But even all that aside, what made even less sense was what she had said to him. Her anger, he understood, but her words… *'How could you fight for them?'*

He just couldn't work out what she'd meant. When Rist had first awakened in the palace in Al'Nasla, there had been no fighting between the Lorian Empire and the people of the South. At least, not fighting he had known about. That had started after. But it had been the rising factions that had caused the fighting. And Rist, so far, had only fought elves. But in truth, he could still understand her anger. The way the soldiers had begun to talk about the 'rebels', as though they were lesser, hadn't sat right with him either.

No, what baffled him was what she'd meant when she said, *'You're meant to be his closest friend. How could you turn on him, Rist?'*

"Turn on who?" he whispered, squeezing on Trusil's reins. "Calen? Dann?" Those two were the only people Rist considered his closest friends, but he would never turn on them. He never had, and he never would. So then what was she talking about?

"Rist?" Neera's voice held that irritated tone. He'd drifted off into his thoughts again.

"Sorry." He gave Neera a weak smile. "Everything's just… It's not what I thought it would be."

Neera nodded, shifting in her saddle. "I understand that."

"I can't believe he's gone," Lena said, staring ahead. She'd barely said a word since Tommin's death. She'd barely even spent any time with Rist or Neera, instead choosing to bury herself in work with Brother Halmak. Rist understood. Lena and Tommin had been particularly close. "The two of us were meant to be the safe ones."

Since Rist had first met Lena, Neera, and Tommin, Lena had always been the calm one. She'd always been so sure of herself. But now, as they rode, the army marching around them, she sobbed.

Rist squeezed his fingers around Trusil's reins, pushing his tongue against the roof of his mouth. He wanted to cry. He wanted to weep for his friend. Tommin had always been so genuine. From the start, he had treated Rist like a true friend. And beneath the wit and jokes, he truly cared – being a Healer had suited him perfectly. It wasn't fair that Tommin had died. It should have been Rist. And so, Rist wanted to cry, but he didn't. Instead, he allowed Lena her chance to feel.

ONCE THE SUN HAD SET over the Lodhar Mountains in the distance, the army had stopped to set up camp for the night. Rist couldn't help but notice how much smaller the camp was than when they were marching the other direction. *So many dead…*

After Rist had helped in pitching the tents and setting up the cots, he'd slipped out into the night air in search of Garramon, who had asked Rist to meet him by the edge of the camp when he was done. Rist found Garramon atop a flat rock, his gaze lost in the flames of a small campfire. The man had been different since the battle, much like everyone had – except for Magnus and Anila, those two were just as they'd been before.

"It's warm tonight." Rist smiled at Garramon as he approached.

Garramon lifted his head, his hard stare softening as he saw Rist. He gestured for Rist to sit next to him. "That it is."

Rist walked in front of the fire, feeling the heat through his trousers, then perched himself on the rock beside Garramon. The two sat in silence for a while, the crackling of the wood blending with the lazy sounds of the camp setting down for the night.

"Thank you," Rist said, not turning his gaze from the fire. "For saving my life. I only realised today that I hadn't thanked you." Memories flashed through Rist's mind of the worry in Garramon's eyes when the man had tackled him out of the path of the dragonfire, the concern in his voice. "I don't know what happened... I just..."

"Froze," Garramon said. "Fear does that. There's no shame in it, Rist. The sight of dragonfire is a fear like no other. Many train and train. They hone their skills with a blade or the Spark, they learn what it is to fight in practice yards and tournaments. But true warriors aren't born in practice yards, they're forged on battlefields. The most skilled swordsman can freeze at the first sight of battle. And then, even with all that training, they still lie dead in the mud. What I need you to do, Rist, is take that fear and learn from it. Pick at it, poke at it, learn it and understand it the way you do with everything else. There is far more to be learned from fear than courage. A courageous heart can falter. A heart that overcomes fear is like hardened steel."

"I will. I promise."

"I know you will." Garramon smiled as he turned his gaze back to the camp, looking out over it. "I told you before, I was proud of you. My pride has only grown."

"Grown? I almost got myself killed, and you in the process."

"You acquitted yourself well on the battlefield. You are young and untested. Most Battlemages are not sent into the fray until they have seen many years more than you have. And what you experienced was not simply a battle. It was the beginning of a cataclysm. You stood against elves and dragonfire. There are mages who have lived a hundred years and not seen battle on that scale." The man shifted in his place. "Which brings me to why I asked you here – the dagger."

The words caught Rist by surprise. They shouldn't have, but they did. In the haze of everything that had happened, he had forgotten what filling the gemstone meant within the Circle. It was the last step to receiving his full colours. Rist swallowed as he dropped his hand to where the dagger hung on the left side of his belt. He'd covered the gemstone set into the pommel with a folded over piece of cotton, tied with string; it had felt strange to see the stone glow with its red light. Slowly, Rist slipped the dagger from its sheath, resting it on his lap.

Garramon gave Rist an amused grin at the sight of the tied cotton.

Rist undid the knot, stuffing the piece of cotton into his pocket as the stone's red glow washed over the black fabric of his trousers.

"The final step." Garramon gazed down at the glowing gemstone set into the pommel of the dagger. "How did it feel?"

"Honestly?" Rist wasn't sure what he was meant to say – he wasn't sure what an Acolyte *should* say. He decided to go with candour. "Horrible." He swallowed, biting at the corner of his lip, unwilling to meet Garramon's gaze. "When it happened, it took the pain from my body, sent a chill through me. But I could see the fear in her eyes – the terror as she grabbed at her neck." Rist had to stop himself from reaching for his own neck, feeling his throat tighten. "It felt… wrong."

Rist kept his head down, his gaze fixed on a patch of trampled grass near the fire.

"Good," Garramon said, his tone level.

"Good?" Rist turned, finding himself looking directly at Garramon. The man's lips were turned in a sympathetic smile that only confused Rist even more. "How is that good?"

"Because that feeling – that wrongness – does not come from filling the vessel, Rist. It comes from death itself. Both from the witnessing of it, and the causing of it. If that wrongness ever fades, you will have become a different man entirely. One should never take pleasure in killing. It is done only because it needs to be done. We are Battlemages. It is our duty to protect those who cannot protect themselves. Death is part of who we are. You need to consider this. If you had killed that elf with a regular dagger, or a sword, or a bow, or the Spark, or anything else at all, do you think you would be free of the wrongness – of the guilt?"

Rist looked down at the dagger, running his finger along the smooth, steel blade. "No…"

"The gemstone salvaged something from her death. Had you killed her in any other way, her Essence would have been wasted, floating in the void. And she still would have been dead. You still would have killed her. But now, her Essence is not wasted – it can be used. Perhaps to save your life, or the life of another. From death comes life anew."

Rist lifted the dagger, carefully wrapping his fingers around the blade and angling it so the gemstone sat just in front of his face. He watched as the gemstone glowed, its red light washing over his hands. Thinking of the elf still twisted his gut, but he couldn't argue with Garramon's logic. Thousands had died at the battle of The Three Sisters. Rist himself had killed others, their Essence left to fade into the wind. At least in this singular death, there could be some form of light. In this singular death, something good could maybe be found.

Garramon reached across and gestured for Rist to hand him the dagger. The man took the hilt, looking over the gemstone one last time before pulling on threads of Fire and Earth, funnelling them into the gold band that held the stone in place, heating the metal just enough to cause it to expand. As he did, he pulled the gemstone free and set the dagger down on his lap.

Garramon produced a gold chain and wire from his pocket. He held the gemstone in one hand, the chain in the other, then lifted the wire with threads of Air, using Fire and Earth to make it malleable. He twisted the wire with Air, wrapping it around the gemstone, binding it, before coiling the wire about the chain and locking it tight, fusing the two metals together with Fire and Earth.

He pulled the excess heat from the newly-formed pendant with threads of Fire, dissipating it into the night air. He gripped the chain on either side, then lifted it. "Here."

Rist hesitated but bowed his head and allowed Garramon to place the pendant around his neck. The metal was cool against his skin as he held the pendant out in front of him, the red light glowing softly.

"When we reach Berona, we will procure your robes and cloak from the High Tower, Battlemage Havel. And, I could be wrong, but I believe you are the youngest ever mage to achieve that rank, though Neera has only seen a summer more. You have worked tirelessly. Your dedication has been whole-hearted and single-minded, but it does not stop now. This is only the beginning. Your forging is far from over. As my apprentice, and then my sponsored acolyte, you have brought me pride beyond measure. And now, I hope, you will do me the honour of spending many years fighting by my side as a Battlemage – as a Brother."

Rist, as seemed to be common lately, had no idea what to say Pride swelled within him, elation, disbelief – he was a Battlemage. But at the same time, his mind drifted to home, to Ella's words. *'How could you fight for them?'*

He drew in a long, steadying breath, pushing Ella's voice to the back of his mind. She had left him there, and he had no way of getting home, not yet. "Thank you, Garramon. It's difficult to believe…"

Garramon patted Rist on the back. "Magnus has asked if we would do him the honour of officially joining the Battlemages of the First Army. He's extended the same offer to Neera and Anila, and they have accepted. New Battlemages will be assigned to bolster the ranks once we reach Berona, but he said, and I'm quoting, 'I'd rather fight beside you two bastards. As long as you don't leave me trapped beneath a horse again'."

Rist laughed at that, shaking his head. He tucked the gemstone pendant beneath his shirt. "It would be an honour."

"Good," Garramon said with a smile. "Because if you'd said no, it would've been a very awkward march back to Berona." Garramon let a silence settle between them before his demeanour changed, growing more serious. "What happened the other night, in the interrogation tent…"

Rist's breath caught in his chest, his throat constricting. "I'm sorry, Exarch, I… I didn't know what to do. I…"

"I understand, Rist. She was your own. Where I come from, you look after your own. That's why I didn't have you put in shackles. But…" Garramon pursed his lips, his brows furrowing. "You put us all in danger. We are your Brothers and Sisters. Me, Anila, Magnus, Neera, Lena, and all the others. The soldiers are one thing, but the mages are another. We are bonded by something greater. That girl was your own. But so are we, and I need to know that you understand that. I need to know I can trust you. Trust is everything."

Garramon's words cut through Rist like a knife. Not only had the man been there for Rist every step of the way through this journey, pushing him forwards, teaching him, but Garramon had also risked his life to save Rist's on the battlefield. Garramon had charged towards dragonfire, with little thought for himself. And he was right, Rist going to set Ella free had put all the others in danger – Neera, Lena, Magnus, Anila. He hadn't given any of them even a fleeting thought. The newfound guilt clawed at him. It was an unwinnable scenario. He could never have not helped Ella. That was just not who he was. But at the same time, he now understood he couldn't endanger the lives of those he cared for.

"You can trust me."

Garramon stared into Rist's eyes, the light of the fire illuminating the angles of his face. He could have pushed Rist further, could have asked him to swear an oath, could have asked him for some kind of assurance, but he didn't. He simply nodded and said, "Good."

They sat for a while, Rist content with the silence until he remembered the letter in his pocket. He reached in and produced an envelope, holding it out to Garramon. "Before I forget, when we get to Berona, could you send this? With everything that's been happening, I haven't written back in a while. I don't want them to get worried."

Garramon's fingers lingered on the envelope before he took it from Rist, and even then he stared at it a few moments before nodding. "I will see that it's sent."

CHAPTER SIXTY-NINE

THE COST OF A CROWN

Dayne breathed in the warm night air of the new summer, dirt crunching beneath his feet as he, Mera, Marlin, and the others strode through the camp.

"How long until we're ready?" Dayne asked Tyr Arnen, High Commander of the Valtaran armies. After Alina's coronation and the events that unfolded, the decision was made to delay the attack on Achyron's Keep by a few weeks in order to allow reinforcements to arrive from Ironcreek, Skyfell, and Stormwatch. Some ten thousand souls had joined the camp over the past week, but they were still short.

"We're expecting another five thousand within the next three days, my lord." Tyr was a short man, with broad shoulders and a thick neck. His head was devoid of hair, while his beard was snow white and thick as a lion's mane. In Dayne's father's time, he'd been Redstone's master at arms. He was a simple man, and Dayne liked that. "There're another three hundred Wyndarii to be expected by midday tomorrow. They were patrolling the sea between Skyfell and Stormwatch, but as those waters are now firmly under our control, I thought it wise to call them in. I've also received word that Tordokal of House Inderes is sailing three ships along the coast filled with another four hundred warriors."

"Good. We'll need every length of steel we can find."

"That still puts our numbers at almost three thousand less than Loren has at Achyron's Keep." Ileeri, one of the Andurii captains, walked to Dayne's left alongside Barak and Urica of House Gurdur, who had been promoted to fill Odys's place. "And they have imperial forces bolstering their numbers."

"This is true," Dayne said, nodding. "But they fight for the pride of their lord and to keep the grey walls of Achyron's Keep under Lorian control. Is that worth dying for? Our warriors fight for freedom, Ileeri. We fight for our home. Never underestimate the power of a cause. That and we have something they don't have."

"What's that, my lord?"

"Wyverns, Ileeri." Mera, who walked to Dayne's right, gestured upwards, where wyverns soared over the camp, their scales glittering in the moonlight. "We have wyverns."

Ileeri gave Mera a broad smile, inclining her head. "That we do, Wyndarii."

Dayne cast his gaze over the camp as they walked. In all his days, he'd never seen something so massive. Just short of thirty-seven thousand Valtarans filled the camp. The day before, he'd climbed atop one of the ledges that overlooked the tents. The sight took his breath away, tents and campfires stretching as far as the eye could see, bronzed cuirasses glistening, wyverns soaring overhead. It was in the logistics of managing such a force that Dayne truly appreciated Tyr Arnen's expertise. Until that point, Dayne would never have believed the hardest thing about mustering an army that size would have been something as simple as putting food in their bellies. Tyr seemed to spend far more time organising supply lines than he did drilling soldiers.

"Ileeri, Urica. See to it at least half the Andurii are armoured and ready. Set up a guard rotation around the central camp throughout the night. We'll do so every night until we're ready to march." Dayne could see Tyr about to protest. "I'm not questioning your guards, Tyr. We are only days away from one of the biggest battles in Valtaran history, and we're too close to Achyron's Keep to take chances. Not to mention, after the coronation, I don't feel particularly trusting. I would rather be safe than sorry."

Tyr nodded in acquiescence, and Urica and Ileeri set off to make their arrangements.

"Alina is in the main tent?" Dayne asked Marlin. It was strange to see the man not garbed in the armour of the Andurii. But when Alina had asked Marlin to become her Archilius, she'd given him little choice but to accept, and he could not perform both roles.

Marlin inclined his head, his white-flecked hair oiled and pressed back. "She is."

"I'm assuming they're all there?" Since the coronation, Alina had kept the heads of the other Major Houses – and those of some of the larger Minor Houses – close, plying them with the finest wines and foods that could be procured. On the outside it may have looked as though she was trying to curry favour, but the truth of it was she was watching. Dayne wasn't particularly happy about it. He didn't trust most of the House heads – besides Senya Deringal and Vhin Herak – but he saw the logic in keeping them close. Wine led to loose lips, and loose lips would be needed to determine the truth of where allegiances truly lay. None of the heads of the Major Houses had shown Dayne open support during the stunt at the coronation, but just because they didn't side with him didn't mean they were happy to follow Alina. The new Valtaran nation was at a vulnerable stage. Extra care needed to be taken.

"Indeed they are."

"Guards?"

"Thirty-four within the tent, my lord," Tyr answered. "Eight at the entrance, and sixteen more stationed outside."

Dayne nodded, clasping his hands behind his back as he walked, his arm pressing against the hilt of his sword. "All Redstone guards?"

"As requested, my lord."

"Good. Mera, the Wyndarii?"

"Six guard Alina – including Amari and Lukira. One hundred are stationed atop the cliffs that overlook the camp. Sixty patrol the skies. The remainder are resting."

"All right. Let's go mingle with vipers."

THE SOUND OF MUSIC DRIFTED on the wind as Dayne and the others approached the main tent – a lute, drums, and a flute by the sound of it. Bards and musicians always reminded Dayne of Belina. He hadn't heard from her in a while, which would have worried him if it were anyone else. Hopefully he'd see her soon; he'd never admit to Belina's face, but he noticed her absence every day.

As Tyr had said, eight guards stood at the entrance of the main tent, each garbed in the bronzed armour and burnt orange skirts of Skyfell's Redstone guard. When they had marched on the campaign across Valtara, they had left a garrison at Redstone, but they had brought most with them. The Redstone guards were some of the only warriors Dayne trusted, and trust was a commodity in short supply.

"Smile," Mera whispered as they walked into the tent.

Dayne twisted his lips into a mock grin, which drew a laugh from Mera.

The tent was easily sixty feet long, maybe forty across, and over a hundred people stood about talking, eating, and drinking. There were no chairs for sitting, but small circular tables sat about the space with trays of cheeses, cold meats, and fresh fruit resting atop them. Two large casks of wine stood in the corner near the door, an attendant watching over them and filling cups. Dayne cast his gaze about, counting the guards that stood along the tent walls – thirty-four.

"They're all there, my lord." Tyr raised his bushy white eyebrows, a knowing smile on his face. "You used to do that when you were a child as well. Always counting, always checking. I once watched you walk length and breadth of the gardens, counting your steps aloud. I'm going to speak with Yulin Karine. House Karine have been breeding some of the best horses in Valtara for almost a decade now."

As Tyr walked off towards the far end of the tent, Marlin nodded to Dayne. "I promised Senya a word. I'll speak with you both later." Marlin placed his hand on Dayne's shoulder, leaning in. "She's your sister. She'll come around. You know how strong headed she is. Just have patience, and try not to say anything stupid."

"Anything stupid?"

Marlin raised an eyebrow and tilted his head, taking a few steps past Dayne. "You know exactly what I mean, Dayne."

Dayne let out a heavy sigh as Marlin walked away. After the coronation, when everything had quietened down and night had fallen, both Alina and Marlin had been furious with Dayne. They weren't the only ones, but they were the ones that mattered. He'd tried to explain, tried to tell them how he couldn't have told them what was going to happen because he couldn't have risked Turik finding out what he was doing.

Marlin had understood – eventually. He'd seen the reasoning behind Dayne's plan and agreed if Turik had found out Dayne was planning to betray him, it all might have turned out very differently. Though, he'd also pulled Dayne aside and told him he should have gone about it another way – which Dayne agreed with, in part.

Alina, however, had barely spoken to Dayne since. Even as a child, she'd always been stubborn as a mule. She stood near the centre of the tent, talking with Rinek Larka; Vhin Herak and her wife, Sara; along with a number of other members of House Deringal and Herak. Amari, Lukira, and four other Wyndarii stood around Alina, swords belted their hips. Dayne did nothing to wipe the smile from his face as he looked at Alina in her long orange and white dress, the golden sunstone crown atop her head, the markings of the blade and spear on her arms, the black ink of the Wyndarii colouring her fingers and hands. The Wyvern Queen, he'd heard some of the soldiers calling her. What their mother would have given to hear that.

As one of the attendants handed Dayne and Mera a cup of wine each, Alina lifted her head and spotted them. A smile touched her lips as she nodded to Mera but evaporated as her gaze moved to Dayne. She gave him a barely perceptible nod, then turned back to her conversation.

"I told you she wouldn't like not being told," Mera said as she plucked a grape from a tray on one of the tables, popping it into her mouth.

"I had no choice. You know that." Dayne sipped his wine, frowning as he did. It held a bit of sweetness to it, but was far too dry and sharp for his tastes. "I needed her reaction to be genuine. She's never been a good actor."

Mera nodded absently, nibbling on a small block of cheese. She eyed Dayne askance. "What are you staring at?"

"Nothing," Dayne said, smiling.

Mera knocked her hip into his, causing him to stumble. "If you keep staring at me like a puppy, I'll have to take you back to bed."

"I wouldn't argue." Dayne kept a straight face as he sipped on his wine.

Mera narrowed her eyes, then shook her head, turning back to look over the tent's occupants. "I see Rogal Baleer has finally shown his face."

Dayne followed Mera's gaze to the right side of the tent, where young Rogal Baleer stood talking to two men and women Dayne didn't recognise – likely members of some of the Minor Houses. He let out a sigh, draining the contents of his cup and gesturing for an attendant to refill it . "He's head of House Baleer now."

"You did what needed to be done, Dayne. We couldn't allow Turik to continue spreading doubts and garnering support. The man's ambition knew no bounds. He used you as a figurehead, but had you not returned, he would have challenged Alina anyway. You protected your sister. You protected Valtara, Dayne."

Dayne nodded, his gaze shifting from Rogal to Aldon Thebal – the new head of House Thebal. Dayne had killed Aldon's father, Miron, during the siege of Myrefall. Dayne held no love for Miron – the man was a coward and had sold out his people to the empire – but Aldon was not his father. The boy had seen only sixteen summers. "I've killed the fathers of two young men in this room. Two young Valtarans – the people I swore to protect."

"Miron opened docks in Myrefall to imperial ships. He called Alina a warmonger. He was as much our enemy as the Lorian Empire. Again, you did what needed to be done."

"Why is it that what needs to be done is always killing?" Dayne glanced at Mera, raising an eyebrow, then looked at his hands. The hands that would never be clean.

Mera's expression softened, and she reached up, resting her hand atop his, sliding her fingers between the gaps. "That won't always be the way, Dayne. There will be a day where we sit at the edge of the Abaddian cliffs, the sunset glistening off the water, the sweet smell of oranges in the air, our ears filled with the sound of children playing. That is why we fight. So that one day we don't have to."

Tears wet Dayne's eyes, but none fell. He pulled Mera's hand to his lips and kissed her fingers. "You said children – more than one."

"It was a figure of speech, Dayne."

"You said it." Dayne smiled, squeezing Mera's hand softly before letting it go.

"Dayne Ateres, Andurios. And Mera Vardas. How is the night treating you?" Dayne had been so distracted by Mera he hadn't seen Tula Vakira approach. The woman stood with her arms folded, a cup of wine in her right hand. She wore a black tunic tied with a white leather belt. Her blonde hair was tied back into a ponytail, black spiral tattoos covered the shaved sides of her head.

Dayne and Mera both greeted Tula, inclining their heads.

"The night is well, I hope it is the same for you." Dayne held the woman's gaze.

"It is, it is. This much wine and cheese would make any night a good one." She picked up a slice of hard Gadeer cheese, breaking it in half with her teeth. Once she'd finished the first half, she tossed the second half into her mouth. "I know you're not much of a talker. But I came to say what you did at the coronation… I want you to know that House Vakira will stand behind you no matter what."

Dayne looked at Tula curiously. "You took your time to come to Alina's side, Tula. In fact, I believe it took a siege on your city for you to make up your mind. What has changed?"

"I took my time, young Ateres, because I had a Lorian blade at my throat." Tula frowned, narrowed her gaze at Dayne, then let out a sigh. "What has changed is that for the first time in my life I truly feel that a free Valtara is possible. Your sister is a woman who will do anything to bring these Houses together. And you are a man who will do anything to keep her alive. The problem our people have always faced is our unwillingness to come together. The Houses have always fought – even before The Fall. While we are divided we can never be strong. And so, long live the Wyvern Queen."

Tula raised her cup, and Dayne and Mera followed.

"Long live the Wyvern Queen."

Tula turned and said something to Mera, but the words faded to the back of Dayne's mind as a man passed him in the armour and skirts of the Redstone guard.

"Dayne?" Mera tapped him on the shoulder. "Dayne, what do you think?"

"Who's that?" Dayne nodded towards the Redstone guard who was making his way through the crowd towards the other side of the tent.

"I don't know. What does it matter?"

"I don't recognise his face." Dayne placed his cup on the table beside him and took a step forward.

"Why does that matter?" Tula asked

"I know all the Redstone guards." When Dayne finally came back to Redstone, he made a personal promise to learn the names and faces of each member of the Redstone guard. The night his parents died, two imposters had posed as Redstone guards and tried to sweep Alina away into the night. He had vowed to never let anything like that happen again. Dayne turned back to Mera. "Tell one of the guards outside to rouse the Andurii."

"Dayne, I—"

"Mera, don't question me." Dayne's voice was firmer than he'd intended, but he made no apologies. "Go."

Mera's face hardened. She nodded, then made for the tent's entrance.

Tula said something to Dayne, but he ignored her and walked after the guard, who was now making his way towards Alina. Dayne picked up his pace, dropping his right hand low so it hovered near his sword. His heart thumped, the skin on his arms prickling. He pushed past a man and woman having an argument. The sounds of the music and the talking became muffled, fading to the back of Dayne's mind as he drew closer to the guard.

He placed his hand on the man's shoulder. "Guard, your name?"

As the man turned, a shriek erupted from behind Dayne. Cries and gasps rang out. Dayne turned to see Senya Deringal clutching her throat, blood spilling down over green and gold robes. The woman stumbled backwards, eyes wide, veins bulging in her face. She collapsed backwards, smashing through a table.

There was a moment when everything went quiet and nobody moved. Dayne's gaze fell on the woman who stood where Senya had been standing, a bloody knife grasped in her fist – Reinan Sarr. She had been one of those Mera had warned Dayne about the day he'd announced his return.

Another shriek and the tent descended into chaos. Everywhere Dayne looked, knives and swords were being pulled, throats slit, lives ended.

"Death to House Ateres!"

Dayne spun. The man who had been posing as a Redstone guard stabbed at him with a knife. Dayne jerked back. He snatched at the man's knife hand, then rammed a closed fist down into his jaw. Bone crunched beneath the weight of Dayne's strike. He brought his fist down, hammering it into the pit of the man's knife arm while peeling back the fingers and prying the knife free. Shock painted the man's face as Dayne drove the knife up through the bottom of his jaw. Dayne yanked the blade free, and the body dropped to the ground.

Alina.

Dayne ripped his sword from its scabbard, keeping the knife in his left hand. Alina stood at the centre of the tent, her six Wyndarii standing about her with their swords drawn.

"No!" Alina cried, pushing through her Wyndarii and pulling a knife from somewhere within her dress.

Dayne followed Alina's gaze to watch as the young Rogal Baleer drove a sword through Vhin Herak's gut, twisting as he pushed it through. Beside him, one of Reinan Sarr's sisters stabbed a knife into Sara Herak's neck, pulling it free in spurts of blood, then ramming it back in.

Cries rang out from the front of the tent, the eight guards stationed outside charging in. But as the guards entered, Dayne felt a tingle on the back of his neck – the sensation of someone drawing from the Spark. Threads of Air gathered on the far side of the tent, and then, faster than Dayne's eyes could follow, small metallic objects streaked across the tent and punched through the guards in plumes of bloodmist. All eight of them fell, their bodies sluicing blood.

Dayne had seen that same manoeuvre enough times to know the weapons used were Hand throwing stars. He broke into a sprint, twisting as a blade was thrust towards him. He stabbed his knife into the neck of his attacker without halting his run, leaving the blade lodged in place. Another tingle of the Spark and Dayne threw himself to the floor, hearing the *whoosh* as the throwing stars sliced through the air above him. He scrambled to his feet, finding himself staring into the eyes of a man who wore the green and gold of House Deringal, but was quite clearly no Valtaran.

The assassin sent a whip of Air towards Dayne's legs, but Dayne sliced through the threads with Spirit. He closed the distance between them in two heartbeats. The man pulled a long knife free from a sheath at his hip and swung.

Dayne pushed forwards, moving inside the assassin's guard. He threw his left arm forwards, ramming his fist into the man's gut. As the assassin lurched forwards, Dayne leaned back and drove his sword up through the bottom of the man's chin. The blade burst up and out through the man's mouth, bone scraping, teeth snapping, blood spurting. Dayne ripped his sword free, shivering involuntarily at the sound of steel screeching off bone.

He turned to feel a battering ram of Air slam into his chest. The force of the blow lifted him off his feet and sent him careening into a tent pole, feeling the wood snap from the impact. Dayne groaned, rolling on his back, the coppery taste of blood on his tongue. *Get up.* He clenched his jaw, pulling himself to an upright position to see two women standing over him, blades in their hands, threads of Air and Earth whirling around them.

Dayne reached for the Spark, but as he did, the steel tip of a spear burst through the neck of the woman on the right, a second spear punching through the other woman's gut. As the spears were wrenched free and the bodies collapsed, two warriors in the armour of the Andurii stepped forwards: Iloen Akaida and Juna Toradin – the woman Alina had once set to watch over Dayne.

Iloen hauled Dayne to his feet. "Andurios." He gave a sharp nod, switching his spear to his shield hand and shrugging another shield from his back, handing it to Dayne.

Dayne slid his arm through the leather strap of his father's shield, gripping the handle near the rim. "My thanks, Iloen."

"Dayne!"

Dayne turned at the sound of Mera's voice. She marched into the tent, tossing him a spear which he snatched out of the air. A glance around the tent told him the attackers were all dead, but so were many others. Tables were shattered, bodies littered the ground, and blood fed the earth.

Dayne moved to where Alina and her Wyndarii still stood at the centre of the tent, swords drawn. Marlin, Tula Vakira, Rinek Larka, and a number of other nobles from both Major and Minor Houses stood around them. "Are you hurt?"

"I'm fine." The tremble in Alina's voice told Dayne his sister was far from fine. Her gaze trailed over the dead bodies. "Senya… Vhin… Tyr… they're all dead. So many dead."

Dayne moved his spear into his shield hand and stepped past Lukira, clasping his hand to Alina's cheek. He turned his sister's head towards him, meeting her gaze. "But you're still alive. We will mourn later. Now we need to take control of the situation. Understood?"

Alina nodded, her usual confidence and surety drained from her. Senya had been like a second mother to Alina. The woman had even helped to deliver her.

"I'm here, Alina." Dayne pulled her face closer, staring into her eyes. "I'm here. By blade and by blood I am your sword. Now we need to move." Dayne turned to see more Andurii flooding into the tent. Two of his captains – Ileeri and Dinekes – pushed to the front. "What's our situation?"

"Attacks all over the camp, Andurios." Blood was splattered across Dinekes's helm and shield. "Thebalan and Koraklon colours mostly, but many of the Minor Houses as well. Lorian mages are inside the boundary – Hand assassins by the looks of it. And…" Dinekes hesitated.

"What?"

"Wyverns, Andurios. I can't tell how many, but they're fighting in the sky."

"Hera Malik," Alina hissed. The muscles in her jaw twitched, and she started forwards.

Dayne put his hand on Alina's shoulder. "Where are you going?"

"I'm going to mount Rynvar and tear that bitch from the sky. You were right, I should have killed her. A mistake I won't make again."

"I can't keep you safe in the sky, Alina."

"I don't need you to keep me safe, Dayne. You're my sword, not my shield. I need you to make them bleed. My Wyndarii and I will clear the skies. You clear the ground." She moved closer. "Together."

"Together," Dayne said with a nod.

The shrieks and cries of wyverns filled the skies as Dayne and the others emerged from the main tent. All three hundred and fifty of Dayne's Andurii stood in the space before the tent, ordo shields and valynas gripped in their fists.

Dayne could see fire blazing all about the camp, the sound of colliding steel blending with shouts and screams.

"I will bleed them slow for this," Alina growled, looking about at the chaos. "Why? We are so close to what we've been fighting for. Why now?"

"Some can't see past their own desires, my Queen." Marlin rested his hand on Alina's shoulder. "This is your first test. Show them who you are."

Alina nodded slowly. "By blade and by blood. Dayne you—"

A piercing shriek cut Alina short as a wyvern with dark brown scales dropped from the sky and hurtled towards them, talons outstretched.

Dayne opened himself to the Spark, pulling on threads of Air. He threw back his shoulder and made to launch his spear, but as he did, a roar erupted from behind him.

Rynvar's orange scales glinted in the light of the fires as he swept overhead and crashed into the brown wyvern. Rynvar wrapped one talon around the creature's neck, the other slicing into its side. As he ripped the wyvern from the sky, Rynvar opened his jaws and tore the rider clean in half, blood sprinkling down like crimson rain. A cloud of dust plumed as Rynvar slammed the other wyvern into the ground, tearing out its throat.

Five more wyverns dropped around Rynvar. Two with Wyndarii on their backs, three riderless. Dayne recognised the riderless wyverns as Syndil, Urin, and Audin – those bonded to Amari, Lukira, and Mera.

Alina ran towards Rynvar, Dayne and the others following after her.

"My Queen!" One of the Wyndarii called from the back of her wyvern. "Koraklon and Lorian forces are advancing from the east. Tens of thousands."

"Fuck!" Alina roared. "That's what they've done? They've cut a deal with Loren and the empire. Burn them all. Cowards!"

"Alina." Dayne moved his head to catch Alina's gaze. "Alina, we need to sound the retreat. We can't organise in this chaos. It will be a slaughter."

"Retreat?" Alina glared at Dayne, fury pulsing from her in waves, her voice growing louder. "Retreat? Have you lost your mind? We will not let them win here."

"They've already won, Alina. Senya is dead, as is Vhin, Tyr, and countless others. They've only won the battle, not the war. If you let them goad you into fighting here, they will take everything."

"Dayne is right." Marlin gestured at the burning tents. "If we stay and fight, we play into their hands. This move was calculated, my Queen. They targeted you and your allies. They've thrown us into disarray, cut the heads off House Deringal and Herak. We need to be smart. Sound the retreat, fall back through the pass between the cliffs on the west. You clear the skies, we'll light the way for our forces. Our task now is keeping as many alive as we can. It's simple, Alina. Fight and die, or fall back, lose the battle, but have a chance at winning the war."

"Fuck." Alina clenched her jaw, shaking her head. "Gods dammit. All right. Go." Alina gestured towards Tula Vakira and the other nobles – among which were Tula's son, Vhin Herak's three sisters, and Senya's niece. "Keep them safe, Dayne."

Dayne nodded. "By blade and by blood."

As Alina marched off to mount Rynvar, Mera pulled at Dayne's shoulder. She cupped her hands around his cheeks and pulled him in, pressing her lips against his. "Remember," she said, pulling away. "We fight so that one day we don't have to. I love you, Dayne."

"With all my heart." Dayne kissed Mera on the forehead, and she ran to Audin, climbing up his back and buckling herself in before he lifted into the air.

Dayne drew in a calming breath. He could feel the rage rising within him, simmering in his blood. Everything felt like it did the night Loren betrayed them all those years ago. Once again, Valtarans were turning their backs on each other, spilling their own blood, and the only one who benefitted was the empire. He would not let it break his House again. Dayne didn't push the rage away, he embraced it, letting it burn in his heart.

"Andurii," Dayne bellowed at the top of his lungs, beating his spear off his shield.

The Andurii all stood to attention, spears smacking off shields, followed by the response, "Andurios."

The flickering light of the burning tents shimmered off the Andurii shields, the wyvern of House Ateres emblazoned across their front in white. "The lines have been drawn! Those who would stand against us, those who would stand against a free Valtara, have stepped from the shadows." Dayne walked closer to the front line of the Andurii, casting his gaze over the warriors who had slowly grown to be like brothers and sisters to him. Men and women he would be proud to die beside. "You are the Andurii of House Ateres. You are the spears of Valtara. The Lorians will learn to fear your name!"

"AH-OOH!"

The response sent a shiver through Dayne, spears cracking off shields. He remembered watching the Andurii when he was a child, remembered hearing the stories of legend. Now they were his Andurii. He stood where his father once stood. "We march for the western pass. Protect all who stand in Alina's name. Those who stand against us, die. Valtara will be free by blade and by blood." Dayne reached out to one of his captains, Barak, who stood with what looked to be Dayne's helmet beneath the crook of his arm. Barak handed Dayne the white-crested helmet, and Dayne slid it into place, the steel cool against his skin. He dropped his voice. "Do not hesitate. Do not contemplate mercy."

THE HORNS OF RETREAT BELLOWED in the night as Dayne, Marlin, the other nobles, and the Andurii cut their way through the camp.

Sweat slicked Dayne's body, covering his arms and dripping off his nose. He drew in long, slow breaths, his feet hammering against the ground. As they moved, Dayne reached out to the Spark, pulling on threads of Air and Spirit, feeling the cool touch of Air tickle his skin. He weaved the threads into his voice, calling out, "We make for the western pass! Fall back!"

His voice boomed through the air, loud as thunder, echoing off the cliffs that overlooked the camp. The horns were well enough, but in the midst of chaos, the clearer the retreat the more lives would be saved.

"Andurios!" Ileeri pointed to the left, where a group of men and women clutching ordo shields and valynas charged from between a clutch of tents. Their skirts were the green and gold of House Deringal.

Dayne tightened his fingers around the haft of his valyna. "Declare yourselves!"

"House Deringal." A tall woman stepped forwards, a bronzed cuirass guarding her chest, the markings of spearmaster on her right arm. "We are going to Senya Deringal. Then we make for the western pass."

"Senya is dead," Dayne called back. "Killed by the traitors. Anda is now head of House Deringal." Dayne gestured to Senya's niece, Anda.

Anda Deringal stepped forwards, tears streaking down her face, her eyes raw from crying. She was Alina's age, with two markings of the spear and shield. She was kind but timid. Though Dayne realised she had just watched her entire family die: her mother, her father, her sister, her aunt. "It is true. My aunt is dead. They're all dead."

"Then we follow you, my lady." The tall woman looked over Dayne and the Andurii, a recognition in her eyes. "Andurios. I am Olivian of House Arnon. We are the Queen's spears, we're with you."

Dayne nodded. "Then let's keep moving."

More stragglers joined as Dayne and the others made their way across the enormous camp towards the western pass. Though not all that approached them were friends, and those who weren't now lay dead in the dirt.

"It looks as though many of the Wyndarii favour the queen." Dayne followed Tula Vakira's gaze to the sky. Rynvar was twice the size of most other wyverns, and his orange scales glittered in the firelight as he soared overhead. Even from the ground it was clear to see that far more wyverns flew at Rynvar's back than against him.

"Hera had maybe sixty to her cause," Marlin said, studying the sky as they moved. "And Reinan Sarr had garnered favour with many of the Minor Houses."

"Their blood will feed the earth," Dayne said with a growl, pulling his gaze from the sky. He could see the western pass ahead, a clear strip of open ground between it and them with tents rising on either side. *Only about six hundred feet.*

A high pitched screech stung Dayne's ears.

"Wyverns!" one of the Andurii called out.

Dayne turned to see a blue scaled wyvern drop from the sky and snatch two Andurii in its talons, shredding them like parchment. The creature cracked its wings, rising again without ever touching the ground. A second wyvern plummeted, ripping one of the Deringal spearmen in half with its jaws, then caving in a noble's skull with a flick of its tail. The creature cut through five of the Deringal warriors before it made to rise, but the Andurii spears plunged through its scaled hide. Steel sliced again and again, the creature shrieking and howling as it collapsed, crushing two men beneath it.

The Wyndarii, still buckled to the wyvern's saddle, howled and groaned. She pulled at her buckles, blood pouring from a wound in her leg.

Dayne looked at the woman, then to Iloen, who stood over her. "Do not hesitate. Do not contemplate mercy."

Iloen nodded, then drove his spear down into the woman's chest, stopping her cries.

More screeches and roars rang out, and Dayne saw a number of wyverns turn in the sky, angling downwards towards them.

"Must be the white crests," Marlin said leaning in. "We're moving targets for them."

"Let them come," Barak said, shifting his spear into an overhand grip. "I don't have wings, so it's easier to kill them if they come to me." The big man rolled his neck side to side, bones cracking.

Three wyverns swooped down in formation, staying close, then spreading. One banked left, the other right.

"Barak, Thuram, Tarine, aim for the middle one. The rest of you hold your spears. We can't afford to lose them."

As the wyverns drew closer, Thuram launched his spear into the air. The spear swept past the middle wyvern's flank as the creature rolled in the air. Barak and Tarine threw at the same time. Barak's spear skittered off the wyvern's scales, but as the creature swept left to avoid it, Tarine's spear punched clean through its neck. The wyvern spun and tumbled in the air, its wings flapping in the wind, blood spurting as it shrieked. And then, by some divine intervention, it collided with the second wyvern that moved to attack the group from the left. Both beasts slammed into a blazing tent, shrieks and cries ringing out as the sparks burst upwards.

As the Andurii cheered, the third wyvern, with scales of bright green, crashed down. Its talons tore through three Andurii, ripping the life from their bodies. A swing of its tail caught Thuram in the ribs, his body dropping limp. The Wyndarii on the wyvern's back launched a javelin, taking one of Vhin Herak's sisters through the chest. A second sweep of its tail and three more warriors fell, and then, with a crack of its wings, the wyvern lifted into the air.

Another roar. Dayne looked up to see Mera's wyvern, Audin, soaring overhead. The creature's red scales shimmered, its wings spreading wide. Dayne's heart clenched as his gaze fell on Mera sitting at the nape of Audin's neck, a javelin gripped in her fist. Audin collided with the green wyvern, tearing it from the air in a cloud of blood. Talons raked and jaws snapped. Dayne watched as Mera twisted, a javelin soaring past her head. She pulled herself upright in her saddle, then launched her own javelin in return. The weapon slammed into the other Wyndarii's face, bursting through her eye. She went limp, flopping backwards in her saddle, only held in place by her straps.

Audin slammed the green scaled wyvern into the dirt, clamped his jaws around its head, and ripped its lower jaw free in a spray of blood. The wyvern stood over his prey for a fleeting moment, then unleashed a monstrous roar, blood and spit spraying from his maw.

The Andurii and the others with them all cheered, roaring as they thrust their spears in the air. Pride swelled in Dayne's chest as he looked at Mera. She looked like the Wyndarii of old.

"Keep moving," Mera shouted as Audin climbed off the body of the dead wyvern. Mera looked to Dayne. "The way to the pass is clear. The

Lorian and Koraklon forces are still moving across the camp from the east. We'll try and keep the wyverns off you."

Without waiting for a response, Mera and Audin lifted into the air, spirals of dust sweeping up in their wake.

Dayne and the others hadn't made it fifty feet before another piercing shriek erupted and a wyvern swept towards them from behind. Dayne recognised the green-tinged yellow scales of Hera Malik's wyvern, Yarsil. The creature's eyes gleamed in the firelight as he soared towards them, but then at the last second, Yarsil pulled up, letting out a high pitched shriek as he did. Dayne followed the creature's flight, a gust of wind sweeping over him.

"They're coming back around!" Dayne called out.

"Dayne!"

Dayne turned at the sound of Tula Vakira's voice. His blood turned to ice.

He dropped his shield and spear to the dirt, his legs feeling like lead as he took a step forwards. Marlin knelt on the ground, his hands clasped around the shaft of a javelin that protruded from his chest. Blood spilled around the wood, seeping into Marlin's robes, staining them crimson.

Dayne crashed to the ground beside Marlin, catching the man before he fell on his side. He held the back of Marlin's head with his left hand, his right hand keeping the man steady. "Marlin, it's all right. It's…"

Marlin's head lolled in Dayne's hand, the life gone from his eyes. Around him, Dayne heard screams and shouts as more wyverns descended, but his sole focus was on Marlin. He wanted to speak, but all his lips did was tremble. Memories flooded his mind: Marlin handing him his first practice sword, teaching him his first form, picking him up every time he fell. Marlin Arkon had been a second father to Dayne. He had never faltered. He'd saved Dayne and Alina's life in Redstone. He brought Alina and Baren to safety. He watched over Alina all these years, guided her, protected her, taught her. He deserved better. Tears streaked through the dirt and blood that coated Dayne's face. Tears of sorrow. Tears of rage. He reached his hand forward and closed Marlin's eyes. "I swear to you, I will kill them all. I will tear them apart, and I will feed Valtara with their blood. We *will* be free, Marlin. I promise. Thank you. Thank you for always believing in me… even when I didn't."

Marlin's words echoed in Dayne's ears as he laid the man on his side. *It doesn't matter what anyone thinks of you. Show them who you are.*

Dayne rested his hand on Marlin's shoulder. He took one last look at the man who'd helped raise him, then rose to his feet, his blood turning to fire in his veins. Hera Malik's wyvern, Yarsil, swept across the sky overhead, circling back around for another pass.

A hand grasped at Dayne's shoulder. Barak's lips were moving, but Dayne heard nothing apart from the beating of his heart and the screeching of the wyverns. He moved past Barak and snatched up his shield and spear, walking towards the approaching wyvern.

Dayne drew in slow breaths as he stared at the yellow-scaled creature hurtling towards him. He pulled back his shoulder and launched his spear through the air. Yarsil rolled, but the steel still cut a bloody furrow through his flank.

Yarsil dropped lower, unleashing a monstrous shriek, eyes fixed on Dayne. Hera Malik sat at the nape of the wyvern's neck, a javelin in her hand. Yarsil dipped his head, and Hera launched the javelin.

Dayne watched the weapon's flight, then shifted his feet and hefted his shield at an angle. A thud vibrated through his arm as the javelin bounced off the shield's rim, skittering away. Lowering the shield, Dayne kept his eyes fixed on Yarsil. *'A hunter never looks away,'* he could hear Belina saying.

Dayne opened himself to the Spark. He let his anger simmer and boil, his jaw clenching, fingers twisting into a fist so tight it pained him. *I will not run again.* Dayne let out a breath. *I am Dayne Ateres.* He pulled on each elemental strand, letting them flow through him like rivers. He funnelled the threads into his hand: Earth, Fire, Water, Air, Spirit. The power of the Spark thrummed through him, pulsing in waves. "This is my home."

Energy surged through Dayne as the words left his lips. Tendrils of white light burst from his hand in both directions, winding around themselves. Energy crackled over his skin like lightning as the tendrils weaved together, leaving a solid form in their wake. Within moments, Dayne held a spear of coruscating white light in his hand. A níthral. *A Soulblade.*

Yarsil let out a shriek at the sight of the níthral and tried to pull up, but Dayne stepped forwards, rolled his shoulder back, and launched his níthral through the air. The white spear plunged into the wyvern's chest as he tried to rise, bursting out the other side in a mist of blood and gore. As the wyvern dropped from the sky and the spear of white glistened in the dark, Dayne released his hold on the níthral.

As soon as the spear faded from existence, Dayne summoned it once more, drawing deeper on threads of each element. The white spear burst into life in his hand once more as Yarsil crashed to the ground before him.

Dirt and dust lifted as the wyvern slid across the earth, the life drained from his body. His soul sheared.

Dayne walked forwards, watching as Hera scrambled to undo her straps. The woman fumbled with the buckles, glancing up towards Dayne with every step he took. She undid the last buckle and fell from the creature's back, gasping as she hit the ground. Hera tried to push herself to her feet, but Dayne stepped forwards and planted his foot square in her chest, knocking her onto her back.

Dayne moved so he stood over Hera, the white light of his níthral illuminating her blood splattered face. "You deserve nothing, Hera Malik. May your soul wander the void until time breaks."

Hera lifted her hands, but Dayne drove his níthral down through her chest, staring into her eyes as the light left them. He pulled the spear free, releasing it, then turned back towards the others.

Dayne stood there for a moment, looking at the shock and awe on the faces of the Andurii, the nobles, and the other warriors who had joined them. "Make for the pass," he called out. "This war has only begun."

Chapter Seventy

To Learn Your Place

Antigan Ocean – Summer, Year 3081 After Doom

Ella looked out over the glistening water of the Antigan Ocean, the summer sun blazing overhead, the ship swaying beneath her. The sound of waves breaking against the ship's bow was cut by the sharp squawks of gulls overhead. It had taken over a month to cross Loria and get a riverboat from Catagan to the coast. Another two weeks had passed since then. The journey would have been easier if she wasn't travelling with two groups who refused to talk.

A low rumble sounded to Ella's right, and she leaned her head sideways without looking, feeling the rough brush of Faenir's fur against her cheek. The wolfpine was so large now his head stood almost at a measure with Ella's. She smiled as he rested his chin on the ship's rail, staring out at the ocean with her. "We'll see him soon, boy." She had to reach her hand up to scratch the crown of his head, receiving a grumble of satisfaction. "I promise."

Footsteps clapped against the wooden deck, and Yana appeared to Ella's left. She folded her arms across the rail and rested her chin atop her hands, mimicking Faenir. The woman looked at the wolfpine, pursing her lips. Faenir didn't move, but his eyes shifted to look at her. He let out a low growl.

"Stop being so grumpy," Yana said, scratching him on the nose. She stood to her full height, resting her palms on the rails. After a moment, she turned and leaned back, looking over the other side of the ship. "You know, if you look starboard you can see the outline of Wolfpine Ridge in the distance."

Ella nodded, smiling. "Honestly, I'd rather not look. It's easier to be so close if I don't look."

Yana reached her left hand over and rested it atop Ella's. "Your parents would have been proud of the person you've become, Ella. I know that for a fact because I am, and I've not known you nearly as long as they have."

Yana let out a sigh, then rested her hand on Ella's shoulder and kissed her cheek. "We'll get you to Calen, don't worry. But just remember—"

"If any harm comes to Tanner, you'll kill me in my sleep – I know."

"What? No, that big idiot's old enough to be responsible for his own safety for once. No, what I was going to say was to remember that no matter what, you're not alone. Now, Ilyain is on cooking duty tonight. And I know Tanner and Farda are doing that whole 'broody no talking' thing, but you remember what happened the last time we left the blind elf to cook alone. We don't need another fire. And seeing as Farda and Hala don't seem interested in helping him, I'm going to go be his eyes."

"What's for supper?" Ella asked as Yana walked away.

"Same thing as every night for the last two weeks. Fish, potatoes, an apple, and an orange. Smuggling ships aren't known for their cuisine."

Ella laughed as Yana walked towards the other end of the ship, disappearing below deck. Despite what had happened in the Lorian camp, Ella had actually come to appreciate Ilyain's company. The elf spoke twice as much as Farda and Hala combined. Over the course of their journey, he had spent many a night talking to Ella of druids and of his 'Ayar Elwyn', Andras. *Ayar Elwyn – One Heart*. That phrase only ever made Ella think of Rhett. There were days when she missed him so desperately her lungs refused to draw breath, and her heart ached. Sometimes when she closed her eyes she could feel his thumb rubbing her cheek; she could see the way he smiled with his eyes.

Ella sniffed, wiping her tears away. "Were you just waiting for her to leave?"

She didn't have to look to know Farda stood behind her; his scent filled Faenir's nostrils.

"Honestly?" Farda didn't move. "She scares me."

"*She* scares *you*?" Ella shook her head, then turned to face Farda, leaning against the rail. She put on her best Farda impression, dropping her voice low and talking as though she'd spent her life gargling stones. "My name is Farda Kyrana, Justicar of the Imperial Battlemages. I can't feel any pain and I like to stand around being dark and broody. I'm also scared of a woman half my size."

Farda looked past Ella, his gaze fixed on the shifting waves. After a few moments, a half-smile cracked through his stony expression. "She's not half my size," he said as he moved towards the rail to Ella's left. "And she's the type of woman who'd cut you to pieces in your sleep for crossing her."

Ella smiled weakly as she looked at Farda, who stared out at the water with his hands clasped behind his back. The man had said a lot to her that night Yana, Tanner, and Farwen had found them – and then barely anything since.

'I don't know what it is you've done to me, but when you're near, I don't feel so fucking broken.'

Those words had twisted Ella's heart and shaken her to her core. For the first time since she'd met the man, she'd actually seen *him* and not the armour he wore every day to shield himself from the world. And it was in that moment of pure vulnerability, as he trembled and shook, she had seen how appropriate that title – Rakina – truly was.

'You're shattered. Your soul is shredded and splintered, its many fragments thrown to the wind. You are nothing, you are nobody. All you feel is empty, and cold, and wrong.'

"Farda?"

Farda raised an eyebrow.

"Back in Loria, when you, Ilyain, and Hala decided to come with me, you told them that they didn't need to come. You told them 'this journey does not end happily'. What did you mean? What are you not telling me?"

Farda sighed through his nose, looking at the waves that crashed against the ship's hull. "You know the stories, Ella. Now that you know who I am, *what* I am, I'm sure you can piece it together."

"I don't want stories. I want the truth."

Farda nodded. "I betrayed the people who trusted me. I killed many of them. When we get to where we're going, they're going to want to return the favour."

Ella stared at Farda, her gaze unwavering. Her throat tightened, and a fist clenched in her chest. She wasn't naïve enough to believe she could see something in Farda that others couldn't. She knew he was a man capable of great anger and terrible things. But she also knew he was capable of good. She remembered how Coren had told her that Farda had once been the Draleid her master held up as an example of what a warrior should be. *'Not in how they should fight, but in how they should carry themselves, in how they should treat those they protect.'* But she also remembered Coren had said that a year before The Fall, Farda changed. *What happened to you?*

"Why?"

"Why what?"

"Why did you betray them if they were your friends, if they trusted you?"

Farda glanced at Ella, his gaze lingering for a moment before he looked back at the ocean. "They took something from me. Something they had no right to take."

❧

RIST SAT WITH ONE LEG folded over the other at the top of a small hill that overlooked the Beronan Lake. His back rested against a satchel and a blanket roll as he watched the reflection of the setting sun paint the water a mesmerising shade of orange. He'd been there for a few hours, reading. While travelling to Steeple before the battle at The Three Sisters, he'd not had much opportunity to read, but on the journey to Berona, and the weeks they'd been waiting, he'd made sure to find the time.

He'd been on the last page of *Druids, a Magic Lost* since just before the sun had begun to set behind the Lodhar Mountains to the west. Rist always found there was something bittersweet about finishing a book. The sense of achievement and joy was often tarnished by the realisation that he could never read it the same way again. He could, of course, start from page one and read through to the end, but it wouldn't be the same. His preconceptions and notions were irrevocably altered by the first read. It was simply the way of things.

And so, Rist delayed reading the last page. Instead, he sat forward, folded over the corner of the page, laid the book down on the satchel behind him, and turned to look at the landscape. Tents of varying sizes skirted the edges of the Beronan lake for miles, stretching from the walls of Berona to the southern edge of the water. Garramon had said sixteen armies had already arrived with another five more on their way. That would make one hundred and five thousand soldiers. Not only that, but Rist had seen three of the Dragonguard flying over the city – Ilkya, Voranur, and Jormun judging by the colouring of the dragons' scales.

Whatever the emperor had called them all to Berona for, it was something enormous. After what had happened at The Three Sisters, Rist logically would have thought it would have something to do with the elves. But if that was the case, surely the armies would be marching towards Steeple, not Berona. What's more, Rist had heard from one of the cavalrymen that eighty thousand had been sent south from Al'Nasla to Gisa only a few weeks back while the First Army was still marching to Berona. That meant the emperor was planning a major move in both the North and the South.

"You've finished it then?"

Rist turned to see Garramon walking up the other side of the hill, Magnus and Anila at his side. For some reason Magnus had committed to not shaving the unburnt half of his beard, and strangely it was kind of starting to suit him.

"What is it with you two and books?" Magnus snatched up *Druids, a Magic Lost* and flicked disinterestedly through the pages. "He was always the same, you know?" Magnus tilted his head towards Garramon. "His head stuck in books." Magnus lay the book back on the satchel and strolled down the hill a few feet, gesturing out towards the lake which, in the light of the setting sun, now looked like sparkling fire. "If you lift your head from the pages, there's much more interesting things to look at."

"You're just bitter because you can't read," Anila said, picking up a stick and throwing it at the back of Magnus's head. She turned to Rist, a half-smile touching her lips. "The robes suit you, *Brother Havel*."

Rist looked down at the black robes draped over his shoulders, running his hand along the soft fabric. Garramon had only been able to get them from the High Tower the day before last. Rist had actually forgotten he was wearing them. "Thank you, Sister."

Anila inclined her head, her smile lingering as she moved to join Magnus where he looked out at the water.

Rist cupped his hand over his eyes to block out the sunlight as he looked up at Garramon. The man raised an eyebrow, and Rist realised he'd never answered his question. "Last page."

"What do you think then? All babble by the end?"

Rist picked up the book, tapping his finger off the cover. "I think it would be easy to believe so, without the proper context."

Garramon smiled. "And what is the proper context?"

"That druids are not dead. Ella is a druid. Everything Ella was capable of doing – her eyes changing, her teeth sharpening, the way she controlled the owl – reinforced what Duran claimed about Aldruids. And so that fact lends validity to some of Duran's other claims."

"Very good," Garramon said with a nod before turning to look at the sunset. "Reading without context is like eating without swallowing. I may have to read it again." Garramon let out a soft sigh. "We have just come from a council with Fane. Once the Forty-Second, Twenty-First, Eighteenth, Eleventh, and Eighth armies arrive, we will be moving to the Dead Tower."

"What are we going there for?"

"The Blood Moon is almost upon us. With its coming, The Saviour will provide everything we need to drive back the elves and the Uraks. We will end this war, Rist. Swiftly and without hesitation. Then we can return to keeping the peace."

Rist looked up at Garramon. There was a fervour in the man's eyes, an intensity that sparkled in the light of the setting sun. "Garramon, what precisely does 'provide everything we need' mean? What are we doing?"

Garramon lowered himself to the grass beside Rist. He pulled his knees towards his chest and leaned forwards. "As the Blood Moon draws closer, the veil between our world and the world of the gods grows thinner. The heralds are Efialtír's warriors in the gods' world. But they are no more than simple soldiers. There are others more powerful, who, with the right aid, can cross over into this world. The Chosen. When the Blood Moon rises, we can be the ones to aid in their crossing. We can be the ones who earn their trust." Garramon looked to Rist, raising his eyebrow. "You're unsure?"

Rist looked out over the sparkling water and let out a sigh. "There's too much I don't know." Talking about the gods was always a precarious topic in the North. Rist still remembered Tommin's furious response when Rist referred to Efialtír as The Traitor and not The Saviour. But Garramon had always encouraged him to talk openly. The man was a creature of logic, like Rist. "I've never cared much for gods," he said. "Their existence has always mattered little. They don't affect where I sleep or what I eat, or the things I care about. What's more, I've always known Efialtír as The Traitor. But this…" Rist reached beneath his robes and pulled out the glowing gemstone that sat around his neck. "This changes everything."

"What have you seen of Efialtír?" Garramon held Rist's gaze.

"What do you mean?"

"What have you seen? Have you seen a single thing in your entire life that would earn the name traitor? I would wager not. Yet, while you've been here, you've seen how his gift of Essence allows the recycling of life. You've seen how after the battle, many of the Healers used Essence harnessed from the fighting to heal the wounded. Yes, you've seen the destruction it can cause, but that is no different than the Spark or dragonfire."

Rist nodded slowly, letting Garramon's words percolate.

"You saw what the elves are capable of at The Three Sisters. You saw the power they had. And you've seen the refugees from the Urak attacks, seen the death and carnage. This isn't about the North or the South, Rist. This is about all human lives. The Chosen can help us stand against the elves and Uraks, help us protect those who cannot protect themselves."

Rist didn't answer; he just continued to nod, staring off into the distance. He didn't like not understanding. He'd seen what Essence could do, the good that could be done with it. But he needed time to think. He was a long way from believing Efialtír was The Saviour, but Efialtír was the only god who seemed to have any tangible impact on the world.

"Take your time," Garramon said, standing. "I know it can be a lot to wrap your mind around. In the meantime, Magnus has procured a few casks of wine in celebration of you and Neera receiving your full colours. We came to get you"

Rist gave Garramon a weak smile and inclined his head. "I just want to finish this last page, then I'll come down."

Garramon nodded, and he, Anila, and Magnus made their way down to the First Army's camp, which lay on the other side of the hill. Neera was in the camp with Lena, enjoying the downtime before they marched again. He would enjoy sharing some wine with them later, but he was also glad for his own time.

Once more, Rist leaned back against the satchel and blanket roll, shifting in place to get comfortable. He opened *Druids, a Magic Lost* to the last page, unfolding the corner.

"All good things must come to an end," he said as he looked at the page.

Duran Linold, Ark-Mage, Year 2340 After Doom

This book is the culmination of my life's work. It is a result of centuries of research and dedication. And so, I thank you for reaching this final page and for dedicating the one thing that cannot be earned, bought, or found – time.

No matter what anyone tells you, the druids are not simply legend. They are not dead, they only wish you to believe as much. They play a larger part in this game of games than anyone dares to whisper. The Seerdruids are the puppeteers. The Aldruids are the warriors. The Skydruids are the instruments of change. The Aetherdruids are the movers. And most importantly, their gods walk among us.

CHAPTER SEVENTY-ONE

BY OUR OWN WILL

Aravell – Winter, Year 3081 After Doom

Calen pressed himself low against Valerys's scales, the rain sheeting down so thick it was almost a fog. With every beat of the dragon's wings, a vibration drummed through Calen. If it wasn't for the warmth of the Spark flowing through him, he had no doubt his teeth would be chattering and his hands shaking. The months had come and gone, late spring fading into summer then turning to winter, and in that time all Calen had done, day and night, was practice and drill.

As they approached the mouth of the valley, Calen reached his mind out to Valerys's, pulling them together as Chora had taught him instead of allowing them to drift into place. The sensation was instant. The world around him sharpened. The air became crisp, the freshness of the rain breaking on Valerys's scales filling their nostrils. A thrum resonated through their body as the wind crashed over their scales. They were one.

No hesitation.

They folded their wings, dropping, before opening them once more at the touch of a rapid air current. They ripped through the sky towards the valley so fast Calen had to close his own eyes and rely solely on Valerys's. The valley was made up of cliff faces that jutted out like jagged teeth, a river raging hundreds of feet below.

Calen and Valerys angled their wings so they flew parallel to the serrated cliff face, pressed tight to the rock as it jutted out and fell back. They stayed as close as possible without crashing. That was what Chora had asked of them. *'Control, Calen. You must fly until it is as effortless as breathing. Until Valerys can turn and move quicker than his heart can beat.'*

The rain crashed over them, the wind tugging them left and right, pushing them closer to the cliff before pulling them back away. As they moved, Calen could feel the fire within Valerys, the primal need to fly. There was something within the dragon's core that yearned to push every boundary, break every limit.

A tingling sensation pulled at the back of their mind, and Valerys reacted in a beat, shifting in the air as a spear of stone shattered against the rock beside them. Four more spears sliced through the rain, one missing Calen's head by a hair's breadth.

Switch sides.

Valerys let out a roar and cracked his wings, spiralling in the air to avoid more stone spears before plummeting downwards and sweeping across the rock face on the opposite side of the valley.

Light shimmered from a cliff on the side of the canyon they had just come from. Calen and Valerys pulled away from the rock face, pressure building within them, fury swelling. A raging pillar of dragonfire poured forth, illuminating the valley and consuming the flurry of ice spheres that had been launched towards them.

From there, they swept forth, executing a myriad of aerial manoeuvres that had been drilled into them over the past months. They climbed, rolled, and dropped, sweeping backwards into inverted loops and plummeting towards the river below at deadly speeds.

As they rounded a jagged cliff and neared the end of the valley, an enormous plateau came into view – the next section. Chora had told Calen and Valerys that in battle they were always stronger together. Their strength was in the bond. The only times she'd said they should separate were when the area they needed to get to was either too small for Valerys, or if Valerys would be too vulnerable or likely to cause unacceptable collateral damage. This task was precisely that situation.

Through Valerys's eyes, Calen could see Tarmon, Vaeril, and Erik waiting on the plateau. Atara, Harken, Aeson, Chora, and Asius stood around them, weapons drawn.

As Valerys approached, Calen drew in a long breath, readying himself. The dragon swept low, picking up speed, then spread his wings, caught the air, and rose, streaking upwards like an arrow.

Chora had taught Calen a number of diving techniques, but the one they were to use today was the catapult. As they neared the plateau, Valerys angled himself upwards, and Calen pulled on threads of air, pushing back, willing the dragon's scales to release him.

His stomach lurched at the sensation of falling, fear clawing at him. But he pushed the fear back and spread the threads out like a canopy behind him. The rushing wind behind Calen crashed against the canopy of Air and launched him forwards.

Calen moved at such speeds his eyes watered and his bones shook. He fortified his body with Earth and Spirit as he soared over the lip of the plateau, Erik, Vaeril, and Tarmon beneath him. He wrapped himself in threads of Air, slowing his descent just enough to not break bones.

Fractions of a second before his feet touched the plateau, Calen pushed down with his threads of Air. He felt the white stone crack beneath him as he landed and unleashed an arc of Air, harnessing the momentum behind him as he swept it outwards towards Aeson, Chora, Atara, Harken, and Asius.

The arc caught Harken in the chest, lifting him off his feet. Aeson and Atara leapt over it while Chora split it with her own threads, and Asius took it head on without flinching.

Calen stumbled forwards, trying to keep his balance; he was still working on his landings. Within a matter of seconds, Tarmon, Vaeril, and Erik were at his side, weapons drawn. They pulled tight together.

"That was the best yet," Erik said, nodding towards a number of large cracks in the stone where Calen had previously fumbled his landings.

"Focus!" Tarmon roared as Aeson and the others fell upon them.

Calen turned away a swipe from Atara's curved elven blade, jerking backwards as one of Aeson's swords almost tore straight across his abdomen. Aeson arced his second blade towards Calen's head, only for Erik to block the strike, sweeping his father's blade aside and smashing Aeson in the jaw with his pommel.

The smile was immediately wiped off Erik's face as Chora wheeled around the outside and hammered a ball of Air into Erik's legs, knocking him off his feet. They moved like that, sweeping about the platform, trading blow after blow, holding back nothing but killing strikes. The thrum of the Spark rippled in the air. As steel collided, so too did threads of Fire, Air, and Spirit. Calen and Vaeril did all they could to hold back the onslaught that came from Asius and the Rakina.

Atara had insisted that if they were to march to war, they must train as though war was already upon them. They had plenty of Healers and any wounds could be seen to.

Calen let out a gasp as Atara's blade sliced through the flesh on his left forearm, but he pressed forwards, moving through the forms of svidarya. He forced Atara back, shifting from Howling Wolf, to Raging Tempest, to Striking Dragon, his heart pounding. He had never so much as landed a scratch on Atara. The elf was even quicker than Aeson. But there, on the plateau as his sword collided with hers, he felt Valerys pushing him forwards, felt the dragon's familiar rage burning through him. His mind dulled to a singular focus, the vibrations of each blow jarring his arms.

He brought his sword up, catching Atara's blade in its downward arc. Countering, Calen swept his sword back across his body, hoping to catch the elf in the chest. But Atara was too quick. Her feet moved in a blur as she leaned back, avoiding the strike, swinging her own blade so its tip sliced through Calen's chin. The steel burned like fire.

Calen caught himself on his back foot, then lunged, pushing the pain down. He drove his blade forwards but only met air as Atara sidestepped with ease. He turned back to reengage but found Asius's enormous frame barrelling towards him. Calen only had a second to understand what was happening before the Jotnar lifted his foot and kicked.

Calen dragged threads of Earth and Spirit into his bones. He lifted his arm, using threads of Air to form a shield between himself and Asius. The Jotnar's foot crashed into the shield of Air with the force of a raging bull, sending Calen careening backwards and knocking the air from his lungs. As he hit the stone, Calen rolled backwards, catching himself on his feet.

His lungs heaved, pulling in air with a thirst. He tried to move his left arm, but it hung limp by his side, pain screaming. Before he could think, the sensation of the Spark rippled through him, and arcs of lightning hurtled towards him from Atara, Aeson, and Chora.

Instinctively, Calen pulled Valerys's mind into his, the dragon's fury raging through the bond. He pulled on threads of Fire, Spirit, and Air, weaving them together and encasing himself in a sphere as Therin had taught him – a Sparkward. The drain sapped at Calen as soon as the arcs of lightning collided with the Sparkward, the ward pulling the energy from his body to fuel itself.

Calen dropped to one knee, slowing his breathing, trying to focus on nothing but the bond, Chora's voice echoing in his mind. *The bond is your strength. A Draleid not only draws the Spark through himself, but also through the dragon to which he is bonded. It is what makes Draleid so powerful in the Spark. The well of strength you draw from is far greater than most mages can dream of.*

Calen clenched his jaw, his teeth grinding, the Spark burning through him. A gust of wind swirled around him as Valerys dropped, alighting on the platform behind him. Together, Calen and Valerys unleashed a thunderous roar of defiance, power surging through their shared soul, crackling over skin and scales.

Seeing through Valerys, Calen looked down over himself. Wisps of incandescent purple light misted from his eyes, the glow reflecting in the sheeting rain around him. Across the plateau, Tarmon was down, and Erik and Vaeril stood back to back with Harken and Asius approaching from either side. All the while arcs of lightning from Atara, Chora, and Aeson crashed against Calen's Sparkward, rippling over its surface.

He could feel Valerys's rage swelling, urging to push himself to his feet, demanding he fight back.

Dragons are fire and fury, Calen could hear Chora saying in his mind. *In battle, never fight Valerys's rage, feed on it.*

Calen opened himself fully to the Spark, letting it blaze with Valerys's anger, burning in his veins like molten fire. As he did, he clenched his jaw and heaved himself upright. "Draleid n'aldryr."

Calen sent a pulse of Spirit through his ward, surging outwards. Through Valerys's eyes, he watched as the Spirit pulsed through the arcs of lightning, sending Aeson and Atara stumbling backwards and releasing their hold on the Spark.

Keep pushing.

Only Chora remained. She sat forward in her wheelchair, her face contorted in focus, the Spark pulsing from her in rippling waves energy.

A warning from Valerys flashed in the back of Calen's mind. More arcs of lightning crashed against Calen's Sparkward. He cried out, dropping to his knees as the ward pulled the energy from his bones to counteract the renewed attack.

Aeson and Atara had rejoined Chora, along with Asius, while Harken stood and watched.

Calen shook, his body convulsing with the strain of holding the ward in place, his lungs gasping for air. The Spark ignited in his veins, pain searing through him.

"Yield!" Aeson roared.

Calen clenched his jaw, closing his eyes and pulling deeper from the Spark, ignoring the pain that screamed from within.

"Calen! Yield!"

"No," Calen growled through gritted teeth. The pain rose to a point where it felt as though his body had been hollowed out and filled with fire.

As the agony intensified, Calen remembered what Vaeril had said all that time ago in Drifaien: *'When you reach out to the Spark, you open a door… The longer that door stays open, the more of the Spark can flow through. Leave it open too long…'* The elf had drawn on Fire, blades of grass disintegrating to charred dust in his hands. *'If you are new to the Spark, you will often simply lose consciousness before you can get to that point. But once you are strong enough to hold more of it, the danger increases. As the drain affects you less and less, the risk of burning out rises… the Spark will not hesitate to consume your soul.'*

In a heartbeat, the Valerys's rage turned to icy fear at the thought of Vaeril's words. The dragon's fear pulled at Calen, dragging the last vestiges of strength from his body. He let go of the Spark, slumping forwards onto the white stone. He rolled onto his back, drifting in and out of consciousness as the cold rain drummed against his face. He felt Valerys's snout pushing against his ribs, a low rumble in the dragon's throat.

A hand rested on his chest, and he felt threads of the Spark weaving through him, easing the pain. A warmth spread through his body and his vision settled. Asius knelt over him, a sympathetic smile on his face.

Ryan Cahill

Calen tried to lift himself upright but gasped as a twinge ignited in his left arm. With the all-consuming pain of the Spark burning through him, he had forgotten Asius's kick. "I think it's dislocated again."

"My apologies, Calen Bryer." Asius weaved threads of each elemental strand into Calen's arm, then pushed.

"Fuck!" Calen shouted, feeling his arm click back into place. He dropped his head against the stone, panting.

"Don't apologise for his recklessness, Asius." Atara stood behind Asius, her arms folded, her hair tacked to her face by the rain.

Calen glared at the elf. He let out a sigh, then heaved himself upright, his sword still gripped in his fist. Asius tried to help him to his feet, but Calen pushed away the Jotnar's hand, hauling himself up – much to his body's complaints.

Erik sat on the ground a few feet away, one of the elven Healers tending to a wound in his arm. Tarmon and Vaeril were both on their feet, but Calen could see by the looks on their faces they had taken a similar beating to him. Calen also spotted Valdrin sitting atop a rock on the far side of the plateau, watching – as he always did.

"You were reckless and stupid," Atara said, folding her arms. "If we were Eltoar, Lyina, or Jormun – if we were any of them – you would be dead." She gestured to the others. "All of you."

"I'd be dead a hundred times at this stage, Atara. And I'll keep dying." Calen slid his sword into its scabbard, then ran his hand through his saturated hair. "Go again."

"I don't think you understand," the elf said, meeting Calen's gaze. "It doesn't matter how many times we do this. You die. You will always die."

"Atara, stop." Aeson stepped between Atara and Calen, holding up his hand. "We're all tired. That's enough for today."

"No." Calen shook his head, moving towards Atara. "What is your point, Atara? Do you want me to give up like you did?"

Aeson put his hand on Calen's chest, trying to push him back. His stare was cold and hard. "Calen, stop."

Calen swiped Aeson's hand away, pushing past the man so he stood less than a foot from Atara. He didn't have to look to know Valerys loomed behind him, his neck craned forwards, wings spread wide, anger swelling within their shared soul. "Tell me," he said, glaring into Atara's eyes. "Is that what you want?"

Atara didn't flinch. To Calen's surprise, his own anger wasn't met in kind. Atara's eyes held a deep melancholy, her expression softening. "I don't want you to die. Too many of us have died."

"That's not your choice."

"The Dragonguard will tear you apart, Calen. Piece by piece. They have killed hundreds of our kind. Draleid far older and wiser than you. And now from the reports we're hearing, more Draleid survived in Lynalion. I would hold happiness in my heart were they not joined to the *Astyrlina*." Atara spit the word out as though it were poison. 'The Faithless', the name the elves of Aravell had given to their kin in Lynalion. "If the Lynalion elves have emerged, it is for nothing but war and death. They despise humans, and they despise us for standing by you. The landscape is changing too quickly, and you're not ready."

Calen's breaths trembled. He had to force his hand to not clench into a fist at his side. He leaned forwards, seeing the incandescent purple glow of his eyes reflecting in Atara's. "You can stay here and keep hiding, but I won't. I've lost too much to keep running and hiding. Not anymore."

"I'm done." Atara shook her head, pursing her lips. She turned to Aeson. "I'm done, Aeson. I thought I could do it, but I can't. I'm not training him only to watch him die. I can't do it."

Atara took one last look at Calen, then turned and left.

Calen looked around the plateau. Aeson was right, everyone did look tired, their chests rising and falling in heavy sweeps as the rain pelted down over them. They could sleep later. He turned to Aeson, the wind sweeping his sopping hair across his face. "Again."

Valerys bowed, dropping low to the ground and splaying out his fore-limb as Calen climbed onto his back. As he hauled himself into position at the nape of Valerys's neck, Calen heard his father's voice in his head. *'The sun will set, and it will rise again, and it will do so the next day and the next. The gods are in charge of such things, but it is by our own will that we pick ourselves up when we fall.'*

Calen filled his lungs with heavy, damp air, pressing his hands against the scales of Valerys's neck. "I will not yield."

Valerys cracked his wings and lifted into the air.

CHAPTER SEVENTY-TWO

THE WHEEL TURNS

Arden folded his arms as the rain hammered down, the sun barely visible behind the dark thunderclouds overhead. He stood atop a low platform that looked over an enormous courtyard where thousands of men and elves stood together in close formations, moving through the sword forms Aeson Virandr had assigned.

Calen had yet to meet with any of the major rebel leaders, thanks to the elven rulers' refusal until Calen had been properly drilled in the formalities and Valdrin had finished his armour. But even at that, more and more rebels had made their way to Aravell over the passing months, answering the call Calen had sent out through the Angan. On the last count, they numbered over two thousand. Funnily enough, upon seeing the rebels grow in size, each of the elven rulers had also committed warriors specifically to Calen's cause. Arden and Lyrin had found no end of amusement in watching as each ruler attempted to outdo the next by offering an ever increasing number. As it stood, all three Kingdoms had committed a thousand elves, each of them swearing oaths of fealty to Calen. Calen hadn't been particularly happy about the oaths, but he couldn't rightly do as he'd done with Vaeril, Gaeleron, Alea, Lyrei, and the others; he couldn't swear an oath to three thousand elves.

And just like that, fewer than fifty rebels marching across the Burnt Lands had become a veritable army in a matter of months. Two thousand humans. Three thousand elves.

"Not too shabby," Lyrin said, stepping up beside Arden, his arms folded, his hair tacked to his face by the rain. Arden and the other Knights of Achyron had been asked to assist in training and drills – Ruon and Ildris in particular had hundreds upon hundreds of years of experience. Both had fought in a number of wars and knew what it was to lead soldiers into battle.

"Not at all." Arden nodded in agreement, looking down to where Ildris, Ruon, and Varlin strode between the practicing groups. Ingvat and Surin had been chosen as captains of the newly formed forces, along with three elves by the names of Narthil, Allinín, and Sylehna.

The elves had been well drilled from the start; they looked and moved like an army should, equipped with the finest of swords and armour. But the rebels were the opposite. They had arrived broken and disparate from all corners of the South. Some bore weapons and armour that would not have looked out of place in the finest armoury, but most carried old, worn equipment and whatever they had been able to salvage. Each and every one of them looked as though they were well accustomed to fighting, no strangers to death and blood. But they were the furthest thing from an army. Over the months, Arden had taken no small amount of pride in watching that slowly change. Every morning they rose with the sun, trained until they could barely stand, ate, and then slept. He had never seen such a large group so singular in their dedication. Aeson Virandr had picked his allies wisely. "We just need to get them some decent equipment."

"What news from the temple?" Arden asked, knowing Lyrin had just come from giving his report to Kallinvar.

Lyrin let out a long sigh. "Pure, untamed chaos." The man shook his head, clicking his tongue off the roof of his mouth. "The elves of Lynalion still haven't moved any further west than Steeple. Their numbers are impossible to determine with that fog always shrouding them – as are the numbers of their dragons. But the reports are telling us they moved north, taking both Khergan and Highpass, as well as Dead Rock's Hold."

"I've heard things of Dead Rock's Hold…"

"Whatever you've heard is likely true. The hold is built around an enormous iron mine. For the past four centuries, the empire have used elves as forced labour to mine the iron. Not only will finding their kin enslaved in a mine piss off those Lynalion elves to no end, Dead Rock's Hold is also the empire's largest iron mine. You better believe that's going to have a major impact on their weapons production."

Arden's jaw clenched. "Or they'll shift the burden to the South," he said, thinking back on how the empire used to pay his dad half of what his armour and weapons were worth – if they bothered to pay at all. "That's always the way. The North doesn't struggle, it stumbles, then uses the South as a crutch."

"True enough." Lyrin nodded, letting out a soft sigh. Before becoming a knight, Lyrin had been born in Loria in a small town south-west of Catagan. "Should we go and help?" Lyrin gestured to where Ruon, Ildris, and Varlin were walking through the ranks of warriors, elven and human captains marching along beside them.

"Actually, Calen is to meet Valdrin soon. His armour is ready. I told him I'd be there."

A smile touched Lyrin's lips. "I'm happy for you. You're still an arse-hole, but I'm happy for you."

Before Arden could respond, a roar rippled through the skies above. He lifted his gaze to see Valerys emerge from behind the dense canopy of trees that framed the training yard, black-veined wings of white spread wide. The dragon swept upwards, soaring over the heads of the practicing warriors below. Cheers and chants rang out from both elves and humans, swords clanging off shields – they did that any time Valerys soared overhead. Arden would have thought they would lose interest after a while, but he had been proven sorely mistaken.

He smiled as he watched the dragon sweep across the sky. Even in the few months that had passed, Valerys had grown further. The dragon's body was almost seventy feet in length, his muscles dense, chest deep. Arden reckoned Valerys was easily big enough to take a second on his back, possibly even a third. As he looked up, Arden dropped his hand to his hip, feeling the soft almost-waxy touch of the scarf Calen had given him. Calen said he'd bought it in the markets at Milltown and that he'd intended to give it to their mam before everything happened. It was now tied between the loops on Arden's sword belt, just as it had been Calen's. His throat clenched as he rubbed the autumn-red scarf between his thumb and forefinger, tracing over the gold and cream leaves that wove through the fabric.

It was strange how such a small thing could pull at Arden so heavily. That scarf was the only thing he had to remind him of his mam; it reminded him of her warmth, her love, her soft, sweet voice... and she'd never even touched it. No words existed in the Common Tongue that could ever explain to Calen how much that meant to him, but somehow he thought Calen already knew.

"You all right?" Lyrin turned his gaze from Calen and Valerys, raising an eyebrow.

"Yeah," Arden said, nodding as he rubbed the heel of his palm into his eye. "Just tired. I need to go to Valdrin's forge. I'll see you in a few hours."

"I see what you're doing," Lyrin called as Arden descended the steps from the platform. "Any excuse to get out of sword forms!"

"You know me too well!"

∽◎

"PLEASE DON'T DIE, PLEASE DON'T die, please don't die." Dann squeezed his arms around Calen's waist, his hands trembling and his head pressed against Calen's back. The wind and rain whipped at him from all sides as the dragon swooped and soared through the many interconnected valleys of Aravell. Walkways, bridges, and platforms of white stone flitted past, barely more than a blur.

From the ground, riding a dragon looked as though it was one of the most incredible things a person could do. It was a thing of legend, a thing of bards' tales and stories told around campfires. But sitting on the dragon's back, clinging on for dear life, damp scales chafing his thighs, and his teeth chattering, Dann decided there were some things best left in stories.

"Stop being such a baby!" Calen called out, his voice muffled by the wind. With his head pressed against Calen's back, Dann could feel the vibrations of his friend's laughter. "You said you wanted to see what it was like. I'm showing you."

"That's easy for you to say!" Dann roared back. "Valerys might be holding you in place, but if I let go I'm dead!"

"Don't let go!"

"I hate you!"

Calen roared laughing. "The forge is up ahead." He turned, the wind whipping his hair back and forth, his eyes misting with an incandescent lavender light. Dann didn't think he would ever get used to that – especially the glowing. "Can you hold on that long?"

Dan interlocked his fingers, clamping his legs tighter to Valerys. *Please don't die. Please don't die.* "I miss my horse!"

"What did you say?" Calen shouted. "Faster?"

Before Dann could respond, Valerys curled his wings, dropping into a dive. Dann felt himself lift, a weightlessness filling his stomach, his entire body feeling as though it were floating. Then the dragon spread his wings once more, and Dann slammed back down, a splitting pain spreading from his arse to his stones. *Never again.*

THE RAIN HAD STOPPED BY the time Valerys alighted on the plateau before Valdrin's forge, his talons depressing into the sodden grass.

Vaeril, Erik, Tarmon, Alea, Lyrei, Haem and Gaeleron all stood to the left of the forge, while Asius, Baldon, Aeson, Therin, Aruni, and a number of the Rakina all waited before the forge's doors.

"Never again," Dann said, releasing his bear hug on Calen's waist. He panted as though he had just run five miles. "Not without a saddle, at least." He let out a groan of relief as he shifted. "I'm not sure I'll be able to have children after that."

"Is that really a bad thing?" Calen laughed, turning to see Dann looking left and right, droplets of water flicking from his hair, a curiosity in his eyes. "Everything all right, Dann?"

"How in the gods do I get down from here?"

"You jump. Watch." Calen tried to keep as straight a face as he could manage. Without another word, he swung his leg over, wrapped himself in threads of Air and leapt from Valerys's back. He was so well practiced at that stage that his feet barely pressed into the sodden grass as he landed, the threads of Air softening his descent. He turned around, looking up at Dann. "You next!"

Dann's eyes widened. "You better be fucking joking."

"Do you want me to catch you?" Therin called up to Dann as he strolled towards Valerys, a beaming smile on his face. He leaned in to Calen, whispering, "You're cruel."

"He'd have done the same to me."

"He'd have done worse," Therin said with a laugh. "Get Valerys to let him down though, Valdrin's waiting, and you know what he's like at this stage."

"Fair enough." *Let him down.*

Valerys shook his head and neck, spraying water in all directions like Faenir had once done when coming inside after being in the rain. The dragon leaned low to the ground, stretching his neck and angling his forelimbs so Dann could climb down.

Climb, Calen discovered, would be too elegant a word for the method Dann used to dismount from Valerys.

Splat.

Mud and water sprayed up into Calen and Therin's faces as Dann clambered from Valerys's back, then slipped on the dragon's forelimb, dropping down face-first into the sodden grass.

"*Ooph.*" Erik grimaced at Dann in the mud as he, Tarmon, and Vaeril, Alea, and Lyrei walked over. "That's got to hurt. Who had him for face first?"

Lyrei raised a hand, a wicked grin spreading from ear to ear. Erik, Tarmon, Aeson, Vaeril, Chora, and Haem all placed a copper mark in Lyrei's open palm. The elf shook the coppers in her hand, then dropped them into a pocket within her cloak.

Dann wiped the mud from his face as Calen helped him to his feet, but he was still filthy from head to toe. He glared at Erik. "Did you all bet if I'd fall?"

"No." Erik raised his open palm defensively. "We didn't bet *if* you'd fall. We bet *how* you would fall. If it's any consolation, I had you landing on your feet."

"It is, actually."

"Well, your feet then your face. The grass is slippery."

"I hate you." Dann narrowed his gaze, turning to Calen. "Never. Again."

"Do you remember the first night in The Proving? When you led us to the cave with the bear. You danced across the stones in the river like a kat while I fell in and got soaked?" Calen clapped Dann and the back, motioning him towards the forge. "Well, this is payback."

"Not your most graceful moment, Pimm." Calen saw Tarmon holding back a laugh as he shook his head at Dann's mud-stained clothes. Since arriving in Aravell, and in the last months in particular, Tarmon, Erik, and Vaeril had treated Dann as though he was a brother. It was something Calen appreciated more than he had the ability to articulate.

"What way did you have me falling?" Dann scraped mud from his cheek as he raised an eyebrow at Tarmon.

"I had you trying to slide down Valerys's wing."

Dann gave an upturn of his bottom lip. "That was actually my next option."

"So close," Tarmon said, clicking his fingers.

They approached the forge, and Calen said his greetings to all who had come. As he made to greet Aruni, the elf pulled him into a warm hug. She squeezed him, then pulled back, pinching his cheek. "Have you been sleeping? Not enough by the looks of it." She examined his eyes. "I have a tea. It should help."

Calen smiled, suppressing a laugh as he nodded his thanks. "That would be lovely."

While Valdrin had been working on Calen's armour, Calen and Haem had come to visit Aruni numerous times with Therin. She reminded him of home, or, more specifically, she reminded him of his mam. She looked nothing like Freis, of course, but she had the same warmth, the same caring eyes. She also had better tea.

"Come!" Valdrin's voice rang out from within the forge.

Erik, Tarmon, Vaeril, and Dann all turned their heads towards the doors of the forge, curious expressions on their faces.

"Did he just summon us like hounds?" Erik asked, laughing.

"I believe so," Tarmon said.

"He summoned *you* like a hound." Dann shrugged, turning so he walked backwards towards the doors. "I'm going of my own free will." As Dann turned, his foot slipped from under him, and he fell into the muddy grass to a chorus of laughter.

"Come on," Therin said, motioning for the others to move inside the forge. "Before this idiot hurts himself." He reached down and hauled Dann to his feet.

"Don't say it." Dann pursed his lips, then let out a long, heavy sigh. "Don't say a word."

The heat from the forge felt like an age-old friend, washing over Calen as he stepped through the doors. He closed his eyes for a moment, letting his mind drift back to those days in the forge with his dad and Haem.

"Well." Calen opened his eyes at the sound of Valdrin's voice. The elf stood before Calen, a dirty cloth clasped in his hands, his leather apron draped over a deep blue cotton shirt. Valdrin's face, arms, hair, and clothes were covered in a mixture of soot, coal, grease, and sweat. In fact, the only part of him that was in any way clean were his hands, which he had clearly scrubbed meticulously. "What are all these people doing here?" Valdrin raised an eyebrow, looking about the group, his gaze stopping on Therin. "I specifically said Calen, Erik, Tarmon, Arden, Alea, Lyrei, Gaeleron, Vaeril and that one." Valdrin pointed to Dann. "Though..." He scrunched his lips. "He's a bit dirty."

Dann was incredulous. He raised his hands, palms out. "Hold on. I know I'm covered in mud. I fell off a dragon. How many of you can say that? But I mean—" He gestured at Valdrin "—this is the pot calling the kettle black... and in this case, the pot really is black. I mean it's all over you. How do you get coal in your hair?"

Valdrin stared at Dann, his eyes narrowing for a moment. "I like you. You can stay. As for the others, out."

Therin sighed heavily. "Valdrin."

Valdrin stared back at Therin curiously. "Therin?"

"Can we not do this?"

A broad smile crept across Valdrin's face. "All right."

"Thank you."

"You can stay – the others can wait outside. It's too crowded in here, and you know I get anxious when it's crowded."

Chora wheeled forwards, dirt and char crunching beneath her chair. She looked from Therin to Aeson. "He's not serious, is he? It's already started raining again."

"You won't melt," Valdrin said with a shrug. "Now, out."

"He's never not serious." Therin's mouth was a thin line.

"All right, all right." Aruni clasped her hands together, rubbing at the scars around her wrists. "How about I take you all into the house for a cup of tea. Valdrin can call us when they're ready."

Baldon bowed. "It would be my pleasure, Aruni Heartsteel. Do you have any more tea of the Tarveenan Starlet?"

"I do, Baldon, I do. Come, come. Follow me." Aruni placed her hand on Baldon's fur-covered back, herding the Angan out the door, gesturing for the others to follow. Asius, Harken, Atara, and the other Rakina followed after Aruni and Baldon with little complaint, barring a few grumbles.

"This better be some damn good tea." Chora frowned, then began to leave before stopping and raising her eyebrows at Aeson. "You're coming too, young Virandr… well…" She looked to Erik, letting out a laugh. "Not so young Virandr. Not anymore."

As Aeson and Chora left, Valdrin closed the door behind them. He puffed out his cheeks. "Finally. Twenty three is far too many to have in here. It's also not an even number." He looked at something in the corner of the workshop. "I don't like odd numbers. They're just… odd. Ten is perfect."

"But there's eleven of us?" Dann said, counting with his finger.

"Very quick mathematics, but I don't count myself because I can't see myself." Valdrin stared at Dann as though daring Dann to challenge him. Dann looked as though he were going to do just that, but eventually shook his head and shrugged. Valdrin rubbed his hands into the cloth one more time, then stuffed it into the pocket at the top of his apron. "Now that is sorted, follow me. Everything's ready."

Valdrin led Calen and the others through the workshop towards the archway at the far end that divided the building in half – where Valdrin had shown him the armour previously. This time, though, a long black curtain was draped over the arch.

Valdrin stopped before the arch, turning to Calen and folding his arms. He bit his lip, his gaze moving over Calen's body. He held out his hands, moving them closer and further apart as though measuring Calen. After a minute, he gave an downturn of his bottom lip, seemingly satisfied.

"The curtain's a little dramatic, no?" Dann asked, looking behind Valdrin at the black curtain.

"Some would say falling off a dragon is a little dramatic," Valdrin said without missing a beat.

"Fair. Carry on."

Without so much as a smile, Valdrin nodded to Dann and turned back to Calen. "I'll still have to watch you train in it, but I think it's going to be perfect. Your shoulders and arms have grown in the last few months, but I've been accounting for that." Valdrin nodded to himself for a few moments as though doing calculations in his head, then turned on his heels and pulled the curtain across, stepping through.

Just as Calen and Haem had done when they had first walked through the arch months ago, both Dann and Erik let out gasps, looking about at the suits and segments of armour that were mounted on stand and hooks around the room.

"Arn elwyn Hafaesiríl." *By Hafaesir's heart.* Vaeril looked about, wide-eyed, Alea, Lyrei, and Gaeleron walking at his side. "Your work

859

is truly an art, Valdrin. For years I've heard of the young smith who rivals the weapons and armour crafts of old. I've heard you forge using the Spark?"

"Among other things," Valdrin said as he walked towards the other side of the room.

Calen stopped in his tracks as his gaze fell on a suit of armour suspended on a stand that Valdrin now stood beside. "That can't be…"

"Your armour."

"By the gods…" Dann stepped up beside Calen, speechless for the first time.

The breastplate was pure white, a trim of gold around its edges. Runes were etched around the collar, smooth and sweeping, inlaid with a whitish metal. At first glance there seemed to be no sigil or markings emblazoned across the breastplate's front, but as Calen looked closer, his breath caught in his chest. He reached out and traced his fingers across vines of gold that swept from left to right, delicate etchings of leaves blowing in the wind – the same as the scarf he had bought his mam. The one he had given to Haem. Calen looked to Valdrin, tears wetting his eyes. "How did you…?"

"It seemed important to you," Valdrin said, a genuine smile touching his lips. "Aeson Virandr and the others had asked that I mark the breast with the old symbol of The Order. They were quite insistent. But this seemed more appropriate." He looked back at the armour, then at the floor, before his gaze finally rested on Haem. "When I saw that you had given the scarf to your brother, my decision was made."

"Valdrin…" Calen couldn't take his fingers away from the golden leaves etched into the plate. It was one of the most thoughtful things anyone had ever done for him. "It's beautiful."

"Why thank you. I'm rather proud of it myself. I did it by hand, which is why it took a bit longer. The Spark can do many things, but when it comes to the finer details, it can be a bit clumsy."

Calen took a step back. The breastplate flowed down into thin articulated panels of white steel that protected the stomach and sides, connecting to a pair of ornately carved tassets on either side. Sections of white cloth were pulled up beneath the tassets and pinned in place. Smooth plate covered the legs, flowing seamlessly into armoured boots. As Calen's gaze moved upwards, it fell on the pauldrons. Each pauldron consisted of a base layer of rounded white steel which was then ornamented with overlapping segments of plate that mimicked the peaks of dragon wings. More overlapping plates of white steel flowed outwards from the pauldrons, covering the arms and joining to a pair of vambraces and gauntlets on either side.

"The cloth is for ornamentation," Valdrin said, circling the armour. "I don't see a point in wasting time on something so impractical, but King Galdra insisted, while Queen Uthrían was quite forceful about the gold trim. It was actually King Silmiryn who suggested the pauldrons mimic Valerys's wings. I know you prefer a simple aesthetic, but I think it works quite well." Valdrin traced his hand over the right pauldron, his eyes narrowing as he inspected his craftsmanship. "The armour itself though is made from an alloy of Antherin steel – the metal used to make the armour worn by the old Draleid. This new alloy is light and flexible but can take a hit from a warhammer without caving. It will move with you instead of against you."

Valdrin stepped back, rubbing his chin with his right hand. Therin had told Calen he'd rescued Valdrin, along with Aruni, from a Lorian prison six years ago. The elf had only seen eighteen summers. Calen had never seen such a natural gift.

"You can thank Queen Uthrían for the Antherin steel. She offered her son's old armour to be melted down – which I used to create this new alloy. Luckily Antherin steel has very few impurities. The process was quite simple. I call this new metal Antherium."

Calen listened to Valdrin, but his thoughts drifted to Uthrían and to the vision he had seen when she had touched his arm. Her son's words as he stood before her. '*Myia'nari. Il vyara… myia'kara… é dauva. Il raethír er veinier.*' *My queen, the princes… my brothers… are dead. The battle is lost.*

Calen hadn't seen as much of the elven rulers as he had thought he would, which was a good thing in general – he had little patience for all the back and forth. But for Uthrían to offer her son's armour so that Calen's could be forged was special.

"Oh, I almost forgot." Valdrin scurried back through the arch, disappearing for a minute before remerging with a helmet in his hand. He placed the helmet on top of the armour stand so it rested just above the breastplate. "I was working on the finishing touches. I wasn't sure what style you'd prefer, but I wanted to give you as much visibility as I could while also offering some protection from the wind while you're flying. I've taken inspiration from the Valtaran style, as well as that of the Lunithíran elves and the old Draleid helmets."

The helmet was smooth and sleek, more gold leaves and vines inlaid across its white steel surface. The faceplate held a singular opening, split by a guard that extended down over the nose while two angular side plates covered the cheeks and jawline. The eye slits were narrow but spread wide, allowing for good lateral vision.

"Jotnar runecraft." Calen could hear the awe in Vaeril's voice as the elf dropped to his haunches to examine the legs.

It was only as Vaeril spoke that Calen noticed that the collar of the breastplate wasn't the only piece of the armour inscribed with the rune markings. He looked closer, staring at the runes that ran down the sides of the breastplate and those along the arms and legs.

"You have come a long way in a short time," Therin said, resting his hand on Valdrin's shoulder.

Valdrin shuffled awkwardly, giving Therin a half smile before moving to stand by Calen. He folded his left arm across his body and pointed at a set of runes. "I haven't tested these particular runes before." He glanced at Haem. "I've tried to make them mimic Arden's Sentinel armour. Not in the way it melts and recedes – though give me a few decades – but a more simplified version. When the runesets are activated, the armour should – theoretically – melt the joints together, eliminating the weak points, or at least reducing them. The points where the armour fuses will be softer and more malleable than the faces of the plate. Otherwise you wouldn't be able to move. But it should provide far greater protection than normal plate while being lighter and more flexible."

"Question," Dann said, folding his arms as he stood beside Valdrin.

"Here we go." Therin raised an expectant eyebrow.

Dann glared at Therin before turning back to Valdrin. "You said 'theoretically'. What happens if your theory is wrong?"

"Honestly? I'm not sure." Valdrin scrunched up his lips. "I've never used runes like this before – I don't believe anyone has. They're a bit of an experiment. But given the intention of the runes, the energy required, and potential variance in translation – the ancient Jotnar runic script is older than the Blodvar – the wearer could melt, burst into flames…" Varlin pressed his fingers into his cheeks. "Possibly even be fused to the armour itself."

"Did you say melt?"

"Potentially."

"How do we test it?" Calen swallowed hard, his mouth drier than the dunes of the Burnt Lands.

Valdrin pursed his lips. "You have to try it… There's not really any other way. These kinds of runes can only be activated by the corresponding master binding runes – which can only be inscribed on a single wearer."

Calen made to ask what master binding runes were when the last part of Valdrin's sentence clicked in his head. "Inscribed?"

Valdrin pursed his lips, then folded his arms. "These runes are crafted from a subset of runes known as binding runes. For lack of a deeper explanation, they bind the armour, or whatever you're marking, to one specific master – in this case, you. The master runes would need to be inscribed on your body using ink that's made from the bones of horned

Krakalun – a type of mountain goat that was common in the old Jotnar lands. Lucky for you, some Krakalun still live near the peaks of Lodhar, and I already have some ink."

"There's the L word again," Erik said with a laugh.

Calen puffed out his cheeks, nodding. "How long does the inscribing take?"

"You're actually going to do it?" Dann looked at Calen in shock. "What if you melt? That's not a good word, Calen. *Melt.*"

Calen looked to Valdrin. "How confident are you that the runes are right?"

The elf shrugged. "Eighty-three… eighty-four percent? The inscribing will take less than an hour with the Spark."

"All right." Calen let out a heavy sigh, nodding, resigned to what needed to be done. "Let's get it over with."

"Oh." Valdrin straightened his back, his eyes widening as though he'd just remembered something. He stuck his index finger in the air. "One moment. There's one other thing."

Valdrin walked over to the left side of the room, where six stands of armour had been covered by sheets. One by one, Valdrin ripped the sheets off. He looked to Gaeleron. "I will craft one for you when you recover."

"I'm not wearing that." Dann folded his arms, shaking his head with his bottom lip turned out. "There's no way I'm… Is that a hood? Actually, it's not that bad. I could just… Wait, no. Is *that* mine?"

Haem moved beside Calen, scratching at his stubble. "How long would it take to make five thousand more of those?"

AESON LEANED BACK AGAINST THE trunk of the tree, his arms folded. The rain had come back with a vengeance, hammering down against the leaves overhead and forming puddles in the grass.

He didn't like being made to wait outside. But the boy, Valdrin, had been through a lot, and Aeson knew what he was like. He remembered when Therin had come to him six years ago with Dayne and Belina. Aruni and Valdrin had been with them, freshly dragged from the dungeons of Kragsdenford and whatever malicious experiments the empire had been running in those dark depths. Valdrin had only seen about twelve summers at that stage. He'd come a long way since then.

As he stood there, he let his mind wander to the reports they'd received from the battle at Steeple. When rumours had spread about elven dragons, Aeson had dismissed them out of hand. Surely there was no possible way they were true. If the elves of Lynalion had kept Draleid alive this long, why had they hidden? But when more and more news came in, Aeson slowly understood. They had been waiting for this precise moment; waiting for the Dragonguard's numbers to dwindle and the continent to drift into chaos. Had the Draleid come from any other place, Aeson would have rejoiced. But the elves of Lynalion were not friends. In the years before they secluded themselves in the woodland, their hatred of humankind, the elves of Aravell, and the Draleid who had betrayed them had become all consuming. He would need to attempt communication, but he held little hope. The last time the Draleid had flown behind banners of kingdoms and not The Order, the Blodvar had raged for centuries.

A loud puff of air brought Aeson from his thoughts. He looked to the left of the forge where Valerys lay in the damp grass, his bulk taking up most of the platform between the forge and the house. The rain crashed down over the dragon, splattering off his scales. In the past few months alone, the dragon had grown more than twice what any other would have. He was still nothing but a plaything compared to the likes of Helios, but he was a devastating creature nonetheless. Aeson had no doubt that if Valerys had flown the skies four centuries ago, he would have been a jewel of The Order.

"How long does it take to try on armour?" Harken let out a sigh. The mountain of a man scratched at the back of his head.

"Patience is a virtue." Chora's eyes were fixed on the forge door as she spoke.

"I have enough virtues," Harken said. "I don't need another one."

Aeson looked to his left, just outside the cover of the tree's branches. Asius sat cross-legged in the rain, his elbows on his knees. Even seated, the Jotnar's head still reached Aeson's shoulders. Asius had spent many a day over the past few months visiting Valdrin in the forge. Apparently the boy was a prodigy when it came to runecraft. Even amongst the Jotnar, rune crafting had been a rare and sought-after skill. Before The Fall, Asius had been one of only six Jotnar Aeson had known to be proficient at the craft, and Asius would never have considered himself particularly adept. But from everything Aeson had heard since arriving back in Aravell, Valdrin was proving to be a prodigy with pretty much everything that involved his hands. As he was not born under the banners of Lunithír, Ardurän, or Vaelen, none of the three Inari claimed him as their own, but many seemed to consider him a multi-generational talent.

"Here we are." Aruni fixed her rain-damp dress as the doors to the forge opened. With the rain weighing the fabric down, Aeson could see the outlines of the rune markings the imperial mages in Kragsdenford had carved into her chest. The elf had barely survived. She wouldn't have if it hadn't been for Therin.

Erik and Tarmon were the first to step from the forge. Each wore flowing suits of burnished plate. Their steel breastplates were smooth, ornamented with delicate gold leaves blowing from left to right and white dragons emblazoned across the front. White pauldrons, gilded along the edges, protected their shoulders while tassets of white steel scales covered their hips and groins. They both held sharp, fitted helmets in the crooks of their arms.

Vaeril and Dann came next, with Alea and Lyrei walking behind them. Vaeril wore the same style armour as the others, but Dann, Alea, and Lyrei's armour was lighter, half-plate. Their breastplates were similar to the others, though sleeker. Smooth pauldrons armoured their left shoulders, smaller less obtrusive spaulders protecting their right, with sets of vambraces on their forearms. But what drew Aeson's attention was the white wood bow slung over Dann's back. *Shit. He's never going to shut up about that.*

"I thought the Triarchy had only arranged for Calen's armour?" Harken asked, looking from Chora to Aeson.

"They did," Chora answered.

"Valdrin's been working night and day. He used the steel from other projects." Aruni gave Aeson a soft smile. "He won't ever tell you, but he was honoured to be asked."

"Well, fuck…" Chora's eyes widened, her lips pursing.

Aeson stared at Chora in shock but then realised what she had seen. Calen strode from the forge, a helmet gripped in his hands, Valdrin, Arden, Gaeleron, and Therin walking behind him.

Aeson had never seen anything like the armour that Calen wore. It was impossibly smooth and flowing, seeming to have no splits or gaps whatsoever. It looked more like the Sentinel armour the Knights of Achyron wore.

"Il nära un'il Enkara vírnae ove'ae." *The light of the Enkara shines upon us.* Asius unfolded his legs and stood, a rare smile touching his lips.

It was then that Aeson saw the soft glow of purple light that drifted from the rune markings on Calen's armour. Those markings must have been how the plate flowed so seamlessly. Rumours of Valdrin's skills had not been exaggerated.

Valerys rose from where he lay, a deep rumble resonating in his throat. The dragon moved forwards, leaning his neck down. Calen rested his hand on Valerys's scaled snout, rain crashing down over them.

"He looks…" Atara shook her head as she tried to find the words.

"He looks like a Draleid."

Chapter Seventy-Three

The Fate of Lies and Loss

Calen sat by the stream in the Eyrie, a few feet from where the water tumbled over the cliff. Dann, Therin, Vaeril, Tarmon, Haem, Lyrin, and Erik sat around him, talking in the firelight, while Valerys was curled up at Calen's back with his head resting on Ithrax's tail. The enormous green dragon did little more than eat, sleep, and fly. Even still, that was more than any of the other five Rakina dragons; most barely moved. In the past few months, Valerys had taken to following Ithrax like a shadow. It broke Calen's heart to feel Valerys's sorrow and the strange loneliness that filled him. Somehow finding the dragons as they were had left Valerys feeling even more alone than he previously had.

Calen pulled in a long breath through his nose, letting it out slowly as he lifted his arms. Having the master runes inscribed into his skin hadn't hurt as much as he'd anticipated, but they'd still pained him. Valdrin had tattooed the runes in four circles, two wrapped around each of Calen's forearms, just below the wrist. The ink was silvery in colour, glimmering when it caught the light.

He traced the index finger of his right hand along the first circle of runes on his left forearm, whispering the phrase Valdrin had taught him – words in the ancient Jotnar tongue, "Dreskyr mit huartan. Dreskr mit hnokle. Bante er vi, measter og osvarthe."

Protect my heart. Protect my bones. Bound are we, master and oath.

The runes ignited, glowing with a faint purple light, and Calen could *feel* his armour where it rested on the stand in his chambers.

"What does it feel like?" Calen lifted his head to see Vaeril looking at him, curiosity in his eyes. "I've seen rune marked weapons and tools before, but I've never seen anything like that."

Calen looked at his arms, staring at the runes that glowed with a dim purple light. "It's almost like the runes are alive. When I ignite them, I can *feel* the armour like it's a part of me – an extension of my body. It's difficult to describe."

"I'm just happy you didn't melt," Dann said with a shrug, shifting the white wood bow in his lap. Calen didn't think he'd seen Dann without the bow since Valdrin had given it to him.

"Really, Dann?" Haem gave Dann a disapproving look, shaking his head.

"What? Are you not happy he didn't melt?"

"Three years." Haem tilted his head, staring at Dann. "Three years and you haven't changed in the slightest. I don't even think you've gotten taller."

"Hey." Dann held a finger. "No need to bring height into it. I'm six foot, I'll have you know."

Haem raised his eyebrows, a knowing smile on his lips.

"Five foot and eleven inches at most," Erik said. "And I'm being generous."

"You know what?" Dann puffed out his bottom lip. "If you're going to give me this much abuse, I'm going to make you listen to my new valúr." Dann pulled a satchel up onto his lap, undid the buckles, and started rooting around inside.

"New valúr? What happened to the carvings?" Erik looked to Therin and Vaeril. "Can he do that? I mean, can you just switch?"

Therin shrugged. "It's not usually done that way, but there's no rule. The concept is more about the understanding of what it takes to create something before you learn to destroy. Although, I'm not going to lie, my interest is piqued."

Dann stopped rummaging, pulling sheets of paper from within the satchel. "I was shit at those sculptures. Baldon told me so more than once – I think, in his own way, he was trying to encourage me? But that Angan is brutally honest." He waved a folded piece of paper in the air. "But I've found something I'm better at."

"I honestly thought your sculpture of Vaeril was fantastic." Tarmon looked to Vaeril, a smile sweeping across his face from ear to ear. "I keep it in my satchel in the room and take it out any time I want to laugh."

Vaeril glared at Tarmon.

Calen scratched at the stubble on his chin, eyeing the paper in Dann's hand. "I think you might be missing the point of a valúr, Dann. The idea isn't to find something you're good at, it's about dedicating yourself to something and appreciating the time and effort it takes to truly create something."

"Yeah…" Dann scrunched his mouth, pondering. He shook his head. "No, that doesn't sound right." Dann unfolded the piece of paper and held it out in front of him. He cracked his neck from side to side, then drew in a long, slow breath, letting it out in an overly dramatic fashion. "I call this one 'You might ride a dragon, but I'm still better.' Agh-hem."

"You may be tall, you may be strong
You may ride a dragon, be sung in song.
You may wield a sword, I'll give you that,
But when you last shot a bow, you killed a cat."

The echoes of Dann's last word faded, and the group sat in silence for a moment before both Dann and Calen burst out laughing. Calen laughed so hard tears rolled down his cheeks, and his stomach hurt. But as the laughter subsided, he looked to see that it was only he and Dann who had been laughing. Everyone else – Haem, Tarmon, Erik, Therin and Vaeril – just stared at the both of them as though they were mad.

"He…" Dann straightened, drawing a settling breath in through his nose, only to start laughing again. "Calen…" Dann exhaled sharply, composing himself. "Calen is terrible with a bow and arrow. Now, I don't mean when someone says they're terrible and they're actually quite good. You know like how Tarmon said he was a terrible singer and then we got him drunk two weeks ago, and he had a voice like a six-foot-five nightingale? No, not like that. Calen is the worst archer I've ever seen in my life."

"All right, Dann." Calen said, raising his hands "Try not to stick the knife in too deep."

"Sorry." Another laugh caught in Dann's throat. "But it's true. Anyway, one time when Rist and I were poking fun at Calen, he started complaining about the size of the target and how far it was. So we bet him he couldn't hit a barn door. He did that thing he does when he's challenged and got all grumpy, put a face on, puffed his chest out, and stomped over to the barn. And then he pulled back the string and loosed the arrow. Not only did the arrow soar past the left side of the barn – never mind the door – it flew into a nearby bush. All we heard was a screech. He'd hit a fucking cat. The only time he'd ever hit anything was by accident." Dann started laughing again, pressing his hand to his stomach. "He missed a literal barn door."

The others all exchanged glances.

"That's not funny," Vaeril said, his expression unchanging. "That's horrible."

Therin pursed his lips. "Even for you, that one's a bit strange."

"I mean…" Dann drew in a short breath, lifting a finger. He closed his hand into a fist and pressed it to his lips. "Well… All right, out of context like that, it's not as funny as it was at the time. I think you had to be there."

"Yeah…" Erik nodded, laughing. "Sure. Whatever helps you sleep at night, Pimm."

Tarmon shrugged. "I mean… your rhyming couplets were strong, at least."

All eyes turned to Tarmon, and everyone, including Vaeril, erupted in laughter.

"What?" Tarmon looked about nervously. "What did I say?"

Erik shook his head, pushing back his laugh. "It's just… do you write poetry, Tarmon?"

"I've tried my hand, what about it? Everyone needs a way to relax."

"It's just the idea of a big man like you writing poems. You look as though you could crush a skull with your bare hands. Now I can't shake the image of you hunched over a small table with a pen in hand writing the sweetest love poems the world has ever seen. You're full of surprises, Tarmon Hoard." Erik leaned closer to Tarmon, tilting his head and batting his eyelashes. He put on a sultry voice. "Would you write a love poem for me, Lord Captain?"

"Oh, fuck off!" Tarmon pushed Erik onto his back, but Erik just laughed, the others joining in.

Calen allowed himself a laugh as well, but his mind kept drifting. In four days, the High Lord of Illyanara, Castor Kai, was to come to Aravell. Due to an increase in Lorian forces in the South, the High Lord was travelling by side-road with little more than a few guards. Aeson, Chora, and the others wanted Calen to fly out on Valerys to meet Castor Kai at the front gates of the city; they wanted him to put on a show. But the thought of doing such a thing for Castor Kai turned Calen's stomach after the story Therin had told of what the man had done with Vars and the Angan.

Even with those thoughts pushed to the back of his mind, Calen was restless. According to Grandmaster Kallinvar, the Blood Moon – the same thing that had aided in the destruction of The Order – was only a matter of days or weeks away. Calen and the others had agreed to aid the knights in whatever was to come. But even with everything Calen had learned from Chora, Harken, Thacia, Atara, and the other Rakina, he couldn't fight the doubts in his mind. Each of them had been Draleid for decades or centuries before The Fall. There had been thousands of them, and still they had failed. What chance did Calen have against the empire and the Dragonguard, against Efialtír himself?

He'd tried to push Atara's words to the darkest corners of his mind, but still, they plagued him. *'The Dragonguard will tear you apart, Calen. Piece by piece. They have killed hundreds of our kind. Draleid far older and wiser than you.'*

A warning from Valerys flashed in Calen's mind, and the dragon shifted. As their minds pulled together, Calen could see Baldon approaching through Valerys's eyes. Calen turned, and as he did, Baldon placed his right palm over his forehead, nodding to both Calen and Haem. "Sons of the Chainbreaker, Therin Silverfang. You are needed immediately."

Calen groaned as he heaved himself to a standing position, his muscles aching from the non-stop training. "What is it, Baldon? What's wrong?"

The Angan pulled his hand away from his forehead. "Aneera has reached out to me. The daughter of the Chainbreaker is at the western gates."

～⊕～

ELLA STOOD AT THE EDGE of an enormous white stone courtyard, Farda, Ilyain, and Hala to her left, Tanner and Yana at her right. The Darkwood rose at Ella's back while before her, across the courtyard, city walls spread left and right, blending seamlessly into the cliffs on either side. The walls were split by gates that looked as though they had been hewn from the bones of a giant stag, their tips like antlers twisting upwards. And, as though everything wasn't already surreal enough, veins of soft azure light wound through the stone of the courtyard and the walls, painting the scene in an ethereal light. She remembered a time she almost let herself be run over by a cart when staring up at the white towers of Midhaven. How insignificant they seemed now.

Faenir brushed against Ella's side, his ears pricked as he stared at the two Angan who stood before them – Ella had recognised them from Ilyain's descriptions. Over the course of their journey through Loria to Catagan and then around the western and southern coasts of Epheria by ship, Ilyain had spent many hours teaching Ella as much of the Angan and the druids as he knew. Each word he'd spoken had been like a weight lifted from her shoulders. Each detail he'd shared of Andras had helped her to better understand small fragments of herself and to better understand what she was.

The first of the two Angan, who had said his name was Gavrien, stood only a few feet in front of Ella. He was covered in short white fur. His legs were double hinged, he had hooves instead of feet, and black antlers laced with gold grew from his head. From what Ilyain had taught her, Gavrien was of Clan Dvalin – the clan of the stag.

It was Gavrien who had found them wandering the outer reaches of the Darkwood. Once Ella had told him that Calen was her brother, he'd brought them straight to Aneera, who was clearly of Clan Fenryr – the god to which Ilyain believed Ella was tied. Her grey fur was thicker and rougher than Gavrien's, and her nails looked more akin to claws. Her face was harsh, and her teeth were sharp like a wolf's. Aneera sat on the ground with her legs crossed and her eyes closed.

Just as Ella had heard and felt the message sent across Loria, so too could she feel the one Aneera was now sending. Her fingers curled inwards, and a high-pitched noise pierced her ears. She drew in slow breaths, trying to focus. Images of a giant wolf wrapped in chains flashed through her mind. The chains snapped and were replaced by three children standing beneath a tree, broken links at their feet. She understood the intention of the message. *Come. Unite. Pack.* There was more; she could feel it, but she couldn't understand it. It was as though Ella was only seeing fragments of the whole message.

"How long does this take?" Hala asked, her voice wrought with impatience. That was one thing Ella had learned about the woman whilst travelling on the ship: for someone who had seen as many summers as Hala, she had as much patience as a four-year-old child and a temperament to match.

"It takes as long as it takes." Farda stood with the hood of his black mantle drawn up over his head. "Do not wish for this journey to end so quickly, Hala."

"You never know," Hala answered back. "Maybe they'll welcome us back as prodigal siblings."

"I think they will sooner hang us from the city gates." Ilyain's tone was flat and level, as it always tended to be.

The three of them had talked that way for most of the last leg of the journey. It made no sense to Ella. If they knew that coming here would mean the end of them, then why had they come? She had asked them to leave her at Kingspass, to let her and Faenir make the last leg of the journey alone. Ilyain and Hala had contemplated it, but Farda had flat out refused. In the end, Ilyain and Hala had committed themselves to going where Farda went.

Aneera let out a low rumble as she opened her eyes and stood. She bowed her head to Ella, leaning back on her left leg. "Baldon Stormseeker has informed the sons of the Chainbreaker that you are here."

The Angan's voice sounded unnatural; she paused on each word as though pondering it, a distinct gruffness painting every syllable. *Wait, sons?*

Ella was about to ask Aneera what she meant when the Angan pressed the palm of her right hand to her forehead – Ilyain had told Ella the gesture was a sign of respect amongst the Angan clans. "Please, daughter of the Chainbreaker, I must ask your forgiveness, for myself and for all of clan Fenryr. Had we known you yet lived, we would have come for you."

Ella wasn't sure what to say. She had no idea why Aneera kept referring to her and Calen as the son and daughter of the Chainbreaker. What did their dad have to do with any of this?

"I'm sorry." Ella looked into Aneera's golden eyes. "I don't know what you mean. You don't need forgiveness for anything. I've never met you before."

"No. We have not before met, daughter of the Chainbreaker. But there is much you do not know. Therin Silverfang will explain. I am sorry we were not there for you, as we should have been. Though it warms my heart to see the Blessed One has kept you safe." Aneera bowed to Faenir, a low growl resonating in her throat. She reached out her hand, and to Ella's surprise Faenir nuzzled against her with the familiarity of a cub and his mother.

Aneera's golden eyes shimmered as she stared into Faenir's, then looked back to Ella. "And you are of the warrior blood, a guardian of Fenryr, an Aldruid. I can feel it in you." Aneera's mouth twisted into a grin that revealed rows of razor-sharp teeth, two fangs protruding from the top and bottom. "Today is a day of celebration."

Ella didn't know what to say. Aneera was speaking as though she knew more about Ella than Ella did herself. She was about to speak when the Dvalin Angan, Gavrien, turned his antlered head towards the gates.

"They come."

As Gavrien spoke, Ella's jaw dropped, her eyes widening. A dragon covered in gleaming white scales soared over the walls. It looked smaller than the ones she had seen with the imperial armies, but it was far closer than they had ever been. The creature's body was enormous. Its wings, spread wide like the sails of a ship, were a pale white with veins of black running through them. Its neck was long and muscular, horns the length of her arms framed its jaw and the side of its face, while its talons looked as though they could tear a horse in half with ease.

The creature swept over the courtyard, appearing larger the closer it got.

Ella's heart stopped as something – no, someone – fell from the dragon's back. *Calen?* Ella took a step forward, then broke into a run, watching as her brother plummeted towards the ground. Panic jolted through her. Her body shook as she ran, Faenir bounding beside her. She screamed so loudly her voice cracked "Calen!"

As the figure approached the ground, they slowed, a gust of wind sweeping around them. The instant their feet touched the white stone of the courtyard, they broke into a run, the dragon alighting behind them.

How is that possible? The questions were swept from Ella's mind as the figure looked up, and she saw her little brother's face looking back at her. She kept running. "Calen!"

Calen crashed into her so hard he nearly knocked her off her feet. He wrapped his arms around her and squeezed as though he was trying to push the air from her lungs. "You're alive." He buried his head in the crook of her neck, and she felt the wet touch of tears. "Ella."

Ella pulled him in even tighter. "Of course I'm alive."

As though she hadn't spoken, Calen kept saying the same thing. "You're alive."

Ella gripped the back of Calen's shirt, hugging him so tightly she was worried he might break. Then she pulled away, clasping her hands either side of his face. Tears rolled down his cheeks.

"I thought you were dead. That day… I thought you were in the house when it caught fire."

Ella's breath caught in her chest. *Was that how they died?*

"I'm here." Ella pulled Calen close, stroking the back of his head, her fingers running through his hair. He trembled against her. He was bigger than the last time she'd seen him – his shoulders were broader, his muscles denser. His face had changed too; it looked harder, colder. But with it all, the biggest change was the way he hugged her. He'd never hugged her like that before, as though he'd never let go. Tears burned in Ella's eyes as she pulled her brother even tighter, pulling his head to her shoulder. "I'm here, I'm here, I'm here."

A low growl sounded to the right. Ella pulled away, wiping a tear from Calen's cheek. "I'm not the only one who's here."

"No… Faen—"

Calen had almost finished saying Faenir's name before the wolfpine crashed into his chest and tackled him to the ground. Ella smiled as she watched Faenir roll around the stone with Calen, licking her brother's face like he'd done since he was a pup.

"Hello, little sister."

Ella's body seized, her muscles tensing. Her blood went cold in her veins. She didn't want to lift her head. *That voice… it can't be.* She drew in a long breath, then looked.

Ella's heart thumped and fluttered at the same time, her stomach turned, and her legs gave way. She dropped to the ground, trembling, tears in freefall as she looked up at a face she had known she would never see again. "No…" Ella shook her head, her vision blurring from the tears. "It's not possible… It can't be you. It can't."

Haem reached down and slid his arms around Ella, lifting her gently. She trembled as he held her, her legs struggling to hold her own weight. Haem looked her in the eyes. "It is."

He pulled her into a tight embrace and she broke. She sobbed and convulsed, burying her head against her brother's shoulder, shaking it back and forth. "It can't be you… Please, please don't let this be a trick."

"It's not a trick," Haem whispered as he held her, his arms wrapping around her with ease, his hand holding the back of her head as she had just held Calen's.

Ella sniffled and sobbed, tears mixing with snot as she pulled her head away, looking up at her brother's face. Her voice quivered as she spoke. "Haem?"

Haem nodded, a weak smile touching his lips, and that was all it took for Ella to break down again. She stayed like that, crying in his arms for what felt like an eternity, and he held her. Once she'd managed to stop the tears, she leaned back to see Haem smiling down at her – she'd forgotten how tall he was. Only one question filled her mind. "How?"

Haem pulled his hand from her back and brushed a tear from cheek. "That is an answer that will require some time. Once we get inside, we can have some mead and sit by a fire. I'll tell you everything."

Ella tried to muster a smile as she sniffed through her now blocked nose. "They have mead?"

Haem laughed, pulling Ella into one more hug. "Lower your expectations."

He gave her one last squeeze, then stepped back, looking at where Calen was still trying – and failing – to push Faenir away. "That... that can't be Faenir?"

"It's Faenir." Ella wiped the tears and snots from her face with the back of her hand, then rubbed them into her trousers; the trousers needed a wash anyway.

"He's almost as big as a horse."

"There's a lot I have to tell, too." Ella stared at Haem, tracing every line of his face, ever wrinkle and crease. In case that portal, or barrier, or whatever they had stepped through to reveal this place was manipulating her mind. It felt real. It looked real. But even if it was some illusion, she didn't care; she had gotten to see her brother one last time. That was everything.

"All right. That's enough, Faenir." Calen laughed, which only encouraged Faenir even more.

After a moment, the wolfpine allowed Calen to get to his feet. The sense of elation – the sense of pack, of family – that flashed from Faenir's mind to Ella's made her heart glow. Pure, unfettered happiness blazed within him, and that joy only grew greater when Faenir turned to see Haem.

Even Haem with all his bulk and muscle couldn't stay upright as Faenir tackled him to the stone.

"I can't believe it's you." Ella turned to see Calen staring into her eyes. It was only then she realised the green of his irises was gone, supplanted by a pale lavender.

"It's me." A soft smile rested on Ella's lips as she looked at her little brother – though, little didn't quite apply anymore. "You've grown." She touched his cheek, looking at his eyes. "Changed."

Calen lifted his hand to his face and rested it atop Ella's. "So have you." He leaned in a bit closer. "You've hit your nose a few times." He tilted his head to the side, his eyes narrowing as he looked at the scar the Urak claw had left on the side of her head. He reached up to touch the mark. "And what in the gods happened there?"

"I think you'll find somebody else hit my nose." Ella pulled away, frowning.

A deep, visceral growl rose beside Ella, and she could feel Faenir's hackles rising. Ella turned to see the white dragon standing before her. Up close, it was enormous. Its shoulders were three times as broad as a horse's, and its jaws looked as though they could rip through Faenir in a single bite.

The dragon leaned its head down, scaled nostrils flaring. It regarded her with pale lavender eyes that gleamed with intelligence. In a sense, the dragon looked almost regal, while at the same time seeming as though it was a creature of complete and utter destruction.

"Ella, this is Valerys."

The dragon snorted a puff of warm air over Ella, blowing her hair up and back.

Ella extended her open hand, and Valerys pressed the tip of his snout against her palm. His scales were cool to the touch at first, but then a warmth radiated from them. They felt as hard as stone. "He's incredible…"

In all the things she had seen since leaving The Glade – the Uraks, the Angan, mages, armies of elves – Ella had never seen anything quite like Valerys. *A dragon. A true, living, breathing dragon.*

"He is." Calen stared at the dragon with pride. He gave a soft smile, then looked to Faenir, who had moved from Haem and was drawing ever closer to Valerys, hackles raised, a deep growl rumbling in his throat. "I don't think Faenir is so sure."

Valerys's eyes shifted to Faenir, and he brought his snout down just in front of the prowling wolfpine. Even with how large Faenir had grown, he looked like a pup next to the dragon. The two creatures watched each other, both waiting for the other to make a move. Ella could feel Faenir's apprehension. This was a creature he knew could kill him with as little effort as Faenir might kill a mouse, and yet the wolfpine would stand between Ella and the dragon without a moment's pause.

"Does this remind anyone of the time Faenir stared down the horse when he was only a pup?" Haem folded his arms, smiling as he watched Faenir and Valerys.

"I don't think this is going to end the same way," Calen said, folding his arms the same way Haem had. "Valerys doesn't scare as easily as a horse."

Valerys leaned his head forwards and nudged Faenir in the side with his snout, which only elicited a deeper growl from the wolfpine. Calen and Haem burst out laughing as the wolfpine almost leapt from his fur when Valerys blew a puff of hot air over him.

Ella just stood there for a moment, watching her brothers as they watched Faenir and Valerys. Tears once again burned at the corners of her eyes, while a smile curled on her lips. She could have stood there forever in that perfect moment, and she would have if she hadn't seen figures emerging from the city gates. A group of seven. She looked to Calen. "Who's that?"

"Friends," Calen said with a wry smile.

As the group drew closer, Ella could make out faces. One was an Angan of clan Fenryr. Another was as tall as Haem, with shoulders to match. But then she saw someone else. "Calen, is that…"

"Ella Bryer." The smile on Dann Pimm's face spread from ear to ear. Ella saw the glint in his eye that always meant he was about to say something stupid. "Finally missed me too much to stay away?"

Yup. Stupid. Ella shook her head and laughed. Pulling Dann into a warm hug. He was a menace, always had been. Not a word popped into his head that didn't leave his mouth. When they had all been younger, Ella's mam, Ylinda Pimm, and Elia Havel had always asked Ella and Haem to watch over Calen, Rist, and Dann. Even then, Dann had been a pain. But he had always looked out for Calen – always. And Ella loved him for that. "It's good to see you too, Dann."

The strength of Dann's embrace took Ella a bit by surprise. But then he pulled away, looked at her and said, "Gods, that nose has seen better days."

"You want one to match?"

"Easy, easy." Dann raised his open hands defensively. "I was only saying."

Ella shook her head at Dann, then looked past him to see a face she truly had not expected. "Therin?"

The elf gave Ella a weak smile. She'd only talked to him once or twice before, but she'd sat in awe and listened to his stories more times than she could count. To her surprise, Therin pulled her into a hug. It wasn't as warm an embrace as Calen, Haem, or Dann had given her, but she hadn't expected any embrace at all from the elf.

"It's good to see you are well."

There was something about the way Therin looked at her that scratched at Ella. His words were genuine, but there was something else – a sadness.

"Ella," Calen moved over to join Ella, Therin, and Dann, the other newcomers standing a few feet back. Calen looked at her as though seeing a ghost – which she supposed he was. He shook his head, smiling. "I still can't believe you're here. I have so many questions. What happened? How did you get here? Who is with you?"

"I think Haem's suggestion…" Ella let her gaze linger on Haem for a second. She was waiting for this illusion to drop, for him to vanish. But he was still there, scratching Faenir's head. "Sorry," she said to Calen, gathering herself. "I think Haem's suggestion of a warm fire and a mead would go down well if we're to tell stories. We've been a long time travelling." Ella gestured to Yana, Tanner, Farda, Ilyain, and Hala, who stood twenty or so feet back where she'd left them when she'd run to Calen. "We sent a letter to Aeson Virandr. Months ago. We sent it to his contact in Argona. I thought he would have gotten it while we were travelling. Coren said you would be with him. Is he here?"

Calen looked from Ella to Therin. "He is here, but we never got a letter…" Calen's voice trailed off as he stared at Therin. The elf was looking at the ground. Something shifted in Calen's expression, and Ella thought she saw a glow emanating from his eyes. Behind him, Valerys pulled away from Faenir, fixing his stare on Therin and Calen. "Therin, we got letters from Arem months ago. I remember. Aeson got a letter from Dahlen telling us what had happened in Durakdur. And we've gotten plenty since."

Therin nodded slowly. "He did, and we have…"

Calen's jaw tensed, and Ella could see an anger in him. It wasn't the petulant anger of the boy she'd known; there was a harshness in this anger, a violence. Calen had always been quick to anger, but at heart he was a sweet boy. Ella saw none of that sweetness now. "Therin, what are you not saying?"

The elf sucked at the sides of his cheeks, then lifted his gaze to meet Calen's. "I'm sorry, Calen."

Ella took a step back as Calen's eyes radiated a deep purple light, wisps of luminescent mist rising into the air. *What in the gods?* Valerys had moved so he stood over Calen, a low rumble in his throat. Calen took a step closer to Therin; his entire demeanour had shifted in a matter of moments. His voice was sharp, his body taut. "Sorry for what, Therin?"

Haem looked to Ella, worry in his eyes.

Therin swallowed hard, but held Calen's gaze. "After you went north in search of Rist… when we got the letter, we decided not to tell you. If you went after her, Calen, the Dragonguard would have ripped you to shreds. I… I'm sorry. We thought it best to wait and bring her to you when it was safe. I didn't want to keep it from you… I'm sorry, Calen."

Calen stared at Therin, his eyes glowing. Valerys mirrored Calen, looming over him, lips pulling back to show rows of razor-sharp teeth. "You knew Ella was alive." There was something cold in Calen's voice that set Ella's hairs on end. "You knew she was alive, and you let me think she was dead." A tremble set into Calen's words, and a single tear rolled down his cheek, glistening in the purple light of his eyes. "What gave you the right? What if she had died, Therin?"

"I…"

Calen moved so his face was only inches from Therin's. "What if she had died?" The muscles in his jaw tensed, his hands curling into fists at his side. "I trusted you. Aeson has always been trying to tie strings around me. But you… you, I trusted." A short silence followed, before Calen's voice dropped to a deep growl. "Where is he?"

"Calen, don't. It will only—"

"Where is he?" Calen roared, his voice blending with the primal thunder that erupted from Valerys's jaws. Together, their roars shook the air.

Therin stared back at Calen but didn't speak. The sorrow and guilt in the elf's eyes was all-consuming.

Another young man, who had come with Dann from the city, stepped forwards. His hair was dark blond, and he was built like a soldier, the pommels of two swords jutting over his shoulders. "Calen, breathe. All right. Don't let him twist you like this."

Calen turned his head. "No, Erik. This time he's gone too far." He looked to the Angan who stood beside Erik. "Baldon, where is Aeson Virandr?"

Aeson stood in the main chamber of Mythníril, his arms folded and his back to the doors. He looked over the white stone table at the centre of the space, the moonlight drifting in from the oculus overhead augmenting the soft glow of the erinian stone that marked the cities and provinces of the map carved into the table.

He'd been there for hours as the Triarchy and the Ephorí argued back and forth over how many warriors each of the kingdoms would contribute for the welcome ceremony when Castor Kai arrived in four days. He'd spent so long away from Aravell he'd forgotten what the elven rulers were truly like.

Two of the knights – Ildris and Sister-Captain Ruon – stood on the opposite side of the table, rows of arched windows set into the wall behind them. Kallinvar wanted the knights to be part of the welcome for each of the major leaders, and so Ruon and Ildris had been asked to join the discussions. Ildris's expression hadn't changed even once, but Aeson could see the ever-growing frustration on Ruon's face. In the short time he'd known her, he'd learned she was not the kind of person who abided needless back and forth.

"What of those pledged to the Draleid?" Thurivîr looked to Aeson, his silvery hair sitting still against his crimson and gold robes.

"What of them?" Aeson said with a sigh, trying his best to conceal his frustration.

"We must have equal representation from the three kingdoms. All three have gifted him oathbound warriors. I would say two hundred from each kingdom should be on display. And then an equal number of humans. Lunithír has granted the young smith, Valdrin, fifty-three of our own smiths to aid in the production of the new armour."

"Ardurän has provided fifty-five smiths," Baralas added.

"What the fuck does it matter?"

Gasps spread through the gathered Ephorí at Ruon's outburst. The woman stood in her smooth green Sentinel armour, her hands outstretched before her. The only two people in the room who hadn't been shocked were the other knight– Ildris – and Queen Uthrían, who stood with her mouth twisted into a grin.

The two kings, Silmiryn and Galdra stared at Ruon, a picture of shock and irritation evident in their expressions. Even they knew better than to think they held any sway over a knight of Achyron.

"Sister-Captain Ruon." The second Ardurän Ephori, Liritháin, took a step closer to Ruon but instead, found herself staring up at the broad-shouldered frame of Ildris. The man had a cold intensity about him. It looked as though Liritháin were about to challenge him, but a loud crash sounded in the hallway outside.

Aeson turned towards the door, the hairs on the back of his neck pricking up as he felt the sensation of someone drawing from the Spark. Around him, he saw the Ephorí and the elven rulers all exchange glances.

"Step aside."

Aeson recognised Calen's voice as it boomed in the hallway. A few seconds passed, and then the doors to the main chamber swung open with such force they cracked against the walls. The six elven guards stood to either side, their eyes fixed on Calen as he strode into the chamber towards Aeson. A roar rolled through the night sky outside.

The young man's eyes glowed with a purple light that misted outwards, trailing after him as he moved. Calen stared at Aeson, his gaze unwavering. Aeson could *feel* the fury in him. Waves of energy pulsed from Calen, rippling outwards, his body thrumming with the Spark.

"Calen, what's wrong?"

"You knew she was alive." Calen rammed his hands into Aeson's chest. The Spark-augmented strike sent Aeson careening backwards. He slammed into the stone table, the air fleeing his lungs.

Fury rising within him, Aeson heaved himself upright. He opened himself to the Spark, pulling at threads of Air. "How dare you—" Aeson cut his sentence short. The Spark was gone. Calen had warded him.

"How dare I?" Calen roared. He moved so he stood only inches from Aeson, nostrils flaring, chest heaving. "You let me believe my sister was dead so I would play along with your games. All I've ever been to you is a puppet. Was any of what you said to me true?" Calen shook his head, a wicked smile on his lips. "I can't believe I let you twist me. I fucking trusted you!"

Aeson stared into the pulsating light of Calen's eyes. There was nothing he could say. Therin must have told Calen. Aeson hadn't wanted to keep the news of Ella from Calen, but he'd had no choice. Calen had already proven that he was reckless when the people he loved were in danger. If Aeson had told him Ella was alive, Calen would have flown right into the Dragonguard's hands. But even that knowledge didn't scrub the guilt that marred Aeson's heart as he looked back at Calen.

"I'm done with you, Aeson. I'll fight because there are people who need me. But I'm done being your puppet." Calen's voice was level, but an icy rage radiated from him. He'd always been quick to temper, but Aeson knew this – this was a dragon's fury. "I hate you for proving Artim Valdock right."

Calen stared at Aeson for a moment longer, then walked around the stone table, ignoring everyone else. He strode past Ruon and Ildris and over towards the arched windows.

"Calen. Stop. Where are you going? You can't go after her."

"To try and find the truth," Calen called back. He stopped at one of the arched windows. "Tell Ella I'm sorry, and I'll be back in a few days."

She's here.

"Calen! Where are you going? Don't be an idiot!"

Without another word, Calen jumped from the window ledge, threads of Air whirling around him, and Valerys's roar tore through the sky.

Aeson stood on the bridge that joined Alura to the rest of the city. The flames of the lanterns set along the parapet cast flickering shadows over the stone. He drew in a slow, level breath, watching as Therin and the others approached.

"I had to, Aeson."

Aeson could see the weight of the guilt in Therin's eyes. He'd never wanted to put Therin in that position. It would have been so much easier if it had been him and not Therin who'd picked up that letter. Aeson had no problem with Calen hating him as long as Calen was alive; he could bear that burden. "It's all right. I understand."

"Where is he?"

"Gone. I don't know where. He said he'll be back in a few days."

As Therin started to speak, Calen's brother, Arden, pushed past him. Liquid metal poured from his chest and swept over his body, rolling across his arms and legs, forming into Sentinel armour. Aeson barely had time to react before the man rammed his fists into Aeson's chest, then grasped Aeson's shirt with both hands. Arden lifted him into the air with the ease of a man lifting a child and slammed him against the parapet of the bridge. Aeson grimaced and gasped for air as a piercing pain erupted through his back, and the air was knocked from his lungs. He reached for the Spark, but as he did, Arden tightened his armoured fists around Aeson's shirt.

"Try it. I'll break your neck before any of that magic leaves your body." Since Calen's brother had emerged with Calen from the Burnt Lands, all Aeson had seen him be was calm and measured. But then, as Arden held Aeson aloft, all he saw in the man's eyes was pure hatred. "If you ever think about lying to my brother again, about using him, or twisting him, or manipulating him, I will break you." Arden's grasp tightened again. His stare was unyielding. "Do you understand?"

Aeson stared back at the man, meeting his gaze. The pain in his back burned up his spine and down through his legs, but he kept his face steady.

Arden pulled his face closer. "I don't think you understand. I don't care who you are. I don't care what your name is. The only people who matter to me in this world are the one you just hurt, and the one you were happy to leave for dead. I need you to listen to me very carefully. I will fucking kill you. I will ram my Soulblade through your cold, black heart." Arden moved his head closer. "Do you fucking understand now?"

There, on that bridge, was the first time in a very long time that Aeson felt fear in his heart. The look in Arden's eyes was not that of a man who was making an idle threat. Aeson didn't fear death; death was inevitable. But if his life was taken by a Soulblade, he would never feel the touch of Lyara's mind again.

"I'm going to need you to speak." A tremble slipped through Arden's level tone.

"I understand."

Arden let out a sigh through his nostrils, nodding slowly. "Good." The knight lowered Aeson to the stone, staring into his eyes. "Don't come near my sister."

With that, Arden walked past Aeson as though nothing had happened.

Aeson let out a sharp breath, his heart pounding.

"There's something else," Therin said, barely giving Aeson a chance to catch his breath. The elf's expression was a sombre one. He gestured behind him to where Tarmon, Erik, Vaeril, Baldon, and Aneera stood. Beside them was a young woman with golden hair and a wolf that was almost the size of a horse. He had no doubt the woman was Ella. She stared at Aeson with an unwavering intensity. Beside her, the wolf's hackles lifted, and a his nose crinkled into a snarl, revealing his fangs.

But it wasn't Ella who Therin had gestured to. Beside her stood a man and a woman side by side, along with three others, their hoods drawn.

Aeson recognised the man Immediately. "Tanner."

"Aeson." Tanner nodded. Aeson saw the disappointment etched into the man's face.

One of the three hooded figures let out a sigh. "Better to get this over with."

A fury swelled within Aeson's chest as the figure drew down their hood, and Aeson's gaze fell on the face of Farda Kyrana.

CHAPTER SEVENTY-FOUR

THE PAST, IT RIPPLES

The vibrations of Valerys's wingbeats thrummed through Calen, his face and hands pressed against the dragon's scales. Valerys's warmth held the bite of the icy wind at bay, but Calen still felt his fingers growing numb. They'd flown for hours after leaving Aravell. Calen hadn't been sure of Dracaldryr's precise location, but he'd seen it on maps, and he knew to follow the Lodhar mountains to the ocean and to look for a massive island covered in snow-capped mountain peaks a couple hundred miles from the Lorian coast. Valerys had flown at such speeds Calen's only choices had been to close his eyes or deflect the wind with the Spark. Considering the lack of sleep he'd had, closing his eyes had seemed the simpler option. Through the dragon's eyes, he watched as the ocean sparkled with the red-orange glow of the rising sun. Ahead, the peaks of Dracaldryr jutted from the ocean, coated in a blanket of white.

No matter how hard he tried to push it down, anger still simmered in Calen's blood. Both Aeson and Therin had been willing to let him think Ella was dead. If something had happened, he would never have seen her again. It had taken every ounce of his strength to step away from Aeson. The rage within him had wanted him to draw his blade, but he'd held it back. His fingers curled into fists at the thought of it.

The last thing he'd wanted to do after finally finding Ella alive was to leave her. Doing so had felt wrong, but it was what he needed to do. Calen needed to hear what Pellenor had to say. He needed to know more about who he was, about what had truly happened to cause The Fall. He couldn't wait any longer. All he knew of the Dragonguard was what Aeson and the other Rakina had told him. But the image they painted was at odds with the words Pellenor had spoken. And now he knew Aeson had no qualms about lying to his face. *'We're not hunting you, Calen. We've been trying to find you, to protect you. You are the last hope for the survival of our kind… There is a temple atop the highest peak of Dracaldryr. When you are ready, light the beacon on the temple's roof.'*

A deep rumble resonated through Valerys in response to Calen's thoughts, and the dragon cracked his wings, rising higher. After a few moments, Valerys spotted an enormous column-fronted temple nestled into the side of a great mountain towards the centre of the island. As soon as the temple came into view, Valerys angled his wings and plummeted. Calen let out a breath at the feeling of weightlessness that he had grown used to whenever Valerys dropped into steep dives. The dragon descended towards the island at such speeds Calen's body shook, the icy wind snapping at his exposed skin.

Calen shifted in his place at the nape of Valerys's neck, anticipating the movement as the dragon spread his wings and changed direction in a heartbeat, swooping towards the island, the force of the world against them. All those hours, days, weeks, and months of training, and it was only that moment that Calen truly understood what Chora had been telling him all along. *'You must fly until it is as effortless as breathing.'*

Calen opened his eyes as Valerys slowed, the ocean disappearing beneath them to be replaced by rocks, trees, and rivers. Calen leaned backwards, sitting upright on Valerys's back as the dragon soared through the valleys that filled the island, sweeping along the rock face, twisting and turning, skirting the forest canopies below. He opened his arms, the frigid air crashing over him and filling his lungs. Pure joy rippled from Valerys to Calen. This was what it meant to be free. This is what it meant to fly. For a few brief minutes, both Calen and Valerys allowed themselves to forget the troubles and darkness of the world.

That calm was shattered when a monstrous roar ripped through the valley, echoing against the rising peaks on either side.

Dread coiled within them. They looked about frantically, searching for the source of the roar. Atop a ledge that jutted out from a nearby mountainside, Calen watched as an enormous dragon unfurled their wings, purple scales glittering like precious gems. Even from a distance, Calen could see that the creature was almost twice Valerys's size. The dragon watched for a moment, then stepped forwards and dropped from the ledge.

Calen's heart drummed against his ribs, beating faster and faster as the dragon plummeted down the rock face. The slightest shift in the dragon's wings and the creature pulled away from the rock, hurtling towards them.

Valerys's body rippled like a wave, and then he was diving. He dropped so fast Calen thought he might be torn from the dragon's back. Calen leaned forwards, pressing his body tight to Valerys. Vibrations swept through him, causing his teeth to chatter.

As Valerys dropped, he spread his wings and angled his body, rounding the base of a nearby cliff and emerging into a valley five times as wide as any they had passed through. Thick forests were split by a wide river, all leading towards a mountain that rose so high it looked as though it pierced the sky itself. *The Temple.*

The wind crashed against Valerys, thick like waves, fighting against every beat of his wings. Calen pushed back, looking over each shoulder, scanning the sky for any sight of the purple dragon. Over his left, he saw nothing but rock face and clouds. Over his right, the sun rested in the icy blue sky.

Panic turned his blood to ice as a shadow swept across the sun. The purple dragon soared above, a deep rumble resonating in their throat. Calen's heartbeat slowed as the creature glided in the air above, wings wide and still. In that moment he felt both calm and dread, for he knew if that dragon had wanted to tear them from the sky they could have done so with ease.

Up close, the dragon was even larger than Calen had first thought. An ocean of purple scales washed over slabs of dense muscle. The scales grew lighter at the edges, turning to cream along the dragon's underbelly.

With inimitable grace, the massive creature shifted in the air and swept left, swirling around Valerys like a leaf caught in the wind, its size belying a deft elegance. Purple scales faded to white along the dragon's snout, horns as large as Calen's legs framing their face. Warmth spilled over from Valerys's mind as the dragon soared in the air beside him. Through Valerys, Calen could feel that this dragon was different to those that hid in the Aravell. This dragon was whole.

With a crack of their wings, the dragon streaked forwards, twisting and spiralling in the air. A fire ignited within Valerys, and he surged after the purple scaled dragon, throwing all caution to the wind. Calen pulled their minds together, a rush of pure elation flooding him. Valerys was not alone. *They* were not alone. This dragon was bound.

Valerys followed after the purple dragon, mimicking their every move. Calen's joy came with a bitter aftertaste. This feeling was what Valerys deserved; such a simple thing, to not feel alone. Calen had been told of the elven dragons at the battle near Steeple. But from what Therin and the others had told him, any Draleid that fought alongside the Lynalion elves would not consider Calen and Valerys to be kin. Though, given every-thing, that could be lies too.

The dragons soared through the valley, their tails creating ripples along the river before they swept upwards, climbing towards the temple that was nestled into the rock of the mountain ahead.

The enormous purple dragon surged past the stone platform that jutted from the rock before looping backwards in the air and alighting on the stone.

Valerys slowed as he reached the platform, unwilling to attempt the same feat of aerial acrobatics. He rose past the platform's edge, then hung for a moment, a beat of his wings carrying him forwards, his talons clicking against stone as he landed.

The purple-scaled dragon stood before them, forelimbs pressed against the stone, head bowed. An elf stood before the dragon, hair dark and robes darker. Her forehead was pressed to the dragon's snout.

Calen slid from Valerys's back, softening his landing with threads of Air. He could feel Valerys looming over him as the elf approached. She was a few inches shorter than he was. Her skin was pale, eyes dark and sunken. A scar cleft her lip on the right side. She stared at Calen with an unsettling intensity as she walked. The purple-scaled dragon moved behind her, shimmering yellow eyes watching.

"I am Calen Bryer." Calen took a step towards the elf, trying to push any of his lingering fear down. He fought his instinct to drop his hand to his sword as she walked towards him wordlessly. This was a Dragonguard – one of those who had turned their back on The Order. At least, that was the story he'd been told. He'd come here to find the truth. Pellenor had not tried to kill him. He needed to have faith. If he didn't try, then he would have wasted his time in coming here. "I've come because—"

The elf crashed into him like a sack of stones, wrapping her arms around him, squeezing him like a long-lost friend. "I'd prayed you'd come, brother. I'd prayed, but I dared not hope."

Calen froze, unsure how to respond.

The elf pulled away and touched her fingers tenderly against Calen's left cheek, smiling. "Draleid n'aldryr, Calen. Laël Tivar Savinír. Din närvarvin gryrr haydria til myia elwyn." *Dragonbound by fire, Calen. I am Tivar Savinír. Your presence brings honour to my heart.*

"Draleid n'aldryr," Calen repeated. He had not expected her to be so open. "Det er diar acea gryrr haydria til myialí." *It is yours that brings honour to mine.*

The smile on Tivar's lips spread even wider as Calen spoke the Old Tongue. Her touch lingered on his cheek before she pulled her hand away and looked to Valerys. "He is the most beautiful sight I have set eyes on in four hundred years." Her voice was almost a whisper, laced with awe and reverence. "His name?"

"Valerys."

Valerys lowered his head, pressing his snout against Tivar's open palm. Comfort and belonging filled the dragon's mind.

"Ice," Tivar whispered as she rested her palm against Valerys's scales. "It's perfect." She pressed her forehead against Valerys's snout, then gestured to the purple dragon. "Valerys, anarie myia nithríen, Avandeer."

Valerys, meet my soulkin, Avandeer.

Valerys lifted his head, his lavender eyes studying Avandeer. Warmth spread through Valerys, tempered only by a thin layer of caution as he stretched his neck towards the larger dragon. A low rumble in Valerys's throat was echoed by Avandeer. The purple dragon nuzzled the side of her scaled snout into Valerys's jaw. The sound that resonated in Avandeer's chest was something Calen could only compare to a purr.

As Calen let his mind slip into Valerys's, he could feel Avandeer's scales against his. The feeling of belonging that spread through Valerys brought Calen a kind of joy that he had not felt in years.

Avandeer nudged her snout into Valerys, then lowered her head, her eyes – the colour of liquid marigold – staring into Calen's. The dragon's snout was twice the width of Calen's shoulders, her nostrils as large as his head. The blending of purple and white along the scales of her face reminded Calen of the petals of the gloxinia flowers Vars had brought back for Freis from one of his visits to Camylin. The dragon was one of the single most beautiful creatures Calen had ever laid eyes on. Her nostrils flared, and she blew a puff of warm air over Calen's face, her head tilting sideways.

Calen reached out his hand, and Avandeer extended her neck. She rested her snout into his palm, then pushed forwards and pressed into his chest, blowing another puff of warm air. Calen spread his arms wide, resting his palms either side of the dragon's snout, his fingers tracing over the furrows and fused scars.

None of the dragons in Aravell had ever greeted him this way. They had barely paid him a passing glance. They had lost their reason to seek joy. Avandeer was whole. Her soulkin was at her side, and the world still held meaning. The dragons in Aravell had lost everything they loved. They were Rakina.

As Avandeer lifted her head and once again nuzzled against Valerys's snout, Calen looked to Tivar. "I hadn't expected anyone to be here."

"I have not left this island in a hundred years." Tivar gave Calen a melancholy-touched smile. "I assume you have come for answers?"

"Truthfully? I don't know what I've come for. Pellenor told me that if I came here, if I lit the beacon on the temple's roof, that he would come. I…" Calen wondered what he could truly say or, rather, what he should say. Could he really trust this elf? "I want to know what happened to The Order. I want to know *why*."

A tear glistened on Tivar's cheek. She let it fall and shook her head. "Pellenor is dead."

The words cut through Calen like a knife. There was no possible way they could be true. The man Calen had met in the Inquisition dungeons was not someone who could die. Calen had heard a Dragonguard had died in the battle near Steeple. But he'd not even considered it could have been Pellenor. The man had held himself as though he were a god.

"He and Meranta fell in the Battle of The Three Sisters. Slain by those we once called kin." Tivar looked past Calen, towards the horizon. "Pellenor was special. He was one of the kindest souls I ever knew."

Calen swallowed. He still couldn't process everything. "Why did you do it? I need to know why."

Tivar took a step closer and rested her hand on his shoulder. "Come, I will tell you whatever you want to know. But not here. I will take you to a place where the blood of your kin flows through the stone."

CALEN AND VALERYS FOLLOWED TIVAR and Avandeer through the valleys of Dracaldryr. As they flew, Tivar pointed towards ancient eyries that were carved into the mountainsides – cavities in the rock large enough to fit Valerys five times over. According to Tivar, the eyries had once been the homes of the first dragons, and after that the entire island had been a sanctuary for the Draleid of The Order, a place where dragons could truly be free.

Avandeer and Tivar alighted on a platform that had clearly been carved from the mountainside using the Spark. The platform was semi-circular in shape and large enough to fit almost ten dragons of Avandeer's size. Its surface was impossibly smooth with rune markings carved around its rim.

On the other side of the platform, two enormous dragon statues framed an opening that Valerys could have walked through with his wings spread to his fullest. The statues rose at least a hundred feet, every scale looking as though it had been carved by the hand of the most delicate sculptor the world had ever seen. The two stone dragons faced out towards the platform, their wings close to their chests, their neck stretched high.

Calen slid from Valerys's back, his boots clicking against the stone.

"They can come," Tivar said, gesturing to Avandeer and Valerys. "But I believe it would be best to allow Valerys to experience what it is to truly fly free. I promise you, not only will his joy be unmatched, but your heart will shine too."

Calen turned as a rumble resonated in Valerys's chest. The dragon bowed his head, and Calen nodded. Without hesitation, both Valerys and Avandeer dove from the edge of the platform, their tails whipping back and forth, their wings spreading wide.

"This place is known as Üvrian un'Aldryr – Cradle of Fire."

Calen followed Tivar through the entranceway, staring up at the stone dragons as he did. A tunnel lay on the other side, as wide as the entrance. The walls of the tunnel were smooth as polished steel, veins of glowing azure erinian stone rippling through them. A staircase of hewn stone descended into the mountain, dropping so deep Calen thought it had no end.

A smile spread across Tivar's face as she gazed up at the veins of erinian stone. "In the time of The Order, this was where the dragon eggs of the great draconian lines were cared for. In each mortal generation, only hundreds were brought here from each race. And of those hundreds, we would be lucky if even four or five heard the Calling. Often, not a single egg would hatch."

Tivar led Calen down the staircase, their steps echoing through the tunnel, the glow of the erinian stone growing dimmer as they descended. When they finally reached the bottom, they stepped out into a large circular chamber that rose to a dome at the ceiling. The chamber was mostly shrouded in dark, only the residual glow of the tunnel's erinian stone providing any light.

"The sun's light isn't strong enough here to charge the erinian stone," Tivar explained, her footsteps echoing as she walked to the centre of the shadow-obscured chamber. Calen felt her reach out to the Spark and draw in threads of Fire, Air, and Spirit. A baldír burst into life beside her, illuminating the chamber in a pure white light.

With the shadows pushed back to the far corners of the chamber, Calen could see that Tivar stood atop a black stone symbol of The Order – a central triangle, with the smaller triangles placed at the sides. A number of alcoves were built into the walls of the chamber, each holding statues of figures in plate armour, The Order's sigil on the breast.

"The first Archons." Tivar cast her gaze around the chamber before walking towards the far well, which was devoid of statues. "The Archons could only hold their title for ten years at a time." Her voice echoed as she walked, bouncing off the high ceiling. "At the end of the Archon's time, each of the Draleid would vote on who would lead them."

Calen followed Tivar, stopping beside her at the far wall. An elaborately carved semi-circle of runes decorated the outer rim of what looked to be a large doorway, but the centre was filled with stone. Calen thought he could hear the sound of crashing water coming from the other side.

"The last Archon, Alvira Serris—" Tivar pulled a small yellow stone from her pocket. Veins of red and blue ran across its surface. She channelled threads of Fire and Spirit into the stone "—had served two terms by The Fall. Had her eyes been open to the rot within our people, perhaps she would still be here."

Calen was about to speak when the stone glowed a bright yellow, and the wall before them vanished leaving only the outer rune markings. "A glamour."

"Indeed." Tivar gestured for Calen to follow her through the now-open passage.

"Tivar, what happened..." Calen stopped speaking as he walked through the passage.

Before him a walkway of smooth stone stretched towards an open chamber that lay a few hundred feet away. A waterfall crashed on either side of the entrance Calen had just walked through, rivers bracketing the walkway. But what pulled the air from Calen's lungs were the dragon statues carved from the rock on either side. The statues rose for hundreds of feet, every detail as crisp as the living breathing creatures from which the statues gained their likeness. Calen counted five on each side of the walkway. Veins of glowing erinian stone rippled through them, accented by the warm sunlight that poured into the cavern from openings in the ceiling that lay hundreds of feet in the air.

When Calen pulled his gaze from the statues, he found himself looking into Tivar's eyes.

"We failed, Calen. That's what happened. I don't know what you've been told. Eltoar said it was Aeson Virandr who brought Valerys's egg to these shores." Tivar shook her head, sorrow marked in every line of her face. "The events he told you are likely true, Aeson is an honourable man, but the hows and the whys will differ from mine. I will give you the only thing I can. The only thing that matters – honesty. I will not shy away from what we did."

"We were meant to protect," she said, as she started off towards the chamber at the other end of the walkway. "We were supposed to be guardians. But we lost our way. The Order was founded after the Blodvar, after the Doom at Haedr. The Jotnar and my ancestors banded together for the first time in recorded history. Before that, all our people knew was death and war. The Order was meant to be something separate. It was meant to be untethered from the powers of the continent. But as the centuries past and turned to millennium, the world shifted. The Order's council slowly gained more power than the Archon and elders of the Draleid.

"It had been suggested that the Draleid had too much power and increasing the council's authority would be safer for the people. But where our ancestors lived to see centuries pass, the council members were fleeting. Ideals changed, nations rose and fell, and with it at all, the council and The Order itself became nothing more than a power broker. It no longer stood for honour or for duty – it no longer stood for anything. The Draleid had become little more than the enforcers of the richest kings and queens. If a nation could put gold in The Order's coffers, the Draleid flew at their backs." Tivar let out a long sigh. "Eventually, it grew to the point we didn't wait for gold or coin or power, we sought it out."

Tivar stopped. She stared up at one of the dragon statues, the muscles in her jaw tensing. Her breaths trembled. Calen could *feel* her pain – hear it in every word, see it in her eyes. She turned to him, her eyes wet with tears. "We started wars. The Lyonin War, the Ingdrin War, and many others. If someone spoke against The Order, they were silenced in the name of peace. If there was gold to be made, people burned. Alvira always stood against it. She was…" Tivar's voice caught in her throat, silent tears rolling down her cheeks. "She was special – the most honourable soul I've ever known. But she couldn't, or wouldn't, allow herself to see what was broken. That is honour's fatal flaw – it blinds us. She disagreed with the council at every turn, yet she rode Vyldrar to war on their orders. We still believed ourselves to be guardians, but we were nothing more than mercenaries and tyrants."

Tivar went silent, her gaze focused on something Calen could not see. "It all changed when Fane came back from Mar Dorul. He fed off our division. You need to understand, people were dying by our hand, cities were burning. We had tried to speak out, tried to fix The Order from within, but it was like trying to put out a fire with our bare hands. Fane was a revolutionary. He stoked the flames in our hearts, convinced us that if we truly were the guardians we believed we were, then we needed to have the courage to stand against the tyranny of The Order and of our own kind. What fools we were."

Tivar drew in a long breath and continued along the walkway. Ahead Calen could see the chamber was cylindrical in shape, hundreds of alcoves set into its walls, rising higher and higher. An opening was carved into the ceiling in the shape of The Order's sigil.

"Fane filled our hearts with hate and our ears with lies. He could weave stories like the greatest bards. It was as though he could see into people's souls. He knew precisely what you wanted and precisely how to twist you. But as charismatic and convincing as Fane was, if he had not turned Eltoar to his side, I do not believe the others would have followed. But he did, and we did. After a time, he began whispering of Efilatír – not The Traitor, but The Saviour. At first, his words found no home. But then he showed us the power Efialtír possessed. The power we would need to win – Essence, or Blood Magic as you might know it. But Essence seeps into your soul, Calen. Efialtír's touch clouds your mind and your heart. Its effect is slow and poisonous. It makes you capable of things you would never have contemplated… Such horrible things. It hungers…" Tivar's eyes glassed over for a moment, lost in a memory. "I swear to you we believed we were doing the right thing. The night Ilnaen fell was the darkest night in the history of our people." Tivar stopped as the pathway joined to the floor of the cylindrical chamber. "And for the atrocities we committed, for our betrayal, for our hubris, this is what the gods have left us."

Tivar gestured towards the walls of the cylindrical chamber, her gaze tracing across the many alcoves. "In four hundred years, not one has hatched."

Calen stepped forwards, every hair standing on end. He could feel Valerys's pulse quicken with his own as the dragon alighted on a cliff. Their minds drifted together as Calen looked about the chamber. "Are they all dragon eggs? There must be hundreds."

"Four hundred and seventy-three. Not a single one has hatched since Ilnaen. At first we thought it coincidence. Maybe the trauma or the change in the world had affected something. But when weeks turned to months, turned to years, decades, centuries, we knew something was wrong. Eltoar has brought tens of thousands of people here over the years – nothing. But..." Calen turned at the glimmer of hope that crept into Tivar's voice. "Perhaps, with Valerys. If his egg hatched, maybe the others will? Maybe the gods have forgiven us?"

"No." Calen's heart twisted for dashing the one sliver of brightness he had seen in Tivar. "The elves have been trying for months. Nothing."

Calen saw the hope die in Tivar's eyes. She nodded slowly. "The dragons suffer for the things we've done." Tivar lifted her gaze to meet Calen's. "If Valerys's egg hatched... that has to mean something. It has to."

"What about the elven dragons, the ones that fought at Steeple?"

Tivar shook his head. "Eltoar said they were too old, too hardened. They are survivors of The Fall. New life does not come with them. They bring only death, as we did."

Calen walked over towards the nearest alcove in the wall. The egg within was coated in scales that were crimson at their root but slowly transitioned to cream at the edges. He brushed his thumb over the cream edge of one of the scales. "Would you make the same decision again?"

"No. We should have tried harder. We should have been better. We let Fane's lies twist us."

"Tell me of the others – the Dragonguard. Pellenor said there are those I shouldn't trust." Aeson, Therin, and the Rakina had told Calen of the Dragonguard, gone through them one by one, but he couldn't trust anything anymore.

"Jormun, Ilkya, and Voranur." Not a heartbeat had passed before Tivar spoke the names. Calen turned to see her walking towards the river that flowed through the right of the cavern. He followed.

Tivar sat on the edge of the walkway and folded her legs, staring at the rushing water. Calen sat beside her.

"Four hundred years is a long time to spend reliving every decision you've ever made – especially as you watch more and more of your kin die until there's barely any of you left. That time affected each of us differently. Jormun, Voranur, and Ilkya grew apathetic towards life. Death and power became them. Of the eight of us that are left, they are the only three I believe still fight for Fane and Efialtír in their hearts. Eltoar is still blinded by his friendship to Fane, just as Alvira was by honour. He doesn't see that we are simply pawns, but I believe he is truly trying to find a way back to what we once were. And his left wing, Lyina, she is a shimmering gem. She's one of the few who would ever challenge him – she and Pellenor." Tivar went silent for a moment, staring down at the water. "My companions, Erdin and Luka, left the continent decades ago, unable to cope with the world we had helped create."

They sat there talking of what the world had once been like. Chora, Harken, and the other Rakina had told Calen their version of The Order, but through Tivar's eyes, he saw the other side – the darkness, the power lust, the tyranny. After hours had passed, Tivar pulled herself to her feet. "Come. I'm not sure how long you intend to stay. We should eat."

As they made their way to the staircase that led to the platform, Calen asked the question that had been lingering in his mind. "What was Aeson Virandr like, before?"

Tivar gave a weak smile. "I could feel the uncertainty in you the moment you arrived. I told you I would be honest, and I will. Aeson was one of the greatest warriors the Draleid had seen in centuries, and he was exactly like Alvira. He idolised her." Tivar stopped at the entrance to the chamber that fronted the stairs, letting out a breath. She turned to look Calen in the eyes. "Aeson lost everything because of what we did. *Everything.* I'm not sure who he is now, but I can tell you he was someone I respected." Once more, tears welled in Tivar's eyes. She wiped them away with the back of her hand. "If he is even half the man he once was, he is better than most."

Calen nodded, sighing. He went to speak, but a shiver swept over his skin, fear and dread pouring into him from Valerys like molten fire. He saw from the look in Tivar's eyes that she was seeing the same thing through Avandeer as he was through Valerys: the sunlight fading, a red glow sweeping across the sky.

They both turned to look back into the cavern. The light that drifted through the openings in the ceiling turned red as blood and dripped down the walls and into the alcoves that held the dragon eggs.

Without a word, Calen and Tivar broke into a run. Calen's heart pounded like a hammer on an anvil, his chest heaving, his lungs dragging in air. His legs burned as he charged up through the chamber and up the seemingly endless staircase.

Crimson light poured down the tunnel, blending with the azure glow of the erinian stone. Calen's lungs felt as though they had been set on fire by the time he'd reached the top of the stairs. It had been only the start of the new day when he and Tivar had descended into the cradle, but now the world had darkened as though it were the dead of night. A crimson moon hung in the sky, its light spreading across the horizon, tainting everything it touched. As Avandeer and Valerys swept past the ledge and alighted on the platform that jutted from the mountainside, Valerys's scales shimmered with a pink hue.

"The Blood Moon," Tivar whispered, dread in her voice.

Calen stared out at the blood-tinted sky, trying to muster words. "I need to go," he said. "I can't leave the others alone."

"I understand." Tivar's face was a sombre one, a deep sorrow in her eyes. "It was a true honour to meet you, Calen Bryer. I only wish it could have been for longer."

"Come with me." The words left Calen's mouth before he'd truly thought on them. What would Aeson, Chora, and the others do if he brought Tivar back?

The shock on Tivar's face was briefly replaced by a quiet contemplation. She shook her head. "I cannot. I am not what I once was, Calen. I am not a Draleid. I am a monster. The things I have done can never be undone. The stains on my soul can never be cleansed. I am darkness."

"I'll come back, I promise."

"Don't make promises you can't keep." Tivar pulled Calen into an embrace, her hands clasping his back. "Thank you."

"For what?"

"For showing me our kind still has a chance."

Calen squeezed a bit tighter, then pulled away and mounted Valerys. "'We were supposed to be guardians'. Those were your words." He looked to the crimson moon, then back to Tivar. "I've been told that what is coming is worse than anything we've ever seen. You might never forgive yourself for what you did. You might not deserve to be forgiven. But if you truly believe what you said, then guardians are what we should be, no matter what we deserve. I *will* come back. But if you change your mind, I will be in the Aravell. Draleid n'aldryr, Tivar Savinír."

"Draleid n'aldryr, Calen Bryer."

Calen drew in a short breath, nodded, and then Valerys dove from the platform.

CHAPTER SEVENTY-FIVE

THE VEIL THINS, THE HAND REACHES

Temple of Achyron – Winter, Year 3081 After Doom

Are you sure you don't want one of the others to go with you?" Watcher Poldor asked, a frown etched into his face. He stood before the desk in Verathin's study. Kallinavar knew he would eventually have to start thinking of the study as his own, but not yet.

"There's not enough to spare." Kallinvar rose from his seat and pushed the chair in behind the desk.

"Watcher Poldor is right, Kallinvar. Aryana Torval flies the banner of Old Amendel, your home." Watcher Gildrick leaned against the stone alcoves by the door, white-trimmed green robes draped over his shoulders. His new charge, Watcher Tallia, stood at this side. Her dark hair fell over her robes, her keen eyes never leaving Kallinvar.

"I'm well aware of my homeland, Gildrick. I do not need a lesson." Kallinvar cursed himself for being so harsh. Since seeing Achyron, he'd not been able to focus; his temper had been short and his mood dark. *'You cannot stop Efialtir's harbinger from widening the tear in the veil. Too much has been set in motion. But you must meet him when he does… The Alignment is only the beginning.'* Kallinvar had spent many weeks grappling with those words. For nearly four centuries, he had prepared for the Blood Moon. It had consumed him. Now, with the Blood Moon so close, Achyron tells him it is only the beginning. *What does that mean?*

"I simply meant it can be difficult for a knight to face his past, Grandmaster."

Kallinvar scowled at Gildrick. The Watcher knew Kallinvar was uncomfortable with the title. He also knew that he particularly hated it when Gildrick used the word. He had known Gildrick since the man was a child – they were past titles and formalities.

Gildrick smiled, which only made Kallinvar scowl deeper. The man always knew when he'd gotten underneath Kallinvar's skin. "You saw it with Arden. It is not a simple thing. To see the banner of your homeland may not be as easy as you think. Take Brother Tarron with you, and perhaps Sister Mirken. They are back from Arkalen."

"I told you," Kallinvar said as he moved past Gildrick and Tallia, opening the door and stepping out into the corridor beyond. "I don't have knights to spare. The elven attacks in northern Loria have driven hordes of refugees to the west and south. The Bloodspawn slaughter them as they march. Have you seen the war table? There are more red markers than I can count."

Polder, Tallia, and Gildrick followed Kallinvar into the corridor.

"Lensa and Yarrin are gone, burned to char and cinder. The Bloodspawn hordes grow stronger with each passing day, Gildrick. I…" A pulse rippled through Kallinvar's Sigil. "I…" He tried to speak but couldn't focus.

"Kallinvar, what's wrong?" Gildrick grabbed Kallinvar by the shoulders, moving his head to keep their gazes locked. "Look at me, Kallinvar."

Kallinvar pushed Gildrick away. The sickly sensation of the Taint seeped into his mind, snatching the air from his lungs and the strength from his legs. His consciousness recoiled, but he could feel the darkness pulsing, throbbing like a beating heart; it turned his blood cold and sent a shiver across his skin.

"The time has come, my child."

Kallinvar pulled himself upright, then set off down the corridor. Gildrick, Poldor, and Tallia followed him. They grabbed at his shoulders and demanded he stop, but he ignored them like a wolf would a fly. As he moved, he picked up pace, stopping short of a jog.

Tarron and Mirken emerged from a corridor on the right, panic on their faces. "Kallinvar!"

"I know." Kallinvar didn't stop. Tarron and Mirken ran to his side, Brother Daynin joining them a few moments later. As they moved through corridors, passing the sleeping quarters, the library, and the watcher's chambers, Sister-Captain Olyria and Sister-Captain Arlena joined them.

"Kallinvar!" Gildrick roared. "What is going on? Answer me, Kallinvar. You…" Gildrick's voice trailed off as they rounded a corner and came to the front doors of the temple. The wicket gate was open, and a thick slice of red light shone through.

Kallinvar stopped a few feet from the wicket gate, his gaze fixed on the red light. The sounds of chatter and murmurs drew his attention behind him. He'd not realised how many others had joined them: knights, priests, porters, cooks, chambermaids. They all looked to Kallinvar, fear and expectation in their eyes. He turned to Tarron, holding his old friend's gaze. Tarron nodded.

Kallinvar drew in a long breath, then strode towards the great doors. He stepped out onto the top of the stone staircase that descended from the temple into Ardholm.

More knights, priests, and citizens of Ardholm stood on the steps. Each of them looked up, their mouths open, their eyes wide as they stared at the crimson moon that dominated the sky. The Blood Moon's light made the horizon look as though it were on fire, the clouds emitting an incandescent glow.

Whispers filled the air as more people stepped out through the wicket gate behind Kallinvar.

"The Blood Moon," Kallinvar heard someone whisper.

Tarron moved beside Kallinvar, his stare fixed on the moon. "And so it begins again, brother. Thirty days of night. Thirty days when Efialtír's hand can reach through the veil."

Kallinvar allowed his gaze to linger on the moon. Four centuries he had waited for this day yet hoped it would never come.

It is not the storm we must fear, but what comes after.

Kallinvar nodded to Tarron. He looked back at Watcher Gildrick. "Gildrick, we must recall the knights at once. Have the beds turned and the kitchens stocked. Give everyone a task. Do not let their minds dwell. We go to war."

Kallinvar turned his back on the Blood Moon and stepped through the wicket gate, Tarron, Mirken, and Daynin behind him.

And so it begins.

CHAPTER SEVENTY-SIX

PLANS LONG LAID

The Burnt Lands – Winter, Year 3081 After Doom

Fane stood on the roof of a damaged building, his arms folded. He brushed his foot across the ground, sweeping the sand aside to reveal white stone. He looked down into the central plaza where hundreds of mages and priests of Efialtír were preparing for the crossing ritual. A pit sat at the centre of the plaza, multiple runic rings marked about its circumference. The pit was filled with thousands of Essence vessels that had been gathered across the centuries. The red glow was almost as strong as that of the Blood Moon itself. Even from where he stood atop the building, he could feel the pull of so much Essence gathered in one place. He would need every last drop.

He lifted his gaze from the plaza and looked at the beauty of the crimson sky. The light of the Blood Moon washed over the ruined city, the sand glittering pink and red in the air.

"We are so close now," the voice whispered in his mind. *"My Chosen will start the next step. Achyron will send his knights, but you have prepared well. I have faith."*

Footsteps sounded behind Fane. Garramon clasped his hands behind his back, looking up towards the Blood Moon as he moved next to Fane. "Brother Pirnil reports the inscriptions are almost complete."

"Good. We must begin the ritual as soon as possible. The armies are in position?"

"They are. All eighty thousand. A herald has been placed with each army. The other armies and their mages should all be in their positions by now as well, and our forces should be moving in the South."

"Good. That should keep the knights busy and thin out their numbers. This is the next step. We've waited a long time for this day, Garramon."

Garramon let out a sigh, staring up at the sky. "That we have, brother."

Fane pulled his gaze from the spectacle above, looking instead to his old friend. "What is it?"

Garramon shook his head. "Nothing. Just thinking."

"A lot has changed across the years. But I would like to think you still trust me enough to speak your mind."

Garramon glanced at Fane before looking back towards the horizon. "Do you ever doubt?"

"Doubt what?"

"Anything?"

Fane smiled, letting a short laugh escape. "What's brought this on? Have you lost faith in Efialtír?"

"Of course not. It's just… Hundreds have already volunteered to become hosts for the Chosen. And so many of them have seen no more than twenty summers. They're only children. It's a heavy burden."

"They are true believers, Garramon. They choose to be servants of their god. Strengthening Efialtír's hand in this world has always been our cause. You've always known this was coming. Not only will he reward us, but he will give us the strength to keep our people safe." Fane clasped his hands behind his back. Primarch Touran had accelerated the training of over a thousand Battlemage apprentices at Fane's instruction. Fane would have done so for the other affinities, but he'd wanted to ensure the strength of the candidates. The weaker the host, the lower the chance of a successful bonding, so said the conclusions of Kiralla Halflower's research. Though, Brother Pirnil's experiments since then had proved rather enlightening.

"I've been in the preparation tents." Garramon tensed his jaw, shaking his head. "Barely half are surviving their inscriptions."

"They knew the risks, Garramon. The survival rates as well as the process were explained to each and every one of them. All great things require sacrifice. From what Brother Pirnil tells me, those who do not survive do so because they lose their faith and their nerve. The runes feed off true belief as well as Essence."

"They're just so young."

Fane sighed. Garramon truly was his oldest friend. And 'friend' was not a word he liked to use. The man had strong faith in Efialtír, but he was also easily swayed by sentimentality.

Fane had no doubt Garramon's uncertainty in some way came from his son, Malyn. Malyn had seen only twenty-three summers when Garramon had come to Fane and told him that Malyn had been spotted providing information to the other side in the years following the fall of Ilnaen. He'd never seen Garramon so distraught. There'd been no choice, of course. The Arbiter could not be seen to deal with any situation in any way other than with impartiality – Fane told him as such. Fane had made sure to stand by Garramon's side at the headsman's block; it was the least he could have done. Fulya had never forgiven either of them, which Fane understood.

"The other gods care little for this world. You know this. They watch as we move through a cycle of endless, meaningless death. Varyn created dragons that could burn flesh from bones with their breath. What kind of god creates such things? Efialtír will grant us the power to bring true peace and to ensure that death is not meaningless. Would you stop someone from being a part of that because of their youth? Do the young not have a place in great deeds?"

"You always have an answer, old friend."

"And you always have questions." Fane let a silence fall between them before speaking again. "Your apprentice has risen to the rank of Battlemage. That is good. How is his commitment?"

"Strong," Garramon said. "He still questions Efialtír, but he is slowly understanding."

"That's to be expected. He is a young man much as I was – full of questions and thirsting for knowledge. Once he sees the ritual, he will not question again."

Garramon let out a sharp breath. "The letters…"

"Are a necessary evil, Garramon. We needed him to feel comfortable. But there will be no more. His parents were taken from Berona, along with another captive."

Garramon turned his head to Fane, shock on his face. "What… what do we tell him?"

"For now? Nothing."

"Why is he so important, Fane? We know the Draleid is with the elves in the Darkwood. We have our eyes and ears. Rist is exceptional, but I don't understand."

Fane smiled. Garramon was not an idiot, and neither was Fane. It was clear Garramon saw his son in the young man. It was better to be honest. "There is a saying by Sumara Tuzan that states 'keep your friends close and your enemies closer'."

"I know the saying, Fane." Irritation crept into Garramon's words. "Rist is not an enemy. He's one of us."

Fane allowed his smile to grow wider, turning his gaze towards the sparkling sand that swept overhead. "I've always felt there was something missing from that saying. 'Keep your friends close, your enemies closer, and the friends of your enemies closest.' Eltoar Daethana is the reason The Order fell. Turning him to our side was our greatest triumph. Without Eltoar, we never would have gotten to Alvira. Without Alvira dead, The Order would not have fallen. If the Draleid survives tonight, your apprentice will be our next greatest triumph. We're all pawns in the great game of games. We all have our parts to play."

Garramon grew silent, and he and Fane stood for a few minutes, looking down over the plaza, until the light around them dimmed as though it had been pulled from the air. Fane and Garramon both turned to see a herald standing before them. A black cloak was draped around its shoulders, its skin white as snow. Fane had always been curious as to how the heralds drew in the light around them. He'd not, as of yet, found a satisfactory answer.

Garramon turned inclining his head. "Herald, the saviour's light upon you."

"Klinzen." Fane folded his arms. "How far?"

"The Uraks will be here in hours. They march with a host of over a hundred thousand souls."

Garramon turned to Fane, concern evident in his expression. "Should we recall some of the Dragonguard?"

"No, old friend. Eltoar and Lyina are needed to keep the elves in check up north while we are here. Besides, this is not a place he and Lyina would return to. The others are needed in the South. More Uraks means more Essence for Efialtír. He tests us still, and we will not fail. Klinzen, what word from Azrim?"

"All is in motion," the Fade hissed. "The city is no more, and the armies march."

"Good. We will rip this rebellion out root and stem. Come, Garramon. It is time."

Rist, Neera, Magnus, Anila, and the other Battlemages of the First Army, along with those of the Nineteenth Army, stood at the western edge of the central plaza. They'd arrived in the ruined city only a few hours previous, and the priests and Craftsmages had immediately begun preparing for the ritual.

The plaza was enormous, a few hundred feet in length and breadth. The pit at the centre had been dug by the Craftsmages and then filled with more glowing gemstones than Rist had thought existed. As he looked towards the pit, he became increasingly aware of the pendant beneath his armour, its touch cold against his skin.

Sixteen armies occupied the city – eighty thousand soldiers in total. While the infantry, cavalry, and archers had been set to defend the outer bounds and midsections of the city, all sixteen hundred Battlemages were gathered around the eight entrances of the central plaza, two hundred at each entrance. Their task would be to provide threads of Spirit for the ritual. Garramon had explained the core concept of the ritual to Rist, but not the intricacies of its inner workings, which irritated him to no end: with the Blood Moon risen, they would widen a tear in the veil between worlds, proving their dedication to Efialtír. And in doing so, they would allow the Chosen to pass through, granting them the strength needed to defeat the elves and Uraks.

In the past, Rist wouldn't have believed a word of it. But Efialtír was the only god who'd shown any proof of their own existence. Rist had seen what Essence could do. He had seen how what he had been told to call 'Blood Magic' was not as he had once thought. In his mind he could see the small hummingbird's wing snap back into place, *feel* the life flood its body as Fane healed it using Essence. According to Garramon, it was also that same Essence that had kept the madness at bay while the armies had crossed the Burnt Lands. That was not the power of a dark god. He still held reservations, but he trusted Garramon. The man had risked his own life to save Rist and had even lied for him when Ella and Farda had escaped. Garramon had stood by Rist at every turn. He'd earned his trust.

"I hate sand." Anila's voice shook Rist from his thoughts. He turned his head to see her leaning against a sand-dusted wall, her boot in her hand. She held the boot upside down, frowning as a thin stream of sand flowed from within, disappearing on the breeze. "It gets everywhere."

Magnus turned at Anila's words, his thumbs tucked behind his sword belt. The man's beard had grown back fully, thicker and blacker than before. "You're not the only one, Uraksplitter. Made love to a woman on a beach once, couldn't piss right for days."

"Shut up, Magnus." Anila pulled her boot back on, sand crunching beneath the sole. Rist watched in awe as she tied the boot's laces quicker with one hand than he could with two. When he'd first met Anila, he'd been curious as to how she could fight with only one hand – a question that had quickly been answered – but he'd never considered how she would have had to adapt the smaller things in her life, such as tying boot laces.

Magnus leaned in closer to Rist. "When I say that shit gets everywhere lad, I mean fucking everywhere. No matter what she suggests—" he nodded at Neera "—avoid the sand."

Neera glared at Rist.

"What did I do?" He raised his open palms in defence.

"You know what you did."

"Thanks, Magnus." Rist frowned at the big man, shaking his head.

"I meant what I said. Whatever you do, don't fuck in the sand."

Rist puffed out his cheeks, then looked back over the plaza. He'd found sometimes it was best to just not respond. "Have you seen Garramon?"

"He went to report Brother Pirnil's progress to the Emperor."

The mention of Brother Pirnil caused Rist to wince. The man's name seemed to reignite the pain in the many scars that laced Rist's back. Of course Brother Pirnil had been the Scholar selected to lead the inscription of the runes for the Chosens' hosts; the man would have delighted in causing the pain.

Rist tried to hold his tongue, but the question he wanted to ask was one that had been scratching at him since the priests had sought out volunteers to be hosts for the Chosen. Garramon had explained the Chosen were warriors of Efialtír who were too powerful to pass into this world in the way Fades did. But with tears in the veil created during the last Blood Moon, they could potentially pass into the world now, as long as they had willing hosts. Though according to the priests, the bodies of those willing participants would not be strong enough to sustain the Chosen without the aid of rune markings.

"Why would someone volunteer to have runes carved into their skin? It just seems…" Rist searched for the word.

"Really fucking painful," Magnus said with a grimace. "I agree with you on that. Look, lad. I'm a believer like everyone else, but you wouldn't catch me putting myself forward to become a host for one of these 'Chosen' or for ascension, for that matter. I don't even like sharing food, never mind my body. But faith is a strange thing. It manifests in many forms. Some, like me and you, are willing to fight for it but maybe not die for it. While others will give everything – body, mind, and soul."

Rist nodded slowly. He wasn't raised with Efialtír as The Saviour, but the others often forgot that. He wasn't fighting for Efialtír, he was fighting to keep people safe, but he understood what Magnus meant.

"It's an honour," Neera said, the slightest of irritations in her voice.

Rist turned his head sharply, eyebrows raised.

"Don't look at me like that." She narrowed her gaze at Rist. "I know your nods. That's the 'I don't know what you're saying, but I'm going to pretend I do' nod. I know you didn't grow up with Efialtír as your god the way we did, but if Achyron came down and asked you to be a vessel for his chosen warriors, what would you say?"

"Honestly? I—"

"Say it and I swear I'll set your books on fire. You know what I'm trying to say. There is no greater honour among those who are truly devout than to be a vessel for their god. I'm not in there having runes inscribed into my skin. But I understand."

"See, Uraksplitter," Magnus turned to Anila, elbowing her in the ribs. "Aren't they adorable? Like I've said, if you ever need someone to warm your bed…" Magnus winked.

"I'll set myself on fire."

Magnus laughed loud enough to draw the attention of the other mages nearby. "What?" he said, narrowing his eyes at a young mage who had only recently been assigned to the First Army in Berona as a replacement for those lost during the Battle of the Three Sisters. "You be careful, or I'll stick you at the front."

Magnus held the young man's gaze for a few more moments before winking again. He turned and looked as though he was about to say something when the light around them dimmed, and a chill swept over Rist. He'd grown so accustomed to the sensation during the journey from Berona he barely flinched. After a moment, a Fade turned the corner from a street ahead and started towards them, its black hood flapping in the wind. The creature's pale skin and brittle, bluish lips made Rist uneasy, but not as much as the black wells of emptiness that acted as the Fade's eyes. Rist had counted twelve of the creatures over the past few weeks though he was sure there were more.

"It must have heard us talking about it," Magnus whispered.

A moment after the Fade stepped into the street, Garramon followed, the wind blowing the hood off his head.

The mages of the First and Nineteenth armies stepped aside as the Fade walked through their ranks. The creature glanced at Magnus as it passed, light-drinking wells for eyes fixing on the man. As much as the power of Essence seemed that of a benevolent god, the Fades seemed the exact opposite. Just their presence alone caused Rist to shift uncomfortably.

Once the creature was through, Garramon approached. He nodded to Rist, Anila, and Neera, before stopping in front of Magnus.

"What'd he say?"

"Once the last inscriptions are finished, we begin."

BROTHER PIRNIL SAT BACK IN his chair, letting out a long sigh. He looked at the lifeless body strapped to the cot before him, then back to the black, leatherbound book that had once belonged to Kiralla Halflower but now sat on the table at his side. He tapped his finger on the last note Kiralla had scribed within the book.

Note – the results of this runeset seem promising. Subject four hundred and fifty-three showed increased aggression and strength, lasting four days longer than the previous subject before expiration. Though it seems the elven constitution is not

*as suited to the gift as that of the Uraks, I maintain strong
belief that this is the path to the Chosen. Sufficient information
has been gathered to progress to the next stage. Subjects four
hundred and fifty-four, four hundred and fifty-five, and four
hundred and fifty-six will be trialled. The remaining subjects
are to be terminated.*

"That was what you missed, Sister," Brother Pirnil whispered. "They need
to be willing. Unfortunately, even most of those who start the process
willingly lose their nerve after the first few cuts."

Pirnil flicked the pages of the book back to his own notes, picked up
the pen that sat beside the table, and marked down his, now definitive,
observation. He had carried out enough of these inscriptions to be confident of his results.

Winter, Year 3081 After Doom, High Scholar Drakus Pirnil

Observation:

*The success of the rune markings hinges not only upon the
willingness of the host, but also on the continued willingness
throughout the inscription. If the host's faith or conviction wa-
vers, the runes begin to consume their Essence. If the host's
willingness diminishes entirely, the runes will consume the life
shortly after inscription is complete, or in some cases, before.*

*The creation of these Urak Bloodmarked shows a greater men-
tal and physical fortitude that is lacking in humans. Though,
the runeset used for inscribing Bloodmarked clearly differs from
that used to mark a host for the Chosen. If a Bloodmarked
body can be captured and the runeset mimicked, perhaps it can
be recreated. It is likely, however, that there is more to Bloodmarked runesets than simply the inscription itself.*

*Note of clarification: Incorrect marking of runesets can result
in blackening of skin, breaking of bones, and other undesired
disfigurations.*

Pirnil looked back at the body. It was that of a young man, hair dark
brown, body gangly. He held about as much muscle as a mouse. All

fifty-three necessary runes were carved along his chest, arms, and neck, the flesh red and bleeding. Pirnil looked back at his notes to check the man's name. *Darran Maseker.* Darran had held his screams in for eight minutes before Pirnil had had to offer him a gag. The runes had drained the young man of Essence. He wished there were an easier way to weed out the weak minded; so much time wasted.

He coughed, lifting phlegm from his chest and spitting it on the floor. He gestured to two of the servants who stood behind them, their faces pale. "To the fire."

The two servants picked up the young man by his shoulders and legs, carrying him from the room. Shortly after, a woman entered, naked as a newborn babe. Her muscles were thick, shoulders broad, and she had a scowl on her face that looked to be a permanent fixture.

Good. Pirnil gestured for the woman to lie on the cot. He'd made a mental note that the younger volunteers had a far higher mortality rate than the older ones. The eagerness of youth faded quickly when faced with the fleeting nature of life. The hardened warriors, like this woman, were more at peace with their choices. It was more conjecture than fact, but he was quite certain. If the trend continued he would add it to the book.

Pirnil went to close the straps around the woman's legs, but she shook her head. "There's no need, High Scholar. I am committed to Efialtír, mind and body. I am prepared to be his vessel. I am prepared to protect my homeland."

"Admirable," Pirnil said, smiling as he fixed the buckle in place. "But the straps are for my safety, not yours."

CHAPTER SEVENTY-SEVEN

MONSTERS AT THE GATES AND WITHIN

Rumbling in Valerys's chest woke Calen from his slumber; he'd not had the chance to sleep much since leaving Aravell. He peeled his eyes open at the feeling of urgency that spilled over from the dragon. "What is it?"

In his daze, Calen looked down from Valerys's back to see the mountains of Lodhar blending into the green ocean of woodland that was the Darkwood. He still couldn't get used to the red haze of the Blood Moon that painted the world. "We're back. Good."

Another flash of urgency filled the dragon's mind, and it took Calen a moment to realise it wasn't the mountains or the woodland that Valerys had been looking at. Far in the distance, past the Darkwood, a great fire burned, flames blazing, dark smoke pluming into the air. "What is that? Surely that can't be Argona…"

Calen's pulse quickened at the thought. "Faster, Valerys. We need to get to Aravell."

Before Valerys could react to the words, a roar thundered through the sky, answered by a second, and then a third. In the distance, three figures emerged from within the cover of the woodland. The figures soared through the air, flying towards the flames in the distance, then swept back around. A moment passed and the world seemed to grow still before all three dragons unleashed columns of fire down over the Darkwood.

"Dive!"

Valerys folded his wings and plummeted towards the mountains. Just as he dropped into the mountains' cover, he unfurled his wings and surged forwards. With the shock of what he had just seen and the weariness from travel, Calen had forgotten to adjust his body position to Valerys's movements and was nearly torn from the dragon's back. The intrinsic magic that moulded Valerys's scales to Calen's presence could only do so much.

Calen's heart pounded like a galloping horse, his chest fluttering. He pushed the panic down and tried to settle himself. "Did they see us? No, I don't think so."

He drew in a long breath, panting, then leaned forwards, pressing his hands against Valerys's scales. Without a word between them, Valerys cracked his wings and broke into a speed that pulled Calen backwards. The dragon tore through the valleys of the Lodhar Mountains like an bolt of lightning, angling himself to best use the currents of air as Chora had taught them. It wasn't long before they had traded mountains around them for the forest canopy. Looking ahead to the right, Calen could still see the three dragons rising high, circling, then turning and unleashing rivers of dragonfire down into the forest. *They're carving a path towards Aravell. How do they know?*

Calen had no idea in which direction he and Valerys needed to fly. Finding Aravell behind the glamour hadn't been something he'd accounted for when he'd left. Forward thinking had always been one of Rist's strengths, not his. But Valerys streaked over the woodland, not hesitating for even a moment. The dragon flew as low as he could without crashing down into the forest below. After a while, a warning flashed in Calen's mind, and he shifted his weight as Valerys banked left, then angled his wings and swooped downwards.

Calen clamped his eyes shut as they passed through the glamour, and the world erupted in a flash of blinding white light. He'd barely had a second to recover before panic poured from Valerys. Calen swung to the left as Valerys spun and twisted in the air, arrows whistling past them. He pulled his and Valerys's minds together, pushing away the panic that threatened them. *Draleid n'aldryr, Valerys.*

The sensation of the Spark pulsed and they dropped, arcs of lightning soaring past them. The wind crashed against Calen from the left, then the right, his stomach turning as Valerys spun.

Steel glinted in the pinkish light of the blood moon as more arrows cut through the air.

Calen pulled on threads of Air and Fire. He reached out, sensing the shifts in the air. He snapped at the arrow shafts with the threads of Fire, watching as the projectiles burst into flames. Calen and Valerys's hearts thumped together, hammering like war drums, blood burning through their veins. Through Valerys's eyes, Calen saw the arrows and lightning had come from one of Aravell's walls. Another flurry cut the air. Valerys folded his wings and dropped, Calen using threads of Air to shield them as they fell. *They think we're the Dragonguard.*

With a mighty crack of his wings, Valerys dropped and alighted on the edge of a cliff that overlooked the Aravell walls. The dragon lifted himself to full height and pulled his chest back. Valerys's dense muscles rippled beneath Calen. A low rumble sounded in the dragon's chest, and then he threw his head forward and unleashed a roar that shook the air. Calen's skin prickled, his breath catching at the sheer power in Valerys's roar.

The rumbles in Valerys's chest and throat subsided slowly, and the echoes of his roar lingered in the air. Calen could hear his own heart beating in the silence that followed. He drew in threads of Air and Spirit weaving them through his voice. "It is Calen Bryer and Valerys."

More silence. Calen sensed the Spark, and his body tensed, preparing for what might come.

"Pass freely, Draleid." The voice carried on threads of Spirit and Air.

"To Alura."

CALEN'S HEART STILL POUNDED AS he and Valerys soared over the bridge that separated Alura from the main city of Aravell. As they flew over the trees that topped the arched passageway, he looked down and saw people gathered in the central courtyard by the thicket of trees that occupied its centre.

"Land near the edge of the main platform."

Shouts rang out from below as Valerys dropped from the sky. Just as they reached the platform, Valerys spread his wings and alighted on a clear patch of stone, people rushing to get out of the way.

As Calen dismounted, he saw Ella, Dann, Erik, Therin, Alea, Lyrei, Tarmon, and Vaeril striding towards him. Faenir bolted past them all, his legs eating the ground. Calen readied himself for the wolfpine to tackle him to the ground, as Faenir had always done, but instead Faenir stopped a foot or so from Calen, hackles raised, face twisted in a snarl.

"Faenir, what's wrong?" Calen reached out his hand but yanked it back when Faenir snapped at him. There was a savagery in the wolfpine's eyes that Calen had never witnessed before.

Valerys moved over Calen, dropped his neck, and swung his head at Faenir. The dragon hooked his snout beneath the wolfpine's body and flung him through the air.

"Valerys, no!" Calen rounded on the dragon, but Valerys ignored him. Instead, he shifted his body so he stood over Calen protectively, wings spread, chest puffed out.

Faenir crashed to the ground a few feet away, hauling himself back to his feet as soon as he'd hit stone. The wolfpine charged at Valerys.

A familiar pressure built in the back of Calen's head, and he frantically pulled his and Valerys's minds together, trying to soothe the dragon's anger. The rumblings of dragonfire faded, but Valerys craned his head over Calen and unleashed a roar that stopped Faenir in his tracks and turned the heads of everyone in the courtyard.

To Calen's surprise, Faenir hadn't run or whimpered, he'd simply slowed. Faenir's hackles were still raised, his nose wrinkled in a snarl as he took cautious steps towards Valerys.

Calen looked to his left to see Ella and Dann had broken into a run, others behind them.

"What's going on?" Calen roared, gesturing at Faenir.

"You left us!" Ella shouted back, anger burning in her voice. As she reached Calen, she slammed her hands into his chest. "That's what happened. We crossed the continent to find you, and you just left!"

Calen stumbled backwards, just managing to stop himself from falling. He made to speak but stopped when he saw Ella's eyes flashing amber, her teeth looking as though they'd sharpened to fangs. "I... I didn't mean to do it like that. I just—"

"You what?" Dann strode past Ella, stopping only inches from Calen. His breaths trembled, and his clenched hands shook at his sides. "Tell me, Calen. Explain to me why you just fucking left us here."

"Aeson lied to me, he lied about everything. There's things I haven't told you, about the Dragonguard. About everything."

Dann's breathing slowed, and he leaned forwards so Calen could feel his breath against his face. "You left me after Durakdur. You had a chance to come back." He shook his head. "We were meant to go after Rist together. That's what we said – together, Calen. But you charged off and left me alone." Dann clenched his jaws, the muscles twitching. His voice rose to a roar. "You left me alone!"

"Dann..."

"Don't you tell me you're sorry. When you finally stumbled out of the Burnt Lands, all I cared was that you were all right. We rode from Durakdur to Argona and all the way to the Burnt Lands trying to find you. You know what I was thinking the whole time?" Tears of anger welled in Dann's eyes. "All I was thinking was what if the only two true friends I have in this world are dead? What if I never see their faces again?" Dann stood there in silence for a moment, his breaths slow. "You're a selfish bastard, Calen."

Calen made to speak, but Dann pulled him into a tight embrace.

"Don't you dare tell me you're sorry. I'm sick of apologies. Don't even think about doing that again." He squeezed tighter. "I'm happy you're all right."

"I won't," Calen said, reciprocating Dann's embrace. As he pulled away he saw a tall, broad-shouldered man and a woman with dark hair standing beside Ella – he thought he remembered them from outside the gates.

"Well," Erik said with a shrug. "That's pretty good timing. At least you're back in time for the fun."

"What's happened? I saw Dragonguard setting fire to the Darkwood."

"Argona is gone." Tarmon's voice was level as he spoke, but Calen heard the ache in it.

"What do you mean it's gone?"

"It's gone," Therin said. "We don't know what happened, but after you left, another message came through to Baldon. We think the empire found out that Castor Kai was intending to meet with us."

"So they burned an entire city?" Calen's shock turned to rage, then dropped to sorrow. "Why in the gods would anyone do that?"

"That's how the empire deals with rebellions." People moved out of the way as Chora approached, threads of Air moving the wheels of her chair. She held his gaze as she approached, her face all hard lines. "I'm not going to ask where you went. We'll have time for that later. You're an idiot. For now, the elves have summoned us for a war council in Mythníril. The long and short of it is that the Dragonguard have burned Argona to the ground, and they are using their fire to carve a path towards Aravell. The Aldithmar won't stray outside the boundaries of the wood. It's a clever tactic, but we'll see what they do when they reach the Nithrandír. Before you ask, no, we don't know how they discovered us or why they've chosen to attack now, though their mages will likely be stronger under the Blood Moon's light. We've long suspected they knew we were here. It was a matter of numbers. The elves stayed put, so there was no reason for the empire to waste lives trying to attack the city. According to the Dvalin Angan, the imperial forces number near eighty thousand, with several Fades among their ranks. Add the three Dragonguard and it's not looking fantastic." Chora looked to Dann, Calen, Erik, Tarmon, and Vaeril. "I suggest you go and put your pretty armour on. Between the rebels and the elves who've sworn to you, you've an army to lead now. Best you look the part."

Calen nodded. "Where's Aeson and Haem?"

"Haem's gone to get your soldiers ready," Ella said, stepping closer. "The other knights left as soon as the Blood Moon rose. They said they'd be back."

"I really fucking hope they come back." Erik let out a puff of air. "After what they did at Kingspass I think we're going to need them."

Calen drew in a short breath, settling himself. This was everything he'd been training for. He was ready. "All right. Dann, Vaeril, Tarmon, Erik. Let's get to it." He turned to Ella. Faenir moved to her side, his shoulder brushing hers. Calen still couldn't believe how enormous the wolfpine had grown, and he was absolutely certain it wasn't natural.

"We're fighting with you." Ella's eyes flashed amber as she spoke, flickering to molten gold. It appeared Calen wasn't the only one who had changed since they'd left The Glade. He would ask her about it all, but at that moment, he looked back at her, and he could see the hardness in her stare.

"We go where Ella goes," the big man standing behind her said. His hair was dark as night, and as Calen looked at him, he couldn't help but think the man reminded him a little of Rhett. The man extended his hand, and Calen reached out and grasped his forearm. "Tanner Fjorn," he said with a gruff nod and gestured towards the woman beside him. "This is Yana."

"Calen Bryer." Calen looked at the man, Tanner, as he spoke. "You're not Rhett's uncle Tanner, are you? He spoke of you."

"That I am. Heraya embrace him."

Calen's heart dropped into his stomach, and he looked to Ella.

The amber in her eyes faded back to blue as she looked at him. Faenir whimpered. "On the road to Gisa. Empire soldiers."

"Ella... I..."

"There'll be time to talk later."

Tanner rested his hand on Ella's shoulder, and Yana placed her hand atop his.

Calen wanted to pull Ella into an embrace, but he could see by the look in her eyes that was not what she wanted or needed, so instead he just nodded and turned to Chora. "We'll get our armour and meet you in Mythníril."

Before Chora answered, a flash of movement in Valerys's vision near the trees at the centre of the courtyard caught Calen's attention. "What's going on over there?"

"Dragonguard Rakina – or 'Imperial Justicars' as they like to call themselves now." The words left Chora's mouth as though they were poison. "They arrived with your sister. Thacia and Asius are fitting them with runecrafted manacles to block their connection to the Spark while we fight. We can deal with them after."

"They're the only reason I got here alive." Ella's stare hardened as she looked at Chora. "If not for Farda, I'd still be chained in that tent, or more likely, dead."

Calen snapped his head around to look at Ella. He could feel fury swelling in Valerys, but he tried to soothe the dragon, tried to temper the flames, at least for the moment. "Farda? Farda Kyrana?"

Speaking the man's name aloud caused Calen's hands to shake. Memories flooded his mind of Freis crashing through the wall of their home, Farda's fist clenching, the flames. He now knew Farda had been using the Spark that day – the day he killed Calen's mam. *Varyn, I pray to you. Let it be him.*

Ella must have seen something in Calen's stare because she tensed. "Why?"

The tone of her voice told Calen everything he needed to know. He saw the purple light of his eyes glowing off the faces of those around him, the wisps of mist drifting into the air as he let Valerys's fury in. He turned away from Ella and pushed through the gathered crowd. Hands pulled at him, and voices called, but he kept walking. Valerys lifted into the air and soared towards the trees at the centre of the courtyard – they were one, their fury and rage all consuming.

As Calen approached, Asius, Senas, and Thacia turned to look at him. He saw their lips moving, but no sounds touched his ears. Three people knelt beside the Jotnar, steel manacles clamped around their wrists. The manacles glowed with a blue light and were connected to chains that had been fused into the white-stone ground with the Spark. The prisoner on the left was a dark-skinned elf, his head drooping. The one in the middle was a woman with hair as white as snow.

"Farda!" Calen's chest and throat scratched as he roared at the top of his lungs, Valerys alighting beside him. A deep, vicious growl resonated in the dragon's throat.

The third prisoner, the man on the right, lifted his head at Calen's roar. As Calen's gaze fell on the bruised and bloody face of Farda Kyrana, his steps slowed. For a moment, his anger froze, his heart twisting as he relived that day in The Glade. Then his anger roared back like a blazing inferno. The way Farda stared back at him only drove Calen's rage further.

Calen strode forwards and, in one sweep of his hands, wrapped his fingers around Farda's neck and heaved the man to his feet. Farda stopped with a sudden jerk as his chains pulled against him. Calen tightened his hand around the man's neck, clenching his jaw as Farda stared back at him, eyes cold and unyielding.

Valerys loomed over Calen, the dragon's fury blending with his own. The sense of loss that rang clear in the dragon's mind only fuelled the fire within Calen. Farda had taken Freis from Valerys before the dragon had ever had a chance to meet her. Valerys had not been there when Calen killed Rendall, but now all the dragon wanted to do was bathe Farda in a river of fire.

"Calen!" Ella grabbed Calen's shoulder, but he shrugged her away.

Farda's stare never left Calen's, and the man made no motions to free his throat from Calen's grasp.

"Calen, you'll kill him!"

Ella grasped Calen's arm, trying to pull it down, but he held firm, muscles burning. She slammed her fist into the pit of his elbow at the same time as a pair of arms wrapped around his chest from behind and pulled him back. His grip slipped from Farda's throat as the man fell to the ground gasping.

Calen thrashed, breaking free of the arms that held him. He turned to find himself staring at Aeson. "Get your fucking hands off me!"

"Do you not think I want him dead? I want to watch the life drain from his eyes for what he has done. But we have enemies at the gates who aren't bound in chains."

Calen shook, his hands, his chest, his whole body. "He killed my mam, Aeson. Like she was nothing." Calen dropped his hand to his hip, needing to rub the fabric of his mam's scarf between his thumbs. For that brief moment, he'd forgotten he'd given it to Haem. Its absence only drove the hurt deeper. "It would only take a second."

Aeson leaned forwards as though he was about to speak, but Ella cut across him. "What did you say?"

The rush of anger was slowly ebbing, but Calen's voice still trembled as he turned to Ella. He pointed at Farda, who still knelt before them. "He killed mam." Calen's words caught in his throat. "He set her on fire... I thought you and Faenir were inside the house when he did."

Ella's eyes shifted from blue to molten gold. Her lips pulled back in a snarl. She spun on her heels and screamed, slapping Farda across the face. "You coward! You bastard!"

Calen looked on in awe as blood poured from four claw marks that sliced through Farda's face from his ear to his jaw, the flesh torn and twisted. The man didn't even flinch, he just stared back at Ella with what Calen could only describe as sorrow in his eyes.

Calen looked down at Ella's hand to see her fingernails had thickened and lengthened, blood pooling at their sharpened tips before dripping onto the white stone. She stared back at Farda, her breaths trembling. Faenir moved beside her, a low growl rumbling in his throat, his lips twisting in a snarl.

Calen's anger still simmered, but he pushed it down, or at least, he tried. He rested his hand on his sister's shoulder, which elicited a snarl. She turned her head, eyes glimmering gold.

"Aeson is right." They were not words Calen enjoyed speaking, but they were true. "He will be here when all this is done. We need to focus on what's in front of us."

A curl of Ella's lip revealed a wolf-like fang. "What if we lose? What if the city falls?"

"We'll cross that bridge if it comes to it."

"He needs to die for what he did, Calen." A low growl crept into Ella's voice, her jaw clenching. "He needs to die."

"He will."

Ella stared at Calen for a moment, then dropped to one knee. She clasped her hand around Farda's jaw, her sharp nails pressing against the wounds on his face. Again, the man didn't flinch. "When this is over, I'll come back here." The tremble in Ella's voice pulled at Calen's heart. "What kind of monster are you?"

Ella pushed Farda backwards, then rose. Her eyes softened a little as she looked at Calen. "I'm sorry, I didn't know. I would never have brought him here."

"As much as I'm loving this family moment," Chora said, pushing her wheelchair level with Calen, "we don't have the time. We'll move them, keep them chained, and place a guard on watch. Now go."

As the courtyard emptied and everyone moved off to prepare for the battle to come, a hand wrapped around Calen's arm, and he turned to see Aeson staring back at him.

"I did what I had to do," Aeson said.

"You did what was easiest."

"Would you have gone, if you knew? Would you have flown on Valerys to find your sister?"

Calen bit the inside of his lip. He decided to be honest. "Yes."

"Then I made the right choice. Did you find the answers you were looking for?"

"Not enough of them. Tivar Savinír."

"You went to Dracaldryr then…" Aeson looked at the ground. "How is she?"

"Haunted."

Aeson nodded slowly, ran his tongue across his front teeth, then let out a sigh. "Before we walk into that war council, I need to ask you to do something, Calen."

"You have some nerve to ask anything from me."

Aeson lifted his gaze to meet Calen's, his blue eyes piercing. "I ask you to run."

That was the last thing Calen had expected. "Sorry, what? You want me to run? Now, when the empire is at the gates?"

"You are the last of us, Calen. The last of our race."

"The Dragonguard, the elven Draleid—"

"They are the reason you are the last of us." Aeson's voice was harsh as he cut across Calen, a vein bulging in his neck. "The Dragonguard do not deserve to call themselves Draleid. And the Draleid who side with the Lynalion elves will be as bloodthirsty now as the Dragonguard were then. They will destroy each other. So yes, you are the last. And not only that, Valerys is the first dragon that's hatched since The Fall. I know you know that, but I need you to understand the significance." Aeson looked at Valerys, who had moved so he now stood over them both. "Valerys is impossible. He should not exist, and yet he does. I had always hoped that maybe whatever had stopped the Epherian dragons from hatching hadn't affected the dragons of Valacia. We sent many expeditions. None ever came back. That's why I went myself. Even if we could trust the elven Draleid, there's no signs to say their eggs are hatching either. If they had been, the elves of Lynalion would have come out from hiding a long time ago. Eventually they will wither and die. Valerys is unique. He must survive. *You* must survive."

As Aeson spoke, a moment of realisation clicked in Calen's head: if it wasn't for Aeson, Valerys wouldn't exist. It was a simple thought, one that Calen had already known, and yet in the midst of everything, he had allowed himself to forget it.

"Take whomever you need. Take them and leave through the eastern gate. Erik can lead you through the pass to Lodhar and the Southern Fold Gate of Durakdur." Aeson took a step closer to Calen, resting a hand on Calen's shoulder. "I don't know if we will survive this, Calen. The elven armies in Aravell are strong, but against three grown dragons and gods know how many Fades... But not if you run. If you live on, the rebellion lives on. The Draleid live on."

The two men stood in silence, only the rustle of the trees passing between them.

"No." Calen shook his head. "All I've done since the start is run. Everywhere we have gone, people have died. In the villages, in Belduar, Durakdur, Drifaien... I keep running, and people keep dying. A friend once told me that the only thing within our control is what we choose to do with the short time we have. He told me that in a world where nothing matters, what matters to us means everything. That if we forget about the ones we love, everything loses meaning. That is why I went after Rist, and it's also why I'm not running. Except for Rist, everyone and everything I love is in this city. The people I am willing to die for – they are here. And this fight, this rebellion, all of those people who have come here – I believe in it. After Valerys hatched, you said to me that this might not have been my cause, but it is now. You were right."

Aeson let out a heavy sigh as he stared back at Calen. "So be it. All things come to an end. If this is that day, we'll face it with our swords in our hands staring into the eyes of those who would send us to the void."

CALEN LOOKED DOWN AS HE traced his hand along the vines of gold that swept across the breastplate of his armour, a smile touching his lips as his skin pressed against the ornate leaves Valdrin had worked into the metal. Aeson and the others hadn't been impressed with the fact that The

Order symbol hadn't been marked across the breast. But Calen didn't think there would be a point in his life when he would be able to explain to Valdrin how much that small detail meant to him.

Footsteps sounded at the door, and Calen turned to see Lasch Havel resting his hand on the doorframe. The man had slowly recovered over the months but still looked gaunt and weary. His beard and hair were trimmed tight, though both remained brittle and grey. "You definitely look the part." Lasch's smile was weak as he stepped into the room. He looked over Calen from head to toe. "A Draleid. Who'd have thought it?"

Calen sighed softly, looking at the white steel armour that covered his body. All he was missing were the two gauntlets that rested on the bed behind him. "How are you feeling? How's Elia?"

"Good," Lasch said with a smile. The man's hands shook as he lifted them and rested them on Calen's pauldrons. "If Vars had seen you like this, he'd have smiled ear-to-ear. He never shut up about you. You know that, right?"

Calen nodded, turning his gaze to the floor.

"It feels like it was only yesterday we were sending you boys into Ölm Forest for The Proving."

Calen lifted his head to see Lasch biting at his lip hard enough that blood was trickling down his chin. The man had done that since being freed from Berona.

"I'll find him, Lasch. I promise."

A brief smile touched Lasch's lips, but he shook his head. "Your father also had a habit of making promises he couldn't keep, or at least, promises he shouldn't have been able to keep. Somehow, he always seemed to find a way." Lasch drew in a deep breath, then let it out slow. "You and Dann were the best thing to ever happen to Rist. You know when you were younger, he barely spoke when you two weren't around, but when he was with you, we couldn't shut him up."

"I think that's Dann's doing," Calen said with a laugh.

Lasch leaned in and rested his forehead against Calen's. "Thank you for everything you've done for him and what you did for us. Vars and Freis might be gone, Calen, but you'll always have a family."

Calen pressed his tongue against the roof of his mouth, holding back the tears that burned at the corner of his eyes.

"May The Mother embrace you," Lasch whispered.

"And The Father protect you," Calen added.

"May The Warrior guide your hand, and The Maiden guide your mind," they both said together.

"May The Smith keep your blade sharp." Dann's voice rang out from the doorway. Calen lifted his head to see Dann wore his new armour, the depiction of the white dragon emblazoned across the breastplate, a white hooded cloak flowing between his pauldron and spaulder. "Am I intentionally being left out?"

"Come here, Dann." Lasch wrapped his arm Dann's head and tugged him close, pulling their heads together. "May The Smith keep both your blades sharp and The Sailor see you to safe shores." Lasch held them for a moment. "I'd be out there with you if I thought I'd be anything more than a hindrance. You two look after each other, you hear? That's what people of The Glade do." A tear trickled down Lasch's cheek. He sniffed, then stood back and patted Dann and Calen's shoulders. "Come on, Elia's waiting downstairs. Be gentle with her, she's having a rough day."

"I'll be down in a second," Calen said as Lasch and Dann stepped out of the room.

Calen turned to the bed, looking down at everything he'd splayed across it, everything he'd carried with him: a purse of coins Alleron had given him, the brass-backed obsidian pendant and Alvira's letter he'd found in Vindakur, the polished metal disk and riddle Rokka had given him, and his two gauntlets.

He let out a heavy sigh, then picked up his left gauntlet, sliding his hand inside. He did the same with his right, then looked at the two circles of runes that ran around the outside of the vambraces matching the ones now inscribed on his forearms.

The last time he was preparing for a battle like this was in Belduar. He'd failed then. Belduar had burned to the ground, and thousands had died as he and the others fled down the Wind Tunnels. But he was a different man now, and Valerys was a far more powerful dragon. A rumble of agreement sounded in the back of his mind. *No matter what, we will not run. We will not yield.* Valerys's rumble turned into a roar of defiance.

Calen dropped his gauntleted hand to the coin pommel of the sword his dad had given him, the sword that had slain Durin Longfang, Taran Shadesmire, and Rayce Garrin. The sword that had been forged over a thousand years ago. The sword that had been wielded by the Chainbreaker – Vars Bryer. Calen remembered what his dad had said to him the day he gave Calen that sword. *'There is no need to thank me, Calen. You have filled me with more pride than I ever thought possible. The man you have become is thanks enough.'*

"I will not let you down. I promise."

Calen lifted his hand from the sword and held his arms out in front of himself. "Dreskyr mit huartan. Dreskr mit hnokle. Bante er vi, measter og osvarthe." *Protect my heart. Protect my bones. Bound are we, master and oath.*

The runes on Calen's armour ignited into life, glowing with a bright purple light. Calen watched as the metal on his vambraces and gauntlets melded together. The rest of his armour followed suit until he was covered in smooth, flowing plate, and the light of the runes had dulled to a pale glow. He could *feel* the runes, feel their power. Once he spoke the rune words, he could link and unlink the armour at will.

Calen picked up his helmet from the bed, casting his eyes over the runes that shimmered along the side plates. He drew in a long breath, then strode from the room.

CHAPTER SEVENTY-EIGHT

AND SO IT BEGINS

Kallinvar stood at the war table, his hands gripping the edge. Every soul in the knighthood, except for Arden, stood around him in silence, watching, as they had since the Blood Moon first tainted the sky. He drew in slow breaths as he studied the stone map carved into the table. As Gildrick had taught him, he had layered the convergences and pulsing of the Taint over the map in his mind.

Small glowing patches of red dotted the continent – convergences where Bloodspawn were gathering and harvesting Essence. On any other day, he would have sent his knights straight through the Rift, but not this day. This day, it wasn't the small glowing patches that concerned him. As he looked at the map, he could see and *feel* the tears in the veil between worlds. They manifested in his mind as black tears with a red glow at their edges, the sickly, oily sensation of the Taint seeping from them. One was torn across a small section of Mar Dorul where the mountains sloped towards Gildor, another near Copperstille, one just north of Catagan, one on Driftstone, and several more about the continent. The largest was stretched across the entirety of the Burnt Lands, shrouding it in black.

"While we wait, people are dying." Brother-Captain Illarin spoke calmly, his words simply a matter of fact. "The Bloodspawn are stronger under the light of this moon – the people don't stand a chance."

"I know, brother." Kallinvar didn't lift his gaze from the table.

Out of the corner of his eye, he saw Tarron step up beside him, arms folded. He didn't speak, but he held Illarin's gaze.

"I know it's hard," Kallinvar said, watching as the black tear above the Burnt Lands pulsed. "But you must remember. 'No decision is straightforward. Black and white do not exist. We live in a world of ever-shifting grey.'"

"I do not need reminding of those words, Kallinvar. I have lived by them."

"And you must live by them again today, Illarin. We must let the lesser evils pass. You know as well as I that we must be ready to strike like a hammer when Fane Mortem or a Bloodspawn Shaman tries to reach through the veil."

"We could be here for weeks," Sister-Captain Airdaine said, moving towards the left side of the table and casting her gaze over Varsund. "I understand your words, Grandmaster. But it's hard to stand by and wait while so much blood is spilled. Ilnaen did not fall until the twenty-fifth day of the last Blood Moon."

"That was different. Fane and the Bloodspawn were working together. That is no longer the case. At Ilnaen they waited until the perfect moment, but now they race against each other. Both seek to win Efialtír's favour. They cannot afford to wait, lest the other succeeds in their stead. I will know when an attempt is made to widen the tears. Be ready."

Kallinvar glanced up to see Illarin with his arms folded, nodding as he looked over the stone map.

"Here." Ruon handed Kallinvar a wooden cup.

"What's this?" Kallinvar brought the cup to his nose and sniffed, puffing out his cheeks and recoiling at the sharp botanical smell.

"Dragon's Tears," Ruon said, producing a second cup and tipping it off Kallinvar's. "Got it off a dwarf about a century ago. Been saving it. Drink up. It'll take the edge off."

"Hey," Tarron said, leaning in. "I thought we spoke about holding out?"

Ruon glared at him but handed over her cup. She pulled a small flask from a satchel that rested atop one of the folding tables the Watchers had brought in. She pulled the stopper, then tipped some of the blue liquid into a third cup. "There's not enough to go around, so—"

"Ahem."

Kallinvar smiled as he looked up to see Ildris standing behind Ruon.

"Fuck sake. Keep it down, or Lyrin will drink the whole flask."

Ruon poured another cup, and they drank.

The last time Kallinvar had drank Dragon's Tears, he'd thought he'd drank liquid fire; this was no different. He clenched his jaw and held a cough in his chest as the spirit burned its way down. "Fuck…" He let out a puff of air, shaking his head.

"I told you it would take the edge off," Ruon said as she collected the four cups. "Any word from Arden?"

Kallinvar looked down at the stone map where a single green counter rested in the Darkwood. As Kallinvar stared at the counter, a green glow encased it. Not only could he feel the thrum of Arden's Sigil, but he could also sense the blend of fear and resolve in the young man's heart. A small patch of glowing red rested just southwest of Arden, moving ever closer. Kallinvar pushed himself away from the table, then reached through his Sigil to Arden's, sending a pulse to let the young man know he was needed.

The Sigil fused with Kallinvar's chest, ignited with a burning fire as he summoned the Rift. The fire flowed through his veins as ice swept over his skin. The juxtaposition of the two sensations always sent a jolt of panic through him. As he drew in a slow breath, he pictured Arden in his mind, feeling the man's Sigil, sensing his surroundings. Seconds later, the core of the rift materialised in the shape of a glowing green sphere a few feet from Kallinvar. The gathered knights turned their heads as the green sphere flattened and spread, its centre turning to a pool of rippling black. Normally he wouldn't summon the Rift in the war room, but this night was no normal night, and Kallinvar could focus better when he could see the war table.

Within moments, Arden stepped through. His helm receded into the collar of his Sentinel armour as the Rift vanished behind him.

"Brother." Kallinvar reached out his hand and clasped Arden's forearm.

"Grandmaster. An army of eighty thousand strong marches through the Darkwood. Three dragons fly with them, and the Angan have reported several Fades amongst the armies."

"Fane must have known of Aravell for a long time." Kallinvar folded his arms, turning to the war table, the other knights moving closer. "He's waited until now to strike, until the prize was more than just the elves. He's splitting us, dividing our attention between the Draleid and the tears in the veil."

"Does the Draleid really matter when placed against the veil itself, Grandmaster?" Sister-Captain Olyria stood on the opposite of the war table, her palms resting against the stone. "Like you said, we must let the lesser evils pass."

"No matter what happens today, this war is only beginning, Olyria. What happened at Ilnaen all those years ago was only the first step."

"What makes you so certain, Kallinvar? What makes you so certain there will even be a time after this? What if we allow Efialtír to push his will into this world and he destroys everything we love?"

Achyron's words echoed in Kallinvar's mind. *'What I have brought you here to tell you is that the Alignment will happen, my child. It is inevitable. You cannot stop Efialtír's harbinger from widening the tear in the veil. Too much has been set in motion. But you must meet him when he does. You must limit the crossing, and then continue to do as you have done – prepare the world for the war to come… The Alignment is only the beginning – only a single step in the Great Deceiver's plan.'*

How did Kallinvar explain that he had spoken to the warrior god himself, that his soul had been brought to the realm of the gods? Gildrick knew – Kallinvar had told him that day but had asked the Watcher to keep it a secret. Faith was a strange thing. Every man and woman in the war room knew Achyron existed; they were alive solely by his grace. The Sigils fused with their chests imbued them with his will and power. And yet, none had ever seen him or heard the sound of his voice. If Kallinvar told them, he risked them thinking him a mad man. He needed to know more before he did. Now was not a time to have a crisis of leadership. Verathin had never spoken of hearing Achyron's voice, and from what Kallinvar had read in the journals of the other Grandmasters, neither had any before him.

"Do you trust me, Olyria?"

The woman stared at Kallinvar from across the table, her Sentinel armour shimmering in the light of the candles that sat about the room. She nodded. "I would follow you to the void, Grandmaster."

"Good. You may have to." Kallinvar summoned the Rift once more, feeling the ripple of fire and ice through his blood and over his skin. As the Rift opened, he turned to Arden. "Take Lyrin and Varlin with you. Ildris and Ruon will stay here."

"Thank you, Grandmaster."

Kallinvar looked back at Arden, taking the young man in. *The last Sigil Bearer. The first time in four centuries the knighthood had been complete.* He remembered finding Arden that day in Ölm Forest. Even then, as the blood had poured through Arden's fingers, Kallinvar had seen something in him. Since then, Arden had become a knight and a man Kallinvar was proud to call brother. He could have sent any knight to protect the Draleid; they were all fine warriors. But he knew none would fight harder than Arden. "The duty of the strong is to protect the weak, brother. Never forget that."

"Never."

Lyrin and Varlin moved to Arden's side, nodding at Kallinvar. He could feel the sense of guilt radiating from their Sigils. He knew the weight of what he asked – to protect the Draleid while the rest of their brothers and sisters readied themselves to stand against the Shadow. It was not an easy thing. He stepped forwards. "Achyron asks much of us." He gestured around the room to the other knights. "But no matter where you hold your blade tonight, you will be at our sides. We fight the Shadow wherever it rises. We fight as one. For Achyron."

The knights of the other chapters echoed the words.

"For Achyron," Lyrin, Varlin, and Arden repeated.

Lyrin and Arden stepped through the Rift, the black pool rippling as they did. Varlin stopped for a moment, turning back. "Good hunting, Grandmaster."

The Rift collapsed on itself as Varlin stepped through, and silence settled in the chamber.

Moments later the doors of the war chamber creaked open and the Watchers, along with some priests and servants, swept into the room, laying out more trays of food and water. As the food was set down, the Watchers moved about the chamber, speaking to the knights and making sure all was well. Each knight may have been imbued with Achyron's strength, but behind it all, they were still human; they still felt fear and worry.

Gildrick approached Kallinvar with his hands clasped behind his back, his gaze tracing the stone map carved into the war table. Watcher Tallia walked behind him, her gaze also fixed on the table. The man stopped beside Kallinvar and stood in silence for a moment before speaking. "Have you heard anything?"

Kallinvar shook his head. Gildrick's words needed no explanation. Kallinvar hadn't heard Achyron's voice since the Blood Moon had risen. It unsettled him.

"He will speak when he needs to," Gildrick whispered. Beside him, Kallinvar saw Tallia's head turn, her keen eyes watching. Had Gildrick told her what Kallinvar had seen?

Kallinvar nodded to Gildrick but didn't speak. As he looked down at the stone map, an almost imperceptible red glow pulsed in the Burnt Lands, momentarily breaking through the blackness of the tear that stretched across the waste. It was so faint he'd barely felt it in his Sigil. Then it pulsed again, stronger, and the oily sensation of the Taint probed at Kallinvar's mind.

The knights around Kallinvar shifted. He felt the weight of expectation in their gazes, the thrum of their Sigils resonating through him. They could feel the heady mix of fear and fervour in his blood.

The red glow pulsed for a third time, piercing through the black that shrouded the wasteland. But this time the pulse didn't sink back into the darkness, it remained, Taint oozing from it.

And so it begins now.

Drawing a deep breath, Kallinvar moved to the end of the table and called to his Sigil, feeling it burn in his chest as he summoned the Rift once more. Knights, Watchers, and servants moved out of the way as the green sphere materialised and flattened out into the rippling pool of black, a bright green light shimmering at its edges. A number of pulses ignited in Kallinvar's Sigil as some of the knights who had been in plain clothes called forth their Sentinel armour. As they moved to stand before Kallinvar, liquid metal poured from the Sigils fused with their chests, flowing over their clothes and bodies, protecting them in Achyron's spirit.

The Watchers, servants, and priests moved to the edges of the chamber, allowing the knights to take position in the war room's centre, standing ready for Kallinvar's words.

The knights of The Second who hadn't gone with Arden stood to his right, looking ready to walk through fire.

"There's not much I can say that you haven't already heard." Kallinvar looked about the room, his gaze meeting those of Armites, Illarin, Olyria, and Emalia – four of seventeen who had survived The Fall. "Some of you have been here before, seen the light of the Blood Moon. But most of you have not. Efailtír's hand reaches through the veil. The Bloodmarked will be stronger than you've ever faced. The Shamans and imperial mages will wield powers far greater than you have come to know. Steel yourselves. Ignite the fires in your hearts. The Shadow has taken from us. It has taken our sisters, our brothers. It took Verathin. But this day, we will make them bleed. We will make their god shake."

A murmur rippled through the knights, some slamming their gauntleted fists against their breastplates.

"I need you to hear me now. We will not just face Bloodspawn or imperial mages when we step through the rift. There will be men and women wielding nothing but sharp steel – men and women who, on another night, we would fight to defend. But there will be no mercy this night of all nights. When we step through the Rift, nothing can keep us from destroying the Shadow. If you hesitate, for even a moment, it will not just be you who suffers, not just your brothers and sisters, but every soul on this mortal plane. Tonight is a night of death. I know what I ask is not easy. That weight will stay with you, but we bear it so others do not have to – it is our burden. Take no more lives than are needed, but do not hesitate in the taking. Where possible, save your Soulblades for the Bloodspawn and mages. Use your steel to take the lives of those not touched by the Taint, but if it comes to it, tonight of all nights, do what must be done. Do you understand, brothers and sisters?"

A murmur of 'Grandmaster' answered. Kallinvar looked to Ruon, who returned his stare with a sombre nod. They had talked of this already, and she had been in agreement – there could be no hesitation this night. They could not allow Efialtír to reach his hand further into the world.

Kallinvar pulled his sword from its sheath at his side. "Each one of us was snatched from the jaws of death for a single purpose." He slammed the handle of his sword against his breastplate. "We were chosen by the warrior god himself. To be his sword and shield in this world. To protect those who cannot protect themselves." Kallinvar once more beat his sword against his armoured chest, a number of the others following suit. He had always found that no matter how many battles a warrior had fought, the fire in their hearts always needed stoking. To kill is no easy task. To sever a soul from the world was even harder. "When you step through the Rift, think of what you fight for. Think of *who* you fight for – the ones you love and the ones you loved. Are you with me, brothers and sisters? Will you follow me to the void and back?"

"To the void and back," Ruon, Ildris, and Tarron responded. A chorus of the words rippled across the knights, and Kallinvar could feel the fire burning in their Sigils.

"Will you allow the Shadow to take our world?"

"No!" Came the reply.

"Will you allow the Great Deceiver to twist the minds of our people?"

"No!"

"Then once more I ask you to follow me into the fires of battle. Once more, I ask you to live and die by my side. For Achyron!"

"For Achyron!" the knights roared, swords beating off armoured chests, veins bulging, voices burning with fervour.

Kallinvar nodded to Ruon and the other knights of The Second. Each of them stepped forwards.

"To the void and back, brother," Ildris said, grasping Kallinvar's forearm. "It has been my honour to fight by your side."

"And mine yours."

Kallinvar turned, drew in a short breath, and charged through the Rift. A chill swept over him, sinking into his core. Every moment in the Rift felt like a lifetime, silence swallowing all sound. He burst through, the icy chill leeching from his bones as his armoured feet *thumped* into the sand.

Before him, hundreds of soldiers were spread about in the red and black of Loria, billowing cloaks flapping behind them. The oily sickness of the Taint pulsed like an infection in the world, emanating from what looked to be hundreds of mages standing in a large circle behind the soldiers. Runic inscriptions in the sand glowed with a red light.

The soldiers nearest to Kallinvar charged, screaming as they did. A man swung his sword towards Kallinvar's side, but the blade skittered off his Sentinel armour. Kallinvar pushed forwards and drove his sword through the man's gut, wrenching it free in a spray of blood. He swung his arm back, slicing through the neck of the second soldier who charged over his companion's corpse. Steel collided against bone and then sliced through, the soldier's head dropping into the sand.

Kallinvar's Sigil pulsed as Ruon, Ildris, Tarron, and Mirken emerged from the Rift behind him, Daynin and Sylven following.

He dropped his shoulder, feeling bones crunch as he hammered into the chest of a charging Lorian. Blood sprayed as his sword carved through limbs and opened chests. He fixed his gaze on the mages at the centre of the circle.

"For Achyron!"

CHAPTER SEVENTY-NINE

SPIRITS AND FIRE

Let them come and crash against our walls." King Galdra of Lunithír stood with his arms folded, looking over the erinian-inlaid table in the main chamber of Mythníril. The king's silvery hair coruscated in the pinkish-red light of the Blood Moon that drifted in through the oculus overhead. Through the arched windows in the walls behind him, Calen could see storm clouds brewing, glowing with a crimson light. "We can teach them to once again fear elven steel."

The other two rulers of Aravell, along with the six Ephorí stood either side of Galdra, all with their arms either folded or clasped behind their backs. A number of elven commanders stood around them wearing smooth silver plate and flowing cloaks the colours of the various kingdoms.

Varthon, the Matriarch of Clan Dvalin, stood to the left of the table, Baldon and Aneera beside her.

"Walls mean nothing to dragons," Aeson said, leaning over the table. "One pass and every warrior you put on those ramparts will be char and ash."

"Agreed." Harken had one arm across his chest, propping up the other, his hand scratching at his chin. The man's long, dark hair was tied into a braid that ran down his back.

"Well—" Queen Uthrían raised an eyebrow at Aeson "—what do you suggest then, Rakina?"

"If I may?" Chora raised a finger.

Uthrían nodded, and Aeson gestured for Chora to carry on.

Chora lifted herself up in her chair, her eyes scanning the map on the table. "The dragons are burning a path through the Aravell, and the armies are walking across the ash. Once the dragons push through the glamour, they will simply burn everything in their path. What I suggest is we take the dragons out of the battle."

Towering behind Chora, Thacia nodded with a broad smile stretching from ear to ear. The Jotnar's blood-red hair glistened in the crimson light.

"With all due respect, Rakina," one of the elven commanders said, "if that was such an easy thing to do, we wouldn't be having this discussion."

"We don't let them reach the walls." All eyes turned to Ella as she moved past Calen and closer the table.

"And who, may I ask, are you?" Baralas, one of the two Ephorí from Ardurän shook his head and gestured at Ella. In the short time Calen had spent in Aravell, he'd found Baralas, of all the Ephorí, to possess a level of arrogance that set his blood boiling.

"She is a guardian of Fenryr." Baldon's voice remained low and level, a rumbling growl reverberating in his throat as he looked at Baralas. "She is an Aldruid of the warrior blood, and she is the daughter of the Chainbreaker."

"My apologies," Baralas inclined his head towards Baldon and gestured for Ella to continue, the colour draining from his face.

Dann leaned in close to Calen, and Calen could sense the smirk on his face just by the tone of his voice as he whispered. "I fucking love Baldon."

Ella gave Baldon a soft smile and a nod. She turned to Chora. "Forgive me, I spoke out of turn."

"Speaking out of turn is what I pride myself on. Continue. I already know my plan. I'd prefer to hear yours."

Ella inclined her head, passing her gaze around the table before she continued. She leaned forwards pointing at Aravell on the map. "If we sit and wait, we're doing exactly what they want. But if we could get closer, if we could move through the woods and bring the fight to them before they knew we were coming, we would negate the dragons' fire. If we get close enough, the dragons wouldn't be able to burn us without burning their own. And if we could somehow drag them into the woods, then not only would we even the odds a little, but maybe those spirits – the Aldithmar? Maybe they could help us." Ella looked to Varthon who stood at the end of the table with strips of black fabric draped over her white fur, the veins of gold in her black antlers glimmering. "Gavrien guided me and my friends through the woodland. He said you have a pact of sorts with the spirits?"

"Of a sort," Varthon replied, her deer-like eyes fixed on Ella.

"We can use that," Ella said, tapping on the table. "If we keep the Dvalin Angan close and draw the imperial soldiers into the wood."

"I like the way your brain works," Chora said. "That's a better plan than I had."

Calen could do nothing to hold back the smile that touched his lips as he looked at Ella, a pride swelling within.

"They would still overrun us." The Ephorí Calen knew as Ara of Lunithír stood with arms folded. She bit at the corner of her lip, raising an eyebrow as she looked up from the map. "And then they could pull back, and the dragons would lay waste to our forces."

"My rangers could go." The elf who spoke was Thalanil, High Captain of the Aravell Rangers. It was he who had recused Calen and the others from the Uraks when they were last in the Darkwood. His left eye was a milky white, and a myriad of scars latticed his face. "We can take galdrín and Dvalin with us, move light. We take up positions on both sides of the path they're burning, split their attention. We wait by the line of Nithrandír. Once the dragons do a pass, we cut through the soldiers with arrows from both sides. Then the galdrín can pull the soldiers into the woods for the Aldithmar to take. They won't know what's happening. We can thin the herd, then lure them in."

It took Calen a moment to remember the word 'galdrín' meant 'mage' in the Old Tongue.

"We can set up the main army here, here, and here." Aeson pointed to three spots on the map: one behind the line of Nithrandír, one to the left, and one to the right. "Once you've dealt your damage, fall back. The empire will give chase, and the Nithrandír will cut them down. As soon as the Nithrandír take form, we will charge. We hit them hard and fast from all three sides." He dragged two fingers in a long line. "We need to make use of the forest, let it cover us as we stretch our forces outside the path they're carving, let them walk willingly into our grasp, then cut them to shreds." Aeson looked up towards Ella. "Like Ella said, if we get in close, quickly, we'll negate the dragonfire – for the most part. It will be chaos. But chaos is our best chance."

"As good a plan as any," Queen Uthrían said, nodding. "It has my support."

"And mine." King Silmiryn, who had remained mostly quiet, inclined his head towards Aeson. "I will provide my royal galdrín to accompany the rangers."

"As will I." King Galdra's chin rose a little higher in the air. Calen had yet to see a time when the two kings hadn't tried to outdo each other.

"My thanks, King Galdra, King Silmiryn." Thalanil inclined his head. "They will be most welcome amongst our number."

"I will go with the rangers." Therin hadn't spoken the entire time. In fact, Therin rarely ever spoke around the other elves at all. And now, as he did, most didn't even turn to acknowledge his words except for Queen Uthrían and one of the Vaelen Ephorí, Ithilin.

Thalanil stared at the stone map for a few moments, then lifted his gaze. He nodded at Therin.

Aeson looked to Haem, who stood to Calen's right along with Lyrin and Varlin. "Arden, will Ruon and Ildris be returning?"

Haem shook his head. "This is all we could spare." Haem gestured towards Lyrin and Varlin, who stood either side of him. "With the Blood Moon, our brothers and sisters must be ready to push back the Shadow. Efialtír is splitting us on purpose."

There was weight in Haem's eyes, loss.

Aeson nodded, then turned to Calen. "Valerys will need to stay in the city."

"What?"

"If he takes to the sky outside the glamour, the Dragonguard will rip you both to pieces. And the woodland is too dense for him to be anything other than a target. If he holds back, he can protect the city from anything that slips through." Calen didn't have to speak. Valerys's roar thundered through the sky outside, echoing in the chamber. But as much as Calen hated the idea, it was true. "He will get his chance," Aeson said, holding Calen's gaze. "But there is no sense in throwing his life away." Aeson drew in a long breath, then looked around the table. "Gather what you need and say whatever you need to say to whomever you need to say it to. We march immediately."

As the room emptied, Ella pulled at Calen's arm. "Tanner, Yana, and I are going with the rangers. Don't argue. It's where we're best suited."

Calen looked into Ella's eyes, seeing the blue shift to amber. In his heart, all he wanted to do was put her somewhere safe, but nowhere was safe. As he stared back at his sister, Ingvat's words in the Burnt Lands rang in his ears. *'Take away their choice and you take away who they are.'*

Those words had found a new meaning in Calen's mind when he'd discovered Aeson had known Ella was alive all this time. Aeson had taken away Calen's choice, taken away his ability to keep his sister safe, and Calen refused to do the same to others. He drew in a sharp breath, nodded, then pulled Ella into a hug. "We'll get through this, I promise."

Ella squeezed, then pulled away, a soft smile on her lips. "Whatever happens, we're together."

"I'll go with her," Dann said, moving to Calen and Ella's side.

"I don't need you to protect me, Dann Pimm," Ella said with a frown. "I'm not some damsel."

"Protect you?" Dann raised his eyebrows. "No, I want you to protect me."

⊘

THE WINTER AIR WAS ICE in Dann's lungs, his breath misting as he exhaled. He held his new white wood bow in his left hand, his heart thumping as his fingers brushed the fletching of the arrows in the quiver at his hip. The drum of feet and howls of instructions and commands from the imperial soldiers echoed through the forest like a landslide. The smell of burning wood filled his nostrils, and smoke clouded the air.

About two hundred feet ahead, the light of the Blood Moon washed down through the clearing created by the Lorian dragonfire. The clouds of smoke from the fires shone with an incandescent pink glow, casting the wood in an eerie light. That was the one benefit Dann had found of the dragons burning their way through the Darkwood: the forest itself was no longer a sea of darkness. A few hundred feet along the clearing, a column of torches marched forwards, shadows dancing across the wood as the imperial forces moved towards the ambush point.

All about Dann, Aravell rangers crouched low, hooded green cloaks draped over their shoulders, white wood bows gripped in their fists. Dvalin Angan were interspersed amongst the elves, strips of black fabric covering their white fur. Alea and Lyrei were crouched to Dann's left, the hoods of their dark green cloaks pulled over their heads, their bows held tight. Ella, Tanner, Yana, Faenir, and Baldon were on his right. Dann barely recognised Ella, and not because of the broken nose or the scars on the side of her head – or even because of her eyes that seemed to shift from blue to gold. But because of the way she held herself, the way she talked, and the way she moved.

The Ella Dann knew was sharp and quick witted. She had always been able to hold a sword and, most importantly for Dann, she could trade insults with the best of them. But *this* Ella was colder. Her wit was sharper, her humour curbed. Dann had been in Aravell for months, and there was no way he would have been caught dead speaking in that chamber in front of those Ephorí and the Kings and Queen. Ella had stepped forwards and spoken as though she were a veteran of a hundred battles. And besides Ella, Faenir looked like he'd gotten in a fight with a bear and then eaten the bear. The wolfpine was enormous.

"You think you might have left the white cloak in the city?" Ella whispered as they creeped through the wood, her gaze focused on the marching imperial soldiers ahead.

Dann looked down at his new armour that Valdrin had made for him. He rubbed the white cloak between the thumb and forefinger of his right hand as he ducked under a low branch. "It kind of completes the look."

Ella turned her head, the faint light of the torches ahead casting shadows across her face. "Really?"

"You're just jealous," Dann whispered back.

"Shh." Lyrei slapped at Dann's hand, glaring at him. Her finger was pressed against her lips. Both Lyrei and Alea had left their white cloaks in

Aravell. Now that Dann thought about it, it probably would have been a good idea.

Dann frowned and stuck out his tongue at Lyrei, which only drew a sharper glare from the elf. He cursed himself for his reaction – it was childish, but fear tended to find the child in him. Strangely, it wasn't fear of the fighting to come that gripped him. It was the fear of what he was about to do. Killing Uraks or trying to kill the spirits that lurked in the Darkwood – the ones he could see drifting through the night around them – was one thing. But Dann had only ever killed eight humans. One in Milltown, three in Camylin, and four at Belduar. And each of those had been with his blood hot in his veins. The first time he'd taken a life had been to save Calen. When he closed his eyes, he could still feel the vibrations as the sword crunched against the bones of the soldier's neck. He could still see the blood on his hands.

Dann looked at the bow clenched in his hands, seeing that he had been subconsciously gripping the wood so tight his knuckles were pale. He loosened his grip, drawing in a slow breath. He knew that for the first time he was about to take a human life not in direct fear of his own but simply because it needed to be done. And the soldier he killed would never know how or why they had died. The thought twisted a knot in Dann's stomach. He wouldn't shy away from what he needed to do, but that didn't mean he would allow himself to accept it peacefully.

The howl of a wolf rippled through the night, rising above the marching feet. All about Dann, the rangers pulled arrows from their quivers and nocked them. Dann drew a short breath, then followed suit, the touch of the fletching calming him before he pulled the arrow free from the quiver.

"Remember," Lyrei whispered, "as soon as the signal is given, run."

Dann nodded, holding Lyrei's gaze for a moment. "I'm not going to have to carry you out of here again, am I?"

The elf sucked in her cheeks, then shook her head and turned back towards the clearing ahead. As Lyrei turned, Dann could see Alea staring at him, her golden eyes shimmering in the light of the Blood Moon.

"What?" he mouthed. Just like her sister, Alea shook her head and looked back towards the clearing.

"I see you have as much success with the elven women as you do with the human ones." Ella's lips widened to a grin as she slipped two short swords the elves had given her from her belt.

"You know, I liked you better when we thought you were dead." A moment passed, and Dann grimaced. "No, wait. That was a bit too mean."

"Yeah." Ella pursed her lips. "It was a bit much."

"I'm working on it."

"No, you're not."

"No, I'm not."

"Shh," Lyrei hushed again. She nodded towards the clearing where the torches were drawing closer, the imperial soldiers marching.

Dann nodded, then dropped to one knee, wet leaves shifting beneath him. One of the greatest things about his new armour was that it didn't hurt his knees when he knelt. *Relax. Let yourself breathe.* The smell of burning wood redoubled in his nostrils as he drew a long breath, and he let out a cough as the smoke caught in his chest.

Lyrei glared at him again as he gave her an apologetic smile.

He let his breath out slow, cracking his neck to the side. The wait was what was killing him. He counted his heartbeats as the column of Lorian soldiers drew closer in the clearing ahead. It was hard to tell in the pale crimson light of the Blood Moon, but it looked as though the column was hundreds of soldiers wide and stretched back until the night swallowed it.

Minutes passed, each more tense than the last. Dann's heartbeat had blocked out almost all other sounds, thumping like a drum. The soldiers were directly ahead of him now, their torches scattering the criss-cross shadows of trees through the undergrowth.

Dann's heart clenched as shapes shifted in the forest between the line of elves and the column of soldiers. Twisted shapes of roots and bark, black smoke illuminated only by the Blood Moon's light. *Aldithmar.* Part of the plan was to draw the imperial soldiers out from the clearing and into trees, exposing them to the Aldithmar's wrath. Dann was all too aware, however, that the Aldithmar would just as easily snap his bones as they would any imperial soldier's if he strayed too far from a Dvalin Angan.

I could really use a drink.

He rolled his shoulders, loosening himself, then slowed his breathing. Little was more important when using a bow and arrow than staying loose and breathing.

The voices of the soldiers drifted on the breeze. Dann could hear them clearly now, chatting, throwing insults back and forth, totally unaware of the blood that was about to be spilt. Dann clenched his jaw, swallowing. Beneath the mask of the 'evil empire', these were just men and women. They had homes and parents, and friends, likely siblings, maybe even children. *You can feel the guilt later. They're here to kill you.* Dann thought back to that night in Ölm Forest during The Proving – the night he had killed the bear. He imagined himself to be that bear now. These men and women had marched into his den, and if he didn't kill them first, they would kill him.

Another howl echoed in the night, and Dann saw the elves around him tense, their fingers ready to draw. He drew in a deep breath and pulled back the bow string, feeling the pressure against his fingers.

A few grumbles rose amongst the soldiers in the clearing, a few curious shouts, but they marched on.

Dann glanced at Ella to his right, the big man, Tanner, and his partner, Yana, standing beside her. None held bows, but Dann had no doubt they would carve the soldiers apart when they got close. Baldon was now in his wolf-like form, standing on all fours beside Faenir, both their eyes glistening. Despite Faenir's growth, the Angan still towered over the wolfpine, though Dann would not want to run into either of them in a dark wood – or *the* Darkwood, as it happened.

He looked back towards the column of soldiers marching past them. His heart beat with a *thump*.

The last howl rang out in the night, and Dann loosed. The snapping of bow strings sounded all around him, the whistle of arrows cutting through the air. Even in the pale red light, Dann followed the flight of his arrow, watching as it soared between the trees and punched into the head of a Lorian soldier.

Cries and screams rang out as the arrows sliced through the column, and soldiers dropped like sacks of stones. Dann didn't think he'd ever seen so many lives taken in a single second. So quick were the elves that the Lorian soldiers hadn't had time to draw their swords before another volley of arrows cut through them like blades of grass. Dann nocked and loosed, allowing himself to find a rhythm as his hand moved from his quiver to his bow. *The more we kill now, the fewer will try to kill us later.* It was a simple thought, but the reality was more complex. With each arrow that landed, his jaw clenched, and he felt a twist in his heart.

The soldiers were forming into lines, hefting shields and screaming orders. Arrows cut into their ranks from both sides, unceasing. Dann watched as something unseen ripped men and women from the forming shield wall, hurling them through the air and into the forest. Even though he wasn't the victim, the helplessness of facing magic always made Dann uncomfortable. No matter how much he trained or prepared, a mage could end his life in a heartbeat.

A blood-chilling cry pierced the night, and Dann followed the sound to see a clutch of Aldithmar tearing through the Lorian soldiers who had been dragged into the woodlands. One of the spirits grabbed a woman by the shoulders and ripped her apart, her body splitting, blood spraying. Another soldier screamed as roots burst from the ground and tore into his skin like laces through a boot, erupting from his mouth. A third Aldithmar had punched its hand through a soldier's gut and now held the man in the air. Dann knocked an arrow and loosed. The arrow slammed into the man's head, his body going limp as the Aldithmar held him.

"Heraya embrace you," Dann whispered. He'd seen those Aldithmar up close, felt the fear of looking into their eyes. He wished that on nobody.

As Dann made to knock another arrow, pillars of fire plumed into the woods, illuminating the forest with the light of a raging sun. The strange pitch of the shrieks and hisses of the Aldithmar as the fire consumed them set Dann's hairs on end. Bolts of purple lightning flashed through the air, and Dann watched as several Aldithmar burst into flames.

Seconds passed, and then Lorian soldiers were charging through the fire, howling war cries. Soldiers on horseback charged amongst them, the horses leaping over thick roots and dense foliage.

As the Lorians charged, the elves unleashed a storm of arrows. Men and women dropped in plumes of blood, vanishing into the dark.

The whistle of an arrow passed Dann's head.

"Down!" he roared, grabbing Lyrei and pulling them both down. Alea, Tanner, Yana, and Ella had done the same, but down the line, Dann saw a number of elves dropping with arrow shafts embedded in their chest.

Another wolf howl cut through the din of charging soldiers.

"Fall back!" One of the elves bellowed as more bolts of purple lightning crashed into trees in explosions of fire.

A series of roars erupted overhead like claps of thunder.

"Please not the fucking dragons," Dann whispered, a bolt of lightning flashing above him.

"Go!" Lyrei grabbed Dann's shoulder and threw him forwards. "We need to get back to the Nithrandír!"

He looked back to see Alea and Lyrei following him. Ella, Tanner, Yana, Faenir, and Baldon were moving as well.

Hooves thundered to Dann's right, and a Lorian rider leapt over the trunk of a fallen tree, spear raised, eyes locking with Dann's. But as the man heaved his shoulder back, Faenir leapt into the air. The wolfpine wrapped his jaws around the rider's throat and ripped him from the saddle. The horse thundered forwards, shrieks ringing out.

"Keep running!" Ella yelled. She moved through the dense wood with as much ease as Alea, Lyrei, running with the loping gait of a wolf, her eyes shifting with a golden glimmer.

Dann made to turn his head, but before he did, his gaze fell on something amidst the flames of the wood. A man plunging a black sword through the midsection of an Aldithmar. The black smoke that shrouded the Aldithmar's body dispersed in a cloud, its white eyes misting upwards. The man turned his head, and Dann recognised the pale sickly skin and the black, light-drinking eyes. Even the blue swirls on his cloak matched those of the Fade they had fought in Belduar.

As he stared, Dann's foot hit something on the forest floor, and he went tumbling sideways. His armour softened the blow as his elbow slammed off a root, but he managed to catch himself with his face. A burst of pain smashed through his head, and stars flitted across his eyes. A hand grabbed him by the hood of his cloak, heaving up. He scrambled to his feet, slipping in the dirt.

"Go! Go!" Ella roared, pushing him forwards.

An arrow sliced past his head, a tree trunk splintering to his right. He blinked furiously, trying to clear his vision. The fingers of his left hand were still wrapped around his bow. He kicked another root as he staggered but kept himself upright. Ahead, the rangers were dropping to one knee, loosing arrows behind them before breaking into sprints again.

Dann touched his hand to the arrows in his quiver, glancing over his shoulder to see Lorian soldiers in full chase, columns of fire pluming from mages' hands as the Aldithmar approached.

Fuck that. He pulled his hand away from his quiver and pushed his legs harder, his balance returning to him. Ella, Tanner, and Yana sprinted beside him, but Faenir and Baldon looped backwards, ripping soldiers from horses, tearing men and women limb from limb.

Why did I say I'd do this?

CHAPTER EIGHTY

CHAOS

Dann's heart pounded, and his legs burned. He would never admit it to Ella, but as he ran for his life with Lorian archers and mages hurling arrows and lightning after him, he truly did regret wearing the white cloak.

He heaved out a breath as he leapt over the trunk of a fallen tree, landing heavy. Ahead, the elves slowed, pulling arrows from their quivers and stopping. It took Dann a moment to realise why, but then he saw the hulking shapes of two Nithrandír.

The enormous figures were ten or eleven feet tall, vines and roots forming their bodies. They had no heads, and their chests were broad and deep. Thick plates of silver armour covered their vine-wrought shapes.

'The souls of old elves who gave themselves to protect their descendants.'

Baldon and Faenir bounded past him on his right, Ella on his left. Dann heaved air into his burning lungs, his legs feeling as though they were going to give way. One downside to wearing plates of armour was how damn heavy they were.

The only light that reached him as he passed the enormous shapes of the Nithrandír was that of the torches and the Blood Moon behind him.

"Down!" Alea roared, standing at the front of the line of elves.

Dann didn't need any convincing. He grabbed Ella's arm and heaved her to the ground with him. They slammed into the dirt and leaves as hundreds of arrows ripped through the air over their heads.

Dann grabbed at the dirt, lifting his gaze in time to see the flurry of steel and wood hammer into the Lorians like a wave. But even as the soldiers fell in their tens, more charged onwards, some on foot, some on horseback.

As two riders moved close together, racing through a clear patch in the wood, a brilliant blue light burst into life on both Dann's left and his right. He watched in awe as the light traced over the vines and roots that composed the Nithrandír bodies. It washed over the legs, glowing and shimmering, then swept up through the chest and arms. Runes glowed across the thick plates of silver that coated the vines, igniting with the same blue light. Then, a tremor ran through the ground, and both Nithrandír before him ripped their legs free of the forest floor. As the riders drew closer, the Nithrandír on Dann's left drew back its enormous arms, and strands of pure blue light burst from its hands, twisting and turning over themselves until they formed the shape of an axe larger than Dann's entire body. The Nithrandír heaved the axe backwards, then swung, cleaving both riders in half with a single swipe.

Tremors shook the earth again, and Dann watched as more bursts of blue light ignited in the darkness of the forest.

⤫

IN THE DARK OF THE woodland, the faint purple light of the runes in Calen's armour washed over the forest floor and glowed off the tree trunk he leaned against. He watched as Lorian soldiers flooded through the trees before him. Torches flickered in the darkness as they chased the rangers into the forest towards the Nithrandír. The column of torchlight, stretched off into the distance on the right, howls, screams, and clinking steel echoing. He gripped the hilt of his sword so tightly he could feel the pressure building in his knuckles. His mind drifted to Ella, Dann, Alea, Lyrei, and Faenir. *Please be all right.*

All he wanted to do was charge in and keep them safe. But they needed to wait until the rangers reached the Nithrandír, until the Lorians had committed. And so he waited, his heart beating like a hammer, his nerves fraying.

He stood on the western flank of the charging Lorian forces. Tarmon, Vaeril, and Erik were on his right, while Haem, Lyrin, Varlin, Asius, and Senas stood to Calen's left; the two Jotnar towered over even the knights in their green Sentinel armour. Crucially, two and a half thousand warriors stood at their back, one thousand humans and one and a half thousand elves. Ingvat, Surin, and an elf by the name of Narthil – all three of whom were now officially captains of the newly formed rebellion – were spread out along the lines, each assigned their warriors. Along with those sworn to the rebellion, another twenty thousand Triarchy elves in smooth silver plate, curved blades gripped in their fists, were lined out through the forest, parallel to the Lorians who charged after the rangers. They'd spread their lines thin, to prevent clusters forming for the Dragonguard to target.

The same number waited on the eastern flank, with Therin, Aeson, and the other Rakina at the head of the rebellion forces. Some of the Rakina who had refused to train Calen, including Atara, had stepped forwards to fight.

A further thirty thousand elves led by the three rulers of Aravell waited to meet the Lorians head on. This was different to anything Calen had faced before. It wasn't just him, Erik, Tarmon, and Vaeril anymore. This was a true battle – one in which thousands looked to him.

"Together," Erik whispered, clinking his vambrace off Calen's. It was strange to see the man in steel armour, evens stranger to see the white dragon emblazoned across his chest.

Screams and shouts rang out, horses snorting and squealing, and Calen lifted his gaze to see torches soaring through the air and setting foliage alight as elven arrows sliced into the charging Lorians. Horses reared and collapsed backwards, arrows shredding them.

"Hold," Tarmon called out, his voice hushed. He'd left his greatsword in Aravell in favour of a short sword and shield due to the confined space in the woods. "Wait until the Nithrandír form."

"What did Aeson say it looked like again?" Calen whispered.

"He said we'd know it when we saw it."

"That sounds like my father," Erik muttered.

As Erik spoke, a series of blue lights burst into life before the Lorian charge, one after the next, stretching into the distance. Calen watched in awe as the Nithrandír took shape, the blue light scattering through the trees, sending shadows dancing across the woodland. Within seconds, the enormous statue-like shapes of the Nithrandír had come to life, thick silver armour covering limbs of blue light. In much the way Calen had seen nithrál form, axes, swords, and spears took shape in the Nithrandírs' hands, cleaving through the charging soldiers.

Calen's heartbeat rose to a deafening drum. He drew in a long breath, letting it swell in his chest before releasing it. This was it. This was the start of everything. This was where he stopped running. *Aravell will not fall.*

Calen reached out to Valerys, pulling their minds together. The dragon could not fight in the forest, but Calen needed him nonetheless. Even as Calen called to Valerys, he could feel the dragon unleash a visceral roar from where he stood in the Eyrie. Calen let out a gasp as Valerys's mind and soul collided with his, power surging through his veins. They were one – as it always should be. All doubt and fear flooded from him, supplanted by the dragon's rage. These people had come to kill their family, to burn their new home to the ground, to end their bond. The empire would find nothing but blood and fire. Calen opened himself to the fury, to the fire, allowing the lightning to crackle through his veins. There was no holding back, not anymore. Aeson wanted a symbol, and Calen would give him one. *Draleid n'aldryr, Valerys. Ayar nithír.* Dragonbound by fire, Valerys. One soul.

He pulled in a lungful of air, imbued it with every drop of his and Valerys's rage, and bellowed, "Forwards!"

Calen reached out to the Spark, pushing Spirit into his legs, willing himself to move faster. Behind him, roars and shouts thundered. Ahead, Lorians turned, the fear on their faces illuminated by torchlight as Calen and his army charged towards them.

More roars rang out on the other side of the Lorian lines and again near the Nithrandír.

Death cannot be beautiful. Vibrations jarred Calen's legs with each pounding step. *But sometimes it is necessary.*

He pulled on threads of Air, wrapping them around a clutch of Lorian soldiers who stood closest to him. He pulled, launching the Lorians through the air. As he did, a Dvalin Angan charged past him in the shape of an enormous stag, twice the size of any Calen had ever seen. The Angan's white fur glistened in the purple light of Calen's eyes and armour, seeming almost ethereal. The creature leapt and threw its head forwards, impaling two soaring Lorians with its black antlers. Bones snapped, and blood sprayed as the antlers burst through the two bodies, piercing legs, arms, and chests at the same time, blood splattering the Angan's white fur. In the same motion, Calen pulled back his sword and swung, funnelling threads of Earth into his bones as his sword sliced through the ribs of one of the soldiers he'd launched into the air. The blade cut clean through, and the soldier crumpled as they hit the ground. Calen kept charging forwards, Vaeril, Tarmon, and Erik at his side.

The Spark thrummed, setting all Calen's hairs on end, as whips of Fire and Air stretched outwards from the Lorian lines. Somewhere to his right he heard the cry, "Dragon's Maw!"

Within moments, a pillar of fire illuminated the woodland like a beacon. Calen let himself stare in awe for just a moment as his gaze passed over the line of charging elves that stretched off endlessly into the forest, their silver armour scintillating in the light of the fire.

This night would be spoken of for centuries. It would be sung in taverns and told around fires. It would be legend. All he needed to do was be around to hear it told.

Calen looked towards the Lorian lines, pulling in threads of Spirit, Fire, and Air, knotting them together, swirling them in his hand. He shifted his shoulder as an arrow sliced past, a second skittering off his pauldron. Power pulsed through him as he held the threads in his palm, Valerys's fury – their fury – blazing in his heart. He separated out thin threads of

Air and Spirit, weaving them into his voice as he had in Kingspass. "For Aravell! For Epheria!"

The words left his lips without thought, the fire inside him calling them forth. And as he spoke, he reached out his hand and unleashed the threads of Fire, Air, and Spirit, sending arcs of blue lightning crashing towards the Lorian lines.

∞

THE WOLF HOWLED IN ELLA's blood as she charged, the elves rushing around her like a raging river splitting across a rock. Dann, Tanner, Yana, and the two elves – Alea and Lyrei – ran beside her, steel glinting in the blue light of the enormous Nithrandír, whose light-forged weapons carved through the Lorian forces like scythes through grass. The massive things were like nothing Ella had ever laid eyes on.

The clang of steel on steel filled the woodland, crashing against the screams and howls, blending with the crackling of fire and burning wood. Blood, loam, iron, and the acrid smell of burning flesh and fur filled Ella's nostrils. A shiver ran over her skin, the wolf hungering within. 'It will be chaos,' Aeson Virandr had said. 'But chaos is our best chance.'

Ella bounded over a thick gnarled root, then used her momentum to leap atop a large rock. About her, elves and humans tore at each other, steel swinging, blood spraying. Through the firelight she could see both Calen and Aeson's forces had successfully charged the Lorian flanks. In the distance, towards the back end of the Lorian column, she could see where the Blood Moon poured over the path burned through the woods by the dragons, glinting off steel. The sheer number of bodies crashing together pulled Ella momentarily from the fervour that clawed in her mind. More would die this night than the entire population of The Glade hundreds of times over.

The momentary lament was shattered as soldiers crashed into Yana, Tanner, Dann, and the elves. The wolf within snarled and snapped. She set it free and hurled herself from the rock. Ella lifted her knee as she leapt, feeling the crunch of bone and cartilage as it slammed into a soldier's nose. As they both fell, Ella stabbed downwards with one of her swords, driving it between the man's neck and shoulder, twisting and ripping. She landed on the soldier's chest as he hit the ground with a *thud,* branches and twigs snapping beneath their weight. Blood spurted as she pulled her blade free, the red mist clouding her eyes. Something slammed into her back, and she stumbled, twisting to see a woman staggering with an arrow embedded in her throat. Ella flipped the sword in her left hand to underhand grip and snapped her arm like a viper, plunging the blade into the side of the woman's head.

More soldiers rushed at them, only for Faenir to leap from the crush of battle, his fur soaked in blood. The wolfpine clamped his jaws around the head of the closest soldier, snapping her neck in a single twist, teeth and fangs ripping through flesh. He let the body fall, then grabbed hold of a man's legs, thrashing his head left and right, bones crunching. Faenir's anger and bloodlust only fuelled the wolf within Ella, their bond burning like a signal fire.

A roar sounded behind her, and she spun, knocking aside the flailing swipe of a sword with the blade in her left hand. She drove her second blade through the soldier's gut. The man clasped his hand around the blade in his stomach, pulling it free from Ella's grasp. She swung her hand and raked her claws across his face, feeling flesh come away beneath her nails. The man collapsed, spluttering and gurgling. Ella reached down and pulled the sword free from his gut, snarling as she turned to see a rider on an obsidian mount charging her. The horse's nostrils flared as it reared, kicking its hooves forward, its rider striking down with a spear. Before Ella had the chance to react, the Fenryr Angan, Baldon, crashed into the horse's side with such force the enormous animal floundered, falling sideways with a shriek. The Angan tore through the horse's ribs, his jaws ripping and thrashing. With the wolf flooding Ella's veins, she could taste the iron tang, feel the crunch of bones. There wasn't a doubt in her mind that Fenryr connected her and the Angan.

Then Faenir and Baldon circled her, snapping out at any imperial soldiers that came close, ripping through flesh and armour, soaking the ground in Lorian blood.

"Ella!" Ella lifted her head to see Tanner take an arrow through his leg. She charged forwards, Faenir and Baldon loping at her side, the wolf howling in her blood.

HOT RAGE POURED THROUGH VALERYS and Calen's shared soul as Calen moved through the forms of the svidarya, flowing from Howling Wolf, into Patient Wind, into Striking Dragon. With each movement, steel split flesh and cleaved bone. Erik, Tarmon, and Vaeril moved beside him, never straying too far in the crush of bodies. Erik and Vaeril moved like wolves, steel glinting in smooth swipes, blood soaking the ground. Tarmon had dropped his short sword and now held two axes decorated with the black lion of Loria. The man was a maelstrom of death; everywhere the axes swung, bones snapped and bodies broke.

Calen brought his blade up, angling the swipe of Lorian steel to his right. He brought his own sword back across, drawing blood as he slashed through the man's leather armour. As the soldier stumbled backwards, Calen drove his sword through their gut, yanked it free, then open their throat. He pulled on threads of Earth as two Varsundi Blackthorns thundered through a clearing, riding straight for them. But as Calen drew in the threads, a green light flashed, and Varlin swirled. Her Soulblade flickered from existence as she dropped her shoulder and charged into the lead horse's ribs, sending the animal careening through the air. She continued her spin, pulling her sword from its sheath and slicing through the second horse's neck. As the horse collapsed to the ground, squealing, the rider scrambled to his feet only to catch a boot in the chest from Lyrin in his Sentinel armour. Calen heard bones snap from feet away.

In the middle of the chaos, Lyrin turned and gripped his sword with both hands. Calen saw him mouth the words, "Heraya embrace you, poor soul," as he drove the blade down through the wailing horse's head.

The knight ripped his sword free, the horse lying lifeless.

"It's never right," Lyrin said, raising his sword to a guard position as he and Varlin joined Calen and the others. "Animals dying in our wars. We destroy everything we touch."

A shriek sounded behind Calen, and he turned to see his brother driving a shimmering green nithrál through the chest of a Fade, the creature's brittle lips twisting in agony as the otherworldly wail left its throat. The world around the creature seemed to ripple as Haem pulled the nithrál free, and the Fade fell lifeless onto the forest floor.

"Calen Bryer." Asius and Senas carved their way through a swathe of Lorian soldiers, both swinging axes forged of shimmering red light. The two Jotnar towered over Calen and the others, a myriad of small cuts lacing the lower halves of their bodies. "The battle goes well, the front of the Lorian column has collapsed beneath the weight of the combined elven armies, but Lorian forces are holding us back further down the line. We must keep pushing lest we lose momentum."

Calen looked around. Just as Aeson had promised, it was chaos. Elves in flowing silver plate mingled with rebels who wore whatever they could get their hands on, all crashing against the black and red of Loria. It was precisely what they wanted. The more chaotic, the more blended everything was, the more protected from dragonfire they were.

"Advance!" Aeson's voice bellowed through the night, augmented by threads of Air and Spirit. There was no need for horns when the Spark could work so easily in their place.

"To me!" Calen called out, weaving threads of Air and Spirit through his voice as Aeson did. "Keep pushing forward!

"We can't let ourselves get separated from the main body," Tarmon said, grabbing Calen's arm.

"You heard the man." Erik spun his twin blades as he walked backwards. Without turning, he swung his left hand back and drove his blade into the gut of a soldier rushing up behind him. He pulled the sword free and let the man fall past him. "Kill with caution. Now come on, he's right. We need to push the advantage."

Tarmon frowned at Erik but nodded. Calen called, urging the army forwards. As they carved their way through the chaos, drawing closer to where the Blood Moon washed down over the path the dragons had burned through the wood, Calen felt an enormous surge of the Spark. It crackled over his skin, tingling on the back of his neck. Threads of Air, Fire, and Spirit wound through the air ahead, whirling and spinning with ferocious speed.

Howls rang out as the threads of Air slammed through Lorian and rebel bodies alike, lifting men, women, and elves off their feet and smashing them off tree trunks and rocks. Ahead, Calen saw a thread slam into an elf's leg, snapping the bone in a spray of blood. Another elf was sent careening through the air, the branch of a fallen tree bursting through his chest. More bones shattered, and blood sprayed as the threads of Air whipped back and forth, the power of the Spark pulsing through the air.

For a brief moment, the wails and groans of the dying filled the air, and the threads stopped whirling. Then a voice bellowed, "Second phase!"

Threads of Fire and Spirit blended with threads of Air. Calen brought his hand to his eyes as the world erupted in a series of blinding flashes. Arcs of lightning ripped roots and dirt from the ground, tearing through bodies and crashing into tree trunks in bursts of flames.

"Calen!" Before Calen could turn at the sound of Erik's voice, something hammered into him. The world spun. He crashed into the trunk of a tree, ringing filling his head.

"Are you all right?" Erik knelt over Calen. His voice was distorted, rising and falling in Calen's ears. Calen's vision shifted, blurring. The harsh smell of charred flesh and burnt earth filled his nostrils. Behind Erik, the ground smouldered where Calen had been standing.

"No... Erik..." Amidst the smoke and ash, and humans and elves stumbling back and forth, Calen saw the large frame of Senas drop to one knee, her silvery-blonde hair shimmering in the firelight. Smoke drifted from holes in Senas's chest and legs. The Jotnar hauled herself upright and swung her shimmering red nithrál. The axe sliced through the torso of a Lorian Battlemage, stripping the life from his bones. Another swing and two more fell.

Calen pushed Erik off him and scrambled to his feet. More Battlemages were emerging from a mass of bodies, black cloaks billowing behind them. There had to be almost a hundred. They drew so much of the Spark the air around them rippled.

One of the mages unleashed a column of fire from his hand, only for Senas to split it with threads of Air, then use those same threads to haul the man through the air. Senas heaved her axe. The man's torsos swung forward as the axe's head sank into his skull. The Jotnar released the nithrál, the mage's body falling lifeless to the forest floor. But as tendrils of red light began to burst from Senas's hand once more, an arrow slammed into her neck. She stumbled, a second arrow lodging in her gut.

A roar thundered in the air as Asius swept forwards, his red nithrál carving through any Lorian who stepped in his path.

Calen called to Erik, then charged. As he moved, Vaeril and Tarmon fell in it at his side, the white dragon on their breastplates barely visible through the blood.

Calen's heart twisted as he charged towards Asius, Senas, and the Lorian Battlemages. Asius stood over Senas, his axe swinging in a fury, threads of Earth lifting spikes of clay from the ground. Senas had been kind when Calen had first met her in Ölm Forest, gentle even. *'It is a pleasure to share our fire with you this night. I am Senas, daughter of Iliria…'*

The sight of her lying in the dirt, arrows jutting from her body, ignited a hot rage in Calen. Valerys roared in the back of his mind, urging him to feed from the fury, to harness it.

Calen drew in a long breath, then opened himself to Valerys, pulling their minds together and letting the dragon's rage pour through him like blazing fire.

Draleid n'aldryr. Ayar elwyn, ayar nithír, ayar ileid. Dragonbound by fire. One heart, one soul, one bond.

Strength flooded Calen's muscles, power crackling over his skin. He surged forwards, Erik, Vaeril, and Tarmon at his back.

The first Battlemage didn't see him coming. The man turned in time to have his stomach opened by Calen's blade, steam wafting as intestines spilled. Calen moved past him, Valerys's strength pushing him forwards. Erik, Vaeril, and Tarmon whirled around him, slicing through Lorian leather and flesh. They had all fought together so long their movements were effortless.

The sensation of the Spark ignited to Calen's left. He pulled on threads of Fire, Spirit, and Air, weaving them together into a minor Sparkward

– as Therin had taught him. He held his hand out, catching the lightning with the ward, the drain instantly pulling at him.

Vaeril stepped past Calen. As the elf moved, he wrapped threads of Air around a dropped spear and launched it towards the mage. The spear slammed into the man's face, tearing open his mouth and nose and bursting through the back of his head in an eruption of bone, brain, and blood.

As Calen nodded at the elf, he spotted a mage charging towards Vaeril's back. He pulled on threads of Air and wrapped them around the mage's torso, dragging the man towards him. Calen reached forwards, wrapping his gauntleted hand around the mage's throat while knocking the man's sword free. Calen made to drive his blade through the mage's gut, but the man pulled on threads of Fire and Spirit, pushing them into Calen. Instantly Calen's veins felt like they had been set aflame, burning from the inside out. It was as though the mage was trying to rip Calen's soul from his body.

Calen squeezed his fist with every ounce of strength he had. *'A Draleid not only draws the Spark through himself but also through the dragon to which he is bonded.'* Chora's words echoed in Calen's mind as the mage continued to push threads of Fire and Spirit into Calen's body. *'It is what makes Draleid so powerful in the Spark. The well of strength you draw from is far greater than most mages can dream of.'*

Valerys's roar was thunder in Calen's mind. Power surged through Calen's body. The purple light of his eyes glowed across the mage's face, wisps of incandescent mist rising into the air, the runes on Calen's vambrace and gauntlet shining like stars. He opened himself to the Spark and pushed back. The mage thrashed and howled, slapping at the white plate that covered Calen's arm. But Calen only pushed harder, feeling the pull on his soul evaporate. He understood what was happening. The mage had tried to push Calen to his limits, tried to force him to burn himself out. At the thought of someone trying to harm his soulkin, Valerys's fury redoubled, and the dragon pushed through Calen's mind, the Spark blazing in Calen's veins.

The mage continued to push back with threads of Fire and Spirit, but there came a point when Calen felt something snap in the tug between himself and the mage. The mage's scream was so visceral it sent chills down Calen's spine. His eyes began to glow, a pure white light bursting forth, and smoke rose into the air as the skin around the mage's eyes blackened and bubbled.

Calen let the mage drop to the ground, watching as he writhed and twisted, the light in his eyes fading, leaving behind nothing but sockets of charred flesh. Calen stumbled backwards, his hand shaking. *That's what it looks like to be burned out.*

Calen turned to find Tarmon and Erik rushing towards him, worry etched into their faces.

"What in the gods was that?" Erik looked down at the mage who now lay shaking with his knees curled to his chest, smoke drifting from his eye sockets. Erik looked backed towards Calen, slapping him on the side of the helmet. "Are you all right? Are you hurt?" An arrow whistled through the air and glanced off Erik's pauldron, slicing upwards. "I'm never taking this off."

"The others need us." Tarmon nodded to where Vaeril, Asius, and several elven mages were weaving through the company of Lorian Battlemages, threads of each elemental strand whirling through the air.

Calen nodded, tightening his grip on the hilt of his sword. He turned, lifted the sword, then drove the blade down through the shaking mage's head. He watched as the body twitched, then went still. There was nothing heroic about battle. There was nothing inspiring about death. As he stood there, Calen decided that if the bards did tell tales of this day, he would have no heart to hear them.

He gave the man's body one last look, then charged towards the Lorian Battlemages. Elves and rebels moved around him, howling as they hacked their steel into the Lorians. Aeson wanted chaos, and he had found it.

Just as the man's name came into Calen's head, Aeson, Therin, Harken, and Thacia came charging through the dense wood on the opposite side of the Battlemages; rebels and silver-armoured elves rushed at their side.

A whip of Fire slammed into Calen's side, knocking him off balance. He caught himself and pivoted, pulling on threads of Earth. He found the mage who had struck at him and pushed the threads into the woman's breastplate. The metal collapsed inwards, blood spraying in a mist as her ribs snapped.

Calen fell into the svidarya, dropping into Crouching Bear. His muscles burned from exertion, but the touch of Valerys's mind kept him warm, ebbing the pain.

A pulse of the Spark rippled through the air, and Calen looked up, his jaw hanging as he watched Chora rise over the battle. Threads of Air moved the wheels of her chair along a bridge of roots that formed before her, created by threads of Earth and Spirit. In a flash, the threads of Earth and Spirit evaporated and the woman's soared. Plumes of fire erupted from her hands, illuminating the forest in an incandescent light. Chora softened her landing with threads of Air, stabilising herself. As soldiers charged her, she snapped bones with Air, ignited flesh with Fire, and pulled roots from the ground with threads of Earth and Spirit.

Erik stopped beside Calen, pointing at Chora with one of his swords. "Did she just... I've seen it all now, and I can die happy. That was beautiful."

Calen looked around him, watching as the elves and rebels cut through the Lorians, pushing them back. The elven and Lorian mages crashed together in explosions of the Spark. But everywhere Calen looked, one thing was clear: they were winning.

To his right, Calen watched as a Nithrandír stepped through a gap in the trees, its thick silver armour shimmering in the blue light that flowed around its root wrought limbs. The Nithrandír's axe carved through two or three soldiers with each swing. Calen could even see the black-smoke-shrouded forms of Aldithmar drifting into the fray wherever Dvalin Angan's presence wasn't felt.

"Calen!"

Calen spun at the sound of Ella's voice. He saw her standing atop the broken body of a Nithrandír about a hundred feet closer to the clearing where the Blood Moon washed down.

A monstrous roar thundered through the sky above the forest. Leaves fell from the canopy, and both humans and elves stopped for a brief moment. Ahead, where the dragonfire had carved a path through the woodland and the crimson light of the Blood Moon washed down, shadows flickered.

A second roar shook the canopy, followed by a third.

"Surely they wouldn't…" Tarmon's voice trailed off as he looked upwards. "They'd torch their own."

Another roar ripped through the night – closer than the last.

Calen's heartbeat slowed, and a wave of fear flowed through him from Valerys. The dragon's panic turned Calen's blood to ice, sending a shiver over his skin and twisting knots in his stomach. He could feel Valerys shifting, moving, cracking his wings against the air. But before he could tell Valerys to stay where he was, a sound like a crashing waterfall filled the forest. Barely a moment passed before a column of dragonfire tore through the canopy overhead, carving a path through the forest battlefield. Lorians, rebels, and elves alike screamed as they burned.

"Calen, Erik!" Aeson sprinted towards Calen and Erik. Therin, Thacia, Harken, and Chora moved with him. "Spiritward, Calen! Now!"

Another column of dragonfire poured down into the forest, followed by a third. The rivers of flame fell with such force that clay was lifted and roots were torn from the ground, the fires illuminating the depths of the Aravell in a blazing light.

"By the gods…" Calen heart slowed to a rhythmic thump as he looked around, sparks and smoke filling the air, warriors burning, screaming and thrashing. The smell of char and ash mixed with the stench of burning flesh and leather. An elf dropped to the ground beside Calen, his armour melted on the left side, his skin bursting into flames as the liquid metal moved across him.

Another roar erupted, and a torrent of dragonfire ripped through the canopy above, carving a path towards Calen and the others. He pulled Erik, Vaeril, and Tarmon close and drew in threads of Fire, Air, and Spirit.

Valerys roared in the back of Calen's mind and took flight.

CHAPTER EIGHTY-ONE

THE TIME IS NOW

The whistling of sand-laden wind was all that could be heard in the central plaza of the ruined city. The air sparkled in a mix of reds, pinks, and silver as the crimson light of the Blood Moon reflected off the sand.

Rist drew a slow breath in through his nose, releasing it from pursed lips and watching as it misted in front of him. His left hand rested on the lion-head pommel of the sword at his hip which Garramon had given him after he'd lost his first sword at the Battle of The Three Sisters. His right hand was beneath his robes, grasping the pendant that hung from his neck. He clenched his jaws to stop his teeth from chattering as he looked out at the rune-marked men and women who stood around the pit of glowing gemstones wearing nothing but the skin they were born in. The runes covered their chests, arms, and backs, glowing with a dull red light. A number of mages stood around the plaza garbed in the grey robes of the Scholars, most with pens and notebooks in hand. Further out, towards the edges of the plaza, Fades lurked, the light bending around them.

The Battlemages of the other armies stood at the eight entrances of the plaza, two hundred at each, lined and ready.

"Fuck me," Magnus whispered to Garramon, though loud enough for Rist to hear. "If they'd told us how cold it was in this forsaken place, I would have brought another set of robes."

Both Garramon and Anila threw sideways glances at Magnus.

"You know, Uraksplitter," Magnus whispered, turning to Anila, his breath misting, "body heat keeps you warm just as well as a fire."

"Magnus, as I've said many times, I'd sooner set myself on fire," Anila whispered back, keeping her eyes forward as the Scholars walked about the central plaza.

A murmur swept through the mages, and Rist looked forwards to see a man stepping from a doorway of one of the ruined buildings. If Rist hadn't already known the man was Emperor Fane Mortem by the red trim of his black robes, the shift in the other mages around him would have given it away.

More men and women followed in Fane's wake, crimson robes draped over their shoulders with white circles marked on each breast. Rist hadn't spent much time around priests of Efialtír, but he'd heard enough about them. Their leader, Radavan Harten – the Divine – along with most of their order resided in the city of Highpass, which was now under elven control, or from what Rist had heard, burned to the ground. He'd read in *A Study of Divinity* by Halban Fandil that each of them were selected at the age of ten. As a sign of devotion to Efialtír, the men were castrated, and the women drank a special tea, known as Devotion's Knot, that would render them unable to bear children. Rist understood the reasoning – the one thing that often superseded all others was a burning loyalty to family, and removing that loyalty made room for devotion to Efialtír – but the concept still turned his stomach. He was sure of one thing: he would never become a priest.

Something brushed against Rist's hand as it sat atop the pommel of his sword, and he turned his gaze from the plaza to see Neera staring past him, her hand on his. He lifted his fingers and wrapped them around hers, turning his gaze back towards the plaza.

The priests spread in a circle behind the rune-marked men and women. The tingle of the Spark ran down Rist's neck as threads of Air and Spirit wove around Emperor Mortem, weaving through his throat and whipping outwards in patterns Rist didn't recognise.

"Tonight is the night we change the world." Fane's voice boomed, amplified by the threads. The echoes of his words lingered far longer than should have been possible. Fane reached into his pocket and produced a smooth, spherical gemstone five times as large as any Rist had laid eyes on. The glowing vessel barely fit in Fane's hand. The emperor held the gemstone in the air. "Efialtír sacrificed his place amongst the gods to ensure that death was not simply wasted life. For his devotion to us, the other gods cast Efialtír from their halls and created the veil so he could not rejoin those who loved him."

Fane released the sphere from his grasp, threads of Air wrapping around it, holding it in place above the ground. A second passed, and then the stone pulsed, the air swirling around it. As though in response, the gemstone around Rist's neck vibrated, and he looked down to see its glow intensifying. Beside him, he could see Neera's gemstone reacting the same way, along with those of the other mages.

"Our god wishes to walk among us once more." Gasps rang out in response, murmurs rising. "Calm yourselves. There is still much to be done before that day, my brothers and sisters. But tonight we widen the tears in the veil. We call forth Efialtír's Chosen. His emissaries, his champions." Fane opened his arms and gestured towards the rune-marked men and women who stood around the pit. "Before you stand those whose devotion knows no equal. After this night, they will no longer be mere mortals. They will be the Chosen, body, mind, and soul. Their loyalty is marked in their flesh, their belief unquestionable."

The gemstone that floated in the air in front of Fane moved towards the pit, threads winding around it. As the gemstone hovered above the thousands that filled the pit, cries rang out in the distance, steel clashing against steel, roars and howls ripping through the night.

"The Uraks have come," Fane called. "They seek to be the ones who strengthen Efialtír's hand in this world. They seek to be the recipients of his power. But that is something we cannot allow. So hear me now, brothers and sisters, when I begin, you are to push the Essence in your vessels towards me, you are to wrap me in threads of Spirit. Give me your strength, and together we will drive both the elves and the Uraks from these lands. We will bring forth the Chosen. We will keep our people safe. This is our time. All we have to do is seize it."

As the screams of men and Uraks rang out in the distance, Fane turned towards the pit. The emperor began to speak aloud in a tongue Rist had never heard. Another pulse rippled outwards from Fane, and the spherical gemstone that hovered above the pit ignited in a brilliant red light. After a moment, the rings of runes that had been marked around the pit in chalk began to glow, red light bursting forth as though it were spraying through cracks in the ground.

The stone thrummed, and the air seemed to shift and shimmer.

"Open yourselves to the Spark," Magnus bellowed, the commander of the Nineteenth Army doing the same. "Push your threads of Spirit towards the emperor. Be his strength as he has been yours. Stand together, for together we can never be broken."

Rist let out a gasp as the power of the Spark pulsed through the air. Threads of Spirit surged from the mages who stood at each entrance to the plaza, all connecting to Fane. As they did, a vivid red light erupted from the thousands of gemstones that filled the pit at the plaza's centre.

Rist squeezed Neera's hand, and she squeezed back.

"Don't be scared," she whispered. "Together."

"Together."

Rist opened himself to the Spark and pulled on threads of Spirit, feeling their cool touch against his mind. He felt Neera do the same, and they both added their threads to the others. Wisps of sand flicked back and forth around the emperor, the wind swirling at his feet.

"Tap into your vessels," Magnus called out. "Give back the gift you were granted. From death comes life anew."

"From death comes life anew." Hundreds of voices chorused the reply as the power of each mage's vessel rippled through the air like a shockwave.

The combined force of Essence and the Spark thrummed through Rist. Neera's grip grew so tight it hurt. Rist listened to the beating of his heart, trying desperately to drown out the deafening roar of the Essence and the Spark. He took in a short breath and tapped into the gemstone around his neck. The blood in his veins froze, blackness consuming his vision and drowning out all sound. For just a moment he was nothing and nowhere. Then the world crashed into him. The red lights of the gemstones and rune markings around the pit glittered, reflected by the sand that swept through the air. The screams and shrieks of battle from the outer edges of the city pounded in his ears like drums. Each breath he drew swelled in his lungs.

The two halves of his mind argued, one telling him to stop, to run and never look back, the other telling him to keep going, keep pushing. He looked to Neera beside him, her hand still squeezing his. Then he looked to Garramon, and Magnus, and Anila. Each of them had believed in him, each of them accepting him for who he was and teaching him to accept himself. They were a family of a sort. A flawed family, but a family, nonetheless.

And finally he thought of his true family: his mother and father, Calen and Dann, and all those in The Glade. Rist had never been the fighter. The idea of protecting others had never been part of who he was; he was the one who needed protecting. But now as he stood there in the middle of the Burnt Lands, gripped by a blend of fear and awe, he finally understood. He had seen what the elves and their dragons could do, seen the fire and death. He'd heard of how the Uraks had slaughtered entire towns, villages, and even cities without a shred of mercy. Rist could not allow the same thing to happen to The Glade. If Efialtír could grant the power to stop the elves and the Uraks, then Rist needed to try. He took in one last long breath and pushed the Essence outwards towards Fane.

The earth shook as a black tear ripped through the air above the pit, like a fissure spreading through rock. And with the tear, the rune-marked men and women lifted into the air, the runes in their skin glistening with a red light.

KALLINVAR LEANED AGAINST THE WAR table, sweat tacking his hair to his head and dripping from his nose and chin.

Gildrick handed him a waterskin. Kallinvar took a long mouthful, then handed the skin back to the Watcher.

"They were good souls," Gildrick said softly, resting his hand on Kallinvar's shoulder before moving away. The knights had carved through the Lorians on the other side of the Rift after Kallinvar had sensed the first pulse of the Taint. It had been too easy. Once they had returned to the temple, more pulses had signalled across Epheria– some in the Burnt Lands, others where small tears had already been made across the continent. It hadn't taken Kallinvar long to realise that Fane was scattering them on purpose. The man had sent armies and mages across the length and breadth of Epheria, from the island of Driftstone to the heart of the Aonan wood. In each location, the mages numbered no more than a hundred. But that was enough to widen the tears in the veil if left unchecked.

Combined with the Lorian armies, Urak Shamans in Mar Dorul, Kolmir, and the Marin Mountains had all attempted to widen the tears. Mirken fell in Mar Dorul to the claw of a Bloodmarked. Daynin lost his life on Driftstone to the black fire Soulblade of a Fade, his soul destined to drift in the void. They had lost others – eight in total.

Kallinvar was given no choice but to split the chapters. As he looked over the stone map carved into the table, he could see the pulses of green light spread about the continent. Olyria and The Third were fifty miles south of Vaerleon. Armites and The Sixth fought Uraks at the foothills of Mar Dorul, near Arginwatch. The Eighth fought on the eastern edge of the Burnt Lands, though Kallinvar had felt Brother-Captain Rivick fall, his loss burning through the Sigil. All in all, only four chapters remained at the Temple – The First, The Second, The Seventh, and The Ninth. Among them, only thirty-six of forty still drew breath.

He had underestimated Fane. The knights had four centuries to pre-pare, and they were still failing. If Verathin had been standing at their head, Kallinvar had no doubt the man would have learned better from the past than Kallinvar had. Verathin never made the same mistakes twice. Kallinvar's mind drifted back to The Fall, to the brothers and sisters he lost, to the people he failed. He raised his armoured hand, clenched his fingers, and slammed his fist down on the stone table, cracks spreading.

A hand rested on his shoulder, and he turned to see Ruon looking back at him, green eyes flickering in the chamber's candlelight. "Pain is the path to strength."

Kallinvar drew in a breath and nodded, turning his gaze back to the table.

"We will not fail, Kallinvar. We *cannot*."

As Ruon spoke, a new red glow pulsed near the centre of the Burnt Lands. Kallinvar turned towards the war table, staring at the light.

"What is it?" Ruon leaned over the table. He'd explained to her how he had layered the convergences of the Taint over the map in his mind, how he had used the technique to help him visualise everything.

The spot pulsed again, but this time it pierced straight through the blackness that coated the Burnt Lands. The oily sensation of the Taint grew stronger and stronger, pulses turning to ripples, the red light spreading.

Kallinvar stepped back, the realisation setting in. "Ilnaen."

Ruon looked at him with narrowed eyes.

"He's gone back to Ilnaen." The words drifted through Kallinvar's mind. The Taint had always covered the Burnt Lands so completely it had been impossible to determine the point where the tear in the veil was the widest. But now that he saw it, he felt a fool for not realising. "He's gone back to where it started."

"The time is now, my child." Achyron's voice rang in Kallinvar's mind for the first time since the Blood Moon had risen. *"I will give you my strength. You must close the tear before too many cross."*

Kallinvar stepped away from the table. Fire burned in his veins, ice swept over his skin. The green light of the Rift burst into existence a few feet from the table's edge, spreading and growing.

"Knights of Achyron," he roared. The knights moved towards Kallinvar, some dragging themselves to their feet, weariness and loss evident in each step they took. "The time is now. I know where Fane hides. Once more we go to Ilnaen."

Ilnaen's name drew whispers.

"This is our purpose, brothers and sisters. This is the reason for our existence. We are the Knights of Achyron, and we will hold back the Shadow." Kallinvar turned towards the rippling pool of black that hung in the air. "Once more into the Rift."

Chapter Eighty-Two

Of War and Ruin

Dann choked and coughed, ash falling from his head as he hauled himself upright. His vision was blurred, painted with a vivid orange hue, shadows flickering back and forth. Muted shouts and howls broke the ringing in his ears.

His eyes stung as he pushed his fingers into the creases, rubbing away the ash and dirt. With his sight clearing, he saw the orange hue came from the blazing fires that consumed the woodland. The flames burned through the dense foliage, climbing up trees and turning the canopy overhead to nothing more than sparks and ash, the light of the Blood Moon shining through. Dann covered his nose and mouth with his cloak. If the dragonfire hadn't ripped holes in the canopy, he'd likely have suffocated from the smoke.

He staggered sideways, his foot hitting something. A tree trunk stopped him from falling. He looked down to see the thing he had kicked was the lower half of a Lorian soldier, their body shorn in two, intestines and blood covering the ground. He shook his head, coughing, his lips and throat dry.

A hand rested on his shoulder, and he jerked away, panic flaring in his blood. He stumbled backwards, a jarring vibration running through his spine as he landed on a thick root, ashes swirling in the air. He found himself staring back at Lyrei. Her hair was matted with blood and ash, her face blackened. She hauled him to his feet.

"Are you hurt?" Lyrei touched his cheek with a gentleness he'd never seen in the elf, her golden eyes studying him.

"I'm all right." Dann looked about at the blazing fires and burning bodies, his eyelids scratching as he blinked. "Alea, the others?"

Dann looked past Lyrei to see that Alea knelt over the body of an elf whose left side was nothing but melted armour and charred skin. She stroked the hair on the right of the elf's head, whispering something as she looked into his eyes.

"One of the mages who saved us." Lyrei's voice was nothing but sorrow. She nodded towards three more elves who stood around them, each wearing crimson cloaks. They all had the curved swords drawn, but dark circles hung beneath their eyes, and their shoulders drooped. "There were a lot more of them. They shielded us from the worst of it. At least, they tried."

Dann saw Tanner leaning against a tree, his hand clasped to a wound in his leg. Yana stood beside him, checking over his face for cuts and burns. Several other elves and rebels lay about in the circular clearing that remained mostly untouched by the fire thanks to the elven mages.

"Fall back!" A voice bellowed from somewhere amidst the flames and chaos, rising above the crackling flames and the wails and howls of the dying. "To the city. Fall back!"

Something caught Dann's eye, and he turned to see a Lorian soldier rising to his feet and drawing his blade behind one of the elven mages. Dann dropped his hand to his sword belt, but he'd dropped the blade when the dragonfire had rained down. He leapt past Lyrei, pulling an arrow from his quiver as he did. He clamped his hand around the man's arm, then drove the head of the arrow through the leather that protected the soldier's gut. As the man gasped, Dann tried to pull the arrow free, but the head was wedged in the man's flesh. He let go and struck his palm up into the man's jaw.

The soldier staggered backwards, blood spilling over his lips from where he'd bitten through his tongue. The soldier lifted his sword, but as he did, a snarl sounded behind him, and Faenir leapt onto his back. The wolfpine's weight knocked the soldier forwards, crashing to the ground. Faenir ripped at the side of his neck, blood spurting.

"You're all right," Ella said as she appeared behind Faenir, Baldon walking beside her in his human-like form.

The Angan nodded to Dann. "Sureheart, it is good to see you well." His lips pulled back into a sharp-toothed smile. The Angan's eyes gleamed in the firelight, but Dann saw nothing but loss within his gaze. "So many souls extinguished in the blink of an eye."

"They probably killed more of their own than they did ours," Dann said, looking around. "Most of ours were further back, or on the flanks. It doesn't make any sense." A knot formed in Dann's throat as he took in the sheer loss of life. Amidst it all, it wasn't the cries of the dying or the charred husks of the dead that really pulled at him, it was the soft sound of sobbing that rose above the crackling flames.

"We were winning," Tanner said, groaning as he lifted himself from the tree trunk, Yana propping him up. The man limped over towards Dann, Ella, and Baldon. "Now we're dead or running, and their forces have a chance to regroup. The Dragonguard are hammers, and every scenario is a nail. Collateral damage means little to them. It's difficult to factor a lack of morality into a battle plan."

"We need to fall back with the others," Yana said, shifting herself to better take Tanner's weight. "It won't take long for the Lorians to regroup, and we're easy pickings out here."

"But there's survivors," Dann said, looking from Yana out into the flames. He could see some of the rebels still moving, elves in smooth silver plate dragging themselves across the ground.

"If they can stand and walk, they don't need us." Tanner pulled his arm from around Yana's shoulder. He groaned as he dropped to one knee, pushed aside the body of a dead Lorian and picked up a white wood bow from beneath. *My bow.* He hauled himself to his feet and pushed the bow into Dann's hands. "If they can't stand or walk, we can't help them. The Lorians will cut through here once they regroup. They'll kill any of us left alive."

Dann looked to Lyrei. She glanced towards Alea, who was now pulling a knife from the temple of the charred elf she had been cradling. "This is the way of war, Dann. Tanner is right."

"What? What about all your talk of honour?"

Lyrei's eyes narrowed, and she rounded on Dann. "My honour is intact." Lyrei's nostrils flared, her breathing heavy.

"I'm sorry. I didn't mean it like that, it's just…"

"I understand." She looked out at the dead and the fires. "I said it was the way of war. I didn't say it was simple or easy."

"What's that?" Ella's eyes shimmered amber as she stepped past Dann and stared into the flames. Faenir moved beside her, his nose raised in the air, his snout wrinkling.

"A herald." Fear grasped Tanner's voice. He pulled his sword from the scabbard at his hip. "A Fade."

As Dann looked into the flames, wisps of air swished back and forth, parting the fire. A Fade walked through the flames, a long black cloak draped over its shoulders. The cloak seemed to drink in the light of the fire, dimming the air around it. Blue swirls decorated the cloak, shimmering as it billowed behind the creature. The Fade walked as though it were strolling through a field of flowers, slow and purposefully, its gaze moving about the bodies.

For a moment, Dann thought it was the Fade who had attacked Belduar; it had the same blue swirls on its cloak, but its face was different, its hair white as snow. Without thinking, Dann brought his hand up to his shoulder, tracing his fingers over the steel plate that rested over the scarred flesh from the Fade's lightning.

The Fade's head snapped sideways in response to something Dann couldn't see. Black fire plumed from either side of the Fade's right hand, the flames twisting into themselves, flickering. In a heartbeat, the black flames had forged into the shape of a sword – the same weapon the Fade had used in Belduar.

An elf leapt from amidst the raging fires to the Fade's left, and the creature swung its black fire sword with inhuman speed. A cloud of ash rose as the elf's head and body hit the ground. The Fade lifted its gaze and locked eyes with Dann. The creature's thin lips cracked into an eerie smile.

"We need to get the fuck out of here." As Dann turned back to the others, the flames around them grew and swirled as though being born anew, cutting off their retreat. "What in all the gods?"

"Can that thing be killed?" Ella's amber eyes flitted from the Fade to Dann, to Tanner.

"Ella, we need to run." Dann slung his white wood bow over his shoulder, his fingers reflexively brushing the fletching of the arrows in his quiver. *Seven.*

"Where, Dann?" Ella gestured to the wall of flames that had redoubled around them.

"It can be killed," one of the three elven mages said, eyes narrowed as it looked towards the approaching Fade. "Either by the Spark or by taking its head."

Ella turned to Tanner and Yana. "Stay here. If the fire wanes, run." Both Tanner and Yana made to argue, but Ella cut them off. "He's in no shape to fight," she said gesturing to Tanner. "And he'll need you to get back. Please, listen." Ella turned to the three elven mages. "We'll distract it. You kill it, all right?"

The elves nodded. "Death or honour," they chorused.

"Death or honour," Lyrei repeated, inclining her head towards the mages. She slung her bow across her back and drew her curved blade. "We're with you," she said to Ella, gesturing at Alea.

"This is a really fucking bad idea." Dann shrugged his bow from his back. He looked back towards the Fade, who was now only twenty feet away, its empty, black eyes stark against its pale white skin. A shiver ran through Dann's body as he stared back at the creature. "A *really* bad idea."

Without another word, Ella charged, Faenir bounding at her side. Alea and Lyrei moved after her, their curved blades shimmering in the firelight.

"Have faith, Sureheart." Baldon inclined his head at Dann, then surged after Ella and the others. The Angan's body shifted as he moved, his torso elongating, shoulders widening, bones crunching and twisting. Dann watched as Baldon grew, his muscles thickening, his shape changing into that of a giant wolf.

Dann drew an arrow, nocked it, then loosed it in one smooth motion. He watched it sink into the Fade's chest before sprinting, drawing another arrow as he did. The last time he stayed still after sticking a Fade with an arrow, he'd taken a bolt of lightning to the shoulder.

His second arrow pierced through the Fade's bicep as the creature struck out at Ella. The Fade moved with inhuman speed, its black fire blade sweeping through the air, meeting every strike Alea, Lyrei, and Ella swung at it. Faenir leapt through the air, wrapping his enormous jaws around the Fade's sword arm. The wolfpine thrashed his head side to side, ripping and tearing. As the Fade turned to Faenir, Baldon charged into its chest, wrapping his jaws around its neck.

Dann's heartbeat thumped in his veins, a surge of hope rushing through him. He drew another arrow. A flash ignited beside him, and arcs of lightning streaked through the air towards the Fade. Even with Baldon and Faenir hanging from him, the Fade swirled out of the way of the lightning which flashed past into the night. Ella charged, but the creature swung his arm and launched Faenir through the air. The wolfpine slammed into Ella, knocking them both to the ground.

Baldon still clung to the creature, his jaws wrapped around its neck. But as Dann nocked his arrow, a howl cut through the night. Dann's heart clenched, his legs losing strength.

The tip of the Fade's black fire sword jutted from the Angan's back, black flames flickering. The Fade wrapped its pale fingers around the back of Baldon's neck, then pulled its blade free, tossing the Angan into the raging flames beside it.

Dann's breaths quickened, his chest fluttering, heart twisting as he watched the fire consume Baldon's body. *'It is the name you have earned. As Therin Eiltris is Silverfang, Aeson Virandr is Broken One, you are Sureheart.'* Tears welled in his eyes, but he charged forwards. He loosed his third arrow, watched it sink into the torn flesh of the Fade's neck. He leapt over a burning log, drawing, nocking, loosing. The arrow sliced through the Fade's neck less than an inch from the other one. The Fade fixed its gaze on Dann and snarled, its mouth opening wider than should have been possible.

Spikes of clay rose from the ground and hurtled towards the Fade, but the creature spun, cutting them from the air with his black fire blade. It extended its hand, and arcs of purple lightning streaked forwards, ripping through roots and dead bodies, tearing up chunks clay. Dann glanced over his shoulder to see the lightning punch smouldering holes through the chests of all three elven mages.

Lyrei and Alea surged forward, attacking from two sides. Their blades sliced through cloth and flesh but came out clean, no blood spilling. The

Fade smashed Lyrei in the face with its elbow, then drove its blade towards Alea's chest. Dann loosed a fifth arrow.

The Fade howled, reeling backwards as the arrow sank into the black well of its left eye, bursting out the back of its head.

Dann charged, and Faenir lunged. The Fade swung its arm, and Faenir froze in the air as though suspended from ropes. Dann nocked and loosed another arrow. The Fade shrieked, the arrow bursting through its other eye. As though invisible ropes had been cut, Faenir collapsed to the ground.

Dann continued his charge, drawing his last arrow. He saw Ella moving to his left, her blades glinting in the light of the fires all around them.

Ahead, Alea traded blows with the creature, the black flames of its blade bursting outwards with each strike.

Dann nocked his last arrow and loosed. The Fade howled as the arrow sliced through its sword hand, its black fire blade vanishing into the air inches from taking Alea's head from her shoulders. It was only then Dann realised he was still charging towards the creature, but he now had no arrows and no sword. *Well, fuck.*

All thoughts and fear fled him as the Fade reached back and unleashed a wave of black fire over Alea. Dann's heart stopped as the elf's shrieks filled the air. *No…*

Ice filled his veins, and he stumbled. Ella and Faenir charged, but the Fade swiped them away with its magic. Dann put one foot forward, but staggered, shaking. His gaze fell to where Alea lay, wisps of black fire still flickering on her charred corpse. He clenched his jaw and moved forwards, a fire burning in him.

The Fade eyed him with curiosity, its lips twisting into a grin.

Dann leaned down and snatched up an arrow that protruded from a body tangled in the forest roots and smouldering shrubs. He charged at the Fade, howling as he did. Arcs of purple lightning hurtled towards him. He twisted as he ran, feeling the heat of the lightning flash past his face. He nocked the arrow, drawing and loosing in a single motion.

The arrow sliced into the Fade's neck, lodging beside the other two. He ducked a swipe of the Fade's black fire sword as it reformed in the creature's other hand. As he passed, Dann reached back and grabbed the shaft of an arrow that jutted through the Fade's neck and yanked it free. The effort caused him to tumble, crashing to the ground as the Fade turned to face him.

Dann scrambled as he hit the ground, his hands shaking, his heart pounding. He nocked the arrow he'd pulled from the Fade, then loosed it. The Fade's head bounced back as the arrow punched up under its chin and through into its head. The creature cracked its neck from side to side, then turned its head down towards Dann. An arrow jutted from each eye, three from its neck, one up through its jaw, one in its hand, and one in its arm.

Dann panted heavily, every muscle in his body aching. "Why the fuck won't you die?"

Something unseen wrapped around Dann's throat and lifted him into the air. At the same time, each of the arrows lodged in the Fade's body pulled free, floating in the air around the creature before dropping to the ground. The Fade wrapped its pale fingers around Dann's neck, replacing the unseen grip.

"Ahh," the Fade let out a long hissing breath, tilting its head to the side. Its cavernous black eyes stared into Dann's, bearing no signs of the arrows that had just been pulled from their depths. It lifted its other hand, running its pale white fingers along the pauldron on Dann's shoulder. It drew a deep, almost longing breath in through its nose. "I thought it might be you." The sound that left the creature's mouth was rough and harsh, almost like two voices talking over each other. "I never forget a face – or a mark."

The creature continued to stare into Dann's eyes as the flames raged around it, the forest burning. Dann kicked and thrashed, the Fade's fingers closing around his throat. Here and there, Dann saw elves and rebels running back towards the city, bloody, burned, and charred. Not a single one of them paid him or the Fade any heed.

"These bodies are so frail," it hissed, its fingers tightening. "Nothing but flesh and bone. Pity. Hopefully I will be free of it soon."

Dann slammed his fists into the Fade's arm, but the creature didn't flinch. His vision blurred, his lungs burning. His arms became heavy, his breaths short and rasped. The pressure around his throat closed tighter and tighter. As he choked, he looked past the Fade. There, through his hazy vision, he saw a purple glow pierce the smoke and flames.

CALEN CHARGED THROUGH THE FLAMES, whipping threads of Air around himself. Rebels, elves, and Dvalin Angan alike swarmed around him, Tarmon, Vaeril, Erik, and the others sprinting at his side.

Flames swirled about the Fade as it held Dann in the air, its fingers wrapped around his throat.

Above, Valerys streaked across the canopy towards Calen. Through Valerys's eyes, Calen could see the shapes of the three dragons swooping high in the dark skies, their scales glittering in the red light of the Blood Moon. They hadn't seen Valerys yet.

Stay low.

A rumble of response sounded in Calen's mind.

He rushed forwards, pulling on threads of Air, feeling Valerys's power surge through him. He needed to move fast. He wove the threads around a spear that lay on the ground by his side and whipped it through the air as hard as he could. Flames swirled around the weapon as it careened through the air and slammed into the side of the Fade's head. The force of the strike lifted the Fade off its feet. Dann collapsed to the ground.

Calen pushed harder, his legs burning. He slid his sword into its scabbard, dropping to the ground beside Dann, grabbing the back of his friend's head, shaking him. "Dann! Dann!"

Fear held Calen's heart in its cold fingers. He shook Dann frantically, hands trembling. "Dann, please. I can't lose you too."

Dann gasped, and relief flooded through Calen. Dann's eyes peeled open as he drew in a lungful of air. He looked up at Calen, dried blood coating his face, his eyes red from the smoke and fire. "It's about fucking time," he croaked.

Calen let out a laugh, tears rolling down his cheeks. "I hate you," he said, letting out a breath.

"You couldn't hate me if you tried. Now, help me up."

Calen heaved Dann to his feet, only for something to hammer into both of them. The world spun as Calen crashed to the ground. Pain seared through his back, and his ears rang. Something wrapped around him and hauled him through the air, fingers curling around his throat. As his vision cleared, he found himself staring back at the Fade. A hole pierced through the side of the creature's head where the spear had hit, the side of its face mangled, but Fade seemed otherwise unhindered.

"I've been looking for you," the creature hissed. It studied him. Calen tried to pull his sword from its scabbard, but he was frozen in the air, something unseen holding him in place. *Blood Magic.* He felt the Fade pulling at the Spark, but before the creature could ward him, Calen drove a spike of Spirit upwards – as Vaeril had taught him. As soon as the spike of Spirit had pushed through the ward the Fade had tried to form, Calen forged threads of Air into a ball and slammed them into the creature's chest.

The Fade careened backwards, Calen falling to the dirt. Hands hauled him upright. He ripped his sword from his scabbard to see Haem, Varlin, and Lyrin charging at the Fade, green lights shimmering as they swung their nithráls through the air. The Fade matched the strokes of their blades, moving with terrifying speed, the black fire of its nithrál swallowing the bursts of green light.

As Calen charged, Asius and Thacia appeared to his right, Aeson and the other Rakina just behind them. The Spark thrummed in the air, threads of each element weaving all around.

The Fade moved in a blur. Arcs of purple lightning erupted from its fingertips, burning holes through four elves as they charged. It blocked a strike from Lyrin, then sent the man careening through the air with unseen Blood Magic. It spun, its black fire blade slicing through the neck of a Dvalin Angan that charged in its stag form. The Angan's headless body dropped to the ground in a cloud of ash.

Black fire plumed from the Fade's open palm, swallowing two rebels in its flames.

As Calen charged towards the creature, he dropped into Striking Dragon, letting the forms of svidarya drift through his mind. He swung his blade upwards, meeting the flame-wrought nithrál.

A howl rang out, and Ella appeared behind the Fade. She leapt onto the creature's back, her eyes shimmering amber, her teeth sharpened and elongated to fangs. She bit into the Fade's neck, thrashing her head from side to side, tearing at flesh. As she did, Faenir bounded from the flames, ripping into the creature's leg.

The Fade reached back, grabbed Ella by the hair and hurled her over its shoulder. Tarmon leapt forwards and cleaved the creature's arm at the elbow, the black fire nithrál flickering from existence. Erik and Vaeril swept in close, steel shimmering, taking the creature's other arm and its left leg in quick succession. Before Calen could even move, Dann charged past him, a curved elven blade in his hand. Dann launched himself at the Fade, driving the blade through its chest.

The Fade fell backwards, and Dann hauled the sword from the creature's chest, swung it behind his head, Moments after the Fade had hit the forest floor, Dann threw his weight forward and took the creature's head from its shoulder, the steel embedding in a thick root behind the Fade's neck.

Dann let go of the blade and dropped to his knees, shoulders trembling. He started sobbing, shaking his head.

"Dann, its dead. You killed it." Calen slid his sword into its scabbard as he approached Dann. His friend's new white cloak was tarnished with blood, char, and dirt.

"We should have killed it with a Soulblade," Lyrin said, glaring at the Fade's beheaded corpse.

Dann turned towards Calen, eyes red. "It took Alea and Baldon."

The words were like a punch to Calen's gut. Behind him a howl split the night. He turned to see Aneera kneeling beside a charred, blackened body, her head tilted towards the sky.

"We need to keep moving," Aeson said, his face illuminated by the pinkish light of the Blood Moon that drifted into the woodland through the gaping chasm in the canopy created by the dragonfire. The other Rakina, along with Asius and Therin, followed him, casting their gazes over the desolation. "At least two thirds of the Lorian army still stands and will be marching through here to get to the city."

Therin pushed past Aeson and dropped to one knee beside Dann. The elf pulled his and Dann's foreheads together as tears streaked through the dirt and blood on Dann's face. "We will mourn later, Dann. We honour them now by standing."

Tears also glistened in Therin's eyes. Calen had forgotten how long Baldon had been a friend to the elf.

"Dann?"

Calen turned his head to see Lyrei stumbling towards them, her nose broken, blood splattered across her face. Most of the elf's green cloak had been devoured by the fires.

The tremble in Dann's shoulders redoubled as he looked to Lyrei. "I'm sorry," he said, shaking his head. "I couldn't do anything."

Loss ached in Calen's chest as he saw the myriad of emotions that passed across Lyrei's face in mere moments.

The elf's lip quivered, but she held herself upright. "Her body?"

Dann shook his head.

Lyrei nodded solemnly. "Myia nithír til diar, vésani. La'uva niassa du i denir viël are altinua. Må Heraya tael du ia'sine ael. Indil vir anarai andin."

My soul to yours, sister. I will love you in this life and always. May Heraya take you into her arms. Until we meet again.

"Indil vir anarai andin," Therin whispered. He rose to his feet and touched his fingers against Lyrei's cheek, giving her a weak smile.

Calen echoed the words.

Aeson stepped closer, looking from Therin to Calen, to Lyrei. "Indil vir anarai andin." He reached out and clasped Lyrei's arm. "Alea dauvin val haydria en sine elwyn ar en sine nithír. Anis, dia aluras."

Alea died with honour in her heart and in her soul. Now, she rests.

Tears streaked down Lyrei's cheeks as she nodded, her lips spread into a weak smile.

As Aeson turned and started to urge everyone onwards, a shadow spread over the ground and the pinkish light of the Blood Moon disappeared.

Valerys descended through the dragonfire-wrought opening in the canopy, his white scales glimmering in the light of the blazing fires. The dragon cracked his wings, flames, ash, and brittle leaves swirling in the air as he landed.

The elves and rebels who had been retreating stopped in their tracks looking up at the white dragon.

Valerys craned his neck down, pressing the tip of his snout into Calen's outstretched hands, a soft rumble resonating from the dragon's throat. Calen rested his forehead against the scales of Valerys's snout and ran his hands over the long horns that framed the dragon's jaw.

"I'm all right."

Images of Alea and Baldon flashed across the dragon's mind, followed by a sense of loss that pulled at Calen's heart. More family lost.

After a few moments, a feeling of urgency pushed from Valerys's mind into Calen's, images of what the dragon had seen flashing between their minds. Calen turned to Aeson and the others. "The glamour has fallen, and the Dragonguard are flying towards the city."

"How is that possible?" Aeson looked to Therin.

"I'm not sure. Unless someone shattered one of the lockstones."

"It doesn't matter," Calen cut across. "It doesn't matter how or why. They're flying towards the city, and we need to stop them." Calen looked around. So many people he cared for in one place. Dann, Ella, Haem, Tarmon, Vaeril, Erik, Therin. Lyrei's eyes were red and raw, tear marks carving through the dirt on her face. Asius stood in silence, his bluish skin seeming to shimmer in the light of the Blood Moon and the fires. The Jotnar's eyes were still filled with loss from Senas's death. Calen looked to Aeson. "Get them all back and get what's left of our forces ready for the Lorian charge. We need to stand with the elves."

Aeson's eyes narrowed as he understood what Calen was implying. "You're not going up there, Calen. They'll rip you apart."

"I've no choice. I can't let them burn the city."

"Calen, you need to use your head. There's over sixty thousand Lorians marching this way. Hundreds of mages. Fades. The Dragonguard are too strong for you. We need to think about—"

"I will not run!" Calen roared, Valerys looming over him. The dragon's rage burned hot, searing through them both. "You've survived all this time by doing what you had to do. You built rebellions, stoked fires. You're a survivor, Aeson. But I don't want to survive anymore, I want to fight." Calen gestured at all those around them. "This is it. This is where we make our choice. The choice to stand, because if we keep running we'll run forever." A low rumble resonated in Valerys's chest, and Calen looked to the dragon. "We're done running. If we die up there, then so be it. But we couldn't live with ourselves knowing we ran when we could have done something." Calen looked from Ella to Haem. "There's no point in living if we don't fight for what we love. We're meant to be Draleid. We're meant to be guardians, not survivors."

Calen's breaths trembled, his hands shaking. He pushed all the anger and loss down and looked to Aneera, who still knelt by Baldon's charred corpse. "Aneera, another of Clan Fenryr arrived in the city not long ago, yes?"

Aneera hauled herself upright, her eyes gleaming. "Yes, son of the Chainbreaker. Diango. He was hurt. He rests in Alura."

"Contact him. I need the elves to send mages to the highest towers and the cliffsides across Aravell. Tell them I'll bring the Dragonguard low, and I'll need support."

"It will be done." Aneera bowed, then dropped to the ground, closing her eyes.

Calen turned back to Aeson. "If I can keep them occupied, lead them through the valleys, can you win on the ground?"

Chora wheeled herself over, her stare fixed on Calen. "We'll have to hit them with everything we have. We won't be able to just hide behind the walls and wait. But if you can keep them away, we'll have a chance."

"I'll ride with you," Vaeril said, stepping forwards. The white dragon emblazoned on his breastplate took on a pinkish hue in the light of the Blood Moon, his hair coruscating. "I can use the Spark from Valerys's back."

"Easy." Therin rested his hand on Vaeril's chest. "The way he needs to fly, you'll never be able to hold on. Your honour is intact, Vaeril."

In contrast to most of the other elves, Vaeril had always looked at Therin with great respect, but at the moment Calen could see only disgust in his eyes. "It's nothing to do with honour."

"Regardless," Therin's voice stayed level, "the fact remains."

As Therin argued with Vaeril, Ella stepped closer to Calen. Haem and Faenir were at her side.

"I'm going, Ella."

Ella didn't answer. She just pulled Calen into a hug, pressing her chin into the crook of his neck. She pulled away and looked him in the eye. "I love you."

"I love you too."

"Come back to us, all right?"

Calen nodded, giving her a weak smile. He scratched Faenir below the chin, receiving a satisfied grumble on return.

Haem pulled him into an embrace, their armour clinking together.

"Keep them safe," Calen said, looking around at the others.

Haem nodded, then looked past Calen to Valerys. "You look after each other."

The dragon lowered his head, tilting it sideways as Haem's gauntleted hand brushed his scales. Warmth drifted from Valerys to Calen as the dragon looked down over Haem, Ella, and Faenir. A deep urge to protect swept through his mind.

"I believe in you, little brother. I'll see you soon." Liquid metal flowed from the collar of Haem's Sentinel armour, forming into a helmet as he turned back towards Lyrin and Varlin.

"I'll make sure Erik doesn't do anything stupid," Tarmon said as he grasped Calen's forearm.

"And I'll make sure he doesn't do anything too sensible." Erik clapped his hands on the side of Calen's helmet. "Give them fucking fire, Calen. Give them fire and blood. We'll do the same down here."

Calen clenched his jaw. He clasped the back of Erik's helmet and pulled their heads even tighter together. With each farewell his stomach twisted and turned, his throat constricting, his chest clenching. He knew in all likelihood he would never lay eyes on any of them again. But if he could buy them enough time, if he and Valerys could get lucky enough to kill one of the Dragonguard, then maybe, just maybe, they could make the difference.

As Erik pulled away and he and the others gathered themselves and readied to follow the rest of the retreating army towards the city, Dann wrapped his arms around Calen and clapped him on the back.

"I'll see you when you're back," Dann said, giving Calen a weak smile. His eyes were still red, and tears had carved paths through the dirt, ash, and blood that marred his face. He held Calen's gaze for a moment, then pulled him back into another embrace, squeezing tight before turning and walking back towards Therin and the others.

Valerys bowed his head, stretching out his forelimb. Calen climbed up and positioned himself on the nape of the dragon's neck. A sense of sorrow ached in their shared soul as they looked over the raging fires, charred bodies, and their friends trudging back towards the city.

"This is it," Calen whispered, running his gauntleted hand along Valerys's scales. "Vir solian katar, vir dauv katar. Laël unira diar. Draleid n'aldryr, Rakina nai dauva." *We live together, we die together. I am always yours. Dragonbound by fire, broken by death.*

A deep rumble resonated through the dragon as he spread his wings and shook his neck. Memories passed through Valerys: breaking from the shell, travelling across Epheria, flying in Belduar, fighting at Kingspass. Faces followed: Arthur, Elissar, Korik, Lopir, Falmin, Alwen, Heldin, Baldon, Alea, Rist, Freis, Vars. All those the empire had taken from them. The family they had found and earned, the family they had lost, and the family Valerys had never gotten to meet.

As the images faded, it wasn't sorrow that washed over from Valerys's mind, it was rage. Pure unfettered fury. If tonight was the night they died, they would take every soul with them they could. Valerys shifted, cracking his wings against the air, lifting them up through the open chasm in the canopy where flames still blazed. The open air swept across them as Valerys surged upwards and unleashed a roar that shook the air like claps of thunder.

CHAPTER EIGHTY-THREE

FAITH AND WILL

ist watched as the rune-marked men and women floated in the air, their arms spread wide, the runes carved into their skin shimmering with a vivid red light. The gemstones in the pit at the centre of the plaza glowed furiously. The black tear in the veil above the pit had spread so its centre was now at least ten feet wide with cracks snaking outwards

The light in Rist's gemstone had faded minutes before, and the Essence had fled his body, leaving an emptiness where the strength had been. But he still drew on the Spark, still pulled thin threads of Spirit and weaved them into the emperor. He could feel the drain pulling at him, sapping the strength from his legs, but he pushed it away, ignoring the pain. *Pain is simply an obstacle to be overcome.* He squeezed Neera's hand, giving her a weak smile.

She looked back at him, the power of the Spark radiating from her, threads of Spirit weaving around her.

"Don't overextend," Magnus called. He turned to Garramon. "How much longer?"

"As long as it takes."

A few moments passed, and then horns bellowed, two sharp bursts, a pause, then one more burst followed by a pause and two short bursts again. Rist ran the pattern through his mind, flicking across the pages of the book he had read on alarms. *Enemy behind the lines; imminent attack.*

"Battle ready!" Magnus roared, pulling his sword from its scabbard.

A ripple of panic spread through the mages around Rist. He could see the weariness in their faces. Funnelling the threads of Spirit into Fane had left most of them tired and weak; they were vulnerable. Magnus turned to Garramon. "How are they behind the lines already? Where are the damn warnings? We need to disengage the threads."

"Do it. Fane can complete the ritual alone." Garramon turned and looked to Rist and Neera, studying their faces. "The first Urak you kill, harness its Essence. Essence is more potent under the light of the Blood Moon, it will replace what the Spark has taken from you. Understood?"

Rist nodded, as did Neera.

"I need you to say it." Garramon clamped his hand down on Rist's shoulder. "I know the hesitation in your heart, but I need you to understand, Rist. Essence will be the difference between life and death here. This isn't a game."

"I understand." Rist pulled his hand away from Neera's and touched his fingers against the cold surface of the gemstone that sat around his neck.

"Good." Garramon slid his sword from his scabbard.

"Bloodmarked!" A voice bellowed into the night.

Rist watched as an enormous Urak charged across one of the rooftops that overlooked the central plaza. The creature was far larger than either of the two Rist, Calen, and Dann had found in Ölm Forest, and its body was covered in glowing red runes that spewed dark smoke. The creature leapt from the building's roof, a pulse of Essence rippling outwards as it landed and slammed its fists into the ground. A shockwave of black fire streaked from the creature's fists, splitting a priest in two and setting both halves aflame. The shockwave carried on igniting two Scholars in a black inferno. Battlemages charged from the street on the right, but the giant Urak turned on its heels and swung a clawed hand, tearing through flesh and bone. Spears pierced its hide as it sent another shockwave slicing through a clutch of mages. More rune-marked Uraks – Bloodmarked – leapt from the rooves around the central plaza. Rist had read of the creatures but had never seen them. They were as terrifying as the accounts claimed, more so.

"Forward!" Magnus roared, charging into the plaza. "Don't let them stop the ritual!"

The mages around Rist charged, their weariness overcome by the battle rush. But Rist's feet remained planted, his gaze fixed on the rooftop the first Bloodmarked had leapt from. Another Urak had walked to the edge of the roof but hadn't jumped. It was smaller than the Bloodmarked but was still layered in muscle. It held a long wooden staff in its right hand with a glowing gemstone set into the top. Horns protruded from the creature's head, winding around into a shape that almost looked like a crown. It just stared down into the plaza, its face expressionless.

"Rist!"

Rist snapped out of his haze to see Garramon roaring at him. The man turned, swinging his blade up to carve through the arm of a Bloodmarked, but the creature lifted its foot and kicked Garramon in the chest, sending him careening across the plaza.

"Garramon!" Rist bolted forwards, ripping his sword from its scabbard. He charged at the Bloodmarked that had kicked Garramon, but it was only as the creature saw him and surged forwards that he realised he had no idea how to kill it, and the Spark had already pulled the energy from his bones. *Think. Page one hundred and twelve from A Study of Control.* He pulled on a single thread of Earth and weaved it into the ground before the Bloodmarked, pulling the stone into a small lump.

The Bloodmarked kicked the lump, staggering. Rist swung his sword with as much force as he could, cleaving the beast's arm just above the elbow.

The Bloodmarked howled, the runes carved into its flesh igniting with a furious light. The beast turned towards him, blood spurting from the stump of its arm. *How in the gods do I kill this thing?* Rist studied the creature as it charged. It was bigger than him, stronger than him, and faster than him.

'*What separates a good Battlemage from a great one are their choices.*' Garramon's words echoed in Rist's mind.

Once more, Rist funnelled a single thread into the ground and formed a lump of stone. The creature shifted, stepping past the lump and hurtling towards Rist, but as it did, he pulled a second lump from the ground and forged it into a spike. The spike burst through the Bloodmarked's foot, ripping through flesh as the creature's momentum carried it forwards.

As the Bloodmarked howled and looked down to see its bloody mess of a clawed foot, Rist sliced through its shin, a vibration jarring his arm as bone gave way to steel. The creature roared, stumbling and falling. As it collapsed, Rist weaved a last thread of Earth into the ground and forged a thin spike where the Urak's head was about to land. The spike pierced the creature's skull, erupting from its eye in a spray of blood. Smoke billowed from the runes in the Bloodmarked's skin as they burned with a bright light.

As the life fled the creature's body, Rist felt a pull from the pendant around his neck. He was weak, his body drained. '*Essence will be the difference between life and death, Rist.*' He opened himself and allowed the gemstone to draw in the Essence. Barely a second passed before he saw the red glow of the gemstone radiate from beneath his breastplate.

"Rist!" Garramon appeared by Rist's side, Neera next to him. The man was limping slightly but was otherwise unharmed. He looked down at the body of the Bloodmarked and gave a gruff nod.

Around them, Bloodmarked and smaller Uraks were still pouring into plaza, leaping from the rooves. The Battlemages were weakened from pushing so much of their power into Fane, but with each Urak killed, their vessels glowed with strength and they pushed back.

A howl erupted to Rist's left, and a Bloodmarked ripped through four Battlemages in quick succession, its claws snapping bones and rending steel.

Rist looked back towards the roof to see the crown-horned Urak staring at Fane. A number of Uraks now stood beside the one who bore the crown. Runes were carved into their chests and arms, though the creatures weren't as big as the Bloodmarked. As Rist stared, he noticed the pattern of the runes; they were identical to the ones carved into the Chosen hosts who floated in the air.

Rist pointed to the crowned Urak, yelling to Garramon, but as he did, a bright green orb emerged from thin air just above the roof to the left. The orb pulsed, then swept outwards, spreading into a circle twenty feet in diameter. The centre of the circle faded to a deep black, rippling like water, while the edges glimmered green.

A moment passed in which the circle simply hung in the air, then the surface of the circle rippled and a warrior garbed in smooth green plate burst through, followed by another and another.

The warriors dropped to the ground, stone cracking beneath their feet, blades of shimmering green light bursting to life in their hands.

Rist watched in horror as the warriors carved through everything in their path, slaughtering humans and Uraks alike, shimmering blades cleaving bone and slicing through armour as though it were paper. As they spread out, more came through the portal, blades of light igniting in their hands.

KALLINVAR DROPPED HIS SHOULDER AND charged into an Urak's chest, feeling bones snap beneath the weight of the strike. He stepped back and swung his Soulblade, slicing through the beast's chest. As the creature howled, Kallinvar drove his Soulblade forward and plunged it into the Urak's gut, heaving it free as the creature collapsed.

A pulse of the taint erupted behind him, and he turned to see two Lorian mages with glowing gemstones hanging around their necks. The oily sensation of the Taint radiated from the mages, flowing outwards in ripples. They charged him. Ruon surged past, taking the first mage's head from his shoulders before swinging her Soulblade back around in the same motion and cleaving the second mage in half.

The Taint clung so heavily to the air it left a tangible pain in Kallinvar's mind, disorienting him. He looked around, watching as the knights of The Ninth, The Seventh, The Second, and The First carved through the Lorians and Bloodspawn, Soulblades shimmering as they moved.

A sharp vibration erupted in his Sigil, stealing his breath. He turned his head to see Brother Lumikes of the Seventh impaled on a Bloodmarked's clawed hand. The creature held him suspended in the air, before flinging its arm outwards and sending Lumikes's lifeless body colliding with Sister Rindil.

Kallinvar looked towards the centre of the plaza where the tear in the veil was a tangible thing; a wound of pure black carved in the fabric world. The Taint swirled around it like a whirlpool. Below the tear, a red, spherical stone hung in the air above a pit of glowing gemstones.

His gaze fell on the men and women who floated in the air around the pit, their arms spread wide, runes carved into their flesh. There had to be a hundred of them.

"They are his Chosen, my child," Achyron's voice boomed. *"Warriors far more powerful than the Urithnilim. Efialtir tries to bring their souls into the world. They are the next step to his forging in the mortal plane. You must strike down as many as you can and close the tear."*

Achyron's voice bellowed in Kallinvar's mind just as Kallinvar spotted a man standing before the pit and ignoring all the chaos around him. The Taint flowed from the man in waves, and Kallinvar had not a doubt in his mind as to who it was. Fane Mortem.

"Illarin!" Kallinvar roared to Brother-Captain Illarin, who was weaving his way through a clutch of Uraks. "The rune-marked! We must end them."

Illarin drove his blade through an Urak's chest, spun, then took the head of a Battlemage with a single swipe. He looked to Kallinvar and nodded. "Knights of The Seventh, with me!"

Kallinvar roared the same command to Sister-Captains Arlena and Airdaine.

"Kallinvar." Ruon pulled at Kallinvar's shoulder and pointed towards a Shaman that stood on one of the rooftops, overlooking the plaza. A number of Uraks stood around the beast, their hides were marked with runes, and yet they were not Bloodmarked.

As Ruon pointed, a pulse signalled in Kallinvar's Sigil. He drew in a breath and summoned the Rift, fire and ice sweeping through him. The Rift burst into life above the roof, Brother-Captain Armites and The Sixth surging through from Mar Dorul.

Kallinvar turned to Ruon, Ildris, Tarron, and Sylven. "We need to close the tear in the veil."

POWER SURGED THROUGH EVERY MUSCLE in Rist's body. With the Essence flowing through him, he felt as though he could tear through steel with his bare hands and soar over mountains with a single leap. He swung his blade, slicing open an Urak's chest before drawing more Essence from his vessel and pulling the beast's chin down onto his steel. The sword tore upwards, bursting from the Urak's skull. Rist drew in a sharp breath, more Essence flooding his vessel.

Beside him Neera crushed an Urak's chest with Essence, then followed through with her sword. Magnus, Garramon, and Anila, and several other mages fought beside them. They all stood around Fane and the Chosen, holding back the Uraks and the new warriors in green plate. The warriors were strong and savage, chanting Achyron's name as they tore through men and Uraks alike, blood spraying wherever their green blades swept. Rist had never seen such merciless carnage.

"Hold them back," Fane roared, turning to look at Garramon. The man's eyes glowed with a vibrant red light. "They are almost here."

"Nothing passes us!" Magnus roared, taking the head from a Bloodmarked's shoulders.

As Magnus spoke, another portal opened on the western edge of the plaza and more of the warriors streamed forth, the dark green armour shimmering in the light of the Blood Moon.

"Those fuckers just keep coming." Magnus pulled his blade from an Urak's chest, glaring at the armoured warriors who stormed from the rippling black portal. He glanced towards Rist. "Anila!"

Rist turned to see Sister Anila looking at Magnus in confusion, a sword gripped in her hand, a second strapped to her hip. Anila's confusion turned to shock as a glowing green blade swung down from above and hacked into her, carving through her shoulder, chest, and hip, ripping her into two pieces. Intestines spilled out into the dirt, blood spraying as Anila's body slopped to the ground, a warrior in green plate standing in her place.

A moment of strange silence passed as the warrior stood there, broken only by Magnus's grief-stricken roar. Essence radiated from Magnus as the man stormed towards the warrior. Their blades collided in bursts of green light before Magnus sent a pulse of Essence into the knight's chest.

As the knight careened backwards, Rist, Garramon, Neera, and two other Battlemages surged to Magnus's side. A swing of the shimmering green blade and one of the other mages was cleaved in half.

The knight turned to Rist, towering over him in a monstrous suit of green plate, a white sigil of a downward facing sword emblazoned across the chest. Rist blocked the first strike of the green blade with an upward swing. The power of the Essence surging through him was the only reason his bones didn't snap from the force of the blow. The knight lifted his blade once more but pivoted and swung towards Magnus.

Rist watched as the green blade sliced through Magnus's arm just below the shoulder, severing it in a spray of blood. Magnus howled, surging forwards, somehow ignoring the loss of a limb. He ducked, leaning to the right as the knight's blade swept over his head. Magnus roared again, dropping his sword. Strands of red light burst from his hand, wrapping around themselves until they formed a solid blade. Magnus lunged forwards and drove the red blade up through the knight's chest.

As Magnus heaved the blade free, a tremor of Essence shook through the world, rippling outwards as though a star had crashed to the ground.

THE GROUND SHOOK BENEATH KALLINVAR'S feet as the Taint erupted outwards from the tear in the veil, sweeping through the air like a shockwave. As it did, black tendrils burst forth, anchoring to the chests of the rune-marked men and women who floated around the pit of gemstones. The runes carved into their flesh ignited with a blazing red light.

More tendrils burst from the tear and streaked towards the rooftops, connecting to the chests of the rune-marked Uraks who stood by the Shaman.

"*The Chosen.*" Achyron's voice boomed in Kallinvar's mind. "*This is why you are here, my child. You must kill as many of the hosts as you can. The survival of this world depends on it. Sever the connections and close the tear.*"

"Tear them down!" Kallinvar roared, sending a pulse through his Sigil to the other knights.

Kallinvar charged towards the tear, carving a path through the Lorian mages, Ildris, Tarron, Ruon, and Sylven moving by his side.

Around the plaza, the Bloodspawn ceased their assault on the Lorians and focused on the knights. Pulses swept through Kallinvar's Sigil as his brothers and sisters fell to Efialtír's servants. With each step his mind flickered back to the night of The Fall, to this very city. In the distance, he could see what remained of the Tower of Faith, shattered and broken, the remnants of the bridge jutting forwards. That had been the tower in which Alvira Serris died, the tower in which the world changed.

He pushed the memories to the back of his mind and surged forwards like the harbinger of death. With each swing of his Soulblade, blood sprayed and bones split. He took solace in knowing that every soul he severed was tarnished by the Taint. Above, another pulse rippled from the tear, energy surging through the black tendrils that were anchored into the rune-marked men and women.

"We need to close the tear and kill the hosts!" he roared. "Ildris, Tarron, Sylven. Take the right! Ruon, with me."

Ildris, Tarron, and Sylven swept forwards, leaping through the air in great bounds. Kallinvar watched as Idris's Soulblade sliced one of the hosts in half at the waist. As the body dropped, a violent ripple shook the air, the black tendril snapping back into the tear.

Kallinvar bent his knees and launched himself towards the rune-marked hosts that hung in the air. He swung his Soulblade, slicing through two of the hosts in a single arc, black tendrils snapping backwards. Around him, more of the knights poured forth, carving through the Lorians and Uraks, leaping through the air to rip the hosts from the world. With each host that fell, the tendril to which they were anchored snapped back into the tear like a severed chord.

Kallinvar drew closer, Ruon at his side. A man stood before him, one arm severed below the shoulder, a red Soulblade gripped in his right fist. The man charged at Kallinvar, moving with the speed and strength only Blood Magic could provide. Their blades collided in bursts of green and red light, each matching the other stroke for stroke. But as Kallinvar made to swing low, Ruon charged from the left, raised her leg and planted her foot in the man's chest, sending him soaring through the air.

Kallinvar didn't hesitate, he surged forwards, his eyes fixed on the tear. He bent his knees and launched himself through the air, his green Soulblade shimmering at his side. The tear floated above the pit, black as night. Kallinvar lifted his Soulblade above his head. As he made to drive his Soulblade through the tear in the veil, a pulse of the Taint rippled and something wrapped around his ankle.

For a moment he hung there, motionless in the air, and then he was spinning. He slammed into the ground, a searing pain burning through his back. Stars flitted across his eyes, and his head spun, but he hauled himself upright, stumbling sideways.

A man stood before him in black robes, Taint seeping from him, eyes burning with a crimson light: Fane Mortem. "Here we are again, knight. I have come to believe your god simply enjoys watching you die."

Fane stared down at Kallinvar, his cloak billowing in the wind, knights, Uraks, and mages battling around them. A flash of green light erupted to Kallinvar's right and Brother-Captain Illarin surged forwards, leaping through the air, Soulblade shimmering.

The Taint pulsed from Fane, and Illarin stopped in the air, suspended within arm's reach of the emperor.

Kallinvar staggered forwards, summoning his Soulblade.

Black fire burst from Fane's hand, forging itself into a dark Soulblade. The man glanced at Kallinvar, then drove the blade through Illarin's chest, pulling it free in the same motion. As Illarin's body fell, oily strands of the Taint slammed on Kallinvar's shoulder and dropped him to his knees.

Fane looked at Kallinvar, eyes glowing with a red light. "You are too late once again, knight."

Behind Fane, the tear in the veil shimmered and rippled. The ground shook beneath Kallinvar, and all those in the plaza stopped in their tracks. A pulse surged through the tendrils of black connected to the rune-marked hosts and Uraks. The runes ignited once more, a fierce red light bursting forth, black smoke pluming. Molten steel poured from the runes, flowing over the hosts' skin, spreading across their backs, over their shoulders, and along their arms and legs. As the steel moved, it took shape, folding over muscles and bones, forming into flowing silver armour. It was like a twisted Sentinel armour.

As the armour solidified, the hosts lowered to the ground. The light of the runes on their backs, chests, and arms, shone through the newly-formed steel, glowing bright red.

"Efialtir's Chosen have crossed," Achyron's voice whispered. *"You must close the tear."*

Kallinvar's heart thundered, each beat sending tremors through his bones. For a moment, nothing and nobody moved. Not a sound echoed through the plaza but the whipping of the wind. Then the Chosen swept outwards, moving with a fury, Soulblades of shimmering red bursting from their hands.

The knights held their ground, but the combined weight of the Chosen, the imperial mages, and the Bloodspawn was too much. Kallinvar's Sigil pulsed and ached as the souls of his brothers and sisters were torn from the world.

Fane stepped forwards, his red Soulblade flickering. "Your god branded him The Traitor," Fane said, staring down at Kallinvar. "But now you will see the truth."

Kallinvar made to charge Fane, but Tarron ripped through one of the Chosen and leapt towards the tear in the veil, his Soulblade coruscating.

Fane turned, crying out, the Taint pulsing from him. But Tarron reached forwards and drove his blade into the heart of the tear.

The world shook. A tremor swept through the ground beneath Kallinvar's feet, and the air trembled. Then, in a single motion, the tear collapsed in on itself, and Tarron was gone.

Kallinvar's Sigil didn't pulse or burn; it didn't react at all. Tarron was just gone. "Tarron…"

Fane turned to Kallinvar, red mist wafting from his eyes, a fury etched into his face.

But as the man approached Kallinvar, the Sigil in Kallinvar's chest surged with energy, and he watched as multiple Rifts opened in the world, bursting into life across the plaza beside the surviving knights.

"Take my children home, Kallinvar. You have done what you could. The tear is closed."

Kallinvar hesitated, the fire within him urging him to charge. But as he looked around at his knights, he saw how few still stood and how broken they were. And it was then, with his heart aching, he called out, "Fall back!"

"Pain is the path to strength, my child."

He took a step backwards towards the Rift he knew was open behind him, waiting as the others fell back through the multiple Rifts that were now open. He felt Ruon's hands tugging at him, pulling him, and then the icy embrace of the Rift washed over him.

CHAPTER EIGHTY-FOUR

CHILDREN OF THE CHAINBREAKER

C alen leaned forwards, pressing his gauntleted hands against Valerys's neck as the dense canopy of the Aravell blurred below. The dragon streaked through the air, the wind crashing over his scales.

Above, the crimson light of the moon bled across the night sky, staining dark clouds with a red hue. With the glamour gone, Calen could see the white peaks of Aravell's towers in the distance, rising from the basin within which the city had been built.

Three enormous shapes tore across the sky over the city, wings black against the light of the moon. Rage surged through Valerys at the sight of dragonfire pouring down over the city. The dragon angled his wings, sweeping upwards, blood burning.

Take them from below, deal as much pain as we can, then lead them towards the valleys. The others need time.

A deep rumble resonated through Valerys. The dragon soared through the sky, moving from air current to air current, keeping his wingbeats to a minimum. With each torrent of fire that poured over Aravell, their shared rage swelled until it blazed like the sun. Calen could see the purple light of his eyes glowing against Valerys's scales.

As they drew closer, the city of Aravell coming into view below, the sheer size of the other three dragons became clear. Calen tensed. He stopped himself from drawing on the Spark. Surprise was their only advantage. In the bleeding light of the Blood Moon, it was difficult to make out the colours of the dragons' scales, but it looked as though the largest of the three was brown. *Hrothmundar.* Chora had said that of the living Dragonguard, only Hrothmundar and Meranta had brown scales. Meranta was dead now.

The dragon who flew on Hrothmundar's left was two thirds the size of the larger dragon, scales shimmering blue in the Blood Moon's light. *Seleraine.* That meant the last dragon, with black wings and scales of polished silver, was Eríthan, soulkin of Ilkya.

Calen drew in a short breath, a strange sense of calm overcoming him. *Solian ata'yar. Dauv ata'yar. Nur temen vie'ryn valana.*

Live as one. Die as one. For those we've lost.

Rage, loss, and defiance radiated from Valerys, and the dragon cracked his wings and swept upwards. As the wind thundered past, Calen pulled their minds together, their hearts beating as one, their thoughts colliding, rage and fury igniting through their shared soul.

Chora had said Eríthan was the quickest of the three, and so that was who Valerys streaked towards.

The three dragons lifted higher, flames raging in the city below, and then Valerys angled his wings and tore through the air like an arrow.

The world shook as Valerys crashed upwards into Eríthan's underbelly, talons ripping and tearing, teeth cracking through scales. The dragon was easily twice Valerys's size, but they'd caught him off guard and now Eríthan shrieked in pain as blood sprayed into the air. Before the other dragons could react, Valerys released his talons from Eríthan's belly. The wind hammered against Calen like a crashing waterfall, his stomach turning as Valerys rolled through the air. Valerys crashed into Hrothmundar. He raked his forelimbs across the enormous dragon's back, using his momentum to carve furrows through Hrothmundar's scales.

Valerys stretched his neck forwards and snapped his jaws shut, coming inches from ripping Jormun from his soulkin's back. Valerys's talons came loose, and he hurtled through the air.

Calen pushed himself deeper into Valerys's mind, closing his own eyes and instead seeing only through the dragon's. They rolled and spun, fighting against the force of the wind. Then Valerys unfurled his wings. Inertia pushed back at Calen as Valerys changed direction with immense speed. He clamped his legs down, leaning forwards.

Monstrous roars tore through the sky. Calen opened his eyes and looked back to see the three Dragonguard hurtling towards them. Through Valerys's nostrils, he could smell the iron tang of blood, taste it. Eríthan wobbled in the sky, his motions uncertain next to the other two.

"Dive!" Calen roared, pressing himself close to Valerys in anticipation. Weightlessness swelled in Calen's stomach as Valerys curled his wings inward and plummeted, the force of the world trying to pull Calen from the dragon's back. As they swept down past one of the city's many white towers, Valerys shifted and changed direction. Calen's muscles burned as he held himself in place. A column of dragonfire poured down after them, illuminating the night as it crashed into the side of the tower. The force of the fire sent white stone tumbling into the city below.

Calen and Valerys's shared heart pounded like a drum, its beat thumping through their veins. As Valerys rolled towards the mouth of an open valley, an arc of purple lightning streaked past them, crashing into the mountainside in a spray of rock. Calen hadn't felt the Spark. *Blood Magic.*

Valerys cracked his wings, shifted, then dove again, sweeping down to catch an upwards current of air, soaring into the mouth of the valley. With each movement, Calen pulled himself tight, pressing his armoured chest against Valerys's scales. They had flown these valleys almost every day for months. They knew every curve, every peak, every jagged cliff. *'You must fly until it is as effortless as breathing.'* Chora's words echoed in Calen's mind. *'Until Valerys can turn and move quicker than his own heart can beat.'*

Calen leaned forwards. "Fly."

As though chains had been pulled from the dragon's wings, Valerys surged forwards, rising and falling, swerving around cliffs and below bridges of stone. As he flew, rain began to fall, droplets at first, then turning to a downpour so heavy it clouded the path ahead. Calen looked back to see the three Dragonguard still following, growing closer with each wingbeat, the light of the Blood Moon scattering in the rain. Two rivers of fire poured forth, and Valerys banked left, the flames crashing against the mountainside.

They moved as one, diving and swerving, bolts of lightning and pillars of fire illuminating the night.

Calen felt a pulse of the Spark, threads of Water, Spirit, and Air, swirling. The rain coalesced, clinging to Valerys's wings like a paste. Within moments, the water on Valerys's wings froze, and panic jolted through the dragon's veins as they fell from the sky, wind and rain crashing against them like a tempest.

Calen opened himself to the Spark, scrambling as he dragged at threads of Fire, pushing them into the ice that held Valerys's wings. A sense of relief flooded Valerys as the ice fragmented and shattered. He unfurled his wings, arresting their fall and sweeping them forwards.

Not a moment had passed before threads of Earth, Spirit, and Air whipped at them. Pressure closed around Calen's breastplate. Terror gripped him as the steel pressed inwards against his chest and ribs. He pushed his fear away and sliced through the threads of Earth with Spirit, gasping for air when the pressure dissipated.

As the Dragonguard drew closer, more threads clawed at Calen and Valerys, threatening to break bones, snap wings, and rip them from the air. Calen drew as deeply as he could from the Spark, feeling it burn in his veins. He let Valerys fly free, rain hammering down as he did everything he could to counter the threads hurled at them. But with each passing second, the drain pulled more and more from him, sapping his energy, leaching his strength.

'The Dragonguard will tear you apart, Calen. Piece by piece. They have killed hundreds of our kind. Draleid far older and wiser than you.'

Calen pushed Atara's words to the back of his mind. They didn't need to kill the Dragonguard. They just needed to give the others a chance.

As the pinkish light of the Blood Moon sprayed through the deluge, Valerys banked hard around a cliff, turning back through the valleys towards the city. If Aneera's message had gotten through, the mages might be in position. It was their only chance.

Valerys tore through the valley, clinging to the mountainside, following its curves. Calen glanced over his shoulder, rain drumming against his helmet and dripping into his eyes. Two shapes closed on them, illuminated by a flash of lightning. Calen scanned the valley frantically for the third dragon, only for a thunderous roar to sound overhead. He turned just in time to see one of the Dragonguard dropping over the cliff's edge, blue scales glinting.

Seleraine crashed into Valerys with the force of a landslide. The world spun as the two dragons hurtled through the air, claws ripping and tearing, jaws snapping.

Valerys let out a shriek. Pain burned in Calen as Seleraine's talon raked a gash through Valerys side. As they spun through the air, Calen turned to see Seleraine's head snaking towards him. The dragon's ice-blue eyes shone as she snapped her jaws, trying to rip Calen from Valerys's back. Calen swung himself to the side, teeth as large as swords ripping through the air beside his head. He pulled on threads of Air, Fire, and Spirit, sending an arc of lightning smashing into the side of the dragon's head. Seleraine roared, reeling backwards. At the same time, Valerys clamped his jaws around the blue dragon's neck and bit down. Scales cracked and blood sprayed, but before Valerys could do any more damage, Seleraine kicked at him with her talons, sending both Calen and Valerys careening through the air.

Once more, the world spun, the wind crashing against Valerys, pinning his wings to his sides. Calen pressed himself against the dragon's neck, his hands gripped tight to Valerys's scales. Valerys's panic scratched at him, but he drew in short breaths, focusing, then pulled on threads of Air. He whipped them around himself and Valerys in much the same way he had done with the Wind Runner in Durakdur, creating a sphere of air. All they needed was a moment's relief, and then Valerys opened his wings, caught the air and swept forwards, his talons raking the mountain, tearing rocks free.

The wound in Valerys's side, along with several others that Seleraine had gouged into him, burned with a fury. Ahead, he saw the white stone of Aravell's western towers. "Come on. Keep going," Calen whispered, grimacing. Seleraine's forelimb had sliced a tear through Valerys's left wing, and Calen could feel the pain with each beat. "The longer we keep them away from the battle, the more chance the others have. We need to protect our family, Valerys. We need to keep them safe."

Valerys let out a roar in response. Power surged through the dragon's mind, pouring into Calen. Threads of each elemental strand snapped at Valerys and Calen from all sides as the Dragonguard tried to pull them from the air, but Calen continued to fight back, countering spikes of ice with Fire, slicing threads of Earth with Spirit.

A bolt of purple lightning collided with the cliff to Valerys's left, a cloud of rock and dust bursting outwards. Debris smashed into Valerys, sending him spinning sideways. Calen whipped his head around to see a stream of dragonfire pouring through the dust and rock. Valerys folded his wings and dove, the flames washing over the dragon's tail and side. As Valerys dove, Hrothmundar and Eríthan burst through the cloud after him, Eríthan's wings shimmering with a pink hue.

"Faster!" Calen roared. He pulled on threads of Water, Fire, and Air. He used the threads of Water to forge the rain around them into hundreds of small spikes, pulling the heat from the spikes with threads of Fire. As the spikes froze, Calen launched them backwards with the threads of Air, roaring as he did.

Eríthan and Hrothmundar unleashed pillars of dragonfire, vaporising the projectiles. But shrieks followed as some of the spikes slipped past and sliced through the dragons' sides and wings.

Valerys soared over the western towers of Aravell, and Calen felt pulses of the Spark below. Arcs of blue lightning streaked upwards from the towers, followed by thick spears launched with threads of Air.

The lightning and spears soared past Valerys, hurtling towards the Dragonguard. But the sense of elation that surged through Calen was short-lived as Hrothmundar, Seleraine, and Eríthan spun and twisted in the air, then dropped and bathed the towers in dragonfire.

Calen's heart wrenched as he watched elves fall from the towers, consumed by flames.

More bolts of lightning streaked upwards from tower tops and cliff sides, more spears were hurled. But wherever lightning or spears rose, dragonfire fell and Aravell burned.

Through Valerys's eyes, Calen could see that further south, the Lorian and elven forces had crashed together outside the walls, fireballs and flashes of lightning streaking through the air.

Calen looked back at the three Dragonguard who were soaring towards them, pouring fire over the city as they went. He leaned against Valerys's neck, running his gauntleted hand across the dragon's scales. "We need to pull them away. We need to—"

An air-shaking roar cut Calen short. Valerys swerved in the air, craning his neck around to see a fourth dragon emerge above the Darkwood and soar over the city. A glint of purple caught in the pinkish light of the moon, and then the dragon dropped towards Seleraine, Eríthan, and Hrothmundar.

"Avandeer… Tivar." Every hair on Calen's body stood on end as he watched the purple dragon tear through the sky towards the others. "They'll die on their own."

Valerys cracked his wings against the air and surged back towards the other dragons. A rage swelled within Valerys, a burning, searing rage that consumed everything. Calen pushed his mind into Valerys's, willing his strength into the dragon. He closed his eyes, seeing through Valerys's. Each beat of their wings resonated through their body. Each beat of their heart thundered in their mind.

Ahead, Avandeer collided with Hrothmundar in a flurry of fire and talons. The two dragons careened into Seleraine, roars echoing through the valley. The silver-scaled Eríthan swooped towards the three dragons who were ripping each other to pieces. Threads of Fire, Air, and Spirit rippled around Eríthan and his Soulkin Ilkya.

"Solian ata'yar. Dauv ata'yar!" Calen roared, repeating the words he had spoken to Valerys earlier. "Nur temen vie'ryn valana!"

Live as one. Die as one. For those we've lost.

A tremor shook through Valerys and Calen as they smashed into Eríthan, jaws snapping, talons raking. Pure, white-hot rage blazed within them. Nothing existed outside of that moment. The two dragons tumbled through the air, spinning with such force Calen thought he would be ripped from Valerys's back. Pain seared in Calen's mind as a talon ripped through Valerys's right wing, another tearing into the muscle on his hind leg. Valerys bit into the larger dragon's forelimb, bones snapping beneath the force.

The two dragons came apart enough for Calen to see Avandeer and Tivar plummeting towards the city, blood streaking across the air in their wake. Coils of dread twisting in his chest as Hrothmundar and Seleraine soared towards him and Valerys, Eríthan roaring above them.

"I hope we gave them enough time." Calen clasped his arms around Valerys's neck as the dragon spread his wings and spiralled away from Eríthan, the energy draining from his bones. They wouldn't be able to keep it up for long. "Draleid n'aldryr, Valerys. Myia elwyn er unira diar."

Dragonbound by fire, Valerys. My heart is always yours.

ELLA PULLED HER ARM ACROSS her face as a fireball crashed into a tower behind her, shattered stone raining down into the courtyard before the walls. The ground shook as the debris fell, humans and elves crushed beneath.

Tanner and Yana had managed to get back inside the city, and Ella and Faenir fought beside Dann, Haem, Lyrin, Varlin, Lyrei, and Aneera, rebels and elves all around. Aeson and the others were spread out through the chaos.

A monstrous roar tore through the skies overhead, and Ella lifted her gaze to see Valerys soaring above, the three Dragonguard pouring fire over the towers and cliffs as they streaked after him. But as she looked, a fourth dragon, scales shimmering purple, appeared in the skies and crashed into the Dragonguard.

All around, elves, rebels, and Lorians stared towards the sky as the dragons tore at each other. Valerys joined the fray, and Ella's heart twisted. He was less than half the size of the others.

A hand brushed against Ella's, and she looked down to see Haem's fingers cupping hers, his green metal gauntlet gone. Her brother squeezed her hand as the dragons ripped each other to pieces, roaring and shrieking, flames pluming into the night.

Ella couldn't look away. Calen was going to die up there. After everything, after all they had gone through, she had only found him, and now she could do nothing but watch him die. When the purple dragon fell, her breath caught in her chest. Beside her, Faenir whimpered, rubbing his head against her shoulder. The fear that permeated the wolfpine's mind flooded into Ella, serving only to exacerbate her own. With each shriek and each plume of fire, her hands shook harder, and her jaw clenched tighter, a cold emptiness filling her chest. Then she remembered something and squeezed Haem's hand.

"I can help him."

"What?" Haem looked at her as though she were crazy.

"I don't have the time to explain. I need you to trust me."

Haem nodded, his expression shifting to a hard stare. "What do you need me to do?"

"Carry me somewhere safe." Ella looked up to where Valerys was streaking across the sky, the other three dragons soaring after him, one of them lagging behind. *Please, Calen. Keep going.* Faenir let out a rumble as he brushed against Ella's side. She looked at Haem, who was just staring back at her. "No matter what happens, trust me, Haem."

Haem nodded. Dann and the others moved around them, but their questions faded into the back of Ella's mind as she closed her eyes, a calm settling over her. As she felt Haem's arms wrap around her body, she tried to remember what she had done that night in the Lorian camp, how her mind had separated, how she Shifted with the owl.

The wolf howled in her blood, the sound echoing through her mind, growing louder and louder until all else capitulated, and then there was silence and darkness.

Ella opened her eyes to an endless sea of black. The armies, the dragons, and the city were gone. Just as before, she floated in the darkness. Her body was no longer flesh and bone, but shimmering white light. She knew it was not her true body; that was cradled in Haem's arms. When travelling, Ilyain told her that his Ayar Elwyn, Andras, called this place Níthianelle – the Sea of Spirits. It was a world between worlds.

Within moments, the darkness was illuminated by thousands of small spheres of glowing white light. The spheres glittered across the darkness around her, each radiating their own thoughts and emotions. Each sphere was the soul of an animal. The more she focused on a particular sphere, the more it took shape: birds, horses, deer, goats, and a wide variety of creatures she had never seen before. Ella pushed her ethereal body through the darkness of Níthianelle, drifting past sphere after sphere, searching. After what felt like an eternity, she found what she had been looking for: six enormous spheres of light, one larger than the other five. Now that she saw them, their presence dominated everything. Rage, loss, fear, sorrow. The myriad of emotions that radiated from the spheres pulled at Ella, scratching at her mind. As she drew closer, the spheres took shape, forms wrought from ethereal white light, massive wings, bodies covered in overlapping scales, jaws framed with horns as long as her arms – dragons.

These dragons were different to the two Ella had felt in the Lorian camp near Steeple. She didn't know how or why, but they were… empty. Like the others had, these dragons sensed her presence – she could feel it. But they didn't instil in her the same fear the others had. She pulled her mind closer to the largest of them, its eyes shifting like pools of molten steel.

The ethereal dragon, wrought in a white light, rose to its feet, its head tilting side to side as it felt the touch of Ella's mind. It knew what she was, but it didn't push her away.

A series of thunderous roars ripped through the sky above Ella's true body in the mortal plane, sending a shiver across her mind.

Ella couldn't deny the panic and fear that pounded in her veins. She remembered the pure terror that had wracked her when she'd Shifted with the owl and felt the unseen force crush her wings and ribs – when she'd felt herself die. But she didn't have time for fear. Calen needed her. As she made to push her mind towards the large dragon before her, she felt the others dragons moving closer, felt their pain and their fury. The sheer volume of agony that poured from them took Ella's breath away. Their minds were little more than empty caverns touched only by the aching torment of loss. She could feel the tears rolling down her cheeks as Haem held her true body in his arms, running.

She pushed everything to the back of her mind and reached out. *I'm coming, Calen.*

⸎

VALERYS SHRIEKED AS HROTHMUNDAR CLAMPED his jaws on Valerys's hind leg. Fury and pain burned through Calen like fire. He twisted to avoid an arc of lightning that ripped past him, then pushed threads of Earth into the scales on Valerys's leg, trying to stop them from shattering. Valerys kicked at Hrothmundar's face, talons slashing across the larger dragon's snout, blood spraying into the air.

Valerys spiralled as Hrothmundar released him, only for Seleraine to crash into his chest. The blue dragon snapped at Valerys's neck, talons sinking into his underbelly. The high pitched cry that left Valerys's throat ignited an anger in Calen so overwhelming it felt as though lightning flowed in his veins. He opened himself to the Spark, and the drain pulled at him, carving through him like a sharp steel; it felt as though his soul was being ripped from his body. Images of the Lorian mage's burning eyes flashed across his mind. Even still, he pulled on threads of Fire, Water, and Air and launched a spear of ice towards Seleraine's exposed belly.

Before the spear connected, Voranur, Seleraine's soulkin, snapped at it with a thread of Fire. At the same time, Seleraine kicked Valerys away.

Calen and Valerys hurtled through the air, wings laced with long gashes, blood streaming behind them. Calen's right hand was numb with pain from where one of the Dragonguard had sent a thin lance of stone straight through his gauntlet. They slammed into something hard, Valerys roaring in pain, rocks coming free.

Valerys fought through the pain and spread his wings, rocks cracking off his scales. Calen looked behind them to see the silver scales and black wings of Eríthan dropping towards them, and then a flash crossed Calen's vision, and Eríthan was gone.

Shrieks and roars echoed through the sky. Both Calen and Valerys looked around to see dragons careening past them. Scales of yellow, grey, blue, pink.

Calen shifted his gaze at the sound of a blood-chilling shriek. He looked down to see an enormous green dragon dashing Eríthan's sil-ver-scaled head off a cliff. *Ithrax.* Calen and Valerys watched as the blind dragon tossed Eríthan through the air. Ithrax roared, then caught the silver dragon in her jaws once more, ripping and tearing until the rain turned crimson.

"What's happening?"

Valerys swerved in the air, looking back to see the other four dragons tearing strips from Seleraine and Hrothmundar. It was the Rakina dragons from Aravell. The only one missing was Sardakes, the black-scaled dragon who had lost his flight.

As Calen watched, Hrothmundar clamped his jaws around the neck of the pink dragon, Thurial, and ripped his head clean from his body, dropping the pieces into the city below. At the same time, arcs of purple lightning streaked from Seleraine's back and seared holes through the chest of the grey dragon, Onymia.

Another monstrous roar echoed through the sky, and Ithrax soared towards Hrothmundar, crashing into the brown dragon's back, tearing and ripping. Aradanil, the large yellow dragon who had barely moved in the Eyrie, clamped his jaws around Hrothmundar's wing only to have his underbelly opened from the neck to tail by one of the larger dragon's talons.

A wave of agony consumed Valerys at the sight of the carnage. Four dragons had been torn from the world in a matter of minutes.

Valerys tore across the sky, rain crashing against his scales. But all he and Calen could do was watch in horror as Hrothmundar sank his talons into Ithrax's chest. Then, in one mighty pull, Hrothmander bit down and ripped Ithrax's lower jaw free, roaring triumphantly as he dashed the green dragon against the mountainside.

Rage consumed everything. Valerys pulled Calen's mind into his, their vision blending, their souls intertwining. The only sensations that touched Calen's mind were wrath and fury. An earth-shattering roar left Valerys's jaws as the dragon slammed into Hrothmundar with the speed of a shooting star. Valerys tore and ripped, his talons slicing, jaws cracking through scales. The larger dragon was weakened and injured. He didn't have time to understand what was happening before Valerys gouged his talons into Hrothmundar's belly and unleashed a torrent of raging dragonfire down over Jormun, who sat at the nape of the massive dragon's neck.

Lightning coursed through Calen's blood, the power of the bond surging within him. He felt no pain, no aches, no sorrow – only rage. He opened himself to the Spark, pulling in threads of Fire and Spirit. He weaved the threads into Valerys. The Spark pulled at his soul, but the bond held him in place. He pushed harder as the flames cascaded down over Jormun.

Hrothmundar's talons sliced through Valerys's side and leg, his jaws snapping at Valerys's throat. Calen could feel the panic and fear in the dragon, and for a moment a pang of sympathy twisted in his chest. But then he remembered Avandeer falling and Ithrax's bloody corpse slamming against the mountain.

Calen leaned into Valerys's rage, adding his own, feeding the bond with pure fury. The blood-curdling shriek that left Hrothmundar's jaws told Calen that Jormun had succumbed to Valerys's flames.

"Solian ata'yar. Dauv ata'yar," Calen whispered. *Live as one. Die as one.*

In response to Calen's words, Valerys took advantage of Hrothmundar's loss to clamp his jaws around the larger dragon's throat. Scales snapped and cracked, blood sliucing as Valerys bit down with every shred of strength left in his body. Even through the crashing wind and the hammering rain, Calen heard the sharp *snap* as the scales on Hrothmundar's neck gave way, and Valerys ripped out the dragon's throat.

Calen watched as the Hrothmundar's body fell, lifeless, to the city below, Jormun's blackened corpse dropping beside it.

All Calen's pain and aches returned, the rage dissipating from his and Valerys's mind. He turned his head to see the last remaining Dragonguard flying awkwardly over the canopy of dark green to the north – Seleraine. The dragon barely managed to stay in the air, her wings torn and bloody.

Only one of the Rakina dragons had survived: the blue-scaled dragon, Varthear. She descended back towards the Eyrie, blood drifting in the air behind her.

Every beat of Valerys's wings resulted in piercing pain. Tears had been raked through the membrane, and more than a few bones had been broken. The dragon's entire body was a tapestry of gashes, wounds, and broken scales. Simply staying in the air was not something that would be possible for too much longer. But as Valerys turned back towards city, towards the torches and glistening armour of the Lorian armies that flooded the land before Aravell, Calen knew there was still one more task for them.

"ELLA! ELLA!" WHEN ELLA'S BODY had gone still, Arden had carried her through the fighting and back into the city, finding a building to keep her safe. He knelt on the floor of the small room, holding Ella in his arms as she convulsed, screaming at the top of her lungs. He'd never heard anything like it. She shrieked and thrashed, tears streaming down her cheeks.

Beside her, Faenir nuzzled his snout into her chest, alternating between whimpering and howling.

Dann burst into the room, the cries of battle drifting in through the open door. "What's wrong?" He took one look at Arden and Ella and turned back, screaming. "We need a Healer! Lyrei, a Healer *now*!" He dropped to his knees beside Arden, cupping Ella's cheeks as she wept. "Haem, what happened?"

Arden shook his head, his heart pounding. "I don't know. She just started screaming."

Ella curled her knees to her chest, screaming and screaming until it sounded as though her throat might tear open.

Aneera, the Angan, sprinted into the room, her long fur-covered legs clearing the ground with enormous strides. She knelt beside Arden, her amber eyes gleaming. "Son of the Chainbreaker, are you harmed?"

Again, Arden shook his head, panic freezing his blood. "Ella, she just…" He looked at his little sister who curled up in his arms. *I'm so sorry, Ella. I'm sorry I haven't been there.*

Aneera leaned over Ella, her head tilting from side to side. Dann moved out of the way as the Angan pressed her hands against the sides of Ella's face. It was only then, as Aneera held Ella's head in place, that Arden's saw Ella's eyes were white from edge to edge, no pupils or irises. Tears still streamed down her cheeks, her body convulsing.

"What's happening to her?" Arden's voice trembled.

Aneera stared into Ella's eyes, then looked up at Arden. "Her mind is fragmented."

CALEN GRUNTED, LIFTING HIMSELF UPRIGHT on Valerys's back as the dragon soared towards the city gates. He held his right hand to his chest, trying his best to block out the pain. He'd wanted to cauterise the wound, but he'd feared doing lasting damage to his hand.

In the distance, the fires the Dragonguard had ripped through the Darkwood still raged, the light of the Blood Moon dripping over the forest canopy. Below, fires blazed in the city as the Lorian and elven armies battled before the walls. Through Valerys's eyes, he could sense the warmth of tens of thousands more Lorian soldiers stretching back into the woodland.

Even with the Dragonguard gone, the Lorian army, along with its Fades, could still burn Aravell to the ground. Both Calen and Valerys knew what they needed to do, but that didn't make it any easier.

'The path you are on will bring death beyond your wildest dreams. I say this not to steer you from it, but to steel you for it.'

Calen drew in a rasping breath, his chest aching and lungs burning, Rokka's words echoing in his mind. He knew now what the old druid had meant.

Valerys dropped, his wings aching. That familiar pressure built at the back of Calen's mind. He leaned forwards, stroking his hand down the scales of Valerys's neck. "We do what we must to protect the ones we love."

He looked down at the Lorian soldiers who had now seen Valerys diving towards them and were screaming at the tops of their lungs. "May Heraya embrace you all."

Valerys kicked back his head and unleashed a raging river of dragonfire down over the Lorian forces.

CHAPTER EIGHTY-FIVE

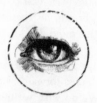

THE PATH

Mountains overlooking Aravell – Winter, Year 3081 After Doom

Rokka ran his fingers over the coarse, wet silver scales that covered the mutilated head of the dragon before him. The creature's body had been ripped to shreds and scattered across the mountain. He'd found the Draleid, dead, over two hundred feet away. The Aldruid, Calen Bryer's sister, as fate would have it, was powerful – one of the most powerful Aldruids Rokka had seen in a very long time – but she had overextended herself. Still, this was the right path.

Rokka rose to his feet, looking out over the city of Aravell from the cliff where he stood. The rain was lighter now, only drizzling. Fires still burned in the forest beyond, but most of those within the city had been quelled.

All the pieces were falling into place. Two more Dragonguard were dead. Only six remained now, though one dwelled in Karvos and another in Ardan. He would have them seen to shortly. There was no reason to leave loose ends untied.

He took a deep breath, filling his lungs with the cool, crisp air.

"There is still much left to do," he whispered, his voice swallowed by the wind. Then he turned and walked back into the woods.

Chapter Eighty-Six

The Exile and The Huntress

One hundred miles east of Lostwren – Winter, Year 3081 After Doom

Candles flickered in the tent as Dayne stood at the edge of the table, flipping the round-backed knife Therin had given him across his fingers.

Alina and Tula Vakira were arguing, as they had done many nights since the betrayal near Achyron's Keep. They'd had seven battles since then, six victories, one loss. Not a bad record, all in all, but the taste from that night still lingered.

Almost a third of the Koraklon warriors who had declared for Alina had turned back to Loren. Aldon Thebal had also defected, taking the vast majority of House Thebal with him. Not a week had passed since Achyron's Keep before the news had spread that 'High Lord' Loren had declared House Baleer as a new Major House, promising them Redstone and all House Ateres lands once the rebellion was crushed. Turik Baleer's son, Rogal, was named as head of the House. Nearly a fifth of the Wyndarii had turned as well, but Alina had seen to it that few of them had seen the light of the next sun.

"Tula is right," Dayne said finally, glancing at Alina, who looked far from impressed. "Skyfell is secure, as is Lostwren. Vhin Herak's sister, Hakari supports you from Ironcreek, but her position is weak. We need to block the pass by sea and stop Lorian ships sailing into the harbour. Miron's army marches along this path." Dayne traced his finger along the rough drawn map pinned to the table. "We must have patience. If we wait and meet Miron's force's here," Dayne rested his finger fifty or so miles northwest of the Rolling Mountains, "where the Lost Hills are at their highest, we will catch them when they're exhausted. We need to be careful, my Queen."

Silence passed through the tent as all eyes moved from Alina to Dayne. Some of Dayne's Andurii captains stood around the tent, along with

Mera, Lukira, Amari, Anda Deringal, Olivian of House Arnon – who had been elevated to the newly formed Royal Guard – and the new High Commander, Joros of House Myr. Alina had offered the position to Dayne, but he had declined in favour of someone who understood the logistics of armies better than he. Joros had served in the Redstone guard for many years, and he was a trustworthy man, something that was more important than almost anything else at that particular time.

After a few moments, the tension drained from the room as Alina nodded. "All right. We will do as you say, brother. Joros, our supply lines from Ironcreek to Skyfell, what's our most recent update?"

Dayne faded out as talk of logistics and supply lines began. He'd never had a head for those things, and he'd had even less of an inclination. Instead, Dayne's mind drifted to Marlin's lifeless eyes as the man lay in the dirt, Hera Malik's javelin jutting from his stomach. Hera's brother, Rexin, numbered among Dayne's Andurii. Dann hadn't enjoyed questioning the man, but he'd been satisfied with Rexin's answers. Saying that, he'd still had Ileeri set someone to watch him.

As Dayne was thinking, Iloen marched into the tent. Dayne had selected Iloan as Marlin's replacement among the Andurii captains. Iloen was young and relatively untested, but there were few Dayne trusted more. Iloen would die for Dayne. Of that, he was certain. Dayne raised an eyebrow in question.

"There's a woman asking for you by name, Andurios."

"A woman?"

"She said to tell you she's come to see her exile."

Before Dayne could answer, Belina walked into the tent behind Iloen with two guards chasing her.

Her hair was longer than when they'd last seen each other, braided as it once was. The woman opened her arms wide, a broad smile touching her lips. "Dayne Ateres, as I live and breathe."

Dayne cleared the distance between him and Belina in a heartbeat, sweeping her into his arms and squeezing tight.

"Down boy, down." Belina slapped at his shoulder, her voice taking on a mock tone. "Sit, stay."

Dayne laughed as he lowered her to the ground.

"Good boy." Belina's smile widened, and she cupped his cheeks. "You look like a sack of shit."

"It's good to see you too, Belina."

"I know it is. I'm fantastic. I would have been here sooner, but traipsing across a continent with a train of refugees takes time. And wait until you meet Dahlen Virandr. You two are like peas in a pod. Anyway, I'm here now. You can thank me for me coming later, preferably over a drink and some hot food." She narrowed her eyes as she scanned the room, her gaze stopping on Alina, Mera, Lukira, and Amari. "And I wouldn't be upset if you brought some of these fine warriors with you. If you'd told me these were the kinds of women Valtara produced, I would've left the refugees in a ditch." Belina raised an eyebrow as Alina and her Wyndarii approached.

"Dayne?" Alina's voice was full of curiosity.

"Alina, this is Belina Louna. She is my closest friend. I trust her with my life and yours." Dayne turned to Belina. "Belina, this is my sister, Alina Ateres, First of the Wyndarii, Queen of Valtara."

The two women stared at each other for a moment. Then Belina laughed. "Those are some impressive titles, my Queen." She gave a bow that, surprisingly, didn't seem mocking at all. "Dayne has told me much about you. You and whoever 'Mera' is, are the only things he loves more than complaining. There's only one problem."

"And that is?" Alina raised an eyebrow, still studying Belina.

"It wasn't until right now I realised how irritatingly similar our names are. Belina and Alina is going to be quite confusing. How about I call you Lini?"

Alina's expression didn't change, she simply continued to stare at Belina. "Ali?"

"If my name is too much trouble you can simply call me 'my Queen'."

"Oh, believe you me." Belina gave a wry smile. "I would call you my queen every morning and every night." She nodded to Dayne. "I just don't think he'd appreciate it very much."

Belina strode over to the table, leaving Alina standing there with more than a touch of crimson her cheeks.

"Well, my exile," Belina said, looking down at the map, then turning back to Dayne. "I'm here now. Who are we killing?"

Dayne stared back, his voice cold. "All of them."

CHAPTER EIGHTY-SEVEN

TREMORS OF CHANGE

Durakdur, Dwarven Freehold – Winter, Year 3081 After Doom

Kira leaned back in her chair. Using her tongue, she picked at a shred of meat stuck between her teeth.

"We need to consider forcing open the Wind Tunnels to Volkur." Elenya sat opposite Kira, her fire-red hair falling loose over her shoulders, her stare unwavering.

The newly elected ruler of Azmar, King Lakar, sat to Kira's right. By all accounts, he seemed an honest dwarf, if in his later years. Both his beard and moustache were thick and grey, though neither held any gold rings, only copper and a splattering of silver. *Not much of a warrior.*

"I'm not so certain that is the wisest course of action, Elenya." Lakar plucked at a roasted potato with his fingers and tossed it into his mouth, dabbing his lips with a cloth. "The Freehold has seen a lot of uncertainty in these times. My people elected me to re-establish a period of stability and prosperity. Entering into more military action with another member kingdom of the Freehold would not fit into that remit."

"There will be no military action if we enter Volkur with enough strength, Lakar. With all due respect, it was your predecessor who played a fundamental part in the uncertainty and instability of this Freehold. We…" Elenya stopped, narrowing her gaze at the sound of footsteps outside the chamber.

Kira heard voices, then silence. She turned her head, though the high back of the chair stopped her from seeing the door. "Mirlak?"

Elenya shook her head, looking back to Lakar. "We cannot allow uncertainty within the Freehold. The Volkur Wind Tunnels have been closed for too long. We must establish control within our borders."

"Are you suggesting we absorb Volkur into our kingdoms? That is a dangerous path, Elenya."

"It is the right path," Elenya insisted. "As you said, the Freehold needs certainty. Volkur represents the exact opposite. With Volkur's resources and people spread between our kingdoms and Belduar established at our gates, we will once again be secure."

Kira drew in a long breath, moving her gaze from Elenya to Lakar. She was not yet sure on which side she fell. Both spoke sense, but Kira was so tired of blood and death. Behind her, the steel doors creaked open. "Mirlak, is all well?"

No answer came, but footsteps tapped against stone.

Kira shifted in her seat, turning her head so she could see dwarves approaching in her periphery. "Mirlak?"

Elenya gasped and leapt to her feet, only for something to slam her back down with a *crack*.

"Mirlak is a little indisposed," a voice said.

Something soared past Kira's face and dropped down on the table, rolling across the stone until it hit a bowl of warm meat. Kira's jaw clenched, and she grabbed a knife from the table at the sight of Mirlak's severed head, blood dripping from his neck. She made to leap from her chair, but panic set in when her body didn't respond. It was as though invisible ropes were holding her to the chair. A glance around the table told her the same was true of both Lakar and Elenya as well.

Kira struggled against her invisible bonds as a dwarf walked around the table, a horned helmet obscuring his face, a black and yellow cloak knotted at the shoulders of sharp-cut armour. He held a heavy double-bladed axe over his shoulder. "I'm truly sorry it has to be this way," the dwarf said, his voice familiar. He nodded to a figure that now stood on the opposite side of the table. A human. *A mage.*

Kira's invisible bonds pulled tighter. The dwarf scratched at his ring-laden beard with his left hand as he walked to stand beside Lakar, then lifted his helmet and rested it on the table.

"Hoffnar?" Kira could do nothing to hide the shock in her voice as she looked at the stern, angular face of King Hoffnar of Volkur. "We thought you were dead."

"Yes," Hofnarr said, tapping his finger on the top of the helmet. More footsteps sounded behind Kira, and armoured dwarves bearing the black and yellow cloaks of Volkur lined the chamber. "That was part of it. It's easier to move around when you're dead." He let out a sigh and walked towards Elenya. "Our people have spent too long hiding beneath this mountain," he said, his dark eyes studying Kira. "Now is our time, Kira. Everything is in chaos. The empire is scrambling, the humans in the South are in open rebellion, the elves and Uraks are killing everything they can find. Now is the time for a strong dwarven hand."

Hoffnar gripped the shaft of the double-bladed axe with both hands, and before Kira could even think, the dwarf swung. Elenya's scream lasted only a fraction of a second before the thick steel hit her just below the nose and split her face. Teeth snapped and bones cracked, blood pouring in freefall. Hoffnar grunted as he heaved the axe free, the top half of Elenya's head sliding onto the floor.

Kira wanted to scream, but her voice held in her throat, trapped by shock as Elenya's body slumped forwards, her mutilated head *thumping* off the table, blood pouring over the stone.

"I'm not going to waste my time telling you the particulars," Hoffnar said as though nothing had happened. "Pulroan *did* instigate the civil war. She wanted Elenya and me dead while having Daymon indebted to you both. From what I know, she actually wanted to raise you, Kira, as the sole queen of the Freehold. I've got to admire her ambition. But needless to say, I didn't agree with her plan, and it's unsurprising how quickly assassins are willing to change allegiances when you pay them more gold." Hoffnar looked at Lakar, who stared back at him in terror. "Apologies, new king."

"No, please, you don't—"

Hoffnar's axe cleaved through Lakar's neck, blood spurting as the king's head rolled to the ground. Hoffnar lay the bloody axe on the table, then walked towards Kira. "I didn't want it this way. It was Pulroan who tried to have me killed. I'm just seizing opportunity." He shook his head. "Don't worry, Kira. I'm not going to kill you. Not yet. If I killed you now, too many would question me. No, I exercised great control in not killing you when I came here to inform you of my survival only to find you had slaughtered Elenya, Lakar, and all their guards. You were thirsty for blood and desired the Freehold for yourself. I kept you alive so the people could see the traitor you truly were." Hoffnar leaned close enough for Kira to feel the warmth of his breath on her face. "And while you are left starving and dying slowly in a cell below the keep of Volkur, I will bind our people and lead them from this mountain. I will crush your little Belduaran pets, and I will give the dwarves of Lodhar the future they deserve."

CHAPTER EIGHTY-EIGHT

THE BOUND AND THE BROKEN

Aravell – Winter, Year 3081 After Doom

Calen knelt by Ella's bed, his fingers wrapped in hers. She had stopped convulsing, but her eyes were still clouded from edge to edge. She lay there, still. Aneera had said it was Ella who had stirred the Rakina dragons, she who had saved Calen's life, and Valerys's, and likely all those in Aravell. *And this is her reward.*

He rested his hand on top of hers, brushing his thumb across her knuckles. A low whimper sounded from the end of the bed. Calen leaned over, scratching the crown of Faenir's head. "She'll be all right, boy."

The wolfpine barely fit in the bed but had managed to curl himself in such a way that only his tail fell off the end. He whimpered again, lifting his head and tilting it into Calen's palm. He touched his wet nose against the side of Calen's hand, then licked Calen's knuckles and rested his chin on Ella's feet.

The door creaked open behind Calen, footsteps clicking against stone. Calen turned his head to see the woman, Yana. "How is she?"

"The same."

Yana drew in a short breath then knelt beside Ella's bed. The woman ran her hand through Ella's hair so tenderly that had Calen not known any better he would have thought Ella her child. "She is made of stronger things than the rest of us." There was no hint of a question in Yana's words. It was a statement of fact, nothing more. She looked up at Calen, sympathy in her eyes. "You can go. I will watch over her a while."

Calen shook his head. Tears burned at the corners of his eyes. "I've been gone too long already."

Yana gave Calen a weak smile, then looked back to Ella, resting her palm on Ella's forehead. "She loves you more than anything in the world. Do you know that? Finding you is all she ever spoke about. She would have carved a path through the Burnt Lands itself just to get to you. And no matter what happens to her now, I know she would make the same decision again without even a moment's doubt." Yana turned back to Calen. "Go, eat, sleep. I will watch her."

CALEN HAD TRIED TO ARGUE with Yana, but he'd soon realised it was an exercise in futility. Even still, after thanking her for watching over Ella, he didn't feel like sleeping. Every time he had tried to close his eyes since the battle, all he had seen was death, and blood, and fire. And so that is how he found himself in the Eyrie, resting against Valerys's scales, gazing up towards the dark sky that was still tinged with a crimson hue.

Less than a day had passed since the battle. King Silmiryn had been slain during the fighting, but King Galdra and Queen Uthrían had sent every Healer under their banners to aid in the mending of Valerys's wounds – along with those of the injured Varthear. But the wounds the Dragonguard had inflicted were deep and would take longer to mend even with the help of Healers.

Calen let his mind drift with Valerys's, pushing his warmth into the dragon. A rumble resonated through Valerys's chest in response. They sat in silence until a voice called out, "Calen."

Calen waited a moment, then heaved himself to his feet, using Valerys as leverage. He looked behind the dragon to see Aeson along with all the Rakina in Aravell, those who had agreed to train him along with those who had refused. "What's wrong?"

Chora wheeled herself forwards, a half-smile on her face. "Nothing is wrong. How is your sister?"

"No change." Calen looked across the other Rakina, trying to gauge their expressions.

"Your brother?"

"He had to leave with the other knights." Calen didn't mean to be so short, but he couldn't help the anger that rose within him. "They took heavy losses. He'll be back in a few days, I think. What is this, Chora? You didn't come to ask about my family. Why is everyone here?"

"No." Atara stepped forwards, her gaze fixed on Calen, her long hair tucked behind her tapered ears. She had aided in the fighting and now bore a new scar across her chin. "I came..." She looked back at the other Rakina, glancing towards Aeson, Thacia, and Chora before settling on the others. "*We* came to say that we were wrong."

"Wrong about what?" Calen took a step forward.

"We were wrong for turning our backs on you." Atara extended her arm, holding it in front of Calen.

Calen hesitated for a moment, then grasped Atara's forearm, looking into her eyes.

"For hundreds of years we have hidden here. We have hidden from the world and hidden from our duty. Fane Mortem and the empire ripped us apart. They tore our soulkin from us, and they burned everything we loved. What you said in the forest, 'We're meant to be guardians', you were right. Whether we are Draleid or Rakina, we're meant to be guardians. Not survivors, guardians. That is our purpose. That is the reason for our existence. And in our loss, we forgot that. Even in the times long gone, you would have been a Draleid I would have been proud to fly beside. Skill in the sword and the Spark can be earned, but what you have, that fire in your heart, that unwillingness to stop. That is one of the rarest qualities a soul can possess. And so I ask, Calen Bryer, will you let us stand by your side in the war to come? Will you let us be guardians again? Because it is time for The Bound and The Broken to stand together once more."

Ryan Cahill

EPILOGUE

Dead Rock's Hold – Winter, Year 3081 After Doom

Salara Ithan looked down at the man garbed in crimson robes, white circles marked on each breast with a black trim around the edges. His hair was black, greying around his temples, and his face was marred by the passage of time. He knelt in the dust and dirt, his gaze fixed on the dead bodies that lay behind Queen Vandrien.

"You are the one they call the Divine, yes?" The queen stood over the man, blood streaked through her long, loose hair. Her golden armour scintillated in the bleeding light of Efialtír's moon.

The human looked up at her, dazed. He nodded.

"You have a name, I assume?"

He nodded again, his stare moving back to the dead bodies before looking at Vandrien. "Rad… Radavan Ha… Harten," he stuttered. "I am not a man of war. Please, spare me. I know of elves and their honour. I ask you now to spare my life."

Queen Vandrien smiled at that. "You are not a man of war? You are a priest of Efialtír, are you not? The Traitor, the Great Deceiver, the Devourer of Souls. Efialtír is the herald of war, he is the merchant of death." Vandrien walked to the nearest body and picked up the clumsy human blade that lay on the ground beside it. "You say you are not a man of war, Radavan Harten, Divine of Efialtír, but you are no stranger to torture, cruelty, death, and pain. It was in the name of your god that my people were slaughtered. In the name of your god that we were driven from our homes, our kin enslaved." She pointed the sword towards the mines erected around the hold. "Your priests oversaw these mines, did they not?"

"I…" The man's words caught in his throat as he looked from the mines to the corpses in the dirt. Hundreds of elves stood around them, some in the golden armour of Numillíon, others in rags, their faces covered in dirt, their bodies marred by sores and scabs.

"You took my people here. You treated them like rats. Forced them to work your mines until their bodies gave way. You may not be a warrior, but you are most certainly a man of war. Twisting your words won't change the truth. My ancestors should have rid the world of your kind when you first landed on these shores. They should have killed you to the last and set fire to your bloodlines. Humans are war incarnate. You are consumption. You are misery. You are death. I will do now what my ancestors should have done then, what my brother and those cowards refused to do all those years ago." She tossed the sword into the dirt before Radavan. "In the name of honour, I give you the same opportunity as I gave your companions. The right of Alvadrû. If you strike me down, you will be allowed to leave without harm."

The man hesitated for only a moment, looking back at the other priests' lifeless bodies, then snatched up the sword and leapt at Vandrien. Humans were always like that, always feigning weakness and innocence only to turn to savagery in the blink of an eye. Treachery and deceit was in their blood. They had no honour.

Radavan lunged towards Vandrien. The queen sidestepped and extended her foot, sending the man crashing to the ground in a heap, a cloud of dust rising around him.

Vandrien turned to Salara, inclining her head. "Narvír." *Commander.*

Salara bowed and handed Vandrien her axe. She watched as the human priest got to his feet behind the queen. Vandrien gripped her axe with both hands and spun. The blade sliced into Radavan's belly. The man dropped his sword and looked into Vandrien's eyes. She heaved the axe free, and Radavan fell to his knees, blood spilling out over the dirt.

"You have been given the honour of dying like a warrior," Vandrien said, looking down at Radavan. "An honour you did not give the elves who died in this mine." She looked up towards Efialtír's moon. "I hope your god is forgiving." Vandrien hefted her axe, then took the man's head from his shoulders.

She handed the axe back to Salara as Radavan's body collapsed, and his head rolled along the dirt. Salara wiped the blood from the axe blade and handed the weapon to the queen's attendant.

The queen turned to where her two sisters, Cala and Ervian, stood beside the druid, Boud. The woman was taller than both sisters, her dark hair tied in a number of plaits. The runes on the collar around her neck glowed with a vivid blue light.

"Rain, Boud. This place has not seen rain for a long time, and it would go some way towards washing away the blood." The queen raised an eyebrow at the woman who looked about the bodies of the dead. "Is there a problem? Do you object to us killing your kind?"

"They are not my kind," Boud said as she stared at the dead. "They hunted my kind just as they did yours." Boud tilted her head back and her eyes turned white as mist. Clouds formed overhead, dark and thick, glowing with the pinkish light of the moon. After a few moments, cool drops of rain tickled Salara's neck and hands, slowly turning to a downpour.

"We will wait for Efialtír's Moon to set." As Vandrien spoke, roars sounded overhead, and Salara watched as the dragons soared across the sky. She could feel Vyrmír's heart beating. "Then we will take back what is ours."

**The End
of the Third Book of
The Bound and The Broken**

ACKNOWLEDGMENTS

A lot of people will tell you they've put blood, sweat, and tears into something – except for chefs, because that would just be unhygienic. Though, now that I think about it I don't see any place that blood, sweat, and tears isn't an unhygienic mixture. Sorry, I got a little side-tracked. What I wanted to say was a lot of people might say it, but I mean it. It's been so hot here in Middle Earth that I've been sweating almost every day while writing this book, I have most definitely cried a little during some of the emotion scenes, and I cut my hand on a piece of paper (I'm counting it).

All this is to say that a little piece of my heart is in this book. Writing *Of War and Ruin* was one of the most challenging experiences of my entire life, and I would never have been able to write it without the support of this around me.

Amy. If I didn't mention you, you'd likely kill me in my sleep. You truly are the kindest soul on this earth. Myia nithír til diar, I denír viël ar altinua. *My soul to yours, in this life and always.*

Séamus. My best friend. Without our constant phone calls about my numerous writing blocks, I'm not sure where I'd be. Often you don't even have to say much, but you just listening to me blather on means more than you know.

My parents. I know I'm about 11,000 miles away now (18,000km) but I'm still right there beside you just as you've always been beside me. Never stop asking all those annoying questions.

My brother, Aron. Shithead. What more can I say? A lot more, in fact, but this book is big enough already. I'll always look out for you, even when you don't want me to.

Sarah, my editor. Well, shit. This was a labour of love from us both. Thank you to the ends of the earth for pushing this book over the line. You are a champion.

Taya, my proofreader. You are a machine. You are the Terminator. You are the Tayanator. Thank you for cleaning up my mess.

My Beta readers: Jann, Viv, Brent, Colin, Carrie, Alicia, Kristin, Dorothy, Claudia, Jonica, Kate, Corey, Will, Adam, Sannie, Blaise, John, Gina, and Brian. This was a beast. Thank you for slogging through the different parts of this Beta read, and for pushing through til they end. I will be forever grateful.

My Advance Readers: Kristin, Brian, Viv, Rachael, Nathaniel, Dorothy, Arundeepak, Chuck, Michael, Nikki, Kate, Melissa, Steve, Sean, Linda, Rashmi, Andy, Alicia, Spencer, Ant, Omar, Graham, Debbie, Jann, Craig, Izzy, Vignesh, Mike, Max, Timothy, Alisha, Marc, Pat, Tom, Joe, David, Charla, Eddie, Terry, Nick, Dylan, Aaron, Joe, Donna, Taylor, Jonathon, Jamie, Wendy, Tianna, Adam, Ethan, Elli, Esmay, Dale, Alex, Sandra, Lisa, Ariana, Susan, June, Melissa, Alicia, and Dom. Well, I didn't give you a lot of time to get this one read, did I? Nevertheless, you smashed through it. Your unwavering support means the world. By blade and by blood.

To every single one of you readers out there, thank you. Your generosity in the time that you donate to my books is truly inspiring. Thank you for joining me on this journey, for passionately shouting at the top of your lungs, and for allowing me to spend my days weaving my imagination into reality.

This is one more step, but it's a long path.

GLOSSARY

The Seasons

The beginning of a new year in Epheria is marked by the passing of the Winter Solstice. There are five seasons that divide the year: earlywinter, spring, summer, autumn, winter.

The Glade

Calen Bryer (Kay-lin BRY-ER): Son of Vars and Freis, brother of Ella and Haem. Villager of The Glade. The first new Draleid free of the empire in four hundred years.

Haem Bryer (HAYM BRY-ER): Son of Vars and Freis, brother of Ella and Calen. Villager of The Glade. Thought to be killed while defending The Glade from Uraks in the year 3078 After Doom, but found to be alive after being granted the Sigil of Achyron and taking on the name 'Arden'.

Ella Bryer (EL-AH BRY-ER): Daughter of Vars and Freis, sister of Haem and Calen. Villager of The Glade. Currently fleeing from Berona.

Freis Bryer (Fr-EHY-s BRY-ER): Wife of Vars, mother of Calen, Haem, and Ella. Herbalist and healer of The Glade. Killed by Farda Kyrana.

Vars Bryer (VARS BRY-ER): Husband of Freis, father of Calen, Haem, and Ella. Blacksmith of The Glade. Killed by Inquisitor Rendall.

Faenir (FAY-near): A wolfpine who was raised by the Bryer family. Currently travelling with Ella Bryer.

Rhett Fjorn (Ret Fy-orn): Captain of The Glade's town guard. Lover of Ella. Killed on the merchant's road to Gisa. Erdhardt

Hammersmith (ERD-Heart Hammer-smith): Husband of Aela. Village elder of The Glade.

Aela Hammersmith (AY-LAH Hammer-smith): Wife of Erdhardt, jeweller of The Glade. Killed during the Urak attack on The Glade in the year 3080 After Doom.

Dann Pimm (Dan-Pim): Son of Tharn and Ylinda, close friend of Calen's. Currently searching for Calen.

Tharn Pimm (TH-ARN Pim): Husband of Ylinda, father of Dann. Fletcher of The Glade.

Ylinda Pimm (Yuh-Lin-Dah Pim): Wife of Tharn, mother of Dann. Weaver of The Glade.

Rist Havel (Ri-st Hah-vul): Son of Lasch and Ylinda, close friend of Calen's. Apprentice Battlemage in the Circle of Magii. Sponsored by Exarch Garramon.

Lasch Havel (Lash Hah-vul): Husband of Elia, father of Rist. Innkeeper of The Gilded Dragon.

Elia Havel (EH-lee-AH Hah-vul): Wife of Lash, mother of Rist. Beekeeper.

Verna Gritten (Ver-NAH GRIT-in): Mother of Anya. Village elder of The Glade. Killed during the Urak attack on The Glade in the year 3080 After Doom.

Anya Gritten (AHN-YA GRIT-in): Daughter of Verna, close friend of Calen's.

Fritz Netly (F-Ritz Net-lee): Childhood rival of Calen's. Betrays Ella's survival to Farda. Apprentice Inquisitor of the Circle of Magii.

Belina Louna (BELL-eena lauw-NAH): A bard, and also a former Hand Assassin, now working alongside Aeson and his rebellion. Close friend of Dayne Ateres.

Therin Eiltris (Theh-RIN EHL-treece): Renowned Bard who performs in The Glade. Former elven ambassador to The Order. Powerful mage.

Belduar

Arthur Bryne (Are-THUR BRINE): Father of Daymon. Murdered king of Belduar.

Daymon Bryne (DAY-MON BRINE): Son of Arthur, newly crowned king of Belduar.

Ihvon Arnell (EYE-VON ARE-nell): Close friend and advisor to Arthur. Betrayed Arthur and allowed the Fade and the empire into Belduar. Advisor to the new king, Daymon.

Oleg Marylin (OH-leg Mar-IH-lin): Belduaran emissary to the Dwarven Freehold.

Conal Braker (CUN-UL BRAH-ker): Young porter in Belduar.

Lumeera Arian (Loo-MEER-AH ARE-EE-an): Belduaran Kingsguard.

Dwarven Freehold

Kira (KEE-RAH): Queen of Durakdur.

Pulroan (PULL-ROW-AN): Queen of Azmar.

Elenya (EL-EN-YA): Queen of Ozryn.

Hoffnar (Hoff-NAR): King of Volkur.

Falmin Tain (FAHL-min TAIN): Member of the Wind Runners Guild, navigator of the Crested Wave.

Nimara (Nih-MAR-AH): Dwarven warrior from Durakdur who aided in the search for Calen and Erik.

Mirlak (Mihr-LAK): Commander of the Durakduran Queensguard.

Almer (Al-MER): Dwarven warrior who fought beside Dahlen in the battle of Belduar.

Yoring (Yor-ING): Dwarven warrior who fought beside Dahlen in the battle of Belduar. Took an arrow to the knee.

Valtara

Dayne Ateres (DAIN AH-Teer-eece): Son of Arkin and Ilya Ateres, brother of Alina, Baren, and Owain. Heir to House Ateres. Exiled from Valtara in the year 3068 After Doom.

Alina Ateres (AH-leen-AH AH-teer-eece): Daughter of Arkin and Ilya Ateres, sister of Dayne, Baren, and Owain. Wyvern rider of Valtara. Wing-Sister of Lukira, Mera, and Amari. Rider of Rynvar. Leader of the Valtaran rebellion.

Baren Ateres (BAH-REN Ah-teer-eece): Son of Arkin and Ilya Ateres, brother of Alina, Dayne, and Owain. Whereabouts currently unknown after Dayne released him following the retaking of Skyfell.

Owain Ateres (OH-AY-in Ah-teer-eece): Son of Arkin and Ilya Ateres, brother of Alina, Dayne, and Baren. Given over to the empire as a child.

Mera (MEH-RAH): Aligned with House Ateres. Wyvern Rider of Valtara. Wing-Sister of Alina, Lukira, and Amari. Rider of Audin. Close friend of Alina, past lover of Dayne.

Marlin Arkon (Mar-lin ARE-kon): Steward of House Ateres.

Loren (Loh-REN): High Lord of Valtara.

Rinda (RIN-dah): Consul of the Lorian Empire. Stationed in Valtara.

Amari (AH-mar-EEE): Wing-Sister of Alina, Mera, and Lukira. Wyvern Rider of Valtara. Rider of Syndil

Lukira (Loo-keer-AH): Wing-Sister of Alina, Mera, and Amari. Wyvern rider of Valtara. Rider of Urin.

Tyr Arnen (Teer ARE-NEN): High Commander of the Valtaran armies.

Senya Deringal (SEN-YAH DER-in-GAHL): Head of House Deringal.

Vhin Herak (VHIN HER-AK): Head of House Herak.

Tula Vakira (TOO-lah VAH-keer-AH): Head of House Vakira

Miron Thebal (Meer-ON THEB-AL): Head of House Thebal.

Turik Baleer (TURE-IK BAH-leer): Head of the Minor House, Baleer.

Reinan Sarr (RAY-NAN SAR): Head of the Minor House, Sarr.

Hera Malik (heh-RAH MAH-lik): Head of the Minor House, Malik. Wyvern rider of Valtara. Rider of Yarsil.

Iloen Akaida (IH-low-EN AH-kay-DAH): Former porter in the Redstone kitchens. Son of Sora and Aren Akaida.

Sylvan Anura: Rakina. Former member of the Dragonguard.

The Lorian Empire

Farda Kyrana (Far-DAH Kie-RAH-nah): Justicar of the Lorian empire and Exarch of the Imperial Battlemages. Killed Freis Bryer. Currently travelling to Fort Harken with the Fourth Army.

Rendall (REN-DULL): Imperial Inquisitor. Killed Vars Bryer. Captured a one-handed elf after the Battle of Belduar.

Andelar Touran (AN-DEH-LAR TOO-RAN): Primarch of the Imperial Battlemages

Fane Mortem (FAIN MORE-tem): Emperor of Loria.

Karsen Craine (CAR-sin CRAYNE): Grand Consul of the Circle of Magii.

Garramon (GAR-ah-MON): Exarch of the Imperial Battlemages, sponsor of Rist Havel.

Andelar Touran (AN-deh-LAR Too-RAN): Primarch of the Imperial Battlemages.

Neera (Neer-AH): Apprentice to Sister Ardal.

Tommin (TOM-in): Apprentice to Sister Danwar.

Lena (Leh-NAH): Apprentice to brother Halmak.

Magnus Offa (Mag-NUS OFF-ah): Exarch of the Imperial Battlemages. Mage Commander of the First Army.

Anila (AH-NIL-AH): Exarch of the Imperial Battlemages. Instructing Rist and Neera in swordsmanship.

Taya Tambrel (TAY-AH Tam-BRELL): Supreme Commander of the Lorian Armies.

Ayura Talvare (AY-OO-rah TAL-VARE): Commander of the Fourth Army.

Guthrin Vandimire (Gooth-RIN VAN-DIH-mire): General to Ayura Talvare.

Northern Rebellion

Tanner Fjorn (TAH-ner FY-orn): Uncle to Rhett. High Captain of the Beronan city guard.

Yana (Yah-NAH): Member of the northern rebellion.

Farwen (FAR-win): Member of the northern rebellion. Rakina.

Coren Valmar (CORE-in Val-MAR): Leader of the northern rebellion. Rakina, formerly bound to Aldryn.

Juro (JURE-OH): Head of the scouts in Tarhelm.

Varik (VAH-RIK): Member of the northern rebellion.

Surin (SURE-IN): Member of the northern rebellion. Craftsmage.

Ingvat (ING-VAT): Member of the northern rebellion.

Elves of the Aravell

Thalanil (Tha-lah-nil): High Captain of the Aravell Rangers

Faelen (FAY-lin): Elven Ranger.

Gaeleron (GAY-ler-on): Elven Ranger. Presumed dead after the Battle of Belduar.

Alea (AH-lee-ah): Elven Ranger.

Lyrei (Lie-REE): Elven Ranger.

Ellisar (EHL-is-ARE): Elven Ranger. Killed by the Fade in the first Battle of Belduar.

Vaeril (VAY-ril): Elven Ranger. Close companion of Calen Bryer.

Thurivîr (THOO-RIH-VARE): Lunithíran Ephorí of Aravell.
Ara (AH-RAH): Lunithíran Ephorí of Aravell.

Dumelian (DOO-MEL-ee-AN): Vaelen Ephorí of Vaelen.

Ithilin (ITH-il-in): Vaelen Ephorí of Vaelen.

Baralas (BAR-AH-LAS): Ardurän Ephorí of Aravell.

Liritháin (LIR-ITH-ain): Ardurän Ephorí of Aravell.

Galdra Lunithír (GAL-DRA Loo-nith-ear): King of the Lunithíran elves in Aravell.

Uthrían Ardurän (OOTH-REE-an ARE-DUR-an): Queen of the Ardurän elves in Aravell.

Silmiryn Vaelen (SIL-MIR-IN VAY-LIN): King of the Vaelen elves in Aravell.

The Enkaran Gods

Achyron (Ack-er-on): The warrior God, or simply The Warrior. The protector against the shadow.

Elyara (El-eee-ARE-AH): The Maiden. The wisest of all the gods, creator of consciousness and free thought.

Varyn (Var-in): The Father. The protector of all things and the provider of the sun.

Heraya (HER-eye-AH): The Mother. The giver of life and receiver of the dead.

Hafaesir (Hah-FYE-SEER): The Smith. The Patron god of the dwarves. Builder of the world.

Neron (NEH-ron): The Sailor. Creator of the seas and provider of safe travel.

Efialtír (Ef-EE-ahl-TIER): The Traitor God. Efialtír betrayed the other six gods at the dawn of creation. He turned his back on their ways, claiming his power through offerings of blood.

The Druidic Gods

Fenryr (Fen-reer): The wolf god.

Kaygan (KAY-GAN): The kat god.

Bjorna (BEE-OR-NAH): The bear god.

Vethnir (Veth-NEER): The hawk god.

Dvalin (DVAH-LIN): The stag god.

The Knights of Achyron

Grandmaster Verathin (Ver-AH-thin): Grandmaster of the knights of Achyron. Leader of The First. Survivor of The Fall. Killed in the Battle of Kingspass.

Brother-Captain Kallinvar (KAL-IN-var): Captain of The Second. Survivor of The Fall.

Arden (AR-DIN): Knight of The Second.

Ildris (ILL-dris): Knight of The Second. Survivor of The Fall.

Ruon (REW-ON): Knight of The Second. Survivor of The Fall.

Tarron (TAR-ON): Knight of The Second. Survivor of The Fall.

Sylven (SILL-VEN): Knight of The Second.

Mirken (MUR-KIN): Knight of The Second.

Daynin (DAY-NIN): Knight of The Second.

Varlin (VAR-LIN): Knight of The Second.

Lyrin (LIH-RIN): Knight of The Second.

Sister-Captain Olyria (OH-LEER-ee-AH): Captain of The Third. Survivor of The Fall.

Sister-Captain Valeian (VAL-AY-IN): Captain of The Fourth.

Brother-Captain Darmerian (DAR-MEHR-ee-an): Captain of The Fifth.

Brother-Captain Armites (AR-MIH-teece): Captain of The Sixth. Survivor of The Fall.

Brother-Captain Illarin (ILL-are-IN): Captain of The Seventh. Survivor of The Fall.

Brother-Captain Rivick (RIV-ICK): Captain of The Eight.

Sister-Captain Airdaine (AIR-DAINE): Captain of The Ninth.

Sister-Captain Emalia (EM-AH-lee-AH): Captain of The Tenth. Survivor of The Fall.

Watcher Gildrick (GIL-DRICK): Watcher of the Knights of Achyron.

The Dragonguard

Eltoar Daethana (EL-TWAR Die-THA-NAH): Commander of the Dragonguard. Bonded to Helios. Wing commander of Lyina and Pellenor.

Lyina (Lie-eee-NAH): Member of the Dragonguard. Bonded to Karakes. Eltoar's left wing.

Pellenor (Pel-EH-NOR): Member of the Dragonguard. Bonded to Meranth. Eltoar's right wing.

Jormun (JOR-mun): Member of the Dragonguard. Bonded to Hrothmundar.

Ilkya (IL-kee-AH): Member of the Dragonguard. Bonded to Eríthan.

Voranur (VOR-ah-noor): Member of the Dragonguard. Bonded to Seleraine.

Erdin (ER-DIN): Member of the Dragonguard.

Luka (Loo-KAH): Member of the Dragonguard.

Tivar (Tee-VAR): Member of the Dragonguard. Bonded to Avandeer.

Aeson's Rebellion

Aeson Virandr (Ay-son VIR-an-DUR): Former Draleid whose dragon, Lyara, was slain. Rakina. Father of Dahlen and Erik. Key member of the rebellion.

Dahlen Virandr (DAH-lin VIR-an-DUR): Son of Aeson, brother of Erik.

Erik Virandr (AIR-ICK VIR-an-DUR): Son of Aeson, brother of Dahlen.

Asius (AY-see-US): Jotnar, close friends with Aeson, companion of Larion and Senas.

Larion (LAR-eee-ON): Jotnar, companion of Asius and Senas.

Senas (See-NAS): Jotnar, companion of Asius and Larion.

Baldon (BAL-DON): Angan of the clan Fenryr, shapeshifter.

Aneera (AH-Neer-AH): Angan of the clan Fenryr, shapeshifter.

Arem (AH-REM): Aeson's contact in Argona who directs all correspondence.

Drifaien

Lothal Helmund (Low-THAL HELL-mund): High Lord of Drifaien.

Orlana Helmund (Or-LAH-NAH HELL-mund): Wife of Lothal.

Artim Valdock (ARE-TIM Val-DOCK): Exarch of the imperial battlemages sent to Drifaien in search of the Draleid.

Alleron (Al-ER-ON): Warrior of Drifaien. Met Calen, Dann, and Erik in The Two Barges.

Baird (BARE-D): Warrior of Drifaien. Met Calen, Dann, and Erik in The Two Barges.

Creatures

N'aka (UHN-Ah-KA): Six-limbed creatures with scythe-like talons and blackish-grey hides. Their general body shapes are not dissimilar to that of a kat's, though they are larger.

Virtuk (VIR-TUK): Dwarven war mounts with white hide of leathery skin and hard carapace-covered beaks. Articulated sections of grey, armour-like carapace grows from their skin, covering their backs, sides, and shoulders, along with a section that formed around their heads and necks like helms. Since The Fall, the virtuks have been transitioned into beasts of burden to keep their numbers viable in the time of peace.

Aldithmar (al-DITH-MAR): Ancient spirits.

Places

Epheria (EH-fear-EE-ah): The continent of Epheria is one of the largest continents in the known world.

Karvos (CAR-VOHS): One of the five main continents in the known world. Home to the Karvosi. Karvos is a continent mostly consumed by rainforest. A number of wars have been fought been the Epherians and the Karvosi across the ages.

Ardan (ARE-DAN): One of the five main continents in the known world. Home to the Ardanians. The Ardanians are a powerful seafaring people.

Narvona (NAR-VOH-NAH): One of the five main continents in the known world. Home to the Narvonans. Narvona's climate is far hotter than Epheria's, and it is home to many mineral deposits and precious stones. Due to the wealth provided by these natural resources, the Narvonans are a wealthy and powerful people. There has been conflict between Epheria and Narvona but for the most part the relations between the two continents have been amicable. Due to this amicable relationship, it is not uncommon to see Narvonans who have made their home in Epheria.

Valacia (VAH-lay-see-AH): Meaning Icelands in the Old Tongue. One of the five main continents in the known world. A mostly unexplored wasteland of ice and snow. The dragons of Valacia are widely considered to be things of legend.

Loria (Lor-EE-AH): The province of Loria dominates northern Epheria. It is in this province that the Lorian Empire hold their seat of power, in the capital city of Al'Nasla.

Illyanara (ILLY-ah-NAH-ra): One of the six provinces of southern Epheria, ruled over by High Lord Castor Kai.

Carvahon (Car-VAH-hon): One of the six provinces of southern Epheria, ruled over by High Lord Talia Kar.

Varsund (VAR-SUND): One of the six provinces of southern Epheria, ruled over by High Lord Korim Garrin.

Arkalen (ARE-KAY-LIN): One of the six provinces of southern Epheria, High Lord Syrene Linas.

Drifaien (Drif-AY-IN): One of the six provinces of southern Epheria, ruled over by High Lord Lothal Helmund.

Valtara (Val-TAHR-AH): One of the six provinces of southern Epheria, ruled over by High Lord Loren Koraklon.

Belduar (BELL-DOO-are): The last "free city of men" in Epheria. Belduar is the only city of men that is not under the dominion of the Lorian Empire, and instead has its own king – Arthur Bryne.

Ölm (Ohm): Ölm is a small village that is part of a collective of villages that sit at the base of Wolfpine Ridge. It shares its name with Ölm Forest. Both the village and the forest take their name from the ancient Jotnar city of Ölmur.

Durakdur (Duhr-ack-duhr): The dwarven kingdom of Durakdur is a member of the Dwarven Freehold. It is ruled over by Queen Kira.

Ozryn (Oz-RHIN): The dwarven kingdom of Ozryn is a member of the Dwarven Freehold. It is ruled over by Queen Elenya.

Volkur (Vol-KOOR): The dwarven kingdom of Volkur is a member of the Dwarven Freehold. It is ruled over by King Hoffnar.

Azmar (AZ-mar): The dwarven kingdom of Azmar is a member of the Dwarven Freehold. It is ruled over by Queen Pulroan.

Lynalion (LIN-ahl-EE-on): The woodland of Lynalion stretches for hundreds of miles in all directions. It sits at the base of Mar Dorul and is where a large portion of the elves retreated to after the fall of The Order.

Aravell (ARA-vell): Aravell is a hidden city that acts as the home to a faction of elves that have split from the elves of Lynalion.

The Old Tongue

The Old Tongue is a language passed down from the gods and creators known as the Enkara. Before the arrival of the humans to the continent in the year 306 After Doom, the Old Tongue was the prevalent language spoken amongst the Elves, and Jotnar. After the arrival of the humans, the Common tongue was developed from a blending of the languages spoken by dwarves and humans with the Old Tongue.

Here are a few common phrases that might be found throughout the books.

Draleid (Drah-laid): Dragonbound. Ancient warriors whose souls were bonded to the dragons that hatched for them.

Rakina (Rah-KEEN-ah): One who is broken, or in the elven dialect – 'one who survived'. When a dragon or their Draleid dies, the other earns the title of 'Rakina'.

Du gryr haydria til myia elwyn (DOO Greer HAY-dree-AH till MAYA EHL-win): You bring honour to my heart.

N'aldryr (Nahl-DREAR): By fire.

Valerys (Vah-lair-is): Ice.

Det være myia haydria (Deh-t VAY-air MAYA HAY-dree-AH): *It would be my honour.*

Du haryn myia vrai (Doo Hah-RIN MAYA VRAY): *You have my thanks.*

Myia elwyn er unira diar (**MAYA EHL-win AIR OO-neer-AH Dee-ARE**): *My heart is always yours.*

Din vrai é atuya sin'vala (DIN VRAY Eh AH-too-YAH Sin-VAH-LAH): *Your thanks are welcome here.*

Draleid n'aldryr, Rakina nai dauva (Drah-laid Nahl-DREAR, Rah-KEEN-ah Nay D-ow-VAH):*Dragonbound by fire, broken by death.*

Det er aldin na vëna du (Deh-t AIR Ahl-DIN Nah VAY-na DOO): *It is good to see you.*

Myia nithír til diar (MAYA NIH-theer TILL Dee-ARE): *My soul to yours.*

I denír viël ar altinua (Eee Deh-Neer Vee-EL ARE Al-tin-OO-AH): *In this life and always.*

Vaen (VAY-en): *Truth.*

Drunir (DREW-Neer): *Companion.*

Aldryr (ALL-DREAR): Fire.

Níthral (Nee-TH-ral): Soulblade.

Svidar'Cia (Svih-DAR-see-AH): *Burnt Lands.*

Svidarya (Svih-DAR-eee-AH): *Burning Winds.*

Valacia (VAH-lay-see-AH): *Icelands.*

Nithír (NIH-Theer): *Soul.*

Din haydria er fyrir (DIN HAY-dree-AH AIR Fih-reer): *Your honour is forfeit.*

Bralgír (Brahl-GEER): *Storyteller.*

Ayar Elwyn (Ay-ARE EHL-win): One Heart.

Galdrín (GAHL-DREEN): *Mage.*

Idyn väe (IH-din VAY): *Rest well.*

Solian ata'yar. Dauv ata'yar (SO-Lee-AN ATA-YAR. D-owv ATA-YAR): *Live as one. Die as one.*

Vået (VYE-ET): Time.

Evalian (EH-VAL-ee-AN): *Elves.*

Dracårdare (DRAC-ah-are-dare): *Dragonkeepers*

Races

Humans: Humans first arrived on the continent of Epheria in the year 306 After Doom, fleeing from an unknown cataclysm in their homeland of Terroncia.

Elves: Along with the Jotnar and the dwarves, the elves were one of the first races to inhabit Epheria. After the fall of the Order the elves fought valiantly against the newly formed Lorian Empire, but were eventually defeated and subsequently split into two major factions. One faction blamed the humans for the decimation of Epheria, and retreated into the enormous woodland known as Lynalion, withdrawing themselves from the rest of the continent. The other faction withdrew to the Darkwood, where they built the city of Aravell and continued on the fight in secret by turning the Darkwood into an impassable barrier between the North and South.

Dwarves: Before the fall of The Order, the dwarves occupied territories both above land and below. But after The Fall, the dwarves retreated back to their mountain kingdoms for safety.

Uraks (UH-raks): Creatures whose way of life revolves around bloodshed. Little is known of them outside of battle, other than they serve the traitor God – Efialtír.

Jotnar (Jot-Nar): The Jotnar, known to humans as 'giants', are a race of people who have inhabited Epheria since the dawn of time. They have an intrinsic connection to the Spark, have bluish-white skin, and stand over eight feet tall.

Angan (Ann-GAN): The Angan are a race of humanoid shape-shifters. It is not truly known when they arrived in Epheria, though it is thought that they are as old as the land itself. They divided into five major factions, each devoted to one of the five Angan Gods: Dvalin, Bjorna, Vethnir, Fenryr, and Kaygan.